JULES VERNE

Jules Verne himself served as the model for this illustration of Professor Aronnax, the narrator of *Twenty Thousand Leagues Under the Sea*. It was done in 1870 by the artist Riou.

Contents

Acknowledgment vi
Introduction vii

Twenty Thousand Leagues Under the Sea 1
A Journey to the Center of the Earth 217
From the Earth to the Moon 391
Round the Moon: A Sequel to From the Earth to the Moon 479
Around the World in Eighty Days 589
Short Stories
Doctor Ox's Experiment 733
Master Zacharius 778
A Drama in the Air 805

Acknowledgment

The publishers would like to express their appreciation for the valuable assistance of the collector, Gerald F. Pavano, who contributed his time, scholarship, and his most precious assets—his valued early editions—to this endeavor.

FOREWORD

HALF a dozen generations have felt the fascination of Jules Verne's tales since they were written over a hundred years ago. He wrote stories of marvelous imaginary voyages, filled with such a wealth of careful detail that they still seem real today. Other writers before him had told of fabulous journeys, from Homer's *Odyssey* to Jonathan Swift's *Gulliver's Travels,* but they had written without Verne's awareness of the snowballing achievements of nineteenth-century science. He refined to crystal-ball clarity his notions of what science might and, as it turned out, often did accomplish. Others before him had found a place for science in their stories. Mary Shelley's Dr. Frankenstein had created artificial life, and Edgar Allan Poe's tales of balloon ascensions and world travelers may have given Verne some plot ideas. But in Jules Verne's fiction, science comes to play the major role—often miraculous, often horrific—that it was beginning to play in Verne's world and still plays today. This is why Jules Verne's position as the originator of the scientific romance and the father of modern science fiction is unique.

Jules Verne's father intended his son to become a lawyer like himself, but it was the revolutionary year of 1848 when Jules arrived in Paris to pursue his law studies—just days after the declaration of the second French republic. He also felt more intensely than most the influences of another revolution, the scientific revolution. Once in Paris, Verne quickly joined the literary circle of the elder Dumas, who soon afterward produced a Jules Verne play. While literature was much more attractive to him than the law, it was not to be in the theatre that Verne would find his element. When he was introduced to the publisher Jules Hetzel, they found a common purpose in the popularization of scientific knowledge. Hetzel was starting a quality magazine for children, and Verne had a balloon story that he quickly adapted for this purpose. As a measure of what a discovery Hetzel knew he had in Verne, the contract they signed offered Verne a fee only slightly less than the fees Hetzel paid to his other, well-established authors, Balzac and George Sand.

It was in his stories and novels written for Hetzel that Jules Verne was to express his immense and intense fascination for his world, which continually was being expanded by exploration and experimentation. He felt these expressions to be an urgent need, for if the public had little knowledge or appreciation of what was happening in science, then the whole scientific revolution might falter. Jules Verne and his publisher Hetzel would bring science to the public. Perhaps Verne's sense of possible failure is a key to his appeal. He saw as real possibilities the failure of science, the failure of the liberal republican revolution, and the failure of love. (He had been severely disappointed in love as a youth.) And this sense may be what gives his books their extra dimension of enthralling drama.

Jules Verne's literary reputation portrays him unfairly as a purveyor of simple though thrilling tales for young minds. This reputation, though it has never hurt sales, for Verne has been a best-selling author since his first book was published, is inaccurate, and critical opinion is taking new account of this father of the scientific romance.

Although Verne published much of his fiction first in magazines for children and so was obliged to write what the whole family could read, he was an eager researcher and frequently knew of scientific discoveries before the general public. He knew, for example, of the discovery of the sources of the Nile before all the explorers had returned, and used this bit of news in his first success, *Five Weeks in a Balloon*.

He was an avid seeker of facts, and geography had been one of his chief interests since boyhood, when he had almost succeeded in running away to sea by changing places with a cabin boy. His father caught him at the last moment; and he promised his parents to go adventuring only in his mind from then on. His adventuresome spirit traveled with the aid of his writing. As he mentally traveled, he noted down what he saw, which is why his books are so fact-studded. Not all the facts would meet scientific standards today, but it was Verne's intention that they should scrupulously adhere to the standards of his day. And as modern editors have found, he achieved the goal of scientific accuracy usually to the limit of the knowledge of his time, and sometimes far beyond it. He had the power of mental extrapolation of scientific situations to such an extent that he often seems, in retrospect, a true prophet. When he described his rocket's trip to the Moon and its return, he uncannily had his rocketeers launch a rocket from the same place—Florida; of the same material—aluminum; and of the same height and weight as Apollo 9. Look at the last illustration in *Round the Moon,* drawn in Verne's day, showing the splash-down, and see if it doesn't look familiar. Verne, by the way, had his rocket spiash down a mere two and a half miles from where Apollo 9 actually did.

Yet throughout Jules Verne's writings about science—and all of the writings in this volume touch on science—there runs an undercurrent of darkness about the products of science that seems curiously modern. Verne did not doubt the value of scientific information. He doubted our ability to master ourselves. He was gloomy, like his greatest character, Captain Nemo, about the limitations of human intelligence.

In this collection, along with copious original illustrations, we have the early story of Master Zacharius, who has what might be called an exaggerated scientific conscience. He links the performance of the clocks he has designed with his own life force, and in his old age he has a horror that when he himself runs down and dies, not only his clocks but even time itself, which he has learned to regulate, will come to an end. Here also we have the later story about Doctor Ox. The tone of this satire on the habits of the phlegmatic Flemings is hilarious, but Doctor Ox's experiment nearly does them all in. Doctor Ox treats the inhabitants of the Flemish town who have come to him for help as if they were his laboratory animals. Although the story is humorous, the author's sympathies are with the doctor's victims.

The novels in this volume are all *voyages extraordinaires*. With them, Jules Verne achieved his success and won the hearts of his readers. Around the world, under the sea, down a volcano to the heart of the Earth, and to the Moon and back his characters go. These stories are familiar to millions who have never read the books or even seen the movie adaptations. Verne's stories have become part of the permanent folklore of the scientific age. But although they are all journeys, they are none of them mere travelogues, for the dramatic questions that they pose direct the reader to deeper issues.

Can Captain Nemo in *Twenty Thousand Leagues Under the Sea* keep himself cut off from the human race and continue to act the avenging angel? In Nemo, Jules Verne most closely depicted his own feelings about life and society, a dark vision. Can Phileas Fogg evade unjust accusation, and win his bet and his love within eighty days? In Fogg, Verne showed his love for the character of the English eccentric, although his politics ran counter to British imperialism. Can Axel in *A Journey to the Center of the Earth,* find his way home, to manhood and to his beloved, from the depths of the Earth? Here the satire on the national characteristics of the three companions who travel to the center of the Earth provides comic relief in situations of great suspense. In *From the Earth to the Moon,* Verne gets his characters to the Moon, but will they be able to get back? Horrified at the tremendous advances in military technology displayed in the American Civil War (which he called "The War of the Rebellion")—among which were the submarines *Monitor* and *Merrimack*—Verne dreamed up the plan of helping the United States occupy its terrible machinery of war, after war's end, with his own space program. But he made his readers wait five years before he brought his characters back to Earth again in *Round the Moon*.

These stories stir the mind and fire the imagination. In them, you will find out for yourself what has made Jules Verne one of the most beloved authors of the modern world.

CURTIS CHURCH
New York City,
1983

Editorial Note

These works have been reprinted from the original classic translations, and therefore contain some archaic spelling, terminology and punctuation. The intention has been to present the stories as they were first published in English and to retain the flavor of the originals as closely as possible.

The illustrations also have been reprinted from the early editions. The French artists who created the illustrations are as follows: *Twenty Thousand Leagues Under the Sea,* Riou and Neuville; *A Journey to the Center of the Earth,* Riou; *From the Earth to the Moon,* Montaut; *Round the Moon,* Neuville and Bayard; *Around the World in Eighty Days,* Neuville and Benet; several artists contributed to short stories.

C. B.

Twenty Thousand Leagues Under the Sea

Captain Nemo taking the altitude of the sun.

Part I

CHAPTER 1

A SHIFTING REEF

THE year 1866 was signalized by a remarkable incident, a mysterious and inexplicable phenomenon, which doubtless no one has yet forgotten. Not to mention rumors which agitated the maritime population, and excited the public mind, even in the interior of continents, seafaring men were particularly excited. Merchants, common sailors, captains of vessels, skippers, both of Europe and America, naval officers of all countries, and the governments of several states on the two continents, were deeply interested in the matter.

For some time past, vessels had been met by "an enormous thing," a long object, spindle-shaped, occasionally phosphorescent, and infinitely larger and more rapid in its movements than a whale.

The facts relating to this apparition (entered in various log-books) agreed in most respects as to the shape of the object or creature in question, the untiring rapidity of its movements, its surprising power of locomotion, and the peculiar life with which it seemed endowed. If it was a cetacean, it surpassed in size all those hitherto classified in science. Taking into consideration the mean of observations made at divers times,—rejecting the timid estimate of those who assigned to this object a length of two hundred feet, equally with the exaggerated opinions which set it down as a mile in width and three in length,—we might fairly conclude that this mysterious being surpassed greatly all dimensions admitted by the ichthyologists of the day, if it existed at all. And that it *did* exist was an undeniable fact; and, with that tendency which disposes the human mind in favor of the marvellous, we can understand the excitement produced in the entire world by this supernatural apparition. As to classing it in the list of fables, the idea was out of the question.

On the 20th of July, 1866, the steamer *Governor Higginson,* of the Calcutta and Burnach Steam Navigation Company, had met this moving mass five miles off the east coast of Australia. Captain Baker thought at first that he was in the presence of an unknown sand-bank; he even prepared to determine its exact position, when two columns of water, projected by the inexplicable object, shot with a hissing noise a hundred and fifty feet up into the air. Now, unless the sand-bank had been submitted to the intermittent eruption of a geyser, the *Governor Higginson* had to do neither more nor less than with an aquatic mammal, unknown till then, which threw up from its blow-holes columns of water mixed with air and vapor.

Similar facts were observed on the 23d of July in the same year, in the Pacific

Ocean, by the *Columbus,* of the West India and Pacific Steam Navigation Company. But this extraordinary cetaceous creature could transport itself from one place to another with surprising velocity; as, in an interval of three days, the *Governor Higginson* and the *Columbus* had observed it at two different points of the chart, separated by a distance of more than seven hundred nautical leagues.

Fifteen days later, two thousand miles farther off, the *Helvetia,* of the Compagnie-Nationale, and the *Shannon,* of the Royal Mail Steamship Company, sailing to windward in that portion of the Atlantic lying between the United States and Europe, respectively signalled the monster to each other in 42° 15′ N. lat. and 60° 35′ W. long. In these simultaneous observations, they thought themselves justified in estimating the minimum length of the mammal at more than three hundred and fifty feet, as the *Shannon* and *Helvetia* were of smaller dimensions than it, though they measured three hundred feet over all.

Now the largest whales, those which frequent those parts of the sea round the Aleutian, Kulammak, and Umgullich Islands, have never exceeded the length of sixty yards, if they attain that.

These reports arriving one after the other, with fresh observations made on board the transatlantic ship *Pereira,* a collision which occurred between the *Etna* of the Inman line and the monster, a *procès verbal* directed by the officers of the French frigate *Normandie,* a very accurate survey made by the staff of Commodore Fitz-James on board the *Lord Clyde,* greatly influenced public opinion. Light-thinking people jested upon the phenomenon, but grave practical countries, such as England, America, and Germany, treated the matter more seriously.

In every place of great resort the monster was the fashion. They sang of it in the cafés, ridiculed it in the papers, and represented it on the stage. All kinds of stories were circulated regarding it. There appeared in the papers caricatures of every gigantic and imaginary creature, from the white whale, the terrible "Moby Dick" of hyperborean regions, to the immense kraken whose tentacles could entangle a ship of five hundred tons, and hurry it into the abyss of the ocean. The legends of ancient times were even resuscitated, and the opinions of Aristotle and Pliny revived, who admitted the existence of those monsters, as well as the Norwegian tales of Bishop Pontoppidan, the accounts of Paul Heggede, and, last of all, the reports of Mr. Harrington (whose good faith no one could suspect), who affirmed that, being on board the *Castillan,* in 1857, he had seen this enormous serpent, which had never until that time frequented any other seas but those of the ancient "*Constitutionel.*"

Then burst forth the interminable controversy between the credulous and the incredulous in the societies of savants and scientific journals. "The question of the monster" inflamed all minds. Editors of scientific journals, quarrelling with believers in the supernatural, spilled seas of ink during this memorable campaign, some even drawing blood; for, from the sea-serpent, they came to direct personalities.

For six months war was waged with various fortune in the leading articles of the Geographical Institution of Brazil, the Royal Academy of Science of Berlin, the British Association, the Smithsonian Institution of Washington, in the discussions of the "Indian Archipelago," of the Cosmos of the Abbé Moigno, in the Mittheilungen of Petermann, in the scientific chronicles of the great journals of France and other countries. The cheaper journals replied keenly and with inexhaustible zest. These satirical writers parodied a remark of Linnæus, quoted by the adversaries of the monster, maintaining "that nature did not make fools," and adjured their contemporaries not to give the lie to nature, by admitting the existence of krakens, sea-serpents, "Moby Dicks," and other lucubrations of delirious sailors. At length an article in a well-known satirical journal by a favorite contributor, the chief of the staff, settled the monster, like Hippolytus, giving it the death-blow amidst a universal burst of laughter. Wit had conquered science.

During the first months of the year 1867, the question seemed buried never to revive, when new facts were brought before the public. It was then no longer a scientific problem to be solved, but a real danger seriously to be avoided. The question took quite another shape. The monster became a small island, a rock, a reef, but a reef of indefinite and shifting proportions.

On the 5th of March, 1867, the *Moravian,* of the Montreal Ocean Company, finding herself during the night in 27° 30′ lat. and 72° 15′ long., struck on her starboard quarter a rock, marked in no chart for that part of the sea. Under the combined efforts of the wind and its four hundred horse-power, it was going at the rate of thirteen knots. Had it not been for the superior strength of the hull of the *Moravian,* she would have been broken by the shock, and gone down with the 237 passengers she was bringing home from Canada.

The accident happened about five o'clock in the morning, as the day was breaking. The officers of the quarter-deck hurried to the after-part of the vessel. They examined the sea with the most scrupulous attention. They saw nothing but a strong eddy about three cables' length distant, as if the surface had been violently agitated. The bearings of the place were taken exactly, and the *Moravian* continued its route without apparent damage. Had it struck on a submerged rock, or on an enormous wreck? they could not tell; but on examination of the ship's bottom when undergoing repairs, it was found that part of her keel was broken.

This fact, so grave in itself, might perhaps have been forgotten like many others, if, three weeks after, it had not been re-enacted under similar circumstances. But, thanks to the nationality of the victim of the shock, thanks to the reputation of the company to which the vessel belonged, the circumstances became extensively circulated.

The 13th of April, 1867, the sea being beautiful, the breeze favorable, the *Scotia,* of the Cunard Company's line, found herself in 15° 12′ long. and 45° 37′ lat. She was going at the speed of thirteen knots and a half.

At seventeen minutes past four in the afternoon, whilst the passengers were assembled at lunch in the great saloon, a slight shock was felt on the hull of the *Scotia,* on her quarter, a little aft of the port paddle.

The *Scotia* had not struck, but she had been struck, and seemingly by something rather sharp and penetrating than blunt. The shock had been so slight that no one had been alarmed, had it not been for the shouts of the carpenter's watch, who rushed on to the bridge, exclaiming, "We are sinking! we are sinking!" At first the passengers were much frightened, but Captain Anderson hastened to reassure them. The danger could not be imminent. The *Scotia,* divided into seven compartments by strong partitions, could brave with impunity any leak. Captain Anderson went down immediately into the hold. He found that the sea was pouring into the fifth compartment; and the rapidity of the influx proved that the force of the water was considerable. Fortunately this compartment did not hold the boilers, or the fires would have been immediately extinguished. Captain Anderson ordered the engines to be stopped at once, and one of the men went down to ascertain the extent of the injury. Some minutes afterwards they discovered the existence of a large hole, of two yards in diameter, in the ship's bottom. Such a leak could not be stopped; and the *Scotia,* her paddles half submerged, was obliged to continue her course. She was then three hundred miles from Cape Clear, and after three days' delay, which caused great uneasiness in Liverpool, she entered the basin of the company.

The engineers visited the *Scotia,* which was put in dry-dock. They could scarcely believe it possible: at two yards and a half below water-mark was a regular rent, in the form of an isosceles triangle. The broken place in the iron plates was so perfectly defined, that it could not have been more neatly done by a punch. It was clear, then, that the instrument producing the perforation was not of a common stamp; and after having been driven with prodigious strength, and piercing an iron plate 1⅜ inches thick, had withdrawn itself by a retrograde motion truly inexplicable.

Such was the last fact, which resulted in exciting once more the torrent of public opinion. From this moment all unlucky casualties which could not be otherwise accounted for were put down to the monster.

Upon this imaginary creature rested the responsibility of all these shipwrecks, which unfortunately were considerable; for of three thousand ships whose loss was annually recorded at Lloyds', the number of sailing and steam ships supposed to be totally lost, from the absence of all news, amounted to not less than two hundred.

Now, it was the "monster" who, justly or unjustly, was accused of their disappearance, and, thanks to it, communication between the different continents became more and more dangerous. The public demanded peremptorily that the seas should at any price be relieved from this formidable cetacean.

CHAPTER 2

PRO AND CON

At the period when these events took place, I had just returned from a scientific research in the disagreeable territory of Nebraska, in the United States. In virtue of my office as Assistant Professor in the Museum of Natural History in Paris, the French government had attached me to that expedition. After six months in Nebraska, I arrived in New York towards the end of March, laden with a precious collection. My departure for France was fixed for the first days in May. Meanwhile, I was occupying myself in classifying my mineralogical, botanical, and zoölogical riches, when the accident happened to the *Scotia*.

I was perfectly up in the subject which was the question of the day. How could I be otherwise? I had read and reread all the American and European papers without being any nearer a conclusion. This mystery puzzled me. Under the impossibility of forming an opinion, I jumped from one extreme to the other. That there really was something could not be doubted, and the incredulous were invited to put their finger on the wound of the *Scotia*.

On my arrival at New York, the question was at its height. The hypothesis of the floating island, and the unapproachable sand-bank, supported by minds little competent to form a judgment, was abandoned. And, indeed, unless this shoal had a machine in its stomach, how could it change its position with such astonishing rapidity?

From the same cause, the idea of a floating hull of an enormous wreck was given up.

There remained then only two possible solutions of the question, which created two distinct parties: on one side, those who were for a monster of colossal strength; on the other, those who were for a submarine vessel of enormous motive power.

But this last hypothesis, plausible as it was, could not stand against inquiries made in both worlds. That a private gentleman should have such a machine at his command was not likely. Where, when, and how was it built? and how could its construction have been kept secret? Certainly a government might possess such a destructive machine. And in these disastrous times, when the ingenuity of man has multiplied the power of weapons of war, it was possible that, without the knowledge of others, a state might try to work such a formidable engine. After the chassepots came the torpedoes, after the torpedoes the submarine rams, then—the reaction. At least, I hope so.

But the hypothesis of a war-machine fell before the declaration of governments. As public interest was in question, and transatlantic communications suffered, their veracity could not be doubted. But, how admit that the construction of this submarine boat had escaped the public eye? For a private gentleman to keep the secret under such circumstances would be very difficult, and for a state whose every act is persistently watched by powerful rivals, certainly impossible.

After inquiries made in England; France, Russia, Prussia, Spain, Italy, and America, even in Turkey, the hypothesis of a submarine monitor was definitely rejected.

Upon my arrival in New York several persons did me the honor of consulting me on the phenomenon in question. I had published in France a work in quarto, in two volumes, entitled, "Mysteries of the Great Submarine Grounds." This book, highly approved of in the learned world, gained for me a special reputation in this rather obscure branch of Natural History. My advice was asked. As long as I could deny the reality of the fact, I confined myself to a decided negative. But soon finding myself driven into a corner, I was obliged to explain myself categorically. And even "the Honorable Pierre Aronnax, Professor in the Museum of Paris," was called upon by the *New York Herald* to express a definite opinion of some sort. I did something. I spoke for want of power to hold my tongue. I discussed the question in all its forms, politically and scientifically; and I give here an extract from a carefully studied article which I published in the number of the 30th of April. It ran as follows:—

"After examining one by one the different hypotheses, rejecting all other suggestions, it becomes necessary to admit the existence of a marine animal of enormous power.

"The great depths of the ocean are entirely unknown to us. Soundings cannot reach them. What passes in those remote depths,—what beings live, or can live, twelve or fifteen miles beneath the surface of the waters,—what is the organization of these animals,—we can scarcely conjecture. However, the solution of the problem submitted to me may modify the form of the dilemma. Either we do know all the varieties of beings which people our planet, or we do not. If we do *not* know them all, if Nature has still secrets in ichthyology for us, nothing is more conformable to reason than to admit the existence of fishes, or cetaceans of other kinds, or even of new species, of an organization formed to inhabit the strata inaccessible to soundings, and which an accident of some sort, either fantastical or capricious, has brought at long intervals to the upper level of the ocean.

"If, on the contrary, we *do* know all living kinds, we must necessarily seek for the animal in question amongst those marine beings already classed; and, in that case, I should be disposed to admit the existence of a gigantic narwhal.

"The common narwhal, or unicorn of the sea, often attains a length of sixty feet. Increase its size fivefold or tenfold, give it strength proportionate to its size, lengthen its destructive weapons, and you obtain the animal required. It will have the proportions determined by the officers of the *Shannon,* the instrument required by the perforation of the *Scotia,* and the power necessary to pierce the hull of the steamer.

"Indeed the narwhal is armed with a sort of ivory sword, a halberd, according to the expression of certain naturalists. The principal tusk has the hardness of steel. Some of these tusks have been found buried in the bodies of whales, which the unicorn always attacks with success. Others have been drawn out, not without trouble, from the bottoms of ships, which they had pierced through and through, as a gimlet pierces a barrel. The Museum of the Faculty of Medicine of Paris possesses one of these defensive weapons, two yards and a quarter in length, and fifteen inches in diameter at the base.

"Very well! suppose this weapon to be six times stronger, and the animal ten times more powerful; launch it at the rate of twenty miles an hour, and you obtain a shock capable of producing the catastrophe required. Until further information, therefore, I shall maintain it to be a sea-unicorn of colossal dimensions, armed, not with a halberd, but with a real spur, as the armored frigates, or the "rams" of war, whose massiveness and motive power it would possess at the same time. Thus may this inexplicable phenomenon be explained, unless there be something over and above all that one has ever conjectured, seen, perceived, or experienced; which is just within the bounds of possibility."

These last words were cowardly on my part; but, up to a certain point, I wished to shelter my dignity as Professor, and not give too much cause for laughter to the Americans, who laugh well when they do laugh. I reserved for myself a way of escape. In effect, however, I admitted the existence of the "monster." My article was warmly discussed, which procured it a high reputation. It rallied round it a certain number of partisans. The solution it proposed gave, at least, full liberty to the imagination. The human mind delights in grand conceptions of supernatural beings. And the sea is precisely their best vehicle, the only medium through which these giants (against which terrestrial animals, such as elephants or rhinoceroses, are as nothing) can be produced or developed.

The industrial and commercial papers treated the question chiefly from this point of view. The *Shipping and Mercantile Gazette,* the *Lloyds' List,* the *Packet-Boat,* and the *Maritime and Colonial Review,* all papers devoted to insurance companies which threatened to raise their rates of premium, were unanimous on this point. Public opinion had been pronounced. The United States were the first in the field; and in New York they made preparations for an expedition destined to pursue this narwhal. A frigate of great speed, the *Abraham Lincoln,* was put in commission as soon as possible. The arsenals were opened to Commander Farragut, who hastened the arming of his frigate; but, as it always happens, the moment it was decided to pursue the monster, the monster did not appear. For two months no one heard it spoken of. No ship met with it. It seemed as if this unicorn knew of the plots weaving around it. It had been so much talked of, even through the Atlantic cable, that jesters pretended that this slender fly had stopped a telegram on its passage, and was making the most of it.

So when the frigate had been armed for a long campaign, and provided with formidable fishing apparatus, no one could tell what course to pursue. Impatience grew apace, when, on the 2d of June, they learned that a steamer of the line of San Francisco, from California to Shanghai, had seen the animal three weeks before in the North Pacific Ocean. The excitement caused by this news was extreme. The ship was revictualled and well stocked with coal.

Three hours before the *Abraham Lincoln* left Brooklyn pier, I received a letter worded as follows:—

"To M. Aronnax, *Professor in the Museum of Paris,*
Fifth Avenue Hotel, New York.

"Sir,—If you will consent to join the *Abraham Lincoln* in this expedition, the government of the United States will with pleasure see France represented in the enterprise. Commander Farragut has a cabin at your disposal.

Very cordially yours,
"J. B. Hobson,
"Secretary of Marine."

CHAPTER 3

I FORM MY RESOLUTION

Three seconds before the arrival of J. B. Hobson's letter, I no more thought of pursuing the unicorn than of attempting the passage of the North Sea. Three seconds after reading the letter of the Honorable Secretary of Marine, I felt that my true vocation, the sole end of my life, was to chase this disturbing monster, and purge it from the world.

But I had just returned from a fatiguing journey, weary, and longing for repose. I aspired to nothing more than again seeing my country, my friends, my little lodging by the Jardin des Plantes, my dear and precious collections. But nothing could keep me back! I forgot all—fatigue, friends, and collections—and accepted without hesitation the offer of the American government.

"Besides," thought I, "all roads lead back to Europe; and the unicorn may be amiable enough to hurry me towards the coast of France. This worthy animal may allow itself to be caught in the seas of Europe (for my particular benefit), and I will not bring back less than half a yard of his ivory halberd to the Museum of Natural History." But in the mean while I must seek this narwhal in the North Pacific Ocean, which, to return to France, was taking the road to the antipodes.

"Conseil," I called in an impatient voice.

Conseil was my servant, a true, devoted Flemish boy, who had accompanied me in all my travels. I liked him, and he returned the liking well. He was phlegmatic by nature, regular from principle, zealous from habit, evincing little disturbance at the different surprises of life, very quick with his hands, and apt at any service required of him; and, despite his name, never giving advice,—even when asked for it.

Conseil had followed me for the last ten years wherever science led. Never once did he complain of the length or fatigue of a journey, never make an objection to pack his portmanteau for whatever country it might be, or however far away, whether China or Congo. Besides all this, he had good health, which defied all sickness, and solid muscles, but no nerves; good morals are understood. This boy was thirty years old, and his age to that of his master as fifteen to twenty. May I be excused for saying that I was forty years old?

But Conseil had one fault, he was ceremonious to a degree, and would never speak to me but in a third person, which was sometimes provoking.

"Conseil," said I again, beginning with feverish hands to make preparations for my departure.

Certainly I was sure of this devoted boy. As a rule, I never asked him if it were convenient for him or not to follow me in my travels; but this time the expedition in question might be prolonged, and the enterprise might be hazardous in pursuit of an animal capable of sinking a frigate as easily as a nutshell. Here there was matter for reflection even to the most impassive man in the world. What would Conseil say?

"Conseil," I called a third time.

Conseil appeared.

"Did you call, sir?" said he, entering.

"Yes, my boy; make preparations for me and yourself too. We leave in two hours."

"As you please, sir," replied Conseil, quietly.

"Not an instant to lose; lock in my trunk all travelling utensils, coats, shirts, and stockings,—without counting,—as many as you can, and make haste."

"And your collections, sir?" observed Conseil.

"We will think of them by and by."

"What! the archiotherium, the hyracotherium, the oreodons, the cheropotamus, and the other skins?"

"They will keep them at the hotel."

"And your live Babiroussa, sir?"

"They will feed it during our absence; besides, I will give orders to forward our menagerie to France."

"We are not returning to Paris, then?" said Conseil.

"Oh! certainly," I answered evasively, "by making a curve."

"Will the curve please you, sir?"

"Oh! it will be nothing; not quite so direct a road, that is all. We take our passage in the *Abraham Lincoln*."

"As you think proper, sir," coolly replied Conseil.

"You see, my friend, it had to do with the monster,—the famous narwhal. We are going to purge it from the seas. The author of a work in quarto, in two volumes, on the 'Mysteries of the Great Submarine Grounds' cannot forbear embarking with Commander Farragut. A glorious mission, but a dangerous one!

We cannot tell where we may go; these animals can be very capricious. But we will go whether or no; we have got a captain who is pretty wide awake."

I opened a credit account for Babiroussa, and, Conseil following, I jumped into a cab. Our luggage was transported to the deck of the frigate immediately. I hastened on board and asked for Commander Farragut. One of the sailors conducted me to the poop, where I found myself in the presence of a good-looking officer, who held out his hand to me.

"Monsieur Pierre Aronnax?" said he.

"Himself," replied I; "Commander Farragut?"

"You are welcome, Professor; your cabin is ready for you."

I bowed, and desired to be conducted to the cabin destined for me.

The *Abraham Lincoln* had been well chosen and equipped for her new destination. She was a frigate of great speed, fitted with high-pressure engines which admitted a pressure of seven atmospheres. Under this the *Abraham Lincoln* attained the mean speed of nearly eighteen knots and a third an hour,—a considerable speed, but, nevertheless, insufficient to grapple with this gigantic cetacean.

The interior arrangements of the frigate corresponded to its nautical qualities. I was well satisfied with my cabin, which was in the after-part, opening upon the gun-room.

"We shall be well off here," said I to Conseil.

"As well, by your honor's leave, as a hermit-crab in the shell of a whelk," said Conseil.

I left Conseil to stow our trunks conveniently away, and remounted the poop in order to survey the preparations for departure.

At that moment Commander Farragut was ordering the last moorings to be cast loose which held the *Abraham Lincoln* to the pier of Brooklyn. So in a quarter of an hour, perhaps less, the frigate would have sailed without me. I should have missed this extraordinary, supernatural, and incredible expedition, the recital of which may well meet with some scepticism.

But Commander Farragut would not lose a day nor an hour in scouring the seas in which the animal had been sighted. He sent for the engineer.

"Is the steam full on?" asked he.

"Yes, sir," replied the engineer.

"Go ahead," cried Commander Farragut.

The quay of Brooklyn, and all that part of New York bordering on the East River, was crowded with spectators. Three cheers burst successively from five hundred thousand throats; thousands of handkerchiefs were waved above the heads of the compact mass, saluting the *Abraham Lincoln,* until she reached the waters of the Hudson, at the point of that elongated peninsula which forms the town of New York. Then the frigate, following the coast of New Jersey along the right bank of the beautiful river, covered with villas, passed between the forts, which saluted her with their heaviest guns. The *Abraham Lincoln* answered by hoisting the American colors three times, whose thirty-nine stars shone resplendent from the mizzen-peak; then modifying its speed to take the narrow channel marked by buoys placed in the inner bay formed by Sandy Hook Point, it coasted the long sandy beach, where some thousands of spectators gave it one final cheer. The escort of boats and tenders still followed the frigate, and did not leave her until they came abreast of the light-ship, whose two lights marked the entrance of New York Channel.

Six bells struck, the pilot got into his boat, and rejoined the little schooner which was waiting under our lee, the fires were made up, the screw beat the waves more rapidly, the frigate skirted the low yellow coast of Long Island; and at eight bells, after having lost sight in the northwest of the lights of Fire Island, she ran at full steam on to the dark waters of the Atlantic.

CHAPTER 4

NED LAND

CAPTAIN FARRAGUT was a good seaman, worthy of the frigate he commanded. His vessel and he were one. He was the soul of it. On the question of the cetacean there was no doubt in his mind, and he would not allow the existence of the animal to be disputed on board. He believed in it as certain good women believe in the leviathan,—by faith, not by reason. The monster did exist, and he had sworn to rid the seas of it. He was a kind of Knight of Rhodes, a second Dieudonné de Gozon, going to meet the serpent which desolated the island. Either Captain Farragut would kill the narwhal, or the narwhal would kill the captain. There was no third course.

The officers on board shared the opinion of their chief. They were ever chatting, discussing, and calculating the various chances of a meeting, watching narrowly the vast surface of the ocean. More than one took up his quarters voluntarily in the cross-trees, who would have cursed such a berth under any other circumstances. As long as the sun described its daily course, the rigging was crowded with sailors, whose feet were burnt to such an extent by the heat of the deck as to render it unbearable; still the *Abraham Lincoln* had not yet breasted the suspected waters of the Pacific. As to the ship's company, they desired nothing better than to meet the unicorn, to harpoon it, hoist it on board, and despatch it. They watched the sea with eager attention.

Besides, Captain Farragut had spoken of a certain sum of two thousand dollars, set apart for whoever should first sight the monster, were he cabin-boy, common seaman, or officer.

I leave you to judge how eyes were used on board the *Abraham Lincoln*.

For my own part, I was not behind the others, and left to no one my share of daily observations. The frigate might have been called the *Argus*, for a hundred reasons. Only one amongst us, Conseil, seemed to protest by his indifference against the question which so interested us all, and seemed to be out of keeping with the general enthusiasm on board.

I have said that Captain Farragut had carefully provided his ship with every apparatus for catching the gigantic cetacean. No whaler had ever been better armed. We possessed every known engine, from the harpoon thrown by the hand to the barbed arrows of the blunderbuss, and the explosive balls of the duck-gun. On the forecastle lay the perfection of a breech-loading gun, very thick at the breech, and very narrow in the bore, the model of which had been in the

Exhibition of 1867. This precious weapon of American origin could throw with ease a conical projectile of nine pounds to a mean distance of ten miles.

Thus the *Abraham Lincoln* wanted for no means of destruction; and, what was better still, she had on board Ned Land, the prince of harpooners.

Ned Land was a Canadian, with an uncommon quickness of hand, and who knew no equal in his dangerous occupation. Skill, coolness, audacity, and cunning he possessed in a superior degree, and it must be a cunning whale or a singularly "cute" cachalot to escape the stroke of his harpoon.

Ned Land was about forty years of age; he was a tall man (more than six feet high), strongly built, grave and taciturn, occasionally violent, and very passionate when contradicted. His person attracted attention, but above all the boldness of his look, which gave a singular expression to his face.

Who calls himself Canadian calls himself French; and little communicative as Ned Land was, I must admit that he took a certain liking for me. My nationality drew him to me, no doubt. It was an opportunity for him to talk, and for me to hear, that old language of Rabelais, which is still in use in some Canadian provinces. The harpooner's family was originally from Quebec, and was already a tribe of hardy fishermen when this town belonged to France.

Little by little, Ned Land acquired a taste for chatting, and I loved to hear the recital of his adventures in the polar seas. He related his fishing, and his combats, with natural poetry of expression; his recital took the form of an epic poem, and I seemed to be listening to a Canadian Homer singing the Iliad of the regions of the North.

I am portraying this hardy companion as I really knew him. We are old friends now, united in that unchangeable friendship which is born and cemented amidst extreme dangers. Ah, brave Ned! I ask no more than to live a hundred years longer, that I may have more time to dwell the longer on your memory.

Now, what was Ned Land's opinion upon the question of the marine monster? I must admit that he did not believe in the unicorn, and was the only one on board who did not share that universal conviction. He even avoided the subject, which I one day thought it my duty to press upon him. One magnificent evening, the 25th June,—that is to say, three weeks after our departure,—the frigate was abreast of Cape Blanc, thirty miles to leeward of the coast of Patagonia. We had crossed the tropic of Capricorn, and the Straits of Magellan opened less than seven hundred miles to the south. Before eight days were over, the *Abraham Lincoln* would be ploughing the waters of the Pacific.

Seated on the poop, Ned Land and I were chatting of one thing and another as we looked at this mysterious sea, whose great depths had up to this time been inaccessible to the eye of man. I naturally led up the conversation to the giant unicorn, and examined the various chances of success or failure of the expedition. But seeing that Ned Land let me speak without saying too much himself, I pressed him more closely.

"Well, Ned," said I, "is it possible that you are not convinced of the existence of this cetacean that we are following? Have you any particular reason for being so incredulous?"

The harpooner looked at me fixedly for some moments before answering, struck his broad forehead with his hand (a habit of his), as if to collect himself, and said at last, "Perhaps I have, Mr. Aronnax."

"But, Ned, you, a whaler by profession, familiarized with all the great marine mammalia,—you, whose imagination might easily accept the hypothesis of enormous cetaceans,—*you* ought to be the last to doubt under such circumstances!''

''That is just what deceives you, Professor,'' replied Ned. ''That the vulgar should believe in extraordinary comets traversing space, and in the existence of antediluvian monsters in the heart of the globe, may well be; but neither astronomers nor geologists believe in such chimeras. As a whaler, I have followed many a cetacean, harpooned a great number, and killed several; but, however strong or well-armed they may have been, neither their tails nor their weapons would have been able even to scratch the iron plates of a steamer.''

''But, Ned, they tell of ships which the teeth of the narwhal have pierced through and through.''

''Wooden ships,—that is possible,'' replied the Canadian; ''but I have never seen it done; and, until further proof, I deny that whales, cetaceans, or sea-unicorns could ever produce the effect you describe.''

''Well, Ned, I repeat it with a conviction resting on the logic of facts. I believe in the existence of a mammal powerfully organized, belonging to the branch of vertebrata, like the whales, the cachalots, or the dolphins, and furnished with a horn of defence of great penetrating power.''

''Hum!'' said the harpooner, shaking his head with the air of a man who would not be convinced.

''Notice one thing, my worthy Canadian,'' I resumed. ''If such an animal is in existence, if it inhabits the depths of the ocean, if it frequents the strata lying miles below the surface of the water, it must necessarily possess an organization the strength of which would defy all comparison.''

''And why this powerful organization?'' demanded Ned.

''Because it requires incalculable strength to keep one's self in these strata and resist their pressure. Listen to me. Let us admit that the pressure of the atmosphere is represented by the weight of a column of water thirty-two feet high. In reality the column of water would be shorter, as we are speaking of sea-water, the density of which is greater than that of fresh water. Very well, when you dive, Ned, as many times thirty-two feet of water as there are above you, so many times does your body bear a pressure equal to that of the atmosphere, that is to say 15 lbs. for each square inch of its surface. It follows then, that at 320 feet this pressure = that of 10 atmospheres, of 100 atmospheres at 3,200 feet, and of 1,000 atmospheres at 32,000 feet, that is, about 6 miles; which is equivalent to saying that, if you could attain this depth in the ocean, each square ⅜ of an inch of the surface of your body would bear a pressure of 5,600 lbs. Ah! my brave Ned, do you know how many square inches you carry on the surface of your body?''

''I have no idea, Mr. Aronnax.''

''About 6,500; and, as in reality the atmospheric pressure is about 15 lbs. to the square inch, your 6,500 square inches bear at this moment a pressure of 97,500 lbs.''

''Without my perceiving it?''

''Without your perceiving it. And if you are not crushed by such a pressure, it is because the air penetrates the interior of your body with equal pressure. Hence perfect equilibrium between the interior and exterior pressure, which thus neutralize each other, and which allows you to bear it without inconvenience. But in the water it is another thing.''

Ned Land, the Canadian harpooner.

"Yes, I understand," replied Ned, becoming more attentive; "because the water surrounds me, but does not penetrate."

"Precisely, Ned; so that at 32 feet beneath the surface of the sea you would undergo a pressure of 97,500 lbs.; at 320 feet, ten times that pressure; at 3,200 feet, a hundred times that pressure; lastly, at 32,000 feet, a thousand times that pressure would be 97,500,000 lbs.,—that is to say, that you would be flattened as if you had been drawn from the plates of an hydraulic machine!"

"The devil!" exclaimed Ned.

"Very well, my worthy harpooner, if some vertebrate, several hundred yards long, and large in proportion, can maintain itself in such depths,—of those whose surface is represented by millions of square inches, that is by tens of millions of pounds, we must estimate the pressure they undergo. Consider, then, what must be the resistance of their bony structure, and the strength of their organization to withstand such pressure!"

"Why!" exclaimed Ned Land, "they must be made of iron plates eight inches thick, like the armored frigates."

"As you say, Ned. And think what destruction such a mass would cause, if hurled with the speed of an express train against the hull of a vessel."

"Yes—certainly—perhaps," replied the Canadian, shaken by these figures, but not yet willing to give in.

"Well, have I convinced you?"

"You have convinced me of one thing, sir, which is, that if such animals do exist at the bottom of the seas, they must necessarily be as strong as you say."

"But if they do not exist, mine obstinate harpooner, how explain the accident to the *Scotia*?"

CHAPTER 5

AT A VENTURE

THE voyage of the *Abraham Lincoln* was for a long time marked by no special incident. But one circumstance happened which showed the wonderful dexterity of Ned Land, and proved what confidence we might place in him.

The 30th of June, the frigate spoke some American whalers, from whom we learned that they knew nothing about the narwhal. But one of them, the captain of the *Monroe,* knowing that Ned Land had shipped on board the *Abraham Lincoln,* begged for his help in chasing a whale they had in sight. Commander Farragut, desirous of seeing Ned Land at work, gave him permission to go on board the *Monroe*. And fate served our Canadian so well that, instead of one whale, he harpooned two with a double blow, striking one straight to the heart and catching the other after some minutes' pursuit.

Decidedly, if the monster ever had to do with Ned Land's harpoon, I would not bet in its favor.

The frigate skirted the southeast coast of America with great rapidity. The 3d of July we were at the opening of the Straits of Magellan, level with Cape

Vierges. But Commander Farragut would not take a tortuous passage, but doubled Cape Horn.

The ship's crew agreed with him. And certainly it was possible that they might meet the narwhal in this narrow pass. Many of the sailors affirmed that the monster could not pass there, "that he was too big for that!"

The 6th of July, about three o'clock in the afternoon, the *Abraham Lincoln*, at fifteen miles to the south, doubled the solitary island, this last rock at the extremity of the American continent to which some Dutch sailors gave the name of their native town, Cape Horn. The course was taken towards the northwest, and the next day the screw of the frigate was at last beating the waters of the Pacific.

"Keep your eyes open!" called out the sailors.

And they were opened widely. Both eyes and glasses, a little dazzled, it is true, by the prospect of two thousand dollars, had not an instant's repose. Day and night they watched the surface of the ocean, and even nyctalopes, whose faculty of seeing in the darkness multiplies their chances a hundred-fold, would have had enough to do to gain the prize.

I myself, for whom money had no charms, was not the least attentive on board. Giving but few minutes to my meals, but a few hours to sleep, indifferent to either rain or sunshine, I did not leave the poop of the vessel. Now leaning on the netting of the forecastle, now on the taffrail, I devoured with eagerness the soft foam which whitened the sea as far as the eye could reach; and how often have I shared the emotion of the majority of the crew when some capricious whale raised its black back above the waves! The poop of the vessel was crowded in a moment. The cabins poured forth a torrent of sailors and officers, each with heaving breast and troubled eye watching the course of the cetacean. I looked, and looked, till I was nearly blind, whilst Conseil, always phlegmatic, kept repeating in a calm voice:—

"If, sir, you would not squint so much, you would see better!"

But vain excitement! the *Abraham Lincoln* checked its speed and made for the animal signalled, a simple whale, or common cachalot, which soon disappeared amidst a storm of execration.

But the weather was good. The voyage was being accomplished under the most favorable auspices. It was then the bad season in Australia, the July of that zone corresponding to our January in Europe; but the sea was beautiful and easily scanned round a vast circumference.

The 20th July, the tropic of Capricorn was cut by 105° of longitude, and the 27th of the same month we crossed the equator on the 110th meridian. This passed, the frigate took a more decided westerly direction, and scoured the central waters of the Pacific. Commander Farragut thought, and with reason, that it was better to remain in deep water, and keep clear of continents or islands, which the beast itself seemed to shun (perhaps because there was not enough water for him! suggested the greater part of the crew). The frigate passed at some distance from the Marquesas and the Sandwich Islands, crossed the tropic of Cancer, and made for the China Seas. We were on the theatre of the last diversions of the monster; and to say truth, we no longer *lived* on board. Hearts palpitated, fearfully preparing themselves for future incurable aneurism. The entire ship's crew were undergoing a nervous excitement, of which I can give no idea; they could not eat, they could not sleep: twenty times a day, a misconception or an optical illusion of some sailor seated on the taffrail would cause dreadful perspirations, and these emotions, twenty times repeated, kept us in a state of excitement so violent that a reaction was unavoidable.

And truly, reaction soon showed itself. For three months, during which a day seemed an age, the *Abraham Lincoln* furrowed all the waters of the Northern Pacific, running at whales, making sharp deviations from her course, veering suddenly from one tack to another, stopping suddenly, putting on steam, and backing ever and anon at the risk of deranging her machinery; and not one point of the Japanese or American coast was left unexplored.

The warmest partisans of the enterprise now became its most ardent detractors. Reaction mounted from the crew to the captain himself, and certainly, had it not been for resolute determination on the part of Captain Farragut, the frigate would have headed due southward. This useless search could not last much longer. The *Abraham Lincoln* had nothing to reproach herself with, she had done her best to succeed. Never had an American ship's crew shown more zeal or patience; its failure could not be placed to their charge,—there remained nothing but to return.

This was represented to the commander. The sailors could not hide their discontent, and the service suffered. I will not say there was a mutiny on board, but after a reasonable period of obstinacy, Captain Farragut (as Columbus did) asked for three days' patience. If in three days the monster did not appear, the man at the helm should give three turns of the wheel, and the *Abraham Lincoln* would make for the European seas.

This promise was made on the 2d of November. It had the effect of rallying the ship's crew. The ocean was watched with renewed attention. Each one wished for a last glance in which to sum up his remembrance. Glasses were used with feverish activity. It was a grand defiance given to the giant narwhal, and he could scarcely fail to answer the summons and "appear."

Two days passed, the steam was at half-pressure; a thousand schemes were tried to attract the attention and stimulate the apathy of the animal in case it should be met in those parts. Large quantities of bacon were trailed in the wake of the ship, to the great satisfaction (I must say) of the sharks. Small craft radiated in all directions round the *Abraham Lincoln* as she lay to, and did not leave a spot of the sea unexplored. But the night of the 4th of November arrived without the unveiling of this submarine mystery.

The next day, the 5th of November, at twelve, the delay would (morally speaking) expire; after that time, Commander Farragut, faithful to his promise, was to turn the course to the southeast and abandon forever the northern regions of the Pacific.

The frigate was then in 31° 15′ north latitude and 136° 42′ east longitude. The coast of Japan still remained less than two hundred miles to leeward. Night was approaching. They had just struck eight bells; large clouds veiled the face of the moon, then in its first quarter. The sea undulated peaceably under the stern of the vessel.

At that moment I was leaning forward on the starboard netting. Conseil, standing near me, was looking straight before him. The crew, perched in the ratlines, examined the horizon, which contracted and darkened by degrees. Officers with their night-glasses scoured the growing darkness; sometimes the ocean sparkled under the rays of the moon, which darted between two clouds, then all trace of light was lost in the darkness.

In looking at Conseil, I could see he was undergoing a little of the general influence. At least I thought so. Perhaps for the first time his nerves vibrated to a sentiment of curiosity.

"Come, Conseil," said I, "this is the last chance of pocketing the two thousand dollars."

"May I be permitted to say, sir," replied Conseil, "that I never reckoned on getting the prize; and, had the government of the Union offered a hundred thousand dollars, it would have been none the poorer."

"You are right, Conseil. It is a foolish affair after all, and one upon which we entered too lightly. What time lost, what useless emotions! We should have been back in France six months ago."

"In your little room, sir," replied Conseil, "and in your museum, sir; and I should have already classed all your fossils, sir. And the Babiroussa would have been installed in its cage in the Jardin des Plantes, and have drawn all the curious people of the capital!"

"As you say, Conseil. I fancy we shall run a fair chance of being laughed at for our pains."

"That's tolerably certain," replied Conseil, quietly; "I think they will make fun of you, sir. And, must I say it?"—

"Go on, my good friend."

"Well, sir, you will only get your deserts."

"Indeed!"

"When one has the honor of being a savant as you are, sir, one should not expose one's self to—"

Conseil had not time to finish his compliment. In the midst of general silence a voice had just been heard. It was the voice of Ned Land shouting:—

"Look out there! the very thing we are looking for,—on our weather beam!"

CHAPTER 6

AT FULL STEAM

AT this cry the whole ship's crew hurried towards the harpooner,—commander, officers, masters, sailors, cabin-boys; even the engineers left their engines, and the stokers their furnaces.

The order to stop her had been given, and the frigate now simply went on by her own momentum. The darkness was then profound; and however good the Canadian's eyes were, I asked myself how he had managed to see, and what he had been able to see. My heart beat as if it would break. But Ned Land was not mistaken, and we all perceived the object he pointed to. At two cables' lengths from the *Abraham Lincoln,* on the starboard quarter, the sea seemed to be illuminated all over. It was not a mere phosphoric phenomenon. The monster emerged some fathoms from the water, and then threw out that very intense but inexplicable light mentioned in the report of several captains. This magnificent irradiation must have been produced by an agent of great *shining* power. The luminous part traced on the sea an immense oval, much elongated, the centre of which condensed a burning heat, whose overpowering brillancy died out by successive gradations.

"It is only an agglomeration of phosphoric particles," cried one of the officers.

"No, sir, certainly not," I replied. "Never did pholades or salpæ produce such a powerful light. That brightness is of an essentially electrical nature. Besides, see, see! it moves; it is moving forwards, backwards, it is darting towards us!"

A general cry arose from the frigate.

"Silence!" said the captain; "up with the helm, reverse the engines."

The steam was shut off, and the *Abraham Lincoln,* beating to port, described a semicircle.

"Right the helm, go ahead," cried the captain.

These orders were executed, and the frigate moved rapidly from the burning light.

I was mistaken. She tried to sheer off, but the supernatural animal approached with a velocity double her own.

We gasped for breath. Stupefaction more than fear made us dumb and motionless. The animal gained on us, sporting with the waves. It made the round of the frigate, which was then making fourteen knots, and enveloped it with its electric rings like luminous dust. Then it moved away two or three miles, leaving a phosphorescent track, like those volumes of steam that the express trains leave behind. All at once from the dark line of the horizon whither it retired to gain its momentum, the monster rushed suddenly towards the *Abraham Lincoln* with alarming rapidity, stopped suddenly about twenty feet from the hull, and died out,—not diving under the water, for its brilliancy did not abate,—but suddenly, and as if the source of this brilliant emanation was exhausted. Then it reappeared on the other side of the vessel, as if it had turned and slid under the hull. Any moment a collision might have occurred which would have been fatal to us. However, I was astonished at the manœuvres of the frigate. She fled and did not attack.

On the captain's face, generally so impassive, was an expression of unaccountable astonishment.

"Mr. Aronnax," he said, "I do not know with what formidable being I have to deal, and I will not imprudently risk my frigate in the midst of this darkness. Besides, how attack this unknown thing, how defend one's self from it? Wait for daylight, and the scene will change."

"You have no further doubt, Captain, of the nature of the animal?"

"No, sir; it is evidently a gigantic narwhal, and an electric one."

"Perhaps," added I, "one can only approach it with a gymnotus or a torpedo."

"Undoubtedly," replied the captain, "if it possesses such dreadful power, it is the most terrible animal that ever was created. That is why, sir, I must be on my guard."

The crew were on their feet all night. No one thought of sleep. The *Abraham Lincoln,* not being able to struggle with such velocity, had moderated its pace, and sailed at half speed. For its part, the narwhal, imitating the frigate, let the waves rock it at will, and seemed decided not to leave the scene of the struggle. Towards midnight, however, it disappeared, or, to use a more appropriate term, it "died out" like a large glow-worm. Had it fled? One could only fear, not hope it. But at seven minutes to one o'clock in the morning a deafening whistling was heard, like that produced by a body of water rushing with great violence.

The Captain, Ned Land, and I were then on the poop, eagerly peering through the profound darkness.

"Ned Land," asked the commander, "you have often heard the roaring of whales?"

"Often, sir; but never such whales the sight of which brought me in two thousand dollars. If I can only approach within four harpoon lengths of it!"

"But to approach it," said the commander, "I ought to put a whaler at your disposal?"

"Certainly, sir."

"That will be trifling with the lives of my men."

"And mine too," simply said the harpooner.

Towards two o'clock in the morning, the burning light reappeared, not less intense, about five miles to windward of the *Abraham Lincoln*. Notwithstanding the distance, and the noise of the wind and sea, one heard distinctly the loud strokes of the animal's tail, and even its panting breath. It seemed that, at the moment that the enormous narwhal had come to take breath at the surface of the water, the air was ingulfed in its lungs, like the steam in the vast cylinders of a machine of two thousand horse-power.

"Hum!" thought I, "a whale with the strength of a cavalry regiment would be a pretty whale!"

We were on the *qui vive* till daylight, and prepared for the combat. The fishing implements were laid along the hammock nettings. The second lieutenant loaded the blunderbusses, which could throw harpoons to the distance of a mile, and long duck-guns, with explosive bullets, which inflicted mortal wounds even to the most terrible animals. Ned Land contented himself with sharpening his harpoon,—a terrible weapon in his hands.

At six o'clock, day began to break; and with the first glimmer of light, the electric light of the narwhal disappeared. At seven o'clock the day was sufficiently advanced, but a very thick sea-fog obscured our view, and the best spy-glasses could not pierce it. That caused disappointment and anger.

I climbed the mizzen-mast. Some officers were already perched on the mast-heads. At eight o'clock the fog lay heavily on the waves, and its thick scrolls rose little by little. The horizon grew wider and clearer at the same time. Suddenly, just as on the day before, Ned Land's voice was heard:—

"The thing itself on the port quarter!" cried the harpooner.

Every eye was turned towards the point indicated. There, a mile and a half from the frigate, a long blackish body emerged a yard above the waves. Its tail, violently agitated, produced a considerable eddy. Never did a caudal appendage beat the sea with such violence. An immense track, of a dazzling whiteness, marked the passage of the animal, and described a long curve.

The frigate approached the cetacean. I examined it thoroughly.

The reports of the *Shannon* and of the *Helvetia* had rather exaggerated its size, and I estimated its length at only two hundred and fifty feet. As to its dimensions, I could only conjecture them to be admirably proportioned. While I watched this phenomenon, two jets of steam and water were ejected from its vents, and rose to the height of 120 feet; thus I ascertained its way of breathing. I concluded definitely that it belonged to the vertebrate branch, class mammalia.

The crew waited impatiently for their chief's orders. The latter, after having observed the animal attentively, called the engineer. The engineer ran to him.

"Sir," said the commander, "you have steam up?"

"Yes, sir," answered the engineer.

"Well, make up your fires and put on all steam."

Three hurrahs greeted this order. The time for the struggle had arrived. Some moments after, the two funnels of the frigate vomited torrents of black smoke, and the bridge quaked under the trembling of the boilers.

The *Abraham Lincoln,* propelled by her powerful screw, went straight at the animal. The latter allowed it to come within half a cable's length; then, as if disdaining to dive, it took a little turn, and stopped a short distance off.

This pursuit lasted nearly three quarters of an hour, without the frigate gaining two yards on the cetacean. It was quite evident that at that rate we should never come up with it.

"Well, Mr. Land," asked the captain, "do you advise me to put the boats out to sea?"

"No, sir," replied Ned Land; "because we shall not take that beast easily."

"What shall we do then?"

"Put on more steam if you can, sir. With your leave, I mean to post myself under the bowsprit, and if we get within harpooning distance, I shall throw my harpoon."

"Go, Ned," said the captain.—"Engineer, put on more pressure."

Ned Land went to his post. The fires were increased, the screw revolved forty-three miles a minute, and the steam poured out of the valves. We heaved the log, and calculated that the *Abraham Lincoln* was going at the rate of 18½ miles an hour.

But the accursed animal swam too at the rate of 18½ miles.

For a whole hour, the frigate kept up this pace, without gaining six feet. It was humiliating for one of the swiftest sailers in the American navy. A stubborn anger seized the crew; the sailors abused the monster, who, as before, disdained to answer them; the captain no longer contented himself with twisting his beard,—he gnawed it.

The engineer was again called.

"You have turned full steam on?"

"Yes, sir," replied the engineer.

The speed of the *Abraham Lincoln* increased. Its masts trembled down to their stepping holes, and the clouds of smoke could hardly find way out of the narrow funnels.

They heaved the log a second time.

"Well?" asked the captain of the man at the wheel.

"Nineteen miles and three tenths, sir."

"Clap on more steam."

The engineer obeyed. The manometer showed ten degrees. But the cetacean grew warm itself, no doubt; for, without straining itself, it made 19³⁄₁₀ miles.

What a pursuit! No, I cannot describe the emotion that vibrated through me. Ned Land kept his post, harpoon in hand. Several times the animal let us gain upon it. "We shall catch it! we shall catch it!" cried the Canadian. But just as he was going to strike, the cetacean stole away with a rapidity that could not be estimated at less than thirty miles an hour, and even during our maximum of speed it bullied the frigate, going round and round it. A cry of fury broke from every one!

At noon we were no further advanced than at eight o'clock in the morning.

The captain then decided to take more direct means.

"Ah!" said he, "that animal goes quicker than the *Abraham Lincoln*. Very well! we will see whether it will escape these conical bullets. Send your men to the forecastle, sir."

The forecastle gun was immediately loaded and slewed round. But the shot passed some feet above the cetacean, which was half a mile off.

"Another more to the right," cried the commander, "and five dollars to whoever will hit that infernal beast."

An old gunner with a gray beard,—that I can see now,—with steady eye and grave face, went up to the gun and took a long aim. A loud report was heard, with which were mingled the cheers of the crew.

The bullet did its work; it hit the animal, but not fatally, and, sliding off the sounded surface, was lost in two miles' depth of sea.

The chase began again, and the captain, leaning towards me, said:—

"I will pursue that beast till my frigate bursts up."

"Yes," answered I; "and you will be quite right to do it."

I wished the beast would exhaust itself, and not be insensible to fatigue, like a steam-engine! But it was of no use. Hours passed, without its showing any signs of exhaustion.

However, it must be said in praise of the *Abraham Lincoln,* that she struggled on indefatigably. I cannot reckon the distance she made under three hundred miles during this unlucky day, November the 6th. But night came on, and overshadowed the rough ocean.

Now I thought our expedition was at an end, and that we should never again see the extraordinary animal. I was mistaken. At ten minutes to eleven in the evening, the electric light reappeared three miles to windward of the frigate, as pure, as intense as during the preceding night.

The narwhal seemed motionless; perhaps, tired with its day's work, it slept, letting itself float with the undulation of the waves. Now was a chance of which the captain resolved to take advantage.

He gave his orders. The *Abraham Lincoln* kept up half-steam, and advanced cautiously so as not to awake its adversary. It is no rare thing to meet in the middle of the ocean whales so sound asleep that they can be successfully attacked, and Ned Land had harpooned more than one during its sleep. The Canadian went to take his place again under the bowsprit.

The frigate approached noiselessly, stopped at two cables' length from the animal, and following its track. No one breached; a deep silence reigned on the bridge. We were not a hundred feet from the burning focus, the light of which increased and dazzled our eyes.

At this moment, leaning on the forecastle bulwark, I saw below me Ned Land grappling the martingale in one hand, brandishing his terrible harpoon in the other, scarcely twenty feet from the motionless animal. Suddenly his arm straightened, and the harpoon was thrown; I heard the sonorous stroke of the weapon, which seemed to have struck a hard body. The electric light went out suddenly, and two enormous waterspouts broke over the bridge of the frigate, rushing like a torrent from stem to stern, overthrowing men, and breaking the lashing of the spars. A fearful shock followed, and, thrown over the rail without having time to stop myself, I fell into the sea.

CHAPTER 7

AN UNKNOWN SPECIES OF WHALE

THIS unexpected fall so stunned me that I have no clear recollection of my sensations at the time. I was at first drawn down to a depth of about twenty feet. I am a good swimmer (though without pretending to rival Byron or Edgar Poe, who were masters of the art), and in that plunge I did not lose my presence of mind. Two vigorous strokes brought me to the surface of the water. My first care was to look for the frigate. Had the crew seen me disappear? Had the *Abraham Lincoln* veered round? Would the captain put out a boat? Might I hope to be saved?

The darkness was intense. I caught a glimpse of a black mass disappearing in the east, its beacon-lights dying out in the distance. It was the frigate! I was lost.

"Help, help!" I shouted, swimming towards the *Abraham Lincoln* in desperation.

My clothes encumbered me; they seemed glued to my body, and paralyzed my movements.

I was sinking! I was suffocating!

"Help!"

This was my last cry. My mouth filled with water; I struggled against being drawn down the abyss. Suddenly my clothes were seized by a strong hand, and I felt myself quickly drawn up to the surface of the sea; and I heard, yes, I heard these words pronounced in my ear;—

"If master would be so good as to lean on my shoulder, master would swim with much greater ease."

I seized with one hand my faithful Conseil's arm.

"Is is you?" said I, "you?"

"Myself," answered Conseil; "and waiting master's orders."

"That shock threw you as well as me into the sea?"

"No; but being in my master's service, I followed him."

The worthy fellow thought that was but natural.

"And the frigate?" I asked.

"The frigate?" replied Conseil, turning on his back; "I think that master had better not count too much on her."

"You think so?"

"I say that, at the time I threw myself into the sea, I heard the men at the wheel say, 'The screw and the rudder are broken.' "

"Broken?"

"Yes, broken by the monster's teeth. It is the only injury the *Abraham Lincoln* has sustained. But it is a bad lookout for us,—she no longer answers her helm."

"Then we are lost!"

"Perhaps so," calmly answered Conseil. "However, we have still several hours before us, and one can do a good deal in some hours."

Conseil's imperturbable coolness set me up again. I swam more vigorously;

but, cramped by my clothes, which stuck to me like a leaden weight, I felt great difficulty in bearing up. Conseil saw this.

"Will master let me make a slit?" said he; and slipping an open knife under my clothes, he ripped them up from top to bottom very rapidly. Then he cleverly slipped them off me, while I swam for both of us.

Then I did the same for Conseil, and we continued to swim near to each other.

Nevertheless, our situation was no less terrible. Perhaps our disappearance had not been noticed; and if it had been, the frigate could not tack, being without its helm. Conseil argued on this supposition, and laid his plans accordingly. This phlegmatic boy was perfectly self-possessed. We then decided that, as our only chance of safety was being picked up by the *Abraham Lincoln's* boats, we ought to manage so as to wait for them as long as possible. I resolved then to husband our strength, so that both should not be exhausted at the same time; and this is how we managed: while one of us lay on our back, quite still, with arms crossed, and legs stregched out, the other would swim and push the other on in front. This towing business did not last more than ten minutes each; and relieving each other thus, we could swim on for some hours, perhaps till day-break. Poor chance! but hope is so firmly rooted in the heart of man! Moreover, there were two of us. Indeed I declare (though it may seem improbable) if I sought to destroy all hope, if I wished to despair, I could not.

The collision of the frigate with the cetacean had occurred about eleven o'clock the evening before. I reckoned then we should have eight hours to swim before sunrise,—an operation quite practicable if we relieved each other. The sea, very calm, was in our favor. Sometimes I tried to pierce the intense darkness that was only dispelled by the phosphorescence caused by our movements. I watched the luminous waves that broke over my hand, whose mirror-like surface was spotted with silvery rings. One might have said that we were in a bath of quicksilver.

Near one o'clock in the morning, I was seized with dreadful fatigue. My limbs stiffened under the strain of violent cramp. Conseil was obliged to keep me up, and our preservation devolved on him alone. I heard the poor boy pant; his breathing became short and hurried. I found that he could not keep up much longer.

"Leave me! leave me!" I said to him.

"Leave my master? never!" replied he. "I would drown first."

Just then the moon appeared through the fringes of a thick cloud that the wind was driving to the east. The surface of the sea glittered with its rays. This kindly light reanimated us. My head got better again. I looked at all the points of the horizon. I saw the frigate! She was five miles from us, and looked like a dark mass, hardly discernible. But no boats!

I would have cried out. But what good would it have been at such a distance! My swollen lips could utter no sounds. Conseil could articular some words, and I heard him repeat at intervals, "Help! help!"

Our movements were suspended for an instant; we listened. It might be only a singing in the ear, but it seemed to me as if a cry answered the cry from Conseil.

"Did you hear?" I murmured.

"Yes! yes!"

And Conseil gave one more despairing call.

This time there was no mistake! A human voice responded to ours! Was it the voice of another unfortunate creature, abandoned in the middle of the ocean, some other victim of the shock sustained by the vessel? Or rather was it a boat from the frigate, that was hailing us in the darkness?

Conseil made a last effort, and leaning on my shoulder, while I struck out in a despairing effort, he raised himself half out of the water, then fell back exhausted.

"What did you see?"

"I saw," murmured he,—"I saw—but do not talk—reserve all your strength!"

What had he seen? Then, I know not why, the thought of the monster came into my head for the first time! But that voice? The time is past for Jonahs to take refuge in whales' bellies! However, Conseil was towing me again. He raised his head sometimes, looked before us, and uttered a cry of recognition, which was responded to by a voice that came nearer and nearer. I scarcely heard it. My strength was exhausted; my fingers stiffened; my hand afforded me support no longer; my mouth, convulsively opening, filled with salt water. Cold crept over me. I raised my head for the last time, then I sank.

At this moment a hard body struck me. I clung to it: then I felt that I was being drawn up, that I was brought to the surface of the water, that my chest collapsed: I fainted.

It is certain that I soon came to, thanks to the vigorous rubbings that I received. I half opened my eyes.

"Conseil!" I murmured.

"Does master call me?" asked Conseil.

Just then, by the waning light of the moon, which was sinking down to the horizon, I saw a face which was not Conseil's, and which I immediately recognized.

"Ned!" I cried.

"The same, sir, who is seeking his prize!" replied the Canadian.

"Were you thrown into the sea by the shock of the frigate?"

"Yes, Professor; but more fortunate than you, I was able to find a footing almost directly upon a floating island."

"An island?"

"Or, more correctly speaking, on our gigantic narwhal."

"Explain yourself, Ned!"

"Only I soon found out why my harpoon had not entered its skin and was blunted."

"Why, Ned, why?"

"Because, Professor, that beast is made of sheet-iron."

The Canadian's last words produced a sudden revolution in my brain. I wriggled myself quickly to the top of the being, or object, half out of the water, which served us for a refuge. I kicked it. It was evidently a hard, impenetrable body, and not the soft substance that forms the bodies of the great marine mammalia. But this hard body might be a bony carapace, like that of the antediluvian animals; and I should be free to class this monster among amphibious reptiles, such as tortoises or alligators.

Well, no! the blackish back that supported me was smooth, polished, without scales. The blow produced a metallic sound; and incredible though it may be, it seemed, I might say, as if it was made of riveted plates.

There was no doubt about it! this monster, this natural phenomenon that had puzzled the learned world, and overthrown and misled the imagination of seamen of both hemispheres, was, it must be owned, a still more astonishing phenomenon, inasmuch as it was a simply human construction.

We had no time to lose, however. We were lying upon the back of a sort of submarine boat, which appeared (as far as I would judge) like a huge fish of steel. Ned Land's mind was made up on this point. Conseil and I could only agree with him.

Just then a bubbling began at the back of this strange thing (which was evidently propelled by a screw), and it began to move. We had only just time to seize hold of the upper part, which rose about seven feet out of the water, and happily its speed was not great.

"As long as it sails horizontally," muttered Ned Land, "I do not mind; but if it takes a fancy to dive, I would not give two straws for my life."

The Canadian might have said still less. It became really necessary to communicate with the beings, whatever they were, shut up inside the machine. I searched all over the outside for an aperture, a panel, or a man-hole, to use a technical expression; but the lines of the iron rivets, solidly driven into the joints of the iron plates, were clear and uniform. Besides, the moon disappeared then, and left us in total darkness.

At last this long night passed. My indistinct remembrance prevents my describing all the impressions it made. I can only recall one circumstance. During some lulls of the wind and sea, I fancied I heard several times vague sounds, a sort of fugitive harmony produced by distant words of command. What was then the mystery of this submarine craft of which the whole world vainly sought an explanation? What kind of beings existed in this strange boat? What mechanical agent caused its prodigious speed?

Daybreak appeared. The morning mists surrounded us, but they soon cleared off. I was about to examine the hull, which formed on deck a kind of horizontal platform, when I felt it gradually sinking.

"O, confound it!" cried Ned Land, kicking the resounding plate; "open, you inhospitable rascals!"

Happily the sinking movement ceased. Suddenly a noise, like iron works violently pushed aside, came from the interior of the boat. One iron plate was moved, a man appeared, uttered an odd cry, and disappeared immediately.

Some moments after, eight strong men with masked faces appeared noiselessly, and drew us down into their formidable machine.

CHAPTER 8

MOBILIS IN MOBILL

THIS forcible abduction, so roughly carried out, was accomplished with the rapidity of lightning. I shivered all over. Whom had we to deal with? No doubt some new sort of pirates, who explored the sea in their own way.

Hardly had the narrow panel closed upon me, when I was enveloped in darkness. My eyes, dazzled with the outer light, could distinguish nothing. I felt my naked feet cling to the rings of an iron ladder. Ned Land and Conseil, firmly seized, followed me. At the bottom of the ladder, a door opened, and shut after us immediately with a bang.

We were alone. Where, I could not say, hardly imagine. All was black, and such a dense black that, after some minutes, my eyes had not been able to discern even the faintest glimmer.

Meanwhile, Ned Land, furious at these proceedings, gave free vent to his indignation.

"Confound it!" cried he, "here are people who come up to the Scotch for hospitality. They only just miss being cannibals. I should not be surprised at it, but I declare that they shall not eat me without my protesting."

"Calm yourself, friend Ned, calm yourself," replied Conseil, quietly. "Do not cry out before you are hurt. We are not quite done for yet."

"Not quite," sharply replied the Canadian, "but pretty near, at all events. Things look black. Happily my bowie-knife I have still, and I can always see well enough to use it. The first of these pirates who lays a hand on me—"

"Do not excite yourself, Ned," I said to the harpooner, "and do not compromise us by useless violence. Who knows that they will not listen to us? Let us rather try to find out where we are."

I groped about. In five steps I came to an iron wall, made of plates bolted together. Then turning back I struck against a wooden table, near which were ranged several stools. The boards of this prison were concealed under a thick mat of phormium, which deadened the noise of the feet. The bare walls revealed no trace of window or door. Conseil, going round the reverse way, met me, and we went back to the middle of the cabin, which measured about twenty feet by ten. As to its height, Ned Land, in spite of his own great height, could not measure it.

Half an hour had already passed without our situation being bettered, when the dense darkness suddenly gave way to extreme light. Our prison was suddenly lighted, that is to say, it became filled with a luminous matter, so strong that I could not bear it at first. In its whiteness and intensity I recognized that electric light which played round the submarine boat like a magnificent phenomenon of phosphorescence. After shutting my eyes involuntarily, I opened them and saw that this luminous agent came from a half-globe, unpolished, placed in the roof of the cabin.

"At last one can see," cried Ned Land, who, knife in hand, stood on the defensive.

"Yes," said I; "but we are still in the dark about ourselves."

"Let master have patience," said the imperturbable Conseil.

The sudden lighting of the cabin enabled me to examine it minutely. It only contained a table and five stools. The invisible door might be hermetically sealed. No noise was heard. All seemed dead in the interior of this boat. Did it move, did it float on the surface of the ocean, or did it dive into its depths? I could not guess.

A noise of bolts was now heard, the door opened, and two men appeared.

One was short, very muscular, broad-shouldered, with robust limbs, strong head, an abundance of black hair, thick mustache, a quick penetrating look, and the vivacity which characterizes the population of Southern France.

The second stranger merits a more detailed description. A disciple of Gratiolet or Engel would have read his face like an open book. I made out his prevailing qualities directly: self-confidence,—because his head was well set on his shoulders, and his black eyes looked around with cold assurance; calmness,—for his skin, rather pale, showed his coolness of blood; energy,—evinced by the rapid contraction of his lofty brows; and courage,—because his deep breathing denoted great power of lungs.

Whether this person was thirty-five or fifty years of age, I could not say. He was tall, had a large forehead, straight nose, a clearly cut mouth, beautiful teeth, with fine taper hands, indicative of a highly nervous temperament. This man was certainly the most admirable specimen I had ever met. One particular feature was his eyes, rather far from each other, and which could take in nearly a quarter of the horizon at once.

This faculty—(I verified it later)—gave him a range of vision far superior to Ned Land's. When this stranger fixed upon an object, his eyebrows met, his large eyelids closed around so as to contract the range of his vision, and he looked as if he magnified the objects lessened by distance, as if he pierced those sheets of water so opaque to our eyes, and as if he read the very depths of the seas.

The two strangers, with caps made from the fur of the sea otter and shod with sea boots of seals' skin, were dressed in clothes of a particular texture, which allowed free movement of the limbs. The taller of the two, evidently the chief on board, examined us with great attention, without saying a word: then turning to his companion, talked with him in an unknown tongue. It was a sonorous, harmonious, and flexible dialect, the vowels seeming to admit of very varied accentuation.

The other replied by a shake of the head, and added two or three perfectly incomprehensible words. Then he seemed to question me by a look.

I replied in good French that I did not know his language; but he seemed not to understand me, and my situation became more embarrassing.

"If master were to tell our story," said Conseil, "perhaps these gentlemen may understand some words."

I began to tell our adventures, articulating each syllable clearly, and without omitting one single detail. I announced our names and rank, introducing in person Professor Aronnax, his servant Conseil, and master Ned Land, the harpooner.

The man with the soft calm eyes listened to me quietly, even politely, and with extreme attention; but nothing in his countenance indicated that he had understood my story. When I finished he said not a word.

There remained one resource, to speak English. Perhaps they would know this almost universal language. I knew it, as well as the German language,—well enough to read it fluently, but not to speak it correctly. But, anyhow, we must make ourselves understood.

"Go on in your turn," I said to the harpooner; "speak your best Anglo-Saxon, and try to do better than I."

Ned did not beg off, and recommenced our story.

To his great disgust, the harpooner did not seem to have made himself more intelligible than I had. Our visitors did not stir. They evidently understood neither the language of Arago nor of Faraday.

Very much embarrassed, after having vainly exhausted our philological resources, I knew not what part to take, when Conseil said,—

"If master will permit me, I will relate it in German."

But in spite of the elegant turns and good accent of the narrator, the German language had no success. At last, nonplussed, I tried to remember my first lessons, and to narrate our adventures in Latin, but with no better success. This last attempt being of no avail, the two strangers exchanged some words in their unknown language, and retired.

The door shut.

"It is an infamous shame," cried Ned Land, who broke out for the twentieth time; "we speak to those rogues in French, English, German, and Latin, and not one of them has the politeness to answer!"

"Calm yourself," I said to the impetuous Ned, "anger will do no good."

"But do you see, Professor," replied our irascible companion, "that we shall absolutely die of hunger in this iron cage?"

"Bah," said Conseil philosophically; "we can hold out some time yet."

"My friends," I said, "we must not despair. We have been worse off than this. Do me the favor to wait a little before forming an opinion upon the commander and crew of this boat."

"My opinion is formed," replied Ned Land sharply. "They are rascals."

"Good! and from what country?"

"From the land of rogues!"

"My brave Ned, that country is not clearly indicated on the map of the world; but I admit that the nationality of the two strangers is hard to determine. Neither English, French, nor German, that is quite certain. However, I am inclined to think that the commander and his companion were born in low latitudes. There is southern blood in them. But I cannot decide by their appearance whether they are Spaniards, Turks, Arabians, or Indians. As to their language, it is quite incomprehensible."

"There is the disadvantage of not knowing all languages," said Conseil, "or the disadvantage of not having one universal language."

As he said these words, the door opened. A steward entered. He brought us clothes, coats and trousers, made of a stuff I did not know. I hastened to dress myself, and my companions followed my example. During that time, the steward—dumb, perhaps deaf—had arranged the table, and laid three plates.

"This is something like," said Conseil.

"Bah," said the rancorous harpooner, "what do you suppose they eat here? Tortoise liver, filleted shark, and beefsteaks from sea-dogs."

"We shall see," said Conseil.

The dishes, of bell metal, were placed on the table, and we took our places. Undoubtedly we had to do with civilized people, and had it not been for the electric light which flooded us, I could have fancied I was in the dining-room of the Adelphi Hotel at Liverpool, or at the Grand Hotel in Paris. I must say, however, that there was neither bread nor wine. The water was fresh and clear, but it was water, and did not suit Ned Land's taste. Amongst the dishes which were brought to us, I recognized several fish delicately dressed; but of some, although excellent, I could give no opinion, neither could I tell to what kingdom they belonged, whether animal or vegetable. As to the dinner service, it was elegant, and in perfect taste. Each utensil, spoon, fork, knife, plate, had a letter engraved on it, with a motto above it, of which this is an exact fac-simile.

MOBILIS IN MOBILI.

N.

The two strangers...examined us with great attention.

The letter N was no doubt the initial of the name of the enigmatical person, who commanded at the bottom of the seas.

Ned and Conseil did not reflect much. They devoured the food, and I did likewise. I was, besides, reassured as to our fate; and it seemed evident that our hosts would not let us die of want.

However, everything has an end, everything passes away, even the hunger of people who have not eaten for fifteen hours. Our appetites satisfied, we felt overcome with sleep.

"Faith! I shall sleep well," said Conseil.

"So shall I," replied Ned Land.

My two companions stretched themselves on the cabin carpet, and were soon sound asleep. For my own part, too many thoughts crowded my brain, too many insoluble questions pressed upon me, too many fancies kept my eyes half open. Where were we? What strange power carried us on? I felt—or rather fancied I felt—the machine sinking down to the lowest beds of the sea. Dreadful nightmares beset me; I saw in these mysterious asylums a world of unknown animals, amongst which this submarine boat seemed to be of the same kind, living, moving, and formidable as they. Then my brain grew calmer, my imagination wandered into vague unconsciousness, and I soon fell into a deep sleep.

CHAPTER 9

NED LAND'S TEMPERS

How long we slept I do not know; but our sleep must have lasted long, for it rested us completely from our fatigues. I woke first. My companions had not moved, and were still stretched in their corner.

Hardly roused from my somewhat hard couch, I felt my brain freed, my mind clear. I then began an attentive examination of our cell. Nothing was changed inside. The prison was still a prison; the prisoners, prisoners. However, the steward, during our sleep, had cleared the table. I breathed with difficulty. The heavy air seemed to oppress my lungs. Although the cell was large, we had evidently consumed a great part of the oxygen that it contained. Indeed, each man consumes, in one hour, the oxygen contained in more than 176 pints of air, and this air, charged (as then) with a nearly equal quantity of carbonic acid, becomes unbreathable.

It became necessary to renew the atmosphere of our prison, and no doubt the whole in the submarine boat. That gave rise to a question in my mind. How would the commander of this floating dwelling-place proceed? Would he obtain air by chemical means, in getting by heat the oxygen contained in chlorate of potass, and in absorbing carbonic acid by caustic potash? Or, a more convenient, economical, and consequently more probable alternative, would he be satisfied to rise and take breath at the surface of the water, like a cetacean, and so renew for twenty-four hours the atmospheric provision?

In fact, I was already obliged to increase my respirations to eke out of this cell the little oxygen it contained, when suddenly I was refreshed by a current of pure air, and perfumed with saline emanations. It was an invigorating sea breeze, charged with iodine. I opened my mouth wide, and my lungs saturated themselves with fresh particles.

At the same time I felt the boat rolling. The iron-plated monster had evidently just risen to the surface of the ocean to breathe, after the fashion of whales. I found out from that the mode of ventilating the boat.

When I had inhaled this air freely, I sought the conduit-pipe, which conveyed to us the beneficial whiff, and I was not long in finding it. Above the door was a ventilator, through which volumes of fresh air renewed the impoverished atmosphere of the cell.

I was making my observations, when Ned and Conseil awoke almost at the same time, under the influence of this reviving air. They rubbed their eyes, stretched themselves, and were on their feet in an instant.

"Did master sleep well?" asked Conseil, with his usual politeness.

"Very well, my brave boy. And you, Mr. Land?"

"Soundly, Professor. But I don't know if I am right or not; there seems to be a sea-breeze!"

A seaman could not be mistaken, and I told the Canadian all that had passed during his sleep.

"Good!" said he; "that accounts for those roarings we heard when the supposed narwhal sighted the *Abraham Lincoln*."

"Quite so, Master Land; it was taking breath."

"Only, Mr. Aronnax, I have no idea what o'clock it is, unless it is dinner-time."

"Dinner-time! my good fellow? Say rather breakfast-time, for we certainly have begun another day."

"So," said Conseil, "we have slept twenty-four hours?"

"That is my opinion."

"I will not contradict you," replied Ned Land. "But dinner or breakfast, the steward will be welcome, whichever he brings."

"Master Land, we must conform to the rules on board, and I suppose our appetites are in advance of the dinner-hour."

"That is just like you, friend Conseil," said Ned, impatiently. "You are never out of temper, always calm; you would return thanks before grace, and die of hunger rather than complain!"

Time was getting on, and we were fearfully hungry; and this time the steward did not appear. It was rather too long to leave us, if they really had good intentions towards us. Ned Land, tormented by the cravings of hunger, got still more angry; and notwithstanding his promise, I dreaded an explosion when he found himself with one of the crew.

For two hours more, Ned Land's temper increased; he cried, he shouted, but in vain. The walls were deaf. There was no sound to be heard in the boat: all was still as death. It did not move, for I should have felt the trembling motion of the hull under the influence of the screw. Plunged in the depths of the waters, it belonged no longer to earth:—this silence was dreadful.

I felt terrified, Conseil was calm, Ned Land roared.

Just then a noise was heard outside. Steps sounded on the metal flags. The locks were turned, the door opened, and the steward appeared.

Before I could rush forward to stop him, the Canadian had thrown him down, and held him by the throat. The steward was choking under the grip of his powerful hand.

Conseil was already trying to unclasp the harpooner's hand from his half-suffocated victim, and I was going to fly to the rescue, when suddenly I was nailed to the spot by hearing these words in French,—

"Be quiet, Master Land; and you, Professor, will you be so good as to listen to me?"

CHAPTER 10

THE MAN OF THE SEAS

It was the commander of the vessel who thus spoke.

At these words, Ned Land rose suddenly. The steward, nearly strangled, tottered out on a sign from his master; but such was the power of the commander on board, that not a gesture betrayed the resentment which this man must have felt towards the Canadian. Conseil interested in spite of himself, I stupefied, awaited in silence the result of this scene.

The commander, leaning against a corner of the table with his arms folded, scanned us with profound attention. Did he hesitate to speak? Did he regret the words which he had just spoken in French? One might almost think so.

After some moments of silence, which not one of us dreamed of breaking, "Gentlemen," said he, in a calm and penetrating voice, "I speak French, English, German, and Latin equally well. I could, therefore, have answered you at our first interview, but I wished to know you first, then to reflect. The story told by each one, entirely agreeing in the main points, convinced me of your identity. I know now that chance has brought before me M. Pierre Aronnax, Professor of Natural History at the Museum of Paris, intrusted with a scientific mission abroad; Conseil, his servant; and Ned Land, of Canadian origin, harpooner on board the frigate *Abraham Lincoln* of the navy of the United States of America."

I bowed assent. It was not a question that the commander put to me. Therefore there was no answer to be made. This man expressed himself with perfect ease, without any accent. His sentences were well turned, his words clear, and his fluency of speech remarkable. Yet, I did not recognize in him a fellow-countryman.

He continued the conversation in these terms:—

"You have doubtless thought, sir, that I have delayed long in paying you this second visit. The reason is that, your identity recognized, I wished to weigh maturely what part to act towards you. I have hesitated much. Most annoying circumstances have brought you into the presence of a man who has broken all the ties of humanity. You have come to trouble my existence."

"Unintentionally!" said I.

"Unintentionally?" replied the stranger, raising his voice a little; "was it unintentionally that the *Abraham Lincoln* pursued me all over the seas? Was it unintentionally that you took passage in this frigate? Was it unintentionally that

your cannon-balls rebounded off the plating of my vessel? Was it unintentionally that Mr. Ned Land struck me with his harpoon?''

I detected a restrained irritation in these words. But to these recriminations I had a very natural answer to make, and I made it.

''Sir,'' said I, ''no doubt you are ignorant of the discussions which have taken place concerning you in America and Europe. You do not know that divers accidents, caused by collisions with your submarine machine, have excited public feeling in the two continents. I omit the hypotheses without number by which it was sought to explain the inexplicable phenomenon of which you alone possess the secret. But you must understand that, in pursuing you over the high seas of the Pacific, the *Abraham Lincoln* believed itself to be chasing some powerful sea-monster, of which it was necessary to rid the ocean at any price.''

A half-smile curled the lips of the commander: then, in a calmer tone:—

''M. Aronnax,'' he replied, ''dare you affirm that your frigate would not as soon have pursued and cannonaded a submarine boat as a monster?''

This question embarrassed me, for certainly Captain Farragut might not have hesitated. He might have thought it his duty to destroy a contrivance of this kind, as he would a gigantic narwhal.

''You understand then, sir,'' continued the stranger, ''that I have the right to treat you as enemies?''

I answered nothing, purposely. For what good would it be to discuss such a proposition, when force could destroy the best arguments?

''I have hesitated for some time,'' continued the commander; ''nothing obliged me to show you hospitality. If I chose to separate myself from you, I should have no interest in seeing you again; I could place you upon the deck of this vessel which has served you as a refuge, I could sink beneath the waters, and forget that you had ever existed. Would not that be my right?''

''It might be the right of a savage,'' I answered, ''but not that of a civilized men.''

''Professor,'' replied the commander quickly, ''I am not what you call a civilized man! I have done with society entirely, for reasons which I alone have the right of appreciating. I do not therefore obey its laws, and I desire you never to allude to them before me again!''

This was said plainly. A flash of anger and disdain kindled in the eyes of the Unknown, and I had a glimpse of a terrible past in the life of this man. Not only had he put himself beyond the pale of human laws, but he had made himself independent of them, free in the strictest acceptation of the word, quite beyond their reach! Who then would dare to pursue him at the bottom of the sea, when, on its surface, he defied all attempts made against him? What vessel could resist the shock of his submarine monitor? What cuirass, however thick, could withstand the blows of his spur? No man could demand from him an account of his actions; God, if he believed in one,—his conscience, if he had one,—were the sole judges to whom he was answerable.

These reflections crossed my mind rapidly, whilst the stranger personage was silent, absorbed, and as if wrapped up in himself. I regarded him with fear mingled with interest, as, doubtless, Œdipus regarded the Sphinx.

After rather a long silence, the commander resumed the conversation.

''I have hesitated,'' said he, ''but I have thought that my interest might be reconciled with that pity to which every human being has a right. You will remain on board my vessel, since fate has cast you there. You will be free; and in exchange for this liberty, I shall only impose one single condition. Your word of honor to submit to it will suffice."

"Speak, sir," I answered. "I suppose this condition is one which a man of honor may accept?"

"Yes, sir; it is this. It is possible that certain events, unforeseen, may oblige me to consign you to your cabins for some hours or some days, as the case may be. As I desire never to use violence, I expect from you, more than all the others, a passive obedience. In thus acting, I take all the responsibility: I acquit you entirely, for I make it an impossibility for you to see what ought not to be seen. Do you accept this condition?"

Then things took place on board which, to say the least, were singular, and which ought not to be seen by people who were not placed beyond the pale of social laws. Amongst the surprises which the future was preparing for me, this might not be the least.

"We accept," I answered; "only I will ask your permission, sir, to address one question to you,—one only."

"Speak, sir."

"You said that we should be free on board."

"Entirely."

"I ask you, then, what you mean by this liberty?"

"Just the liberty to go, to come, to see, to observe even all that passes here,—save under rare circumstances,—the liberty, in short, which we enjoy ourselves, my companions and I."

It was evident that we did not understand one another.

"Pardon me, sir," I resumed, "but this liberty is only what every prisoner has of pacing his prison. It cannot suffice us."

"It must suffice you, however."

"What! we must renounce forever seeing our country, our friends, our relations again?"

"Yes, sir. But to renounce that unendurable worldly yoke which men believe to be liberty is not perhaps so painful as you think."

"Well," exclaimed Ned Land, "never will I give my word of honor not to try to escape."

"I did not ask you for your word of honor, Master Land," answered the commander, coldly.

"Sir," I replied, beginning to get angry in spite of myself, "you abuse your situation towards us; it is cruelty."

"No, sir, it is clemency. You are my prisoners of war. I keep you, when I could, by a word, plunge you into the depths of the ocean. You attacked me. You came to surprise a secret which no man in the world must penetrate,—the secret of my whole existence. And you think that I am going to send you back to that world which must know me no more? Never! In retaining you, it is not you whom I guard,—it is myself."

These words indicated a resolution taken on the part of the commander, against which no arguments would prevail.

"So, sir," I rejoined, "you give us simply the choice between life and death?"

"Simply."

"My friends," said I, "to a question thus put, there is nothing to answer. But no word of honor binds us to the master of this vessel."

"None, sir," answered the Unknown.

Then, in a gentler tone, he continued:—

"Now, permit me to finish what I have to say to you. I know you, M. Aronnax. You and your companions will not, perhaps, have so much to complain of in the chance which has bound you to my fate. You will find amongst the books which are my favorite study the work which you have published on 'the depths of the sea.' I have often read it. You have carried your work as far as terrestrial science permitted you. But you do not know all,—you have not seen all. Let me tell you then, Professor, that you will not regret the time passed on board my vessel. You are going to visit the land of marvels."

These words of the commander had a great effect upon me. I cannot deny it. My weak point was touched; and I forgot, for a moment, that the contemplation of these sublime subjects was not worth the loss of liberty. Besides, I trusted to the future to decide this grave question. So I contented myself with saying,—

"By what name ought I to address you?"

"Sir," replied the commander, "I am nothing to you but Captain Nemo; and you and your companions are nothing to me but the passengers of the *Nautilus*."

Captain Nemo called. A steward appeared. The captain gave him his orders in that strange language which I did not understand. Then, turning towards the Canadian and Conseil:—

"A repast awaits you in your cabin," said he. "Be so good as to follow this man."

"And now, M. Aronnax, our breakfast is ready. Permit me to lead the way."

"I am at your service, Captain."

I followed Captain Nemo; and as soon as I had passed through the door, I found myself in a kind of passage lighted by electricity, similar to the waist of a ship. After we had proceeded a dozen yards, a second door opened before me.

I then entered a dining room, decorated and furnished in severe taste. High oaken sideboards, inlaid with ebony, stood at the two extremities of the room, and upon their shelves glittered china, porcelain, and glass of inestimable value. The plate on the table sparkled in the rays which the luminous ceiling shed around while the light was tempered and softened by exquisite paintings.

In the centre of the room was a table richly laid out. Captain Nemo indicated the place I was to occupy.

The breakfast consisted of a certain number of dishes, the contents of which were furnished by the sea alone; and I was ignorant of the nature and mode of preparation of some of them. I acknowledged that they were good, but they had a peculiar flavor, which I easily became accustomed to. These different aliments appeared to me to be rich in phosphorus, and I thought they must have a marine origin.

Captain Nemo looked at me. I asked him no questions, but he guessed my thoughts, and answered of his own accord the questions which I was burning to address to him.

"The greater part of these dishes are unknown to you," he said to me. "However, you may partake of them without fear. They are wholesome and nourishing. For a long time I have renounced the food of the earth, and I am never ill now. My crew, who are healthy, are fed on the same food."

"So," said I, "all these eatables are the produce of the sea?"

"Yes, Professor, the sea supplies all my wants. Sometimes I cast my nets in tow, and I draw them in ready to break. Sometimes I hunt in the midst of this element, which appears to be inaccessible to man, and quarry the game which dwells in my submarine forests. My flocks, like those of Neptune's old shepherds, graze fearlessly in the immense prairies of the ocean. I have a vast property there, which I cultivate myself, and which is always sown by the hand of the Creator of all things."

"I can understand perfectly, sir, that your nets furnish excellent fish for your table; I can understand also that you hunt aquatic game in your submarine forests; but I cannot understand at all how a particle of meat, no matter how small, can figure in your bill of fare."

"This, which you believe to be meat, Professor, is nothing else than fillet of turtle. Here are also some dolphins' livers, which you take to be ragout of pork. My cook is a clever fellow, who excels in dressing these various products of the ocean. Taste all these dishes. Here is a preserve of holothuria, which a Malay would declare to be unrivalled in the world; here is a cream, of which the milk has been furnished by the cetacea, and the sugar by the great fucus of the North Sea; and lastly, permit me to offer you some preserve of anemones, which is equal to that of the most delicious fruits."

I tasted, more from curiosity than as a connoisseur, whilst Captain Nemo enchanted me with his extraordinary stories.

"You like the sea, Captain?"

"Yes; I love it! The sea is everything. It covers seven tenths of the terrestrial globe. Its breath is pure and healthy. It is an immense desert, where man is never lonely, for he feels life stirring on all sides. The sea is only the embodiment of a supernatural and wonderful existence. It is nothing but love and emotion; it is the 'Living Infinite,' as one of your poets has said. In fact, Professor, Nature manifests herself in it by her three kingdoms, mineral, vegetable, and animal. The sea is the vast reservoir of Nature. The globe began with sea, so to speak; and who knows if it will not end with it? In it is supreme tranquillity. The sea does not belong to despots. Upon its surface men can still exercise unjust laws, fight, tear one another to pieces, and be carried away with terrestrial horrors. But at thirty feet below its level, their reign ceases, their influence is quenched, and their power disappears. Ah! sir, live—live in the bosom of the waters! There only is independence! There I recognize no masters! There I am free!"

Captain Nemo suddenly became silent in the midst of this enthusiasm, by which he was quite carried away. For a few moments he paced up and down, much agitated. Then he became more calm, regained his accustomed coldness of expression, and turning towards me:—

"Now, Professor," said he, "if you wish to go over the *Nautilus,* I am at your service."

Captain Nemo rose. I followed him. A double door, contrived at the back of the dining-room, opened, and I entered a room equal in dimensions to that which I had just quitted.

It was a library. High pieces of furniture, of black violet ebony inlaid with brass, supported upon their wide shelves a great number of books uniformly bound. They followed the shape of the room, terminating at the lower part in huge divans, covered with brown leather, which were curved, to afford the greatest comfort. Light movable desks, made to slide in and out at will, allowed one to rest one's book while reading. In the centre stood an immense table, covered with pamphlets, amongst which were some newspapers, already of old date. The electric light flooded everything; it was shed from four unpolished globes half sunk in the volutes of the ceiling. I looked with real admiration at this room, so ingeniously fitted up, and I could scarcely believe my eyes.

"Captain Nemo," said I to my host, who had just thrown himself on one of the divans, "this is a library which would do honor to more than one of the continental palaces, and I am absolutely astounded when I consider that it can follow you to the bottom of the seas."

"Where could one find greater solitude of silence, Professor?" replied Captain Nemo. "Did your study in the Museum afford you such perfect quiet?"

"No, sir; and I must confess that it is a very poor one after yours. You must have six or seven thousand volumes here."

"Twelve thousand, M. Aronnax. These are the only ties which bind me to the earth. But I had done with the world on the day when my *Nautilus* plunged for the first time beneath the waters. That day I bought my last volumes, my last pamphlets, my last papers, and from that time I wish to think that men no longer think or write. These books, Professor, are at your service besides, and you can make use of them freely."

I thanked Captain Nemo, and went up to the shelves of the library. Works on science, morals, and literature abounded in every language; but I did not see one single work on political economy; that subject appeared to be strictly proscribed. Strange to say, all these books were irregularly arranged, in whatever language they were written; and this medley proved that the captain of the *Nautilus* must have read indiscriminately the books which he took up by chance.

"Sir," said I to the captain, "I thank you for having placed this library at my disposal. It contains treasures of science, and I shall profit by them."

"This room is not only a library," said Captain Nemo, "it is also a smoking-room."

"A smoking-room!" I cried. "Then one may smoke on board?"

"Certainly."

"Then, sir, I am forced to believe that you have kept up a communication with Havannah."

"Not any," answered the captain. "Accept this cigar, M. Aronnax; and though it does not come from Havannah, you will be pleased with it, if you are a connoisseur."

I took the cigar which was offered me; its shape recalled the London ones, but it seemed to be made of leaves of gold. I lighted it at a little brazier, which was supported upon an elegant bronze stem, and drew the first whiffs with the delight of a lover of smoking who has not smoked for two days.

"It is excellent," said I, "but it is not tobacco."

"No!" answered the captain, "this tobacco comes neither from Havannah nor from the East. It is a kind of sea-weed, rich in nicotine, with which the sea provides me, but somewhat sparingly."

At that moment Captain Nemo opened a door which stood opposite to that by which I had entered the library, and I passed into an immense drawing-room splendidly lighted.

It was a vast four-sided room, thirty feet long, eighteen wide, and fifteen high. A luminous ceiling, decorated with light arabesques, shed a soft clear light over all the marvels accumulated in this museum. For it was in fact a museum, in which an intelligent and prodigal hand had gathered all the treasures of nature and art, with the artistic confusion which distinguishes a painter's studio. Thirty first-rate pictures, uniformly framed, separated by bright drapery, ornamented the walls, which were hung with tapestry of severe design. I saw works of great value, the greater part of which I had admired in the special collections of Europe, and in the exhibitions of paintings. The several schools of the old masters were represented by a Madonna of Raphael, a Virgin of Leonardo da Vinci, a nymph of Correggio, a woman of Titian, an Adoration of Veronese, an Assumption of Murillo, a portrait of Holbein, a monk of Velasquez, a martyr of Ribeira, a fair of Rubens, two Flemish landscapes of Teniers, three little "genre" pictures of Gérard Dow, Metsu, and Paul Potter, two specimens of Géricault and Prudhon, and some sea-pieces of Backhuysen and Vernet. Amongst the works of modern painters were pictures with the signatures of Delacroix, Ingres, Decamp, Troyon, Meissonnier, Daubigny, etc.; and some admirable statues in marble and bronze, after the finest antique models, stood upon pedestals in the corners of this magnificent museum. Amazement, as the captain of the *Nautilus* had predicted, had already begun to take possession of me.

"Professor," said this strange man, "you must excuse the unceremonious way in which I receive you, and the disorder of this room."

"Sir," I answered, "without seeking to know who you are, I recognize in you an artist."

"An amateur, nothing more, sir. Formerly I loved to collect these beautiful works created by the hand of man. I sought them greedily and ferreted them out indefatigably, and I have been able to bring together some objects of great value. These are my last souvenirs of that world which is dead to me. In my eyes, your modern artists are already old: they have two or three thousand years of existence; I confound them in my own mind. Masters have no age."

"And these musicians?" said I, pointing out some works of Weber, Rossini, Mozart, Beethoven, Haydn, Meyerbeer, Hérold, Wagner, Auber, Gounod, and a number of others scattered over a large model piano organ which occupied one of the panels of the drawing-room.

"These musicians," replied Captain Nemo, "are the contemporaries of Orpheus; for in the memory of the dead all chronological differences are effaced; and I am dead, Professor; as much dead as those of your friends who are sleeping six feet under the earth!"

Captain Nemo was silent, and seemed lost in a profound revery. I contemplated him with deep interest, analyzing in silence the strange expression of his countenance. Leaning on his elbow against an angle of a costly mosaic table, he no longer saw me,—he had forgotten my presence.

I did not disturb this revery, and continued my observation of the curiosities which enriched this drawing-room.

Under elegant glass cases, fixed by copper rivets, were classed and labelled the most precious productions of the sea which had ever been presented to the eye of a naturalist. My delight as a professor may be conceived.

The division containing the zoophytes presented the most curious specimens of the two groups of polypi and echinodermes. In the first group, the tubipores, were gorgones arranged like a fan, soft sponges of Syria, ises of the Moluccas, pennatules, an admirable virgularia of the Norwegian seas, variegated umbellulairæ, alcyonariæ, a whole series of madrepores, which my master Milne-Edwards has so cleverly classified, amongst which I remarked some wonderful flabellinæ, oculinæ of the island of Bourbon, the "Neptune's car" of the Antilles, superb varieties of corals, in short, every species of those curious polypi of which entire islands are formed, which will one day become continents. Of the

"You must have six or seven thousand volumes here."

echinodermes, remarkable for their coating of spines, asteri, sea-stars, pantacrinæ, comatules, astérophons, echini, holothuri, etc., represented individually a complete collection of this group.

A somewhat nervous conchyliologist would certainly have fainted before other more numerous cases, in which were classified the specimens of molluscs. It was a collection of inestimable value, which time fails me to describe minutely. Amongst these specimens, I will quote from memory only the elegant royal hammer-fish of the Indian Ocean, whose regular white spots stood out brightly on a red and brown ground, an imperial spondyle, bright colored, bristling with spines, a rare specimen in the European museums (I estimated its value at not less than £ 1,000); a common hammer-fish of the seas of New Holland, which is only procured with difficulty; exotic buccardia of Senegal; fragile white bivalve shells, which a breath might shatter like a soap-bubble; several varieties of the aspirgillum of Java, a kind of calcareous tube, edged with leafy folds, and much debated by amateurs; a whole series of trochi, some a greenish-yellow, found in the American seas, others a reddish-brown, natives of Australian waters; others from the Gulf of Mexico, remarkable for their imbricated shell; stellari found in the Southern Seas; and last, the rarest of all, the magnificent spur of New Zealand; and every description of delicate and fragile shells to which science has given appropriate names.

Apart, in separate compartments, were spread out chaplets of pearls of the greatest beauty, which reflected the electric light in little sparks of fire; pink pearls, torn from the pinna-marina of the Red Sea; green pearls of the haliotyde iris; yellow, blue, and black pearls, the curious productions of the divers molluscs of every ocean, and certain mussels of the watercourses of the North; lastly, several specimens of inestimable value which had been gathered from the rarest pintadines. Some of these pearls were larger than a pigeon's egg, and were worth as much, and more than that which the traveller Tavernier sold to the Shah of Persia for three millions, and surpassed the one in the possession of the Imaum of Muscat, which I had believed to be unrivalled in the world.

Therefore, to estimate the value of this collection was simply impossible. Captain Nemo must have expended millions in the acquirement of these various specimens, and I was thinking what source he could have drawn from, to have been able thus to gratify his fancy for collecting, when I was interrupted by these words:—

"You are examining my shells, Professor? Unquestionably they must be interesting to a naturalist; but for me they have a far greater charm, for I have collected them all with my own hand, and there is not a sea on the face of the globe which has escaped my researches."

"I can understand, Captain, the delight of wandering about in the midst of such riches. You are one of those who have collected their treasures themselves. No museum in Europe possesses such a collection of the produce of the ocean. But if I exhaust all my admiration upon it, I shall have none left for the vessel which carries it. I do not wish to pry into your secrets; but I must confess that this *Nautilus,* with the motive power which is confined in it, the contrivances which enable it to be worked, the powerful agent which propels it, all excite my curiosity to the highest pitch. I see suspended on the walls of this room instruments of whose use I am ignorant."

"You will find these same instruments in my own room, Professor, where I shall have much pleasure in explaining their use to you. But first come and inspect the cabin which is set apart for your own use. You must see how you will be accommodated on board the *Nautilus*."

I followed Captain Nemo, who, by one of the doors opening from each panel of the drawing-room, regained the waist. He conducted me towards the bow, and there I found, not a cabin, but an elegant room, with a bed, dressing-table, and several other pieces of furniture.

I could only thank my host.

"Your room adjoins mine," said he, opening a door, "and mine opens into the drawing-room that we have just quitted."

I entered the captain's room: it had a severe, almost a monkish, aspect. A small iron bedstead, a table, some articles for the toilet; the whole lighted by a skylight. No comforts, the strictest necessaries only.

Captain Nemo pointed to a seat.

"Be so good as to sit down," he said. I seated myself, and he began thus:—

CHAPTER 11

ALL BY ELECTRICITY

"SIR," said Captain Nemo, showing me the instruments hanging on the walls of his room, "here are the contrivances required for the navigation of the *Nautilus*. Here, as in the drawing-room, I have them always under my eyes, and they indicate my position and exact direction in the middle of the ocean. Some are known to you, such as the thermometer, which gives the internal temperature of the *Nautilus;* the barometer, which indicates the weight of the air and foretells the changes of the weather; the hygrometer, which marks the dryness of the atmosphere; the storm-glass, the contents of which, by decomposing, announce the approach of tempests; the compass, which guides my course; the sextant, which shows the latitude by the altitude of the sun; chronometers, by which I calculate the longitude; and glasses for day and night, which I use to examine the points of the horizon, when the *Nautilus* rises to the surface of the waves."

"These are the usual nautical instruments," I replied, "and I know the use of them. But these others, no doubt, answer to the particular requirements of the *Nautilus*. This dial with the movable needle is a manometer, is it not?"

"It is actually a manometer. But by communication with the water, whose external pressure it indicates, it gives our depth at the same time."

"And these other instruments, the use of which I cannot guess?"

"Here, Professor, I ought to give you some explanations. Will you be kind enough to listen to me?"

He was silent for a few moments, then he said:—

"There is a powerful agent, obedient, rapid, easy, which conforms to every use, and reigns supreme on board my vessel. Everything is done by means of it. It lights it, warms it, and is the soul of my mechanical apparatus. This agent is electricity."

"Electricity?" I cried in surprise.

"Yes, sir."

"Nevertheless, Captain, you possess an extreme rapidity of movement, which does not agree well with the power of electricity. Until now its dynamic force has remained under restraint, and has only been able to produce a small amount of power."

"Professor," said Captain Nemo, "my electricity is not everybody's. You know what sea-water is composed of. In a thousand grammes are found 96½ per cent of water, and about 2⅔ per cent of chloride of sodium; then, in a smaller quantity, chlorides of magnesium and of potassium, bromide of magnesium, sulphate of magnesia, sulphate and carbonate of lime. You see, then, that chloride of sodium forms a large part of it. So it is this sodium that I extract from sea-water, and of which I compose my ingredients. I owe all to the ocean; it produces electricity, and electricity gives heat, light, motion, and, in a word, life to the *Nautilus*."

"But not the air you breathe?"

"O, I could manufacture the air necessary for my consumption, but it is useless, because I go up to the surface of the water when I please. However, if electricity does not furnish me with air to breathe, it works at least the powerful pumps that are stored in spacious reservoirs, and which enable me to prolong at need, and as long as I will, my stay in the depths of the sea. It gives a uniform and unintermittent light, which the sun does not. Now look at this clock; it is electrical, and goes with a regularity that defies the best chronometers. I have divided it into twenty-four hours, like the Italian clocks, because for me there is neither night nor day, sun nor moon, but only that factitious light that I take with me to the bottom of the sea. Look! just now, it is ten o'clock in the morning."

"Exactly."

"Another application of electricity. This dial hanging in front of us indicates the speed of the *Nautilus*. An electric thread puts it in communication with the screw, and the needle indicates the real speed. Look! now we are spinning along with a uniform speed of fifteen miles an hour."

"It is marvellous! and I see, Captain, you were right to make use of this agent that takes the place of wind, water, and steam."

"We have not finished, M. Aronnax," said Captain Nemo, rising; "if you will follow me, we will examine the stern of the *Nautilus*."

Really, I knew already the anterior part of this submarine boat, of which this is the exact division, starting from the ship's head: the dining-room, five yards long, separated from the library by a water-tight partition; the library, five yards long; the large drawing-room, ten yards long, separated from the captain's room by a second water-tight partition; the said room, five yards in length; mine, two and a half yards; and lastly, a reservoir of air, seven and a half yards, that extended to the bows. Total length thirty-five yards, or one hundred and five feet. The partitions had doors that were shut hermetically by means of india-rubber instruments, and they insured the safety of the *Nautilus* in case of a leak.

I followed Captain Nemo through the waist, and arrived at the centre of the boat. There was a sort of well that opened between two partitions. An iron ladder, fastened with an iron hook to the partition, led to the upper end. I asked the captain what the ladder was used for.

"It leads to the small boat," he said.

"What! have you a boat?" I exclaimed, in surprise.

"Of course; an excellent vessel, light and insubmersible, that serves either as a fishing or as a pleasure boat."

"But then, when you wish to embark, you are obliged to come to the surface of the water?"

"Not at all. This boat is attached to the upper part of the hull of the *Nautilus,* and occupies a cavity made for it. It is decked, quite water-tight, and held together by solid bolts. This ladder leads to a man-hole made in the hull of the *Nautilus,* that corresponds with a similar hole made in the side of the boat. By this double opening I get into the small vessel. They shut the one belonging to the *Nautilus,* I shut the other by means of screw pressure. I undo the bolts, and the little boat goes up to the surface of the sea with prodigious rapidity. I then open the panel of the bridge, carefully shut till then; I mast it, hoist my sail, take my oars, and I'm off."

"But how do you get back on board?"

"I do not come back, M. Aronnax; the *Nautilus* comes to me."

"By your orders?"

"By my orders. An electric thread connects us. I telegraph to it, and that is enough."

"Really," I said, astonished at these marvels, "nothing can be more simple."

After having passed by the cage of the staircase that led to the platform, I saw a cabin six feet long, in which Conseil and Ned Land, enchanted with their repast, were devouring it with avidity. Then a door opened into a kitchen nine feet long, situated between the large storerooms. There electricity, better than gas itself, did all the cooking. The streams under the furnaces gave out to the sponges of platina a heat which was regularly kept up and distributed. They also heated a distilling apparatus, which, by evaporation, furnished excellent drinkable water. Near this kitchen was a bath-room comfortably furnished, with hot and cold water taps.

Next to the kitchen was the berth-room of the vessel, sixteen feet long. But the door was shut, and I could not see the management of it, which might have given me an idea of the number of men employed on board the *Nautilus*.

At the bottom was a fourth partition, that separated this office from the engine-room. A door opened, and I found myself in the compartment where Captain Nemo—certainly an engineer of a very high order—had arranged his locomotive machinery. This engine-room, clearly lighted, did not measure less than sixty-five feet in length. It was divided into two parts; the first contained the materials for producing electricity, and the second the machinery that connected it with the screw. I examined it with great interest, in order to understand the machinery of the *Nautilus*.

"You see," said the captain, "I use Bunsen's contrivances, not Ruhmkorff's. Those would not have been powerful enough. Bunsen's are fewer in number, but strong and large, which experience proves to be the best. The electricity produced passes forward, where it works, by electro-magnets of great size, on a system of levers and cog-wheels that transmit the movement to the axle of the screw. This one, the diameter of which is nineteen feet, and the thread twenty-three feet, performs about a hundred and twenty revolutions in a second."

"And you get then?"

"A speed of fifty miles an hour."

"I have seen the *Nautilus* manœuvre before the *Abraham Lincoln,* and I have my own ideas as to its speed. But this is not enough. We must see where we go. We must be able to direct it to the right, to the left, above, below. How do you get to the great depths, where you find an increasing resistance, which is rated by hundreds of atmospheres? How do you return to the surface of the ocean? And how do you maintain yourselves in the requisite medium? Am I asking too much?''

''Not at all, Professor,'' replied the captain, with some hesitation; ''since you may never leave this submarine boat. Come into the saloon, it is our usual study, and there you will learn all you want to know about the *Nautilus*.''

CHAPTER 12

SOME FIGURES

A MOMENT after we were seated on a divan in the saloon smoking. The captain showed me a sketch that gave the plan, section, and elevation of the *Nautilus*. Then he began his description in these words:—

''Here, M. Aronnax, are the several dimensions of the boat you are in. It is an elongated cylinder with conical ends. It is very like a cigar in shape, a shape already adopted in London in several constructions of the same sort. The length of this cylinder, from stem to stern, is exactly 232 feet, and its maximum breadth is twenty-six feet. It is not built quite like your long-voyage steamers, but its lines are sufficiently long, and its curves prolonged enough, to allow the water to slide off easily, and oppose no obstacle to its passage. These two dimensions enable you to obtain by a simple calculation the surface and cubic contents of the *Nautilus*. Its area measures 6,032 feet; and its contents about 1,500 cubic yards; that is to say, when completely immersed it displaces 50,000 feet of water, or weighs 1,500 tons.

''When I made the plans for this submarine vessel, I meant that nine tenths should be submerged; consequently, it ought only to displace nine tenths of its bulk, that is to say, only to weigh that number of tons. I ought not, therefore, to have exceeded that weight, constructing it on the aforesaid dimensions.

''The *Nautilus* is composed of two hulls, one inside, the other outside, joined by T-shaped irons, which render it very strong. Indeed, owing to this cellular arrangement it resists like a block, as if it were solid. Its sides cannot yield; it coheres spontaneously, and not by the closeness of its rivets; and the homogeneity of its construction, due to the perfect union of the materials, enables it to defy the roughest seas.

''These two hulls are composed of steel plates, whose density is from .7 to .8 that of water. The first is not less than two inches and a half thick, and weighs 394 tons. The second envelope, the keel, twenty inches high and ten thick, weighs alone sixty-two tons. The engine, the ballast, the several accessories and apparatus appendages, the partitions and bulkheads, weigh 961.62 tons. Do you follow all this?''

''I do.''

''Then, when the *Nautilus* is afloat under these circumstances, one tenth is

The engine-room of the *Nautilus*.

out of the water. Now, if I have made reservoirs of a size equal to this tenth, or capable of holding 150 tons, and if I fill them with water, the boat, weighing then 1,507 tons, will be completely immersed. That would happen, Professor. These reservoirs are in the lower parts of the *Nautilus*. I turn on taps and they fill, and the vessel sinks that had just been level with the surface."

"Well, Captain, but now we come to the real difficulty. I can understand your rising to the surface; but diving below the surface, does not your submarine contrivance encounter a pressure, and consequently undergo an upward thrust of one atmosphere for every thirty feet of water, just about fifteen pounds per square inch?"

"Just so, sir."

"Then unless you quite fill the *Nautilus,* I do not see how you can draw it down to those depths."

"Professor, you must not confound statics with dynamics, or you will be exposed to grave errors. There is very little labor spent in attaining the lower regions of the ocean, for all bodies have a tendency to sink. When I wanted to find out the necessary increase of weight required to sink the *Nautilus,* I had only to calculate the reduction of volume that sea-water requires according to the depth."

"That is evident."

"Now, if water is not absolutely incompressible, it is at least capable of very slight compression. Indeed, after the most recent calculations this reduction is only .000436 of an atmosphere for each thirty feet of depth. If we want to sink 3,000 feet, I should keep account of the reduction of bulk under a pressure equal to that of a column of water of a thousand feet. The calculation is easily verified. Now, I have supplementary reservoirs capable of holding a hundred tons. Therefore I can sink to a considerable depth. When I wish to rise to the level of the sea, I only let off the water, and empty all the reservoirs if I want the *Nautilus* to emerge from the tenth part of her total capacity."

I had nothing to object to these reasonings.

"I admit your calculations, Captain," I replied; "I should be wrong to dispute them since daily experience confirms them; but I foresee a real difficulty in the way."

"What, sir?"

"When you are about 1,000 feet deep, the walls of the *Nautilus* bear a pressure of 100 atmospheres. If, then, just now you were to empty the supplementary reservoirs, to lighten the vessel, and to go up to the surface, the pumps must overcome the pressure of 100 atmospheres, which is 1,500 lbs. per square inch. From that a power—"

"That electricity alone can give," said the captain, hastily. "I repeat, sir, that the dynamic power of my engines is almost infinite. The pumps of the *Nautilus* have an enormous power, as you must have observed when their jets of water burst like a torrent upon the *Abraham Lincoln*. Besides, I use subsidiary reservoirs only to attain a mean depth of 750 to 1,000 fathoms, and that with a view of managing my machines. Also, when I have a mind to visit the depths of the ocean five or six miles below the surface, I make use of slower but not less infallible means."

"What are they, Captain?"

"That involves my telling you how the *Nautilus* is worked."

"I am impatient to learn."

"To steer this boat to starboard or port, to turn, in a word, following a horizontal plan, I use an ordinary rudder fixed on the back of the stern-post, and with one wheel and some tackle to steer by. But I can also make the *Nautilus* rise and sink, and sink and rise, by a vertical movement by means of two inclined planes fastened to its sides, opposite the centre of flotation, planes that move in every direction, and that are worked by powerful levers from the interior. If the planes are kept parallel with the boat, it moves horizontally. If slanted, the *Nautilus,* according to this inclination, and under the influence of the screw, either sinks diagonally or rises diagonally as it suits me. And even if I wish to rise more quickly to the surface, I ship the screw, and the pressure of the water causes the *Nautilus* to rise vertically like a balloon filled with hydrogen."

"Bravo, Captain! But how can the steersman follow the route in the middle of the waters?"

"The steersman is placed in a glazed box, that is raised above the hull of the *Nautilus,* and furnished with lenses."

"Are these lenses capable of resisting such pressure?"

"Perfectly. Glass, which breaks at a blow, is, nevertheless, capable of offering considerable resistance. During some experiments of fishing by electric light in 1864 in the Northern Seas, we saw plates less than a third of an inch thick resist a pressure of sixteen atmospheres. Now, the glass that I use is not less than thirty times thicker."

"Granted. But, after all, in order to see, the light must exceed the darkness, and in the midst of the darkness in the water, how can you see?"

"Behind the steersman's cage is placed a powerful electric reflector, the rays from which light up the sea for half a mile in front."

"Ah! bravo, bravo, Captain! Now I can account for this phosphorescence in the supposed narwhal that puzzled us so. I now ask you if the boarding of the *Nautilus* and of the *Scotia,* that has made such a noise, has been the result of a chance recontre?"

"Quite accidental, sir. I was sailing only one fathom below the surface of the water when the shock came. It had no bad result."

"None, sir. But now, about your recontre with the *Abraham Lincoln*?"

"Professor, I am sorry for one of the best vessels in the American navy; but they attacked me, and I was bound to defend myself. I contented myself, however, with putting the frigate *hors de combat*: she will not have any difficulty in getting repaired at the next port."

"Ah, Commander! your *Nautilus* is certainly a marvellous boat."

"Yes, Professor; and I love it as if it were part of myself. If danger threatens one of your vessels on the ocean, the first impression is the feeling of an abyss above and below. On the *Nautilus* men's hearts never fail them. No defects to be afraid of, for the double shell is as firm as iron; no rigging to attend to; no sails for the wind to carry away; no boilers to burst; no fire to fear, for the vessel is made of iron, not of wood; no coal to run short, for electricity is the only mechanical agent; no collision to fear, for it alone swims in deep water; no tempest to brave, for when it dives below the water, it reaches absolute tranquillity. There, sir! that is the perfection of vessels! And if it is true that the engineer has more confidence in the vessel than the builder, and the builder than the captain himself, you understand the trust I repose in my *Nautilus*; for I am at once captain, builder, and engineer."

"But how could you construct this wonderful *Nautilus* in secret?"

"Each separate portion, M. Aronnax, was brought from different parts of the globe. The keel was forged at Crensot, the shaft of the screw at Penn & Co.'s, London, the iron plates of the hull at Laird's of Liverpool, the screw itself at Scott's at Glasgow. The reservoirs were made by Cail & Co. at Paris, the engine by Krupp in Prussia, its beak in Motala's workshop in Sweden, its mathematical instruments by Hart Brothers, of New York, etc.; and each of these people had my orders under different names."

"But these parts had to be put together and arranged?"

"Professor, I had set up my workshops upon a desert island in the ocean. There my workmen, that is to say, the brave men that I instructed and educated, and myself have put together our *Nautilus*. Then, when the work was finished, fire destroyed all trace of our proceedings on this island, that I could have jumped over if I had liked."

"Then the cost of this vessel is great?"

"M. Aronnax, an iron vessel costs £ 45 per ton. Now the *Nautilus* weighed 1,500. It came therefore to £ 67,500, and £ 80,000 more for fitting it up, and about £ 200,000 with the works of art and the collections it contains."

"One last question, Captain Nemo."

"Ask it, Professor."

"You are rich?"

"Immensely rich, sir; and I could, without missing it, pay the national debt of France."

I stared at the singular person who spoke thus. Was he playing upon my credulity? The future would decide that.

CHAPTER 13

THE BLACK RIVER

THE portion of the terrestrial globe which is covered by water is estimated at upwards of eighty millions of acres. This fluid mass comprises two billions two hundred and fifty millions of cubic miles, forming a spherical body of a diameter of sixty leagues, the weight of which would be three quintillions of tons. To comprehend the meaning of these figures, it is necessary to observe that a quintillion is to a billion as a billion is to unity; in other words, there are as many billions in a quintillion as there are units in a billion. This mass of fluid is equal to about the quantity of water which would be discharged by all the rivers of the earth in forty thousand years.

During the geological epochs, the igneous period succeeded to the aqueous. The ocean originally prevailed everywhere. Then by degrees, in the silurian period, the tops of the mountains began to appear, the islands emerged, then disappeared in partial deluges, reappeared, became settled, formed continents, till at length the earth became geographically arranged, as we see in the present day. The solid had wrested from the liquid thirty-seven million six hundred and fifty-seven square miles, equal to twelve billions nine hundred and sixty millions of acres.

The shape of continents allows us to divide the waters into five great portions: the Arctic or Frozen Ocean, the Antarctic or Frozen Ocean, the Indian, the Atlantic, and the Pacific Oceans.

The Pacific Ocean extends from north to south between the two polar circles, and from east to west between Asia and America, over an extent of 145 degrees of longitude. It is the quietest of seas; its currents are broad and slow, it has medium tides and abundant rain. Such was the ocean that my fate destined me first to travel over under these strange conditions.

"Sir," said Captain Nemo, "we will, if you please, take our bearings and fix the starting-point of this voyage. It is a quarter to twelve, I will go up again to the surface."

The captain pressed an electric clock three times. The pumps began to drive the water from the tanks; the needle of the manometer marked by a different pressure the ascent of the *Nautilus,* then it stopped.

"We have arrived," said the captain.

I went to the central staircase which opened on to the platform, clambered up the iron steps, and found myself on the upper part of the *Nautilus*.

The platform was only three feet out of the water. The front and back of the *Nautilus* was of that spindle-shape which caused it justly to be compared to a cigar. I notticed that its iron plates, slightly overlaying each other, resembled the shell which clothes the bodies of our large terrestrial reptiles. It explained to me how natural it was, in spite of all glasses, that this boat should have been taken for a marine animal.

Towards the middle of the platform the long-boat, half buried in the hull of the vessel, formed a slight excrescence. Fore and aft rose two cages of medium height with inclined sides, and partly closed by thick lenticular glasses; one destined for the steersman who directed the *Nautilus,* the other containing a brilliant lantern to give light on the road.

The sea was beautiful, the sky pure. Scarcely could the long vehicle feel the broad undulations of the ocean. A light breeze from the east rippled the surface of the waters. The horizon, free from fog, made observation easy. Nothing was in sight. Not a quicksand, not an island. A vast desert.

Captain Nemo, by the help of his sextant, took the altitude of the sun, which ought also to give the latitude. He waited for some moments till its disc touched the horizon. Whilst taking observations not a muscle moved, the instrument could not have been more motionless in a haud of marble.

"Twelve o'clock, sir," said he. "When you like—"

I cast a last look upon the sea, slightly yellowed by the Japanese coast, and descended to the saloon.

"And now, sir, I leave you to your studies," added the captain; "our course is E.N.E., our depth is twenty-six fathoms. Here are maps on a large scale by which you may follow it. The saloon is at your disposal, and with your permission I will retire." Captain Nemo bowed, and I remained alone, lost in thoughts all bearing on the commander of the *Nautilus*.

For a whole hour was I deep in these reflections, seeking to pierce this mystery so interesting to me. Then my eyes fell upon the vast planisphere spread upon the table, and I placed my finger on the very spot where the given latitude and longitude crossed.

The sea has its large rivers like the continents. They are special currents known by their temperature and their color. The most remarkable of these is known by the name of the Gulf Stream. Science has decided on the globe the direction of five principal currents: one in the North Atlantic, a second in the South, a third in the North Pacific, a fourth in the South, and a fifth in the Southern Indian Ocean. It is even probable that a sixth current existed at one time or another in the Northern Indian Ocean, when the Caspian and Aral Seas formed but one vast sheet of water.

At this point indicated on the planisphere one of these currents was rolling, the Kuro-Scivo of the Japanese, the Black River, which, leaving the Gulf of Bengal where it is warmed by the perpendicular rays of a tropical sun, crosses the Straits of Malacca along the coast of Asia, turns into the North Pacific to the Aleutian Islands, carrying with it trunks of camphor-trees and other indigenous productions, and edging the waves of the ocean with the pure indigo of its warm water. It was this current that the *Nautilus* was to follow. I followed it with my eye; saw it lose itself in the vastness of the Pacific, and felt myself drawn with it, when Ned Land and Conseil appeared at the door of the saloon.

My two brave companions remained petrified at the sight of the wonders spread before them.

"Where are we, where are we?" exclaimed the Canadian. "In the museum at Quebec?"

"My friends," I answered, making a sign for them to enter, "you are not in Canada, but on board the *Nautilus,* fifty yards below the level of the sea."

"But, M. Aronnax," said Ned Land, "can you tell me how many men there are on board? Ten, twenty, fifty, a hundred?"

"I cannot answer you, Mr. Land; it is better to abandon for a time all idea of seizing the *Nautilus* or escaping from it. This ship is a masterpiece of modern industry, and I should be sorry not to have seen it. Many people would accept the situation forced upon us, if only to move amongst such wonders. So be quiet and let us try and see what passes around us."

"See!" exclaimed the harpooner, "but we can see nothing in this iron prison! We are walking—we are sailing—blindly."

Ned Land had scarcely pronounced these words when all was suddenly darkness. The luminous ceiling was gone, and so rapidly that my eyes received a painful impression.

We remained mute, not stirring, and not knowing what surprise awaited us, whether agreeable or disagreeable. A sliding noise was heard: one would have said that panels were working at the side of the *Nautilus*.

"It is the end of the end!" said Ned Land.

Suddenly light broke at each side of the saloon, through two oblong openings. The liquid mass appeared vividly lit up by the electric gleam. Two crystal plates separated us from the sea. At first I trembled at the thought that this frail partition might break, but strong bands of copper bound them, giving an almost infinite power of resistance.

The sea was distinctly visible for a mile all round the *Nautilus*. What a spectacle! What pen can describe it? Who could paint the effects of the light through those transparent sheets of water, and the softness of the successive gradations from the lower to the superior strata of the ocean?

We know the transparency of the sea, and that its clearness is far beyond that of rock water. The mineral and organic substances which it holds in suspension

CHAPTER 14

A NOTE OF INVITATION

THE next day was the 9th of November. I awoke after a long sleep of twelve hours. Conseil came, according to custom, to know "how I had passed the night," and to offer his services. He had left his friend the Canadian sleeping like a man who had never done anything else all his life. I let the worthy fellow chatter as he pleased, without caring to answer him. I was preoccupied by the absence of the captain during our sitting of the day before, and hoping to see him to-day.

As soon as I dressed I went into the saloon. It was deserted.

I plunged into the study of the conchological treasures hidden behind the glasses. I revelled also in great herbals filled with the rarest marine plants, which, although dried up, retained their lovely colors. Amongst those precious hydrophytes I remarked some vorticellæ, pavonariæ, delicate ceramies with scarlet tints, some fan-shaped agari, and some natabuli like flat mushrooms, which at one time used to be classed as zoophytes; in short, a perfect series of algæ.

The whole day passed without my being honored by a visit from Captain Nemo. The panels of the saloon did not open. Perhaps they did not wish us to tire of these beautiful things.

The course of the *Nautilus* was E.N.E., her speed twelve knots, the depth below the surface between twenty-five and thirty fathoms.

The next day, 10th of November, the same desertion, the same solitude. I did not see one of the ship's crew: Ned and Conseil spent the greater part of the day with me. They were astonished at the inexplicable absence of the captain. Was this singular man ill? had he altered his intentions with regard to us?

After all, as Conseil said, we enjoyed perfect liberty, we were delicately and abundantly fed. Our host kept to his terms of the treaty. We could not complain, and, indeed, the singularity of our fate reserved such wonderful compensation for us, that we had no right to accuse it as yet.

That day I commenced the journal of these adventures which has enabled me to relate them with more scrupulous exactitude and minute detail. I wrote it on paper made from the zostera marina.

11th November, early in the morning. The fresh air spreading over the interior of the *Nautilus* told me that we had come to the surface of the ocean to renew our supply of oxygen. I directed my steps to the central staircase, and mounted the platform.

It was six o'clock, the weather was cloudy, the sea gray but calm. Scarcely a billow. Captain Nemo, whom I hoped to meet, would he be there? I saw no one but the steersman imprisoned in his glass cage. Seated upon the projection formed by the hull of the pinnace, I inhaled the salt breeze with delight.

By degrees the fog disappeared under the action of the sun's rays, the radiant orb rose from behind the eastern horizon. The sea flamed under its glance like a train of gunpowder. The clouds scattered in the heights were colored with lively tints of beautiful shades, and numerous "mare's tails," which betokened heighten its transparency. In certain parts of the ocean at the An seventy-five fathoms of water, can be seen with surprising clearn sand. The penetrating power of the solar rays does not seem to ceas of one hundred and fifty fathoms. But in this middle fluid travelled *Nautilus* the electric brightness was produced even in the bosom of It was no longer luminous water, but liquid light.

On each side a window opened into this unexplored abyss. The the saloon showed to advantage the brightness outside, and we look this pure crystal had been the glass of an immense aquarium.

"You wished to see, friend Ned; well, you see now."

"Curious! curious!" muttered the Canadian, who, forgetting his seemed to submit to some irresistible attraction; "and one would c than this to admire such a sight!"

"Ah!" thought I to myself, "I understand the life of this man; h a world apart for himself, in which he treasures all his greatest wor

For two whole hours an aquatic army escorted the *Nautilus*. D games, their bounds, while rivalling each other in beauty, brightne locity, I distinguished the green labre; the banded mullet, marked b line of black; the round-tailed goby, of a white color, with violet s back; the Japanese scombrus, a beautiful mackerel of these seas, body and silvery head; the brilliant azurors, whose name alone defies some banded spares, with variegated fins of blue and yellow; some the woodcocks of the seas, some specimens of which attain a yard Japanese salamanders, spider lampreys, serpents six feet long, with and lively, and a huge mouth bristling with teeth; with many other

Our imagination was kept at its height, interjections followed quick other. Ned named the fish, and Conseil classed them. I was in ecs the vivacity of their movements and the beauty of their forms. Never given to me to surprise these animals, alive and at liberty, in their natur I will not mention all the varieties which passed before my dazzled e collection of the seas of China and Japan. These fish, more numerou birds of the air, came, attracted, no doubt, by the brilliant focus of t light.

Suddenly there was daylight in the saloon, the iron panels closed the enchanting vision disappeared. But for a long time I dreamt on ti fell on the instruments hanging on the partition. The compass still s course to be E.N.E., the manometer indicated a pressure of five atn equivalent to a depth of twenty-five fathoms, and the electric log ga of fifteen miles an hour. I expected Captain Nemo, but he did not ap clock marked the hour of five.

Ned Land and Conseil returned to their cabin, and I retired to my My dinner was ready. It was composed of turtle-soup made of the mo hawksbills, of a surmullet served with puff paste (the liver of which by itself, was most delicious), and fillets of the emperor-holocanthus, of which seemed to me superior even to salmon.

I passed the evening reading, writing, and thinking. Then sleep ove me, and I stretched myself on my couch of zostera, and slept profound the *Nautilus* was gliding rapidly through the current of the Black Riv

A window opened into this unexplored abyss.

wind for that day. But what was wind to this *Nautilus,* which tempests could not frighten!

I was admiring this joyous rising of the sun, so gay, and so lifegiving, when I heard steps approaching the platform. I was prepared to salute Captain Nemo, but it was his second (whom I had already seen on the captain's first visit) who appeared. He advanced on the platform, not seeming to see me. With his powerful glass to his eye he scanned every point of the horizon with great attention. This examination over, he approached the panel and pronounced a sentence in exactly these terms. I have remembered it, for every morning it was repeated under exactly the same conditions. It was thus worded:—

"Nautron respoc lorni virch."

What it meant I could not say.

These words pronounced, the second descended. I thought that the *Nautilus* was about to return to its submarine navigation. I regained the panel and returned to my chamber.

Five days sped thus, without any change in our situation. Every morning I mounted the platform. The same phrase was pronounced by the same individual. But Captain Nemo did not appear.

I had made up my mind that I should never see him again, when, on the 16th November, on returning to my room with Ned and Conseil, I found upon my table a note addressed to me. I opened it impatiently. It was written in a bold, clear hand, the characters rather pointed, recalling the German type. The note was worded as follows:—

"TO PROFESSOR ARONNAX, *on board the Nautilus.*

"16th of November, 1867.

"Captain Nemo invites Professor Aronnax to a hunting-party, which will take place to-morrow morning in the forests of the island of Crespo. He hopes that nothing will prevent the Professor from being present, and he will with pleasure see him joined by his companions.

"CAPTAIN NEMO, *Commander of the Nautilus.*"

"A hunt!" exclaimed Ned.

"And in the forests of the island of Crespo!" added Conseil.

"Oh, then the gentleman is going on *terra firma*?" replied Ned Land.

"That seems to me to be clearly indicated," said I, reading the letter once more.

"Well, we must accept," said the Canadian. "But once more on dry ground, we shall know what to do. Indeed, I shall not be sorry to eat a piece of fresh venison."

Without seeking to reconcile what was contradictory between Captain Nemo's manifest aversion to islands and continents, and his invitation to hunt in a forest, I contented myself with replying,—

"Let us first see where the island of Crespo is."

I consulted the planisphere, and in 32° 40′ north lat., and 157° 50′ west long., I found a small island, recognized in 1801 by Captain Crespo, and marked in the ancient Spanish maps as Rocca de la Plata, the meaning of which is "The Silver Rock." We were then about eighteen hundred miles from our starting-point, and the course of the *Nautilus,* a little changed, was bringing it back towards the southeast.

Life in the Black River.

I showed this little rock lost in the midst of the North Pacific to my companions.

"If Captain Nemo does sometimes go on dry ground," said I, "he at least chooses desert islands."

Ned Land shrugged his shoulders without speaking, and Conseil and he left me.

After supper, which was served by the steward, mute and impassible, I went to bed, not without some anxiety.

The next morning, the 17th of November, on awakening I felt the *Nautilus* was perfectly still. I dressed quickly and entered the saloon.

Captain Nemo was there, waiting for me. He rose, bowed, and asked me if it was convenient for me to accompany him. As he made no allusion to his absence during the last eight days, I did not mention it, and simply answered that my companions and myself were ready to follow him.

We entered the dining-room, where breakfast was served.

"M. Aronnax," said the captain, "pray share my breakfast without ceremony; we will chat as we eat. For though I promised you a walk in the forest, I did not undertake to find hotels there. So breakfast as a man who will most likely not have his dinner till very late."

I did honor to the repast. It was composed of several kinds of fish, and slices of holothuridæ (excellent zoöphytes), and different sorts of sea-weed. Our drink consisted of pure water, to which the Captain added some drops of a fermented liquor, extracted by the Kamschatcha method from a sea-weed known under the name of *Rhodomenia palmata*. Captain Nemo ate at first without saying a word. Then he began,—

"Sir, when I proposed to you to hunt in my submarine forest of Crespo, you evidently thought me mad. Sir, you should never judge lightly of any man."

"But, Captain, believe me—"

"Be kind enough to listen, and you will then see whether you have any cause to accuse me of folly and contradiction."

"I listen."

"You know as well as I do, Professor, that man can live under water, providing he carries with him a sufficient supply of breathable air. In submarine works, the workman, clad in an impervious dress, with his head in a metal helmet, receives air from above by means of forcing-pumps and regulators."

"That is a diving apparatus," said I.

"Just so; but under these conditions the man is not at liberty; he is attached to the pump which sends him air through an india-rubber tube, and if we were obliged to be thus held to the *Nautilus,* we could not go far."

"And the means of getting free?" I asked.

"It is to use the Ronquayrol apparatus, invented by two of your own countrymen, which I have brought to perfection for my own use, and which will allow you to risk yourself under these new physiological conditions, without any organ whatever suffering. It consists of a reservoir of thick iron plates, in which I store the air under a pressure of fifty atmospheres. The reservoir is fixed on the back by means of braces, like a soldier's knapsack. Its upper part forms a box in which the air is kept by means of a bellows, and therefore cannot escape unless at its normal tension. In the Ronquayrol apparatus such as we use, two india-rubber pipes leave this box and join a sort of tent which holds the nose and mouth; one is to introduce fresh air, the other to let out the foul, and the tongue closes one or the other according to the wants of the respirator. But I, in encountering great pressures at the bottom of the sea, was obliged to shut my head, like that of a diver, in a ball of copper; and it is to this ball of copper that the two pipes, the inspirator and the expirator, open."

"Perfectly, Captain Nemo; but the air that you carry with you must soon be used; when it only contains fifteen per cent of oxygen, it is no longer fit to breathe."

"Right! but I told you, M. Aronnax, that the pumps of the *Nautilus* allow me to store the air under considerable pressure; and on those conditions, the reservoir of the apparatus can furnish breathable air for nine or ten hours."

"I have no further objections to make," I answered; "I will only ask you one thing, Captain,—how can you light your road at the bottom of the sea?"

"With the Ruhmkorff apparatus, M. Aronnax; one is carried on the back, the other is fastened to the waist. It is composed of a Bunsen pile, which I do not work with bichromate of potash, but with sodium. A wire is introduced which collects the electricity produced, and directs it towards a particularly made lantern. In this lantern is a spiral glass which contains a small quantity of carbonic gas. When the apparatus is at work, this gas becomes luminous, giving out a white and continuous light. Thus provided, I can breathe and I can see."

"Captain Nemo, to all my objections you make such crushing answers, that I dare no longer doubt. But if I am forced to admit the Ronquayrol and Ruhmkorff apparatus, I must be allowed some reservations with regard to the gun I am to carry."

"But it is not a gun for powder," answered the captain.

"Then it is an air-gun."

"Doubtless! How would you have me manufacture gunpowder on board, without either saltpetre, sulphur, or charcoal?"

"Besides," I added, "to fire under water in a medium eight hundred and fifty-five times denser than the air, we must conquer very considerable resistance."

"That would be no difficulty. There exist guns, according to Fulton, perfected in England by Philip Coles and Burley, in France by Furcy, and in Italy by Landi, which are furnished with a peculiar system of closing, which can fire under these conditions. But I repeat, having no powder, I use air under great pressure, which the pumps of the *Nautilus* furnish abundantly."

"But this air must be rapidly used?"

"Well, have I not my Ronquayrol reservoir, which can furnish it at need? A tap is all that is required. Besides, M. Aronnax, you must see yourself that, during our submarine hunt, we can spend but little air and but few balls."

"But it seems to me that in this twilight, and in the midst of this fluid, which is very dense compared with the atmosphere, shots could not go far, nor easily prove mortal."

"Sir, on the contrary, with this gun every blow is mortal; and however lightly the animal is touched, it falls as if struck by a thunderbolt."

"Why?"

"Because the balls sent by this gun are not ordinary balls, but little cases of glass (invented by Leniebroek, an Austrian chemist), of which I have a large supply. These glass cases are covered with a case of steel, and weighted with a pellet of lead; they are real Leyden bottles, into which the electricity is forced to a very high tension. With the slightest shock they are discharged, and the animal, however strong it may be, falls dead. I must tell you that these cases are size number four, and that the charge for an ordinary gun would be ten."

"I will argue no longer," I replied, rising from the table; "I have nothing left me but to take my gun. At all events, I will go where you go."

Captain Nemo then led me aft; and in passing before Ned and Conseil's cabin, I called my two companions, who followed immediately. We then came to a kind of cell near the machinery-room, in which we were to put on our walking-dress.

CHAPTER 15

A WALK ON THE BOTTOM OF THE SEA

THIS cell was, to speak correctly, the arsenal and wardrobe of the *Nautilus*. A dozen diving apparatuses hung from the partition, waiting our use.

Ned Land, on seeing them, showed evident repugnance to dress himself in one.

"But, my worthy Ned, the forests of the Island of Crespo are nothing but submarine forests."

"Good!" said the disappointed harpooner, who saw his dreams of fresh meat fade away. "And you, M. Aronnax, are you going to dress yourself in those clothes?"

"There is no alternative, Master Ned."

"As you please, sir," replied the harpooner, shrugging his shoulders; "but as for me, unless I am forced, I will never get into one."

"No one will force you, Master Ned," said Captain Nemo.

"Is Conseil going to risk it?" asked Ned.

"I follow my master wherever he goes," replied Conseil.

At the captain's call two of the ship's crew came to help us to dress in these heavy and impervious clothes, made of india-rubber without seam, and constructed expressly to resist considerable pressure. One would have thought it a suit of armor, both supple and resisting. This suit formed trousers and waistcoat. The trousers were finished off with thick boots, weighted with heavy leaden soles. The texture of the waistcoat was held together by bands of copper, which crossed the chest, protecting it from the great pressure of the water, and leaving the lungs free to act; the sleeves ended in gloves, which in no way restrained the movement of the hands. There was a vast difference noticeable between these consummate apparatuses and the old cork breastplates, jackets, and other contrivances in vogue during the eighteenth century.

Captain Nemo and one of his companions (a sort of Hercules, who must have possessed great strength), Conseil and myself, were soon enveloped in the dresses. There remained nothing more to be done but to enclose our heads in the metal box. But before proceeding to this operation, I asked the Captain's permission to examine the guns we were to carry.

One of the *Nautilus* men gave me a simple gun, the butt end of which, made of steel hollow in the centre, was rather large. It served as a reservoir for compressed air, which a valve, worked by a spring, allowed to escape into a metal tube. A box of projectiles, in a groove in the thickness of the butt-end, contained about twenty of these electric balls, which by means of a spring were forced into the barrel of the gun. As soon as one shot was fired, another was ready.

"Captain Nemo," said I, "this arm is perfect, and easily handled; I only ask to be allowed to try it. But how shall we gain the bottom of the sea?"

"At this moment, Professor, the *Nautilus* is stranded in five fathoms, and we have nothing to do but to start."

"But how shall we get off?"

"You shall see."

Captain Nemo thrust his head into the helmet, Conseil and I did the same, not without hearing an ironical "Good sport!" from the Canadian. The upper part of our dress terminated in a copper collar, upon which was screwed the metal helmet. Three holes, protected by thick glass, allowed us to see in all directions, by simply turning our heads in the interior of the head-dress. As soon as it was in position, the Rouquayrol apparatus on our backs began to act; and, for my part, I could breathe with ease.

With the Ruhmkorff lamp hanging from my belt, and the gun in my hand, I was ready to set out. But to speak the truth, imprisoned in these heavy garments, and glued to the deck by my leaden soles, it was impossible for me to take a step.

But this state of things was provided for. I felt myself being pushed into a little room contiguous to the wardrobe-room. My companions followed, towed along in the same way. I heard a water-tight door, furnished with stopper-plates, close upon us, and we were wrapped in profound darkness.

After some minutes, a loud hissing was heard. I felt the cold mount from my feet to my chest. Evidently from some part of the vessel they had by means of a tap given entrance to the water, which was invading us, and with which the room was soon filled. A second door cut in the side of the *Nautilus* then opened. We saw a faint light. In another instant our feet trod the bottom of the sea.

And now, how can I retrace the impression left upon me by that walk under the waters? Words are impotent to relate such wonders! Captain Nemo walked in front, his companion followed some steps behind. Conseil and I remained near each other, as if an exchange of words had been possible through our metallic cases. I no longer felt the weight of my clothing, or of my shoes, of my reservoir of air, or my thick helmet, in the midst of which my head rattled like an almond in its shell.

The light, which lit the soil thirty feet below the surface of the ocean, astonished me by its power. The solar rays shone through the watery mass easily, and dissipated all color, and I clearly distinguished objects at a distance of a hundred and fifty yards. Beyond that the tints darkened into fine gradations of ultramarine, and faded into vague obscurity. Truly this water which surrounded me was but another air denser than the terrestrial atmosphere, but almost as transparent. Above me was the calm surface of the sea. We were walking on fine, even sand, not wrinkled, as on a flat shore, which retains the impression of the billows. This dazzling carpet, really a reflector, repelled the rays of the sun with wonderful intensity, which accounted for the vibration which penetrated every atom of liquid. Shall I be believed when I say that, at the depth of thirty feet, I could see as if I was in broad daylight?

For a quarter of an hour I trod on this sand, sown with the impalpable dust of shells. The hull of the *Nautilus*, resembling a long shoal, disappeared by degrees; but its lantern, when darkness should overtake us in the waters, would help to guide us on board by its distinct rays.

Soon forms of objects outlined in the distance were discernible. I recognized magnificent rocks, hung with a tapestry of zoöphytes of the most beautiful kind, and I was at first struck by the peculiar effect of this medium.

It was then ten in the morning; the rays of the sun struck the surface of the waves at rather an oblique angle, and at the touch of their light, decomposed by refraction as through a prism, flowers, rocks, plants, shells, and polypi were shaded at the edges by the seven solar colors. It was marvellous, a feast for the eyes, this complication of colored tints, a perfect kaleidoscope of green, yellow, orange, violet, indigo, and blue; in one word, the whole palette of an enthusiastic colorist! Why could I not communicate to Conseil the lively sensations which were mounting to my brain, and rival him in expressions of admiration? For aught I knew, Captain Nemo and his companion might be able to exchange thoughts by means of signs previously agreed upon. So for want of better, I talked to myself; I declaimed in the copper box which covered my head, thereby expending more air in vain words than was, perhaps, expedient.

Various kinds of isis, clusters of pure tuft-coral, prickly fungi, and anemones, formed a brilliant garden of flowers, enamelled with porphitæ, decked with their collarettes of blue tentacles, sea-stars studding the sandy bottom, together with asterophytons like fine lace embroidered by the hands of naiads, whose festoons were waved by the gentle undulations caused by our walk. It was a real grief to me to crush under my feet the brilliant specimens of molluscs which strewed the ground by thousands of hammerheads, donaciæ (veritable bounding shells), of staircases, and red helmetshells, angel-wings, and many other produced by this inexhaustible ocean. But we were bound to walk, so we went on, whilst above our heads waved shoals of physalides leaving their tentacles to float in their train, medusæ whose umbrellas of opal or rose-pink, escalloped with a band of blue, sheltered us from the rays of the sun and fiery pelagiæ, which, in the darkness, would have strewn our path with phosphorescent light.

All those wonders I saw in the space of a quarter of a mile, scarcely stopping, and following Captain Nemo, who beckoned me on by signs. Soon the nature of the soil changed; to the sandy plain succeeded an extent of slimy mud, which the Americans call "ooze," composed of equal parts of silicious and calcareous shells. We then travelled over a plain of sea-weed of wild and luxuriant vegetation. This sward was of close texture, and soft to the feet, and rivalled the softest carpet woven by the hand of man. But whilst verdure was spread at our feet, it did not abandon our heads. A light network of marine plants, of that inexhaustible family of sea-weeds of which more than two thousand kinds are known, grew on the surface of the water. I saw long ribbons of fucus floating, some globular, others tuberous; laurenciæ and cladostephi of most delicate foliage, and some rhodomeniæ palmatæ, resembling the fan of a cactus. I noticed that the green plants kept nearer the top of the sea, whilst the red were at a greater depth, leaving to the black or brown hydrophytes the care of forming gardens and parterres in the remote beds of the ocean.

We had quitted the *Nautilus* about an hour and a half. It was near noon; I knew by the perpendicularity of the sun's rays, which were no longer refracted. The magical colors disappeared by degrees, and the shades of emerald and sapphire were effaced. We walked with a regular step, which rang upon the

I was ready to set out.

ground with astonishing intensity; the slightest noise was transmitted with a quickness to which the ear is unaccustomed on the earth; indeed, water is a better conductor of sound than air, in the ratio of four to one. At this period the earth sloped downwards; the light took a uniform tint. We were at a depth of a hundred and five yards and twenty inches, undergoing a pressure of six atmospheres.

At this depth I could still see the rays of the sun, though feebly; to their intense brilliancy had succeeded a reddish twilight, the lowest state between day and night; but we could still see well enough; it was not necessary to resort to the Ruhmkorff apparatus as yet. At this moment Captain Nemo stopped; he waited till I joined him, and then pointed to an obscure mass, looming in the shadow, at a short distance.

"It is the forest of the Island of Crespo," thought I;—and I was not mistaken.

CHAPTER 16

A SUBMARINE FOREST

WE had at last arrived on the borders of this forest, doubtless one of the finest of Captain Nemo's immense domains. He looked upon it as his own, and considered he had the same right over it that the first men had in the first days of the world. And, indeed, who would have disputed with him the possession of this submarine property? What other hardier pioneer would come, hatchet in hand, to cut down the dark copses?

This forest was composed of large tree-plants; and the moment we penetrated under its vast arcades, I was struck by the singular position of their branches,—a position I had not yet observed.

Not an herb which carpeted the ground, not a branch which clothed the trees, was either broken or bent, nor did they extend horizontally; all stretched up to the surface of the ocean. Not a filament, not a ribbon, however thin they might be, but kept as straight as a rod of iron. The fuci and llianas grew in rigid perpendicular lines, due to the density of the element which had produced them. Motionless, yet, when bent to one side by the hand, they directly resumed their former position. Truly it was the region of perpendicularity!

I soon accustomed myself to this fantastic position, as well as to the comparative darkness which surrounded us. The soil of the forest seemed covered with sharp blocks, difficult to avoid. The submarine flora struck me as being very perfect, and richer even than it would have been in the arctic or tropical zones, where these productions are not so plentiful. But for some minutes I involuntarily confounded the genera, taking zoöphytes for hydrophytes, animals for plants; and who would not have been mistaken? The fauna and the flora are too closely allied in this submarine world.

These plants are self-propagated, and the principle of their existence is in the water, which upholds and nourishes them. The greater number, instead of leaves, shoot forth blades of capricious shapes comprised within a scale of colors,—

A walk under the waters.

pink, carmine, green, olive, fawn, and brown. I saw there (but not dried up, as our specimens of the *Nautilus* are) pavonari spread like a fan as if to catch the breeze; scarlet ceramies, whose laminaries extended their edible shoots of fern-shaped nereocysti, which grow to a height of fifteen feet; clusters of acetabuli, whose stems increase in size upwards; and numbers of other marine plants, all devoid of flowers!

"Curious anomaly! fantastic element!" said an ingenious naturalist, "in which the animal kingdom blossoms, and the vegatable does not!"

Under these numerous shrubs (as large as trees of the temperature zone), and under their damp shadow, were massed together real bushes of living flowers, hedges of zoöphytes, on which blossomed some zebra-meandrines, with crooked grooves; some yellow caryophylliæ; and to complete the illusion, the fish-flies flew from branch to branch like a swarm of humming birds, whilst yellow lepisacomthi, with bristling jaws, dactylopteri, and monocentrides rose at our feet like a flight of snipes.

In about an hour Captain Nemo gave the signal to halt. I, for my part, was not sorry, and we stretched ourselves under an arbor of alariæ, the long thin blades of which stood up like arrows.

This short rest seemed delicious to me; there was nothing wanting but the charm of conversation; but, impossible to speak, impossible to answer, I only put my great copper head to Conseil's. I saw the worthy fellow's eyes glistening with delight, and to show his satisfaction he shook himself in his breastplate of air, in the most comical way in the world.

After four hours of this walking I was surprised not to find myself dreadfully hungry. How to account for this state of the stomach I could not tell. But instead I felt an insurmountable desire to sleep, which happens to all divers. And my eyes soon closed behind the thick glasses, and I fell into a heavy slumber, which the movement alone had prevented before. Captain Nemo and his robust companion, stretched in the clear crystal, set us the example.

How long I remained buried in this drowsiness, I cannot judge; but, when I woke, the sun seemed sinking towards the horizon. Captain Nemo had already risen, and I was beginning to stretch my limbs, when an unexpected apparition brought me briskly to my feet.

A few steps off, a monster sea-spider, about thirty-eight inches high, was watching me with squinting eyes, ready to spring upon me. Though my diver's dress was thick enough to defend me from the bite of this animal, I could not help shuddering with horror. Conseil and the sailor of the *Nautilus* awoke at this moment. Captain Nemo pointed out the hideous crustacean, which a blow from the butt-end of the gun knocked over, and I saw the horrible claws of the monster writhe in terrible convulsions. This accident reminded me that other animals more to be feared might haunt these obscure depths, against whose attacks my diving-dress would not protect me. I had never thought of it before, but I now resolved to be upon my guard. Indeed, I thought that this halt would mark the termination of our walk; but I was mistaken, for, instead of returning to the *Nautilus,* Captain Nemo continued his bold excursion. The ground was still on the incline, its declivity seemed to be getting greater, and to be leading us to greater depths. It must have been about three o'clock when we reached a narrow valley, between high perpendicular walls, situated about seventy-five fathoms deep. Thanks to the perfection of our apparatus, we were forty-five fathoms

below the limit which nature seems to have imposed on man as to his submarine excursions.

I say seventy-five fathoms, though I had no instrument by which to judge the distance. But I knew that even in the clearest waters the solar rays could not penetrate further. And accordingly the darkness deepened. At ten paces not an object was visible. I was groping my way, when I suddenly saw a brilliant white light. Captain Nemo had just put his electric apparatus into use; his companion did the same, and Conseil and I followed their example. By turning a screw I established a communication between the wire and the spiral glass, and the sea, lit by our four lanterns, was illuminated for a circle of thirty-six yards.

Captain Nemo was still plunging into the dark depths of the forest, whose trees were getting scarcer at every step. I noticed that vegetable life disappeared sooner than animal life. The medusæ had already abandoned the arid soil, from which a great number of animals, zoöphytes, articulata, molluscs, and fishes, still obtained sustenance.

As we walked, I thought the light of our Ruhmkorff apparatus could not fail to draw some inhabitant from its dark couch. But if they did approach us, they at least kept at a respectful distance from the hunters. Several times I saw Captain Nemo stop, put his gun to his shoulder, and after some moments drop it and walk on. At last, after about four hours, this marvellous excursion came to an end. A wall of superb rocks, in an imposing mass, rose before us, a heap of gigantic blocks, an enormous steep granite shore, forming dark grottos, but which presented no practicable slope; it was the prop of the Island of Crespo. It was the earth! Captain Nemo stopped suddenly. A gesture of his brought us all to a halt; and however desirous I might be to scale the wall, I was obliged to stop. Here ended Captain Nemo's domains, and he would not go beyond them. Further on was a portion of the globe he might not trample upon.

The return began. Captain Nemo had returned to the head of his little band, directing their course without hesitation. I thought we were not following the same road to return to the *Nautilus*. The new road was very steep, and consequently very painful. We approached the surface of the sea rapidly. But this return to the upper strata was not so sudden as to cause relief from the pressure too rapidly, which might have produced serious disorder in our organization, and brought on internal lesions, so fatal to divers. Very soon light reappeared and grew, and the sun being low on the horizon, the refraction edged the different objects with a spectral ring. At ten yards and a half deep, we walked amidst a shoal of little fishes of all kinds, more numerous than the birds of the air, and also more agile; but no aquatic game worthy of a shot had as yet met our gaze, when at that moment I saw the captain shoulder his gun quickly, and follow a moving object into the shrubs. He fired;—I heard a slight hissing, and a creature fell stunned at some distance from us. It was a magnificent sea-otter, an enhydrus, the only exclusively marine quadruped. This otter was five feet long, and must have been very valuable. Its skin, chestnut-brown above and silvery underneath, would have made one of those beautiful furs so sought after in the Russian and Chinese markets; the fineness and the lustre of its coat would certainly fetch £ 80. I admired this curious mammal, with its rounded head ornamented with short ears, its round eyes, and white whiskers like those of a cat, with webbed feet and nails, and tufted tail. This precious animal, hunted and tracked by fishermen, has now become very rare, and taken refuge chiefly in the northern parts of the Pacific, or probably its race would soon become extinct.

Captain Nemo's companion took the beast, threw it over his shoulder, and we continued our journey. For one hour a plain of sand lay stretched before us. Sometimes it rose to within two yards and some inches of the surface of the water. I then saw our image clearly reflected, drawn inversely, and above us appeared an identical group reflecting our movements and our actions; in a word, like us in every point, except that they walked with their heads downward and their feet in the air.

Another effect I noticed, which was the passage of thick clouds which formed and vanished rapidly; but on reflection I understood that these seeming clouds were due to the varying thickness of the reeds at the bottom, and I could even see the fleecy foam which their broken tops multiplied on the water, and the shadows of large birds passing above our heads, whose rapid flight I could discern on the surface of the sea.

On this occasion I was witness to one of the finest gun-shots which ever made the nerves of a hunter thrill. A large bird of great breadth of wing, clearly visible, approached, hovering over us. Captain Nemo's companion shouldered his gun and fired, when it was only a few yards above the waves. The creature fell stunned, and the force of its fall brought it within the reach of the dexterous hunter's grasp. It was an albatross of the finest kind.

Our march had not been interrupted by this incident. For two hours we followed these sandy plains, then fields of algæ very disagreeable to cross. Candidly, I could do no more when I saw a glimmer of light, which for a half-mile broke the darkness of the waters. It was the lantern of the *Nautilus*. Before twenty minutes were over we should be on board, and I should be able to breathe with ease; for it seemed that my reservoir supplied air very deficient in oxygen. But I did not reckon on an accidental meeting, which delayed our arrival for some time.

I had remained some steps behind, when I presently saw Captain Nemo coming hurriedly towards me. With his strong hand he bent me to the ground, his companion doing the same to Conseil. At first I knew not what to think of this sudden attack, but I was soon reassured by seeing the captain lie down beside me, and remain immovable.

I was stretched on the ground, just under shelter of a bush of algæ, when, raising my head, I saw some enormous mass, casting phosphorescent gleams, pass blusteringly by.

My blood froze in my veins as I recognized two formidable sharks which threatened us. It was a couple of tintoreas, terrible creatures, with enormous tails and a dull glassy stare, the phosphorescent matter ejected from holes pierced around the muzzle. Monstrous brutes! which would crush a whole man in their iron jaws. I did not know whether Conseil stopped to classify them; for my part, I noticed their silver bellies, and their huge mouths bristling with teeth, from a very unscientific point of view, and more as possible victim than as a naturalist.

Happily the voracious creatures do not see well. They passed without seeing us, brushing us with their brownish fins, and we escaped by a miracle from a danger certainly greater than meeting a tiger full-face in the forest. Half an hour after, guided by the electric light, we reached the *Nautilus*. The outside door had been left open, and Captain Nemo closed it as soon as we had entered the first cell. He then pressed a knob. I heard the pumps working in the midst of the vessel, I felt the water sinking from around me, and in a few moments the cell was entirely empty. The inside door then opened, and we entered the vestry.

There our diving-dress was taken off, not without some trouble; and, fairly worn out from want of food and sleep, I returned to my room, in great wonder at this surprising excursion at the bottom of the sea.

CHAPTER 17

FOUR THOUSAND LEAGUES UNDER THE PACIFIC

THE next morning, the 18th of November, I had quite recovered from my fatigues of the day before, and I went up on to the platform, just as the second lieutenant was uttering his daily phrase.

I was admiring the magnificent aspect of the ocean when Captain Nemo appeared. He did not seem to be aware of my presence, and began a series of astronomical observations. Then, when he had finished, he went and leant on the cage of the watchlight, and gazed abstractedly on the ocean. In the mean time, a number of the sailors of the *Nautilus,* all strong and healthy men, had come up on to the platform. They came to draw up the nets that had been laid all night. These sailors were evidently of different nations, although the European type was visible to all of them. I recognized some unmistakable Irishmen, Frenchmen, some Sclaves, and a Greek or a Candiote. They were civil, and only used that odd language among themselves, the origin of which I could not guess, neither could I question them.

The nets were hauled in. They were a large kind of "chaluts," like those on the Normandy coasts, great pockets that the waves and a chain fixed in the smaller meshes, kept open. These pockets, drawn by iron poles, swept through the water, and gathered in everything in their way. That day they brought up curious specimens from those productive coasts,—fishing frogs that, from their comical movements, have acquired the name of buffoons; black commersons, furnished with antennæ; trigger-fish, encircled with red bands; orthragorisci, with very subtle venom; some olive-colored lampreys; macrorhynci, covered with silvery scales; trichiuri, the electric power of which is equal to that of the gymnotus and cramp-fish; scaly notopteri, with transverse brown bands; greenish cod; several varieties of gobies, etc.; also some larger fish; a caranx with a prominent head a yard long; several fine bonitos, streaked with blue and silver; and three splendid tunnies, which, spite of the swiftness of their motion, had not escaped the net.

I reckoned that the haul had brought in more than nine hundred-weight of fish. It was a fine haul, but not to be wondered at. Indeed, the nets are let down for several hours, and enclose in their meshes an infinite variety. We had no lack of excellent food, and the rapidity of the *Nautilus* and the attraction of the electric light could always renew our supply. These several productions of the sea were immediately lowered through the panel to the steward's room, some to be eaten fresh, and others pickled.

The fishing ended, the provision of air renewed, I thought that the *Nautilus* was about to continue its submarine excursion, and was about to continue its submarine excursion, and was preparing to return to my room, when, without further preamble, the captain turned to me, saying,—

"Professor, is not this ocean gifted with real life? It has its tempers and its gentle moods. Yesterday it slept as we did, and now it has woke after a quiet night. Look!" he continued, "it wakes under the caresses of the sun. It is going to renew its diurnal existence. It is an interesting study to watch the play of its organization. It has a pulse, arteries, spasms; and I agree with the learned Maury, who discovered in it a circulation as real as the circulation of blood in animals.

"Yes, the ocean has indeed circulation, and to promote it, the Creator has caused things to multiply in it,—caloric, salt, and animalculæ."

When Captain Nemo spoke thus, he seemed altogether changed, and aroused an extraordinary emotion in me.

"Also," he added, "true existence is there; and I can imagine the foundations of nautical towns, clusters of submarine houses, which, like the *Nautilus,* would ascend every morning to breathe at the surface of the water,—free towns, independent cities. Yet who knows whether some despot—"

Captain Nemo finished his sentence with a violent gesture. Then, addressing me as if to chase away some sorrowful thought,—

"M. Aronnax," he asked, "do you know the depth of the ocean?"

"I only know, Captain, what the principal soundings have taught us."

"Could you tell me them, so that I can suit them to my purpose?"

"These are some," I replied, "that I remember. If I am not mistaken, a depth of 8000 yards has been found in the North Atlantic, and 2500 yards in the Mediterranean. The most remarkable soundings have been made in the South Atlantic, near the 35th parallel, and they gave 12,000 yards, 14,000 yards, and 15,000 yards. To sum up all, it is reckoned that if the bottom of the sea were levelled, its mean depth would be about one and three quarter leagues."

"Well, Professor," replied the captain, "we shall show you better than that, I hope. As to the mean depth of this part of the Pacific, I tell you it is only 4000 yards."

Having said this, Captain Nemo went towards the panel, and disappeared down the ladder. I followed him, and went into the large drawing-room. The screw was immediately put in motion, and the log gave twenty miles an hour.

During the days and weeks that passed, Captain Nemo was very sparing of his visits. I seldom saw him. The lieutenant pricked the ship's course regularly on the chart, so I could always tell exactly the route of the *Nautilus*.

Nearly every day, for some time, the panels of the drawing-room were opened, and we were never tired of penetrating the mysteries of the submarine world.

The general direction of the *Nautilus* was southeast, and it kept between 100 and 150 yards of depth. One day, however, I do not know why, being drawn diagonally by means of the inclined planes, it touched the bed of the sea. The thermometer indicated a temperature of 4.25 (cent.); a temperature that at this depth seemed common to all latitudes.

At three o'clock on the morning of the 26th of November, the *Nautilus* crossed the tropic of Cancer at 172° longitude. On the 27th instant it sighted the Sandwich Islands, where Cook died, February 14, 1779. We had then gone 4860 leagues from our starting-point. In the morning, when I went on the platform, I saw, two miles to windward, Hawaii, the largest of the seven islands that form the group. I saw clearly the cultivated ranges, and the several mountain-chains that run parallel with the side, and the volcanoes that overtop Monna-Rea, which rise 5000 yards above the level of the sea. Besides other things the nets brought up, were several flabellariæ and graceful polypi, that are peculiar to that part of the ocean. The direction of the *Nautilus* was still to the southeast. It crossed the equator December 1, in 142° longitude; and on the 4th of the same month, after crossing rapidly and without anything particular occurring, we sighted the Marquesas group. I saw, three miles off, at 8° 57′ latitude south, and 139° 32′ west longitude, Martin's peak in Nouka-Hiva, the largest of the group that belongs to France. I only saw the woody mountains against the horizon, because Captain Nemo did not wish to bring the ship to the wind. There the nets brought up beautiful specimens of fish: choryphenes, with azure fins and tails like gold, the flesh of which is unrivalled; hologymnoses, nearly destitute of scales, but of exquisite flavor; ostorhyncs, with bony jaws, and yellow-tinged thasards, as good as bonitos; all fish that would be of use to us. After leaving these charming islands protected by the French flag, from the 4th to the 11th of December the *Nautilus* sailed over about 2000 miles. This navigation was remarkable for the meeting with an immense shoal of calmars, near neighbors to the cuttle. The French fishermen call them *hornets;* they belong to the cephalopod class, and to the dibranchial family, that comprehends the cuttles and the argonauts. These animals were particularly studied by students of antiquity, and they furnished numerous metaphors to the popular orators, as well as excellent dishes for the tables of the rich citizens, if one can believe Athenæus, a Greek doctor, who lived before Galen. It was during the night of the 9th or 10th of December that the *Nautilus* came across this shoal of molluscs, that are peculiarly nocturnal. One could count them by millions. They emigrate from the temperate to the warmer zones, following the track of herrings and sardines. We watched them through the thick crystal panes, swimming down the wind with great rapidity, moving by means of their locomotive tube, pursuing fish and molluscs, eating the little ones, eaten by the big ones, and tossing about in indescribable confusion the ten arms that nature has placed on their heads like a crest of pneumatic serpents. The *Nautilus,* in spite of its speed, sailed for several hours in the midst of these animals, and its nets brought in an enormous quantity, among which I recognized the nine species that D'Orbigny classed for the Pacific. One saw, while crossing, that the sea displays the most wonderful sights. They were in endless variety. The scene changed continually, and we were called upon not only to contemplate the works of the Creator in the midst of the liquid element, but to penetrate the awful mysteries of the ocean.

During the daytime of the 11th of December, I was busy reading in the large drawing-room. Ned Land and Conseil watched the luminous water through the half-open panels. The *Nautilus* wes immovable. While its reservoirs were filled, it kept at a depth of 1000 yards, a region rarely visited in the ocean, and in which large fish were seldom seen.

I was then reading a charming book by Jean Macé, "The Slaves of the Stomach," and I was learning some valuable lessons from it, when Conseil interrupted me.

"Will master come here a moment?" he said, in a curious voice.

"What is the matter, Conseil?"

"I want master to look."

I rose, went and leaned on my elbows before the panes, and watched.

In a full electric light, an enormous black mass, quite immovable, was suspended in the midst of the waters. I watched it attentively, seeking to find out the nature of this gigantic cetacean. But a sudden thought crossed my mind. "A vessel!" I said, half aloud.

"Yes," replied the Canadian, "a disabled ship that has sunk perpendicularly."

Ned Land was right; we were close to a vessel of which the tattered shrouds still hung from their chains. The keel seemed to be in good order, and it had been wrecked at most some few hours. Three stumps of masts, broken off about two feet above the bridge, showed that the vessel had had to sacrifice its masts. But, lying on its side, it had filled, and it was heeling over to port. The skeleton of what it had once been was a sad spectacle as it lay lost under the waves; but sadder still was the sight of the bridge, where some corpses, bound with ropes, were still lying. I counted five,—four men, one of whom was standing at the helm, and a woman standing by the poop holding an infant in her arms. She was quite young. I could distinguish her features, which the water had not decomposed, by the brilliant light from the *Nautilus*. In one despairing effort, she had raised her infant above her head, poor little thing! whose arms encircled its mother's neck. The attitude of the four sailors was frightful, distorted as they were by their convulsive movements, whilst making a last effort to free themselves from the cords that bound them to the vessel. The steersman alone, calm, with a grave, clear face, his gray hair glued to his forehead, and his hand clutching the wheel of the helm, seemed even then to be guiding the three broken masts through the depths of the ocean.

What a scene! We were dumb; our hearts beat fast before this shipwreck, taken as it were from life, and photographed in its last moments. And I saw already, coming towards it with hungry eyes, enormous sharks, attracted by the human flesh.

However, the *Nautilus*, turning, went round the submerged vessel, and in one instant I read on the stern,— "*The Florida, Sunderland.*"

CHAPTER 18

VANIKORO

THIS terrible spectacle was the forerunner of the series of maritime catastrophes that the *Nautilus* was destined to meet with in its route. As long as it went through more frequented waters, we often saw the hulls of shipwrecked vessels that were rotting in the depths, and, deeper down, cannons, bullets, anchors, chains, and a thousand other iron materials eaten up by rust. However, on the 11th of December, we sighted the Pomoton Islands, the old "dangerous group" of Bougainville, that extend over a space of 500 leagues at E.S.E. to W.N.W., from the Island Ducie to that of Lazareff. This group covers an area of 370 square leagues, and it is formed of sixty groups of islands, among which the Gambier group is remarkable, over which France exercises sway. These are coral islands, slowly raised, but continuous, created by the daily work of polypi. Then this new island will be joined later on to the neighboring groups, and a fifth continent will stretch from New Zealand and New Caledonia, and from thence to the Marquesas.

One day, when I was suggesting this theory to Captain Nemo, he replied coldly,—

"The earth does not want new continents, but new men."

Chance had conducted the *Nautilus* towards the island of Clermont-Tonnerre, one of the most curious of the group that was discovered in 1822 by Captain Bell of the *Minerva*. I could study now the madreporal system, to which are due the islands in this ocean.

Madrepores (which must not be mistaken for corals) have a tissue lined with a calcareous crust, and the modifications of its structure have induced M. Milne-Edwards, my worthy master, to class them into five sections. The animalculæ that the marine polypus secretes live by millions at the bottom of their cells. Their calcareous deposits become rocks, reefs, and large and small islands. Here they form a ring, surrounding a little inland lake, that communicates with the sea by means of gaps. There they make barriers of reefs like those on the coasts of New Caledonia and the various Pomotou islands. In other places, like those at Reunion and at Maurice, they raise fringed reefs, high, straight walls, near which the depths of the ocean is considerable.

Some cable-lengths off the shores of the island of Clermont, I admired the gigantic work accomplished by these microscopical workers. These walls are specially the work of those madrepores known as milleporas, porites, madrepores, and astræas. These polypi are found particularly in the rough beds of the sea, near the surface; and consequently it is from the upper part that they begin their operations in which they bury themselves by degrees with the debris of the secretions that support them. Such is, at least, Darwin's theory, who thus explains the formation of the *atolls,* a superior theory (to my mind) to that given of the foundation of the madreporical works, summits of mountains or volcanoes, that are submerged some feet below the level of the sea.

I could observe closely these curious walls, for perpendicularly they were more than 300 yards deep, and our electric sheets lighted up this calcareous matter brilliantly. Replying to a question Conseil asked me as to the time these colossal barriers took to be raised, I astonished him much by telling him that learned men reckoned it about the eighth of an inch in a hundred years.

Towards evening Clermont-Tonnerre was lost in the distance, and the route of the *Nautilus* was sensibly changed. After having crossed the tropic of Capricorn in 135° longitude, it sailed W.N.W., making again for the tropical zone. Although the summer sun was very strong, we did not suffer from heat, for at fifteen or twenty fathoms below the surface the temperature did not rise above from ten to twelve degrees.

On December 15, we left to the east the bewitching group of the Societies and the graceful Tahiti, queen of the Pacific. I saw in the morning, some miles to the windward, the elevated summits of the island. These waters furnished our table with excellent fish, mackerel, bonitos, and albicores, and some varieties of a sea-serpent called munirophis.

On the 25th of December the *Nautilus* sailed into the midst of the New Hebrides, discovered by Quiros in 1606, and that Bougainville explored in 1768, and to which Cook gave its present name in 1773. This group is composed principally of nine large islands, that form a band of 120 leagues N.N.S. to S.S.W., between 15° and 2° south latitude, and 164° and 168° longitude. We passed tolerably near to the Island of Auron, that at noon looked like a mass of green woods surmounted by a peak of great height.

That day being Christmas Day, Ned Land seemed to regret sorely the non-celebration of "Christmas," the family fête of which Protestants are so fond. I had not seen Captain Nemo for a week when, on the morning of the 27th, he came into the large drawing-room, always seeming as if he had seen you five minutes before. I was busily tracing the route of the *Nautilus* on the planisphere. The captain came up to me, put his finger on one spot on the chart, and said this single word,—

"Vanikoro."

The effect was magical! It was the name of the islands on which La Perouse had been lost! I rose suddenly.

"The *Nautilus* has brought us to Vanikoro?" I asked.

"Yes, Professor," said the captain.

"And I can visit the celebrated islands where the *Boussole* and the *Astrolabe* struck?"

"If you like, Professor."

"When shall we be there?"

"We are there now."

Followed by Captain Nemo, I went up on to the platform, and greedily scanned the horizon.

To the N.E. two volcanic islands emerged, of unequal size, surrounded by a coral reef that measured forty miles in circumference.

We were close to Vanikoro, really the one to which Dumont d'Urville gave the name of Isle de la Recherche, and exactly facing the little harbor of Vanou, situated in 16° 4′ south latitude, and 164° 32′ east longitude. The earth seemed covered with verdure from the shore to the summits in the interior, that were crowned by Mount Kapogo, 476 feet high. The *Nautilus*, having passed the outer belt of rocks by a narrow strait, found itself among breakers where the sea was from thirty to forty fathoms deep. Under the verdant shade of some mangroves I perceived some savages, who appeared greatly surprised at our approach. In the long black body, moving between wind and water, did they not see some formidable cetacean that they regarded with suspicion?

Just then Captain Nemo asked me what I knew about the wreck of La Perouse.

"Only what every one knows, Captain," I replied.

"And could you tell me what every one knows about it?" he inquired ironically.

"Easily."

I related to him all that the last works of Dumont d'Urville had made known,—works from which the following is a brief account.

La Perouse, and his second, Captain de Langle, were sent by Louis XVI., in 1785, on a voyage of circumnavigation. They embarked in the corvettes the *Boussole* and the *Astrolabe*, neither of which were again heard of. In 1791 the French government, justly uneasy as to the fate of these two sloops, manned two large merchantmen, the *Recherche* and the *Esperance*, which left Brest the 28th of September, under the command of Bruni d'Entrecasteaux.

Two months after, they learned from Bowen, commander of the *Albemarle*, that the debris of shipwrecked vessels had been seen on the coasts of New Georgia. But D'Entrecasteaux, ignoring this communication,—rather uncertain, besides,—directed his course towards the Admiralty Isles, mentioned in a report of Captain Hunter's as being the place where La Perouse was wrecked.

They sought in vain. The *Esperance* and the *Recherche* passed before Vanikoro without stopping there, and in fact this voyage was most disastrous, as it cost D'Entrecasteaux his life, and those of two of his lieutenants, besides several of his crew.

Captain Dillon, a shrewd old Pacific sailor, was the first to find unmistakable traces of the wrecks. On the 15th of May, 1824, his vessel, the *St. Patrick,* passed close to Tikopia, one of the New Hebrides. There a Lascar came alongside in a canoe, sold him the handle of a sword in silver, that bore the print of characters engraved on the hilt. The Lascar pretended that six years before, during a stay at Vanikoro, he had seen two Europeans that belonged to some vessels that had run aground on the reefs some years ago.

Dillon guessed that he meant La Perouse, whose disappearance had troubled the whole world. He tried to get on to Vanikoro, where, according to the Lascar, he would find numerous debris of the wreck, but winds and tide prevented him.

Dillon returned to Calcutta. There he interested the Asiatic Society and the Indian Company in his discovery. A vessel, to which was given the name of the *Recherche,* was put at his disposal, and he set out, January 23, 1827, accompanied by a French agent.

The *Recherche,* after touching at several points in the Pacific, cast anchor before Vanikoro, July 7, 1827, in this same harbor of Vanou where the *Nautilus* was at this time.

There it collected numerous relics of the wreck,—iron utensils, anchors, pulley-strops, swivel-guns, an 18 lb. shot, fragments of astronomical instruments, a piece of crown-work, and a bronze clock, bearing this inscription,—"*Bazin m'a fait,*" the mark of the foundry of the arsenal at Brest about 1785. There could be no further doubt.

Dillon, having made all inquiries, stayed in the unlucky place till October. Then he quitted Vanikoro, and directed his course towards New Zealand; put into Calcutta, April 7, 1828, and returned to France, where he was warmly welcomed by Charles X.

But at the same time, without knowing Dillon's movements, Dumont d'Urville had already set out to find the scene of the wreck. And they had learned from a whaler that some medals and a cross of St. Louis had been found in the hands of some savages of Louisiade and New Caledonia. Dumont d'Urville, commander of the *Astrolabe,* had then sailed, and two months after Dillon had left Vanikoro, he put into Hobart Town. There he learned the results of Dillon's inquiries, and found that a certain James Hobbs, second lieutenant of the *Union* of Calcutta, after landing on an island situated 8° 18′ south latitude, and 156° 30′ east longitude, had seen some iron bars and red stuffs used by the natives of these parts. Dumont d'Urville, much perplexed, and not knowing how to credit the reports of low-class journals, decided to follow Dillon's track.

On the 10th of February, 1828, the *Astrolabe* appeared off Tikopia, and took as guide and interpreter a deserter found on the island; made his way to Vanikoro, sighted it on the 12th inst., lay among the reefs until the 14th, and not until the 20th did he cast anchor within the barrier in the harbor of Vanou.

On the 23d, several officers went round the island, and brought back some unimportant trifles. The natives, adopting a system of denials and evasions, refused to take them to the unlucky place. This ambiguous conduct led them to believe that the natives had ill-treated the castaways, and indeed they seemed to fear that Dumont d'Urville had come to avenge La Perouse and his unfortunate crew.

However, on the 26th, appeased by some presents, and understanding that they had no reprisals to fear, they led M. Jacquireot to the scene of the wreck.

There, in three or four fathoms of water, between the reefs of Pacou and Vanou, lay anchors, cannons, pigs of lead and iron, embedded in the limy concretions. The large boat and the whaler belonging to the *Astrolabe* were sent to this place, and, not without some difficulty, their crews hauled up an anchor weighing 1800 lbs., a brass gun, some pigs of iron, and two copper swivel-guns.

Dumont d'Urville, questioning the natives, learned, too, that La Perouse, after losing both his vessels on the reefs of this island, had constructed a smaller boat, only to be lost a second time. Where?—no one knew.

But the French government, fearing that Dumont d'Urville was not acquainted with Dillon's movements, had sent the sloop *Bayonnaise,* commanded by Legoarant de Tromelin, to Vanikoro, which had been stationed on the west coast of America. The *Bayonnaise* cast her anchor before Vanikoro some months after the departure of the *Astrolabe,* but found no new document; but stated that the savages had respected the monument to La Perouse. That is the substance of what I told to Captain Nemo.

"So," he said, "no one knows now where the third vessel perished that was constructed by the castaways on the island of Vanikoro?"

"No one knows."

Captain Nemo said nothing, but signed to me to follow him into the large saloon. The *Nautilus* sank several yards below the waves, and the panels were opened.

I hastened to the aperture, and under the crustations of coral, covered with fungi, syphonules, alcyons, madrepores, through myriads of charming fish,—girelles, glyphisidri, pompherides, diacopes, and holocentres,—I recognized certain debris that the drags had not been able to tear up: iron stirrups, anchors, cannons, bullets, capstan-fittings, the stem of a ship,—all objects clearly proving the wreck of some vessel, and now carpeted with living flowers. While I was looking on this desolate scene, Captain Nemo said, in a sad voice,—

"Commander La Perouse set out December 7, 1785, with his vessels *La Bousolle* and the *Astrolabe*. He first cast anchor at Botany Bay, visited the Friendly Isles, New Caledonia, then directed his course towards Santa Cruz, and put into Namouka, one of the Hapaï group. Then his vessels struck on the unknown reefs of Vanikoro. The *Bousolle,* which went first, ran aground on the southerly coast. The *Astrolabe* went to its help, and ran aground too. The first vessel was destroyed almost immediately. The second, stranded under the wind, resisted some days. The natives made the castaways welcome. They installed themselves in the island, and constructed a smaller boat with the debris of the two large ones. Some sailors stayed willingly at Vanikoro; the others, weak and ill, set out with La Perouse. They directed their course towards the Solomon Isles, and there perished, with everything, on the westerly coast of the chief island of the group, between Capes Deception and Satisfaction."

"How do you know that?"

"By this, that I found on the spot where was the last wreck."

Captain Nemo showed me a tin-plate box, stamped with the French arms, and corroded by the salt water. He opened it, and I saw a bundle of papers, yellow but still readable.

They were the instructions of the naval minister to Commander La Perouse, annotated in the margin in Louis XVI.'s handwriting.

"Ah! it is a fine death for a sailor!" said Captain Nemo, at last. "A coral tomb makes a quiet grave; and I trust that I and my comrades will find no other."

CHAPTER 19

TORRES STRAITS

DURING the night of the 27th or 28th of December, the *Nautilus* left the shores of Vanikoro with great speed. Her course was southwesterly, and in three days she had gone over the 750 leagues that separated it from La Perouse's group and the southeast point of Papua.

Early on the 1st of January, 1863, Conseil joined me on the platform.

"Master, will you permit me to wish you a happy new year?"

"What! Conseil; exactly as if I was at Paris in my study at the Jardin des Plantes? Well, I accept your good wishes, and thank you for them. Only, I will ask you what you mean by a 'Happy new year,' under our circumstances? Do you mean the year that will bring us to the end of our imprisonment, or the year that sees us continue this strange voyage?"

"Really, I do not know how to answer, master. We are sure to see curious things, and for the last two months we have not had time for ennui. The last marvel is always the most astonishing; and if we continue this progression, I do not know how it will end. It is my opinion that we shall never again see the like. I think, then, with no offence to master, that a happy year would be one in which we could see everything."

On January 2, we had made 11,340 miles, or 5250 French leagues, since our starting-point in the Japan Seas. Before the ship's head stretched the dangerous shores of the coral sea, on the northeast coast of Australia. Our boat lay along some miles from the redoubtable bank on which Cook's vessel was lost, June 10, 1770. The boat in which Cook was struck on a rock, and if it did not sink, it was owing to a piece of the coral that was broken by the shock, and fixed itself in the broken keel.

I had wished to visit the reef, 360 leagues long, against which the sea, always rough, broke with great violence, with a noise like thunder. But just then the inclined planes drew the *Nautilus* down to a great depth, and I could see nothing of the high coral walls. I had to content myself with the different specimens of fish brought up by the nets. I remarked, among others, some germons, a species of mackerel as large as a tunny, wich bluish sides, and striped with transverse bands, that disappear with the animal's life. These fish followed us in shoals, and furnished us with very delicate food. We took also a large number of giltheads, about one and a half inches long, tasting like dorys; and flying pyrapeds like submarine swallows, which, in dark nights, light alternately the air and water with their phosphorescent light. Among the molluscs and zoöphytes, I found in the meshes of the net several species of alcyonarians, echini, hammers, spurs, dials, cerites, and hyalleæ. The flora was represented by beautiful floating sea-weeds, laminariæ, and macrocystes, impregnated with the mucilage that transudes through their pores; and among which I gathered an admirable *Nemastoma Geliniarois,* that was classed among the natural curiosities of the museum.

Two days after crossing the coral sea, January 4, we sighted the Papuan coasts. On this occasion, Captain Nemo informed me that his intention was to get into the Indian Ocean by the Strait of Torres. His communication ended there.

The Torres Straits are nearly thirty-four leagues wide; but they are obstructed by an innumerable quantity of islands, islets, breakers, and rocks, that make its navigation almost impracticable; so that Captain Nemo took all needful precautions to cross them. The *Nautilus,* floating betwixt wind and water, went at a moderate pace. Her screw, like a cetacean's tail, beat the waves slowly.

Profiting by this, I and my two companions went up on to the deserted platform. Before us was the steersman's cage, and I expected that Captain Nemo was there directing the course of the *Nautilus*. I had before me the excellent charts of the Strait of Torres, made out by the hydrographical engineer Vincendon Dumoulin. These and Captain King's are the best charts that clear the intricacies of this strait, and I consulted them attentively. Round the *Nautilus* the sea dashed furiously. The course of the waves, that went from southeast to northwest at the rate of two and a half miles, broke on the coral that showed itself here and there.

"This is a bad sea!" remarked Ned Land.

"Detestable indeed, and one that does not suit a boat like the *Nautilus*."

"The captain must be very sure of his route, for I see there pieces of coral that would do for its keel if it only touched them slightly."

Indeed the situation was dangerous, but the *Nautilus* seemed to slide like magic off these rocks. It did not follow the routes of the *Astrolabe* and the *Zélée* exactly, for they proved fatal to Dumont d'Urville. It bore more northwards, coasted the Island of Murray, and came back to the southwest towards Cumberland Passage. I thought it was going to pass it by, when, going back to northwest, it went through a large quantity of islands and islets little known, towards the Island Sound and Canal Mauvais.

I wondered if Captain Nemo, foolishly imprudent, would steer his vessel into that pass where Dumont d'Urville's two corvettes touched; when, swerving again, and cutting straight through to the west, he steered for the Island of Gilboa.

It was then three in the afternoon. The tide began to recede, being quite full. The *Nautilus* approached the island, that I still saw, with its remarkable border of screw-pines. He stood off it at about two miles distant. Suddenly a shock overthrew me. The *Nautilus* just touched a rock, and stayed immovable, laying lightly to port side.

When I rose, I perceived Captain Nemo and his lieutenant on the platform. They were examining the situation of the vessel, and exchanging words in their incomprehensible dialect.

She was situated thus: two miles, on the starboard side, appeared Gilboa, stretching from north to west like an immense arm; towards the south and east some coral showed itself, left by the ebb. We had run aground, and in one of those seas where the tides are middling,—a sorry matter for the floating of the

The *Nautilus* in danger.

Nautilus. However, the vessel had not suffered, for her keel was solidly joined. But if she could neither glide off nor move, she ran the risk of being forever fastened to these rocks, and then Captain Nemo's submarine vessel would be done for.

I was reflecting thus, when the captain, cool and calm, always master of himself, approached me.

"An accident?" I asked.

"No; an incident."

"But an incident that will oblige you perhaps to become an inhabitant of this land from which you flee?"

Captain Nemo looked at me curiously, and made a negative gesture, as much as to say that nothing would force him to set foot on *terra firma* again. Then he said,—

"Besides, M. Aronnax, the *Nautilus* is not lost; it will carry you yet into the midst of the marvels of the ocean. Our voyage is only begun, and I do not wish to be deprived so soon of the honor of your company."

"However, Captain Nemo," I replied, without noticing the ironical turn of his phrase, "the *Nautilus* ran aground in open sea. Now the tides are not strong in the Pacific; and if you cannot lighten the *Nautilus*, I do not see how it will be reinflated."

"The tides are not strong in the Pacific: you are right there, Professor; but in Torres Straits, one finds still a difference of a yard and a half between the level of high and low seas. To-day is January 4, and in five days the moon will be full. Now, I shall be very much astonished if that complaisant satellite does not raise these masses of water sufficiently, and render me a service that I should be indebted to her for."

Having said this, Captain Nemo, followed by this lieutenant, re-descended to the interior of the *Nautilus*. As to the vessel, it moved not, and was immovable, as if the coralline polypi had already walled it up with their indestructible cement.

"Well, sir?" said Ned Land, who came up to me after the departure of the captain.

"Well, friend Ned, we will wait patiently for the tide on the 9th instant; for it appears that the moon will have the goodness to put it off again."

"Really?"

"Really."

"And this captain is not going to cast anchor at all, since the tide will suffice?" said Conseil, simply.

The Canadian looked at Conseil, then shrugged his shoulders.

"Sir, you may believe me when I tell you that this piece of iron will navigate neither on nor under the sea again; it is only fit to be sold for its weight. I think, therefore, that the time has come to part company with Captain Nemo."

"Friend Ned, I do not despair of this stout *Nautilus*, as you do; and in four days we shall know what to hold to on the Pacific tides. Besides, flight might be possible if we were in sight of the English or Provençal coasts; but on the Papuan shores, it is another thing; and it will be time enough to come to that extremity if the *Nautilus* does not recover itself again, which I look upon as a grave event."

"But do they know, at least, how to act circumspectly? There is an island; on that island there are trees; under those trees, terrestrial animals, bearers of cutlets and roast-beef, to which I would willingly give a trial."

"In this, friend Ned is right," said Conseil, "and I agree with him. Could not master obtain permission from his friend Captain Nemo to put us on land, if only so as not to lose the habit of treading on the solid parts of our planet?"

"I can ask him, but he will refuse."

"Will master risk it?" asked Conseil, "and we shall know how to rely upon the captain's amiability."

To my great surprise Captain Nemo gave me the permission I asked for, and he gave it very agreeably, without even exacting from me a promise to return to the vessel; but flight across New Guinea might be very perilous, and I should not have counselled Ned Land to attempt it. Better to be a prisoner on board the *Nautilus* than to fall into the hands of the natives.

At eight o'clock, armed with guns and hatchets, we got off the *Nautilus*. The sea was pretty calm; a slight breeze blew on land. Conseil and I rowing, we sped along quickly, and Ned steered in the straight passage that the breakers left between them. The boat was well handled, and moved rapidly.

Ned Land could not restrain his joy. He was like a prisoner that had escaped from prison, and knew not that it was necessary to re-enter it.

"Meat! We are going to eat some meat; and what meat!" he replied. "Real game! no, bread, indeed."

"I do not say that fish is not good; we must not abuse it; but a piece of fresh venison grilled on live coals will agreeably vary our ordinary course."

"Gourmand!" said Conseil; "he makes my mouth water."

"It remains to be seen," I said, "if these forests are full of game, and if the game is not such as will hunt the hunter himself."

"Well said, M. Aronnax," replied the Canadian, whose teeth seemed sharpened like the edge of a hatched; "but I will eat tiger,—loin of tiger,— if there is no other quadruped on this island."

"Friend Ned is uneasy about it," said Conseil.

"Whatever it may be," continued Ned Land, "every animal with four paws without feathers, or with two paws without feathers, will be saluted by my first shot."

"Very well! Master Land's imprudences are beginning."

"Never fear, M. Aronnax," replied the Canadian; "I do not want twenty-five minutes to offer you a dish of my sort."

At half past eight the *Nautilus* boat ran softly aground, on a heavy sand, after having happily passed the coral reef that surrounds the Island of Gilboa.

CHAPTER 20

A FEW DAYS ON LAND

I WAS much impressed on touching land. Ned Land tried the soil with his feet, as if to take possession of it. However, it was only two months before that we had become, according to Captain Nemo, "passengers on board the *Nautilus*," but, in reality, prisoners of its commander.

In a few minutes we were within musket-shot of the coast. The soil was almost entirely madreporical, but certain beds of dried-up torrents strewn with debris of granite showed that this island was of the primary formation. The whole horizon was hidden behind a beautiful curtain of forests. Enormous trees, the trunks of which attained a height of 200 feet, were tied to each other by garlands of bindweed, real natural hammocks, which a light breeze rocked. They were mimosas, ficuses, casuarinæ, teks, hibisci, and palm-trees, mingled together in profusion; and under the shelter of their verdant vault grew orchids, leguminous plants, and ferns.

But without noticing all these beautiful specimens of Papuan flora, the Canadian abandoned the agreeable for the useful. He discovered a cocoanut-tree, beat down some of the fruit, broke them, and we drunk the milk and ate the nut with a satisfaction that protested against the ordinary food on the *Nautilus*.

"Excellent!" said Ned Land.

"Exquisite!" replied Conseil.

"And I do not think," said the Canadian, "that he would object to our introducing a cargo of cocoanuts on board."

"I do not think he would, but he would not taste them."

"So much the worse for him," said Conseil.

"And so much the better for us," replied Ned Land. "There will be more for us."

"One word only, Master Land," I said to the harpooner, who was beginning to ravage another cocoanut-tree. "Cocoanuts are good things, but before filling the canoe with them, it would be wise to reconnoitre and see if the island does not produce some substance not less useful. Fresh vegetables would be welcome on board the *Nautilus*."

"Master is right," replied Conseil; "and I propose to reserve three places in our vessel: one for fruits, the other for vegetables, and the third for the venison, of which I have not yet seen the smallest specimen."

"Conseil, we must not despair," said the Canadian.

"Let us continue," I returned, "and lie in wait. Although the island seems uninhabited, it might still contain some individuals that would be less hard than we on the nature of game."

"Ho! ho!" said Ned Land, moving his jaws significantly.

"Well, Ned!" cried Conseil.

"My word!" returned the Canadian, "I begin to understand the charms of anthropophagy."

"Ned! Ned! what are you saying? You, a man-eater? I should not feel safe with you, especially as I share your cabin. I might perhaps wake one day to find myself half devoured."

"Friend Conseil, I like you much, but not enough to eat you unnecessarily."

"I would not trust you," replied Conseil. "But enough. We must absolutely bring down some game to satisfy this cannibal, or else, one of these fine mornings, master will find only pieces of his servant to serve him."

While we were talking thus, we were penetrating the sombre arches of the forest, and for two hours we surveyed it in all directions.

Chance rewarded our search for eatable vegetables, and one of the most useful products of the tropical zones furnished us with precious food that we missed on board. I would speak of the bread-fruit tree, very abundant in the Island of Gilboa; and I remarked chiefly the variety destitute of seeds, which bears in Malaya the name of "rima."

Ned Land knew these fruits well. He had already eaten many during his numerous voyages, and he knew how to prepare the eatable substance. Moreover, the sight of them excited him, and he could contain himself no longer.

"Master," he said, "I shall die if I do not taste a little of this bread-fruit pie."

"Taste it, friend Ned, taste it as you want. We are here to make experiments,—make them."

"It won't take long," said the Canadian.

And provided with a lentil, he lighted a fire of dead wood, that crackled joyously. During this time, Conseil and I chose the best fruits of the artocarpus. Some had not then attained a sufficient degree of maturity, and their thick skin covered a white but rather fibrous pulp. Others, the greater number yellow and gelatinous, waited only to be picked.

These fruits enclose no kernel. Conseil brought a dozen to Ned Land, who placed them on a coal fire, after having cut them in thick slices, and while doing this repeating,—

"You will see, master, how good this bread is. More so when one has been deprived of it so long. It is not even bread," added he, "but a delicate pastry. You have eaten none, master?"

"No, Ned."

"Very well, prepare yourself for a juicy thing. If you do not come for more, I am no longer the king of harpooners."

After some minutes, the part of the fruits that was exposed to the fire was completely roasted. The interior looked like a white pasty, a sort of soft crumb, the flavor of which was like that of an artichoke.

It must be confessed this bread was excellent, and I ate of it with great relish.

"What time is it now?" asked the Canadian.

"Two o'clock at least," replied Conseil.

"How time flies on firm ground!" sighed Ned Land.

"Let us be off," replied Conseil.

We returned through the forest, and completed our collection by a raid upon the cabbage-palms, that we gathered from the tops of the trees, little beans that I recognized as the "abron" of the Malays, and yams of a superior quality.

We were loaded when we reached the boat. But Ned Land did not find his provision sufficient. Fate, however, favored us. Just as we were pushing off, he perceived several trees, from twenty-five to thirty feet high, a species of palm-tree. These trees, as valuable as the atrocarpus, justly are reckoned among the most useful products of Malaya.

At last, a five o'clock in the evening, loaded with our riches, we quitted the shore, and half an hour after we hailed the *Nautilus*. No one appeared on our arrival. The enormous iron-plated cylinder seemed deserted. The provisions embarked, I descended to my chamber, and after supper slept soundly.

The next day, January 6, nothing new on board. Not a sound inside, not a sign of life. The boat rested along the edge, in the same place in which we had left it. We resolved to return to the island. Ned Land hoped to be more fortunate than on the day before with regard to the hunt, and wished to visit another part of the forest.

At dawn we set off. The boat, carried on by the waves that flowed to shore, reached the island in a few minutes.

We landed, and thinking that it was better to give in to the Canadian, we followed Ned Land, whose long limbs threatened to distance us. He wound up the coast towards the west; then, fording some torrents, he gained the high plain that was bordered with admirable forests. Some kingfishers were rambling along the water-courses, but they would not let themselves be approached. Their circumspection proved to me that these birds knew what to expect from bipeds of our species, and I concluded that, if the island was not inhabited, at least human beings occasionally frequented it.

After crossing a rather large prairie, we arrived at the skirts of a little wood that was enlivened by the songs and flight of a large number of birds.

"There are only birds!" said Conseil.

"But they are eatable," replied the harpooner.

"I do not agree with you, friend Ned, for I see only parrots there."

"Friend Conseil," said Ned, gravely, "the parrot is like pheasant to those who have nothing else."

"And," I added, "this bird, suitably prepared, is worth knife and fork."

Indeed, under the thick foliage of this wood, a world of parrots were flying from branch to branch, only needing a careful education to speak the human language. For the moment, they were chattering with parrots of all colors, and grave cockatoos, who seemed to meditate upon some philosophical problem, whilst brilliant red lories passed like a piece of bunting carried away by the breeze; papuans, with the finest azure colors, and in all a variety of winged things most charming to behold, but few eatable.

However, a bird peculiar to these lands, and which has never passed limits of the Arrow and Papuan islands, was wanting in this collection. But fortune reserved it for me before long.

After passing through a moderately thick copse, we found a plain obstructed with bushes. I saw then those magnificent birds, the disposition of whose long feathers obliges them to fly against the wind. Their undulating flight, graceful aerial curves, and the shading of their colors, attracted and charmed one's looks. I had no trouble in recognizing them.

"Birds of Paradise!" I exclaimed.

The Malays, who carry on a great trade in these birds with the Chinese, have several means that we could not employ for taking them. Sometimes they put snares at the top of high trees that the birds of Paradise prefer to frequent. Sometimes they catch them with a viscous bird-lime that paralyzes their movements. They even go so far as to poison the fountains that the birds generally drink from. But we were obliged to fire at them during flight, which gave us few chances to bring them down; and indeed, we vainly exhausted one half of our ammunition.

About eleven o'clock in the morning, the first range of mountains that form the centre of the island was traversed, and we had killed nothing. Hunger drove us on. The hunters had relied on the products of the chase, and they were wrong. Happily Conseil, to his great surprise, made a double shot and secured breakfast. He brought down a white pigeon and a wood-pigeon, which, cleverly plucked and suspended from a skewer, were roasted before a red fire of dead wood. Whilst these interesting birds were cooking, Ned prepared the fruit of the artocarpus. Then the wood-pigeons were devoured to the bones, and declared excellent. The nutmeg, with which they are in the habit of stuffing their crops, flavors their flesh and renders it delicious eating.

"Now, Ned, what do you miss now?"

"Some four-footed game, M. Aronnax. All these pigeons are only side-dishes, and trifles; and until I have killed an animal with cutlets, I shall not be content."

"Nor I, Ned, if I do not catch a bird of Paradise."

"Let us continue hunting," replied Conseil. "Let us go towards the sea. We have arrived at the first declivities of the mountains, and I think we had better regain the region of forests."

That was sensible advice, and was followed out. After walking for one hour, we had attained a forest of sago-trees. Some inoffensive serpents glided away from us. The birds of Paradise fled at our approach, and truly I despaired of getting near one, when Conseil, who was walking in front, suddenly bent down, uttered a triumphal cry, and came back to me bringing a magnificent specimen.

"Ah! bravo, Conseil!"

"Master is very good."

"No, my boy; you have made an excellent stroke. Take one of these living birds, and carry it in your hand."

"If master will examine it, he will see that I have not deserved great merit."

"Why, Conseil?"

"Because this bird is as drunk as a quail."

"Drunk!"

"Yes, sir; drunk with the nutmegs that it devoured under the nutmeg-tree, under which I found it. See, friend Ned, see the monstrous effects of intemperance!"

"By Jove!" exclaimed the Canadian, "because I have drunk gin for two months, you must needs reproach me!"

However, I examined the curious bird. Conseil was right. The bird, drunk with juice, was quite powerless. It could not fly; it could hardly walk.

This bird belonged to the most beautiful of the eight species that are found in Papua and in the neighboring islands. It was the "large emerald bird, the most rare kind." It measured three feet in length. Its head was comparatively small, its eyes placed near the opening of the beak, and also small. But the shades of color were beautiful, having a yellow beak, brown feet and claws, nut-colored wings with purple tips, pale yellow at the back of the neck and head, and emerald color at the throat, chestnut on the breast and belly. Two horned downy nets rose from below the tail, that prolonged the long light feathers of admirable fineness, and they completed the whole of this marvellous bird, that the natives have poetically named the "bird of the sun."

But if my wishes were satisfied by the possession of the bird of Paradise, the Canadian's were not yet. Happily about two o'clock Ned Land brought down a magnificent hog, from the brood of those the natives call "bari-outang." The animal came in time for us to procure real quadruped meat, and he was well received. Ned Land was very proud of his shot. The hog, hit by the electric ball, fell stone dead. The Canadian skinned and cleaned it properly, after having taken half a dozen cutlets, destined to furnish us with a grilled repast in the evening. Then the hunt was resumed, which was still more marked by Ned and Conseil's exploits.

Indeed, the two friends, beating the bushes, roused a herd of kangaroos, that fled and bounded along on their elastic paws. But these animals did not take flight so rapidly but what the electric capsule could stop their course.

"Ah, Professor!" cried Ned Land, who was carried away by the delights of the chase, "what excellent game! and stewed too! What a supply for the *Nautilus!*

two! three! five down! And to think that we shall eat that flesh, and that the idiots on board shall not have a crumb!"

I think that, in the excess of his joy, the Canadian, if he had not talked so much, would have killed them all. But he contented himself with a single dozen of these interesting marsupians. These animals were small. They were a species of those "kangaroo rabbits" that live habitually in the hollows of trees, and whose speed is extreme; but they are moderately fat, and furnish, at least, estimable food. We were very satisfied with the results of the hunt. Happy Ned proposed to return to this enchanting island the next day, for hs wished to depopulate it of all the eatable quadrupeds. But he reckoned without his host.

At six o'clock in the evening we had regained the shore; our boat was moored to the usual place. The *Nautilus,* like a long rock, emerged from the waves two miles from the beach. Ned Land, without waiting, occupied himself about the important dinner business. He understood all about cooking well. The "bariou-tang," grilled on the coals, soon scented the air with a delicious odor.

Indeed, the dinner was excellent. Two wood-pigeons completed this extraordinary *menu*. The sago pasty, the artocarpus bread, some mangoes, half a dozen pineapples, and the liquor fermented from some cocoanuts, overjoyed us. I even think that my worthy companions' ideas had not all the plainness desirable.

"Suppose we do not return to the *Nautilus* this evening?" said Conseil.

"Suppose we never return?" added Ned Land.

Just then a stone fell at our feet, and cut short the harpooner's proposition.

CHAPTER 21

CAPTAIN NEMO'S THUNDERBOLT

We looked at the edge of the forest without rising, my hand stopping in the action of putting it to my mouth, Ned Land's completing its office.

"Stones do not fall from the sky," remarked Conseil, "or they would merit the name of aerolites."

A second stone, carefully aimed, that made a savory pigeon's leg fall from Conseil's hand, gave still more weight to his observation. We all three arose, shouldered our guns, and were ready to reply to any attack.

"Are they apes?" cried Ned Land.

"Very nearly,—they are savages."

"To the boat!" I said, hurrying to the sea.

It was indeed necessary to beat a retreat, for about twenty natives, armed with bows and slings, appeared on the skirts of a copse that masked the horizon to the right, hardly a hundred steps from us.

Our boat was moored about sixty feet from us. The savages approached us, not running, but making hostile demonstrations. Stones and arrows fell thickly.

Ned Land had not wished to leave his provisions; and, in spite of his imminent danger, his pig on one side, and kangaroos on the other, he went tolerably fast. In two minutes we were on the shore. To load the boat with provisions and

Conseil suddenly bent down, uttered a triumphal cry, and came back, bringing a magnificent specimen.

arms, to push it out to sea, and ship the oars, was the work of an instant. We had not gone two cable-lengths when a hundred savages, howling and gesticulating, entered the water up to their waists. I watched to see if their apparition would attract some men from the *Nautilus* on to the platform. But no. The enormous machine, lying off, was absolutely deserted.

Twenty minutes later we were on board. The panels were open. After making the boat fast, we entered into the interior of the *Nautilus*.

I descended to the drawing-room, from whence I heard some chords. Captain Nemo was there, bending over his organ, and plunged in a musical ecstasy.

"Captain!"

He did not hear me.

"Captain!" I said again, touching his hand.

He shuddered, and, turning round, said, "Ah! it is you, Professor? Well, have you had a good hunt? Have you botanized successfully?"

"Yes, Captain; but we have unfortunately brought a troop of bipeds, whose vicinity troubles me."

"What bipeds?"

"Savages."

"Savages!" he echoes ironically. "So you are astonished, Professor, at having set foot on a strange land and finding savages? Savages! where are there not any? Besides, are they worse than others, these whom you call savages?"

"But, Captain—"

"How many have you counted?"

"A hundred at least."

"M. Aronnax," replied Captain Nemo, placing his fingers on the organ stops, "when all the natives of Papua are assembled on this shore, the *Nautilus* will have nothing to fear from their attacks."

The captain's fingers were then running over the keys of the instrument, and I remarked that he touched only the black keys, which gave to his melodies an essentially Scotch character. Soon he had forgotten my presence, and had plunged into a reverie that I did not disturb. I went up again on to the platform,—night had already fallen; for, in this low latitude, the sun sets rapidly and without twilight. I could only see the island indistinctly; but the numerous fires lighted on the beach showed that the natives did not think of leaving it. I was alone for several hours, sometimes thinking of the natives,—but without any dread of them, for the imperturbable confidence of the captain was catching,—sometimes forgetting them to admire the splendors of the night in the tropics. My remembrances went to France, in the train of those zodiacal stars that would shine in some hours' time. The moon shone in the midst of the constellations of the zenith.

The night slipped away without any mischance, the islanders frightened, no doubt, at the sight of a monster aground in the bay. The panels were open, and would have offered an easy access to the interior of the *Nautilus*.

At six o'clock in the morning of the 8th January, I went up on to the platform. The dawn was breaking. The island soon showed itself through the dissipating fogs,—first the shore, then the summits.

The natives were there, more numerous than on the day before,—500 or 600 perhaps,—some of them, profiting by the low water, had come on to the coral, at less than two cable-lengths from the *Nautilus*. I distinguished them easily; they were true Papuans, with athletic figures; men of good race, large high foreheads,—large, but not broad, and flat,—and white teeth. Their woolly hair, with a reddish tinge, showed off on their black, shining bodies like those of the Nubians. From the lobes of their ears, cut and distended, hung chaplets of bones. Most of these savages were naked. Amongst them I remarked some women dressed from the hips to the knees in quite a crinoline of herbs, that sustained a vegetable waistband. Some chiefs had ornamented their necks with a crescent and collars of glass beads, red and white; nearly all were armed with bows, arrows, and shields, and carried on their shoulders a sort of net containing those round stones which they cast from their slings with great skill. One of these chiefs, rather near to the *Nautilus,* examined it attentively. He was, perhaps, a "mado" of high rank, for he was draped in a mat of banana leaves notched round the edges, and set off with brilliant colors.

I could easily have knocked down this native, who was within a short length; but I thought that it was better to wait for real hostile demonstrations. Between Europeans and savages, it is proper for the Europeans to parry sharply, not to attack.

During low water the natives roamed about near the *Nautilus,* but were not troublesome; I heard them frequently repeat the word "Assai," and by their gestures I understood that they invited me to go on land, an invitation that I declined.

So that, on that day, the boat did not push off, to the great displeasure of Master Land, who could not complete his provisions.

This adroit Canadian employed his time in preparing the viands and meat that he had brought off the island. As for the savages, they returned to the shore about eleven o'clock in the morning, as soon as the coral tops began to disappear under the rising tide; but I saw their numbers had increased considerably on the shore. Probably they came from the neighboring islands, or very likely from Papua. However, I had not seen a single native canoe. Having nothing better to do, I thought of dragging these beautiful limpid waters, under which I saw a profusion of shells, zoöphytes, and marine plants. Moreover, it was the last day that the *Nautilus* would pass in these parts, if it float in open sea the next day, according to Captain Nemo's promise.

I therefore called Conseil, who brought me a little light drag, very like those for the oyster-fishery. Now to work! For two hours we fished unceasingly, but without bringing up any rarities. The drag was filled with midas-ears, harps, melames, and particularly the most beautiful hammers I have ever seen. We also brought up some holothurias, pearl-oysters, and a dozen little turtles, that were reserved for the pantry on board.

But just when I expected it least, I put my hand on a wonder, I might say a natural deformity, very rarely met with. Conseil was just dragging, and his net came up filled with divers ordinary shells, when, all at once, he saw me plunge my arm quickly into the net, to draw out a shell, and heard me utter a conchological cry, that is to say, the most piercing cry that human throat can utter.

"What is the matter, sir?" he asked, in surprise; "has master been bitten?"

"No, my boy; but I would willingly have given a finger for my discovery."

"What discovery?"

"This shell," I said, holding up the object of my triumph.

"It is simply an olive porphyry, genus olive, order of the pectinibranchidæ, class of gasteropods, sub-class of mollusca."

"Yes, Conseil; but instead of being rolled from right to left, this olive turns from left to right."

"Is it possible?"

"Yes, my boy; it is a left shell."

Shells are all right-handed, with rare exceptions; and when by chance their spiral is left, amateurs are ready to pay their weight in gold.

Conseil and I were absorbed in the contemplation of our treasure, and I was promising myself to enrich the museum with it, when a stone, unfortunately thrown by a native, struck against and broke the precious object in Conseil's hand. I uttered a cry of despair! Conseil took up his gun, and aimed at a savage who was poising his sling at ten yards from him. I would have stopped him, but his blow took effect, and broke the bracelet of amulets which encircled the arm of the savage.

"Conseil!" cried I; "Conseil!"

"Well, sir! do you not see that the cannibal has commenced the attack?"

"A shell is not worth the life of a man," said I.

"Ah! the scoundrel!" cried Conseil; "I would rather he had broken my shoulder!"

Conseil was in earnest, but I was not of his opinion. However, the situation had changed some minutes before, and we had not perceived. A score of canoes surrounded the *Nautilus*. These canoes, scooped out of the trunk of a tree, long, narrow, well adapted for speed, were balanced by means of a long bamboo pole, which floated on the water. They were managed by skillful, half-naked paddlers, and I watched their advance with some uneasiness. It was evident that these Papuans had already had dealings with the Europeans, and knew their ships. But this long iron cylinder anchored in the bay, without masts or chimney, what could they think of it? Nothing good, for at first they kept at a respectful distance. However, seeing it motionless, by degrees they took courage, and sought to familiarize themselves with it. Now this familiarity was precisely what it was necessary to avoid. Our arms, which were noiseless, could only produce a moderate effect on the savages, who have little respect for aught but blustering things. The thunderbolt without the reverberations of thunder would frighten man but little, though the danger lies in the lightning, not in the noise.

At this moment the canoes approached the *Nautilus*, and a shower of arrows alighted on her.

I went down to the saloon, but found no one there. I ventured to knock at the door that opened into the captain's room. "Come in," was the answer.

I entered, and found Captain Nemo deep in algebraical calculations of x and other quantities.

"I am disturbing you," said I, for courtesy's sake.

"That is true, M. Aronnax," replied the captain; "but I think you have serious reasons for wishing to see me?"

"Very grave ones; the natives are surrounding us in their canoes, and in a few minutes we shall certainly be attacked by many hundreds of savages."

"Ah!" said Captain Nemo, quietly, "they are come with their canoes?"

"Yes, sir."

"Well, sir, we must close the hatches."

"Exactly, and I came to say to you—"

"Nothing can be more simple," said Captain Nemo. And pressing an electric button, he transmitted an order to the ship's crew.

One of these chiefs, rather near the *Nautilus*, examined it attentively.

"It is all done, sir," said he, after some moments. "The pinnace is ready, and the hatches are closed. You do not fear, I imagine, that these gentlemen could stave in walls on which the balls of your frigate have had no effect?"

"No, Captain; but a danger still exists."

"What is that, sir?"

"It is that to-morrow, at about this hour, we must open the hatches to renew the air of the *Nautilus*. Now, if, at this moment, the Papuans should occupy the platform, I do not see how you could prevent them from entering."

"Then, sir, you suppose that they will board us?"

"I am certain of it."

"Well, sir, let them come. I see no reason for hindering them. After all, these Papuans are poor creatures, and I am unwilling that my visit to the Island of Gueberoan should cost the life of a single one of these wretches."

Upon that I was going away; but Captain Nemo detained me, and asked me to sit down by him. He questioned me with interest about our excursions on shore, and our hunting and seemed not to understand the craving for meat that possessed the Canadian. Then the conversation turned on various subjects, and without being more communicative, Captain Nemo showed himself more amiable.

Amongst other things, we happened to speak of the situation of the *Nautilus,* run aground in exactly the same spot in this strait where Dumont d'Urville was nearly lost. Apropos of this,—

"This D'Urville was one of your great sailors," said the captain to me; "one of your most intelligent navigators. He is the Captain Cook of you Frenchmen. Unfortuunate man of science, after having braved the icebergs of the south pole, the coral reefs of Oceania, the cannibals of the Pacific, to perish miserably in a railway train! If this energetic man could have reflected during the last moments of his life, what must have been uppermost in his last thoughts, do you suppose?"

So speaking, Captain Nemo seemed moved, and his emotion gave me a better opinion of him. Then, chart in hand, we reviewed the travels of the French navigator, his voyages of circumnavigation, his double detention at the south pole, which led to the discovery of Adelaide and Louis Philippe, and fixing the hydrographical bearings of the principal islands of Oceania.

"That which your D'Urville has done on the surface of the seas," said Captain Nemo, "that have I done under them, and more easily, more completely than he. The *Astrolabe* and the *Zelia,* incessantly tossed about by the hurricanes, could not be worth the *Nautilus,* quiet repository of labor that she is, truly motionless in the midst of the waters."

"To-morrow," added the captain, rising, "to-morrow, at twenty minutes to three P.M., the *Nautilus* shall float, and leave the Strait of Torres uninjured."

Having curtly pronounced these words, Captain Nemo bowed slightly. This was to dismiss me, and I went back to my room.

There I found Conseil, who wished to know the result of my interview with the captain.

"My boy," said I, "when I feigned to believe that his *Nautilus* was threatened by the natives of Papua, the captain answered me very sarcastically. I have but one thing to say to you: Have confidence in him, and go to sleep in peace."

"Have you no need of my services, sir?"

"No, my friend. What is Ned Land doing?"

"If you will excuse me, sir," answered Conseil, "friend Ned is busy making a kangaroo-pie, which will be a marvel."

The first native who placed his hand on the staircase, struck from behind by some invisible force, fled.

I remained alone, and went to bed, but slept indifferently. I heard the noise of the savages, who stamped on the platform, uttering deafening cries. The night passed thus, without disturbing the ordinary repose of the crew. The presence of these cannibals affected them no more than the soldiers of a masked battery care for the ants that crawl over its front.

At six in the morning I rose. The hatches had not been opened. The inner air was not renewed, but the reservoirs, filled ready for any emergency, were now resorted to, and discharged several cubic feet of oxygen into the exhausted atmosphere of the *Nautilus*.

I worked in my room till noon, without having seen Captain Nemo, even for an instant. On board no preparations for departure were visible.

I waited still some time, then went into the large saloon. The clock marked half past two. In ten minutes it would be high tide, and if Captain Nemo had not made a rash promise, the *Nautilus* would be immediately detached. If not, many months would pass ere she could leave her bed of coral.

However, some warning vibrations began to be felt in the vessel. I heard the keel grating against the rough, calcareous bottom of the coral feef.

At five-and-twenty minutes to three, Captain Nemo appeared in the saloon.

"We are going to start," said he.

"Ah!" replied I.

"I have given the order to open the hatches."

"And the Papuans?"

"The Papuans?" answered Captain Nemo, slightly shrugging his shoulders.

"Will they not come inside the *Nautilus?*"

"How?"

"Only by leaping over the hatches you have opened."

"M. Aronnax," quietly answered Captain Nemo, "they will not enter the hatches of the *Nautilus* in that way, even if they were open."

I looked at the captain.

"You do not understand?" said he.

"Hardly."

"Well, come and you will see."

I directed my steps toward the central staircase. There Ned Land and Conseil were slyly watching some of the ship's crew, who were opening the hatches, while cries of rage and fearful vociferations resounded outside.

The port lids were pulled down outside. Twenty horrible faces appeared. But the first native who placed his hand on the stair-rail, struck from behind by some invisible force, I know not what, fled, uttering the most fearful cries, and making the wildest contortions.

Ten of his companions followed him. They met with the same fate.

Conseil was in ecstasy. Ned Land, carried away by his violent instincts, rushed on to the staircase. But the moment he seized the rail with both hands, he, in his turn, was overthrown.

"I am struck by a thunderbolt," cried he, with an oath.

This explained all. It was no rail, but a metallic cable, charged with electricity from the deck, communicating with the platform. Whoever touched it felt a powerful shock,—and this shock would have been mortal, if Captain Nemo had discharged into the conductor the whole force of the current. It might truly be said that between his assailants and himself he had stretched a network of electricity which none could pass with impunity.

Meanwhile, the exasperated Papuans had beaten a retreat, paralyzed with terror. As for us, half laughing, we consoled and rubbed the unfortunate Ned Land, who swore like one possessed.

But, at this moment, the *Nautilus,* raised by the last waves of the tide, quitted her coral bed exactly at the fortieth minute fixed by the captain. Her screw swept the waters slowly and majestically. Her speed increased gradually, and sailing on the surface of the ocean, she quitted safe and sound the dangerous passes of the Straits of Torres.

CHAPTER 23

"ÆGRI SOMNIA

THE following day, 10th January, the *Nautilus* continued her course between two seas, but with such remarkable speed that I could not estimate it at less than thirty-five miles an hour. The rapidity of her screw was such that I could neither follow nor count its evolutions. When I reflected that this marvellous electric agent, after having afforded motion, heat, and light to the *Nautilus,* still protected her from outward attack, and transformed her into an ark of safety which no profane hand might touch without being thunderstricken, my admiration was unbounded, and from the structure it extended to the engineer who had called it into existence.

Our course was directed to the west, and on the 11th January we doubled Cape Wessel, situated in 135° longitude and 10° north latitude, which forms the east point of the Gulf of Carpentaria. The reefs were still numerous, but more equalized, and marked on the chart with extreme precision. The *Nautilus* easily avoided the breakers of Money to port, and the Victoria reefs to starboard, placed at 130° longitude, and on the tenth parallel which we strictly followed.

On the 13th January, Captain Nemo arrived in the Sea of Timor, and recognized the island of that name in 122° longitude.

From this point the direction of the *Nautilus* inclined towards the southwest. Her head was set for the Indian Ocean. Where would the fancy of Captain Nemo carry us next? Would he return to the coast of Asia? or would he approach again the shores of Europe? Improbable conjectures both, for a man who fled from inhabited continents. Then, would he descend to the south? Was he going to double the Cape of Good Hope, then Cape Horn, and finally go as far as the antarctic pole? Would he come back at last to the Pacific, where his *Nautilus* could sail free and independently? Time would show.

After having skirted the sands of Cartier, of Hibernia, Seringapatam, and Scott, last efforts of the solid against the liquid element, on the 14th January we lost sight of land altogether. The speed of the *Nautilus* was considerably abated, and with irregular course, she sometimes swam in the bosom of the waters, sometimes floated on their surface.

During this period of the voyage, Captain Nemo made some interesting experiments on the varied temperature of the sea, in different beds. Under ordinary conditions, these observations are made by means of rather complicated instruments, and with somewhat doubtful results, by means of thermometrical sounding-leads, the glasses often breaking under the pressure of the water, or an apparatus grounded on the variations of the resistance of metals to the electric currents. Results so obtained could not be correctly calculated. On the contrary, Captain Nemo went himself to test the temperature in the depths of the sea, and his thermometer, placed in communication with the different sheets of water, gave him the required degree immediately and accurately.

It was thus that, either by overloading her reservoirs, or by descending obliquely by means of her inclined planes, the *Nautilus* successively attained the depth of three, four, five, seven, nine, and ten thousand yards, and the definite result of this experience was, that the sea preserved an average temperature of four degrees and a half, at a depth of five thousand fathoms, under all latitudes.

On the 16th January, the *Nautilus* seemed becalmed, only a few yards beneath the surface of the waves. Her electric apparatus remained inactive, and her motionless screw left her to drift at the mercy of the currents. I supposed that the crew was occupied with interior repairs, rendered necessary by the violence of the mechanical movements of the machine.

My companions and I then witnessed a curious spectacle. The hatches of the saloon were open, and as the beacon light of the *Nautilus* was not in action, a dim obscurity reigned in the midst of the waters. I observed the state of the sea under these conditions, and the largest fish appeared to me no more than scarcely defined shadows, when the *Nautilus* found herself suddenly transported into full light. I thought at first that the beacon had been lighted, and was casting its electric radiance into the liquid mass. I was mistaken, and after a rapid survey perceived my error.

The *Nautilus* floated in the midst of a phosphorescent bed, which, in this obscurity, became quite dazzling. It was produced by myriads of luminous animalculæ, whose brilliancy was increased as they glided over the metallic hull of the vessel. I was surprised by lightning in the midst of these luminous sheets, as though they had been rivulets of lead melted in an ardent furnace, or metallic masses brought to a white heat, so that, by force of contrast, certain portions of light appeared to cast a shade in the midst of the general ignition, from which all shade seemed banished. No; this was not the calm irradiation of our ordinary lightning. There was unusual life and vigor; this was truly living light!

In reality, it was an infinite agglomerration of colored infusoria, of veritable globules of diaphanous jelly, provided with a thread-like tentacle, and of which as many as twenty-five thousand have been counted in less than two cubic half-inches of water; and their light was increased by the glimmering peculiar to the medusæ, starfish, aurelia, and other phosphorescent zoöphytes, impregnated by the grease of the organic matter decomposed by the sea, and, perhaps, the mucus secreted by the fish.

During several hours the *Nautilus* floated in these brilliant waves, and our admiration increased as we watched the marine monsters disporting themselves like salamanders. I saw there, in the midst of this fire that burns not, the swift and elegant porpoise (the indefatigable clown of the ocean), and some swordfish ten feet long, those prophetic heralds of the hurricane, whose formidable sword would now and then strike the glass of the saloon. Then appeared the smaller fish, the variegated balista, the leaping mackerel, wolf-thorntails, and a hundred others which striped the luminous atmosphere as they swam. This dazzling spectacle was enchanting! Perhaps some atmospheric condition increased the intensity of this phenomenon. Perhaps some storm agitated the surface of the waves. But, at this depth of some yards, the *Nautilus* was unmoved by its fury, and reposed peacefully in still water.

So we progressed, incessantly charmed by some new marvel. Conseil arranged and classed his zoöphytes, his articulata, his molluscs, his fishes. The days passed rapidly away, and I took no account of them. Ned, according to habit, tried to vary the diet on board. Like snails, we were fixed to our shells, and I declare it is easy to lead a snail's life.

Thus this life seemed easy and natural, and we thought no longer of the life we led on land; but something happened to recall us to the strangeness of our situation.

On the 18th of January, the *Nautilus* was in 105° longitude and 15° south latitude. The weather was threatening, the sea rough and rolling. There was a strong east wind. The barometer, which had been going down for some days, foreboded a coming storm. I went up on to the platform just as the second lieutenant was taking the measure of the horary angles, and waited, according to habit, till the daily phrase was said. But, on this day, it was exchanged for another phrase not less incomprehensible. Almost directly, I saw Captain Nemo appear, with a glass, looking towards the horizon.

For some minutes he was immovable, without taking his eye off the point of observation. Then he lowered his glass, and exchanged a few words with his lieutenant. The latter seemed to be a victim to some emotion that he tried in vain to repress. Captain Nemo, having more command over himself, was cool. He seemed, too, to be making some objections, to which the lieutenant replied by formal assurances; at least I concluded so by the difference of their tones and gestures. For myself, I had looked carefully in the direction indicated without seeing anything. The sky and water were lost in the clear line of the horizon.

However, Captain Nemo walked from one end of the platform to the other, without looking at me, perhaps without seeing me. His step was firm, but less regular than usual. He stopped sometimes, crossed his arms, and observed the sea. What could he be looking for on that immense expanse?

The *Nautilus* was then some hundreds of miles from the nearest coast.

The lieutenant had taken up the glass, and examined the horizon steadfastly, going and coming, stamping his foot and showing more nervous agitation than his superior officer. Besides, this mystery must necessarily be solved, and before long; for, upon an order from Captain Nemo, the engine, increasing to propelling power, made the screw turn more rapidly.

Just then the lieutenant drew the captain's attention again. The latter stopped walking and directed his glass towards the place indicated. He looked long. I felt very much puzzled, and descended to the drawing-room and took out an excellent telescope that I generally used. Then, leaning on the cage of the watch-light, that jutted out from the front of the platform, set myself to look over all the line of the sky and sea.

But my eye was no sooner applied to the glass, than it was quickly snatched out of my hands.

I turned round. Captain Nemo was before me, but I did not know him. His face was transfigured. His eyes flashed sullenly; his teeth were set; his stiff body, clenched fists, and head shrunk between his shoulders, betrayed the violent agitation that pervaded his whole frame. He did not move. My glass, fallen from his hands, had rolled at his feet.

Had I unwittingly provoked this fit of anger? Did this incomprehensible person imagine that I had discovered some forbidden secret? No; I was not the object of this hatred, for he was not looking at me, his eye was steadily fixed upon the impenetrable point of the horizon. At last Captain Nemo recovered himself. His agitation subsided. He addressed some words in a foreign language to his lieutenant, then turned to me. "M. Aronnax," he said, in rather an imperious tone, "I require you to keep one of the conditions that bind you to me."

"What is it, Captain?"

"You must be confined, with your companions, until I think fit to release you."

"You are the master," I replied, looking steadily at him. "But may I ask you one question?"

"None, sir."

There was no resisting this imperious command; it would have been useless. I went down to the cabin occupied by Ned Land and Conseil, and told them the captain's determination. You may judge how this communication was received by the Canadian.

But there was no time for altercation. Four of the crew waited at the door, and conducted us to that cell where we had passed our first night on board the *Nautilus*.

Ned Land would have remonstrated, but the door was shut upon him.

"Will master tell me what this means?" asked Conseil.

I told my companions what had passed. They were as much astonished as I, and equally at a loss how to account for it.

Meanwhile, I was absorbed in my own reflections, and could think of nothing but the strange fear depicted in the captain's countenance. I was utterly at a loss to account for it, when my cogitations were disturbed by these words from Ned Land,—

"Hallo! breakfast is ready!"

And indeed the table was laid. Evidently Captain Nemo had given this order at the same time that he had hastened the speed of the *Nautilus*.

"Will master permit me to make a recommendation?" asked Conseil.

"Yes, my boy."

"Well, it is that master breakfasts. It is prudent, for we do not know what may happen."

"You are right, Conseil."

"Unfortunately," said Ned Land, "they have only given us the ship's fare."

"Friend Ned," asked Conseil, "what would you have said if the breakfast had been entirely forgotten?"

This argument cut short the harpooner's recriminations.

We sat down to table. The meal was eaten in silence.

Just then, the luminous globe that lighted the cell went out, and left us in total darkness. Ned Land was soon asleep, and what astonished me was that Conseil went off into a heavy sleep. I was thinking what could have caused his irresistible drowsiness, when I felt my brain becoming stupefied. In spite of my efforts to keep my eyes open, they would close. A painful suspicion seized me. Evidently soporific substances had been mixed with the food we had just taken.

Imprisonment was not enough to conceal Captain Nemo's projects from us; sleep was more necessary.

I then heard the panels shut. The undulations of the sea, which caused a slight rolling motion, ceased. Had the *Nautilus* quitted the surface of the ocean? Had it gone back to the motionless bed of water? I tried to resist sleep. It was impossible. My breathing grew weak. I felt a mortal cold freeze my stiffened and half-paralyzed limbs. My eyelids, like leaden caps, fell over my eyes. I could not raise them; a morbid sleep, full of hallucinations, bereft me of my being. Then the visions disappeared, and left me in complete insensibility.

CHAPTER 24

THE CORAL KINGDOM

THE next day I woke with my head singularly clear. To my great surprise I was in my own room. My companions, no doubt, had been reinstated in their cabin, without having perceived it any more than I. Of what had passed during the night they were as ignorant as I was, and to penetrate this mystery I only reckoned upon the chances of the future.

I then thought of quitting my room. Was I free again, or a prisoner? Quite free. I opened the door, went to the half-deck, went up the central stairs. The panels, shut the evening before, were open. I went on to the platform.

Ned Land and Conseil waited there for me. I questioned them; they knew nothing. Lost in a heavy sleep in which they had been totally unconscious, they had been astonished at finding themselves in their cabin.

As for the *Nautilus,* it seemed quiet and mysterious as ever. It floated on the surface of the waves at a moderate pace. Nothing seemed changed on board.

The second lieutenant then came on to the platform, and gave the usual order below.

As for Captain Nemo, he did not appear.

Of the people on board I only saw the impassive steward, who served me with his usual dumb regularity.

About two o'clock, I was in the drawing-room, busied in arranging my notes, when the captain opened the door and appeared. I bowed. He made a slight inclination in return, without speaking. I resumed my work, hoping that he would perhaps give me some explanation of the events of the preceding night. He made none. I looked at him. He seemed fatigued; his heavy eyes had not been refreshed by sleep; his face looked very sorrowful. He walked to and fro, sat down and got up again, took up a chance book, put it down, consulted his instruments without taking his habitual notes, and seemed restless and uneasy. At last, he came up to me, and said,—

"Are you a doctor, M. Aronnax?"

I so little expected such a question, that I stared some time at him without answering.

"Are you a doctor?" he repeated. "Several of your colleagues have studied medicine."

"Well," said I, "I am a doctor and resident surgeon to the hospital. I practised several years before entering the museum."

"Very well, sir."

My answer had evidently satisfied the captain. But not knowing what he would say next, I waited for other questions, reserving my answers according to circumstances.

"M. Aronnax, will you consent to prescribe for one of my men?" he asked.

"Is he ill?"

"Yes."

"I am ready to follow you."

"Come then."

I own my heart beat, I do not know why. I saw a certain connection between the illness of one of the crew and the events of the day before; and this mystery interested me at least as much as the sick man.

Captain Nemo conducted me to the poop of the *Nautilus,* and took me into a cabin situated near the sailors' quarters.

There, on a bed, lay a man about forty years of age, with a resolute expression of countenance, a true type of an Anglo-Saxon.

I leant over him. He was not only ill, he was wounded. His head, swathed in bandages covered with blood, lay on a pillow. I undid the bandages, and the wounded man looked at me with his large eyes and gave no sign of pain as I did it. It was a horrible wound. The skull, shattered by some deadly weapon, left the brain exposed, which was much injured. Clots of blood had formed in the bruised and broken mass, in color like the dregs of wine.

There was both contusion and suffusion of the brain. His breathing was slow, and some spasmodic movements of the muscles agitated his face. I felt his pulse. It was intermittent. The extremities of the body were growing cold already, and I saw death must inevitably ensue. After dressing the unfortunate man's wounds, I readjusted the bandages on his head, and turned to Captain Nemo.

"What caused this wound?" I asked.

"What does it signify?" he replied, evasively. "A shock has broken one of the levers of the engine, which struck myself. But your opinion as to his state?"

I hesitated before giving it.

"You may speak," said the captain. "This man does not understand French."

I gave a last look at the wounded man.

"He will be dead in two hours."

"Can nothing save him?"

"Nothing."

Captain Nemo's hand contracted, and some tears glistened in his eyes, which I thought incapable of shedding any.

For some moments I still watched the dying man, whose life ebbed slowly. His pallor increased under the electric light that was shed over his death-bed. I looked at his intelligent forehead, furrowed with premature wrinkles, produced probably by misfortune and sorrow. I tried to learn the secret of his life from the last words that escaped his lips.

"You can go now, M. Aronnax," said the captain.

I left him in the dying man's cabin, and returned to my room, much affected by this scene. During the whole day, I was haunted by uncomfortable suspicions, and at night I slept badly, and, between my broken dreams, I fancied I heard distant sighs like the notes of a funeral psalm. Were they the prayers of the dead, murmured in that language that I could not understand?

The next morning I went on the bridge. Captain Nemo was there before me. As soon as he perceived me he came to me.

"Professor, will it be convenient to you to make a submarine excursion to-day?"

"With my companions?" I asked.

"If they like."

"We obey your orders, Captain."

"Will you be so good then as to put on your cork-jackets?"

It was not a question of dead or dying. I rejoined Ned Land and Conseil, and told them of Captain Nemo's proposition. Conseil hastened to accept it, and this time the Canadian seemed quite willing to follow our example.

It was eight o'clock in the morning. At half past eight we were equipped for this new excursion, and provided with two contrivances for light and breathing. The double door was open; and accompanied by Captain Nemo, who was followed by a dozen of the crew, we set foot, at a depth of about thirty feet, on the solid bottom on which the *Nautilus* rested.

A slight declivity ended in an uneven bottom, at fifteen fathoms depth. This bottom differed entirely from the one I had visited on my first excursion under the waters of the Pacific Ocean. Here, there was no fine sand, no submarine prairies, no sea-forest. I immediately recognized that marvellous region in which, on that day, the captain did the honors to us. It was the coral kingdom. In the zoöphyte branch and in the alcyon class I noticed the gorgoneæ, the isidiæ, and the corollariæ.

The light produced a thousand charming varieties, playing in the midst of the branches that were so vividly colored. I seemed to see the membraneous and cylindrical tubes tremble beneath the undulation of the waters. I was tempted to gather their fresh petals, ornamented with delicate tentacles, some just blown, the others budding, while small fish, swimming swiftly, touched them slightly, like flights of birds. But if my hand approached these living flowers, these animated sensitive plants, the whole colony took alarm. The white petals re-entered their red cases, the flowers faded as I looked, and the bush changed into a block of stony knobs.

Chance had thrown me just by the most precious specimens of this zoöphyte. This coral was more valuable than that found in the Mediterranean, on the coasts of France, Italy, and Barbary. Its tints justified the poetical names of "Flower of Blood," and "Froth of Blood," that trade has given to its most beautiful productions. Coral is sold for £ 20 per ounce; and in this place, the watery beds would make the fortunes of a company of coral-divers. This precious matter, often confused with other polypi, formed then the inextricable plots called "macciota," and on which I noticed several beautiful specimens of pink coral.

But soon the bushes contract, and the arborizations increase. Real petrified thickets, long joists of fantastic architecture, were disclosed before us. Captain Nemo placed himself under a dark gallery, where by a slight declivity we reached a depth of 100 yards. The light from our lamps produced sometimes magical effects, following the rough outlines of the natural arches, and pendants disposed like lustres, that were tipped with points of fire. Between the coralline shrubs I noticed other polypi not less curious,—melites, and irises with articulated ramifications; also some tufts of coral, some green, others red, like sea-weed incrusted in their calcareous salts, that naturalists, after long discussion, have definitely classed in the vegetable kingdom. But following the remark of a thinking man, "there is perhaps the real point where life rises obscurely from the sleep of a stone, without detaching itself from the rough point of departure."

At last, after walking two hours, we had attained a depth of about 300 yards, that is to say, the extreme limit on which coral begins to form. But there was no isolated bush, nor modest brushwood, at the bottom of lofty trees. It was an immense forest of large mineral vegetations, enormous petrified trees, united by garlands of elegant plumarias, sea bindweed, all adorned with clouds and reflections. We passed freely under their high branches, lost in the shade of the waves, while at our feet, tubipores, meandrines, stars, fungi, and caryophyllidæ formed a carpet of flowers sown with dazzling gems. What an indescribable spectacle!

Captain Nemo had stopped. I and my companions halted, and turning round, I saw his men were forming a semicircle round their chief. Watching attentively, I observed that four of them carried on their shoulders an object of an oblong shape.

We occupied, in this place, the centre of a vast glade surrounded by the lofty foliage of the submarine forest. Our lamps threw over this place a sort of clear twilight that singularly elongated the shadows on the ground. At the end of the glade the darkness increased, and was only relieved by little sparks reflected by the points of coral.

Ned Land and Conseil were near me. We watched, and I thought I was going to witness a strange scene. On observing the ground, I saw that it was raised in certain places by slight excrescences encrusted with limy deposits, and disposed with a regularity that betrayed the hand of man.

In the midst of the glade, on a pedestal of rocks roughly piled up, stood a cross of coral, that extended its long arms that one might have thought were made of petrified blood.

Upon a sign from Captain Nemo, one of the men advanced; and at some feet from the cross, he began to dig a hole with a pickaxe that he took from his belt. I understood all! This glade was a cemetery, this hole a tomb, this oblong object the body of the man who had died in the night! The captain and his men had come to bury their companion in this general resting place, at the bottom of this inaccessible ocean!

The grave was being dug slowly; the fish fled on all sides while their retreat was being thus disturbed; I heard the strokes of the pickaxe, which sparkled when it hit upon some flint lost at the bottom of the waters. The hole was soon large and deep enough to receive the body. Then the bearers approached; the body, enveloped in a tissue of white byssus, was lowered into the damp grave. Captain Nemo, with his arms crossed on his breast, and all the friends of him who had loved them, knelt in prayer.

The grave was then filled in with the rubbish taken from the ground, which formed a slight mound. When this was done, Captain Nemo and his men rose; then, approaching the grave, they knelt again, and all extended their hands in sign of a last adieu. Then the funeral procession returned to the *Nautilus*, passing under the arches of the forest, in the midst of thickets, along the coral bushes, and still on the ascent. At last the fires on board appeared, and their luminous track guided us to the *Nautilus*. At one o'clock we had returned.

A coral cemetery.

As soon as I had changed my clothes, I went up on to the platform, and, a prey to conflicting emotions, I sat down near the binnacle. Captain Nemo joined me. I rose and said to him,—

"So, as I said he would, this man died in the night?"

"Yes, M. Aronnax."

"And he rests now, near his companions, in the coral cemetery?"

"Yes, forgotten by all else, but not by us. We dug the grave, and the polypi undertake to seal our dead for eternity." And burying his face quickly in his hands, he tried in vain to suppress a sob. Then he added,—"Our peaceful cemetery is there, some hundred feet below the surface of the waves."

"Your dead sleep quietly, at least, Captain, out of the reach of sharks."

"Yes, sir, of sharks and *Men,*" gravely replied the captain.

PART II

CHAPTER 1

THE INDIAN OCEAN

We now come to the second part of our journey under the sea. The first ended with the moving scene in the coral cemetery, which left such a deep impression on my mind. Thus, in the midst of this great sea, Captain Nemo's life was passing even to his grave, which he had prepared in one of its deepest abysses. There, not one of the ocean's monsters could trouble the last sleep of the crew of the *Nautilus,* of those friends riveted to each other in death as in life. "Nor any man either," had added the captain. Still the same fierce, implacable defiance towards human society!

I could no longer content myself with the hypothesis which satisfied Conseil.

That worthy fellow persisted in seeing in the commander of the *Nautilus* one of those unknown savants who return mankind contempt for indifference. For him, he was a misunderstood genius, who, tired of earth's deceptions, had taken refuge in this inaccessible medium, where he might follow his instincts freely. To my mind, this hypothesis explained but one side of Captain Nemo's character.

Indeed, the mystery of that last night, during which we had been chained in prison, the sleep, and the precaution so violently taken by the captain of snatching from my eyes the glass I had raised to sweep the horizon, the mortal wound of the man, due to an unaccountable shock of the *Nautilus,* all put me on a new track. No; Captain Nemo was not satisfied with shunning man. His formidable apparatus not only suited his instinct of freedom, but, perhaps, also the design of some terrible retaliation.

At this moment nothing is clear to me; I catch but a glimpse of light amidst all the darkness, and I must confine myself to writing as events shall dictate.

That day, the 24th of January, 1868, at noon, the second officer came to take the altitude of the sun. I mounted the platform, lit a cigar, and watched the operation. It seemed to me that the man did not understand French; for several times I made remarks in a loud voice, which must have drawn from him some involuntary sign of attention, if he had understood them, but he remained undisturbed and dumb.

As he was taking observations with the sextant, one of the sailors of the *Nautilus* (the strong man who had accompanied us on our first submarine excursion to the Island of Crespo) came to clean the glasses of the lantern. I examined the fittings of the apparatus, the strength of which was increased a hundred-fold by lenticular rings, placed similar to those in a lighthouse, and which projected their brilliance in a horizontal plane. The electric lamp was combined in such a way as to give its most powerful light. Indeed it was produced in *vacuo,* which insured both its steadiness and its intensity. This vacuum economized the graphite points, between which the luminous arc was developed,—an important point of economy for Captain Nemo, who could not easily have replaced them; and under these conditions their waste was imperceptible. When the *Nautilus* was ready to continue its submarine journey, I went down to the saloon. The panels were closed and the course marked direct west.

We were furrowing the waters of the Indian Ocean, a vast liquid plain, with a surface of 1,200,000,000 of acres, and whose waters are so clear and transparent, that any one leaning over them would turn giddy. The *Nautilus* usually floated between fifty and a hundred fathoms deep. We went on so for some days. To any one but myself, who had a great love for the sea, the hours would have seemed long and monotonous; but the daily walks on the platform, when I steeped myself in the reviving air of the ocean, the sight of the rich waters through the windows of the saloon, the books in the library, the compiling of my memoirs, took up all my time, and left me not a moment of ennui or weariness.

For some days we saw a great number of aquatic birds, seamews or gulls. Some were cleverly killed, and, prepared in a certain way, made very acceptable water-game. Amongst large winged birds, carried a long distance from all lands, and resting upon the waves from the fatigue of their flight, I saw some magnificent albatrosses, uttering discordant cries like the braying of an ass, and birds belonging to the family of the longipennates. The family of the totipalmates was represented by the sea-swallows, which caught the fish from the surface, and by numerous phaetons, or lepturi; amongst others, the phaeton with red lines, as large as a pigeon, whose white plumage, tinted with pink, shows off to advantage the blackness of its wings.

As to the fish, they always provoked our admiration when we surprised the secrets of their aquatic life through the open panels. I saw many kinds which I never before had a chance of observing.

I shall notice chiefly ostracions peculiar to the Red Sea, the Indian Ocean, and that part which washes the coast of tropical America. These fishes, like the tortoise, the armadillo, the sea hedgehog, and the crustacea, are protected by a breastplate which is neither chalky nor stony, but real bone. In some it takes the form of a solid triangle, in others of a solid quadrangle. Amongst the triangular I saw some an inch and a half in length, with wholesome flesh and a delicious flavor; they are brown at the tail, and yellow at the fins, and I recommend their introduction into fresh water, to which a certain number of sea-fish easily accustom themselves. I would also mention quadrangular ostracions, having on the back four large tubercles; some dotted over with white spots on the lower part of the body, and which may be tamed like birds; trigons provided with spikes formed by the lengthening of their bony shell, and which from their strange gruntings are called "sea-pigs"; also dromedaries with large humps in the shape of a cone, whose flesh is very tough and leathery.

I now borrow from the daily notes of Master Conseil. "Certain fish of the genus petrodon peculiar to those seas, with red backs and white chests, which are distinguished by three rows of longitudinal filaments; and some electrical, seven inches long, decked in the liveliest colors. Then, as specimens of other kinds, some ovoides, resembling an egg of a dark brown color, marked with white bands, and without tails; diodons, real sea-porcupines, furnished with spikes, and capable of swelling in such a way as to look like cushions bristling with darts; hippocampi, common to every ocean; some pegasi with lengthened snouts, which their pectoral fins, being much elongated and formed in the shape of wings, allow, if not to fly, at least to shoot into the air; pigeon spatulæ, with tails covered with many rings of shell; macrognathi with long jaws, an excellent fish, nine inches long, and bright with most agreeable colors; pale-colored calliomores, with rugged heads; and plenty of chætodons, with long and tubular muzzles, which kill insects by shooting them, as from an air-gun, with a single drop of water. These we may call the fly-catchers of the seas.

"In the eighty-ninth genus of fishes, classed by Lacépède, belonging to the second lower class of bony, characterized by opercules and bronchial membranes, I remarked the scorpæna, the head of which is furnished with spikes, and which has but one dorsal fin; these creatures are covered, or not, with little shells, according to the sub-class to which they belong. The second sub-class give us specimens of didactyles fourteen or fifteen inches in length, with yellow rays, and heads of a most fantastic appearance. As to the first sub-class, it gives several specimens of that singular-looking fish appropriately called a "sea-frog," with large head, sometimes pierced with holes, sometimes swollen with protuberances, bristling with spikes, and covered with tubercles; it has irregular and hideous horns; its body and tail are covered with callosities; its sting makes a dangerous wound; it is both repugnant and horrible to look at."

From the 21st to the 23d of January, the *Nautilus* went at the rate of two hundred and fifty leagues in twenty-four hours, being five hundred and forty miles, or twenty-two miles an hour. If we recognized so many different varieties of fish, it was because, attracted by the electric light, they tried to follow us; the greater part, however, were soon distanced by our speed, though some kept their place in the waters of the *Nautilus* for a time. The morning of the 24th, in 12° 5′ south latitude, and 94° 33′ longitude, we observed Keeling Island, a madrepore formation, planted with magnificent cocoas, and which had been visited by Mr. Darwin and Captain Fitzroy. The *Nautilus* skirted the shores of this desert island for a little distance. Its nets brought up numerous specimens of polypi, and curious shells of mollusca. Some precious productions of the species of delphinulæ enriched the treasures of Captain Nemo, to which I added an astræa punctifera, a kind of parasite polypus often found fixed to a shell. Soon Keeling Island disappeared from the horizon, and our course was directed to the northwest in the direction of the Indian Peninsula.

From Keeling Island our course was slower and more variable, often taking us into great depths. Several times they made use of the inclined planes, which certain internal levers placed obliquely to the water-line. In that way we went about two miles, but without ever obtaining the greatest depths of the Indian Sea, which soundings of seven thousand fathoms have never reached. As to the temperature of the lower strata, the thermometer invariably indicated 4° above zero. I only observed that, in the upper regions, the water was always colder in the high levels than at the surface of the sea.

On the 25th of January, the ocean was entirely deserted; the *Nautilus* passed the day on the surface, beating the waves with its powerful screw, and making them rebound to a great height. Who under such circumstances would not have taken it for a gigantic cetacean? Three parts of this day I spent on the platform. I watched the sea. Nothing on the horizon, till about four o'clock a steamer running west on our counter. Her masts were visible for an instant, but she could not see the *Nautilus,* being too low in the water. I fancied this steamboat belonged to the P. O. Company, which runs from Ceylon to Sydney, touching at King George's Point and Melbourne.

At five o'clock in the evening, before that fleeting twilight which binds night to day in tropical zones, Conseil and I were astonished by a curious spectacle.

It was a shoal of argonants travelling along on the surface of the ocean. We could count several hundreds. They belonged to the tubercle kind which are peculiar to the Indian seas.

These graceful molluscs moved backwards by means of their locomotive tube, through which they propelled the water already drawn in. Of their eight tentacles, six were elongated, and stretched out floating on the water, whilst the other two, rolled up flat, were spread to the wind like a light sail. I saw their spiral-shaped and fluted shells, which Cuvier justly compares to an elegant skiff. A boat indeed! It bears the creature which secretes it without its adhering to it.

For nearly an hour the *Nautilus* floated in the midst of this shoal of molluscs. Then I know not what sudden fright they took; but as if at a signal every sail was furled, the arms folded, the body drawn in, the shells turned over, changing their centre of gravity, and the whole fleet disappeared under the waves. Never did the ships of a squadron manœuvre with more unity.

At that moment night fell suddenly, and the reeds, scarcely raised by the breeze, lay peaceably under the sides of the *Nautilus*.

The next day, 26th of January, we cut the equator at the eighty-second meridian, and entered the northern hemisphere. During the day, a formidable troop of sharks accompanied us, terrible creatures, which multiply in these seas, and make them very dangerous. They were "cestracio philippi" sharks, with brown backs and whitish bellies, armed with eleven rows of teeth,—eyed sharks,—their throat being marked with a large black spot surrounded with white like an eye. There were also some Isabella sharks, with rounded snouts marked with dark spots. These powerful creatures often hurled themselves at the windows of the saloon with such violence as to make us feel very insecure. At such times Ned Land was no longer master of himself. He wanted to go to the surface and harpoon the monsters, particularly certain smooth-hound sharks, whose mouth is studded with teeth like a mosaic; and large tiger-sharks nearly six yards long, the last-named of which seemed to excite him more particularly. But the *Nautilus,* accelerating her speed, easily left the most rapid of them behind.

The 27th of January, at the entrance of the vast Bay of Bengal, we met repeatedly a forbidding spectacle,—dead bodies floating on the surface of the water. They were the dead of the Indian villages, carried by the Ganges to the level of the sea, and which the vultures, the only undertakers of the country, had not been able to devour. But the sharks did not fail to help them at their funereal work.

About seven o'clock in the evening, the *Nautilus,* half immersed, was sailing in a sea of milk. At first sight the ocean seemed lactified. Was it the effect of the lunar rays? No; for the moon, scarcely two days old, was still lying hidden under the horizon in the rays of the sun. The whole sky, though lit by the sidereal rays, seemed black by contrast with the whiteness of the waters.

Conseil could not believe his eyes, and questioned me as to the cause of this strange phenomenon. Happily I was able to answer him.

"It is called a milk sea," I explained; "a large extent of white wavelets often to be seen on the coasts of Amboyna, and in these parts of the sea."

"But, sir," said Conseil, "can you tell me what causes such an effect? for I suppose the water is not really turned into milk."

"No, my boy; and the whiteness which surprises you is caused only by the presence of myriads of infusoria, a sort of luminous little worm, gelatinous and without color, of the thickness of a hair, and whose length is not more than the 7/1000 of an inch. These insects adhere to one another sometimes for several leagues."

"Several leagues!" exclaimed Conseil.

"Yes, my boy; and you need not try to compute the number of these infusoria. You will not be able; for, if I am not mistaken, ships have floated on these milk seas for more than forty miles."

Towards midnight the sea suddenly resumed its usual color; but behind us, even to the limits of the horizon, the sky reflected the whitened waves, and for a long time seemed impregnated with the vague glimmerings of an aurora borealis.

CHAPTER 2

A NOVEL PROPOSAL OF CAPTAIN NEMO'S

On the 28th of February, when at noon the *Nautilus* came to the surface of the sea, in 9° 4′ north latitude, there was land in sight about eight miles to westward. The first thing I noticed was a range of mountains about two thousand feet high, the shapes of which were most capricious. On taking the bearings, I knew that we were nearing the Island of Ceylon, the pearl which hangs from the lobe of the Indian Peninsula.

Captain Nemo and his second appeared at this moment. The captain glanced at the map. Then, turning to me, said,—

"The Island of Ceylon, noted for its pearl-fisheries. Would you like to visit one of them. M. Aronnax?"

"Certainly, Captain."

"Well, the thing is easy. Though if we see the fisheries, we shall not see the fishermen. The annual exportation has not yet begun. Never mind, I will give orders to make for the Gulf of Manaar, where we shall arrive in the night."

The captain said something to his second, who immediately went out. Soon the *Nautilus* returned to her native element, and the manometer showed that she was about thirty feet deep.

"Well, sir," said Captain Nemo, "you and your companions shall visit the Bank of Manaar, and if by chance some fisherman should be there, we shall see him at work."

"Agreed, Captain!"

"By the by, M. Aronnax, you are not afraid of sharks?

"Sharks!" exclaimed I.

This question seemed a very hard one.

"Well?" continued Captain Nemo.

"I admit, Captain, that I am not yet very familiar with that kind of fish."

"*We* are accustomed to them," replied Captain Nemo, "and in time you will be too. However, we shall be armed, and on the road we may be able to hunt some of the tribe. It is interesting. So, till to-morrow, sir, and early."

This said in a careless tone, Captain Nemo left the saloon. Now, if you were invited to hunt the bear in the mountains of Switzerland, what would you say? "Very well! to-morrow we will go and hunt the bear." If you were asked to hunt the lion in the plains of Atlas, or the tiger in the Indian jungles, what would you say? "Ha! ha! it seems we are going to hunt the tiger or the lion!" But when you are invited to hunt the shark in its natural element, you would perhaps reflect before accepting the invitation. As for myself, I passed my hand over my forehead, on which stood large drops of cold perspiration. "Let us reflect," said I, "and take our time. Hunting otters in submarine forests, as we did in the Island of Crespo, will pass; but going up and down at the bottom of the sea, where one is almost certain to meet sharks, is quite another thing! I know well that in certain countries, particularly in the Andaman Islands, the negroes never hesitate to attack them with a dagger in one hand and a running noose in the other; but I also know that few who affront those creatures ever return alive. However, I am not a negro, and, if I were, I think a little hesitation in this case would not be ill-timed."

At this moment, Conseil and the Canadian entered, quite composed, and even joyous. They knew not what awaited them.

"Faith, sir," said Ned Land, "your Captain Nemo—the devil take him!—has just made us a very pleasant offer."

"Ah!" said I, "you know?"

"If agreeable to you, sir," interrupted Conseil, "the commander of the *Nautilus* has invited us to visit the magnificent Ceylon fisheries to-morrow, in your company; he did it kindly, and behaved like a real gentleman."

"He said nothing more?"

"Nothing more, sir, except that he had already spoken to you of this little walk."

"Sir," said Conseil, "would you give us some details of the pearl-fishery?"

"As to the fishing itself," I asked, "or the incidents, which?"

"On the fishing," replied the Canadian; "before entering upon the ground, it is as well to know something about it."

"Very well; sit down, my friends, and I will teach you."

Ned and Conseil seated themselves on an ottoman, and the first thing the Canadian asked was:—

"Sir, what is a pearl?"

"My worthy Ned," I answered, "to the poet; a pearl is a tear of the sea; to the Orientals, it is a drop of dew solidified; to the ladies, it is a jewel of an oblong shape, of a brilliancy of mother-of-pearl substance, which they wear on their fingers, their necks, or their ears; for the chemist, it is a mixture of phosphate and carbonate of lime, with a little gelatine; and lastly, for naturalists, it is simply a morbid secretion of the organ that produces the mother-of-pearl amongst certain bivalves."

"Branch of mollusca," said Conseil, "class of acephali, order of testacea."

"Precisely so, my learned Conseil; and, amongst these testacea, the earshell, the tridacnæ, the turbots,—in a word, all those which secrete mother-of-pearl, that is, the blue, bluish, violet, or white substance which lines the interior of their shells, are capable of producing pearls."

"Mussels too?" asked the Canadian.

"Yes, mussels of certain waters in Scotland, Wales, Ireland, Saxony, Bohemia, and France."

"Good! For the future I shall pay attention," replied the Canadian.

"But," I continued, "the particular mollusc which secretes the pearl is the *pearl-oyster,* the *Meleagrina margaritifera,* that precious pintadine. The pearl is nothing but a nacreous formation, deposited in a globular form, either adhering to the oyster shell, or buried in the folds of the creature. On the shell it is fast; in the flesh it is loose; but always has for a kernel a small, hard substance, may be a barren egg, may be a grain of sand, around which the pearly matter deposits itself year after year successively, and by thin concentric layers."

"Are many pearls found in the same oyster?" asked Conseil.

"Yes, my boy. There are some pintadines a perfect casket. One oyster has been mentioned, though I allow myself to doubt it, as having contained no less than a hundred and fifty sharks."

"A hundred and fifty sharks!" exclaimed Ned Land.

"Did I say sharks?" said I, hurriedly. "I meant to say a hundred and fifty pearls. Sharks would not be sense."

"Certainly not," said Conseil; "but will you tell us now by what means they extract these pearls?"

"They proceed in various ways. When they adhere to the shell, the fishermen often pull them off with pincers; but the most common way is to lay the pintadines on mats of the sea-weed which covers the banks. Thus they die in the open air; and at the end of ten days they are in a forward state of decomposition. They are then plunged into large reservoirs of sea-water; then they are opened and washed. Now begins the double work of the sorters. First they separate the layers of pearl, known in commerce by the name of bastard whites and bastard blacks, which are delivered in boxes of two hundred and fifty and three hundred pounds each. Then they take the parenchyma of the oyster, boil it, and pass it through a sieve in order to extract the very smallest pearls."

"The price of these pearls varies according to their size?" asked Conseil.

"Not only according to their size," I answered, "but also according to their shape, their *water* (that is, their color), and their lustre; that is, that bright and diapered sparkle which makes them so charming to the eye. The most beautiful are called virgin pearls or paragons. They are formed alone in the tissue of the mollusc, are white, often opaque, and sometimes have the transparency of an opal; they are generally round or oval. The round are made into bracelets, the oval into pendants; and, being more precious, are sold singly. Those adhering to the shell of the oyster are more irregular in shape, and are sold by weight. Lastly, in a lower order are classed those small pearls known under the name of seed-pearls; they are sold by measure, and are especially used in embroidery for church ornaments."

"But," said Conseil, "is this pearl-fishery dangerous?"

"No," I answered, quickly; "particularly if certain precautions are taken."

"What does one risk in such a calling?" said Ned Land; "the swallowing of some mouthfuls of sea-water?"

"As you say, Ned. By and by," said I, trying to take Captain Nemo's careless tone, "are you afraid of sharks, brave Ned?"

"I!" replied the Canadian; "a harpooner by profession? It is my trade to make light of them."

"But," said I, "it is not a question of fishing for them with an iron swivel, hoisting them into the vessel, cutting off their tails with a blow of a chopper, ripping them up, and throwing their heart into the sea!"

"Then, it is a question of—"

"Precisely."

"In the water?"

"In the water."

"Faith, with a good harpoon! You know, sir, these sharks are ill-fashioned beasts. They must turn on their bellies to seize you, and in that time—"

Ned Land had a way of saying "seize," which made my blood run cold.

"Well, and you, Conseil, what do you think of sharks?"

"Me!" said Conseil. "I will be frank, sir."

"So much the better," thought I.

"If you, sir, mean to face the sharks, I do not see why your faithful servant should not face them with you."

CHAPTER 3

A PEARL OF TEN MILLIONS

THE next morning at four o'clock I was awakened by the steward, whom Captain Nemo had placed at my service. I rose hurriedly, dressed, and went into the saloon.

Captain Nemo was awaiting me.

"M. Aronnax," said he, "are you ready to start?"

"I am ready."

"Then, please to follow me."

"And my companions, Captain?"

"They have been told, and are waiting."

"Are we not to put on our diver's dresses?" asked I.

"Not yet. I have not allowed the *Nautilus* to come too near this coast, and we are some distance from the Manaar Bank; but the boat is ready, and will take us to the exact point of disembarking, which will save us a long way. It carries our diving apparatus, which we will put on when we begin our submarine journey."

Captain Nemo conducted me to the central staircase, which led on to the platform. Ned and Conseil were already there, delighted at the idea of the "pleasure party" which was preparing. Five sailors from the *Nautilus*, with their oars, waited in the boat, which had been made fast against the side.

The night was still dark. Layers of clouds covered the sky, allowing but few stars to be seen. I looked on the side where the land lay, and saw nothing but a dark line enclosing three parts of the horizon, from southwest to northwest. The *Nautilus*, having returned during the night up the western coast of Ceylon, was now west of the bay, or rather gulf, formed by the mainland and the island of Manaar. There, under the dark waters, stretched the pintadine bank, an inexhaustible field of pearls, the length of which is more than twenty miles.

Captain Nemo, Ned Land, Conseil, and I, took our places in the stern of the boat. The master went to the tiller; his four companions leaned on their oars, the painter was cast off, and we sheered off.

The boat went towards the south; the oarsmen did not hurry. I noticed that their strokes, strong in the water, only followed each other every ten seconds, according to the method generally adopted in the navy. Whilst the craft was running by its own velocity, the liquid drops struck the dark depths of the waves crisply like spats of melted lead. A little billow, spreading wide, gave a slight roll to the boat, and some samphire reeds flapped before it.

We were silent. What was Captain Nemo thinking of? Perhaps of the land he was approaching, and which he found too near to him, contrary to the Canadian's opinion, who thought it too far off. As to Conseil, he was merely there from curiosity.

About half past five, the first tints on the horizon showed the upper line of coast more distinctly. Flat enough in the east, it rose a little to the south. Five miles still lay between us, and it was indistinct, owing to the mist on the water. At six o'clock it became suddenly daylight, with that rapidity peculiar to tropical regions, which know neither dawn nor twilight. The solar rays pierced the curtain of clouds piled up on the eastern horizon, and the radiant orb rose rapidly. I saw land distinctly, with a few trees scattered here and there. The boat neared Manaar Island, which was rounded to the south. Captain Nemo rose from his seat and watched the sea.

At a sign from him the anchor was dropped, but the chain scarcely ran, for it was little more than a yard deep, and this spot was one of the highest points of the bank of pintadines.

"Here we are, M. Aronnax," said Captain Nemo. "You see that enclosed bay? Here, in a month, will be assembled the numerous fishing-boats of the exporters, and these are the waters situated for that kind of fishing. It is sheltered from the strongest winds; the sea is never very rough here, which makes it favorable for the diver's work. We will now put on our dresses, and begin our walk."

I did not answer, and while watching the suspected waves, began with the help of the sailors to put on my heavy sea-dress. Captain Nemo and my companions were also dressing. None of the *Nautilus* men were to accompany us on this new excursion.

Soon we were enveloped to the throat in india-rubber clothing; the air apparatus fixed to our backs by braces. As to the Ruhmkorff apparatus, there was no necessity for it. Before putting my head into the copper cap, I had asked the question of the captain.

"They would be useless," he replied. "We are going to no great depth, and the solar rays will be enough to light our walk. Besides, it would not be prudent to carry the electric light in these waters; its brilliancy might attract some of the dangerous inhabitants of the coast most inopportunely."

As Captain Nemo pronounced these words, I turned to Conseil and Ned Land. But my two friends had already encased their heads in the metal cap, and they could neither hear nor answer.

One last question remained to ask of Captain Nemo.

"And our arms?" asked I; "our guns?"

"Guns! what for? Do not mountaineers attack the bear with a dagger in their hand, and is not steel surer than lead? Here is a strong blade; put it in your belt, and we start."

I looked at my companions; they were armed like us, and, more than that, Ned Land was brandishing an enormous harpoon, which he had placed in the boat before leaving the *Nautilus*.

Then, following the captain's example, I allowed myself to be dressed in the heavy copper helmet, and our reservoirs of air were at once in activity. An instant after, we were landed, one after the other, in about two feet of water upon an even sand. Captain Nemo made a sign with his hand, and we followed him by a gentle declivity till we disappeared under the waves.

Over our feet, like coveys of snipe in a bog, rose shoals of fish, of the genus monoptera, which have no other fins but their tail. I recognized the Javanese, a real serpent two and a half feet long, of a livid color underneath, and which might easily be mistaken for a conger eel if it was not for the golden stripes on its sides. In the genus stromateus, whose bodies are very flat and oval, I saw some of the most brilliant colors, carrying their dorsal fin like a scythe; an excellent eating fish, which, dried and pickled, is known by the name of *Karawade;* then some tranquebars, belonging to the genus apsiphoroides, whose body is covered with a shell cuirass of eight longitudinal plates.

The heightening sun lit the mass of waters more and more. The soil changed by degrees. To the fine sand succeeded a perfect causeway of boulders, covered with a carpet of molluscs and zoöphytes. Amongst the specimens of these branches I noticed some placenæ, with thin, unequal shells, a kind of ostracion peculiar to the Red Sea and the Indian Ocean; some orange lucinæ with rounded shells; rock-fish three feet and a half long, which raised themselves under the waves like hands ready to seize one. There were also some panopyres, slightly luminous; and lastly, some oculines, like magnificent fans, forming one of the richest vegetations of these seas.

In the midst of these living plants, and under the arbors of the hydrophytes, were layers of clumsy articulates, particularly some raninæ, whose carapace formed a slightly rounded triangle; and some horrible-looking parthenopes.

At about seven o'clock we found ourselves at last surveying the oyster-banks, on which the pearl-oysters are reproduced by millions.

Captain Nemo pointed with his hand to the enormous heap of oysters; and I could well understand that this mine was inexhaustible, for nature's creative power is far beyond man's instinct of destruction. Ned Land, faithful to his instinct, hastened to fill a net which he carried by his side with some of the finest specimens. But we could not stop. We must follow the captain, who seemed to guide himself by paths known only to himself. The ground was sensibly rising, and sometimes, on holding up my arm, it was above the surface of the sea. Then the level of the bank would sink capriciously. Often we rounded high rocks scarped into pyramids. In their dark fractures huge crustacea, perched upon their high claws like some war-machine, watched us with fixed eyes, and under our feet crawled various kinds of annelides.

At this moment there opened before us a large grotto, dug in a picturesque heap of rocks, and carpeted with all the thick warp of the submarine flora. At first it seemed very dark to me. The solar rays seemed to be extinguished by successive gradations, until its vague transparency became nothing more than drowned light. Captain Nemo entered; we followed. My eyes soon accustomed themselves to this relative state of darkness. I could distinguish the arches springing capriciously from natural pillars, standing broad upon their granite base, like the heavy columns of Tuscan architecture. Why had our incomprehensible guide led us to the bottom of this submarine crypt? I was soon to know. After descending a rather sharp declivity, our feet trod the bottom of a kind of circular pit. There Captain Nemo stopped, and with his hand indicated an object I had not yet perceived. It was an oyster of extraordinary dimensions, a gigantic tridacne, a goblet which could have contained a whole lake of holy water, a basin the breadth of which was more than two yards and a half, and consequently larger than that ornamenting the saloon of the *Nautilus*. I approached this extraordinary mollusc. It adhered by its byssus to a table of granite, and there, isolated, it developed itself in the calm waters of the grotto. I estimated the weight of this tridacne at 600 pounds. Such an oyster would contain thirty pounds of meat; and one must have the stomach of a Gargantua, to demolish some dozens of them.

Captain Nemo was evidently acquainted with the existence of this bivalve, and seemed to have a particular motive in verifying the actual state of this tridacne. The shells were a little open; the captain came near, and put his dagger between to prevent them from closing; then with his hand he raised the membrane with its fringed edges, which formed a cloak for the creature. There, between the folded plaits, I saw a loose pearl, whose size equalled that of a cocoanut. Its globular shape, perfect clearness, and admirable lustre, made it altogether a jewel of inestimable value. Carried away by my curiosity I stretched out my hand to seize it, weigh it, and touch it; but the captain stopped me, made a sign of refusal, and quickly withdrew his dagger, and the two shells closed suddenly. I then understood Captain Nemo's intention. In leaving this pearl hidden in the mantle of the tridacne, he was allowing it to grow slowly. Each year the secretions of the mollusc would add new concentric circles. I estimated its value at £ 500,000 at least.

After ten minutes Captain Nemo stopped suddenly. I thought he had halted previously to returning. No; by a gesture he bade us crouch beside him in a deep fracture of the rock, his hand pointed to one part of the liquid mass, which I watched attentively.

About five yards from me a shadow appeared, and sank to the ground. The disquieting idea of sharks shot through my mind, but I was mistaken; and once again it was not a monster of the ocean that we had anything to do with.

It was a man, a living man, an Indian, a fisherman, a poor devil, who, I suppose, had come to glean before the harvest. I could see the bottom of his canoe anchored some feet above his head. He dived and went up successively. A stone held between his feet, cut in the shape of a sugar-loaf, whilst a rope fastened him to his boat, helped him to descend more rapidly. This was all his apparatus. Reaching the bottom about five yards deep, he went on his knees and filled his bag with oysters picked up at random. Then he went up, emptied it, pulled up his stone, and began the operation once more, which lasted thirty seconds.

The diver did not see us. The shadow of the rock hid us from sight. And how should this poor Indian ever dream that men, beings like himself, should be there under the water watching his movements, and losing no detail of the fishing? Several times he went up in this way, and dived again. He did not carry away more than ten at each plunge, for he was obliged to pull them from the bank to which they adhered by means of their strong byssus. And how many of those oysters for which he risked his life had no pearl in them! I watched him closely; his manœuvres were regular, and, for the space of half an hour, no danger appeared to threaten him.

I was beginning to accustom myself to the sight of this interesting fishing, when suddenly, as the Indian was on the ground, I saw him make a gesture of terror, rise, and make a spring to return to the surface of the sea.

I understood his dread. A gigantic shadow appeared just above the unfortunate diver. It was a shark of enormous size advancing diagonally, his eyes on fire, and his jaws open. I was mute with horror, and unable to move.

The voracious creature shot towards the Indian, who threw himself on one side in order to avoid the shark's fins; but not its tail, for it struck his chest, and stretched him on the ground.

This scene lasted but a few seconds; the shark returned, and, turning on his back, prepared himself for cutting the Indian in two, when I saw Captain Nemo rise suddenly, and then, dagger in hand, walk straight to the monster, ready to fight face to face with him. The very moment the shark was going to snap the unhappy fisherman in two, he perceived his new adversary, and, turning over, made straight towards him.

I can still see Captain Nemo's position. Holding himself well together, he waited for the shark with admirable coolness; and, when it rushed at him, threw himself on one side with wonderful quickness, avoiding the shock, and burying his dagger deep into its side. But it was not all over. A terrible combat ensued.

The shark had seemed to roar, if I might say so. The blood rushed in torrents from its wound. The sea was dyed red, and through the opaque liquid I could distinguish nothing more. Nothing more, until the moment when, like lightning, I saw the undaunted captain hanging on to one of the creature's fins, struggling, as it were, hand to hand with the monster, and dealing successive blows at his enemy, yet still unable to give a decisive one.

The shark's struggles agitated the water with such fury that the rocking threatened to upset me.

I wanted to go to the captain's assistance, but, nailed to the spot with horror, I could not stir.

I saw the haggard eye; I saw the different phases of the fight. The captain fell to the earth, upset by the enormous mass which leant upon him. The shark's jaws opened wide, like a pair of factory shears, and it would have been all over with the captain; but, quick as thought, harpoon in hand, Ned Land rushed towards the shark and struck it with its sharp point.

The waves were impregnated with a mass of blood. They rocked under the shark's movements, which beat them with indescribable fury. Ned Land had not missed his aim. It was the monster's death-rattle. Struck to the heart, it struggled in dreadful convulsions, the shock of which overthrew Conseil.

But Ned Land had disentangled the captain, who, getting up without any wound, went straight to the Indian, quickly cut the cord which held him to his stone, took him in his arms, and, with a sharp blow of his heel, mounted to the surface.

We all three followed in a few seconds, saved by a miracle, and reached the fisherman's boat.

Captain Nemo's first care was to recall the unfortunate man to life again. I

A terrible combat ensued.

did not think he could succeed. I hoped so, for the poor creature's immersion was not long; but the blow from the shark's tail might have been his death-blow.

Happily, with the captain's and Conseil's sharp friction, I saw consciousness return by degrees. He opened his eyes. What was his surprise, his terror even, at seeing four great copper heads leaning over him! And, above all, what must he have thought when Captain Nemo, drawing from the pocket of his dress a bag of pearls, placed it in his hand! This munificent charity from the man of the waters to the poor Cingalese was accepted with a trembling hand. His wondering eyes showed that he knew not to what superhuman beings he owed both fortune and life.

At a sign from the captain we regained the bank, and following the road already traversed, came in about half an hour to the anchor which held the canoe of the *Nautilus* to the earth.

Once on board, we each, with the help of the sailors, got rid of the heavy copper helmet.

Captain Nemo's first word was to the Canadian.

"Thank you, Master Land." said he.

"It was in revenge, Captain," replied Ned Land. "I owed you that."

A ghastly smile passed across the captain's lips, and that was all.

"To the *Nautilus,*" said he.

The boat flew over the waves. Some minutes after, we met the shark's dead body floating. By the black marking of the extremity of its fins, I recognized the terrible melanopteron of the Indian Seas, of the species of shark properly so called. It was more than twenty-five feet long; its enormous mouth occupied one third of its body. It was an adult, as was known by its six rows of teeth placed in an isosceles triangle in the upper jaw.

Conseil looked at it with scientific interest, and I am sure that he placed it, and not without reason, in the cartilaginous class, of the chondropterygian order, with fixed gills, of the selacian family, in the genus of the sharks.

Whilst I was contemplating this inert mass, a dozen of these voracious beasts appeared round the boat; and, without noticing us, threw themselves upon the dead body and fought with one another for the pieces.

At half past eight we were again on board the *Nautilus*. There I reflected on the incidents which had taken place in our excursion to the Manaar Bank.

Two conclusions I must inevitably draw from it,—one bearing upon the unparalleled courage of Captain Nemo, the other upon his devotion to a human being, a representative of that race from which he fled beneath the sea. Whatever he might say, this strange man had not yet succeeded in entirely crushing his heart.

When I made this observation to him, he answered in a slightly moved tone,—

"That Indian, sir, is an inhabitant of an oppressed country; and I am still, and shall be, to my last breath, one of them!"

CHAPTER 4

THE RED SEA

In the course of the day of the 29th of January, the Island of Ceylon disappeared under the horizon, and the *Nautilus,* at a speed of twenty miles an hour, slid into the labyrinth of canals which separate the Maldives from the Laccadives. It coasted even the Island of Kiltan, a land originally madreporic, discovered by Vasco de Gama in 1499, and one of the ninteen principal islands of the Laccadive Archipelago, situated between 10° and 14° 30′ north latitude, and 69° 50′ 72″ east longitude.

We had made 16,220 miles, or 7,500 (French) leagues from our starting point in the Japanese Seas.

The next day (30th January), when the *Nautilus* went to the surface of the ocean, there was no land in sight. Its course was N.N.E., in the direction of the Sea of Oman, between Arabia and the Indian Peninsula, which serves as an outlet to the Persian Gulf. It was evidently a block without any possible egress. Where was Captain Nemo taking us to? I could not say. This, however, did not satisfy the Canadian, who that day came to me asking where we were going.

"We are going where our captain's fancy takes us, Master Ned."

"His fancy cannot take us far, then," said the Canadian. "The Persian Gulf has no outlet; and if we do go in, it will not be long before we are out again."

"Very well, then, we will come out again, Master Land; and if after the Persian Gulf the *Nautilus* would like to visit the Red Sea, the Straits of Bab-el-mandeb are there to give us entrance."

"I need not tell you, sir," said Ned Land, "that the Red Sea is as much closed as the Gulf, as the Isthmus of Suez is not yet cut; and if it was, a boat as mysterious as ours would not risk itself in a canal cut with sluices. And again, the Red Sea is not the road to take us back to Europe."

"But I never said we were going back to Europe."

"What do you suppose, then?"

"I suppose that, after visiting the curious coasts of Arabia and Egypt, the *Nautilus* will go down the Indian Ocean again, perhaps cross the Channel of Mozambique, perhaps off the Mascarenhas, so as to gain the Cape of Good Hope."

"And once at the Cape of Good Hope?" asked the Canadian, with peculiar emphasis.

"Well, we shall penetrate into that Atlantic which we do not yet know. Ah! friend Ned, you are getting tired of this journey under the sea: you are surfeited with the incessantly varying spectacle of submarine wonders. For my part, I shall be sorry to see the end of a voyage which it is given to so few men to make."

For four days, till the 3d of February, the *Nautilus* scoured the Sea of Oman, at various speeds and at various depths. It seemed to go at random, as if hesitating as to which road it should follow, but we never passed the Tropic of Cancer.

In quitting this sea we sighted Muscat for an instant, one of the most important towns of the country of Oman. I admired its strange aspect, surrounded by black rocks upon which its white houses and forts stood in relief. I saw the rounded domes of its mosques, the elegant points of its minarets, its fresh and verdant terraces. But it was only a vision! the *Nautilus* soon sank under the waves of that part of the sea.

We passed along the Arabian coast of Mahrah and Hadramaut, for a distance of six miles, its undulating line of mountains being occasionally relieved by some ancient ruin. The 5th of February we at last entered the Gulf of Aden, a perfect funnel introduced into the neck of Bab-el-mandeb, through which the Indian waters entered the Red Sea.

The 6th of February, the *Nautilus* floated in sight of Aden, perched upon a promontory which a narrow isthmus joins to the mainland, a kind of inaccessible Gibraltar, the fortifications of which were rebuilt by the English after taking possession in 1839. I caught a glimpse of the octagon minarets of this town, which was at one time, according to the historian Edrisi, the richest commercial magazine on the coast.

I certainly thought that Captain Nemo, arrived at this point, would back out again; but I was mistaken, for he did no such thing, much to my surprise.

The next day, the 7th of February, we entered the Straits of Bab-el-mandeb, the name of which, in the Arab tongue, means "The gate of tears."

To twenty miles in breadth, it is only thirty-two in length. And for the *Nautilus*, starting at full speed, the crossing was scarcely the work of an hour. But I saw nothing, not even the island of Perim, with which the British government has fortified the position of Aden. There were too many English or French steamers of the line of Suez to Bombay, Calcutta to Melbourne, and from Bourbon to the Mauritius, furrowing this narrow passage, for the *Nautilus* to venture to show itself. So it remained prudently below. At last, about noon, we were in the waters of the Red Sea.

I would not even seek to understand the caprice which had decided Captain Nemo upon entering the gulf. But I quite approved of the *Nautilus* entering it. Its speed was lessened: sometimes it kept on the surface, sometimes it dived to avoid a vessel, and thus I was able to observe the upper and lower parts of this curious sea.

The 8th of February, from the first dawn of day, Mocha came in sight, now a ruined town, whose walls would fall at a gun-shot, yet which shelters here and there some verdant date-trees; once an important city, containing six public markets, and twenty-six mosques, and whose walls, defended by fourteen forts, formed a girdle of two miles in circumference.

The *Nautilus* then approached the African shore, where the depth of the sea was greater. There, between two waters clear as crystal, through the open panels we were allowed to contemplate the beautiful bushes of brilliant coral, and large blocks of rock clothed with a splendid fur of green algæ and fuci. What an indescribable spectacle, and what variety of sites and landscapes along these sand-banks and volcanic islands which bound the Lybian coast! But where these shrubs appeared in all their beauty was on the eastern coast, which the *Nautilus* soon gained. It was on the coast of Tehama, for there not only did this display of zoöphytes flourish beneath the level of the sea, but they also formed picturesque interlacings which unfolded themselves about sixty feet above the surface, more capricious but less highly colored than those whose freshness was kept up by the vital power of the waters.

What charming hours I passed thus at the window of the saloon! What new specimens of submarine flora and fauna did I admire under the brightness of our electric lantern!

There grew sponges of all shapes, pediculated, foliated, globular, and digital. They certainly justified the names of baskets, cups, distaffs, elk's-horns, lion's-feet, peacock's-tails, and Neptune's-gloves, which have been given to them by the fishermen, greater poets than the savants.

Other zoöphytes which multiply near the sponges consist principally of medusæ of a most elegant kind. The molluscs were represented by varieties of the calmar (which, according to Orbigny, are peculiar to the Red Sea); and reptiles by the virgata turtle, of the genus of cheloniæ, which furnished a wholesome and delicate food for our table.

As to the fish, they were abundant, and often remarkable. The following are those which the nets of the *Nautilus* brought more frequently on board:—

Rays of a red-brick color, with bodies marked with blue spots, and easily recognizable by their double spikes; some superb caranxes, marked with seven transverse bands of jet-black, blue and yellow fins, and gold and silver scales; mullets with yellow heads; gobies, and a thousand other species, common to the ocean which we had just traversed.

The 9th of February, the *Nautilus* floated in the broadest part of the Red Sea, which is comprised between Souakin on the west coast, and Koomfidah, on the east coast, with a diameter of ninety miles.

That day at noon, after the bearings were taken, Captain Nemo mounted the platform, where I happened to be, and I was determined not to let him go down again without at least pressing him regarding his ulterior projects. As soon as he saw me he approached, and graciously offered me a cigar.

"Well, sir, does this Red Sea please you? Have you sufficiently observed the wonders it covers, its fishes, its zoöphytes, its parterres of sponges, and its forests of coral? Did you catch a glimpse of the towns on its borders?"

"Yes, Captain Nemo," I replied; "and the *Nautilus* is wonderfully fitted for such a study. Ah! it is an intelligent boat!"

"Yes, sir, intelligent and invulnerable. It fears neither the terrible tempests of the Red Sea, nor its currents, nor its sand-banks."

"Certainly," said I, "this sea is quoted as one of the worst, and in the time of the ancients, if I am not mistaken, its reputation was detestable."

"Detestable, M. Aronnax. The Greek and Latin historians do not speak favorably of it, and Strabo says it is very dangerous during the Etesian winds, and in the rainy season. The Arabian Edrisi portrays it under the name of the Gulf of Colzoum, and relates that vessels perished there in great numbers on the sand-banks, and that no one would risk sailing in the night. It is, he pretends, a sea subject to fearful hurricanes, strewn with inhospitable islands, and 'which offers nothing good either on its surface or in its depths.' Such, too, is the opinion of Arrian, Agatharcides, and Artemidorus."

"One may see," I replied, "that these historians never sailed on board the *Nautilus*."

"Just so," replied the captain, smiling; "and in that respect moderns are not more advanced than the ancients. It required many ages to find out the mechanical power of steam. Who knows if, in another hundred years, we may not see a second *Nautilus*? Progress is slow, M. Aronnax."

"It is true," I answered; "your boat is at least a century before its time, perhaps an era. What a misfortune that the secret of such an invention should die with its inventor!''

Captain Nemo did not reply. After some minutes' silence he continued,—

''You were speaking of the opinions of ancient historians upon the dangerous navigation of the Red Sea.''

''It is true,'' said I; ''but were not their fears exaggerated?''

''Yes and no, M. Aronnax,'' replied Captain Nemo, who seemed to know the Red Sea by heart. ''That which is no longer dangerous for a modern vessel, well rigged, strongly built, and master of its own course, thanks to obedient steam, offered all sorts of perils to the ships of the ancients. Picture to yourself those first navigators venturing in ships made of planks sewn with the cords of the palm-tree, saturated with the grease of the sea-dog, and covered with powdered resin! They had not even instruments wherewith to take their bearings, and they went by guess amongst currents of which they scarcely knew anything. Under such conditions shipwrecks were, and must have been, numerous. But in our time, steamers running between Suez and the South Seas have nothing more to fear from the fury of this gulf, in spite of contrary trade-winds. The captain and passengers do not prepare for their departure by offering propitiatory sacrifices; and, on their return, they no longer go ornamented with wreaths and gilt fillets to thank the gods in the neighboring temple.''

''I agree with you,'' said I; ''and steam seems to have killed all gratitude in the hearts of sailors. But, Captain, since you seem to have especially studied this sea, can you tell me the origin of its name?''

''There exist several explanations on the subject, M. Aronnax. Would you like to know the opinion of a chronicler of the fourteenth century?''

''Willingly.''

''This fanciful writer pretends that its name was given to it after the passage of the Israelites, when Pharaoh perished in the waves which closed at the voice of Moses.''

''A poet's explanation, Captain Nemo,'' I replied; ''but I cannot content myself with that. I ask you for your personal opinion.''

''Here it is, M. Aronnax. According to my idea, we must see in this appellation of the Red Sea a translation of the Hebrew word 'Edom'; and if the ancients gave it that name, it was on account of the particular color of its waters.''

''But up to this time I have seen nothing but transparent waves and without any particular color.''

''Very likely; but as we advance to the bottom of the gulf, you will see this singular appearance. I remember seeing the Bay of Tor entirely red, like a sea of blood.''

''And you attribute this color to the presence of a microscopic sea-weed?''

''Yes; it is a mucilaginous purple matter, produced by the restless little plants known by the name of trichodesmia, and of which it requires 40,000 to occupy the space of a square .04 of an inch. Perhaps we shall meet some when we get to Tor.''

''So, Captain Nemo, it is not the first time you have overrun the Red Sea on board the *Nautilus?*''

''No, sir.''

''As you spoke a while ago of the passage of the Israelites, and of the catastrophe to the Egyptians, I will ask whether you have met with traces under the water of this great historical fact?''

"No, sir; and for a very good reason."

"What is it?"

"It is, that the spot where Moses and his people passed is now so blocked up with sand, that the camels can barely bathe their legs there. You can well understand that there would not be water enough for my *Nautilus*."

"And the spot?" I asked.

"The spot is situated a little above the Isthmus of Suez, in the arm which formerly made a deep estuary, when the Red Sea extended to the Salt Lakes. Now, whether this passage were miraculous or not, the Israelites, nevertheless, crossed there to reach the Promised Land, and Pharaoh's army perished precisely on that spot; and I think that excavations made in the middle of the sand would bring to light a large number of arms and instruments of Egyptian origin."

"That is evident," I replied; "and for the sake of archæologists let us hope that these excavations will be made sooner or later, when new towns are established on the isthmus, after the construction of the Suez Canal; a canal, however, very useless to a vessel like the *Nautilus*."

"Very likely; but useful to the whole world," said Captain Nemo. "The ancients well understood the utility of a communication between the Red Sea and the Mediterranean for their commercial afffairs; but they did not think of digging a canal direct, and took the Nile as an intermediate. Very probably the canal which united the Nile to the Red Sea was begun by Sesostris, if we may believe tradition. One thing is certain, that in the year 615 before Jesus Christ, Necos undertook the works of an alimentary canal to the waters of the Nile, across the plain of Egypt, looking towards Arabia. It took four days to go up this canal, and it was so wide that two triremes could go abreast. It was carried on by Darius, the son of Hystaspes, and probably finished by Ptolemy II. Strabo saw it navigated; but its decline from the point of departure, near Bubastes, to the Red Sea was so slight, that it was only navigable for a few months in the year. This canal answered all commercial purposes to the age of Antoninus, when it was abandoned and blocked up with sand. Restored by order of the Caliph Omar, it was definitively destroyed in 761 or 762 by Caliph Al-Mansor, who wished to prevent the arrival of provisions to Mohammed-ben-Abdallah, who had revolted against him. During the expedition into Egypt, your General Bonaparte discovered traces of the works in the Desert of Suez; and, surprised by the tide, he nearly perished before regaining Hadjaroth, at the very place where Moses had encamped three thousand years before him."

"Well, Captain, what the ancients dared not undertake, this junction between the two seas, which will shorten the road from Cadiz to India, M. Lesseps has succeeded in doing; and before long he will have changed Africa into an immense island."

"Yes, M. Aronnax; you have the right to be proud of your countryman. Such a man brings more honor to a nation than great captains. He began, like so many others, with disgust and rebuffs; but he has triumphed, for he has the genius of will. And it is sad to think that a work like that, which ought to have been an international work, and which would have sufficed to make a reign illustrious, should have succeeded by the energy of one man. All honor to M. Lesseps!"

"Yes, honor to the great citizen!" I replied, surprised by the manner in which Captain Nemo had just spoken.

"Unfortunately," he continued, "I cannot take you through the Suez Canal;

but you will be able to see the long jetty of Port Said after to-morrow, when we shall be in the Mediterranean.''

''The Mediterranean!'' I exclaimed.

''Yes, sir; does that astonish you?''

''What astonishes me is to think that we shall be there the day after to-morrow.''

''Indeed?''

''Yes, Captain, although by this time I ought to have accustomed myself to be surprised at nothing since I have been on board your boat.''

''But the cause of this surprise?''

''Well! it is the fearful speed you will have to put on the *Nautilus,* if the day after to-morrow she is to be in the Mediterranean, having made the round of Africa, and doubled the Cape of Good Hope!''

''Who told you that she would make the round of Africa, and double the Cape of Good Hope, sir?''

''Well, unless the *Nautilus* sails on dry land, and passes above the isthmus—''

''Or beneath it, M. Aronnax.''

''Beneath it?''

''Certainly,'' replied Captain Nemo, quietly. ''A long time ago nature made under this tongue of land what man has this day made on its surface.''

''What! such a passage exists?''

''Yes; a subterranean passage, which I have named the Arabian Tunnel. It takes us beneath Suez, and opens into the Gulf of Pelusium.''

''But this isthmus is composed of nothing but quicksands?''

''To a certain depth. But at fifty-five yards only, there is a solid layer of rock.''

''Did you discover this passage by chance?'' I asked, more and more surprised.

''Chance and reasoning, sir; and by reasoning even more than by chance. Not only does this passage exist, but I have profited by it several times. Without that I should not have ventured this day into the impassable Red Sea. I noticed that in the Red Sea and in the Mediterranean there existed a certain number of fishes of a kind perfectly identical,—ophidia, fiatoles, girelles, and exocœti. Certain of that fact, I asked myself was it possible that there was no communication between the two seas? If there was, the subterranean current must necessarily run from the Red Sea to the Mediterranean, from the sole cause of difference of level. I caught a large number of fishes in the neighborhood of Suez. I passed a copper ring through their tails, and threw them back into the sea. Some months later, on the coast of Syria, I caught some of my fish ornamented with the ring. Thus the communication between the two was proved. I then sought for it with my *Nautilus;* I discovered it, ventured into it, and before long, sir, you too will have passed through my Arabian tunnel!''

CHAPTER 5

THE ARABIAN TUNNEL

THAT same evening, in 21° 30′ north latitude, the *Nautilus* floated on the surface of the sea, approaching the Arabian coast. I saw Djeddah, the most important counting-house of Egypt, Syria, Turkey, and India. I distinguished clearly enough its buildings, the vessels anchored at the quays, and those whose draught of water obliged them to anchor in the roads. The sun, rather low on the horizon, struck full on the houses of the town, bringing out their whiteness. Outside, some wooden cabins, and some made of reeds, showed the quarter inhabited by the Bedouins. Soon Djeddah was shut out from view by the shadows of night, and the *Nautilus* found herself under water slightly phorphorescent.

The next day, the 10th of February, we sighted several ships running to windward. The *Nautilus* returned to its submarine navigation; but at noon, when her bearings were taken, the sea being deserted, she rose again to her water-line.

Accompanied by Ned and Conseil, I seated myself on the platform. The coast on the eastern side looked like a mass faintly printed upon a damp fog.

We were learning on the sides of the pinnace, talking of one thing and another, when Ned Land, stretching out his hand towards a spot on the sea, said,—

"Do you see anything there, sir?"

"No, Ned," I replied; "but I have not your eyes, you know."

"Look well," said Ned, "there, on the starboard beam, about the height of the lantern! Do you not see a mass which seems to move?"

"Certainly," said I, after close attention; "I see something like a long black body on the top of the water."

And certainly before long the black object was not more than a mile from us. It looked like a great sand-bank deposited in the open sea. It was a gigantic dugong!

Ned Land looked eagerly. His eyes shone with covetousness at the sight of the animal. His hand seemed ready to harpoon it. One would have thought he was awaiting the moment to throw himself into the sea, and attack it in its element.

At this instant Captain Nemo appeared on the platform. He saw the dugong, understood the Canadian's attitude, and addressing him, said,—

"If you held a harpoon just now, Master Land, would it not burn your hand?"

"Just so, sir."

"And you would not be sorry to go back, for one day, to your trade of a fisherman, and to add this cetacean to the list of those you have already killed?"

"I should not, sir."

"Well, you can try."

"Thank you, sir," said Ned Land, his eyes flaming.

"Only," continued the captain, "I advise you for your own sake not to miss the creature."

"Is the dugong dangerous to attack?" I asked, in spite of the Canadian's shrug of the shoulders.

"Yes," replied the captain; "sometimes the animal turns upon its assailants and overturns their boat. But for Master Land, this danger is not to be feared. His eye is prompt, his arm sure."

At this moment seven men of the crew, mute and immovable as ever, mounted the platform. One carried a harpoon and a line similar to those employed in catching whales. The pinnace was lifted from the bridge, pulled from its socket, and let down into the sea. Six oarsmen took their seats, and the coxswain went to the tiller. Ned, Conseil, and I went to the back of the boat.

"You are not coming, Captain?" I asked.

"No, sir; but I wish you good sport."

The boat put off, and lifted by the six rowers, drew rapidly towards the dugong, which floated about two miles from the *Nautilus*.

Arrived some cables' length from the cetacean, the speed slackened, and the oars dipped noiselessly into the quiet waters. Ned Land, harpoon in hand, stood in the fore part of the boat. The harpoon used for striking the whale is generally attached to a very long cord, which runs out rapidly as the wounded creature draws it after him. But here the cord was not more than ten fathoms long, and the extremity was attached to a small barrel, which, by floating, was to show the course dugong took under the water.

I stood, and carefully watched the Canadian's adversary. This dugong, which also bears the name of the halicore, closely resembles the manatee; its oblong body terminated in a lengthened tail, and its lateral fins in perfect fingers. Its difference from the manatee consisted in its upper jaw, which was armed with two long and pointed teeth, which formed on each side diverging tusks.

This dugong, which Ned Land was preparing to attack, was of colossal dimensions; it was more than seven yards long. It did not move, and seemed to be sleeping on the waves, which circumstance made it easier to capture.

The boat approached within six yards of the animal. The oars rested on the rowlocks. I half rose. Ned Land, his body thrown a little back, brandished the harpoon in his experienced hand.

Suddenly a hissing noise was heard, and the dugong disappeared. The harpoon, although thrown with great force, had apparently only struck the water.

"Curse it!" exclaimed the Canadian furiously; "I have missed it!"

"No," said I; "the creature is wounded,—look at the blood; but your weapon has not struck in his body."

"My harpoon! my harpoon!" cried Ned Land.

The sailors rowed on, and the coxswain made for the floating barrel. The harpoon regained, we followed in pursuit of the animal.

The latter came now and then to the surface to breathe. Its wound had not weakened it, for it shot onwards with great rapidity.

The boat, rowed by strong arms, flew on its track. Several times it approached within some few yards, and the Canadian was ready to strike, but the dugong made off with a sudden plunge, and it was impossible to reach it.

Imagine the passion which excited impatient Ned Land! He hurled at the unfortunate creature the most energetic expletives in the English tongue. For my part I was only vexed to see the dugong escape all our attacks.

We pursued it without relaxation for an hour, and I began to think it would prove difficult to capture, when the animal, possessed with the perverse idea of vengeance, of which he had cause to repent, turned upon the pinnace and assailed us in its turn.

Ned Land, stretching out his hand, asked, "Do you see anything there?"

This manœuvre did not escape the Canadian.

"Look out!" he cried.

The coxswain said some words in his outlandish tongue, doubtless warning the men to keep on their guard.

The dugong came within twenty feet of the boat, stopped, sniffed the air briskly with its large nostrils (not pierced at the extremity, but in the upper part of its muzzle). Then taking a spring he threw himself upon us.

The pinnace could not avoid the shock, and half upset, shipped at least two tons of water, which had to be emptied; but thanks to the coxswain, we caught it sideways, not full front, so we were not quite overturned. While Ned Land, clinging to the bows, belabored the gigantic animal with blows from his harpoon, the creature's teeth were buried in the gunwale, and it lifted the whole thing out of the water, as a lion does a roebuck. We were upset over one another, and I know not how the adventure would have ended, if the Canadian, still enraged with the beast, had not struck it to the heart.

I heard its teeth grind on the iron plate, and the dugong disappeared, carrying the harpoon with him. But the barrel soon returned to the surface, and shortly after the body of the animal, turned on its back. The boat came up with it, took it in tow, and made straight for the *Nautilus*.

It required tackle of enormous strength to hoist the dugong on to the platform. It weighed 10,000 lbs.

The next day, February 11th, the larder of the *Nautilus* was enriched by some more delicate game. A flight of sea-swallows rested on the *Nautilus*. It was a species of the Sterna nilotica, peculiar to Egypt; its beak is black, head gray and pointed, the eye surrounded by white spots, the back, wings, and tail of a grayish color, the belly and throat white, and claws red. They also took some dozen of Nile ducks, a wild bird of high flavor, its throat and upper part of the head white with black spots.

About five o'clock in the evening we sighted to the north the Cape of Ras-Mohammed. This cape forms the extremity of Arabia Petræa, comprised between the Gulf of Suez and the Gulf of Acabah.

The *Nautilus* penetrated into the Straits of Jubal, which leads to the Gulf of Suez. I distinctly saw a high mountain, towering between the two gulfs of Ras-Mohammed. It was Mount Horeb, that Sinai at the top of which Moses saw God face to face.

At six o'clock the *Nautilus*, sometimes floating, sometimes immersed, passed some distance from Tor, situated at the end of the bay, the waters of which seemed tinted with red, an observation already made by Captain Nemo. Then night fell in the midst of a heavy silence, sometimes broken by the cries of the pelican and other night-birds, and the noise of the waves breaking upon the shore, chafing against the rocks, or the panting of some far-off steamer beating the waters of the gulf with its noisy paddles.

From eight to nine o'clock the *Nautilus* remained some fathoms under the water. According to my calculation we must have been very near Suez. Through the panel of the saloon I saw the bottom of the rocks brilliantly lit up by our electric lamp. We seemed to be leaving the straits behind us more and more.

At a quarter past nine, the vessel having returned to the surface, I mounted the platform. Most impatient to pass through Captain Nemo's tunnel, I could not stay in one place, so came to breathe the fresh night-air.

Soon in the shadow I saw a pale light, half discolored by the fog, shining about a mile from us.

"A floating lighthouse!" said some one near me.

I turned, and saw the captain.

"It is the floating light of Suez," he continued. "It will not be long before we gain the entrance of the tunnel."

"The entrance cannot be easy?"

"No, sir; and for that reason I am accustomed to go into the steersman's cage, and myself direct our course. And now if you will go down, M. Aronnax, the *Nautilus* is going under the waves, and will not return to the surface until we have passed through the Arabian Tunnel."

Captain Nemo led me towards the central staircase; half-way down he opened a door, traversed the upper deck, and landed in the pilot's cage, which it may be remembered rose at the extremity of the platform. It was a cabin measuring six feet square, very much like that occupied by the pilot on the steamboats of the Mississippi or Hudson. In the midst worked a wheel, placed vertically, and caught to the tiller-rope, which ran to the back of the *Nautilus*. Four light-ports with lenticular glasses, let in a groove in the partition of the cabin, allowed the man at the wheel to see in all directions.

This cabin was dark; but soon my eyes accustomed themselves to the obscurity, and I perceived the pilot, a strong man, with his hands resting on the spokes of the wheel. Outside, the sea appeared vividly lit up by the lantern, which shed its rays from the back of the cabin to the other extremity of the platform.

"Now," said Captain Nemo, "let us try to make our passage."

Electric wires connected the pilot's cage with the machinery-room, and from there the captain could communicate simultaneously to his *Nautilus* the direction and the speed. He pressed a metal knob, and at once the speed of the screw diminished.

I looked in silence at the high straight wall we were running by at this moment, the immovable base of a massive sandy coast. We followed it thus for an hour only some few yards off.

Captain Nemo did not take his eye from the knob, suspended by its two concentric circles in the cabin. At a simple gesture, the pilot modified the course of the *Nautilus* every instant.

I had placed myself at the port-scuttle, and saw some magnificent substructures of coral, zoöphytes, sea-weed, and fucus, agitating their enormous claws, which stretched out from the fissures of the rock.

At a quarter past ten, the captain himself took the helm. A large gallery, black and deep, opened before us. The *Nautilus* went boldly into it. A strange roaring was heard round its sides. It was the waters of the Red Sea, which the incline of the tunnel precipitated violently towards the Mediterranean. The *Nautilus* went with the torrent, rapid as an arrow, in spite of the efforts of the machinery, which, in order to offer more effective resistance, beat the waves with reversed screw.

On the walls of the narrow passage I could see nothing but brilliant rays, straight lines, furrows of fire, traced by the great speed, under the brilliant electric light. My heart beat fast.

At thirty-five minutes past ten, Captain Nemo quitted the helm; and, turning to me, said,—

"The Mediterranean!"

In less than twenty minutes, the *Nautilus,* carried along by the torrent, had passed through the Isthmus of Suez.

CHAPTER 6

THE GRECIAN ARCHIPELAGO

THE next day, the 12th of February, at the dawn of day, the *Nautilus* rose to the surface. I hastened on to the platform. Three miles to the south the dim outline of Pelusium was to be seen. A torrent had carried us from one sea to the other. About seven o'clock Ned and Conseil joined me.

"Well, Sir Naturalist," said the Canadian, in a slightly jovial tone, "and the Mediterranean?"

"We are floating on its surface, friend Ned."

"What!" said Conseil, "this very night."

"Yes, this very night; in a few minutes we have passed this impassable isthmus."

"I do not believe it," replied the Canadian.

"Then you are wrong, Master Land," I continued; "this low coast which rounds off to the south is the Egyptian coast. And you, who have such good eyes, Ned, you can see the jetty of Port Said stretching into the sea."

The Canadian looked attentively.

"Certainly you are right, sir, and your captain is a first-rate man. We are in the Mediterranean. Good! Now, if you please, let us talk of our own little affair, but so that no one hears us."

I saw what the Canadian wanted, and, in any case, I thought it better to let him talk, as he wished it; so we all three went and sat down near the lantern, where we were less exposed to the spray of the blades.

"Now, Ned, we listen; what have you to tell us?"

"What I have to tell you is very simple. We are in Europe; and before Captain Nemo's caprices drag us once more to the bottom of the Polar Seas, or lead us into Oceania, I ask to leave the *Nautilus*."

I wished in no way to shackle the liberty of my companions, but I certainly felt no desire to leave Captain Nemo.

Thanks to him, and thanks to his apparatus, I was each day nearer the completion of my submarine studies; and I was rewriting my book of submarine depths in its very element. Should I ever again have such an opportunity of observing the wonders of the ocean? No, certainly not! And I could not bring myself to the idea of abandoning the *Nautilus* before the cycle of investigation was accomplished.

"Friend Ned, answer me frankly, are you tired of being on board? Are you sorry that destiny has thrown us into Captain Nemo's hands?"

The Canadian remained some moments without answering. Then crossing his arms, he said,—

"Frankly, I do not regret this journey under the seas. I shall be glad to have made it; but now that it is made, let us have done with it. That is my idea."

"It will come to an end, Ned."

"Where and when?"

"Where I do not know, when I cannot say; or, rather, I suppose it will end when these seas have nothing more to teach us."

"Then what do you hope for?" demanded the Canadian.

"That circumstances may occur as well six montths hence as now by which we may and ought to profit."

"O," said Ned Land, "and where shall we be in six months, if you please, Sir Naturalist?"

"Perhaps in China; you know the *Nautilus* is a rapid traveller. It goes through water as swallows through the air, or as an express on the land. It does not fear frequented seas; who can say that it may not beat the coasts of France, England, or America, on which flight may be attempted as advantageously as here."

"M. Aronnax," replied the Canadian, "your arguments are rotten at the foundation. You speak in the future, 'We shall be there! we shall be here!' I speak in the present, 'We are here, and we must profit by it.' "

Ned Land's logic pressed me hard, and I felt myself beaten on that ground. I knew not what argument would now tell in my favor.

"Sir," continued Ned, "let us suppose an impossibility; if Captain Nemo should this day offer you your liberty, would you accept it?"

"I do not know," I answered.

"And if," he added, "the offer he made you this day was never to be renewed, would you accept it?"

"Friend Ned, this is my answer. Your reasoning is against me. We must not rely on Captain Nemo's good-will. Common prudence forbids him to set us at liberty. On the other side, prudence bids us profit by the first opportunity to leave the *Nautilus*."

"Well, M. Aronnax, that is wisely said."

"Only one observation,—just one. The occasion must be serious, and our first attempt must succeed; if it fails, we shall never find another, and Captain Nemo will never forgive us."

"All that is true," replied the Canadian. "But your observation applies equally to all attempts at flight, whether in two years' time, or in two days. But the question is still this: if a favorable opportunity presents itself, it must be seized."

"Agreed! and now, Ned, will you tell me what you mean by a favorable opportunity?"

"It will be that which, on a dark night, will bring the *Nautilus* a short distance from some European coast."

"And you will try and save yourself by swimming?"

"Yes, if we were near enough to the bank, and if the vessel was floating at the time. Not if the bank was far away, and the boat was under the water."

"And in that case?"

"In that case, I should seek to make myself master of the pinnace. I know how it is worked. We must get inside, and the bolts once drawn, we shall come to the surface of the water, without even the pilot, who is in the bows, perceiving our flight."

"Well, Ned, watch for the opportunity; but do not forget that a hitch will ruin us."

"I will not forget, sir."

"And now, Ned, would you like to know what I think of your project?"

"Certainly, M. Aronnax."

"Well I think—I dò not say I hope—I think that this favorable opportunity will never present itself."

"Why not?"

"Because Captain Nemo cannot hide from himself that we have not given up all hope of regaining our liberty, and he will be on his guard, above all, in the seas, and in the sight of European coasts."

"We shall see," replied Ned Land, shaking his head determinedly.

"And now, Ned Land," I added, "let us stop here. Not another word on the subject. The day that you are ready, come and let us know, and we will follow you. I rely entirely upon you."

Thus ended a conversation which, at no very distant time, led to such grave results. I must say here that facts seemed to confirm my foresight, to the Canadian's great despair. Did Captain Nemo distrust us in these frequented seas? or did he only wish to hide himself from the numerous vessels, of all nations, which ploughed the Mediterranean? I could not tell; but we were oftener between waters, and far from the coast. Or, if the *Nautilus* did emerge, nothing was to be seen but the pilot's cage; and sometimes it went to great depths, for, between the Grecian Archipelago and Asia Minor, we could not touch the bottom by more than a thousand fathoms.

Thus I only knew we were near the island of Carpathos, one of the Sporades, by Captain Nemo reciting these lines from Virgil,—

"Est in Carpathio Neptuni gurgite vates,
Cæruleus Proteus,"

as he pointed to a spot on the planisphere.

It was indeed the ancient abode of Proteus, the old shepherd of Neptune's flocks, now the island of Scarpanto, situated between Rhodes and Crete. I saw nothing but the granite base through the glass panels of the saloon.

The next day, the 14th of February, I resolved to employ some hours in studying the fishes of the Archipelago; but for some reason or other, the panels remained hermetically sealed. Upon taking the course of the *Nautilus* I found that we were going towards Candia, the ancient Isle of Crete. At the time I embarked on the *Abraham Lincoln,* the whole of this island had risen in insurrection against the despotism of the Turks. But how the insurgents had fared since that time I was absolutely ignorant, and it was not Captain Nemo, deprived of all land communications, who could tell me.

I made no allusion to this event when that night I found myself alone with him in the saloon. Besides, he seemed to be taciturn and preoccupied. Then, contrary to his custom, he ordered both panels to be opened, and going from one to the other, observed the mass of waters attentively. To what end I could not guess; so, on my side, I employed my time in studying the fish passing before my eyes.

Amongst others, I remarked some gobies, mentioned by Aristotle, and commonly known by the name of sea-braches, which are more particularly met with in the salt waters lying near the Delta of the Nile. Near them rolled some sea-bream, half phosphorescent, a kind of sparus, which the Egyptians ranked amongst their sacred animals, whose arrival in the waters of their river announced a fertile overflow, and was celebrated by religious ceremonies. I also noticed some cheilines about nine inches long, a bony fish with transparent shell, whose livid color is mixed with red spots; they are great eaters of marine vegetation, which gives them an exquisite flavor. These cheilines were much sought after by the epicures of ancient Rome; the inside, dressed with the soft roe of the lamprey, peacocks' brains, and tongues of the phenicoptera, composed that divine dish of which Vitellius was so enamored.

Another inhabitant of these seas drew my attention, and led my mind back to recollections of antiquity. It was the remora, that fastens on to the shark's belly. This little fish, according to the ancients, hooking on to the ship's bottom, could stop its movements; and one of them, by keeping back Antony's ship during the battle of Actium, helped Augustus to gain the victory. On how little hangs the destiny of nations! I observed some fine anthiæ, which belong to the order of lutjans, a fish held sacred by the Greeks, who attributed to them the power of hunting the marine monsters from waters they frequented. Their name signifies *flower,* and they justify their appellation by their shaded colors, their shades comprising the whole gamut of reds, from the paleness of the rose to the brightness of the ruby, and the fugitive tints that clouded their dorsal fin. My eyes could not leave these wonders of the sea, when they were suddenly struck by an unexpected apparition.

In the midst of the waters a man appeared, a diver, carrying at his belt a leathern purse. It was not a body abandoned to the waves; it was a living man, swimming with a strong hand, disappearing occasionally to take breath at the surface.

I turned towards Captain Nemo, and in an agitated voice exclaimed,—

"A man shipwrecked! He must be saved at any price!"

The captain did not answer me, but came and leaned against the panel.

The man had approached, and with his face flattened against the glass, was looking at us.

To my great amazement, Captain Nemo signed to him. The diver answered with his hand, mounted immediately to the surface of the water, and did not appear again.

"Do not be uncomfortable," said Captain Nemo. "It is Nicholas of Cape Matapan, surnamed Pesca. He is well known in all the Cyclades. A bold diver! water is his element, and he lives more in it than on land, going continually from one island to another, even as far as Crete."

"You know him, Captain?"

"Why not, M. Aronnax?"

Saying which, Captain Nemo went towards a piece of furniture standing near the left panel of the saloon. Near this piece of furniture, I saw a chest bound with iron, on the cover of which was a copper plate, bearing the cipher of the *Nautilus* with its device.

At that moment, the captain, without noticing my presence, opened the piece of furniture, a sort of strong box, which held a great many ingots.

They were ingots of gold. From whence came this precious metal, which represented an enormous sum? Where did the captain gather this gold from? and what was he going to do with it?

I did not say one word. I looked. Captain Nemo took the ingots one by one, and arranged them methodically in the chest, which he filled entirely. I estimated the contents at more than 4,000 lbs. weight of gold, that is to say, nearly £ 200,000.

The chest was securely fastened, and the captain wrote an address on the lid, in characters which must have belonged to Modern Greece.

This done, Captain Nemo pressed a knob, the wire of which communicated with the quarters of the crew. Four men appeared, and, not without some trouble, pushed the chest out of the saloon. Then I heard them hoisting it up the iron staircase by means of pulleys.

At that moment, Captain Nemo turned to me.

"And you were saying, sir?" said he.

"I was saying nothing, Captain."

"Then, sir, if you will allow me, I will wish you good night."

Whereupon he turned and left the saloon.

I returned to my room much troubled, as one may believe. I vainly tried to sleep,—I sought the connecting link between the apparition of the diver and the chest filled with gold. Soon, I felt by certain movements of pitching and tossing, that the *Nautilus* was leaving the depths and returning to the surface.

Then I heard steps upon the platform; and I knew they were unfastening the pinnace, and launching it upon the waves. For one instant it struck the side of the *Nautilus,* then all noise ceased.

Two hours after, the same noise, the same going and coming was renewed; the boat was hoisted on board, replaced in its socket, and the *Nautilus* again plunged under the waves.

So these millions had been transported to their address. To what point of the Continent? Who was Captain Nemo's correspondent?

The next day, I related to Conseil and the Canadian the events of the night, which had excited my curiosity to the highest degree. My companions were not less surprised than myself.

"But where does he take his millions to?" asked Ned Land.

To that there was no possible answer. I returned to the saloon after having breakfast, and set to work. Till five o'clock in the evening, I employed myself in arranging my notes. At that moment (ought I to attribute it to some peculiar idiosyncrasy?) I felt so great a heat that I was obliged to take off my coat of byssus! It was strange, for we were not under low latitudes; and even then, the *Nautilus,* submerged as it was, ought to experience no change of temperature. I looked at the manometer; it showed a depth of sixty feet, to which atmospheric heat could never attain.

I continued my work, but the temperature rose to such a pitch as to be intolerable.

"Could there be fire on board?" I asked myself.

I was leaving the saloon, when Captain Nemo entered; he approached the thermometer, consulted it, and turning to me, said,—

"Forty-two degrees."

"I have noticed it, Captain," I replied; "and if it gets much hotter we cannot bear it."

"O, sir, it will not get hotter if we do not wish it!"

"You can reduce it as you please, then?"

"No; but I can go farther from the stove which produces it."

"It is outward then!"

"Certainly; we are floating in a current of boiling water."

"Is it possible!" I exclaimed.

"Look."

The panels opened, and I saw the sea entirely white all round. A sulphurous smoke was curling amid the waves, which boiled like water in a copper. I placed my hand on one of the panes of glass, but the heat was so great that I quickly took it off again.

"Where are we?" I asked.

"Near the Island of Santorin, sir," replied the captain, "and just in the canal which separates Nea Kamenni from Pali Kamenni. I wished to give you a sight of the curious spectacle of a submarine eruption."

"I thought," said I, "that the formation of these new islands was ended."

"Nothing is ever ended in the volcanic parts of the sea," replied Captain Nemo; "and the globe is always being worked by subterranean fires. Already, in the nineteenth year of our era, according to Cassiodorus and Pliny, a new island, Theia (the divine), appeared in the very place where these islets have recently been formed. Then they sank under the waves, to rise again in the year 69, when they again subsided. Since that time to our days, the Plutonian work has been suspended. But, on the 3d of February, 1866, a new island, which they named George Island, emerged from the midst of the sulphurous vapor near Nea Kamenni, and settled again the 6th of the same month. Seven days after, the 13th of February, the Island of Aphroessa appeared, leaving between Nea Kamenni and itself a canal ten yards broad. I was in these seas when the phenomenon occurred, and I was able therefore to observe all the different phases. The Island of Aphroessa, of round form, measured 300 feet in diameter, and thirty feet in height. It was composed of black and vitreous lava, mixed with fragments of felspar. And lastly, on the 10th of March, a smaller island, called Reka, showed itself near Nea Kamenni, and since then these three have joined together, forming but one and the same island."

"And the canal in which we are at this moment?" I asked.

"Here it is," replied Captain Nemo, showing me a map of the Archipelago. "You see I have marked the new islands."

I returned to the glass. The *Nautilus* was no longer moving, the heat was becoming unbearable. The sea, which till now had been white, was red, owing to the presence of salts of iron. In spite of the ship's being hermetically sealed, an insupportable smell of sulphur filled the saloon, and the brilliancy of the electricity was entirely extinguished by bright scarlet flames. I was in a bath, I was choking, I was broiled.

"We can remain no longer in this boiling water," said I to the captain.

"It would not be prudent," replied the impassive Captain Nemo.

An order was given; the *Nautilus* tacked about and left the furnace it could not brave with impunity. A quarter of an hour after we were breathing fresh air on the surface. The thought then struck me that, if Ned Land had chosen this part of the sea for our flight, we should never have come alive out of this sea of fire.

The next day, the 16th of February, we left the basin which, between Rhodes and Alexandria, is reckoned about 1,500 fathoms in depth, and the *Nautilus*, passing some distance from Cerigo, quitted the Grecian Archipelago, after having doubled Cape Matapan.

CHAPTER 7

THE MEDITERRANEAN IN FORTY-EIGHT HOURS

THE Mediterranean, the blue sea *par excellence,* "the great sea" of the Hebrews, "the sea" of the Greeks, the "mare nostrum" of the Romans, bordered by orange-trees, aloes, cacti, and sea-pines; embalmed with the perfume of the myrtle, surrounded by rude mountains, saturated with pure and transparent air, but incessantly worked by underground fires, a perfect battle-field in which Neptune and Pluto still dispute the empire of the world!

It is upon these banks, and on these waters, says Michelet, that man is renewed in one of the most powerful climates of the globe. But, beautiful as it was, I could only take a rapid glance at the basin whose superficial area is two millions of square yards. Even Captain Nemo's knowledge was lost to me, for this enigmatical person did not appear once during our passage at full speed. I estimated the course which the *Nautilus* took under the waves of the sea at about six hundred leagues, and it was accomplished in forty-eight hours. Starting on the morning of the 16th of February from the shores of Greece, we had crossed the Straits of Gibraltar by sunrise on the 18th.

It was plain to me that this Mediterranean, enclosed in the midst of those countries which he wished to avoid, was distasteful to Captain Nemo. Those waves and those breezes brought back too many remembrances, if not too many regrets. Here he had no longer that independence and that liberty of gait which he had when in the open seas, and his *Nautilus* felt itself cramped between the close shores of Africa and Europe.

Our speed was now twenty-five miles an hour. It may be well understood that Ned Land, to his great disgust, was obliged to renounce his intended flight. He could not launch the pinnace, going at the rate of twelve or thirteen yards every second. To quit the *Nautilus* under such conditions would be as bad as jumping from a train going at full speed,—an imprudent thing, to say the least of it. Besides, our vessel only mounted to the surface of the waves at night to renew its stock of air; it was steered entirely by the compass and the log.

I saw no more of the interior of this Mediterranean than a traveller by express train perceives of the landscape which flies before his eyes; that is to say, the distant horizon, and not the nearer objects which pass like a flash of lightning.

In the midst of the mass of waters brightly lit up by the electric light glided some of those lampreys, more than a yard long, common to almost every climate. Some of the oxyrhynchi, a kind of ray five feet broad, with white belly and gray spotted back, spread out like a large shawl carried along by the current. Other rays passed so quickly that I could not see if they deserved the name of eagles which was given to them by the ancient Greeks, or the qualification of rats, toads, and bats, with which modern fishermen have loaded them. A few milander sharks, twelve feet long, and much feared by divers, struggled amongst them. Sea-foxes eight feet long, endowed with wonderful fineness of scent, appeared like large blue shadows. Some dorades of the shark kind, some of which measured seven feet and a half, showed themselves in their dress of blue and silver, encircled by small bands which struck sharply against the sombre tints of their fins, a fish consecrated to Venus, the eyes of which are encased in a socket of gold, a precious species, friend of all waters, fresh or salt, an inhabitant of rivers, lakes, and oceans, living in all climates, and bearing all temperatures; a race belonging to the geological era of the earth, and which has preserved all the beauty of its first days. Magnificent sturgeons, nine or ten yards long, creatures of great speed, striking the panes of glass with their strong tails, displayed their bluish backs with small brown spots; they resemble the sharks, but are not equal to them in strength, and are to be met with in all seas. But of all the diverse inhabitants of the Mediterranean, those I observed to the greatest advantage, when the *Nautilus* approached the surface, belonged to the sixty-third genus of bony fish. They were a kind of tunny, with bluish black backs, and silvery breastplates, whose dorsal fins threw out sparkles of gold. They are said to follow in the wake of vessels, whose refreshing shade they seek from the fire of a tropical sky, and they did not belie the saying, for they accompanied the *Nautilus* as they did in former times the vessel of La Perouse. For many a long hour they struggled to keep up with our vessel. I was never tired of admiring these creatures really built for speed,—their small heads, their bodies lithe and cigar-shaped, which in some were more than three yards long, their pectoral fins, and forked tail endowed with remarkable strength. They swam in a triangle, like certain flocks of birds, whose rapidity they equalled, and of which the ancients used to say that they understood geometry and strategy. But still they do not escape the pursuit of the provençals, who esteem them as highly as the inhabitants of the Propontis and of Italy used to do; and these precious but blind and foolhardy creatures perish by millions in the nets of the Marseillaise.

With regard to the species of fish common to the Atlantic and the Mediterranean the giddy speed of the *Nautilus* prevented me from observing them with any degree of accuracy.

As to marine mammals, I thought, in passing the entrance of the Adriatic, that I saw two or three cachalots, furnished with one dorsal fin, of the genus physetera, some dolphins of the genus globicephali, peculiar to the Mediterranean, the back part of the head being marked like a zebra with small lines; also, a dozen of seals, with white bellies and black hair, known by the name of *monks*, and which really have the air of a Dominican; they are about three yards in length.

As to zoöphytes, for some instants I was able to admire a beautiful orange galeolaria, which had fastened itself to the port panel; it held on by a long filament, and was divided into an infinity of branches, terminated by the finest lace which could ever have been woven by the rivals of Arachne herself. Unfortunately, I could not take this admirable specimen; and doubtless no other Mediterranean zoöphyte would have offered itself to my observation, if, on the night of the 16th, the *Nautilus* had not, singularly enough, slackened its speed, under the following circumstances.

We were then passing between Sicily and the coast of Tunis. In the narrow space between Cape Bon and the Straits of Messina the bottom of the sea rose almost suddenly. There was a perfect bank, on which there was not more than nine fathoms of water, whilst on either side the depth was ninety fathoms.

The *Nautilus* had to manœuvre very carefully so as not to strike against this submarine barrier.

I showed Conseil on the map of the Mediterranean the spot occupied by this reef.

"But if you please, sir," observed Conseil, "it is like a real isthmus joining Europe to Africa."

"Yes, my boy, it forms a perfect bar to the Straits of Lybia, and the soundings of Smith have proved that in former times the continents between Cape Boco and Cape Furina were joined."

"I can well believe it," said Conseil.

"I will add," I continued, "that a similar barrier exists between Gibraltar and Ceuta, which in geological times formed the entire Mediterranean."

"What if some volcanic burst should one day raise these two barriers above the waves?"

"It is not probable, Conseil."

"Well, but allow me to finish, please, sir; if this phenomenon should take place, it will be troublesome for M. Lesseps, who has taken so much pains to pierce the isthmus."

"I agree with you; but I repeat, Conseil, this phenomenon will never happen. The violence of subterranean force is ever diminishing. Volcanoes, so plentiful in the first days of the world, are being extinguished by degrees; the internal heat is weakened, the temperature of the lower strata of the globe is lowered by a perceptible quantity every century to the detriment of our globe, for its heat is its life."

"But the sun?"

"The sun is not sufficient, Conseil. Can it give heat to a dead body?"

"Not that I know of."

"Well, my friend, this earth will one day be that cold corpse; it will become uninhabitable and uninhabited like the moon, which has long since lost all its vital heat."

"In how many centuries?"

"In some hundreds of thousands of years, my boy."

"Then," said Conseil, "we shall have time to finish our journey, that is, if Ned Land does not interfere with it."

And Conseil, reassured, returned to the study of the bank, which the *Nautilus* was skirting at a moderate speed.

There, beneath the rocky and volcanic bottom, lay outspread a living flora of sponges and reddish cydippes, which emitted a slight phosphorescent light, commonly known by the name of sea-cucumbers; and walking comatulæ more than a yard long, the purple of which completely colored the water around.

The *Nautilus* having now passed the high bank in the Lybian Straits returned to the deep waters and its accustomed speed.

From that time no more molluscs, no more articulates, no more zoöphytes; barely a few large fish passing like shadows.

During the night of the 16th and 17th February, we had entered the second Mediterranean basin, the greatest depth of which was 1,450 fathoms. The *Nautilus,* by the action of its screw, slid down the inclined planes, and buried itself in the lowest depths of the sea.

On the 18th of February, about three o'clock in the morning, we were at the entrance of the Straits of Gibraltar. There once existed two currents,—an upper one, long since recognized, which conveys the waters of the ocean into the basin of the Mediterranean; and a lower counter-current, which reasoning has now shown to exist. Indeed, the volume of water in the Mediterranean, incessantly added to by the waves of the Atlantic, and by rivers falling into it, would each year raise the level of this sea, for its evaporation is not sufficient to restore the equilibrium. As it is not so, we must necessarily admit the existence of an under-current, which empties into the basin of the Atlantic, through the Straits of Gibraltar, the surplus waters of the Mediterranean. A fact, indeed; and it was this counter-current by which the *Nautilus* profitted. It advanced rapidly by the narrow pass. For one instant I caught a glimpse of the beautiful ruins of the temple of Hercules, buried in the ground, according to Pliny, and with the low island which supports it; and a few minutes later we were floating on the Atlantic.

CHAPTER 8

VIGO BAY

THE Atlantic! a vast sheet of water, whose superficial area covers twenty-five millions of square miles, the length of which is nine thousand miles, with a mean breadth of two thousand seven hundred,—an ocean whose parallel winding shores embrace an immense circumference, watered by the largest rivers of the world, the St. Lawrence, the Mississippi, the Amazon, the Plata, the Orinoco, the Niger, the Senegal, the Elbe, the Loire, and the Rhine, which carry water from the most civilized, as well as from the most savage countries! Magnificent field of water, incessantly ploughed by vessels of every nation, sheltered by the flags of every nation, and which terminates in those two terrible points so dreaded by mariners, Cape Horn, and the Cape of Tempests!

The *Nautilus* was piercing the water with its sharp spur, after having accomplished nearly ten thousand leagues in three months and a half, a distance greater than the great circle of the earth. Where were we going now? and what was reserved for the future? The *Nautilus,* leaving the Straits of Gibraltar, had gone far out. It returned to the surface of the waves, and our daily walks on the platform were restored to us.

I mounted at once, accompanied by Ned Land and Conseil. At a distance of about twelve miles, Cape St. Vincent was dimly to be seen, forming the south-western point of the Spanish peninsula. A strong southerly gale was blowing. The sea was swollen and billowy; it made the *Nautilus* rock violently. It was almost impossible to keep one's footing on the platform, which the heavy rolls of the sea beat over every instant. So we descended after inhaling some mouthfuls of fresh air.

I returned to my room, Conseil to his cabin; but the Canadian, with a preoccupied air, followed me. Our rapid passage across the Mediterranean had not allowed him to put his project into execution, and he could not help showing his disappointment. When the door of my room was shut, he sat down and looked at me silently.

"Friend Ned," said I, "I understand you; but you cannot reproach yourself. To have attempted to leave the *Nautilus* under the circumstances would have been folly."

Ned Land did not answer; his compressed lips and frowning brow showed with him the violent possession this fixed idea had taken of his mind.

"Let us see," I continued; "we need not despair yet. We are going up the coast of Portugal again; France and England are not far off, where we can easily find refuge. Now, if the *Nautilus,* on leaving the Straits of Gibraltar, had gone to the south, if it had carried us towards regions where there were no continents, I should share your uneasiness. But we know now that Captain Nemo does not fly from civilized seas, and in some days I think you can act with security."

Ned Land still looked at me fixedly; at length his fixed lips parted, and he said, "It is for to-night."

I drew myself up suddenly. I was, I admit, little prepared for this communication. I wanted to answer the Canadian, but words would not come.

"We agreed to wait for an opportunity," continued Ned Land, "and the opportunity has arrived. This night we shall be but a few miles from the Spanish coast. It is cloudy. The wind blows freely. I have your word, M. Aronnax, and I rely upon you."

As I was still silent, the Canadian approached me.

"To-night, at nine o'clock," said he. "I have warned Conseil. At that moment, Captain Nemo will be shut up in his room, probably in bed. Neither the engineers nor the ship's crew can see us. Conseil and I will gain the central staircase, and you, M. Aronnax, will remain in the library, two steps from us, waiting my signal. The oars, the mast, and the sail are in the canoe. I have even succeeded in getting in some provisions. I have procured an English wrench, to unfasten the bolts which attach it to the shell of the *Nautilus*. So all is ready, till to-night."

"The sea is bad."

"That I allow," replied the Canadian; "but we must risk that. Liberty is worth paying for; besides, the boat is strong, and a few miles with a fair wind to carry us is no great thing. Who knows but by to-morrow we may be a hundred leagues away? Let circumstances only favor us, and by ten or eleven o'clock we shall have landed on some spot of *terra firma,* alive or dead. But adieu now till to-night."

With these words the Canadian withdrew, leaving me almost dumb. I had imagined that, the chance gone, I should have time to reflect and discuss the matter. My obstinate companion had given me no time; and, after all, what could I have said to him? Ned Land was perfectly right. There was almost the opportunity to profit by. Could I retract my word, and take upon myself the responsibility of compromising the future of my companions? To-morrow Captain Nemo might take us far from all land.

At that moment a rather loud hissing told me that the reservoirs were filling, and that the *Nautilus* was sinking under the waves of the Atlantic.

A sad day I passed, between the desire of regaining my liberty of action, and of abandoning the wonderful *Nautilus,* and leaving my submarine studies incomplete.

What dreadful hours I passed thus! sometimes seeing myself and companions safely landed, sometimes wishing, in spite of my reason, that some unforeseen circumstances would prevent the realization of Ned Land's project.

Twice I went to the saloon. I wished to consult the compass. I wished to see if the direction the *Nautilus* was taking was bringing us nearer or taking us farther from the coast. But no; the *Nautilus* kept in Portuguese waters.

I must therefore take my part, and prepare for flight. My luggage was not heavy; my notes, nothing more.

As to Captain Nemo, I asked myself what he would think of our escape; what trouble, what wrong it might cause him, and what he might do in case of its discovery or failure. Certainly I had no cause to complain of him; on the contrary, never was hospitality freer than his. In leaving him I could not be taxed with ingratitude. No oath bound us to him. It was on the strength of circumstances he relied, and not upon our word, to fix us forever.

I had not seen the captain since our visit to the Island of Santorin. Would chance bring me to his presence before our departure? I wished it, and I feared it at the same time. I listened if I could hear him walking in the room contiguous to mine. No sound reached my ear. I felt an unbearable uneasiness. This day of waiting seemed eternal. Hours struck too slowly to keep pace with my impatience.

My dinner was served in my room as usual. I ate but little, I was too preoccupied. I left the table at seven o'clock. A hundred and twenty minutes (I counted them) still separated me from the moment in which I was to join Ned Land. My agitation redoubled. My pulse beat violently. I could not remain quiet. I went and came, hoping to calm my troubled spirit by constant movement. The idea of failure in our bold enterprise was the least painful of my anxieties; but the thought of seeing our project discovered before leaving the *Nautilus,* of being brought before Captain Nemo, irritated, or (what was worse) saddened at my desertion, made my heart beat.

I wanted to see the saloon for the last time. I descended the stairs, and arrived in the museum where I had passed so many useful and agreeable hours. I looked at all its riches, all its treasures, like a man on the eve of an eternal exile, who was leaving never to return. These wonders of nature, these masterpieces of art, amongst which, for so many days, my life had been concentrated, I was going to abandon them forever! I should like to have taken a last look through the windows of the saloon into the waters of the Atlantic; but the panels were hermetically closed, and a cloak of steel separated me from that ocean which I had not yet explored.

In passing through the saloon, I came near the door, let into the angle, which opened into the captain's room. To my great surprise, the door was ajar. I drew back, involuntarily. If Captain Nemo should be in his room, he could see me. But, hearing no noise, I drew nearer. The room was deserted. I pushed open the door, and took some steps forward. Still the same monk-like severity of aspect.

Suddenly the clock struck eight. The first beat of the hammer on the bell awoke me from my dreams. I trembled as if an invisible eye had plunged into my most secret thoughts, and I hurried from the room.

There my eye fell upon the compass. Our course was still north. The log indicated moderate speed, the manometer a depth of about sixty feet.

I returned to my room, clothed myself warmly,—sea-boots, an otterskin cap, a great-coat of byssus, lined with sealskin; I was ready, I was waiting. The vibration of the screw alone broke the deep silence which reigned on board. I listened attentively. Would no loud voice suddenly inform me that Ned Land had been surprised in his projected flight? A mortal dread hung over me, and I vainly tried to regain my accustomed coolness.

At a few minutes to nine, I put my ear to the captain's door. No noise. I left my room and returned to the saloon, which was half in obscurity, but deserted. I opened the door communicating with the library. The same insufficient light, the same solitude. I placed myself near the door leading to the central staircase, and there waited for Ned Land's signal.

At that moment the trembling of the screw sensibly diminished, then it stopped entirely. The silence was now only disturbed by the beatings of my own heart. Suddenly a slight shock was felt; and I knew that the *Nautilus* had stopped at the bottom of the ocean. My uneasiness increased. The Canadian's signal did not come. I felt inclined to join Ned Land and beg of him to put off his attempt. I felt that we were not sailing under our usual conditions.

At this moment the door of the large saloon opened, and Captain Nemo appeared. He saw me, and, without further preamble, began in an amiable tone of voice,—

"Ah, sir! I have been looking for you. Do you know the history of Spain?"

Now, one might know the history of one's own country by heart; but in the condition I was at the time, with troubled mind and head quite lost, I could not have said a word of it.

"Well," continued Captain Nemo, "you heard my question? Do you know the history of Spain?"

"Very slightly," I answered.

"Well, here are learned men having to learn," said the captain. "Come, sit down, and I will tell you a curious episode in this history.—Sir, listen well," said he; "this history will interest you on one side, for it will answer a question which doubtless you have not been able to solve."

"I listen, Captain," said I, not knowing what my interlocutor was driving at, and asking myself if this incident was bearing on our projected flight.

"Sir, if you have no objection, we will go back to 1702. You cannot be ignorant that your king, Louis XIV., thinking that the gesture of a potentate was sufficient to bring the Pyrenees under his yoke, had imposed the Duke of Anjou, his grandson, on the Spaniards. This prince reigned more or less badly under the name of Philip V., and had a strong party against him abroad. Indeed, the preceding year, the royal houses of Holland, Austria, and England had concluded a treaty of alliance at the Hague, with the intention of plucking the crown of Spain from the head of Philip V., and placing it on that of an archduke to whom they prematurely gave the title of Charles III.

"Spain must resist this coalition; but she was almost entirely unprovided with either soldiers or sailors. However, money would not fail them, provided that their galleons, laden with gold and silver from America, once entered their ports. And about the end of 1702 they expected a rich convoy which France was escorting with a fleet of twenty-three vessels, commanded by Admiral Château-Renaud, for the ships of the coalition were already beating the Atlantic. This convoy was to go to Cadiz, but the admiral, hearing that an English fleet was cruising in those waters, resolved to make for a French port.

"The Spanish commanders of the convoy objected to this decision. They wanted to be taken to a Spanish port, and if not to Cadiz, into Vigo Bay, situated on the northwest coast of Spain, and which was not blocked.

"Admiral Château-Renaud had the rashness to obey this injunction, and the galleons entered Vigo Bay.

"Unfortunately, it formed an open road which could not be defended in any way. They must therefore hasten to unload the galleons before the arrival of the combined fleet; and time would not have failed them had not a miserable question of rivalry suddenly arisen.

"You are following the chain of events?" asked Captain Nemo.

"Perfectly," said I, not knowing the end proposed by this historical lesson.

"I will continue. This is what passed. The merchants of Cadiz had a privilege by which they had the right of receiving all merchandise coming from the West Indies. Now, to disembark these ingots at the port of Vigo was depriving them of their rights. They complained at Madrid, and obtained the consent of the weak-minded Philip that the convoy, without discharging its cargo, should remain sequestered in the roads of Vigo until the enemy had disappeared.

"But whilst coming to this decision, on the 22d of October, 1702, the English vessels arrived in Vigo Bay, when Admiral Château-Renaud, in spite of inferior forces, fought bravely. But seeing that the treasure must fall into the enemy's hands, he burnt and scuttled every galleon, which went to the bottom with their immense riches."

Captain Nemo stopped. I admit I could not yet see why this history should interest me.

"Well?" I asked.

"Well, M. Aronnax," replied Captain Nemo, "we are in that Vigo Bay; and it rests with yourself whether you will penetrate its mysteries."

The captain rose, telling me to follow him. I had had time to recover. I obeyed. The saloon was dark, but through the transparent glass the waves were sparkling. I looked.

For half a mile around the *Nautilus* the waters seemed bathed in electric light. The sandy bottom was clean and bright. Some of the ship's crew in their diving-dresses were clearing away half-rotten barrels and empty cases from the midst of the blackened wrecks. From these cases and from these barrels escaped ingots of gold and silver, cascades of piastres and jewels. The sand was heaped up with them. Laden with their precious booty the men returned to the *Nautilus*, disposed of their burden, and went back to this inexhaustible fishery of gold and silver.

I understood now. This was the scene of the battle of the 22d of October, 1702. Here on this very spot the galleons laden for the Spanish government had sunk. Here Captain Nemo came, according to his wants, to pack up those millions with which he burdened the *Nautilus*. It was for him and him alone America had given up her precious metals. He was heir direct, without any one to share in those treasures torn from the Incas and from the conquered of Ferdinand Cortez.

"Did you know, sir," he asked, smiling, "that the sea contained such riches?"

"I knew," I answered, "that they value the money held in suspension in these waters at two millions."

"Doubtless; but to extract this money the expense would be greater than the profit. Here, on the contrary, I have but to pick up what man has lost; and not only in Vigo Bay, but in a thousand other spots where shipwrecks have happened, and which are marked on my submarine map. Can you understand now the source of the millions I am worth?"

"I understand, Captain. But allow me to tell you that in exploring Vigo Bay you have only been beforehand with a rival society."

"And which?"

"A society which has received from the Spanish government the privilege of seeking these buried galleons. The shareholders are led on by the allurement of an enormous bounty, for they value these rich shipwrecks at five hundred millions."

"Five hundred millions they were," answered Captain Nemo, "but they are so no longer."

"Just so," said I; "and a warning to those shareholders would be an act of charity. But who knows if it would be well received? What gamblers usually regret above all is less the loss of their money, than of their foolish hopes. After all, I pity them less than the thousands of unfortunates to whom so much riches well distributed would have been profitable, whilst for them they will be forever barren."

I had no sooner expressed this regret, than I felt that it must have wounded Captain Nemo.

"Barren!" he exclaimed, with animation. "Do you think then, sir, that these riches are lost because I gather them? Is it for myself alone, according to your idea, that I take the trouble to collect these treasures? Who told you that I did not make a good use of it? Do you think I am ignorant that there are suffering beings and oppressed races on this earth, miserable creatures to console, victims to avenge? Do you not understand?"

Captain Nemo stopped at these last words, regretting perhaps that he had spoken so much. But I had guessed that whatever the motive which had forced him to seek independence under the sea, it had left him still a man, that his heart still beat for the sufferings of humanity, and that his immense charity was for oppressed races as well as individuals. And I then understood for whom those millions were destined, which were forwarded by Captain Nemo when the *Nautilus* was cruising in the waters of Crete.

CHAPTER 9

A VANISHED CONTINENT

THE next morning, the 19th of February, I saw the Canadian enter my room. I expected this visit. He looked very disappointed.

"Well, sir?" said he.

"Well, Ned, fortune was against us yesterday."

"Yes; that captain must needs stop exactly at the hour we intended leaving his vessel."

"Yes, Ned, he had business at his bankers."

"His bankers!"

"Or rather his banking house; by that I mean the ocean, where his riches are safer than in the chests of the state."

I then related to the Canadian the incidents of the preceding night, hoping to bring him back to the idea of not abandoning the captain; but my recital had no other result than an energetically expressed regret from Ned, that he had not been able to take a walk on the battle-field of Vigo on his own account.

"However," said he, "all is not ended. It is only a blow of the harpoon lost. Another time we must succeed; and to-night, if necessary—"

"In what direction is the *Nautilus* going?" I asked.

"I do not know," replied Ned.

"Well, at noon we shall see the point."

The Canadian returned to Conseil. As soon as I was dressed, I went into the saloon. The compass was not reassuring. The course of the *Nautilus* was S.S.W. We were turning our backs on Europe.

I waited with some impatience till the ship's place was pricked on the chart. At about half past eleven the reservoirs were emptied, and our vessel rose to the surface of the ocean. I rushed towards the platform. Ned Land had preceded me. No more land in sight. Nothing but an immense sea. Some sails on the horizon, doubtless those going to San Roque in search of favorable winds for doubling the Cape of Good Hope. The weather was cloudy. A gale of wind was preparing. Ned raved, and tried to pierce the cloudy horizon. He still hoped that behind all that fog stretched the land he so longed for.

At noon the sun showed itself for an instant. The second profited by this brightness to take its height. Then the sea becoming more billowy, we descended, and the panel closed.

An hour after, upon consulting the chart, I saw the position of the *Nautilus* was marked at 16° 17′ longitude, and 33° 22′ latitude, at 150 leagues from the nearest coast. There was no means of flight, and I leave you to imagine the rage of the Canadian, when I informed him of our situation.

For myself, I was not particularly sorry. I felt lightened of the load which had oppressed me, and was able to return with some degree of calmness to my accustomed work.

That night, about eleven o'clock, I received a most unexpected visit from Captain Nemo. He asked me very graciously if I felt fatigued from my watch of the preceding night. I answered in the negative.

"Then, M. Aronnax, I propose a curious excursion."

"Propose, Captain?"

"You have hitherto only visited the submarine depths by daylight, under the brightness of the sun. Would it suit you to see them in the darkness of the night?"

"Most willingly.

"I warn you, the way will be tiring. We shall have far to walk, and must climb a mountain. The roads are not well kept."

"What you say, Captain, only heightens my curiosity; I am ready to follow you."

"Come then, sir, we will put on our diving-dresses."

Arrived at the robing-room, I saw that neither of my companions nor any of the ship's crew were to follow us on this excursion. Captain Nemo had not even proposed my taking with me either Ned or Conseil.

In a few moments we had put on our diving-dresses; they placed on our backs the reservoirs, abundantly filled with air, but no electric lamps were prepared. I called the captain's attention to the fact.

"They will be useless," he replied.

I thought I had not heard aright, but I could not repeat my observation, for the captain's head had already disappeared in its metal case. I finished harnessing myself, I felt them put an iron-pointed stick into my hand, and some minutes later, after going through the usual form, we set foot on the bottom of the

Atlantic, at a depth of 150 fathoms. Midnight was near. The waters were profoundly dark, but Captain Nemo pointed out in the distance a reddish spot, a sort of large light shining brilliantly, about two miles from the *Nautilus*. What this fire might be, what could feed it, why and how it lit our way, vaguely, it is true, but I soon accustomed myself to the peculiar darkness, and I understood, under such circumstances, the uselessness of the Ruhmkorff apparatus.

As we advanced, I heard a kind of pattering above my head. The noise redoubling, sometimes producing a continual shower. I soon understood the cause. It was rain falling violently, and crisping the surface of the waves. Instinctively the thought flashed across my mind that I should be wet through! By the water! in the midst of the water! I could not help laughing at the odd idea. But indeed, in the thick diving-dress, the liquid element is no longer felt, and one only seems to be in an atmosphere somewhat denser than the terrestrial atmosphere. Nothing more.

After half an hour's walk the soil became stony. Medusæ, microscopic crustacea, and pennatules lit it slightly with their phosphorescent gleam. I caught a glimpse of pieces of stone covered with millions of zoöphytes and masses of sea-weed. My feet often slipped upon this viscous carpet of sea-weed, and without my iron-tipped stick I should have fallen more than once. In turning round, I could still see the whitish lantern of the *Nautilus* beginning to pale in the distance.

But the rosy light which guided us increased and lit up the horizon. The presence of this fire under water puzzled me in the highest degree. Was it some electric effulgence? Was I going towards a natural phenomenon as yet unknown to the savants of the earth? Or even (for this thought crossed my brain) had the hand of man aught to do with this conflagration? Had he fanned this flame? Was I to meet in these depths companions and friends of Captain Nemo whom he was going to visit, and who, like him, led this strange existence? Should I find down there a whole colony of exiles, who, weary of the miseries of this earth, had sought and found independence in the deep ocean? All these foolish and unreasonable ideas pursued me. And in this condition of mind, overexcited by the succession of wonders continually passing before my eyes, I should not have been surprised to meet at the bottom of the sea one of those submarine towns of which Captain Nemo dreamed.

Our road grew lighter and lighter. The white glimmer came in rays from the summit of a mountain about 800 feet high. But what I was was simply a reflection, developed by the clearness of the waters. The source of this inexplicable light was a fire on the opposite side of the mountain.

In the midst of this stony maze, furrowing the bottom of the Atlantic, Captain Nemo advanced without hesitation. He knew this dreary road. Doubtless he had often travelled over it, and could not lose himself. I followed him with unshaken confidence. He seemed to me like a genie of the sea; and, as he walked before me, I could not help admiring his stature, which was outlined in black on the luminous horizon.

It was one in the morning when we arrived at the first slopes of the mountain; but to gain access to them we must venture through the difficult paths of a vast copse.

Yes; a copse of dead trees, without leaves, without sap, trees petrified by the action of the water, and here and there overtopped by gigantic pines. It was like a coal pit, still standing, holding by the roots to the broken soil, and whose branches, like fine black paper cuttings, showed distinctly on the watery ceiling.

Picture to yourself a forest in the Hartz, hanging on to the sides of the mountain, but a forest swallowed up. The paths were encumbered with sea-weed and fucus, between which grovelled a whole world of crustacea. I went along, climbing the rocks, striding over extended trunks, breaking the sea bind-weed, which hung from one tree to the other; and frightening the fishes, which flew from branch to branch. Pressing onward, I felt no fatigue. I followed my guide, who was never tired. What a spectacle! how can I express it? how paint the aspect of those woods and rocks in this medium,—their under parts dark and wild, the upper colored with red tints, by that light which the reflecting powers of the waters doubled? We climbed rocks, which fell directly after with gigantic bounds, and the low growling of an avalanche. To right and left ran long, dark galleries, where sight was lost. Here opened vast glades which the hand of man seemed to have worked; and I sometimes asked myself if some inhabitant of these submarine regions would not suddenly appear to me.

But Captain Nemo was still mounting. I could not stay behind. I followed boldly. My stick gave me good help. A false step would have been dangerous on the narrow passes sloping down to the sides of the gulfs; but I walked with firm step, without feeling any giddiness. Now I jumped a crevice the depth of which would have made me hesitate had it been among the glaciers on the land; now I ventured on the unsteady trunk of a tree, thrown across from one abyss to the other, without looking under my feet, having only eyes to admire the wild sites of this region.

There, monumental rocks, leaning on their regularly cut bases, seemed to defy all laws of equilibrium. From between their stony knees, trees sprang, like a jet under heavy pressure, and upheld others which upheld them. Natural towers, large scarps, cut perpendicularly, like a "curtain," inclined at an angle which the laws of gravitation could never have tolerated in terrestrial regions.

Two hours after quitting the *Nautilus,* we had crossed the line of trees, and a hundred feet above our heads rose the top of the mountain, which cast a shadow on the brilliant irradiation of the opposite slope. Some petrified shrubs ran fantastically here and there. Fishes got up under our feet like birds in the long grass. The massive rocks were rent with impenetrable fractures, deep grottos, and unfathomable holes, at the bottom of which formidable creatures might be heard moving. My blood curdled when I saw enormous antennæ blocking my road, or some frightful claw closing with a noise in the shadow of some cavity. Millions of luminous spots shone brightly in the midst of the darkness. They were the eyes of giant crustacea crouched in their holes; giant lobsters setting themselves up like halberdiers, and moving their claws with the clicking sound of pincers; titanic crabs, pointed like a gun on its carriage; and frightful-looking poulps, interweaving their tentacles like a living nest of serpents.

We had now arrived on the first platform, where other surprises awaited me. Before us lay some picturesque ruins, which betrayed the hand of man, and not that of the Creator. They were vast heaps of stone, amongst which might be traced the vague and shadowy forms of castles and temples, clothed with a world of blossoming zoöphytes, and over which, instead of ivy, sea-weed and fucus threw a thick vegetable mantle. But what was this portion of the globe which had been swallowed by cataclysms? Who had placed those rocks and stones like cromlechs of prehistoric times? Where was I? Whither had Captain Nemo's fancy hurried me?

I would fain have asked him; not being able to, I stopped him,—I seized his arm. But shaking his head, and pointing to the highest point of the mountain, he seemed to say,—

"Come, come along; come higher!"

I followed, and in a few minutes I had climbed to the top, which for a circle of ten yards commanded the whole mass of rock.

I looked down the side we had just climbed. The mountain did not rise more than seven or eight hundred feet above the level of the plain; but on the opposite side it commanded from twice that height the depths of this part of the Atlantic. My eyes ranged far over a large space lit by a violent fulguration. In fact, the mountain was a volcano.

At fifty feet above the peak, in the midst of a rain of stones and scoriæ, a large crater was vomiting forth torrents of lava which fell in a cascade of fire into the bosom of the liquid mass. Thus situated, this volcano lit the lower plain like an immense torch, even to the extreme limits of the horizon. I said that the submarine crater threw up lava, but no flames. Flames require the oxygen of the air to feed upon, and cannot be developed under water; but streams of lava, having in themselves the principles of their incandescence, can attain a white heat, fight vigorously against the liquid element, and turn it to vapor by contact.

Rapid currents bearing all these gases in diffusion, and torrents of lava, slid to the bottom of the mountain like an eruption of Vesuvius on another Terra del Greco.

There, indeed, under my eyes, ruined, destroyed, lay a town,—its roofs open to the sky, its temples fallen, its arches dislocated, its columns lying on the ground, from which one could still recognize the massive character of Tuscan architecture. Farther on, some remains of a gigantic aqueduct; here the high base of an Acropolis, with the floating outline of a Parthenon; there were traces of a quay, as if an ancient port had formerly abutted on the borders of the ocean, and disappeared with its merchant-vessels and its war-galleys. Farther on again, long lines of sunken walls and broad deserted streets,—a perfect Pompeii escaped beneath the waters. Such was the sight that Captain Nemo brought before my eyes.

Where was I? Where was I? I must know at any cost. I tried to speak, but Captain Nemo stopped me by a gesture, and picking up a piece of chalk stone, advanced to a rock of black basalt, and traced the one word,

ATLANTIS.

What a light shot through my mind! Atlantis, the ancient Meropis of Theopompus, the Atlantis of Plato, that continent denied by Origen, Jamblichus, D'Anville, Malte-Brun, and Humboldt, who placed its disappearance amongst the legendary tales admitted by Posidonius, Pliny, Ammianus Marcellinus, Tertullian, Engel, Buffon, and D'Avezac. I had it there now before my eyes, bearing upon it the unexceptionable testimony of its catastrophe. The region thus ingulfed was beyond Europe, Asia, and Lybia, beyond the columns of Hercules, where those powerful people, the Atlantides, lived, against whom the first wars of ancient Greece were waged.

Thus, led by the strangest destiny, I was treading under foot the mountains of this continent, touching with my hand those ruins a thousand generations old, and contemporary with the geological epochs. I was walking on the very spot where the contemporaries of the first man had walked.

There, under my eyes, ruined, destroyed, lay a town.

Whilst I was trying to fix in my mind every detail of this grand landscape, Captain Nemo remained motionless, as if petrified in mute ecstasy, leaning on a mossy stone. Was he dreaming of those generations long since disappeared? Was he asking them the secret of human destiny? Was it here this strange man came to steep himself in historical recollections, and live again this ancient life,—he who wanted no modern one? What would I not have given to know his thoughts, to share them, to understand them! We remained for an hour at this place, contemplating the vast plain under the brightness of the lava, which was sometimes wonderfully intense. Rapid tremblings ran along the mountain caused by internal bubblings, deep noises distinctly transmitted through the liquid medium were echoed with majestic grandeur. At this moment the moon appeared through the mass of waters, and threw her pale rays on the buried continent. It was but a gleam, but what an indescribable effect! The captain rose, cast one last look on the immense plain, and then bade me follow him.

We descended the mountain rapidly, and the mineral forest once passed, I saw the lantern of the *Nautilus* shining like a star. The captain walked straight to it, and we got on board as the first rays of light whitened the surface of the ocean.

CHAPTER 10

THE SUBMARINE COAL-MINES

THE next day, the 20th of February, I awoke very late; the fatigues of the previous night had prolonged my sleep until eleven o'clock. I dressed quickly and hastened to find the course the *Nautilus* was taking. The instruments showed it to be still towards the south, with a speed of twenty miles an hour, and a depth of fifty fathoms.

The species of fishes here did not differ much from those already noticed. There were rays of giant size, five yards long, and endowed with great muscular strength, which enabled them to shoot above the waves; sharks of many kinds, amongst others a glaucus fifteen feet long, with triangular sharp teeth, and whose transparency rendered it almost invisible in the water; brown sagræ; humantins, prism-shaped and clad with a tuberculous hide; sturgeons, resembling their congeners of the Mediterranean; trumpet syngnathes, a foot and a half long, furnished with grayish bladders, without teeth or tongue, and as supple as snakes.

Amongst bony fish, Conseil noticed some blackish makairas, about three yards long, armed at the upper jaw with a piercing sword; other bright-colored creatures, known in the time of Aristotle by the name of the sea-dragon, which are dangerous to capture on account of the spikes on their back; also some coryphænes with brown backs marked with little blue stripes, and surrounded with a gold border; some beautiful dorades; and swordfish four-and-twenty feet long, swimming in troops, fierce animals, but rather herbivorous than carnivorous.

About four o'clock, the soil, generally composed of a thick mud mixed with petrified wood, changed by degrees, and it became more stony, and seemed strewn with conglomerate and pieces of basalt, with a sprinkling of lava and sulphurous obsidian. I thought that a mountainous region was succeeding the long plains; and accordingly, after a few evolutions of the *Nautilus,* I saw the southerly horizon blocked by a high wall which seemed to close all exit. Its summit evidently passed the level of the ocean. It must be a continent, or at least an island,—one of the Canaries, or of the Cape Verd Islands. The bearings not being yet taken, perhaps designedly, I was ignorant of our exact position. In any case, such a wall seemed to me to mark the limits of that Atlantis, of which we had in reality passed over only the smallest part.

Much longer should I have remained at the window, admiring the beauties of sea and sky, but the panels closed. At this moment the *Nautilus* arrived at the side of this high perpendicular wall. What would it do, I could not guess. I returned to my room; it no longer moved. I laid myself down with the full intention of waking after a few hours' sleep; but it was eight o'clock the next day when I entered the saloon. I looked at the manometer. It told me that the *Nautilus* was floating on the surface of the ocean. Besides, I heard steps on the platform. I went to the panel. It was open; but instead of broad daylight, as I expected, I was surrounded by profound darkness. Where were we? Was I mistaken? Was it still night? No; not a star was shining, and night has not that utter darkness.

I knew not what to think, when a voice near me said,—

"It that you, Professor?"

"Ah! Captain," I answered, "where are we?"

"Under ground, sir."

"Under ground!" I exclaimed. "And the *Nautilus* floating still?"

"It always floats."

"But I do not understand."

"Wait a few minutes, our lantern will be lit, and if you like light places, you will be satisfied."

I stood on the platform and waited. The darkness was so complete that I could not even see Captain Nemo; but looking to the zenith, exactly above my head, I seemed to catch an undecided gleam, a kind of twilight filling a circular hole. At this instant the lantern was lit, and its vividness dispelled the faint light. I closed my dazzled eyes for an instant, and then looked again. The *Nautilus* was stationary, floating near a mountain which formed a sort of quay. The lake then supporting it was a lake imprisoned by a circle of walls, measuring two miles in diameter, and six in circumference. Its level (the manometer showed) could only be the same as the outside level, for there must necessarily be a communication between the lake and the sea. The high partitions, leaning forward on their base, grew into a vaulted roof bearing the shape of an immense funnel turned upside down, the height being about five or six hundred yards. At the summit was a circular orifice, by which I had caught the slight gleam of light, evidently daylight.

"Where are we?" I asked.

"In the very heart of an extinct volcano, the interior of which has been invaded by the sea, after some great convulsion of the earth. Whilst you were sleeping, Professor, the *Nautilus* penetrated to this lagoon by a natural canal, which opens about ten yards beneath the surface of the ocean. This is its harbor of refuge, a sure, commodious, and mysterious one, sheltered from all gales. Show me, if you can, on the coasts of any of your continents or islands, a road which can give such perfect refuge from all storms.''

''Certainly,'' I replied, ''you are in safety here, Captain Nemo. Who could reach you in the heart of a volcano? But did I not see an opening at its summit?''

''Yes; its crater, formerly filled with lava, vapor, and flames, and which now gives entrance to the life-giving air we breathe.''

''But what is this volcanic mountain?''

''It belongs to one of the numerous islands with which this sea is strewn,—to vessels a simple sand-bank,—to us an immense cavern. Chance led me to discover it, and chance served me well.''

''But of what use if this refuge, Captain? The *Nautilus* wants no port.''

''No, sir; but it wants electricity to make it move, and the wherewithal to make the electricity,—sodium to feed the elements, coal from which to get the sodium, and a coal-mine to supply the coal. And exactly on this spot the sea covers entire forests embedded during the geological periods, now mineralized, and transformed into coal; for me they are an inexhaustible mine.''

''Your men follow the trade of miners here, then, Captain?''

''Exactly so. These mines extend under the waves like the mines of Newcastle. Here, in their diving-dresses, pickaxe and shovel in hand, my men extract the coal, which I do not even ask from the mines of the earth. When I burn this combustible for the manufacture of sodium, the smoke, escaping from the crater of the mountain, gives it the appearance of a still active volcano.''

''And we shall see your companions at work?''

''No; not this time at least; for I am in a hurry to continue our submarine tour of the earth. So I shall content myself with drawing from the reserve of sodium I already possess. The time for loading is one day only, and we continue our voyage. So if you wish to go over the cavern, and make the round of the lagoon, you must take advantage of to-day, M. Aronnax.''

I thanked the captain, and went to look for my companions, who had not yet left their cabin. I invited them to follow me without saying where we were. They mounted the platform. Conseil, who was astonished at nothing, seemed to look upon it as quite natural that he should wake under a mountain, after having fallen asleep under the waves. But Ned Land thought of nothing but finding whether the cavern had any exit. After breakfast, about ten o'clock, we went down on to the montain.

''Here we are, once more on land,'' said Conseil.

''I do not call this land,'' said the Canadian. ''And besides, we are not on it, but beneath it.''

Between the walls of the mountain and the waters of the lake lay a sandy shore, which, at its greatest breadth, measured five hundred feet. On this soil one might easily make the tour of the lake. But the base of the high partitions was stony ground, with volcanic blocks and enormous pumice-stones lying in picturesque heaps. All these detached masses, covered with enamel, polished by the action of the subterraneous fires, shone resplendent by the light of our electric lantern. The mica-dust from the shore, rising under our feet, flew like a cloud of sparks. The bottom now rose sensibly, and we soon arrived at long circuitous slopes, or inclined planes, which took us higher by degrees; but we were obliged to walk carefully among these conglomerates, bound by no cement, the feet slipping on the glassy trachyte, composed of crystal, felspar, and quartz.

The volcanic nature of this enormous excavation was confirmed on all sides, and I pointed it out to my companions.

"Picture to yourselves," said I, "what this crater must have been when filled with boiling lava, and when the level of the incandescent liquid rose to the orifice of the mountain, as though melted on the top of a hot plate."

"I can picture it perfectly," said Conseil. "But, sir, will you tell me why the Great Architect has suspended operations, and how it is that the furnace is replaced by the quiet waters of the lake?"

"Most probably, Conseil, because some convulsion beneath the ocean produced that very opening which has served as a passage for the *Nautilus*. Then the waters of the Atlantic rushed into the interior of the mountain. There must have been a terrible struggle between the two elements, a struggle which ended in the victory of Neptune. But many ages have run out since then, and the submerged volcano is now a peaceable grotto."

"Very well," replied Ned Land; "I accept the explanation, sir; but, in our own interests, I regret that the opening of which you speak was not made above the level of the sea."

"But, friend Ned," said Conseil, "if the passage had not been under the sea, the *Nautilus* could not have gone through it."

We continued ascending. The steps became more and more perpendicular and narrow. Deep excavations, which we were obliged to cross, cut them here and there; sloping masses had to be turned. We slid upon our knees and crawled along. But Conseil's dexterity and the Canadian's strength surmounted all obstacles. At a height of about thirty-one feet, the nature of the ground changed without becoming more practicable. To the conglomerate and trachyte succeeded black basalt, the first dispread in layers full of bubbles, the latter forming regular prisms, placed like a colonnade supporting the spring of the immense vault, an admirable specimen of natural architecture. Between the blocks of basalt wound long streams of lava, long since grown cold, encrusted with bituminous rays; and in some places there were spread large carpets of sulphur. A more powerful light shone through the upper crater, shedding a vague glimmer over these volcanic depressions forever buried in the bosom of this extinguished mountain. But our upward march was soon stopped at a height of about two hundred and fifty feet by impassable obstacles. There was a complete vaulted arch overhanging us, and our ascent was changed to a circular walk. At the last change vegetable life began to struggle with the mineral. Some shrubs, and even some trees, grew from the fractures of the walls. I recognized some euphorbias, with the caustic sugar coming from them; heliotropes, quite incapable of justifying their name, sadly drooped their clusters of flowers, both their color and perfume half gone. Here and there some chrysanthemums grew timidly at the foot of an aloe with long sickly-looking leaves. But between the streams of lava, I saw some little violets still slightly perfumed, and I admit that I smelt them with delight. Perfume is the soul of the flower, and sea flowers, those splendid hydrophytes, have no soul.

We had arrived at the foot of some sturdy dragon-trees, which had pushed aside the rocks with their strong roots, when Ned Land exclaimed,—

"Ah! sir, a hive! a hive!"

"A hive!" I replied, with a gesture of incredulity.

"Yes, a hive," repeated the Canadian, "and bees humming round it."

I approached, and was bound to believe my own eyes. There, at a hole bored in one of the dragon-trees, were some thousands of these ingenious insects, so common in all the Canaries, and whose produce is so much esteemed. Naturally enough, the Canadian wished to gather the honey, and I could not well oppose his wish. A quantity of dry leaves, mixed with sulphur, he lit with a spark from his flint, and he began to smoke out the bees. The humming ceased by degrees, and the hive eventually yielded several pounds of the sweetest honey, with which Ned Land filled his haversack.

"When I have mixed this honey with the paste of the artocarpus," said he, "I shall be able to offer you a succulent cake."

"Upon my word," said Conseil, "it will be gingerbread."

"Never mind the gingerbread," said I; "let us continue our interesting walk."

At every turn of the path we were following, the lake appeared in all its length and breadth. The lantern lit up the whole of its peaceable surface which knew neither ripple nor wave. The *Nautilus* remained perfectly immovable. On the platform, and on the mountain, the ship's crew were working like black shadows clearly carved against the luminous atmosphere. We were now going round the highest crest of the first layers of rock which upheld the roof. I then saw that bees were not the only representatives of the animal kingdom in the interior of this volcano. Birds of prey hovered here and there in the shadows, or fled from their nests on the top of the rocks. There were sparrow-hawks with white breasts, and kestrels, and down the slopes scampered, with their long legs, several fine fat bustards. I leave any one to imagine the covetousness of the Canadian at the sight of this savory game, and whether he did not regret having no gun. But he did his best to replace the lead by stones, and after several fruitless attempts, he succeeded in wounding a magnificent bird. To say that he risked his life twenty times before reaching it, is but the truth; but he managed so well, that the creature joined the honeycakes in his bag. We were now obliged to descend towards the shore, the crest becoming impracticable. Above us the crater seemed to gape like the mouth of a well. From this place the sky could be clearly seen, and clouds, dissipated by the west wind, leaving behind them, even on the summit of the mountain, their misty remnants,—certain proof that they were only moderately high, for the volcano did not rise more than eight hundred feet above the level of the ocean. Half an hour after the Canadian's last exploit we had regained the inner shore. Here the flora was represented by large carpets of marine crystal, a little umbelliferons plant very good to pickle, which also bears the name of pierce-stone, and sea-fennel. Conseil gathered some bundles of it. As to the fauna, it might be counted by thousands of crustacea of all sorts, lobsters, crabs, palæmons, spider-crabs, chameleon shrimps, and a large number of shells, rockfish, and limpets. Three quarters of an hour later, we had finished our circuitous walk, and were on board. The crew had just finished loading the sodium, and the *Nautilus* could have left that instant. But Captain Nemo gave no order. Did he wish to wait until night, and leave the submarine passage secretly? Perhaps so. Whatever it might be, the next day, the *Nautilus*, having left its port, steered clear of all land at a few yards beneath the waves of the Atlantic.

CHAPTER 11

THE SARGASSO SEA

THAT day the *Nautilus* crossed a singular part of the Atlantic Ocean. No one can be ignorant of the existence of a current of warm water, known by the name of the Gulf Stream. After leaving the Gulf of Mexico, about the twenty-fifth degree of north latitude, this current divides into two arms, the principal one going towards the coast of Ireland and Norway, whilst the second bends to the south about the height of the Azores; then, touching the African shore, and describing a lengthened oval, returns to the Antilles. The second arm—it is rather a collar than an arm—surrounds with its circles of warm water that portion of the cold, quiet, immovable ocean called the Sargasso Sea, a perfect lake in the open Atlantic: it takes no less than three years for the great current to pass round it. Such was the region the *Nautilus* was now visiting, a perfect meadow, a close carpet of sea-weed, fucus, and tropical berries, so thick and so compact that the stem of a vessel could hardly tear its way through it. And Captain Nemo, not wishing to entangle his screw in this herbaceous mass, kept some yards beneath the surface of the waves. The name Sargasso comes from the Spanish word "sargazzo," which signifies kelp. This kelp or varech, or berry-plant, is the principal formation of this immense bank. And this is the reason, according to the learned Maury, the author of "The Physical Geography of the Globe," why these hydrophytes unite in the peaceful basin of the Atlantic. The only explanation which can be given, he says, seems to me to result from the experience known to all the world. Place in a vase some fragments of cork or other floating body, and give to the water in the vase a circular movement, the scattered fragments will unite in a group in the centre of the liquid surface, that is to say, in the part least agitated. In the phenomenon we are considering, the Atlantic is the vase, the Gulf Stream the circular current, and the Sargasso Sea the central point at which the floating bodies unite.

I share Maury's opinion, and I was able to study the phenomenon in the very midst, where vessels rarely penetrate. Above us floated products of all kinds, heaped up among these brownish plants; trunks of trees torn from the Andes or the Rocky Mountains, and floated by the Amazon or the Mississippi; numerous wrecks, remains of keels, or ships' bottoms, side planks stove in, and so weighted with shells and barnacles that they could not again rise to the surface. And time will one day justify Maury's other opinion, that these substances thus accumulated for ages will become petrified by the action of the water, and will then form inexhaustible coal-mines,—a precious reserve prepared by far-seeing nature for the moment when men shall have exhausted the mines of continents.

In the midst of this inextricable mass of plants and sea-weed, I noticed some charming pink halycons and actiniæ, with their long tentacles trailing after them; medusæ, green, red, and blue, and the great rhyostoms of Cuvier, the large umbrella of which was bordered and festooned with violet.

All the day of the 22d of February we passed in the Sargasso Sea, where such fish as are partial to marine plants and fuci find abundant nourishment. The next, the ocean had returned to its accustomed aspect. From this time for nineteen days, from the 23d of February to the 12th of March, the *Nautilus* kept in the middle of the Atlantic, carrying us at a constant speed of a hundred leagues in twenty-four hours. Captain Nemo evidently intended accomplishing his submarine programme, and I imagined that he intended, after doubling Cape Horn, to return to the Australian seas of the Pacific. Ned Land had cause for fear. In these large seas, void of islands, we could not attempt to leave the boat. Nor had we any means of opposing Captain Nemo's will. Our only course was to submit; but what we could neither gain by force nor cunning, I liked to think might be obtained by persuasion. This voyage ended, would he not consent to restore our liberty, under an oath never to reveal his existence?—an oath of honor which we should have religiously kept. But we must consider that delicate question with the captain. But was I free to claim this liberty? Had he not himself said from the beginning, in the firmest manner, that the secret of his life exacted from him our lasting imprisonment on board the *Nautilus?* And would not my four months' silence appear to him a tacit acceptance of our situation? And would not a return to the subject result in raising suspicions which might be hurtful to our projects if at some future time a favorable opportunity offered to return to them?

During the nineteen days mentioned above, no incident of any note happened to signalize our voyage. I saw little of the captain; he was at work. In the library I often found his books left open, especially those on Natural History. My work on submarine depths, conned over by him, was covered with marginal notes, often contradicting my theories and systems; but the captain contented himself with thus purging my work; it was very rare for him to discuss it with me. Sometimes I heard the melancholy tones of his organ; but only at night, in the midst of the deepest obscurity, when the *Nautilus* slept upon the deserted ocean. During this part of our voyage we sailed whole days on the surface of the waves. The sea seemed abandoned. A few sailing-vessels, on the road to India, were making for the Cape of Good Hope. One day we were followed by the boats of a whaler, who, no doubt, took us for some enormous whale of great price; but Captain Nemo did not wish the worthy fellows to lose their time and trouble, so ended the chase by plunging under the water. Our navigation continued until the 13th of March; that day the *Nautilus* was employed in taking soundings, which greatly interested me. We had then made about 13,000 leagues since our departure from the high seas of the Pacific. The bearings gave us 45° 37′ south latitude, and 37° 53′ west longitude. It was the same water in which Captain Denham of the *Herald* sounded 7,000 fathoms without finding the bottom. There, too, Lieutenant Parker, of the American frigate *Congress,* could not touch the bottom with 15,140 yards. Captain Nemo intended seeking the bottom of the ocean by a diagonal sufficiently lengthened by means of lateral planes placed at an angle of forty-five degrees with the water-line of the *Nautilus*. Then the screw set to work at its maximum speed, its four blades beating the waves with indescribable force. Under this powerful pressure the hull of the *Nautilus* quivered like a sonorous chord, and sank regularly under the water.

At 7,000 fathoms I saw some blackish tops rising from the midst of the waters; but these summits might belong to high mountains like the Himalayas or Mount Blanc, even higher; and the depth of the abyss remained incalculable. The *Nautilus* descended still lower, in spite of the great pressure. I felt the steel plates tremble at the fastenings of the bolts; its bars bent, its partitions groaned; the windows of the saloon seemed to curve under the pressure of the waters. And this firm structure would doubtless have yielded, if, as its captain had said, it had not been capable of resistance like a solid block. In skirting the declivity of these rocks, lost under the water, I still saw some shells, some serpulæ and spinorbes, still living, and some specimens of asteriads. But soon this last representative of animal life disappeared; and at the depth of more than three leagues, the *Nautilus* had passed the limits of submarine existence, even as a balloon does when it rises above the respirable atmosphere. We had attained a depth of 16,000 yards (four leagues), and the sides of the *Nautilus* then bore a pressure of 1,600 atmospheres, that is to say, 3,200 pounds to each square two fifths of an inch of its surface.

"What a situation to be in!" I exclaimed. "To overrun these deep regions where man has never trod! Look, Captain, look at these magnificent rocks, these uninhabited grottos, these lowest receptacles of the globe, where life is no longer possible! What unknown sights are here! Why should we be unable to preserve a remembrance of them?"

"Would you like to carry away more than the remembrance?" said Captain Nemo.

"What do you mean by those words?"

"I mean to say that nothing is easier than to take a photographic view of this submarine region."

I had not time to express my surprise at this new proposition, when, at Captain Nemo's call, an objective was brought into the saloon. Through the widely opened panel, the liquid mass was bright with electricity, which was distributed with such uniformity, that not a shadow, not a gradation, was to be seen in our manufactured light. The *Nautilus* remained motionless, the force of its screw subdued by the inclination of its planes: the instrument was propped on the bottom of the oceanic site, and in a few seconds we had obtained a perfect negative. I here give the positive, from which may be seen those primitive rocks, which have never looked upon the light of heaven; that lowest granite which forms the foundation of the globe; those deep grottos, woven in the stony mass whose outlines were of such sharpness, and the border lines of which are marked in black, as if done by the brush of some Flemish artist. Beyond that again a horizon of mountains, an admirable undulating line, forming the prospective of the landscape. I cannot describe the effect of these smooth, black, polished rocks, without moss, without a spot, and of strange forms, standing solidly on the sandy carpet, which sparkled under the jets of our electric light.

But the operation being over, Captain Nemo said, "Let us go up; we must not abuse our position, nor expose the *Nautilus* too long to such great pressure."

"Go up again!" I exclaimed.

"Hold well on."

I had not time to understand why the captain cautioned me thus, when I was thrown forward on to the carpet. At a signal from the captain, its screw was shipped, and its blades raised vertically; the *Nautilus* shot into the air like a balloon, rising with stunning rapidity, and cutting the mass of waters with a sonorous agitation. Nothing was visible; and in four minutes it had shot through the four leagues which separated it from the ocean, and, after emerging like a flying-fish, fell, making the waves rebound to an enormous height.

CHAPTER 12

CACHALOTS AND WHALES

DURING the nights of the 13th and 14th of March, the *Nautilus* returned to its southerly course. I fancied that, when on a level with Cape Horn, he would turn the helm westward, in order to beat the Pacific seas, and so complete the tour of the world. He did nothing of the kind, but continued on his way to the southern regions. Where was he going to? To the pole? It was madness! I began to think that the captain's temerity justified Ned Land's fears. For some time past the Canadian had not spoken to me of his projects of flight; he was less communicative, almost silent. I could see that this lengthened imprisonment was weighing upon him, and I felt that rage was burning within him. When he met the captain, his eyes lit up with suppressed anger; and I feared that his natural violence would lead him into some extreme. That day, the 14th of March, Conseil and he came to me in my room. I inquired the cause of their visit.

"A simple question to ask you, sir," replied the Canadian.

"Speak, Ned."

"How many men are there on board the *Nautilus,* do you think?"

"I cannot tell, my friend."

"I should say that its working does not require a large crew."

"Certainly, under existing conditions, ten men, at the most, ought to be enough."

"Well, why should there be any more?"

"Why?" I replied, looking fixedly at Ned Land, whose meaning was easy to guess. "Because," I added, "if my surmises are correct, and if I have well understood the captain's existence, the *Nautilus* is not only a vessel, it is also a place of refuge for those who, like its commander, have broken every tie upon earth."

"Perhaps so," said Conseil; "but, in any case, the *Nautilus* can only contain a certain number of men. Could not you, sir, estimate their maximum?"

"How, Conseil?"

"By calculation; given the size of the vessel, which you know, sir, and consequently the quantity of air it contains, knowing also how much each man expends at a breath, and comparing these results with the fact that the *Nautilus* is obliged to go to the surface every twenty-four hours."

Conseil had not finished the sentence before I saw what he was driving at.

"I understand," said I; "but that calculation, though simple enough, can give but a very uncertain result."

"Never mind," said Ned Land urgently.

"Here it is, then," said I. "In one hour each man consumes the oxygen contained in twenty gallons of air; and in twenty-four, that contained in 480 gallons. We must, therefore, find how many times 480 gallons of air the *Nautilus* contains."

"Just so," said Conseil.

"Or," I continued, "the size of the *Nautilus* being 1,500 tons, and one ton holding 200 gallons, it contains 300,000 gallons of air, which, divided by 480, gives a quotient of 625. Which means to say, strictly speaking, that the air contained in the *Nautilus* would suffice for 625 men for twenty-four hours."

"Six hundred and twenty-five!" repeated Ned.

"But remember, that all of us, passengers, sailors, and officers included, would not form a tenth part of that number."

"Still too many for three men," murmured Conseil.

The Canadian shook his head, passed his hand across his forehead, and left the room without answering.

"Will you allow me to make one observation, sir?" said Conseil. "Poor Ned is longing for everything that he cannot have. His past life is always present to him; everything that we are forbidden he regrets. His head is full of old recollections. And we must understand him. What has he to do here? Nothing; he is not learned like you, sir; and has not the same taste for the beauties of the sea that we have. He would risk everything to be able to go once into a tavern in his own country."

Certainly the monotony on board must seem intolerable to the Canadian, accustomed as he was to a life of liberty and activity. Events were rare which could rouse him to any show of spirit; but that day an event did happen which recalled the bright days of the harpooner. About eleven in the morning, being on the surface of the ocean, the *Nautilus* fell in with a troop of whales,—an encounter which did not astonish me, knowing that these creatures, hunted to the death, had taken refuge in high latitudes.

We were seated on the platform, with a quiet sea. The month of October in those latitudes gave us some lovely autumnal days. It was the Canadian—he could not be mistaken—who signalled a whale on the eastern horizon. Looking attentively one might see its black back rise and fall with the waves five miles from the *Nautilus*.

"Ah!" exclaimed Ned Land, "if I was on board a whaler now, such a meeting would give me pleasure. It is one of the large size. See with what strength its blow-holes throw up columns of air and steam! Confound it, why am I bound to these steel plates?"

"What, Ned," said I, "you have not forgotten your old ideas of fishing?"

"Can a whale-fisher ever forget his old trade, sir? Can he ever tire of the emotions caused by such a chase?"

"You have never fished in these seas, Ned?"

"Never, sir; in the northern only, and as much in Behring as in Davis Straits."

"Then the southern whale is still unknown to you. It is the Greenland whale you have hunted up to this time, and that would not risk passing through the warm waters of the equator. Whales are localized according to their kinds, in certain seas which they never leave. And if one of these creatures went from Behring to Davis Straits, it must be simply because there is a passage from one sea to the other, either on the American or the Asiatic side."

"In that case, as I have never fished in these seas, I do not know the kind of whale frequenting them."

"I have told you, Ned."

"A greater reason for making their acquaintance," said Conseil.

"Look! look!" exclaimed the Canadian, "they approach; they aggravate me; they know that I cannot get at them!"

Ned stamped his feet. His hand trembled, as he grasped an imaginary harpoon.

"Are these cetacea as large as those of the northern seas?" asked he.

"Very nearly, Ned."

"Because I have seen large whales, sir, whales measuring a hundred feet. I have even been told that those of Hullamoch and Umgallick, of the Aleutian Islands, are sometimes a hundred and fifty feet long."

"That seems to me exaggeration. These creatures are only balænopterons, provided with dorsal fins; and, like the cachalots, are generally much smaller than the Greenland whale."

"Ah!" exclaimed the Canadian, whose eyes had never left the ocean, "they are coming nearer; they are in the same water as the *Nautilus!*"

Then returning to the conversation, he said,—

"You spoke of the cachalot as a small creature. I had heard of gigantic ones. They are intelligent cetacea. It is saie of some that they cover themselves with sea-weed and fucus, and then are taken for islands. People encamp upon them, and settle there; light a fire—"

"And build houses," said Conseil.

"Yes, joker," said Ned Land. "And one fine day the creature plunges, carrying with it all the inhabitants to the bottom of the sea."

"Something like the travels of Sinbad the Sailor," I replied, laughing.

"Ah!" suddenly exclaimed Ned Land, "it is not one whale; there are ten,—there are twenty,—it is a whole troop! And I not able to do anything! hands and feet tied!"

"But, friend Ned," said Conseil, "why do you not ask Captain Nemo's permission to chase them?"

Conseil had not finished his sentence when Ned Land had lowered himself through the panel to seek the captain. A few minutes afterwards the two appeared together on the platform.

Captain Nemo watched the troop of cetacea playing on the waters about a mile from the *Nautilus*.

"They are southern whales," said he; "there goes the fortune of a whole fleet of whalers."

"Well, sir," asked the Canadian, "can I not chase them, if only to remind me of my old trade of harpooner?"

"And to what purpose?" replied Captain Nemo; "only to destroy! We have nothing to do with whale-oil on board."

"But, sir," continued the Canadian, "in the Red Sea you allowed us to follow the dugong."

"Then it was to procure fresh meat for my crew. Here it would be killing for killing's sake. I know that is a privilege reserved for man, but I do not approve of such murderous pastime. In destroying the southern whale (like the Greenland whale, an inoffensive creature), your traders do a culpable action, Master Land. They have already depopulated the whole of Baffin's Bay, and are annihilating a class of useful animals. Leave the unfortunate cetacea alone. They have plenty of natural enemies,—cachalots, swordfish, and sawfish,—without *your* troubling them."

The captain was right. The barbarons and inconsiderate greed of these fishermen will one day cause the disappearance of the last whale in the ocean. Ned Land whistled "Yankee Doodle" between his teeth, thrust his hands into his pockets, and turned his back upon us. But Captain Nemo watched the troop of cetacea, and addressing me said,—

"I was right in saying that whales had natural enemies enough, without

counting man. These will have plenty to do before long. Do you see, M. Aronnax, about eight miles to leeward, those blackish moving points?''

''Yes, Captain,'' I replied.

''Those are cachalots,—terrible animals, which I have sometimes met in troops of two or three hundred. As to *those,* they are cruel, mischievous creatures; they would be right in exterminating them.''

The Canadian turned quickly at the last words.

''Well, Captain,'' said he, ''it is still time, in the interest of the whales.''

''It is useless to expose one's self, Professor. The *Nautilus* will disperse them. It is armed with a steel spur as good as Master Land's harpoon, I imagine.''

The Canadian did not put himself out enough to shrug his shoulders. Attack cetacea with blows of a spur! Who had ever heard of such a thing?

''Wait, M. Aronnax,'' said Captain Nemo. ''We will show you something you have never yet seen. We have no pity for these ferocious creatures. They are nothing but mouth and teeth.''

Mouth and teeth! No one could better describe the macrocephalous cachalot, which is sometimes more than seventy-five feet long. Its enormous head occupies one third of its entire body. Better armed than the whale, whose upper jaw is furnished only with whalebone, it is supplied with twenty-five large tusks, about eight inches long, cylindrical and conical at the top, each weighing two pounds. It is in the upper part of this enormous head, in great cavities divided by cartilages, that is to be found from six to eight hundred pounds of that precious oil called spermaceti. The cachalot is a disagreeable creature, more tadpole than fish, according to Fredol's description. It is badly formed, the whole of its left side being (if we may say it) a ''failure,'' and being only able to see with its right eye. But the formidable troop was nearing us. They had seen the whales and were preparing to attack them. One could judge beforehand that the cachalots would be victorious, not only because they were better built for attack than their inoffensive adversaries, but also because they could remain longer under water without coming to the surface. There was only just time to go to the help of the whales. The *Nautilus* went under water. Conseil, Ned Land, and I took our places before the window in the saloon, and Captain Nemo joined the pilot in his cage to work his apparatus as an engine of destruction. Soon I felt the beatings of the screw quicken, and our speed increased. The battle between the cachalots and the whales had already begun when the *Nautilus* arrived. They did not at first show any fear at the sight of this new monster joining in the conflict. But they soon had to guard against its blows. What a battle! The *Nautilus* was nothing but a formidable harpoon, brandished by the hand of its captain. It hurled itself against the fleshy mass, passing through from one part to the other, leaving behind it two quivering halves of the animal. It could not feel the formidable blows from their tails upon its sides, nor the shock which it produced itself, much more. One cachalot killed, it ran at the next, tacked on the spot that it might not miss its prey, going forwards and backwards, answering to its helm, plunging when the cetacean dived into the deep waters, coming up with it when it returned to the surface, striking it front or sideways, cutting or tearing in all directions, and at any pace, piercing it with its terrible spur. What carnage! What a noise on the surface of the waves! What sharp hissing, and what snorting peculiar to these enraged animals! In the midst of these waters generally so peaceful their tails made perfect billows. For one hour this wholesale massacre continued, from which the cachalots could not escape. Several times ten or twelve united tried to crush the *Nautilus* by their weight. From the window we could see their enormous mouths studded with tusks, and their formidable eyes. Ned Land could not contain himself, he threatened and swore at them. We could feel them clinging to our vessel like dogs worrying a wild boar in a copse. But the *Nautilus,* working its screw, carried them here and there, or to the upper levels of the ocean, without caring for their enormous weight, nor the powerful strain on the vessel. At length, the mass of cachalots broke up, the waves became quick, and I felt that we were rising to the surface. The panel opened, and we hurried on to the platform. The sea was covered with mutilated bodies. A formidable explosion could not have divided and torn this fleshy mass with more violence. We were floating amid gigantic bodies, bluish on the back and white underneath, covered with enormous protuberances. Some terrified cachalots were flying towards the horizon. The waves were dyed red for several miles, and the *Nautilus* floated in a sea of blood. Captain Nemo joined us.

"Well, Master Land?" said he.

"Well, sir," replied the Canadian, whose enthusiasm had somewhat calmed; "it is a terrible spectacle, certainly. But I am not a butcher. I am a hunter, and I call this a butchery."

"It is a massacre of mischievous creatures," replied the captain; "and the *Nautilus* is not a butcher's knife."

"I like my harpoon better," said the Canadian.

"Every one to his own," answered the captain, looking fixedly at Ned Land.

I feared he would commit some act of violence, which would end in sad consequences. But his anger was turned by the sight of a whale which the *Nautilus* had just come up with. The creature had not quite escaped from the cachalot's teeth. I recognized the southern whale by its flat head, which is entirely black. Anatomically, it is distinguished from the white whale and the North Cape whale by the seven cervical vertebræ, and it has two more ribs than its congeners. The unfortunate cetacean was lying on its side, riddled with holes from the bites, and quite dead. From its mutilated fin still hung a young whale which it could not save from the massacre. Its open mouth let the water flow in and out, murmuring like the waves breaking on the shore. Captain Nemo steered close to the corpse of the creature. Two of his men mounted its side, and I saw, not without surprise, that they were drawing from its breasts all the milk which they contained, that is to say, about two or three tons. The captain offered me a cup of the milk, which was still warm. I could not help showing my repugnance to the drink; but he assured me that it was excellent, and not to be distinguished from cow's milk. I tasted it, and was of his opinion. It was a useful reserve to us, for in the shape of salt butter or cheese it would form an agreeable variety from our ordinary food. From that day I noticed with uneasiness that Ned Land's ill-will towards Captain Nemo increased, and I resolved to watch the Canadian's gestures closely.

CHAPTER 13

THE ICEBERG

THE *Nautilus* was steadily pursuing its southerly course, following the fiftieth meridian with considerable speed. Did he wish to reach the pole? I did not think so, for every attempt to reach that point had hitherto failed. Again the season was far advanced; for in the antarctic regions the 13th of March corresponds with the 13th of September of northern regions, which begin at the equinoctial season. On the 14th of March I saw floating ice in latitude 55°, merely pale bits of *débris* from twenty to twenty-five feet long, forming banks over which the sea curled. The *Nautilus* remained on the surface of the ocean. Ned Land, who had fished in the arctic seas, was familiar with its icebergs; but Conseil and I admired them for the first time. In the atmosphere towards the southern horizon stretched a white dazzling band. English whalers have given it the name of "ice blink." However thick the clouds may be, it is always visible, and announces the presence of an ice pack or bank. Accordingly, larger blocks soon appeared, whose brilliancy changed with the caprices of the fog. Some of these masses showed green veins, as if long undulating lines had been traced with sulphate of copper; others resembled enormous amethysts with the light shining through them. Some reflected the light of day upon a thousand crystal facets. Others shaded with vivid calcareous reflections resembled a perfect town of marble. The more we neared the south, the more these floating islands increased both in number and importance.

At the sixtieth degree of latitude, every pass had disappeared. But seeking carefully, Captain Nemo soon found a narrow opening, through which he boldly slipped, knowing, however, that it would close behind him. Thus, guided by this clever hand, the *Nautilus* passed through all the ice with a precision which quite charmed Conseil; icebergs or mountains, ice-fields or smooth plains, seeming to have no limits, drift ice or floating ice packs, or plains broken up, called *palchs* when they are circular, and streams when they are made up of long strips. The temperature was very low; the thermometer exposed to the air marked two or three degrees below zero, but we were warmly clad with fur, at the expense of the sea-bear and seal. The interior of the *Nautilus*, warmed regularly by its electric apparatus, defied the most intense cold. Besides, it would only have been necessary to go some yards beneath the waves to find a more bearable temperature. Two months earlier we should have had perpetual daylight in these latitudes; but already we had three or four hours night, and by and by there would be six months of darkness in these circumpolar regions. On the 15th of March we were in the latitude of New Shetland and South Orkney. The captain told me that formerly numerous tribes of seals inhabited them; but that English and American whalers, in their rage for destruction, massacred both old and young; thus where there was once life and animation, they had left silence and death.

About eight o'clock on the morning of the 16th of March, the *Nautilus*, following the fifty-fifth meridian, cut the antarctic polar circle. Ice surrounded us on all sides, and closed the horizon. But Captain Nemo went from one opening to another, still going higher. I cannot express my astonishment at the beauties of these new regions. The ice took most surprising forms. Here the grouping formed an Oriental town, with innumerable mosques and minarets; there a fallen city thrown to the earth, as it were, by some convulsion of nature. The whole aspect was constantly changed by the oblique rays of the sun, or lost in the grayish fog amidst hurricanes of snow. Detonations and falls were heard on all sides, great overthrows of icebergs, which altered the whole landscape like a diorama. Often seeing no exit, I thought we were definitively prisoners; but instinct guiding him at the slightest indication, Captain Nemo would discover a new pass. He was never mistaken when he saw the thin threads of bluish water trickling along the ice-fields; and I had no doubt that he had already ventured into the midst of these antarctic seas before. On the 16th of March, however, the ice-fields absolutely blocked our road. It was not the iceberg itself, as yet, but vast fields cemented by the cold. But this obstacle could not stop Captain Nemo: he hurled himself against it with frightful violence. The *Nautilus* entered the brittle mass like a wedge, and split it with frightful crackings. It was the battering-ram of the ancients hurled by infinite strength. The ice, thrown high in the air, fell like hail around us. By its own power of impulsion our apparatus made a canal for itself; sometimes carried away by its own impetus it lodged on the ice-field, crushing it with its weight, and sometimes buried beneath it, dividing it by a simple pitching movement, producing large rents in it. Violent gales assailed us at this time, accompanied by thick fogs, through which, from one end of the platform to the other, we could see nothing. The wind blew sharply from all points of the compass, and the snow lay in such hard heaps that we had to break it with blows of a pickaxe. The temperature was always at five degrees below zero; every outward part of the *Nautilus* was covered with ice. A rigged vessel could never have worked its way there, for all the rigging would have been entangled in the blocked-up gorges. A vessel without sails, with electricity for its motive-power, and wanting no coal, could alone brave such high latitudes. At length, on the 18th of March, after many useless assaults, the *Nautilus* was positively blocked. It was no longer either streams, packs, or ice-fields, but an interminable and immovable barrier, formed by mountains soldered together.

"An iceberg!" said the Canadian to me.

I knew that to Ned Land, as well as to all other navigators who had preceded us, this was an inevitable obstacle. The sun appearing for an instant at noon, Captain Nemo took an observation as near as possible, which gave our situation at 51° 30′ longitude and 67° 39′ of south latitude. We had advanced one degree more in this antarctic region. Of the liquid surface of the sea there was no longer a glimpse. Under the spur of the *Nautilus* lay stretched a vast plain, entangled with confused blocks. Here and there sharp points, and slender needles rising to a height of 200 feet; farther on a steep shore, hewn as it were with an axe, and clothed with grayish tints; huge mirrors, reflecting a few rays of sunshine, half drowned in the fog. And over this desolate face of nature a stern silence reigned, scarcely broken by the flapping of the wings of petrels and puffins. Everything was frozen,—even the noise. The *Nautilus* was then obliged to stop in its adventurous course amid these fields of ice. In spite of our efforts, in spite of the powerful means employed to break up the ice, the *Nautilus* remained immovable. Generally, when we can proceed no farther, we have return still open to us; but here return was as impossible as advance, for every pass had closed behind us; and for the few moments when we were stationary, we were likely to be entirely blocked, which did, indeed, happen about two o'clock in the afternoon, the fresh ice forming around its sides with astonishing rapidity. I was obliged to admit that Captain Nemo was more than imprudent. I was on the platform at that moment. The captain had been observing our situation for some time past, when he said to me,—

"Well, sir, what do you think of this?"

"I think that we are caught, Captain."

"So, M. Aronnax, you really think that the *Nautilus* cannot disengage itself?"

"With difficulty, Captain; for the season is already too far advanced for you to reckon on the breaking up of the ice."

"Ah! sir," said Captain Nemo, in an ironical tone, "you will always be the same. You see nothing but difficulties and obstacles. I affirm that not only can the *Nautilus* disengage itself, but also that it can go further still."

"Farther to the south?" I asked, looking at the captain.

"Yes, sir; it shall go to the pole."

"To the pole!" I exclaimed, unable to repress a gesture of incredulity.

"Yes," replied the captain, coldly, "to the antarctic pole, to that unknown point from whence springs every meridian of the globe. *You* know whether I can do as I please with the *Nautilus!*"

Yes, I knew that. I knew that this man was bold, even to rashness. But to conquer those obstacles which bristled round the south pole, rendering it more inaccessible than the north, which had not yet been reached by the boldest navigators,—was it not a mad enterprise, one which only a maniac would have conceived? It then came into my head to ask Captain Nemo if he had ever discovered that pole which had never yet been trodden by a human creature.

"No, sir," he replied; "but we will discover it together. Where others have failed, *I* will not fail. I have never yet led my *Nautilus* so far into southern seas; but, I repeat, it shall go farther yet."

"I can well believe you, Captain," said I, in a slightly ironical tone. "I believe you! Let us go ahead! There are no obstacles for us! Let us smash this iceberg! Let us blow it up; and if it resists, let us give the *Nautilus* wings to fly over it!"

"Over it, sir!" said Captain Nemo, quietly; "no, not *over* it, but *under* it!"

"Under it!" I exclaimed, a sudden idea of the captain's projects flashing upon my mind. I understood the wonderful qualities of the *Nautilus* were going to serve us in this superhuman enterprise.

"I see we are beginning to understand one another, sir," said the captain, half smiling. "You begin to see the possibility—I should say the success—of this attempt. That which is impossible for an ordinary vessel, is easy to the *Nautilus*. If a continent lies before the pole, it must stop before the continent; but if, on the contrary, the pole is washed by open sea, it will go even to the pole."

"Certainly," said I, carried away by the captain's reasoning; "if the surface of the sea is solidified by the ice, the lower depths are free by the providential law which has placed the maximum of density of the waters of the ocean one degree higher than freezing point; and, if I am not mistaken, the portion of this iceberg which is above the water is as one to four to that which is below."

"Very nearly, sir; for one foot of iceberg above the sea there are three below it. If these ice mountains are not more than 300 feet above the surface, they are not more than 900 beneath. And what are 900 feet to the *Nautilus?*"

"Nothing, sir."

"It could even seek at greater depths that uniform temperature of sea-water, and there brave with impunity the thirty or forty degrees of surface cold."

"Just so, sir,—just so," I replied, getting animated.

"The only difficulty," continued Captain Nemo, "is that of remaining several days without renewing our provision of air."

"Is that all? The *Nautilus* has vast reservoirs; we can fill them, and they will supply us with all the oxygen we want."

"Well thought of, M. Aronnax," replied the captain, smiling. "But not wishing you to accuse me of rashness, I will first give you all my objections."

"Have you any more to make?"

"Only one. It is possible, if the sea exists at the south pole, that it may be covered; and, consequently, we shall be unable to come to the surface."

"Good, sir! but do you forget that the *Nautilus* is armed with a powerful spur, and could we not send it diagonally against these fields of ice, which would open at the shock."

"Ah! sir, you are full of ideas to-day."

"Besides, Captain," I added, enthusiastically, "why should we not find the sea open at the south pole as well as at the north? The frozen poles and the poles of the earth do not coincide, either in the southern or in the northern regions; and, until it is proved to the contrary, we may suppose either a continent or an ocean free from ice at these two points of the globe."

"I think so too, M. Aronnax," replied Captain Nemo. "I only wish you to observe that, after having made so many objections to my project, you are now crushing me with arguments in its favor!"

The preparations for this audacious attempt now began. The powerful pumps of the *Nautilus* were working air into the reservoirs and storing it at high pressure. About four o'clock, Captain Nemo announced the closing of the panels on the platform. I threw one last look at the massive iceberg which we were going to cross. The weather was clear, the atmosphere pure enough, the cold very great, being twelve degrees below zero; but the wind having gone down, this temperature was not so unbearable. About ten men mounted the sides of the *Nautilus,* armed with pickaxes to break the ice around the vessel, which was soon free. The operation was quickly performed, for the fresh ice was still very thin. We all went below. The usual reservoirs were filled with the newly liberated water, and the *Nautilus* soon descended. I had taken my place with Conseil in the saloon; through the open window we could see the lower beds of the Southern Ocean. The thermometer went up, the needle of the compass deviated on the dial. At about 900 feet, as Captain Nemo had foreseen, we were floating beneath the undulating bottom of the iceberg. But the *Nautilus* went lower still,—it went to the depth of four hundred fathoms. The temperature of the water at the surface showed twelve degrees, it was now only ten; we had gained two. I need not say the temperature of the *Nautilus* was raised by its heating apparatus to a much higher degree; every manœuvre was accomplished with wonderful precision.

"We shall pass it, if you please, sir," said Conseil.

"I believe we shall," I said, in a tone of firm conviction.

In this open sea, the *Nautilus* had taken its course direct to the pole, without leaving the fifty-second meridian. From 67° 30′ to 90°, twenty-two degrees and

In spite of the means employed to break up the ice,
the *Nautilus* remained immovable.

a half of latitude remained to travel; that is, about five hundred leagues. The *Nautilus* kept up a mean speed of twenty-six miles an hour,— the speed of an express train. If that was kept up, in forty hours we should reach the pole.

For a part of the night the novelty of the situation kept us at the window. The sea was lit with the electric lantern; but it was deserted; fishes did not sojourn in these imprisoned waters; they only found there a passage to take them from the antarctic ocean to the open polar sea. Our progress was rapid; we could feel it by the quivering of the long steel body. About two in the morning, I took some hours' repose, and Conseil did the same. In crossing the waist I did not meet Captain Nemo: I supposed him to be in the pilot's cage. The next morning, the 19th of March, I took my post once more in the saloon. The electric log told me that the speed of the *Nautilus* had been slackened. It was then going towards the surface, but prudently emptying its reservoirs very slowly. My heart beat fast. Were we going to emerge and regain the open polar atmosphere? No! A shock told me that the *Nautilus* had struck the bottom of the iceberg, still very thick, judging from the deadened sound. We had indeed "struck," to use a sea expression, but in an inverse sense, and at a thousand feet deep. This would give three thousand feet of ice above us; one thousand being above the water-mark. The iceberg was then higher than at its borders,—not a very re-assuring fact. Several times that day the *Nautilus* tried again, and every time it struck the wall which lay like a ceiling above it. Sometimes it met with but 900 yards, only 200 of which rose above the surface. It was twice the height it was when the *Nautilus* had gone under the waves. I carefully noted the different depths, and thus obtained a submarine profile of the chain as it was developed under the water. That night no change had taken place in our situation. Still ice between four and five hundred yards in depth! It was evidently diminishing, but still what a thickness between us and the surface of the ocean! It was then eight. According to the daily custom on board the *Nautilus*, its air should have been renewed four hours ago; but I did not suffer much, although Captain Nemo had not yet made any demand upon his reserve of oxygen. My sleep was painful that night; hope and fear besieged me by turns: I rose several times. The groping of the *Nautilus* continued. About three in the morning, I noticed that the lower surface of the iceberg was only about fifty feet deep. One hundred and fifty feet now separated us from the surface of the waters. The iceberg was by degrees becoming an ice-field, the mountain a plain. My eyes never left the manometer. We were still rising diagonally to the surface, which sparkled under the electric rays. The iceberg was stretching both above and beneath into lengthening slopes; mile after mile it was getting thinner. At length, at six in the morning of that memorable day, the 19th of March, the door of the saloon opened, and Captain Nemo appeared.

"The sea is open!" was all he said.

CHAPTER 14

THE SOUTH POLE

I RUSHED on to the platform. Yes! the open sea, with but a few scattered pieces of ice and moving icebergs;—a long stretch of sea; a world of birds in the air, and myriads of fishes under those waters, which varied from intense blue to olive green, according to the bottom. The thermometer marked three degrees centigrade above zero. It was comparatively spring, shut up as we were behind this iceberg, whose lengthened mass was dimly seen on our northern horizon.

"Are we at the pole?" I asked the captain, with a beating heart.

"I do not know," he replied. "At noon I will take our bearings."

"But will the sun show himself through this fog?" said I, looking at the leaden sky.

"However little it shows, it will be enough," replied the captain.

About ten miles south, a solitary island rose to a height of one hundred and four yards. We made for it, but carefully, for the sea might be strewn with banks. One hour afterwards we had reached it, two hours later we had made the round of it. It measured four or five miles in circumference. A narrow canal separated it from a considerable stretch of land, perhaps a continent, for we could not see its limits. The existence of this land seemed to give some color to Maury's hypothesis. The ingenious American has remarked, that between the south pole and the sixtieth parallel, the sea is covered with floating ice of enormous size, which is never met with in the North Atlantic. From this fact he has drawn the conclusion that the antarctic circle encloses considerable continents, as icebergs cannot form in open sea, but only on the coasts. According to these calculations, the mass of ice surrounding the southern pole forms a vast cap, the circumference of which must be, at least, 2,500 miles. But the *Nautilus,* for fear of running aground, had stopped about three cables' length from a strand over which reared a superb heap of rocks. The boat was launched; the captain, two of his men bearing instruments, Conseil, and myself were in it. It was ten in the morning. I had not seen Ned Land. Doubtless the Canadian did not wish to admit the presence of the south pole. A few strokes of the oar brought us to the sand, where we ran ashore. Conseil was going to jump on to the land, when I held him back.

"Sir," said I to Captain Nemo, "to you belongs the honor of first setting foot on this land."

"Yes, sir," said the captain; "and if I do not hesitate to tread this south pole, it is because, up to this time, no human being has left a trace there."

Saying this, he jumped lightly on to the sand. His heart beat with emotion. He climbed a rock, sloping to a little promontory; and there, with his arms crossed, mute and motionless, and with an eager look, he seemed to take possession of these southern regions. After five minutes passed in this ecstasy, he turned to us.

"When you like, sir."

I landed, followed by Conseil, leaving the two men in the boat. For a long way the soil was composed of a reddish, sandy stone, something like crushed brick, scoriæ, streams of lava, and pumice-stones. One could not mistake its volcanic origin. In some parts, slight curls of smoke emitted a sulphurous smell, proving that the internal fires had lost nothing of their expansive powers, though, having climbed a high acclivity, I could see no volcano for a radius of several miles. We know that in those antarctic countries, James Ross found two craters, the Erebus and Terror, in full activity, on the 167th meridian, latitude 77° 32′. The vegetation of this desolate continent seemed to me much restricted. Some lichens of the species usnea melanoxantha lay upon the black rocks; some microscopic plants, rudimentary diatomas, a kind of cells, placed between two quartz shells; long purple and scarlet fucus, supported on little swimming bladders, which the breaking of the waves brought to the shore. These constituted the meagre flora of this region. The shore was strewn with molluscs, little mussels, limpets, smooth bucards in the shape of a heart, and particularly some clios, with oblong membraneous bodies, the head of which was formed of two rounded lobs. I also saw myriads of northern clios, one and a quarter inches long, of which a whale would swallow a whole world at a mouthful; and some charming pteropods, perfect sea-butterflies, animating the waters on the skirts of the shore.

Amongst other zoöphytes, there appeared on the high bottoms some coral shrubs, of that kind which, according to James Ross, live in the antarctic seas to the depth of more than 1,000 yards. Then there were little kingfishers, belonging to the species procellaria pelagica, as well as a large number of asteriads, peculiar to these climates, and starfish studding the soil. But where life abounded most was in the air. There thousands of birds fluttered and flew of all kinds, deafening us with their cries; others crowded the rocks, looking at us as we passed by without fear, and pressing familiarly close by our feet. There were penguins, so agile in the water that they have been taken for the rapid bonitos, heavy and awkward as they are on the ground; they were uttering harsh cries, a large assembly, sober in gesture, but extravagant in clamor. Amongst the birds I noticed the chionis, of the long-legged family, as large as pigeons, white, with a short conical beak, and the eye framed in a red circle. Conseil laid in a stock of them, for these winged creatures, properly prepared, make an agreeable meat. Albatrosses passed in the air (the expanse of their wings being at least four yards and a half), and justly called the vultures of the ocean; some gigantic petrels, and some damiers, a kind of small duck, the under part of whose body is black and white; then there were a whole series of petrels, some whitish with brown-bordered wings, others blue, peculiar to the antarctic seas, and so oily, as I told Conseil, that the inhabitants of the Ferroe Islands had nothing to do before lighting them, but to put a wick in.

"A little more," said Conseil, "and they would be perfect lamps! After that, we cannot expect nature to have previously furnished them with wicks!"

About half a mile farther on, the soil was riddled with ruff's nests, a sort of laying ground, out of which many birds were issuing. Captain Nemo had some hundreds hunted. They uttered a cry like the braying of an ass, were about the size of a goose, slate color on the body, white beneath, with a yellow line round their throats; they allowed themselves to be killed with a stone, never trying to escape. But the fog did not lift, and at eleven the sun had not yet shown itself. Its absence made me uneasy. Without it no observations were possible. How then could we decide whether we had reached the pole? When I rejoined Captain Nemo, I found him leaning on a piece of rock, silently watching the sky. He seemed impatient and vexed. But what was to be done? This rush and powerful man could not command the sun as he did the sea. Noon arrived without the orb of day showing itself for an instant. We could not even tell its position behind the curtain of fog; and soon the fog turned to snow.

"Till to-morrow," said the captain quietly, and we returned to the *Nautilus* amid these atmospheric disturbances.

The tempest of snow continued till the next day. It was impossible to remain on the platform. From the saloon, where I was taking notes of incidents happening during this excursion to the polar continent, I could hear the cries of petrels and albatrosses sporting in the midst of this violent storm. The *Nautilus* did not remain motionless, but skirted the coast, advancing ten miles more to the south in the half-light left by the sun as it skirted the edge of the horizon. The next day, the 20th of March, the snow had ceased. The cold was a little greater, the thermometer showing two degrees below zero. The fog was rising, and I hoped that that day our observations might be taken. Captain Nemo not having yet appeared, the boat took Conseil and myself to land. The soil was still of the same volcanic nature; everywhere were traces of lava, scoriæ, and basalt; but the crater which had vomited them I could not see. Here, as lower down, this continent was alive with myriads of birds; but their rule was now divided with large troops of sea-mammals, looking at us with their soft eyes. There were several kinds of seals, some stretched on the earth, some on flakes of ice, many going in and out of the sea. They did not flee at our approach, never having had anything to do with man; and I reckoned that there were provisions there for hundreds of vessels.

"Sir," said Conseil, "will you tell me the names of these creatures?"

"They are seals and morses."

It was now eight in the morning. Four hours remained to us before the sun could be observed with advantage. I directed our steps towards a vast bay cut in the steep granite shore. There, I can aver that earth and ice were lost to sight by the numbers of sea-mammals covering them, and I involuntarily sought for old Proteus, the mythological shepherd who watched these immense flocks of Neptune. There were more seals than anything else, forming distinct groups, male and female, the father watching over his family, the mother suckling her little ones, some already strong enough to go a few steps. When they wished to change their place, they took little jumps, made by the contraction of their bodies, and helped awkwardly enough by their imperfect fin, which, as with the lamantin, their congener, forms a perfect forearm. I should say that, in the water, which is their element,—the spine of these creatures is flexible,—with smooth and close skin and webbed feet, they swim admirably. In resting on the earth they take the most graceful attitudes. Thus the ancients, observing their soft and expressive looks, which cannot be surpassed by the most beautiful look a woman can give, their clear voluptuous eyes, their charming positions, and the poetry of their manners, metamorphosed them, the male into a triton and the female into a mermaid. I made Conseil notice the considerable development of the lobes of the brain in those interesting cetaceans. No mammal, except man, has such a quantity of cerebral matter; they are also capable of receiving a certain amount of education, are easily domesticated, and I think, with other naturalists, that, if properly taught, they would be of great service as fishing-dogs. The greater part of them slept on the rocks or on the sand. Amongst these seals, properly so called, which have no external ears (in which they differ from the otter, whose ears are prominent), I noticed several varieties of stenorhynchi about three yards long, with a white coat, bulldog heads, armed with teeth in both jaws, four incisors at the top and four at the bottom, and two large canine teeth in the shape of a "fleur de lis." Amongst them glided sea-elephants, a kind of seal, with short flexible trunks. The giants of this species measured twenty feet round, and ten yards and a half in length; but they did not move as we approached.

"These creatures are not dangerous?" asked Conseil.

"No; not unless you attack them. When they have to defend their young, their rage is terrible, and it is not uncommon for them to break the fishing boats to pieces."

"They are quite right," said Conseil.

"I do not say they are not."

Two miles farther on we were stopped by the promontory which shelters the bay from the southerly winds. Beyond it we heard loud bellowings such as a troop of ruminants would produce.

"Good!" said Conseil; "a concert of bulls!"

"No; a concert of morses."

"They are fighting!"

"They are either fighting or playing."

We now began to climb the blackish rocks, amid unforeseen stumbles, and over stones which the ice made slippery. More than once I rolled over, at the expense of my loins. Conseil, more prudent or more steady, did not stumble, and helped me up, saying,—

"If, sir, you would have the kindness to take wider steps, you would preserve your equilibrium better."

Arrived at the upper ridge of the promontory, I saw a vast white plain covered with morses. They were playing amongst themselves, and what we heard were bellowings of pleasure, not of anger.

As I passed near these curious animals, I could examine them leisurely, for they did not move. Their skins were thick and rugged, of a yellowish tint, approaching to red; their hair was short and scant. Some of them were four yards and a quarter long. Quieter and less timid than their congeners of the north, they did not, like them, place sentinels round the outskirts of their encampment. After examining this city of morses, I began to think of returning. It was eleven o'clock, and if Captain Nemo found the conditions favorable for observations, I wished to be present at the operation. We followed a narrow pathway running along the summit of the steep shore. At half past eleven we had reached the place where we landed. The boat had run aground bringing the captain. I saw him standing on a block of basalt, his instruments near him, his eyes fixed on the northern horizon, near which the sun was then describing a lengthened curve. I took my place beside him, and waited without speaking. Noon arrived, and, as before, the sun did not appear. It was a fatality. Observations were still wanting. If not accomplished to-morrow, we must give up all idea of taking any. We were indeed exactly at the 20th of March. To-morrow, the 21st, would be the equinox; the sun would disappear behind the horizon for six months, and with its disappearance the long polar night would begin. Since the September equinox it had emerged from the northern horizon, rising by lengthened spirals up to the 21st of December. At this period, the summer solstice of the northern regions, it had begun to descend, and to-morrow was to shed its last rays upon them. I communicated my fears and observations to Captain Nemo.

"You are right, M. Aronnax," said he; "if to-morrow I cannot take the altitude of the sun, I shall not be able to do it for six months. But precisely because chance has led me into these seas on the 21st of March, my bearings will be easy to take, if at twelve we can see the sun."

"Why, Captain?"

"Because then the orb of day describes such lengthened curves, that it is difficult to measure exactly its height above the horizon, and grave errors may be made with instruments."

"What will you do then?"

"I shall only use my chronometer," replied Captain Nemo. "If to-morrow, the 21st of March, the disc of the sun, allowing for refraction, is exactly cut by the northern horizon, it will show that I am at the south pole."

"Just so," said I. "But this statement is not mathematically correct, because the equinox does not necessarily begin at noon."

"Very likely, sir; but the error will not be a hundred yards, and we do not want more. Till to-morrow then!"

Captain Nemo returned on board. Conseil and I remained to survey the shore, observing and studying until five o'clock. Then I went to bed, not, however, without invoking, like the Indian, the favor of the radiant orb. The next day, the 21st of March, at five in the morning, I mounted the platform. I found Captain Nemo there.

"The weather is lightening a little," said he. "I have some hope. After breakfast we will go on shore, and choose a post for observation."

That point settled, I sought Ned Land. I wanted to take him with me. But the obstinate Canadian refused, and I saw that his taciturnity and his bad humor grew day by day. After all I was not sorry for his obstinacy under the circumstances. Indeed, there were too many seals on shore, and we ought not to lay such temptation in this unreflecting fisherman's way. Breakfast over, we went on shore. The *Nautilus* had gone some miles farther up in the night. It was a whole league from the coast, above which reared a sharp peak above five hundred yards high. The boat took with me Captain Nemo, two men of the crew, and the instruments, which consisted of a chronometer, a telescope, and a barometer. While crossing, I saw numerous whales belonging to the three kinds peculiar to the southern seas: the whale, or the English "right whale," which has no dorsal fin; the "humpback," or balænopteron, with reeved chest, and large whitish fins, which, in spite of its name, do not form wings; and the fin-back, of a yellowish brown, the liveliest of all the cetacea. This powerful creature is heard a long way off when he throws to a great height columns of air and vapor, which look like whirlwinds of smoke. Those different mammals were disporting themselves in troops in the quiet waters; and I could see that this basin of the antarctic pole served as a place of refuge to the cetacea too closely tracked by the hunters. I also noticed long whitish lines of salpæ, a kind of gregarious mollusc, and large medusæ floating between the reeds.

At nine we landed; the sky was brightening, the clouds were flying to the south, and the fog seemed to be leaving the cold surface of the waters. Captain Nemo went towards the peak, which he doubtless meant to be his observatory. It was a painful ascent over the sharp lava and the pumice-stones, in an atmosphere often impregnated with a sulphurous smell from the smoking cracks. For a man unaccustomed to walk on land, the captain climbed the steep slopes with an agility I never saw equalled, and which a hunter would have envied. We were two hours getting to the summit of this peak, which was half porphyry and half basalt. From thence we looked upon a vast sea, which, towards the north, distinctly traced its boundary line upon the sky. At our feet lay fields of dazzlnig whiteness. Over our heads a pale azure, free from fog. To the north the disc of the sun seemed like a ball of fire, already horned by the cutting of the horizon. From the bosom of the water rose sheaves of liquid jets by hundreds. In the distance lay the *Nautilus* like a cetacean asleep on the water. Behind us, to the south and east, an immense country, and a chaotic heap of rocks and ice, the limits of which were not visible. On arriving at the summit, Captain Nemo carefully took the mean height of the barometer, for he would have to consider that in taking his observations. At a quarter to twelve, the sun, then seen only by refraction, looked like a golden disc shedding its last rays upon this deserted continent, and seas which never man had yet ploughed. Captain Nemo, furnished with a lenticular glass, which, by means of a mirror, corrected the refraction, watched the orb sinking below the horizon by degrees, following a lengthened diagonal. I held the chronometer. My heart beat fast. If the disappearance of the half-disc of the sun coincided with twelve o'clock on the chronometer, we were at the pole itself.

"Twelve!" I exclaimed.

"The South Pole!" replied Captain Nemo, in a grave voice, handing me the glass, which showed the orb cut in exactly equal parts by the horizon.

I looked at the last rays crowning the peak, and the shadows mounting by degrees up its slopes. At that moment Captain Nemo, resting with his hand on my shoulder, said,—

"I, Captain Nemo, on this 21st day of March, 1868, have reached the south pole on the ninetieth degree; and I take possession of this part of the globe, equal to one sixth of the known continents."

"In whose name, Captain?"

"In my own, sir!"

Saying which, Captain Nemo unfurled a black banner, bearing an N in gold quartered on its bunting. Then turning towards the orb of day, whose last rays lapped the horizon of the sea, he exclaimed,—

"Adieu, sun! Disappear, thou radiant orb! rest beneath this open sea, and let a night of six months spread its shadows over my new domains!"

CHAPTER 15

ACCIDENT OR INCIDENT?

THE next day, the 22d of March, at six in the morning, preparations for departure were begun. The last gleams of twilight were melting into night. The cold was great; the constellations shone with wonderful intensity. In the zenith glittered that wondrous Southern Cross,—the polar bear of antarctic regions. The thermometer showed twelve degrees below zero, and when the wind freshened, it was most biting. Flakes of ice increased on the open water. The sea seemed everywhere alike. Numerous blackish patches spread on the surface, showing the formation of fresh ice. Evidently the southern basin, frozen during the six winter months, was absolutely inaccessible. What became of the whales in that time? Doubtless they went beneath the icebergs, seeking more practicable seas. As to the seals and morses, accustomed to live in a hard climate, they remained on these icy shores. These creatures have the instinct to break holes in the ice-fields, and to keep them open. To these holes they come for breath; when the birds, driven away by the cold, have emigrated to the north, these sea mammals remain sole masters of the polar continent. But the reservoirs were filling with water, and the *Nautilus* was slowly descending. At 1,000 feet deep it stopped; its screw beat the waves, and it advanced straight towards the north, at a speed of fifteen miles an hour. Towards night it was already floating under the immense body of the iceberg. At three in the morning I was awakened by a violet shock. I sat up in my bed and listened in the darkness, when I was thrown into the middle of the room. The *Nautilus,* after having struck, had rebounded violently. I groped along the partition, and by the staircase to the saloon, which was lit by the luminous ceiling. The furniture was upset. Fortunately the windows were firmly set, and had held fast. The pictures on the starboard-side, from being no longer vertical, wore clinging to the paper, whilst those of the port-side were hanging at least a foot from the wall. The *Nautilus* was lying on its starboard-side perfectly motionless. I heard footsteps, and a confusion of voices; but Captain Nemo did not appear. As I was leaving the saloon, Ned Land and Conseil entered.

"What is the matter?" said I, at once.

"I came to ask you, sir," said Conseil.

"Confound it!" exclaimed the Canadian, "I know well enough! The *Nautilus* has struck; and judging by the way she lies, I do not think she will right herself as she did the first time in Torres Straits."

"But," I asked, "has she at least come to the surface of the sea?"

"We do not know," said Conseil.

"It is easy to decide," I answered. I consulted the manometer. To my great surprise it showed a depth of more than 180 fathoms. "What does that mean?" I exclaimed.

"We must ask Captain Nemo," said Conseil.

"But where shall we find him?" said Ned Land.

"Follow me," said I to my companions.

We left the saloon. There was no one in the library. At the centre staircase, by the berths of the ship's crew, there was no one. I thought that Captain Nemo must be in the pilot's cage. It was best to wait. We all returned to the saloon. For twenty minutes we remained thus, trying to hear the slightest noise which might be made on board the *Nautilus,* when Captain Nemo entered. He seemed not to see us; his face, generally so impassive, showed signs of uneasiness. He watched the compass silently, then the manometer; and going to the planisphere, placed his finger on a spot representing the southern seas. I would not interrupt him; but, some minutes later, when he turned towards me, I said, using one of his own expressions in the Torres Straits,—

"An incident, Captain?"

"No, sir; an accident this time."

"Serious?"

"Perhaps."

"Is the danger immediate?"

"No."

"The *Nautilus* has stranded?"

"Yes."

"And this has happened—how?"

"From a caprice of nature, not from the ignorance of man. Not a mistake has been made in the working. But we cannot prevent equilibrium from producing its effects. We may brave human laws, but we cannot resist natural ones."

Captain Nemo had chosen a strange moment for uttering this philosophical reflection. On the whole, his answer helped me little.

"May I ask, sir, the cause of this accident?"

"An enormous block of ice, a whole mountain, has turned over," he replied. "When icebergs are undermined at their base by warmer water or reiterated shocks, their centre of gravity rises, and the whole thing turns over. This is what has happened; one of these blocks, as it fell, struck the *Nautilus,* then, gliding under its hull, raised it with irresistible force, bringing it into beds which are not so thick, where it is lying on its side."

"But can we not get the *Nautilus* off by emptying its reservoirs, that it may regain its equilibrium?"

"That, sir, is being done at this moment. You can hear the pump working. Look at the needle of the manometer; it shows that the *Nautilus* is rising, but the block of ice is rising with it; and, until some obstacle stops its ascending motion, our position cannot be altered."

Indeed, the *Nautilus* still held the same position to starboard; doubtless it would right itself when the block stopped. But at this moment who knows if we may not strike the upper part of the iceberg, and if we may not be frightfully crushed between the two glassy surfaces? I reflected on all the consequences of our position. Captain Nemo never took his eyes off the manometer. Since the fall of the iceberg, the *Nautilus* had risen about a hundred and fifty feet, but it still made the same angle with the perpendicular. Suddenly a slight movement was felt in the hold. Evidently it was righting a little. Things hanging in the saloon were sensibly returning to their normal position. The partitions were nearing the upright. No one spoke. With beating hearts we watched and felt the straightening. The boards became horizontal under our feet. Ten minutes passed.

"At last we have righted!" I exclaimed.

"Yes," said Captain Nemo, going to the door of the saloon.

"But are we floating?" I asked.

"Certainly," he replied; "since the reservoirs are not empty; and, when empty, the *Nautilus* must rise to the surface of the sea."

We were in open sea; but at a distance of about ten yards, on either side of the *Nautilus,* rose a dazzling wall of ice. Above and beneath the same wall. Above, because the lower surface of the iceberg stretched over us like an immense ceiling. Beneath, because the overturned block, having slid by degrees, had found a resting-place on the lateral walls, which kept it in that position. The *Nautilus* was really imprisoned in a perfect tunnel of ice more than twenty yards in breadth, filled with quiet water. It was easy to get out of it by going either forward or backward, and then make a free passage under the iceberg, some hundreds of yards deeper. The luminous ceiling had been extinguished, but the saloon was still resplendent with intense light. It was the powerful reflection from the glass partition sent violently back to the sheets of the lantern. I cannot

The Captain exclaimed, "Adieu, sun! Disappear, thou radiant orb!"

describe the effect of the voltaic rays upon the great blocks so capriciously cut; upon every angle, every ridge, every facet, was thrown a different light, according to the nature of the veins running through the ice; a dazzling mine of gems, particularly of sapphires, their blue rays crossing with the green of the emerald. Here and there were opal shades of wonderful softness, running through bright spots like diamonds of fire, the brilliancy of which the eye could not bear. The power of the lantern seemed increased a hundred-fold, like a lamp through the lenticular plates of a first-class lighthouse.

"How beautiful! how beautiful!" cried Conseil.

"Yes," I said, "it is a wonderful sight. Is it not, Ned?"

"Yes, confound it! Yes," answered Ned Land, "it is superb! I am mad at being obliged to admit it. No one has ever seen anything like it; but the sight may cost us dear. And if I must say all, I think we are seeing here things which God never intended man to see."

Ned was right, it was too beautiful. Suddenly a cry from Conseil made me turn.

"What is it?" I asked.

"Shut your eyes, sir! do not look, sir!" Saying which, Conseil clapped his hands over his eyes.

"But what is the matter, my boy?"

"I am dazzled, blinded."

My eyes turned involuntarily towards the glass, but I could not stand the fire which seemed to devour them. I understood what had happened. The *Nautilus* had put on full speed. All the quiet lustre of the ice walls was at once changed into flashes of lightning. The fire from these myriads of diamonds was blinding. It required some time to calm our troubled looks. At last the hands were taken down.

"Faith, I should never have believed it," said Conseil.

It was then five in the morning; and at that moment a shock was felt at the bows of the *Nautilus*. I knew that its spur had struck a block of ice. It must have been a false manœuvre, for this submarine tunnel, obstructed by blocks, was not very easy navigation. I thought that Captain Nemo, by changing his course, would either turn these obstacles, or else follow the windings of the tunnel. In any case, the road before us could not be entirely blocked. But, contrary to my expectations, the *Nautilus* took a decided retrograde motion.

"We are going backwards?" said Conseil.

"Yes," I replied. "This end of the tunnel can have no egress."

"And then?"

"Then," said I, "the working is easy. We must go back again, and go out at the southern opening. That is all."

In speaking thus, I wished to appear more confident than I really was. But the retrograde motion of the *Nautilus* was increasing; and, reversing the screw, it carried us at great speed.

"It will be a hindrance," said Ned.

"What does it matter, some hours more or less, provided we get out at last?"

"Yes," repeated Ned Land, "provided we do get out at last!"

For a short time I walked from the saloon to the library. My companions were silent. I soon threw myself on an ottoman, and took a book, which my eyes overran mechanically. A quarter of an hour after, Conseil, approaching me, said, "Is what you are reading very interesting, sir?"

"Very interesting!" I replied.

"I should think so, sir. It is your own book you are reading."

"My book?"

And indeed I was holding in my hand the work on the "Great Submarine Depths." I did not even dream of it. I closed the book, and returned to my walk. Ned and Conseil rose to go.

"Stay here, my friends," said I, detaining them. "Let us remain together until we are out of this block."

"As you please, sir," Conseil replied.

Some hours passed. I often looked at the instruments hanging from the partition. The manometer showed that the *Nautilus* kept at a constant depth of more than three hundred yards; the compass still pointed to the south; the log indicated a speed of twenty miles an hour, which, in such a cramped space, was very great. But Captain Nemo knew that he could not hasten too much, and that minutes were worth ages to us. At twenty-five minutes past eight a second shock took place, this time from behind. I turned pale. My companions were close by my side. I seized Conseil's hand. Our looks expressed our feelings better than words. At this moment the captain entered the saloon. I went up to him.

"Our course is barred southward?" I asked.

"Yes, sir. The iceberg has shifted, and closed every outlet."

"We are blocked up, then?"

"Yes."

CHAPTER 16

WANT OF AIR

THUS, around the *Nautilus*, above and below, was an impenetrable wall of ice. We were prisoners to the iceberg. I watched the captain. His countenance had resumed its habitual imperturbability.

"Gentlemen," he said, calmly, "there are two ways of dying in the circumstances in which we are placed." (This inexplicable person had the air of a mathematical professor lecturing to his pupils.) "The first is to be crushed; the second is to die of suffocation. I do not speak of the possibility of dying of hunger, for the supply of provisions in the *Nautilus* will certainly last longer than we shall. Let us then calculate our chances."

"As to suffocation, Captain," I replied, "that is not to be feared, because our reservoirs are full."

"Just so; but they will only yield two days' supply of air. Now, for thirty-six hours we have been hidden under the water, and already the heavy atmosphere of the *Nautilus* requires renewal. In forty-eight hours our reserve will be exhausted."

"Well, Captain, can we be delivered before forty-eight hours?"

"We will attempt it, at least, by piercing the wall that surrounds us."

"On which side?"

"Sound will tell us. I am going to run the *Nautilus* aground on the lower bank, and my men will attack the iceberg on the side that is least thick."

Captain Nemo went out. Soon I discovered by a hissing noise that the water was entering the reservoirs. The *Nautilus* sank slowly, and rested on the ice at a depth of 350 yards, the depth at which the lower bank was immersed.

"My friends," I said, "our situation is serious, but I rely on your courage and energy."

"Sir," replied the Canadian, "I am ready to do anything for the general safety."

"Good! Ned," and I held out my hand to the Canadian.

"I will add," he continued, "that being as handy with the pickaxe as with the harpoon, if I can be useful to the captain, he can command my services."

"He will not refuse your help. Come, Ned!"

I led him to the room where the crew of the *Nautilus* were putting on their cork-jackets. I told the captain of Ned's proposal, which he accepted. The Canadian put on his sea-costume, and was ready as soon as his companions. When Ned was dressed, I re-entered the drawing-room, where the panes of glass were open, and, posted near Conseil, I examined the ambient beds that supported the *Nautilus*. Some instants after, we saw a dozen of the crew set foot on the bank of ice, and among them Ned Land, easily known by his stature. Captain Nemo was with them. Before proceeding to dig the walls, he took the soundings, to be sure of working in the right direction. Long sounding lines were sunk in the side walls, but after fifteen yards they were again stopped by the thick wall. It was useless to attack it on the ceiling-like surface, since the iceberg itself measured more than 400 yards in height. Captain Nemo then sounded the lower surface. There ten yards of wall separated us from the water, so great was the thickness of the ice-field. It was necessary, therefore, to cut from it a piece equal in extent to the water-line of the *Nautilus*. There were about 6,000 cubic yards to detach, so as to dig a hole by which we could descend to the ice-field. The work was begun immediately, and carried on with indefatigable energy. Instead of digging round the *Nautilus*, which would have involved greater difficulty, Captain Nemo had an immense trench made at eight yards from the port quarter. Then the men set to work simultaneously with their screws, on several points of its circumference. Presently the pickaxe attacked this compact matter vigorously, and large blocks were detached from the mass. By a curious effect of specific gravity, these blocks, lighter than water, fled, so to speak, to the vault of the tunnel, that increased in thickness at the top in proportion as it diminished at the base. But that mattered little, so long as the lower part grew thinner. After two hours' hard work, Ned Land came in exhausted. He and his comrades were replaced by new workers, whom Conseil and I joined. The second lieutenant of the *Nautilus* superintended us. The water seemed singularly cold, but I soon got warm handling the pickaxe. My movements were free enough, although they were made under a pressure of thirty atmospheres. When I re-entered, after working two hours, to take some food and rest, I found a perceptible difference between the pure fluid with which the Rouquayrol engine supplied me, and the atmosphere of the *Nautilus*, already charged with carbonic acid. The air had not been renewed for forty-eight hours, and its vivifying qualities were considerably enfeebled. However, after a lapse of twelve hours, we had only raised a block of ice one yard thick, on the marked surface, which was about 600 cubic yards! Reckoning that it took twelve hours to accomplish this much, it would take five nights and four days to bring this enterprise to a satisfactory conclusion. Five nights and four days! And we have only air enough for two days in the reservoirs! "Without taking into account," said Ned, "that, even if we get out of this infernal prison, we shall also be imprisoned under the iceberg, shut out from all possible communication with the atmosphere." True enough! Who could then foresee the minimum of time necessary for our deliverance? We might be suffocated before the *Nautilus* could regain the surface of the waves! Was it destined to perish in this icetomb, with all those it enclosed? The situation was terrible. But every one had looked the danger in the face, and each was determined to do his duty to the last.

As I expected, during the night a new block a yard square was carried away, and still further sank the immense hollow. But in the morning when, dressed in my cork-jacket, I traversed the slushy mass at a temperature of six or seven degrees below zero, I remarked that the side walls were gradually closing in. The beds of water farthest from the trenth, that were not warmed by the men's mere work, showed a tendency to solidification. In presence of this new and imminent danger, what would become of our chances of safety, and how hinder the solidification of this liquid medium, that would burst the partitions of the *Nautilus* like glass?

I did not tell my companions of this new danger. What was the good of damping the energy they displayed in the painful work of escape? But when I went on board again, I told Captain Nemo of this grave complication.

"I know it," he said, in that calm tone which could counteract the most terrible apprehensions. "It is one danger more; but I see no way of escaping it; the only chance of safety is to go quicker than solidification. We must be beforehand with it, that is all."

On this day for several hours I used my pickaxe vigorously. The work kept me up. Besides, to work was to quit the *Nautilus,* and breathe directly the pure air drawn from the reservoirs, and supplied by our apparatus, and to quit the impoverished and vitiated atmosphere. Towards evening the trench was dug one yard deeper. When I returned on board, I was nearly suffocated by the carbonic acid with which the air was filled—ah! if we had only the chemical means to drive away this deleterious gas. We had plenty of oxygen; all this water contained a considerable quantity, and by dissolving it with our powerful piles, it would restore the vivifying fluid. I had thought well over it; but of what good was that, since the carbonic acid produced by our respiration had invaded every part of the vessel? To absorb it, it was necessary to fill some jars with caustic potash, and to shake them incessantly. Now this substance was wanting on board, and nothing could replace it. On that evening, Captain Nemo ought to open the taps of his reservoirs, and let some pure air into the interior of the *Nautilus;* without this precaution, we could not get rid of the sense of suffocation. The next day, March 26, I resumed my miner's work in beginning the fifth yard. The side walls and the lower surface of the iceberg thickened visibly. It was evident that they would meet before the *Nautilus* was able to disengage itself. Despair seized me for an instant, my pickaxe nearly fell from my hands. What was the good of digging if I must be suffocated, crushed by the water, that was turning into stone?—a punishment that the ferocity of the savages even would not have invented! Just then Captain Nemo passed near me. I touched his hand and showed him the walls of our prison. The wall to port had advanced to at least four yards from the hull of the *Nautilus*. The captain understood me, and signed to me to follow him. We went on board. I took off my cork-jacket, and accompanied him into the drawing-room.

"M. Aronnax, we must attempt some desperate means, or we shall be sealed up in this solidified water as in cement."

"Yes; but what is to be done?"

"Ah! if my *Nautilus* were strong enough to bear this pressure without being crushed!"

"Well?" I asked, not catching the captain's idea.

"Do you not understand," he replied, "that this congelation of water will help us? Do you not see that, by its solidification, it would burst through this field of ice that imprisons us, as, when it freezes, it bursts the hardest stones? Do you not perceive that it would be an agent of safety instead of destruction?"

"Yes, Captain, perhaps. But whatever resistance to crushing the *Nautilus* possesses, it could not support this terrible pressure, and would be flattened like an iron plate."

"I know it, sir. Therefore we must not reckon on the aid of nature, but on our own exertions. We must stop this solidification. Not only will the side walls be pressed together; but there is not ten feet of water before or behind the *Nautilus*. The congelation gains on us on all sides."

"How long will the air in the reservoirs last for us to breathe on board?"

The Captain looked in my face. "After to-morrow they will be empty!"

A cold sweat came over me. However, ought I to have been astonished at the answer? On March 22, the *Nautilus* was in the open polar seas. We were at 26°. For five days we had lived on the reserve on board. And what was left of the respirable air must be kept for the workers. Even now, as I write, my recollection is still so vivid, that an involuntary terror seizes me, and my lungs seem to be without air. Meanwhile Captain Nemo reflected silently, and evidently an idea had struck him; but he seemed to reject it. At last, these words escaped his lips,—

"Boiling water!" he mutteed.

"Boiling water?" I cried.

"Yes, sir. We are enclosed in a space that is relatively confined. Would not jets of boiling water, constantly injected by the pumps, raise the temperature in this part, and stay the congelation?"

"Let us try it," I said, resolutely.

"Let us try, Professor."

The thermometer then stood at seven degrees outside. Captain Nemo took me to the galleys, where the vast distillatory machines stood that furnished the drinkable water by evaporation. They filled these with water, and all the electric heat from the piles was thrown through the worms bathed in the liquid. In a few minutes this water reached a hundred degrees. It was directed towards the pumps, while fresh water replaced it in proportion. The heat developed by the troughs was such that cold water, drawn up from the sea, after only having gone through the machines, came boiling into the body of the pump. The injection was begun, and three hours after the thermometer marked six degrees below zero outside. One degree was gained. Two hours later, the thermometer only marked four degrees.

"We shall succeed," I said to the captain, after having anxiously watched the result of the operation.

"I think," he answered, "that we shall not be crushed. We have no more suffocation to fear."

During the night the temperature of the water rose to one degree below zero. The injections could not carry it to a higher point. But as the congelation of the sea-water produces at least two degrees, I was at last reassured against the dangers of solidification.

The next day, March 27, six yards of ice had been cleared, four yards only remaining to be cleared away. There was yet forty-eight hours' work. The air could not be renewed in the interior of the *Nautilus*. And this day would make it worse. An intolerable weight oppressed me. Towards three o'clock in the evening, this feeling rose to a violent degree. Yawns dislocated my jaws. My lungs panted as they inhaled this burning fluid, which became rarefied more and more. A moral torpor took hold of me. I was powerless, almost unconscious. My brave Conseil, though exhibiting the same symptoms and suffering in the same manner, never left me. He took my hand and encouraged me, and I heard him murmur, "O, if I could only not breathe, so as to leave more air for my master!"

Tears came into my eyes on hearing him speak thus. If our situation to all was intolerable in the interior, with what haste and gladness would we put on our cork-jackets to work in our turn! Pickaxes sounded on the frozen ice-beds. Our arms ached, the skin was torn off our hands. But what were these fatigues, what did the wounds matter? Vital air came to the lungs! we breathed! we breathed!

All this time no one prolonged his voluntary task beyond the prescribed time. His task accomplished, each one handed in turn to his panting companions the apparatus that supplied him with life. Captain Nemo set the example, and submitted first to this severe discipline. When the time came he gave up his apparatus to another, and returned to the vitiated air on board, calm, unflinching, unmurmuring.

On that day the ordinary work was accomplished with unusual vigor. Only two yards remained to be raised from the surface. Two yards only separated us from the open sea. But the reservoirs were nearly emptied of air. The little that remained ought to be kept for the workers; not a particle for the *Nautilus*. When I went back on board, I was half suffocated. What a night! I know not how to describe it. The next day my breathing was oppressed. Dizziness accompanied the pain in my head, and made me like a drunken man. My companions showed the same symptoms. Some of the crew had rattling in the throat.

On that day, the sixth of our imprisonment, Captain Nemo, finding the pickaxes work too slowly, resolved to crush the ice-bed that still separated us from the liquid sheet. This man's coolness and energy never forsook him. He subdued his physical pains by moral force.

By his orders the vessel was lightened, that is to say, raised from the ice-bed by a change of specific gravity. When it floated they towed it so as to bring it above the immense trench made on the level of the water-line. Then filling his reservoirs of water, he descended and shut himself up in the hole.

Just then all the crew came on board, and the double door of communication was shut. The *Nautilus* then rested on the bed of ice, which was not one yard thick, and which the sounding leads had perforated in a thousand places. The taps of the reservoirs were then opened, and a hundred cubic yards of water was let in, increasing the weight of the *Nautilus* to 1800 tons. We waited, we listened, forgetting our sufferings in hope. Our safety depended on this last chance. Notwithstanding the buzzing in my head, I soon heard the humming sound under the hull of the *Nautilus*. The ice cracked with a singular noise, like tearing paper, and the *Nautilus* sank.

"We are off!" murmured Conseil in my ear.

I could not answer him. I seized his hand, and pressed it convulsively. All at once, carried away by its frightful overcharge, the *Nautilus* sank like a bullet under the waters, that is to say, it fell as if it was in a vacuum. Then all the electric force was put on the pumps, that soon began to let the water out of the reservoirs. After some minutes our fall was stopped. Soon, too, the manometer indicated an ascending movement. The screw, going at full speed, made the iron hull tremble to its very bolts, and drew us towards the north. But if this floating under the iceberg is to last another day before we reach the open sea, I shall be dead first.

Half stretched upon a divan in the library, I was suffocating. My face was purple, my lips blue, my faculties suspended. I neither saw nor heard. All notion of time had gone from my mind. My muscles could not contract. I do not know how many hours passed thus, but I was conscious of the agony that was coming over me. I felt as if I was going to die. Suddenly I came to. Some breaths of air penetrated my lungs. Had we risen to the surface of the waves? Were we free of the iceberg? No; Ned and Conseil, my two brave friends, were sacrificing themselves to save me. Some particles of air still remained at the bottom of one apparatus. Instead of using it, they had kept it for me, and while they were being suffocated, they gave me life drop by drop. I wanted to push back the thing; they held my hands, and for some moments I breathed freely. I looked at the clock; it was eleven in the morning. It ought to be the 28th of March. The *Nautilus* went at a frightful pace, forty miles an hour. It literally tore through the water. Where was Captain Nemo? Had he succumbed? Were his companions dead with him? At the moment, the manometer indicated that we were not more than twenty feet from the surface. A mere plate of ice separated us from the atmosphere; could we not break it? Perhaps. In any case the *Nautilus* was going to attempt it. I felt that it was in an oblique position, lowering the stern, and raising the bows. The introduction of water had been the means of disturbing its equilibrium. Then, impelled by its powerful screw, it attacked the ice-field from beneath like a formidable battering-ram. It broke it by backing and then rushing forward against the field, which gradually gave way; and at last, dashing suddenly against it, shot forwards on the icy field, that crushed beneath its weight. The panel was opened,—one might say torn off,—and the pure air came in in abundance to all parts of the *Nautilus*.

CHAPTER 17

FROM CAPE HORN TO THE AMAZON

How I got on to the platform, I have no idea; perhaps the Canadian had carried me there. But I breathed, I inhaled the vivifying sea-air. My two companions were getting drunk with the fresh particles. The other unhappy men had been so long without food, that they could not with impunity indulge in the simplest ailments that were given them. We, on the contrary, had no need to restrain

I breathed, I inhaled the vivifying sea-air.

ourselves; we could draw this air freely into our lungs, and it was the breeze, the breeze alone, that filled us with this keen enjoyment.

"Ah!" said Conseil, "how delightful this oxygen is! Master need not fear to breathe it. There is enough for everybody."

Ned Land did not speak, but he opened his jaws wide enough to frighten a shark. Our strength soon returned, and when I looked round me, I saw we were alone on the platform. The foreign seamen in the *Nautilus* were contented with the air that circulated in the interior; none of them had come to drink in the open air.

The first words I spoke were words of gratitude and thankfulness to my two companions. Ned and Conseil had prolonged my life during the last hours of this long agony. All my gratitude could not repay such devotion.

"My friends," said I, "we are bound one to the other forever, and I am under infinite obligations to you."

"Which I shall take advantage of," exclaimed the Canadian.

"What do you mean?" said Conseil.

"I mean that I shall take you with me when I leave this infernal *Nautilus*."

"Well," said Conseil, "after all this, are we going right?"

"Yes," I replied, "for we are going the way of the sun, and here the sun is in the north."

"No doubt," said Ned Land; "but it remains to be seen whether he will bring the ship into the Pacific or the Atlantic Ocean, that is, into frequented or deserted seas."

I could not answer that question, and I feared that Captain Nemo would rather take us to the vast ocean that touches the coasts of Asia and America at the same time. He would thus complete the tour round the submarine world, and return to those waters in which the *Nautilus* could sail freely. We ought, before long, to settle this important point. The *Nautilus* went at a rapid pace. The polar circle was soon passed, and the course shaped for Cape Horn. We were off the American point, March 31, at seven o'clock in the evening. Then all our past sufferings were forgotten. The remembrance of that imprisonment in the ice was effaced from our minds. We only thought of the future. Captain Nemo did not appear again either in the drawing-room or on the platform. The point shown each day on the planisphere, and marked by the lieutenant, showed me the exact direction of the *Nautilus*. Now, on that evening, it was evident, to my great satisfaction, that we were going back to the north by the Atlantic. The next day, April 1, when the *Nautilus* ascended to the surface, some minutes before noon, we sighted land to the west. It was Terra del Fuego, which the first navigators named thus from seeing the quantity of smoke that rose from the natives' huts. The coast seemed low to me, but in the distance rose high mountains. I even thought I had a glimpse of Mount Sarmiento, that rises 2,070 yards above the level of the sea, with a very pointed summit, which, according as it is misty or clear, is a sign of fine or of wet weather. At this moment, the peak was clearly defined against the sky. The *Nautilus,* diving again under the water, approached the coast, which was only some few miles off. From the glass windows in the drawing-room, I saw long sea-weeds, and gigantic fuci, and varech, of which the open polar sea contains so many specimens, with their sharp polished filaments; they measured about 300 yards in length,—real cables, thicker than one's thumb; and having great tenacity, they are often used as ropes for vessels. Another weed known as velp, with leaves four feet long, buried in the coral concretions, hung at the bottom. It served as nest and food for myriads of crustacea and molluscs, crabs and cuttle-fish. There seals and otters had splendid repasts, eating the flesh of fish with sea-vegetables, according to the English fashion. Over this fertile and luxuriant ground the *Nautilus* passed with great rapidity. Towards evening, it approached the Falkland group, the rough summits of which I recognized the following day. The depth of the sea was moderate. On the shores, our nets brought in beautiful specimens of sea-weed, and particularly a certain fucus, the roots of which were filled with the best mussels in the world. Geese and ducks fell by dozens on the platform, and soon took their places in the pantry on board. With regard to fish, I observed especially specimens of the goby species, some two feet long, all over white and yellow spots. I admired also numerous medusæ, and the finest of the sort, the crysaora, peculiar to the sea about the Falkland Isles. I should have liked to preserve some specimens of these delicate zoöphytes; but they are only like clouds, shadows, apparitions, that sink and evaporate, when out of their native element.

When the last heights of the Falklands had disappeared from the horizon, the *Nautilus* sank to between twenty and twenty-five yards, and followed the American coast. Captain Nemo did not show himself. Until the 3d of April we did not quit the shores of Patagonia, sometimes under the ocean, sometimes at the surface. The *Nautilus* passed beyond the large estuary formed by the mouth of the Plata, and was, on the 4th of April, fifty-six miles off Uruguay. Its direction was northwards, and followed the long windings of the coast of South America. We had then made 16,000 miles since our embarkation in the seas of Japan. About eleven o'clock in the morning the Tropic of Capricorn was crossed on the thirty-seventh meridian, and we passed Cape Frio standing out to sea. Captain Nemo, to Ned Land's great displeasure, did not like the neighborhood of the inhabited coasts of Brazil, for we went at a giddy speed. Not a fish, not a bird of the swiftest kind could follow us, and the natural curiosities off these seas escaped all observation.

This speed was kept up for several days, and in the evening of the 9th of April we sighted the most easterly point of South America that forms Cape San Roque. But then the *Nautilus* swerved again, and sought the lowest depth of a submarine valley which is between this cape and Sierra Leone on the African coast. This valley bifurcates to the parallel of the Antilles, and terminates at the north by the enormous depression of 9,000 yards. In this place, the geological basin of the ocean forms, as far as the Lesser Antilles, a cliff of three and a half miles perpendicular in height, and at the parallel of the Cape Verd Islands, another wall not less considerable, that encloses thus all the sunk continent of the Atlantic. The bottom of this immense valley is dotted with some mountains, that give to these submarine places a picturesque aspect. I speak, moreover, from the manuscript charts that were in the library of the *Nautilus*,—charts evidently due to Captain Nemo's hand, and made after his personal observations. For two days the desert and deep waters were visited by means of the inclined planes. The *Nautilus* was furnished with long diagonal broadsides which carried it to all elevations. But, on the 11th of April, it rose suddenly, and land appeared at the mouth of the Amazon River, a vast estuary, the embouchure of which is so considerable that it freshens the sea-water for the distance of several leagues.

The equator was crossed. Twenty miles to the west were the Guianas, a French territory, on which we could have found an easy refuge; but a stiff breeze was blowing, and the furious waves would not have allowed a single boat to face them. Ned Land understood that, no doubt, for he spoke not a word about it. For my part, I made no allusion to his schemes of flight, for I would not urge him to make an attempt that must inevitably fail. I made the time pass pleasantly by interesting studies. During the days of April 11th and 12th, the *Nautilus* did not leave the surface of the sea, and the net brought in a marvellous haul of zoöphytes, fish and reptiles. Some zoöphytes had been fished up by the chain of the nets; they were for the most part beautiful phyctallines, belonging to the actinidian family, and among other species the phyctalis protexta, peculiar to that part of the ocean, with a little cylindrical trunk, ornamented with vertical lines, speckled with red dots, crowning a marvellous blossoming of tentacles. As to the molluscs, they consisted of some I had already observed,—turritellas, olive porphyras, with regular lines intercrossed, with red spots standing out plainly against the flesh; odd peteroceras, like petrified scorpions; translucid hyaleas, argonauts, cuttle-fish (excellent eating), and certain species of calmars that naturalists of antiquity have classed amongst the flying-fish, and that serve principally for bait for cod fishing. I had not an opportunity of studying several species of fish on these shores. Amongst the cartilaginous ones, petromyzons-pricka, a sort of eel, fifteen inches long, with a greenish head, violet fins, gray-blue back, brown belly, silvered and sown with bright spots, the pupil of the eye encircled with gold,—a curious animal, that the current of the Amazon had drawn to the sea, for they inhabit fresh waters,—tuberculated streaks, with pointed snouts, and a long loose tail, armed with a long jagged sting; little sharks, a yard long, gray and whitish skin, and several rows of teeth, bent back, that are generally known by the name of pantouffles; vespertilios, a kind of red isosceles triangle, half a yard long, to which pectorals are attached by fleshy prolongations that make them look like bats, but that their horny appendage, situated near the nostrils, has given them the name of sea-unicorns; lastly, some species of balistæ, the curassavian, whose spots were of a brilliant gold color, and the capriscus of clear violet, and with varying shades like a pigeon's throat.

I end here this catalogue, which is somewhat dry perhaps, but very exact, with a series of bony fish that I observed in passing belonging to the apteronotes, and whose snout is white as snow, the body of a beautiful black, marked with a very long loose fleshy strip; odontognathes, armed with spikes; sardines, nine inches long, glittering with a bright silver light; a species of mackerel provided with two anal fins; centronotes of a blackish tint, that are fished for with torches, long fish, two yards in length, with fat flesh, white and firm, which, when they are fresh, taste like eel, and when dry, like smoked salmon; labres, half red, covered with scales only at the bottom of the dorsal and anal fins; chrysoptera, on which gold and silver blend their brightness with that of the ruby and topaz; golden-tailed spares, the flesh of which is extremely delicate, and whose phosphorescent properties betray them in the midst of the waters; orange-colored spares with a long tongue; maigres, with gold caudal fins, dark thorn-tails, anableps of Surinam, etc.

Notwithstanding this "etcetera," I must not omit to mention fish that Conseil will long remember, and with good reason. One of our nets had hauled up a sort of very flat rayfish, which, with the tail cut off, formed a perfect disk, and weighed twenty ounces. It was white underneath, red above, with large round spots of dark blue encircled with black, very glossy skin, terminating in a bilobed fin. Laid out on the platform, it struggled, tried to turn itself by convulsive movements, and made so many efforts, that one last turn had nearly sent it into the sea. But Conseil, not wishing to let the fish go, rushed to it, and, before I could prevent him, had seized it with both hands. In a moment he was overthrown, his legs in the air, and half his body paralyzed, crying,—

"O master, master! come to me!"

It was the first time the poor boy had not spoken to me in the third person. The Canadian and I took him up, and rubbed his contracted arms till he became sensible. The unfortunate Conseil had attacked a crampfish of the most dangerous kind, the cumana. This odd animal, in a medium conductor like water, strikes fish at several yards' distance, so great is the power of its electric organ, the two principal surfaces of which do not measure less than twenty-seven square feet. The next day, April 12, the *Nautilus* approached the Dutch coast, near the mouth of the Maroni. There several groups of sea-cows herded together; they were manatees, that, like the dugong and the stellera, belong to the sirenian order. These beautiful animals, peaceable and inoffensive, from eighteen to twenty-one feet in length, weigh at least sixteen hundredweight. I told Ned Land and Conseil that provident nature had assigned an important *rôle* to these mammalia. Indeed, they, like the seals, are designed to graze on the submarine prairies, and thus destroy the accumulation of weed that obstructs the tropical rivers.

"And do you know," I added, "what has been the result since men have almost entirely annihilated this useful race? That the putrified weeds have poisoned the air, and the poisoned air causes the yellow fever, that desolates these beautiful countries. Enormous vegetations are multiplied under the torrid seas, and the evil is irresistibly developed from the mouth of the Rio de la Plata to Florida. If we are to believe Toussenel, this plague is nothing to what it would be if the seas were cleared of whales and seals. Then, infested with poulps, medusæ, and cuttle-fish, they would become immense centres of infection, since their waves would not possess 'these vast stomachs that God had charged to infest the surface of the seas.' "

However, without disputing these theories, the crew of the *Nautilus* took possession of half a dozen manatees. They provisioned the larders with excellent flesh, superior to beef and veal. This sport was not interesting. The manatees allowed themselves to be hit without defending themselves. Several thousand pounds of meat were stored up on board to be dried. On this day, a successful haul of fish increased the stores of the *Nautilus,* so full of game were these seas. They were echeneides belonging to the third family of the malacopterygiens; their flattened disks were composed of transverse movable cartilaginous plates, by which the animal was enabled to create a vacuum, and so to adhere to any object like a cupping-glass. The remora that I had observed in the Mediterranean belongs to this species. But the one of which we are speaking was the echeneis osteochera, peculiar to this sea.

The fishing over, the *Nautilus* neared the coast. About here a number of sea-turtles were sleeping on the surface of the water. It would have been difficult to capture these precious reptiles, for the least noise awakens them, and their solid skull is proof against the harpoon. But the echeneis effects their capture with extraordinary precision and certainty. This animal is, indeed, a living fish-hook, which would make the fortune of an inexperienced fisherman. The crew of the *Nautilus* tied a ring to the tail of these fish, so large as not to encumber their movements, and to this ring a long cord, lashed to the ship's side by the other end. The echeneids, thrown into the sea, directly began their game, and fixed themselves to the breastplate of the turtles. Their tenacity was such, that they were torn rather than let go their hold. The men hauled them on board, and with them the turtles to which they adhered. They took also several cacouannes a yard long, which weighed 400 lbs. Their carapace covered with large horny plates, thin, transparent, brown, with white and yellow spots, fetch a good price in the market. Besides, they were excellent in an edible point of view, as well as the fresh turtles, which have an exquisite flavor. This day's fishing brought to a close our stay on the shores of the Amazon, and by nightfall the *Nautilus* had regained the high seas.

CHAPTER 18

THE POULPS

FOR several days the *Nautilus* kept off from the American coast. Evidently it did not wish to risk the tides of the Gulf of Mexico, or of the sea of the Antilles. April 16th, we sighted Martinique and Guadaloupe from a distance of about thirty miles. I saw their tall peaks for an instant. The Canadian, who counted on carrying out his projects in the Gulf, by either landing, or hailing one of the numerous boats that coast from one island to another, was quite disheartened. Flight would have been quite practicable, if Ned Land had been able to take possession of the boat without the captain's knowledge. But in the open sea it could not be thought of. The Canadian, Conseil, and I had a long conversation on this subject. For six months we had been prisoners on board the *Nautilus*. We had travelled 17,000 leagues; and, as Ned Land said, there was no reason why it should not come to an end. We could hope nothing from the captain of the *Nautilus,* but only from ourselves. Besides, for some time past he had become graver, more retired, less sociable. He seemed to shun me. I met him rarely. Formerly, he was pleased to explain the submarine marvels to me; now, he left me to my studies, and came no more to the saloon. What change had come over him? For what cause? For my part, I did not wish to bury with me my curious and novel studies. I had now the power to write the true book of the sea; and this book, sooner or later, I wished to see daylight. Then again, in the water by the Antilles, ten yards below the surface of the waters, by the open panels, what interesting products I had to enter on my daily notes! There were, among other zoöphytes, those known under the name of physalis pelagica, a sort of large oblong bladder with mother-of-pearl rays, holding out their membranes to the wind, and letting their blue tentacles float like threads of silk; charming medusæ to the eye, real nettles to the touch, that distil a corrosive fluid. There were also annelides, a yard and a half long, furnished with a pink horn, and with 1,700 locomotive organs, that wind through the waters, and throw out in passing all the light of the solar spectrum. There were, in the fish category, some Malabar rays, enormous gristly things, ten feet long, weighing 600 pounds, the pectoral fin triangular in the midst of a slightly humped back, the eyes fixed in the extremities of the face, beyond the head, and which floated like weft, and looked sometimes like an opaque shutter on our glass window. There were American balistæ, which nature had only dressed in black and white; gobies, with yellow fins and prominent jaw; mackerel sixteen feet long, with short-pointed teeth, covered with small scales, belonging to the albicore species. Then, in swarms, appeared gray mullet, covered with stripes of gold from the head to the tail, beating their resplendent fins, like masterpieces of jewelry, consecrated formerly to Diana, particularly sought after by rich Romans, and of which the proverb says, "Whoever takes them does not eat them." Lastly, pomacanthe dorees, ornamented with emerald bands, dressed in velvet and silk, passed before our eyes like Veronese lords; spurred spari passed with their pectoral fins; clupanodons fifteen inches long, enveloped in their phosphorescent light; mullet beat the sea with their large jagged tail; red vendaces seemed to mow the waves with their showy pectoral fins; and silvery selenes, worthy of their name, rose on the horizon of the waters like so many moons with whitish rays. April 20th, we had risen to a mean height of 1,500 yards. The land nearest us then was the archipelago of the Bahamas. There rose high submarine cliffs covered with large woods, giant laminariæ and fuci, a perfect espalier of hydrophytes worthy of a Titan world. It was about eleven o'clock when Ned Land drew my attention to a formidable pricking, like the sting of an ant, which was produced by means of large sea-weeds.

"Well," I said, "these are proper caverns for poulps, and I should not be astonished to see some of these monsters."

"What!" said Conseil; "cuttle-fish, real cuttle-fish, of the cephalopod class?"

"No," I said; "poulps of huge dimensions."

"I will never believe that such animals exist," said Ned.

"Well," said Conseil, with the most serious air in the world, "I remember perfectly to have seen a large vessel drawn under the waves by a cephalopod's arm."

"You saw that?" said the Canadian.

"Yes, Ned."

"With your own eyes?"

"With my own eyes."

"Where, pray, might that be?"

"At St. Malo," answered Conseil.

"In the port?" said Ned, ironically.

"No; in a church," replied Conseil.

"In a church!" cried the Canadian.

"Yes; friend Ned. In a picture representing the poulp in question."

"Good!" said Ned Land, bursting our laughing.

"He is quite right," I said. "I have heard of this picture; but the subject represented is taken from a legend, and you know what to think of legends in the matter of natural history. Besides, when it is a question of monsters, the imagination is apt to run wild. Not only is it supposed that these poulps can draw down vessels, but a certain Olaüs Magnus speaks of a cephalopod a mile long, that is more like an island than an animal. It is also said that the Bishop of Nidros was building an altar on an immense rock. Mass finished, the rock began to walk, and returned to the sea. The rock was a poulp. Another bishop, Pontoppidan, speaks also of a poulp on which a regiment of cavalry could manœuvre. Lastly, the ancient naturalists speak of monsters whose mouths were like gulfs, and which were too large to pass through the Straits of Gibraltar."

"But how much is true of these stories?" asked Conseil.

"Nothing, my friends; at least of that which passes the limit of truth to get to fable or legend. Nevertheless, there must be some ground for the imagination of the story-tellers. One cannot deny that poulps and cuttle-fish exist of a large species, inferior, however, to the cetaceans. Aristotle has stated the dimensions of a cuttle-fish as five cubits, or nine feet two inches. Our fishermen frequently see some that are more than four feet long. Some skeletons of poulps are preserved in the museums of Trieste and Montpelier, that measure two yards in length. Besides, according to the calculations of some naturalists, one of these animals, only six feet long, would have tentacles twenty-seven feet long. That would suffice to make a formidable monster."

"Do they fish for them in these days?" asked Ned.

"If they do not fish for them, sailors see them at least. One of my friends, Captain Paul Bos of Havre, has often affirmed that he met one of these monsters, of colossal dimensions, in the Indian seas. But the most astonishing fact, and which does not permit of the denial of the existence of these gigantic animals, happened some years ago, in 1861."

"What is the fact?" asked Ned Land.

"This is it. In 1861, to the northeast of Teneriffe, very nearly in the same latitude we are in now, the crew of the despatch-boat *Alector* perceived a monstrous cuttle-fish swimming in the waters. Captain Bouguer went near to the animal, and attacked it with harpoons and guns, without much success, for balls and harpoons glided over the soft flesh. After several fruitless attempts, the crew tried to pass a slip-knot round the body of the mollusc. The noose slipped as far as the caudal fins, and there stopped. They tried then to haul it on board, but its weight was so considerable that the tightness of the cord separated the tail from the body, and, deprived of this ornament, he disappeared under the water."

"Indeed! is that a fact?"

"An indisputable fact, my good Ned. They proposed to name this poulp 'Bouguer's cuttle-fish.' "

"What length was it?" asked the Canadian.

"Did it not measure about six yards?" said Conseil, who, posted at the window, was examining again the irregular windings of the cliff.

"Precisely," I replied.

"Its head," rejoined Conseil, "was it not crowned with eight tentacles, that beat the water like a nest of serpents?"

"Precisely."

"Had not its eyes, placed at the back of its head, considerable development?"

"Yes, Conseil."

"And was not its mouth like a parrot's beak?"

"Exactly, Conseil."

"Very well! no offence to master," he replied, quietly; "if this is not Bouguerr's cuttle-fish, it is, at least, one of its brothers."

I looked at Conseil. Ned Land hurried to the window.

"What a horrible beast!" he cried.

I looked in my turn, and could not repress a gesture of disgust. Before my eyes was a horrible monster, worthy to figure in the legends of the marvellous. It was an immense cuttle-fish, being eight yards long. It swam crossways in the direction of the *Nautilus* with great speed, watching us with its enormous staring

green eyes. Its eight arms, or rather feet, fixed to its head, that have given the name of cephalopod to these animals, were twice as long as its body, and were twisted like the Furies' hair. One could see the 250 air-holes on the inner side of the tentacles. The monster's mouth, a horned beak like a parrot's, opened and shut vertically. Its tongue, a horned substance, furnished with several rows of pointed teeth, came out quivering from this veritable pair of shears. What a freak of nature, a bird's beak on a mollusc! Its spindle-like body formed a fleshy mass that might weigh 4,000 to 5,000 lbs.; the varying color changing with great rapidity, according to the irritation of the animal, passed successively from livid gray to reddish brown. What irritated this mollusc? No doubt the presence of the *Nautilus,* more formidable than itself, and on which its suckers or its jaws had no hold. Yet, what monsters these poulps are! what vitality the Creator has given them! what vigor in their movements! and they possess three hearts! Chance had brought us in presence of this cuttle-fish, and I did not wish to lose the opportunity of carefully studying this specimen of cephalopods. I overcame the horror that inspired me; and, taking a pencil, began to draw it.

"Perhaps this is the same which the *Alector* saw," said Conseil.

"No," replied the Canadian; "for this is whole, and the other had lost its tail."

"That is no reason," I replied. "The arms and tails of these animals are reformed by redintegration; and, in seven years, the tail of Bouguer's cuttle-fish has no doubt had time to grow."

By this time other poulps appeared at the port light. I counted seven. They formed a procession after the *Nautilus,* and I heard their beaks gnashing against the iron hull. I continued my work. These monsters kept in the water with such precision, that they seemed immovable. Suddenly the *Nautilus* stopped. A shock made it tremble in every plate.

"Have we struck anything?" I asked.

"In any case," replied the Canadian, "we shall be free, for we are floating."

The *Nautilus* was floating, no doubt, but it did not move. A minute passed. Captain Nemo, followed by his lieutenant, entered the drawing-room. I had not seen him for some time. He seemed dull. Without noticing or speaking to us, he went to the panel, looked at the poulps, and said something to his lieutenant. The latter went out. Soon the panels were shut. The ceiling was lighted. I went towards the captain.

"A curious collection of poulps?" I said.

"Yes, indeed, Mr. Naturalist," he replied; "and we are going to fight them, man to beast."

I looked at him. I thought I had not heard aright.

"Man to beast?" I repeated.

"Yes, sir. The screw is stopped. I think that the horny jaw of one of the cuttle-fish is entangled in the blades. That is what prevents our moving."

"What are you going to do?"

"Rise to the surface, and slaughter this vermin."

"A difficult enterprise."

"Yes, indeed. The electric bullets are powerless against the soft flesh, where they do not find resistance enough to go off. But we shall attack them with the hatchet."

"And the harpoon, sir," said the Canadian, "if you do not refuse my help."

"I will accept it, Master Land."

"We will follow you," I said; and following Captain Nemo, we went towards the central staircase.

There, about ten men with boarding hatchets were ready for the attack. Conseil and I took two hatchets; Ned Land seized a harpoon. The *Nautilus* had then risen to the surface. One of the sailors, posted on the top ladder step, unscrewed the bolts of the panels. But hardly were the screws loosed, when the panel rose with great violence, evidently drawn by the suckers of a poulp's arm. Immediately one of these arms slid like a serpent down the opening, and twenty others were above. With one blow of the axe, Captain Nemo cut this formidable tentacle, that slid wriggling down the ladder. Just as we were pressing one on the other to reach the platform, two other arms, lashing the air, came down on the seaman placed before Captain Nemo, and lifted him up with irresistible power. Captain Nemo uttered a cry, and rushed out. We hurried after him.

What a scene! The unhappy man, seized by the tentacle, and fixed to the suckers, was balanced in the air at the caprice of this enormous trunk. He rattled in his throat, he was stifled, he cried, "Help! help!" These words, *spoken in French,* startled me! I had a fellow-countryman on board, perhaps several! That heart-rending cry! I shall hear it all my life. The unfortunate man was lost. Who could rescue him from that powerful pressure? However, Captain Nemo had rushed to the poulp, and with one blow of the axe had cut through one arm. His lieutenant struggled furiously against other monsters that crept on the flanks of the *Nautilus*. The crew fought with their axes. The Canadian, Conseil, and I buried our weapons in the fleshy masses; a strong smell of musk penetrated the atmosphere. It was horrible!

For one instant, I thought the unhappy man entangled with the poulp would be torn from its powerful suction. Seven of the eight arms had been cut off. One only wriggled in the air, brandishing the victim like a feather. But just as Captain Nemo and his lieutenant threw themselves on it, the animal ejected a stream of black liquid. We were blinded with it. When the cloud dispersed, the cuttle-fish had disappeared, and my unfortunate countryman with it. Ten or twelve poulps now invaded the platform and sides of the *Nautilus*. We rolled pell-mell into the midst of this nest of serpents, that wriggled on the platform in the waves of blood and ink. It seemed as though these slimy tentacles sprang up like the hydra's heads. Ned Land's harpoon, at each stroke, was plunged into the staring eyes of the cuttle-fish. But my bold companion was suddenly overturned by the tentacles of a monster he had not been able to avoid.

Ah! how my heart beat with emotion and horror! The formidable beak of a cuttle-fish was open over Ned Land. The unhappy man would be cut in two. I rushed to his succor. But Captain Nemo was before me; his axe disappeared between the two enormous jaws, and, miraculously saved, the Canadian, rising, plunged his harpoon deep into the triple heart of the poulp.

"I owed myself this revenge!" said the captain to the Canadian.

Ned bowed without replying. The combat had lasted a quarter of an hour. The monsters, vanquished and mutilated, left us at last, and disappeared under the waves. Captain Nemo, covered with blood, nearly exhausted, gazed upon the sea that had swallowed up one of his companions, and great tears gathered in his eyes.

Only one of its arms wriggled in the air, brandishing the victim like a feather.

CHAPTER 19

THE GULF STREAM

THIS terrible scene of the 20th of April none of us can ever forget. I have written it under the influence of violent emotion. Since then I have revised the recital; I have read it to Conseil and to the Canadian. They found it exact as to facts, but insufficient as to effect. To paint such pictures, one must have the pen of the most illustrious of our poets, the author of "The Toilers of the Deep."

I have said that Captain Nemo wept while watching the waves; his grief was great. It was the second companion he had lost since our arrival on board, and what a death! That friend, crushed, stifled, bruised by the dreadful arms of a poulp, pounded by his iron jaws, would not rest with his comrades in the peaceful coral cemetery! In the midst of the struggle, it was the despairing cry uttered by the unfortunate man that had torn my heart. The poor Frenchman, forgetting his conventional language, had taken to his own mother tongue, to utter a last appeal! Amongst the crew of the *Nautilus,* associated with the body and soul of the captain, recoiling like him from all contact with men, I had a fellow-countryman. Did he alone represent France in this mysterious association, evidently composed of individuals of divers nationalities? It was one of these insoluble problems that rose up unceasingly before my mind!

Captain Nemo entered his room, and I saw him no more for some time. But that he was sad and irresolute I could see by the vessel, of which he was the soul, and which received all his impressions. The *Nautilus* did not keep on in its settled course; it floated about like a corpse at the will of the waves. It went at random. He could not tear himself away from the scene of the last struggle, from this sea that had devoured one of his men. Ten days passed thus. It was not till the 1st of May that the *Nautilus* resumed its northerly course, after having sighted the Bahamas at the mouth of the Bahama Canal. We were then following the current from the largest river to the sea, that has its banks, its fish, and its proper temperatures. I mean the Gulf Stream. It is really a river, that flows freely to the middle of the Atlantic, and whose waters do not mix with the ocean waters. It is a salt river, salter than the surrounding sea. Its mean depth is 1,500 fathoms, its mean breadth ten miles. In certain places the current flows with the speed of two miles and a half an hour. The body of its waters is more considerable than that of all the rivers in the globe. It was on this ocean river that the *Nautilus* then sailed.

This current carried with it all kinds of living things. Argonauts, so common in the Mediterranean, were there in quantities. Of the gristly sort, the most remarkable were the turbot, whose slender tails form nearly the third part of the body, and that looked like large lozenges twenty-five feet long; also, small sharks a yard long, with large heads, short rounded muzzles, pointed teeth in several rows, and whose bodies seemed covered with scales. Among the bony fish I noticed some gray gobies, peculiar to these waters; black giltheads, whose iris shone like fire; sirenes a yard long, with large snouts thickly set with little teeth, that uttered little cries; blue coryphænes, in gold and silver; parrots, like the rainbows of the ocean, that could rival in color the most beautiful tropical birds;

blennies with triangular heads; bluish rhombs destitute of scales; batrachoides covered with yellow transversal bands like a Greek τ; heaps of little gobies spotted with yellow; dipterodons with silvery heads and yellow tails; several specimens of salmon, mugilomores slender in shape, shining with a soft light that Lacépède consecrated to the service of his wife; and lastly, a beautiful fish, the American-knight, that, decorated with all the orders and ribbons, frequents the shores of this great nation, that esteems orders and ribbons so little.

I must add that, during the night, the phosphorescent waters of the Gulf Stream rivalled the electric power of our watch-light, especially in the stormy weather that threatened us so frequently. May 8th, we were still crossing Cape Hatteras, at the height of the North Caroline. The width of the Gulf Stream there is seventy-five miles, and its depth 210 yards. The *Nautilus* still went at random; all supervision seemed abandoned. I thought that, under these circumstances, escape would be possible. Indeed, the inhabited shores offered anywhere an easy refuge. The sea was incessantly ploughed by the steamers that ply between New York or Boston and the Gulf of Mexico, and overrun day and night by the little schooners coasting about the several parts of the American coast. We could hope to be picked up. It was a favorable opportunity, notwithstanding the thirty miles that separated the *Nautilus* from the coasts of the Union. One unfortunate circumstance thwarted the Canadian's plans. The weather was very bad. We were nearing those shores where tempests are so frequent, that country of waterspouts and cyclones actually engendered by the current of the Gulf Stream. To tempt the sea in a frail boat was certain destruction. Ned Land owned this himself. He fretted, seized with nostalgia that flight only could cure.

"Master," he said that day to me, "this must come to an end. I must make a clean breast of it. This Nemo is leaving land and going up to the north. But I declare to you, I have had enough of the South Pole, and I will not follow him to the North."

"What is to be done, Ned, since flight is impracticable just now?"

"We must speak to the captain," said he; "you said nothing when we were in your native seas. I will speak, now we are in mine. When I think that before long the *Nautilus* will be by Nova Scotia, and that there near Newfoundland is a large bay, and into that bay the St. Lawrence empties itself, and that the St. Lawrence is my river, the river by Quebec, my native town,—when I think of this I feel furious, it makes my hair stand on end. Sir, I would rather throw myself into the sea! I will not stay here! I am stifled!"

The Canadian was evidently losing all patience. His vigorous nature could not stand this prolonged imprisonment. His face altered daily; his temper became more surly. I knew what he must suffer, for I was seized with nostalgia myself. Nearly seven months had passed without our having had any news from land; Captain Nemo's isolation, his altered spirits, especially since the fight with the poulps, his taciturnity, all made me view things in a different light.

"Well, sir?" said Ned, seeing I did not reply.

"Well, Ned! do you wish me to ask Captain Nemo his intentions concerning us?"

"Yes, sir."

"Although he has already made them known?"

"Yes; I wish it settled finally. Speak for me, in my name only, if you like."

"But I so seldom meet him. He avoids me."

"That is all the more reason for you to go to see him."

I went to my room. From thence I meant to go to Captain Nemo's. It would not do to let this opportunity of meeting him slip. I knocked at the door. No answer. I knocked again, then turned the handle. The door opened, I went in. The captain was there. Bending over his work-table, he had not heard me. Resolved not to go without having spoken, I approached him. He raised his head quickly, frowned, and said roughly, "You here! What do you want?"

"To speak to you, Captain."

"But I am busy, sir; I am working. I leave you at liberty to shut yourself up; cannot I be allowed the same?"

This reception was not encouraging; but I was determined to hear and answer everything.

"Sir," I said, coldly, "I have to speak to you on a matter that admits of no delay."

"What is that, sir?" he replied, ironically. "Have you discovered something that has escaped me, or has the sea delivered up any new secrets?"

We were at cross-purposes. But before I could reply, he showed me an open manuscript on his table, and said, in a more serious tone, "Here, M. Aronnax, is a manuscript written in several languages. It contains the sum of my studies of the sea; and, if it please God, it shall not perish with me. This manuscript, signed with my name, completed with the history of my life, will be shut up in a little insubmersible case. The last survivor of all of us on board the *Nautilus* will throw this case into the sea, and it will go whither it is borne by the waves."

This man's name! his history written by himself! His mystery would then be revealed some day.

"Captain," I said, "I can but approve of the idea that makes you act thus. The result of your studies must not be lost. But the means you employ seem to me to be primitive. Who knows where the winds will carry this case, and in whose hands it will fall? Could you not use some other means? Could not you, or one of yours—"

"Never, sir!" he said, hastily interrupting me.

"But I and my companions are ready to keep this manuscript in store; and, if you will put us at liberty—"

"At liberty?" said the captain, rising.

"Yes, sir; that is the subject on which I wish to question you. For seven months we have been here on board, and I ask you to-day, in the name of my companions, and in my own, if your intention is to keep us here always?"

"M. Aronnax, I will answer you to-day as I did seven months ago; whoever enters the *Nautilus* must never quit it."

"You impose actual slavery on us!"

"Give it what name you please."

"But everywhere the slave has the right to regain his liberty."

"Who denies you this right? Have I ever tried to chain you with an oath?"

He looked at me with his arms crossed.

"Sir," I said, "to return a second time to this subject will be neither to your nor to my taste; but as we have entered upon it, let us go through with it. I repeat, it is not only myself whom it concerns. Study is to me a relief, a diversion, a passion that could make me forget everything. Like you, I am willing to live obscure in the frail hope of bequeathing one day, to future time, the result of my labors. But it is otherwise with Ned Land. Every man, worthy of the name, deserves some consideration. Have you thought that love of liberty, hatred of slavery, can give rise to schemes of revenge in a nature like the Canadian's; that he could think, attempt, and try—"

I was silenced; Captain Nemo rose.

"Whatever Ned Land thinks of, attempts, or tries, what does it matter to me? I did not seek him! It is not for my pleasure that I keep him on board! As for you, M. Aronnax, you are one of those who can understand everything, even silence. I have nothing more to say to you. Let this first time you have come to treat of this subject be the last; for a second time I will not listen to you."

I retired. Our situation was critical. I related my conversation to my two companions.

"We know now," said Ned, "that we can expect nothing from this man. The *Nautilus* is nearing Long Island. We will escape, whatever the weather may be."

But the sky became more and more threatening. Symptoms of a hurricane became manifest. The atmosphere was becoming white and misty. On the horizon fine streaks of cirrhous clouds were succeeded by masses of cumuli. Other low clouds passed swiftly by. The swollen sea rose in huge billows. The birds disappeared, with the exception of the petrels, those friends of the storm. The barometer fell sensibly, and indicated an extreme tension of the vapors. The mixture of the storm-glass was decomposed under the influence of the electricity that pervaded the atmosphere. The tempest burst on the 18th of May, just as the *Nautilus* was floating off Long Island, some miles from the port of New York. I can describe this strife of the elements! for, instead of fleeing to the depths of the sea, Captain Nemo, by an unaccountable caprice, would brave it at the surface. The wind blew from the southwest at first. Captain Nemo, during the squalls, had taken his place on the platform. He had made himself fast, to prevent being washed overboard by the monstrous waves. I had hoisted myself up, and made myself fast also, dividing my admiration between the tempest and this extraordinary man who was coping with it. The raging sea was swept by huge cloud-drifts, which were actually saturated with the waves. The *Nautilus,* sometimes lying on its side, sometimes standing up like a mast, rolled and pitched terribly. About five o'clock a torrent of rain fell, that lulled neither sea nor wind. The hurricane blew nearly forty leagues an hour. It is under these conditions that it overturns houses, breaks iron gates, displaces twenty-four pounders. However, the *Nautilus,* in the midst of the tempest, confirmed the words of a clever engineer, "There is no well-constructed hull that cannot defy the sea." This was not a resisting rock; it was a steel spindle, obedient and movable, without rigging or masts, that braved its fury with impunity. However, I watched these raging waves attentively. They measured fifteen feet in height, and 150 to 175 yards long, and their speed of propagation was thirty feet per second. Their bulk and power increased with the depth of the water. Such waves as these at the Hebrides have displaced a mass weighing 8,400 lbs. They are they which, in the tempest of December 23, 1864, after destroying the town of Yeddo, in Japan, broke the same day on the shores of America. The intensity of the tempest increased with the night. The barometer, as in 1860 at Reunion during a cyclone, fell seven tenths at the close of day. I saw a large vessel pass the horizon struggling painfully. She was trying to lie to under half steam, to keep up above the waves. It was probably one of the steamers of the line from New York to Liverpool, or Havre. It soon disappeared in the gloom. At ten o'clock in the evening the sky was on fire. The atmosphere was streaked with vivid lightning.

I could not bear the brightness of it; while the captain, looking at it, seemed to envy the spirit of the tempest. A terrible noise filled the air, a complex noise, made up of the howls of the crushed waves, the roaring of the wind, and the claps of thunder. The wind veered suddenly to all points of the horizon; and the cyclone, rising in the east, returned after passing by the north, west, and south, in the inverse course pursued by the circular storms of the southern hemisphere. Ah, that Gulf Stream! It deserves its name of the King of Tempests. It is that which causes those formidable cyclones, by the difference of temperature between its air and its currents. A shower of fire had succeeded the rain. The drops of water were changed to sharp spikes. One would have thought that Captain Nemo was courting a death worthy of himself, a death by lightning. As the *Nautilus,* pitching dreadfully, raised its steel spur in the air, it seemed to act as a conductor, and I saw long sparks burst from it. Crushed and without strength, I crawled to the panel, opened it, and descended to the saloon. The storm was then at its height. It was impossible to stand upright in the interior of the *Nautilus*. Captain Nemo came down about twelve. I heard the reservoirs filling by degrees, and the *Nautilus* sank slowly beneath the waves. Through the open windows in the saloon I saw large fish, terrified, passing like phantoms in the water. Some were struck before my eyes. The *Nautilus* was still descending. I thought that at about eight fathoms deep we should find a calm. But no! the upper beds were too violently agitated for that. We had to seek repose at more than twenty-five fathoms in the bowels of the deep. But there, what quiet, what silence, what peace! Who could have told that such a hurricane had been let loose on the surface of that ocean?

CHAPTER 20

FROM LATITUDE 47° 24′ TO LONGITUDE 17° 28′

In consequence of the storm, we had been thrown eastward once more. All hope of escape on the shores of New York or St. Lawrence had faded away; and poor Ned, in despair, had isolated himself like Captain Nemo. Conseil and I, however, never left each other. I said that the *Nautilus* had gone aside to the east. I should have said (to be more exact), the northeast. For some days it wandered, first on the surface, and then beneath it, amid those fogs so dreaded by sailors. What accidents are due to these thick fogs! What shocks upon these reefs when the wind drowns the breaking of the waves! What colisions between vessels, in spite of their warning lights, whistles, and alarm-bells! And the bottoms of these seas look like a field of battle, where still lie all the conquered of the ocean; some old and already incrusted, others fresh and reflecting from their iron bands and copper plates the brilliancy of our lantern.

On the 15th of May we were at the extreme south of the Bank of Newfoundland. This bank consists of alluvia, or large heaps of organic matter, brought either from the Equator by the Gulf Stream, or from the North Pole by the counter-current of cold water which skirts the American coast. There also are heaped up those erratic blocks which are carried along by the broken ice; and close by, a vast charnel-houose of molluscs or zoöphytes, which perish here by millions. The depth of the sea is not great at Newfoundland,—not more than some hundreds of fathoms; but towards the south is a depression of 1,500 fathoms. There the Gulf Stream widens. It loses some of its speed and some of its temperature, but it becomes a sea.

It was on the 17th of May, about 500 miles from Heart's Content, at a depth of more than 1,400 fathoms, that I saw the electric cable lying on the bottom. Conseil, to whom I had not mentioned it, thought at first that it was a gigantic sea-serpent. But I undeceived the worthy fellow, and by way of consolation related several particulars in the laying of this cable. The first one was laid in the years 1857 and 1858; but, after transmitting about 400 telegrams, would not act any longer. In 1863, the engineers constructed another one, measuring 2,000 miles in length, and weighing 4,500 tons, which was embarked on the *Great Eastern*. This attempt also failed.

On the 25th of May the *Nautilus,* being at a depth of more than 1,918 fathoms, was on the precise spot where the rupture occurred which ruined the enterprise. It was within 638 miles of the coast of Ireland; and at half past two in the afternoon they discovered that communication with Europe had ceased. The electricians on board resolved to cut the cable before fishing it up, and at eleven o'clock at night they had recovered the damaged part. They made another point and spliced it, and it was once more submerged. But some days after it broke again, and in the depths of the ocean could not be recaptured. The Americans, however, were not discouraged. Cyrus Field, the bold promoter of the enterprise, as he had sunk all his own fortune, set a new subscription on foot, which was at once answered, and another cable was constructed on better principles. The bundles of conducting wires were each enveloped in gutta-percha, and protected by a wadding of hemp, contained in a metallic covering. The *Great Eastern* sailed on the 13th of July, 1866. The operation worked well. But one incident occurred. Several times in unrolling the cable they observed that nails had been recently forced into it, evidently with the motive of destroying it. Captain Anderson, the officers and engineers, consulted together, and had it posted up that if the offender was surprised on board, he would be thrown without further trial into the sea. From that time the criminal attempt was never repeated.

On the 23d of July the *Great Eastern* was not more than 500 miles from Newfoundland, when they telegraphed from Ireland news of the armistice concluded between Prussia and Austria after Sadowa. On the 27th, in the midst of heavy fogs, they reached the port of Heart's Content. The enterprise was successfully terminated; and for its first despatch young America addressed old Europe in these words of wisdom so rarely understood,—"Glory to God in the highest, and on earth peace, good-will towards men."

I did not expect to find the electric cable in its primitive state, such as it was on leaving the manufactory. The long serpent, covered with the remains of shells, bristling with foraminiferæ, was incrusted with a strong coating which served as a protection against all boring molluscs. It lay quietly sheltered from the motions of the sea, and under a favorable pressure for the transmission of the electric spark which passes from Europe to America in .32 of a second. Doubtless this cable will last for a great length of time, for they find that the gutta-percha covering is improved by the sea-water. Besides, on this level, so well chosen, the cable is never so deeply submerged as to cause it to break. The

Nautilus followed it to the lowest depth, which was more than 2,212 fathoms, and there it lay without any anchorage; and then we reached the spot where the accident had taken place in 1863. The bottom of the ocean then formed a valley about 100 miles broad, in which Mont-Blanc might have been placed without its summit appearing above the waves. This valley is closed at the east by a perpendicular wall more than 2,000 yards high. We arrived thee on the 28th of May, and the *Nautilus* was then not more than 120 miles from Ireland.

Was Captain Nemo going to land on the British Isles? No. To my great surprise he made for the south, once more coming back towards European seas. In rounding the Emerald Isle, for one instant I caught sight of Cape Clear, and the light which guides the thousands of vessels leaving Glasgow or Liverpool. An important question then arose in my mind. Did the *Nautilus* dare entangle itself in the Mauch? Ned Land, who had reappeared since we had been nearing land, did not cease to question me. How could I answer? Captain Nemo remained invisible. After having shown the Canadian a glimpse of American shores, was he going to show me the coast of France?

But the *Nautilus* was still going southward. On the 30th of May, it passed in sight of the Land's End, between the extreme point of England and the Scilly Isles, which were left to starboard. If he wished to enter the Mauch he must go straight to the east. He did not do so.

During the whole of the 31st of May, the *Nautilus* described a series of circles on the water, which greatly interested me. It seemed to be seeking a spot it had some trouble in finding. At noon, Captain Nemo himself came to work the ship's log. He spoke no word to me, but seemed gloomier than ever. What could sadden him thus? Wat it his proximity to European shores? Had he some recollections of his abandoned country? If not, what did he feel? Remorse or regret? For a long while this thought haunted my mind, and I had a kind of presentiment that before long chance would betray the captain's secrets.

The next day, the 1st of June, the *Nautilus* continued the same process. It was evidently seeking some particular spot in the ocean. Captain Nemo took the sun's altitude as he had done the day before. The sea was beautiful, the sky clear. About eight miles to the east, a large steam-vessel could be discerned on the horizon. No flag fluttered from its mast, and I could not discover its nationality. Some minutes before the sun passed the meridian, Captain Nemo took his sextant, and watched with great attention. The perfect rest of the water greatly helped the operation. The *Nautilus* was motionless; it neither rolled nor pitched.

I was on the platform when the altitude was taken, and the captain pronounced these words,—"It is here."

He turned and went below. Had he seen the vessel which was changing its course and seemed to be nearing us? I could not tell. I returned to the saloon. The panels closed, I heard the hissing of the water in the reservoirs. The *Nautilus* began to sink, following a vertical line, for its screw communicated no motion to it. Some minutes later it stopped at a depth of more than 420 fathoms, resting on the ground. The luminous ceiling was darkened, then the panels were opened, and through the glass I saw the sea brilliantly illuminated by the rays of our lantern for at least half a mile round us.

I looked to the port side, and saw nothing but an immensity of quiet waters. But to starboard, on the bottom appeared a large protuberance, which at once attracted my attention. One would have thought it a ruin buried under a coating of white shells, much resembling a covering of snow. Upon examining the mass attentively, I could recognize the ever-thickening form of a vessel bare of its masts, which must have sunk. It certainly belonged to past times. This wreck, to be thus incrusted with the lime of the water, must already be able to count many years passed at the bottom of the ocean.

What was this vessel? Why did the *Nautilus* visit its tomb? Could it have been aught but a shipwreck which had drawn it under the water? I knew not what to think, when near me in a slow voice I heard Captain Nemo say,—

"At one time this ship was called the *Marseillais*. It carried seventy-four guns, and was launched in 1762. In 1778, the 13th of August, commanded by La Poype-Vertrieux, it fought boldly against the *Preston*. In 1779, on the 4th of July, it was at the taking of the Grenada, with the squadron of Admiral Estaing. In 1781, on the 5th of September, it took part in the battle of Comte de Grasse, in Chesapeake Bay. In 1794, the French Republic changed its name. On the 16th of April, in the same year, it joined the squadron of Villaret Joyeuse, at Brest, being intrusted with the escort of a cargo of corn coming from America, under the command of Admiral Van Stabel. On the 11th and 12th Prairal of the second year, this squadron fell in with an English vessel. Sir, to-day is the 13th Prairal, the 1st of June, 1868. It is now seventy-four years ago, day for day on this very spot, in latitude 47° 24′, longitude 17° 28′, that this vessel, after fighting heroically, losing its three masts, with the water in its hold, and the third of its crew disabled, preferred sinking with its 356 sailors to surrendering; and nailing its colors to the poop, disappeared under the waves to the cry of 'Long live the Republic!' "

"The *Avenger!*" I exclaimed.

"Yes, sir, the *Avenger!* A good name!" muttered Captain Nemo, crossing his arms.

CHAPTER 21

A HECATOMB

THE way of describing this unlooked-for scene, the history of the patriot ship, told at first so coldly, and the emotion with which this strange man pronounced the last words, the name of the *Avenger,* the significance of which could not escape me, all impressed itself deeply on my mind. My eyes did not leave the captain; who, with his hand stretched out to sea, was watching with a glowing eye the glorious wreck. Perhaps I was never to know who he was, from whence he came, or where he was going to, but I saw the man move, and apart from the savant. It was no common misanthropy which had shut Captain Nemo and his companions within the *Nautilus,* but a hatred, either monstrous or sublime, which time could never weaken. Did this hatred still seek for vengeance? The future would soon teach me that. But the *Nautilus* was rising slowly to the surface of the sea, and the form of the *Avenger* disappeared by degrees from my sight. Soon a slight rolling told me that we were in the open air. At that moment a dull boom was heard. I looked at the captain. He did not move.

"Captain?" said I.

He did not answer. I left him and mounted the platform. Conseil and the Canadian were already there.

"Where did that sound come from?" I asked.

"It was a gunshot," replied Ned Land.

I looked in the direction of the vessel I had already seen. It was nearing the *Nautilus,* and we could see that it was putting on steam. It was within six miles of us.

"What is that ship, Ned?"

"By its rigging, and the height of its lower masts," said the Canadian, "I bet she is a ship of war. May it reach us; and, if necessary, sink this cursed *Nautilus.*"

"Friend Ned," replied Conseil, "what harm can it do to the *Nautilus?* Can it attack it beneath the waves? Can it cannonade us at the bottom of the sea?"

"Tell me, Ned," said I, "can you recognize what country she belongs to?"

The Canadian knitted his eyebrows, dropped his eyelids, and screwed up the corners of his eyes, and for a few moments fixed a piercing look upon the vessel.

"No, sir," he replied; "I cannot tell what nation she belongs to, for she shows no colors. But I can declare she is a man-of-war, for a long pennant flutters from her main-mast."

For a quarter of an hour we watched the ship which was steaming towards us. I could not, however, believe that she could see the *Nautilus* from that distance, and still less that she could know what this submarine engine was. Soon the Canadian informed me that she was a large armored two-decker ram. A thick black smoke was pouring from her two funnels. Her closely furled sails were stopped to her yards. She hoisted no flag at her mizzen-peak. The distance prevented us from distinguishing the colors of her pennant, which floated like a thin ribbon. She advanced rapidly. If Captain Nemo allowed her to approach, there was a chance of salvation for us.

"Sir," said Ned Land, "if that vessel passes within a mile of us, I shall throw myself into the sea, and I should advise you to do the same."

I did not reply to the Canadian's suggestion, but continued watching the ship. Whether English, French, American, or Russian, she would be sure to take us in if we could only reach her. Presently a white smoke burst from the forepart of the vessel; some seconds after the water, agitated by the fall of a heavy body, splashed the stern of the *Nautilus,* and shortly afterwards a loud explosion struck my ear.

"What! they are firing at us!" I exclaimed.

"So please you, sir," said Ned, "they have recognized the unicorn, and they are firing at us."

"But," I exclaimed, "surely they can see that there are men in the case?"

"It is, perhaps, because of that," replied Ned Land, looking at me.

A whole flood of light burst upon my mind. Doubtless they knew now how to believe the stories of the pretended monster. No doubt, on board the *Abraham Lincoln,* when the Canadian struck it with the harpoon, Commander Farragut had recognized in the supposed narwhal a submarine vessel, more dangerous than a supernatural cetacean. Yes, it must have been so; and on every sea they were now seeking this engine of destruction. Terrible indeed! if, as we supposed, Captain Nemo employed the *Nautilus* in works of vengeance. On the night when we were imprisoned in that cell, in the midst of the Indian Ocean, had he not

"The *Avenger!*" I exclaimed.

attacked some vessel? The man buried in the coral cemetery, had he not been a victim to the shock caused by the *Nautilus*? Yes, I repeat it, it must be so. One part of the mysterious existence of Captain Nemo had been unveiled; and, if his identity had not been recognized, at least, the nations united against him were no longer hunting a chimerical creature, but a man who had vowed a deadly hatred against them. All the formidable past rose before me. Instead of meeting friends on board the approaching ship, we could only expect pitiless enemies. But the shot rattled about us. Some of them struck the sea and ricochetted, losing themselves in the distance. But none touched the *Nautilus*. The vessel was not more than three miles from us. In spite of the serious cannonade, Captain Nemo did not appear on the platform; but, if one of the conical projectiles had struck the shell of the *Nautilus,* it would have been fatal. The Canadian then said, "Sir, we must do all we can to get out of this dilemma. Let us signal them. They will then, perhaps, understand that we are honest folks."

Ned Land took his handkerchief to wave in the air; but he had scarcely displayed it, when he was struck down by an iron hand, and fell, in spite of his great strength, upon the deck.

"Fool!" exclaimed the captain, "do you wish to be pierced by the spur of the *Nautilus* before it is hurled at this vessel?"

Captain Nemo was terrible to hear; he was still more terrible to see. His face was deadly pale, with a spasm at his heart. For an instant it must have ceased to beat. His pupils were fearfully contracted. He did not *speak,* he *roared,* as, with his body thrown forward, he wrung the Canadian's shoulders. Then, leaving him, and turning to the ship of war, whose shot was still raining around him, he exclaimed, with a powerful voice, "Ah, ship of an accursed nation, you know who I am! I do not want your colors to know you by! Look! and I will show you mine!"

And on the forepart of the platform Captain Nemo unfurled a black flag, similar to the one he had placed at the South Pole. At that moment a shot struck the shell of the *Nautilus* obliquely, without piercing it; and, rebounding near the captain, was lost in the sea. He shrugged his shoulders; and addressing me, said shortly, "Go down, you and your companions, go down!"

"Sir," I exclaimed, "are you going to attack this vessel?"

"Sir, I am going to sink it."

"You will not do that?"

"I shall do it," he replied, coldly. "And I advise you not to judge me, sir. Fate has shown you what you ought not to have seen. The attack has begun; go down."

"What is this vessel?"

"You do not know? Very well! so much the better! its nationality to you, at least, will be a secret. Go down!"

We could but obey. About fifteen of the sailors surrounded the captain, looking with implacable hatred at the vessel nearing them. One could feel that the same desire of vengeance animated every soul. I went down at the moment another projectile struck the *Nautilus,* and I heard the captain exclaim,—

"Strike, mad vessel! Shower your useless shot! And then, you will not escape the spur of the *Nautilus*. But it is not here that you shall perish! I would not have your ruins mingle with those of the *Avenger!*"

I reached my room. The captain and his second had remained on the platform. The screw was set in motion, and the *Nautilus,* moving with speed, was soon beyond the reach of the ship's guns. But the pursuit continued, and Captain Nemo contented himself with keeping his distance.

About four in the afternoon, being no longer able to contain my impatience, I went to the central staircase. The panel was open, and I ventured on to the platform. The captain was still walking up and down with an agitated step. He was looking at the ship, which was five or six miles to leeward.

He was going round it like a wild beast, and drawing it eastward, he allowed them to pursue. But he did not attack. Perhaps he still hesitated? I wished to mediate once more. But I had scarcely spoken, when Captain Nemo imposed silence, saying,—

"I am the law, and I am the judge! I am the oppressed, and there is the oppressor! Through him I have lost all that I loved, cherished, and venerated,—country, wife, children, father, and mother. I saw all perish! All that I hate is there! Say no more!"

I cast a last look at the man-of-war, which was putting on steam, and rejoined Ned and Conseil.

"We will fly!" I exclaimed.

"Good!" said Ned. "What is this vessel?"

"I do not know; but whatever is it, it will be sunk before night. In any case, it is better to perish with it, than be made accomplices in a retaliation, the justice of which we cannot judge."

"That is my opinion too," said Ned Land, coolly. "Let us wait for night."

Night arrived. Deep silence reigned on board. The compass showed that the *Nautilus* had not altered its course. It was on the surface, rolling slightly. My companions and I resolved to fly when the vessel should be near enough either to hear us or to see us; for the moon, which would be full in two or three days, shone brightly. Once on board the ship, if we could not prevent the blow which threatened it, we could, at least we would, do all that circumstances would allow. Several times I thought the *Nautilus* was preparing for attack; but Captain Nemo contented himself with allowing his adversary to approach, and then fled once more before it.

Part of the night passed without any incident. We watched the opportunity for action. We spoke little, for we were too much moved. Ned Land would have thrown himself into the sea, but I forced him to wait. According to my idea, the *Nautilus* would attack the ship at her water-line, and then it would not only be possible, but easy to fly.

At three in the morning, full of uneasiness, I mounted the platform. Captain Nemo had not left it. He was standing at the forepart near his flag, which a slight breeze displayed above his head. He did not take his eyes from the vessel. The intensity of his look seemed to attract, and fascinate, and draw it onward more purely than if he had been towing it. The moon was then passing the meridian. Jupiter was rising in the east. Amid this peaceful scene of nature, sky and ocean rivalled each other in tranquillity, the sea offering to the orbs of night the finest mirror they could ever have in which to reflect their image. As I thought of the deep calm of these elements, compared with all those passions brooding imperceptibly within the *Nautilus,* I shuddered.

The vessel was within two miles of us. It was ever nearing that phosphorescent light which showed the presence of the *Nautilus*. I could see its green and red lights, and its white lantern hanging from the large mizzen-mast. An indistinct vibration quivered through its rigging, showing that the furnaces were heated to the uttermost. Sheaves of sparks and red ashes flew from the funnels, shining in the atmosphere like stars.

I remained thus until six in the morning, without Captain Nemo noticing me. The ship stood about a mile and a half from us, and with the first dawn of day the firing began afresh. The moment could not be far off when, the *Nautilus* attacking its adversary, my companions and myself should forever leave this man. I was preparing to go down to remind them, when the second mounted the platform, accompanied by several sailors. Captain Nemo either did not or would not see them. Some steps were taken which might be called the signal for action. They were very simple. The iron balustrade around the platform was lowered, and the lantern and pilot-cages were pushed within the shell until they were flush with the deck. The long surface of the steel cigar no longer offered a single point to check its manœuvres. I returned to the saloon. The *Nautilus* still floated; some streaks of light were filtering through the liquid beds. With the undulations of the waves the windows were brightened by the red streaks of the rising sun, and this dreadful day of the 2d of June had dawned.

At five o'clock, the log showed that the speed of the *Nautilus* was slackening, and I knew that it was allowing them to draw nearer. Besides, the reports were heard more distinctly, and the projectiles, laboring through the ambient water, were extinguished with a strange hissing noise.

"My friends," said I, "the moment is come. One grasp of the hand, and may God protect us!"

Ned Land was resolute, Conseil calm, myself so nervous that I knew not how to contain myself. We all passed into the library; but the moment I pushed the door opening on to the central staircase, I heard the upper panel close sharply. The Canadian rushed on to the stairs, but I stopped him. A well-known hissing noise told me that the water was running into the reservoirs, and in a few minutes the *Nautilus* was some yards beneath the surface of the waves. I understood the manœuvre. It was too late to act. The *Nautilus* did not wish to strike at the impenetrable cuirass, but below the water-line, where the metallic covering no longer protected it.

We were again imprisoned, unwilling witnesses of the dreadful drama that was preparing. We had scarcely time to reflect; taking refuge in my room, we looked at each other without speaking. A deep stupor had taken hold of my mind: thought seemed to stand still. I was in that painful state of expectation preceding a dreadful report. I waited, I listened, every sense was merged in that of hearing! The speed of the *Nautilus* was accelerated. It was preparing to rush. The whole ship trembled. Suddenly I screamed. I felt the shock, but comparatively light. I felt the penetrating power of the steel spur. I heard rattlings and scrapings. But the *Nautilus*, carried along by its propelling power, passed through the mass of the vessel, like a needle through sail-cloth!

I could stand it no longer. Mad, out of my mind, I rushed from my room into the saloon. Captain Nemo was there, mute, gloomy, implacable; he was looking through the port panel. A large mass cast a shadow on the water; and that it might lose nothing of her agony, the *Nautilus* was going down into the abyss with her. Ten yards from me I saw the open shell through which the water was rushing with the noise of thunder, then the double line of guns and the netting. The bridge was covered with black agitated shadows.

The water was rising. The poor creatures were crowding the ratlings, clinging to the masts, struggling under the water. It was a human ant-heap overtaken by the sea. Paralyzed, stiffened with anguish, my hair standing on end, my eyes wide open, panting, without breath and without voice, I too was watching! An irresistible attraction glued me to the glass! Suddenly an explosion took place. The compressed air blew up her decks, as if the magazines had caught fire. Then the unfortunate vessel sunk more rapidly. Her topmast, laden with victims, now appeared; then her spars, bending under the weight of men; and last of all, the top of her mainmast. Then the dark mass disappeared, and with it the dead crew, drawn down by the strong eddy.

I turned to Captain Nemo. That terrible avenger, a perfect archangel of hatred, was still looking. When all was over, he turned to his room, opened the door, and entered. I followed him with my eyes. On the end wall beneath his heroes, I saw the portrait of a woman still young, and two little children. Captain Nemo looked at them for some moments, stretched his arms towards them, and kneeling down burst into deep sobs.

CHAPTER 22

THE LAST WORDS OF CAPTAIN NEMO

THE panels had closed on this dreadful vision, but light had not returned to the saloon: all was silence and darkness within the *Nautilus*. At wonderful speed, a hundred feet beneath the water, it was leaving this desolate spot. Whither was it going? To the north or south? Where was the man flying to after such dreadful retaliation? I had returned to my room, where Ned and Conseil had remained silent enough. I felt an insurmountable horror for Captain Nemo. Whatever he had suffered at the hands of these men, he had no right to punish thus. He had made me, if not an accomplice, at least a witness of his vengeance. At eleven the electric light reappeared. I passed into the saloon. It was deserted. I consulted the different instruments. The *Nautilus* was flying northward at the rate of twenty-five miles an hour, now on the surface, and now thirty feet below it. On taking the bearings by the chart, I saw that we were passing the mouth of the Manche, and that our course was hurrying us towards the northern seas at a frightful speed. That night we had crossed two hundred leagues of the Atlantic. The shadows fell, and the sea was covered with darkness until the rising of the moon. I went to my room, but could not sleep. I was troubled with dreadful nightmare. The horrible scene of destruction was continually before my eyes. From that day, who could tell into what part of the North Atlantic basin the *Nautilus* would take us? Still with unaccountable speed. Still in the midst of these northern fogs. Would it touch at Spitzbergen, or on the shores of Nova Zembla? Should we explore these unknown seas, the White Sea, the Sea of Kara, the Gulf of Obi, the Archipelago of Liarrov, and the unknown coast of Asia? I could not say. I could no longer judge of the time that was passing. The clocks had been stopped on board. It seemed, as in polar countries, that night and day no longer followed their regular course. I felt myself being drawn into that strange region where the foundered imagination of Edgar Poe roamed at will. Like the fabulous Gordon

Pym, at every moment I expected to see "that veiled human figure, of larger proportions than those of any inhabitant of the earth, thrown across the cataract which defends the approach to the pole." I estimated (though perhaps, I may be mistaken)—I estimated this adventurous course of the *Nautilus* to have lasted fifteen or twenty days. And I know not how much longer it might have lasted, had it not been for the catastrophe which ended this voyage. Of Captain Nemo I saw nothing whatever now, nor of his second. Not a man of the crew was visible for an instant. The *Nautilus* was almost incessantly under water. When we came to the surface to renew the air, the panels opened and shut mechanically. There were no more marks on the planisphere. I knew not where we were. And the Canadian, too, his strength and patience at an end, appeared no more. Conseil could not draw a word from him, and fearing that, in a dreadful fit of madness, he might kill himself, watched him with constant devotion. One morning (what date it was I could not say), I had fallen into a heavy sleep towards the early hours, a sleep both painful and unhealthy, when I suddenly awoke. Ned Land was leaning over me, saying in a low voice, "We are going to fly."

I sat up.

"When shall we go?" I asked.

"To-morrow night. All inspection on board the *Nautilus* seems to have ceased. All appear to be stupefied. You will be ready, sir?"

"Yes; where are we?"

"In sight of land. I took the reckoning this morning in the fog,—twenty miles to the east."

"What country is it?"

"I do not know; but whatever it is, we will take refuge there."

"Yes, Ned, yes. We will fly to-night, even if the sea should swallow us up."

"The sea is bad, the wind violent, but twenty miles in that light boat of the *Nautilus* does not frighten me. Unknown to the crew, I have been able to procure food and some bottles of water."

"I will follow you."

"But," continued the Canadian, "if I am surprised, I will defend myself; I will force them to kill me."

"We will die together, friend Ned."

I had made up my mind to all. The Canadian left me. I reached the platform, on which I could with difficulty support myself against the shock of the waves. The sky was threatening; but as land was in those thick brown shadows, we must fly. I returned to the saloon, fearing and yet hoping to see Captain Nemo, wishing and yet not wishing to see him. What could I have said to him? Could I hide the involuntary horror with which he inspired me? No. It was better that I should not meet him face to face; better to forget him. And yet—How long seemed that day, the last that I should pass in the *Nautilus*. I remained alone. Ned Land and Conseil avoided speaking, for fear of betraying themselves. At six I dined, but I was not hungry; I forced myself to eat in spite of my disgust, that I might not weaken myself. At half past six Ned Land came to my room saying, "We shall not see each other again before our departure. At ten the moon will not be risen. We will profit by the darkness. Come to the boat; Conseil and I will wait for you."

The Canadian went out without giving me time to answer. Wishing to verify the course of the *Nautilus,* I went to the saloon. We were running N.N.E. at frightful speed, and more than fifty yards deep. I cast a last look on these wonders of nature, on the riches of art heaped up in this museum, upon the unrivalled collection destined to perish at the bottom of the sea, with him who had formed it. I wished to fix an indelible impression of it in my mind. I remained an hour thus, bathed in the light of that luminous ceiling, and passing in review those treasures shining under their glasses. Then I returned to my room.

I dressed myself in strong sea clothing. I collected my notes, placing them carefully about me. My heart beat loudly. I could not check its pulsations. Certainly my trouble and agitation would have betrayed me to Captain Nemo's eyes. What was he doing at this moment? I listened at the door of his room. I heard steps. Captain Nemo was there. He had not gone to rest. At every moment I expected to see him appear, and ask me why I wished to fly. I was constantly on the alert. My imagination magnified everything. The impression became at last so poignant, that I asked myself if it would not be better to go to the captain's room, see him face to face, and brave him with look and gesture.

It was the inspiration of a madman; fortunately I resisted the desire, and stretched myself on my bed to quiet my bodily agitation. My nerves were somewhat calmer, but in my excited brain I saw over again all my existence on board the *Nautilus;* every incident, either happy or unfortunate, which had happened since my disappearance from the *Abraham Lincoln;*—the submarine hunt, the Torres Straits, the savages of Papua, the running ashore, the coral cemetery, the passage of Suez, the Island of Santorin, the Cretan diver, Vigo Bay, Atlantis, the iceberg, the South Pole, the imprisonment in the ice, the fight among the poulps, the storm in the Gulf Stream, the *Avenger,* and the horrible scene of the vessel sunk with all her crew. All these events passed before my eyes like scenes in a drama. Then Captain Nemo seemed to grow enormously, his features to assume superhuman proportions. He was no longer my equal, but a man of the waters, the genie of the sea.

It was then half past nine. I held my head between my hands to keep it from bursting. I closed my eyes, I would not think any longer. There was another half-hour to wait, another half-hour of a nightmare, which might drive me mad.

At that moment I heard the distant strains of the organ, a sad harmony to an undefinable chant, the wail of a soul longing to break these earthly bonds. I listened with every sense, scarcely breathing; plunged, like Captain Nemo, in that musical ecstasy, which was drawing him in spirit to the end of life.

Then a sudden thought terrified me. Captain Nemo had left his room. He was in the saloon, which I must cross to fly. There I should meet him for the last time. He would see me, perhaps speak to me. A gesture of his might destroy me, a single word chain me on board.

But ten was about to strike. The moment had come for me to leave my room and join my companions.

I must not hesitate, even if Captain Nemo himself should rise before me. I opened my door carefully; and even then, as it turned on its hinges, it seemed to me to make a dreadful noise. Perhaps it only existed in my own imagination.

I crept along the dark stairs of the *Nautilus,* stopping at each step to check the beating of my heart. I reached the door of the saloon, and opened it gently. It was plunged in profound darkness. The strains of the organ sounded faintly. Captain Nemo was there. He did not see me. In the full light I do not think he would have noticed me, so entirely was he absorbed in the ecstasy.

I crept along the carpet, avoiding the slightest sound which might betray my presence. I was at least five minutes reaching the door, at the opposite side, opening into the library.

I was going to open it, when a sigh from Captain Nemo nailed me to the spot. I knew that he was rising. I could even see him, for the light from the library came through to the saloon. He came towards me silently, with his arms crossed, gliding like a spectre rather than walking. His breast was swelling with sobs; and I heard him murmur these words (the last which ever struck my ear),—

"Almighty God! enough! enough!"

Was it a confession of remorse which thus escaped from this man's conscience?

In desperation I rushed through the library, mounted the central staircase, and following the upper flight reached the boat. I crept through the opening, which had already admitted my two companions.

"Let us go! let us go!" I exclaimed.

"Directly!" replied the Canadian.

The orifice in the plates of the *Nautilus* was first closed, and fastened down by means of a false key, with which Ned Land had provided himself; the opening in the boat was also closed. The Canadian began to loosen the bolts which still held us to the submarine boat.

Suddenly a noise within was heard. Voices were answering each other loudly. What was the matter? Had they discovered our flight? I felt Ned Land slipping a dagger into my hand.

"Yes," I murmured, "we know how to die!"

The Canadian had stopped in his work. But one word many times repeated, a dreadful word, revealed the cause of the agitation spreading on board the *Nautilus*. It was not we the crew were looking after!

"The maëlstrom! the maëlstrom!" I exclaimed.

The maëlstrom! Could a more dreadful word in a more dreadful situation have sounded in our ears! We were then upon the dangerous coast of Norway. Was the *Nautilus* being drawn into this gulf at the moment our boat was going to leave its sides? We knew that at the tide the pent-up waters between the islands of Ferroe and Loffoden rush with irresistible violence, forming a whirlpool from which no vessel ever escapes. From every point of the horizon enormous waves were meeting, forming a gulf justly called the "Navel of the Ocean," whose power of attraction extends to a distance of twelve miles. There, not only vessels, but whales, are sacrificed, as well as white bears from the northern regions.

It is thither that the *Nautilus,* voluntarily or involuntarily, had been run by the captain.

It was describing a spiral, the circumference of which was lessening by degrees, and the boat, which was still fastened to its side, was carried along with giddy speed. I felt that sickly giddiness which arises from long-continued whirling round.

We were in dread. Our horror was at its height, circulation had stopped, all nervous influence was annihilated, and we were covered with cold sweat, like a sweat of agony! And what noise around our frail bark! What roarings repeated by the echo miles away! What an uproar was that of the waters broken on the sharp rocks at the bottom, where the hardest bodies are crushed, and trees worn away, "with all the fur rubbed off," according to the Norwegian phrase!

What a situation to be in! We rocked frightfully. The *Nautilus* defended itself like a human being. Its steel muscles cracked. Sometimes it seemed to stand upright, and we with it!

When I returned to consciousness, I was lying in a fisherman's hut.

"We must hold on," said Ned, "and look after the bolts. We may still be saved if we stick to the *Nautilus*—"

He had not finished the words, when we heard a crashing noise, the bolts gave way, and the boat, torn from its groove, was hurled like a stone from a sling into the midst of the whirlpool.

My head struck on a piece of iron, and with the violent shock I lost all consciousness.

CHAPTER 23

CONCLUSION

THUS ends the voyage under the seas. What passed during that night—how the boat escaped from the eddies of the maëlstrom, how Ned Land, Conseil, and myself ever came out of the gulf—I cannot tell.

But when I returned to consciousness, I was lying in a fisherman's hut, on the Loffoden Isles. My two companions, safe and sound, were near me holding my hands. We embraced each other heartily.

At that moment we could not think of returning to France. The means of communication between the north of Norway and the south are rare, and I am therefore obliged to wait for the steamboat running monthly from Cape North.

And among the worthy people who have so kindly received us I revised my record of these adventures once more. Not a fact has been omitted, not a detail exaggerated. It is a faithful narrative of this incredible expedition in an element inaccessible to man, but to which Progress will one day open a road.

Shall I be believed? I do not know. And it matters little, after all. What I now affirm is, that I have a right to speak of these seas, under which, in less than ten months, I have crossed 20,000 leagues in that submarine tour of the world, which has revealed so many wonders.

But what has become of the *Nautilus?* Did it resist the pressure of the maëlstrom? Does Captain Nemo still live? And does he still follow under the ocean those frightful retaliations? Or did he stop after that last hecatomb?

Will the waves one day carry to him this manuscript containing the history of his life? Shall I ever know the name of this man? Will the missing vessel tell us by its nationality that of Captain Nemo?

I hope so. And I also hope that his powerful vessel has conquered the sea and its most terrible gulf, and that the *Nautilus* has survived where so many other vessels have been lost! If it be so, if Captain Nemo still inhabits the ocean, his adopted country, may hatred be appeased in that savage heart! May the contemplation of so many wonders extinguish forever the spirit of vengeance! May the judge disappear, and the philosopher continue the peaceful exploration of the sea! If his destiny be strange, it is also sublime. Have I not understood it myself? Have I not lived ten months of this unnatural life? And to the question asked by Ecclesiastes 3,000 years ago, "That which is far off and exceeding deep, who can find it out?" two men alone of all now living have the right to give an answer,—

CAPTAIN NEMO AND MYSELF.

A Journey to the Center of the Earth

The outlet: the rock must be blasted.

CHAPTER 1

MY UNCLE MAKES A GREAT DISCOVERY

LOOKING back to all that has occurred to me since that eventful day, I am scarcely able to believe in the reality of my adventures. They were truly so wonderful that even now I am bewildered when I think of them.

My uncle was a German, having married my mother's sister, an Englishwoman. Being very much attached to his fatherless nephew, he invited me to study under him in his home in the fatherland. This home was in a large town, and my uncle a Professor of philosophy, chemistry, geology, mineralogy, and many other ologies.

One day, after passing some hours in the laboratory—my uncle being absent at the time—I suddenly felt the necessity of renovating the tissues—*i.e.*, I was hungry, and was about to rouse up our old French cook, when my uncle, Professor Von Hardwigg, suddenly opened the street door, and came rushing up stairs.

Now Professor Hardwigg, my worthy uncle, is by no means a bad sort of man; he is, however, choleric and original. To bear with him means to obey; and scarcely had his heavy feet resounded within our joint domicile than he shouted for me to attend upon him.

"Harry—Harry—Harry——"

I hastened to obey, but before I could reach his room, jumping three steps at a time, he was stamping his right foot upon the landing.

"Harry!" he cried, in a frantic tone, "are you coming up?"

Now to tell the truth, at that moment I was far more interested in the question as to what was to constitute our dinner than in any problem of science; to me soup was more interesting than soda, an omelette more tempting than arithmetic, and an artichoke of ten times more value than any amount of asbestos.

But my uncle was not a man to be kept waiting; so adjourning therefore all minor questions, I presented myself before him.

He was a very learned man. Now most persons in this category supply themselves with information, as pedlars do with goods, for the benefit of others, and lay up stores in order to diffuse them abroad for the benefit of society in general. Not so my excellent uncle, Professor Hardwigg; he studied, he consumed the midnight oil, he pored over heavy tomes, and digested large quartos and folios in order to keep the knowledge acquired to himself.

There was a reason, and it may be regarded as a good one, why my uncle objected to display his learning more than was absolutely necessary; he stammered; and when intent upon explaining the phenomena of the heavens, was apt to find himself at fault, and allude in such a vague way to sun, moon, and stars, that few were able to comprehend his meaning. To tell the honest truth, when the right word would not come, it was generally replaced by a very powerful adjective.

In connection with the sciences there are many almost unpronounceable names—names very much resembling those of Welsh villages; and my uncle being very fond of using them, his habit of stammering was not thereby improved. In fact, there were periods in his discourse when he would finally give up, and swallow his discomfiture—in a glass of water.

As I said, my uncle, Professor Hardwigg, was a very learned man; and I now add a most kind relative. I was bound to him by the double ties of affection and interest. I took deep interest in all his doings, and hoped some day to be almost as learned myself. It was a rare thing for me to be absent from his lectures. Like him, I preferred mineralogy to all the other sciences. My anxiety was to gain *real knowledge of the earth*. Geology and mineralogy were to us the sole objects of life, and in connection with these studies many a fair specimen of stone, chalk, or metal did we break with our hammers.

Steel rods, loadstone, glass pipes, and bottles of various acids were oftener before us than our meals. My uncle Hardwigg was once known to classify six hundred different geological specimens by their weight, hardness, fusibility, sound, taste, and smell.

He corresponded with all the great, learned, and scientific men of the age. I was therefore in constant communication with, at all events the letters of, Sir Humphrey Davy, Captain Franklin, and other great men.

But before I state the subject on which my uncle wished to confer with me, I must say a word about his personal appearance. Alas! my readers will see a very different portrait of him at a future time, after he has gone through the fearful adventures yet to be related.

My uncle was fifty years old; tall, thin, and wiry. Large spectacles hid, to a certain extent, his vast, round and goggle eyes, while his nose was irreverently compared to a thin file. So much indeed did it resemble that useful article, that a compass was said in his presence to have made considerable N* deviation.

The truth being told, however, the only article really attracted to my uncle's nose was tobacco.

Another peculiarity of his was, that he always stepped a yard at a time, clenched his fists as if he were going to hit you, and was, when in one of his peculiar humours, very far from a pleasant companion.

It is further necessary to observe that he lived in a very nice house, in that very nice street, the Königstrasse at Hamburg. Though lying in the centre of a town, it was perfectly rural in its aspect—half wood, half bricks, with old-fashioned gables—one of the few old houses spared by the great fire of 1842.

When I say a nice house, I mean a handsome house—old, tottering, and not exactly comfortable to English notions: a house a little off the perpendicular and inclined to fall into the neighbouring canal; exactly the house for a wandering artist to depict; all the more that you could scarcely see it for ivy and a magnificent old tree which grew over the door.

My uncle was rich; his house was his own property, while he had a considerable private income. To my notion the best part of his possessions was his god-

* (?) Nasal.

daughter Gretchen. And the old cook, the young lady, the Professor and I were the sole inhabitants.

I loved mineralogy, I loved geology. To me there was nothing like pebbles—and if my uncle had been in a little less of a fury, we should have been the happiest of families. To prove the excellent Hardwigg's impatience, I solemnly declare that when the flowers in the drawing-room pots began to grow, he rose every morning at four o'clock to make them grow quicker by pulling the leaves!

Having described my uncle, I will now give an account of our interview.

He received me in his study; a perfect museum, containing every natural curiosity that can well be imagined—minerals, however, predominating. Every one was familiar to me, having been catalogued by my own hand. My uncle, apparently oblivious of the fact that he had summoned me to his presence, was absorbed in a book. He was particularly fond of early editions, tall copies, and unique works.

"Wonderful!" he cried, tapping his forehead. "Wonderful—wonderful!"

It was one of those yellow-leaved volumes now rarely found on stalls, and to me it appeared to possess but little value. My uncle, however, was in raptures.

He admired its binding, the clearness of its characters, the ease with which it opened in his hand, and repeated aloud, half-a-dozen times, that it was very, very old.

To my fancy he was making a great fuss about nothing, but it was not my province to say so. On the contrary, I professed considerable interest in the subject, and asked him what it was about.

"It is the Heims-Kringla of Snorre Tarleson," he said, "the celebrated Icelandic author of the twelfth century—it is a true and correct account of the Norwegian princes who reigned in Iceland."

My next question related to the language in which it was written. I hoped at all events it was translated into German. My uncle was indignant at the very thought, and declared he wouldn't give a penny for a translation. His delight was to have found the original work in the Icelandic tongue, which he declared to be one of the most magnificent and yet simple idioms in the world—while at the same time its grammatical combinations were the most varied known to students.

"About as easy as German?" was my insidious remark.

My uncle shrugged his shoulders.

"The letters at all events," I said, "are rather difficult of comprehension."

"It is a Runic manuscript, the language of the original population of Iceland, invented by Odin himself," cried my uncle, angry at my ignorance.

I was about to venture upon some misplaced joke on the subject, when a small scrap of parchment fell out of the leaves. Like a hungry man snatching at a morsel of bread, the Professor seized it. It was about five inches by three, and was scrawled over in the most extraordinary fashion.

The lines on page 222 are exact fac-simile of what was written on the venerable piece of parchment—and have wonderful importance, as they induced my uncle to undertake the most wonderful series of adventures which ever fell to the lot of human beings.

My uncle looked keenly at the document for some moments and then declared that it was Runic. The letters were similar to those in the book, but then what did they mean? This was exactly what I wanted to know.

Now as I had a strong conviction that the Runic alphabet and dialect were simply an invention to mystify poor human nature, I was delighted to find that my uncle knew as much about the matter as I did—which was nothing. At all events, the tremulous motion of his fingers made me think so.

"And yet," he muttered to himself, "it is old Icelandic, I am sure of it."

And my uncle ought to have known, for he was a perfect polyglot dictionary in himself. He did not pretend, like a certain learned pundit, to speak the two thousand languages and four thousand idioms made use of in different parts of the globe, but he did know all the more important ones.

It is a matter of great doubt to me now, to what violent measures my uncle's impetuosity might have led him, had not the clock struck two, and our old French cook called out to let us know that dinner was on the table.

"Bother the dinner!" cried my uncle.

But as I was hungry, I sallied forth to the dining room, where I took up my usual quarters. Out of politeness I waited three minutes, but no sign of my uncle, the Professor. I was surprised. He was not usually so blind to the pleasures of a good dinner. It was the acme of German luxury—parsley soup, a ham omelette with sorrel trimmings, an oyster of veal stewed with prunes, delicious fruit, and sparkling Moselle. For the sake of poring over this musty old piece of parchment, my uncle forbore to share our meal. To satisfy my conscience, I ate for both.

The old cook and housekeeper was nearly out of her mind. After taking so much trouble, to find her master not appear at dinner was to her a sad disappointment—which, as she occasionally watched the havoc I was making on the viands, became also alarm. If my uncle were to come to table after all?

Suddenly, just as I had consumed the last apple and drank the last glass of wine, a terrible voice was heard at no great distance. It was my uncle roaring for me to come to him. I made very nearly one leap of it—so loud, so fierce was his tone.

CHAPTER 2

THE MYSTERIOUS PARCHMENT

"I DECLARE," cried my uncle, striking the table fiercely with his fist, "I declare to you it is Runic—and contains some wonderful secret, which I must get at, at any price."

I was about to reply when he stopped me.

Professor Von Hardwigg.

"Sit down," he said, quite fiercely, "and write to my dictation."

I obeyed.

"I will substitute," he said, "a letter of our alphabet for that of the Runic: we will then see what that will produce. Now, begin and make no mistakes."

The dictation commenced with the following incomprehensible result:—

m.rnlls	*esruel*	*seecJde*
sgtssmf	*unteief*	*niedrke*
kt,samn	*atrateS*	*Saodrrn*
emtnael	*nuaect*	*rrilSa*
Atvaar	*.nscrc*	*ieaabs*
ccdrmi	*eeutul*	*frantu*
dt,iac	*vseibo*	*KediiI*

Scarcely giving me time to finish, my uncle snatched the document from my hands and examined it with the most rapt and deep attention.

"I should like to know what it means," he said, after a long period.

I certainly could not tell him, nor did he expect me to—his conversation being uniformly answered by himself.

"I declare it puts me in mind of a cryptograph," he cried, "unless, indeed, the letters have been written without any real meaning; and yet why take so much trouble? Who knows but I may be on the verge of some great discovery?"

My candid opinion was that it was all rubbish! But this opinion I kept carefully to myself, as my uncle's choler was not pleasant to bear. All this time he was comparing the book and the parchment.

"The manuscript volume and the smaller document are written in different hands," he said, "the cryptograph is of much later date than the book; there is an undoubted proof of the correctness of my surmise. [An irrefragable proof I took it to be.] The first letter is a double M, which was only added to the Icelandic language in the twelfth century—this makes the parchment two hundred years posterior to the volume."

The circumstance appeared very probable and very logical, but it was all surmise to me.

"To me it appears probable that this sentence was written by some owner of the book. Now who was the owner, is the next important question. Perhaps by great good luck it may be written somewhere in the volume."

With these words Professor Hardwigg took off his spectacles, and, taking a powerful magnifying glass, examined the book carefully.

On the fly leaf was what appeared to be a blot of ink, but on examination proved to be a line of writing almost effaced by time. This was what he sought; and, after some considerable time, he made out these letters:

"Arne Saknussemm!" he cried in a joyous and triumphant tone, "that is not only an Icelandic name, but of a learned professor of the sixteenth century, a celebrated alchemist."

I bowed as a sign of respect.

"These alchemists," he continued, "Avicena, Bacon, Lully, Paracelsus, were the true, the only learned men of the day. They made surprising discoveries. May not this Saknussemm, nephew mine, have hidden on this bit of parchment some astounding invention? I believe the cryptograph to have a profound meaning—which I must make out."

My uncle walked about the room in a state of excitement almost impossible to describe.

"It may be so, sir," I timidly observed, "but why conceal it from posterity, if it be a useful, a worthy discovery?"

"Why—how should I know? Did not Galileo make a secret of his discoveries in connection with Saturn? But we shall see. Until I discover the meaning of this sentence I will neither eat nor sleep."

"My dear uncle——" I began.

"Nor you neither," he added.

It was lucky I had taken double allowance that day.

"In the first place," he continued, "there must be a clue to the meaning. If we could find that, the rest would be easy enough."

I began seriously to reflect. The prospect of going without food and sleep was not a promising one, so I determined to do my best to solve the mystery. My uncle, meanwhile, went on with his soliloquy.

"The way to discover it is easy enough. In this document there are one hundred and thirty-two letters, giving seventy-nine consonants to fifty-three vowels. This is about the proportion found in most southern languages, the idioms of the north being much more rich in consonants. We may confidently predict, therefore, that we have to deal with a southern dialect."

Nothing could be more logical.

"Now," said Professor Hardwigg, "to trace the particular language."

"As Shakespeare says, 'that is the question,' " was my rather satirical reply.

"This man Saknussemm," he continued, "was a very learned man: now as he did not write in the language of his birth-place, he probably, like most learned men of the sixteenth century, wrote in Latin. If, however, I prove wrong in this guess, we must try Spanish, French, Italian, Greek, and even Hebrew. My own opinion, though, is decidedly in favour of Latin."

This proposition startled me. Latin was my favourite study, and it seemed sacrilege to believe this gibberish to belong to the country of Virgil.

"Barbarous Latin, in all probability," continued my uncle, "but still Latin."

"Very probably," I replied, not to contradict him.

"Let us see into the matter," continued my uncle; "here you see we have a series of one hundred and thirty-two letters, apparently thrown pell-mell upon paper, without method or organisation. There are words which are composed wholly of consonants, such as *m.rnlls,* others which are nearly all vowels, the fifth, for instance, which is *unteief,* and one of the last *oseibo*. This appears an extraordinary combination. Probably we shall find that the phrase is arranged according to some mathematical plan. No doubt a certain sentence has been written out and then jumbled up—some plan to which some figure is the clue. Now, Harry, to show your English wit—what is that figure?"

I could give him no hint. My thoughts were indeed far away. While he was speaking I had caught sight of the portrait of my cousin Gretchen, and was wondering when she would return.

We were affianced, and loved one another very seriously. But my uncle, who never thought even of such sublunary matters, knew nothing of this. Without noticing my abstraction, the Professor began reading the puzzling cryptograph all sorts of ways, according to some theory of his own. Presently, rousing my wandering attention, he dictated one precious attempt to me.

I mildly handed it over to him. I read as follows:—

mmessunkaSenrA.icefdoK.segnittamurtn
ecertserrette,rotaivsadua,ednecsedsadne
lacartniiiluJsiratracSarbmutabiledmek
meretarcsilucoIsleffenSnI.

I could scarcely keep from laughing, while my uncle, on the contrary, got in a towering passion, struck the table with his fist, darted out of the room, out of the house, and then taking to his heels was presently lost to sight.

CHAPTER 3

AN ASTOUNDING DISCOVERY

"WHAT is the matter?" cried the cook, entering the room; "when will master have his dinner?"

"Never."

"And his supper?"

"I don't know. He says he will eat no more, neither shall I. My uncle has determined to fast and make me fast until he makes out this abominable inscription," I replied.

"You will be starved to death," she said.

I was very much of the same opinion, but not liking to say so, sent her away, and began some of my usual work of classification. But boy as I made myself, nothing could keep me from thinking alternately of the stupid manuscript and of the pretty Gretchen.

Several times I thought of going out, but my uncle would have been angry at my absence. At the end of an hour, my allotted task was done. How to pass the time? I began by lighting my pipe. Like all other students, I delighted in tobacco; and, seating myself in the great armchair, I began to think.

Where was my uncle? I could easily imagine him tearing along some solitary road, gesticulating, talking to himself, cutting the air with his cane, and still thinking of the absurd bit of hieroglyphics. Would he hit upon some clue? Would he come home in better humour? While these thoughts were passing through my brain, I mechanically took up the execrable puzzle and tried every imaginable way of grouping the letters. I put them together by twos, by threes, fours, and fives—in vain. Nothing intelligible came out, except that the fourteenth, fifteenth and sixteenth made *ice* in English; the eighty-fourth, eighty-fifth and eighty-sixth, the word *sir;* then at last I seemed to find the Latin words *rota, mutabile, ira, nec, atra.*

"Ha! there seems to be some truth in my uncle's notion," thought I.

Then again I seemed to find the word *luco,* which means sacred wood. Then in the third line I appeared to make out *labiled,* a perfectly Hebrew word, and at the last the syllables *mère, are, mer,* which were French.

It was enough to drive one mad. Four different idioms in this absurd phrase. What connection could there be between ice, sir, anger, cruel, sacred wood, changing, mother, are and sea? The first and the last might, in a sentence connected with Iceland, mean sea of ice. But what of the rest of this monsrous cryptograph?

I was, in fact, fighting against an insurmountable difficulty; my brain was almost on fire; my eyes were strained with staring at the parchment; the whole absurd collection of letters appeared to dance before my vision in a number of black little groups. My mind was possessed with temporary hallucination—I was stifling. I wanted air. Mechanically I fanned myself with the document, of which now I saw the back and then the front.

Imagine my surprise when glancing at the back of the wearisome puzzle, the ink having gone through, I clearly made out Latin words, and among others *craterem* and *terrestre.*

I had discovered the secret!

It came upon me like a flash of lightning. I had got the clue. All you had to do to understand the document was to read it backwards. All the ingenious ideas of the Professor were realised; he had dictated it rightly to me; by a mere accident I had discovered what he so much desired.

My delight, my emotion may be imagined, my eyes were dazzled and I trembled so that at first I could make nothing of it. One look, however, would tell me all I wished to know.

"Let me read," I said to myself, after drawing a long breath.

I spread it before me on the table, I passed my finger over each letter, I spelt it through; in my excitement I read it out.

What horror and stupefaction took possession of my soul. It was like a man who had received a knock-down blow. Was it possible that I really read the terrible secret, and it had really been accomplished! A man had dared to do—what?

No living being should ever know.

"Never!" cried I, jumping up; "Never shall my uncle be made aware of the dread secret. He would be quite capable of undertaking the terrible journey. Nothing would check him, nothing stop him. Worse, he would compel me to accompany him, and we should be lost for ever. But no; such folly and madness cannot be allowed.

I was almost beside myself with rage and fury.

"My worthy uncle is already nearly mad," I cried aloud. "This would finish him. By some accident he may make the discovery; in which case, we are both lost. Perish the fearful secret—let the flames for ever bury it in oblivion."

I snatched up book and parchment, and was about to cast them into the fire, when the door opened and my uncle entered.

I had scarcely time to put down the wretched documents before my uncle was by my side. He was profoundly absorbed. His thoughts were evidently bent on the terrible parchment. Some new combination had probably struck him while taking his walk.

He seated himself in his armchair, and with a pen began to make an algebraical calculation. I watched him with anxious eyes. My flesh crawled as it became probable that he would discover *the* secret.

His combinations I knew now were useless, I having discovered the one only clue. For three mortal hours he continued without speaking a word, without raising his head, scratching, re-writing, calculating over and over again. I knew that in time he must hit upon the right phrase. The letters of every alphabet have only a certain number of combinations. But then years might elapse before he would perhaps arrive at the correct solution.

Still time went on; night came, the sounds in the streets ceased—and still my uncle went on, not even answering our worthy cook when she called us to supper.

I did not dare to leave him, so waved her away, and at last fell asleep on the sofa.

When I awoke my uncle was still at work. His red eyes, his pallid countenance, his matted hair, his feverish hands, his hecticly flushed cheeks, showed how terrible had been his struggle with the impossible, and what fearful fatigue he had undergone during that long sleepless night. It made me quite ill to look at him. Though he was rather severe with me, I loved him, and my heart ached at his sufferings. He was so overcome by one idea that he could not even get in a passion! All his energies were focused on one point. And I knew that by speaking one little word all this suffering would cease. I could not speak it.

My heart was, nevertheless, inclining towards him. Why, then, did I remain silent? In the interest of my uncle himself.

"Nothing shall make me speak," I muttered. "He will want to follow in the footsteps of the other! I know him well. His imagination is a perfect volcano, and to make discoveries in the interests of geology, he would sacrifice his life. I will therefore be silent and strictly keep the secret I have discovered. To reveal it would be suicidal. He would not only rush, himself, to destruction but drag me with him."

I crossed my arms, looked another way and smoked—resolved never to speak.

When our cook wanted to go out to market, or on any other errand, she found the front door locked and the key taken away. Was this done purposely or not? Surely Professor Hardwigg did not intend the old woman and myself to become martyrs to his obstinate will. Were we to be starved to death? A frightful recollection came to my mind. Once we had fed on bits and scraps for a week while he sorted some curiosities. It gave me the cramp even to think of it!

I wanted my breakfast, and saw no way of getting it. Still my resolution held good. I would starve rather than yield. But the cook began to take me seriously to task. What was to be done? She could not go out; and I dared not.

My uncle continued counting and writing; his imagination seemed to have translated him to the skies. He neither thought of eating nor drinking. In this way twelve o'clock came round. I was hungry, and there was nothing in the house. The cook had eaten the last bit of bread. This could not go on. It did, however, until two, when my sensations were terrible. After all, I began to think the document very absurd. Perhaps it might only be a gigantic hoax. Besides, some means would surely be found to keep my uncle back from attempting any such absurd expedition. On the other hand, if he did attempt anything so Quixotic, I should not be compelled to accompany him. Another line of reasoning partially decided me. Very likely he would make the discovery himself when I should have suffered starvation for nothing. Under the influence of hunger this reasoning appeared admirable. I determined to tell all.

The question now arose as to how it was to be done. I was still dwelling on the thought, when he rose and put on his hat.

What! go out and lock us in? Never!

"Uncle," I began.

He did not appear even to hear me.

"Professor Hardwigg," I cried.

"What," he retorted, "did you speak?"

"How about the key?"

"What key—the key of the door?"

"No—of these horrible hieroglyphics?"

He looked at me from under his spectacles, and started at the odd expression of my face. Rushing forward, he clutched me by the arm and keenly examined my countenance. His very look was an interrogation.

I simply nodded.

With an incredulous shrug of the shoulders, he turned upon his heel. Undoubtedly he thought I had gone mad.

"I have made a very important discovery."

His eyes flashed with excitement. His hand was lifted in a menacing attitude. For a moment neither of us spoke. It is hard to say which was most excited.

"You don't mean to say that you have any idea of the meaning of the scrawl?"

"I do," was my desperate reply. "Look at the sentence as dictated by you."

"Well, but it means nothing," was the angry answer.

"Nothing if you read from left to right, but mark, if from right to left——"

"Backwards!" cried my uncle, in wild amazement. "Oh most cunning Saknussemm; and I to be such a blockhead!"

He snatched up the document, gazed at it with haggard eye, and read it out as I had done.

It read as follows:—

In Sneffels yoculis craterem kem delebat
Umbra Scartaris Julii intra calendas descende.
Audas viator, et terrestre centrum attinges,
Kod feci. Arne Saknussemm.

Which dog-Latin being translated, reads as follows:—

"Descend into the crater of Yocul of Sneffels, which the shade of Scartaris caresses, before the kalends of July, audacious traveller, and you will reach the centre of the earth. I did it. ARNE SAKNUSSEMM."

My uncle leaped three feet from the ground with joy. He looked radiant and handsome. He rushed about the room wild with delight and satisfaction. He knocked over tables and chairs. He threw his books about until at last, utterly exhausted, he fell into his armchair.

"What's o'clock?" he asked.

"About three."

"My dinner does not seem to have done me much good," he observed, "Let me have something to eat. We can then start at once. Get my portmanteau ready."

"What for?"

"And your own," he continued. "We start at once."

My horror may be conceived. I resolved however to show no fear. Scientific reasons were the only ones likely to influence my uncle. Now, there were many against this terrible journey. The very idea of going down to the centre of the earth was simply absurd. I determined therefore to argue the point after dinner.

My uncle's rage was now directed against the cook for having no dinner ready. My explanation however satisfied him, and giving her the key she soon contrived to get sufficient to satisfy our voracious appetites.

During the repast my uncle was rather gay than otherwise. He made some of those peculiar jokes which belong exclusively to the learned. As soon however as dessert was over, he called me to his study. We each took a chair on opposite sides of the table.

"Henry," he said, in a soft and winning voice; "I have always believed you ingenious, and you have rendered me a service never to be forgotten. Without you, this great, this wondrous discovery would never have been made. It is my duty, therefore, to insist on your sharing the glory."

"He is in a good humour," thought I; "I'll soon let him know my opinion of glory."

"In the first place," he continued, "you must keep the whole affair a profound secret. There is no more envious race of men than scientific discoverers. Many would start on the same journey. At all events, we will be the first in the field."

"I doubt your having many competitors," was my reply.

"A man of real scientific acquirements would be delighted at the chance. We should find a perfect stream of pilgrims on the traces of Arne Saknussemm, if this document were once made public."

"But, my dear sir, is not this paper very likely to be a hoax?" I urged.

"The book in which we find it is sufficient proof of its authenticity," he replied.

"I thoroughly allow that the celebrated Professor wrote the lines, but only, I believe, as a kind of mystification," was my answer.

Scarcely were the words out of my mouth, when I was sorry I had uttered them. My uncle looked at me with a dark and gloomy scowl, and I began to be alarmed for the results of our conversation. His mood soon changed, however, and a smile took the place of a frown.

"We shall see," he remarked, with decisive emphasis.

"But see, what is all this about Yocul, and Sneffels, and this Scartaris? I have never heard anything about them."

"The very point to which I am coming. I lately received from my friend, Augustus Peterman, of Leipzig, a map. Take down the third atlas from the second shelf, series Z, plate 4.

I rose, went to the shelf, and presently returned with the volume indicated.

"This," said my uncle, "is one of the best maps of Iceland. I believe it will settle all your doubts, difficulties and objections."

With a grim hope to the contrary, I stooped over the map.

Tracing our route.

CHAPTER 4

WE START ON THE JOURNEY

"YOU see, the whole island is composed of volcanoes," said the Professor, "and remark carefully that they all bear the name of Yokul. The word is Icelandic, and means a glacier. In most of the lofty mountains of that region the volcanic eruptions come forth from icebound caverns. Hence the name applied to every volcano on this extraordinary island."

"But what does this word Sneffels mean?"

To this question I expected no rational answer. I was mistaken.

"Follow my finger to the western coast of Iceland, there you see Reykjawik, its capital. Follow the direction of one of its innumerable fjords or arms of the sea, and what do you see below the sixty-fifth degree of latitude?"

"A peninsula—very like a thigh-bone in shape."

"And in the centre of it——?"

"A mountain."

"Well, that's Sneffels."

I had nothing to say.

"That is Sneffels—a mountain about five thousand feet in height, one of the most remarkable in the whole island, and certainly doomed to be the most celebrated in the world, for through its crater we shall reach the Centre of the Earth."

"Impossible!" cried I, startled and shocked at the thought.

"Why impossible?" said Professor Hardwigg in his severest tones.

"Because its crater is choked with lava, by burning rocks—by infinite dangers."

"But if it be extinct?"

"That would make a difference."

"Of course it would. There are about three hundred volcanoes on the whole surface of the globe—but the greater number are extinct. Of these Sneffels is one. No eruption has occurred since 1219—in fact, it has ceased to be a volcano at all."

After this what more could I say? Yes—I thought of another objection.

"But what is all this about Scartaris and the kalends of July——?"

My uncle reflected deeply. Presently he gave forth the result of his reflections in a sententious tone.

"What appears obscure to you, to me is light. This very phrase shows how particular Saknussemm is in his directions. The Sneffels' mountain has many craters. He is careful therefore to point the exact one which is the highway into the Interior of the Earth. He lets us know, for this purpose, that about the end of the month of June, the shadow of Mount Scartaris falls upon the one crater. There can be no doubt about the matter."

My uncle had an answer for everything.

"I accept all your explanations," I said, "and Saknussemm is right. He found out the entrance to the bowels of the earth, he has indicated correctly, but that he or any one else ever followed up the discovery, is madness to suppose."

"Why so, young man?"

"All scientific teaching, theoretical and practical, shows it to be impossible."

"I care nothing for theories," retorted my uncle.

"But is it not well-known that heat increases one degree for every seventy feet you descend into the earth? which gives a fine idea of the central heat. All the matters which compose the globe are in a state of incandescence; even gold, platinum, and the hardest rocks are in a state of fusion. What would become of us?"

"Don't be alarmed at the heat, my boy."

"How so?"

"Neither you nor anybody else know anything about the real state of the earth's interior. All modern experiments tend to explode the older theories. Were any such heat to exist, the upper crust of the earth would be shattered to atoms, and the world would be at an end."

A long, learned and not uninteresting discussion followed, which ended in this wise:—

"I do not believe in the dangers and difficulties which you, Henry, seem to multiply; and the only way to learn, is like Arne Saknussemm, to go and see."

"Well," cried I, overcome at last, "let us go and see. Though how we can do that in the dark is another mystery."

"Fear nothing. We shall overcome these, and many other difficulties. Besides, as we approach the Centre, I expect to find it luminous—"

"Nothing is impossible."

"And now that we have come to a thorough understanding, not a word to any living soul. Our success depends on secrecy and despatch."

Thus ended our memorable conference, which roused a perfect fever in me. Leaving my uncle, I went forth like one possessed. Reaching the banks of the Elbe, I began to think. Was all I had heard really and truly possible? Was my uncle in his sober senses, and could the interior of the earth be reached? Was I the victim of a madman, or was he a discoverer of rare courage and grandeur of conception?

To a certain extent I was anxious to be off. I was afraid my enthusiasm would cool. I determined to pack up at once. At the end of an hour, however, on my way home, I found that my feelings had very much changed.

"I'm all abroad," I cried; " 'tis a nightmare—I must have dreamed it."

At this moment I came face to face with Gretchen, whom I warmly embraced.

"So you have come to meet me," she said; "how good of you. But what is the matter?"

Well, it was no use mincing the matter, I told her all. She listened with awe, and for some minutes she could not speak.

"Well?" I at last said, rather anxiously.

"What a magnificent journey. If I were only a man! A journey worthy of the nephew of Professor Hardwigg. I should look upon it as an honour to accompany him."

"My dear Gretchen, I thought you would be the first to cry out against this mad enterprise."

"No; on the contrary, I glory in it. It is magnificent, splendid—an idea worthy of my father. Henry Lawson, I envy you."

This was, as it were, conclusive. The final blow of all.

When we entered the house we found my uncle surrounded by workmen and porters, who were packing up. He was pulling and hauling at a bell.

"Where have you been wasting your time? Your portmanteau is not packed—my papers are not in order—the precious tailor has not brought my clothes, nor my gaiters—the key of my carpet bag is gone!"

I looked at him stupefied. And still he tugged away at the bell.

"We are really off, then?" I said.

"Yes—of course, and yet you go out for a stroll, unfortunate boy!"

"And when do we go?"

"The day after to-morrow, at daybreak."

I heard no more; but darted off to my little bed-chamber and locked myself in. There was no doubt about it now. My uncle had been hard at work all the afternoon. The garden was full of ropes, rope-ladders, torches, gourds, iron clamps, crow-bars, alpenstocks, and pickaxes—enough to load ten men.

I passed a terrible night. I was called early the next day to learn that the resolution of my uncle was unchanged and irrevocable. I also found my cousin and affianced wife as warm on the subject as was her father.

Next day, at five o'clock in the morning, the post chaise was at the door. Gretchen and the old cook received the keys of the house; and, scarcely pausing to wish anyone good-bye, we started on our adventurous journey into the Centre of the Earth.

CHAPTER 5

FIRST LESSONS IN CLIMBING

At Altona, a suburb of Hamburg, is the Chief Station of the Kiel railway, which was to take us to the shores of the Belt. In twenty minutes from the moment of our departure we were in Holstein, and our carriage entered the station. Our heavy luggage was taken out, weighed, labelled, and placed in a huge van. We then took our tickets, and exactly at seven o'clock were seated opposite each other in a first-class railway carriage.

My uncle said nothing. He was too busy examining his papers, among which of course was the famous parchment, and some letters of introduction from the Danish consul, which were to pave the way to an introduction to the Governor of Iceland. My only amusement was looking out of the window. But as we passed through a flat though fertile country, this occupation was slightly monotonous. In three hours we reached Kiel, and our baggage was at once transferred to the steamer.

We had now a day before us, a delay of about ten hours. Which fact put my uncle in a towering passion. We had nothing to do but to walk about the pretty town and bay. At length, however, we went on board, and at half past ten were steaming down the Great Belt. It was a dark night, with a strong breeze and a rough sea, nothing being visible but the occasional fires on shore, with here and there a lighthouse. At seven in the morning we left Korsör, a little town on the western side of Seeland.

Here we took another railway, which in three hours brought us to the capital,

Copenhagen, where, scarcely taking time for refreshment, my uncle hurried out to present one of his letters of introduction. It was to the director of the Museum of Antiquities, who having been informed that we were tourists bound for Iceland, did all he could to assist us. One wretched hope sustained me now. Perhaps no vessel was bound for such distant parts.

Alas! a little Danish schooner, the *Valkyrie*, was to sail on the second of June for Reykjawik. The captain, M. Bjarne, was on board, and was rather surprised at the energy and cordiality with which his future passenger shook him by the hand. To him a voyage to Iceland was merely a matter of course. My uncle, on the other hand, considered the event of sublime importance. The honest sailor took advantage of the Professor's enthusiasm to double the fare.

"On Tuesday morning at seven o'clock be on board," said M. Bjarne, handing us our receipts.

"Excellent! Capital! Glorious!" remarked my uncle as we sat down to a late breakfast; "refresh yourself, my boy, and we will take a run through the town."

Our meal concluded, we went to the Kongens-Nye-Torw; to the king's magnificent palace; to the beautiful bridge over the canal near the Museum; to the immense cenotaph of Thorwaldsen with its hideous naval groups; to the Castle of Rosenberg; and to all the other lions of the place,—none of which my uncle even saw, so absorbed was he in his anticipated triumphs.

But one thing struck his fancy, and that was a certain singular steeple situated on the Island of Amak, which is the south-east quarter of the city of Copenhagen. My uncle at once ordered me to turn my steps that way, and accordingly we went on board the steam ferry boat which does duty on the canal, and very soon reached the noted dockyard quay.

In the first instance we crossed some narrow streets, where we met numerous groups of galley slaves, with parti-coloured trousers, grey and yellow, working under the orders and the sticks of severe task-masters, and finally reached the Vor-Frelser's-Kirk.

This church exhibited nothing remarkable in itself; in fact, the worthy Professor had only been attracted to it by one circumstance, which was, that its rather elevated steeple started from a circular platform, after which there was an exterior staircase, which wound round to the very summit.

"Let us ascend," said my uncle.

"But I never could climb church towers," I cried, "I am subject to dizziness in my head."

"The very reason why you should go up. I want to cure you of a bad habit."

"But my good sir——"

"I tell you to come. What is the use of wasting so much valuable time?"

It was impossible to dispute the dictatorial commands of my uncle. I yielded with a groan. On payment of a fee, a verger gave us the key. He, for one, was not partial to the ascent. My uncle at once showed me the way, running up the steps like a schoolboy. I followed as well as I could, though no sooner was I outside the tower, than my head began to swim. There was nothing of the eagle about me. The earth was enough for me, and no ambitious desire to soar ever entered my mind. Still things did not go badly until I had ascended 150 steps, and was near the platform, when I began to feel the rush of cold air. I could scarcely stand, when clutching the railings, I looked upwards. The railing was frail enough, but nothing to those which skirted the terrible winding staircase, that appeared, from where I stood, to ascend to the skies.

"Now then, Henry."

"I can't do it!" I cried, in accents of despair.

"Are you, after all, a coward, sir?" said my uncle in a pitiless tone. "Go up, I say!"

To this there was no reply possible. And yet the keen air acted violently on my nervous system; sky, earth, all seemed to swim round; while the steeple rocked like a ship. My legs gave way like those of a drunken man. I crawled upon my hands and knees; I hauled myself up slowly, crawling like a snake. Presently I closed my eyes, and allowed myself to be dragged upwards.

"Look around you," said my uncle, in a stern voice, "heaven knows what profound abysses you may have to look down. This is excellent practice."

Slowly, and shivering all the while with cold, I opened my eyes. What then did I see? My first glance was upwards at the cold fleecy clouds, which as by some optical delusion appeared to stand still, while the steeple, the weathercock, and our two selves were carried swiftly along. Far away on one side could be seen the grassy plain, while on the other lay the sea bathed in translucent light. The Sund, or Sound as we call it, could be discovered beyond the point of Elsinore, crowded with white sails, which, at that distance, looked like the wings of seagulls; while to the east could be made out the far-off coast of Sweden. The whole appeared a magic panorama.

But faint and bewildered as I was, there was no remedy for it. Rise and stand up I must. Despite my protestations my first lesson lasted quite an hour. When, nearly two hours later, I reached the bosom of mother earth, I was like a rheumatic old man bent double with pain.

"Enough for one day," said my uncle, rubbing his hands, "we will begin again to-morrow."

There was no remedy. My lessons lasted five days, and at the end of that period, I ascended blithely enough, and found myself able to look down into the depths below, without even winking, and with some degree of pleasure.

CHAPTER 6

OUR VOYAGE TO ICELAND

THE hour of departure came at last. The night before, the worthy Mr. Thomson brought us the most cordial letters of introduction for Count Trampe, Governor of Iceland, for M. Pictursson, coadjutor to the bishop, and for M. Finsen, mayor of the town of Reykjawik. In return, my uncle nearly crushed his hands, so warmly did he shake them.

On the second of the month, at two in the morning, our precious cargo of luggage was taken on board the good ship *Valkyrie*. We followed, and were very politely introduced by the captain to a small cabin with two standing bed places, neither very well ventilated nor very comfortable. But in the cause of science men are expected to suffer.

"Well, and have we a fair wind?" cried my uncle, in his most mellifluous accents.

"An excellent wind!" replied Captain Bjarne; "we shall leave the Sound, going free with all sails set."

A few minutes afterwards, the schooner started before the wind, under all the canvas she could carry, and entered the channel. An hour later, the capital of Denmark seemed to sink into the waves, and we were at no great distance from the coast of Elsinore. My uncle was delighted; for myself, moody and dissatisfied, I appeared almost to expect a glimpse of the ghost of Hamlet.

"Sublime madman," thought I, "you, doubtless, would approve our proceedings. You might perhaps even follow us to the centre of the earth, there to resolve your eternal doubts."

But no ghost, or anything else appeared upon the ancient walls. The fact is, the castle is much later than the time of the heroic prince of Denmark. It is now the residence of the keeper of the Strait of the Sound, and through that Sound more than fifteen thousand vessels of all nations pass every year.

The castle of Kronborg soon disappeared in the murky atmosphere, as well as the tower of Helsinborg, which raises its head on the Swedish Bank. And here the schooner began to feel in earnest the breezes of the Cattegat. The *Valkyrie* was swift enough, but with all sailing boats there is the same uncertainty. Her cargo was coal, furniture, pottery, woollen clothing, and a load of corn. As usual, the crew was small, five Danes doing the whole of the work.

"How long will the voyage last?" asked my uncle.

"Well, I should think about ten days," replied the skipper, "unless, indeed, we meet with some north-east gales among the Faroe Islands."

"At all events, there will be no very considerable delay," cried the impatient Professor.

"No, Mr. Hardwigg," said the captain, "no fear of that. At all events, we shall get there some day."

Towards evening the schooner doubled Cape Skagen, the northernmost part of Denmark, crossed the Skager-Rak during the night—skirted the extreme point of Norway through the gut of Cape Lindness, and then reached the Northern Seas. Two days later we were not far from the coast of Scotland, somewhere near what Danish sailors call Peterhead, and then the *Valkyrie* stretched out direct for the Faroe Islands, between Orkney and Shetland. Our vessel now felt the full force of the ocean waves, and the wind shifting, we with great difficulty made the Faroe Isles. On the eighth day, the captain made out Myganness, the westernmost of the Isles, and from that moment headed direct for Portland, a cape on the southern shores of the singular island for which we were bound.

The voyage offered no incidents worthy of record. I bore it very well, but my uncle to his great annoyance, and even shame, was remarkably sea-sick! This *mal de mer* troubled him the more, that it prevented him from questioning Captain Bjarne as to the subject of Sneffels, as to the means of communication, and the facilities of transport. All these explanations he had to adjourn to the period of his arrival. His time meanwhile was spent lying in bed groaning, and dwelling anxiously on the hoped-for-termination of the voyage. I didn't pity him.

On the eleventh day we sighted Cape Portland, over which towered Mount Myrdals Yokul, which, the weather being clear, we made out very readily. The cape itself is nothing but a huge mount of granite standing naked and alone to meet the Atlantic waves. The *Valkyrie* kept off the coast, steering to the westward. On all sides were to be seen whole "schools" of whales and sharks. After some hours we came in sight of a solitary rock in the ocean, forming a mighty vault, through which the foaming waves poured with intense fury. The islets of Westman appeared to leap from the ocean, being so low in the water as scarcely to be seen until you were right upon them. From that moment the schooner was steered to the westward in order to round Cape Reykjaness, the western point of Iceland.

My uncle, to his great disgust, was unable even to crawl on deck, so heavy a sea was on, and thus lost the first view of the Land of Promise. Forty-eight hours later, after a storm which drove us far to sea under bare poles, we came once more in sight of land, and were boarded by a pilot, who, after three hours of dangerous navigation, brought the schooner safely to an anchor in the bay of Faxa before Reykjawik.

My uncle came out of his cabin pale, haggard, thin, but full of enthusiasm, his eyes dilated with pleasure and satisfaction. Nearly the whole population of the town was on foot to see us land. The fact was, that scarcely any one of them but expected some goods by the periodical vessel.

Professor Hardwigg was in haste to leave his prison, or rather as he called it, his hospital; but before he attempted to do so, he caught hold of my hand, led me to the quarterdeck of the schooner, took my arm with his left hand, and pointed inland with his right, over the northern part of the bay, to where rose a high two-peaked mountain—a double cone covered with eternal snow.

"Behold," he whispered in an awe-stricken voice, "behold—Mount Sneffels!"

Then without further remark, he put his finger to his lips, frowned darkly, and descended into the small boat which awaited us. I followed, and in a few minutes we stood upon the soil of mysterious Iceland!

Scarcely were we fairly on shore when there appeared before us a man of excellent appearance, wearing the costume of a military officer. He was, however, but a civil servant, a magistrate, the governor of the island—Baron Trampe. The Professor knew whom he had to deal with. He therefore handed him the letters from Copenhagen, and a brief conversation in Danish followed, to which I of course was a stranger, and for a very good reason, for I did not know the language in which they conversed. I afterwards heard, however, that Baron Trampe placed himself entirely at the beck and call of Professor Hardwigg.

My uncle was most graciously received by M. Finsen, the mayor, who as far as costume went, was quite as military as the governor, but also from character and occupation quite as pacific. As for his coadjutor M. Pictursson, he was absent on an episcopal visit to the northern portion of the diocese. We were therefore compelled to defer the pleasure of being presented to him. His absence was, however, more than compensated by the presence of M. Fridriksson, Professor of natural sciences in the college of Reykjawik, a man of invaluable ability. This modest scholar spoke no languages save Icelandic and Latin. When, therefore, he addressed himself to me in the language of Horace, we at once came to understand one another. He was, in fact, the only person that I did thoroughly understand during the whole period of my residence in this benighted island.

Out of three rooms of which his house was composed, two were placed at our service, and in a few hours we were installed with all our baggage, the amount of which rather astonished the simple inhabitants of Reykjawik.

"Now, Harry," said my uncle, rubbing his hands, "all goes well, the worst difficulty is now over."

"How the worst difficulty over?" I cried in fresh amazement.

"Doubtless. Here we are in Iceland. Nothing more remains but to descend into the bowels of the earth."

"Well, sir, to a certain extent you are right. We have only to go down—but, as far as I am concerned, that is not the question. I want to know how we are to get up again."

"That is the least part of the business, and does not in any way trouble me. In the meantime, there is not an hour to lose. I am about to visit the public library. Very likely I may find there some manuscripts from the hand of Saknussemm. I shall be glad to consult them."

"In the meanwhile," I replied, "I will take a walk through the town. Will you not likewise do so?"

"I feel no interest in the subject," said my uncle. "What for me is curious in this island, is not what is above the surface, but what is below."

I bowed by way of reply, put on my hat and furred cloak, and went out.

It was not an easy matter to lose oneself in the two streets of Reykjawik; I had therefore no need to ask my way. The town lies on a flat and marshy plain, between two hills. A vast field of lava skirts it on one side, falling away in terraces towards the sea. On the other hand is the large bay of Faxa, bordered on the north by the enormous glacier of Sneffels, and in which bay the *Valkyrie* was then the only vessel at anchor. Generally there were one or two English or French gunboats, to watch and protect the fisheries in the offing. They were now, however, absent on duty.

The longest of the streets of Reykjawik runs parallel to the shore. In this steet the merchants and traders live in wooden huts made with beams of wood, painted red,—mere log huts, such as you find in the wilds of America. The other street, situated more to the west, runs towards a little lake between the residences of the bishop and the other personages not engaged in commerce.

I had soon seen all I wanted of these weary and dismal thoroughfares. Here and there was a strip of discoloured turf, like an old worn-out bit of woollen carpet; and now and then a bit of kitchen garden, in which grew potatoes, cabbages, and lettuces, almost diminutive enough to suggest the idea of Lilliput.

In the centre of the new commercial street, I found the public cemetery, enclosed by an earthen wall. Though not very large, it appeared not likely to be filled for centuries. From hence I went to the house of the Governor—a mere hut in comparison with the Mansion House of Hamburg—but a palace alongside the other Icelandic houses. Between the little lake and the town was the church, built in simple Protestant style, and composed of calcined stones, thrown up by volcanic action. I have not the slightest doubt that in high winds, its red tiles were blown about, to the great annoyance of the pastor and congregation. Upon an eminence close at hand was the national school, in which were taught Hebrew, English, French and Danish.

In three hours my tour was complete. The general impression upon my mind was sadness. No trees, no vegetation, so to speak—on all sides volcanic peaks—the huts of turf and earth—more like roofs than houses. Thanks to the heat of these residences, grass grows on the roof, which grass is carefully cut for hay. I saw but few inhabitants during my excursion, but I met a crowd on the beach, drying, salting and loading cod-fish, the principal article of exportation. The men appeared robust but heavy; fairhaired like Germans, but of pensive mien—exiles of a higher scale in the ladder of humanity than the Esquimaux, but, I thought, much more unhappy, since with superior perceptions they are compelled to live within the limits of the Polar Circle.

Sometimes they gave vent to a convulsive laugh, but by no chance did they smile. Their costume consists of a coarse capote of black wool, known in Scandinavian countries as the "vadmel," a broad brimmed hat, trousers of red serge, and a piece of leather tied with strings for a shoe—a coarse kind of moccasin. The women, though sad-looking and mournful, had rather agreeable features, without much expression. They wear a boddice and petticoat of sombre vadmel. When unmarried they wear a little brown knitted cap over a crown of plaited hair; but when married, they cover their heads with a coloured handkerchief, over which they tie a white scarf.

CHAPTER 7

CONVERSATION AND DISCOVERY

WHEN I returned, dinner was ready. This meal was devoured by my worthy relative with avidity and voracity. His shipboard diet had turned his interior into a perfect gulf. The repast, which was more Danish than Icelandic, was in itself nothing, but the excessive hospitality of our host made us enjoy it doubly.

The conversation turned upon scientific matters, and M. Fridriksson asked my uncle what he thought of the public library.

"Library, sir?" cried my uncle; "it appears to me a collection of useless odd volumes, and a beggarly amount of empty shelves."

"What!" cried M. Fridriksson; "why, we have eight thousand volumes of most rare and valuable works—some in the Scandinavian language, besides all the new publications from Copenhagen."

"Eight thousand volumes, my dear sir—why, where are they?" cried my uncle.

"Scattered over the country, Professor Hardwigg. We are very studious, my dear sir, though we do live in Iceland. Every farmer, every labourer, every fisherman can both read and write—and we think that books instead of being locked up in cupboards, far from the sight of students, should be distributed as widely as possible. The books of our library are therefore, passed from hand to hand without returning to the library shelves perhaps for years."

"Then when foreigners visit you, there is nothing for them to see?"

"Well, sir, foreigners have their own libraries, and our first consideration is, that our humbler classes should be highly educated. Fortunately, the love of study is innate in the Icelandic people. In 1816 we founded a Literary Society and Mechanics' Institute; many foreign scholars of eminence are honorary members; we published books destined to educate our people, and these books have rendered valuable services to our country. Allow me to have the honour, Professor Hardwigg, to enrol you as an honorary member?"

My uncle, who already belonged to nearly every literary and scientific institution in Europe, immediately yielded to the amiable wishes of good M. Fridriksson.

"And now," he said, after many expressions of gratitude and good-will, "if you will tell me what books you expected to find, perhaps I may be of some assistance to you."

I watched my uncle keenly. For a minute or two he hesitated, as if unwilling to speak; to speak openly was, perhaps, to unveil his projects. Nevertheless, after sone reflection, he made up his mind.

"Well, M. Fridriksson," he said, in an easy unconcerned kind of way. "I was desirous of ascertaining, if among other valuable works, you had any of the learned Arne Saknussemm."

"Arne Saknussemm!" cried the Professor of Reykjawik; "you speak of one of the most distinguished scholars of the sixteenth century, of the great naturalist, the great alchemist, the great traveller.'

"Exactly so."

"One of the most distinguished men connected with Icelandic science and literature."

"As you say, sir——"

"A man illustrious above all."

"Yes, sir, all this is true, but his works?"

"We have none of them."

"Not in Iceland?"

"There are none in Iceland or elsewhere," answered the other, sadly.

"Why so?"

"Because Arne Saknussemm was persecuted for heresy, and in 1573 his works were publicly burnt at Copenhagen, by the hands of the common hangman."

"Very good! capital!" murmured my uncle, to the great astonishment of the worthy Icelander.

"You said, sir——"

"Yes, yes, all is clear, I see the link in the chain; everything is explained, and I now understand why Arne Saknussemm, put out of court, forced to hide his magnificent discoveries, was compelled to conceal beneath the veil of an incomprehensible cryptograph, the secret——"

"What secret?"

"A secret—which," stammered my uncle.

"Have you discovered some wonderful manuscript?" cried M. Fridriksson.

"No, no, I was carried away by my enthusiasm. A mere supposition."

"Very good, sir. But, really, to turn to another subject, I hope you will not leave our island without examining into its mineralogical riches."

"Well, the fact is, I am rather late. So many learned men have been here before me."

"Yes, yes, but there is still much to be done," cried M. Fridriksson.

"You think so," said my uncle, his eyes twinkling with hidden satisfaction.

"Yes, you have no idea how many unknown mountains, glaciers, volcanoes there are which remain to be studied. Without moving from where we sit, I can show you one. Yonder on the edge of the horizon, you see Sneffels."

"Oh yes, Sneffels," said my uncle.

"One of the most curious volcanoes in existence, the crater of which has been rarely visited.

"Extinct?"

"Extinct, any time these five hundred years," was the ready reply.

"Well," said my uncle, who dug his nails into his flesh, and pressed his knees tightly together to prevent himself from leaping up with joy. "I have a great mind to begin my studies with an examination of the geological mysteries of this Mount Seffel—Feisel—what do you call it?"

"Sneffels, my dear sir."

This portion of the conversation took place in Latin, and I had therefore understood all that had been said. I could scarcely keep my countenance when I found my uncle so cunningly concealing his delight and satisfaction. I must confess that his artful grimaces, put on to conceal his happiness, made him look like a new Mephistopheles.

"Yes, yes," he continued, "your proposition delights me. I will endeavour to climb to the summit of Sneffels, and, if possible, will descend into its crater."

"I very much regret," continued M. Fridriksson, "that my occupation will entirely preclude the possibility of my accompanying you. It would have been both pleasurable and profitable if I could have spared the time."

"No, no, a thousand times no," cried my uncle. "I do not wish to disturb the serenity of any man. I thank you, however, with all my heart. The presence of one so learned as yourself, would no doubt have been most useful, but the duties of your office and profession before everything."

In the innocence of his simple heart, our host did not perceive the irony of these remarks.

"I entirely approve your project," continued the Icelander, after some further remarks. "It is a good idea to begin by examining this volcano. You will make a harvest of curious observations. In the first place, how do you propose to get to Sneffels?"

"By sea. I shall cross the bay. Of course that is the most rapid route."

"Of course. But still it cannot be done."

"Why?"

"We have not an available boat in all Reykjawik," replied the other.

"What is to be done?"

"You must go by land along the coast. It is longer, but much more interesting."

"Then I must have a guide."

"Of course; and I have your very man."

"Somebody on whom I can depend?"

"Yes, an inhabitant of the peninsula on which Sneffels is situated. He is a very shrewd and worthy man, with whom you will be pleased. He speaks Danish like a Dane."

"When can I see him—to-day?"

"No, to-morrow; he will not be here before."

"To-morrow be it," replied my uncle, with a deep sigh.

The conversation ended by compliments on both sides. During the dinner my uncle had learned much as to the history of Arne Saknussemm, the reasons for his mysterious and hieroglyphical document. He also became aware that his host would not accompany him on his adventurous expedition, and that next day we should have a guide.

CHAPTER 8

THE EIDER-DOWN HUNTER—OFF AT LAST

THAT evening I took a brief walk on the shore near Reykjawik, after which I returned to an early sleep on my bed of coarse planks, where I slept the sleep of the just. When I awoke I heard my uncle speaking loudly in the next room. I rose hastily and joined him. He was talking in Danish with a man of tall stature, and of perfectly Herculean build. This man appeared to be possessed of very great strength. His eyes, which started rather prominently from a very large head, the face belonging to which was simple and naïve, appeared very quick and intelligent. Very long hair, which even in England would have been accounted exceedingly red, fell over his athletic shoulders. This native of Iceland was active and supple in appearance, though he scarcely moved his arms, being in fact one of those men who despise the habit of gesticulation common to southern people.

Everything in this man's manner revealed a calm and phlegmatic temperament. There was nothing indolent about him, but his appearance spoke of tranquillity. He was one of those who never seemed to expect anything from anybody, who liked to work when he thought proper, and whose philosophy nothing could astonish or trouble.

I began to comprehend his character, simply from the way in which he listened to the wild and impassioned verbiage of my worthy uncle. While the excellent Professor spoke sentence after sentence, he stood with folded arms, utterly still, motionless to all my uncle's gesticulations. When he wanted to say No he moved his head from left to right; when he acquiesced he nodded, so slightly that you could scarcely see the undulation of his head. This economy of motion was carried to the length of avarice.

Judging from his appearance I should have been a long time before I had suspected him to be what he was, a mighty hunter. Certainly his manner was not likely to frighten the game. How, then, did he contrive to get at his prey?

My surprise was slightly modified when I knew that this tranquil and solemn personage, was only a hunter of the eider-duck, the down of which is, after all, the greatest source of the Icelanders' wealth.

In the early days of summer, the female of the eider, a pretty sort of duck, builds its nest amid the rocks of the fjords—the name given to all narrow gulfs in Scandinavian countries—with which every part of the island is indented. No sooner has the eider duck made her nest than she lines the inside of it with the softest down from her breast. Then comes the hunter or trader, taking away the nest; the poor bereaved female begins her task over again, and this continues as long as any eider-down is to be found.

When she can find no more the male bird sets to work to see what he can do. As, however, his down is not so soft, and has therefore no commercial value, the hunter does not take the trouble to rob him of his nest-lining. The nest is accordingly finished, the eggs are laid, the little ones are born, and next year the harvest of eider-down is again collected.

Now, as the eider-duck never selects steep rocks or aspects to build its nest, but rather sloping and low cliffs near to the sea, the Icelandic hunter can carry on his trade operations without much difficulty. He is like a farmer who has neither to plough, to sow, nor to harrow, only to collect his harvest.*

This grave, sententious, silent person, as phlegmatic as an Englishman on the French stage, was named Hans Bjelke. He had called upon us in consequence of the recommendation of M. Fridriksson. He was, in fact, our future guide. It struck me that had I sought the world over, I could not have found a greater contradiction to my impulsive uncle.

They, however, readily understood one another. Neither of them had any thought about money; one was ready to take all that was offered him, the other ready to offer anything that was asked. It may readily be conceived, then, that an understanding was soon come to between them.

Now, the understanding was, that he was to take us to the village of Stapi, situated on the southern slope of the peninsula of Sneffels, at the very foot of the volcano. Hans, the guide, told us the distance was about twenty-two miles, a journey which my uncle supposed would take about two days.

But when my uncle came to understand that they were Danish miles, of eight thousand yards each, he was obliged to be more moderate in his ideas, and, considering the horrible roads we had to follow, to allow eight or ten days for the journey.

Four horses were prepared for us, two to carry the baggage, and two to bear the important weight of myself and uncle. Hans declared that nothing ever would make him climb on the back of any animal. He knew every inch of that part of the coast, and promised to take us the very shortest way.

His engagement with my uncle was by no means to cease with our arrival at Stapi; he was further to remain in his service during the whole time required for the completion of his scientific investigations, at the fixed salary of three rix-dollars a week, being exactly fourteen shillings and twopence, minus one farthing, English currency. One stipulation, however, was made by the guide—the money was to be paid to him every Saturday night, failing which, his engagement was at an end.

The day of our departure was fixed. My uncle wished to hand the eider-down hunter an advance, but he refused in one emphatic word—

"*Efter*."

Which being translated from Icelandic into plain English means—After.

The treaty concluded, our worthy guide retired without another word.

"A splendid fellow," said my uncle; "only he little suspects the marvellous part he is about to play in the history of the world."

"You mean, then," I cried in amazement, "that he should accompany us?"

"To the Interior of the Earth, yes;" replied my uncle. "Why not?"

There were yet forty-eight hours to elapse before we made our final start. To my great regret, our whole time was taken up in making preparations for our journey. All our industry and ability were devoted to packing every object in

* The birds, however, are not always so accommodating. They are found in the southern part of England as a winter visitant, but in the more northern part of our isle, and in the north of Scotland remain all the year. One of our ablest naturalists says: "Taking these nests is a regular business not unattended with risk, on account of the precipitous localities in which the eider-duck often breeds." Again, "The eider is a shy, retiring bird, placing its nest on islands and rocks projecting well into the sea."

Hans Bjelke, the guide.

the most advantageous manner—the instruments on one side, the arms on the other, the tools here and the provisions there. There were, in fact, four distinct groups.

The instruments were of course of the best manufacture:—

1. A centigrade thermometer of Eizel, counting up to 150 degrees, which to me did not appear half enough—or too much. Too hot by half, if the degree of heat was to ascend so high—in which case we should certainly be cooked—not enough, if we wanted to ascertain the exact temperature of springs or metal in a state of fusion.

2. A *manometer* worked by compressed air, an instrument used to ascertain the upper atmospheric pressure on the level of the ocean. Perhaps a common barometer would not have done as well, the atmospheric pressure being likely to increase in proportion as we descended below the surface of the earth.

3. A first-class chronometer made by Boissonnas, of Geneva, set at the meridian of Hamburg, from which Germans calculate, as the English do from Greenwich, and the French from Paris.

4. Two compasses, one for horizontal guidance, the other to ascertain the dip.

5. A night glass.

6. Two Ruhmkorff's coils, which, by means of a current of electricity, would ensure us a very excellent, easy carried, and certain means of obtaining light.

7. A voltaic battery on the newest principle.*

Our arms consisted of two rifles, with two revolving six-shooters. Why these arms were provided it was impossible for me to say. I had every reason to believe that we had neither wild beasts nor savage natives to fear. My uncle, on the other hand, was quite as devoted to his arsenal as to his collection of instruments, and above all was very careful with his provision of fulminating or gun cotton, warranted to keep in any climate, and of which the expansive force was known to be greater than that of ordinary gunpowder.

Our tools consisted of two pickaxes, two crowbars, a silken ladder, three iron-shod Alpine poles, a hatchet, a hammer, a dozen wedges, some pointed pieces of iron, and a quantity of strong rope. You may conceive that the whole made a tolerable parcel, especially when I mention that the ladder itself was three hundred feet long!

* Thermometer (*thermos*, hot, and *metron*, measure); an instrument for measuring the temperature of the air.—Manometer (*manos*, rare, and *metron*, measure); an instrument to show the density or rarity of gases.—Chronometer (*chronos*, time, and *metron*, measure) a time measurer, or superior watch.—Ruhmkorff's coil, an instrument for producing currents of induced electricity of great intensity. It consists of a coil of copper wire, insulated by being covered with silk, surrounded by another coil of fine wire, also insulated, in which a momentary current is induced when a current is passed through the inner coil from a voltaic battery. When the apparatus is in action, the gas becomes luminous, and produces a white and continued light. The battery and wire are carried in a leather bag, which the traveller fastens by a strap to his shoulders. The lantern is in front, and enables the benighted wanderer to see in the most profound obscurity. He may venture without fear of explosion into the midst of the most inflammable gases, and the lantern will burn beneath the deepest waters. M. Ruhmkorff, an able and learned chemist, discovered the induction coil. In 1864 he obtained the great French prize of £2,000 for this ingenious application of electricity.—A voltaic battery, so called from Volta, its designer, is an apparatus consisting of a series of metal plates arranged in pairs and subjected to the action of saline solutions for producing currents of electricity.

Then there came the important question of provisions. The hamper was not very large but tolerably satisfactory, for I knew that in concentrated essence of meat and biscuit there was enough to last six months. The only liquid provided by uncle was scheidam. Of water, not a drop. We had, however, an ample supply of gourds, and my uncle counted on finding water, and enough to fill them, as soon as we commenced our downward journey.

My remarks as to the temperature, the quality, and even as to the possibility of none being found, remained wholly without effect.

To make up the exact list of our travelling gear—for the guidance of future travellers—I will add, that we carried a medicine and surgical chest with all apparatus necessary for wounds, fractures and blows; lint, scissors, lancets—in fact, a perfect collection of horrible-looking instruments; a number of phials containing ammonia, alcohol, ether, goulard water, aromatic vinegar, in fact, every possible and impossible drug—finally, all the materials for working the Ruhmkorff coil!

My uncle had also been careful to lay in a goodly supply of tobacco, several flasks of very fine gunpowder, boxes of tinder, besides a large black belt crammed full of notes and gold. Good boots rendered water-tight were to be found to the number of six in the tool-box.

"My boy, with such clothing, with such boots, and such general equipments," said my uncle, in a state of rapturous delight; "we may hope to travel far."

It took a whole day to put all these matters in order. In the evening we dined with Baron Trampe, in company with the Mayor of Reykjawik, and Doctor Hyaltalin, the great medical man of Iceland. M. Fridriksson was not present, and I was afterwards sorry to hear that he and the governor did not agree on some matters connected with the administration of the island. Unfortunately, the consequence was, that I did not understand a word that was said at dinner—a kind of semi-official reception. One thing I can say, my uncle never left off speaking.

The next day our labour came to an end. Our worthy host delighted my uncle, Professor Hardwigg, by giving him a good map of Iceland, a most important and precious document for a mineralogist.

Our last evening was spent in a long conversation with M. Fridriksson, whom I liked very much—the more that I never expected to see him or any one else again. After this agreeable way of spending an hour or so, I tried to sleep. In vain; with the exception of a few dozes, my night was miserable.

At five o'clock in the morning I was awakened from the only real half hour's sleep of the night, by the loud neighing of horses under my window. I hastily dressed myself and went down into the street. Hans was engaged in putting the finishing stroke to our baggage, which he did in a silent, quiet way that won my admiration, and yet he did it admirably well. My uncle wasted a great deal of breath in giving him directions, but worthy Hans took not the slightest notice of his words.

At six o'clock all our preparations were completed, and M. Fridriksson shook hands heartily with us. My uncle thanked him warmly, in the Icelandic language, for his kind hospitality, speaking truly from the heart.

As for myself, I put together a few of my best Latin phrases and paid him the highest compliments I could. This fraternal and friendly duty performed, we salled forth and mounted our horses.

As soon as we were quite ready, M. Fridriksson advanced, and by way of farewell, called after me in the words of Virgil—words which appeared to have been made for us, travellers starting for an uncertain destination:—

"*Et quacunque viam dederit fortuna sequamur.*"

("And whichsoever way thou goest, may fortune follow!")

CHAPTER 9

OUR START—WE MEET WITH ADVENTURES BY THE WAY

THE weather was overcast but settled, when we commenced our adventurous and perilous journey. We had neither to fear fatiguing heat nor drenching rain. It was, in fact, real tourist weather.

As there was nothing I liked better than horse exercise, the pleasure of riding through an unknown country, caused the early part of our enterprise to be particularly agreeable to me.

I began to enjoy the exhilarating delight of travelling, a life of desire, gratification and liberty. The truth is, that my spirits rose so rapidly, that I began to be indifferent to what had once appeared to be a terrible journey.

"After all," I said to myself, "what do I risk? Simply to take a journey through a curious country, to climb a remarkable mountain, and if the worst comes to the worst, to descend into the crater of an extinct volcano."

There could be no doubt that this was all this terrible Saknussemm had done. As to the existence of a gallery, or of subterraneous passages leading into the interior of the earth, the idea was simply absurd, the hallucination of a distempered imagination. All, then, that may be required of me I will do cheerfully, and will create no difficulty.

It was just before we left Reykjawik that I came to this decision.

Hans, our extraordinary guide, went first, walking with a steady, rapid, and unvarying step. Our two horses with the luggage followed of their own accord, without requiring whip or spur. My uncle and I came behind, cutting a very tolerable figure upon our small but vigorous animals.

Iceland is one of the largest islands in Europe. It contains thirty thousand square miles of surface, and has about seventy thousand inhabitants. Geographers have divided it into four parts, and we had to cross the South-west quarter which in the vernacular is called Sudvestr Fjordùngr.

Hans, on taking his departure from Reykjawik, had followed the line of the sea. We took our way through poor and sparse meadows, which made a desperate effort every year to show a little green. They very rarely succeed in a good show of yellow.

The rugged summits of the rocky hills were dimly visible on the edge of the horizon, through the misty fogs; every now and then some heavy flakes of snow showed conspicuous in the morning light, while certain lofty and pointed rocks were first lost in the grey low clouds, their summits clearly visible above, like jagged reefs rising from a troublous sea.

Every now and then a spur of rock came down through the arid ground, leaving us scarcely room to pass. Our horses, however, appeared not only well acquainted with the country, but by a kind of instinct, knew which was the best road. My uncle had not even the satisfaction of urging forward his steed by whip, spur, or voice. It was utterly useless to show any signs of impatience. I could not help smiling to see him look so big on his little horse; his long legs now and then touching the ground made him look like a six-footed centaur.

"Good beast, good beast," he would cry. "I assure you, Henry, that I begin to think no animal is more intelligent than an Icelandic horse. Snow, tempest, impracticable roads, rocks, icebergs—nothing stops him. He is brave; he is sober; he is safe; he never makes a false step; never glides or slips from his path. I dare to say that if any river, any fjord has to be crossed—and I have no doubt there will be many—you will see him enter the water without hesitation like an amphibious animal, and reach the opposite side in safety. We must not, however, attempt to hurry him; we must allow him to have his own way, and I will undertake to say that between us we shall do our ten leagues a day."

"We may do so," was my reply, "but what about our worthy guide?"

"I have not the slightest anxiety about him: those sort of people go ahead without knowing even what they are about. Look at Hans. He moves so little that it is impossible for him to become fatigued. Besides, if he were to complain of weariness, he could have the loan of my horse. I should have a violent attack of the cramp if I were not to have some sort of exercise. My arms are right—but my legs are getting a little stiff.

All this while we were advancing at a rapid pace. The country we had reached was already nearly a desert. Here and there could be seen an isolated farm, some solitary boër, or Icelandic house, built of wood, earth, fragments of lava—looking like beggars on the highway of life. These wretched and miserable huts excited in us such pity that we felt half disposed to leave alms at every door. In this country there are no roads, paths are nearly unknown, and vegetation, poor as it was, slowly as it reached perfection, soon obliterated all traces of the few travellers who passed from place to place.

Nevertheless, this division of the province, situated only a few miles from the capital, is considered one of the best cultivated and most thickly peopled in all Iceland. What, then, must be the state of the less known and more distant parts of the island? After travelling fully half a Danish mile, we had met neither a farmer at the door of his hut, nor even a wandering shepherd with his wild and savage flock.

A few stray cows and sheep were only seen occasionally. What, then, must we expect when we come to the upheaved regions—to the districts broken and roughened from volcanic eruptions and subterraneous commotions?

We were to learn this all in good time. I saw, however, on consulting the map, that we avoided a good deal of this rough country, by following the winding and desolate shores of the sea. In reality, the great volcanic movement of the island, and all its attendant phenomena, is concentrated in the interior of the island; there, horizontal layers or strata of rocks, piled one upon the other, eruptions of basaltic origin, and streams of lava, have given this country a kind of supernatural reputation.

Little did I expect, however, the spectacle which awaited us when we reached the peninsula of Sneffels, where agglomerations of nature's ruins form a kind of terrible chaos.

Some two hours or more after we had left the city of Reykjawik, we reached the little town called Aoalkirkja, or the principal church. It consists simply of a few houses—not what in England or Germany we should call a hamlet.

Hans stopped here one half hour. He shared our frugal breakfast, answered *yes* and *no* to my uncle's questions as to the nature of the road, and at last when asked where we were to pass the night was as laconic as usual.

"Gardar!" was his one-worded reply.

I took occasion to consult the map, to see where Gardar was to be found. After looking keenly I found a small town of that name on the borders of the Hvalfjord, about four miles from Reykjawik. I pointed this out to my uncle, who made a very energetic grimace.

"Only four miles out of twenty-two? Why it is only a little walk."

He was about to make some energetic observation to the guide, but Hans, without taking the slightest notice of him, went in front of the horses, and walked ahead with the same imperturbable phlegm he had always exhibited.

Three hours later, still travelling over those apparently interminable and sandy prairies, we were compelled to go round the Kollafjord, an easier and shorter cut than crossing the gulfs. Shortly after we entered a place of communal jurisdiction called Ejulberg, and the clock of which would then have struck twelve, if any Icelandic church had been rich enough to possess so valuable and useful an article. These sacred edifices are, however, very much like these people, who do without watches—and never miss them.

Here the horses were allowed to take some rest and refreshment, then following a narrow strip of shore between high rocks and the sea, they took us without farther halt to the "aoalkirkja" of Brantar, and after another mile to "Saurboer Annexia," a chapel of ease, situated on the southern bank of the Hvalfjord.

It was four o'clock in the evening and we had travelled four Danish miles, about equal to twenty English.

The fjord was in this place about half-a-mile in width. The sweeping and broken waves came rolling in upon the pointed rocks; the gulf was surrounded by rocky walls—a mighty cliff, three thousand feet in height, remarkable for its brown strata, separated here and there by beds of tufa of a reddish hue. Now, whatever may have been the intelligence of our horses, I had not the slightest reliance upon them, as a means of crossing a stormy arm of the sea. To ride over salt water upon the back of a little horse seemed to me absurd.

"If they are really intelligent," I said to myself, "they will certainly not make the attempt. In any case, I shall trust rather to my own intelligence than theirs."

But my uncle was in no humour to wait. He dug his heels into the sides of his steed, and made for the shore. His horse went to the very edge of the water, sniffed at the approaching wave and retreated.

My uncle, who was, sooth to say, quite as obstinate as the beast he bestrode, insisted on his making the desired advance. This attempt was followed by a new refusal on the part of the horse which quietly shook its head. This demonstration of rebellion was followed by a volley of words and a stout application of whipcord; also followed by kicks on the part of the horse, which threw its head and heels upwards and tried to throw his rider. At length the sturdy little pony, spreading out his legs, in a stiff and ludicrous attitude, got from under the professor's legs, and left him standing, with both feet on a separate stone, like the Colossus of Rhodes.

"Wretched animal!" cried my uncle, suddenly transformed into a foot passenger—and as angry and ashamed as a dismounted cavalry officer on the field of battle.

"Farja," said the guide, tapping him familiarly on the shoulder.

"What, a ferry boat!"

"*Der,*" answered Hans, pointing to where lay the boat in question—"there."

"Well," I cried, quite delighted with the information; "so it is."

"Why did you not say so before," cried my uncle; "why not start at once?"

"Tidvatten," said the guide.

"What does he say?" I asked, considerably puzzled by the delay and the dialogue.

"He says tide," replied my uncle, translating the Danish word for my information.

"Of course I understand—we must wait till the tide serves."

"*For bida?*" asked my uncle.

"*Ja,*" replied Hans.

My uncle frowned, stamped his feet and then followed the horses to where the boat lay.

I thoroughly understood and appreciated the necessity for waiting, before crossing the fjord, for that moment when the sea at its highest point is in a state of slack water. As neither the ebb nor flow can then be felt, the ferry boat was in no danger of being carried out to sea, or dashed upon the rocky coast.

The favourable moment did not come until six o'clock in the evening. Then my uncle, myself, and guide, two boatmen and the four horses got into a very awkward flat-bottomed boat. Accustomed as I had been to the steam ferry-boats of the Elbe, I found the long oars of the boatmen but sorry means of locomotion. We were more than an hour in crossing the fjord; but at length the passage was concluded without accident.

Half-an-hour later we reached Gardar.

CHAPTER 10

TRAVELLING IN ICELAND—THE LEPERS

It ought, one would have thought, to have been night, even in the sixty-fifth parallel of latitude; but still the nocturnal illumination did not surprise me. For in Iceland, during the months of June and July, the sun never sets.

The temperature, however, was very much lower than I expected. I was cold, but even that did not affect me so much as ravenous hunger. Welcome indeed, therefore, was the hut which hospitably opened its doors to us.

It was merely the house of a peasant, but in the matter of hospitality, it was worthy of being the palace of a king. As we alighted at the door the master of the house came forward, held out his hand, and without any further ceremony, signaled to us to follow him.

We followed him, for to accompany him was impossible. A long, narrow, gloomy passage led into the interior of this habitation, made from beams roughly squared by the axe. This passage gave ingress to every room. The chambers were four in number—the kitchen, the workshop, where the weaving was carried on, the general sleeping chamber of the family, and the best room, to which strangers were specially invited. My uncle, whose lofty stature had not been taken into consideration when the house was built, contrived to knock his head against the beams of the roof.

We were introduced into our chamber, a kind of large room with a hard earthern floor, and lighted by a window, the panes of which were made of a sort of parchment from the intestines of sheep—very far from transparent.

The bedding was composed of dry hay thrown into two long red wooden boxes, ornamented with sentences painted in Icelandic. I really had no idea that we should be made so comfortable. There was one objection to the house, and that was, the very powerful odour of dried fish, of macerated meat, and of sour milk, which three fragrances combined, did not at all suit my olfactory nerves.

As soon as we had freed ourselves from our heavy travelling costume, the voice of our host was heard calling to us to come into the kitchen, the only room in which the Icelanders ever make any fire, no matter how cold it may be.

My uncle, nothing loth, hastened to obey this hospitable and friendly invitation. I followed.

The kitchen chimney was made on an antique model. A large stone standing in the middle of the room was the fireplace, above, in the roof, was a hole for the smoke to pass through. This apartment was kitchen, parlour and dining-room all in one.

On our entrance, our worthy host, as if he had not seen us before, advanced ceremoniously, uttered a word which means "be happy," and then kissed each of us on the cheek.

His wife followed, pronounced the same word, with the same ceremonial, then the husband and wife, placing their right hands upon their hearts, bowed profoundly.

This excellent Icelandic woman was the mother of nineteen children, who, little and big, rolled, crawled, and walked about in the midst of volumes of smoke arising from the angular fireplace in the middle of the room. Every now and then I could see a fresh white head, and a slightly melancholy expression of countenance, peering at me through the vapour.

Both my uncle and myself, however, were very friendly with the whole party, and before we were aware of it, there were three or four of these little ones on our shoulders, as many on our boxes, and the rest hanging about our legs. Those who could speak kept crying out *sællvertu* in every possible and impossible key. Those who did not speak only made all the more noise.

This concert was interrupted by the announcement of supper. At this moment our worthy guide, the eider-duck hunter, came in after seeing to the feeding and stabling of the horses—which consisted in letting them loose to browse on the stunted green of the Icelandic prairies. There was little for them to eat, but moss and some very dry and innutritious grass; next day they were ready before the door, some time before we were.

"Welcome," said Hans.

Then tranquilly, with the air of an automaton, without any more expression in one kiss than another, he embraced the host, the hostess and their nineteen children.

This ceremony concluded to the satisfaction of all parties, we all sat down to table, that is twenty-four of us, somewhat crowded. Those who were best off had only two juveniles on their knees.

As soon, however, as the inevitable soup was placed on the table, the natural taciturnity, common even to Icelandic babies, prevailed over all else. Our host filled our plates with a portion of *Lichen* soup of Iceland moss, of by no means disagreeable flavour, an enormous lump of fish floating in sour butter. After that there came some "skyr," a kind of curds and whey, served with biscuits and juniper-berry juice. To drink, we had blanda, skimmed milk with water. I was hungry, so hungry, that by way of dessert I finished up with a basin of thick oaten porridge.

As soon as the meal was over, the children disappeared, whilst the grown people sat round the fireplace, on which was placed turf, heather, cow dung and dried fish-bones. As soon as everybody was sufficiently warm, a general dispersion took place, all retiring to their respective couches. Our hostess offered to pull off our stockings and trousers, according to the custom of the country, but as we graciously declined to be so honoured, she left us to our bed of dry fodder.

Next day, at five in the morning, we took our leave of these hospitable peasants. My uncle had great difficulty in making them accept a sufficient and proper remuneration.

Hans then gave the signal to start.

We had scarcely got a hundred yards from Gardar, when the character of the country changed. The soil began to be marshy and boggy, and less favourable to progress. To the right, the range of mountains was prolonged indefinitely like a great system of natural fortifications, of which we skirted the glacis. We met with numerous streams and rivulets which it was necessary to ford, and that without wetting our baggage. As we advanced, the deserted appearance increased, and yet now and then we could see human shadows flitting in the distance. When a sudden turn of the track brought us within easy reach of one of these spectres, I felt a sudden impulse of disgust at the sight of a swollen head, with shining skin, utterly without hair, and whose repulsive and revolting wounds could be seen through his rags. The unhappy wretches never came forward to beg; on the contrary, they ran away; not so quick, however, but that Hans was able to salute them with the universal Sællvertu.

"Spetelsk," said he.

"A leper," explained my uncle.

The very sound of such a word caused a feeling of repulsion. The horrible affection known as leprosy, which has almost vanished before the effects of modern science, is common in Iceland. It is not contagious but hereditary, so that marriage is strictly prohibited to these unfortunate creatures.

These poor lepers did not tend to enliven our journey, the scene of which was inexpressibly sad and lonely. The very last tufts of grassy vegetation appeared to die at our feet. Not a tree was to be seen, except a few stunted willows about as big as blackberry bushes. Now and then we watched a falcon soaring in the grey and misty air, taking his flight towards warmer and sunnier regions. I could not help feeling a sense of melancholy come over me. I sighed for my own Native Land, and wished to be back with Gretchen.

We were compelled to cross several little fjords, and at last came to a real gulf. The tide was at its height, and we were able to go over at once, and reach the hamlet of Alftanes, about a mile farther.

That evening, after fording the Alfa and the Heta, two rivers rich in trout and pike, we were compelled to pass the night in a deserted house, worthy of being haunted by all the fays of Scandinavian mythology. The King of Cold had taken up his residence there, and made us feel his presence all night.

The following day was remarkable by its lack of any particular incidents. Always the same damp and swampy soil; the same dreary uniformity; the same sad and monotonous aspect of scenery. In the evening, having accomplished the half of our projected journey, we slept at the Annexia of Krosolbt.

For a whole mile we had under our feet nothing but lava. This disposition of the soil is called *hraun:* the crumbled lava on the surface was in some instances like ship cables stretched out horizontally, in others coiled up in heaps; an immense field of lava came from the neighbouring mountains, all extinct volcanoes, but whose remains showed what once they had been. Here and there could be made out the steam from hot water springs.

There was no time, however, for us to take more than a cursory view of these phenomena. We had to go forward with what speed we might. Soon the soft and swampy soil again appeared under the feet of our horses, while at every hundred yards we came upon one or more small lakes. Our journey was now in a westernly direction; we had, in fact, swept round the great bay of Faxa, and the twin white summits of Sneffels rose to the clouds at a distance of less than five miles.

The horses now advanced rapidly. The accidents and difficulties of the soil no longer checked them. I confess that fatigue began to tell severely upon me; but my uncle was as firm and as hard as he had been on the first day. I could not help admiring both the excellent Professor and the worthy guide; for they appeared to regard this rugged expedition as a mere walk!

On Saturday, the 20th June, at six o'clock in the evening, we reached Budir, a small town picturesquely situated on the shore of the ocean; and here the guide asked for his money. My uncle settled with him immediately. It was now the family of Hans himself, that is to say, his uncles, his cousins-german, who offered us hospitality. We were exceedingly well received, and without taking too much advantage of the goodness of these worthy people, I should have liked very much to have rested with them after the fatigues of the journey. But my uncle, who did not require rest, had no idea of anything of the kind; and despite the fact that next day was Sunday, I was compelled once more to mount my steed.

The soil was again affected by the nieghbourhood of the mountains, whose granite peered out of the ground like tops of an old oak. We were skirting the enormous base of the mighty volcano. My uncle never took his eyes from off it; he could not keep from gesticulating, and looking at it with a kind of sullen defiance, as much us to say, "that is the giant I have made up my mind to conquer."

After four hours of steady travelling, the horses stopped of themselves before the door of the presbytery of Stapi.

CHAPTER 11

WE REACH MOUNT SNEFFELS—THE "REYKIR"

STAPI is a town consisting of thirty huts, built on a large plain of lava, exposed to the rays of the sun, reflected from the volcano. It stretches its humble tenements along the end of a little fjord, surrounded by a basaltic wall of the most singular character.

Basalt is a brown rock of igneous origin. It assumes regular forms, which astonish by their singular appearance. Here we found Nature proceeding geometrically, and working quite after a human fashion, as if she had employed the plummet line, the compass, and the rule. If elsewhere she produces grand artistic effects by piling up huge masses without order or connection—if elsewhere we see truncated cones, imperfect pyramids, with an odd succession of lines; here, as if wishing to give a lesson in regularity, and preceding the architects of the early ages, she has erected a severe order of architecture, which neither the splendours of Babylon nor the marvels of Greece ever surpassed.

I had often heard of the Giants' Causeway in Ireland, the Grotto of Fingal in one of the Hebrides, but the grand spectacle of a real basaltic formation had never yet come before my eyes.

This at Stapi gave us an idea of one in all its wonderful beauty and grace.

The wall of the fjord, like nearly the whole of the peninsula, consisted of a series of vertical columns, in height about thirty feet. These upright pillars of stone, of the finest proportions, supported an archivault of horizontal columns which formed a kind of half-vaulted roof above the sea. At certain intervals, and below this natural basin, the eye was pleased and surprised by the sight of oval openings through which the outward waves came thundering in volleys of foam. Some banks of basalt, torn from their fastenings by the fury of the waves, lay scattered on the ground like the ruins of an ancient temple—ruins eternally young, over which the storms of ages swept without producing any perceptible effect!

This was the last stage of our journey. Hans had brought us along with fidelity and intelligence, and I began to feel somewhat more comfortable when I reflected that he was to accompany us still farther on our way.

When we halted before the house of the Rector, a small and incommodious cabin, neither handsome nor more comfortable than those of his neighbours, I saw a man in the act of shoeing a horse, a hammer in his hand, and a leathern apron tied round his waist.

"Be happy," said the eider-down hunter, using his national salutation in his own language.

"*Good-dag*—good day!" replied the former, in excellent Danish.

"Kyrkoherde," cried Hans, turning round and introducing him to my uncle.

"The Rector," repeated the worthy Professor; "it appears, my dear Harry, that this worthy man is the Rector, and is not above doing his own work."

During the speaking of these few words the guide intimated to the Kyrkoherde what was the true state of the case. The good man, ceasing from his occupation, gave a kind of halloo, upon which a tall woman, almost a giantess, came out of the hut. She was at least six feet high, which in that region is something considerable.

My first impression was one of horror. I thought she had come to give us the Icelandic kiss. I had however, nothing to fear, for she did not even show much inclination to receive us into her house.

The room devoted to strangers appeared to me to be by far the worst in the presbytery; it was narrow, dirty, and offensive. There was, however, no choice about the matter. The Rector had no notion of practising the usual cordial and antique hospitality. Far from it. Before the day was over, I found we had to deal with a blacksmith, a fisherman, a hunter, a carpenter—anything but a clergyman. It must be said in his favour that we had caught him on a week day: probably he appeared to greater advantage on the Sunday.

These poor priests receive from the Danish Government a most ridiculously inadequate salary, and collect one quarter of the tithe of their parish—not more than sixty marks current, or about £3 10*s*. sterling. Hence the necessity of working to live. In truth, we soon found that our host did not count civility among the cardinal virtues.

My uncle soon became aware of the kind of man he had to deal with. Instead of a worthy and learned scholar, he found a dull ill-mannered peasant. He therefore resolved to start on his great expedition as soon as possible. He did not care about fatigue, and resolved to spend a few days in the mountains.

The preparations for our departure were made the very next day after our arrival at Stapi; Hans now hired three Icelanders to take the place of the horses—which could no longer carry our luggage. When, however, these worthy islanders had reached the bottom of the crater, they were to go back and leave us to ourselves. This point was settled before they would agree to start.

On this occasion, my uncle partially confided in Hans, the eider-duck hunter, and gave him to understand that it was his intention to continue his exploration of the volcano to the last possible limits.

Hans listened calmly, and then nodded his head. To go there, or elsewhere, to bury himself in the bowels of the earth, or to travel over its summits, was all the same to him! As for me, amused and occupied by the incidents of travel, I had begun to forget the inevitable future; but now I was once more destined to realise the actual state of affairs. What was to be done? Run away? But if I really had intended to leave Professor Hardwigg to his fate, it should have been at Hamburg and not at the foot of Sneffels.

One idea, above all others, began to trouble me: a very terrible idea, and one calculated to shake the nerves of a man even less sensitive than myself.

"Let us consider the matter," I said to myself; "we are going to ascend the Sneffels mountain. Well and good. We are about to pay a visit to the very bottom of the crater. Good, still. Others have done it and did not perish from that course.

"That, however, is not the whole matter to be considered. If a road does really present itself by which to descend into the dark and subterraneous bowels of Mother Earth, if this thrice unhappy Saknussemm has really told the truth, we shall be most certainly lost in the midst of the labyrinth of subterraneous galleries of the volcano. Now, we have no evidence to prove that Sneffels is really extinct. What proof have we that an eruption is not shortly about to take place? Because the monster has slept soundly since 1229, does it follow that he is never to wake?

"If he does wake what is to become of us?"

These were questions worth thinking about, and upon them I reflected long and deeply. I could not lie down in search of sleep without dreaming of eruptions. The more I thought, the more I objected to be reduced to the state of dross and ashes.

I could stand it no longer: so I determined at last to submit the whole case to my uncle, in the most adroit manner possible, and under the form of some totally irreconcilable hypothesis.

I sought him. I laid before him my fears, and then drew back in order to let him get his passion over at his ease.

"I have been thinking about the matter," he said, in the quietest tone in the world.

What did he mean? Was he at last about to listen to the voice of reason? Did he think of suspending his projects? It was almost too much happiness to be true.

I however made no remark. In fact, I was only too anxious not to interrupt him, and allowed him to reflect at his leisure. After some moments he spoke out.

"I have been thinking about the matter," he resumed. "Ever since we have been at Stapi, my mind has been almost solely occupied with the grave question which has been submitted to me by yourself—for nothing would be unwiser and more inconsistent than to act with imprudence."

"I heartily agree with you, my dear uncle," was my somewhat hopeful rejoinder.

"It is now six hundred years since Sneffels has spoken—but though now reduced to a state of utter silence, he may speak again. New volcanic eruptions are always preceded by perfectly well-known phenomena. I have closely examined the inhabitants of this region; I have carefully studied the soil, and I beg to tell you emphatically, my dear Harry, there will be no eruption at present."

As I listened to his positive affirmations, I was stupefied and could say nothing.

"I see you doubt my word," said my uncle; "follow me."

I obeyed mechanically.

Leaving the presbytery, the Professor took a road through an opening in the basaltic rock, which led far away from the sea. We were soon in open country, if we could give such a name to a place all covered with volcanic deposits. The whole land seemed crushed under the weight of enormous stones—of trap, of basalt, of granite, of lava, and of all other volcanic substances.

I could see many spouts of steam rising in the air. These white vapours, called in the Icelandic language "reykir," come from hot water fountains, and indicate by their violence the volcanic activity of the soil. Now the sight of these appeared to justify my apprehension. I was, therefore, all the more surprised and mortified when my uncle thus addressed me.

"You see all this smoke, Harry, my boy?"

"Yes, sir."

"Well, as long as you see them thus, you have nothing to fear from the volcano."

"How can that be?"

"Be careful to remember this," continued the Professor. "At the approach of an eruption these spouts of vapour redouble their activity—to disappear altogether during the period of volcanic eruption; for the elastic fluids, no longer having the necessary tension, seek refuge in the interior of the crater, instead of escaping through the fissures of the earth. If, then, the steam remains in its normal or habitual state, if their energy does not increase, and if you add to this, the remark, that the wind is not replaced by heavy atmospheric pressure and dead calm, you may be quite sure that there is no fear of any immediate eruption."

"But——"

"Enough, my boy. When science has sent forth her fiat—it is only to hear and obey."

I came back to the house quite downcast and disappointed. My uncle had completely defeated me with his scientific arguments. Nevertheless, I had still one hope, and that was, when once we were at the bottom of the crater, that it would be impossible in default of a gallery or tunnel, to descend any deeper; and this, despite all the learned Saknussemms in the world.

I passed the whole of the following night with a nightmare on my chest! and, after unheard of miseries and tortures, found myself in the very depths of the earth, from which I was suddenly launched into planetary space, under the form of an eruptive rock!

Next day, the 23rd June, Hans calmly awaited us outside the presbytery with his two companions loaded with provisions, tools, and instruments. Two iron-shod poles, two guns, and two large game bags, were reserved for my uncle and myself. Hans, who was a man who never forgot even the minutest precautions, had added to our baggage a large skin full of water, as an addition to our gourds. This assured us water for eight days.

It was nine o'clock in the morning when we were quite ready. The rector and his huge wife or servant, I never knew which, stood at the door to see us off. They appeared to be about to inflict on us the usual final kiss of the Icelanders. To our supreme astonishment their adieu took the shape of a formidable bill, in which they even counted the use of the pastoral house, really and truly the most abominable and dirty place I ever was in. The worthy couple cheated and robbed us like a Swiss innkeeper, and made us feel, by the sum we had to pay, the splendours of their hospitality.

My uncle, however, paid without bargaining. A man who had made up his mind to undertake a voyage into the Interior of the Earth, is not the man to haggle over a few miserble rix-dollars.

This important matter settled, Hans gave the signal for departure, and some few moments later we had left Stapi.

CHAPTER 12

THE ASCENT OF MOUNT SNEFFELS

THE huge volcano which was the first stage of our daring experiment, is above five thousand feet high. Sneffels is the termination of a long range of rocky volcanic mountains, of a different character to the system of the island itself. One of its peculiarities is its two huge pointed summits. From whence we started it was impossible to make out the real outlines of the peak against the grey field

The "Reykir."

of sky. All we could distinguish was a vast dome of white, which fell downwards from the head of the giant.

The commencement of the great undertaking filled me with awe. Now that we had actually started, I began to believe in the reality of the undertaking!

Our party formed quite a procession. We walked in single file, preceded by Hans, the imperturbable eider-duck hunter. He calmly led us by narrow paths where two persons could by no possibility walk abreast. Conversation was wholly impossible. We had all the more opportunity to reflect and admire the awful grandeur of the scene around.

Beyond the extraordinary basaltic wall of the fjord of Stapi we found ourselves making our way through fibrous turf, over which grew a scanty vegetation of grass, the residuum of the ancient vegetation of the swampy peninsula. The vast mass of this combustible, the field of which as yet is utterly unexplored, would suffice to warm Iceland for a whole century. This mighty turf pit, measured from the bottom of certain ravines, is often not less than seventy feet deep, and presents to the eye, the view of successive layers of black burned-up rocky detritus, separated by thin streaks of porous sandstone.

The grandeur of the spectacle was undoubted, as well as its arid and deserted air.

As a true nephew of the great Professor Hardwigg, and despite my preoccupation and doleful fears of what was to come, I observed with great interest the vast collection of mineralogical curiosities spread out before me in this vast museum of natural history. Looking back to my recent studies, I went over in thought the whole geological history of Iceland.

This extraordinary and curious island must have made its appearance from out the great world of waters at a comparatively recent date. Like the coral islands of the Pacific, it may, for aught we know, be still rising by slow and imperceptible degrees.

If this really be the case, its origin can be attributed to only one cause—that of the continued action of subterranean fires.

This was a happy thought.

If so, if this were true, away with the theories of Sir Humphrey Davy; away with the authority of the parchment of Arne Saknussemm; the wonderful pretensions to discovery on the part of my uncle—and to our journey!

All must end in smoke.

Charmed with the idea, I began more carefully to look about me. A serious study of the soil was necessary to negative or confirm my hypothesis. I took in every item of what I saw, and I began to comprehend the succession of phenomena which had preceded its formation.

Iceland, being absolutely without sedimentary soil, is composed exclusively of volcanic tufa; that is to say, of an agglomeration of stones and of rocks of a porous texture. Long before the existence of volcanoes, it was composed of a solid body of massive trap-rock lifted bodily and slowly out of the sea, by the action of the centrifugal force at work in the interior of the earth.

The internal fires, however, had not as yet burst their bounds and flooded the exterior cake of Mother Earth with hot and raging lava.

My readers must excuse this brief and somewhat pedantic geological lecture. But it is necessary to the complete understanding of what follows.

At a later period in the world's history, a huge and mighty fissure must, reasoning by analogy, have been dug diagonally from the south-west to the north-east of the island, through which by degrees flowed the volcanic crust. The great and wondrous phenomenon then went on without violence—the outpouring was enormous, and the seething fused matter, ejected from the bowels of the earth, spread slowly and peacefully in the form of vast level plains, or what are called mamelons or mounds.

It was at this epoch that the rocks called feldspars, syenites, and porphyries appeared.

But as a natural consequence of this overflow, the depth of the island increased. It can readily be believed what an enormous quantity of elastic fluids were piled up within its centre, when at last it afforded no other openings, after the process of cooling the crust had taken place.

At length a time came when despite the enormous thickness and weight of the upper crust, the mechanical forces of the combustible gases below became so great, that they actually upheaved the weighty back and made for themselves huge and gigantic shafts. Hence the volcanoes which suddenly arose through the upper crust, and next the craters, which burst forth at the summit of these new creations.

It will be seen that the first phenomena in connexion with the formation of the island were simply eruptive; to these, however, shortly succeeded the volcanic phenomena.

Through the newly-formed openings, escaped the marvellous mass of basaltic stones with which the plain we were now crossing was covered. We were trampling our way over heavy rocks of dark grey colour, which, while cooling, had been moulded into six-sided prisms. In the "back distance" we could see a number of flattened cones, which formerly were so many fire-vomiting mouths.

After the basaltic eruption was appeased and set at rest, the volcano, the force of which increased with that of the extinct craters, gave free passage to the fiery overflow of lava, and to the mass of cinders and pumice-stone, now scattered over the sides of the mountain, like dishevelled hair on the shoulders of a Bacchante.

Here, in a nutshell, I had the whole history of the phenomena from which Iceland arose. All take their rise in the fierce action of interior fires, and to believe that the central mass did not remain in a state of liquid fire, white hot, was simply and purely madness.

This being satisfactorily proved, *(q.e.d.)* what insensate folly to pretend to penetrate into the interior of the mighty earth!

This mental lecture delivered to myself while proceeding on my journey, did me good. I was quite re-assured as to the fate of our enterprise; and therefore went, like a brave soldier mounting a bristling battery, to the assault of old Sneffels.

As we advanced, the road became every moment more difficult. The soil was broken and dangerous. The rocks broke and gave way under our feet, and we had to be scrupulously careful in order to avoid dangerous and constant falls.

Hans advanced as calmly as if he had been walking over Salisbury Plain; sometimes he would disappear behind huge blocks of stone, and we momentarily lost sight of him. There was a little period of anxiety and then there was a shrill whistle, just to tell us where to look for him.

Occasionally he would take it into his head to stop to pick up lumps of rock, and silently pile them up into small heaps, *in order that we might not lose our way on our return.*

He had no idea of the journey we were about to undertake.

At all events, the precaution was a good one; though how utterly useless and unnecessary—but I must not anticipate.

Three hours of terrible fatigue, walking incessantly, had only brought us to the foot of the great mountain. This will give some notion of what we had still to undergo.

Suddenly, however, Hans cried a halt—that is, he made signs to that effect—and a summary kind of breakfast was laid out on the lava before us. My uncle, who now was simply Professor Hardwigg, was so eager to advance, that he bolted his food like a greedy clown. This halt for refreshment was also a halt for repose. The Professor was therefore compelled to wait the good pleasure of his imperturbable guide, who did not give the signal for departure for a good hour.

The three Icelanders, who were as taciturn as their comrade, did not say a word; but went on eating and drinking very quietly and soberly.

From this, our first real stage, we began to ascend the slopes of the Sneffels volcano. Its magnificent snowy night-cap, as we began to call it, by an optical delusion very common in mountains, appeared to me to be close at hand; and yet how many long weary hours must elapse before we reached its summit. What unheard of fatigue must we endure!

The stones on the mountain side, held together by no cement of soil, bound together by no roots or creeping herbs, gave way continually under our feet, and went rushing below into the plains, like a series of small avalanches.

In certain places the sides of this stupendous mountain were at an angle so steep that it was impossible to climb upwards, and we were compelled to get round these obstacles as best we might.

Those who understand Alpine climbing will comprehend our difficulties. Often we were obliged to help each other along by means of our climbing poles.

I must say this for my uncle, that he stuck as close to me as possible. He never lost sight of me, and on many occasions his arm supplied me with firm and solid support. He was strong, wiry, and apparently insensible to fatigue. Another great advantage with him was that he had the innate sentiment of equilibrium—for he never slipped or failed in his steps. The Icelanders, though heavily loaded, climbed with the agility of mountaineers.

Looking up, every now and then, at the height of the great volcano of Sneffels, it appeared to me wholly impossible to reach to the summit on that side; at all events, if the angle of inclination did not speedily change.

Fortunately, after an hour of unheard of fatigues, and of gymnastic exercises that would have been trying to an acrobat, we came to a vast field of ice, which wholly surrounded the bottom of the cone of the volcano. The natives called it the table cloth, probably from some such reason as the dwellers in the Cape of Good Hope call their mountain Table Mountain, and their roads Table Bay.

Here, to our mutual surprise, we found an actual flight of stone steps, which wonderfully assisted our ascent. This singular flight of stairs was, like everything else, volcanic. It had been formed by one of those torrents of stones cast up by the eruptions, and of which the Icelandic name is stinâ. If this singular torrent had not been checked in its descent by the peculiar shape of the flanks of the mountain, it would have swept into the sea, and would have formed new islands.

Such as it was, it served us admirably. The abrupt character of the slopes momentarily increased, but these remarkable stone steps, a little less difficult than those of the Egyptian pyramids, were the one simple natural means by which we were enabled to proceed.

About seven in the evening of that day, after having clambered up two thousand of these rough steps, we found overselves over-looking a kind of spur or projection of the mountain—a sort of buttress upon which the cone-like crater, properly so called, leaned for support.

The ocean lay beneath us at a depth of more than three thousand two hundred feet—a grand and mighty spectacle. We had reached the region of eternal snows.

The cold was keen, searching and intense. The wind blew with extraordinary violence. I was utterly exhausted.

My worthy uncle, the Professor, saw clearly that my legs refused further service, and that, in fact, I was utterly exhausted. Despite his hot and feverish impatience, he decided, with a sigh, upon a halt. He called the eider-duck hunter to his side. That worthy, however, shook his head.

"Ofvanfor," was his sole spoken reply.

"It appears," says my uncle with a woebegone look, "that we must go higher."

He then turned to Hans, and asked him to give some reason for this decisive response.

"Mistour," replied the guide.

"*Ja mistour*—yes, the mistour," cried one of the Islandic guides in a terrified tone.

It was the first time he had spoken.

"What does this mysterious word signify?" I anxiously enquired.

"Look," said my uncle.

I looked down upon the plain below, and I saw a vast, a prodigious volume of pulverised pumice-stone, of sand, of dust, rising to the heavens in the form of a mighty water-spout. It resembled the fearful phenomenon of a similar character known to travellers in the desert of the great Sahara.

The wind was driving it directly towards that side of Sneffels on which we were perched. This opaque veil standing up between us and the sun projected a deep shadow on the flanks of the mountain. If this sand-spout broke over us, we must all be infallibly destroyed, crushed in its fearful embraces. This extraordinary phenomenon, very common when the wind shakes the glaciers, and sweeps over the arid plains, is in the Icelandic tongue called *mistour*.

"Hastigt, Hastigt!" cried our guide.

Now I certainly knew nothing of Danish, but I thoroughly understood that his gestures were meant to quicken us.

The guide turned rapidly in a direction which would take us to the back of the crater, all the while ascending slightly.

We followed rapidly, despite our excessive fatigue.

A quarter of an hour later Hans paused to enable us to look back. The mighty whirlwind of sand was spreading up the slope of the mountain to the very spot where we had proposed to halt. Huge stones were caught up, cast into the air, and thrown about as during an eruption. We were happily a little out of the direction of the wind, and therefore out of reach of danger. But for the precaution and knowledge of our guide, our dislocated bodies, our crushed and broken limbs, would have been cast to the wind, like dust from some unknown meteor.

Hans, however, did not think it prudent to pass the night on the bare side of the cone. We therefore continued our journey in a zigzag direction. The fifteen hundred feet which remained to be accomplished took us at least five hours. The turnings and windings, the no-thoroughfares, the marches and marches, turned that insignificant distance into at least three leagues. I never felt such misery, fatigue and exhaustion in my life. I was ready to faint from hunger and cold. The rarified air at the same time painfully acted upon my lungs.

At last, when I thought myself at my last gasp, about eleven at night, it being in that region quite dark, we reached the summit of Mount Sneffels! It was in an awful mood of mind, that despite my fatigue, before I descended into the crater which was to shelter us for the night, I paused to behold the sun rise at midnight on the very day of its lowest declension, and enjoyed the spectacle of its ghastly pale rays cast upon the isle which lay sleeping at our feet!

I no longer wondered at people travelling all the way from England to Norway, to behold this magical and wondrous spectacle.

CHAPTER 13

THE SHADOW OF SCARTARIS

OUR supper was eaten with ease and rapidity, after which everybody did the best he could for himself within the hollow of the crater. The bed was hard, the shelter unsatisfactory, the situation painful—lying in the open air, five thousand feet above the level of the sea!

Nevertheless, it has seldom happened to me to sleep so well as I did on that particular night. I did not even dream. So much for the effects of what my uncle called "wholesome fatigue."

Next day, when we awoke under the rays of a bright and glorious sun, we were nearly frozen by the keen air. I left my granite couch and made one of the party to enjoy a view of the magnificent spectacle which developed itself, panorama-like, at our feet.

I stood upon the lofty summit of Mount Sneffels' southern peak. Thence I was able to obtain a view of the greater part of the island. The optical delusion, common to all lofty heights, raised the shores of the island, while the central portions appeared depressed. It was by no means too great a flight of fancy to believe that a giant picture was stretched out before me. I could see the deep valleys that crossed each other in every direction. I could see precipices looking like sides of wells, lakes that seemed to be changed into ponds, ponds that looked like puddles, and rivers that were transformed into petty brooks. To my right were glaciers upon glaciers, and multiplied peaks, topped with light clouds of smoke.

The undulation of these infinite numbers of mountains, whose snowy summits made them look as if covered by foam, recalled to my remembrance the surface of a storm-beaten ocean. If I looked towards the west, the ocean lay before me in all its majestic grandeur, a continuation as it were, of these fleecy hill tops.

Where the earth ended and the sea began it was impossible for the eye to distinguish.

I soon felt that strange and mysterious sensation which is awakened in the mind when looking down from lofty hill tops, and now I was able to do so without any feeling of nervousness, having fortunately hardened myself to that kind of sublime contemplation.

I wholly forgot who I was, and where I was. I became intoxicated with a sense of lofty sublimity, without thought of the abysses into which my daring was soon about to plunge me. I was presently, however, brought back to the realities of life, by the arrival of the Professor and Hans, who joined me upon the lofty summit of the peak.

My uncle, turning in a westerly direction, pointed out to me a light cloud of vapour, a kind of haze, with a faint outline of land rising out of the waters.

"Greenland!" said he.

"Greenland?" cried I, in reply.

"Yes," continued my uncle, who always when explaining anything spoke as if he were in a Professor's chair; "we are not more than thirty-five leagues distant from that wonderful land. When the great annual break up of the ice takes place, white bears come over to Iceland, carried by the floating masses of ice from the north. This, however, is a matter of little consequence. We are now on the summit of the great, the transcendent Sneffels, and here are its two peaks, north and south. Hans will tell you the name by which the people of Iceland call that on which we stand."

My uncle turned to the imperturbable guide, who nodded, and spoke as usual—one word.

"*Scartaris.*"

My uncle looked at me with a proud and triumphant glance.

"A crater," he said, "you hear?"

I did hear, but I was totally unable to make reply.

The crater of Mount Sneffels represented an inverted cone, the gaping orifice apparently half a mile across; the depth indefinite feet. Conceive what this *hole* must have been like when full of flame and thunder and lightning. The bottom of the funnel-shaped hollow was about five hundred feet in circumference, by which it will be seen that the slope from the summit to the bottom was very gradual, and we were therefore clearly able to get there without much fatigue or difficulty. Involuntarily, I compared this crater to an enormous loaded cannon; and the comparison completely terrified me.

"To descend into the interior of a cannon," I thought to myself, "when perhaps it is loaded, and will go off at the least shock, is the act of a madman."

But there was no longer any opportunity for me to hesitate. Hans, with a perfectly calm and indifferent air, took his usual post at the head of the adventurous little band. I followed without uttering a syllable.

I felt like the lamb led to the slaughter.

In order to render the descent less difficult, Hans took his way down the interior of the cone in rather a zigzag fashion, making, as the sailors say, long tacks to the eastward, followed by equally long ones to the west. It was necessary to walk through the midst of eruptive rocks, some of which, shaken in their balance, went rolling down with thundering clamour to the bottom of the abyss. These continual falls awoke echoes of singular power and effect.

Many portions of the cone consisted of interior glaciers. Hans, whenever he met with one of these obstacles advanced with a great show of precaution, sounding the soil with his long iron pole in order to discover fissures and layers of deep soft snow. In many doubtful or dangerous places, it became necessary for us to be tied together by a long rope in order that should any one of us be unfortunate enough to slip, he would be supported by his companions. This connecting link was doubtless a prudent precaution, but not by any means unattended with danger.

Nevertheless, and despite all the manifold difficulties of the descent, along slopes with which our guide was wholly unacquainted, we made considerable progress without accident. One of our great parcels of rope slipped from one of the Iceland porters, and rushed by a short cut to the bottom of the abyss.

By mid-day we were at the end of our journey. I looked upwards, and saw only the upper orifice of the cone, which served as a circular frame to a very small portion of the sky—a portion which seemed to me singularly beautiful. Should I ever again gaze on that lovely sunlit sky!

The only exception to this extraordinary landscape, was the Peak of Scartaris, which seemed lost in the great void of the heavens.

The bottom of the crater was composed of three separate shafts, through which, during periods of eruption, when Sneffels was in action, the great central furnace sent forth its burning lava and poisonous vapours. Each of these chimneys or shafts gaped open-mouthed in our path. I kept as far away from them as possible, not even venturing to take the faintest peep downwards.

As for the Professor, after a rapid examination of their disposition and characteristics, he became breathless and panting. He ran from one to the other like a delighted schoolboy, gesticulating wildly, and uttering incomprehensible and disjointed phrases in all sorts of languages.

Hans, the guide, and his humbler companions seated themselves on some piles of lava and looked silently on. They clearly took my uncle for a lunatic; and—waited the result.

Suddenly the Professor uttered a wild, unearthly cry. At first I imagined he had lost his footing, and was falling headlong into one of the yawning gulfs. Nothing of the kind. I saw him, his arms spread out to their widest extent, his legs stretched apart, standing upright before an enormous pedestal, high enough and black enough to bear a gigantic statue of Pluto. His attitude and mien were that of a man utterly stupefied. But his stupefaction was speedily changed to the wildest joy.

"Harry! Harry! come here!" he cried; "make haste—wonderful—wonderful!"

Unable to understand what he meant, I turned to obey his commands. Neither Hans, nor the other Icelanders moved a step.

"Look!" said the Professor, in something of the manner of the French general, pointing out the pyramids to his army.

And fully partaking his stupefaction, if not his joy, I read on the eastern side of the huge block of stone, the same characters, half eaten away by the corrosive action of time, the name, to me a thousand times accursed—

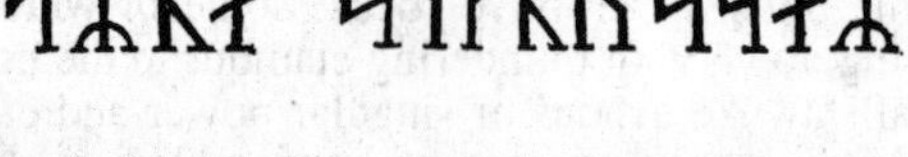

"Arne Saknussemm!" cried my uncle, "now, unbeliever, do you begin to have faith?"

Arne Saknussemm.

It was totally impossible for me to answer a single word. I went back to my pile of lava, in a state of silent awe. The evidence was unanswerable, overwhelming!

In a few moments, however, my thoughts were far away, back in my German home, with Gretchen and the old cook. What would I have given for one of my cousin's smiles, for one of the ancient domestic's omelettes, and for my own feather bed!

How long I remained in this state I know not. All I can say is that when at last I raised my head from between my hands, there remained at the bottom of the crater only myself, my uncle and Hans. The Icelandic porters had been dismissed and were now descending the exterior slopes of Mount Sneffels, on their way to Stapi. How heartily did I wish myself with them!

Hans slept tranquilly at the foot of a rock in a kind of rill of lava, where he had made himself a rough and ready bed. My uncle was walking about the bottom of the crater like a wild beast in a cage. I had no desire, neither had I the strength, to move from my recumbent position. Taking example by the guide, I gave way to a kind of painful somnolency, during which I seemed both to hear and feel continued heavings and shudderings in the mountain.

In this way we passed our first night in the interior of a crater.

Next morning, a grey, cloudy, heavy sky hung like a funeral-pall over the summit of the volcanic cone. I did not notice it so much from the obscurity that reigned around us, as from the rage with which my uncle was devoured.

I fully understood the reason, and again a glimpse of hope made my heart leap with joy. I will briefly explain the cause.

Of the three openings which yawned beneath our steps, only one could have been followed by the adventurous Saknussemm. According to the words of the learned Icelander, it was only to be known by that one particular mentioned in the cryptograph, that the shadow of Scartaris fell upon it, just touching its mouth in the last days of the month of June.

We were, in fact, to consider the pointed peak as the *stylus* of an immense sun-dial, the shadow of which pointed on one given day, like the inexorable finger of fate, to the yawning chasm which led into the interior of the earth.

Now, as often happens in these regions, should the sun fail to burst through the clouds, no shadow. Consequently, no chance of discovering the right aperture. We had already reached the 25th June. If the kindly heavens would only remain densely clouded for six more days, we should have to put off our voyage of discovery for another year, when certainly there would be one person fewer in the party. I already had sufficient of the mad and monstrous enterprise.

It would be utterly impossible to depict the impotent rage of Professor Hardwigg. The day passed away, and not the faintest outline of a shadow could be seen at the bottom of the crater. Hans the guide never moved from his place. He must have been curious to know what we were about, if indeed he could believe we were about anything. As for my uncle, he never addressed a word to me. He was nursing his wrath to keep it warm! His eyes fixed on the black and foggy atmosphere, his complexion hideous with suppressed passion. Never had his eyes appeared so fierce, his nose so aquiline, his mouth so hard and firm.

On the 26th no change for the better. A mixture of rain and snow fell during the whole day. Hans very quietly built himself a hut of lava into which he retired like Diogenes into his tub. I took a malicious delight in watching the thousand little cascades that flowed down the side of the cone, carrying with them at times a stream of stones into the "vasty deep" below.

My uncle was almost frantic: to be sure it was enough to make even a patient man angry. He had reached to a certain extent the goal of his desires, and yet he was likely to be wrecked in port.

But if the heavens and the elements are capable of causing us much pain and sorrow, there are two sides to a medal. And there was reserved for Professor Hardwigg a brilliant and sudden surprise which was to compensate him for all his sufferings.

Next day the sky was still overcast, but on Sunday the 29th, the last day but one of the month, with a sudden change of wind and a new moon there came a change of weather. The sun poured its beaming rays to the very bottom of the crater.

Each hillock, every rock, every stone, every asperity of the soil had its share of the luminous effulgence, and its shadow fell heavily on the soil. Among others, to his insane delight, the shadow of Scartaris was marked and clear, and moved slowly with the radiant star of day.

My uncle moved with it in a state of mental ecstacy.

At twelve o'clock exactly, when the sun had attained its highest altitude for the day, the shadow fell upon the edge of the central pit!

"Here it is," gasped the Professor in an agony of joy, "here it is—we have found it. Forward, my friends, into the Interior of the Earth."

I looked curiously at Hans to see what reply he would make to this terrific announcement.

"Forüt," said the guide tranquilly.

"Forward it is," answered my uncle, who was now in the seventh heaven of delight.

When we were quite ready, our watches indicated thirteen mintues past one!

CHAPTER 14

THE REAL JOURNEY COMMENCES

OUR real journey had now commenced.

Hitherto our courage and determination had overcome all difficulties. We were fatigued at times; and that was all. Now, unknown and fearful dangers we were about to encounter.

I had not as yet ventured to take a glimpse down the horrible abyss into which in a few mintues more I was about to plunge. The fatal moment had, however, at last arrived. I had still the option of refusing or accepting a share in this foolish and audacious enterprise. But I was ashamed to show more fear than the eider-duck hunter. Hans seemed to accept the difficulties of the journey so tranquilly, with such calm indifference, with such perfect recklessness of all danger, that I actually blushed to appear less of a man than he!

Had I been alone with my uncle, I should certainly have sat down and argued the point fully; but in the presence of the guide I held my tongue. I gave one moment to the thought of my charming cousin, and then I advanced to the mouth of the central shaft.

It measured about a hundred feet in diameter, which made about three hundred in circumference. I leaned over a rock which stood on its edge, and looked down. My hair stood on end, my teeth chattered, my limbs trembled, I seemed utterly to lose my centre of gravity, while my head was in a sort of whirl, like that of a drunken man. There is nothing more powerful than this attraction towards an abyss. I was about to fall headlong into the gaping well, when I was drawn back by a firm and powerful hand. It was that of Hans. I had not taken lessons enough at the Frelser's-kirk of Copenhagen in the art of looking down from lofty eminences without blinking!

However, few as the minutes were during which I gazed down this tremendous and even wondrous shaft, I had a sufficient glimpse of it to give me some idea of its physical conformation. Its sides, which were almost as perpendicular as those of a well, presented numerous projections which doubtless would assist our descent.

It was a sort of wild and savage staircase, without bannister or fence. A rope fastened above, near the surface, would certainly support our weight and enable us to reach the bottom, but how, when we had arrived at its utmost depths, were we to loosen it above? This was, I thought, a question of some importance.

My uncle, however, was one of those men who are nearly always prepared with expedients. He hit upon a very simple method of obviating this difficulty. He unrolled a cord about as thick as my thumb, and at least four hundred feet in length. He allowed about half of it to go down the pit and catch in a hitch over a great block of lava which stood on the edge of the precipice. This done, he threw the second half after the first.

Each of us could now descend by catching the two cords in one hand. When about two hundred feet below, all the explorer had to do was to let go one end and pull away at the other, when the cord would come falling at his feet. In order to go down farther, all that was necessary was to continue the same operation.

This was a very excellent proposition, and no doubt a correct one. Going down appeared to me easy enough, it was the coming up again that now occupied my thoughts.

"Now," said my uncle, as soon as he had completed this important preparation, "let us see about the baggage. It must be divided into three separate parcels, and each of us must carry one on his back. I allude to the more important and fragile articles.

My worthy and ingenious uncle did not appear to consider that we came under that denomination.

"Hans," he continued, "you will take charge of the tools and some of the provisions; you, Harry, must take possession of another third of the provisions and of the arms. I will load myself with the rest of the eatables, and with the more delicate instruments."

"But," I exclaimed, "our clothes, this mass of cord and ladders—who will undertake to carry them down?"

"They will go down of themselves."

"And how so?" I asked.

"You shall see."

My uncle was not fond of half measures, nor did he like anything in the way of hesitation. Giving his orders to Hans he had the whole of non-fragile articles made up into one bundle; and the packet, firmly and solidly fastened, was simply pitched over the edge of the gulph.

I heard the moaning of the suddenly displaced air, and the noise of falling stones. My uncle leaning over the abyss followed the descent of his luggage with a perfectly self-satisfied air, and did not rise until it had completely disappeared from sight.

"Now then," he cried, "it is our turn."

I put it in good faith to any man of common sense—was it possible to hear this energetic cry without a shudder?

The Professor fastened his case of instruments on his back, Hans took charge of the tools, I of the arms. The descent then commenced in the following order. Hans went first, my uncle followed, and I went last. Our progress was made in profound silence—a silence only troubled by the fall of pieces of rock, which breaking from the jagged sides, fell with a roar into the depths below.

I allowed myself to slide, so to speak, holding frantically on to the double cord with one hand and with the other keeping myself off the rocks by the assistance of my iron-shod pole. One idea was all the time impressed upon my brain. I feared that the upper support would fail me. The cord appeared to me far too fragile to bear the weight of three such persons as we were, with our luggage. I made as little use of it as possible, trusting to my own agility and doing miracles in the way of feats of dexterity and strength upon the projecting shelves and spurs of lava which my feet seemed to clutch as strongly as my hands.

The guide went first I have said, and when one of the slippery and frail supports broke from under his feet he had recourse to his usual monosyllabic way of speaking.

"Gifakt——."

"Attention—look out," repeated my uncle.

In about half an hour we reached a kind of small terrace formed by a fragment of rock projecting some distance from the sides of the shaft.

Hans now began to haul upon the cord on one side only, the other going as quietly upward as the other came down. It fell at last, bringing with it a shower of small stones, lava and dust, a disagreeable kind of rain or hail.

While we were seated on this extraordinary bench I ventured once more to look downwards. With a sigh I discovered that the bottom was still wholly invisible. Were we, then, going direct to the interior of the earth?

The performance with the cord recommenced, and a quarter of an hour later, we had reached to the depth of another two hundred feet.

I have very strong doubts if the most determined geologist would, during that descent have studied the nature of the different layers of earth around him. I did not trouble my head much about the matter; whether we were among the combustible carbon, silurians, or primitive soil, I neither knew nor cared to know.

Not so the inveterate Professor. He must have taken notes all the way down, for, at one of our halts, he began a brief lecture.

"The farther we advance," said he, "the greater is my confidence in the result. The disposition of these volcana strata absolutely confirms the theories of Sir Humphrey Davy. We are still within the region of the primordial soil, the soil in which took place the chemical operation of metals becoming inflamed by coming in contact with air and water. I at once regret the old and now for ever exploded theory of a central fire. At all events, we shall soon know the truth."

Such was the everlasting conclusion to which he came. I, however, was very far from being in a humour to discuss the matter. I had something else to think of. My silence was taken for consent; and still we continued to go down.

At the expiration of three hours, we were, to all appearance, as far off as ever from the bottom of the well. When I looked upwards, however, I could see that the upper orifice was every minute decreasing in size. The sides of the shaft were getting closer and closer together, we were approaching the regions of eternal night!

And still we continued to descend!

At length, I noticed that when pieces of stone were detached from the sides of this stupendous precipice, they were swallowed up with less noise than before. The final sound was sooner heard. We were approaching the bottom of the abyss!

As I had been very careful to keep account of all the changes of cord which took place, I was able to tell exactly what was the depth we had reached, as well as the time it had taken.

We had shifted the rope twenty-eight times, each operation taking a quarter of an hour, which in all made seven hours. To this had to be added twenty-eight pauses; in all ten hours and a-half. We started at one, it was now, therefore, about eleven o'clock at night.

It does not require great knowledge of arithmetic to know that twenty-eight times two hundred feet makes five thousand six hundred feet in all (more than an English mile).

While I was making this mental calculation a voice broke the dreary silence. It was the voice of Hans.

"Halt!" he cried.

I checked myself very suddenly, just at the moment when I was about to kick my uncle on the head.

"We have reached the end of our journey," said the worthy Professor in a satisfied tone.

"What, the interior of the earth?" said I, slipping down to his side.

"No, you stupid fellow! but we have reached the bottom of the well."

"And I suppose there is no farther progress to be made?" I hopefully exclaimed.

"Oh, yes, I can dimly see a sort of tunnel, which turns off obliquely to the right. At all events, we must see about that to-morrow. Let us sup now, and seek slumber as best we may."

I thought it time, but made no observations on that point. I was fairly launched on a desperate course, and all I had to do was to go forward hopefully and trustingly.

It was not even now quite dark, the light filtering down in a most extraordinary manner.

We opened the provision bag, ate a frugal supper, and each did his best to find a bed amid the pile of stones, dirt, and lava which had accumulated for ages at the bottom of the shaft.

I happened to grope out the pile of ropes, ladders, and clothes which we had thrown down; and upon them I stretched myself. After such a day's labour, my rough bed seemed as soft as down!

For awhile I lay in a sort of pleasant trance.

Presently, after lying quietly for some minutes, I opened my eyes and looked upwards. As I did so I made out a brilliant little dot, at the extremity of this long, gigantic telescope.

It was a star without scintillating rays. According to my calculation, must be β in the constallation of the Little Bear.

After this bit of astronomical recreation, I dropped into a sound sleep.

CHAPTER 15

WE CONTINUE OUR DESCENT

At eight o'clock the next morning, a faint kind of dawn of day awoke us. The thousand and one prisms of the lava, collected the light as it passed and brought it to us like a shower of sparks.

We were able with ease to see objects around us.

"Well, Harry, my boy," cried the delighted Professor, rubbing his hands together, "what say you now? Did you ever pass a more tranquil night in our house in the König Strasse? No deafening sounds of cart-wheels, no cries of hawkers, no bad language from boatmen or watermen!"

"Well, uncle, we are very quiet at the bottom of this well—but to me there is something terrible in this calm."

"Why," said the Professor, hotly, "one would say you were already beginning to be afraid. How will you get on presently? Do you know, that as yet, we have not penetrated one inch into the bowels of the earth."

"What can you mean, sir?" was my bewildered and astonished reply.

"I mean to say that we have only just reached the soil of the island itself. This long vertical tube, which ends at the bottom of the crater of Sneffels, ceases here just about on a level with the sea."

"Are you sure, sir?"

"Quite sure. Consult the barometer."

It was quite true that the mercury, after rising gradually in the instrument, as long as our descent was taking place, had stopped precisely at twenty-nine degrees.

"You perceive," said the Professor, "we have as yet only to endure the pressure of air. I am curious to replace the barometer by the manometer.

The barometer, in fact, was about to become useless—as soon as the weight of the air was greater than what was calculated as above the level of the ocean.

"But," said I, "is it not very much to be feared that this ever-increasing pressure may not in the end turn out very painful and inconvenient?"

"No," said he. "We shall descend very slowly, and our lungs will be gradually accustomed to breathe compressed air. It is well known that aëronauts have gone so high as to be nearly without air at all—why, then, should we not accustom ourselves to breathe when we have, say, a little too much of it? For myself, I am certain I shall prefer it. Let us not lose a moment. Where is the packet which preceded us in our descent?"

I smilingly pointed it out to my uncle. Hans had not seen it, and believed it caught somewhere above us: "huppe" as he phrased it.

"Now," said my uncle, "let us breakfast, and break fast like people who have a long day's work before them."

Biscuit and dried meat, washed down by some mouthfuls of water flavoured with schiedam, was the material of our luxurious meal.

As soon as it was finished, my uncle took from his pocket a note-book destined to be filled by memoranda of our travels. He had already placed his instruments in order, and this is what he wrote:—

Monday, July 1st.

Chronometer, 8h. 17m. morning.
Barometer, 29 degrees.
Thermometer, 43° Fahr.
Direction, E.S.E.

This last observation referred to the obscure gallery, and was indicated to us by the compass.

"Now Harry," cried the Professor, in an enthusiastic tone of voice, "we are truly about to take our first step into the Interior of the Earth; never before visited by man since the first creation of the world. You may consider, therefore, that at this precise moment our travels really commence."

As my uncle made this remark, he took in one hand the Ruhmkorff coil apparatus, which hung round his neck, and with the other he put the electric current into communication with the worm of the lantern. And a bright light at once illumined that dark and gloomy tunnel!

The effect was magical!

Hans, who carried the second apparatus, had it also put into operation. This ingenious application of electricity to practical purposes enabled us to move along by the light of an artificial day, amid even the flow of the most inflammable and combustible gases.

"Forward!" cried my uncle. Each took up his burden. Hans went first, my uncle followed, and I going third, we entered the sombre gallery!

Just as we were about to engulph ourselves in this dismal passage, I lifted up my head, and through the tube-like shaft saw that Iceland sky I was never to see again!

Was it the last I should ever see of any sky?

The stream of lava flowing from the bowels of the earth in 1229, had forced itself a passage through the tunnel. It lined the whole of the inside with its thick and brilliant coating. The electric light added very greatly to the brilliancy of the effect.

The great difficulty of our journey now began. How were we to prevent ourselves from slipping down the steeply-inclined plane? Happily some cracks, abrasures of the soil, and other irregularities, served the place of steps; and we descended slowly; allowing our heavy luggage to slip on before, at the end of a long cord.

But that which served as steps under our feet, became in other places stalactites. The lava, very porous in certain places, took the form of little round blisters. Crystals of opaque quartz, adorned with limpid drops of natural glass suspended to the roof like lustres, seemed to take fire as we passed beneath them. One

would have fancied that the genii of romance were illuminating their underground palaces to receive the sons of men.

"Magnificent, glorious!" I cried in a moment of involuntary enthusiasm, "what a spectacle, uncle! Do you not admire these variegated shades of lava, which run through a whole series of colours, from reddish brown to pale yellow—by the most insensible degrees. And these crystals, they appear like luminous globes."

"You are beginning to see the charms of travel, Master Harry," cried my uncle. "Wait a bit, until we advance farther. What we have as yet discovered is nothing—onwards, my boy, onwards!"

It would have been a far more correct and appropriate expression, had he said, "let us slide," for we were going down an inclined plane with perfect ease. The compass indicated that we were moving in a south-easterly direction. The flow of lava had never turned to the right or the left. It had the inflexibility of a straight line.

Nevertheless, to my great surprise, we found no perceptible increase in heat. This proved the theories of Humphrey Davy to be founded on truth, and more than once I found myself examining the thermometer in silent astonishment.

Two hours after my departure it only marked 54 degrees Fahrenheit. I had every reason to believe from this that our descent was far more horizontal than vertical. As for discovering the exact depth to which we had attained, nothing could be easier. The Professor, as he advanced measured the angles of deviation and inclination; but he kept the result of his observations to himself.

About eight o'clock in the evening, my uncle gave the signal for halting. Hans seated himself on the ground. The lamps were hung to fissures in the lava rock. We were now in a large cavern where air was not wanting. On the contrary, it abounded. What could be the cause of this—to what atmospheric agitation could be ascribed this draught? But this was a question which I did not care to discuss just then. Fatigue and hunger made me incapable of reasoning. An unceasing march of seven hours had not been kept up without great exhaustion. I was really and truly worn out; and delighted enough I was to hear the word Halt.

Hans laid out some provisions on a lump of lava, and we each supped with keen relish. One thing, however, caused us great uneasiness—our water reserve was already half exhausted. My uncle had full confidence in finding subterranean sources, but hitherto we had completely failed in so doing. I could not help calling my uncle's attention to the circumstance.

"And you are surprised at this total absence of springs?" he said.

"Doubtless—I am very uneasy on the point. We have certainly not enough water to last us five days."

"Be quite easy on that matter," continued my uncle. "I answer for it we shall find plenty of water—in fact, far more than we shall want."

"But when?"

"When we once get through this crust of lava. How can you expect springs to force their way through these solid stone walls?"

"But what is there to prove that this concrete mass of lava does not extend to the centre of the earth? I don't think we have as yet done much in a vertical way."

"What puts that into your head, my boy?" asked my uncle, mildly.

"Well, it appears to me that if we had descended very far below the level of the sea—we should find it rather hotter than we have."

"According to your system," said my uncle; "but what does the thermometer say?"

"Scarcely 15 degrees by Reaumur, which is only an increase of 9 since our departure."

"Well, and what conclusion does that bring you to?" enquired the Professor.

"The deduction I draw from this is very simple. According to the most exact observations, the augmentation of the temperature of the interior of the earth is 1 degree for every hundred feet. But certain local causes may considerably modify this figure. Thus at Yakoust in Siberia, it has been remarked that the heat increases a degree every thirty-six feet. The difference evidently depends on the conductibility of certain rocks. In the neighbourhood of an extinct volcano, it has been remarked that the elevation of temperature was only 1 degree on every five-and-twenty feet. Let us, then, go upon this calculation—which is the most favourable—and calculate."

"Calculate away, my boy."

"Nothing easier," said I, pulling out my note-book and pencil. "Nine times one hundred and twenty-five feet, make a depth of eleven hundred and twenty-five feet."

"Archimedes could not have spoken more geometrically."

"Well?"

"Well, according to my observations, we are at least ten thousand feet below the level of the sea."

"Can it be possible?"

"Either my calculation is correct, or there is no truth in figures."

The calculations of the Professor were perfectly correct. We were already six thousand feet deeper down in the bowels of the earth than any one had ever been before. The lowest known depth to which man had hitherto penetrated was in the mines of Kitz-Bahl, on the Tyrol, and those of Wuttemburg in Bohemia.

The temperature, which should have been eight-one, was in this place only fifteen. This was a matter for serious consideration.

CHAPTER 16

THE EASTERN TUNNEL

THE next day was Tuesday, the 2nd of July—and at six o'clock in the morning we resumed our journey.

We still continued to follow the gallery of lava, a perfect natural pathway, as easy of descent as some of those inclined planes which, in very old German houses, serve the purpose of staircases. This went on until seventeen minutes past twelve, the precise instant at which we rejoined Hans, who having been somewhat in advance, had suddenly stopped.

"At last," cried my uncle, "we have reached the end of the shaft."

I looked wonderingly about me. We were in the centre of four cross paths—

sombre and narrow tunnels. The question now arose as to which it was wise to take; and this of itself was no small difficulty.

My uncle, who did not wish to appear to have any hesitation about the matter before myself or the guide, at once made up his mind. He pointed quietly to the eastern tunnel; and, without delay, we entered within its gloomy recesses.

Besides, had he entertained any feeling of hesitation it might have been prolonged indefinitely, for there was no indication by which to determine on a choice. It was absolutely necessary to trust to chance and good fortune!

The descent of this obscure and narrow gallery was very gradual and winding. Sometimes we gazed through a succession of arches, its course very like the aisles of a Gothic cathedral. The great artistic sculptors and builders of the middle ages might have here completed their studies with advantage. Many most beautiful and suggestive ideas of architectural beauty would have been discovered by them. After passing through this phase of the cavernous way, we suddenly came, about a mile farther on, upon a square system of arch, adopted by the early Romans, projecting from the solid rock, and keeping up the weight of the roof.

Suddenly we would come upon a series of low subterranean tunnels which looked like beaver holes, or the work of foxes. Through whose narrow and winding ways we had literally to crawl!

The heat still remained at quite a supportable degree. With an involuntary shudder, I reflected on what the heat must have been when the volcano of Sneffels was pouring its smoke, flames, and streams of boiling lava—all of which must have come up by the road we were now following. I could imagine the torrents of hot seething stone darting on, bubbling up with accompaniments of smoke, steam, and sulphurous stench!

"Only to think of the consequence," I mused, "if the old volcano were once more to set to work."

I did not communicate these rather unpleasant reflections to my uncle. He not only would not have understood them, but would have been intensely disgusted. His only idea was to go ahead. He walked, he slid, he clambered over piles of fragments, he rolled down heaps of broken lava, with an earnestness and conviction it was impossible not to admire.

At six o'clock in the evening, after a very wearisome journey, but one not so fatiguing as before, we had made six miles towards the southward, but had not gone more than a mile downwards.

My uncle, as usual gave the signal to halt. We ate our meal in thoughtful silence, and then retired to sleep.

Our arrangements for the night were very primitive and simple. A travelling rug, in which each rolled himself, was all our bedding. We had no necessity to fear cold or any unpleasant visit. Travellers who bury themselves in the wilds and depths of the African desert, who seek profit and pleasure in the forests of the New World, are compelled to take it in turn to watch during the hours of sleep; but in this region of the earth absolute solitude and complete security, reigned supreme.

We had nothing to fear either from savages or from wild beasts.

After a night's sweet repose, we awoke fresh and ready for action. There being nothing to detain us, we started on our journey. We continued to burrow through the lava tunnel as before. It was impossible to make out through what soil we were making way. The tunnel, moreover, instead of going down into the bowels of the earth, became absolutely horizontal.

I even thought, after some examination, that we were actually tending upwards. About ten o'clock in the day this state of things became so clear, that finding the change very fatiguing I was obliged to slacken my pace and finally to come to a halt.

"Well," said the Professor, impatiently, "what is the matter?"

"The fact is, I am dreadfully tired," was my earnest reply.

"What," cried my uncle, "tired after a three hours' walk, and by so easy a road?"

"Easy enough, I daresay, but very fatiguing."

"But how can that be, when all we have to do is to go downwards?"

"I beg your pardon, sir. For some time I have noticed that we are going upwards."

"Upwards," cried my uncle, shrugging his shoulders, "how can that be?"

"There can be no doubt about it. For the last half hour the slopes have been upward—and if we go on in this way much longer we shall find ourselves back in Iceland."

My uncle shook his head with the air of a man who does not want to be convinced. I tried to continue the conversation. He would not answer me, but once more gave the signal for departure. His silence I thought was only caused by concentrated ill-temper.

However this might be, I once more took up my load, and boldly and resolutely followed Hans, who was now in advance of my uncle. I did not like to be beaten or even distanced. I was naturally anxious not to lose sight of my companions. The very idea of being left behind, lost in that terrible labyrinth, made me shiver as with the ague.

Besides, if the ascending path was more arduous and painful to clamber, I had one source of secret consolation and delight. It was to all appearance taking us back to the surface of the earth. That of itself was hopeful. Every step I took confirmed me in my belief, and I began already to build castles in the air in relation to my marriage with my pretty little cousin.

About twelve o'clock there was a great and sudden change in the aspect of the rocky sides of the gallery. I first noticed it from the diminution of the rays of light which cast back the reflection of the lamp. From being coated with shining and resplendent lava, it became living rock. The sides were sloping walls, which sometimes became quite vertical.

We were now in what the geological professors call a state of transition, in the period of Silurian stones, so called because this specimen of early formation is very common in England in the counties formerly inhabited by the Celtic nation known as Silures.

"I can see, clearly now," I cried; "the sediment from the waters which once covered the whole earth, formed during the second period of its existence, these schists and these calcareous rocks. We are turning our backs on the granitic rocks, and are like people from Hamburg who would go to Lübeck by way of Hanover."

I might just as well have kept my observations to myself. My geological enthusiasm got the better, however, of my cooler judgment, and Professor Hardwigg heard my observations.

"What is the matter now?" he said, in a tone of great gravity.

The crossroads.

"Well," cried I, "do you not see these different layers of calcareous rocks and the first indication of slate strata?"

"Well; what then?"

"We have arrived at that period of the world's existence when the first plants and the first animals made their appearance."

"You think so?"

"Yes, look; examine and judge for yourself."

I induced the Professor with some difficulty to cast the light of his lamp on the sides of the long winding gallery. I expected some exclamation to burst from his lips. I was very much mistaken. The worthy Professor never spoke a word.

It was impossible to say whether he understood me or not. Perhaps it was possible that in his pride—my uncle and a learned professor—he did not like to own that he was wrong in having chosen the eastern tunnel, or was he determined at any price to go to the end of it. It was quite evident we had left the region of lava, and that the road by which we were going could not take us back to the great crater of Mount Sneffels.

As we went along I could not help ruminating on the whole question, and asked myself if I did not lay too great a stress on these sudden and peculiar modifications of the earth's crust.

After all, I was very likely to be mistaken—and it was within the range of probability and possibility, that we were not making our way through the strata of rocks which I believed I recognised piled on the lower layer of granitic formation.

"At all events, if I am right," I thought to myself, "I must certainly find some remains of primitive plants, and it will be absolutely necessary to give way to such indubitable evidence. Let us have a good search."

I accordingly lost no opportunity of searching, and had not gone more than about a hundred yards, when the evidence I sought for cropped up in the most incontestable manner before my eyes. It was quite natural that I should expect to find these signs, for during the Silurian period the seas contained no fewer than fifteen hundred different animal and vegetable species. My feet, so long accustomed to the hard and arid lava soil, suddenly found themselves treading on a kind of soft dust, the remains of plants and shells.

Upon the walls themselves I could clearly make out the outline, as plain as a sun picture, of the fucus and the lycopodes. The worthy and excellent Professor Hardwigg could not of course make any mistake about the matter; but I believe he deliberately closed his eyes, and continued on his way with a firm and unalterable step.

I begin to think that he was carrying his obstinacy a great deal too far. I could no longer act with prudence or composure. I stooped on a sudden and picked up an almost perfect shell, which had undoubtedly belonged to some animal very much resembling some of the present day. Having secured the prize, I followed in the wake of my uncle.

"Do you see this?" I said.

"Well," said the Professor, with the most imperturbable tranquillity, "it is the shell of a crustaceous animal of the extinct order of the trilobites; nothing more I assure you."

"But," cried I, much troubled at his coolness, "do you draw no conclusion from it?"

"Well, if I may ask, what conclusion do you draw from it yourself?"

"Well, I thought——"

"I know, my boy, what you would say, and you are right, perfectly and incontestably right. We have finally abandoned the crust of lava and the road by which the lava ascended. It is quite possible that I may have been mistaken, but I shall be unable to discover my error until I get quite to the end of this gallery."

"You are quite right as far as that is concerned," I replied, "and I should highly approve of your decision, if we had not to fear the greatest of all dangers."

"And what is that?"

"Want of water."

"Well, my dear Henry, it can't be helped. We must put ourselves on rations."

And on he went.

CHAPTER 17

DEEPER AND DEEPER—THE COAL MINE

In truth, we were compelled to put ourselves upon rations. Our supply would certainly last not more than three days. I found this out about supper time. The worst part of the matter was, that in what is called the transition rocks, it was hardly to be expected we should meet with water!

I had read of the horrors of thirst, and I knew that where we were, a brief trial of its sufferings would put an end to our adventures—and our lives! But it was utterly useless to discuss the matter with my uncle. He would have answered by some axiom from Plato.

During the whole of next day we proceeded on our journey through this interminable gallery, arch after arch, tunnel after tunnel. We journeyed without exchanging a word. We had become as mute and reticent as Hans our guide.

The road had no longer an upward tendency; at all events, if it had, it was not to be made out very clearly. Sometimes there could be no doubt that we were going downwards. But this inclination was scarcely to be distinguished, and was by no means reassuring to the Professor, because the character of the strata was in no wise modified, and the transition character of the rocks became more and more marked.

It was a glorious sight to see how the electric light brought out the sparkles in the walls of the calcareous rocks, and the old red sandstone. One might have fancied oneself in one of those deep cuttings in Devonshire, which have given their name to this kind of soil. Some magnificent specimens of marble projected from the sides of the gallery; some of an agate grey with white veins of variegated character, others of a yellow spotted colour, with red veins; farther off might be seen samples of colour in which cherry-tinted seams were to be found in all their brightest shades.

The greater number of these marbles were stamped with the marks of primitive animals. Since the previous evening, nature and creation had made considerable progress. Instead of the rudimentary trilobites, I perceived the remains of a more perfect order. Among others, the fish in which the eye of a geologist has been able to discover the first form of the reptile.

The Devonian seas were inhabited by a vast number of animals of this species, which were deposited in tens of thousands in the rocks of new formation.

It was quite evident to me that we were ascending the scale of animal life of which man forms the summit. My excellent uncle, the Professor, appeared not to take notice of these warnings. He was determined at any risk to proceed.

He must have been in expectation of one of two things; either that a vertical well was about to open under his feet, and thus allow him to continue his descent, or that some insurmountable obstacle would compel us to stop and go back by the road we had so long travelled. But evening came again, and, to my horror, neither hope was doomed to be realised!

On Friday, after a night when I began to feel the gnawing agony of thirst, and when in consequence appetite decreased, our little band rose and once more followed the turnings and windings, the ascents and descents, of this interminable gallery. All were silent and gloomy. I could see that even my uncle had ventured too far.

After about ten hours of further progress,—a progress dull and monotonous to the last degree—I remarked that the reverberation, and reflection of our lamps upon the sides of the tunnel had singularly diminished. The marble, the schist, the calcareous rocks, the red sandstone, had disappeared, leaving in their places a dark and gloomy wall, sombre and without brightness. When we reached a remarkably narrow part of the tunnel, I leaned my left hand against the rock.

When I took my hand away, and happened to glance at it, it was quite black. We had reached the coal strata of the Central Earth.

"A coal mine!" I cried.

"A coal mine without miners," responded my uncle, a little severely.

"How can we tell?"

"I can tell," replied my uncle, in a sharp and doctorial tone. "I am perfectly certain that this gallery through successive layers of coal, was not cut by the hand of man. But whether it is the work of nature or not is of little concern to us. The hour for our evening has come—let us sup."

Hans, the guide, occupied himself in preparing food. I had come to that point when I could no longer eat. All I cared about were the few drops of water which fell to my share. What I suffered it is useless to record. The guide's gourd, not quite half full, was all that was left for us three!

Having finished their repast, my two companions laid themselves down upon their rugs, and found in sleep a remedy for their fatigue and sufferings. As for me, I could not sleep, I lay counting the hours until morning.

The next morning, Saturday, at six o'clock, we started again. Twenty minutes later we suddenly came upon a vast excavation. From its mighty extent I saw at once that the hand of man could have had nothing to do with this coal mine; the vault above would have fallen in; as it was, it was only held together by some miracle of nature.

This mighty natural cavern was about a hundred feet wide, by about a hundred and fifty high. The earth had evidently been cast apart by some violent subterranean commotion. The mass, giving way to some prodigious upheaving of nature, had split in two, leaving the vast gap into which we inhabitants of the earth had penetrated for the first time.

The whole singular history of the coal period was written on those dark and gloomy walls. A geologist would have been able easily to follow the different phases of its formation. The seams of coal were separated by strata of sandstone, a compact clay, which appeared to be crushed down by the weight from above.

At that period of the world which preceeded the secondary epoch, the earth was covered by a coating of enormous and rich vegetation, due to the double action of tropical heat and perpetual humidity. A vast atmospheric cloud of vapour surrounded the earth on all sides, preventing the rays of the sun from ever reaching it.

Hence the conclusion that these intense heats did not arise from this new source of caloric.

Perhaps even the star of day was not quite ready for its brilliant work—to illumine a universe. Climates did not as yet exist, and a level heat pervaded the whole surface of the globe—the same heat existing at the north pole as at the equator.

Whence did it come? From the interior of the earth?

In spite of all the learned theories of Professor Hardwigg, a fierce and vehement fire certainly burned within the entrails of the great spheroid. Its action was felt even to the very topmost crust of the earth; the plants then in existence being deprived of the vivifying rays of the sun, had neither buds, nor flowers, nor odour, but their roots drew a strong and vigorous life from the burning earth of early days.

There were but few of what may be called trees—only herbaceous plants, immense turfs, briers, mosses, rare families, which however in those days were counted by tens and tens of thousands.

It is entirely to this exuberant vegetation that coal owes its origin. The crust of the vast globe still yielded under the influence of the seething, boiling mass, which was for ever at work beneath. Hence arose numerous fissures, and continual falling in of the upper earth. The dense mass of plants being beneath the waters, soon formed themselves into vast agglomerations.

Then came about the action of natural chemistry; in the depths of the ocean the vegetable mass at first became turf, then, thanks to the influence of gases and subterranean fermentation, they underwent the complete process of mineralisation.

In this manner, in early days, were formed those vast and prodigious layers of coal, which an ever increasing consumption must utterly use up in about three centuries more, if people do not find some more economic light than gas, and some cheaper motive power than steam.

All these reflections, the memories of my school studies, came to my mind while I gazed upon these mighty accumulations of coal, whose riches however are scarcely likely to be ever utilised. The working of these mines could only be carried out at an expense that would never yield a profit.

The matter, however, is scarcely worthy consideration, when coal is scattered over the whole surface of the globe, within a few yards of the upper crust. As I looked at these untouched strata, therefore, I knew they would remain as long as the world lasts.

While we still continued our journey, I alone forgot the length of the road, by giving myself up wholly to these geological considerations. The temperature continued to be very much the same as while we were travelling amid the lava and the schists. On the other hand my sense of smell was much affected by a very powerful odour. I immediately knew that the gallery was filled to overflowing with that dangerous gas the miners call fire-damp, the explosion of which has caused such fearful and terrible accidents, making a hundred widows, and hundreds of orphans in a single hour.

Happily, we were able to illumine our progress by means of the Ruhmkorff apparatus. If we had been so rash and imprudent as to explore this gallery, torch in hand, a terrible explosion would have put an end to our travels, simply because no travellers would be left.

Our excusion through this wondrous coal mine in the very bowels of the earth lasted until evening. My uncle was scarcely able to conceal his impatience and dissatisfaction at the road continuing still to advance in a horizontal direction.

The darkness, dense and opaque, a few yards in advance and in the rear, rendered it impossible to make out what was the length of the gallery. For myself, I began to believe that it was simply interminable, and would go on in the same manner for months.

Suddenly, at six o'clock, we stood in front of a wall. To the right, to the left, above, below, nowhere was there any passage. We had reached a spot where the rocks said in unmistakeable accents—No Throughfare.

I stood stupefied. The guide simply folded his arms. My uncle was silent.

"Well, well, so much the better," cried my uncle, at last, "I now know what we are about. We are decidedly not upon the road followed by Saknussemm. All we have to do is to go back. Let us take one night's good rest, and before three days are over, I promise you we shall have regained the point where the galleries divided.

"Yes, we may, if our strength lasts as long," I cried, in a lamentable voice.

"And why not?"

"To-morrow, among us three, there will not be a drop of water. It is just gone."

"And your courage with it," said my uncle, speaking in a severe tone.

What could I say? I turned round on my side, and from sheer exhaustion fell into a heavy but troubled sleep. Dreams of water! And I awoke unrefreshed.

I would have bartered a diamond mine for a glass of pure spring water!

CHAPTER 18

THE WRONG ROAD!

NEXT day, our departure took place at a very early hour. There was no time for the least delay. According to my account, we had five days' hard work to get back to the place where the galleries divided.

I can never tell all the sufferings we endured upon our return. My uncle bore them like a man who has been in the wrong—that is, with concentrated and suppressed anger; Hans, with all the resignation of his pacific character; and I—I confess that I did nothing but complain, and despair. I had no heart for this bad fortune.

But there was one consolation. Defeat at the outset would probably upset the whole journey!

As I had expected from the first, our supply of water gave completely out on our first day's march. Our provision of liquids was reduced to our supply of schiedam; but this horrible—nay, I will say it—this infernal liquor burnt the throat, and I could not even bear the sight of it. I found the temperature to be stifling. I was paralysed with fatigue. More than once I was about to fall insensible to the ground. The whole party then halted, and the worthy Icelander and my excellent uncle did their best to console and comfort me. I could, however, plainly see that my uncle was contending painfully against the extreme fatigues of our journey, and the awful torture generated by the absence of water.

At length a time came when I ceased to recollect anything—when all was one awful, hideous, fantastic dream!

At last, on Tuesday, the eighth of the month of July, after crawling on our hands and knees for many hours, more dead than alive, we reached the point of junction between the galleries. I lay like a log, an inert mass of human flesh on the arid lava soil. It was then ten in the morning.

Hans and my uncle, leaning against the wall, tried to nibble away at some pieces of biscuit, while deep groans and sighs escaped from my scorched and swollen lips. Then I fell off into a kind of deep lethargy.

Presently I felt my uncle approach, and lift me up tenderly in his arms.

"Poor boy," I heard him say in a tone of deep commiseration.

I was profoundly touched by these words, being by no means accustomed to signs of womanly weakness in the Professor. I caught his trembling hands in mine and gave them a gentle pressure. He allowed me to do so without resistance, looking at me kindly all the time. His eyes were wet with tears.

I then saw him take the gourd which he wore at his side. To my surprise, or rather to my stupefaction, he placed it to my lips.

"Drink, my boy," he said.

Was it possible my ears had not deceived me? Was my uncle mad? I looked at him, with, I am sure, quite an idiotic expression. I would not understand him. I too much feared the counteraction of disappointment.

"Drink," he said again.

Had I heard aright? Before, however, I could ask myself the question a second time, a mouthful of water cooled my parched lips and throat—one mouthful, but I do believe it brought me back to life.

I thanked my uncle by clasping my hands. My heart was too full to speak.

"Yes," said he, "one mouthful of water, the very last—do you hear, my boy—the very last! I have taken care of it at the bottom of my bottle as the apple of my eye. Twenty times, a hundred times, I have resisted the fearful desire to drink it. But—no—no, Harry, I saved it for you."

"My dear uncle," I exclaimed, and the big tears rolled down my hot and feverish cheeks.

"Yes, my poor boy, I knew that when you reached this place, this cross road in the earth, you would fall down half dead, and I saved my last drop of water in order to restore you."

"Thanks," I cried; "thanks from my heart."

As little as my thirst was really quenched, I had nevertheless partially recovered my strength. The contracted muscles of my throat relaxed—and the inflammation of my lips in some measure subsided. At all events, I was able to speak.

"Well," I said, "there can be no doubt now as to what we have to do. Water has utterly failed us; our journey is therefore at an end. Let us return."

While I spoke thus, my uncle evidently avoided my face: he held down his head; his eyes were turned in every possible direction but the right one.

"Yes," I continued, getting excited by my own words, "we must go back to Sneffels. May heaven give us strength to enable us once more to revisit the light of day. Would that we now stood on the summit of the crater."

"Go back," said my uncle speaking to himself—"and must it be so?"

"Go back—yes, and without losing a single moment," I vehemently cried.

For some moments there was silence under that dark and gloomy vault.

"So, my dear Harry," said the Professor in a very singular tone of voice, "those few drops of water have not sufficed to restore your energy and courage."

"Courage!" I cried.

"I see that you are quite as downcast as before—and still give way to discouragement and despair."

What, then, was the man made of, and what other projects were entering his fertile and audacious brain!

"You are not discouraged, sir?"

"What! give up just as we are on the verge of success," he cried, "never, never shall it be said that Professor Hardwigg retreated."

"Then we must make up our minds to perish," I cried with a helpless sigh.

"No, Harry, my boy, certainly not. Go, leave me, I am very far from desiring your death. Take Hans with you. *I will go on alone*."

"You ask us to leave you?"

"Leave me, I say. I have undertaken this dangerous and perilous adventure. I will carry it to the end—or I will never return to the surface of Mother Earth. Go,—Harry—once more I say to you—go!"

My uncle as he spoke was terribly excited. His voice, which before had been tender, almost womanly, became harsh and menacing. He appeared to be struggling with desperate energy against the impossible. I did not wish to abandon him at the bottom of that abyss, while, on the other hand, the instinct of preservation told me to fly.

Meanwhile, our guide was looking on with profound calmness and indifference. He appeared to be an unconcerned party, and yet he perfectly well knew what was going on between us. Our gestures sufficiently indicated the different roads each wished to follow—and which each tried to influence the other to undertake. But Hans appeared not to take the slightest interest in what was really a question of life and death for us all, but waited quite ready to obey the signal which should say go aloft, or to resume his desperate journey into the interior of the earth.

How then I wished with all my heart and soul that I could make him understand my words. My representations, my sighs and groans, the earnest accents in which I should have spoken would have convinced that cold hard nature. Those fearful dangers and perils of which the stolid guide had no idea, I would have pointed them out to him—I would have, as it were, made him see and feel. Between us, we might have convinced the obstinate Professor. If the worst had come to the worst, we could have compelled him to return to the summit of Sneffels.

I quietly approached Hans. I caught his hand in mine. He never moved a muscle. I indicated to him the road to the top of the crater. He remained motionless. My panting form, my haggard countenance, must have indicated the extent of my sufferings. The Icelander gently shook his head and pointed to my uncle.

"*Master,*" he said.

The word is Icelandic as well as English.

"The master!" I cried, beside myself with fury—"madman! no—I tell you he is not the master of our lives; we must fly! we must drag him with us! do you hear me? Do you understand me, I say?"

I have already explained that I held Hans by the arm. I tried to make him rise from his seat. I struggled with him and tried to force him away. My uncle now interposed.

"My good Henry, be calm," he said. "You will obtain nothing from my devoted follower; therefore, listen to what I have to say."

I folded my arms, as well as I could, and looked my uncle full in the face.

"This wretched want of water," he said, "is the sole obstacle to the success of my project. In the entire gallery, composed of lava, schist, and coal, it is true we found not one liquid molecule. It is quite possible that we may be more fortunate in the western tunnel."

My sole reply was to shake my head with an air of incredulity.

"Listen to me to the end," said the Professor in his well-known lecturing voice. "While you lay yonder without life or motion, I undertook a reconnoitering journey into the conformation of this other gallery. I have discovered that it goes directly downwards into the bowels of the earth, and in a few hours will take us to the old granitic formation. In this we shall undoubtedly find innumerable springs. The nature of the rock makes this a mathematical certainty, and instinct agrees with logic to say that it is so. Now, this is the serious proposition which I have to make to you. When Christopher Columbus asked of his men three days to discover the land of promise, his men ill, terrified, and hopeless, yet gave him three days—and the New World was discovered. Now I, the Christopher Columbus of this subterranean region, only ask of you one more day. If, when that time is expired, I have not found the water of which we are in search, I swear to you, I will give up my mighty enterprise and return to the earth's surface."

Despite my irritation and despair, I knew how much it cost my uncle to make this proposition, and to hold such conciliatory language. Under the circumstances, what could I do, but yield?

"Well," I cried, "let it be as you wish, and may heaven reward your superhuman energy. But as, unless we discover water, our hours are numbered, let us lose no time, but go ahead."

CHAPTER 19

THE WESTERN GALLERY—A NEW ROUTE

OUR descent was now resumed by means of the second gallery. Hans took up his post in front as usual. We had not gone more than a hundred yards when the Professor carefully examined the walls.

"This is the primitive formation—we are on the right road—onwards is our hope!"

When the whole earth got cool in the first hours of the world's morning, the diminution of the volume of the earth produced a state of dislocation in its upper crust, followed by ruptures, crevasses and fissures. The passage was a fissure of this kind, through which, ages ago, had flowed the eruptive granite. The thousand windings and turnings formed an inextricable labyrinth through the ancient soil.

As we descended, successions of layers composing the primitive soil appeared with the utmost fidelity of detail. Geological science considers this primitive soil as the base of the mineral crust, and it has recognised that it is composed of three different strata or layers, all resting on the immoveable rock known as granite.

No mineralogists had ever found themselves placed in such a marvellous position to study nature in all her real and naked beauty. The sounding rod, a mere machine, could not bring to the surface of the earth the objects of value for the study of its internal structure, which we were about to see with our own eyes, to touch with our own hands.

Remember that I am writing this *after* the journey.

Across the streak of the rocks, coloured by beautiful green tints, wound metallic threads of copper, of manganese, with traces of platinum and gold. I could not help gazing at these riches buried in the entrails of mother earth, and of which no man would have the enjoyment to the end of time! These treasures—mighty and inexhaustible, were buried in the morning of the earth's history, at such awful depths, that no crowbar or pickaxe will ever drag them from their tomb!

The light of our Ruhmkorff's coil, increased tenfold by the myriad of prismatic masses of rock, sent their jets of fire in every direction, and I could fancy myself travelling through a huge hollow diamond, the rays of which produced myriads of extraordinary effects.

Towards six o'clock, this festival of light began sensibly and visibly to decrease, and soon almost ceased. The sides of the gallery assumed a crystallized tint, with a sombre hue; white mica began to commingle more freely with feldspar and quartz, to form what may be called the true rock—the stone which is hard above all, that supports, without being crushed, the four stories of the earth's soil.

We were walled by an immense and wondrous prison of granite!

It was now eight o'clock, and still there was no sign of water. The sufferings I endured were horrible. My uncle kept at the head of our little column. Nothing could induce him to stop. I, meanwhile, had but one real thought. My ear was keenly on the watch to catch the sound of a spring. But no pleasant sound of falling water fell upon my listening ear.

But at last the time came when my limbs refused to longer carry me. I contended heroically against the terrible tortures I endured, because I did not wish to compel my uncle to halt. To him I knew this would be the last fatal stroke.

Suddenly I felt a deadly faintness come over me. My eyes could no longer see; my knees shook. I gave one despairing cry—and fell!

"Help, help, I am dying!"

My uncle turned and slowly retraced his steps. He looked at me with folded arms, and then allowed one sentence to escape, in hollow accents, from his lips—

A diamond mine.

"All is over."

The last thing I saw was a face fearfully distorted with pain and sorrow; and then my eyes closed.

When I again opened them, I saw my companions lying near me, motionless, wrapped in their huge travelling rugs. Were they asleep or dead? For myself, sleep was wholly out of the question. My fainting fit over, I was wakeful as the lark. I suffered too much for sleep to visit my eyelids—the more, that I thought myself sick unto death—dying. The last words spoken by my uncle seemed to be buzzing in my ears—*all is over!* And it was probable that he was right. In the state of prostration to which I was reduced, it was madness to think of ever again seeing the light of day.

Above were miles upon miles of the earth's crust. As I thought of it, I could fancy the whole weight resting on my shoulders. I was crushed, annihilated! and exhausted myself in vain attempts to turn in my granite bed.

Hours upon hours passed away. A profound and terrible silence reigned around us—a silence of the tomb. Nothing could make itself heard through these gigantic walls of granite. The very thought was stupendous.

Presently, despite my apathy, despite the kind of deadly calm into which I was cast, something aroused me. It was a slight but peculiar noise. While I was watching intently, I observed that the tunnel was becoming dark. Then gazing through the dim light that remained, I thought I saw the Icelander taking his departure, lamp in hand.

Why had he acted thus? Did Hans the guide mean to abandon us? My uncle lay fast asleep—or dead. I tried to cry out, and arouse him. My voice, feebly issuing from my parched and fevered lips, found no echo in that fearful place. My throat was dry, my tongue stuck to the roof of my mouth. The obscurity had by this time become intense, and at last even the faint sound of the guide's footsteps was lost in the blank distance. My soul seemed filled with anguish, and death appeared welcome, only let it come quickly.

"Hans is leaving us," I cried. "Hans—Hans, if you are a man, come back."

These words were spoken to myself. They could not be heard aloud. Nevertheless, after the first few moments of terror were over, I was ashamed of my suspicions against a man, who hitherto had behaved so admirably. Nothing in his conduct or character justified suspicion. Moreover, a moment's reflection reassured me. His departure could not be a flight. Instead of ascending the gallery, he was going deeper down into the gulf. Had he had any bad design, his way would have been upwards.

This reasoning calmed me a little and I began to hope!

The good, and peaceful, and imperturbable Hans would certainly not have arisen from his sleep without some serious and grave motive. Was he bent on a voyage of discovery? During the deep, still silence of the night had he at last heard that sweet murmur about which we were all so anxious?

CHAPTER 20

WATER, WHERE IS IT? A BITTER DISAPPOINTMENT

DURING a long, long, weary hour, there crossed my wildly delirious brain all sorts of reasons as to what could have aroused our quiet and faithful guide. The most absurd and ridiculous ideas passed through my head, each more impossible than the other. I believe I was either half or wholly mad.

Suddenly, however, there arose, as it were from the depths of the earth, a voice of comfort. It was the sound of footsteps! Hans was returning.

Presently the uncertain light began to shine upon the walls of the passage, and then it came in view far down the sloping tunnel. At length Hans himself appeared.

He approached my uncle, placed his hand upon his shoulder, and gently awakened him. My uncle, as soon as he saw who it was, instantly rose.

"Well!" exclaimed the Professor.

"*Vatten,*" said the hunter.

I did not know a single word of the Danish language, and yet by a sort of mysterious instinct I understood what the guide had said.

"Water, water!" I cried, in a wild and frantic tone, clapping my hands, and gesticulating like a madman.

"Water!" murmured my uncle, in a voice of deep emotion and gratitude. "Hvar?" (where.)

"Nedat" (below.)

"Where? below!" I understood every word. I had caught the hunter by the hands, and I shook them heartily, while he looked on with perfect calmness.

The preparations for our departure did not take long, and we were soon making a rapid descent into the tunnel.

An hour later we had advanced a thousand yards, and descended two thousand feet.

At this moment I heard an accustomed and well-known sound running along the floors of the granite rock—a kind of dull and sullen roar, like that of a distant waterfall.

During the first half-hour of our advance, not finding the discovered spring, my feelings of intense suffering appeared to return. Once more I began to lose all hope. My uncle, however, observing how downhearted I was again becoming, took up the conversation.

"Hans was right," he exclaimed, enthusiastically; "that is the dull roaring of a torrent."

"A torrent," I cried, delighted at even hearing the welcome words.

"There's not the slightest doubt about it," he replied, "a subterranean river is flowing beside us."

I made no reply, but hastened on, once more animated by hope. I began not even to feel the deep fatigue which hitherto had overpowered me. The very sound of this glorious murmuring water already refreshed me. We could hear it increasing in volume every moment. The torrent, which for a long time could be heard flowing over our heads, now ran distinctly along the left wall, roaring, rushing, spluttering, and still falling.

Several times I passed my hand across the rock hoping to find some trace of humidity—of the slightest percolation. Alas! in vain.

Again a half hour elapsed in the same weary toil. Again we advanced.

It now became evident that the hunter, during his absence, had not been able to carry his researches any farther. Guided by an instinct peculiar to the dwellers in mountain regions and water finders, he "smelt" the living spring through the rock. Still he had not seen the precious liquid. He had neither quenched his own thirst, nor brought us one drop in his gourd.

Moreover, we soon made the disastrous discovery, that if our progress continued, we should soon be moving away from the torrent, the sound of which gradually diminished. We turned back. Hans halted at the precise spot where the sound of the torrent appeared nearest.

I could bear the suspense and suffering no longer, and seated myself against the wall, behind which I could hear the water seething and effervescing not two feet away. But a solid wall of granite still separated us from it!

Hans looked keenly at me, and, strange enough, for once I thought I saw a smile on his imperturbable face.

He rose from a stone on which he had been seated, and took up the lamp. I could not help rising and following. He moved slowly along the firm and solid granite wall. I watched him with mingled curiosity and eagerness. Presently he halted and placed his ear against the dry stone, moving slowly along and listening with the most extreme care and attention. I understood at once that he was searching for the exact spot where the torrent's roar was most plainly heard. This point he soon found in the lateral wall on the left side, about three feet above the level of the tunnel floor.

I was in a state of intense excitement. I scarcely dared believe what the eider-duck hunter was about to do. It was, however, impossible in a moment more not to both understand and applaud, and even to smother him in my embraces, when I saw him raise the heavy crowbar and commence an attack upon the rock itself.

"Saved," I cried.

"Yes," cried my uncle, even more excited and delighted than myself; "Hans is quite right. Oh, the worthy, excellent man! We should never have thought of such an idea."

And nobody else, I think, would have done so. Such a process, simple as it seemed, would most certainly not have entered our heads. Nothing could be more dangerous than to begin to work with pickaxes in that particular part of the globe. Supposing while he was at work a break-up were to take place, and supposing the torrent once having gained an inch were to take an ell, and come pouring bodily through the broken rock!

Not one of these dangers were chimerical. They were only too real. But at that moment no fear of falling in of roof, or even of inundation was capable of stopping us. Our thirst was so intense, that to quench it we would have dug below the bed of old Ocean itself.

Hans went quietly to work—a work which neither my uncle nor I would have undertaken at any price. Our impatience was so great, that if we had once begun with pickaxe and crowbar, the rock would soon have split into a hundred fragments. The guide, on the contrary, calm, ready, moderate, wore away the hard rock by little steady blows of his instrument, making no attempt at a larger hole than about six inches. As I stood, I heard, or I thought I heard, the roar of the torrent momentarily increasing in loudness, and at times I almost felt the pleasant sensation of water upon my parched lips.

At the end of what appeared an age, Hans had made a hole, which enabled his crowbar to enter two feet into the solid rock. He had been at work exactly an hour. It appeared a dozen. I was getting wild with impatience. My uncle began to think of using more violent measures. I had the greatest difficulty in checking him. He had indeed just got hold of his crowbar when a loud and welcome hiss was heard. Then a stream, or rather jet of water burst through the wall and came out with such force as to hit the opposite side!

Hans, the guide, who was half upset by the shock, was scarcely able to keep down a cry of pain and grief. I understood his meaning when plunging my hands into the sparkling jet I myself gave a wild and frantic cry. The water was scalding hot!

"Boiling," I cried, in bitter disappointment.

"Well, never mind," said my uncle, "it will soon get cool."

The tunnel began to be filled by clouds of vapour, while a small stream ran away into the interior of the earth. In a short time we had some sufficiently cool to drink. We swallowed it in huge mouthfuls.

Oh what exalted delight—what rich and incomparable luxury! What was this water, whence did it come? To us what was that? The simple fact was—it was water; and, though still with a tinge of warmth about it, it brought back to the heart, that life which, but for it, must surely have faded away. I drank greedily, almost without tasting it.

When, however, I had almost quenched my ravenous thirst, I made a discovery.

"Why, it is ferruginous water."

"Most excellent stomachic," replied my uncle, "and highly mineralised. Here is a journey worth twenty to Spa."

"It's very good," I replied.

"I should think so. Water found six miles under ground. There is a peculiarly inky flavour about it, which is by no means disagreeable. Hans may congratulate himself on having made a rare discovery. What do you say, nephew, according to the usual custom of travellers, to name the stream after him?"

"Good," said I.

And the name of "Hans-bach" was at once agreed upon.

Hans was not a bit more proud after hearing our determination than he was before. After having taken a very small modicum of the welcome refreshment, he had seated himself in a corner with his usual imperturbable gravity.

"Now," said I, "it is not worth while letting this water run to waste."

"What is the use," replied my uncle, "the source from which this river rises is inexhaustible."

"Never mind," I continued, "let us fill our goat skin and gourds, and then try to stop the opening up."

My advice, after some hesitation, was followed or attempted to be followed. Hans picked up all the broken pieces of granite he had knocked out, and using some tow he happened to have about him, tried to shut up the fissure he had made in the wall. All he did was to scald his hands. The pressure was too great, and all our attempts were utter failures.

"It is evident," I remarked, "that the upper surface of these springs is situated at a very great height above—as we may fairly infer from the great pressure of the jet."

"That is by no means doubtful," replied my uncle, "if this column of water is about thirty-two thousand feet high, the atmospheric pressure must be something enormous. But a new idea has just struck me."

"And what is that?"

"Why be at so much trouble to close this aperture?"

"Because——"

I hesitated and stammered, having no real reason.

"When our water bottles are empty, we are not at all sure that we shall be able to fill them," observed my uncle.

"I think that is very probable."

"Well, then, let this water run. It will, of course, naturally follow in our track, and will serve to guide and refresh us."

"I think the idea a good one," I cried, in reply, "and with this rivulet as a companion, there is no further reason why we should not succeed in our marvellous project."

"Ah, my boy," said the professor, laughing, "after all, you are coming round."

"More than that, I am now confident of ultimate success. Forward."

"One moment, nephew mine. Let us begin by taking some hours of repose."

I had utterly forgotten that it was night. The chronometer, however, informed me of the fact. Soon we were sufficiently restored and refreshed, and had all fallen into a profound sleep.

CHAPTER 21

UNDER THE OCEAN

BY the next day we had nearly forgotten our past sufferings. The first sensation I experienced was surprise at not being thirsty, and I actually asked myself the reason. The running stream, which flowed in rippling wavelets at my feet, was the satisfactory reply.

We breakfasted with a good appetite, and then drank our fill of the excellent water. I felt myself quite a new man, ready to go anywhere my uncle chose to lead. I began to think. Why should not a man as seriously convinced as my uncle, succeed, with so excellent a guide as worthy Hans, and so devoted a nephew as myself? These were the brilliant ideas which now invaded my brain. Had the proposition now been made to go back to the summit of Mount Sneffels, I should have declined the offer in a most indignant manner.

But fortunately there was no question of going up. We were about to descend farther into the interior of the earth.

"Let us be moving," I cried, awakening the echoes of the old world.

We resumed our march on Thursday at eight o'clock in the morning. The great granite tunnel going round by sinuous and winding ways, presented every now and then sharp turns, and in fact had all the appearance of a labyrinth. Its direction, however, was in general towards the south-west. My uncle made several pauses in order to consult his compass.

The gallery now began to trend downwards in a horizontal direction, with about two inches of fall in every furlong. The murmuring stream flowed quietly at our feet. I could not but compare it to some familiar spirit, guiding us through the earth, and I dabbled my fingers in its tepid water, which sang like a naiad as we progressed. My good humour began to assume a mythological character.

As for my uncle he began to complain of the horizontal character of the road. His route he found began to be indefinitely prolonged, instead of "sliding down the celestial ray," according to his expression.

But we had no choice; and as long as our road lead towards the centre—however little progress we made, there was no reason to complain.

Moreover, from time to time the slopes were much greater; the naiad sang more loudly, and we began to dip downwards in earnest.

As yet, however, I felt no painful sensation. I had not got over the excitement of the discovery of water.

That day and the next we did a considerable amount of horizontal, and relatively very little vertical, travelling.

On Friday evening, the tenth of July, according to our estimation, we ought to have been thirty leagues to the south-east of Reykjawik, and about two leagues and a half deep. We now received a rather startling surprise.

Under our feet there opened a horrible well. My uncle was so delighted that he actually clapped his hands—as he saw how steep and sharp was the descent.

"Ah, ah!" he cried, in rapturous delight; "this will take us a long way. Look at the projections of the rock. Hah!" he exclaimed, "it's a fearful staircase!"

Hans, however, who in all our troubles had never given up the ropes, took care so to dispose of them as to prevent any accidents. Our descent then began. I dare not call it a perilous descent, for I was already too familiar with that sort of work to look upon it as anything but a very ordinary affair.

This well was a kind of narrow opening in the massive granite of the kind known as a fissure. The contraction of the terrestrial scaffolding, when it suddenly cooled, had been evidently the cause. If it had ever served in former times as a kind of funnel through which passed the eruptive masses vomited by Sneffels, I was at a loss to explain how it had left no mark. We were, in fact, descending a spiral, something like those winding staircases in use in modern houses.

We were compelled every quarter of an hour or thereabouts to sit down in order to rest our legs. Our calves ached. We then seated ourselves on some projecting rock with our legs hanging over, and gossipped while we ate a mouthful—drinking still from the pleasantly-warm running stream which had not deserted us.

It is scarcely necessary to say, that in this curiously-shaped fissure the Hansbach had become a cascade to the detriment of its size. It was still however sufficient, and more, for our wants. Besides we knew that, as soon as the declivity ceased to be so abrupt, the stream must resume its peaceful course. At this moment it reminded me of my uncle, his impatience and rage, while when it flowed more peacefully, I pictured to myself the placidity of the Icelandic guide.

During the whole of two days, the sixth and seventh of July, we followed the extraordinary spiral staircase of the fissure, penetrating two leagues farther into the crust of the earth, which placed us five leagues below the level of the sea.

On the eighth, however, at twelve o'clock in the day, the fissure suddenly assumed a much more gentle slope still trending in a south-east direction.

The road now became comparatively easy, and at the same time dreadfully monotonous. It would have been difficult for matters to have turned out otherwise. Our peculiar journey had no chance of being diversified by landscape and scenery. At all events, such was my idea.

At length, on Wednesday the fifteenth, we were actually seven leagues (twenty-one miles,) below the surface of the earth, and fifty leagues distant from the mountain of Sneffels. Though, if the truth be told, we were very tired, our health had resisted all suffering, and was in a most satisfactory state. Our traveller's box of medicaments had not even been opened.

My uncle was careful to note every hour the indications of the compass, of the chronometer, of the manometer, and of the thermometer, all which he afterwards published in his elaborate philosophical and scientific account of our remarkable voyage. He was therefore able to give an exact relation of the situation. When, therefore, he informed me that we were fifty leagues in a horizontal direction distant from our starting point, I could not suppress a loud exclamation.

"What is the matter now?" cried my uncle.

"Nothing very important, only an idea has entered my head," was my reply.

"Well, out with it, my boy."

"It is my opinion that if your calculations are correct we are no longer under Iceland."

"Do you think so?"

"We can very easily find out," I replied, pulling out the map and compasses.

"You see," I said, after careful measurement, "that I am not mistaken. We are far beyond Cape Portland; and those fifty leagues to the south-east will take us into the open sea."

"Under the open sea," cried my uncle, rubbing his hands with a delighted air.

"Yes," I cried, "no doubt old ocean flows over our heads."

"Well, my dear boy, what can be more natural. Do you not know that in the neighbourhood of Newcastle there are coal mines which have been worked far out under the sea?"

Now my worthy uncle the Professor, no doubt regarded this discovery as a very simple fact, but to me the idea was by no means a pleasant one. And yet when one came to think the matter over seriously, what mattered it whether the plains and mountains of Iceland were suspended over our devoted heads, or the mighty billows of the Atlantic Ocean? The whole question rested on the solidity of the granite roof above us. However, I soon got used to the idea, for the passage now level, now running down, and still always to the south-east, kept going deeper and deeper into the profound abysses of Mother Earth.

Three days later, on the eighteenth day of July, on a Saturday, we reached a kind of vast grotto. My uncle here paid Hans his usual rix-dollars, and it was decided that the next day should be a day of rest.

A vertical descent.

CHAPTER 22

SUNDAY BELOW GROUND

I AWOKE on Sunday morning without any sense of hurry and bustle attendant on an immediate departure. Though the day to be devoted to repose and reflection was spent under such strange circumstances, and in so wonderful a place, the idea was a pleasant one. Besides, we all began to get used to this kind of existence. I had almost ceased to think of the sun, of the moon, of the stars, of the trees, houses, and towns; in fact, about any terrestrial necessities. In our peculiar position we were far above such reflections.

The grotto was a vast and magnificent hall. Along its granitic soil the stream flowed placidly and pleasantly. So great a distance was it now from its fiery source, that its water was scarcely lukewarm, and could be drank without delay or difficulty.

After a frugal breakfast, the Professor made up his mind to devote some hours to putting his notes and calculations in order.

"In the first place," he said, "I have a good many to verify and prove, in order that we may know our exact position. I wish to be able on our return to the upper regions, to make a map of our journey, a kind of a vertical section of the globe, which will be as it were the profile of the expedition."

"That would indeed be a curious work, uncle; but can you make your observations with anything like certainty and precision?"

"I can. I have never on one occasion failed to note with great care the angles and slopes. I am certain as to having made no mistake. Take the compass and examine how she points."

I looked at the instrument with care.

"East one quarter south-east."

"Very good," resumed the Professor, noting the observation, and going through some rapid calculations. "I make out that we have journeyed two hundred and fifty miles from the point of our departure."

"Then the mighty waves of the Atlantic are rolling over our heads?"

"Certainly."

"And at this very moment it is possible that fierce tempests are raging above, and that men and ships are battling against the angry blasts just over our heads?"

"It is quite within the range of possibility," rejoined my uncle smiling.

"And that whales are playing in shoals, thrashing the bottom of the sea, the roof of our adamantine prison?"

"Be quite at rest on that point; there is no danger of their breaking through. But to return to our calculations. We are to the south-east, two hundred and fifty miles from the base of Sneffels, and according to my preceding notes, I think we have gone sixteen leagues in a downward direction."

"Sixteen leagues—fifty miles!" I cried.

"I am sure of it."

"But that is the extreme limit allowed by science for the thickness of the earth's crust," I replied, referring to my geological studies.

"I do not contravene that assertion," was his quiet answer.

"And at this stage of our journey, according to all known laws on the increase of heat, there should be here a temperature of *fifteen hundred* degrees of Reaumur."

"There should be—you say, my boy."

"In which case this granite would not exist, but be in a state of fusion."

"But you perceive, my boy, that it is not so, and that facts, as usual, are very stubborn things, overruling all theories."

"I am forced to yield to the evidence of my senses, but I am nevertheless very much surprised."

"What heat does the thermometer really indicate?" continued the philosopher.

"Twenty-seven six-tenths."

"So that science is wrong by fourteen hundred and seventy-four degrees and four-tenths. According to which, it is demonstrated that the proportional increase in the temperature is an exploded error. Humphrey Davy here shines forth in all his glory. He is right, and I have acted wisely to believe him. Have you any answer to make to this statement?"

Had I chosen to have spoken, I might have said a great deal. I in no way admitted the theory of Humphrey Davy—I still held out for the theory of proportional increase of heat, though I did not feel it.

I was far more willing to allow that this chimney of an extinct volcano was covered by lava of a kind refractory to heat—in fact a bad conductor—which did not allow the great increase of temperature to percolate through its sides. The hot water jet supported my view of the matter.

But without entering on a long and useless discussion, or seeking for new arguments to controvert my uncle, I contented myself with taking up facts as they were.

"Well, sir, I take for granted that all your calculations are correct, but allow me to draw from them a rigorous and definite conclusion."

"Go on, my boy—have your say," cried my uncle, good-humouredly.

"At the place where we now are, under the latitude of Iceland, the terrestrial depth is about fifteen hundred and eighty-three leagues."

"Fifteen hudnred, eighty-three and a quarter."

"Well, suppose we say sixteen hundred in round numbers. Now, out of a voyage of sixteen hundred leagues we have completed sixteen."

"As you say, what then?"

"At the expense of a diagonal journey of no less than eighty-five leagues."

"Exactly."

"We have been twenty days about it."

"Exactly twenty days."

"Now sixteen is the hundredth part of our contemplated expedition. If we go on in this way we shall be two thousand days, that is about five years and a half going down."

The Professor folded his arms, listened, but did not speak.

"Without counting that if a vertical descent of sixteen leagues costs us a horizontal of eighty-five, we shall have to go about eight thousand leagues to the south-east, and we must therefore come out somewhere in the circumference long before we can hope to reach the centre."

"Bother your calculations," cried my uncle in one of his old rages. "On what bases do they rest? How do you know that this passage does not take us direct to the end we require? Moreover, I have in my favour, fortunately, a precedent. What I have undertaken to do, another has done, and he having succeeded, why should I not be equally successful?"

"I hope, indeed, you will, but still, I suppose I may be allowed to——"

"You are allowed to hold your tongue," cried Professor Hardwigg, "when you talk so unreasonably as this."

I saw at once that old doctorial Professor was still alive in my uncle—and fearful to rouse his angry passions, I dropped the unpleasant subject.

"Now, then," he explained, "consult the manometer. What does that indicate?"

"A considerable amount of pressure."

"Very good. You see, then, that by descending slowly, and by gradually accustoming ourselves to the density of this lower atmosphere, we shall not suffer.

"Well, I suppose not, except it may be a certain amount of pain in the ears," was my rather grim reply.

"That, my dear boy, is nothing, and you will easily get rid of that source of discomfort by bringing the exterior air in communication with the air contained in your lungs."

"Perfectly," said I, for I had quite made up my mind in no wise to contradict my uncle. "I should fancy almost that I should experience a certain amount of satisfaction in making a plunge into this dense atmosphere. Have you taken note of how wonderfully sound is propagated?"

"Of course I have. There can be no doubt that a journey into the interior of the earth would be an excellent cure for deafness."

"But then, uncle," I ventured mildly to observe, "this density will continue to increase."

"Yes—according to a law which, however, is scarcely defined. It is true that the intensity of weight will diminish just in proportion to the depth to which we go. You know very well that it is on the surface of the earth that its action is most powerfully felt, while on the contrary, in the very centre of the earth bodies cease to have any weight at all."

"I know that is the case, but as we progress will not the atmosphere finally assume the density of water?"

"I know it; when placed under the pressure of seven hundred and ten atmospheres," cried my uncle with imperturbable gravity.

"And when we are still lower down?" I asked with natural anxiety.

"Well, lower down, the density will become even greater still."

"Then how shall we be able to make our way through this atmospheric fog?"

"Well, my worthy nephew, we must ballast ourselves by filling our pockets with stones," said Professor Hardwigg.

"Faith, uncle, you have an answer for everything," was my only reply.

I began to feel that it was unwise in me to go any farther into the wide field of hypotheses for I should certainly have revived some difficulty, or rather impossibility that would have enraged the Professor.

It was evident, nevertheless, that the air under a pressure which might be multiplied by thousands of atmospheres, would end by becoming perfectly solid, and that then admitting our bodies resisted the pressure, we should have to stop, in spite of all the reasonings in the world. Facts overcome all arguments.

But I thought it best not to urge this argument. My uncle would simply have quoted the example of Saknussemm. Supposing the learned Icelander's journey ever really to have taken place—there was one simple answer to be made:—

In the sixteenth century neither the barometer nor the manometer had been invented—how, then, could Saknussemm have been able to discover when he did reach the centre of the earth?

This unanswerable and learned objection, I, however, kept to myself, and bracing up my courage awaited the course of events—little aware of how adventurous yet were to be the incidents of our remarkable journey.

The rest of the day of leisure and repose was spent in calculation and conversation. I made it a point to agree with the Professor in everything; but I envied the perfect indifference of Hans, who without taking any such trouble about cause and effect, went blindly onwards wherever destiny chose to lead him.

CHAPTER 23

ALONE

It must in all truth be confessed, things as yet had gone on well, and I should have acted in bad taste to have complained. If the true medium of our difficulties did not increase, it was within the range of possibility that we might ultimately reach the end of our journey. Then what glory would be ours! I began in the newly-aroused ardour of my soul to speak enthusiastically to the Professor. Well, was I serious? The whole state in which we existed was a mystery—and it was impossible to know whether or not I was in earnest.

For several days after our memorable halt, the slopes became more rapid—some were even of a most frightful character—almost vertical, so that we were for ever going down into the solid interior mass. During some days, we actually descended a league and a-half, even two leagues towards the centre of the earth. The descents were sufficiently perilous, and while we were engaged in them we learned fully to appreciate the marvellous coolness of our guide Hans. Without him we should have been wholly lost. The grave and impassible Icelander devoted himself to us with the most incomprehensible *sang froid* and ease; and, thanks to him, many a dangerous pass was got over, where, but for him, we should inevitably have stuck fast.

His silence increased every day. I think that we began to be influenced by this peculiar trait in his character. It is certain that the inanimate objects by which you are surrounded have a direct action on the brain. It must be that a man who shuts himself up between four walls must lose the faculty of associating ideas and words. How many persons condemned to the horrors of solitary confinement have gone mad—simply because the thinking faculties have lain dormant!

During the two weeks that followed our last interesting conversation, there occurred nothing worthy of being especially recorded.

I have, while writing these memoirs, taxed my memory in vain for one incident of travel during this particular period.

But the next event to be related is indeed terrible. Its very memory, even now, makes my soul shudder, and my blood run cold.

It was on the seventh of August. Our constant and successive descents had taken us quite thirty leagues into the interior of the earth, that is to say that there were above us thirty leagues, nearly a hundred miles, of rocks, and oceans and continents and towns, to say nothing of living inhabitants. We were in a south-easterly direction, about two hundred leagues from Iceland.

On that memorable day the tunnel had begun to assume an almost horizontal course.

I was on this occasion walking on in front. My uncle had charge of one of the Ruhmkorff coils, I had possession of the other. By means of its light I was busily examining the different layers of granite. I was completely absorbed in my work.

Suddenly halting and turning round, I found that I was alone!

"Well," thought I to myself, "I have certainly been walking too fast—or else Hans and my uncle have stopped to rest. The best thing I can do is to go back and find them. Luckily, there is very little ascent to tire me."

I accordingly retraced my steps, and while doing so, walked for at least a quarter of an hour. Rather uneasy, I paused and looked eagerly around. Not a living soul. I called aloud. No reply. My voice was lost amid the myriad cavernous echoes it aroused!

I began for the first time to feel seriously uneasy. A cold shiver shook my whole body, and perspiration, chill and terrible, burst upon my skin.

"I must be calm," I said, speaking aloud, as boys whistle to drive away fear. "There can be no doubt that I shall find my companions. There cannot be two roads. It is certain that I was considerably ahead; all I have to do is to go back."

Having come to this determination I ascended the tunnel for at least half an hour, unable to decide if I had ever seen certain landmarks before. Every now and then I paused to discover if any loud appeal was made to me, well knowing that in that dense and intensified atmosphere I should hear it a long way off. But no. The most extraordinary silence reigned in this immense gallery. Only the echoes of my own footsteps could be heard.

At last I stopped. I could scarcely realise the fact of my isolation. I was quite willing to think that I had made a mistake, but not that I was lost. If I had made a mistake, I might find my way: if lost—I shuddered to think of it.

"Come, come," said I to myself, "since there is only one road, and they must come by it, we shall at last meet. All I have to do is still to go upwards. Perhaps, however, not seeing me, and forgetting I was ahead, they may have gone back in search of me. Still even in this case, if I make haste, I shall get up to them. There can be no doubt about the matter."

But as I spoke these last words aloud, it would have been quite clear to any listener—had there been one—that I was by no means convinced of the fact. Moreover, in order to associate together these simple ideas and to reunite them under the form of reasoning, required some time. I could not all at once bring my brain to think.

Then another dread doubt fell upon my soul. After all, was I ahead? Of course I was. Hans was no doubt following behind preceded by my uncle. I perfectly recollected his having stopped for a moment to strap his baggage on his shoulder. I now remembered this trifling detail. It was, I believed, just at that very moment that I had determined to continue my route.

"Again," thought I, reasoning as calmly as was possible, "there is another sure means of not losing my way, a thread to guide me thorugh the labyrinthine subterraneous retreat,—one which I had forgotten—my faithful river."

This course of reasoning roused my drooping spirits, and I resolved to resume my journey without further delay. No time was to be lost.

It was at this moment that I had reason to bless the thoughtfulness of my uncle, when he refused to allow the eider hunter to close the orifice of the hot spring—that small fissure in the great mass of granite. This beneficent spring after having saved us from thirst during so many days would now enable me to regain the right road.

Having come to this mental decision, I made up my mind, before I started upwards, that ablution would certainly do me a great deal of good.

I stopped to plunge my hands and forehead in the pleasant water of the Hansbach stream, blessing its presence as a certain consolation.

Conceive my horror and stupefaction!—I was treading a hard, dusty, shingly road of granite. The stream on which I reckoned had wholly disappeared!

CHAPTER 24

LOST!

No words in any human language can depict my utter despair. I was literally buried alive; with no other expectation before me but to die in all the slow horrible torture of hunger and thirst.

Mechanically I crawled about, feeling the dry and arid rock. Never to my fancy had I ever felt anything so dry.

But, I frantically asked myself, how had I lost the course of the flowing stream? There could be no doubt it had ceased to flow in the gallery in which I now was. Now I began to understand the cause of the strange silence which prevailed when last I tried if any appeal from my companions might perchance reach my ear.

It so happened that when I first took an imprudent step in the wrong direction, I did not perceive the absence of the all-important stream.

It was now quite evident that when we halted, another tunnel must have received the waters of the little torrent, and that I had unconsciously entered a different gallery. To what unknown depths had my companions gone? Where was I?

How to get back! Clue or landmark there was absolutely none! My feet left no signs on the granite and shingle. My brain throbbed with agony as I tried to discover the solution of this terrible problem. My situation, after all sophistry and reflection, had finally to be summed up in three awful words—

Lost! LOST!! LOST!!!

Lost at a depth which, to my finite understanding, appeared to be immeasurable.

These thirty leagues of the crust of the earth weighed upon my shoulders like the globe on the shoulders of Atlas. I felt myself crushed by the awful weight. It was indeed a position to drive the sanest man to madness!

I tried to bring my thoughts back to the things of the world so long forgotten. It was with the greatest difficulty that I succeeded in doing so. Hamburg, the house on the Königstrasse, my dear cousin Gretchen—all that world which had before vanished like a shadow floated before my now vivid imagination.

There they were before me, but now unreal. Under the influence of a terrible hallucination I saw the whole incidents of our journey pass before me like the scenes of a panorama. The ship and its inmates, Iceland, M. Fridriksson, and the great summit of Mount Sneffels! I said to myself that if in my position, I retained the most faint and shadowy outline of a hope it would be a sure sign of approaching delirium. It were better to give way wholly to despair!

In fact, did I but reason with calmness and philosophy, what human power was there in existence able to take me back to the surface of the earth, and ready too, to split asunder, to rend in twain, those huge and mighty vaults which stand above my head? Who could enable me to find my road—and regain my companions?

Insensate folly and madness to entertain even a shadow of hope!

"Oh, uncle!" was my despairing cry.

This was the only word of reproach which came to my lips; for I thoroughly understood how deeply and sorrowfully the worthy Professor would regret my loss, and how in his turn he would patiently seek for me.

When I at last began to resign myself to the fact that no further aid was to be expected from man, and knowing that I was utterly powerless to do anything for my own salvation, I kneeled with earnest fervour and asked assistance from Heaven. The remembrance of my innocent childhood, the memory of my mother, known only in my infancy, came welling forth from my heart. I had recourse to prayer. And little as I had a right to be remembered by Him whom I had forgotten in the hour of prosperity, and whom I so tardily invoked, I prayed earnestly and sincerely.

This renewal of my youthful faith brought about a much greater amount of calm, and I was enabled to concentrate all my strength and intelligence on the terrible realities of my unprecedented situation.

I had about me that which I had at first wholly forgotten—three days' provisions. Moreover, my water bottle was quite full. Nevertheless, the one thing which it was impossible to do was to remain alone. Try to find my companions I must, at any price. But which course should I take? Should I go upwards, or again descend? Doubtless it was right to retrace my steps in an upward direction.

By doing this with care and coolness, I must reach the point where I had turned away from the rippling stream. I must find the fatal bifurcation or fork. Once at this spot, once the river at my feet, I could, at all events, regain the awful crater of Mount Sneffels. Why had I not thought of this before? This, at last, was a reasonable hope of safety. The most important thing, then, to be done was to discover the bed of the Hansbach.

After a slight meal and a draught of water, I rose like a giant refreshed. Leaning heavily on my pole, I began the ascent of the gallery. The slope was very rapid and rather difficult. But I advanced hopefully and carefully, like a man who at last is making his way out of a forest, and knows there is only one road to follow.

During one whole hour nothing happened to check my progress. As I advanced I tried to recollect the shape of the tunnel—to recall to my memory certain projections of rocks—to persuade myself that I had followed certain winding

"Lost! Lost!"

routes before. But no one particular sign could I bring to mind, and I was soon forced to allow that this gallery would never take me back to the point at which I had separated myself from my companions. It was absolutely without issue—a mere blind alley in the earth.

The moment at length came when, facing the solid rock, I knew my fate, and fell inanimate on the arid floor!

To describe the horrible state of despair and fear into which I then fell would now be vain and impossible. My last hope, the courage which had sustained me, drooped before the sight of this pitiless granite rock!

Lost in a vast labyrinth, the sinuosities of which spread in every direction, without guide, clue or compass, it was a vain and useless task to attempt flight. All that remained to me was to lie down and die. To lie down and die the most cruel and horrible of deaths!

In my state of mind, the idea came into my head that one day perhaps, when my fossil bones were found, their discovery so far below the level of the earth might give rise to solemn and interesting scientific discussions.

I tried to cry aloud, but hoarse, hollow and inarticulate sounds alone could make themselves heard through my parched lips. I literally panted for breath.

In the midst of all these horrible sources of anguish and despair, a new horror took possession of my soul. My lamp, by falling down, had got out of order. I had no means of repairing it. Its light was already becoming paler and paler, and soon would expire.

With a strange sense of resignation and despair, I watched the luminous current in the coil getting less and less. A procession of shadows moved flashing along the granite wall. I scarcely dared to lower my eyelids, fearing to lose the last spark of this fugitive light. Every instant it seemed to me that it was about to vanish and to leave me for ever—in utter darkness!

At last, one final trembling flame remained in the lamp; I followed it with all my power of vision; I gasped for breath; I concentrated upon it all the power of my soul, as upon the last scintillation of light I was ever destined to see: and then I was to be lost for ever in Cimmerian and tenebrous shades.

A wild and plaintive cry escaped my lips. On earth during the most profound and comparatively complete darkness, light never allows a complete destruction and extinction of its power. Light is so diffuse, so subtle, that it permeates everywhere, and whatever little may remain, the retina of the eye will succeed in finding it. In this place nothing—not the faintest ray of light. It amazed me!

My head was now wholly lost. I raised my arms, trying the effect of the feeling in getting against the cold stone wall. It was painful in the extreme. Madness must have taken possession of me. I knew not what I did. I began to run, to fly, rushing at haphazard in this inextricable labyrinth, always going downwards, running wildly underneath the terrestrial crust, like an inhabitant of the subterranean furnaces, screaming, roaring, howling, until bruised by the pointed rocks, falling and picking myself up all covered with blood, seeking madly to drink the blood which dripped from my torn features, mad because this blood only trickled over my face, and watching always for this horrid wall which ever presented to me the fearful obstacle against which I could not dash my head.

Where was I going? It was impossible to say. I was perfectly ignorant of the matter.

Several hours passed in this way. After a long time, having utterly exhausted my strength, I fell, a heavy inert mass along the side of the tunnel, and lost all consciousness of existence!

CHAPTER 25

THE WHISPERING GALLERY

WHEN at last I came back to a sense of life and being, my face was wet; but wet as I soon knew with tears. How long this state of insensibility lasted, it is quite impossible for me now to say. I had no means left to me of taking any account of time. Never since the creation of the world, had such a solitude as mine existed. I was completely abandoned.

After my fall, I lost much blood. I felt myself flooded with the life-giving liquid. My first sensation was perhaps a natural one. Why was I not dead? Because I was alive, there was something left to do. I tried to make up my mind to think no longer. As far as I was able, I drove away all ideas, and utterly overcome by pain and grief, I crouched against the granite wall.

I just commenced to feel the fainting coming on again, and the sensation that this was the last struggle before complete annihilation,—when, on a sudden, a violent uproar reached my ears. It had some resemblance to the prolonged rumbling voice of thunder, and I clearly distinguished sonorous voices, lost one after the other, in the distant depths of the gulf.

Whence came this noise? Naturally, it was to be supposed from new phenomena which were taking place in the bosom of the solid mass of Mother Earth! The explosion of some gaseous vapours, or the fall of some solid, of the granitic or other rock.

Again I listened with deep attention. I was extremely anxious to hear if this strange and inexplicable sound was likely to be renewed! A whole quarter of an hour elapsed in painful expectation. Deep and solemn silence reigned in the tunnel. So still that I could hear the beatings of my own heart! I waited, waited, waited with a strange kind of hopefulness.

Suddenly my ear, which leant accidentally against the wall, appeared to catch as it were the faintest echo of a sound. I thought that I heard vague, incoherent and distant voices. I quivered all over with excitement and hope!

"It must be hallucination," I cried. "It cannot be! it is not true!"

But no! By listening more attentively, I really did convince myself that what I heard was truly the sound of human voices. To make any meaning out of the sound, however, was beyond my power. I was too weak even to hear distinctly. Still it was a positive fact that some one was speaking. Of that I was quite certain.

There was a moment of fear. A dread fell upon my soul that it might be my own words brought back to me by a distant echo. Perhaps without knowing it, I might have been crying aloud. I resolutely closed my lips, and once more placed my ear to the huge granite wall.

Yes, for certain. It was in truth the sound of human voices.

I now by the exercise of great determination dragged myself along the sides of the cavern, until I reached a point where I could hear more distinctly. But though I could detect the sound, I could only make out uncertain, strange, and incomprehensible words. They reached my ear as if they had been spoken in a low tone—murmured, as it were, afar off.

At last, I made out the word *förlorad* repeated several times in a tone betokening great mental anguish and sorrow.

What could this word mean, and who was speaking it? It must be either my uncle or the guide Hans! If, therefore, I could hear them, they must surely be able to hear me.

"Help," I cried at the top of my voice; "help, I am dying!"

I then listened with scarcely a breath; I panted for the slightest sound in the darkness—a cry, a sigh, a question! But silence reigned supreme. No answer came! In this way some minutes passed. A whole flood of ideas flashed through my mind. I began to fear that my voice weakened by sickness and suffering could not reach my companions who were in search of me.

"It must be them," I cried; "what other men can by possibility be buried a hundred miles below the level of the earth?" The mere supposition was preposterous.

I began, therefore, to listen again with the most breathless attention. As I moved my ears along the side of the place I was in, I found a mathematical point as it were, where the voices appeared to attain their maximum of intensity. The word *förlorad* again distinctly reached my ear. Then came again that rolling noise like thunder which had awakened me out of torpor.

"I begin to understand," I said to myself after some little time devoted to reflection; "it is not through the solid mass that the sound reaches my ears. The walls of my cavernous retreat are of solid granite, and the most fearful explosion would not make uproar enough to penetrate them. The sound must come along the gallery itself. The place I was in must possess some peculiar acoustic properties of its own.

Again I listened; and this time—yes, this time—I heard my name distinctly pronounced: cast as it were into space.

It was my uncle the Professor who was speaking. He was in conversation with the guide, and the word which had so often reached my ears, *förlorad,* was a Danish expression.

Then I understood it all. In order to make myself heard, I too must speak as it were along the side of the gallery, which would carry the sound of my voice just as the wire carries the electric fluid from point to point.

But there was no time to lose. If my companions were only to remove a few feet from where they stood, the acoustic effect would be over, my Whispering Gallery would be destroyed. I again therefore crawled towards the wall, and said as clearly and distinctly as I could—

"Uncle Hardwigg."

I then awaited a reply.

Sound does not possess the property of travelling with such extreme rapidity. Besides, the density of the air at that depth from light and motion, was very far from adding to the rapidity of circulation. Several seconds elapsed, which to my excited imagination, appeared ages; and these words reached my eager ears, and moved my wildly beating heart—

"Harry, my boy, is that you?"

A short delay between question and answer.

"Yes—yes."

"Where are you?"

"Lost!"

"And your lamp?"

"Out."

"But the guiding stream?"

"Is lost!"

"Keep your courage, Harry. We will do our best."

"One moment, my uncle," I cried; "I have no longer strength to answer your questions. But—for heaven's sake—do you—continue—to speak—to me!"

Absolute silence I felt, would be annihilation.

"Keep up your courage," said my uncle. "As you are so weak do not speak. We have been searching for you in all directions, both by going upwards and downwards in the gallery. My dear boy, I had begun to give over all hope—and you can never know what bitter tears of sorrow and regret I have shed. At last, supposing you to be still on the road beside the Hansbach we again descended, firing off guns as signals. Now, however, that we have found you, and that our voices reach each other, it may be a long time before we actually meet. We are conversing by means of some extraordinary acoustic arrangement of the labyrinth. But do not despair, my dear boy. It is something gained even to hear each other."

While he was speaking my brain was at work reflecting. A certain undefined hope, vague and shapeless as yet, made my heart beat wildly. In the first place, it was absolutely necessary for me to know one thing. I once more therefore leaned my head against the wall, which I almost touched with my lips, and again spoke.

"Uncle."

"My boy," was his ready answer.

"It is of the utmost consequence that we should know how far we are asunder."

"That is not difficult."

"You have your chronometer at hand?" I asked.

"Certainly."

"Well, take it into your hand. Pronounce my name, noting exactly the second at which you speak. I will reply as soon as I hear your words—and you will then note exactly the moment at which my reply reaches you."

"Very good; and the mean time between my question and your answer will be the time occupied by my voice in reaching you."

"That is exactly what I mean, uncle," was my eager reply.

"Are you ready?"

"Yes."

"Well, make ready, I am about to pronounce your name," said the Professor.

I applied my ear close to the sides of the cavernous gallery, and as soon as the word Harry reached my ear, I turned round, and placing my lips to the wall, repeated the sound. "Forty seconds," said my uncle. "There has elapsed forty seconds between the two words. The sound, therefore, takes twenty seconds to ascend. Now, allowing a thousand and twenty feet for every second—we have twenty thousand four hundred feet—a league and a half and one-eighth."

These words fell on my soul like a kind of death-knell.

"A league and a-half," I muttered in a low and despairing voice.

"It shall be got over, my boy," cried my uncle in a cheery tone; "depend on us."

"But do you know whether to ascend or descend?" I asked faintly enough.

"We have to descend, and I will tell you why. You have reached a vast open space, a kind of bare cross road, from which galleries diverge in every direction. That in which you are now lying, must necessarily bring you to this point, for it appears that all these mighty fissures, these fractures of the globe's interior radiate from the vast cavern which we at this moment occupy. Rouse yourself, then, have courage and continue your route. Walk if you can, if not drag yourself along—slide, if nothing else is possible. The slope must be rather rapid—and you will find strong arms to receive you at the end of your journey. Make a start, like a good fellow."

These words served to rouse some kind of courage in my sinking frame.

"Farewell for the present, good uncle, I am about to take my departure. As soon as I start, our voices will cease to commingle. Farewell, then, until we meet again.'

"Adieu, Harry—until we say Welcome." Such were the last words which reached my anxious ears, before I commenced my weary and almost hopeless journey.

This wonderful and surprising conversation which took place through the vast mass of the earth's labyrinth, these words exchanged, the speakers being about five miles apart—ended with hopeful and pleasant expressions. I breathed one more prayer to Heaven, I sent up words of thanksgiving—believing in my inmost heart that He had led me to the only place where the voices of my friends could reach my ears.

This apparently astounding acoustic mystery is easily explainable by simple natural laws; it arose from the peculiar formation of the gallery and from the conductibility of the rock. There are many instances of this singular propagation of sound which are not perceptible in its less mediate positions. In the interior gallery of St. Paul's, and amid the curious caverns in Sicily, these phenomena are observable. The most marvellous of them all is known as the Ear of Dionysius.

These memories of the past, of my early reading and studies, came fresh to my thoughts. Moreover, I began to reason that if my uncle and I could communicate at so great a distance, no serious obstacle could exist between us. All I had to do was to follow the direction whence the sound had reached me; and, logically putting it, I must reach him if my strength did not fail.

I accordingly rose to my feet. I soon found, however, that I could not walk; that I must drag myself along. The slope as I expected, was very rapid; but I allowed myself to slip down.

Soon the rapidity of the descent began to assume frightful proportions; and menanced a fearful fall. I clutched at the sides; I grasped at projections of rocks; I threw myself backwards. All in vain. My weakness was so great I could do nothing to save myself.

Suddenly earth failed me.

I was first launched into a dark, and gloomy void. I then struck against the projecting asperities of a vertical gallery, a perfect well. My head bounded against a pointed rock, and I lost all knowledge of existence. As far as I was concerned, death had claimed me for his own.

The whisper heard.

CHAPTER 26

A RAPID RECOVERY

When I returned to the consciousness of existence, I found myself surrounded by a kind of semi-obscurity, lying on some thick and soft coverlids. My uncle was watching—his eye fixed intently on my countenance, a grave expression on his face; a tear in his eye. At the first sigh which struggled from my bosom he took hold of my hand. When he saw my eyes open and fix themselves upon his, he uttered a loud cry of joy.

"He lives! he lives!"

"Yes, my good uncle," I whispered.

"My dear boy," continued the grim Professor, clasping me to his heart, "you are saved!"

I was deeply and unaffectedly touched by the tone in which these words were uttered, and even more by the kindly care which accompanied them. The Professor, however, was one of those men who must be severely tried in order to induce any display of affection or gentle emotion. At this moment our friend, Hans, the guide joined us. He saw my hand in that of my uncle, and I venture to say that, taciturn as he was, his eyes beamed with lively satisfaction.

"*God dag,*" he said.

"Good day, Hans, good day," I replied, in as hearty a tone as I could assume, "and now, uncle, that we are together, tell me where we are. I have lost all idea of our position, as of everything else."

"To-morrow, Harry, to-morrow," he replied. "To-day you are far too weak. Your head is surrounded with bandages and poultices that must not be touched. Sleep, my boy, sleep, and to-morrow you will know all that you require."

"But," I cried, "let me know what o'clock it is—what day it is?"

"It is now eleven o'clock at night, and this is once more Sunday. It is now the ninth of the month of August. And I distinctly prohibit you from asking any more questions until the tenth of the same."

I was, if the truth be told, very weak indeed, and my eyes soon closed, involuntarily. I did require a good night's rest, and I went off reflecting at the last moment that my perilous adventure in the interior of the earth, in total darkness, had lasted four days!

On the morning of the next day, at my awakening, I began to look around me. My sleeping place, made of all our travelling bedding, was in a charming grotto, adorned with magnificent stalagmites, glittering in all the colours of the rainbow, the floor of soft and silvery sand.

A dim obscurity prevailed. No torch, no lamp was lighted, and yet certain unexplained beams of light penetrated from without, and made their way through the opening of the beautiful grotto.

I, moreover, heard a vague and indefinite murmur, like the ebb and flow of waves upon a strand, and sometimes I verily believed I could hear the sighing of the wind.

I began to believe that, instead of being awake, I must be dreaming. Surely my brain had not been affected by my fall, and all that occurred during the last twenty-four hours was not the frenzied visions of madness? And yet after some reflection, a trial of my faculties, I came to the conclusion that I could not be mistaken. Eyes and ears could not surely both deceive me.

"It is a ray of the blessed daylight," I said to myself, "which has penetrated through some mighty fissure in the rocks. But what is the meaning of this murmur of waves, this unmistakable moaning of the salt sea billows? I can hear, too, plainly enough, the whistling of the wind. But can I be altogether mistaken? If my uncle, during my illness, has but carried me back to the surface of the earth! Has he, on my account, given up his wondrous expedition, or in some strange manner has it come to an end?"

I was puzzling my brain over these and other questions, when the Professor joined me.

"Good-day, Harry," he cried, in a joyous tone. "I fancy you are quite well."

"I am very much better," I replied, actually sitting up in my bed.

"I knew that would be the end of it, as you slept both soundly and tranquilly. Hans and I have each taken turn to watch, and every hour we have seen visible signs of amelioration."

"You must be right, uncle," was my reply, "for I feel as if I could do justice to any meal you could put before me. I am really hungry."

"You shall eat, my boy, you shall eat. The fever has left you. Our excellent friend Hans has rubbed your wounds and bruises, with I know not what ointment, of which the Icelanders alone possess the secret. And they have healed your bruises in the most marvellous manner. Ah, he's a wise fellow, is Master Hans."

While he was speaking, my uncle was placing before me several articles of food, which despite his earnest injunctions, I readily devoured. As soon as the first rage of hunger was appeased, I overwhelmed him with questions, to which he now no longer hesitated to give answers.

I then learned, for the first time, that my providential fall had brought me to the bottom of an almost perpendicular gallery. As I came down, amidst a perfect shower of stones, the least of which falling on me would have crushed me to death, they came to the conclusion that I had carried with me an entire dislocated rock. Riding as it were on this terrible chariot, I was cast headlong into my uncle's arms. And into them I fell, insensible and covered with blood.

"It is indeed a miracle," was the Professor's final remark, "that you were not killed a thousand times over. But let us take care never to separate; for surely we should risk never meeting again."

These words fell with a sort of chill upon my heart. The journey, then, was not over. I looked at my uncle with surprise and astonishment. My uncle, after an instant's examination of my countenance, said—

"What is the matter, Harry?"

"I want to ask you a serious question. You say that I am all right in health?"

"Certainly you are."

"And all my limbs are sound and capable of new exertion?" I asked.

"Most undoubtedly."

"But what about my head?" was my next anxious question.

"Well, your head, except that you have one or two contusions, is exactly where it ought to be—on your shoulders," said my uncle, laughing.

"Well, my own opinion is that my head is not exactly right. In fact, I believe myself slightly delirious."

"What makes you think so?"

"I will explain why I fancy I have lost my senses," I cried; "have we not returned to the surface of mother earth?"

"Certainly not."

"Then truly I must be mad, for do I not see the light of day? do I not hear the whistling of the wind? and can I not distinguish the wash of a great sea?"

"And that is all that makes you uneasy?" said my uncle, with a smile.

"Can you explain?"

"I will not make any attempt to explain; for the whole matter is utterly inexplicable. But you shall see and judge for yourself. You will then find that geological science is as yet in its infancy—and that we are doomed to enlighten the world."

"Let us advance, then," I cried eagerly, no longer able to restrain my curiosity.

"Wait a moment, my dear Harry," he responded; "you must take precautions after your illness before going into the open air."

"The open air?"

"Yes, my boy. I have to warn you that the wind is rather violent—and I have no wish for you to expose yourself without necessary precautions."

"But I beg to assure you that I am perfectly recovered from my illness."

"Have just a little patience, my boy. A relapse would be inconvenient to all parties. We have no time to lose—as our approaching sea voyage may be of long duration."

"Sea voyage?" I cried, more bewildered than ever.

"Yes. You must take another day's rest, and we shall be ready to go on board by to-morrow," replied my uncle, with a peculiar smile.

Go on board! The words utterly astonished me.

Go on board—what and how? Had we come upon a river, a lake, had we discovered some inland sea? Was a vessel lying at anchor in some part of the interior of the earth?

My curiosity was worked up to the very highest pitch. My uncle made vain attempts to restrain me. When at last, however, he discovered that my feverish impatience would do more harm than good—and that the satisfaction of my wishes could alone restore me to a calm state of mind, he gave way.

I dressed myself rapidly—and then taking the precaution to please my uncle, of wrapping myself in one of the coverlets, I rushed out of the grotto.

CHAPTER 27

THE CENTRAL SEA

At first I saw absolutely nothing. My eyes, wholly unused to the effulgence of light, could not bear the sudden brightness; and I was compelled to close them. When I was able to re-open them, I stood still, far more stupefied than astonished. Not all the wildest effects of imagination could have conjured up such a scene!

"The sea—the sea," I cried.

"Yes," replied my uncle, in a tone of pardonable pride; "The Central Sea.

No future navigator will deny the fact of my having discovered it; and hence of acquiring a right of giving it a name.''

It was quite true. A vast, limitless expanse of water, the end of a lake if not of an ocean, spread before us, until it was lost in the distance. The shore which was very much indented, consisted of a beautiful soft golden sand, mixed with small shells, the long deserted home of some of the creatures of a past age. The waves broke incessantly, and with a peculiarly sonorous murmur—to be found in underground localities.—A slight frothy flake arose as the wind blew along the pellucid waters; and many a dash of spray was blown into my face. The mighty superstructure of rock which rose above to an inconceivable height, left only a narrow opening—but where we stood, there was a large margin of strand. On all sides were capes and promontories and enormous cliffs, partially worn by the eternal breaking of the waves, through countless ages! And as I gazed from side to side, the mighty rocks faded away like a fleecy film of cloud.

It was in reality an ocean, with all the usual characteristics of an inland sea, only horribly wild—so rigid, cold and savage.

One thing startled and puzzled me greatly. How was it that I was able to look upon that vast sheet of water instead of being plunged in utter darkness? The vast landscape before me was lit up like day. But there was wanting the dazzling brilliancy, the splendid irradiation of the sun; the pale cold illumination of the moon; the brightness of the stars. The illuminating power in this subterraneous region, from its trembling and flickering character, its clear dry whiteness, the very slight elevation of its temperature, its great superiority to that of the moon, was evidently electric; something in the nature of the aurora borealis, only that its phenomena were constant, and able to light up the whole of the ocean cavern.

The tremendous vault above our heads, the sky, so to speak, appeared to be composed of a conglomeration of nebulous vapours, in constant motion. I should originally have supposed, that under such an atmospheric pressure as must exist in that place, the evaporation of water could not really take place, and yet from the action of some physical law, which escaped my memory, there were heavy and dense clouds rolling along that mighty vault, partially concealing the roof. Electric currents produced astonishing play of light and shade in the distance, especially around the heavier clouds. Deep shadows were cast beneath, and then suddenly, between two clouds, there would come a ray of unusual beauty, and remarkable intensity. And yet it was not like the sun, for it gave no heat.

The effect was sad and excruciatingly melancholy. Instead of a noble firmament of blue, studded with stars, there was above me a heavy roof of granite, which seemed to crush me.

Gazing around, I began to think of the theory of the English captain, who compared the earth to a vast hollow sphere in the interior of which the air is retained in a luminous state by means of atmospheric pressure, while two stars, Pluto and Proserpine, circled there in their mysterious orbits. After all, suppose the old fellow was right!

In truth, we were imprisoned—bound as it were, in a vast excavation. Its width it was impossible to make out; the shore, on either hand, widening rapidly until lost to sight; while its length was equally uncertain. A haze on the distant horizon bounded our view. As to its height we could see that it must be many miles to the roof. Looking upward, it was impossible to discover where the stupendous roof began. The lowest of the clouds must have been floating at an elevation of two thousand yards, a height greater than that of terrestrial vapours, which circumstance was doubtless owing to the extreme density of the air.

I use the word cavern in order to give an idea of the place. I cannot describe its awful grandeur; human language fails to convey an idea of its savage sublimity. Whether this singular vacuum had or had not been caused by the sudden cooling of the earth when in a state of fusion, I could not say. I had read of most wonderful and gigantic caverns—but none in any way like this.

The great grotto of Guachara, in Colombia, visited by the learned Humboldt; the vast and partially explored Mammoth Cave in Kentucky; what were these holes in the earth to that in which I stood in speechless admiration! with its vapoury clouds, its electric light, and the mighty ocean slumbering in its bosom! Imagination, not description, can alone give an idea of the splendour and vastness of the cave.

I gazed at these marvels in profound silence. Words were utterly wanting to indicate the sensations of wonder I experienced. I seemed, as I stood upon that mysterious shore, as if I were some wandering inhabitant of a distant planet, present for the first time at the spectacle of some terrestrial phenomena belonging to another existence. To give body and existence to such new sensations, would have required the coinage of new words—and here my feeble brain found itself wholly at fault. I looked on, I thought, I reflected, I admired, in a state of stupefaction not altogether unmingled with fear!

The unexpected spectacle restored some colour to my pallid cheeks. I seemed to be actually getting better under the influence of this novelty. Moreover, the vivacity of the dense atmosphere, reanimated my body, by inflating my lungs with unaccustomed oxygen.

It will be readily conceived that after an imprisonment of forty-seven days, in a dark and miserable tunnel, it was with infinite delight that I breathed this saline air. It was like the genial, reviving influence of the salt sea waves.

My uncle had already got over the first surprise.

With the Latin poet Horace his idea was that—

"Not to admire is all the art I know,
To make man happy and to keep him so."

"Well," he said, after giving me time thoroughly to appreciate the marvels of this underground sea, "do you feel strong enough to walk up and down?"

"Certainly," was my ready answer, "nothing would give me greater pleasure."

"Well then, my boy," he said, "lean on my arm, and we will stroll along the beach."

I accepted his offer eagerly, and we began to walk along the shores of this extraordinary lake. To our left were abrupt rocks, piled one upon the other,—a stupendous titanic pile; down their sides leapt innumerable cascades, which at last, becoming limpid and murmuring streams, were lost in the waters of the lake. Light vapours, which rose here and there, and floated in fleecy clouds from rock to rock, indicated hot springs, which also poured their superfluity into the vast reservoir at our feet.

Among them I recognised our old and faithful stream, the Hansbach, which, lost in that wild basin, seemed as if it had been flowing since the creation of the world.

"We shall miss our excellent friend," I remarked, with a deep sigh.

"Bah!" said my uncle, testily, "what matters it. That or another, it is all the same."

I thought the remark ungrateful, and felt almost inclined to say so; but I forebore.

At this moment my attention was attracted by an unexpected spectacle. After we had gone about five hundred yards, we suddenly turned a steep promontory, and found ourselves close to a lofty forest! It consisted of straight trunks with tufted tops, in shape like parasols. The air seemed to have no effect upon these trees—which in spite of a tolerable breeze remained as still and motionless as if they had been petrified.

I hastened forward. I could find no name for these singular formations. Did they not belong to the two thousand and more known trees—or were we to make the discovery of a new growth? By no means. When we at last reached the forest, and stood beneath the trees, my surprise gave way to admiration.

In truth, I was simply in the presence of a very ordinary product of the earth, of singular and gigantic proportions. My uncle unhesitatingly called them by their real names.

"It is only," he said, in his coolest manner, "a forest of mushrooms."

On close examination I found that he was not mistaken. Judge of the development attained by this product of damp hot soils. I had heard that the *lycoperdon giganteum* reaches nine feet in circumference, but here were white mushrooms, nearly forty feet high, and with tops of equal dimensions. They grew in countless thousands—the light could not make its way through their massive substance, and beneath them reigned a gloomy and mystic darkness.

Still I wished to go forward. The cold in the shades of this singular forest was intense. For nearly an hour we wandered about in this darkness visible. At length I left the spot, and once more returned to the shores of the lake, to light and comparative warmth.

But the amazing vegetation of subterraneous land was not confined to gigantic mushrooms. New wonders awaited us at every step. We had not gone many hundred yards, when we came upon a mighty group of other trees with discoloured leaves—the common humble trees of mother earth, of an exorbitant and phenomenal size: lycopodes a hundred feet high; flowering ferns as tall as pines; gigantic grasses!

"Astonishing, magnificent, splendid!" cried my uncle; "here we have before us the whole Flora of the second period of the world, that of transition. Behold the humble plants of our gardens, which in the first ages of the world were mighty trees. Look around you, my dear Harry. No botanist ever before gazed on such a sight!"

My uncle's enthusiasm, always a little more than was required, was now excusable.

"You are right, uncle," I remarked. "Providence appears to have designed the preservation in this vast and mysterious hot-house of antediluvian plants, to prove the sagacity of learned men in figuring them so marvellously on paper."

"Well said, my boy—very well said; it is indeed a mighty hot-house;—but you would also be within the bounds of reason and common sense, if you also added—a vast menagerie."

I looked rather anxiously around. If the animals were as exaggerated as the plants, the matter would certainly be serious.

"A menagerie?"

"Doubtless. Look at the dust we are treading under foot—behold the bones with which the whole soil of the sea shore is covered——."

"Bones," I replied, "yes, certainly, the bones of antediluvian animals."

I stooped down as I spoke, and picked up one or two singular remains, relics of a by-gone age. It was easy to give a name to these gigantic bones, in some instances as big as trunks of trees.

"Here is, clearly, the lower jaw-bone of a mastodon," I cried, almost as warmly and enthusiastically as my uncle, "here are the molars of the dinotherium; here is a leg-bone which belonged to the megatherium. You are right, uncle, it is indeed a menagerie; for the mighty animals to which these bones once belonged, have lived and died on the shores of this subterranean sea, under the shadow of these plants. Look, yonder are whole skeletons—and yet——"

"And yet, nephew?" said my uncle, noticing that I suddenly came to a full stop.

"I do not understand the presence of such beasts in granite caverns, however vast and prodigious," was my reply.

"Why not?" said my uncle, with very much of his old professional impatience.

"Because it is well known that animal life only existed on earth during the secondary period, when the sedimentary soil was formed by the alluviums, and thus replaced the hot and burning rocks of the primitive age."

"I have listened to you earnestly and with patience, Harry, and I have a simple and clear answer to your objections: and that is, that this itself is a sedimentary soil."

"How can that be at such enormous depths from the surface of the earth?"

"The fact can be explained both simply and geologically. At a certain period, the earth consisted only of an elastic crust, liable to alternative upward and downward movements in virtue of the law of attraction. It is very probable that many a landslip took place in those days, and that large portions of sedimentary soil were cast into huge and mighty chasms."

"Quite possible," I drily remarked. "But uncle, if these antediluvian animals formerly lived in these subterranean regions, what more likely that one of these huge monsters may at this moment be concealed behind one of yonder mighty rocks."

As I spoke, I looked keenly around, examining with care every point of the horizon; but nothing alive appeared to exist on these deserted shores.

I now felt rather fatigued, and told my uncle so. The walk and the excitement were too much for me in my weak state. I therefore seated myself at the end of a promontory, at the foot of which the waves broke in incessant rolls. I looked round a bay formed by projections of vast granitic rocks. At the extreme end was a little port protected by huge pyramids of stones. A brig and three or four schooners might have lain there with perfect ease. So natural did it seem, that every minute my imagination induced me to expect a vessel coming out under all sail and making for the open sea under the influence of a warm southerly breeze.

But the fantastic illusion never lasted more than a minute. We were the only living creatures in this subterranean world!

During certain periods there was an utter cessation of wind, when a silence deeper, more terrible than the silence of the desert fell upon these solitary and arid rocks—and seemed to hang like a leaden weight upon the waters of this singular ocean. I sought, amid the awful stillness, to penetrate through the distant

The first bather in these waters.

fog, to tear down the veil which concealed the mysterious distance. What unspoken words were murmured by my trembling lips—what questions did I wish to ask and did not! Where did this sea end—to what did it lead? Should we ever be able to examine its distant shores?

But my uncle had no doubts about the matter. He was convinced that our enterprise would in the end be successful. For my part, I was in a state of painful indecision—I desired to embark on the journey and to succeed, and still I feared the result.

After we had passed an hour or more in silent contemplation of the wondrous spectacle, we rose and went down towards the bank on our way to the grotto, which I was not sorry to gain. After a slight repast, I sought refuge in slumber, and at length, after many and tedious struggles, sleep came over my weary eyes.

CHAPTER 28

LAUNCHING THE RAFT

ON the morning of the next day, to my great surprise, I awoke completely restored. I thought a bath would be delightful after my long illness and sufferings. So, soon after rising, I went and plunged into the waters of this new Mediterranean. The bath was cool, fresh and invigorating.

I came back to breakfast with an excellent appetite. Hans, our worthy guide, thoroughly understood how to cook such eatables as we were able to provide; he had both fire and water at discretion, so that he was enabled slightly to vary the weary monotony of our ordinary repast.

Our morning meal was like a capital English breakfast, with coffee by way of a wind up. And never had this delicious beverage been so welcome and refreshing.

My uncle had sufficient regard for my state of health not to interrupt me in the enjoyment of the meal, but he was evidently delighted when I had finished.

"Now then," said he, "come with me. It is the height of the tide, and I am anxious to study its curious phenomena."

"What," I cried, rising in astonishment, "did you say the tide, uncle?"

"Certainly I did."

"You do not mean to say," I replied, in a tone of respectful doubt, "that the influence of the sun and moon is felt here below."

"And pray why not? Are not all bodies influenced by the law of universal attraction? Why should this vast underground sea be exempt from the general law, the rule of the universe? Besides, there is nothing like that which is proved and demonstrated. Despite the great atmospheric pressure down here, you will notice that this inland sea rises and falls with as much regularity as the Atlantic itself."

As my uncle spoke, we reached the sandy shore, and saw and heard the waves breaking monotonously on the beach. They were evidently rising.

"This is truly the flood," I cried looking at the water at my feet.

"Yes, my excellent nephew," replied my uncle, rubbing his hands with the gusto of a philosopher, "and you see by these several streaks of foam, that the tide rises at least ten or twelve feet."

"It is indeed marvellous."

"By no means," he responded; "on the contrary, it is quite natural."

"It may appear so in your eyes, my dear uncle," was my reply, "but the whole phenomena of the place appear to me to partake of the marvellous. It is almost impossible to believe that which I see. Who in his wildest dreams could have imagined that, beneath the crust of our earth, there could exist a real ocean, with ebbing and flowing tides, with its changes of winds, and even its storms. I for one should have laughed the suggestion to scorn."

"But, Harry, my boy, why not?" enquired my uncle, with a pitying smile, "is there any physical reason in opposition to it?"

"Well, if we give up the great theory of the central heat of the earth, I certainly can offer no reasons why anything should be looked upon as impossible."

"Then you will own," he added, "that the system of Sir Humphrey Davy is wholly justified by what we have seen?"

"I allow that it is—and that point once granted, I certainly can see no reason for doubting the existence of seas and other wonders, even countries, in the interior of the globe."

"That is so—but of course these varied countries are uninhabited?"

"Well, I grant that it is more likely than not: still, I do not see why this sea should not have given shelter to some species of unknown fish."

"Hitherto we have not discovered any, and the probabilities are rather against our ever doing so," observed the Professor.

I was losing my scepticism in the presence of these wonders.

"Well, I am determined to solve the question. It is my intention to try my luck with my fishing line and hook."

"Certainly; make the experiment," said my uncle, pleased with my enthusiasm. "While we are about it, it will certainly be only proper to discover all the secrets of this extraordinary region."

"But, after all, where are we now?" I asked; "all this time I have quite forgotten to ask you a question, which, doubtless, your philosophical instruments have long since answered."

"Well," replied the Professor, "examining the situation from only one point of view, we are now distant three hundred and fifty leagues from Iceland."

"So much?" was my exclamation.

"I have gone over the matter several times, and am sure not to have made a mistake of five hundred yards," replied my uncle positively.

"And as to the direction—are we still going to the south-east?"

"Yes, with a western declination* of nineteen degrees, forty-two minutes, just as it is above. As for the inclination† I have discovered a very curious fact."

"And what may that be, uncle? Your information interests me."

"Why that the needle, instead of dipping towards the pole as it does on earth, in the northern hemisphere, has an upward tendency."

"This proves," I cried, "that the great point of magnetic attraction lies some-

* The declination is the variation of the needle from the true meridian of a place.

† Inclination is the dip of the magnetic needle with a tendency to incline towards the earth.

where between the surface of the earth and the spot we have succeeded in reaching."

"Exactly, my observant nephew," exclaimed my uncle, elated and delighted, "and it is quite probable that if we succeed in getting towards the polar regions—somewhere near the seventy-third degree of latitude, where Sir James Ross discovered the magnetic pole, we shall behold the needle point directly upward. We have therefore discovered by analogy, that this great centre of attraction is not situated at a very great depth."

"Well," said I, rather surprised, "this discovery will astonish experimental philosophers. It was never suspected."

"Science, great, mighty and in the end unerring," replied my uncle dogmatically, "science has fallen into many errors—errors which have been fortunate and useful rather than otherwise, for they have been the stepping stones to truth."

After some further discussion, I turned to another matter.

"Have you any idea of the depth we have reached?"

"We are now," continued the Professor, "exactly thirty-five leagues—above a hundred miles—down into the interior of the earth."

"So," said I, after measuring the distance on the map, "we are now beneath the Scottish Highlands, and have over our heads the lofty Grampian hills."

"You are quite right," said the Professor laughing, "it sounds very alarming, the weight being heavy—but the vault which supports this vast mass of earth and rock is solid and safe—the mighty Architect of the Unvierse has constructed it of solid materials. Man, even in his highest flights of vivid and poetic imagination, never thought of such things! What are the finest arches of our bridges, what the vaulted roofs of our cathedrals, to that mighty dome above us, and beneath which floats an ocean with its storms and clams and tides!"

"I admire it all as much as you can, uncle, and have no fear that our granite sky will fall upon our heads. But now that we have discussed matters of science and discovery, what are your future intentions? Are you not thinking of getting back to the surface of our beautiful earth?"

This was said móre as a feeler than with any hope of success.

"Go back, nephew," cried my uncle in a tone of alarm, "you are not surely thinking of anything so absurd or cowardly. No; my intention is to advance and continue our journey. We have as yet been singularly fortunate, and henceforth I hope we shall be more so."

"But," said I, "how are we to cross yonder liquid plain?"

"It is not my intention to leap into it head foremost, or even to swim across it, like Leander over the Hellespont. But as oceans are, after all, only great lakes, inasmuch as they are surrounded by land, so does it stand to reason, that this central sea is circumscribed by granite surroundings."

"Doubtless," was my natural reply.

"Well, then, do you not think that when once we reach the other end, we shall find some means of continuing our journey?"

"Probably, but what extent do you allow to this internal ocean?"

"Well, I should fancy it to extend about forty or fifty leagues—more or less."

"But even supposing this approximation to be a correct one—what then?" I asked.

"My dear boy, we have no time for further discussion. We shall embark tomorrow."

I looked around with surprise and incredulity. I could see nothing in the shape of boat or vessel.

"What!" I cried, "we are about to launch out upon an unknown sea; and where, if I may ask, is the vessel to carry us?"

"Well, my boy, it will not be exactly what you would call a vessel. For the present we must be content with a good and solid raft."

"A raft," I cried, incredulously, "but down here a raft is as impossible of construction as a vessel—and I am at a loss to imagine—"

"My good Harry—if you were to listen instead of talking so much, you would hear," said my uncle, waxing a little impatient.

"I should hear?"

"Yes—certain knocks with the hammer, which Hans is now employing to make the raft. He has been at work for many hours."

"Making a raft?"

"Yes."

"But where has he found trees suitable for such a construction?"

"He found the trees all ready to his hand. Come, and you shall see our excellent guide at work."

More and more amazed at what I heard and saw, I followed my uncle like one in a dream.

After a walk of about a quarter of an hour, I saw Hans at work on the other side of the promontory which formed our natural port. A few mintues more and I was beside him. To my great surprise, on the sandy shore lay a half-finished raft. It was made from beams of a very peculiar wood, and a great number of limbs, joints, boughs and pieces lay about, sufficient to have constructed a fleet of ships and boats.

I turned to my uncle, silent with astonishment and awe.

"Where did all this wood come from?" I cried; "what wood is it?"

"Well, there is pine-wood, fir, and the palms of the northern regions, mineralised by the action of the sea," he replied, sententiously.

"Can it be possible?"

"Yes," said the learned Professor, "what you see is called fossil wood."

"But then," cried I, after reflecting for a moment, "like the lignites, it must be as hard and heavy as iron, and therefore will certainly not float."

"Sometimes that is the case. Many of these woods have become true anthracites, but others again, like those you see before you, have only undergone one phase of fossil transformation. But there is no proof like demonstration," added my uncle, picking one or two of these precious waifs and casting them into the sea.

The piece of wood, after having disappeared for a moment, came to the surface, and floated about with the oscillation produced by wind and tide.

"Are you convinced?" said my uncle, with a self-satisfied smile.

"I am convinced," I cried, "that what I see is incredible."

The fact was that my journey into the interior of the earth was rapidly changing all preconceived notions, and day by day preparing me for the marvellous.

I should not have been surprised to have seen a fleet of native canoes afloat upon that silent sea.

The very next evening, thanks to the industry and ability of Hans, the raft was finished. It was about ten feet long and five feet wide. The beams bound together with stout ropes, were solid and firm, and once launched by our united efforts, the improvised vessel floated tranquilly upon the waters of what the Professor had well named the Central Sea.

CHAPTER 29

ON THE WATERS—A RAFT VOYAGE

ON the 13th of August we were up betimes. There was no time to be lost. We now had to inaugurate a new kind of locomotion, which would have the advantage of being rapid and not fatiguing.

A mast, made of two pieces of wood fastened together, to give additional strength, a yard made from another one, the sail a linen sheet from our bed. We were fortunately in no want of cordage, and the whole on trial appeared solid and seaworthy.

At six o'clock in the morning, when the eager and enthusiastic Professor gave the signal to embark, the victuals, the luggage, all our instruments, our weapons, and a goodly supply of sweet water, which we had collected from springs in the rocks, were placed on the raft.

Hans had, with considerable ingenuity, contrived a rudder, which enabled him to guide the floating apparatus with ease. He took the tiller, as a matter of course. The worthy man was as good a sailor as he was a guide and duck-hunter. I then let go the painter which held us to the shore, the sail was brought to the wind, and we made a rapid offing.

Our sea voyage had a length commenced; and once more we were making for distant and unknown regions.

Just as we were about to leave the little port where the raft had been constructed, my uncle, who was very strong as to geographic nomenclature, wanted to give it a name, and among others, suggested mine.

"Well," said I, "before you decide I have another to propose."

"Well; out with it."

"I should like to call it Gretchen. Port Gretchen will sound very well on our future map."

"Well then, Port Gretchen let it be," said the Professor.

And thus it was that the memory of my dear girl was attached to our adventurous and memborable expedition.

When we left the shore the wind was blowing from the northward and eastward. We went directly before the wind at a much greater speed than might have been expected from a raft. The dense layers of atmosphere at that depth had great propelling power and acted upon the sail with considerable force.

At the end of an hour, my uncle, who had been taking careful observations, was enabled to judge of the rapidity with which we moved. It was far beyond anything seen in the upper world.

"If," he said, "we continue to advance at our present rate, we shall have travelled at least thirty leagues in twenty-four hours. With a mere raft this is an almost incredible velocity."

I certainly was surprised, and without making any reply went forward upon the raft. Already the northern shore was fading away on the edge of the horizon. The two shores appeared to separate more and more, leaving a wide and open space for our departure. Before me I could see nothing but the vast and apparently limitless sea—upon which we floated—the only living objects in sight.

Huge and dark clouds cast their grey shadows below—shadows which seemed to crush that colourless and sullen water by their weight. Anything more suggestive of gloom and of regions of nether darkness I never beheld. Silvery rays of electric light, reflected here and there upon some small spots of water, brought up luminous sparkles in the long wake of our cumbrous bark. Presently we were wholly out of sight of land, not a vestige could be seen, nor any indication of where we were going. So still and motionless did we seem without any distant point to fix our eyes on, that but for the phosphoric light at the wake of the raft I should have fancied that we were still and motionless.

But I knew that we were advancing at a very rapid rate.

About twelve o'clock in the day, vast collections of seaweed were discovered surrounding us on all sides. I was aware of the extraordinary vegetative power of these plants, which have been known to creep along the bottom of the great ocean, and stop the advance of large ships. But never were seaweeds ever seen, so gigantic and wonderful as those of the Central Sea. I could well imagine how, seen at a distance, tossing and heaving on the summit of the billows, the long lines of Algæ have been taken for living things, and thus have been the fertile sources of the belief in sea serpents.

Our raft swept past great specimens of fucæ or sea-wrack, from three to four thousand feet in length, immense, incredibly long, looking like snakes that stretched out far beyond our horizon. It afforded me great amusement to gaze on their variegated ribbon-like endless lengths. Hour after hour passed without our coming to the termination of these floating weeds. If my astonishment increased, my patience was well-nigh exhausted.

What natural force could possibly have produced such abnormal and extraordinary plants? What must have been the aspect of the globe, during the first centuries of its formation, when under the combined action of heat and humidity, the vegetable kingdom occupied its vast surface to the exclusion of everything else?

These were considerations of never-ending interest for the geologist and the philosopher.

All this while we were advancing on our journey; and at length night came; but as I had remarked the evening before, the luminous state of the atmosphere was in nothing diminished. Whatever was the cause, it was a phenomenon upon the duration of which we could calculate with certainty.

As soon as our supper had been disposed of, and some little speculative conversation indulged in, I stretched myself at the foot of the mast, and presently went to sleep.

Hans remained motionless at the tiller, allowing the raft to rise and fall on the waves. The wind being aft, and the sail square, all he had to do was to keep his oar in the centre.

Ever since we had taken our departure from the newly-named Port Gretchen, my worthy uncle had directed me to keep a regular log of our day's navigation, with instructions to put down even the most minute particulars, every interesting and curious phenomenon, the direction of the wind, our rate of sailing, the distance we went; in a word, every incident of our extraordinary voyage.

From our log, therefore, I tell the story of our voyage on the Central Sea.

Friday, August 14th. A steady breeze from the north-west. Raft progressing with extreme rapidity, and going perfectly straight. Coast still dimly visible about thirty leagues to leeward. Nothing to be seen beyond the horizon in front.

The extraordinary intensity of the light neither increases nor diminishes. It is singularly stationary. The weather remarkably fine; that is to say, the clouds have ascended very high, and are light and fleecy, and surrounded by an atmosphere resembling silver in fusion.

Thermometer +32 degrees centigrade.

Above twelve o'clock in the day our guide Hans having prepared and baited a hook, cast his line into the subterranean waters. The bait he used was a small piece of meat, by means of which he concealed his hook. Anxious as I was, I was for a long time doomed to disappointment. Were these waters supplied with fish or not? That was the important question. No—was my decided answer. Then there came a sudden and rather hard tug. Hans coolly drew it in, and with it a fish, which struggled violently to escape.

"A fish," cried my uncle, putting on his spectacles to examine it.

"It is a sturgeon!" I cried, "certainly a small sturgeon."

The Professor examined the fish carefully, noting every characteristic; and he did not coincide in my opinion. The fish had a flat head, round body, and the lower extremities covered with bony scales; its mouth was wholly without teeth, the pectoral fins, which were highly developed, sprouted direct from the body, which properly speaking had no tail. The animal certainly belonged to the order in which naturalists class the sturgeon, but it differed from that fish in many essential particulars.

My uncle, after all, was not mistaken. After a long and patient examination he said—

"This fish, my dear boy, belongs to a family which has been extinct for ages, and of which no trace has ever been found on earth, except fossil remains in the Devonian strata."

"You do not mean to say," I cried, "that we have captured a live specimen of a fish belonging to the primitive stock that existed before the deluge?"

"We have," said the Professor, who all this time was continuing his observations, "and you may see by careful examination that these fossil fish have no identity with existing species. To hold in one's hand, therefore, a living specimen of the order, is enough to make a naturalist happy for life."

"But," cried I, "to what family does it belong?"

"To the order of Ganoides—an order of fish having angular scales, covered with bright enamel—forming one of the family of the Cephalaspides, of the genus——"

"Well, sir," I remarked, as I noticed my uncle hesitated to conclude.

"To the Genus Pterychtis—yes, I am certain of it. Still, though I am confident of the correctness of my surmise, this fish offers to our notice a remarkable peculiarity, never known to exist in any other fish but those which are the natives of subterranean waters, wells, lakes in caverns, and such like hidden pools."

"And what may that be?"

"It is blind."

"Blind!" I cried, much surprised.

"Not only blind," continued the Professor, "but absolutely without organs of sight."

I now examined our discovery for myself. It was singular, to be sure, but it was really a fact. This, however, might be a solitary instance, I suggested. The hook was baited again and once more thrown into the water. This subterranean ocean must have been tolerably well supplied with fish, for in two hours we

The antediluvian world.

took a large number of Pterychtis, as well as other fish belonging to another supposed extinct family—the Dipterides (a genus of fish, furnished with two fins only, whence the name,) though my uncle could not class it exactly. All, without exception, however, were blind. This unexpected capture enabled us to renew our stock of provisions in a very satsifactory way.

We were now convinced that this Subterranean Sea contained only fish known to us as fossil specimens—and fish and reptiles alike, were all the more perfect the farther back they dated their origin.

We began to hope that we should find some of those Saurians which science has succeeded in reconstructing from bits of bone or cartilage.

I took up the telescope and carefully examined the horizon—looked over the whole sea; it was utterly and entirely deserted. Doubtless we were still too near the coast.

After an examination of the ocean, I looked upward, towards the strange and mysterious sky. Why should not one of the birds, reconstructed by the immortal Cuvier, flap his stupendous wings aloft in the dull strata of subterranean air? It would, of course, find quite sufficient food from the fish in the sea. I gazed for some time upon the void above. It was as silent and as deserted as the shores we had but lately left.

Nevertheless, though I could neither see nor discover anything, my imagination carried me away into wild hypotheses. I was in a kind of waking dream. I thought I saw on the surface of the water those enormous antediluvian turtles as big as floating islands. Upon those dull and sombre shores passed a spectral row of the mammifers of early days, the great Leptotherium found in the cavernous hollow of the Brazilian hills, the Mesicotherium, a native of the glacial regions of Siberia.

Farther on, the pachydermatous Lophrodon, that gigantic tapir, which concealed itself behind rocks, ready to do battle for its prey with the Anoplotherium, a singular animal partaking of the nature of the rhinoceros, the horse, the hippopotamus and the camel.

There was the giant Mastodon, twisting and turning his horrid trunk, with which he crushed the rocks of the shore to powder, while the Megatherium—his back raised like a cat in a passion, his enormous claws stretched out, dug into the earth for food, at the same time that he awoke the sonorous echoes of the whole place with his terrible roar.

Higher up still, the first monkey ever seen on the face of the globe clambered, gambling and playing up the granite hills. Still farther away, ran the Pterodactyl, with the winged hand, gliding or rather sailing through the dense and compressed air like a huge bat.

Above all, near the leaden granitic sky, were immense birds, more powerful than the casoar, giants to the ostrich, which spread their mighty wings and fluttered against the huge stone vault of the inland sea.

I thought, such was the effect of my imagination, that I saw this whole tribe of antediluvian creatures. I carried myself back to far ages, long before man existed—when, in fact, the earth was in too imperfect a state for him to live upon it.

My dream was of countless ages before the existence of man. The mammifers first disappeared, then the mighty birds, then the reptiles of the secondary period, presently the fish, the crustacea, the molluscs, and finally the vertebrata. The zoophytes of the period of transition in their turn sank into annihilation.

The whole panorama of the world's life before the historic period, seemed to be born over again, and mine was the only human heart that beat in this unpeopled world! There were no more seasons; there were no more climates; the natural heat of the world increased unceasingly, and neutralised that of the great radiant Sun.

Vegetation was exaggerated in an extraordinary manner. I passed like a shadow in the midst of brushwood as lofty as the giant trees of California, and trod underfoot the moist and humid soil, reeking with a rank and varied vegetation.

I leaned against the huge column-like trunks of giant trees, to which those of Canada were as ferns. Whole ages passed, hundreds upon hundreds of years were concentrated into a single day.

Next, unrolled before me like a panorama, came the great and wondrous series of terrestrial transformations. Plants disappeared; the granitic rocks lost all trace of solidity; the liquid state was suddenly substituted for that which had before existed. This was caused by intense heat acting on the organic matter of the earth. The waters flowed over the whole surface of the globe; they boiled; they were volatilised, or turned into vapour; a kind of steam-cloud wrapped the whole earth, the globe itself becoming at last nothing but one huge sphere of gas, indescribable in colour, between white heat and red, as big and as brilliant as the sun.

In the very centre of this prodigious mass, fourteen hundred thousand times as large as our globe, I was whirled round in space, and brought into close conjunction with the planets. My body was subtilised, or rather became volatile, and commingled in a state of atomic vapour, with the prodigious clouds, which rushed forward like a mighty comet into infinite space!

What an extraordinary dream! Where would it finally take me? My feverish hand began to write down the marvellous details—details more like the imaginings of a lunatic than anything sober and real. I had during this period of hallucination forgotten everything—the Professor, the guide, and the raft on which we were floating. My mind was in a state of semi-oblivion.

"What is the matter, Harry?" said my uncle, suddenly.

My eyes, which were wide open like those of a somnambulist, were fixed upon him, but I did not see him, nor could I clearly make out anything around me.

"Take care, my boy," again cried my uncle, "you will fall into the sea."

As he uttered these words, I felt myself seized on the other side by the firm hand of our devoted guide. Had it not been for the presence of mind of Hans, I must infallibly have fallen into the waves and been drowned.

"Have you gone mad?" cried my uncle shaking me on the other side.

"What—what is the matter?" I said at last, coming to myself.

"Are you ill, Henry?" continued the Professor in an anxious tone.

"No—no; but I have had an extraordinary dream. It, however, has passed away. All now seems well," I added, looking around me with strangely puzzled eyes.

"All right," said my uncle; "a beautiful breeze, a splendid sea. We are going along at a rapid rate, and if I am not out in my calculations we shall soon see land. I shall not be sorry to exchange the narrow limits of our raft for the mysterious strand of the Subterranean Ocean."

As my uncle uttered these words, I rose and carefully scanned the horizon. But the line of water was still confounded with the lowering clouds that hung aloft, and in the distance appeared to touch the edge of the water.

CHAPTER 30

TERRIFIC SAURIAN COMBAT

SATURDAY, August 15. The sea still retains its uniform monotony. The same leaden hue, the same eternal glare from above. No indication of land being in sight. The horizon appears to retreat before us, more and more as we advance.

My head still dull and heavy from the effects of my extraordinary dream, which I cannot as yet banish from my mind.

The Professor, who has not dreamed, is, however, in one of his morose and unaccountable humours. Spends his time in scanning the horizon, at every point of the compass. His telescope is raised every moment to his eyes, and when he finds nothing to give any clue to our whereabouts, he assumes a Napoleonic attitude and walks anxiously.

I remarked that my uncle, the Professor, had a strong tendency to resume his old impatient character, and I could not but make a note of this disagreeable circumstance in my Journal. I saw clearly that it had required all the influence of my danger and suffering, to extract from him one scintillation of humane feeling. Now that I was quite recovered, his original nature had conquered and obtained the upper hand.

And, after all, what had he to be angry and annoyed about, now more than at any other time? Was not the journey being accomplished under the most favourable circumstances? Was not the raft progressing with the most marvellous rapidity?

What, then, could be the matter? After one or two preliminary hems, I determined to inquire.

"You seem uneasy, uncle," said I, when for about the hundredth time he put down his telescope and walked up and down, muttering to himself.

"No, I am not uneasy," he replied in a dry harsh tone, "by no means."

"Perhaps I should have said impatient," I replied, softening the force of my remark.

"Enough to make me so, I think."

"And yet we are advancing at a rate seldom attained by a raft," I remarked.

"What matters that?" cried my uncle. "I am not vexed at the rate we go at, but I am annoyed to find the sea so much vaster than I expected."

I then recollected that the Professor, before our departure, had estimated the length of this Subterranean Ocean, as at most about thirty leagues. Now we had travelled at least over thrice that distance without discovering any trace of the distant shore. I began to understand my uncle's anger.

"We are not going down," suddenly exclaimed the Professor. "We are not progressing with our great discoveries. All this is utter loss of time. After all, I did not come from home to undertake a party of pleasure. This voyage on a raft over a pond annoys and wearies me."

He called his adventurous journey a party of pleasure, and this great Inland Sea a pond!

"But," argued I, "if we have followed the route indicated by the great Saknussemm, we cannot be going far wrong."

" 'That is the question,' as the great, the immortal Shakespeare, has it. Are we following the route indicated by that wondrous sage? Did Saknussemm ever fall in with this great sheet of water? If he did, did he cross it? I begin to fear that the rivulet we adopted for a guide has led us wrong."

"In any case, we can never regret having come thus far. It is worth the whole journey to have enjoyed this magnificent spectacle—it is something to have seen."

"I care nothing about seeing, nor about magnificent spectacles. I came down into the interior of the earth with an object, and that object I mean to attain. Don't talk to me about admiring scenery, or any other sentimental trash."

After this I thought it well to hold my tongue, and allow the Professor to bite his lips until the blood came, without further remark.

At six o'clock in the evening, our matter-of-fact guide, Hans, asked for his week's salary, and receiving his three rix-dollars, put them carefully in his pocket. He was perfectly contented and satisfied.

Sunday, 16th August. Nothing new to record. The same weather as before. The wind has a slight tendency to freshen up, with signs of an approaching gale. When I awoke, my first observation was in regard to the intensity of the light. I keep on fearing, day after day, that the extraordinary electric phenomenon should become first obscured, and then go wholly out, leaving us in total darkness. Nothing, however, of the kind occurs. The shadow of the raft, its mast and sails, is clearly distinguished on the surface of the water.

This wondrous sea is, after all, infinite in its extent. It must be quite as wide as the Mediterranean—or perhaps even as the great Atlantic Ocean. Why, after all, should it not be so?

My uncle has on more than one occasion tried deep sea soundings. He tied the cross of one of our heaviest crowbars to the extremity of a cord, which he allowed to run out to the extent of two hundred fathoms. We had the greatest difficulty in hoisting in our novel kind of lead.

When the crowbar was finally dragged on board, Hans called my attention to some singular marks upon its surface. The piece of iron looked as if it had been crushed between two very hard substances.

I looked at our worthy guide with an inquiring glance.

"Tänder," said he.

Of course I was at a loss to understand. I turned round towards my uncle, absorbed in gloomy reflections. I had little wish to disturb him from his reverie. I accordingly turned once more towards our worthy Icelander.

Hans very quietly and significantly opened his mouth once or twice, as if in the act of biting, and in this way made me understand his meaning.

"Teeth!" cried I, with stupefaction, as I examined the bar of iron with more attention.

Yes. There can be no doubt about the matter. The indentations on the bar of iron are the marks of teeth! What jaws must the owner of such molars be possessed of! Have we, then, come upon a monster of unknown species, which still exists within the vast waste of waters—a monster more voracious than a shark, more terrible and bulky than the whale. I am unable to withdraw my eyes, from the bar of iron, actually half crushed!

Is, then, my dream about to come true—a dread and terrible reality?

All day my thoughts were bent upon these speculations, and my imagination scarcely regained a degree of calmness and power of reflection until after a sleep of many hours.

This day, as on other Sundays, we observed as a day of rest and pious meditation.

Monday, August 17th. I have been trying to realise from memory the particular instincts of those antediluvian animals of the secondary period, which succeeding to the mollusca, to the crustacea, and to the fish, preceded the appearance of the race of mammifers. The generation of reptiles then reigned supreme upon the earth. These hideous monsters ruled everything in the seas of the secondary period, which formed the strata of which the Jura mountains are composed. Nature had endowed them with perfect organisation. What a gigantic structure was theirs; what vast and prodigious strength they possessed!

The existing Saurians, which include all such reptiles as lizards, crocodiles, and alligators, even the largest and most formidable of their class, are but feeble imitations of their mighty sires, the animals of ages long ago. If there were giants in the days of old, there were also gigantic animals.

I shuddered as I evolved from my mind the idea and recollection of these awful monsters. No eye of man had seen them in the flesh. They took their walks abroad upon the face of the earth thousands of ages before man came into existence, and their fossil bones, discovered in the limestone, have allowed us to reconstruct them anatomically, and thus to get some faint idea of their colossal formation.

I recollect once seeing in the great Museum of Hamburg the skeleton of one of these wonderful Saurians. It measured no less than thirty feet from the nose to the tail. Am I, then, an inhabitant of the earth of the present day, destined to find myself face to face with a representative of this antediluvian family? I can scarcely believe it possible; can hardly believe it true. And yet these marks of powerful teeth upon the bar of iron! can there be a doubt from their shape that the bite is the bite of a crocodile?

My eyes stare wildly and with terror upon the subterranean sea. Every moment I expect one of these monsters to rise from its vast cavernous depths.

I fancy that the worthy Professor in some measure shares my notions, if not my fears, for, after an attentive examination of the crowbar, he cast his eyes rapidly over the mighty and mysterious ocean.

"What could possess him to leave the land," I thought, "as if the depth of this water was of any importance to us. No doubt he has disturbed some terrible monster in his watery home, and perhaps we may pay dearly for our temerity."

Anxious to be prepared for the worst, I examined our weapons, and saw that they were in a fit state for use. My uncle looked on at me and nodded his head approvingly. He, too, has noticed what we have to fear.

Already the uplifting of the waters on the surface indicates that something is in motion below. The danger approaches. It comes nearer and nearer. It behoves us to be on the watch.

Tuesday, August 18. Evening came at last, the hour, when the desire for sleep caused our eyelids to be heavy. Night there is not, properly speaking, in this place, any more than there is in summer in the arctic regions. Hans, however, is immovable at the rudder. When he snatches a moment of rest I really cannot say. I take advantage of his vigilance to take some little repose.

But two hours after I was awakened from a heavy sleep by an awful shock. The raft appeared to have struck upon a sunken rock. It was lifted right out of

These animals fought with fury.

the water by some wondrous and mysterious power, and then started off twenty fathoms distant.

"Eh, what is it?" cried my uncle starting up, "are we shipwrecked, or what?"

Hans raised his hand and pointed to where, about two hundred yards off, a huge black mass was moving up and down. I looked with awe. My worst fears were realised.

"It is a colossal monster!" I cried clasping my hands.

"Yes," cried the agitated Professor, "and there yonder is a huge sea lizard of terrible size and shape."

"And farther on behold a prodigious crocodile. Look at his hideous jaws, and that row of monstrous teeth. Ha! he has gone."

"A whale! a whale!" shouted the Professor, "I can see her enormous fins. See, see how she blows air and water!"

Two liquid columns rose to a vast height above the level of the sea, into which they fell with a terrific crash, waking up the echoes of that awful place. We stood still—surprised, stupefied, terror-stricken at the sight of this group of fearful marine monsters, more hideous in the reality than in my dream. They were of supernatural dimensions; the very smallest of the whole party could with ease have crushed our raft and ourselves with a single bite.

Hans seizing the rudder which had flown out of his hand, puts it hard a-weather in order to escape from such dangerous vicinity; but no sooner does he do so, then he finds he is flying from Scylla to Charybdis. To leeward is a turtle about forty feet wide, and a serpent quite as long, with an enormous and hideous head peering from out the waters.

Look which way we will, it is impossible for us to fly. The fearful reptiles advanced upon us; they turned and twisted about the raft with awful rapidity. They formed around our devoted vessel a series of concentric circles. I took up my rifle in desperation. But what effect can a rifleball produce upon the armour scales with which the bodies of these horrid monsters are covered?

We remain still and dumb from utter horror. They advance upon us, nearer and nearer. Our fate appears certain, fearful and terrible. On one side the mighty crocodile, on the other the great sea serpent. The rest of the fearful crowd of marine prodigies have plunged beneath the briny waves and disappeared!

I am about at all risks to fire, and try the effect of a shot. Hans the guide, however, interfered by a sign to check me. The two hideous and ravenous monsters passed within fifty fathoms of the raft, and then made a rush at one another—their fury and rage preventing them from seeing us.

The combat commenced. We distinctly make out every action of the two hideous monsters.

But to my excited imagination the other animals appeared about to take part in the fierce and deadly struggle—the monster, the whale, the lizard, and the turtle. I distinctly saw them every moment. I pointed them out to the Icelander. But he only shook his head.

"Tva," he said.

"What—two only does he say? Surely he is mistaken," I cried, in a tone of wonder.

"He is quite right," replied my uncle coolly and philosophically, examining the terrible duel with his telescope and speaking as if he were in a lecture room.

"How can that be?"

"Yes, it is so. The first of these hideous monsters has the snout of a porpoise, the head of a lizard, the teeth of a crocodile; and it is this that has deceived us. It is the most fearful of all antediluvian reptiles, the world-renowned Ichthyosaurus or Great Fish Lizard."

"And the other?"

"The other is a monstrous serpent, concealed under the hard vaulted shell of the turtle, the terrible enemy of its fearful rival, the Plesiosaurus, or Sea Crocodile."

Hans was quite right. The two monsters only, disturbed the surface of the sea!

At last have mortal eyes gazed upon two reptiles of the great primitive ocean! I see the flaming red eyes of the Ichthyosaurus, each as big, or bigger than a man's head. Nature in its infinite wisdom had gifted this wondrous marine animal with an optical apparatus of extreme power, capable of resisting the pressure of the heavy layers of water which rolled over him in the depth of the ocean where he usually fed. It has by some authors truly been called the whale of the Saurian race, for it is as big and quick in its motions as our king of the seas. This one measures not less than a hundred feet in length, and I can form some idea of his girth, when I see him lift his prodigious tail out of the waters. His jaw is of awful size and strength, and according to the best-informed naturalists, it does not contain less than a hundred and eighty-two teeth.

The other was the mighty Plesiosaurus, a serpent with a cylindrical trunk, with a short stumpy tail, with fins like a bank of oars in a Roman galley.

Its whole body covered by the carapace or shell, and its neck, as flexible as that of a swan, rose more than thirty feet above the waves, a tower of animated flesh!

These animals attacked one another with inconceivable fury. Such a combat was never *seen* before by mortal eyes, and to us who did see it, it appeared more like the phantasmagoric creation of a dream than anything else. They raised mountains of water, which dashed in spray over the raft, already tossed to and fro by the waves. Twenty times we seemed on the point of being upset and hurled headlong into the waves. Hideous hisses appeared to shake the gloomy granite roof of that mighty cavern—hisses which carried terror to our hearts. The awful combatants held each other in a tight embrace. I could not make out one from the other. Still the combat could not last for ever; and woe unto us, whichsoever became the victor.

One hour, two hours, three hours passed away, without any decisive result. The struggle continued with the same deadly tenacity, but without apparent result. The deadly opponents now approached, now drew away from the raft. Once or twice we fancied they were about to leave us altogether, but instead of that, they came nearer and nearer.

We crouched on the raft ready to fire at them at a moment's notice, poor as the prospect of hurting or terrifying them was. Still we were determined not to perish without a struggle.

Suddenly the Ichthyosaurus and the Plesiosaurus disappeared beneath the waves, leaving behind them a maelstrom in the midst of the sea. We were very nearly drawn down by the indraught of the water!

Several minutes elapsed before anything was again seen. Was this wonderful combat to end in the depths of the ocean? Was the last act of this terrible drama to take place without spectators?

It was impossible for us to say.

Suddenly, at no great distance from us, an enormous mass rises out of the waters—the head of the great Plesiosaurus. The terrible monster is now wounded unto death. I can see nothing now of his enormous body. All that could be distinguished was his serpent-like neck, which he twisted and curled in all the agonies of death. Now he struck the waters with it as if it had been a gigantic whip, and then again wriggled like a worm cut in two. The water was spurted up to a great distance in all directions. A great portion of it swept over our raft and nearly blinded us. But soon the end of the beast approached nearer and nearer; his movements slackened visibly; his contortions almost ceased; and at last the body of the mighty snake lay an inert, dead mass on the surface of the now calm and placid waters.

As for the Ichthyosaurus, has he gone down to his mighty cavern under the sea to rest, or will he reappear to destroy us?

This question remained unanswered. And we had breathing time.

CHAPTER 31

THE SEA MONSTER

WEDNESDAY, August 19. Fortunately the wind, which at the present blows with great violence, has allowed us to escape from the scene of the unparalleled and extraordinary struggle. Hans with his usual imperturbable calm remained at the helm. My uncle, who for a short time had been withdrawn from his absorbing reverie by the novel incidents of this sea-fight, fell back again apparently into a brown study. All this time, however, his eyes were fixed impatiently on the wide-spread ocean.

Our voyage now became monotonous and uniform. Dull as it has become, I have no desire to have it broken by any repetition of the perils and adventures of yesterday.

Thursday, August 20. The wind is now N.N.E., and blows very irregularly. It has changed to fitful gusts. The temperature is exceedingly high. We are now progressing at the average rate of about ten miles and a half per hour.

About twelve o'clock a distant sound as of thunder fell upon our ears. I make a note of the fact without even venturing a suggestion as to its cause. It was one continued roar as of a sea falling over mighty rocks.

"Far off in the distance," said the Professor dogmatically, "there is some rock or some island against which the sea, lashed to fury by the wind, is breaking violently."

Hans, without saying a word, clambered to the top of the mast, but could make out nothing. The ocean was level in every direction as far as the eye could reach.

Three hours passed away without any sign to indicate what might be before us. The sound began to assume that of a mighty cataract.

I expressed my opinion on this point strongly to my uncle. He merely shook his head. I, however, am strongly impressed by a conviction that I am not wrong. Are we advancing towards some mighty waterfall which shall cast us into the abyss? Probably this mode of descending into the abyss may be agreeable to the Professor, because it would be something like the vertical descent he is so eager to make. I entertain a very different opinion.

Whatever be the truth, it is certain that not many leagues distant there must be some very extraordinary phenomenon, for as we advance the roar becomes something mighty and stupendous. Is it in the water, or in the air?

I cast hasty glances aloft at the suspended vapours, and I seek to penetrate their mighty depths. But the vault above is tranquil. The clouds, which are now elevated to the very summit, appear utterly still and motionless, and completely lost in the irradiation of electric light. It is necessary, therefore, to seek for the cause of this phenomenon elsewhere.

I examine the horizon, now perfectly calm, pure and free from all haze. Its aspect still remains unchanged. But if this awful noise proceeds from a cataract—if, so to speak in plain English, this vast interior ocean is precipitated into a lower basin—if these tremendous roars are produced by the noise of falling waters, the current would increase in activity, and its increasing swiftness would give me some idea of the extent of the peril with which we are menaced. I consult the current. It simply does not exist: there is no such thing. An empty bottle cast into the water lies to leeward without motion.

About four o'clock Hans rises, clambers up the mast and reaches the truck itself. From this elevated position his looks are cast around. They take in a vast circumference of the ocean. At last, his eyes remain fixed. His face expresses no astonishment, but his eyes slightly dilate.

"He has seen something at last," cried my uncle.

"I think so," I replied.

Hans came down, stood beside us and pointed with his right hand to the south.

"Der nere," he said.

"There," replied my uncle.

And seizing his telescope he looked at it with great attention for about a minute, which to me appeared an age. I knew not what to think or expect.

"Yes, yes," he cried in a tone of considerable surprise, "there it is."

"What?" I asked.

"A tremendous spurt of water rising out of the waves."

"Some other marine monster," I cried, already alarmed.

"Perhaps."

"Then let us steer more to the westward, for we know what we have to expect from antediluvian animals," was my eager reply.

"Go ahead," said my uncle.

I turned towards Hans. Hans was at the tiller steering with his usual imperturbable calm.

Nevertheless, if from the distance which separated us from this creature, a distance which must be estimated at not less than a dozen leagues, and this spurting of water proceeded from the pranks of some antediluvian animal, his dimensions must be something preternatural. To fly is, therefore, the course to be suggested by ordinary prudence. But we have not come into that part of the world to be prudent. Such is my uncle's determination.

We, accordingly, continued to advance. The nearer we come, the loftier is the spouting water. What monster can fill himself with such huge volumes of water, and then unceasingly spout them out in such lofty jets?

At eight o'clock in the evening, reckoning as above ground, where there is day and night, we are not more than two leagues from the mighty beast. Its long, black, enormous, mountainous body, lies on the top of the water like an island. But then sailors have been said to have gone ashore on sleeping whales, mistaking them for land. Is it illusion, or is it fear? Its length cannot be less than a thousand fathoms. What, then, is this cetaceous monster of which no Cuvier ever thought?

It is quite motionless and presents the appearance of sleep. The sea seems unable to lift him upwards; it is rather the waves which break on his huge and gigantic frame. The water-spout, rising to a height of five hundred feet, breaks in spray with a dull, sullen roar.

We advance, like senseless lunatics, towards this mighty mass.

I honestly confess that I was abjectly afraid. I declared that I would go no farther. I threatened in my terror to cut the sheet of the sail. I attacked the Professor with considerable acrimony, calling him foolhardy, mad, I know not what. He made no answer.

Suddenly the imperturbable Hans once more pointed his finger to the menacing object.

"*Holme!*"

"An island!" cried my uncle.

"An island?" I replied, shrugging my shoulders at this poor attempt at deception.

"Of course it is," cried my uncle, bursting into a loud and joyous laugh.

"But the water spout?"

"Geyser," said Hans.

"Yes, of course—a geyser," replied my uncle, still laughing, "a geyser like those common in Iceland. Jets like this are the great wonders of the country."

At first I would not allow that I had been so grossly deceived. What could be more ridiculous than to have taken an island for a marine monster? But kick as one may, one must yield to evidence, and I was finally convinced of my error. It was nothing, after all, but a natural phenomenon.

As we approached nearer and nearer, the dimensions of the liquid sheaf of waters became truly grand and stupendous. The island had, at a distance, presented the appearance of an enormous whale, whose head rose high above the waters. The geyser, a word the Icelanders pronounce geysir, and which signfies fury, rose majestically from its summit. Dull detonations are heard every now and then, and the enormous jet, taken as it were with sudden fury, shakes its plume of vapour, and bounds into the first layer of the clouds. It is alone. Neither spurts of vapour not hot springs surround it, and the whole volcanic power of that region is concentrated in one sublime column. The rays of electric light mix with this dazzling sheaf, every drop as it falls assuming the prismatic colours of the rainbow.

"Let us go on shore," said the Professor, after some minutes of silence.

It is necessary, however, to take great precaution, in order to avoid the weight of falling waters, which would cause the raft to founder in an instant. Hans, however, steers admirably, and brings us to the other extremity of the island.

I was the first to leap on the rock. My uncle followed, while the eider-duck hunter remained still, like a man above any childish sources of astonishment. We were now walking on granite mixed with silicious sandstone; the soil shivered under our feet like the sides of boilers in which over-heated steam is forcibly confined. It is burning. We soon came in sight of the little central bason from which rose the geyser. I plunged a thermometer into the water which ran bubbling from the centre, and it marked a heat of a hundred and sixty-three degrees!

This water, therefore, came from some place where the heat was intense. This was singularly in contradiction with the theories of Professor Hardwigg. I could not help telling him my opinion on the subject.

"Well," said he sharply, "and what does this prove against my doctrine?"

"Nothing," replied I drily, seeing that I was running my head agianst a foregone conclusion.

Nevertheless, I am compelled to confess that until now we have been most remarkably fortunate, and that this voyage is being accomplished in most favourable conditions of temperature; but it appears evident, in fact, certain, that we shall sooner or later arrive at one of those regions, where the central heat will reach its utmost limits, and will go far beyond all the possible gradations of thermometers.

Visions of the Hades of the ancients, believed to be in the centre of the earth, floated through my imagination.

We shall however see what we shall see. That is the Professor's favourite phrase now. Having christened the volcanic island by the name of his nephew, the leader of the expedition turned away and gave the signal for embarkation.

I stood still, however, for some minutes, gazing upon the magnificent geyser. I soon was able to perceive that the upward tendency of the water was irregular; now it diminished in intensity, and then, suddenly it regained new vigour, which I attributed to the variation of the pressure of the accumulated vapours in its reservoir.

At last we took our departure, going carefully round the projecting, and rather dangerous, rocks of the southern side. Hans had taken advantage of this brief halt to repair the raft. Not before it was required.

Before we took our final departure from the island, however, I made some observations to calculate the distance we had gone over, and I put them down in my Journal. Since we left Port Gretchen, we had travelled two hundred and seventy leagues—more than eight hundred miles—on this great inland sea; we were therefore six hundred and twenty leagues from Iceland, and exactly under England.

CHAPTER 32

THE BATTLE OF THE ELEMENTS

FRIDAY, August 21st. This morning the magnificent geyser had wholly disappeared. The wind had freshened up, and we were fast leaving the neighbourhood of Henry's Island. Even the roaring sound of the mighty column was lost to the ear.

The weather, if, under the circumstances, we may use such an expression, is about to change very suddenly. The atmosphere is being gradually loaded with vapours, which carry with them the electricity formed by the constant evaporation of the saline waters; the clouds are slowly but sensibly falling towards the sea, and are assuming a dark olive texture; the electric rays can scarcely pierce through the opaque curtain which has fallen like a drop-scene before this wondrous theatre, on the stage of which another and terrible drama is soon to be enacted. This time it is no fight of animals; it is the fearful battle of the elements.

I feel that I am very peculiarly influenced, as all creatures are on land when a deluge is about to take place.

The cumuli, a perfectly oval kind of cloud, piled upon the south, presented a most awful and sinister appearance; with the pitiless aspect often seen before a storm. The air is extremely heavy; the sea is comparatively calm.

In the distance, the clouds have assumed the appearance of enormous balls of cotton, or rather pods, piled one above the other in picturesque confusion. By degrees, they appear to swell out, break, and gain in number what they lose in grandeur; their heaviness is so great that they are unable to lift themselves from the horizon; but under the influence of the upper currents of air, they are gradually broken up, become much darker, and then present the appearance of one single layer of a formidable character; now and then a lighter cloud, still lit up from above, rebounds upon this grey carpet, and is lost in the opaque mass.

There can be no doubt that the entire atmosphere is saturated with electric fluid; I am myself wholly impregnated; my hairs literally stand on end as if under the influence of a galvanic battery. If one of my companions ventured to touch me, I think he would receive rather a violent and unpleasant shock.

About ten o'clock in the morning, the symptoms of the storm became more thorough and decisive; the wind appeared to soften down as if to take breath for a renewed attack; the vast funereal pall above us looked like a huge bag—like the cave of Æolus, in which the storm was collecting its forces for the attack.

I tried all I could not to believe in the menacing signs of the sky, and yet I could not avoid saying, as it were involuntarily—

"I believe we are going to have bad weather."

The Professor made me no answer. He was in a horrible, in a detestable humour—to see the ocean stretching interminably before his eyes. On hearing my words he simply shrugged his shoulders.

"We shall have a tremendous storm," I said again, pointing to the horizon. "These clouds are falling lower and lower upon the sea, as if to crush it."

A great silence prevailed. The wind wholly ceased. Nature assumed a dead calm, and ceased to breathe. Upon the mast, where I noticed a sort of slight *ignis fatuus,* the sail hangs in loose heavy folds. The raft is motionless in the midst of a dark heavy sea—without undulation, without motion. It is as still as glass. But as we are making no progress, what is the use of keeping up the sail, which may be the cause of our perdition if the tempest should suddenly strike us without warning.

"Let us lower the sail," I said, "it is only an act of common prudence."

"No—no," cried my uncle, in an exasperated tone, "a hundred times, no. Let the wind strike us and do its worst, let the storm sweep us away where it will—only let me see the glimmer of some coast—of some rocky cliffs, even if they dash our raft into a thousand pieces. No! keep up the sail—no matter what happens."

These words were scarcely uttered, when the southern horizon underwent a sudden and violent change. The long accumulated vapours were resolved into water, and the air required to fill up the void produced became a wild and raging tempest.

It came from the most distant corners of the mighty cavern. It raged from every point of the compass. It roared; it yelled; it shrieked with glee as of demons let loose. The darkness increased and became indeed darkness visible.

The raft rose and fell with the storm, and bounded over the waves. My uncle was cast headlong upon the deck. I with great difficulty dragged myself towards him. He was holding on with might and main to the end of a cable, and appeared to gaze with pleasure and delight at the spectacle of the unchained elements.

Hans never moved a muscle. His long hair driven hither and thither by the tempest and scattered wildly over his motionless face, gave him a most extraordinary appearance—for every single hair was illuminated by little sparkling sprigs.

His countenance presents the extraordinary appearance of an antediluvian man, a true contemporary of the megatherium.

Still the mast holds good against the storm. The sail spreads out and fills like a soap bubble about to burst. The raft rushes on at a pace impossible to estimate, but still less swiftly than the body of water displaced beneath it, the rapidity of which may be seen by the lines which fly right and left in the wake.

"The sail, the sail!" I cried, making a trumpet of my hands, and then endeavouring to lower it.

"Let it alone!" said my uncle, more exasperated than ever.

"*Nej,*" said Hans, gently shaking his head.

Nevertheless, the rain formed a roaring cataract before this horizon of which we were in search, and to which we were rushing like madmen.

But before this wilderness of waters reached us, the mighty veil of cloud was torn in twain; the sea began to foam wildly; and the electricity, produced by some vast and extraordinary chemical action in the upper layer of cloud, is brought into play. To the fearful claps of thunder are added dazzling flashes of lightning, such as I had never seen. The flashes crossed one another, hurled from every side; while the thunder came pealing like an echo. The mass of vapour becomes incandescent; the hail stones which strike the metal of our boots and our weapons, are actually luminous; the waves as they rise appear to be fire-eating monsters, beneath which seethes an intense fire, their crests surmounted by combs of flame.

My eyes are dazzled, blinded by the intensity of light, my ears are deafened by the awful roar of the elements. I am compelled to hold on to the mast, which bends like a reed beneath the violence of the storm, to which none ever before seen by mariners bore any resemblance.

* * * * *

Here my travelling notes become very incomplete, loose, and vague. I have only been able to make out one or two fugitive observations, dotted down in a mere mechanical way. But even their brevity, even their obscurity, show the emotions which overcame me.

* * * * *

Sunday, August 23. Where have we got to? In what region are we wandering? We are still carried forward with inconceivable rapidity.

The night has been fearful, something not to be described. The storm shows no signs of cessation. We exist in the midst of an uproar which has no name. The detonations as of artillery are incessant. Our ears literally bleed. We are unable to exchange a word, or hear each other speak.

The lightning never ceases to flash for a single instant. I can see the zigzags after a rapid dart, strike the arched roof of this mightiest of mighty vaults. If it were to give way and fall upon us! Other lightnings plunge their forked streaks in every direction, and take the form of globes of fire, which explode like bomb shells over a beleaguered city. The general crash and roar do not apparently increase; it has already gone far beyond what human ear can appreciate. If all the powder magazines in the world were to explode together, it would be impossible for us to hear worse noise.

There is a constant emission of light from the storm-clouds; the electric matter is incessantly released; evidently the gaseous principles of the air are out of order; innumerable columns of water rush up like waterspouts, and fall back upon the surface of the ocean in foam.

Whither are we going? My uncle still lies at full length upon the raft, without speaking—without taking any note of time.

The heat increases. I look at the thermometer, to my surprise it indicates—*The exact figure is here rubbed out in my manuscript.*

Monday, August 24. This terrible storm will never end. Why should not this state of the atmosphere, so dense and murky, once modified, again remain definitive?

We are utterly broken and harassed by fatigue. Hans remains just as usual. The raft runs to the south-east invariably. We have now already run two hundred leagues from the newly-discovered island.

About twelve o'clock the storm became worse than ever. We are obliged now to fasten every bit of cargo tightly on the deck of the raft, or everything would be swept away. We tie ourselves to the mast, each man lashing the other. The waves drive over us, so that several times we are actually under water.

We had been under the painful necessity of abstaining from speech for three days and three nights. We opened our mouths, we moved our lips, but no sound came. Even when we placed our mouths to each other's ears it was the same.

The wind carried the voice away.

My uncle once contrived to get his head close to mine after several almost vain endeavours. He appeared to my nearly exhausted senses to articulate some word. I had a notion, more from intuition than anything else, that he said to me, "we are lost."

I took out my note book, from which under the most desperate circumstances I never parted, and wrote a few words as legibly as I could——

"Take in sail."

With a deep sigh he nodded his head and acquiesced.

His head had scarcely time to fall back in the position from which he had momentarily raised it, than a disc or ball of fire appeared on the very edge of the raft—our devoted, our doomed craft. The mast and sail are carried away bodily, and I see them swept away to a prodigious height like a kite.

We were frozen, actually shivered with terror. The ball of fire, half white, half azure coloured, about the size of a ten-inch bomb-shell, moved along, turning with prodigious rapidity to leeward of the storm. It ran about here, there and everywhere, it clambered up one of the bulwarks of the raft, it leaped upon the sack of provisions, and then finally descended lightly, fell like a foot ball and landed on our powder barrel.

Horrible situation. An explosion of course was now inevitable.

By heaven's mercy, it is not so.

The dazzling disc moves on one side, it approaches Hans, who looked at it with singular fixity; then it approached my uncle, who cast himself on his knees to avoid it; it came towards me, as I stood pale and shuddering in the dazzling light and heat; it pirouetted round my feet, which I endeavoured to withdraw.

An odour of nitrous gas filled the whole air; it penetrated to the throat, to the lungs. I felt ready to choke.

Why is it that I cannot withdraw my feet? Are they rivetted to the flooring of the raft?

No.

The fall of the electric globe has turned all the iron on board into loadstones—the instruments, the tools, the arms are clanging together with awful and horrible noise; the nails of my heavy boots adhere closely to the plate of iron incrustated in the wood. I cannot withdraw my foot.

It is the old story over again of the mountain of adamant.

At last, by a violent and almost superhuman effort, I tear it away just as the ball which is still executing its gyratory motions is about to run round it and drag me with it—if—

O what intense stupendous light! The globe of fire bursts—we are enveloped in cascades of living fire, which floods the space around with luminous matter.

Then all went out and darkness once more fell upon the deep! I had just time to see my uncle once more cast apparently senseless on the flooring of the raft, Hans at the helm, "spitting fire" under the influence of the electricity which seemed to have gone thorugh him.

Whither are we going, I ask? and echo answers, Whither?

Tuesday, Ausgust 25. I have just come out of a long fainting fit. The awful and hideous storm still continues; the lightning has increased in vividness, and pours out its fiery wrath like a brood of serpents let loose in the atmosphere.

Are we still upon the sea? Yes, and being carried along with incredible velocity.

We have passed under England, under the Channel, under France, probably under the whole extent of Europe.

* * * * *

Another awful clamour in the distance. This time it is certain that the sea is breaking upon the rocks at no great distance. Then——

CHAPTER 33

OUR ROUTE REVERSED

HERE ends what I call My Journal of our voyage on board the raft, which Journal was happily saved from the wreck. I proceed with my narrative as I did before I commenced my daily notes.

What happened when the terrible shock took place, when the raft was cast upon the rocky shore, it would be impossible for me now to say. I felt myself precipitated violently into the boiling waves, and if I escaped from a certain and cruel death, it was wholly owing to the determination of the faithful Hans, who clutching me by the arm, saved me from the yawning abyss.

The courageous Icelander then carried me in his powerful arms, far out of reach of the waves, and laid me down upon a burning expanse of sand, where I found myself some time afterwards in the company of my uncle the Professor.

Then he quietly returned towards the fatal rocks, against which the furious waves were beating, in order to save any stray waifs from the wreck. This man was always practical and thoughtful. I could not utter a word; I was quite overcome with emotion; my whole body was broken and bruised with fatigue; it took hours before I was anything like myself.

Meanwhile, there fell a fearful deluge of rain, drenching us to the skin. Its very violence, however, proclaimed the approaching end of the storm. Some over-hanging rocks, afforded us a slight protection from the torrents.

Under this shelter, Hans prepared some food, which, however, I was unable to touch; and, exhausted by the three weary days and nights of watching, we fell into a deep and painful sleep. My dreams were fearful, but at last exhausted nature asserted her supremacy, and I slumbered.

Next day when I awoke the change was magical. The weather was magnificent. Air and sea, as if by mutual consent, had regained their serenity. Every trace of the storm, even the faintest, had disappeared. I was saluted on my awakening by the first joyous tones I had heard from the Professor for many a day. His gaiety, indeed, was something terrible.

"Well, my lad," he cried, rubbing his hands together, "have you slept soundly?"

Might it not have been supposed that we were in the old house on the Königstrasse; that I had just come down quietly to my breakfast, and that my marriage with Gretchen was to take place that very day? My uncle's coolness was exasperating.

Alas, considering how the tempest had driven us in an easterly direction, we had passed under the whole of Germany, under the city of Hamburg where I had been so happy, under the very street which contained all I loved and cared for in the world.

It was a positive fact that I was only separated from her by a distance of forty leagues. But these forty leagues were of hard impenetrable granite!

All these dreary and miserble reflections passed through my mind, before I attempted to answer my uncle's question.

"Why, what is the matter?" he cried, "cannot you say whether you have slept well or not?"

"I have slept very well," was my reply, "but every bone in my body aches. I suppose that will lead to nothing."

"Nothing at all, my boy. It is only the result of the fatigue of the last few days—that is all."

"You appear—if I may be allowed to say so—to be very jolly this morning," I said.

"Delighted, my dear boy, delighted. Was never happier in my life. We have at last reached the wished-for port."

"The end of our expedition?" cried I, in a tone of considerable surprise.

"No; but to the confines of that sea which I began to fear would never end, but go round the whole world. We will now tranquilly resume our journey by land, and once again endeavour to dive into the centre of the Earth."

"My dear uncle," I began, in a hesitating kind of way, "allow me to ask you one question?"

"Certainly, Harry; a dozen, if you think proper."

"One will suffice. How about getting back?" I asked.

"How about getting back? What a question to ask. We have not as yet reached the end of our journey."

"I know that. All I want to know is, how you propose we shall manage the return voyage?"

"In the most simple manner in the world," said the imperturbable Professor. Once we reach the exact centre of this sphere, either we shall find a new road by which to ascend to the surface, or we shall simply turn round and go back by the way we came. I have every reson to believe that while we are travelling forward, it will not close behind us."

"Then one of the first matters to see to will be to repair the raft," was my rather melancholy response.

"Of course. We must attend to that above all things," continued the Professor.

"Then comes the all-important question of provisions," I urged. "Have we anything like enough left to enable us to accomplish such great, such amazing, designs as you contemplate carrying out?"

"I have seen into the matter, and my answer is in the affirmative. Hans is a very clever fellow, and I have reason to believe that he has saved the greater part of the cargo. But the best way to satisfy your scruples, is to come and judge for yourself."

Saying which, he led the way out of the kind of open grotto in which we had taken shelter. I had almost begun to hope that which I should rather have feared, and this was the impossibility of such a shipwreck leaving even the slightest signs of what it had carried as freight. I was, however, thoroughly mistaken.

As soon as I reached the shores of this inland sea, I found Hans standing gravely in the midst of a large number of things laid out in complete order. My uncle wrung his hands with deep and silent gratitude. His heart was too full for speech.

This man, whose superhuman devotion to his employers, I not only never saw surpassed, nor even equalled, had been hard at work all the time we slept, and at the risk of his life had succeeded in saving the most precious articles of our cargo.

Of course, under the circumstances, we necessarily experienced several severe losses. Our weapons had wholly vanished. But experience had taught us to do without them. The provision of powder had, however, remained intact, after having narrowly escaped blowing us all to atoms in the storm.

"Well," said the Professor, who was now ready to make the best of everything, "as we have no guns, all we have to do is to give up all idea of hunting."

"Yes, my dear sir, we can do without them, but what about all our instruments?"

"Here is the manometer, the most useful of all, and which I gladly accept in lieu of the rest. With it alone I can calculate the depth as we proceed; by its means alone I shall be able to decide when we have reached the centre of the earth. Ha, ha! but for this little instrument we might make a mistake, and run the risk of coming out at the antipodes!"

All this was said amid bursts of unnatural laughter.

"But the compass!" I cried, "without that what can we do?"

"Here it is safe and sound!" he cried, with real joy, "ah, ah, and here we have the chronometer and the thermometers. Hans the hunter is indeed an invaluable man!"

It was impossible to deny this fact. As far as the nautical and other instruments were concerned, nothing was wanting. Then on further examination, I found ladders, cords, pickaxes, crowbars, and shovels, all scattered about on the shore.

There was, however, finally the most important question of all, and that was, provisions.

"But what are we to do for food?" I asked.

"Let us see to the commissariat department," replied my uncle gravely.

The boxes which contained our supply of food for the voyage were placed in a row along the strand, and were in a capital state of preservation; the sea had in every case respected their contents, and to sum up in one sentence, taking into consideration, biscuits, salt meat, schiedam and dried fish, we could still calculate on having about four months' supply, if used with prudence and caution.

"Four months," cried the sanguine Professor, in high glee, "then we shall have plenty of time both to go and to come, and with what remains I undertake to give a grand dinner to my colleagues of the Johanneum."

I sighed. I should by this time have used myself to the temperament of my uncle, and yet this man astonished me more and more every day. He was the greatest human enigma I ever had known.

"Now," said he, "before we do anything else we must lay in a stock of fresh water. The rain has fallen in abundance, and filled the hollows of the granite. There is a rich supply of water, and we have no fear of suffering from thirst, which in our circumstances is of the last importance. As for the raft, I shall recommend Hans to repair it to the best of his abilities; though I have every reason to believe we shall not require it again."

"How is that?" I cried, more amazed than ever at my uncle's style of reasoning.

"I have an idea, my dear boy; it is none other than this simple fact: we shall not come out by the same opening as that by which we entered."

I began to look at my uncle with vague suspicion. An idea had more than once taken possession of me; and this was, that he was going mad. And yet, little did I know how true and prophetic his words were doomed to be.

"And now," he said, "having seen to all these matters of detail, to breakfast."

I followed him to a sort of projecting cape, after he had given his last instructions to our guide. In this original position, with dried meat, biscuit, and a delicious cup of tea, we made a satisfactory meal—I may say one of the most

The ball of fire.

welcome and pleasant I ever remember. Exhaustion, the keen atmosphere, the state of calm after so much agitation, all contributed to give me an excellent appetite. Indeed, it contributed very much to producing a pleasant and cheerful state of mind.

While breakfast was in hand, and between the sips of warm tea, I asked my uncle if he had any idea of how we now stood in relation to the world above.

"For my part," I added, "I think it will be rather difficult to determine."

"Well, if we were compelled to fix the exact spot," said my uncle, "it might be difficult, since during the three days of that awful tempest I could keep no account either of the quickness of our pace, or of the direction in which the raft was going. Still, we will endeavour to approximate to the truth. We shall not, I believe, be so very far out."

"Well, if I recollect rightly," I replied, "our last observation was made at the Geyser island."

"Harry's Island, my boy! Harry's Island. Do not decline the honour of having named it; given your name to an island discovered by us, the first human beings who trod it since the creation of the world!"

"Let it be so, then. At Harry's Island we had already gone over two hundred and seventy leagues of sea, and we were, I believe, about six hundred leagues, more or less from Iceland."

"Good. I am glad to see that you remember so well. Let us start from that point, and let us count four days of storm, during which our rate of travelling must have been very great. I should say that our velocity must have been about eighty leagues to the twenty-four hours."

I agreed that I thought this a fair calculation. There were then three hundred leagues to be added to the grand total.

"Yes, and the Central Sea must extend at least six hundred leagues from side to side. Do you know, my boy, Harry, that we have discovered an inland lake larger than the Mediterranean?"

"Certainly, and we only know of its extent in one way. It may be hundreds of miles in length."

"Very likely."

"Then," said I, after calculating for some minutes, "if your previsons are right, we are at this moment exactly under the Mediterranean itself."

"Do you think so?"

"Yes, I am almost certain of it. Are we not nine hundred leagues distant from Reykjawik?"

"That is perfectly true, and a famous bit of road we have travelled, my boy. But why we should be under the Mediterranean more than under Turkey or the Atlantic Ocean can only be known when we are sure of not having deviated from our course; and of this we know nothing."

"I do not think we were driven very far from our course: the wind appears to me to have been always about the same. My opinion is that this shore must be situated to the south-east of Port Gretchen."

"Good—I hope so. It will, however, be easy to decide the matter by taking the bearings from our departure by means of the compass. Come along, and we will consult that invaluable invention."

The Professor now walked eagerly in the direction of the rock where the indefatigable Hans had placed the instruments in safety. My uncle was gay and light-hearted; he rubbed his hands, and assumed all sorts of attitudes. He was to all appearance once more a young man. Since I had known him never had he been so amiable and pleasant. I followed him, rather curious to know whether I had made any mistake in my estimation of our position.

As soon as we had reached the rock, my uncle took the compass, placed it horizontally before him and looked keenly at the needle.

As he had at first shaken it to give it vivacity, it oscillated considerably, and then slowly assumed its right position under the influence of the magnetic power.

The Professor bent his eyes curiously over the wondrous instrument. A violent start immediately showed the extent of his emotion.

He closed his eyes, rubbed them, and took another and a keener survey.

Then he turned slowly round to me, stupefaction depicted on his countenance.

"What is the matter?" said I, beginning to be alarmed.

He could not speak. He was too overwhelmed for words. He simply pointed to the instrument.

I examined it eagerly according to his mute directions, and a loud cry of surprise escaped my lips. The needle of the compass pointed due north, in the direction we expected was the south!

It pointed to the shore instead of to the high seas.

I shook the compass; I examined it with a curious and anxious eye. It was in a state of perfection. No blemish in any way explained the phenomenon. Whatever position we forced the needle into, it returned invariably to the same unexpected point.

It was useless attempting to conceal from ourselves the fatal truth.

There could be no doubt about it, unwelcome as was the fact, that during the tempest, there had been a sudden slant of wind, of which we had been unable to take any account and thus the raft had carried us back to the shores we had left, apparently for ever, so many days before!

CHAPTER 34

A VOYAGE OF DISCOVERY

IT would be altogether impossible for me to give any idea of the utter astonishment which overcame the Professor on making this extraordinary discovery. Amazement, incredulity, and rage were blended in such a way as to alarm me.

During the whole course of my life I had never seen a man at first so chapfallen; and then so furiously indignant.

The terrible fatigues of our sea voyage, the fearful dangers we had passed through, had all, all, gone for nothing. We had to begin them all over again.

Instead of progressing, as we fondly expected, during a voyage of so many days, we had retreated. Every hour of our expedition on the raft had been so much lost time!

Presently, however, the indomitable energy of my uncle overcame every other consideration.

"So," he said, between his set teeth, "fatality will play me these terrible tricks. The elements themselves conspire to overwhelm me with mortification. Air, fire, and water combine their united efforts to oppose my passage. Well, they shall see what the earnest will of a determined man can do. I will not yield, I will not retreat even one inch; and we shall see who shall triumph in this great contest—man or nature."

Standing upright on a rock, irritated and menacing, Professor Hardwigg, like the ferocious Ajax, seemed to defy the fates. I, however, took upon myself to interfere, and to impose some sort of check upon such insensate enthusiasm.

"Listen to me, uncle," I said, in a firm but temperate tone of voice, "there must be some limit to ambition here below. It is utterly useless to struggle against the impossible. Pray listen to reason. We are utterly unprepared for a sea voyage; it is simple madness to think of performing a journey of five hundred leagues upon a wretched pile of beams, with a counterpane for a sail, a paltry stick for a mast, and a tempest to contend with. As we are totally incapable of steering our frail craft, we shall become the mere plaything of the storm, and it is acting the part of madmen if we, a second time, run any risk upon this dangerous and treacherous Central Sea."

These are only a few of the reasons and arguments I put together—reasons and arguments which to me appeared unanswerable. I was allowed to go on without interruption for about ten minutes. The explanation to this I soon discovered. The Professor was not even listening, and did not hear a word of all my eloquence.

"To the raft!" he cried, in a hoarse voice, when I paused for a reply.

Such was the result of my strenuous effort to resist his iron will. I tried again; I begged and implored him; I got into a passion; but I had to deal with a will more determined than my own. I seemed to feel like the waves which fought and battled against the huge mass of granite at our feet, which had smiled grimly for so many ages at their puny efforts.

Hans, meanwhile, without taking part in our discussion, had been repairing the raft. One would have supposed that he instinctively guessed at the further projects of my uncle.

By means of some fragments of cordage, he had again made the raft seaworthy.

While I had been speaking he had hoisted a new mast and sail, the latter already fluttering and waving in the breeze.

The worthy Professor spoke a few words to our imperturbable guide, who immediately began to put our baggage on board, and to prepare for our departure. The atmosphere was now tolerably clear and pure, and the north-east wind blew steadily and serenely. It appeared likely to last for some time.

What, then, could I do? Could I undertake to resist the iron will of two men? It was simply impossible; if even I could have hoped for the support of Hans. This, however, was out of the question. It appeared to me that the Icelander had set aside all personal will and identity. He was a picture of abnegation.

I could hope for nothing from one so infatuated with and devoted to his master. All I could do, therefore, was to swim with the stream.

In a mood of stolid and sullen resignation, I was about to take my accustomed place on the raft, when my uncle placed his hand upon my shoulder.

"There is no hurry, my boy," he said, "we shall not start until to-morrow."

I looked the picture of resignation to the dire will of fate.

"Under the circumstances," he said, "I ought to neglect no precautions. As fate has cast me upon these shores, I shall not leave without having completely examined them."

In order to understand this remark, I must explain that though we had been driven back to the northern shore, we had landed at a very different spot from that which had been our starting point.

Port Gretchen must, we calculated, be very much to the westward. Nothing, therefore, was more natural and reasonable than that we should reconnoitre this new shore upon which we had so unexpectedly landed.

"Let us go on a journey of discovery," I cried.

And leaving Hans to his important operation, we started on our expedition. The distance between the foreshore at high-water and the foot of the rocks was considerable. It would take about half-an-hour's walking to get from one to the other.

As we trudged along, our feet crushed innumerable shells of every shape and size—once the dwelling-places of animals of every period of creation.

I particularly noticed some enormous shells—carapaces (turtle and tortoise species) the diameter of which exceeded fifteen feet.

They had in past ages belonged to those gigantic glyptodons of the pliocene period, of which the modern turtle is but a minute specimen. In addition, the whole soil was covered by a vast quantity of stony relics, having the appearance of flints worn by the action of the waves, and lying in successive layers one above the other. I came to the conclusion that in past ages the sea must have covered the whole district. Upon the scattered rocks, now lying far beyond its reach, the mighty waves of ages had left evident marks of their passage.

On reflection, this appeared to me partially to explain the existence of this remarkable ocean, forty leagues below the surface of the earth's crust. According to my new, and perhaps fanciful, theory, this liquid mass must be gradually lost in the deep bowels of the earth. I had also no doubt that this mysterious sea was fed by infiltration of the ocean above, through imperceptible fissures.

Nevertheless, it was impossible not to admit that these fissures must now be nearly chocked up, for if not, the cavern, or rather the immense and stupendous reservoir would have been completely filled in a short space of time. Perhaps even this water, having to contend against the accumulated subterraneous fires of the interior of the earth, had become partially vaporised. Hence the explanation of those heavy clouds suspended over our heads, and the super-abundant display of that electricity which occasioned such terrible storms in this deep and cavernous sea.

This lucid explanation of the phenomena we had witnessed appeared to me quite satisfactory. However great and mighty the marvels of nature may seem to us, they are always to be explained by physical reasons. Everything is subordinate to some great law of nature.

It now appeared clear that we were walking upon a kind of sedimentary soil, formed like all the soils of that period, so frequent on the surface of the globe, by the subsidence of the waters. The Professor, who was now in his element, carefully examined every rocky fissure. Let him only find an opening and it directly became important to him to examine its depth.

For a whole mile we followed the windings of the Central Sea, when suddenly an important change took place in the aspect of the soil. It seemed to have been rudely cast up, convulsionised, as it were, by a violent upheaving of the lower strata. In many places, hollows here, and hillocks there, attested great dislocations at some other period of the terrestrial mass.

We advanced with great difficulty over the broken masses of granite mixed with flint, quartz and alluvial deposits, when a large field, more even than a field, a plain of bones, appeared suddenly before our eyes! It looked like an immense cemetery, where generation after generation had mingled their mortal dust.

Lofty barrows of early remains rose at intervals. They undulated away to the limits of the distant horizon and were lost in a thick and brown fog.

On that spot, some three square miles in extent, was accumulated the whole history of animal life—scarcely one creature upon the comparatively modern soil of the upper and inhibited world had there existed.

Nevertheless, we were drawn forward by an all-absorbing and impatient curiosity. Our feet crushed with a dry and crackling sound the remains of these prehistoric fossils, for which the museums of great cities quarrel, even when they obtain only rare and curious morsels. A thousand such naturalists as Cuvier would not have sufficed to recompose the skeletons of the organic beings which lay in this magnificent osseous collection.

I was utterly confounded. My uncle stood for some minutes with his arms raised on high towards the thick granite vault which served us for a sky. His mouth was wide open; his eyes sparkled wildly behind his spectacles (which he had fortunately saved), his head bobbed up and down and from side to side, while his whole attitude and mien expressed unbounded astonishment.

He stood in the presence of an endless, wondrous and inexhaustibly rich collection of antediluvian monsters, piled up for his own private and peculiar satisfaction.

Fancy an enthusiastic lover of books carried suddenly into the very midst of the famous library of Alexandria burned by the sacrilegious Omar, and which some miracle had restored to its pristine splendour! Such was something of the state of mind in which uncle Hardwigg was now placed.

For some time he stood thus, literally aghast at the magnitude of his discovery.

But it was even a greater excitement when, darting wildly over this mass of organic dust, he caught up a naked skull and addressed me in a quivering voice—

"Harry, my boy—Harry—this is a human head!"

"A human head, uncle!" I said, no less amazed and stupefied than himself.

"Yes, nephew. Ah! Mr. Milne-Edwards—ah! Mr. De Quatrefages—why are you not where I am—I, Professor Hardwigg!"

CHAPTER 35

DISCOVERY UPON DISCOVERY

In order fully to understand the exclamation made by my uncle, and his allusions to these illustrious and learned men, it will be necessary to enter into certain explanations in regard to a circumstance of the highest importance to palæontology or the science of fossil life, which had taken place a short time before our departure from the upper regions of the earth.

On the 28th of March, 1863, some navigators under the direction of M. Boucher de Perthes, were at work in the great quarries of Moulin-Quignon, near Abbeville, in the department of the Somme, in France. While at work, they unexpectedly came upon a human jawbone buried fourteen feet below the surface of the soil. It was the first fossil of the kind that had ever been brought to the light of day. Near this unexpected human relic were found stone hatchets and carved flints, coloured and clothed by time in one uniform brilliant tint of verdigris.

The report of this extraordinary and unexpected discovery spread not only all over France, but over England and Germany. Many learned men belonging to various scientific bodies, and noteworthy among others, Messrs. Milne-Edwards and De Quatrefages, took the affair very much to heart, demonstrated the incontestible authenticity of the bone in question, and became—to use the phrase then recognised in England—the most ardent supporters of the "jawbone question."

To the eminent geologists of the United Kingdom who looked upon the fact as certain—Messrs. Falconer, Buck, Caarpenter and others—were soon united the learned men of Germany, and among those in the first rank, the most eager, the most enthusiastic, was my worthy uncle, Professor Hardwigg.

The authenticity of a human fossil of the quaternary period seemed then to be incontestably demonstrated, and even to be admitted by the most sceptical.

This system or theory, call it what you will, had, it is true, a bitter adversary in M. Elie de Beaumont. This learned man, who holds such a high place in the scientific world, holds that the soil of Moulin-Quignon does not belong to the diluvium, but to a much less ancient strata, and, in accordance with Cuvier in this respect, he would by no means admit that the human species was cotemporary with the animals of the quaternary epoch. My worthy uncle, Professor Hardwigg, in concert with the great majority of geologists, had held firm, had disputed, discussed, and finally, after considerable talking and writing, M. Elie de Beaumont had been pretty well left alone in his opinions.

We were familiar with all the details of this discussion, but were far from being aware then that since our departure the matter had entered upon a new phase. Other similar jawbones, though belonging to individuals of varied types and very different natures, had been found in the movable gray sands of certain grottoes in France, Switzerland, and Belgium; together with arms, utensils, tools, bones of children, of men in the prime of life, and of old men. The existence of men in the quaternary period became, therefore, more positive every day.

But this was far from being all. New remains, dug up from the pliocene or tertiary deposits, had enabled the more far-seeing or audacious among learned men to assign even a far greater degree of antiquity to the human race. These remains, it is true, were not those of men; that is, were not the bones of men, but objects decidedly having served the human race, shin bones, thigh bones of fossil animals, regularly scooped out, and in fact sculptured—bearing the unmistakable signs of human handy-work.

By means of these wondrous and unexpected discoveries, man ascended endless centuries in the scale of time; he, in fact, preceded the mastodon; became the cotemporary of the *elephas meridionalis*—the southern elephant; acquired an antiquity of over a hundred thousand years—since that is the date given by the most eminent geologists to the pliocene period of the earth. Such was then the state of palæontologic science, and what we moreover knew, sufficed to explain our attitude before this great cemetery of the plains of the Hardwigg Ocean.

It will now be easy to understand the Professor's mingled astonishment and joy when, on advancing about twenty yards, he found himself in the presence of, I may say face to face with, a specimen of the human race actually belonging to the quaternary period!

It was indeed a human skull, perfectly recognisable. Had a soil of very peculiar nature, like that of the cemetery of St. Michel at Bordeaux, preserved it during countless ages? This was the question I asked myself, but which I was wholly unable to answer. But this head with stretched and parchmenty skin, with the teeth whole, the hair abundant, was before our eyes as in life!

I stood mute, almost paralysed with wonder and awe before this dread apparition of another age. My uncle, who on almost every occasion was a great talker, remained for a time completely dumbfounded. He was too full of emotion for speech to be possible. After a while, however, we raised up the body to which the skull belonged. We stood it on end. It seemed, to our excited imaginations, to look at us with its terrible hollow eyes.

After some minutes of silence, the man was vanquished by the Professor. Human instincts succumbed to scientific pride and exultation. Professor Hardwigg, carried away by his enthusiasm, forgot all the circumstances of our journey, the extraordinary position in which we were placed, the immense cavern which stretched far away over our heads. There can be no doubt that he thought himself at the Institution addressing his attentive pupils, for he put on his most doctorial style, waved his hand, and began—

"Gentlemen, I have the honour on this auspicious occasion to present to you a man of the quaternary period of our globe. Many learned men have denied his very existence, while other able persons, perhaps of even higher authority, have affirmed their belief in the reality of his life. If the St. Thomases of palæontology were present, they would reverentially touch him with their fingers and believe in his existence—thus acknowledging their obstinate heresy. I know that science should be careful in relation to all discoveries of this nature. I am not without having heard of the many Barnums and other quacks who have made a trade of such like pretended discoveries. I have, of course, heard of the discovery of the knee-bones of Ajax, of the pretended finding of the body of Orestes by the Spartiates, and of the body of Asterius, ten spans long—fifteen feet—of which we read in Pausanias.

"I have read everything in relation to the skeleton of Trapani, discovered in the fourteenth century, and which many persons chose to regard as that of Polyphemus, and the history of the giant dug up during the sixteenth century in the environs of Palmyra. You are as well aware as I am, gentlemen, of the existence of the celebrated analysis made near Lucerne, in 1577, of the great bones which the celebrated Doctor Felix Plater declared belonged to a giant about nineteen feet high. I have devoured all the treatises of Cassanion, and all those memoirs, pamphlets, speeches, and replies, published in reference to the skeleton of Teutobochus, king of the Cimbri, the invader of Gaul, dug out of a gravel pit in Dauphiny, in 1613. In the eighteenth century I should have denied, with Peter Campet, the existence of the preadamites of Scheuchzer. I have had in my hands the writing called Gigans——"

Here my uncle was afflicted by the natural infirmity which prevented him

Human or not?

from pronouncing difficult words in public. It was not exactly stuttering, but a strange sort of constitutional hesitation.

"The writing named Gigans——" he repeated.

He, however, could get no further.

"Giganteo——"

Impossible! The unfortunate word would not come out. There would have been great laugher at the Institution, had the mistake happened there.

"Gigantosteology!" at last exclaimed Professor Hardwigg, between two savage growls.

Having got over our difficulty, and getting more and more excited—

"Yes, gentlemen, I am well acquainted with all these matters, and know, also, that Cuvier and Blumenbach fully recognised in these bones, the undeniable remains of mammoths of the quaternary period. But after what we now see, to allow a doubt is to insult scientific inquiry. There is the body; you can see it; you can touch it. It is not a skeleton, it is a complete and uninjured body, preserved with an anthropological object."

I did not attempt to controvert this singular and astounding assertion.

"If I could but wash this corpse in a solution of sulphuric acid," continued my uncle, "I would undertake to remove all the earthy particles, and these resplendent shells, which are incrusted all over his body. But I am without this precious dissolving medium. Nevertheless, such as it is, this body will tell its own history."

Here the Professor held up the fossil body, and exhibited it with rare dexterity. No professional showman could have shown more activity.

"As on examination you will see," my uncle continued, "it is only about six feet in length, which is a long way from the pretended giants of early days. As to the particular race to which it belonged, it is incontestably Caucasian. It is of the white race, that is, of our own. The skull of this fossil being is a perfect ovoid without any remarkable or prominent development of the cheek bones, and without any projection of the jaw. It presents no indication of the prognathism which modifies the facial angle.* Measure the angle for yourselves, and you will find that it is just ninety degrees. But I will advance still farther on the road of inquiry and deduction, and I dare venture to say that this human sample or specimen belongs to the Japhetic family, which spread over the world from India to the uttermost limits of western Europe. There is no occasion, gentlemen, to smile at my remarks."

Of course nobody smiled. But the excellent Professor was so accustomed to beaming countenances at his lectures, that he believed he saw all his audience laughing during the delivery of his learned dissertation.

"Yes," he continued, with renewed animation, "this is a fossil man, a contemporary of the mastodons, with the bones of which this whole amphitheatre is covered. But if I am called on to explain how he came to this place, how these various strata by which he is covered have fallen into this vast cavity, I can undertake to give you no explanation. Doubtless, if we carry ourselves back to the quaternary epoch, we shall find that great and mighty convulsions took

* The facial angle is formed by two planes—one more or less vertical, which is in a straight line with the forehead and the incisors; the other, horizontal, which passes through the organs of hearing, and the lower nasal bone. Prognathism, in anthropological language, means that particular projection of the jaw which modifies the facial angle.

place in the crust of the earth; the continually cooling operation, through which the earth had to pass, produced fissures, landslips, and chasms, through which a large portion of the earth made its way. I come to no absolute conclusion, but there is the man, surrounded by the works of his hands, his hatchets, his carved flints, which belong to the stony period; and the only rational supposition is, that, like myself, he visited the centre of the earth as a travelling tourist, a pioneer of science. At all events, there can be no doubt of his great age, and his being one of the oldest race of human beings."

The Professor with these words ceased his oration, and I burst forth into loud and "unanimous" applause. Besides, after all, my uncle was right. Much more learned men than his nephew would have found it rather hard to refute his facts and arguments.

Another circumstance soon presented itself. This fossilised body was not the only one in this vast plain of bones—the cemetery of an extinct world. Other bodies were found, as we trod the dusty plain, and my uncle was able to choose the most marvellous of these specimens in order to convince the most incredulous.

In truth, it was a surprising spectacle, the successive remains of generations and generations of men and animals confounded together in one vast cemetery. But a great question now presented itself to our notice, and one we were actually afraid to contemplate in all its bearings.

Had these once animated beings been buried so far beneath the soil by some tremendous convulsion of nature, after they had been earth to earth and ashes to ashes, or had they lived here below, in this subterranean world, under this factitious sky, born, married, and given in marriage, and dying at last, just like ordinary inhabitants of the earth?

Up to the present moment, marine monsters, fish, and such like animals, had alone been seen alive!

The question, which rendered us rather uneasy, was a pertinent one. Were any of these men of the abyss wandering about the deserted shores of this wondrous sea of the centre of the earth?

This was a question which rendered me very uneasy and uncomfortable. How, should they really be in existence, would they receive us men from above?

CHAPTER 36

WHAT IS IT

For a long and weary hour we tramped over this great bed of bones. We advanced regardless of everything, drawn on by ardent curiosity. What other marvels did this great cavern contain—what other wondrous treasures for the scientific man? My eyes were quite prepared for any number of surprises, my imagination lived in expectation of something new and wonderful.

The borders of the great Central Ocean had for some time disappeared behind the hills that were scattered over the ground occupied by the plain of bones. The imprudent and enthusiastic Professor, who did not care whether he lost himself or not, hurried me forward. We advanced silently, bathed in waves of electric fluid.

By reason of a phenomenon which I cannot explain, and thanks to its extreme diffusion, now complete, the light illumined equally the sides of every hill and rock. Its seat appeared to be nowhere, in no determined force, and produced no shade whatever.

The appearance presented was that of a tropical country at midday in summer—in the midst of the equatorial regions and under the vertical rays of the sun.

All sign of vapour had disappeared. The rocks, the distant mountains, some confused masses of far-off forests, assumed a weird and mysterious aspect under this equal distribution of the luminous fluid!

We resembled to a certain extent the mysterious personage in one of Hoffmann's fantastic tales—the man who lost his shadow.

After we had walked about a mile farther, we came to the edge of a vast forest, not however one of the vast mushroom forests we had discovered near Port Gretchen.

It was the glorious and wild vegetation of the tertiary period, in all its superb magnificence. Huge palms, of a species now unknown, superb palmacites—a genus of fossil palms from the coal formation—pines, yews, cypress, and conifers or cone-bearing trees, the whole bound together by an inextricable and complicated mass of creeping plants.

A beautiful carpet of mosses and ferns grew beneath the trees. Pleasant brooks murmured beneath umbrageous boughs, little worthy of this name, for no shade did they give. Upon their borders grew small tree-like shrubs, such as are seen in the hot countries on our inhabited globe.

The one thing wanted to these plants, these shrubs, these trees—was colour! For ever deprived of the vivifying warmth of the sun, they were vapid and colourless. All shade was lost in one uniform tint, of a brown and faded character. The leaves were wholly devoid of verdure, and the flowers, so numerous during the tertiary period which gave them birth, were without colour and without perfume, something like paper discoloured by long exposure to the atmosphere.

My uncle ventured beneath the gigantic groves. I followed him, though not without a certain amount of apprehension. Since nature had shown herself capable of producing such stupendous vegetable productions, why might we not meet with mammals (animals with breasts) as large, and therefore dangerous.

I particularly remarked, in the clearings left by trees that had fallen and been partially consumed by time, many leguminous (beanlike) shrubs, such as the maple and other eatable trees, dear to ruminating animals. Then there appeared confounded together and intermixed, the trees of such varied lands, specimens of the vegetation of every part of the globe; there was the oak near the palm tree, the Australian eucalyptus, an interesting class of the order *Myrtaceæ*—leaning against the tall Norwegian pine, the poplar of the north, mixing its branches with those of the New Zealand kauris. It was enough to drive the most ingenious classifier of the upper regions out of his mind, and to upset all his received ideas about botany.

Suddenly I stopped short and restrained my uncle.

The extreme diffuseness of the light enabled me to see the smallest objects in the distant copses. I thought I saw—no, I really did see with my own eyes—immense, gigantic animals moving about under the mighty trees. Yes, they were truly gigantic animals, a whole herd of mastodons, not fossils, but living, and exactly like those discovered in 1801, on the marshy banks of the great Ohio, in North America!

Yes, I could see these enormous elephants, whose trunks were tearing down large boughs, and working in and out the trees like a legion of serpents. I could hear the sounds of the mighty tusks uprooting huge trees!

The boughs crackled, and whole masses of leaves and green branches went down the capacious throats of these terrible monsters!

That wondrous dream, when I saw the ante-historical times revivified, when the tertiary and quaternary periods passed before me, was now realised!

And there we were alone, far down in the bowels of the earth, at the mercy of its ferocious inhabitants!

My uncle paused, full of wonder and astonishment.

"Come," he said at last, when his first surprise was over, "come along, my boy, and let us see them nearer."

"No," replied I, restraining his efforts to drag me forward, "we are wholly without arms. What should we do in the midst of that flock of gigantic quadrupeds? Come away, uncle, I implore you. No human creature can with impunity brave the ferocious anger of these monsters."

"No human creature," said my uncle, suddenly lowering his voice to a mysterious whisper, "you are mistaken, my dear Henry. Look! look yonder! It seems to me that I behold a human being—a being like ourselves—a man!"

I looked, shrugging my shoulders, decided to push incredulity to its very last limits. But whatever might have been my wish, I was compelled to yield to the weight of ocular demonstration.

Yes—not more than a quarter of a mile off, leaning against the trunk of an enormous tree, was a human being—a Proteus of these subterranean regions, a new son of Neptune keeping this innumerable herd of mastodons.

*Immanis pecoris custos, immanis ipse!**

Yes—it was no longer a fossil whose corpse we had raised from the ground in the great cemetery, but a giant capable of guiding and driving these prodigious monsters. His height was above twelve feet. His head, as big as the head of a buffalo, was lost in a mane of matted hair. It was indeed a huge mane, like those which belonged to the elephants of the earlier ages of the world.

In his hand was a branch of a tree, which served as crook for this antediluvian shepherd.

We remained profoundly still, speechless with surprise.

But we might at any moment be seen by him. Nothing remained for us but instant flight.

"Come, come!" I cried, dragging my uncle along; and, for the first time, he made no resistance to my wishes.

A quarter of an hour later we were far away from that terrible monster!

Now that I think of the matter calmly, and that I reflect upon it dispassionately; now that months, years, have passed since this strange and unnatural adventure befell us,—what am I to think, what am I to believe?

No, it is utterly impossible! Our ears must have deceived us, and our eyes have cheated us! we have not seen what we believed we had seen. No human being could by any possibility have existed in that subterranean world! No generation of men could inhabit the lower caverns of the globe without taking

* The keeper of gigantic cattle, himself a giant!

note of those who peopled the surface, without communication with them. It was folly, folly, folly! nothing else!

I am rather inclined to admit the existence of some animal resembling in structure the human race—of some monkey of the first geological epochs, like that discovered by M. Lartet in the ossiferous deposit of Sansan.

But this animal, or being, whichsoever it was, surpassed in height all things known to modern science. Never mind. However unlikely it may be, it might have been a monkey—but a man, a living man, and with him a whole generation of gigantic animals, buried in the entrails of the earth—it was too monstrous to be believed!

CHAPTER 37

THE MYSTERIOUS DAGGER

DURING this time, we had left the bright and transparent forest far behind us. We were mute with astonishment, overcome by a kind of feeling which was next door to apathy. We kept running in spite of ourselves. It was a perfect flight, which resembled one of those horrible sensations we sometimes meet with in our dreams.

Instinctively we made our way towards the Central Sea, and I cannot now tell what wild thoughts passed through my mind, nor of what follies I might have been guilty, but for a very serious pre-occupation which brought me back to practical life.

Though I was aware that we were treading on a soil quite new to us, I, however, every now and then noticed certain aggregations of rock, the shape of which forcibly reminded me of those near Port Gretchen.

This confirmed, moreover, the indications of the compass and our extraordinary and unlooked for, as well as involuntary, return to the north of this great Central Sea. It was so like our starting point, that I could scarcely doubt the reality of our position. Streams and cascades, fell in hundreds over the numerous projections of the rocks.

I actually thought I could see our faithful and monotonous Hans and the wonderful grotto in which I had come back to life after my tremendous fall.

Then, as we advanced still farther, the position of the cliffs, the appearance of a stream, the unexpected profile of a rock, threw me again into a state of bewildering doubt.

After some time, I explained my state of mental indecision to my uncle. He confessed to a similar feeling of hesitation. He was totally unable to make up his mind in the midst of this extraordinary but uniform panorama.

"There can be no doubt," I insisted, "that we have not landed exactly at the place whence we first took our departure; but the tempest has brought us above our starting point. I think, therefore, that if we follow the coast we shall once more find Port Gretchen."

"In that case," cried my uncle, "it is useless to continue our exploration.

The very best thing we can do is to make our way back to the raft. Are you quite sure, Harry, that you are not mistaken?''

''It is difficult,'' was my reply, ''to come to any decision, for all these rocks are exactly alike. There is no marked difference between them. At the same time, the impression on my mind is, that I recognise the promontory at the foot of which our worthy Hans constructed the raft. We are, I am nearly convinced, near the little port: if this be not it,'' I added, carefully examining a creek which appeared singularly familiar to my mind.

''My dear Harry—if this were the case, we should find traces of our own footsteps, some signs of our passage; and I can really see nothing to indicate our having passed this way.''

''But I see something,'' I cried, in an impetuous tone of voice, as I rushed forward and eagerly picked up something which shone in the sand under my feet.

''What is it?'' cried the astonished and bewildered Professor.

''This,'' was my reply.

And I handed to my startled relative a rusty dagger, of singular shape.

''What made you bring with you so useless a weapon?'' he exclaimed. ''It was needlessly hampering yourself.''

''I bring it?—it is quite new to me. I never saw it before—are you sure it is not out of your collection?''

''Not that I know of,'' said the Professor, puzzled. ''I have no recollection of the circumstance. It was never my property.''

''This is very extraordinary,'' I said, musing over the novel and singular incident.

''Not at all. There is a very simple explanation, Harry. The Icelanders are known to keep up the use of these antiquated weapons, and this must have belonged to Hans, who has let it fall without knowing it.''

I shook my head. That dagger had never been in the possession of the pacific and taciturn Hans. I knew him and his habits too well.

''Then what can it be—unless it be the weapon of some antediluvian warrior,'' I continued, ''of some living man, a contemporary of that mighty shepherd from whom we have just escaped? But no—mystery upon mystery—this is no weapon of the stony epoch, nor even of the bronze period. It is made of excellent steel——''

Ere I could finish my sentence, my uncle stopped me short from entering upon a whole train of theories, and spoke in his most cold and decided tone of voice.

''Calm yourself, my dear boy, and endeavour to use your reason. This weapon, upon which we have fallen so unexpectedly, is a true *dague,* one of those worn by gentlemen in their belts during the sixteenth century. Its use was to give the *coup de grâce,* the final blow, to the foe who would not surrender. It is clearly of Spanish workmanship. It belongs neither to you, nor to me, nor the eider-down hunter, nor to any of the living beings who may still exist so marvellously in the interior of the earth.''

''What can you mean, uncle?'' I said, now lost in a host of surmises.

''Look closely at it,'' he continued; these jagged edges were never made by the resistance of human blood and bone. The blade is covered with a regular coating of iron-mould and rust, which is not a day old, not a year old, not a century old, but much more——''

The Professor began to get quite excited, according to custom, and was allowing himself to be carried away by his fertile imagination. I could have said something. He stopped me.

"Harry," he cried, "we are now on the verge of a great discovery. This blade of a dagger you have so marvellously discovered, after being abandoned upon the sand for more than a hundred, two hundred, even three hundred years, has been indented by some one endeavouring to carve an inscription on these rocks."

"But this poignard never got here of itself," I exclaimed, "it could not have twisted itself. Some one, therefore, must have preceded us upon the shores of this extraordinary sea."

"Yes, a man."

"But what man has been sufficiently desperate to do such a thing."

"A man who has somewhere written his name with this very dagger—a man who had endeavoured once more to indicate the right road to the interior of the earth. Let us look around, my boy. You know not the importance of your singular and happy discovery."

Prodigiously interested, we walked along the wall of rock, examining the smallest fissures, which might finally expand into the much wished for gully or shaft.

We at last reached a spot where the shore became extremely narrow. The sea almost bathed the foot of the rocks, which were here very lofty and steep. There was scarcely a path wider than two yards at any point. At last, under a huge overhanging rock, we discovered the entrance of a dark and gloomy tunnel.

There, on a square tablet of granite, which had been smoothed by rubbing it with another stone, we could see two mysterious, and much worn letters, the two initials of the bold and extraordinary traveller who had preceded us on our adventurous journey.

'A. S.," cried my uncle; "you see I was right. Arne Saknussemm, always Arne Saknussemm!"

CHAPTER 38

NO OUTLET—BLASTING THE ROCK

EVER since the commencement of our marvellous journey, I had experienced many surprises, had suffered from many illusions. I thought that I was case-hardened against all surprises and could neither see nor hear anything to amaze me again.

I was like a man who, having been round the world, finds himself wholly *blasé* and proof against the marvellous.

When, however, I saw these two letters, which had been engraven three hundred years before, I stood fixed in an attitude of mute surprise.

Not only was there the signature of the learned and enterprising alchemist written in the rock, but I held in my hand the very identical instrument with which he had laboriously engraved it.

It was impossible, without showing an amount of incredulity scarcely becoming a sane man, to deny the existence of the traveller, and the reality of that voyage which I believed all along to have been a myth—the mystification of some fertile brain.

While these reflections were passing through my mind, my uncle, the Professor, gave way to an access of feverish and poetical excitement.

"Wonderful and glorious Genius, great Saknussemm," he cried, "you have left no stone unturned, no resource omitted, to show to other mortals the way into the interior of our mighty globe, and your fellow creatures can find the trail left by your illustrious footsteps, three hundred years ago, at the bottom of these obscure subterranean abodes. You have been careful to secure for others the contemplation of these wonders and marvels of creation. Your name engraved at every important stage of your glorious journey, leads the hopeful traveller direct to the great and mighty discovery to which you devoted such energy and courage. The audacious traveller, who shall follow your footsteps to the last, will doubtless find your initials engraved with your own hand upon the centre of the earth. *I* will be that audacious traveller—*I,* too, will sign my name upon the very same spot, upon the central granite stone of this wondrous work of the Creator. But in justice to your devotion, to your courage, and to your being the first to indicate the road, let this Cape, seen by you upon the shores of this sea discovered by you, be called of all time, Cape Saknussemm."

This is what I heard, and I began to be roused to the pitch of enthusiasm indicated by those words. A fierce excitement roused me. I forgot everything. The dangers of the voyage, and the perils of the return journey, were now as nothing!

What another man had done in ages past, could I felt be done again; I was determined to do it myself, and now nothing that man had accomplished appeared to me impossible.

"Forward—forward," I cried in a burst of genuine and hearty enthusiasm.

I had already started in the direction of the sombre and gloomy gallery, when the Professor stopped me; he, the man so rash and hasty, he, the man so easily roused to the highest pitch of enthusiasm, checked me, and asked me to be patient and show more calm.

"Let us return to our good friend, Hans," he said; "we will then bring the raft down to this place."

I must say that though I at once yielded to my uncle's request, it was not without dissatisfaction, and I hastened along the rocks of that wonderful coast.

"Do you know, my dear uncle," I said, as we walked along, "that we have been singularly helped by a concurrence of circumstances, right up to this very moment?"

"So you begin to see it, do you, Harry?" said the Professor, with a smile.

"Doubtless," I responded, "and strangely enough, even the tempest has been the means of putting us on the right road. Blessings on the tempest! It brought us safely back to the very spot from which fine weather would have driven us for ever. Supposing we had succeeded in reaching the southern and distant shores of this extraordinary sea, what would have become of us? The name of Saknussemm would never have appeared to us, and at this moment we should have been cast away upon an inhospitable coast, probably without an outlet.''

''Yes, Harry, my boy, there is certainly something providential in that wandering at the mercy of wind and waves towards the south: we have come back exactly north; and what is better still, we fall upon this great discovery of Cape Saknussemm. I mean to say, that it is more than surprising; there is something in it which is far beyond my comprehension. The coincidence is unheard of, marvellous!''

''What matter! It is not our duty to explain facts, but to make the best possible use of them.''

''Doubtless, my boy; but if you will allow me——'' said the really-delighted Professor.

''Excuse me, sir, but I see exactly how it will be; we shall take the northern route; we shall pass under the northern regions of Europe, under Sweden, under Russia, under Siberia, and who knows where—instead of burying ourselves under the burning plains and deserts of Africa, or beneath the mighty waves of the ocean; and that is all, at this stage of our journey, that I care to know. Let us advance, and Heaven will be our guide!''

''Yes, Harry, you are right, quite right; all is for the best. Let us abandon this horizontal sea, which could never have led to anything satisfactory. We shall descend, descend, and everlastingly descend. Do you know, my dear boy, that to reach the interior of the earth we have only five thousand miles to travel!''

''Bah!'' I cried, carried away by a burst of enthusiasm, ''the distance is scarcely worth speaking about. The thing is to make a start.''

My wild, mad, and incoherent speeches continued until we rejoined our patient and phlegmatic guide. All was, we found, prepared for an immediate departure. There was not a single parcel but what was in its proper place. We all took up our posts on the raft, and the sail being hoisted, Hans received his directions, and guided the frail barque towards Cape Saknussemm, as we had definitely named it.

The wind was very unfavourable to a craft that was unable to sail close to the wind. It was constructed to go before the blast. We were continually reduced to pushing ourselves forward by means of poles. On several occasions the rocks ran far out into deep water and we were compelled to make a long round. At last, after three long and weary hours of navigation, that is to say, about six o'clock in the evening, we found a place at which we could land.

I jumped on shore first. In my present state of excitement and enthusiasm, I was always first. My uncle and the Icelander followed. The voyage from the port to this point of the sea had by no means calmed me. I had rather produced the opposite effect. I even proposed to burn our vessel, that is to destroy our raft, in order to completely cut off our retreat. But my uncle sternly opposed this wild project. I began to think him particularly lukewarm and unenthusiastic.

''At any rate, my dear uncle,'' I said, ''let us start without delay.''

''Yes, my boy, I am quite as eager to do so as you can be. But, in the first place, let us examine this mysterious gallery, in order to find if we shall need to prepare and mend our ladders.''

My uncle now began to see to the efficiency of our Ruhmkorff's coil, which would doubtless soon be needed; the raft, securely fastened to a rock, was left alone. Moreover, the opening into the new gallery was not twenty paces distant from the spot. Our little troop, with myself at the head, advanced.

The orifice, which was almost circular, presented a diameter of about five feet; the sombre tunnel was cut in the living rock, and coated on the inside by the different material which had once passed through it in a state of fusion. The lower part was above level with the water, so that we were able to penetrate to the interior without difficulty.

We followed an almost horizontal direction; when, at the end of about a dozen paces, our further advance was checked by the interposition of an enormous block of granite rock.

"Accursed stone!" I cried, furiously, on perceiving that we were stopped by what seemed an insurmountable obstacle.

In vain we looked to the right, in vain we looked to the left; in vain examined it above and below. There existed no passage, no sign of any other tunnel. I experienced the most bitter and painful disappointment. So enraged was I that I would not admit the reality of any obstacle. I stooped to my knees; I looked under the mass of stone. No hole, no interstice. I then looked above. The same barrier of granite! Hans, with the lamp, examined the sides of the tunnel in every direction. But all in vain! It was necessary to renounce all hope of passing through.

I had seated myself upon the ground. My uncle walked angrily and hopelessly up and down. He was evidently desperate.

"But," I cried after some moments' thought, "what about Arne Saknussemm?"

"You are right," replied my uncle, "he can never have been checked by a lump of rock."

"No—ten thousand times, no," I cried with extreme vivacity. "This huge lump of rock, in consequence of some singular concussion, or process, one of those magnetic phenomena which have so often shaken the terrestrial crust, has in some unexpected way closed up the passage. Many and many years have passed away since the return of Saknussemm, and the fall of this huge block of granite. Is it not quite evident that this gallery was formerly the outlet for the pent-up lava in the interior of the earth, and that these eruptive matters then circulated freely? Look at these recent fissures in the granite roof; it is evidently formed of pieces of enormous stone, placed here as if by the hand of a giant, who had worked to make a strong and substantial arch. One day, after an unusually strong shock, the vast rock which stands in our way, and which was doubtless the key of a kind of arch, fell through to a level with the soil and has barred our further progress. We are right, then, in thinking that this is an unexpected obstacle, with which Saknussemm did not meet; and if we do not upset it in some way, we are unworthy of following in the footsteps of the great discoverer; and incapable of finding our way to the Centre of the Earth!"

In this wild way I addressed my uncle. The zeal of the Professor, his earnest longing for success, had become part and parcel of my being. I wholly forgot the past; I utterly despised the future. Nothing existed for me upon the surface of this spheroid in the bosom of which I was engulphed, no towns, no country, no Hamburg, no König-strasse, not even my poor Gretchen, who by this time would believe me utterly lost in the interior of the earth!

"Well," cried my uncle, roused to enthusiasm by my words, "let us go to work with pickaxes, with crowbars, with anything that comes to hand—but down with these terrible walls."

"It is far too tough and too big to be destroyed by a pickaxe or crowbar," I replied.

"What then?"

"As I said, it is useless to think of overcoming such a difficulty by means of ordinary tools."

"What then?"

"What else but gunpowder, a subterranean mine? Let us blow up the obstacle that stands in our way."

"Gunpowder!"

"Yes; all we have to do is to get rid of this paltry obstacle."

"To work, Hans, to work!" cried the Professor.

The Icelander went back to the raft, and soon returned with a huge crowbar, with which he began to dig a hole in the rock, which was to serve as a mine. It was by no means a slight task. It was necessary for our purpose to make a cavity large enough to hold fifty pounds of fulminating gun cotton, the expansive power of which is four times as great as that of ordinary gunpowder.

I had now roused myself to an almost mircaculous state of excitement. While Hans was at work, I actively assisted my uncle to prepare a long wick, made from damp gunpowder, the mass of which we finally enclosed in a bag of linen.

"We are bound to go through," I cried, enthusiastically.

"We are bound to go through," responded the Professor, tapping me on the back.

At midnight, our work as miners was completely finished; the charge of fulminating cotton was thrust into the hollow, and the match, which we had made of considerable length, was ready.

A spark was now sufficient to ignite this formidable engine, and to blow the rock to atoms!

"We will now rest until to-morrow."

It was absolutely necessary to resign myself to my fate, and to consent to wait for the explosion for six weary hours!

CHAPTER 39

THE EXPLOSION AND ITS RESULTS

THE next day, which was the twenty-seventh of August, was a date celebrated in our wondrous, subterranean journey.

I never think of it even now, but I shudder with horror. My heart beats wildly at the very memory of that awful day.

From this time forward, our reason, our judgment, our human ingenuity, have nothing to do with the course of events. We are about to become the plaything of the great phenomena of the earth!

At six o'clock we were all up and ready. The dreaded moment was arriving when we were about to seek an opening into the interior of the earth by means of gunpowder. What would be the consequences of breaking through the crust of the earth?

I begged that it might be my duty to set fire to the mine. I looked upon it as an honour. This task once performed, I could rejoin my friends upon the raft, which had not been unloaded. As soon as we were all ready, we were to sail away to some distance to avoid the consequences of the explosion, the effects of which would certainly not be concentrated in the interior of the earth.

The slow match we calculated to burn for about ten minutes, more or less, before it reached the chamber in which the great body of powder was confined. I should therefore have plenty of time to reach the raft and put off to a safe distance.

I prepared to execute my self-allotted task—not, it must be confessed, without considerable emotion.

After a hearty repast, my uncle and the hunter-guide embarked on board the raft, while I remained alone upon the desolate shore.

I was provided with a lantern which was to enable me to set fire to the wick of the infernal machine.

"Go, my boy," said my uncle, "and Heaven be with you. But come back as soon as you can. I shall be all impatience."

"Be easy on that matter," I replied, "there is no fear of my delaying on the road."

Having said this, I advanced towards the opening of the sombre gallery. My heart beat wildly. I opened my lantern and seized the extremity of the wick.

The Professor, who was looking on, held his chronometer in his hand.

"Are you ready?" cried he.

"Quite ready."

"Well, then, fire away!"

I hastened to put the light to the wick, which crackled and sparkled, hissing and spitting like a serpent; then, running as fast as I could, I returned to the shore.

"Get on board my lad, and you, Hans, shove off," cried my uncle.

By a vigorous application of his pole Hans sent us flying over the water. The raft was quite twenty fathoms distant.

It was a moment of palpitating interest, of deep anxiety. My uncle, the Professor, never took his eyes off the chronometer.

"Only five minutes more," he said, in a low tone, "only four, only three."

My pulse went a hundred to the minute. I could hear my heart beating.

"Only two, one! Now, then, mountains of granite, crumble beneath the power of man!"

What happened after that? As to the terrific roar of the explosion, I do not think I heard it. But the form of the rocks completely changed in my eyes—they seemed to be drawn aside like a curtain. I saw a fathomless, a bottomless abyss, which yawned beneath the turgid waves. The sea, which seemed suddenly to have gone mad, then became one great mountainous mass, upon the top of which the raft rose perpendicularly.

We were all thrown down. In less than a second the light gave place to the most profound obscurity. Then I felt all solid support give way, not to my feet, but the raft itself, I thought it was going bodily down a tremendous well. I tried to speak, to question my uncle. Nothing could be heard but the roaring of the mighty waves. We clung together in utter silence.

Despite the awful darkness, despite the noise, the surprise, the emotion, I thoroughly understood what had happened.

Beyond the rock which had been blown up, there existed a mighty abyss. The explosion had caused a kind of earthquake in this soil, broken by fissures and rents. The gulf, thus suddenly thrown open, was about to swallow the inland sea, which, transformed into a mighty torrent, was dragging us with it.

One only idea filled my mind. We were utterly and completely lost!

One hour, two hours—what more I cannot say, passed in this manner. We sat close together, elbow touching elbow, knee touching knee! We held one another's hands not to be thrown off the raft. We were subjected to the most violent shocks, whenever our sole dependence, a frail wooden raft struck against the rocky sides of the channel. Fortunately for us, these concussions became less and less frequent, which made me fancy that the gallery was getting wider and wider. There could be now no doubt that we had chanced upon the road once followed by Saknussemm, but instead of going down in a proper manner, we had, through our own imprudence, drawn a whole sea with us!

These ideas presented themselves to my mind in a very vague and obscure manner. I felt rather than reasoned. I put my ideas together only confusedly, while spinning along like a man going down a waterfall. To judge by the air which, as it were, whipped my face, we must have been rushing at a perfectly lightning rate.

To attempt under these circumstances to light a torch was simply impossible, and the last remains of our electric machine, of our Ruhmkorff's coil, had been destroyed during the fearful explosion.

I was therefore very much confused to see at last a bright light shining close to me. The calm countenance of the guide seemed to gleam upon me. The clever and patient hunter had succeeded in lighting the lantern; and though, in the keen and thorough draught, the flame flickered and vacillated and was nearly put out, it served partially to dissipate the awful obscurity.

The gallery into which we had entered was very wide. I was, therefore, quite right in that part of my conjecture. The insufficient light did not allow us to see both of the walls at the same time. The slope of waters, which was carrying us away, was far greater than that of the most rapid river of America. The whole surface of the stream seemed to be composed of liquid arrows, darted forward with extreme violence and power. I can give no idea of the impression it made upon me.

The raft, at times, caught in certain whirlpools, and rushed forward, yet turned on itself all the time. How it did not upset I shall never be able to understand. When it approached the sides of the gallery, I took care to throw upon them the light of the lantern, and I was able to judge of the rapidity of motion by looking at the projecting masses of rock, which as soon as seen were again invisible. So rapid was our progress, the points of rock, at a considerable distance one from the other, appeared like portions of transverse lines, which enclosed us in a kind of net, like that of a line of telegraphic wires.

I believe we were now going at a rate of not less than a hundred miles an hour.

My uncle and I looked at one another with wild and haggard eyes; we clung convulsively to the stump of the mast, which, at the moment when the catastrophe took place, had snapped short off. We turned our backs as much as possible to the wind, in order not to be stifled by a rapidity of motion which nothing human could face and live.

And still the long monotonous hours went on. The situation did not change in the least, though a discovery I suddenly made seemed to complicate it very much.

When we had slightly recovered our equilibrium, I proceeded to examine our cargo. I then made the unsatisfactory discovery that the greater part of it had utterly disappeared.

I became alarmed, and determined to discover what were our resources. My heart beat at the idea, but it was absolutely necessary to know on what we had to depend. With this view, I took the lantern and looked around.

Of all our former collection of nautical and philosophical instruments there remained only the chronometer and the compass. The ladders and ropes were reduced to a small piece of rope fastened to the stump of the mast. Not a pickaxe, not a crowbar, not a hammer, and, far worse than all, no food—not enough for one day!

This discovery was a prelude to a certain and horrible death.

Seated gloomily on the raft, clasping the stump of the mast mechanically, I thought of all I had read as to sufferings from starvation.

I remembered everything that history had taught me on the subject, and I shuddered at the remembrance of the agonies to be endured.

Maddened at the prospect of enduring the miseries of starvation, I persuaded myself that I must be mistaken. I examined the cracks in the raft; I poked between the joints and beams; I examined every possible hole and corner. The result was—simply nothing!

Our stock of provisions consisted of nothing but a piece of dry meat and some soaked and half-mouldy biscuits.

I gazed around me scared and frightened. I could not understand the awful truth. And yet of what consequence was it in regard to any new danger? Supposing that we had had provisions for months, and even for years, how could we ever get out of the awful abyss into which we were being hurled by the irresistible torrent we had let loose?

Why should we trouble ourselves about the sufferings and tortures to be endured from hunger, when death stared us in the face under so many other swifter and perhaps even more horrid forms?

It was very doubtful, under the circumstances in which we were placed, if we should have time to die of inanition.

But the human frame is singularly constituted.

I knew not how it was; but, from some singular hallucination of the mind, I forgot the real, serious and immediate danger to which we were exposed, to think of the menaces of the future, which appeared before us in all their naked terror. Besides, after all, suggested Hope, perhaps we might finally escape the fury of the raging torrent, and once more revisit the glimpses of the moon, on the surface of our beautiful mother earth.

How was it to be done? I had not the remotest idea. Where were we to come out? No matter, so that we did.

One chance in a thousand is always a chance, while death from hunger gave us not even the faintest glimpse of hope. It left to the imagination nothing but blank horror, without the faintest chance of escape!

I had the greatest mind to reveal all to my uncle, to explain to him the extraordinary and wretched position to which we were reduced, in order that, between the two, we might make a calculation as to the exact space of time which remained for us to live.

It was, it appeared to me, the only thing to be done. But I had the courage to hold my tongue, to gnaw at my entrails like the Spartan boy. I wished to leave him all his coolness.

At this moment, the light of the lantern slowly fell, and at last went out!

The wick had wholly burnt to an end. The obscurity became absolute. It was no longer possible to see through the impenetrable darkness! There was one torch left, but it was impossible to keep it alight. Then, like a child, I shut my eyes, that I might not see the darkness.

After a great lapse of time, the rapidity of our journey increased. I could feel it by the rush of air upon my face. The slope of the waters was excessive. I began to feel that we were no longer going down a slope; we were falling. I felt as one does in a dream, going down bodily—falling; falling; falling!

I felt that the hands of my uncle and Hans were vigorously clasping my arms.

Suddenly, after a lapse of time scarcely appreciable, I felt something like a shock. The raft had not struck a hard body, but had suddenly been checked in its course. A waterspout, a liquid column of water, fell upon us. I felt suffocating. I was being drowned.

Still the sudden inundation did not last. In a few seconds I felt myself once more able to breathe. My uncle and Hans pressed my arms, and the raft carried us all three away.

CHAPTER 40

THE APE GIGANS

It is difficult for me to determine what was the real time, but I should suppose, by after calculation, that it must have been ten at night.

I lay in a stupor, a half dream, during which I saw visions of astounding character. Monsters of the deep were side by side with the mighty elephantine shepherd. Gigantic fish and animals seemed to form strange conjunctions.

The raft took a sudden turn, whirled round; entered another tunnel; this time illumined in a most singular manner. The roof was formed of porous stalactite, through which a moon-lit vapour appeared to pass, casting its brilliant light upon our gaunt and haggard figures. The light increased as we advanced, while the roof ascended; until at last, we were once more in a kind of water cavern, the lofty dome of which disappeared in a luminous cloud!

A rugged cavern of small extent appeared to offer a halting place to our weary bodies.

My uncle and the guide moved as men in a dream. I was afraid to waken them, knowing the danger of such a sudden start. I seated myself beside them to watch.

As I did so, I became aware of something moving in the distance, which at once fascinated my eyes. It was floating, apparently, upon the surface of the water, advancing by means of what at first appeared paddles. I looked with glaring eyes. One glance told me that it was something monstrous.

But what?

It was the great *Shark Crocodile* of the early writers on geology. About the size of an ordinary whale, with hideous jaws and two gigantic eyes, it advanced. Its eyes fixed on me with terrible sternness. Some indefinite warning told me that it had marked me for its own.

I attempted to rise—to escape, no matter where, but my knees shook under me; my limbs trembled violenty; I almost lost my senses. And still the mighty monster advanced. My uncle and the guide made no effort to save themselves.

With a strange noise, like none other I had ever heard, the beast came on. His jaws were at least seven feet apart, and his distended mouth looked large enough to have swallowed a boatful of men.

We were about ten feet distant, when I discovered that much as his body resembled that of a crocodile, his mouth was wholly that of a shark.

His twofold nature now became apparent. To snatch us up at a mouthful it was necessary for him to turn on his back, which motion necessarily caused his legs to kick up helplessly in the air.

I actually laughed even in the very jaws of death!

But next minute, with a wild cry, I darted away into the interior of the cavern, leaving my unhappy comrades to their fate! This cavern was deep and dreary. After about a hundred yards, I paused and looked around.

The whole floor, composed of sand and malachite, was strewn with bones, freshly-gnawed bones of reptiles and fish, with a mixture of mammalia. My very soul grew sick as my body shuddered with horror. I had truly, according to the old proverb, fallen out of the frying-pan into the fire. Some beast larger and more ferocious even than the Shark-Crocodile inhabited this den.

What could I do? The mouth of the cave was guarded by one ferocious monster, the interior was inhabited by something too hideous to contemplate. Flight was impossible!

One only resource remained, and that was to find some small hiding place to which the fearful denizen of the cavern could not penetrate. I gazed wildly around, and at last discovered a fissure in the rock, to which I rushed in the hope of recovering my scattered senses.

Crouching down, I waited shivering as in an ague fit. No man is brave in presence of an earthquake, or a bursting boiler, or an exploding torpedo. I could not be expected to feel much courage in presence of the fearful fate that appeared to await me.

An hour passed. I heard all the time a strange rumbling outside the cave.

What was the fate of my unhappy companions? It was impossible for me to pause to inquire. My own wretched existence was all I could think of.

Suddenly a groaning, as of fifty bears in a fight, fell upon my ears—hisses, spitting, moaning, hideous to hear—and then I saw—

Never, were ages to pass over my head, shall I forget the horrible apparition.

It was the Ape Gigans!

Fourteen feet high, covered with coarse hair, of a blackish brown, the hair on the arms, from the shoulder to the elbow joints, pointing downwards, while that from the wrist to the elbow pointed upwards, it advanced. Its arms were as long as its body, while its legs were prodigious. It had thick, long, and sharply-pointed teeth—like a mammoth saw.

It struck its breast as it came on smelling and sniffing, reminding me of the stories we read in our early childhood of giants who ate the flesh of men and little boys!

Suddenly it stopped. My heart beat wildly, for I was conscious that, somehow or other, the fearful monster had smelt me out and was peering about with his hideous eyes to try and discover my whereabouts.

My reading, which as a rule is a blessing, but which on this occasion, seemed momentarily to prove a curse, told me the real truth. It was the Ape Gigans, the Antediluvian Gorilla.

Yes! This awful monster, confined by good fortune to the interior of the earth, was the progenitor of the hideous monster of Africa.

He glared wildly about, seeking something—doubtless myself. I gave myself up for lost. No hope of safety or escape seemed to remain.

At this moment, just as my eyes appeared to close in death, there came a strange noise from the entrance of the cave; and turning, the Gorilla evidently recognised some enemy more worthy his prodigious size and strength. It was the huge Shark-Crocodile, which perhaps having disposed of my friends, was coming in search of further prey.

The Gorilla placed himself on the defensive, and clutching a bone some seven or eight feet in length, a perfect club, aimed a deadly blow at the hideous beast, which reared upwards and fell with all its weight upon its adversary.

A terrible combat, the details of which it is impossible to give, now ensued. The struggle was awful and ferocious. I, however, did not wait to witness the result. Regarding myself as the object of contention, I determined to remove from the presence of the victor. I slid down from my hiding-place, reached the ground, and gliding against the wall, strove to gain the open mouth of the cavern.

But I had not taken many steps when the fearful clamour ceased, to be followed by a mumbling and groaning which appeared to be indicative of victory.

I looked back and saw the huge ape, gory with blood, coming after me with glaring eyes, with dilated nostrils that gave forth two columns of heated vapour. I could feel his hot and fetid breath on my neck; and with a horrid jump—awoke from my nightmare sleep.

Yes—it was all a dream. I was still on the raft with my uncle and the guide.

The relief was not instantaneous, for under the influence of the hideous nightmare my senses had become numbed. After a while, however, my feelings were tranquillised. The first of my perceptions which returned in full force was that of hearing. I listened with acute and attentive ears. All was still as death. All I comprehended was silence. To the roaring of the waters, which had filled the gallery with awful reverberations, succeeded perfect peace.

After some little time my uncle spoke, in a low and scarcely audible tone—

"Harry, boy, where are you?"

"I am here," was my faint rejoinder.

"Well, don't you see what has happened? We are going upwards."

"My dear uncle, what can you mean?" was my half delirious reply.

"Yes, I tell you we are ascending rapidly. Our downward journey is quite checked."

I held out my hand, and, after some little difficulty, succeeded in touching the wall. My hand was in an instant covered with blood. The skin was torn from the flesh. We were ascending with extraordinary rapidity.

"The torch—the torch!" cried the Professor, wildly; "it must be lighted."

Hans, the guide, after many vain efforts, at last succeeded in lighting it, and the flame having now nothing to prevent its burning, shed a tolerably clear light. We were enabled to form an approximate idea of the truth.

"It is just as I thought," said my uncle, after a moment or two of silent attention. "We are in a narrow well about four fathoms square. The waters of the great inland sea, having reached the bottom of the gulf, are now forcing themselves up the mighty shaft. As a natural consequence, we are being cast up on the summit of the waters."

"That I can see," was my lugubrious reply; "but where will this shaft end, and to what fall are we likely to be exposed?"

"Of that I am as ignorant as yourself. All I know is, that we should be prepared for the worst. We are going up at a fearfully rapid rate. As far as I can judge, we are ascending at the rate of two fathoms a second, of a hundred and twenty fathoms a minute, or rather more than three and a-half leagues an hour. At this rate, our fate will soon be a matter of certainty."

"No doubt of it," was my reply. "The great concern I have now, however, is to know whether this shaft has any issue. It may end in a granite roof—in which case we shall be suffocated by compressed air, or dashed to atoms against the top. I fancy, already, that the air is beginning to be close and condensed. I have a difficulty in breathing."

This might be fancy, or it might be the effect of our rapid motion, but I certainly felt a great oppression of the chest.

"Henry," said the Professor, "I do believe that the situation is to a certain extent desperate. There remain, however, many chances of ultimate safety, and I have, in my own mind, been revolving them over, during your heavy but agitated sleep. I have come to this logical conclusion—whereas we may at any moment perish, so at any moment we may be saved! We need, therefore, prepare ourselves for whatever may turn up in the great chapter of accidents."

"But what would you have us do?" I cried; "are we not utterly helpless?"

"No! While there is life there is hope. At all events, there is one thing we can do—eat, and thus obtain strength to face victory or death."

As he spoke, I looked at my uncle with a haggard glance. I had put off the fatal communication as long as possible. It was now forced upon me, and I must tell him the truth. Still I hesitated.

"Eat," I said, in a deprecating tone as if there were no hurry.

"Yes, and at once. I feel like a starving prisoner," he said, rubbing his yellow and shivering hands together.

And, turning round to the guide, he spoke some hearty, cheering words, as I judged from his tone, in Danish. Hans shook his head in a terribly significant manner. I tried to look unconcerned.

"What!" cried the Professor, "you do not mean to say that all our provisions are lost?"

"Yes," was my lowly-spoken reply, as I held out something in my hand, "this morsel of dried meat is all that remains for us three."

My uncle gazed at me as if he could not fully appreciate the meaning of my words. The blow seemed to stun him by its severity. I allowed him to reflect for some moments.

"Well," said I, after a short pause, "what do you think now? Is there any chance of our escaping from our horrible subterranean dangers? Are we not doomed to perish in the great hollows of the Centre of the Earth?"

But my pertinent questions brought no answer. My uncle either heard me not, or appeared not to do so.

And in this way a whole hour passed. Neither of us cared to speak. For myself, I began to feel the most fearful and devouring hunger. My companions, doubtless, felt the same horrible tortures, but neither of them would touch the wretched morsel of meat that remained. It lay there, a last remnant of all our great preparations for the mad and senseless journey!

I looked back, with wonderment, to my own folly. Fully was I aware that, despite his enthusiasm, and the ever-to-be-hated scroll of Saknussemm, my uncle should never have started on his perilous voyage. What memories of the happy past, what previsions of the horrible future, now filled my brain!

CHAPTER 41

HUNGER

HUNGER, prolonged, is temporary madness!

The brain is at work without its required food, and the most fantastic notions fill the mind. Hitherto I had never known what hunger really meant. I was likely to understand it now.

And yet, three months before I could tell my terrible story of starvation, as I thought it. As a boy I used to make frequent excursions in the neighbourhood of the Professor's house.

My uncle always acted on system, and he believed that, in addition to the day of rest and worship, there should be a day of recreation. In consequence, I was always free to do as I liked on a Wednesday.

Now, as I had a notion to combine the useful and the agreeable, my favourite pastime was birds' nesting. I had one of the best collections of eggs in all the town. They were classified, and under glass cases.

There was a certain wood, which, by rising at early morn, and taking the cheap train, I could reach at eleven in the morning. Here I would botanise or geologise at my will. My uncle was always glad of specimens for his herbarium, and stones to examine. When I had filled my wallet, I proceeded to search for nests.

After about two hours of hard work, I, one day, sat down by a stream to eat my humble but copious lunch. How the remembrance of the spiced sausage, the wheaten loaf, and the beer, made my mouth water now! I would have given every prospect of worldly wealth for such a meal. But to my story.

While seated thus at my leisure, I looked up at the ruins of an old castle, at no great distance. It was the remains of an historical dwelling, ivy clad, and now falling to pieces.

While looking, I saw two eagles circling about the summit of a lofty tower.

I soon became satisfied that there was a nest. Now, in all my collection, I wanted eggs of the native eagle and the large owl.

My mind was made up. I would reach the summit of that tower, or perish in the attempt. I went nearer, and surveyed the ruins. The old staircase, years before, had fallen in. The outer walls were, however, intact. There was no chance that way, unless I looked to the ivy solely for support. This was, as I soon found out, futile.

There remained the chimney, which still went up to the top, and had once served to carry off the smoke from every story of the tower.

Up this I determined to venture. It was narrow, rough, and therefore the more easily climbed. I took off my coat and crept into the chimney. Looking up, I saw a small, light opening, proclaiming the summit of the chimney.

Up—up I went, for some time using my hands and knees, after the fashion of a chimney sweep. It was slow work, but, there being continual projections, the task was comparatively easy. In this way, I reached half way. The chimney now became narrower. The atmosphere was close, and, at last, to end the matter, I stuck fast. I could ascend no higher.

There could be no doubt of this, and there remained no resource but to descend, and give up my glorious prey in despair. I yielded to fate and endeavoured to descend. But I could not move. Some unseen and mysterious obstacle intervened and stopped me. In an instant the full horror of my situation seized me.

I was unable to move either way, and was doomed to a terrible and horrible death, that of starvation. In a boy's mind, however, there is an extraordinary amount of elasticity and hope, and I began to think of all sorts of plans to escape my gloomy fate.

In the first place, I required no food just at present, having had an excellent meal, and was therefore allowed time for reflection. My first thought was to try and move the mortar with my hand. Had I possessed a knife, something might have been done, but that useful instrument I had left in my coat pocket.

I soon found that all efforts of this kind were vain and useless, and that all I could hope to do was to wriggle downwards.

But though I jerked and struggled, and strove to turn, it was all in vain. I could not move an inch, one way or the other. And time flew rapidly. My early rising probably contributed to the fact that I felt sleepy, and gradually gave way to the sensation of drowsiness.

I slept, and awoke in darkness, ravenously hungry.

Night had come, and still I could not move. I was tight bound, and did not succeed in changing my position an inch. I groaned aloud. Never since the days of my happy childhood, when it was a hardship to go from meal to meal without eating, had I really experienced hunger. The sensation was as novel as it was painful. I began now to lose my head and to scream and cry out in my agony. Something appeared, startled by my noise. It was a harmless lizard, but it appeared to me a loathsome reptile. Again I made the old ruins resound with my cries, and finally so exhausted myself that I fainted.

How long I lay in a kind of trance or sleep I cannot say, but when again I recovered consciousness it was day. How ill I felt, how hunger still gnawed at me, it would be hard to say. I was too weak to scream now, far too weak to struggle.

Suddenly I was startled by a roar.

"Are you there, Henry?" said the voice of my uncle; "are you there, my boy?"

I could only faintly respond, but I also made a desperate effort to turn. Some mortar fell. To this I owed my being discovered. When the search took place, it was easily seen that mortar and small pieces of stone had recently fallen from above. Hence my uncle's cry.

"Be calm," he cried, "if we pull down the whole ruin, you shall be saved."

They were delicious words, but I had little hope.

Soon however, about a quarter of an hour later, I heard a voice *above me,* at one of the upper fireplaces.

"Are you below, or above?"

"Below," was my reply.

In an instant a basket was lowered with milk, a biscuit, and an egg. My uncle was fearful to be too ready with his supply of food. I drank the milk first, for thirst had nearly deadened hunger. I then, much refreshed, ate my bread and hard egg.

They were now at work at the wall, I could hear a pickaxe. Wishing to escape all danger from this terrible weapon I made a desperate struggle, and the belt, which surrounded my waist and which had been hitched on a stone, gave way. I was free, and only escaped falling down by a rapid motion of my hands and knees.

In ten minutes more I was in my uncle's arms, after being two days and nights in that horrible prison. My occasional delirium prevented me from counting time.

I was weeks recovering from that awful starvation adventure; and yet what was that to the hideous sufferings I now endured?

After dreaming for some time, and thinking of this and other matters, I once more looked around me. We were still ascending with fearful rapidity. Every now and then the air appeared to check our respiration as it does that of aëronauts when the ascension of the balloon is too rapid. But if they feel a degree of cold in proportion to the elevation they attain in the atmosphere, we experienced quite a contrary effect. The heat began to increase in a most threatening and exceptional manner. I cannot tell exactly the mean, but I think it must have reached 122 degrees of Fahrenheit.

What was the meaning of this extraordinary change in the temperature? As far as we had hitherto gone, facts had proved the theories of Davy and of Lidenbrock to be correct. Until now, all the peculiar conditions of refractory rocks, of electricity of magnetism, had modified the general laws of nature, and had created for us a moderate temperature; for the theory of the central fire, remained, in my eyes, the only explainable one.

Were we, then, going to reach a position in which these phenomena were to be carried out in all their rigour, and in which the heat would reduce the rocks to a state of fusion?

Such was my not unnatural fear, and I did not conceal the fact from my uncle. My way of doing so might be cold and heartless, but I could not help it.

"If we are not drowned, or smashed into pancakes, and if we do not die of starvation, we have the satisfaction of knowing that we must be burned alive."

My uncle, in presence of this brusque attack, simply shrugged his shoulders, and resumed his reflections—whatever they might be.

An hour passed away, and except that there was a slight increase in the temperature, no incident modifed the situation. My uncle at last, of his own accord, broke silence.

"Well Henry my boy," he said, in a cheerful way, "we must make up our minds."

"Make up our minds to what?" I asked, in considerable surprise.

"Well—to something. We must at whatever risk recruit our physical strength. If we make the fatal mistake of husbanding our little remnant of food, we may probably prolong our wretched existence a few hours—but we shall remain weak to the end."

"Yes," I growled, "to the end. That, however, will not keep us long waiting."

"Well, only let a chance of safety present itself,—only allow that a moment of action be necessary,—where shall we find the means of action if we allow ourselves to be reduced to physical weakness by inanition?"

"When this piece of meat is devoured, uncle, what hope will there remain unto us?"

"None, my dear Henry, none. But will it do you any good to devour it with your eyes? You appear to me to reason like one without will or decision, like a being without energy."

"Then," cried I, exasperated to a degree which is scarcely to be explained, "you do not mean to tell me—that you—that you—have not lost all hope?"

"Certainly not," replied the Professor, with consummate coolness.

"You mean to tell me, uncle, that we shall get out of this monstrous subterranean shaft?"

"While there is life there is hope. I beg to assert, Henry, that as long as a man's heart beats, as long as a man's flesh quivers, I do not allow that a being gifted with thought and will can allow himself to despair."

What a nerve! The man placed in a position like that we occupied must have been very brave to speak like this.

"Well," I cried, "what do you mean to do?"

"Eat what remains of the food we have in our hands; let us swallow the last crumb. It will be, heaven willing, our last repast. Well, never mind—instead of being exhausted skeletons, we shall be men."

"True," muttered I in a despairing tone, "let us take our fill."

"We must," replied my uncle, with a deep sigh—"call it what you will."

My uncle took a piece of the meat that remained, and some crusts of biscuit which had escaped the wreck. He divided the whole into three parts.

Each had one pound of food to last him as long as he remained in the interior of the earth.

Each now acted in accordance with his own private character.

My uncle, the Professor, ate greedily, but evidently without appetite, eating simply from some mechanical motion. I put the food inside my lips, and hungry as I was, chewed my morsel without pleasure, and without satisfaction.

Hans the guide, just as if he had been eider-down hunting, swallowed every mouthful, as though it were a usual affair. He looked like a man equally prepared to enjoy superfluity or total want.

Hans, in all probability, was no more used to starvation than ourselves, but his hardy Icelndic nature had prepared him for many sufferings. As long as he received his three rix-dollars every Saturday night, he was prepared for anything.

The fact was, Hans never troubled himself about much except his money. He had undertaken to serve a certain man at so much per week, and no matter what evils befell his employer or himself, he never found fault or grumbled, so long as his wages were duly paid.

Suddenly my uncle roused himself. He had seen a smile on the face of our guide. I could not make it out.

"What is the matter?" said my uncle.

"Schiedam," said the guide, producing a bottle of this precious fluid.

We drank. My uncle and myself will own to our dying day that hence we derived strength to exist until the last bitter moment. That precious bottle of Hollands was in reality only half-full; but, under the circumstances, it was nectar.

It took some minutes for myself and my uncle to form a decided opinion on the subject. The worthy Professor swallowed about half a pint and did not seem able to drink any more.

"Förtrafflig," said Hans, swallowing nearly all that was left.

"Excellent—very good," said my uncle with as much gusto as if he had just left the steps of the club at Hamburg.

I had begun to feel as if there had been one gleam of hope. Now all thought of the future vanished!

We had consumed our last ounce of food, and it was five o'clock in the morning!

CHAPTER 42

THE VOLCANIC SHAFT

MAN's constitution is so peculiar, that his health is purely a negative matter. No sooner is the rage of hunger appeased, than it becomes difficult to comprehend the meaning of starvation. It is only when you suffer that you really understand.

As to any one who has not endured privation having any notion of the matter, it is simply absurd.

With us, after a long fast, some mouthfuls of bread and meat, a little mouldy-biscuit and salt beef triumphed over all our previous gloomy and saturnine thoughts.

Nevertheless, after this repast each gave way to his own reflections. I wondered what were those of Hans—the man of the extreme north, who was yet gifted with the fatalistic resignation of Oriental character. But the utmost stretch of the imagination would not allow me to realise the truth. As for my individual self, my thoughts had ceased to be anything but memories of the past, and were all connected with that upper world which I never should have left. I saw it all now, the beautiful house in the Königstrasse, my poor Gretchen, the good Martha; they all passed before my mind like visions of the past. Every time any of the lugubrious groanings which were to be distinguished in the hollows around fell upon my ears, I fancied I heard the distant murmur of the great cities above my head.

As for my uncle, always thinking of his science, he examined the nature of the shaft be means of a torch. He closely examined the different strata one above the other, in order to recognise his situation by geological theory. This calculation, or rather this estimation, could by no means be anything but approximate. But a learned man, a philosopher, is nothing if not a philosopher, when he keeps his ideas calm and collected; and certainly the Professor possessed this quality to perfection.

I heard him, as I sat in silence, murmuring words of geological science. As I understood his object and his meaning, I could not but interest myself despite my pre-occupation in that terrible hour.

"Eruptive granite," he said to himself, "we are still in the primitive epoch. But we are going up—going up, still going up. But who knows? Who knows?"

Then he still hoped. He felt along the vertical sides of the shaft with his hand, and some few minutes later, he would go on again in the following style—

"This is gniess. This is mocashites—silicious mineral. Good again; this is the epoch of transition, at all events, we are close to them—and then and then—"

What could the Professor mean? Could he, by any conceivable means, measure the thickness of the crust of the earth suspended above our heads? Did he possess any possible means of making any approximation to this calculation? No.

The manometer was wanting and no summary estimation could take the place of it.

And yet, as we progressed, the temperature increased in the most extraordinary degree, and I began to feel as if I were bathed in a hot and burning atmosphere. Never before had I felt anything like it. I could only compare it to the hot vapour from an iron foundry, when the liquid iron is in a state of ebullition and runs over. By degrees, and one after the other, Hans, my uncle, and myself had taken off our coats and waistcoats. They were unbearable. Even the slightest garment was not only uncomfortable, but the cause of extreme suffering.

"Are we ascending to a living fire?" I cried; when, to my horror and astonishment, the heat became greater than before.

"No, no," said my uncle, "it is simply impossible, quite impossible."

"And yet," said I, touching the side of the shaft with my naked hand, "this wall is literally burning."

At this moment, feeling as I did that the sides of this extraordinary well were red hot, I plunged my hands into the water to cool them. I drew them back with a cry of despair.

"The water is boiling!" I cried.

My uncle, the Professor, made no reply other than a gesture of rage and despair.

Something very like the truth had probably struck his imagination.

But I could take no share in either what was going on, or in his speculations. An invincible dread had taken possession of my brain and soul. I could only look forward to an immediate catastrophe, such a catastrophe as not even the most vivid imagination could have thought of. An idea, at first vague and uncertain, was gradually being changed into certainty.

I tremulously rejected it at first, but it forced itself upon me by degrees with extreme obstinacy. It was so terrible an idea that I scarcely dared to whisper it to myself.

And yet all the while certain, and as it were, involuntary observations determined my convictions. By the doubtful glare of the torch, I could make out some singular changes in the granitic strata; a strange and terrible phenomenon was about to be produced, in which electricity played a part.

Then this boiling water, this terrible and excessive heat? I determined as a last resource to examine the compass.

The compass had gone mad!

Yes, wholly stark staring mad. The needle jumped from pole to pole with sudden and surprising jerks, ran round, or as it is said, boxed the compass, and then ran suddenly back again as if it had the vertigo.

I was aware that, according to the best acknowledged theories, it was a received notion that the mineral crust of the globe is never, and never has been, in a state of complete repose.

The modifications caused by the decomposition of internal matter, the agitation consequent on the flowing of extensive liquid currents, the excessive action of magnetism which tends to shake it incessantly, at a time when even the multitudinous beings on its surface do not suspect the seething process to be going on.

Still this phenomenon would have not alarmed me alone; it would not have aroused in my mind a terrible, an awful idea.

Terrible detonations, like heaven's artillery, began to multiply themselves with fearful intensity. I could only compare them with the noise made by hundreds of heavily-laden chariots being madly driven over a stone pavement. It was a continuous roll of heavy thunder.

And then the mad compass, shaken by the wild electric phenomena, confirmed me in my rapidly-formed opinion. The mineral crust was about to burst, the heavy granite masses were about to be filled up, and we poor atoms to be crushed in its awful embrace!

"Uncle, uncle!" I cried, "we are wholly, irretrievably lost!"

"What, then, my young friend, is your new cause of terror and alarm?" he said, in his calmest manner. "What fear you now?"

"What do I fear now!" I cried, in fierce and angry tones. "Do you not see that the walls of the shaft are in motion? do you not see that the solid granite masses are cracking? do you not feel the terrible, torrid heat? do you not observe the awful boiling water on which we float? do you not remark this mad needle? every sign and portent of an awful earthquake?"

My uncle coolly shook his head.

"An earthquake," he replied in the most calm and provoking tone.

"Yes."

"My nephew, I tell you that you are utterly mistaken," he continued.

"Do you not, can you not, recognise all the well-known symptoms——"

"Of an earthquake? by no means. I am expecting something far more important."

"My brain is strained beyond endurance—what, what do you mean?" I cried.

"An eruption, Harry."

"An eruption," I gasped. "We are, then, in the volcanic shaft of a crater in full action and vigour."

"I have every reason to think so," said the Professor in a smiling tone, "and I beg to tell you that it is the most fortunate thing that could happen to us."

The most fortunate thing! Had my uncle really and truly gone mad? What did he mean by these awful words—what did he mean by this terrible calm, this solemn smile?

"What!" cried I, in the height of my exasperation, "we are on the way to an eruption, are we? Fatality has cast us into a well of burning and boiling lava, of rocks on fire, of boiling water, in a word, filled with every kind of eruptive matter? We are about to be expelled, thrown up, vomited, spit out of the interior of the earth, in common with huge blocks of granite, with showers of cinders and scoria, in a wild whirlwind of flame, and you say—the most fortunate thing which could happen to us."

"Yes," replied the Professor, looking at me calmly from under his spectacles, "it is the only chance which remains to us of ever escaping from the interior of the earth to the light of day."

It is quite impossible that I can put on paper the thousand strange, wild thoughts which followed this extraordinary announcement.

But my uncle was right, quite right, and never had he appeared to me so audacious and so convinced as when he looked me calmly in the face and spoke of the chances of an eruption—of our being cast upon mother earth once more through the gaping crater of a volcano!

Nevertheless, while we were speaking we were still ascending; we passed the whole night going up, or to speak more scientifically, in an ascensional motion. The fearful noise redoubled; I was ready to suffocate. I seriously believed that my last hour was approaching, and yet, so strange is imagination, all I thought of was some childish hypothesis or other. In such circumstances you do not choose your own thoughts. They overcome you.

It was quite evident that we were being cast upwards by eruptive matter; under the raft there was a mass of boiling water, and under this was a heaving mass of lava, and an aggregate of rocks which on reaching the summit of the water would be dispersed in every direction.

That we were inside the chimney of a volcano there could no longer be the shadow of a doubt. Nothing more terrible could be conceived!

But on this occasion, instead of Sneffels, an old and extinct volcano, we were inside a mountain of fire in full activity. Several times I found myself asking, what mountain was it, and on what part of the world we should be shot out. As if it were of any consequence!

In the northern regions, there could be no reasonable doubt about that. Before it went decidedly mad, the compass had never made the slightest mistake. From the cape of Saknussemm, we had been swept away to the northward many hundreds of leagues. Now the question was, were we once more under Iceland—should we be belched forth on to the earth through the crater of Mount Hecla, or should we re-appear through one of the other seven fire-funnels of the island? Taking in my mental vision a radius of five hundred leagues to the westward, I could see under this parallel only the little-known volcanoes of the north-west coast of America.

To the east one only existed somewhere above the eightieth degree of latitude, the Esk, upon the island of Jean Mayen, not far from the frozen regions of Spitzbergen.

It was not craters that were wanting, and many of them were big enough to vomit a whole army; all I wished to know was the particular one towards which we were making with such fearful velocity.

I often think now of my folly: as if I should ever have expected to escape!

Towards morning, the ascending motion became greater and greater. If the degree of heat increased instead of decreasing, as we approached the surface of the earth, it was simply because the causes were local and wholly due to volanic influence. Our very style of locomotion left in my mind no doubt upon the subject. An enormous force, a force of some hundred of combined atmospheres produced by vapours accumulated and long compressed in the interior of the earth, were hoisting us upwards with irresistible power.

But though we were approaching the light of day, to what fearful dangers were we about to be exposed?

Instant death appeared the only fate which we could expect or contemplate.

Soon a dim, sepulchral light penetrated the vertical gallery, which became wider and wider. I could make out to the right and left long dark corridors like immense tunnels, from which awful and horrid vapours poured out. Tongues of fire, sparkling and crackling, appeared about to lick us up.

The hour had come!

"Look, uncle, look!" I cried.

"Well, what you see are the great sulphurous flames. Nothing more common in connection with an eruption."

"But if they lap us round!" I angrily replied.

"They will not lap us round," was his quiet and serene answer.

"But it will be all the same in the end if they stifle us," I cried.

"We shall not be stifled. The gallery is rapidly becoming wider and wider, and if it be necessary, we will presently leave the raft and take refuge in some fissure in the rock."

"But the water, the water, which is continually ascending!" I despairingly replied.

"There is no longer any water, Harry," he answered, "but a kind of lava paste, which is heaving us up, in company with itself, to the mouth of the crater."

In truth, the liquid column of water had wholly disappeared to give place to dense masses of boiling eruptive matter. The temperature was becoming utterly insupportable, and a thermometer exposed to this atmosphere would have marked between 189 and 190 degrees Fahrenheit.

Perspiration rushed from every pore. But for the extraordinary rapidity of our ascent we should have been stifled.

Nevertheless, the Professor did not carry out his proposition of abandoning the raft; and he did quite wisely. Those few ill-joined beams offered, any way, a solid surface—a support which elsewhere must have utterly failed us.

Towards eight o'clock in the morning a new incident startled us. The ascensional movement suddenly ceased. The raft became still and motionless.

"What is the matter now?" I said, querulously, very much startled by this change.

"A simple halt," replied my uncle.

"Is the eruption about to fail?" I asked.

"I hope not."

Without making any reply, I rose. I tried to look around me. Pehaps the raft, checked by some projecting rock, opposed a momentary resistance to the eruptive mass. In this case, it was absolutely necessary to release it as quickly as possible.

Nothing of the kind had occurred. The column of cinders, or scoriæ, of broken rocks and earth, had wholly ceased to ascend.

"I tell you, uncle, that the eruption has stopped," was my oracular decision.

"Ah," said my uncle, "you think so, my boy. You are wrong. Do not be in the least alarmed; this sudden moment of calm will not last long, be assured. It has already endured five minutes, and before we are many minutes older we shall be continuing our journey to the mouth of the crater."

All the time he was speaking the Professor continued to consult his chronometer, and he was probably right in his prognostics. Soon the raft resumed its motion, in a very rapid and disorderly way, which lasted two minutes or thereabout; and then again it stopped as suddenly as before.

"Good," said my uncle, observing the hour, "in ten minutes we shall start again."

"In ten minutes?"

"Yes—precisely. We have to do with a volcano, the eruption of which is intermittent. We are compelled to breathe just as it does."

Nothing could be more true. At the exact minute he had indicated, we were again launched on high with extreme rapidity. Not to be cast off the raft, it was necessary to hold on to the beams. Then the hoist again ceased.

Many times since have I thought of this singular phenomenon without being able to find for it any satisfactory explanation. Nevertheless, it appeared quite clear to me, that we were not in the principal chimney of the volcano, but in an accessory conduit, where we felt the counter shock of the great and principal tunnel filled by burning lava.

It is impossible for me to say how many times this manœuvre was repeated. All that I can remember is, that on every ascensional motion, we were hoisted up with ever-increasing velocity, as if we had been launched from a huge projectile. During the sudden halts we were nearly stifled; during the moments of projection the hot air took away our breath.

I thought for a moment of the voluptuous joy of suddenly finding myself in the hyperborean regions with the cold 30 degrees below zero!

My exalted imagination pictured to itself the vast snowy plains of the arctic regions, and I was impatient to roll myself on the icy carpet of the north pole.

By degrees my head, utterly overcome by a series of violent emotions, began to give way to hallucination. I was delirious. Had it not been for the powerful arms of Hans the guide, I should have broken my head against the granite masses of the shaft.

I have, in consequence, kept no account of what followed for many hours. I have a vague and confused remembrance of continual detonations, of the shaking of the huge granitic mass, and of the raft going round and round like a spinning-top. It floated on the stream of hot lava, amidst a falling cloud of cinders. The huge flames roaring, wrapped us around.

A storm of wind which appeared to be cast forth from an immense ventilator roused up the interior fires of the earth. It was a hot incandescent blast!

At last I saw the figure of Hans as if enveloped in the huge halo of burning blaze, and no other sense remained to me but that sinister dread which the condemned victim may be supposed to feel when led to the mouth of a cannon, at the supreme moment when the shot is fired and his limbs are dispersed into empty space.

CHAPTER 43

DAYLIGHT AT LAST

WHEN I opened my eyes I felt the hand of the guide clutching me firmly by the belt. With his other hand he supported my uncle. I was not grievously wounded, but bruised all over in the most remarkable manner.

After a moment I looked around, and found that I was lying down on the slope of a mountain not two yards from a yawning gulf into which I should have fallen had I made the slightest false step. Hans had saved me from death, while I rolled insensible on the flanks of the crater.

"Where are we?" dreamily asked my uncle, who literally appeared to be disgusted at having returned to earth.

The eider down hunter simply shrugged his shoulders as a mark of total ignorance.

"In Iceland?" said I, not positively but interrogatively.

"Nej," said Hans.

"How do you mean?" cried the Professor; "no—what are your reasons?"

"Hans is wrong," said I, rising.

After all the innumerable surprises of this journey, a yet more singular one was reserved to us. I expected to see a cone covered by snow, by extensive and wide-spread glaciers, in the midst of the arid deserts of the extreme northern regions, beneath the full rays of a polar sky, beyond the highest latitudes.

But contrary to all our expectations, I, my uncle, and the Icelander, were cast upon the slope of a mountain calcined by the burning rays of a sun which was literally baking us with its fires.

I could not believe my eyes, but the actual heat which affected my body allowed me no chance of doubting. We came out of the crater half naked, and the radiant star from which we had asked nothing for two months, was good enough to be prodigal to us of light and warmth—a light and warmth we could easily have dispensed with.

When our eyes were accustomed to the light we had lost sight so long, I used them to rectify the errors of my imagination. Whatever happened, we should have been at Spitzbergen, and I was in no humour to yield to anything but the most absolute proof.

After some delay, the Professor spoke.

"Hem!" he said, in a hesitating kind of way, "it really does not look like Iceland."

"But supposing it were the island of Jean Mayen?" I ventured to observe.

"Not in the least, my boy. This is not one of the volcanoes of the north, with its hills of granite and its crown of snow."

"Nevertheless——"

"Look, look, my boy," said the Professor, as dogmatically as usual.

Right above our heads, at a great height, opened the crater of a volcano from which escaped, from one quarter of an hour to the other, with a very loud explosion, a lofty jet of flame mingled with pumice stone, cinders, and lava. I could feel the convulsions of nature in the mountain, which breathed like a huge whale, throwing up from time to time fire and air through its enormous vents.

Below, and floating along a slope of considerable angularity, the stream of eruptive matter spread away to a depth which did not give the volcano a height of three hundred fathoms.

Its base disappeared in a perfect forest of green trees, among which I perceived olives, fig trees, and vines loaded with rich grapes.

Certainly this was not the ordinary aspect of the Arctic regions. About that there could not be the slightest doubt.

When the eye was satisfied at its glimpse of this verdant expanse, it fell upon the waters of a lovely sea or beautiful lake, which made of this enchanted land an island of not many leagues in extent.

On the side of the rising sun was to be seen a little port, crowded with houses, and near which boats and vessels of peculiar build were floating upon azure waves.

Beyond, groups of islands rose above the liquid plain, so numerous and close together as to resemble a vast bee-hive.

Towards the setting sun, some distant shores were to be made out on the edge of the horizon. Some presented the appearance of blue mountains of harmonious conformation; upon others, much more distant, there appeared a prodigiously lofty cone, above the summit of which hung dark and heavy clouds.

Towards the north, an immense expanse of water sparkled beneath the solar rays, occasionally allowing the extremity of a mast or the convexity of a sail bellying to the wind, to be seen.

The unexpected character of such a scene added an hundredfold to its marvellous beauties.

"Where can we be?" I asked, speaking in a low and solemn voice.

Hans shut his eyes with an air of indifference, and my uncle looked on without clearly understanding.

"Whatever this mountain may be," he said, at last, "I must confess it is rather warm. The explosions do not leave off, and I do not think it is worth while to have left the interior of a volcano and remain here to receive a huge piece of rock upon one's head. Let us carefully descend the mountain and discover the real state of the case. To confess the truth, I am dying of hunger and thirst."

Decidedly the Professor was no longer a truly reflective character. For myself, forgetting all my necessities, ignoring my fatigues and sufferings, I should have remained still for several hours longer—but it was necessary to follow my companions.

The slope of the volcano was very steep and slippery; we slid over piles of ashes, avoiding the streams of hot lava which glided about like fiery serpents. Still, while we were advancing, I spoke with extreme volubility, for my imagination was too full not to explode in words.

"We are in Asia!" I exclaimed; "we are on the coast of India, in the great Malay islands, in the centre of Oceana. We have crossed the one half of the globe to come out right at the antipodes of Europe!"

"But the compass!" exclaimed my uncle; "explain that to me!"

"Yes,—the compass," I said, with considerable hesitation; "I grant that is a difficulty. According to it, we have always been going northward."

"Then it lied."

"Hem—to say it lied is rather a harsh word," was my answer.

"Then we are at the north pole—"

"The pole—no—well—well I give it up," was my reply.

The plain truth was, that there was no explanation possible. I could make nothing of it.

And all the while we were approaching this beautiful verdure, hunger and thirst tormented me fearfully. Happily, after two long hours' march, a beautiful country spread out before us, covered by olives, pomegranates, and vines, which appeared to belong to anybody and everybody.

In the state of destitution into which we had fallen, we were not particular to a grape.

What delight it was to press these delicious fruits to our lips, and to bite at grapes and pomegranates fresh from the vine. Not far off, near some fresh and mossy grass, under the delicious shade of some trees, I discovered a spring of fresh water, into which we voluptuously laved our faces, hands, and feet.

While we were all giving way to the delights of new-found pleasures, a little child appeared between two tufted olive trees.

"Ah," cried I, "an inhabitant of this happy country."

The little fellow was poorly dressed, weak and suffering, and appeared terribly alarmed at our appearance. Half naked, with tangled, matted and ragged beards, we did look supremely ill-favoured; and unless the country was a bandit land, we were not unlikely to alarm the inhabitants!

Just as the boy was about to take to his heels, Hans ran after him, and brought him back, despite his cries and kicks.

My uncle tried to look as gentle as possible, and then spoke in German.

"What is the name of this mountain, my friend?"

The child made no reply.

"Good," said my uncle, with a very positive air of conviction, "we are not in Germany."

He then made the same demand in English, of which language he was an excellent scholar.

The child shook its head and made no reply. I began to be considerably puzzled.

"Is he dumb?" cried the Professor, who was rather proud of his polyglot knowledge of languages, and making the same demand in French.

The boy only stared in his face.

"I must perforce try him in Italian," said my uncle, with a shrug.

"Dove noi siamo?"

"Yes, tell me where we are?" I added, impatiently and eagerly.

Again the boy remained silent.

"My fine fellow, do you or do you not mean to speak?" cried my uncle, who began to get angry. He shook him, and spoke another dialect of the Italian language.

"Come si noma questa isola?"—what is the name of this island?

"Stromboli," replied the rickety little shepherd, dashing away from Hans and disappearing in the olive groves.

We thought little enough about him.

Stromboli! What effect on the imagination did these few words produce! We were in the centre of the Mediterranean; amidst the Eastern archipelago of mythological memory; in the ancient Strongylos, where Æolus kept the wind

and the tempest chained up. And those blue mountains, which rose towards the rising of the sun, were the mountains of Calabria.

And that mighty volcano which rose on the southern horizon was Etna, the fierce and celebrated Etna!

"Stomboli! Stromboli!" I repeated to myself.

My uncle played a regular accompaniment to my gestures and words. We were singing together like an ancient chorus.

Ah—what a journey—what a marvellous and extraordinary journey! Here we had entered the earth by one volcano, and we had come out by another. And this other was situated more than twelve hundred leagues from Sneffels, from that dear country of Iceland cast away on the confines of the earth. The wondrous chances of this expedition had transported us to the most harmonious and beautiful of earthly lands. We had abandoned the region of eternal snows for that of infinite verdure, and had left over our heads the grey fog of the icy regions to come back to the azure sky of Sicily!

After a delicious repast of fruits and fresh water, we again continued our journey in order to reach the port of Stromboli. To say how we had reached the island would scarcely have been prudent. The superstitious character of the Italians would have been at work, and we should have been called demons vomited from the infernal regions. It was therefore necessary to pass for humble and unfortunate shipwrecked travellers. It was certainly less striking and romantic, but it was decidedly safer.

As we advanced, I could hear my worthy uncle muttering to himself—

"But the compass. The compass most certainly marked north. This is a fact I cannot explain in any way."

"Well, the fact is," said I, with an air of disdain, "we must not explain anything. It will be much more easy."

"I should like to see a professor of the Johannæum Institution, who is unable to explain a cosmic phenomenon—it would indeed be strange."

And speaking thus; my uncle, half naked, his leathern purse round his loins, and his spectacles upon his nose, became once more the terrible Professor of Mineralogy.

An hour after leaving the wood of olives, we reached the fort of San Vicenza, where Hans demanded the price of his thirteenth week of service. My uncle paid him, with very many warm shakes of the hand.

At that moment, if he did not indeed quite share our natural emotion, he allowed his feelings so far to give way as to indulge in an extraordinary expression for him.

With the tips of two fingers he gently pressed our hands and smiled.

CHAPTER 44

THE JOURNEY ENDED

THIS is the final conclusion of a narrative which will be probably disbelieved even by people who are astonished at nothing. I am, however, armed at all points against human incredulity.

We were kindly received by the Strombolite fishermen, who treated us as shipwrecked travellers. They gave us clothes and food. After a delay of forty-eight hours, on the 31st of September a little vessel took us to Messina, where a few days of delightful and complete repose restored us to ourselves.

On Friday, the 4th October, we embarked in the Volturus, one of the postal packets of the Imperial Messagerie of France; and three days later we landed at Marseilles, having no other care on our minds but that of our precious but erratic compass. This inexplicable circumstance tormented me terribly. On the 9th of October, in the evening, we reached Hamburg.

What was the astonishment of Martha, what the joy of Gretchen! I will not attempt to define it.

"Now then, Harry, that you really are a hero," she said, "there is no reason why you should ever leave me again."

I looked at her. She was weeping tears of joy.

I leave it to be imagined if the return of Professor Hardwigg made or did not make a sensation in Hamburg. Thanks to the indiscretion of Martha, the news of his departure for the Interior of the Earth had been spread over the whole world.

No one would believe it—and when they saw him come back in safety they believed it all the less.

But the presence of Hans and many stray scraps of information by degrees modified public opinion.

Then my uncle became a great man, and I the nephew of a great man; which, at all events, is something. Hamburg gave a festival in our honour. A public meeting of the Johannæum Institution was held, at which the Professor related the whole story of his adventures, omitting only the facts in connection with the compass.

That same day he deposited in the archives of the town the document he had found written by Saknussemm, and he expressed his great regret that circumstances, stronger than his will, did not allow him to follow the Icelandic traveller's track into the very Centre of the Earth. He was modest in his glory, but his reputation only increased.

So much honour necessarily created for him many envious enemies. Of course they existed, and as his theories, supported by certain facts, contradicted the system of science upon the question of central heat, he maintained his own views both with pen and speech against the learned of every country. Although I still believe in the theory of central heat, I confess that certain circumstances, hitherto very ill defined, may modify the laws of such natural phenomena.

At the moment when these questions were being discussed with interest, my uncle received a rude shock—one that he felt very much. Hans, despite everything he could say to the contrary, quitted Hamburg; the man to whom we owed so much would not allow us to pay our deep debt of gratitude. He was taken with nostalgia; a love for his Icelandic home.

"*Farval,*" said he, one day, and with this one short word of adieu, he started for Reykjawik, which he soon reached in safety.

We were deeply attached to our brave eider-duck hunter. His absence will never cause him to be forgotten by those whose lives he saved, and I hope, at some not distant day, to see him again.

To conclude, I may say that our Journey into the Interior of the Earth created an enormous sensation throughout the civilised world. It was translated and printed in many languages. All the leading journals published extracts from it, which were commentated, discussed, attacked, and supported with equal ani-

Our condition at the end of the journey.

mation by those who believed in its episodes, and by those who were utterly incredulous.

Wonderful! My uncle enjoyed during his lifetime all the glory he deserved; and he was even offered a large sum of money, by Mr. Barnum, to exhibit himself in the United States; while I am credibly informed by a traveller that he is to be seen in waxwork at Madame Tussaud's!

But one care preyed upon his mind, a care which rendered him very unhappy. One fact remained inexplicable—that of the compass. For a learned man to be baffled by such an inexplicable phenomenon was very aggravating. But heaven was merciful, and in the end my uncle was happy.

One day, while he put some minerals belonging to his collection in order, I fell upon the famous compass and examined it keenly.

For six months it had lain unnoticed and untouched.

I looked at it with curosity, which soon became surprise. I gave a loud cry. The Professor, who was at hand, soon joined me.

"What is the matter?" he cried.

"The compass!"

"What then?"

"Why its needle points to the south and not to the north."

"My dear boy, you must be dreaming."

"I am not dreaming. See the poles are changed."

"Changed!"

My uncle put on his spectacles, examined the instrument, and leaped with joy, shaking the whole house.

A clear light fell upon our minds.

"Here it is!" he cried, as soon as he had recovered the use of his speech, "after we had once passed Cape Saknussemm, the needle of this compass pointed to the southward instead of the northward."

"Evidently."

"Our error is now easily explained. But to what phenomenon do we owe this alteration in the needles?"

"Nothing more simple."

"Explain yourself, my boy. I am on thorns."

"During the storm, upon the Central Sea, the ball of fire which made a magnet of the iron in our raft, turned our compass topsy turvy."

"Ah!" cried the Professor, with a loud and ringing laugh, "it was a trick of that inexplicable electricity."

From that hour my uncle was the happiest of learned men, and I the happiest of ordinary mortals. For my pretty Virland girl, abdicating her position as ward, took her place in the house in King Street (König Strasse) in the double quality of niece and wife.

We need scarcely mention that her uncle was the illustrious Professor Hardwigg, corresponding member of all the scientific, geographical, mineralogical and geological societies of the five quarters of the globe.

From the Earth to the Moon

Projectile trains for the moon.

CHAPTER 1

THE GUN CLUB

DURING the War of the Rebellion, a new and influential club was established in the city of Baltimore in the State of Maryland. It is well known with what energy the taste for military matters became developed amongst that nation of ship-owners, shopkeepers, and mechanics. Simple tradesmen jumped their counters to become extemporized captains, colonels, and generals, without having ever passed the School of Instruction at West Point: nevertheless, they quickly rivalled their compeers of the old continent, and, like them, carried off victories by dint of lavish expenditure in ammunition, money, and men.

But the point in which the Americans singularly distanced the Europeans was in the science of *gunnery*. Not, indeed, that their weapons retained a higher degree of perfection than theirs, but that they exhibited unheard-of dimensions, and consequently attained hitherto unheard-of ranges. In point of grazing, plunging, oblique, or enfilading, or point-blank firing, the English, French, and Prussians have nothing to learn; but their cannon, howitzers, and mortars are mere pocket-pistols compared with the formidable engines of the American artillery.

This fact need surprise no one. The Yankees, the first mechanicians in the world, are engineers—just as the Italians are musicians and the Germans metaphysicians—by right of birth. Nothing is more natural, therefore, than to perceive them applying their audacious ingenuity to the science of gunnery. Witness the marvels of Parrott, Dahlgren, and Rodman. The Armstrong, Palliser, and Beaulieu guns were compelled to bow before their transatlantic rivals.

Now when an American has an idea, he directly seeks a second American to share it. If there be three, they elect a president and two secretaries. Given *four*, they name a keeper of records, and the office is ready for work; *five*, they convene a general meeting, and the club is fully constituted. So things were managed in Baltimore. The inventor of a new cannon associated himself with the caster and the borer. Thus was formed the nucleus of the "Gun Club." In a single month after its formation it numbered 1833 effective members and 30,565 corresponding members.

One condition was imposed as a *sine quâ non* upon every candidate for admission into the association, and that was the condition of having designed, or (more or less) perfected a cannon; or, in default of a cannon, at least a firearm of some description. It may, however, be mentioned that mere inventions of revolvers, five-shooting carbines, and similar small arms, met with but little consideration. Artillerists always commanded the chief place of favour.

The estimation in which these gentlemen were held, according to one of the most scientific exponents of the Gun Club, was "proportional to the masses of their guns, and in the direct ratio of the square of the distances attained by their projectiles."

The Gun Club once founded, it is easy to conceive the result of the inventive genius of the Americans. Their military weapons attained colossal proportions, and their projectiles, exceeding the prescribed limits, unfortunately occasionally cut in two some unoffending pedestrians. These inventions, in fact, left far in the rear the timid instruments of European artillery.

It is but fair to add that these Yankees, brave as they have ever proved themselves to be, did not confine themselves to theories and formulæ, but that they paid heavily, *in propriâ personâ,* for their inventions. Amongst them were to be counted officers of all ranks, from lieutenants to generals; military men of every age, from those who were just making their *début* in the profession of arms up to those who had grown old on the gun-carriage. Many had found their rest on the field of battle whose names figured in the "Book of Honour" of the Gun Club; and of those who made good their return the greater proportion bore the marks of their indisputable valour. Crutches, wooden legs, artificial arms, steel hooks, caoutchouc jaws, silver craniums, platinum noses, were all to be found in the collection; and it was calculated by the great statistician Pitcairn that throughout the Gun Club there was not quite one arm between four persons, and exactly two legs between six.

Nevertheless, these valiant artillerists took no particular account of these little facts, and felt justly proud when the despatches of a battle returned the number of victims at tenfold the quantity of the projectiles expended.

One day, however—sad and melancholy day!—peace was signed between the survivors of the war; the thunder of the guns gradually ceased, the mortars were silent, the howitzers were muzzled for an indefinite period, the cannon, with muzzles depressed, were returned into the arsenal, the shot were repiled, all bloody reminiscences were effaced; the cotton-plants grew luxuriantly in the well-manured fields, all mourning garments were laid aside, together with grief; and the Gun Club was relegated to profound inactivity.

Some few of the more advanced and inveterate theorists set themselves again to work upon calculations regarding the laws of projectiles. They reverted invariably to gigantic shells and howitzers of unparalleled calibre. Still, in default of practical experience, what was the value of mere theories? Consequently, the club-rooms became deserted, the servants dozed in the ante-chambers, the newspapers grew mouldy on the tables, sounds of snoring came from dark corners, and the members of the Gun Club, erstwhile so noisy in the séances, were reduced to silence by this disastrous peace and gave themselves up wholly to dreams of a Platonic kind of artillery.

"This is horrible!" said Tom Hunter one evening, while rapidly carbonizing his wooden legs in the fire-place of the smoking-room; "nothing to do! nothing to look forward to! what a loathsome existence! When again shall the guns arouse us in the morning with their delightful reports?"

"Those days are gone by," said jolly Bilsby, trying to extend his missing arms. "It was delightful once upon a time! One invented a gun, and hardly was it cast, when one hastened to try it in the face of the enemy! Then one returned to camp with a word of encouragement from Sherman or a friendly shake of the hand from M'Clellan. But now the generals are gone back to their counters; and

The artillery men of the Gun Club.

in place of projectiles, they despatch bales of cotton. By Jove, the future of gunnery in America is lost!''

''Ay! and no war in prospect!'' continued the famous James T. Maston, scratching with his steel hook his gutta-perchacranium. ''Not a cloud in the horizon! and that too at such a critical period in the progress of the science of artillery! Yes, gentlemen! I who address you have myself this very morning perfected a model (plan, section, elevation, &c.) of a mortar destined to change all the conditions of warfare!:

''No! is it possible?'' replied Tom Hunter, his thoughts reverting involuntarily to a former invention of the Hon. J. T. Maston, by which, at its first trial, he had succeeded in killing three hundred and thirty-seven people.

''Fact!'' replied he. ''Still, what is the use of so many studies worked out, so many difficulties vanquished? It's mere waste of time! The New World seems to have made up its mind to live in peace; and our bellicose *Tribune* predicts some approaching catastrophes arising out of this scandalous increase of population.''

''Nevertheless,'' replied Colonel Blomsberry, ''they are always struggling in Europe to maintain the principle of nationalities.''

''Well?''

''Well, there might be some field for enterprise down there; and if they would accept our services—''

''What are you dreaming of?'' screamed Bilsby; ''work at gunnery for the benefit of foreigners?''

''That would be better than doing nothing here,'' returned the colonel.

''Quite so,'' said J. T. Maston; ''but still we need not dream of that expedient.''

''And why not?'' demanded the colonel.

''Because their ideas of progress in the Old World are contrary to our American habits of thought. Those fellows believe that one can't become a general without having served first as an ensign; which is as much as to say that one can't point a gun without having first cast it oneself!''

''Ridiculous!'' replied Tom Hunter, whittling with his bowie-knife the arms of his easy-chair; ''but if that be the case there, all that is left for us is to plant tobacco and distil whale-oil.''

''What!'' roared J. T. Maston, ''shall we not employ these remaining years of our life in perfecting fire-arms? Shall there never be a fresh opportunity of trying the ranges of projectiles? Shall the air never again be lighted with the glare of our guns? No international difficulty ever arise to enable us to declare war against some transatlantic power? Shall not the French sink one of our steamers, or the English, in defiance of the rights of nations, hang a few of our countrymen?''

''No such luck,'' replied Colonel Blomsberry; ''nothing of the kind is likely to happen; and even if it did, we should not profit by it. American susceptibility is fast declining, and we are all going to the dogs.''

''It is too true,'' replied J. T. Maston, with fresh violence; ''there are a thousand grounds for fighting, and yet we don't fight. We save up our arms and legs for the benefit of nations who don't know what to do with them! But stop—without going out of one's way to find a cause for war—did not North America once belong to the English?''

''Undoubtedly,'' replied Tom Hunter, stamping his crutch with fury.

"Well then," replied J. T. Maston, "why should not England in her turn belong to the Americans?"

"It would be but just and fair," returned Colonel Blomsberry.

"Go and propose it to the President of the United States," cried J. T. Maston, "and see how he will receive you."

"Bah!" growled Bilsby between the four teeth which the war had left him; "that will never do!"

"By Jove!" cried J. T. Maston, "he mustn't count on my vote at the next election!"

"Nor on ours," replied unanimously all the bellicose invalids.

"Meanwhile," replied J.T.M., "allow me to say that, if I cannot get an opportunity to try my new mortars on a real field of battle, I shall say good-bye to the members of the Gun Club, and go and bury myself in the prairies of Arkansas!"

"In that case we will accompany you," cried the others.

Matters were in this unfortunate condition, and the club was threatened with approaching dissolution, when an unexpected circumstance occurred to prevent so deplorable a catastrophe.

On the morrow after this conversation every member of the association received a sealed circular couched in the following terms:—

"BALTIMORE, *Oct.* 3.

"The President of the Gun Club has the honour to inform his colleagues that, at the meeting of the 5th instant, he will bring before them a communication of an extremely interesting nature. He requests, therefore, that they will make it convenient to attend in accordance with the present invitation.—Very cordially,

"IMPEY BARBICANE, P.G.C."

CHAPTER 2

PRESIDENT BARBICANE'S COMMUNICATION

ON the 5th of October, at 8 p.m., a dense crowd pressed towards the saloons of the Gun Club at No. 21, Union Square. All the members of the association resident in Baltimore attended the invitation of their president. As regards the corresponding members, notices were delivered by hundreds throughout the streets of the city, and, large as was the great hall, it was quite inadequate to accommodate the crowd of *savants*. They overflowed into the adjoining rooms, down the narrow passages, into the outer courtyards. There they ran against the vulgar herd who pressed up to the doors, each struggling to reach the front ranks, all eager to learn the nature of the important communication of President Barbicane; all pushing, squeezing, crushing with that perfect freedom of action which is peculiar to the masses when educated in ideas of "self-government."

On that evening a stranger who might have chanced to be in Baltimore could not have gained admission for love or money into the great hall. That was reserved exclusively for resident or corresponding members; no one else could possibly have obtained a place; and the city magnates, municipal councillors, and "select men" were compelled to mingle with the mere townspeople in order to catch stray bits of news from the interior.

Nevertheless the vast hall presented a curious spectacle. Its immense area was singularly adapted to the purpose. Lofty pillars formed of cannon, superposed upon huge mortars as a base, supported the fine ironwork of the arches, a perfect piece of cast-iron lacework. Trophies of blunderbuses, matchlocks, arquebuses, carbines, all kinds of fire-arms, ancient and modern, were picturesquely interlaced against the walls. The gas lit up in full glare myriads of revolvers grouped in the form of lustres, whilst groups of pistols, and candelabra formed of muskets bound together, completed this magnificent display of brilliance. Models of cannon, bronze castings, sights covered with dents, plates battered by the shots of the Gun Club, assortments of rammers and sponges, chaplets of shells, wreaths of projectiles, garlands of howitzers—in short, all the apparatus of the artillerist, enchanted the eye by this wonderful arrangment and induced a kind of belief that their real purpose was ornamental rather than deadly.

At the further end of the saloon the president, assisted by four secretaries, occupied a large platform. His chair, supported by a carved gun-carriage, was modelled upon the ponderous proportions of a 32-inch mortar. It was pointed at an angle of ninety degrees, and suspended upon trunnions, so that the president could balance himself upon it as upon a rocking-chair, a very agreeable fact in the very hot weather. Upon the table (a huge iron plate supported upon six carronnades) stood an inkstand of exquisite elegance, made of a beautifully chased Spanish piece, and a sonnette, which, when required, could give forth a report equal to that of a revolver. During violent debates this novel kind of bell scarcely sufficed to drown the clamour of these excitable artillerists.

In front of the table benches arranged in zigzag form, like the circumvallations of a retrenchment, formed a succession of bastions and curtains set apart for the use of the members of the club; and on this especial evening one might say, "All the world was on the ramparts." The president was sufficiently well known, however, for all to be assured that he would not put his colleagues to discomfort without some very strong motive.

Impey Barbicane was a man of forty years of age, calm, cold, austere; of a singularly serious and self-contained demeanour, punctual as a chronometer, of imperturbable temper and immovable character; by no means chivalrous, yet adventurous withal, and always bringing practical ideas to bear upon the very rashest enterprises; and essentially New-Englander, a Northern colonist, a descendant of the old anti-Stuart Roundheads, and the implacable enemy of the gentlemen of the South, those ancient Cavaliers of the mother-country. In a word, he was a Yankee to the backbone.

Barbicane had made a large fortune as a timber-merchant. Being nominated Director of Artillery during the war, he proved himself fertile in invention. Bold in his conceptions, he contributed powerfully to the progresss of that arm and gave an immense impetus to experimental researches.

He was a personage of the middle height, having, by a rare exception in the Gun Club, all his limbs complete. His strongly-marked features seemed drawn by square and rule; and if it be true that, in order to judge of a man's character one must look at his profile, Barbicane, so examined, exhibited the most certain indications of energy, audactity, and *sang-froid*.

At this moment he was sitting in his armchair, silent, absorbed, lost in reflection, sheltered under his high-crowned hat—a kind of black silk cylinder which always seems firmly screwed upon the head of an American.

Just when the deep-toned clock in the great hall struck eight, Barbicane, as if he had been set in motion by a spring, raised himself up. A profound silence ensued, and the speaker, in a somewhat emphatic tone of voice, commenced as follows:—

"My brave colleagues, too long already a paralyzing peace has plunged the members of the Gun Club in deplorable inactivity. After a period of years full of incidents we have been compelled to abandon our labours, and to stop short on the road of progress. I do not hesitate to state, boldly, that any war which should recall us to arms would be welcome!" (*Tremendous applause!*)"But war, gentlemen, is impossible under existing circumstances; and, however we may desire it, many years may elapse before our cannon shall again thunder in the field of battle. We must make up our minds, then, to seek in another train of ideas some field for the activity which we all pine for."

The meeting felt that the president was now approaching the critical point, and redoubled their attention accordingly.

"For some months past, my brave colleagues," continued Barbicane, "I have been asking myself whether, while confining ourselves to our own particular objects, we could not enter upon some grand experiment worthy of the nineteenth century; and whether the progress of artillery science would not enable us to carry it out to a successful issue. I have been considering, working, calculating; and the result of my studies is the conviction that we are safe to succeed in an enterprise which to any other country would appear wholly impracticable. This project, the result of long elaboration, is the object of my present communication. It is worthy of yourselves, worthy of the antecedents of the Gun Club; and it cannot fail to make some noise in the world."

A thrill of excitement ran through the meeting.

Barbicane, having by a rapid movement firmly fixed his hat upon his head, calmly continued his harangue:—

"There is no one among you, my brave colleagues, who has not seen *the Moon*, or, at least, heard speak of it. Don't be surprised if I am about to discourse to you regarding this Queen of the Night. It is perhaps reserved for us to become the Columbuses of this unknown world. Only enter into my plans, and second me with all your power, and I will lead you to its conquest, and its name shall be added to those of the thirty-six States which compose this Great Union."

"Three cheers for the Moon!" roared the Gun Club, with one voice.

"The moon, gentlemen, has been carefully studied," continued Barbicane; "her mass, density, and weight; her constitution, motions, distance, as well as her place in the solar system, have all been exactly determined. Selenographic charts have been constructed with a perfection which equals, if it does not even surpass, that of our terrestrial maps. Photography has given us proofs of the incomparable beauty of our satellite; in short, all is known regarding the moon which mathematical science, astronomy, geology, and optics can learn about her. But up to the present moment no direct communication has been established with her."

A violent movement of interest and surprise here greeted this remark of the speaker.

''Permit me,'' he continued, ''to recount to you briefly how certain ardent spirits, starting on imaginary journeys, have penetrated the secrets of our satellite. In the seventeenth century a certain David Fabricius boasted of having seen with his own eyes the inhabitants of the moon. In 1649 a Frenchman, one Jean Baudoin, published a 'Journey performed from the Earth to the Moon by Domingo Gonzales,' a Spanish Adventurer. At the same period Cyrano de Bergerac published that celebrated 'Journeys in the Moon' which met with such success in France. Somewhat later another Frenchman, named Fontenelle, wrote 'The Plurality of Worlds,' a *chef-d'œuvre* of its time. About 1835 a small treatise, translated from the *New York American*, related how Sir John Herschell, having been despatched to the Cape of Good Hope for the purpose of making there some astronomical calculations, had, by means of a telescope brought to perfection by means of internal lighting, reduced the apparent distance of the moon to eighty yards! He then distinctly perceived caverns frequented by hippopotami, green mountains bordered by golden lace-work, sheep with horns of ivory, a white species of deer, and inhabitants with membranous wings, like bats. This *brochure*, the work of an American named Locke, had a great sale. But, to bring this rapid sketch to a close, I will only add that a certain Hans Pfaal, of Rotterdam, launching himself in a balloon filled with a gas extracted from nitrogen, thirty-seven times lighter than hydrogen, reached the moon after a passage of nineteen hours. This journey, like all the previous ones, was purely imaginary; still, it was the work of a popular American author—I mean, Edgar Poe!''

''Cheers for Edgar Poe!'' roared the assemblage, electrified by their president's words.

''I have now enumerated,'' said Barbicane, ''the experiments which I call purely paper ones, and wholly insufficient to establish serious relations with the Queen of Night. Nevertheless, I am bound to add that some practical geniuses have attempted to establish actual communication with her. Thus, a few years ago, a German geometrician proposed to send a scientific expedition to the steppes of Siberia. There, on those vast plains, they were to describe enormous geometric figures, drawn in characters of reflecting luminosity, amongst which was the prop. regarding the 'square of the hypothenuse,' commonly called the '*Ass's bridge*' by the French. 'Every intelligent being,' said the geometrician, 'must understand the scientific meaning of that figure. The selenites, do they exist, will respond by a similar figure; and, a communication being thus once established, it will be easy to form an alphabet which shall enable us to converse with the inhabitants of the moon.' So spoke the German geometrician; but his project was never put into practice, and up to the present day there is no bond in existence between the earth and her satellite. It is reserved for the practical genius of Americans to establish a communication with the sidereal world. The means of arriving thither are simple, easy, certain, infallible—and that is the purpose of my present proposal.''

A storm of acclamations greeted these words. There was not a single person in the whole audience who was not overcome, carried away, lifted out of himself by the speaker's words!

Long continued applause resounded from all sides.

President Barbicane.

As soon as the excitement had partially subsided, Barbicane resumed his speech in a somewhat graver voice.

"You know," said he, "what progress artillery science has made during the last few years, and what a degree of perfection fire-arms of every kind have reached. Moreover, you are well aware that, in general terms, the resisting power of cannon and the expansive force of gunpowder are practically unlimited. Well! starting from this principle, I ask myself whether, supposing sufficient apparatus could be obtained constructed upon the conditions of ascertained resistance, it might not be possible to project a shot up to the moon?"

At these words a murmur of amazement escaped from a thousand panting chests; then succeeded a moment of perfect silence, resembling that profound stillness which preceeds the bursting of a tunderstorm. In point of fact, a thunderstorm did peal forth, but it was the thunder of applause, of cries, and of uproar which made the very hall tremble. The president attempted to speak, but could not. It was fully ten minutes before he could make himself heard.

"Suffer me to finish," he calmly continued. "I have looked at the question in all its bearings, I have resolutely attacked it, and by incontrovertible calculations I find that a projectile endowed with an initial velocity of 12,000 yards per second, and aimed at the moon, must necessarily reach it. I have the honour my brave colleagues, to propose a trial of this little experiment."

CHAPTER 3

EFFECT OF THE PRESIDENT'S COMMUNICATION

IT is impossible to describe the effect produced by the last words of the hon. president—the cries, the shouts, the succession of roars, hurrahs, and all the varied vociferations which the American language is capable of supplying. It was a scene of indescribable confusion and uproar. They shouted, they clapped, they stamped on the floor of the hall. All the weapons in the museum discharged at once could not have more violently set in motion the waves of sound. One need not be surprised at this. There are some cannoneers nearly as noisy as their own guns.

Barbicane remained calm in the midst of this enthusiastic clamour; perhaps he was desirous of addressing a few more words to his colleagues, for by his gestures he demanded silence, and his powerful alarum was worn out by its violent reports. No attention, however, was paid to his request. He was presently torn from his seat and passed from the hands of his faithful colleagues into the arms of a no less excited crowd.

Nothing can astound an American. It has often been asserted that the word "impossible" is not a French one. People have evidently been deceived by the dictionary. In America, all is easy, all is simple; and as for mechanical difficulties, they are overcome before they arise. Between Barbicane's proposition and its realization no true Yankee would have allowed even the semblance of a difficulty to be possible. A thing with them is no sooner said than done.

The triumphal progress of the president continued throughout the evening. It was a regular torchlight procession. Irish, Germans, French, Scotch, all the heterogeneous units which make up the population of Maryland shouted in their respective vernaculars; and the "vivas," "hurrahs," and "bravos" were intermingled in inexpressible enthusiasm.

Just as this crisis, as though she comprehended all this agitation regarding herself, the Moon shone forth with serene splendour, eclipsing by her intense illumination all the surrounding lights. The Yankees all turned their gaze towards her resplendent orb, kissed their hands, called her by all kinds of endearing names. Between eight o'clock and midnight one optician in Jones'-Fall Street made his fortune by the sale of opera-glasses.

Midnight arrived, and the enthusiasm showed no signs of diminution. It spread equally among all classes of citizens—men of science, shopkeepers, merchants, porters, chair-men, as well as "greenhorns," were stirred in their innermost fibres. A national enterprise was at stake. The whole city, high and low, the quays bordering the Patapsco, the ships lying in the basins, disgorged a crowd drunk with joy, gin, and whisky. Every one chattered, argued, discussed, disputed, applauded, from the gentleman lounging upon the bar-room settee with his tumbler of sherry-cobbler before him down to the waterman who got drunk upon his "knock-me-down" in the dingy taverns of Fell Point.

About 2 a.m., however, the excitement began to subside. President Barbicane reached his house, bruised, crushed, and squeezed almost to a mummy. A Hercules could not have resisted a similar outbreak of enthusiasm. The crowd gradually deserted the squares and streets. The four railways from Philadelphia and Washington, Harrisburg and Wheeling, which converge at Baltimore, whirled away the heterogeneous population to the four corners of the United States, and the city subsided into comparative tranquillity.

On the following day, thanks to the telegraphic wires, five hundred newspapers and journals, daily, weekly, monthly, or bi-monthly, all took up the question. They examined it under all its different aspects, physical, meteorological, economical, or moral, up to its bearings on politics or civilization. They debated whether the moon was a finished world, or whether it was destined to undergo any further transformation. Did it resemble the earth at the period when the latter was destitute as yet of an atmosphere? What kind of spectacle would its hidden hemisphere present to our terrestrial spheroid? Granting that the question at present was simply that of sending a projectile up to the moon, every one must see that that involved the commencement of a series of experiments. All must hope that some day America would penetrate the deepest secrets of that mysterious orb; and some even seemed to fear lest its conquest should not sensibly derange the equilibrium of Europe.

The project once under discussion, not a single paragraph suggested a doubt of its realization. All the papers, pamphlets, reports—all the journals published by the scientific, literary, and religious societies enlarged upon its advantages; and the Society of Natural History of Boston, the Society of Science and Art of Albany, the Geographical and Statistical Society of New York, the Philosophical Society of Philadelphia, and the Smithsonian of Washington sent innumerable letters of congratulation to the Gun Club, together with offers of immediate assistance and money.

From that day forward Impay Barbicane became one of the greatest citizens of the United States, a kind of Washington of Science. A single trait of feeling, taken from many others, will serve to show the point which this homage of a whole people to a single individual attained.

Some few days after this memorable meeting of the Gun Club, the manager of an English company announced, at the Baltimore theatre, the production of "Much ado about Nothing." But the populace, seeing in that title an allusion damaging to Barbicane's project, broke into the auditorium, smashed the benches, and compelled the unlucky director to alter his playbill. Being a sensible man, he bowed to the public will and replaced the offending comedy by "As you like it;" and for many weeks he realized fabulous profits.

CHAPTER 4

REPLY FROM THE OBSERVATORY OF CAMBRIDGE

BARBICANE, however, lost not one moment amidst all the enthusiasm of which he had become the object. His first care was to reassemble his colleagues in the board-room of the Gun Club. There, after some discussion, it was agreed to consult the astronomers regarding the astronomical part of the enterprize. Their reply once ascertained, they could then discuss the mechanical means, and nothing should be wanting to ensure the success of this great experiment.

A note couched in precise terms, containing special interrogatories, was then drawn up and addressed to the Observatory of Cambridge in Massachusetts. This city, where the first University of the United States was founded, is justly celebrated for its astronomical staff. There are to be found assembled all the most eminent men of science. Here is to be seen at work that powerful telescope which enabled Bond to resolve the nebula of Andromeda, and Clarke to discover the satellite of Sirius. This celebrated institution fully justified on all points the confidence reposed in it by the Gun Club.

So, after two days, the reply so impatiently awaited was placed in the hands of President Barbicane.

It was couched in the following terms:—

"*The Director of the Cambridge Observatory to the President of the Gun Club at Baltimore.*

"CAMBRIDGE, Oct. 7.

"On the receipt of your favour of the 6th inst., addressed to the Observatory of Cambridge in the name of the Members of the Baltimore Gun Club, our staff was immediately called together, and it was judged expedient to reply as follows:—

"The questions which have been proposed to it are these,—

" '1. Is it possible to transmit a projectile up to the moon?

" '2. What is the exact distance which seperates the earth from its satellite?

" '3. What will be the period of transit of the projectile when endowed with sufficient initial velocity? and, consequently, at what moment ought it to be discharged in order that it may touch the moon at a particular point?

" '4. At what precise moment will the moon present herself in the most favourable position to be reached by the projectile?

" '5. What point in the heavens ought the cannon to be aimed at which is intended to discharge the projectile?

" '6. What place will the moon occupy in the heavens at the moment of the projectile's departure?'

Regarding the *first* question, 'Is it possible to transmit a projectile up to the moon?'

"*Answer.*—Yes; provided it possess an initial velocity of 1200 yards per second; calculations prove that to be sufficient. In proportion as we recede from the earth the action of gravitation diminishes in the inverse ratio of the square of the distance; that is to say, *at three times a given distance the action is nine times less*. Consequently, the weight of a shot will decrease, and will become reduced to *zero* at the instant that the attraction of the moon exactly counterpoises that of the earth; that is to say, at 47/52 of its passage. At that instant the projectile will have no weight whatever; and, if it passes that point, it will fall into the moon by the sole effect of the lunar attraction. The *theoretical possibility* of the experiment is therefore absolutely demonstrated; its *success* must depend upon the power of the engine employed.

"As to the *second* question, 'What is the exact distance which separates the earth from its satellite?'

"*Answer.*—The moon does not describe a *circle* round the earth, but rather an *ellipse*, of which our earth occupies one of the *foci*; the consequence, therefore, is, that at certain times it approaches nearer to, and at others it recedes farther from, the earth; in astronomical language, it is at one time in *apogee*, at another in *perigee*. Now the difference between its greatest and its least distance is too considerable to be left out of consideration. In point of fact, in its apogee the moon is 247,552 miles, and in its perigee, 218,657 miles only distant; a fact which makes a difference of 28,895 miles, or more than one ninth of the entire distance. The perigee distance, therefore, is that which ought to serve as the basis of all calculations.

"To the *third* question:—

"*Answer.*—If the shot should preserve continuously its initial velocity of 12,000 yards per second, it would require little more than nine hours to reach its destination; but, inasmuch as that initial velocity will be continually decreasing, it results that, taking everything into consideration, it will occupy 300,000 seconds, that is 83hrs. 20m. in reaching the point where the attraction of the earth and moon will be *in equilibrio*. From this point it will fall into the moon in 50,000 seconds, or 13hrs. 53m. 20sec. It will be desirable, therefore, to discharge it 97hrs. 13m. 20sec. before the arrival of the moon at the point aimed at.

"Regarding guestion *four*, 'At what precise moment will the moon present herself in the most favourable position, &c.?'

"*Answer.*—After what has been said above, it will be necessary, first of all, to choose the period when the moon will be in perigee, and *also* the moment when she will be crossing the zenith, which latter event will further diminish the entire distance by a length equal to the radius of the earth, i.e. 3919 miles; the result of which will be that the final passage remaining to be accomplished will be 214,976 miles. But although the moon passes her perigee every month, she does not reach the zenith always at *exactly the same moment*. She does not appear under these two conditions simultaneously, except at long intervals of time. It will be necessary, therefore, to wait for the moment when her passage in perigee shall coincide with that in the zenith. Now, by a fortunate circumstance, on the 4th December in the ensuing year the moon *will* present these two conditions. At midnight she will be in perigee, that is, at her shortest distance from the earth, and at the same moment she will be crossing the zenith.

"On the *fifth* question, 'At what point in the heavens ought the cannon to be aimed?'

"*Answer*.—The preceding remarks being admitted, the cannon ought to be pointed to the zenith of the place. Its fire, therefore, will be perpendicular to the plane of the horizon; and the projectile will soonest pass beyond the range of the terrestrial attraction. But, in order that the moon should reach the zenith of a given place, it is necessary that the place should not exceed in latitude the declination of the luminary; in other words, it must be comprised within the degrees 0° and 28° of lat. N. or S. In every other spot the fire must necessarily be oblique, which would seriously militate against the success of the experiment.

"As to the *sixth* question, 'What place will the moon occupy in the heavens at the moment of the projectile's departure?'

"*Answer*.—At the moment when the projectile shall be discharged into space, the moon, which travels daily forward 13° 10′ 35″, will be distant from the zenith point by four times that quantity, i.e. by 52° 42′ 20″, a space which corresponds to the path which she will describe during the entire journey of the projectile. But, inasmuch as it is equally necessary to take into account the deviation which the rotary motion of the earth will impart to the shot, as the shot cannot reach the moon until after a deviation equal to 16 radii of the earth, which, calculated upon the moon's orbit are equal to about eleven degrees, it becomes necessary to add these eleven degrees to those which express the retardation of the moon just mentioned: that is to say, in round numbers, about 64 degrees. Consequently, at the moment of firing the visual radius applied to the moon will describe, with the vertical line of the place, an angle of sixty-four degrees.

"These are our answers to the questions proposed to the Observatory of Cambridge by the members of the Gun Club:—

"To sum up,—

"1st. The cannon ought to be planted in a country situated between 0° and 28° of N. or S. lat.

"2ndly. It ought to be pointed directly towards the zenith of the place.

"3rdly. The projectile ought to be propelled with an initial velocity of 12,000 yards per second.

"4thly. It ought to be discharged at 10hrs. 46m. 40sec. of the 1st December of the ensuing year.

"5thly. It will meet the moon four days after its discharge, precisely at midnight on the 4th December, at the moment of its transit across the zenith.

"The members of the Gun Club ought, therefore, without delay, to commence the works necessary for such an experiment, and to be prepared to set to work at the moment determined upon; for, if they should suffer this 4th December to go by, they will not find the moon again under the same conditions of perigee and of zenith until eighteen years and eleven days afterwards.

"The Staff of the Cambridge Observatory place themsèlves entirely at their disposal in respect of all questions of theoretical astronomy; and herewith add their congratulations to those of all the rest of America.

"For the Astronomical Staff,

"J. M. Belfast,

"Director of the Observatory of Cambridge."

CHAPTER 5

THE ROMANCE OF THE MOON

An observer endued with an infinite rage of vision, and placed in that unknown centre around which the entire world revolves, might have beheld myriads of atoms filling all space during the chaotic epoch of the universe. Little by little, as ages went on, a change took place; a general law of attraction manifested itself, to which the hitherto errant atoms became obedient: these atoms combined together chemically according to their affinities, formed themselves into molecules, and composed those nebulous masses with which the depths of the heavens are strewed.

These masses became immediately endued with a rotary motion around their own central point. This centre, formed of indefinite molecules, began to revolve round its own axis during its gradual condensation; then, following the immutable laws of mechanics, in proportion as its bulk diminished by condensation, its rotary motion became accelerated, and these two effects continuing, the result was the formation of one principal star, the centre of the nebulous mass.

By attentively watching, the observer would then have perceived the other molecules of the mass, following the example of this central star, become likewise condensed by gradually accelerated rotation, and gravitating round it in the shape of innumerable stars. Thus was formed the *Nebulæ,* of which astronomers have reckoned up nearly 5000.

Amongst these 5000 nebulæ there is one which has received the name of the Milky Way, and which contains eighteen millions of stars, each of which has become the centre of a solar world.

If the observer had then specially directed his attention to one of the more humble and less brilliant of these stellar bodies, a star of the fourth class, that which is arrogantly called the Sun, all the phenomena to which the formation of the Universe is to be ascribed would have been successively fulfilled before his eyes. In fact, he would have perceived this sun, as yet in the gaseous state, and composed of moving molecules, revolving round its axis in order to accomplish its work of concentration. This motion, faithful to the laws of mechanics, would have been accelerated with the diminution of its volume; and a moment would have arrived when the centrifugal force would have overpowered the centripetal, which causes the molecules all to tend towards the centre.

Another phenomenon would now have passed before the observer's eye, and the molecules situated on the plane of the equator escaping, like a stone from a sling of which the cord had suddenly snapped, would have formed around the sun sundry concentric rings resembling that of Saturn. In their turn, again, these rings of cosmical matter, excited by a rotary motion round the central mass, would have been broken up and decomposed into secondary nebulosities, that is to say, into planets. Similarly he would have observed these planets throw off one or more rings each, which became the origin of the secondary bodies which we call satellites.

Thus, then, advancing from atom to molecule, from molecule to nebulous mass, from that to a principal star, from star to sun, from sun to planet, and hence to satellite, we have the whole series of transformations undergone by the heavenly bodies during the first days of the world.

Now, of those attendant bodies which the sun maintains in their elliptical orbits by the great law of gravitation, some few in their turn possess satellites. Uranus has eight, Saturn eight, Jupiter four, Neptune possibly three, and the Earth *one*. This last, one of the least important of the entire solar system, we call *the Moon*; and it is she whom the daring genius of the Americans professed their intention of conquering.

The moon, by her comparative proximity, and the constantly varying appearances produced by her several phases, has always occupied a considerable share of the attention of the inhabitants of the earth.

From the time of Thales of Miletus, in the fifth century B.C., down to that of Copernicus in the fifteenth and Tycho Brahé in the sixteenth century A.D., observations have been from time to time carried on with more or less correctness, until in the present day the altitudes of the lunar mountains have been determined with exactitude. Galileo explained the phenomena of the lunar light produced during certain of her phases by the existence of mountains, to which he assigned a mean altitude of 27,000 feet. After him Hévelius, an astronomer of Dantzic, reduced the highest elevations to 15,000 feet; but the calculations of Riccioli brought them up again to 21,000 feet.

At the close of the eighteenth century Herschell, armed with a powerful telescope, considerably reduced the preceding measurements. He assigned a height of 11,400 feet to the maximum elevations, and reduced the mean of the different altitudes to little more than 2400 feet. But Herschell's calculations were in their turn corrected by the observations of Halley, Nasmyth, Bianchini, Gruithuysen, and others; but it was reserved for the labours of Bœer and Mædler finally to solve the question. They succeeded in measuring 1905 different elevations, of which six exceed 15,000 feet, and twenty-two exceed 14,400 feet. The highest summit of all towers to a height of 22,606 feet above the surface of the lunar disc. At the same period the examination of the moon was completed. She appeared completely riddled with *craters*, and her essentially volcanic character was apparent at each observation. By the absence of refraction in the rays of the planets occulted by her we conclude that she is absolutely devoid of an atmosphere. The absence of air entails the absence of water. It became, therefore, manifest that the Selenites, to support life under such conditions, must possess a special organization of their own, must differ remarkably from the inhabitants of the earth.

At length, thanks to modern art, instruments of still higher perfection searched the moon without intermission, not leaving a single point of her surface unex-

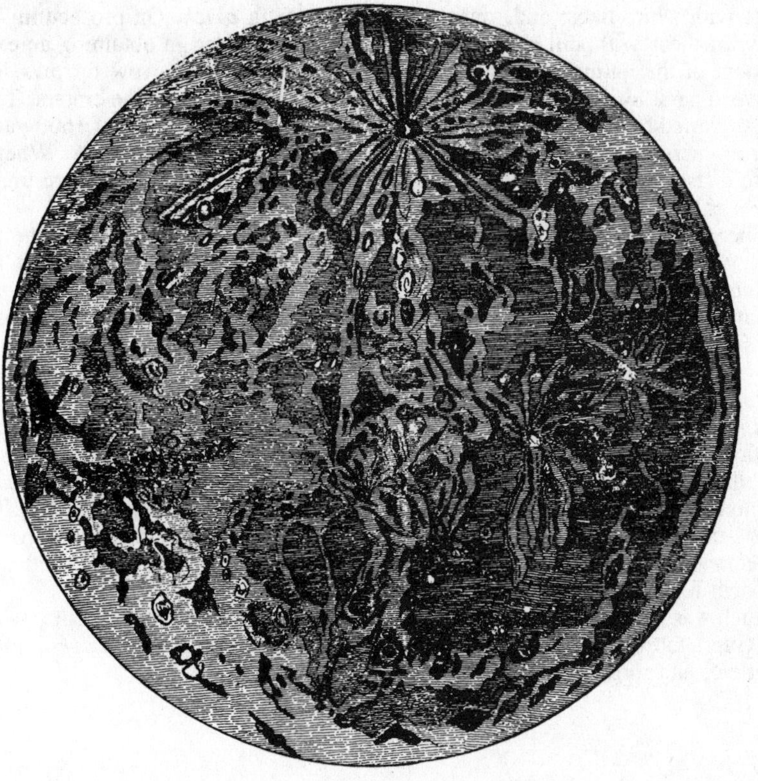

The moon's disc.

plored; and notwithstanding that her diameter measures 2150 miles, her surface equals the 1-15th part of that of our globe, and her bulk the 1-49th part of that of the terrestrial spheroid—not one of her secrets was able to escape the eyes of the astronomers; and these skilful men of science carried to even greater degree their prodigious observations.

Thus they remarked that, during full moon, the disc appeared scored in certain parts with *white* lines; and, during the phases, with *black*. On prosecuting the study of these with still greater precision, they succeeded in obtaining an exact account of the nature of these lines. They were long and narrow furrows sunk between parallel ridges, bordering generally upon the edges of the craters. Their length varied between ten and 100 miles, and their width was about 1600 yards. Astronomers called them chasms, but they could not get any farther. Whether these chasms were the dried-up beds of ancient rivers or not they were unable thoroughly to ascertain.

The Americans, amongst others, hoped one day or other to determine this geological question. They also undertook to examine the true nature of that system of parallel ramparts discovered on the moon's surface by Gruithuysen, a learned professor of Munich, who considered them to be "a system of fortifications thrown up by the Selenitic engineers." These two points, yet obscure, as well as others, no doubt, could not be definitively settled except by direct communication with the moon.

Regarding the degree of intensity of its light, there was nothing more to learn on this point. It was known that it is 300,000 times weaker than that of the sun, and that its heat has no appreciable effect upon the thermometer. As to the phenomenon known as the "ashy light," it is explained naturally by the effect of the transmission of the solar rays from the earth to the moon, which give the appearance of completeness to the lunar disc, while it presents itself under the crescent form during its first and last phases.

Such was the state of knowledge acquired regarding the earth's satellite, which the Gun Club undertook to perfect in all its aspects, cosmographic, geological, political, and moral.

CHAPTER 6

THE PERMISSIVE LIMITS OF IGNORANCE AND BELIEF IN THE UNITED STATES

THE immediate result of Barbicane's proposition was to place upon the orders of the day all the astronomical facts relative to the Queen of Night. Everybody set to work to study assiduously. One would have thought that the moon had just appeared for the first time, and that no one had ever before caught a glimpse of her in the heavens. The papers revived all the old anecdotes in which the "sun of the wolves" played a part; they recalled the influences which the ignorance of past ages ascribed to her; in short, all America was seized with selenomania, or had become moon-mad.

The scientific journals, for their part, dealt more especially with the questions which touched upon the enterprise of the Gun Club. The letter of the Observatory of Cambridge was published by them, and commented upon with unreserved approval.

Until that time most people had been ignorant of the mode in which the distance which separates the moon from the earth is calculated. They took advantage of this fact to explain to them that this distance was obtained by measuring the parallax of the moon. The term parallax proving "caviare to the general," they further explained that it meant the angle formed by the inclination of two straight lines drawn from either extremity of the earth's radius to the moon. On doubts being expressed as to the correctness of this method, they immediately proved that not only was this mean distance 234,347 miles, but that astronomers could not possibly be in error in their estimate by more than 70 miles either way.

To those who were not familiar with the motions of the moon, they demonstrated that she possesses two distinct motions, the first being that of rotation upon her axis, the second that of revolution round the earth, accomplishing both together in an equal period of time, that is to say, in 27⅓ days.

The motion of rotation is that which produces day and night on the surface of the moon; save that there is only one day and one night in the lunar month, each lasting 354⅓ hours. But, happily for her, the face turned towards the terrestrial globe is illuminated by it with an intensity equal to the light of fourteen moons. As to the other face, always invisible to us, it has of necessity 354 hours of absolute night, tempered only by the "pale glimmer which falls upon it from the stars."

Some well-intentioned but rather obstinate persons, could not at first comprehend how, if the moon displays invariably the same face to the earth during her revolution, she can describe one turn round herself. To such they answered, "Go into your dining-room, and walk round the table in such a way as always to keep your face turned towards the centre; by the time you will have achieved one complete round you will have completed one turn round yourself, since your eye will have traversed successively every point of the room. Well, then, the room is the heavens, the table is the earth, and the moon is yourself." And they would go away delighted.

So, then, the moon displays invariably the same face to the earth; nevertheless, to be quite exact, it is necessary to add that, in consequence of certain fluctuations of north and south, and of west and east, termed her libration, she permits rather more than the half, that is to say, five-sevenths, to be seen.

As soon as the ignoramuses came to understand as much as the Director of the Observatory himself knew, they began to worry themselves regarding her revolution round the earth, whereupon twenty scientific reviews immediately came to the rescue. They pointed out to them then that the firmament, with its infinitude of stars, may be considered as one vast dial-plate, upon which the moon travels, indicating the true time to all the inhabitants of the earth; that it is during this movement that the Queeen of Night exhibits her different phases; that the moon is *full* when she is in *opposition* with the sun, that is, when the three bodies are on the same straight line, the earth occupying the centre; that she is *new* when she is in *conjunction* with the sun, that is, when she is between it and the earth; and lastly, that she is in her *first* or *last* quarter, when she makes with the sun and the earth an angle of which she herself occupies the apex.

Regarding the altitude which the moon attains above the horizon, the letter of the Cambridge Observatory had said all that was to be said in that respect. Every one knew that this altitude varies according to the latitude of the observer. But the only zones of the globe in which the moon passes the zenith, that is, the point directly over the head of the spectator, are of necessity comprised between the twenty-eighth parallels and the equator. Hence the importance of the advice to try the experiment upon some point of that part of the globe, in order that the projectile might be discharged perpendicularly, and so the soonest escape the action of gravitation. This was an essential condition to the success of the enterprise, and continued actively to engage the public attention.

Regarding the path described by the moon in her revolution round the earth, the Cambridge Observatory had demonstrated that this path is a re-entering curve, not a perfect circle, but an ellipse, of which the earth occupies one of the *foci*. It was also well understood that it is farthest removed from the earth during its *apogee*, and approaches most nearly to it at its *perigee*.

Such then was the extent of knowledge possessed by every American on the subject, and of which no one could decently profess ignorance. Still, while these true principles were being rapidly disseminated many errors and illusory fears proved less easy to eradicate.

For instance, some worthy persons maintained that the moon was an ancient comet which, in describing its elongated orbit round the sun, happened to pass near the earth, and became confined within her circle of attraction. These drawing-room astronomers professed so to explain the charred aspect of the moon—a disaster which they attributed to the intensity of the solar heat; only, on being reminded that comets have an atmosphere, and that the moon has little or none, they were fairly at a loss for a reply.

Others again, belonging to the doubting class expressed certain fears as to the postion of the moon. They had heard it said that, according to observations made in the time of the Caliphs, her revolution had become accelerated in a certain degree. Hence they concluded, logically enough, that an acceleration of motion ought to be accompanied by a corresponding diminution in the distance separating the two bodies; and that, supposing the double effect to be continued to infinity, the moon would end by one day falling into the earth. However, they became reassured as to the fate of future generations on being apprised that, according to the calculations of Laplace, this acceleration of motion is confined within very restricted limits, and that a proportional diminution of speed will be certain to succeed it. So, then, the stability of the solar system would not be deranged in ages to come.

Their remains but the third class, the superstitious. These worthies were not content merely to rest in ignorance; they must know all about things which had no existence whatever, and as to the moon, they had long known all about her. One set regarded her disc as a polished mirror, by means of which people could see each other from different points of the earth and interchange their thoughts. Another set pretended that out of one thousand new moons that had been observed, nine hundred and fifty had been attended with remarkable disturbances, such as cataclysms, revolutions, earthquakes, the deluge, &c. Then they believed in some mysterious influence exercised by her over human destinies—that every Selenite was attached to some inhabitant of the earth by a tie of sympathy; they maintained that the entire vital system is subject to her control, &c., &c. But in time the majority renounced these vulgar errors, and espoused the true side of the question. As for the Yankees, they had no other ambition than to take possession of this new continent of the sky, and to plant upon the summit of its highest elevation the star-spangled banner of the United States of America.

CHAPTER 7

THE HYMN OF THE CANNON-BALL

THE Observatory of Cambridge in its memorable letter had treated the question from a purely astronomical point of view. The mechanical part still remained.

President Barbicane had, without loss of time, nominated a Working Committee of the Gun Club. The duty of this Committee was to resolve the three grand questions of the cannon, the projectile, and the powder. It was composed of four members of great technical knowledge, Barbicane (with a casting vote in case of equality), General Morgan, Major Elphinstone, and J. T. Maston, to whom were confided the functions of secretary. On the 8th of October the Committee met at the house of President Barbicane, 3, Republican Street. The meeting was opened by the president himself.

"Gentlemen," said he, "we have to resolve one of the most important problems in the whole of the noble science of gunnery. It might appear, perhaps, the most logical course to devote our first meeting to the discussion of the engine to be employed. Nevertheless, after mature consideration, it has appeared to me that the question of the projectile must take precedence of that of the cannon, and that the dimensions of the latter must necessarily depend upon those of the former."

"Suffer me to say a word," here broke in J. T. Maston. Permission having been granted, "Gentlemen," said he, with an inspired accent, "our president is right in placing the question of the projectile above all others. The ball we are about to discharge at the moon is our ambassador to her, and I wish to consider it from a moral point of view. The cannon-ball, gentlemen, to my mind, is the most magnificent manifestation of human power. If Providence has created the stars and the planets, man has called the cannon-ball into existence. Let Providence claim the swiftness of electricity and of light, of the stars, the comets, and the planets, of wind and sound—we claim to have invented the swiftness of the cannon-ball, a hundred times superior to that of the swiftest horses or railway train. How glorious will be the moment when, infinitely exceeding all hitherto attained velocities, we shall launch our new projectile with the rapidity of seven miles a second! Shall it not, gentlemen—shall it not be received up there with the honours due to a terrestrial ambassador?"

Overcome with emotion the orator sat down and applied himself to a huge plate of sandwiches before him.

"And now," said Barbicane, "let us quit the domain of poetry and come direct to the question."

"By all means," replied the members, each with his mouth full of sandwich.

"The problem before us," continued the president, "is how to communicate to a projectile a velocity of 12,000 yards per second. Let us at present examine the velocities hitherto attained. General Morgan will be able to enlighten us on this point."

"And the more easily," replied the general, "that during the war I was a member of the Committee of experiments. I may say, then, that the 100-pounder Dahlgrens, which carried a distance of 5000 yards, impressed upon their projectile an initial velocity of 500 yards a second. The Rodman Columbiad threw a shot weighing half a ton a distance of six miles, with a velocity of 800 yards per second—a result which Armstrong and Palisser have never obtained in England."

"This," replied Barbicane, "is, I believe, the maximum velocity ever attained?"

"It is so," replied the general.

"Ah!" groaned J. T. Maston, "if my mortar had not burst—"

"Yes," quietly replied Barbicane, "but it did burst. We must take, then, for our starting-point this velocity of 800 yards. We must increase it twenty-fold. Now, reserving for another discussion the means of producing this velocity, I will call your attention to the dimensions which it will be proper to assign to the shot. You understand that we have nothing to do here with projectiles weighing at most but half a ton."

"Why not?" demanded the major.

"Because the shot," quickly replied J. T. Maston, "must be big enough to attract the attention of the inhabitants of the moon, if there are any?"

"Yes," replied Barbicane, "and for another reason more important still."

"What mean you?" asked the major.

"I mean that it is not enough to discharge a projectile, and then take no further notice of it; we must follow it throughout its course, up to the moment when it shall reach its goal."

"What?" shouted the general and the major in great surprise.

"Undoubtedly," replied Barbicane, composedly, "or our experiment would produce no result."

"But then," replied the major, "you will have to give this projectile enormous dimensions."

"No! Be so good as to listen. You know that optical instruments have acquired great perfection; with certain telescopes we have succeeded in obtaining enlargements of 6000 times and reducing the moon to within forty miles' distance. Now, at this distance, any objects sixty feet square would be perfectly visible. If, then, the penetrative power of telescopes has not been further increased, it is because that power detracts from their light; and the moon, which is but a reflecting mirror, does not give back sufficient light to enable us to perceive objects of lesser magnitude."

"Well, then, what do you propose to do?" asked the general, "Would you give your projectile a diameter of sixty feet?"

"Not so."

"Do you intend, then, to increase the luminous power of the moon?"

"Exactly so. If I can succeed in diminishing the density of the atmosphere through which the moon's light has to travel I shall have rendered her light more intense. To effect that object it will be enough to establish a telescope on some elevated mountain. That is what we will do."

"I give it up," answered the major. "You have such a way of simplifying things. And what enlargement do you expect to obtain in this way?"

"One of 48,000 times, which should bring the moon within an apparent distance of five miles; and, in order to be visible, objects need not have a diameter of more than nine feet."

"So, then," cried J. T. Maston, "our projectile need not be more than nine feet in diameter."

"Let me observe, however," interrupted Major Elphinstone, "this will involve a weight such as—"

"My dear major," replied Barbicane, "before discussing its weight, permit me to enumerate some of the marvels which our ancestors have achieved in this respect. I don't mean to pretend that the science of gunnery has not advanced, but it is as well to bear in mind that during the middle ages they obtained results more surprising, I will venture to say, than ours. For instance, during the siege of Constantinople by Mahomet II., in 1453, stone shot of 1900lbs weight were employed. At Malta, in the time of the knights, there was a gun of the fortress of St. Elmo which threw a projectile weighing 2500lbs. And, now, what is the extent of what we have seen ourselves? Armstrong guns discharging shot of 500lbs., and the Rodman guns projectiles of half a ton! It seems, then, that if projectiles have gained in range, they have lost far more in weight. Now, if we turn our efforts in that direction, we ought to arrive, with the progress of science, at ten times the weight of the shot of Mahomet II. and the Knights of Malta."

"Clearly," replied the major; "but what metal do you calculate upon employing?"

"Simply cast iron," said General Morgan.

"But," interrupted the major, "since the weight of a shot is proportionate to its volume, an iron ball of nine feet in diameter would be of tremendous weight."

"Yes, if it were solid, not if it were hollow."

"Hollow? then it would be a shell?"

"Yes, a shell," replied Barbicane; "decidely it must be. A solid shot of 108 inches would weight more than 200,000lbs., a weight evidently far too great. Still, as we must reserve a certain stability for out projectile, I propose to give it a weight of 20,000lbs."

"What, then, will be the thickness of the sides?" asked the major.

"If we follow the usual proportion," replied Morgan, "a diameter of 108 inches would require sides of two feet thickness, or less."

"That would be too much," replied Barbicane; "for you will observe that the question is not that of a shot intended to pierce an iron plate: it will suffice, therefore to give it sides strong enough to resist the pressure of the gas. The problem, therefore, is this—What thickness ought a cast-iron shell to have in order not to weigh more than 20,000lbs.? Our clever secretary will soon enlighten us upon this point."

"Nothing easier," replied the worthy secretary of the Committee; and, rapidly tracing a few algebraical formulæ upon paper, among which n^2 and x^2 frequently appeared, he presently said,—

"The sides will require a thickness of less than two inches."

"Will that be enough?" asked the major doubtfully.

"Clearly not!" replied the president.

"What is to be done, then?" said Elphinstone, with a puzzled air.

"Employ another metal instead of iron."

"Copper?" said Morgan.

"No; that would be too heavy. I have better than that to offer."

"What then?" said the major.

"Aluminium!" replied Barbicane.

"Aluminium?" cried his three colleagues in chorus.

"Unquestionably, my friends. This valuable metal possesses the whiteness of silver, the indestructibility of gold, the tenacity of iron, the fusibility of copper, the lightness of glass. It is easily wrought, is very widely distributed, forming the base of most of the rocks, is three times lighter than iron, and seems to have been created for the express purpose of furnishing us with the material for our projectile."

"But, my dear president," said the major, "is not the cost price of aluminium extremely high?"

"It was so at its first discovery, but it has fallen now to nine dollars a pound."

"But still, nine dollars a pound!" replied the major, who was not willing readily to give in; "even that is an enourmous price."

"Undoubtedly, my dear major; but not beyond our reach."

"What will the projectile weigh then?" asked Morgan.

"Here is the result of my calculations," replied Barbicane. "A shot of 108 inches in diameter, and 12 inches in thickness, would weigh, in cast-iron, 67,440lbs.; cast in aluminium, its weight will be reduced to 19,250lbs."

"Capital!" cried the major; "but do you know that, at nine dollars the pound, this projectile will cost—"

"One hundred and seventy-three thousand and fifty dollars ($173,050). I know it quite well. But fear not, my friends; the money will not be wanting for our enterprise, I will answer for it. Now what say you to aluminium, gentlemen?"

"Adopted!" replied the three members of the Committee.

So ended the first meeting. The question of the projectile was definitively settled.

CHAPTER 8

HISTORY OF THE CANNON

THE resolutions passed at the last meeting produced a great effect out of doors. Timid people took fright at the idea of a shot weighing 20,000lbs. being launched into space; they asked what cannon could ever transmit a sufficient velocity to such a mighty mass. The minutes of the second meeting were destined triumphantly to answer such questions. The following evening the discussion was renewed.

"My dear colleagues," said Barbicane, without further preamble, "the subject now before us is the construction of the engine, its length, its composition, and its weight. It is probable that we shall end by giving it gigantic dimensions; but however great may be the difficulties in the way, our mechanical genius will readily surmout them. Be good enough, then, to give me your attention, and do not hesitate to make objections at the close. I have no fear of them. The problem before us is how to communicate an initial force of 12,000 yards per second to a shell of 108 inches in diameter, weighing 20,000lbs. Now when a projectile is launched into space, what happens to it? It is acted upon by three independent forces, the resistance of the air, the attraction of the earth, and the force of impulsion with which it is endowed. Let us examine these three forces. The resistance of the air is of little importance. The atmosphere of the earth does not exceed forty miles. Now, with the given rapidity, the projectile will have traversed this in five seconds, and the period is too brief for the resistance of the medium to be regarded otherwise than as insignificant. Proceeding, then, to the attraction of the earth, that is, the weight of the shell, we know that this weight will dimish in the inverse ratio of the square of the distance. When a body left to itself falls to the surface of the earth, it falls five feet in the first second; and if the same body were removed 257,542 miles farther off, in other words, to the distance of the moon, its fall would be reduced to about half a line in the first second. That is almost equivalent to a state of perfect rest. Our business, then, is to overcome progressively this action of gravitation. The mode of accomplishing that is by the force of impulsion."

"There's the difficulty," broke in the major.

"True," replied the president; "But we will overcome that, for this force of impulsion will depend upon the length of the engine and the powder employed, the latter being limited only by the resisting power of the former. Our business, then, to-day is with the dimensions of the cannon."

"Now, up to the present time," said Barbicane, "our longest guns have not exceeeded twenty-five feet in length. We shall therefore astonish the world by the dimensions we shall be obliged to adopt. It must evidently be, then, a gun of great range, since the length of the piece will increase the detention of the gas accumulated behind the projectile; but there is no advantage in passing certain limits."

"Quite so," said the major. "What is the rule in such a case?"

"Ordinarily the length of a gun is 20 to 25 times the diameter of the shot, and its weight 235 to 240 times that of the shot."

"That is not enough," cried J. T. Maston impetuously.

"I agree with you, my good friend; and, in fact, following this proportion for a projectile nine feet in diameter, weighing 30,000lbs., the gun would only have a length of 225 feet, and a weight of 7,200,000lbs."

"Ridiculous!" rejoined Maston. "As well take a pistol."

"I think so too," replied Barbicane; "that is why I propose to quadruple that length, and to construct a gun of 900 feet."

The general and the major offered some objections; nevertheless, the proposition, actively supported by the secreatry, was definitively adopted.

"But," said Elphinstone, "what thickness must we give it?"

"A thickness of six feet," replied Barbicane.

"You surely don't think of mounting a mass like that upon a carriage?" asked the major.

"It would be a superb idea, though," said Maston.

"But impracticable," replied Barbicane. "No; I think of sinking this engine in the earth alone, binding it with hoops of wrought iron, and finally surrounding it with a thick mass of masonry of stone and cement. The piece once cast, it must be bored with great precision, so as to preclude any possible windage. So there will be no loss whatever of gas, and all the expansive force of the powder will be employed in the propulsion."

"One simple question," said Elphinstone: "is our gun to be rifled?"

"No, certainly not," replied Barbicane; "we require an enormous initial velocity; and you are well aware that a shot quits a rifled gun less rapidly than it does a smooth-bore."

"True," rejoined the major.

The Committee here adjourned for a few minutes to tea and sandwiches.

On the discussion being renewed, "Gentlemen," said Barbicane, "we must now take into consideration the metal to be employed. Our cannon must be possessed of great tenacity, great hardness, be infusible by heat, indissoluble, and inoxydable by the corrosive action of acids."

"There is no doubt about that," replied the major; "and as we shall have to employ an immense quantity of metal, we shall not be at a loss for choice."

"Well, then," said Morgan, "I propose the best alloy hitherto known, which consists of 100 parts of copper, 12 of tin, and 6 of brass."

"I admit," replied the president, "that this composition has yielded excellent results, but in the present cast it would be too expensive, and very difficult to work. I think, then, that we ought to adopt a material excellent in its way and of low price, such as cast iron. What is your advice, major?"

"I quite agree with you," replied Elphinstone.

"In fact," continued Barbicane, "cast iron cost ten times less than bronze; it is easy to cast, it runs readily from the moulds of sand, it is easy of manipulation, it is at once economical of money and of time. In addition, it is excellent as a material, and I well remember that during the war, at the siege of Atlanta, some iron guns fired one thousand rounds at intervals of twenty minutes without injury."

"Cast iron is very brittle, though," replied Morgan.

"Yes, but it possesses great resistance. I will now ask our worthy secretary to calculate the weight of a cast-iron gun with a bore of nine feet and thickness of six feet of metal."

"In a moment," replied Maston. Then, dashing off some algebraical formulæ with marvellous facility, in a minute or two he declared the following result:—

"The cannon will weigh 68,040 tons. And, at two cents a pound, it will cost—?"

"2,510,701 dollars."

Maston, the major, and the general regarded Barbicane with uneasy looks.

"Well, gentlemen," replied the president, "I repeat what I said yesterday. Make yourselves easy; the millions will not be wanting."

With this assurance of their president the Committee separated, after having fixed their third meeting for the following evening.

Ideal sketch of J. T. Maston's gun.

CHAPTER 9

THE QUESTION OF THE POWDERS

THERE remained for consideration merely the question of powders. The public awaited with interest its final decision. The size of the projectile, the length of the cannon being settled, what would be the quantity of powder necessary to produce impulsion?

It is generally asserted that gunpowder was invented in the fourteenth century by the monk Schwartz, who paid for his grand discovery with his life. It is, however, pretty well proved that this story ought to be ranked amongst the legends of the middle ages. Gunpowder was not invented by any one; it was the lineal successor of the Greek fire, which, like itself, was composed of sulphur and saltpetre. Few persons are acquainted with the mechanical power of gunpowder. Now this is precisely what is necessary to be understood in order to comprehend the importance of the question submitted to the committee.

A litre of gunpowder weighs about 2lbs.; during combustion it produces 400 litres of gas. This gas, on being liberated and acted upon by a temperature raised to 2400 degrees, occupies a space of 4000 litres: consequently the volume of powder is to the volume of gas produced by its combustion as 1 to 4000. One may judge, therefore, of the trmendous pressure of this gas when compressed with a space 4000 times too confined. All this was, of course, well known to the members of the committee when they met on the following evening.

The first speaker on this occasion was Major Elphinstone, who had been the director of the gunpowder factories during the war.

"Gentlemen," said this distinguished chemist, "I begin with some figures which will serve as the basis of our calculation. The old 24-pounder shot required for its discharge 16lbs. of powder."

"You are certain of the amount?" broke in Barbicane.

"Quite certain," replied the major. "The Armstrong cannon employs only 75lbs. of powder for a projectile of 800lbs., and the Rodman Columbiad uses only 160lbs. of powder to send its half-ton shot a distance of six miles. These facts cannot be called in question, for I myself raised the point during the depositions taken before the Committee of Artillery."

"Quite true," said the general.

"Well," replied the major, "these figures go to prove that the quantity of powder is not increased with the weight of the shot; that is to say, if a 24-pounder shot requires 16lbs of powder;—in other words, if in ordinary guns we employ a quantity of powder equal to two-thirds of the weight of the projectile, this proportion is not constant. Calculate, and you will see that in place of 333lbs. of powder, the quantity is reduced to no more than 160lbs."

"What are you aiming at?" asked the president.

"If you push your theory to extremes, my dear major," said J. T. Maston, "you will get to this, that as soon as your shot becomes sufficiently heavy you will not require any powder at all."

"Our friend Maston is always at his jokes, even in serious matters," cried the major; "but let him make his mind easy, I am going presently to propose gunpowder enough to satisfy his artillerist's propensities. I only keep to statistical facts when I say that during the war, and for the very largest guns, the weight of powder was reduced, as the result of experience, to a tenth part of the weight of the shot."

"Perfectly correct," said Morgan; "but before deciding the quantity of powder necessary to give the impulse, I think it would be as well—"

"We shall have to employ a large-grained powder," continued the major, "its combustion is more rapid than that of the small."

"No doubt about that," replied Morgan, "but it is very destructive, and ends by enlarging the bore of the pieces."

"Granted; but that which is injurious to a gun destined to perform long service is not so to our Columbiad. We shall run no danger of an explosion; and it is necessary that our powder should take fire instantaneously in order that its mechanical effect may be complete."

"We must have," said Maston, "several touch-holes, so as to fire it at different points at the same time."

"Certainly," replied Elphinestone; "but that will render the working of the piece more difficult. I return then to my large-grained powder, which removes those difficulties. In his Columbiad charges Rodman employed a powder as large as chestnuts, made of willow charcoal, simply dried in cast-iron pans. This powder was hard and glittering, left no trace upon the hand, contained hydrogen and oxygen in large proportion, took fire instantaneously, and, though very destructive, did not sensibly injure the mouthpiece."

Up to this point Barbecane had kept aloof from the discussion; he left the others to speak while he himself listened; he had evidently got an idea. He now simply said, "Well, my friends, what quantity of powder do your propose?"

The three members look at one another.

"Two hundred thousand pounds," at last said Morgan.

"Five hundred thousand," added the major.

"Eight hundred thousand," screamed Maston.

A moment of silence followed this triple proposal; it was at last broken by the president.

"Gentlemen," he quietly said, "I start from this principle, that the resistance of a gun, constructed under the given conditions, is unlimited. I shall surprise our friend Maston, then, by stigmatizing his calculations as timid; and I propose to double his 800,000lbs. of powder."

"Sixteen hundred thousand pounds?" shouted Maston, leaping from his seat.

"Just so."

"We shall have to come then to my ideal of a cannon half a mile long; for you see 1,600,000lbs. will occupy a space of about 20,000 cubic feet; and since the contents of your cannon do not exceed 54,000 cubic feet, it would be half full; and the bore will not be more than long enough for the gas to communicate to the projectile sufficient impulse."

"Nevertheless," said the president, "I hold to that quantity of powder. Now, 1,600,000lbs. of powder will create 6,000,000,000 of litres of gas. Six thousand millions! You quite understand?"

"What is to be done then?" said the general.

"The thing is very simple; we must reduce this enormous quantity of powder, while preserving to it its mechanical power."

"Good; but by what means?"

"I am going to tell you," replied Barbicane quietly. "Nothing is more easy than to reduce this mass to one quarter of its bulk. You know that curious cellular matter which constitutes the elementary tissues of vegetables? This substance is found quite pure in many bodies, especially in cotton, which is nothing more than the down of the seeds of the cotton plant. Now cotton, combined with cold nitric acid, becomes transformed into a substance eminently insoluble, combustible, and explosive. It was first discovered in 1832 by Branconnot, a French chemist, who called it xyloidine. In 1838 another Frenchman, Pelouze, investigated its different properties, and finally, in 1846, Schonbein, Professor of Chemistry at Bâle, proposed its employment for purposes of war. This powder, now called pyroxyle, or fulminating cotton, is prepared with great facility by simply plunging cotton for fifteen minutes in nitric acid, then washing it in water, then drying it, and it is ready for use."

"Nothing could be more simple," said Morgan.

"Moreover, pyroxyle is unaltered by moisture—a valuable property to us, inasmuch as it would take several days to charge the cannon. It ignites at 170 degrees in place of 240, and its combustion is so rapid that one many set light to it on the top of ordinary powder, without the latter having time to ignite."

"Perfect!" exclaimed the major.

"Only it is more expensive."

"What matter?" cried J. T. Maston.

"Finally, it imparts to projectiles a velocity four times superior to that of gunpowder. I will even add, that if we mix with it one-eighth of its own weight of nitrate of potass, its expansive force is again considerably augmented."

"Will that be necessary?" asked the major.

"I think not," replied Barbicane. "So, then, in place of 1,600,000lbs. of powder, we shall have but 400,000lbs. of fulminating cotton; and since we can, without danger, compress 500lbs. of cotton into 27 cubic feet, the whole quantity will not occupy a height of more than 180 feet within the bore of the Columbiad. In this way the shot will have more than 700 feet of bore to traverse under a force of 6,000,000,000 litres of gas before taking its flight towards the moon."

At this junction J. T. Maston could not repress his emotion; he flung himself into the arms of his friend with the violence of a projectile, and Barbicane would have been stove in if he had not been bomb-proof.

This incident terminated the third meeting of the Committee.

Barbicane and his bold colleagues, to whom nothing seemed impossible, had succeeded in solving the complex problems of projectile, cannon, and powder. Their plan was drawn up, and it only remained to put it in execution.

"A mere matter of detail, a bagatelle," said J. T. Maston.

CHAPTER 10

ONE ENEMY *v.* TWENTY-FIVE MILLIONS OF FRIENDS

THE American public took a lively interest in the smallest details of the enterprise of the Gun Club. It followed day by day the discussions of the committee. The most simple preparation for the great experiment, the questions of figures which it involved, the mechanical difficulties to be resolved—in one word, the entire plan of work—roused the popular excitement to the highest pitch.

Captain Nicholl.

The purely scientific attraction was suddenly intensified by the following incident:—

We have seen what legions of admirers and friends Barbicane's project rallied round its author. There was, however, one single individual alone in all the States of the Union who protested against the attempt of the Gun Club. He attacked it furiously on every opportunity, and human nature is such that Barbicane felt more keenly the opposition of that one man than he did the applause of all the others. He was well aware of the motive of this antipathy, the origin of this solitary enmity, the cause of its personality and old standing, and in what rivalry of self-love it had its rise.

This persevering enemy the President of the Gun Club had never seen. Fortunate that it was so, for a meeting between the two men would certainly have been attended with serious consequences. This rival was a man of science, like Barbicane himself, of a fiery, daring, and violent disposition; a pure Yankee. His name was Captain Nicholl; he lived at Philadelphia.

Most people are aware of the curious struggle which arose during the Federal war between the guns and the armour of iron-plated ships. The results was the entire reconstruction of the navy of both the continents; as the one grew heavier, the other became thicker in proportion. The "Merrimac," the "Monitor," the "Tennessee," the "Weehawken" discharged enormours projectiles themselves, after having been armour-clad against the projectiles of others. In fact they did to others that which they would *not* they should do to them—that grand principle of immorality upon which rests the whole art of war.

Now if Barbicane was a great founder of shot, Nicholl was a great forger of plates; the one cast night and day at Baltimore, the other forged day and night at Philadelphia. As soon as ever Barbicane invented a new shot, Nicholl invented a new plate, each followed a current of ideas essentially opposed to the other. Happily for these citizens, so useful to their country, a distance of from fifty to sixty miles separated them from one another, and they had never yet met. Which of these two inventors had the advantage over the other it was difficult to decide from the results obtained. By last accounts, however, it would seem that the armour-plate would in the end have to give way to the shot; nevertheless, there were competent judges who had their doubts on the point.

At the last experiment the cylindro-conical projectiles of Barbicane stuck like so many pins in the Nicholl plates. On that day the Philadelphian iron-forger then believed himself victorious, and could not evince contempt enough for his rival; but when the other afterwards substituted for conical shot simple 600lb. shells, at very moderate velocity, the captain was obliged to give in. In fact, these projectiles knocked his best metal plate to shivers.

Matters were at this stage, and victory seemed to rest with the shot, when the war came to an end on the very day when Nicholl had completed a new armour-plate of wrought steel. It was a masterpiece of its kind, and bid defiance to all the projectiles in the world. The captain had it conveyed to the Polygon at Washington, challenging the President of the Gun Club to break it. Barbicane, peace having been declared, declined to try the experiment.

Nicholl, now furious, offered to expose his plate to the shock of any shot, solid, hollow, round, or conical. Refused by the president, who did not choose to compromise his last success.

Nicholl, disgusted by this obstinacy, tried to tempt Barbicane by offering him every chance. He proposed to fix the plate within two hundred yards of the gun. Barbicane still obstinate in refusal. A hundred yards? Not even *seventy-five!*

"At fifty then!" roared the captain through the newspapers. "At twenty-five yards!! and I'll stand behind!!!"

Barbicane returned for answer that, even if Captain Nicholl would be so good as to stand in front, he would not fire any more.

Nicholl could not contain himself at this reply; threw out hints of cowardice; that a man who refused to fire a cannon-shot was pretty near being afraid of it; that artillerists who fight at six miles' distance are substituting mathematical formulæ for individual courage.

To these insinuations Barbicane returned no answer; perhaps he never heard of them, so absorbed was he in the calculations for his great enterprise.

When his famous communication was made to the Gun Club, the captain's wrath passed all bounds; with his intense jealousy was mingled a feeling of absolute impotence. How was he to invent anything to beat this 900-feet Columbiad? What armour-plate could ever resist a projectile of 30,000lbs. weight? Overwhelmed at first under this violent shock, he by and by recovered himself, and resolved to crush the proposal by the weight of his arguments.

He then violently attacked the labours of the Gun Club, published a number of letters in the newspapers, endeavoured to prove Barbicane ignorant of the first principles of gunnery. He maintained that it was absolutely impossible to impress upon any body whatever a velocity of 12,000 yards per second; that even with such a velocity a projectile of such a weight could not transcend the limits of the earth's atmosphere. Further still, even regarding the velocity to be acquired, and granting it to be sufficient, the shell could not resist the pressure of the gas developed by the ignition of 1,600,000lbs. of powder; and supposing it to resist that pressure, it would be the less able to support that temperature; it would melt on quitting the Columbiad, and fall back in a red-hot shower upon the heads of the imprudent spectators.

Barbicane continued his work without regarding these attacks.

Nicholl then took up the question in its other aspects. Without touching upon its uselessness in all points of view, he regarded the experiment as fraught with extreme danger, both to the citizens, who might sanction by their presence so reprehensible a spectacle, and also to the towns in the neighbourhood of this deplorable cannon. He also observed that if the projectile did not succeed in reaching its destination (a result absolutely impossible), it must inevitably fall back upon the earth, and that the shock of such a mass, multiplied by the square of its velocity, would seriously endanger every point of the globe. Under the circumstances, therefore, and without interfering with the rights of free citizens, it was a case for the intervention of Government, which ought not to endanger the safety of all for the pleasure of one individual.

Spite of all his arguments, however, Captain Nicholl remained alone in his opinion. Nobody listened to him, and he did not succeed in alienating a single admirer from the President of the Gun Club. The latter did not even take the pains to refute the arguments of his rival.

Nicholl, driven into his last entrenchments, and not able to fight personally in the cause, resolved to fight with money. He published, therefore, in the *Richmond Inquirer* a series of wagers, conceived in these terms, and on an increasing scale:—

No. 1 (1000 dols.).—That the necessary funds for the experiment of the Gun Club will not be forthcoming.

No. 2 (2000 dols.).—That the operation of casting a cannon of 900 feet is impracticable, and cannot possibly succeed.

No. 3 (3000 dols.).—That it is impossible to load the Columbiad, and that the pyroxyle will take fire spontaneously under the pressure of the projectile.

No. 4 (4000 dols.).—That the Columbiad will burst at the first fire.

No. 5 (5000 dols.).—That the shot will not travel farther than six miles, and that it will fall back again a few seconds after its discharge.

It was an important sum, therefore, which the captain risked in his invincible obstinacy. He had no less than 15,000 dollars at stake.

Notwithstanding the importance of the challenge, on the 19th of May he received a sealed packet containing the following superbly laconic reply:—

"BALTIMORE, *Oct.* 19.
"Done.
BARBICANE."

Chapter 11

FLORIDA AND TEXAS

ONE question yet reamined to be decided: it was necessary to choose a favourable spot for the experiment. According to the advice of the Observatory of Cambridge, the gun must be fired perpendicularly to the plane of the horizon, that is to say, towards the zenith. Now the moon does not traverse the zenith, except in places situated between 0° and 28′ of latitude. It became, then, necessary to determine exactly that spot on the globe where the immense Columbiad should be cast.

On the 20th of October, at a general meeting of the Gun Club, Barbicane produced a magnificent map of the United States. "Gentlemen," said he, in opening the discussion, "I presume that we are all agreed that this experiment cannot and ought not to be tried anywhere but within the limits of the soil of the Union. Now, by good fortune, certain frontiers of the United States extend downwards as far as the 28th parallel of the north latitude. If you will cast your eye over this map, you will see that we have at our disposal the whole of the southern portion of Texas and Florida."

It was finally agreed, then, that the Columbiad must be cast on the soil of either Texas or Florida. The result, however, of this decision was to create a rivalry entirely without precedent between the different towns of these two states.

The 28th parallel, on reaching the American coast, traverses the peninsula of Florida, dividing it into two nearly equal portions. Then, plunging into the Gulf of Mexico, it subtends the arc formed by the coast of Alabama, Mississippi, and Louisiana; then skirting Texas, off which it cuts an angle, it continues its course over Mexico, crosses the Sonora, Old California, and loses itself in the Pacific Ocean. It was, therefore, only those portions of Texas and Florida which were situated below this parallel which came within the prescribed conditions of latitude.

Florida, in its southern part, reckons no cities of importance; it is simply studded with forts raised against the roving Indians. One solitary town, Tampa Town, was able to put in a claim in favour of its situation.

In Texas, on the contrary, the towns are much more numerous and important. Corpus Christi, in the county of Nuaces, and all the cities situated on the Rio Bravo, Laredo, Comalites, San Ignacio on the Web, Rio Grande city on the Starr, Edinburgh in the Hidalgo, Santa Rita, Elpanda, Brownsville in the Cameron, formed an imposing league against the pretensions of Florida. So, scarcely was the decision known, when the Texian and Floridan deputies arrived at Baltimore in an incredibly short space of time. From that very moment President Barbicane and the influential members of the Gun Club were besieged day and night by formidable claims. If seven cities of Greece contended for the honour of having given birth to Homer, here were two entire states threatening to come to blows about the question of a cannon.

The rival parties promenaded the streets with arms in their hands; and at every occasion of their meeting a collision was to be apprehended which might have been attended with disastrous results. Happily the prudence and address of President Barbicane averted the danger. These personal demonstrations found a division in the newpapers of the different states. The *New York Herald* and the *Tribune* supported Texas, while the *Times* and the *American Review* espoused the cause of the Floridan Deputies. The members of the Gun Club could not decide to which to give the preference.

Texas produced its array of twenty-six counties; Florida replied that twelve counties were better than twenty-six in a country only one-sixth part of the size.

Texas plumed itself upon its 330,000 natives; Florida with a far smaller territory, boasted of being much more densely populated with 56,000.

The Texians, through the columns of the *Herald*, claimed that some regard should be had to a state which grew the best cotton in all America, produced the best green oak for the service of the navy, and contained the finest oil, besides iron mines, in which the yield was 50 per cent. of pure metal.

To this the *American Review* replied that the soil of Florida, although not equally rich, afforded the best conditions for the moulding and casting of the Columbiad, consisting as it did of sand and argillaceous earth.

"That may be all very well," replied the Texians; "but you must first get to this country. Now the communications with Florida are difficult, while the coast of Texas offers the bay of Galveston, which possesses a circumference of fourteen leagues, and is capable of containing the navies of the entire world!"

"A pretty notion truly," replied the papers in the interest of Florida, "that of Galveston Bay, *below the 29th parallel!* Have *we* not got the bay of Espiritu Santo, opening precisely upon *the 28th degree*, and by which ships can reach Tampa Town by direct route?"

"A fine bay! half choked with sand!" "Choked yourselves!" returned the others.

Thus the war went on for several days, when Florida endeavoured to draw her adversary away on to fresh ground; and one morning the *Times* hinted that, the enterpirse being essentially American, it ought not to be attempted upon other than purely American territory.

To these words Texas retorted, "American! are we not as much so as you? Were not Texas and Florida both incorporated into the Union in 1845?"

"Undoubtedly," replied the *Times*; "but we have belonged to the Americans ever since 1820."

"Yes!" returned the *Tribune*; "after having been Spaniards or English for 200 years, you were sold to the United States for five million dollars!"

"Well! and why need we blush for that? Was not Louisiana bought from Napoleon in 1803 at the price of sixteen million dollars?"

"Scandalous!" roared the Texian deputies. "A wretched little strip of country like Florida to dare to compare itself to Texas, who, in place of selling herself, asserted her own independence, drove out the Mexicans in March 2, 1836, and declared herself a federal republic after the victory gained by Samuel Houston, on the banks of the San Jacinto, over the troops of Santa Anna!—a country, in fine, which voluntarily annexed itself to the United States of America!"

"Yes; because it was afraid of the Mexicans!" replied Florida.

"Afraid!" From this moment the state of things became intolerable. A sanguinary encounter seemed daily imminent between the two parties in the streets of Baltimore. It became necessary to keep an eye upon the deputies.

President Barbicane knew not which way to look. Notes, documents, letters full of menaces showered down upon his house. Which side ought he to take? As regarded the appropriation of the soil, the facility of communication, the rapidity of transport, the claims of both states were evenly balanced. As for political prepossessions, they had nothing to do with the question.

This dead block had existed for some little time, when Barbicane resolved to get rid of it at once. He called a meeting of his colleagues, and laid before them a proposition which, it will be seen, was profoundly sagacious.

"On carefully considering," he said, "what is going on now between Florida and Texas, it is clear that the same difficulties will recur with all the towns of the favoured state. The rivalry will descend from state to city, and so on downwards. Now Texas possesses *eleven* towns within the prescribed conditions, which will further dispute the honour and create us new enemies, while Florida has only *one*. I go in, therefore, for Florida and Tampa Town."

This decision, on being made known, utterly crushed the Texian deputies. Seized with an indescribable fury, they addressed threatening letters to the different members of the Gun Club by name. The magistrates had but one course to take, and they took it. They chartered a special train, forced the Texians into it whether they would or no; and they quitted the city with a speed of thirty miles an hour.

Quickly, however, as they were despatched, they found time to hurl one last and bitter sarcasm at their adversaries.

Alluding to the extent of Florida, a mere peninsula confined between two seas, they pretended that it could never sustain the shock of the discharge, and that it would "bust up" at the very first shot.

"Very well, let it bust up!" replied the Floridans, with a brevity worthy of the days of ancient Sparta.

CHAPTER 12

URBI ET ORBI

THE astronomical, mechanical, and topographical difficulties resolved, finally came the question of finance. The sum required was far too great for any individual, or even any single state, to provide the requisite millions.

President Barbicane undertook, despite of the matter being a purely American affair, to render it one of universal interest, and to request the financial co-operation of all peoples. It was, he maintained, the right and the duty of the whole earth to interfere in the affairs of its satellite. The subscription opened at Baltimore extended properly to the whole world—*Urbi et orbi*.

This subscription was successful beyond all expectation; notwithstanding that it was a question not of *lending* but of *giving* the money. It was a purely disinterested operation in the strictest sense of the term, and offered not the slightest chance of profit.

The effect, however, of Barbicane's communication was not confined to the frontiers of the United States; it crossed the Atlantic and Pacific, invading simultaneously Asia and Europe, Africa and Oceania. The observatories of the Union placed themselves in immediate communication with those of foreign countries. Some, such as those of Paris, Peterburgh, Berlin, Stockholm, Hamburg, Malta, Lisbon, Benares, Madras, and others, transmitted their good wishes; the rest maintained a prudent silence, quietly awaiting the result. As for the observatory at Greenwich, seconded as it was by the twenty-two astronomical establishments of Great Britain, it spoke plainly enough. It boldly denied the possibility of success, and pronounced in favour of the theories of Captain Nicholl. But this was nothing more than mere English jealousy.

On the 8th of October President Barbicane published a manifesto full of enthusiasm, in which he made an appeal to "all persons of good will upon the face of the earth." This document, translated into all languages, met with immense success.

Subscription lists were opened in all the principal cities of the Union, with a central office at the Baltimore Bank, 9, Baltimore Street.

In addition, subscriptions were received at the following banks in the different states of the two continents:—

At Vienna, with S. M. de Rothschild.
,, Petersburg, Stieglitz and Co.
,, Paris, The Crédit Mobilier.
,, Stockholm, Tottie and Arfuredson.
,, London, N. M. Rothschild and Son.
,, Turin, Ardouin and Co.
,, Berlin, Mendelssohn.
,, Geneva, Lombard, Odier, and Co.
,, Constantinople, The Ottoman Bank.
,, Brussels, J. Lambert.
,, Madrid, Daniel Weisweller.

,, Amsterdam, Netherlands Credit Co.
,, Rome, Torlonia and Co.
,, Lisbon, Lecesne.
,, Copenhagen, Private Bank.
,, Rio Janeiro, do.
,, Monte Video, do.
,, Valparaiso and Lima, Thomas la Chambre and Co.
,, Mexico, Martin Daran and Co.

Three days after the manifesto of President Barbicane 4,000,000 of dollars were paid into the different towns of the Union. With such a balance the Gun Club might begin operations at once. But some days later advices were received to the effect that the foreign subscriptions were being eagerly taken up. Certain countries distinguished themselves by their liberality; others untied their purse-strings with less facility—matter of temperament. Figures are, however, more eloquent than words, and here is the official statement of the sums which were paid in to the credit of the Gun Club at the close of the subscription.

Russia paid in as her contingent the enourmous sum of 368,733 roubles. No one need be surprised at this, who bears in mind the scientific taste of the Russians, and the impetus which they have given to astronomical studies—thanks to their numerous observatories.

France began by deriding the pretentions of the Americans. The moon served as a pretext for a thousand stale puns and a score of ballads, in which bad taste contested the palm with ignorance. But as formerly the French paid before singing, so now they paid after having had their laugh, and they subscribed for a sum of 1,253,930 francs. At that price they had a right to enjoy themselves a little.

Austria showed herself generous in the midst of her financial crisis. Her public contributions amounted to the sum of 216,000 florins—a perfect godsend.

52,000 rix-dollars were the remittance of Sweden and Norway; the amount is large for the country, but it would undoubtedly have been considerably increased had the subscription been opened in Christiania simultaneously with that of Stockholm. For some reason or other the Norwegians do not like to send their money to Sweden.

Prussia, by a remittance of 250,000 thalers, testified her high approval of the enterprise.

Turkey behaved generously; but she had a personal interest in the matter. The moon, in fact, regulates the cycle of her years and her fast of Ramadan. She could not do less than give 1,372,640 piastres; and she gave then with an eagerness which denoted, however, some pressure on the part of the Government.

Belgium distinguished herself among the second-rate states by a grant of 513,000 francs—about two centimes per head of her population.

Holland and her colonies interested themselves to the extent of 110,000 florins, only demanding an allowance of five percent discount for paying ready money.

Denmark, a little contracted in territory, gave nevertheless 9000 ducats, proving her love for scientific experiments.

The Germanic Confederation pledged itself to 34,285 florins. It was impossible to ask for more; besides, they would not have given it.

Though very much crippled, Italy found 200,000 lire in the pockets of her people. If she had had Venetia she would have done better; but she not *not*.

The subscription was opened.

The States of the Church thought that they could not send less than 7040 Roman crowns; and Portugal carried her devotion to science as far as 30,000 cruzados. It was the widow's mite—eighty-six piastres; but self-constituted empires are always rather short of money.

257 francs, this was the modest contribution of Switzerland to the American work. One must freely admit that she did not see the practical side of the matter. It did not seem to her that the mere despatch of a shot to the moon could possibly establish any relation of affairs with her; and it did not seem prudent to her to embark her capital in so hazardous an enterprise. After all, perhaps she was right.

As to Spain, she could not scrape together more than 110 reals. She gave as an excuse that she had her railways to finish. The truth is, that science is not favourably regarded in that country, it is still in a backward state; and, moreover, certain Spaniards, not by any means the least educated, did not form a correct estimate of the bulk of the projectile compared with that of the moon. They feared that it would disturb the established order of things. In that case it were better to keep aloof; which they did to the tune of some reals.

There remained but England; and we know the contemptuous antipathy with which she received Barbicane's proposition. The English have but one soul for the whole twenty-six millions of inhabitants which Great Britain contains. They hinted that the enterprise of the Gun Club was contrary to the "principle of non-intervention." And they did not subscribe a single farthing.

At this intimation the Gun Club merely shrugged its shoulders and returned to its great work. When South America, that is to say, Peru, Chili, Brazil, the provinces of La Plata and Columbia, had poured forth their quota into their hands, the sum of 300,000 dollars, it found itself in possession of a considerable capital, of which the following is a statement:—

United States subscriptions	4,000,000	dollars.
Foreign subscriptions	1,446,675	,,
Total	5,446,675	,,

Such was the sum which the public poured into the treasury of the Gun Club.

Let no one be surprised at the vastness of the amount. The work of casting, boring, masonry, the transport of workmen, their establishment in an almost uninhabited country, the construction of furnaces and workshops, the plant, the powder, the projectile, and incidental expenses, would according to the estimates, absorb nearly the whole. Certain cannon shots in the Federal war cost 1000 dollars a-piece. This one of President Barbicane, unique in the annals of gunnery, might well cost five thousand times more.

On the 20th of October a contract was entered into with the manufactory at Coldspring, near New York, which during the war had furnished the largest Parrott cast-iron guns. It was stipulated between the contracting parties that the manufactory of Coldspring should engage to transport to Tampa Town, in southern Florida, the necessary materials for casting the Columbiad. The work was bound to be completed at latest by the 15th of October following, and the cannon delivered in good condition under penalty of a forfeit of 100 dollars a day to the moment when the moon should again present herself under the same conditions—that is to say, in eighteen years and eleven days.

The engagement of the workmen, their pay, and all the necessary details of the work, devolved upon the Coldspring Company.

This contract, executed in duplicate, was signed by Barbicane, President of the Gun Club, of the one part, and T. Murphison, director of the Coldspring manufactory, of the other, who thus executed the deed on behalf of their respective principals.

CHAPTER 13

STONES HILL

WHEN the decision was arrived at by the Gun Club, to the disparagement of Texas, every one in America, where reading is an universal acquirement, set to work to study the geography of Florida. Never before had there been such a sale for works like *Bertram's Travels in Florida, Roman's Natural History of East and West Florida, William's Territory of Florida,* and *Cleland on the Cultivation of the Sugar-Cane in Florida*. It became necessary to issue fresh editions of these works.

Barbicane had something better to do than to read. He desired to see things with his own eyes, and to mark the exact position of the proposed gun. So, without a moment's loss of time, he placed at the disposal of the Cambridge Observatory the funds necessary for the construction of a telescope, and entered into negotiations with the house of Breadwill and Co., of Albany, for the construction of an aluminium projectile of the required size. He then quitted Baltimore, accompanied by J. T. Maston, Major Elphinstone, and the manager of the Coldspring Factory.

On the following day, the four fellow-travellers arrived at New Orleans. There they immediately embarked on board the "Tampico," a despatch-boat belonging to the Federal navy, which the Government had placed at their disposal; and, getting up steam, the banks of the Louisiana speedily disappeared from sight.

The passage was not long. Two days after starting, the "Tampico," having made four hundred and eighty miles, came in sight of the coast of Florida. On a nearer approach Barbicane found himself in view of a low, flat country of somewhat barren aspect. After coasting along a series of creeks abounding in lobsters and oysters, the "Tampico" entered the bay of Espiritu Santo, where she finally anchored in a small natural harbour, formed by the *embouchure* of the River Hillisborough, at seven p.m., on the 22nd October.

Our four passengers disembarked at once. "Gentlemen," said Barbicane, "we have no time to lose; to-morrow we must obtain horses, and proceed to reconnoitre the country."

Barbicane had scarcely set his foot on shore when three thousand of the inhabitants of Tampa Town came forth to meet him, an honour due to the president who had signalized their country by his choice.

Declining, however, every kind of ovation, Barbicane ensconced himself in a room of the Franklin Hotel.

On the morrow some of those small horses of the Spanish breed, full of vigour and of fire, stood snorting under his windows; but instead of *four* steeds, here were *fifty*, together with their riders. Barbicane descended with his three fellow-travellers; and much astonished were they all to find themselves in the midst of such a cavalcade. He remarked that every horseman carried a carbine slung across his shoulders and pistols in his holsters.

On expressing his surprise at these preparations, he was speedily enlightened by a young Floridan, who quietly said,—

"Sir, there are Seminoles there."

"What do you mean by Seminoles?"

"Savages who scour the prairies. We thought it best, therefore, to escort you on your road."

"Pooh!" cried J. T. Maston, mounting his steed.

"All right," said the Floridan; "but it is true enough, nevertheless."

"Gentlemen," answered Barbicane, "I thank you for your kind attention; but it is time to be off."

It was five a.m. when Barbicane and his party, quitting Tampa Town, made their way along the coast in the direction of Alifia Creek. This little river falls into Hillisborough Bay twelve miles above Tampa Town. Barbicane and his escort coasted along its right bank to the eastward. Soon the waves of the bay disappeared behind a bend of rising ground, and the Floridan "champagne" alone offered itself to view.

Florida, dicovered on Palm Sunday, in 1512, by Juan Ponce de Leon, was originally named *Pascha Florida*. It little deserved that designation with its dry and parched coasts. But after some few miles of tract the nature of the soil gradually changes and the country shows itself worthy of the name. Cultivated plains soon appear, where are united all the productions of the northern and tropical floras, terminating in prairies abounding with pineapples and yams, tobacco, rice, cotton-plants, and sugar-canes, which extend beyond reach of sight, flinging their riches broadcast with careless prodigality.

Barbicane appeared highly pleased on observing the progressive elevation of the land; and in answer to a question of J. T. Maston, replied,—

"My worthy friend, we cannot do better than sink our Columbiad in these high grounds."

"To get nearer to the moon, perhaps?" said the secretary of the Gun Club.

"Not exactly," replied Barbicane, smiling; "do you not see that amongst these elevated plateaus we shall have a much easier work of it? No struggles with the water-springs, which will save us long and expensive tubings; and we shall be working in daylight instead of down a deep and narrow well. Our business, then, is to open our trenches upon ground some hundreds of yards above the level of the sea."

"You are right, sir," struck in Murchison, the engineer; "and, if I mistake not, we shall ere long find a suitable spot for our purpose."

"I wish we were at the first stroke of the pickaxe," said the president.

"And I wish we were at the *last*," cried J. T. Maston.

About ten a.m. the little band had crossed a dozen miles. To fertile plains succeeded a region of forests. There perfumes of the most varied kinds mingled together in tropical profusion. These almost impenetrable forests were composed of pomegranates, orange-trees, citrons, figs, olives, apricots, bananas, huge vines, whose blossoms and fruits rivalled each other in colour and perfume.

Beneath the odorous shade of these magnificent trees fluttered and warbled a little world of brilliantly plumaged birds.

J. T. Maston and the major could not repress their admiration on finding themselves in presence of the glorious beauties of this wealth of nature. President Barbicane, however, less sensitive to these wonders, was in haste to press forward; the very luxuriance of the country was displeasing to him. They hastened onwards, therefore, and were compelled to ford several rivers, not without danger, for they were infested with huge alligators from fifteen to eighteen feet long. Maston courageously menaced them with his steel hook, but he only succeeded in frightening some pelicans and teal, while tall flamingos stared stupidly at the party.

At length these denizens of the swamps disappeared in their turn; smaller trees became thinly scattered among less dense thickets—a few isolated groups detached in the midst of endless plains over which ranged herds of startled deer.

"At last," cried Barbicane, rising in his stirrups, "here we are at the region of pines!"

"Yes! and of savages too," replied the major.

In fact, some Seminoles had just come in sight upon the horizon; they rode violently backwards and forwards on their fleet horses, brandishing their spears or discharging their guns with a dull report. These hostile demonstrations, however, had no effect upon Barbicane and his companions.

They were then occupying the centre of a rocky plain, which the sun scorched with its parching rays. This was formed by a considerable elevation of the soil, which seemed to offer to the members of the Gun Club, all the conditions requisite for the construction of their Columbiad.

"Halt!" said Barbicane, reining up. "Has this place any local appellation?"

"It is called Stones Hill," replied one of the Floridans.

Barbicane, without saying a word, dismounted, seized his instruments, and began to note his position with extreme exactness. The little band, drawn up in rear, watched his proceedings in profound silence.

At this moment the sun passed the meridian. Barbicane, after a few moments, rapidly wrote down the result of his observations, and said,—

"This spot is situated 1800 feet above the level of the sea, in 27° 7′ N. lat. and 5° 7′ W. long. of the meridian of Washington. It appears to me by its rocky and barren character to offer all the conditions requsite for our experiment. On that plain will be raised our magazines, workshops, furnaces, and workmen's huts; and here, from this very spot," said he, stamping his foot on the summit of Stones Hill, "hence shall our projectile take its flight into the regions of the Solar World."

CHAPTER 14

PICKAXE AND TROWEL

THE same evening Barbicane and his companions returned to Tampa Town; and Murchison, the engineer, re-embarked on board the "Tampico" for New Orleans. His object was to enlist an army of workmen, and to collect together the greater part of the materials. The members of the Gun Club remained at Tampa Town, for the purpose of setting on foot the preliminary works by the aid of the people of the country.

Eight days after its departure, the "Tampico" returned into the bay of Espiritu Santo, with a whole flotilla of steamboats. Murchison had succeeded in assembling together fifteen hundred artisans. Attracted by the high pay and considerable bounties offered by the Gun Club, he had enlisted a choice legion of stokers, iron-founders, lime-burners, miners, brickmakers, and artisans of every trade, without distinction of colour. As many of these people brought their families with them, their departure resembled a perfect emigration.

On the 31st October, at ten o'clock in the morning, the troop disembarked on the quays of Tampa Town; and one may imagine the activity which pervaded that little town, whose population was thus doubled in a single day.

During the first few days they were busy discharging the cargo brought by the flotilla, the machines, and the rations, as well as a large number of huts constructed of iron plates, separately pieced and numbered. At the same period Barbicane laid the first sleepers of a railway fifteen miles in length, intended to unite Stones Hill with Tampa Town. On the first of November Barbicane quitted Tampa Town with a detachment of workmen; and on the following day the whole town of huts was erected round Stones Hill. This they enclosed with palisades; and in respect of energy and activity, it might have shortly been mistaken for one of the great cities of the Union. Everything was placed under a complete system of dicipline, and the works were commenced in most perfect order.

The nature of the soil having been carefully examined, by means of repeated borings, the work of excavation was fixed for the 4th of November.

On that day Barbicane called together his foremen and addressed them as follows:—"You are well aware, my friends, of the object with which I have assembled you together in this wild part of Florida. Our business is to construct a cannon measuring nine feet it its interior diameter, six feet thick, and with a stone revetment of nineteen and a half feet in thickness. We have, therefore, a well of sixty feet in diameter to dig down to a depth of nine hundred feet. This great work must be completed *within eight months*, so that you have 2,543,400 cubic feet of earth to excavate in 255 days; that is to say, in round numbers, 2000 cubic feet per day. That which would present no difficulty to a thousand navvies working in open country will be of course more troublesome in a comparatively confined space. However, the thing must be done, and I reckon for its accomplishment upon your courage as much as upon your skill.

At eight o'clock in the morning the first stroke of the pickaxe was struck upon the soil of Florida; and from that moment that prince of tools was never inactive for one moment in the hands of the excavators. The gangs relieved each other every three hours.

On the 4th of November fifty workmen commenced digging, in the very centre of the enclosed space on the summit of Stones Hill, a circular hole sixty feet in diameter. The pickaxe first struck upon a kind of black earth, six inches in thickness, which was speedily disposed of. To this earth succeeded two feet of fine sand, which was carefully laid aside as being valuable for serving for the casting of the inner mould. After the sand appeared some compact white clay, resembling the chalk of Great Britain, which extended down to a depth of four feet. Then the iron of the picks struck upon the hard bed of the soil; a kind of rock formed of petrified shells, very dry, very solid, and which the picks could with difficulty penetrate. At this point the excavation exhibited a depth of six feet and a half, and the work of the masonry was begun.

At the bottom of this excavation they constructed a wheel of oak, a kind of circle strongly bolted together, and of immense strength. The centre of this wooden disc was hollowed out to a diameter equal to the exterior diameter of the Columbiad. Upon this wheel rested the first layers of the masonry, the stones of which were bound together by hydraulic cement, with irresistible tenacity. The workmen, after laying the stones from the circumference to the centre, were thus enclosed within a kind of well twenty-one feet in diameter. When this work was accomplished, the miners resumed their picks and cut away the rock from underneath the *wheel* itself, taking care to support it as they advanced upon blocks of great thickness. At every two feet which the hole gained in depth they successively withdrew the blocks. The *wheel* then sank little by little, and with it the massive ring of masonry, on the upper bed of which the masons laboured incessantly, always reserving some vent holes to permit the escape of gas during the operation of casting.

This kind of work required on the part of the workmen extreme nicety and minute attention. More than one, in digging underneath the wheel, was dangerously injured by the splinters of stone. But their ardour never relaxed, night or day. By day they worked under the rays of the scorching sun; by night, under the gleam of the electric light. The sounds of the picks against the rock, the bursting of mines, the grinding of the machines, the wreaths of smoke scattered through the air, traced around Stones Hill a circle of terror which the herds of buffaloes and the war parties of the Seminoles never ventured to pass. Nevertheless, the works advanced regularly, as the steam-cranes actively removed the rubbish. Of unexpected obstacles there was little account; and with regard to foreseen difficulties, they were speedily disposed of.

At the expiration of the first month the well had attained the depth assigned for that lapse of time, viz. 112 feet. This depth was doubled in December, and trebled in January.

During the month of February the workmen had to contend with a sheet of water which made its way right across the outer soil. It became necessary to employ very powerful pumps and compressed air-engines to drain it off, so as to close up the orifice from whence it issued; just as one stops a leak on board ship. They at last succeeded in getting the upper hand of these untoward streams; only, in consequence of the loosening of the soil, the wheel partly gave way, and a slight partial settlement ensued. This accident cost the life of several workmen.

No fresh occurrence thenceforward arrested the progress of the operation; and on the 10th of June, twenty days before the expiration of the period fixed by Barbicane, the well, lined throughout with its facing stone, had attained the depth of 900 feet. At the bottom the masonry rested upon a massive block measuring thirty feet in thickness, whilst on the upper portion it was level with the surrounding soil.

President Barbicane and the members of the Gun Club warmly congratulated their engineer Murchison; the cyclopean work had been accomplished with extraordinary rapidity.

During these eight months Barbicane never quitted Stones Hill for a single instant. Keeping ever close by the work of excavation, he busied himself incessantly with the welfare and health of his workpeople, and was singularly fortunate in warding off the epidemics common to large communities of men, and so disastrous in those regions of the globe which are exposed to the influences of tropical climates.

Many workmen, it is true, paid with their lives for the rashness inherent in these dangerous labours; but these mishaps are impossible to be avoided, and they are classed amongst details with which the Americans trouble themselves but little. They have in fact more regard for human nature in general than for the individual in particular.

Nevertheless, Barbicane professed opposite principles to these, and put them in force at every opportunity. So, thanks to his care, his intelligence, his useful intervention in all difficulties, his prodigious and humane sagacity, the average of accidents did not exceed that of transatlantic countries, noted for their excessive precautions, France, for instance, among others, where they reckon about one accident for every two hundred thousand francs of work.

CHAPTER 15

THE FÊTE OF THE CASTING

DURING the eight months which were employed in the work of excavation the preparatory works of the casting had been carried on simultaneously with extreme rapidity. A stranger arriving at Stones Hill would have been surprised at the spectacle offered to his view.

At 600 yards from the well, and circularly arranged around it as a central point, rose 1200 reverberating ovens, each six feet in diameter, and separated from each other by an interval of three feet. The circumference occupied by these 1200 ovens presented a length of two miles. Being all constructed on the same plan, each with its high quadrangular chimney, they produced a most singular effect.

It will be remembered that on their third meeting the Committee had decided to use cast-iron for the Columbiad, and in particular the *white* description. This metal in fact is the most tenacious, the most ductile, and the most malleable, and consequently suitable for all moulding operations; and when smelted with pit coal, is of superior quality for all engineering works requiring great resisting power, such as cannon, steam-boilers, hydraulic presses, and the like.

Cast-iron, however, if subjected to only one single fusion, is rarely sufficiently homogeneous; and it requres a second fusion completely to refine it by dispossessing it of its last earthly deposits. So before being forwarded to Tampa Town, the iron ore, molten in the great furnaces of Coldspring, and brought into contact with coal and silicium heated to a high temperature, was carburized and transformed into cast-iron. After this first operation, the metal was sent on to Stones Hill. They had, however, to deal with 136,000,000lbs. of iron, a quantity far too costly to send by railway. The cost of transport would have been double that of material. It appeared preferable to freight vessels at New York, and to load them with the iron in bars. This, however, required not less than sixty-eight vessels of 1000 tons, a veritable fleet, which, quitting New York on the 3rd of May, on the 10th of the same month ascended the Bay of Espiritu Santo, and discharged their cargoes, without dues, in the port at Tampa Town. Thence the iron was transported by rail to Stones Hill, and about the middle of January this enormous mass of metal was delivered at its destination.

It will be easily understood that 1200 furnaces were not too many to melt simultaneously these 60,000 tons of iron. Each of these furnaces contained nearly 140,000lbs.weight of metal. They were all built after the model of those which served for the casting of the Rodman gun, they were trapezoidal in shape, with a height elliptical arch. These furnaces, constructed of fireproof brick, were especially adapted for burning pit coal, with a flat bottom upon which the iron bars were laid. This bottom, inclined at an angle of 25°, allowed the metal to flow into the receiving troughs; and the 1200 converging trenches carried the molten metal down to the central well.

The day following that on which the works of the masonry and boring had been completed, Barbicane set to work upon the central mould. His object now was to raise within the centre of the well, and with a coincident axis, a cylinder 900 feet high, and 9 feet in diameter, which should exactly fill up the space reserved for the bore of the Columbiad. This cylinder was composed of a mixture of clay and sand, with the addition of a little hay and straw. The space left between the mould and the masonry was intended to be filled up by the molten metal, which would thus form the walls six feet in thickness. This cylinder, in order to maintain its equilibrium, had to be bound by iron bands, and firmly fixed at certain intervals by cross-clamps fastened into the stone lining; after the castings these would be buried in the block of metal, leaving no external projection.

This operation was completed on the 8th of July, and the run of the metal was fixed for the following day.

"This fête of the casting will be a grand ceremony," said J. T. Maston to his friend Barbicane.

"Undoubtedly," said Barbicane; "but it will not be a public fête."

"What! will you not open the gates of the enclosure to all comers?"

"I must be very careful, Maston. The casting of the Columbiad is an extremely delicate, not to say a dangerous, operation, and I should prefer its being done privately. At the discharge of the projectile, a feté if you like—till then, no!"

The president was right. The operation involved unforeseen dangers, which a great influx of spectators would have hindered him from averting. It was necessary to preseve complete freedom of movement. No one was admitted within the enclosure except a delegation of members of the Gun Club, who had made the voyage to Tampa Town. Among these was the brisk Bilsby, Tom Hunter, Colonel Blomsberry, Major Elphinstone, General Morgan, and the rest of the lot to whom the casting of the Columbiad was a matter of personal interst. J. T. Maston became their cicerone. He omitted no point of detail; he conducted them throughout the magazines, workshops, through the midst of the engines, and compelled them to visit the whole 1200 furnaces one after the other. At the end of the twelve-hundredth visit they were pretty well knocked up.

The casting was to take place at 12 o'clock precisely. The previous evening each furnace had been charged with 114,000lbs weight of metal in bars disposed cross-ways to each other, so as to allow the hot air to circulate freely between them. At daybreak the 1200 chimneys vomited their torrents of flame into the air, and the ground was agitated with dull tremblings. As many pounds of metal as there were to *cast*, so many pounds of coal were there to *burn*. Thus there were 68,000 tons of coal which projected in the face of the sun a thick curtain of smoke. The heat soon became insupportable within the circle of furnaces, the rumbling of which resembled the rolling of thunder. The powerful ventilators added their continuous blasts and saturated with oxygen the glowing plates. The operation, to be successful, required to be conducted with great rapidity. On a signal given by a cannon-shot each furnace was to give vent to the molten iron and completely to empty itself. These arrangements made, foremen and workmen waited the preconcerted moment with an impatience mingled with a certain amount of emotion. Not a soul remained within the enclosure. Each superintendent took his post by the aperture of the run.

Barbicane and his colleagues, perched on a neighbouring eminence, assisted at the operation. In front of them was a piece of artillery ready to give fire on the signal from the engineer. Some minutes before midday the first drivlets of metal began to flow; the reservoirs filled little by little; and, by the time that the whole melting was completely accomplished, it was kept in abeyance for a few minuites in order to facilitate the separation of foreign substances.

Twelve o'clock struck! A gun-shot suddenly pealed forth and shot its flame into the air. Twelve hundred melting-troughs were simultaneously opened and twelve hundred fiery serpents crept towards the central well, unrolling their incandescent curves. There, down they plunged with a terrific noise into a depth of 900 feet. It was an exciting and a magnificent spectacle. The ground trembled, while these molten waves, launching into the sky their wreaths of smoke, evaporated the moisture of the mould and hurled it upwards through the vent-holes of the stone lining in the form of dense vapour-clouds. These artificial clouds unrolled their thick spirals to a height of 1000 yards into the air. A savage, wandering somehwere beyond the limits of the horizon, might have believed that some new crater was forming in the bosom of Florida, although there was neither any eruption, nor typhoon, nor storm, nor struggle of the elements, nor any of those terrible phenomena which nature is capable of producing. No, it was man alone who had produced these reddish vapours, these gigantic flames worthy of a volcano itself, these tremendous vibrations resembling the shock of an earthquake, these reverberations rivalling those of hurricanes and storms; and it was his hand which precipitated into an abyss, dug by himself, a whole Niagara of molten metal!

CHAPTER 16

THE COLUMBIAD

HAD the casting succeeded? They were reduced to mere conjecture. There was indeed every reason to expect success, since the mould had absorbed the entire mass of the molten metal; still some considerable time must elapse before they could arrive at any certainty upon the matter.

The patience of the members of the Gun Club was sorely tried during this period of time. But they could do nothing. J. T. Maston escaped roasting by a miracle. Fifteen days after the casting an immense column of smoke was still rising in the open sky, and the ground burnt the soles of the feet within a radius of 200 feet round the summit of Stones Hill. It was impossible to approach nearer. All they could do was to wait with what patience they might.

"Here we are at the 10th August," exclaimed J. T. Maston one morning, "only four months to the 1st of December! We shall never be ready in time!" Barbicane said nothing, but his silence covered serious irritation.

However, daily observations revealed a certain change going on in the state of the ground. About the 15th August the vapours ejected had sensibly diminished in intensity and thickness. Some days afterwards the earth exhaled only a slight puff of smoke, the last breath of the monster enclosed within its circle of stone. Little by little the belt of heat contracted, until on the 22nd August Barbicane, his colleagues, and the engineer were enabled to set foot on the iron sheet which lay level upon the summit of Stones Hill.

"At last!" exclaimed the President of the Gun Club, with an immense sigh of relief.

The work was resumed the same day. They proceeded at once to extract the interior mould, for the purpose of clearing out the boring of the piece. Pickaxes and boring irons were set to work without intermission. The clayey and sandy soils had acquired extreme hardness under the action of the heat; but by the aid of the machines, the rubbish on being dug out was rapidly carted away on railway wagons; and such was the ardour of the work, so persuasive the arguments of Barbicane's dollars, that by the 3rd of September all traces of the mould had entirely disappeared.

Immediately the operation of boring was commenced; and by the aid of powerful machines, a few weeks later, the inner surface of the immense tube had been rendered perfectly cylindrical, and the bore of the piece had acquired a thorough polish.

At length, on the 22nd of September, less than a twelvemonth after Barbicane's original proposition, the enormous weapon, accurately bored, and exactly vertically pointed, was ready for work. There was only the moon now to wait for; and they were pretty sure that she would not fail in the rendezvous.

The ecstacy of J. T. Maston knew no bounds, and he narrowly escaped a frightful fall while staring down the tube. But for the strong hand of Colonel Blomsberry, the worthy secretary, like a modern Erostratus, would have found his death in the depths of the Columbiad.

The cannon was then finished; there was no possible doubt as to its perfect completion. So, on the 6th of October, Captain Nicholl opened an account between himself and President Barbicane, in which he debited himself to the latter in the sum of 2000 dollars. One may believe that the Captain's wrath was increased to it highest point, and must have made him seriously ill. However, he had still three bets of three, four, and five thousand dollars, respectively; and if he gained two out of these, his position would not be very bad. But the money question did not enter into his caluclations; it was the success of his rival in casting a cannon against which iron plates sixty feet thick would have been ineffectual, that dealt him a terrible blow.

After the 23rd of September the enclosure of Stones Hill was thrown open to the public; and it will be easily imagined what was the concourse of visitors to this spot! There was an incessant flow of people to and from Tampa Town and the place, which resembled a procession, or rather, in fact, a pilgrimage.

It was already clear to be seen that, on the day of the experiment itself, the aggregate of spectators would be counted by millions; for they were already arriving from all parts of the earth upon this narrow strip of promontory. Europe was emigrating to America.

Up to that time, however, it must be confessed, the curiosity of the numerous comers was but scantily gratified. Most had counted upon witnessing the spectacle of the casting, and they were treated to nothing but smoke. This was sorry food for hungry eyes; but Barbicane would admit no one to that operation. Then ensued grumbling, discontent, murmurs; they blamed the President, taxed him with dictatorial conduct. His proceedings were declared "un-American." There was very nearly a riot round Stones Hill; but Barbicane remained inflexible. When, however, the Columbiad was entirely finished, this state of closed doors could no longer be maintained; besides it would have been bad taste, and even imprudence, to affront the public feeling. Barbicane, therefore, opened the enclosure to all comers; but, true to his practical disposition, he determined to coin money out of the public curiosity.

It was something, indeed, to be enabled to contemplate this immense Columbiad; but to descend into its depths, this seemed to the Americans the *ne plus ultra* of earthly felicity. Consequently, there was not one curious spectator who was not willing to give himself the treat of visiting the interior of this metallic abyss. Baskets suspended from steam-cranes permitted them to satisfy their curiosity. There was a perfect mania. Women, children, old men, all made it a point of duty to penetrate the mysteries of the colassal gun. The fare for the descent was fixed at five dollars per head; and, despite this high charge, during the two months which preceded the experiment, the influx of visitors enabled the Gun Club to pocket nearly 500,000 dollars!

It is needless to say that the first visitors of the Columbiad were the members of the Gun Club. This privilege was justly reserved for that illustrious body. The ceremony took place on the 25th September. A basket of honour took down the President, J. T. Maston, Major Elphinstone, General Morgan, Colonel Blomsberry, and other members of the club, to the number of ten in all. How hot it was at the bottom of that long tube of metal! They were half suffocated. But what delight! What ecstacy! A table had been laid with six covers on the massive stone which formed the bottom of the Columbiad, and lighted by a jet of electric light resembling that of day itself. Numerous exquisite dishes, which seemed to descend from heaven, were placed successively before the guests, and the richest wines of France flowed in profusion during this splendid repast, served nine hundred feet beneath the surface of the earth!

The festival was animated, not to say somewhat noisy. Toasts flew backwards and forwards. They drank to the earth and to her satellite, to the Gun Club, the Union, the moon, Diana, Phœbe, Selene, the "peaceful courier of the night"! All the hurrahs, carried upwards upon the sonorous waves of the immense acoustic tube, arrived with the sound of thunder at its mouth; and the multitude ranged round Stones Hill heartily united their shouts with those of the ten revellers hidden from view at the botton of the gigantic Columbiad.

J. T. Maston was no longer master of himself. Whether he shouted or gesticulated, ate or drank most, would be a difficult matter to determine. At all events, he would not have given his place up for an empire, "not even if the cannon—loaded, primed, and fired at that very moment—were to blow him in pieces into the planetary world."

CHAPTER 17

A TELEGRAPHIC DESPATCH

THE great works undertaken by the Gun Club had now virtually come to an end; and two months still remained before the day for the discharge of the shot to the moon. To the general impatience these two months appeared as long as years! Hitherto the smallest details of the operation had been daily chronicled by the journals, which the public devoured with eager eyes.

Just at this moment a circumstance, the most unexpected, the most extraordinary and incredible, occurred to rouse afresh their panting spirits, and to throw every mind into a state of the most violent excitement.

One day, the 30th September, at 3.47 p.m., a telegram, transmitted by cable from Valentia (Ireland) to Newfoundland and the American mainland, arrived at the address of President Barbicane.

The President tore open the envelope, read the despatch, and, despite his remarkable powers of self-control, his lips turned pale and his eyes grew dim, on reading the twenty words of this telegram.

Here is the text of the despatch, which figures now in the archives of the Gun Club:—

"FRANCE, PARIS,

"30 *September, 4 a.m.*

"Barbicane, Tampa Town, Florida, United States.

"Substitute for your spherical shell a cylindro-conical projectile. I shall go inside. Shall arrive by steamer 'Atlanta.'

"MICHEL ARDAN."

CHAPTER 18

THE PASSENGER OF THE "ATLANTA"

IF this astounding news, instead of flying through the electric wires, had simply arrived by post in the ordinary sealed envelope, Barbicane would not have hesitated a moment. He would have held his tongue about it, both as a measure of prudence, and in order not to have to reconsider his plans. This telegram might be a cover for some jest, especially as it came from a Frenchman. What human being would ever have conceived the idea of such a journey? and, if such a person really existed, he must be an idiot, whom one would shut up in a lunatic ward, rather than within the walls of the projectile.

The contents of the despatch, however, speedily became known; for the telegraphic officials possessed but little discretion, and Michel Ardan's proposition ran at once throughout the several States of the Union. Barbicane had, therefore, no further motive for keeping silence. Consequently, he called together such of his colleagues as were at the moment in Tampa Town, and without any expression of his own opinions simply read to them the laconic text itself. It was received with every possible variety of expressions of doubt, incredulity, and derision from every one, with the exception of J. T. Maston, who exclaimed, "It is a grand idea, however!"

When Barbicane originally proposed to send a shot to the moon every one looked upon the enterprise as simple and practicable enough—a mere question of gunnery; but when a person, professing to be a reasonable being, offered to take passage within the projectile, the whole thing became a farce, or, in plainer language,a *humbug*.

One question, however, remained. Did such a being exist? This telegram flashed across the depths of the Atlantic, the designation of the vessel on board which he was to take his passage, the date assigned for his speedy arrival, all combined to impart a certain character of reality to the proposal. They must get some clearer notion of the matter. Scattered groups of inquirers at length condensed themselves into a compact crowd, which made straight for the residence of President Barbicane. That worthy individual was keeping quiet with the intention of watching events as they arose. But he had forgotten to take into account the public impatience; and it was with no pleasant countenance that he watched the population of Tampa Town gathering under his windows. The murmurs and vociferations below presently obliged him to appear. He came forward, therefore, and on silence being procured, a citizen put point-blank to him the following question:—"Is the person mentioned in the telegram, under the name of Michel Ardan, on his way here ? Yes or no."

"Gentlemen," replied Barbicane, "I know no more than you do."

"We must know," roared the impatient voices.

"Time will show," calmly replied the President.

"Time has no business to keep a whole country in suspense," replied the orator. "Have you altered the plans of the projectile according to the request of the telegram?"

"Not yet, gentlemen; but you are right! we must have better information to go by. The telegraph must complete its information."

"To the telegraph!" roared the crowd.

Barbicane descended; and heading the immense assemblage, led the way to the telegraph office. A few minutes later a telegram was despatched to the secretary of the underwriters at Liverpool, requesting answers to the following queries:—

"About the ship 'Atlanta'—when did she leave Europe? Had she on board a Frenchman named Michel Ardan?"

Two hours afterwards Barbicane received information too exact to leave room for the smallest reamining doubt.

"The steamer 'Atlanta' from Liverpool put to sea on the 2nd October, bound for Tampa Town, having on board a Frenchman borne on the list of passengers by the name of Michel Ardan."

That very evening he wrote to the house of Breadwill and Co., requesting them to suspend the casting of the projectile until the receipt of further orders. On the 20th October, at 9 a.m., the semaphores of the Bahama Canal signalled a thick smoke on the horizon. Two hours later a large steamer exchanged signals

Michel Ardan.

with them. The name of the "Atlanta" flew at once over Tampa Town. At four o'clock the English vessel entered the Bay of Espiritu Santo. At five it crossed the passage of Hillisborough Bay at full steam. At six she cast anchor at Port Tampa. The anchor had scarcely caught the sandy bottom when 500 boats surrounded the "Atlanta," and the steamer was taken by assault. Barbicane was the first to set foot on deck, and in a voice of which he vainly tried to conceal the emotion, called "Michel Ardan."

"Here!" replied an individual perched on the poop.

Barbicane, with arms crossed, looked fixedly at the passenger of the "Atlanta."

He was a man of about 42 years of age, of large build, but slightly round-shouldered. His massive head momentarily shook a shock of reddish hair, which resembled a lion's mane. His face was short with a broad forehead, and furnished with a moustache as bristly as a cat's, and little patches of yellowish whisker upon full cheeks. Round, wildish eyes, slightly near-sighted, completed a physiognomy essentially *feline*. His nose was firmly shaped, his mouth particularly sweet in expression, high forehead, intelligent and furrowed with wrinkles like a newly-ploughed field. The body was powerfully developed and firmly fixed upon long legs. Muscular arms, and a general air of decision gave him the appearance of a hardy, jolly companion. He was dressed in a suit of ample dimensions, loose neckerchief, open shirt-collar, disclosing a robust neck; his cuffs were invariably unbuttoned,through which appeared a pair of red hands.

On the bridge of the steamer, in the midst of the crowd, he bustled to and fro, never still for a moment, "Dragging his anchors," as the sailors say, gesticulating, making free with everybody, biting his nails with nervous avidity. He was one of those originals which nature sometimes invents in the freak of a moment, and of which she then breaks the mould.

Amongst other peculiarities, this curiosity gave himself out for a sublime ignoramus, "like Shakespeare," and professed supreme contempt for all scientific men. Those "fellows," as he called them, "are only fit to mark the points, while we play the game." He was, in fact, a thorough Bohemian, adventurous, but not an adventurer; a hair-brained fellow, a kind of Icarus, only possessing relays of wings. For the rest, he was ever in scrapes, ending invariably by falling on his feet, like those little pith figures which they sell for children's toys. In two words, his motto was "I have my opinions," and the love of the impossible constituted his ruling passion.

Such was the passenger of the "Atlantic," always excitable, as if boiling under the action of some internal fire by the character of his physical organization. If ever two individuals offered a striking contrast to each other, these were certainly Michel Ardan and the Yankee Barbicane; both, moreover, being equally enterprising and daring, each in his own way.

The scrutiny which the President of the Gun Club had instituted regarding this new rival was quickly interrupted by the shouts and hurrahs of the crowd. The cries became at last so uproarious, and the popular enthusiasm assumed so personal a form, that Michel Ardan, after having shaken hands some thousands of times, at the imminent risk of leaving his fingers behind him, was fain at last to make a bolt for his cabin.

Barbicane followed him without uttering a word.

"You are Barbicane, I suppose?" said Michel Ardan in a tone of voice in which he would have addressed a friend of twenty years' standing.

"Yes," replied the President of the G. C.

"All right! how d'ye do, Barbicane? how are you getting on—pretty well? that's right."

"So," said Barbicane, without further preliminary, "you are quite determined to go."

"Quite decided."

"Nothing will stop you?"

"Nothing. Have you modified your projectile according to my telegram."

"I waited for your arrival. But," asked Barbicane again, "have you carefully reflected?"

"Reflected? have I any time to spare? I find an opportunity of making a tour in the moon, and I mean to profit by it. There is the whole gist of the matter."

Barbicane looked hard at this man who spoke so lightly of his project with such complete absence of anxiety. "But, at least," said he, "you have some plans, some means of carrying your project into execution?"

"Excellent, my dear Barbicane; only permit me to offer one remark:—My wish is to tell my story once for all, to everybody, and then to have done with it; then there will be no need for recapitulation. So, if you have no objection, assemble your friends, colleagues, the whole town, all Florida, all America if you like, and to-morrow I shall be ready to explain my plans and answer any objections whatever that may be advanced. You may rest assured I shall wait without stirring. Will that suit you?"

"All right," replied Barbicane.

So saying, the President left the cabin and informed the crowd of the proposal of Michel Ardan. His words were received with clappings of hands and shouts of joy. They had removed all difficulties. To-morrow every one would contemplate at his ease this European hero. However, some of the spectators, more infatuated than the rest, would not leave the deck of the "Atlanta." They passed the night on board. Amongst others, J. T. Maston got his hook fixed in the combing of the poop, and it pretty nearly required the capstan to get it out again.

"He is a hero! a hero!" he cried, a theme of which he was never tired of ringing the changes; "and we are only like weak, silly women, compared with this European!"

As to the president, after having suggested to the visitors it was time to retire, he re-entered the passenger's cabin, and remained there till the bell of the steamer made it midnight.

But then the two rivals in popularity shook hands heartily and parted on terms of intimate friendship.

CHAPTER 19

A MONSTER MEETING

On the following day Barbicane, fearing that indiscreet questions might be put to Michel Ardan, was desirous of reducing the number of the audience to a few of the initiated, his own colleagues for instance. He might as well have tried to check the Falls of Niagara! He was compelled, therefore, to give up the idea, and to let his new friend run the chances of a public conference. The place chosen for this monster meeting was a vast plain situated in the rear of the town. In a few hours, thanks to the help of the shipping in port, an immense roofing of canvas was stretched over the parched prairie, and protected it from the burning rays of the sun. There 300,000 people braved for many hours the stifling heat while awaiting the arrival of the Frenchman. Of this crowd of spectators a first set could both see and hear; a second set saw badly and heard nothing at all; and as for the third, it could neither see nor hear anything at all. At three o'clock Michel Ardan made his appearance, accompanied by the principal members of the Gun Club. He was supported on his right by President Barbicane, and on his left by J. T. Maston, more radiant than the midday sun and nearly as ruddy. Ardan mounted a platform, from the top of which his view extended over a sea of black hats. He exhibited not the slightest embarrassment; he was just as gay, familiar, and pleasant as if he were at home. To the hurrahs which greeted him he replied by a graceful bow; then, waving his hand to request silence, he spoke in perfectly correct English as follows:—

"Gentlemen, despite the very hot weather I request your patience for a short time while I offer some explanations regarding the projects which seem to have so interested you. I am neither an orator nor a man of science, and I had no idea of addressing you in public; but my friend Barbicane has told me that you would like to hear me, and I am quite at your service. Listen to me, therefore, with your 600,000 ears, and please to excuse the faults of the speaker. Now pray do not forget that you see before you a perfect ignoramus, whose ignorance goes so far that he cannot even understand the difficulties! It seemed to him that it was a matter quite simple, natural, and easy to take one's place in a projectile and start for the moon! That journey must be undertaken sooner or later; and, as for the mode of locomotion adopted, it follows simply the law of progress. Man began by walking on all-fours; then, one fine day, on two feet; then in a carriage; then in a stage-coach; and lastly by railway. Well, the projectile is the vehicle of the future, and the planets themselves are nothing else! Now some of you, gentlemen, may imagine that the velocity we propose to impart to it is extravagant. It is nothing of the kind. All the stars exceed it in rapidity, and the earth herself is at this moment carrying us round the sun at three times as rapid a rate, and yet she is a mere lounger on the way compared with many other of the planets! And her velocity is constantly *decreasing*. Is it not evident, then, I ask you, that there will some day appear velocities far greater than these, of which light or electricity will probably be the mechanical agent?

"Yes, gentlemen," continued the orator, "in spite of the opinions of certain narrow-minded people, who would shut up the human race upon this globe, as within some magic circle which it must never outstep, we shall one day travel to the moon, the planets, and the stars, with the same facility, rapidity, and certainty as we now make the voyage from Liverpool to New York! Distance is but a relative expression, and must end by being reduced to zero."

The assembly, strongly predisposed as they were in favour of the French hero, were slightly staggered at this bold theory. Michel Ardan perceived the fact.

"Gentlemen," he continued with a pleasant smile, "you do not seem quite convinced. Very good! Let us reason the matter out. Do you know how long it would take for an *express train* to reach the moon? Three hundred days; no more! And what is that? The distance is no more than nine times the circumference of the earth; and there are no sailors or travellers, of even moderate activity, who have not made longer journeys than that in their lifetime. And now consider that I shall be only ninety-seven hours on my journey. Ah! I see you are reckoning that the moon is a long way off from the earth, and that one must think twice before making the experiment. What would you say, then, if we were talking of going to Neptune, which revolves at a distance of more than two thousand seven hundred and twenty millions of miles from the sun! And yet what is that compared with the distance of the fixed stars, some of which, such as Areturus, are at billions of miles distant from us? And then you talk of the *distance* which seperates the planets from the sun! And there are people who affirm that such a thing as distance exists. Absurdity, folly, idiotic nonsense! Would you know what *I* think of our own solar universe? Shall I tell you my theory? It is very simple! In my opinion the solar system is a solid, homogeneous body; the planets which compose it are in *actual contact* with each other; and whatever space exists between them is nothing more than the space which separates the molecules of the densest metal, such as silver, iron, or platinum! I have the right, therefore, to affirm, and I repeat, with the conviction which must penetrate all your minds, 'Distance is but an empty name; distance does not really exist!' "

"Hurrah!" Cried one voice (need it be said it was that of J. T. Maston?). "Distance does not exist!" And overcome by the energy of his movements, he nearly fell from the platform to the ground. He just escaped a severe fall, which would have proved to him that distance was by no means *an empty name*.

"Gentlemen," resumed the orator, "I repeat that the distance between the earth and her satellite is mere trifle, and undeserving of serious consideration. I am conviced that before twenty years are over one half of our earth will have paid a visit to the moon. Now, my worthy friends, if you have any question to put to me, you will, I fear, sadly embarrass a poor man like myself; still I will do my best to answer you."

Up to this point the President of the Gun Club had been satisfied with the turn which the discussion had assumed. It became now, however, desirable to divert Ardan from questions of a practical nature, with which he was doubtless far less conversant. Barbicane, therefore, hastened to get in a word, and began by asking his new friend whether he thought that the moon and the planets were inhabited.

"You put before me a great problem, my worthy President," replied the orator, smiling. "Still, men of great intelligence, such as Plutarch, Swedenborg, Bernardin de St. Pierre, and other have, if I mistake not, pronounced in the affirmative. Looking at the question from the natural philosopher's point of view, I should say that *nothing useless* existed in the world; and, replying to your question by another, I should venture to assert, that if these worlds are *habitable*, they either are, have been, or will be inhabited."

"No one could answer more logically or fairly," replied the president. "The question then reverts to this: *Are* these worlds habitable? For my own part I believe they are."

"For myself, I feel certain of it," said Michel Ardan.

"Nevertheless," retorted one of the audience, "there are many arguments *against* the habitability of the worlds. The conditions of life must evidently be greatly modified upon the majority of them. To mention only the planets, we should be either broiled alive in some, or frozen to death in others, according as they are more or less removed from the sun."

"I regret," replied Michel Ardan, "that I have not the honour of personally knowing my contradictor, for I would have attempted to answer him. His objection has its merits, I admit; but I think we may successfully combat it, as well as all others which affect the habitability of the other worlds. If I were a *natural philospher*, I would tell him that if less of caloric were *set in motion* upon the planets which are nearest to the sun, and more, on the contrary, upon those which are farthest removed from it, this simple fact would alone suffice to equalize the heat, and to render the temperature of those worlds supportable by beings organized like ourselves. If I were a *naturalist*, I would tell him that, according to some illustrious men of science, nature has furnished us with instances upon the earth of animals existing under very varying conditions of life; that fish respire in a medium fatal to other animals; that amphibious creatures possess a double existence very difficult of explanation; that certain denizens of the seas maintain life at enormous depths, and there support a pressure equal to that of fifty or sixty atmospheres without being crushed; that several aquatic insects, insensible to temperature, are met with equally among boiling springs and in the frozen plains of the Polar Sea; in fine, that we cannot help recognizing in nature a diversity of means of operation oftentimes incomprehensible, but not the less real. If I were a *chemist*, I would tell him that the aerolites, bodies evidently formed exteriorly of our terrestrial globe, have, upon analysis, revealed indisputable traces of carbon, a substance which owes its origin solely to organized beings, and which, according to the experiments of Reichenbach, must necessarily itself have been *endured with animation*. And lastly, were I a theologian, I would tell him that the scheme of the Divine Redemption, according to St. Paul, seems to be applicable, not merely to the earth, but to all the celestial worlds. But, unfortunately I am neither theologian, nor chemist, nor naturalist, nor philosopher; therefore, in my absolute ignorance of the great laws which govern the universe, I confine myself to saying in reply, 'I do not know whether the worlds are inhabited or not; and since I do not know, *I am going to see!*'"

Whether Michel Ardan's antagonist hazarded any further arguments or not it is impossible to say, for the uproarious shouts of the crowd would not allow any expression of opinion to gain a hearing. On silence being restored, the triumphant orator contented himself with adding the following remarks:—

"Gentlemen, you will observe that I have but slightly touched upon this great question. There is another altogether different line of arguments in favour of the habitability of the starts, which I omit for the present. I only desire to call attention to one point. To those who maintain that the planets are *not* inhabited one may reply:—You might be perfectly in the right, if you could only show that the earth is the *best possible world*, spite of what Valtaire has said. She has but *one* satellite, while Jupiter, Uranus, Saturn, Neptune have each several, an advantage by no means to be despised. But that which renders our own globe so uncomfortable to the inclination of its axis to the plane of its orbit. Hence the inequality of days and nights; hence the disagreeable diversity of the seasons. On the surface of our unhappy spheroid we are always either too hot or too cold; we are frozen in winter, broiled in summer; it is the planet of rheumatism, coughs, bronchitis; while on the surface of Jupiter, for example, where the axis is but slightly inclined, the inhabitants may enjoy uniform temperatures. It possesses zones of perpetual springs, summers, autumns, and winters; every Jovian may choose for himself what climate he likes, and there spend the whole of his life in security from all variations of temperature. You will, I am sure, readily admit this superiority of Jupiter over our own planet, to say nothing of his years, which each equal twelve of ours! Under such auspices, and such marvellous conditions of existence, it appears to me that the inhabitants of so fortunate a world must be in every respect superior to ourselves. All we require, in order to attain to such perfection, is the mere trifle of having an axis of rotation less inclined to the plane of its orbit!"

"Hurrah!" roared an energetic voice, "let us unite our efforts, invent the necessary machines, and rectify the earth's axis!"

A thunder of applause followed this proposal, the author of which was, of course, no other than J. T. Maston. And, in all probability, if the truth must be told, if the Yankees could only have found a point of application for it, they would have constructed a lever capable of raising the earth and rectifying its axis. It was just this deficiency which baffled these daring mechanicians.

CHAPTER 20

ATTACK AND RIPOSTE

As soon as the excitement had subsided, the following words were heard uttered in a strong and determined voice:—

"Now that the speaker has favoured us with so much imagination, would he be so good as to return to his subject, and give us a little practical view of the question?"

All eyes were directed towards the person who spoke. He was a little dried-up man, of an active figure, with an American "goatee" beard. Profiting by the different movements in the crowd, he had managed by degrees to gain the front row of spectators. There, with arms crossed and stern gaze, he watched the hero of the meeting. After having put his question he remained silent, and appeared to take no notice of the thousands of looks directed towards himself, nor of the murmur of disapprobation excited by his words. Meeting at first with no reply, he repeated his question with marked emphasis, adding, "We are here to talk about the *moon* and not about the *earth*."

"You are right, sir," replied Michel Ardan; "the discussion has become irregular. We will return to the moon."

"Sir," said the unknown, "you pretend that our satellite is inhabited. Very good; but if Selenites do exist, that race of beings assuredly must live without breathing, for—I warn you for your own sake—there is not the smallest particle of air on the surface of the moon."

At this remark Ardan pushed up his shock of red hair; he saw that he was on the point of being involved in a struggle with this person upon the very gist of the whole question. He looked sternly at him in his turn and said,—

"Oh! so there is no air in the moon? And pray, if you are so good, who ventures to affirm that?"

"The men of science."

"Really?"

"Really."

"Sir," replied Michel, "pleasantry apart, I have a profound respect for men of science who do possess science, but a profound contempt for men of science who do not.''

''Do you know any who belong to the latter category?''

''Decidedly. In France there are some who maintain that, mathematically, a bird cannot possibly fly; and others who demonstrate theoretically that fishes were never made to live in water.''

''I have nothing to do with persons of that description, and I can quote, in support of my statement, names which you cannot refuse deference to.''

''Then, sir, you will sadly embarrass a poor ignorant, who, besides, asks nothing better than to learn.''

''Why, then, do you introduce scientific questions if you have never studied them?'' asked the unknown somewhat coarsely.

''For the reason that 'he is always brave who never suspects danger.' I know nothing, it is true; but it is precisely my very weakness which constitutes my strength.''

''Your weakness amounts to folly,'' retorted the unknown in a passion.

''All the better,'' replied our Frenchman, ''if it carries me up to the *moon*.''

Barbicane and his colleagues devoured with their eyes the intruder who had so boldly placed himself in antagonism to their enterprise. Nobody knew him, and the president, uneasy as to the result of so free a discussion, watched his new friend with some anxiety. The meeting began to be somewhat fidgetty also, for the contest directed their attention to the dangers, if not the actual impossibilities, of the proposed expedition.

''Sir,'' replied Ardan's antagonist, ''there are many and incontrovertible reasons which prove the absence of an atmostphere in the moon. I might say that, *à priori*, if one ever did exist, it must have been absorbed by the earth; but I prefer to bring forward indisputable facts.''

''Bring them forward then, sir, as many as you please.''

''You know,'' said the stranger, ''that when any luminous rays cross a medium such as the air, they are deflected out of the straight line; in other words, they undergo *refraction*. Well! When stars are occulted by the moon, their rays, on grazing the edge of her disc, exhibit not the least deviation, nor offer the slightest indication of refraction. It follows, therefore, that the moon cannot be surrounded by an atmosphere.''

''In point of fact,'' replied Ardan, ''this is your chief, if not your *only* argument; and a really scientific man might be puzzled to answer it. For myself, I will simply say that it is defective, because it assumes that the angular diameter of the moon has been completely determined, which is not the case. But let us proceed. Tell me, my dear sir, do you admit the existence of volcanoes on the moon's surface?''

''*Extinct*, yes! In activity, no!''

''These volcanoes, however, were at one time in a state of activity?''

''True! but, as they furnished themselves the oxygen necessary for combustion, the mere fact of their eruption does not prove the presence of an atmosphere.''

''Proceed again, then; and let us set aside this class of arguments in order to come to direct observations. In 1715 the astronomers Louville and Halley, watching the eclipse of the 3rd May, remarked some very extraordinary scintillations. These jets of light, rapid in nature, and of frequent recurrence, they attributed to thunderstorms generated in the lunar atmosphere.''

''In 1715,'' replied the unknown, ''the astronomers Louville and Halley mistook for lunar phenomena some which were purely terrestrial, such as meteoric or other bodies which are generated in our own atmosphere. This was the scientific explanation at the time of the facts; and that is my answer now."

"On again, then," replied Ardan; "Herschel, in 1787, observed a great number of luminous points on the moon's surface, did he not?"

"Yes! but without offering any solution of them. Herschel himself never inferred from them the necessity of a lunar atmosphere. And I may add that Bæer and Maedler, the two great authorities upon the moon, are quite agreed as to the entire absence of air on its surface."

A movement was here manifest among the assemblage, who appeared to be growing excited by the arguments of this singular personage.

"Let us proceed," replied Ardan, with perfect coolness, "and come to one important fact. A skilful French astronomer, M. Laussedat, in watching the eclipse of July 18, 1860, proved that the horns of the solar crescent were *rounded and truncated*. Now, this appearance could only have been produced by a deviation of the solar rays in traversing the atmosphere of the moon. There is no other possible explanation of the fact."

"But is this established as a fact?"

"Absolutely certain!"

A counter-movement here took place in favour of the hero of the meeting, whose opponent was now reduced to silence. Ardan resumed the conversation; and, without exhibiting any exultation at the advantage he had gained, simply said,—

"You see, then, my dear sir, we must not pronounce with absolute positiveness against the existence of an atmosphere in the moon. That atmosphere is, probably, of extreme rarity; nevertheless at the present day science generally admits that it exist."

"Not in the mountains, at all events," returned the unknown, unwilling to give in.

"No! but at the bottom of the valleys, and not exceeding a few hundred feet in height."

"In any case you do well to take every precaution, for the air will be terribly rarified."

"My good sir, there will always be enough for a solitary individual; besides, once arrived up there, I shall do my best to economize, and not to breathe except on grand occasions!"

A tremendous roar of laughter rang in the ears of the mysterious interlocutor, who glared fiercely round upon the assembly.

"Then," continued Ardan, with a careless air, "since we are in accord regarding the presence of a certain atmosphere, we are forced to admit the presence of a certain quantity of water. This is a happy consequence for me. Moreover, my amiable contradictor, permit me to submit to you one further observation. We only know *one* side of the moon's disc; and if there is but little air on the face presented to us, it is possible that there is plenty on the one turned away from us."

"And for what reason?"

"Because the moon, under the action of the earth's attraction, has assumed the form of an egg, which we look at from the smaller end. Hence it follows, by Hausen's calculations, that its centre of gravity is situated in the other hemisphere. Hence it results that the great mass of air and water must have been drawn away to the other face of our satellite during the first days of its creation."

"Pure fancies!" cried the unknown.

"No! Pure theories! which are based upon the laws of mechanics, and it seems difficult to me to refute them. I appeal then to this meeting, and I put it to them whether life, such as exists upon the earth, is possible on the surface of the moon?"

Three hundred thousand auditors at once applauded the proposition. Ardan's opponent tried to get in another word, but he could not obtain a hearing. Cries and menaces fell upon him like hail.

"Enough! enough!" cried some.

"Drive the intruder off!" shouted others.

"Turn him out!" roared the exasperated crowd.

But he, holding firmly on to the platform, did not budge an inch, and let the storm pass on, which would soon have assumed formidable proportions, if Michel Ardan had not quieted it by a gesture. He was too chivalrous to abandon his opponent in an apparent extremity.

"You wished to say a few more words?" he asked, in a pleasant voice.

"Yes, a thousand; or rather, no, only one! If you perservere in your enterprise, you must be a—"

"Very rash person! How can you treat me as such? me, who have demanded a cylindro-conical projectile, in order to prevent turning round and round on my way like a squirrel?"

"But, unhappy man, the dreadful recoil will smash you to pieces at your starting."

"My dear contradictor, you have just put your finger upon the true and the only difficulty; nevertheless, I have too good an opinion of the industrial genius of the Americans not to believe that they will succeed in overcoming it."

"But the heat developed by the rapidity of the projectile in crossing the strata of air?"

"Oh! the walls are thick, and I shall soon have crossed the atmosphere."

"But victuals and water?"

"I have calculated for a twelve month's supply, and I shall be only four days on the journey."

"But for air to breath on the road?"

"I shall make it by chemical process."

"But your fall on the moon, supposing you ever reach it?"

"It will be six times less dangerous than a sudden fall upon the earth, because the weight will be only one-sixth as great on the surface of the moon."

"Still it will be enough to smash you like glass!"

"What is to prevent my retarding the shock by means of rockets conveniently placed, and lighted at the right moment?"

"But after all, supposing all difficulties surmounted, all obstacles removed, supposing everything combined to favour you, and granting that you may arrive safe and sound in the moon, how will you come back?"

"I am not coming back!"

At this reply, almost sublime in its very simplicity, the assembly became silent. But its silence was more eloquent than could have been its cries of enthusiasm. The unknown profited by the opportunity and once more protested,—

"You will inevitably kill yourself!" he cried; "and your death will be that of a madman, useless even to science!"

"Go on, my dear unknown, for truly your prophecies are most agreeable!"

"It really is too much!" cried Michel Ardan's adversary. "I do not know why I should continue so frivolous a discussion! Please yourself about this insane expedition! We need not trouble ourselves about *you*!"

"Pray don't stand upon ceremony!"

"No! another person is responsible for your act."

"Who, may I ask?" demanded Michel Ardan in an imperious tone.

"The ignoramus who organized this equally absurd and impossible experiment!"

The attack was direct. Barbicane, ever since the interference of the unknown, had been making fearful efforts of self-control; now, however, seeing himself directly attacked, he could restrain himself no longer. He rose suddenly, and was rushing upon the enemy who thus braved him to the face, when all at once he found himself separated from him.

The platform was lifted by a hundred strong arms, and the President of the Gun Club shared with Michel Ardan triumphal honours. The shield was heavy, but the bearers came in continuous relays, disputing, struggling, even fighting among themselves in their eagerness to lend their shoulders to this demonstration.

However, the unknown had not profited by the tumult to quit his post. Besides, he could not have done it in the midst of that compact crowd. There he held on in the front row, with crossed arms, glaring at President Barbicane.

The shouts of the immense crowd continued at their highest pitch throughout this triumphant march. Michel Ardan took it all with evident pleasure. His face gleamed with delight. Several times the platform seemed seized with ptiching and rolling like a weather-beaten ship. But the two heroes of the meeting had good sea-legs. They never stumbled; and their vessel arrived without dues at the port of Tampa Town.

Michel Ardan managed fortunately to escape from the last embraces of his vigorous admirers. He made for the Hotel Franklin, quickly gained his chamber, and slid under the bedclothes, while an army of a hundred thousand men kept watch under his windows.

During this time a scene, short, grave, and decisive, took place between the mysterious personage and the President of the Gun Club.

Barbicane, free at last, had gone straight at his adversary.

"Come!" he said shortly.

The other followed him on to the quay; and the two presently found themselves alone at the entrance of an open wharf on Jones' Fall.

The two enemies, still mutually unknown, gazed at each other.

"Who are you?" asked Barbicane.

"Captain Nicholl!"

"So I suspected. Hitherto chance has never thrown you in my way."

"I am come for that purpose."

"You have insulted me!"

"Publicly!"

"And you will answer to me for this insult?"

"At this very moment."

"No! I desire that all that passes between us shall be secret. There is a wood situated three miles from Tampa, the wood of Skersnaw. Do you know it?"

"I know it."

"Will you be so good as to enter it to-morrow morning at five o'clock, on one side?"

"Yes! if you will enter at the other side at the same hour."

"And you will not forget your rifle?" asked Barbicane.

"No more than you will forget yours," replied Nicholl.

These words having been coldly spoken, the President of the Gun Club and the captain parted. Barbicane returned to his lodging; but, instead of snatching a few hours of repose, he passed the night in endeavouring to discover a means of evading the recoil of the projectile, and resolving the difficult problem proposed by Michel Ardan during the discussion at the meeting.

CHAPTER 21

HOW A FRENCHMAN MANAGES AN AFFAIR

WHILE the contract of this duel was being discussed by the president and the captain—this dreadful savage duel, in which each adversary became a man-hunter—Michel Ardan was resting from the fatigues of his triumph. *Resting* is hardly an appropriate expression, for American beds rival marble or granite tables for hardness.

Ardan was sleeping, then, badly enough, tossing about between the cloths which served him for sheets, and he was dreaming of making a more comfortable couch in his projectile when a frightful noise disturbed his dreams. Thundering blows shook his door. They seemed to be caused by some iron instrument. A great deal of loud talking was distinguishable in this racket, which was rather too early in the morning. "Open the door," some one shrieked, "for Heaven's sake!" Ardan saw no reason for complying with a demand so roughly expressed. However, he got up and opened the door just as it was giving way before the blows of this determined visitor. The secretary of the Gun Club burst into the room. A bomb could not have made more noise or have entered the room with less ceremony.

"Last night," cried J. T. Maston, *ex abrupto*, "our president was publicly insulted during the meeting. He provoked his adversary, who is none other than Captain Nicholl! They are fighting this morning in the wood of Skersnaw. I heard all particulars from the mouth of Barbicane himself. If he is killed, then our scheme is at end. We must prevent this duel; and one man alone has enough influence over Barbicane to stop him, and that man is Michel Ardan."

While J. T. Maston was speaking, Michel Ardan, without interrupting him, had hastily put on his clothes; and, in less than two minutes, the two friends were making for the suburbs of Tampa Town with rapid strides.

It was during this walk that Maston told Ardan the state of the case. He told him the real cuases of the hostility between Barbicane and Nicholl; how it was of old date, and why, thanks to unknown friends, the president and the captain had, as yet, never met face to face. He added that it arose simply from a rivalry between iron plates and shot, and, finally, that the scene at the meeting was only the long-wished-for opportunity for Nicholl to pay off an old grudge.

Nothing is more dreadful than private duels in America. The two adversaries attack each other like wild beasts. Then it is that they might well covet those wonderful properties of the Indians of the prairies—their quick intelligence, their ingenious cunning, their scent of the enemy. A single mistake, a moment's hesitation, a single false step may cause death. On these occasions Yankees are often accompanied by their dogs, and keep up the struggle for hours.

"What demons you are!" cried Michel Ardan, when his companion had depicted this scene to him with much energy.

"Yes we are," replied J. T. modestly; "but we had better make haste."

Though Michel Ardan and he had crossed the plain still wet with dew, and had taken the shortest route over creeks and rice-fields, they could not reach Skersnaw under five hours and a half.

Barbicane must have passed the border half an hour ago.

There was an old bushman working there, occupied in selling faggots from the trees that had been levelled by his axe.

Maston ran towards him, saying, "Have you seen a man go into the wood, armed with a rifle? Barbicane, the president, my best friend?"

The worthy secretary of the Gun Club thought that his president must be known by all the world. But the bushman did not seem to understand him.

"A hunter?" said Ardan.

"A hunter? Yes," replied the bushman.

"Long ago?"

"About an hour."

"Too late!" cried Maston.

"Have you heard any gun-shots?" asked Ardan.

"No!"

"Not one?"

"Not one! that hunter did not look as if he knew how to hunt!"

"What is to be done?" said Maston.

"We must go into the wood, at the risk of getting a ball which is not intended for us."

"Ah!" cried Maston, in a tone which could not be mistaken, "I would rather have twenty balls in my own head than one in Barbicane's."

"Forward, then," said Ardan, pressing his companion's hand.

A few moments later the two friends had disappeared in the copse. It was a dense thicket, in which rose huge cypresses, sycamores, tulip-trees, olives, tamarinds, oaks, and magnolias. These different trees had interwoven their branches into an inextricable maze, through which the eye could not penetrate. Michel Ardan and Maston walked side by side in silence through the tall grass, cutting themselves a path through the strong creepers, casting curious glances on the bushes, and momentarily expecting to hear the sound of rifles. As for the traces which Barbicane ought to have left of his passage through the wood, there was not a vestige of them visible: so they followed the barely perceptible paths along which Indians had tracked some enemy, and which the dense foliage darkly overshadowed.

After an hour spent in vain pursuit the two stopped, in intensified anxiety.

"It must be all over," said Maston, discouraged. "A man like Barbicane would not dodge with his enemy, or ensnare him, would not even manœuvre!

He is too open, too brave. He has gone straight ahead, right into the danger, and doubtless far enough from the bushman for the wind to prevent his hearing the report of the rifles."

"But surely," replied Michel Ardan, "since we entered the wood we should have heard!"

"And what if we came too late?" cried Maston in tones of despair.

For once Ardan had no reply to make, he and Maston resuming their walk in silence. From time to time, indeed, they raised great shouts, calling alternately Barbicane and Nicholl, neither of whom, however, answered their cries. Only the birds, awakened by the sound, flew past them and disappeared among the branches, while some frightened deer fled precipitately before them.

For another hour their search was continued. The greater part of the wood had been explored. There was nothing to reveal the presence of the combatants. The information of the bushman was after all doubtful, and Ardan was about to propose their abandoning this useless pursuit, when all at once Maston stopped.

"Hush!" said he, "there is some one down there!"

"Some one?" repeated Michel Ardan.

"Yes; a man! He seems motionless. His rifle is not in his hands. What can he be doing?"

"But can you recognize him?" asked Ardan, whose short sight was of little use to him in such circumstances.

"Yes! yes! He is turning towards us," answered Maston.

"And it is?"

"Captain Nicholl!"

"Nicholl?" cried Michel Ardan, feeling a terrible pang of grief.

"Nicholl unarmed! He has, then, no longer any fear of his adversary!"

"Let us go to him," said Michel Ardan, "and find out the truth."

But he and his companion had barely taken fifty steps, when they paused to examine the captain more attentively. They expected to find a bloodthirsty man, happy in his revenge.

On seeing him, they remained stupefied.

A net, composed of very fine meshes, hung between two enormous tulip-trees, and in the midst of this snare, with its wings entangled, was a poor little bird, uttering pitiful cries, while it vainly struggled to escape. The bird-catcher who had laid this snare was no human being, but a venomous spider, peculiar to that country, as large as a pigeon's egg, and armed with enormous claws. The hideous creature, instead of rushing on its prey, had beaten a sudden retreat and taken refuge in the upper branches of the tulip-tree, for a formidable enemy menaced its stronghold.

Here, then, was Nicholl, his gun on the ground, forgetful of danger, trying if possible to save the victim from its cobweb prison. As last it was accomplished, and the little bird flew joyfully away and disappeared.

Nicholl lovingly watched its flight, when he heard these words pronounced by a voice full of emotion,—

"You are indeed a brave man!"

He turned. Michel Ardan was before him, repeating in a different tone,—

"And a kindhearted one!"

"Michel Ardan!" cried the captain. "Why are you here?"

"To press your hand, Nicholl, and to prevent you from either killing Barbicane or being killed by him."

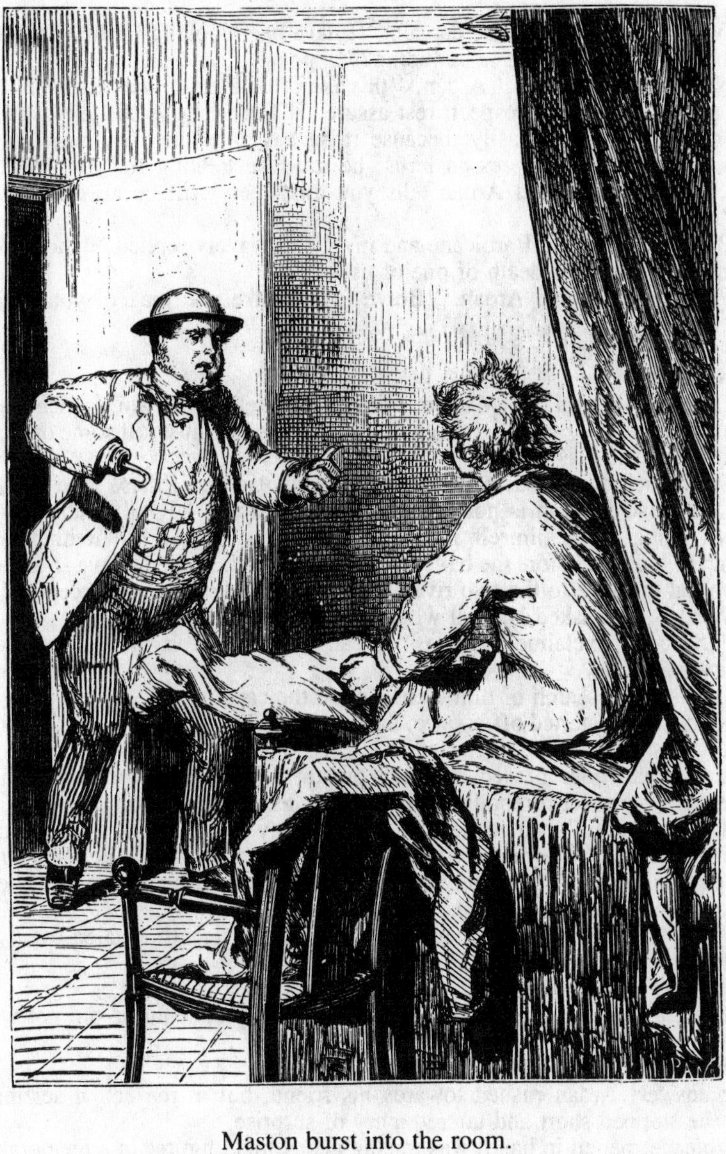

Maston burst into the room.

"Barbicane!" returned the captain. "I have been looking for him for the last two hours in vain. Where is he hiding?"

"Nicholl!" said Michel Ardan, "this is not courteous! we ought always to treat an adversary with respect; rest assured if Barbicane is still alive we shall find him all the more easily; because if he has not, like you, been amusing himself with freeing oppressed birds, he must be looking for *you*. When we have found him, Michel Ardan tells you this, there will be no duel between you."

"Between President Barbicane and myself," gravely replied Nicholl, "there is a rivalry which the death of one of us—"

"Pooh, pooh!" said Ardan. "Brave fellows like you indeed! you shall not fight!"

"I will fight, sir!"

"No!"

"Captain," said J. T. Maston, with much feeling, "I am a friend of the president's, his *alter ego*, his second self; if you really must kill some one, *shoot me!* it will do just as well!"

"Sir," Nicholl replied, seizing his rifle convulsively, "these jokes—"

"Our friend Maston is not joking," replied Ardan. "I fully understand his idea of being killed himself in order to save his friend. But neither he nor Barbicane will fall before the balls of Captain Nicholl. Indeed I have so attractive a proposal to make to the two rivals, that both will be eager to accept it."

"What is it?" asked Nicholl with manifest incredulity.

"Patience!" exclaimed Ardan. "I can only reveal it in the presence of Barbicane."

"Let us go in search of him then!" cried the captain.

The three men started off at once; the captain having discharged his rifle threw it over his shoulder, and advanced in silence.

Another half-hour passed, and the pursuit was still fruitless. Maston was oppressed by sinister forebodings. He looked fiercely at Nicholl, asking himself whether the captain's vengeance had been already satisfied, and the unfortunate Barbicane, shot, was perhaps lying dead on some bloody track. The same thought seemed to occur to Ardan; and both were casting inquiring glances on Nicholl, when suddenly Maston paused.

The motionless figure of a man leaning against a gigantic catalpa twenty feet off appeared, half-veiled by the foliage.

"It is he!" said Maston.

Barbicane never moved. Ardan looked at the captain, but he did not wince. Ardan went forward crying,—

"Barbicane, Barbicane!"

No answer! Ardan rushed towards his friend; but in the act of seizing his arms, he stopped short and uttered a cry of surprise.

Barbicane, pencil in hand, was tracing geometrical figures in a memorandum book, whilst his unloaded rifle lay beside him on the ground.

Absorbed in his studies, Barbicane, in his turn forgetful of the duel, had seen and heard nothing.

When Ardan took his hand, he looked up and stared at his visitor in astonishment.

"Ah, it is you!" he cried at last, "I have found it, my friend, I have found it!"

"What?"

"My plan!"

"What plan?"

"The plan for counteracting the effect of the shock at the departure of the projectile!"

"Indeed?" said Michel Ardan, looking at the captain out of the corner of his eye.

"Yes! water! simply water, which will act as a spring—ah! Maston," cried Barbicane, "you here also?"

"Himself," replied Ardan; "and permit me to introduce to you at the same time the worthy Captain Nicholl!"

"Nicholl!" cried Barbicane, who jumped up at once. "Pardon me, captain, I had quite forgotten—I am ready!"

Michel Ardan interfered, without giving the two enemies time to say anything more.

"Thank Heaven!" said he. "It is a happy thing that brave men like you two did not meet sooner! we should now have been mourning for one or other of you. But, thanks to Providence, which has interfered, there is now no further cause for alarm. When one forgets one's anger in mechanics or in cobwebs, it is a sign that the anger is not dangerous."

Michel Ardan then told the president how the captain had been found occupied.

"I put it to you now," said he in conclusion, "are two such good fellows as you are made on purpose to smash each other's skulls with shot?"

There was in "the situation" somewhat of the ridiculous, something quite unexpected; Michel Ardan saw this, and determined to effect a reconciliation.

"My good friends," said he, with his most bewitching smile, "this is nothing but a misunderstanding. Nothing more! well! to prove that it is all over between you, accept frankly the proposal I am going to make to you."

"Make it," said Nicholl.

"Our friend Barbicane believes that his projectile will go straight to the moon?"

"Yes, certainly," replied the president.

"And our friend Nicholl is persuaded it will fall back upon the earth?"

"I am certain of it," cried the captain.

"Good!" said Ardan. "I cannot pretend to make you agree; but I suggest this:—Go with me, and so see whether we are stopped on our journey."

"What?" exclaimed J. T. Maston, stupefied.

The two rivals, on this sudden proposal, looked steadily at each other. Barbicane waited for the captain's answer. Nicholl watched for the decision of the president.

"Well?" said Michel. "There is now no fear of the shock!"

"Done!" cried Barbicane.

But quickly as he pronounced the word, he was not before Nicholl.

"Hurrah! bravo! hip! hip! hurrah!" cried Michel, giving a hand to each of the late adversaries. "Now that it is all settled, my friends, allow me to treat you after French fashion. Let us be off to breakfast!"

CHAPTER 22

THE NEW CITIZEN OF THE UNITED STATES

THAT same day all America heard of the affair of Captain Nicholl and President Barbicane, as well as its singular *dénouement*. From that day forth, Michel Ardan had not one moment's rest. Deputations from all corners of the Union harassed him without cessation on intermission. He was compelled to receive them all, whether he would or no. How many hands he shook, how many people he was "hail-fellow-well-met" with, it is impossible to guess! Such a triumphal result would have intoxicated any other man; but he managed to keep himself in a state of delightful *semi*-tipsiness.

Among the deputations of all kinds which assailed him, that of "The Lunatics" were careful not to forget what they owed to the future conqueror of the moon. One day, certain of these poor people, so numerous in American, came to call upon him, and requested permission to return with him to their native country.

"Singular hallucination!" said he to Barbicane, after having dismissed the deputation with promises to convey numbers of messages to friends in the moon. "Do you believe in the influence of the moon upon distempers?"

"Scarcely!"

"No more do I, despite some remarkable recorded facts of history. For instance, during an epidemic in 1693, a large number of persons died at the very moment of an eclipse. The celebrated Bacon always fainted during an eclipse. Charles VI. relapsed six times into madness during the year 1399, sometimes during the new, sometimes during the full moon. Gall observed that insane persons underwent an accession of their disorder twice in every month, at the epochs of new and full moon. In fact, numerous observations made upon fevers, somnambulisms, and other human maladies, seem to prove that the moon does exercise some mysterious influence upon man."

"But the how and the wherefore?" asked Barbicane.

"Well, I can only give you the answer which Arago borrowed from Plutarch, which is nineteen centuries old. 'Perhaps the stories are not true!'"

In the height of his triumph, Michel Ardan had to encounter all the annoyances incidental to a man of celebrity. Managers of entertainments wanted to exhibit him. Barnum offered him a million dollars to make the tour of the United States in his show. As for his photographs, they were sold of all sizes, and his portrait taken in every imaginable posture. More than half a million copies were disposed of in an incredibly short space of time.

But it was not only the men who paid him homage, but the women also. He might have married well a hundred times over, if he had been willing to settle in life. The old maids, in particular, of forty years and upwards, and dry in proportion, devoured his photographs day and night. They would have married him by hundreds, even if he had imposed upon them the condition of accompanying him into space. He had, however, no intention of transplating a race of Franco-Americans upon the surface of the moon.

He therefore declined all offers.

As soon as he could withdraw from these somewhat embarrassing demonstrations, he went, accompanied by his friends, to pay a visit to the Columbiad. He was highly gratified by his inspection, and made the descent to the bottom of the tube of this gigantic machine which was presently to launch him to the regions of the moon.

It is necessary here to mention a proposal of J. T. Maston's. When the secretary of the Gun Club found that Barbicane and Nicholl accepted the proposal of Michel Ardan, he determined to join then, and make one of a snug party of four. So one day he determined to be admitted as one of the travellers. Barbicane, pained at having to refuse him, gave him clearly to understand that the projectile could not possibly contain so many passengers. Maston, in despair, went in search of Michel Ardan, who counselled him to resign himself to the situation, adding one or two arguments *ad hominem*.

"You see, old fellow," he said, "you must not take what I say in bad part; but really, between ourselves, you are in too incomplete a condition to appear in the moon!"

"Incomplete?" shrieked the valiant invalid.

"Yes, my dear fellow! imagine our meeting some of the inhabitants up there! Would you like to give them such a melancholy notion of what goes on down here? to teach them what war is, to inform them that we employ our time chiefly in devouring each other, in smashing arms and legs, and that too on a globe which is capable of supporting a hundred billions of inhabitants, and which actually does contain nearly two hundred millions? Why, my worthy friend, we should have to turn you out of doors!"

"But still, if you arrive there in pieces, you will be as *incomplete* as I am."

"Unquestionably," replied Michel Ardan; "but we shall not."

In fact, a preparatory experiment, tried on the 18th October, had yielded the best results and caused the most well-grounded hopes of success. Barbicane, desirous of obtaining some notion of the effect of the shock at the moment of the projectile's departure, had procured a 38-inch mortar from the arsenal of Pensacola. He had this placed on the bank of Hillisborough Roads, in order that the shell might fall back into the sea, and the shock be thereby destroyed. His object was to ascertain the extent of the shock of departure, and not that of the return.

A hollow projectile had been prepared for this curious experiment. A thick padding fastened upon a kind of elastic network, made of the best steel, lined the inside of the walls. It was a veritable *nest* most carefully wadded.

"What a pity I can't find room in there," said J. T. Maston, regretting that his height did not allow of his trying the adventure.

Within this shell were shut up a large cat, and a squirrel belonging to J. T. Maston, and of which he was particularly fond. They were desirous, however, of ascertaining how this little animal, least of all others subject to giddiness, would endure this experimental voyage.

The mortar was charged with 160lbs. of powder, and the shell placed in the chamber. On being fired, the projectile rose with great velocity, described a majestic parabola, attained a height of about a thousand feet, and with a graceful curve descended in the midst of the vessels that lay there at anchor.

Without a moment's loss of time a small boat put off in the direction of its fall; some active divers plunged into the water and attached ropes to the handles of the shell, which was quickly dragged on board. Five minutes did not elapse between the moment of enclosing the animals and that of unscrewing the coverlid of their prison.

Ardan, Barbicane, Maston, and Nicholl were present on board the boat, and assisted at the operation with an interest which may readily be comprehended. Hardly had the shell been opened when the cat leaped out, slightly bruised, but full of life, and exhibiting no signs whatever of having made an aerial expedition. No trace, however, of the squirrel could be discovered. The truth at last became apparent;—the cat had eaten its fellow-traveller!

J. T. Maston grieved much for the loss of his poor squirrel, and proposed to add its case to that of other martyrs to science.

After this experiment all hesitation, all fear disappeared. Besides, Barbicane's plans would ensure greater perfection for his projectile, and go far to annihilate altogether the effects of the shock. Nothing now remained but to go!

Two days later Michel Ardan received a message from the President of the United States, an honour of which he showed himself especially sensible.

After the example of his illustrious fellow-countryman, the Marquis de la Fayette, the Goverment had decreed to him the title of "Citizen of the United States of America."

CHAPTER 23

THE PROJECTILE VEHICLE

ON the completion of the Columbiad the public interest centred in the projectile itself, the vehicle which was destined to carry the three hardy adventurers into space.

The new plans had been sent to Breadwill and Co., of Albany, with the request for their speedy execution. The projectile was consequently cast on the 2nd November, and immediately forwarded by the Eastern Railway to Stones Hill, which it reached without accident on the 10th of that month, where Michel Ardan, Barbicane, and Nicholl were waiting impatiently for it.

The projectile had now to be filled to the depth of three feet with a bed of water, intended to support a watertight wooden disc, which worked easily within the walls of the projectile. It was upon this kind of raft that the travellers were to take their place. This body of water was divided by horizontal partitions, which the shock of the departure would have to break in succession. Then each sheet of the water, from the lowest to the highest running off into escape tubes towards the top of the projectile, constituted a kind of spring; and the wooden disc, supplied with extremely powerful plugs, could not strike the lowest plate except after breaking successively the different partitions. Undoubtedly the travellers would still have to encounter a violent *recoil* after the complete escapement of the water; but the first shock would be almost entirely destroyed by this powerful spring. The upper part of the walls were lined with a thick padding of leather, fastened upon springs of the best steel, behind which the escape tubes were completely concealed; thus all imaginable precautions had been taken for

The arrival of the projectile at Stone's Hill.

averting the first shock; and if they *did* get crushed, they must, as Michel Ardan said, be made of very bad materials.

The entrance into this metallic tower was by a narrow aperture contrived in the wall of the cone. This was hermetically closed by a plate of aluminium, fastened internally be powerful screw-pressure. The travellers could therefore quit their prison at pleasure, as soon as they should reach the moon.

Light and view were given by means of four thick lenticular glass scuttles, two pierced in the circular wall itself, the third in the bottom, the fourth in the top. These scuttles then were protected against the shock of departure by plates let into solid grooves, which could easily be opened outwards by unscrewing them from the inside. Reservoirs firmly fixed contained water and the necessary provisions; and fire and light were procurable by means of gas, contained in a special reservoir under a pressure of several atmospheres. They had only to turn a tap, and for six hours the gas would light and warm this comfortable vehicle.

There now remained only the question of air; for allowing for the consumption of air by Barbicane, his two companions, and two dogs which he purposed taking with him, it was necessary to renew the air of the projectile. Now air consists principally of twenty-one parts of oxygen and seventy-nine of nitrogen. The lungs absorb the oxygen, which is indispensable for the support of life, and reject the nitrogen. The air expired loses nearly five percent, of the former and contains nearly an equal volume of carbonic acid, produced by the combustion of the elements of the blood. In an air-tight enclosure, then, after a certain time, all the oxygen of the air will be replaced by the carbonic acid—a gas fatal to life. There were two things to be done then—first, to replace the absorbed oxygen; secondly, to destroy the expired carbonic acid; both easy enough to do, by means of chlorate of potass and caustic potash. The former is a salt which appears under the form of white crystals; when raised to a temperature of 400° it is transformed into chlorure of potassium, and the oxygen which it contains is entirely liberated. Now twenty-eight pounds of chlorate of potass produce seven pounds of oxygen, or 2400 *litres*—the quantity necessary for the travellers during twenty-four hours.

Caustic potash has a great affinity for carbonic acid; and it is sufficient to shake it in order for it to seize upon the acid and form bi-carbonate of potass. By these two means they would be enabled to restore to the vitiated air its life-supporting properties.

It is necessary, however, to add that the experiments had hitherto been made *in anima vili*. Whatever its scientific accuracy was, they were at present ignorant how it would answer with human beings. The honour of putting it to the proof was energetically claimed by J. T. Maston.

"Since I am not to go," said the brave artillerist, "I may at least live for a week in the projectile."

It would have been hard to refuse him; so they consented to his wish. A sufficient quantity of chlorate of potass and of caustic potash was placed at his disposal, together with provisions for eight days. And having shaken hands with his friends, on the 12th November, at six o'clock a.m., after strictly informing them not to open his prison before the 20th, at six o'clock p.m., he slid down the projectile, the plate of which was at once hermetically sealed. What did he do with himself during that week? They could get no information. The thickness of the walls of the projectile prevented any sound reaching from the inside to the outside. On the 20th November, at six p.m. exactly, the plate was opened.

The friends of J. T. Maston had been all along in a state of much anxiety; but they were promptly reassured on hearing a jolly voice shouting a boisterous hurrah.

Presently afterwards the secretary of the Gun Club appeared at the top of the cone in a triumphant attitude. He had grown fat!

CHAPTER 24

THE TELESCOPE OF THE ROCKY MOUNTAINS

On the 20th October in the preceding year, after the close of the subscription, the president of the Gun Club had credited the Observatory of Cambridge with the necessary sums for the construction of a gigantic optical instrument. This instrument was designed for the purpose of rendering visible on the surface of the moon any object exceeding nine feet in diameter.

At the period when the Gun Club essayed their great experiment, such instruments had reached a high degree of perfection, and produced some magnificent results. Two telescopes in particular, at this time, were possessed of remarkable power and of gigantic dimension. The first, constructed by Herschel, was thirty-six feet in length, and had an object-glass of four feet six inches; it possessed a magnifying power of 6000. The second was raised in Ireland, in Parsonstown Park, and belongs to Lord Rosse. The glass six feet; it magnifies 6400 times, and required an immense erection of brickwork and masonry for the purpose of working it, its weight being twelve tons and a half.

Still, despite these colassal dimensions, the actual enlargements scarcely exceeded 6000 times in round numbers; consequently, the moon was brought within no nearer an apparent distance than thirty-nine miles; and objects of less than sixty feet in diameter, unless they were of very considerable length, were still imperceptible.

In the present case, dealing with a projectile nine feet in diameter and fifteen feet long, it became necessary to bring the moon within an apparent distance of five miles at most; and, for that purpose, to establish a magnifying power of 48,000 times.

Such was the question proposed to the Observatory of Cambridge. There was no lack of funds; the difficulty was purely one of construction.

After considerable discussion as to the best form and principle of the proposed instrument the work was finally commenced. According to the calculations of the Observatory of Cambridge, the tube of the new reflector would require to be 280 feet in length, and the object-glass sixteen feet in diameter. Colassal as these dimensions may appear, they were diminutive in comparison with the 10,000 foot telescope proposed by the astonomer Hooke only a few years ago!

Regarding the choice of locality, that matter was promptly determined. The object was to select some lofty mountain, and there are not many of these in the United States. In fact there are but two chains of moderate elevation, between which runs the magnificent Mississippi, the "king of rivers," as these Republican Yankees delight to call it.

Eastwards rise the Apalachians, the very highest point of which, in New Hampshire, does not exceed the very moderate altitude of 5600 feet.

On the west, however, rise the Rocky Mountains, that immense range which, commencing at the Straits of Magellan, follows the western coast of Southern America under the name of the Andes or the Cordilleras, until it crosses the Isthmus of Panama, and runs up the whole of North America to the very borders of the Polar Sea. The highest elevation of this range still does not exceed 10,700 feet. With this elevation, nevertheless, the Gun Club were compelled to be content, inasmuch as they had determined that both telescope and Columbiad should be erected within the limits of the Union. All the necessary apparatus was consequently sent on to the summit of Long's Peak, in the territory of Missouri.

Neither pen nor language can describe the difficulties of all kinds which the American engineers had to surmount, or the prodigies of daring and skill which they accomplished. They had to raise enormous stones, massive pieces of wrought iron, heavy corner-clamps and huge portions of cylinder, with an object-glass weighing nearly 30,000lbs., above the line of perpetual snow for more than 10,000 feet in height, after crossing desert prairies, impenetrable forests, fearful rapids, far from all centres of population, and in the midst of savage regions, in which every detail of life becomes an almost insoluble problem. And yet, notwithstanding these innumerable obstacles, American genius triumphed. In less than a year after the commencement of the works, towards the close of September, the gigantic reflector rose into the air to a height of 280 feet. It was raised by means of an enormous iron crane; an ingenious mechanism allowed it to be easily worked towards all the points of the heavens, and to follow the stars from the one horizon to the other during their journey through the heavens.

It had cost 400,000 dollars. The first time it was directed towards the moon, the observers evinced both curiosity and anxiety. What were they about to discover in the field of this telescope which magnified objects 48,000 times? Would they perceive peoples, herds of lunar animals, towns, lakes seas? No! there was nothing which science had not already discovered! and on all the points of its disc the volcanic nature of the moon became determinable with the utmost precision.

But the telescope of the Rocky Mountains, before doing its duty to the Gun Club, rendered immense services to astronomy. Thanks to its penetrative power, the depths of the heavens were sounded to the utmost extent; the apparent diameter of a great number of stars was accurately measured; and Mr. Clark, of the Cambridge staff, resolved the Crab nebula in Taurus, which the reflector of Lord Rosse had never been able to decompose.

CHAPTER 25

FINAL DETAILS

It was the 22nd of November; the departure was to take place in ten days. One operation alone reamined to be accomplished to bring all to a happy termination; an operation delicate and perilous, requiring infinite precautions, and against the success of which Captain Nicholl had laid his third bet. It was, in fact, nothing less than the loading of the Columbiad, and the introduction into it of 400,000 pounds of gun-cotton. Nicholl had thought, not perhaps without reason, that the handling of such formidable quantities of pyroxyle would, in all probability, involve a grave catastrophe; and at any rate, that this immense mass of eminently inflammable matter would inevitably ignite when submitted to the pressure of the projectile.

There were indeed dangers accruing as before from the carelessness of the Americans, But Barbicane had set his heart on success, and took all possible precautions. In the first place, he was very careful as to the transportation of the gun-cotton to Stones Hill. He had it conveyed in small quantities, carefully packed in sealed cases. These were brought by rail from Tampa Town to the camp, and from thence were taken to the Columbiad by barefooted workmen, who deposited them in their places by means of cranes placed at the orifice of the cannon. No steam-engine was permitted to work, and every fire was extinguished within two miles of the works.

Even in November they feared to work by day, lest the sun's rays acting on the gun-cotton might lead to unhappy results. This led to their working at night, by light produced in a vacuum by means of Rühmkorff's apparatus, which threw an artificial brightness into the depths of the Columbaid. There the cartridges were arranged with the utmost regularity, connected by a metallic thread, destined to communicate to them all simultaneously the electric spark, by which means this mass of gun-cotton was eventually to be ignited.

By the 28th of November, 800 cartridges had been placed in the bottom on the Columbiad. So far the operation had been successful! But what confusion, what anxieties, what struggles were undergone by President Barbicane! In vain had he refused admission to Stones Hill; every day the inquisitive neighbours scaled the palisades, some even carrying their imprudence to the point of smoking, while surrounded by bales of gun-cotton. Barbicane was in a perpetual state of alarm. J. T. Maston seconded him to the best of his ability, by giving vigorous chase to the intruders, and carefully picking up the still lighted cigar ends which the Yankees threw about. A somewhat difficult task! seeing that more than 300,000 persons were gathered round the enclosure. Michel Ardan had volunteered to superintend the transport of the cartridges to the mouth of the Columbiad; but the president, having surprised him with an enormous cigar in his mouth, while he was hunting out the rash spectators to whom he himself offered so dangerous an example, was that he could not trust this fearless smoker, and was therefore obliged to mount a special guard over him.

At last, Providence being propitious, this wonderful loading came to a happy termination, Captain Nicholl's third bet being thus lost. It remained now to introduce the projectile into the Columbiad, and to place it on its soft bed of gun-cotton.

But before doing this, all those things necessary for the journey had to be carefully arranged in the projectile-vehicle. These necessaries were numerous; and had Ardan been allowed to follow his own wishes, there would have been no space remaining for the travellers. It is impossible to conceive of half the things this charming Frenchman wished to convey to the moon. A veritable stock of useless trifles! But Barbicane interfered and refused admission to anything not absolutely needed. Several thermometers, barometers, and telescopes were packed in the instrument case.

The travellers being desirous of examining the moon carefully during their voyage, in order to facilitate their studies, they took with them Bœer and Moëller's excellent *Mappa Selenographica*, a masterpiece of patience and observation, which they hoped would enable them to identify those physical features in the moon, with which they were acquainted. This map reproduced with scrupulous fidelity the smallest details of the lunar surface which faces the earth; the mountains, valleys, craters, peaks, and ridges were all represented, with their exact dimensions, relative positions, and names; from the mountains Doërfel and Leibnitz on the eastern side of the disc, to the *Mare frigoris* of the North Pole.

They took also three rifles and three fowling-pieces, and a large quantity of balls, shot, and powder.

"We cannot tell whom we shall have to deal with," said Michel Ardan. "Men or beasts may possibly object to our visit. It is only wise to take all precautions."

These defensive weapons were accompanied by pickaxes, crowbars, saws, and other useful implements, not to mention clothing adapted to every temperature, from that of the polar regions to that of the torrid zone.

Ardan wished to convey a number of animals of different sorts (not indeed a pair of every known species), as he could not see the necessity of acclimatizing serpents, tigers, alligators, or any other noxious beasts in the moon. "Nevertheless," he said to Barbicane, "some valuable and useful beasts, bullocks, cows, horses, and donkeys, would bear the journey very well, and would also be very useful to us."

"I dare say, my dear Ardan," replied the President, "but out projectile-vehicle is no Noah's ark, from which it differs both in dimensions and object. Let us confine ourselves to possibilities."

After a prolonged discussion, it was agreed that the travellers should restrict themselves to a sporting-dog belonging to Nicholl, and to a large Newfoundland. Several packets of seeds were also included among the necessaries. Michel Ardan, indeed, was anxious to add some sacks full of earth to sow them in; as it was, he took a dozen shrubs carefully wrapped up in straw to plant in the moon.

The important question of provisions still remained; it being necessary to provide against the possiblity of their finding the moon absolutely barren. Barbicane managed so successfully, that he supplied them with sufficient rations for a year. These consisted of perserved meats and vegetables, reduced by strong hydraulic pressure to the smallest possible dimensions. They were also supplied with brandy, and took water enough for two months, being confident, from astronomical observations, that there was no lack of water on the moon's surface. As to provisions, doubtless the inhabitants of the *earth* would find nourishment

The interior of the projectile.

somewhere in the *moon*. Ardan never questioned this; indeed, had he done so, he would never have undertaken the journey.

"Besides," he said one day to his friends, "we shall not be completely abandoned by our terrestrial friends; they will take care not to forget us."

"No, indeed!" replied J. T. Maston.

"What do you mean?" asked Nicholl.

"Nothing would be simpler," replied Ardan; "the Columbiad will be always there. Well! whenever the moon is in a favourable condition as to the zenith, if not to the perigee, that is to say about once a year, could you not send us a shell packed with provisions, which we might expect on some appointed day?"

"Hurrah! hurrah!" cried J. T. Maston; "what an ingenious fellow! what a splendid idea! Indeed, my good friends, we shall not forget you!"

"I shall reckon upon you! Then, you see, we shall receive news regularly from the earth, and we shall indeed be stupid if we hit upon no plan for communicating with our good friends here!"

These words inspired such confidence, that Michel Ardan carried all the Gun Club with him in his enthusiasm. What he said seemed so simple and so easy, so sure of success, that none could be so sordidly attached to this earth, as to hesitate to follow the three travellers on their lunar expedition.

All being ready at last, it remained to place the projectile in the Columbiad, an operation abundantly accompanied by dangers and difficulties.

The enormous shell was conveyed to the summit of Stones Hill. There, powerful cranes raised it, and held it suspended over the mouth of the cylinder.

It was a fearful moment! What if the chains should break under its enormous weight? The sudden fall of such a body would inevitably cause the gun-cotton to explode!

Fortunately this did not happen; and some hours later the projectile-vehicle descended gently into the heart of the cannon and rested on its couch of pyroxyle, a veritable bed of explosive eider-down. Its pressure had no result, other than the more effectual ramming down of the charge of the Columbiad.

"I have lost," said the Captain, who forthwith paid President Barbicane the sum of 3000 dollars.

Barbicane did not wish to accept the money from one of his fellow-travellers, but gave way at last before the determination of Nicholl, who wished before leaving the earth to fulfill all his engagements.

"Now," said Michel Ardan, "I have only one thing more to wish for you, my brave Captain."

"What is that?" asked Nicholl.

"It is that you may lose your two other bets! Then we shall be sure not to be stopped on our journey!"

CHAPTER 26

FIRE!

THE first of December had arrived! the fatal day! for, if the projectile were not discharged that very night at 10h. 46m. 40s. p.m., more than eighteen years must roll by before the moon would again present herself under the same conditions of zenith and perigee.

The weather was magnificent. Despite the approach of winter, the sun shone brightly, and bathed in its radiant light that earth which three of its denizens were about to abandon for a new world.

How many persons lost their rest on the night which preceded this long-expected day! All hearts beat with disquietude, save only the heart of Michel Ardan. That imperturbable personage came and went with his habitual business-like air, while nothing whatever denoted that any unusual matter preoccupied his mind.

After dawn, an innumerable multitude covered the prairie which extends as far as the eye can reach, round Stones Hill. Every quarter of an hour the railway brought fresh accessions of sightseers; and, according to the statement of the *Tampa Town Observer*, not less than five millions of spectators thronged the soil of Florida.

For a whole month previously, the mass of these persons had bivouacked round the enclosure, and laid the foundations for a town which was afterwards called "Ardan's Town." The whole plain was covered with huts, cottages, and tents. Every nation under the sun was represented there; and every language might be heard spoken at the same time. It was a perfect Babel re-enacted. All the various classes of American society were mingled together in terms of absolute equality. Bankers, farmers, sailors, cotton-planters, brokers, merchants, watermen, magistrates, elbowed each other in the most free-and-easy way. Louisiana Creoles fraternised with farmers from Indiana; Kentucky and Tennessee gentlemen and haughty Virginians conversed with trappers and the half-savages of the lakes and butchers from Cincinnati. Broad-brimmed white hats and Panamas, blue cotton trowsers, light coloured stockings, cambrie frills, were all here displayed; while upon shirt-fronts, wristbands and neckties, upon every finger, even upon the very *ears*, they wore an assortment of rings, shirt-pins, brooches, and trinkets, of which the value only equalled the execrable taste. Women, children, and servants, in equally expensive dress, surrounded their husbands, fathers, or masters, who resembled the patriarchs of tribes in the midst of their immense households.

At meal-times, all fell to work upon the dishes peculiar to the Southern States, and consumed with an appetite that threatened speedy exhaustion of the victualling powers of Florida, fricasseed frogs, stuffed monkey, fishchowder, underdone 'possum, and racoon steaks. And as for the liquors which accompanied this indigestible repast! The shours, the bociferations that resounded through the bars and taverns decorated with glasses, tankards, and bottles of marvellous shape, mortars for pounding sugar, and bundles of straws! "Mint-julep!" roars one of the barmen; "Claret Sangaree!" shouts another; "Cocktail!" "Brandy-smash!" "Real mint-julep in the new style!" All these cries intermingled produced a bewildering and deafening hubbub.

But on this day, 1st December, such sounds were rare. No one thought of eating or drinking, and at four p.m. there were vast numbers of spectators who had not even taken their customary lunch! And, a still more significant fact, even the national passion forplay seemed quelled for the time under the general excitement of the hour.

Up till nightfall, a dull, noiseless agitation, such as precedes great catastrophes, ran through the anxious multitide. An indescribable uneasiness pervaded all minds, an indefinable sensation which oppressed the heart. Every one wished it was over.

However, about seven o'clock, the heavy silence was dissipated. The moon rose above the horizon. Millions of hurrahs hailed her appearance. She was punctual to the rendezvous, and shouts of welcome greeted her on all sides, as her pale beams shone gracefully in the clear heavens. At this moment the three intrepid travellers appeared. This was the signal for renewed cries of still greater intensity. Instantly the vast assemblage, as with one accord, struck up the national hymn of the United States, and "Yankee Doodle," sung by five millions of hearty throats, rose like a roaring tempest to the farthest limits of the atmosphere. Then a profound silence reigned throughout the crowd.

The Frenchman and the two Americans had by this time entered the enclosure reserved in the centre of the multitude. They were accompanied by the members of the Gun Club, and by deputations sent from all the European Observatories. Barbicane, cool and collected, was giving his final directions. Nicholl, with compressed lips, his arms crossed behind his back, walked with a firm and measured step. Michel Ardan, always easy, dressed in thorough traveller's costume, leathern gaiters on his legs, pouch by his side, in loose velvet suit, cigar in mouth, was full of inexhaustible gaiety, laughing, joking, playing pranks with J. T. Maston. In one word, he was the thorough "Frenchman" (and worse, a "Parisian") to the last moment.

Ten o'clock struck! The moment had arrived for taking their places in the projectile! The necessary operations for the descent, and the subsequent removal of the cranes and scaffolding that inclined over the mouth of the Columbiad, required a certain period of time.

Barbicane had regulated his chronometer to the tenth part of a second by that of Murchison the engineer, who was charged with the duty of firing the gun by means of an electric spark. Thus the travellers enclosed within the projectile, were enabled to follow with their eyes the impassive needle which marked the precise moment of their departure.

The moment had arrived for saying "Good-bye!" The scene was a touching one. Despite his feverish gaiety, even Michel Ardan was touched. J. T. Maston had found in his own dry eyes one ancient tear, which he had doubtless reserved for the occasion. He dropped it on the forehead of his dear president.

"Can I not go?" he said, "there is still time!"

"Impossible, old fellow!" replied Barbicane. A few moments later, the three fellow-travellers had ensconced themselves in the projectile, and screwed down the plate which covered the entrance-aperture. The mouth of the Columbiad, now completely disencumbered, was open entirely to the sky.

The moon advanced upwards in a heaven of the purest clearness, outshining in her passage the twinkling light of the stars. She passed over the constellation of the Twins, and was now nearing the half-way point between the horizon and the zenith. A terrible silence weighed upon the entire scene! Not a breath of wind upon the earth! not a sound of breathing from the countless chests of the spectators! Their hearts seemed afraid to beat! All eyes were fixed upon the yawning mouth of the Columbiad.

Murchison followed with his eye the hand of his chronometer. It wanted scarce forty seconds to the moment of departure, but each second seemed to last an age! At the twentieth there was a general shudder, as it occurred to the minds of that vast assemblage that the bold travellers shut up within the projectile were also counting those terrible seconds. Some few cries here and there escaped the crowd.

"Thirty-five!—thirty-six!—thirty-seven!—thirty-eight!—Thirty-nine!—forty! FIRE!!!"

Instantly Murchison pressed with his finger the key of the electric battery, restored the current of the fluid, and discharged the spark into the breach of the Columbiad.

An appalling, unearthly report followed instantly, such as can be compared to nothing whatever known, not even to the roar of thunder, or the blast of volcanic explosions! No words can convey the slightest idea of the terrific sound! An immense spount of fire shot up from the bowels of the earth as from a crater. The earth heaved up, and with great difficulty some few spectators obtained a momentary glimpse of the projectile victoriously cleaving the air in the midst of the fiery vapours!

CHAPTER 27

FOUL WEATHER

AT the moment when that pyramid of fire rose to a prodigious height into the air, the glare of the flame lit up the whole of Florida; and for a moment day superseded night over a considerable extent of the country. This immense canopy of fire was perceived at a distance of 100 miles out at sea, and more than one ship's captain entered in his log the appearance of this gigantic meteor.

The discharge of the Columbiad was accompanied by a perfect earthquake. Florida was shaken to its very depths. The gases of the powder, expanded by heat, forced back the atmospheric strata with tremedous violence, and this artificial hurricane rushed like a waterspout through the air.

Not a single spectator remained on his feet! Men, women, children, all lay prostrate like ears of corn under a tempest. There ensued a terrible tumult; a large number of persons were seriously injured. J. T. Maston, who, despite of all dictates of prudence had kept in advance of the mass, was pitched back 120 feet, shooting like a projectile over the heads of his fellow-citizens. Three hundred thousand persons remained deaf for a time, and as though struck stupefied.

As soon as the first effects were over, the injured, the deaf, and lastly, the crowd in general, woke up with frenzied cries. "Hurrah for Ardan! Hurrah for Barbicane! Hurrah for Nicholl!" rose to the skies. Thousands of persons, noses in air, armed with telescopes and race-glasses, were questioning space, forgetting all contusions and emotions in the one idea of watching for the projectile. They looked in vain! It was no longer to be seen, and they were obliged to wait for telegrams from Long's Peak. The Director of the Cambridge Observatory was at his post on the Rocky Mountains; and to him, as a skilful and persevering astronomer, all observations had been confided.

But an unforeseen phenomenon came in to subject the public impatience to a severe trial.

The weather, hitherto so fine, suddenly changed; the sky became heavy with clouds. It could not have been otherwise after the terrible derangement of the atmospheric strata, and the dispersion of the enormous quantity of vapour arising from the combustion of 200,000lbs. of pyroxyle!

On the morrow the horizon was covered with clouds—a thick and impenetrable curtain between earth and sky, which unhappily extended as far as the Rocky Mountains. It was a fatality! But since man had chosen so to disturb the atmosphere, he was bound to accept the consequences of his experiment.

Supposing, now, that the experiment had succeeded, the travellers having started on the 1st of December, at 10h. 46m. 40s. p.m., were due on the 4th at 0h. p.m. at their destination.So that up to that time it would have been very difficult after all to have observed, under such conditions, a body so small as the shell. Therefore they waited with what patience they might.

From the 4th to the 6th of December inclusive, the weather remaining much the same in America, the great European instruments of Herschel, Rosse, and Foucault, were constantly directed towards the moon, for the weather was then magnificent; but the comparative weakness of their glasses prevented any trustworthy observations being made.

On the 7th the sky seemed to lighten. They were in hopes now, but their hope was of but short duration, and at night again thick clouds hid the starry vault from all eyes.

Matters were now becoming serious, when on the 9th, the sun reappeared for an instant, as if for the purpose of teasing the Americans. It was received with hisses; and wounded, no doubt, by such a reception, showed itself very sparing of its rays.

On the 10th, no change! J. T. Maston went nearly mad, and great fears were entertained regarding the brain of this worthy individual, which had hitherto been so well perserved within his gutta-percha cranium.

But on the 11th one of those inexplicable tempests peculiar to those intertropical regions, was let loose in the atmosphere. A terrific east wind swept away the groups of clouds which had been so long gathering, and at night the semidisc of the orb of night rode majestically amidst the soft constellations of the sky.

CHAPTER 28

A NEW STAR

THAT very night, the startling news so impatiently awaited, burst like a thunderbold over the United States of the Union, and thence, darting across the ocean, ran through all the telegraphic wires of the globe. The projectile had been detected, thanks to the gigantic reflector of Long's Peak! Here is the note received by the Director of the Observatory of Cambridge. It contains the scientific conclusion regarding this great experiment of the Gun Club.

"LONG'S PEAK, *December* 12.

"To the Officers of the Observatory of Cambridge.

"The projectile discharged by the Columbiad at Stones Hill has been detected by Messrs. Belfast and J. T. Maston, 12th December, at 8.47 p.m., the moon having entered her last quarter. This projectile has not arrived at its destination. It has passed by the side; but sufficiently near to be retained by the lunar attraction.

"The rectilinear movement has thus become changed into a circular motion of extreme velocity, and it is now pursuing an elliptical orbit round the moon, of which it has become a true satellite.

"The elements of this new star we have as yet been unable to determine; we do not yet know the velocity of its passage. The distance which separates it from the surface of the moon may be estimated at about 2833 miles.

"However, two hypothesis come here into our consideration.

"1. Either the attraction of the moon will end by drawing them into itself, and the travellers will attain their destination; or,—

"2. The projectile, following an immutable law, will continue to gravitate round the moon till the end of time.

"At some future time, our observations will be able to determine this point, but till then the experiment of the Gun Club can have no other result than to have provided our solar system with a new star.

"J. BELFAST."

To how many questions did this unexpected denouement give rise? What mysterious results was the future reserving for the investigations of science? At all events, the names of Nicholl, Barbicane, and Michel Ardan were certain to be immortalized in the annals of astronomy!

When the despatch from Long's Peak had once become known, there was but one universal feeling of surprise and alarm. Was it possible to go to the aid of these bold travellers? No! for they had placed themselves beyond the pale of humanity, by crossing the limits imposed by the Creator on his earthly creatures. They had air enough for *two* months; they had victuals enough for *twelve;—but after that*? There was only one man who would not admit that the situation was desperate,—he alone had confidence; and that was their devoted friend J. T. Maston.

Besides, he never let them get out of sight. His home was henceforth the post at Long's Peak; his horizon, the mirror of that immense reflector. As soon as the moon rose above the horizon, he immediately caught her in the field of the telescope; he never let her got for an instant out of his sight, and followed her assiduously in her course through the stellar spaces. He watched with untiring patience the passage of the projectile across her silvery disc, and really the worthy man remained in perpetual communication with his three friends, whom he did not despair of seeing again some day.

"Those three men," said he, "have carried into space all the resources of art, science, and industry. With that, one can do anything; and you will see that, some day, they will come out all right."

Round the Moon

A Sequel to

FROM THE EARTH TO THE MOON

Ardan applied the lighted match.

PRELIMINARY CHAPTER

RECAPITULATING THE FIRST PART OF THIS WORK, AND SERVING AS A PREFACE TO THE SECOND

DURING the year 186—, the whole world was greatly excited by a scientific experiment unprecedented in the annals of science. The members of the Gun Club, a circle of artillerymen formed at Baltimore after the American war, conceived the idea of putting themselves in communication with the moon!—yes, with the moon,—by sending to her a projectile. Their president, Barbicane, the promoter of the enterprise, having consulted the astronomers of the Cambridge Observatory upon the subject, took all necessary means to ensure the success of this extraordinary enterprise, which had been declared practicable by the majority of competent judges. After setting on foot a public subscription, which realized nearly 1,200,000*l*., they began the gigantic work.

According to the advice forwarded from the members of the Observatory, the gun destined to launch the projectile had to be fixed in a country situated between the 0 and 28th degrees of north or south latitude, in order to aim at the moon when at the zenith; and its initiatory velocity was fixed at twelve thousand yards to the second. Launched on the 1st of December, at 10hrs. 46m. 40s. p.m., it ought to reach the moon four days afters its departure, that is on the 5th of December, at midnight precisely, at the moment of her attaining her *perigee*, that is her nearest distance from the earth, which is exactly 86,410 leagues (French), or 238,833 miles *mean distance* (English).

The principal members of the Gun Club, President Barbicane, Major Elphinstone, the secretary Joseph T. Maston, and other learned men, held several meetings, at which the shape and composition of the projectile were discussed, also the position and nature of the gun, and the quality and quantity of the powder to be used. It was decided: 1st, that the projectile should be a shell made of aluminium with a diameter of 108 inches and a thickness of twelve inches to its walls; and should weight 19,250lbs. 2ndly, that the gun should be a Columbiad cast in iron, 900 feet long, and run perpendicularly into the earth. 3rdly, that the charge should contain 400,000 pounds of gun-cotton, which, giving out six billions of litres of gas in rear of the projectile, would easily carry it towards the orb of night.

These questions determined President Barbicane, assisted by Murchison the engineer, to choose a spot situated in Florida, in 27° 7′ North latitude, and 77° 3′ W. (Greenwich) longitude. It was on this spot, after stupendous labour, that the Columbiad was cast with full success. Things stood thus, when an incident took place which increased the interest attached to this great enterprise a hundredfold.

A Frenchman, an enthusiastic Parisian, as witty as he was bold, asked to be enclosed in the projectile, in order that he might reach the moon, and reconnoitre this terrestial satellite. The name of this intrepid adventurer was Michel Ardan. He landed in America, was received with enthusiasm, held meetings, saw himself carried in triumph, reconciled President Barbicane to his mortal enemy, Captain Nicholl, and, as a token of reconciliation, persuaded them both to start with him in the projectile. The proposition being accepted, the shape of the projectile was slightly altered. It was made of a cylindro-conical form. This species of aerial car was lined with strong springs and partitions to deaden the shock of departure. It was provided with food for a year, water for some months, and gas for some days. A self-acting apparatus supplied the three travellers with air to breathe. At the same time, on one of the highest points of the Rocky Mountains, the Gun Club had a gigantic telescope erected, in order that they might be able to follow the course of the projectile through space. All was then ready.

On the 30th November, at the hour fixed upon, from the midst of an extraordinary crowd of spectators, the departure took place; and for the first time, three human beings quitted the terrestial globe, and launched into interplanetary space with almost a certainty of reaching their destination. These bold travellers, Michel Ardan, President Barbicane, and Captain Nicholl, ought to make the passage in ninety-seven hours, thirteen minutes, and twenty seconds. Consequently, their arrival on the lunar disc could not take place until the 5th December at twelve at night, at the exact moment when the moon should be full, and not on the 4th, as some badly-informed journals had announced.

But an unforeseen circumstance, viz., the detonation produced by the Columbiad, had the immediate effect of troubling the terrestial atmosphere, by accumulating a large quantity of vapour, a phenomenon which excited universal indignation, for the moon was hidden from the eyes of the watchers for several nights.

The worthy Joseph T. Maston, the staunchest friend of the three travellers, started for the Rocky Mountains, accompanied by the Hon. J. Belfast, director of the Cambridge Observatory, and reached the station of Long's Peak, where the telescope was erected which brought the moon within an apparent distance of two leagues. The hon. secretary of the Gun Club wished himself to observe the vehicle of his daring friends.

The accumulation of clouds in the atmosphere prevented all observations on the 5th, 6th, 7th, 8th, 9th, and 10th of December. Indeed it was thought that all observations would have to be put off to the 3rd of January in the following year; for the moon entering its last quarter on the 11th, would then only present an ever-decreasing portion of her disc, insufficient to allow of their following the course of the projectile.

At length, to the general satisfaction, a heavy storm cleared the atmosphere on the night of the 11th and 12th December, and the moon, with half illuminated disc, was plainly to be seen upon the black sky.

That very night, a telegram was sent from the station of Long's Peak by Joseph T. Maston and Belfast to the gentlemen of the Cambridge Observatory, announcing that, on the 11th of December at 8h. 47m. p.m., the projectile launched by the Columbiad of Stones Hill had been detected by Messrs. Belfast and

Maston,—that it had deviated from its course from some unknown cause, and had not reached its destination; but that it had passed near enough to be retained by the lunar attraction; that is rectilinear movement had been changed to a circular one, and that following an elliptical orbit round the star of night it had become *its satellite*. The telegram added that the elements of this new star had not yet been calculated; and indeed three observations made upon a star in three different positions, are necessary to determine these elements. Then it showed that the distance seperating the projectile from the lunar surface "might" be reckoned at about 2833 miles.

It ended with this double hypothesis; either the attraction of the moon would draw it to herself and the travellers thus attain their end; or that the projectile, held in one immutable orbit, would gravitate around the lunar disc to all eternity.

With such alternatives, what would be the fate of the travellers? Certainly they had food for some time. But supposing they did succeed in their rash enterprise, how would they return? *Could* they ever return? Should they hear from them? These questions, debated by the most learned pens of the day, strongly engrossed the public attention.

It is advisable here to make a remark which ought to be well considered by hasty observers. When a purely speculative discovery is announced to the public, it cannot be done with too much prudence. No one is obliged to discover either a planet, a comet, or a satellite; and whoever makes a mistake in such a case exposes himself justly to the derision of the mass. Far better it is to wait; and that is what the impatient Joseph T. Maston should have done before sending this telegram forth to the world, which, according to his idea, told the whole result of the enterprise. Indeed this telegram contained two sorts of errors, as was proved eventually. 1st, errors of observation, concerning the distance of the projectile from the surface of the moon, for on the 11th December it was impossible to see it; and what Joseph T. Maston had seen, or thought he saw, could not have been the projectile of the Columbiad. 2ndly, errors of theory on the fate in store for the said projectile; for in making it a satellite of the moon, it was putting it in direct contradiction to all mechanical laws.

One single hypothesis of the observers of Long's Peak could ever be realized, that which foresaw the case of the travellers (if still alive) uniting their efforts with the lunar attraction to attain the surface of the disc.

Now these men, as clever as they were daring, *had* survived the terrible shock consequent on their departure, and it is their journey in the projectile car which is here related in its most dramatic as well as in its most singular details. This recital will destroy many illusions and surmises; but it will give a true idea of the singular changes in store for such an enterprise; it will bring out the scientific instincts of Barbicane, the industrious resources of Nicholl, and the audacious humour of Michel Ardan.

Besides this, it will prove that their worthy friend, Joseph T. Maston, was wasting his time, while leaning over the gigantic telescope he watched the course of the moon through the starry space.

[illegible] and [illegible] explained [illegible] and [illegible] became [illegible] [illegible] the [illegible] from the [illegible]

[illegible] the [illegible]

[illegible]

[illegible]

CHAPTER 1

FROM TWENTY MINUTES PAST TEN TO FORTY-SEVEN MINUTES PAST TEN P.M.

As ten o'clock struck, Michel Ardan, Barbicane, and Nicholl, took leave of the numerous friends they were leaving on the earth. The two dogs, destined to propagate the canine race on the lunar continents, were already shut up in the projectile.

The three travellers approached the orifice of the enormous cast-iron tube, and a crane let them down to the conical top of the projectile. There, an opening made for the purpose gave them access to the aluminium car. The tackle belonging to the crane being hauled from outside, the mouth of the Columbiad was instantly disencumbered of its last supports.

Nicholl, once introduced with his companions inside the projectile, began to close the opening by means of a strong plate, held in position by powerful screws. Other plates, closely fitted, covered the lenticular glasses, and the travellers, hermetically enclosed in their metal prison, were plunged in profound darkness.

"And now, my dear companions," said Michel Ardan, "let us make ourselves at home; I am a domesticated man and strong in housekeeping. We are bound to make the best of our new lodgings, and make ourselves comfortable. And first let us try and see a little. Gas was not invented for moles."

So saying, the thoughtless fellow lit a match by striking it on the sole of his boot; and approached the burner fixed to the receptacle, in which the carbonized hydrogen, stored at high pressure, sufficed for the lighting and warming of the projectile for a hundred and forty-four hours, or six days and six nights. The gas caught fire, and thus lighted, the projectile looked like a comfortable room with thickly padded walls, furnished with a circular divan, and a roof rounded in the shape of a dome.

The objects it contained, arms, instruments, and utensils securely fastened against the rounds of wadding, could bear the shock of departure with impunity. Humanly speaking, every possible precaution had been taken to bring this rash experiment to a successful termination.

Michel Ardan examined everything, and declared himself satisfied with his installation.

"It is a prison," said he, "but a travelling prison; and, with the right of putting my nose to the window, I could well stand a lease of a hundred years.

You smile, Barbicane. Have you any *arrière-pensé?* Do you say to yourself, 'This prison may be our tomb'? Tomb, perhaps; still I would not change it for Mahomet's, which floats in space, but never advances an inch!"

Whilst Michel Ardan was speaking, Barbicane and Nicholl were making their last preparations.

Nicholl's chronometer marked twenty minutes past ten p.m. when the three travellers were finally enclosed in their projectile. This chronometer was set within the thenth of a second by that of Murchison the engineer. Barbicane consulted it.

"My friends," said he, "it is twenty minutes past ten. At forty-seven minutes past ten Murchison will launch the electric spark on the wire which communicates with the charge of the Columbiad. At that precise moment we shall leave our spheroid. Thus we have still twenty-seven minutes to remain on the earth."

"Twenty-six minutes thirteen seconds," replied the methodical Nicholl.

"Well!" exclaimed Michel Ardan, in a good-natured tone, "much may be done in twenty-six minutes. The gravest questions of morals and politics may be discussed, and even solved. Twenty-six minutes well employed are worth more than twenty-six years in which nothing is done. Some *seconds* of a Pascal or a Newton are more precious than the whole existence of a crowd of raw simpletons—"

"And you conclude, then, you everlasting talker?" asked Barbicane.

"I conclude that we have twenty-six minutes left," replied Ardan.

"Twenty-four only," said Nicholl.

"Well, twenty-four, if you like, my noble captain," said Ardan; "twenty-four minutes in which to investigate—"

"Michel," said Barbicane, "during the passage we shall have plenty of time to investigate the most difficult questions. For the present we must occupy ourselves with our departure."

"Are we not ready?"

"Doubtless; but there are still some precautions to be taken, to deaden as much as possible the first shock."

"Have we not the water-cushions placed between the partition-breaks, whose elasticity will sufficiently protect us?"

"I *hope* so, Michel," replied Barbicane gently, "but I am not sure."

"Ah, the joker!" exclaimed Michel Ardan. "He hopes!—He is not sure!—and he waits for the moment when we are encased to make this deplorable admission! I beg to be allowed to get out!"

"And how?" asked Barbicane.

"Humph!" said Michel Ardan, "it is not easy; we are in the train, and the guard's whistle will sound before twenty-four minutes are over."

"*Twenty*," said Nicholl.

For some moments the three travellers looked at each other. Then they began to examine the objects imprisoned with them.

"Everything is in its place," said Barbicane. "We have now to decide how we can best place ourselves to resist the shock. Position cannot be an indifferent matter; and we must, as much as possible, prevent the rush of blood to the head."

"Just so," said Nicholl.

"Then," replied Michel Ardan, ready to suit the action to the word, "let us put our heads down and our feet in the air, like the clowns in the grand circus."

The gas caught fire.

"No," said Barbicane, "let us stretch ourselves on our sides; we shall resist the shock better that way. Remember that, when the projectile starts, it matters little whether we are in it or before it; it amounts to much the same thing."

"If it is only 'much the same thing,' I may cheer up," said Michel Ardan.

"Do you approve of my idea, Nicholl?" asked Barbicane.

"Entirely," replied the captain. "We've still thirteen minutes and a half."

"That Nicholl is not a man," exclaimed Michel; "he is a chronometer with seconds, an escape, and eight holes."

But his companions were not listening; they were taking up their last positions with the most perfect coolness. They were like two methodical travellers in a car, seeking to place themselves as comfortably as possible.

We might well ask ourselves of what materials are the hearts of these Americans made, to whom the approach of the most frightful danger added no pulsation.

Three thick and solidly-made couches had been placed in the projectile. Nicholl and Barbicane placed them in the centre of the disc forming the floor. There the three travellers were to stretch themselves some moments before their departure.

During this time, Ardan, not being able to keep still, turned in his narrow prison like a wild beast in a cage, chatting with his friends, speaking to the dogs Diana and Satellite, to whom, as may be seen, he had given significant names.

"Ah, Diana! Ah, Satellite!" he exclaimed, teasing them; "so you are going to show the moon-dogs the good habits of the dogs of the earth! That will do honour to the canine race! If ever we do come down again, I will bring a cross type of 'moon-dogs,' which will make a stir!"

"If there *are* dogs in the moon," said Barbicane.

"There are," said Michel Ardan, "just as there are horses, cows, donkeys, and chickens. I bet that we shall find chickens."

"A hundred dollars we shall find none!" said Nicholl.

"Done, my captain!"replied Ardan, clasping Nicholl's hand. "But, by the bye, you have already lost three bets with out president, as the necessary funds for the enterprise have been found, as the operation of casting has been successful, and lastly, as the Columbiad has been loaded without accident, six thousand dollars."

"Yes," replied Nicholl. "Thirty-seven minutes six seconds past ten."

"It is understood, captain. Well, before another quarter of an hour you will have to count 9000 dollars to the president; 4000 because the Columbiad will not burst, and 5000 because the projectile will rise more than six miles in the air."

"I have the dollars," replied Nicholl, slapping the pocket of his coat. "I only ask to be allowed to pay."

"Come, Nicholl, I see that you are a man of method, which I could never be; but indeed you have made a series of bets of very little advantage to yourself, allow me to tell you."

"And why?" asked Nicholl.

"Because, if you gain the first, the Columbiad will have burst, and the projectile with it; and Barbicane will no longer be there to reimburse your dollars."

"My stake is deposited at the bank in Baltimore," replied Barbicane simply; "and if Nicholl is not there, it will go to his heirs."

"Ah, you practical men!" exclaimed Michel Ardan; "I admire you the more for not being able to understand you."

"Forty-two minutes past ten!" said Nicholl.

"Only five minutes more!" answered Barbicane.

"Yes, five little mintues!" replied Michel Ardan; "and we are enclosed in a projectile, at the bottom of a gun 900 feet long! And under this projectile are rammed 400,000 lbs. of gun-cotton, which is equal to 1,600,000 lbs. of ordinary powder! And friend Murchison, with his chronometer in hand, his eye fixed on the needle, his finger on the electric apparatus, is counting the seconds preparatory to launching us into interplanetary space."

"Enough, Michel, enough!" said Barbicane, in a serious voice; "let us prepare. A few instants alone seperate us from an eventful moment. One clasp of the hand, my friends."

"Yes," exclaimed Michel Ardan, more moved than he wished to appear; and the three bold companions were united in a last embrace.

"God preserve us!" said the religious Barbicane.

Michel Ardan and Nicholl stretched themselves on the couches placed in the centre of the disc.

"Forty seven minutes past ten!" murmured the captain.

"Twenty seconds more!" Barbicane quickly put out the gas and lay down by his companions, and the profound silence was only broken by the ticking of the chronometer marking the seconds.

Suddenly a dreadful shock was felt, and the projectile, under the force of six billions of litres of gas, developed by the combustion of the pyroxyle, mounted into space.

CHAPTER 2

THE FIRST HALF-HOUR

WHAT had happened? What effect had this frightful shock produced? Had the ingenuity of the constructors of the projectile obtained any happy results? Had the shock been deadened, thanks to the springs, the four plugs, the water-cushions, and the partition-breaks? Had they been able to subdue the frightful pressure of the initiatory speed of more than 11,000 yards, which was enough to traverse Paris or New York in a second? This was evidently the question suggested to the thousand spectators of this moving scene. They forgot the aim of the journey, and thought only of the travellers. And if one amongst them—Joseph T. Maston for example—could have cast one glimpse into the projectile, what would he have seen?

Nothing then. The darkness was profound. But its cylindro-conical partitions had resisted wonderfully. Not a rent or a dent anywhere! The wonderful projectile was not even heated under the intense deflagration of the powder, nor liquefied, as they seemed to fear, in a shower of aluminium.

The interior showed but little disorder; indeed, only a few objects had been violently thrown towards the roof; but the most important seemed not to have suffered from the shock at all; their fixtures were intact.

On the movable disc, sunk down to the bottom by the smashing of the partition-breaks and the escape of the water, three bodies lay apparently lifeless. Barbicane, Nicholl, and Michel Ardan—did they still breathe? or was the projectile nothing now but a metal coffin, bearing three corpses into space?

Some minutes after the departure of the projectile, one of the bodies moved, shook its arms, lifted its head, and finally succeeded in getting on its knees. It was Michel Ardan. He felt himself all over, gave a sonorous "Hem!" and then said,—

"Michel Ardan is whole. How about the others?"

The courageous Frenchman tried to rise, but could not stand. His head swam, from the rush of blood; he was blind; he was like a drunken man.

"Bur-r!" said he. "It produces the same effect as two bottles of Corton, though perhaps less agreeable to swallow." Then, passing his hand several times across his forehead and rubbing his temples, he called in a firm voice,—

"Nicholl! Barbicane!"

He waited anxiously. No answer; not even a sigh to show that the hearts of his companions were still beating. He called again. The same silence.

"The devil!" he exclaimed. "They look as if they had fallen from a fifth story on their heads. Bah!" he added, with that imperturbable confidence which nothing could check, "if a Frenchman can get on his knees, two Americans ought to be able to get on their feet. But first let us light up."

Ardan felt the tide of life return by degrees. His blood became calm, and returned to its accustomed circulation. Another effort restored his equilibrium. He succeeded in rising, drew a match from his pocket, and approaching the burner lighted it. The receiver had not suffered at all. The gas had not escaped. Besides, the smell would have betrayed it; and in that case Michel Ardan could not have carried a lighted match with impunity through the space filled with hydrogen. The gas mixing with the air would have produced a detonating mixture, and the explosion would have finished what the shock had perhaps begun. When the burner was lit, Ardan leaned over the bodies of his companions; they were lying one on the other, an inert mass, Nicholl above, Barbicane underneath.

Ardan lifted the captain, propped him up against the divan, and began to rub vigorously. This means, used with judgement, restored Nicholl, who opened his eyes, and instantly recovering his presence of mind, seized Ardan's hand and looked around him.

"And Barbicane?" said he.

"Each in turn," replied Michel Ardan. "I began with you, Nicholl, because you were on the top. Now let us look to Barbicane," Saying which, Ardan and Nicholl raised the president of the Gun Club and laid him on the divan. He seemed to have suffered more than either of his companions; he was bleeding, but Nicholl was reassured by finding that the hæmorrhage came from a slight wound on the shoulder, a mere graze, which he bound up carefully.

Still, Barbicane was a long time coming to himself, which frightened his friends, who did not spare friction.

"He breathes though," said Nicholl, putting his ear to the chest of the wounded man.

"Yes," replied Ardan "he breathes like a man who has some notion of that daily operation. Rub, Nicholl; let us rub harder." And the two improvised practitioners worked so hard and so well that Barbicane recovered his senses. He opened his eyes, sat up, took his two friends by the hands, and his first words were—

"Nicholl, are we moving?"

Nicholl and Barbicane looked at each other; they had not yet troubled themselves about the projectile; their first thought had been for the traveller, not for the car.

"Well, are we really moving?" repeated Michel Ardan.

"Or quietly resting on the soil of Florida?" asked Nicholl.

"Or at the bottom of the Gulf of Mexico?" added Michel Ardan.

"What an idea!" exclaimed the president.

And this double hypothesis suggested by his companions had the effect of recalling him to his senses. In any case the could not yet decide on the position of the projectile. Its apparent immovability, and the want of communication with the outside, prevented them from solving the question. Perhaps the projectile was unwinding its course through space. Perhaps after a short rise it had fallen upon the earth, or even in the Gulf of Mexico—a fall which the narrowness of the peninsula of Florida would render not impossible.

The case was serious, the problem interesting, and one that must be solved as soon as possible. Thus, highly excited, Barbicane's moral energy triumphed over physical weakness, and he rose to his feet. He listened. Outside was perfect silence; but the thick padding was enough to intercept all sounds coming from the earth. But one circumstance struck Barbicane, viz., that the temperature inside the projectile was singularly high. The president drew a thermometer from its case, and consulted it. The instrument showed 81° Fahr.

"Yes," he exclaimed, "yes, we are moving! This stifling heat, penetrating through the partitions of the projectile, is produced by its friction on the atmospheric strata. It will soon diminish, because we are already floating in space, and after having been nearly stifled, we shall have to suffer intense cold.

"What!" said Michel Ardan. "According to your showing, Barbicane, we are already beyond the limits of the terrestrial atmosphere?"

"Without a doubt, Michel. Listen to me. It is fifty-five minutes past ten; we have been gone about eight minutes; and if our initiatory speed has not been checked by the friction, six seconds would be enough for us to pass through the forty miles of atmosphere which surrounds the globe."

"Just so," replied Nicholl; "but in what proportion do you estimate the diminution of speed by friction?"

"In the proportion of one-third, Nicholl. This diminution is considerable, but according to my calculations it is nothing less. If, then, we had an initiatory speed of 12,000 yards, on leaving the atmosphere this speed would be reduced to 9165 yards. In any case we have already passed through this interval, and—"

"And then," said Michel Ardan, "friend Nicholl has lost his two bets: four thousand dollars because the Columbiad did not burst; five thousand dollars because the projectile has risen more than six miles. Now, Nicholl, pay up."

"Let us prove it first," said the captain, "and we will pay afterwards. It is quite possible that Barbicane's reasoning is correct, and that I have lost my nine thousand dollars. But a new hypothesis presents itself to my mind, and it annuls the wager."

"What is that?" asked Barbicane quickly.

"The hypothesis that, for some reason or other, fire was never set to the powder, we have not started at all."

"My goodness, captain," exclaimed Michel Ardan, "that hypothesis is worthy of my brain! It cannot be a serious one. For have we not been half annihilated by the shock? Did I not recall you to life? Is not the president's shoulder still bleeding from the blow it has received?"

"Granted," replied Nicholl; "but one question."

"Well, captain?"

"Did you hear the detonation, which certainly ought to be loud?"

"No," replied Ardan, much surprised; "certainly I did not hear the detonation."

"And you, Barbicane?"

"Very well," said Nicholl.

"Well now," murmured the president, "why did we not hear the detonation?"

The three friends looked at each other with a disconcerted air. It was quite an inexplicable phenomenon. The projectile had started, and consequently there must have been a detonation.

"Let us first find out where we are," said Barbicane, "and let down the panel."

This very simple operation was soon accomplished.

The nuts which held the bolts to the outer plates of the right-hand scuttle gave way under the pressure of the English wrench. These bolts were pushed outside, and buffers covered with india-rubber stopped up the holes which let them through. Immediately the outer plate fell back upon its hinges like a porthole, and the lenticular glass which closed the scuttle appeared. A similar one was let into the thick partition on the opposite side of the projectile, another in the top of the dome, and finally, a fourth in the middle of the base. They could, therefore, make observations in four different directions: the firmament by the side and most direct windows, the earth or the moon by the upper and under openings in the projectile.

Barbicane and his two companions immediately rushed to the uncovered window. But it was lit by no ray of light. Profound darkness surrounded them, which, however, did not prevent the president from exclaiming,—

"No, my friends, we have not fallen back upon the earth; no, nor are we submerged in the Gulf of Mexico. Yes! we are mounting into space. See those stars shining in the night, and that impenetrable darkness heaped up between the earth and us!"

"Hurrah! hurrah!" exclaimed Michel Ardan and Nicholl in one voice.

Indeed, this thick darkness proved that the projectile had left the earth, for the soil, brilliantly lit by the moonbeams, would have been visible to the travellers, if they had been lying on its surface. This darkness also showed that the projectile had passed the atmospheric strata, for the diffused light spread in the air would have been reflected on the metal walls, which reflection was wanting. This light would have lit the window, and the window was dark. Doubt was no longer possible; the travellers had left the earth.

"I have lost," said Nicholl.

"I congratulate you," replied Ardan.

"Here are the nine thousand dollars," said the captain, drawing a roll of paper dollars from his pocket.

"Will you have a receipt for it?" asked Barbicane, taking the sum.

"If you do not mind," answered Nicholl; "it is more business-like."

And coolly and seriously, as if he had been at his strong-box, the president drew forth his note-book, tore out a blank leaf, wrote a proper receipt in pencil, dated and signed it with the usual flourish,* and gave it to the captain, who carefully placed it in his pocketbook. Michel Ardan, taking off his hat, bowed to his two companions without speaking. So much formality under such circumstances left him speechless. He had never before seen anything so "American."

This affair settled, Barbicane and Nicholl had returned to the window, and were watching the constllations. The stars looked like bright points on the black sky. But from that side they could not see the orb of night, which, travelling from east to west, would rise by degrees towards the zenith. Its absence drew the following remark from Ardan.

"And the moon; will she perchance fail at our rendezvous?"

"Do not alarm yourself," said Barbicane; "our future globe is at its post, but we cannot see her from this side; let us open the other."

As Barbicane was about leaving the window to open the opposite scuttle, his attention was attracted by the approach of a brilliant object. It was an enormous disc, whose colossal dimension could not be estimated. Its face, which was turned to the earth, was very bright. One might have thought it a small moon reflecting the light of the larger one. She advanced with great speed, and seemed to describe an orbit round the earth, which would intersect the passage of the projectile. This body revolved upon its axis, and exhibited the phenomena of all celestial bodies abandoned in space.

"Ah!" exclaimed Michel Ardan, "what is that? another projectile?"

Barbicane did not answer. The appearance of this enormous body surprised and troubled him. A collision was possible, and might be attended with deplorable results; either the projectile would deviate from its path, or a shock, breaking its impetus, might precipitate it to the earth; or, lastly, it might be irresistibly drawn away by the powerful asteroid. The president caught at a glance the consequences of these three hypotheses, either of which would, one way or the other, bring their experiment to an unsuccessful and fatal termination. His companions stood silently looking into space. The object grew rapidly as it approached them, and by an optical illusion the projectile seemed to be throwing itself before it.

"By Jove!" exclaimed Michel Ardan, "we shall run into one another!"

Instinctively the travellers drew back. Their dread was great, but it did not last many seconds. The asteroid passed several hundred yards from the projectile and disappeared, not so much from the rapidity of its course, as that its face being opposite the moon, it was suddenly merged into the perfect darkness of space.

"A happy journey to you,"exclaimed Michel Ardan, with a sigh of relief. "Surely infinity of space is large enough for a poor little projectile to walk through without fear. Now, what is this portentous globe which nearly struck us?"

"I know," replied Barbicane.

"Oh indeed! you know everything."

"It is," said Barbicane, "a simple meteorite, but an enormous one, which the attraction of the earth has retained as a satellite."

"Is it possible!" exclaimed Michel Ardan; "the earth then has two moons like Neptune?"

"Yes, my friend, two moons, though it passes generally for having only one;

* This is a purely French habit. (Ed.)

but this second moon is so small, and its speed so great, that the inhabitants of the earth cannot see it. It was by noticing disturbances that a French astronomer, M. Petit, was able to determine the existance of this second satellite and calculate its elements. According to his observations, this meteorite will accomplish its revolution round the earth in three hours and twenty minutes, which implies a wonderful rate of speed."

"Do all astronomers admit the existence of this satellite?" asked Nicholl.

"No," replied Barbicane; "but if, like us, they had met it, they could no longer doubt it. Indeed, I think that this meteorite, which, had it struck the projectile, would have much embarrassed us, will give us the means of deciding what our position in space is."

"How?" asked Ardan.

"Because its distance is known, and when we met it, we were exactly 4650 miles from the surface of the terrestrial globe.

"More than 2000 French leagues," exclaimed Michel Ardan. "That beats the express trains of the pitiful globe called the earth."

"I should think so," replied Nicholl, consulting his chronometer; "it is eleven o'clock, and it is only thirteen minutes since we left the American Continent."

"Only thirteen minutes?"said Barbicane.

"Yes," said Nicholl; "and if our initiatory speed of 12,000 yards has been kept up, we shall have made about 20,000 miles in the hour."

"That is all very well, my friends," said the president, "but the insoluble question still remains. Why did we not hear the detonation of the Columbiad?"

For want of an answer the conversation dropped, and Barbicane began thoughtfully to let down the shutter of the second side. He succeeded; and through the uncovered glass the moon filled the projectile with a brilliant light. Nicholl, as an economical man, put out the gas, now useless, and whose brilliancy prevented any observation of the interplanetary space.

The lunar disc shone with wonderful purity. Her rays, no longer filtered through the vapoury atmosphere of the terrestrial globe, shone through the glass, filling the air in the interior of the projectile with silvery reflections. The black curtain of the firmament in reality heightened the moon's brilliancy, which in this void of ether unfavourable to diffusion did not eclipse the neighbouring stars. The heavens, thus seen, presented quite a new aspect, and one which the human eye could never dream of. One many conceive the interest with which these bold men watched the orb of night, the great aim of their journey.

In its motion the earth's satellite was insensibly nearing the zenith, the mathematical point which it ought to attain ninety-six hours later. Her mountains, her plains, every projection was as clearly discernible to their eyes as if they were observing it from some spot upon the earth; but its light was developed through space with wonderful intensity. The disc shone like a platinum mirror. Of the earth flying from under their feet, the travellers had lost all recollection.

It was Captain Nicholl who first recalled their attention to the vanishing globe.

"Yes,"said Michel Ardan, "do not let us be ungrateful to it. Since we are leaving our country, let our last looks be directed to it. I wish to see the earth once more before it is quite hidden from my eyes."

To satisfy his companions, Barbicane began to uncover the window at the bottom of the projectile, which would allow them to observe the earth direct. The disc, which the force of the projection had beaten down to the base, was removed, not without difficulty. Its fragments, placed carefully against the wall, might serve again upon occasion. Then a circular gap appeared, nineteen inches in diameter, hollowed out of the lower part of the projectile. A glass cover, six inches thick and strengthened with upper fastenings, closed it tightly. Beneath was fixed an aluminium plate, held in place by bolts. The screws being undone, and the bolts let go, the plate fell down, and visible communication was established between the interior and the exterior.

Michel Ardan knelt by the glass. It was cloudy, seemingly opaque.

"Well!" he exclaimed, "and the earth?"

"The earth?" said Barbicane. "There it is."

"What! that little thread; that silver crescent?"

"Doubtless, Michel. In four days, when the moon will be full, at the very time we shall reach it, the earth will be new, and will only appear to us as a slender crescent which will soon disappear, and for some days will be enveloped in utter darkness."

"That the earth?" repeated Michel Ardan, looking with all his eyes at the thin slip of his native planet.

The explanation given by President Barbicane was correct. The earth, with respect to the projectile, was entering its last phase. It was in its octant, and showed a crescent finely traced on the dark background of the sky. Its light, rendered bluish by the thick strata of the atmosphere, was less intense than that of the crescent moon, but it was of considerable dimensions, and looked like an enourmous arch stretched across the firmament. Some parts brilliantly lighted, especially on its concave part, showed the presence of high mountains, often disappearing behind thick spots, which are never seen on the lunar disc. They were rings of clouds placed concentrically round the terrestrial globe.

Whilst the travellers were trying to pierce the profund darkness, a brilliant cluster of shooting stars burst upon their eyes. Hundreds of meteorites, ignited by the friction of the atmosphere, irradiated the shadow of the luminous train, and lined the cloudy parts of the disc with their fire. At this period the earth was in its perihelium, and the month of December is so propitious to these shooting stars, that astronomers have counted as many as twenty-four thousand in an hour. But Michel Ardan, disdaining scientific reasonings, preferred thinking that the earth was thus saluting the departure of her three children with her most brilliant fireworks.

Indeed this was all they saw of the globe lost in the shadow, an inferior orb of the solar world, rising and setting to the great planets like a simple morning or evening star! This globe, where they had left all their affections, was nothing more than a fugitive crescent!

Long did the three friends look without speaking, though united in heart, whilst the projectile sped onward with an ever-decreasing speed. Then an irresistible drowsiness crept over their brain. Was it weariness both of body and mind? No doubt; for after the over-excitement of those last hours passed upon the earth, reaction was inevitable.

"Well," said Nicholl, "since we must sleep, let us sleep."

And stretching themselves on their couches, they were all three soon in a profound slumber.

But they had not forgotten themselves more than a quarter of an hour, when Barbicane sat up suddenly, and rousing his companions with a loud voice, exclaimed,—

"I have found it!"

"What have you found?" asked Michel Ardan, jumping from his bed.
"The reason why we did not hear the detonation of the Columbiad."
"And it is—?" said Nicholl.
"Because our projectile travelled *faster than the sound!*"

CHAPTER 3

THEIR PLACE OF SHELTER

THIS curious but certainly correct explanation once given, the three friends returned to their slumbers. Could they have found a calmer or more peaceful spot to sleep in? On the earth, houses, towns, cottages, and country feel every shock given to the exterior of the globe. On sea, the vessels rocked by the waves are still in motion; in the air, the balloon oscillates incessantly on the fluid strata of divers densities. This projectile alone, floating in perfect space, in the midst of perfect silence, offered perfect repose.

Thus the sleep of our adventurous travellers might have been indefinitely prolonged, if an unexpected noise had not awakened them at about seven o'clock in the morning of the 2nd of December, eight hours after their departure.

This noise was a very natural barking.

"The dogs! it is the dogs!" exclaimed Michel Ardan, rising at once.

"They are hungry," said Nicholl.

"By Jove!" replied Michel, "we have forgotten them."

"Where are they?" asked Barbicane.

They looked, and found one of the animals crouched under the divan. Terrified and shaken by the initiatory shock, it had remained in the corner till its voice returned with the pangs of hunger. It was the amiable Diana, still very confused, who crept out of her retreat, though not without much persuasion, Michel Ardan encouraging her with most gracious words.

"Come, Diana," said he; "come, my girl! thou whose destiny will be marked in the cynegetic annals; thou whom the pagans would have given as companion to the god Anubis, and Christians as friend to St. Roch; thou who art rushing into interplanetary space, and wilt perhaps be the Eve of all Selenite dogs! come, Diana, come here."

Diana, flattered or not, advanced by degrees, uttering plaintive cries.

"Good," said Barbicane; "I see Eve, but where is Adam?"

"Adam?" replied Michel; "Adam cannot be far off; he is there somewhere; we must call him. Satellite! here, Satellite!"

But Satellite did not appear. Diana would not leave off howling. They found, however, that she was not bruised, and they gave her a pie, which silenced her complaints. As to Satellite, he seemed quite lost. They had to hunt a long time before finding him in one of the upper compartments of the projectile, whither some unaccountable shock must have violently hurled him. The poor beast, much hurt, was in a piteous state.

"The devil!" said Michel.

They brought the unfortunate dog down with great care. Its skull had been broken against the roof, and it seemed unlikely that he could recover from such a shock. Meanwhile, he was stretched comfortably on a cushion. Once there, he heaved a sigh.

"We will take care of you," said Michel; "we are responsible for your existence. I would rather lose an arm than a paw of my poor Satellite."

Saying which, he offered some water to the wounded dog, who swallowed it with avidity.

This attention paid, the travellers watched the earth and the moon attentively. The earth was now only discernible by a cloudy disc ending in a crescent, rather more contracted than that of the previous evening; but its expanse was still enormous, compared with that of the moon, which was approaching nearer and nearer to a perfect circle.

"By Jove!" said Michel Ardan, "I am really sorry that we did not start when the earth was full, that is to say, when our globe was in opposition to the sun."

"Why?" asked Nicholl.

"Because we should have seen our continents and seas in a new light,—the first resplendent under the solar rays, the latter cloudy as represented on some maps of the world. I should like to have seen those poles of the earth on which the eye of man has never yet rested.

"I dare say," replied Barbicane; "but if the earth had been *full*, the moon would have been *new*; that is to say, invisible, because of the rays of the sun. It is better for us to see the destination we wish to reach, than the point of departure."

"You are right, Barbicane," replied Captain Nicholl; "and, besides, when we have reached the moon, we shall have time during the long lunar nights to consider at our leisure the globe on which our likenesses swarm."

"Our likenesses!" exclaimed Michel Ardan; "they are no more our likenesses than the Selenites are! We inhabit a new world, peopled by ourselves—the projectile! I am Barbicane's likeness, and Barbicane is Nicholl's. Beyond us, around us, human nature is at an end, and we are the only population of this microcosm until we become pure Selenites."

"In about eighty-eight hours," replied the captain.

"Which means to say?" asked Michel Ardan.

"That it is half-past eight," replied Nicholl.

"Very well," retorted Michel; "then it is impossible for me to find even the shadow of a reason why we should not go to breakfast."

Indeed the inhabitants of the new star could not live without eating, and their stomachs were suffering from the imperious laws of hunger. Michel Ardan, as a Frenchman, was declared chief cook, an important function, which raised no rival. The gas gave sufficient heat for the culinary apparatus, and the provision-box furnished the elements of this first feast.

The breakfast began with three bowls of excellent soup, thanks to the liquefaction in hot water of those precious cakes of Liebig, prepared from the best parts of the ruminants of the Pampas. To the soup succeeded some beefsteaks, compressed by a hydraulic press, as tender and succulent as if brought straight from the kitchen of an English eating-house. Michel, who was imaginative, maintained that they were even "red."

Preserved vegetables ("fresher than nature," said the amiable Michel) succeeded the dish of meat; and was followed by some cups of tea with bread and butter, after the American fashion.

The beverage was declared exquisite, and was due to the infusion of the choicest leaves, of which the Emperor of Russia had given some chests for the benefit of the travellers.

And lastly, to crown the repast, Ardan brought out a fine bottle of Nuits, which was found "by chance" in the provision-box. The three friends drank to the union of the earth and her satellite.

And, as if he had not already done enough for the generous wine which he had distilled on the slopes of Burgundy, the sun chose to be of the party. At this moment the projectile emerged from the conical shadow cast by the terrestrial globe, and the rays of the radiant orb struck the lower disc of the projectile direct, occasioned by the angle which the moon's orbit makes with that of the earth.

"The sun!" exclaimed Michel Ardan.

"No doubt," replied Barbicane; "I expected it."

"But," said Michel, "the conical shadow which the earth leaves in space extends beyond the moon?"

"Far beyond it, if the atmospheric refraction is not taken into consideration," said Barbicane. "But when the moon is enveloped in this shadow, it is because the centres of the three stars, the sun, the earth, and the moon, are all in one and the same straight line. Then the *nodes* coincide with the *phases* of the moon, and there is an eclipse. If we had started when there was an eclipse of the moon, all our passage would have been in the shadow, which would have been a pity."

"Why?"

"Because, though we are floating in space, our projectile, bathed in the solar rays, will receive their light and heat. It economizes the gas, which is in every respect a good economy."

Indeed, under these rays which no atmosphere can temper, either in temperature or brilliancy, the projectile grew warm and bright, as if it had passed suddenly from winter to summer. The moon above, the sun beneath, were inundating it with their fire.

"It is pleasant here," said Nicholl.

"I should think so," said Michel Ardan. "With a little earth spread on our aluminium planet we should have green peas in twenty-four hours. I have but one fear, which is that the walls of the projectile might melt."

"Calm yourself, my worthy friend," replied Barbicane; "the projectile withstood a very much higher temperature than this as it slid through the strata of the atmosphere. I should not be surprised if it did not look like a meteor on fire to the eyes of the spectators in Florida."

"But then Joseph T. Maston will think we are roasted!"

"What astonishes me," said Barbicane, "is that we have not been. That was a danger we had not provided for."

"I feared it," said Nicholl simply.

"And you never mentioned it, my sublime captain," exclaimed Michel Ardan, clasping his friend's hand.

Barbicane now began to settle himself in the projectile as if he was never to leave it. One must remember that this aërial car had a base with a superficies of fifty-four feet. Its height to the roof was twelve feet. Carefully laid out in the inside, and little encumbered by instruments and travelling utensils which each had their particular place, it left the three travellers a certain freedom of movement. The thick window inserted in the bottom could bear any amount of weight, and Barbicane and his companions walked upon it as if it were solid plank; but the sun striking it directly with its rays lit the interior of the projectile from beneath, thus producing singular effects of light.

They began by investigating the state of their store of water and provisions, neither of which had suffered, thanks to the care taken to deaden the shock. Their provisions were abundant, and plentiful enough to last the three travellers for more than a year. Barbicane wished to be cautious, in case the projectile should land on a part of the moon which was utterly barren. As to water and the reserve of brandy, which consisted of fifty gallons, there was only enough for two months; but according to the last observations of astronomers, the moon had a low, dense, and thick atmosphere, at least in the deep valleys, and there springs and streams could not fail. Thus, during their passage, and for the first year of their settlement on the lunar continent, these adventurous explorers would suffer neither hunger nor thirst.

Now about the air in the projectile. There, too, they were secure. Reiset and Regnaut's apparatus, intended for the production of oxygen, was supplied with chlorate of potass for two months. They necessarily consumed a certain quantity of gas, for they were obliged to keep the producing susbstance at a temperature of above 400°. But there again they were all safe. The apparatus only wanted a little care. But it was not enough to renew the oxygen; they must absorb the carbonic acid produced by expiration. During the last twelve hours the atmosphere of the projectile had become charged with this deleterious gas. Nicholl discovered the state of the air by observing Diana panting painfully. The carbonic acid, by a phenomenon similar to that produced in the famous Grotto del Cane, had collected at the bottom of the projectile owing to its weight. Poor Diana, with her head low, would suffer before her masters from the presence of this gas. But Captain Nicholl hastened to remedy this state of things, by placing on the floor several receivers containing caustic potash which he shook about for a time, and this substance, greedy of carbonic acid, soon completely absorbed it, thus purifying the air.

An inventory of instruments was then begun. The thermometers and barometers had resisted, all but one minimum thermometer, the glass of which was broken. An excellent aneroid was drawn from the wadded box which contained it and hung on the wall. Of course it was only affected by and marked the pressure of the air inside the projectile, but it also showed the quantity of moisture which it contained. At that moment its needle oscillated between 25·24 and 25·08.

It was fine weather.

Barbicane had also brought several compasses, which he found intact. One must understand that under present conditions their needles were acting *wildly*, that is without any *constant* direction. Indeed, at the distance they were from the earth, the magnetic pole could have no perceptible action upon the apparatus; but the box placed on the lunar disc might perhaps exhibit some strange phenomena. In any case it would be interesting to see whether the earth's satellite submitted like herself to its magnetic influence.

A hypsometer to measure the height of the lunar mountains, a sextant to take the height of the sun, glasses which would be useful as they neared the moon, all these instruments were carefully looked over, and pronounced good in spite of the violent shock.

As to the pickaxes and different tools which were Nicholl's especial choice; as to the sacks of different kinds of grain and shrubs which Michel Ardan hoped to transplant into Selenite ground, they were stowed away in the upper part of the projectile. There was a sort of granary there, loaded with things which the extravagant Frenchman had heaped up. What they were no one knew, and the good-tempered fellow did not explain. Now and then he climbed up by cramp-irons rivetted to the walls, but kept the inspection to himself. He arranged and rearranged, he plunged his hand rapidly into certain mysterious boxes, singing in one of the falsest of voices an old French refrain to enliven the situation.

Barbicane observed with some interest that his guns and other arms had not been damaged. These were important, because, heavily loaded, they were to help to lessen the fall of the projectile, when drawn by the lunar attraction (after having passed the point of neutral attraction) on to the moon's surface; a fall which ought to be six times less rapid than it would have been on the earth's surface, thanks to the difference of bulk. The inspection ended with general satisfaction, when each returned to watch space through the side windows and the lower glass coverlid.

There was the same view. The whole extent of the celestial sphere swarmed with stars and constellations of wonderful purity, enough to drive an astronomer out of his mind! On one side the sun, like the mouth of a lighted oven, a dazzling disc without a halo, standing out on the dark background of the sky! On the other, the moon returning its fire by reflection, and apparently motionless in the midst of the starry world. Then, a large spot seemingly nailed to the firmament, bordered by a silvery cord: it was the earth! Here and there nebulous masses like large flakes of starry snow; and from the zenith to the nadir, an immense ring formed by an impalpable dust of stars, the "Milky Way," in the midst of which the sun ranks only as a star of the fourth magnitude. The observers could not take their eyes from this novel spectacle, of which no description could give an adequate idea. What reflections it suggested! What emotions hitherto unknown awoke in their souls ! Barbicane wished to begin the relation of his journey while under its first impressions, and hour after hour took notes of all facts happening in the beginning of the enterprise. He wrote quietly, with his large square writing, in a business-like style.

During this time Nicholl, the calculator, looked over the minutes of their passage, and worked out figures with unparalleled dexterity. Michel Ardan chatted first with Barbicane, who did not answer him, and then with Nicholl, who did not hear him, with Diana, who understood none of his theories, and lastly with himself, questioning and answering, going and coming, busy with a thousand details; at one time bent over the lower glass, at another roosting in the heights of the projectile, and always singing. In this microcosm he represented French loquacity and excitability, and we beg you to believe that they were well represented. The day, or rather (for the expression is not correct) the lapse of twelve hours, which forms a day upon earth, closed with a plentiful supper carefully prepared. No accident of any nature had yet happened to shake the travellers' confidence; so, full of hope, already sure of success, they slept peacefully, whilst the projectile under an uniformly decreasing speed was crossing the sky.

CHAPTER 4

A LITTLE ALGEBRA

THE night passed without incident. The word "night," however, is scarcely applicable.

The position of the projectile with regard to the sun did not change. Astronomically, it was daylight on the lower part, and night on the upper; so when during this narrative these words are used, they represent the lapse of time between the rising and setting of the sun upon the earth.

The travellers' sleep was rendered more peaceful by the projectile's excessive speed, for it seemed absolutely motionless. Not a motion betrayed its onward course through space. The rate of progress, however rapid it might be, cannot produce any sensible effect on the human frame when it takes place in a vacuum, or when the mass of air circulates with the body which is carried with it. What inhabitant of the earth perceives its speed, which, however, is at the rate of 68,000 miles per hour? Motion under such conditions is "felt" no more than repose; and when a body is in repose it will remain so as long as no strange force displaces it; if moving, it will not stop unless an obstacle comes in its way. This indifference to motion or repose is called inertia.

Barbicane and his companions might have believed themselves perfectly stationary, being shut up in the projectile; indeed, the effect would have been the same if they had been on the outside of it. Had it not been for the moon, which was increasing above them, they might have sworn that they were floating in complete stagnation.

That morning, the 3rd of December, the travellers were awakened by a joyous but unexpected noise; it was the crowing of a cock which sounded through the ear. Michel Ardan, who was the first on his feet, climbed to the top of the projectile, and shutting a box, the lid of which was partly open, said in a low voice, "Will you hold your tongue? That creature will spoil my design!"

But Nicholl and Barbicane were awake.

"A cock!" said Nicholl.

"Why no, my friends," Michel answered quickly; "it was I who wished to awake you by this rural sound." So saying, he gave vent to a splendid cock-a-doodledoo, which would have done honour to the proudest of poultry-yards.

The two Americans could not help laughing.

"Fine talent that," said Nicholl, looking suspiciously at his companion.

"Yes," said Michel; "a joke in my country. It is very Gallic; they play the cock so in the best society."

Then turning the conversation,—

"Barbicane, do you know what I have been thinking of all night?"

"No," answered the president.

"Of our Cambridge friends. You have already remarked that I am an ignoramus in mathematical subjects; and it is impossible for me to find out how the savants of the Observatory were able to calculate what initiatory speed the projectile ought to have on leaving the Columbiad in order to attain the moon."

"You mean to say," replied Barbicane, "to attain that neutral point where the terrestrial and lunar attractions are equal; for, starting from that point, situated about nine-tenths of the distance travelled over, the projectile would simply fall upon the moon, on account of its weight."

"So be it," said Michel; "but, once more; how could they calculate the initiatory speed?"

"Nothing can be easier," replied Barbicane.

"And you knew how to make that calculation?" asked Michel Ardan.

"Perfectly. Nicholl and I would have made it, if the Observatory had not saved us the trouble."

"Very well, old Barbicane," replied Michel; "they might have cut off my head, beginning at my feet, before they could have made me solve that problem."

"Because you do not know algebra," answered Barbicane quietly.

"Ah, there you are, you eaters of x^1; you think you have said all when you have said 'Algebra.' "

"Michel," said Barbicane, "can you use a forge without a hammer, or plough without a ploughshare?"

"Hardly."

"Well, algebra is a tool, like the plough or the hammer, and a good tool to those who know how to use it."

"Seriously?"

"Quite seriously."

"And can you use that tool in my presence?"

"If it will interest you."

"And show me how they calculated the initiatory speed of our car?"

"Yes, my worthy friend; taking into consideration all the elements of the problem, the distance from the centre of the earth to the centre of the moon, of the radius of the earth, of its bulk, and of the bulk of the moon, I can tell exactly what ought to be the initiatory speed of the projectile, and that by a simple formula."

"Let us see."

"You shall see it; only I shall not give you the real course drawn by the projectile between the moon and the earth in considering their motion round the sun. No, I shall consider these two orbs as perfectly motionless, which will answer all our purpose."

"And why?"

"Because it will be trying to solve the problem called 'the problem of the three bodies,' for which the integral calculus is not yet far enough advanced."

"Then," said Michel Ardan, in his sly tone, "mathematics have not said their last word?"

"Certainly not," replied Barbicane.

"Well, perhaps the Selenites have carried the integral calculus father than you have; and, by the bye, what is this 'integral calculus?' "

"It is a calculation the converse of the differential," replied Barbicane seriously.

"Much obliged; it is all very clear, no doubt."

"And now," continued Barbicane, "a slip of paper and a bit of pencil, and before a half-hour is over I will have found the required formula."

Half an hour had not elapsed before Barbicane, raising his head, showed Michel Ardan a page covered with algebraical signs, in which the general formula for the solution was contained.

"Well, and does Nicholl understand what that means?"

"Of course, Michel," replied the captain. "All these signs, which seem cabalistic to you, form the plainest, the clearest, and the most logical language to those who know how to read it."

"And you pretend, Nicholl," asked Michel, "that by means of these hieroglyphics, more incomprehensible than the Egyptian Ibis, you can find what initiatory speed it was necessary to give to the projectile?"

"Incontestably," replied Nicholl; "and even by this same formula I can always tell you its speed at any point of its transit."

"On your word?"

"On my word."

"Then you are as cunning as our president."

"No, Michel; the difficult part is what Barbicane has done; that is, to get an equation which shall satisfy all the conditions of the problem. The remainder is only a question of arithmetic, requiring merely the knowledge of the four rules."

"That is something!" replied Michel Ardan, who for his life could not do addition right, and who defined the rule as a Chinese puzzle, which allowed one to obtain all sorts of totals.

"The expression ν zero, which you see in that equation, is the speed which the projectile will have on leaving the atmosphere."

"Just so," said Nicholl; "it is from that point that we must calculate the velocity, since we know already that the volocity at departure was exactly one and a half times more than on leaving the atmosphere."

"I understand no more," said Michel.

"It is a very simple calculation," said Barbicane.

"Not as simple as I am," retorted Michel.

"That means, that when our projectile reached the limits of the terrestrial atmosphere it had already lost one-third of its initiatory speed."

"As much as that?"

"Yes, my friend; merely by friction against the atmospheric strata. You understand that the faster it goes the more resistance it meets with from the air."

"That I admit," answered Michel; "and I understand it, although your x's and zero's, and algebraic formulæ, are rattling in my head like nails in a bag."

"First effects of algebra," replied Barbicane; "and now, to finish, we are going to prove the given number of these different expressions, that is, work our their value."

"Finish me!" replied Michel.

Barbicane took the paper, and began again to make his calculations with great rapidity. Nicholl looked over and greedily read the work as it proceeded.

"That's it! that's it" at last he cried.

"Is it clear?" asked Barbicane.

"It is written in letters of fire," said Nicholl.

"Wonderful fellows!" muttered Ardan.

"Do you understand it at last?" asked Barbicane.

"Do I understand it?" cried Ardan; "my head is splitting with it."

"And now," said Nicholl, "to find out the speed of the projectile when it left the atmosphere, we have only to calculate that."

The captain, as a practical man equal to all difficulties, began to write with frightful rapidity. Divisions and multiplications grew under his fingers; the figures were like hail on the white page. Barbicane watched him, whilst Michel Ardan nursed a growing headache with both hands.

"Very well?" asked Barbicane, after some minutes'silence.

"Well!" replied Nicholl; "every calculation made, v zero, that is to say, the speed necessary for the projectile on leaving the atmosphere, to enable it to reach the equal point of attraction, ought to be—"

"Yes?" said Barbicane.

"Twelve thousand yards."

"What!" exclaimed Barbicane, starting; "you say—"

"Twelve thousand yards."

"The devil!" cried the president, making a gesture of despair.

"What is the matter?" asked Michel Ardan, much surprised.

"What is the matter! why, if at this moment our speed had already diminished one-third by friction, the initiatory speed ought to have been—"

"Seventeen thousand yards."

"And the Cambridge Observatory declared that 12,000 yards was enough at starting; and our projectile, which only started with that speed—"

"Well?" asked Nicholl.

"Well, it will not be enough."

"Good."

"We shall not be able to reach the neutral point."

"The deuce!"

"We shall not even get half way."

"In the name of the projectile!" exclaimed Michel Ardan, jumping as if it was already on the point of striking the terrestrial globe.

"And we shall fall back upon the earth!"

CHAPTER 5

THE COLD OF SPACE

THIS revelation came like a thunderbolt. Who could have expected such an error in calculation? Barbicane would not believe it. Nicholl revised his figures: they were exact. As to the formula which had determined them, they could not suspect its truth; it was evident that an initiatory velocity of 17,000 yards in the first second was necessary to enable them to reach the neutral point.

The three friends looked at each other silently. There was no thought of breakfast. Barbicane, with clenched teeth, knitted brows, and hands clasped convulsively, was watching through the window. Nicholl had crossed his arms, and was examining his calculations. Michel Ardan was muttering,—

"That is just like those scientific men: they never do anything else. I would give twenty pistoles if we could fall upon the Cambridge Observatory and crush it, together with the whole lot of dabblers in figures which it contains."

Suddenly a thought struck the captain, which he at once communicated to Barbicane.

"Ah!" said he; "it is seven o'clock in the morning; we have already been

"Do I understand it?" cried Ardan. "My head is splitting with it."

gone thirty-two hours; more than half our passage is over, and we are not falling that I am aware of."

Barbicane did not answer, but, after a rapid glance at the captain, took a pair of compasses wherewith to measure the angular distance of the terrestrial globe; then from the lower window he took an exact observation, and noticed that the projectile was apparently stationary. Then rising and wiping his forehead, on which large drops of perspiration were standing, he put some figures on paper. Nicholl understood that the president was deducting from the terrrestrial diameter the projectile's distance from the earth. He watched him anxiously.

"No," exclaimed Barbicane, after some moments, "no, we are not falling! no, we are already more than 50,000 leagues from the earth. We have passed the point at which the projectile would have stopped if its speed had only been 12,000 yards at starting. We are still going up."

"That is evident," replied Nicholl; "and we must conclude that our initial speed, under the power of the 400,000 lbs. of gun-cotton, must have exceeded the required 12,000 yards. Now I can understand how, after thirteen minutes only, we met the second satellite, which gravitates round the earth at more than 2000 leagues' distance."

"And this explanation is the more probable," added Barbicane, "because, in throwing off the water enclosed between its partition-breaks, the projectile found itself lightened of a considerable weight."

"Just so," said Nicholl.

"Ah, my brave Nicholl, we are saved!"

"Very well, then," said Michel Ardan quietly; "as we are safe, let us have breakfast."

Nicholl was not mistaken. The initial speed had been, very fortunately, much above that estimated by the Cambridge Observatory; but the Cambridge Observatory had nevertheless made a mistake.

The travellers, recovered from this false alarm, breakfasted merrily. If they ate a great deal, they talked more. Their confidence was greater after than before "the incident of the algebra."

"Why should we not succeed?" said Michel Ardan; "why should we not arrive safely? We are launched; we have no obstacle before us, no stones in our way; the road is open, more so than that of a ship battling with the sea; more open than that of a balloon battling with the wind; and if a ship can reach its destination, a balloon go where it pleases, why cannot our projectile attain its end and aim?"

"It *will* attain it," said Barbicane.

"If only to do honour to the Americans," added Michel Ardan, "the only people who could bring such an enterprise to a happy termination, and the only one which could produce a President Barbicane. Ah, now we are no longer uneasy, I begin to think, What will become of us? We shall get right royally weary."

Barbicane and Nicholl made a gesture of denial.

"But I have provided for the contingency, my friends," replied Michel; "you have only to speak, and I have chess, draughts, cards, and dominoes at your disposal; nothing is wanting but a billiard-table."

"What!" exclaimed Barbicane; "you brought away such trifles?"

"Certainly," replied Michel, "and not only to distract ourselves, but also with the laudable intention of endowing the Selenite smoking divans with them."

"My friend," said Barbicane, "if the moon is inhabited, its inhabitants must have appeared some thousands of years before those of the earth, for we cannot doubt that their star is much older than ours. If then these Selenites have existed their hundreds of thousands of years, and if their brain is on the same organization as the human brain, they have already invented all that we have invented, and even what we may invent in future ages. They have nothing to learn from *us*, and we have everything to learn from *them*."

"What!" said Michel; "you believe that they have artists like Phidias, Michael Angelo, or Raphael?"

"Yes."

"Poets like Homer, Virgil, Milton, Lamartine, and Hugo?"

"I am sure of it."

"Philosophers like Plato, Aristotle, Descartes, Kant?"

"I have no doubt of it."

"Scientific men like Archimedes, Euclid, Pascal, Newton?"

"I could swear it."

"Comic writers like Arnal, and photographers like—like Nadar?"

"Certain."

"Then, friend Barbicane, if they are as strong as we are, and even stronger—these Selenites—why have they not tried to communicate with the earth? why have they not launched a lunar projectile to our terrestrial regions?"

"Who told you that they have never done so?" said Barbicane, seriously.

"Indeed," added Nicholl, "it would be easier for them than for us, for two reasons; first, because the attraction on the moon's surface is six times less than on that of the earth, which would allow a projectile to rise more easily; secondly, because it would be enough to send such a projectile only at 8000 leagues instead of 80,000 which would require the force of projection to be ten times less strong."

"Then," continued Michel; "I repeat it, why have they not done it?"

"And I repeat," said Barbicane; "who told you that they have not done it?"

"When?"

"Thousands of years before man appeared on earth."

"And the projectile—where is the projectile? I demand to see the projectile."

"My friend," replied Barbicane; "the sea covers five-sixths of our globe. From that we may draw five good reasons for supposing that the lunar projectile, if ever launched, is now at the bottom of the Atlantic or the Pacific, unless it sped into some crevasse at that period when the crust of the earth was not yet hardened."

"Old Barbicane," said Michel, "you have an answer for everything, and I bow before your wisdom. But there is one hypothesis that would suit me better than all the others, which is, that the Selenties, being older than we, are wiser, and have not invented *gunpowder*.

At this moment Diana joined in the conversation by a sonorous barking. She was asking for her breakfast.

"Ah!" said Michel Ardan, "in our discussion we have forgotten Diana and Satellite."

Immediately a good-sized pie was given to the dog, which devoured it hungrily.

"Do you see, Barbicane," said Michel, "we should have made a second Noah's Ark of this projectile, and borne with us to the moon a couple of every kind of domestic animal."

"I dare say; but room would have failed us."

"Oh!" said Michel, "we might have squeezed a little."

"The fact is," replied Nicholl, "that cows, bulls, and horses, and all reminants, would have been very useful on the lunar continent, but unfortunately the car could neither have been made a stable nor a shed."

"Well, we might at least have brought a donkey, only a little donkey; that courageous beast which old Silenus loved to mount. I love those old donkeys; they are the least favoured animals in creation; they are not only beaten while alive, but even after they are dead."

"How do you make that out?" asked Barbicane.

"Why," said Michel, "they make their skins into drums."

Barbicane and Nicholl could not help laughing at this ridiculous remark. But a cry from their merry companion stopped them. The latter was leaning over the spot where Satellite lay. He rose, saying,—

"My good Satellite is no longer ill."

"Ah!" Said Nicholl.

"No," answered Michel, "he is dead! There," added he, in a piteous tone, "that is embarrassing. I much fear, my poor Diana, that you will leave no progeny in the lunar regions!"

Indeed the unfortunate Satellite had not survived its wound. It was quite dead. Michel Ardan looked at his friends with a rueful countenance.

"One question presents itself," said Barbicane. "We cannot keep the dead body of this dog with us for the next forty-eight hours."

"No! certainly not," replied Nicholl; "but our scuttles are fixed on hinges; they can be let down. We will open one, and throw the body out into space."

The president thought for some moments, and then said,—

"Yes, we must do so, but at the same time taking very great precautions."

"Why?" asked Michel.

"For two reasons which you will understand," answered Barbicane. "The first relates to the air shut up in the projectile, and of which we must lose as little as possible."

"But we manufacture the air?"

"Only in part. We make only the oxygen, my worthy Michel; and with regard to that, we must watch that the apparatus does not furnish the oxygen in too great a quantity; for an excess would bring us very serious physiological troubles. But if we make the oxygen, we do not make the azote, that medium which the lungs do not absorb, and which ought to remain intact; and that azote will escape rapidly through the open scuttles."

"Oh! the time for throwing out poor Satellite?" said Michel.

"Agreed; but we must act quickly."

"And the second reason?" asked Michel.

"The second reason is that we must not let the outer cold, which is excessive, penetrate the projectile, or we shall be frozen to death."

"But the sun?"

"The sun warms our projectile, which absorbs its rays; but it does not warm the vacuum in which we are floating at this moment. Where there is no air, there is no more heat than diffused light; and the same with darkness: it is cold where the sun's rays do not strike direct. This temperature is only the temperature produced by the radiation of the stars; that is to say, what the terrestrial globe would undergo if the sun disappeared one day."

"Which is not to be feared," replied Nicholl.

"Who knows?" said Michel Ardan. "But, in admitting that the sun does not go out, might it not happen that the earth might move away from it?"

"There!" said Barbicane, "there is Michel with his ideas."

"And," continued Michel, "do we not know that in 1861 the earth passed through the tail of a coment? Or let us suppose a comet whose power of attraction is greater than that of the sun. The terrestrial orbit will bend towards the wandering star, and the earth, becoming its satellite, will be drawn such a distance that the rays of the sun will have no action on its surface."

"That *might* happen, indeed," replied Barbicane, "but the consequences of such a displacement need not be so formidable as you suppose."

"And why not?"

"Because the heat and the cold would be equalized on our globe. It has been calculated that, had our earth been carried along in its course by the comet of 1861, at its perihelion, that is, its nearest approach to the sun, it would have undergone a heat 28,000 times greater than that of summer. But this heat, which is sufficient to evaporate the waters, would have formed a thick ring of cloud, which would have modified that excessive temperature; hence the compensation between the cold of the aphelion and the heat of the perihelion."

"At how many degrees," asked Nicholl, "is the temperature of the planetary spaces estimated?"

"Formerly," replied Barbicane, "it was greatly exaggerated; but now, after the calculations of Fourier, of the French Academy of Science, it is not supposed to exceed 60° Centigrade below zero."

"Pooh!" said Michel, "that's nothing!"

"It is very much," replied Barbicane; "the temperature which was observed in the polar regions, at Melville Island and Fort Reliance, that is 76° Fahrenheit below zero."

"If I mistake not," said Nicholl, "M. Pouillet, another savant, estimates the temperature of space at 250° Fahr. below zero. We shall, however, be able to verify these calculations for ourselves."

"Not at present; because the solar rays, beating directly upon our thermometer, would give, on the contrary, a very high temperature. But, when we arrive in the moon, during its fifteen days of night at either face, we shall have leisure to make the experiment, for our satellite lies in a vacuum."

"What do you mean by a *vacuum!*" asked Michel. "Is it perfectly such?"

"It is absolutely void of air."

"And is the air replaced by nothing whatever?"

"By the ether only," replied Barbicane.

"And pray what is the ether?"

"The ether, my friend, is an agglomeration of imponderable atoms, which, relatively to their dimensions, are as far removed from each other as the celestial bodies are in space. It is these atoms which, by their vibratory motion, produce both light and heat in the universe."

They now proceeded to the burial of Satellite. They had merely to drop him into space, in the same way that sailors drop a body into the sea; but, as President Barbicane suggested, they must act quickly, so as to lose as little as possible of that air whose elasticity would rapidly have spread it into space. The bolts of the right scuttle, the opening of which measured about twelve inches across, were carefully drawn, whilst Michel, quite grieved, prepared to launch his dog into space. The glass, raised by a powerful lever, which enabled it to overcome the pressure of the inside air on the walls of the projectile, turned rapidly on its hinges, and Satellite was thrown out. Scarcely a particle of air could have escaped, and the operation was so successful, that later on Barbicane did not fear to dispose of the rubbish which encumbered the car.

CHAPTER 6

QUESTION AND ANSWER

On the 4th of December, when the travellers awoke after fifty-four hours' journey, the chronometer marked five o'clock of the terrestrial morning. In time it was just over five hours and forty minutes, half of that assigned to their sojourn in the projectile; but they had already accomplished nearly seven-tenths of the way. This peculiarity was due to their regularly decreasing speed.

Now when they observed the earth through the lower window, it looked like nothing more than a dark spot, drowned in the solar rays. No more crescent, no more cloudy light! The next day, at midnight, the earth would be *new*, at the very moment when the moon would be full. Above, the orb of night was nearing the line followed by the projectile, so as to meet it at the given hour. All around the black vault was studded with brilliant points, which seemed to move slowly; but, at the great distance they were from them, their relative size did not seem to change. The sun and stars appeared exactly as they do to us upon earth. As to the moon, she was considerably larger; but the travellers' glasses, not very powerful, did not allow them as yet to make any useful observations upon her surface, or reconnoitre her topographically or geologically.

Thus the time passed in never-ending conversations all about the moon. Each one brought forward his own contingent of particular facts; Barbicane and Nicholl always serious, Michel Ardan always enthusiastic. The projectile, its situation, its direction, incidents which might happen, the precautions necessitated by their fall on to the moon, were inexhaustible matters of conjecture.

As they were breakfasting, a question of Michel's, relating to the projectile, provoked rather a curious answer from Barbicane, which is worth repeating. Michel, supposing it to be roughly stopped, whilst still under its formidable initial speed, wished to know what the consequences of the stoppage would have been.

"But," said Barbicane, "I do not see how it could have been stopped."

"But let us suppose so," said Michel.

"It is an impossible supposition," said the practical Barbicane; "unless the impulsive force had failed; but even then its speed would dimish by degrees, and it would not have stopped suddenly."

"Admit that it had struck a body in space."

"What body?"

"Why that enormous meteor which we met."

"Then," said Nicholl, "the projectile would have been broken into a thousand pieces, and we with it."

"More than that," replied Barbicane; "we should have been burnt to death."

"Burnt?" exclaimed Michel, "by Jove! I am sorry it did not happen, 'just to see.'"

"And you would have seen," replied Barbicane. "It is known now that heat is only a modification of motion. When water is warmed—that is to say, when heat is added to it—its particles are set in motion."

"Well," said Michel, "that is an ingenious theory!"

"And a true one, my worthy friend; for it explains every phenomenon of caloric. Heat is but the motion of atoms, a simple oscillation of the particles of a body. When they apply the break to a train, the train comes to a stop; but what becomes of the motion which it had previously possessed? It is transformed into heat, and the brake becomes hot. Why do they grease the axles of the wheels? To prevent their heating, because this heat would be generated by the motion which is thus lost by transformation."

"Yes, I understand," replied Michel, "perfectly. For example, when I have run a long time, when I am swimming, when I am perspiring in large drops, why am I obliged to stop? Simply because my motion is changed into heat."

Barbicane could not help smiling at Michel's reply; then, returning to his theory, said,—

"Thus, in case of a shock, it would have been with our projectile as with a ball which falls in a burning state afer having struck the metal plate; it is its motion which is turned into heat. Consequently I affirm that, if our projectile had struck the meteor, its speed thus suddenly checked would have raised a heat great enough to turn it into vapour instantaneously."

"Then," asked Nicholl, "what would happen if the earth's motion were to stop suddenly?"

"Her temperature would be raised to such a pitch," said Barbicane, "that she would be at once reduced to vapour."

"Well," said Michel, "that is a way of ending the earth which will greatly simplify things."

"And if the earth fell upon the sun?" asked Nicholl.

"According to calculation," replied Barbicane, "the fall would develope a heat equal to that produced by 16,000 globes of coal, each equal in bulk to our terrestrial globe."

"Good additional heat for the sun," replied Michel Ardan, "of which the inhabitants of Uranus or Neptune would doubtless not compalin; they must be perished with cold on their planets."

"Thus, my friends," said Barbicane, "all motion suddenly stopped produces heat. And this theory allows us to infer that the heat of the solar disc is fed by a hail of meteors falling incessantly on its surface. They have even calculated—"

"Oh dear!" murmured Michel, "the figures are coming."

"They have even calculated," contined the imperturbable Barbicane, "that the shock of each meteor on the sun ought to produce a heat equal to that of 4000 masses of coal of an equal bulk."

"And what is the solar heat?" asked Michel.

"It is equal to that produced by the combustion of a stratum of coal surrounding the sun to a depth of forty-seven miles."

"And that heat—"

"Would be able to boil two billions nine hundred millions of cubic myriametres* of water."

"And it does not roast us!" exclaimed Michel.

"No," replied Barbicane, "because the terrrestrial atmosphere absrobs four-tenths of the solar heat; besides, the quantity of heat intercepted by the earth is but a billionth part of the entire radiation."

"I see that all is for the best," said Michel, "and that this atmosphere is a useful invention; for it not only allows us to breath, but it prevents us from roasting."

"Yes!" said Nicholl, "unfortunately, it will not be the same in the moon."

"Bah!" said Michel, always hopeful. "If there are inhabitants, they must breathe. If there are no longer any, they must have left enough oxygen for three people, if only at the bottom of ravines, where its own weight will cause it to accumulate, and we will not climb the mountains; that is all." And Michel, rising, went to look at the lunar disc, which shone with intolerable brilliancy.

"By Jove!" said he, "it must be hot up there!"

"Without considering," replied Nicholl, "that the day lasts 360 hours!"

"And to compensate that," said Barbicane, "the nights have the same length; and as heat is restored by radiation, their temperature can only be that of the planetary space."

"A pretty country, that!" exclaimed Michel. "Never mind! I wish I was there! Ah! my dear comrades, it will be rather curious to have the earth for our moon, to see it rise on the horizon, to recognize the shape of its continents, and to say to oneself, 'There is America, there is Europe;' then to follow it when it is about to lose itself in the sun's rays! By-the-bye, Barbicane, have the Selenites eclipses?"

"Yes, eclipses of the sun," replied Barbicane, "when the centres of the three orbs are on a line, the earth being in the middle. But they are only partial, during which the earth, cast like a screen upon the solar disc, allows the greater portion to be seen."

"And why," asked Nicholl, "is there no total eclipse? Does not the cone of the shadow cast by the earth extend beyond the moon?"

"Yes, if we do not take into consideration the refraction produced by the terrestrial atmosphere. No, if we take that refraction into consideration. Thus let δ be the horizontal parallel, and p the apparent semidiameter—"

"Oh!" said Michel. "Do speak plainly, you man of algebra!"

"Very well;" replied Barbicane, "in popular language the mean distance from the moon to the earth being sixty terrestrial radii, the length of the cone of the shadow, on account of the refraction, is reduced to less than forty-two radii. The result is that when there are eclipses, the moon finds itself beyond the cone of pure shadow, and that the sun sends her rays, not only from its edges, but also from its centre."

"Then," said Michel, in a merry tone, "why are there eclipses, when there ought not to be any?"

"Simply because the solar rays are weakened by this refraction, and the atmosphere through which they pass extinguishes the greater part of them!"

"That reason satisfies me," replied Michel. "Besides we shall see when we

* The myriametre is equal to rather more than 10,936 cubic yards English.—(Ed.)

get there. Now, tell me, Barbicane, do you believe that the moon is an old comet?''

''There's an idea!''

''Yes,'' replied Michel, with an amiable swagger, ''I have a few ideas of that sort.''

''But that idea does not spring from Michel,'' answered Nicholl.

''Well, then, I am a plagiarist.''

''No doubt about it. According to the ancients, the Arcadians pretend that their ancestors inhabited the earth before the moon became her satellite. Starting from this fact, some scientific men have seen in the moon a comet whose orbit will one day bring it so near to the earth that it will be held there by its attraction.''

''Is there any truth in this hypothesis?'' asked Michel.

''None whatever,'' said Barbicane, ''and the proof is, that the moon has preserved no trace of the gaseous envelope which always accompanies comets.''

''But,'' continues Nicholl, ''before becoming the earth's satellite, could not the moon, when in her perihelion, pass so near the sun as by evaporation to get rid of all those gaseous substances?''

''It is possible, friend, Nicholl, but no probable.''

''Why not?''

''Because—Faith I do not know.''

''Ah!'' Exclaimed Michel, ''what hundreds of volumes we might make of all that we do not know!''

''Ah! indeed. What time is it?'' asked Barbicane.

''Three o'clock,'' answered Nicholl.

''How time goes,'' said Michel, ''in the conversation of scientific men such as we are! Certainly, I feel I know too much! I feel that I am becoming a well!''

Saying which, Michel hoisted himself to the roof of the projectile, ''to observe the moon better,'' he pretended. During this time his companions were watching through the lower glass. Nothing new to note!

When Michel Ardan came down, he went to the side scuttle; and suddenly they heard an exclamation of surprise!

''What is it?'' asked Barbicane.

The president approached the window, and saw a sort of flattened sack floating some yards from the projectile. This object seemed as motionless as the projectile, and was consequently animated with the same ascending movement.

''What is that machine?'' continued Michel Ardan. ''Is it one of the bodies of space which our projectile keeps within its attraction, and which will accompany it to the moon?''

''What astonishes me,'' said Nicholl, ''is that the specific weight of the body, which is certainly less than that of the projectile, allows it to keep so perfectly on a level with it.''

''Nicholl,'' replied Barbicane, after a moment's reflection, ''I do not know what the object is, but I do know why it maintains our level.''

''And why?''

''Because we are floating in space, my dear captain, and in space bodies fall or move (which is the same thing) with equal speed whatever be their weight or form; it is the air, which by its resistance creates these differences in weight. When you create a vacuum in a tube, the objects you send through it, grains of dust or grains of lead, fall with the same rapidity. Here in space is the same cause and the same effect.''

"Just so," said Nicholl, "and everything we throw out of the projectile will accompany it until it reaches the moon."

"Ah! fools that we are!" exclaimed Michel.

"Why that expletive?" asked Barbicane.

"Because we might have filled the projectile with useful objects, books, instruments, tools, &c. We could have thrown them all out, and all would have followed in our train. But happy thought! Why cannot we walk ouside like the meteor? Why cannot we launch into space through the scuttle? What enjoyment it would be to feel oneself thus suspended in either, more favoured than the birds who must use their wings to keep themselves up!"

"Granted," said Barbicane, "but how to breathe?"

"Hang the air, to fail so inopportunely!"

"But if it did not fail, Michel, your density being less than that of the projectile, you would soon be left behind."

"Then we must remain in our car?"

"We must!"

"Ah!" exclaimed Michel, in a loud voice.

"What is the matter," asked Nicholl.

"I know, I guess, what this pretended meteor is! It is no asteroid which is accompanying us! It is not a piece of a planet."

"What is it then?" asked Barbicane.

"It is our unfortunate dog! It is Diana's husband!"

Indeed, this deformed, unrecognizable object, reduced to nothing, was the body of Satellite, flattened like a bagpipe without wind, and ever mounting, mounting!

CHAPTER 7

A MOMENT OF INTOXICATION

THUS a phenomenon, curious but explicable, was happening under these strange conditions.

Every object thrown from the projectile would follow the same course and never stop until it did. There was a subject for conversation which the whole evening could not exhaust.

Besides, the excitement of the three travellers increased as they drew near the end of their journey. They expected unforeseen incidents, and new phenomena; and nothing would have astonished them in the frame of mind they then were in. Their over-excited imagination went faster than the projectile, whose speed was evidently diminishing, though insensibly to themselves. But the moon grew larger to their eyes, and they fancied if they stretched out their hands they could seize it.

The next day, the 5th of November, at five in the morning, all three were on foot. That day was to be the last of their journey, if all calculations were true. That very night, at twelve o'clock, in eighteen hours, exactly at the full moon, they would reach its brilliant disc. The next midnight would see that journey ended, the most extraordinary of ancient or modern times. Thus from the first of the morning, through the scuttles silvered by its rays, they saluted the orb of night with a confident and joyous hurrah.

The moon was advancing majestically along the starry firmament. A few more degrees, and she would reach the exact point where her meeting with the projectile was to take place.

According to his own observations, Barbicane reckoned that they would land on her northern hemisphere, where stretch immense planes, and where mountains are rare. A favourable circumstance if, as they thought, the lunar atmosphere was stored only in its depths.

"Besides," observed Michel Ardan, "a plain is easier to disembark upon than a mountain. A Selenite, deposited in Europe on the summit of Mont Blanc, or in Asia on the top of the Himalayas, would not be quite in the right place."

"And," added Captain Nicholl, "on a flat ground, the projectile will remain motionless when it has once touched; whereas on a declivity it would roll like an avalance, and not being squirrels we should not come out safe and sound. So it is all for the best."

Indeed, the success of the audacious attempt no longer appeared doubtful. But Barbicane was preoccupied with one thought; but not wishing to make his companions uneasy, he kept silence on the subject.

The direction the projectile was taking towards the moon's northern hemisphere, showed that her course had been slightly altered. The discharge, mathematically calculated, would carry the projectile to the very centre of the lunar disc. If it did not land there, there must have been some deviation. What had caused it? Barbicane could neither imagine, nor determine the importance of the deviation, for there were no points to go by.

He hoped, however, that it would have no other result than that of bringing them near the upper border of the moon, a region more suitable for landing.

Without imparting his uneasiness to his companions, Barbicane contented himself with constantly observing the moon, in order to see whether the course of the projectile would not be altered; for the situation would have been terrible if it failed in its aim, and being carried beyond the disc should be launched into interplanetary space. At that moment, the moon, instead of appearing flat like a disc, showed its convexity. If the sun's rays had struck it obliquely, the shadow thrown would have brought out the high mountains, which would have been clearly detached. The eye might have gazed into the crater's gaping abysses, and followed the capricious fissures which wound through the immense plains. But all relief was as yet levelled in intense brilliancy. They could scarcely distinguish those large spots which give the the moon the appearance of a human face.

"Face, indeed!" said Michel Ardan; "but I am sorry for the amiable sister of Apollo. A very pitted face!"

But the travellers, now so near the end, were incessantly observing this new world. They imagined themselves walking through its unknown countries, climbing its highest peaks, descending into its lowest depths. Here and there they facied they saw vast seas, scarcely kept together under so rarefied an atmosphere, and watercourses emptying the moutain tributaries. Leaning over the abyss, they hoped to catch some sounds from that orb forever mute in the solitude of space. That last day left them.

They took down the most trifling details. A vague uneasiness took possession of them as they neared the end. This uneasiness would have been doubled had they felt how their speed had decreased. It would have seemed to them quite insufficient to carry them to the end. It was because the projectile then "weighed" almost nothing. Its weight was ever decreasing, and would be entirely annihilated on that line where the lunar and terrestrial attractions would neutralize each other.

But in spite of his preoccupation, Michel Ardan did not forget to prepare the morning repast with his accustomed punctuality. They ate with a good appetite. Nothing was so excellent as the soup liquefied by the heat of the gas; nothing better than the preserved meat. Some glasses of good French wine crowned the repast, causing Michel Ardan to remark that the lunar vines warmed by that ardent sun, ought to distil even more generous wines; that is, if they existed. In any case, the far-seeing Frenchman had taken care not to forget in his collection some precious cuttings of the Médoc and Côte d'Or, upon which he founded his hopes.

Reiset and Regnault's apparatus worked with great regularity. Not an atom of carbonic acid resisted the potash; and as to the oxygen, Captain Nicholl said "it was of the first quality."The little watery vapour enclosed in the projectile mixing with the air tempered the dryness; and many apartments in London, Paris, or New York, and many theatres, were certainly not in such a healthy condition.

But that it might act with regularity, the apparatus must be kept in perfect order; so each morning Michel visited the escape regulators, tried the taps, and regulated the heat of the gas by the pyrometer. Everything had gone well up to that time, and the travellers, imitating the worthy Joseph T. Maston, began to acquire a degree of embonpoint, which would have rendered them unrecognizable if their imprisonment had been prolonged to some months. In a word, they behaved like chickens in a coop; they were getting fat.

In looking through the scuttle Barbicane saw the spectre of the dog, and other divers objects which had been thrown from the projectile obstinately following them. Diana howled lugubriously on seeing the remains of Satellite, which seemed as motionless as if they reposed on the solid earth.

"Do you know, my friends," said Michel Ardan, "that if one of us had succumbed to the shock consequent on departure, we should have had a great deal of trouble to bury him? What an I saying? to *etherize* him, as here ether takes the place of earth. You see the accusing body would have followed us into space like a remorse."

"That would have been sad," said Nicholl.

"Ah!" continued Michel, "what I regret is not being able to take a walk outside. What voluptuousness to float amid this radiant ether, to bathe oneself in it, to wrap oneself in the sun's pure rays. If Barbicane had only thought of furnishing us with a diving apparatus and an air-pump, I could have ventured out and assumed fanciful attitudes of feigned monsters on the top of the projectile."

"Well, old Michel," replied Barbicane, "you would not have made a feigned monster long, for in spite of your diver's dress, swollen by the expansion of air within you, you would have burst like a shell, or rather like a balloon which has risen too high. So do not regret it, and do not forget this—as long as we float in space, all sentimental walks beyond the projectile are forbidden."

Michel Ardan allowed himself to be convinced to a certain extent. He admitted that the thing was difficult but not *impossible*, a word which he never uttered.

It was the body of Satellite.

The conversation passed from this subject to another, not failing for an instant. It seemed to the three friends as though, under present conditions, ideas shot up in their brains as leaves shoot at the first warmth of spring. They felt bewildered. In the middle of the questions and answeres which crossed each other, Nicholl put one question which did not find an immediate solution.

"Ah, indeed!" said he; "it is all very well to go to the moon, but how to get back again?"

His two interlocutors looked surprised. One would have thought that this possibility now occurred to them for the first time.

"What do you mean by that, Nicholl?" asked Barbicane gravely.

"To ask for means to leave a country," added Michel, "when we have not yet arrived there, seems to me rather inopportune."

"I do not say that, wishing to draw back," replied Nicholl; "but I repeat my question, and I ask, 'How shall we return?' "

"I know nothing about it," answered Barbicane.

"And I," said Michel, "if I had known how to return, I would never have started."

"There's an answer!" cried Nicholl.

"I quite approve of Michel's words," said Barbicane; "and add, that the question has no real interest. Later, when we think it advisable to return, we will take counsel together. If the Columbiad is not there, the projectile will be."

"That is a step certainly. A ball without a gun!"

"The gun," replied Barbicane, "can be manufactured. The powder can be made. Neither metals, saltpetre, nor coal can fail in the depths of the moon, and we need only go 8000 leagues in order to fall upon the terrestrial globe by virtue of the mere laws of weight."

"Enough," said Michel with animation. "Let it be no longer a question of returning: we have already entertained it too long. As to communicating with our former earthly colleagues, that will not be difficult."

"And how?"

"By means of meteors launched by lunar volcanos."

"Well thought of, Michel," said Barbicane in a convinced tone of voice. "Laplace has calculated that a force five times greater than that of our gun would suffice to send a meteor from the moon to the earth, and there is not one volcano which has not a greater power of propulsion than that."

"Hurrah!" exclaimed Michel; "these meteors are handy postmen, and cost nothing. And how we shall be able to laugh at the post-office administration. But now I think of it—"

"What do you think of?"

"A capital idea. Why did we not fasten a thread to our projectile, and we could have exchanged telegrams with the earth?"

"The deuce!" answered Nicholl. "Do you consider the weight of a thread 250,000 miles long nothing?"

"As nothing. They could have trebled the Columbiad's charge; they could have quadrupled or quintupled it!" exclaimed Michel, with whom the verb took a higher intonation each time.

"There is but one little objection to make to your proposition," replied Barbicane, "which is that, during the rotary motion of the globe, our thread would have wound itself round it like a chain on a capstan, and that it would inevitably have brought us to the ground."

"I could have ventured out on the top of the projectile."

"By the thirty-nine stars of the Union!" said Michel, "I have nothing but impracticable ideas to-day; ideas worthy of J. T. Maston. But I have a notion that, if we do not return to earth, J. T. Maston will be able to come to us."

"Yes, he'll come," replied Barbicane; "he is a worthy and a courageous comrade. Besides, what is easier? Is not the Columbiad still buried in the soil in Florida? Is cotton and nitric acid wanted wherewith to manufacture the pyroxile? Will not the moon again pass to the zenith of Florida? In eighteen years' time will she not occupy exactly the same place as to-day?"

"Yes," continued Michel, "yes, Maston will come, and with him our friends Elphistone, Blomsberry, all the members of the Gun Club, and they will be well received. And by and by they will run trains of projectiles between the earth and the moon! Hurrah for J. T. Maston!"

It is probable that, if the Hon. J. T. Maston did not hear the hurrahs uttered in his honour, his ears at least tingled. What was he doing then? Doubtless posted in the Rocky Mountains, at the station of Long's Peak, he was trying to find the invisible projectile gravitating in space. If he was thinking of his dear companions, we must allow that they were not far behind him; and that, under the influence of a strange excitement, they were devoting to him their best thoughts.

But whence this excitement, which was evidently growing upon the tenants of the projectile? Their sobriety could not be doubted. This strange irritation of the brain, must it be attributed to the peculiar circumstances under which they found themselves, to their proximity to the orb of night, from which only a few hours seperated them, to some secret influence of the moon acting upon their nervous system? Their faces were as rosy as if they had been exposed to the roaring flames of an oven; their voices resounded in loud accents; their words escaped like a champagne cork driven out by carbonic acid; their gestures became annoying, they wanted so much room to perform them; and, strange to say, that none of them noticed this great tension of the mind.

"Now," said Nicholl, in a short one, "now that I do not know whether we shall ever return from the moon, I want to know what we are going to do there?"

"What we are going to do there?" replied Barbicane, stamping with his foot as if he was in a fencing saloon; "I do not know."

"You do not know!" exclaimed Michel, with a bellow which provoked a sonorous echo in the projectile.

"No, I have not even thought about it," retorted Barbicane, in the same loud tone.

"Well, I know," replied Michel.

"Speak, then," cried Nicholl, who could no longer contain the growling of his voice.

"I shall speak if it suits me," exclaimed Michel, seizing his companions' arms with violence.

"It *must* suit you," said Barbicane, with an eye on fire and a threatening hand. "It was you who drew us into this frightful journey, and we want to know what for."

"Yes," said the captain, "now that I do not know *where* I am going, I want to know *why* I am going."

"Why?" exclaimed Michel, jumping a yard high, "why? To take possession of the moon in the name of the United States; to add a fortieth State to the Union; to colonize the lunar regions; to cultivate them, to people them, to transport thither all the prodigies of art, of science, and industry; to civilize the Selenites, unless they are more civilized than we are; and to constitute them a republic, if they are not already one!"

"And if there are no Selenites?" retorted Nicholl, who, under the influence of this unaccountable intoxication, was very contradictory.

"Who said that there were no Selenites?" exclaimed Michel in a threatening tone.

"I do," howled Nicholl.

"Captain," said Michel, "do not repeat that insolence, or I will knock your teeth down your throat!"

The two adversaries were going to fall upon each other, and the incoherent discussion threatened to merge into a fight, when Barbicane intervened with one bound.

"Stop, miserable men," said he, separating his two companions; "if there are no Selenites, we will do without them."

"Yes," exclaimed Michel, who was not particular; "yes, we will do without them. We have only to make Selenites. Down with the Selenites!"

"The empire of the moon belongs to us," said Nicholl. "Let us three constitute the republic."

"I will be the congress," cried Michel.

"And I the senate," retorted Nicholl.

"And Barbicane, the president," howled Michel.

"Not a president elected by the nation," replied Barbicane.

"Very well, a president elected by the congress," cried Michel; "and as I am the congress, you are unanimously elected!"

"Hurrah! hurrah! hurrah! for President Barbicane," exclaimed Nicholl.

"Hip! hip! hip!" vociferated Michel Ardan.

Then the President and the Senate struck up in a tremendous voice the popular song "Yankee Doodle," whilst from the Congress resounded the masculine tones of the "Marseillaise."

Then they struck up a frantic dance, with maniacal gestures, idiotic stampings, and somersaults like those of the boneless clowns in the circus. Diana, joining in the dance, and howling in her turn, jumped to the top of the projectile. An unaccountable flapping of wings was then heard amidst most fantastic cock-crows, while five or six hens fluttered like bats against the walls.

Then the three travelling companions, acted upon by some unaccountable influence above that of intoxication, inflamed by the air which had set their respiratory apparatus on fire, fell motionless to the bottom of the projectile.

CHAPTER 8

AT SEVENTY-EIGHT THOUSAND FIVE HUNDRED AND FOURTEEN LEAGUES

WHAT had happened? Whence the cause of this singular intoxication, the consequences of which might have been very disastrous? A simple blunder of Michel's, which, fortunately, Nicholl was able to correct in time.

After a perfect swoon, which lasted some minutes, the captain, recovering first, soon collected his scattered senses. Although he had breakfasted only two hours before, he felt a gnawing hunger, as if he had not eaten anything for several days. Everything about him, stomach and brain, were overexcited to the highest degree. He got up and demanded from Michel a supplementary repast. Michel, utterly done up, did not answer.

Nicholl then tried to prepare some tea destined to help the absorption of a dozen sandwiches. He first tried to get some fire, and struck a match sharply. What was his surprise to see the sulphur shine with so extraordinary a brilliancy as to be almost unbearable to the eye. From the gas-burner which he lit rose a flame equal to a jet of electric light.

A revelation dawned on Nicholl's mind. That intensity of light, the physiological troubles which had arisen in him, the overexcitement of all his moral and quarrelsome faculities,—he understood all.

"The oxygen!" he exclaimed.

And leaning over the air apparatus, he saw that the tap was allowing the scentless colourless gas to escape freely, life-giving, by in its pure state producing the gravest disorders in the system. Michel had blunderingly opened the tap of the apparatus to the full.

Nicholl hastened to stop the escape of oxygen with which the atmosphere was saturated, which would have been the death of the travellers, not by suffocation, but by combustion. An hour later, the air less charged with it restored the lungs to their normal condition. By degrees the three friends recovered from their intoxication; but they were obliged to sleep themselves sober over their oxygen, as a drunkard does over his wine.

When Michel learnt his share of the responsiblity of this incident, he was not much disconcerted. This unexpected drunkeness broke the monotony of the journey. Many foolish things had been said while under its influence, but also quickly forgotten.

"And then," added the merry Frenchman, "I am not sorry to have tasted a little of this heady gas. Do you know, my friends, that a curious establishment might be founded with rooms of oxygen, where people whose system is weakened could for a few hours live a more active life. Fancy parties where the room was saturated with this heroic fluid, theatres where it should be kept at high pressure; what passion in the souls of the actors and spectators! what fire, what enthusiasm! And if, instead of an assembly only a whole people could be saturated, what activity in its functions, what a supplement to life it would derive. From an exhausted nation they might make a great and strong one, and I know more than one state in old Europe which ought to put itself under the regime of oxygen for the sake of its health!"

Michel spoke with so much animation, that one might have fancied that the tap was still open. But a few words from Barbicane soon scattered his enthusiasm.

"That is all very well, friend Michel," said he, "but will you inform us where these chickens came from which have mixed themselves up in our concert?'

"Those chickens?"

"Yes."

Indeed, half a dozen chickens and a fine cock were walking about, flapping their wings and chattering.

"Ah, the awkward things!" exclaimed Michel. "The oxygen has made them revolt."

"But what do you want to do with these chickens?" asked Barbicane.

"To acclimatize them in the moon, by Jove!"

"Then why did you hide them?"

"A joke, my worthy president, a simple joke, which has proved a miserable failure. I wanted to set them free on the lunar continent, without saying anything. Oh, what would have been your amazement of seeing these earth-winged animals pecking in the lunar fields!"

"You rascal, you unmitigated rascal," replied Barbicane, "*you* do not want oxygen to mount to the head. You are always what *we* were under the influence of the gas; you are always foolish!"

"Ah, who says that we were not wise then?" replied Michel Ardan.

After this philosophical reflection, the three friends set about restoring the order of the projectile. Chickens and cock were reinstated in their coup. But whilst proceeding with this operation, Barbicane and his two companions had a most desired perception of a new phenomenon. From the moment of leaving the earth, their own weight, that of the projectile, and the objects it enclosed, had been subject to an increasing diminution. If they could not prove this loss of the projectile, a moment would arrive when it would be sensibly felt upon themselves and the utensils and instruments they used.

It is needless to say that a *scale* would not show this loss; for the weight destined to weigh the object would have lost exactly as much as the object itself; but a spring steelyard for example, the tension of which was independent of the attraction, would have given a just estimate of this loss.

We know that the attraction, otherwise called the *weight*, is in proportion to the densities of bodies, and inversely as the squares of the distances. Hence this effect: If the earth had been alone in space, if the other celestial bodies had been suddenly annihilated, the projectile, according to Newton's laws, would weigh less as it got farther from the earth, but without ever losing its weight *entirely*, for the terrestrial attraction would always have made itself felt, at whatever distance.

But, in reality, a time must come when the projectile would no longer be subject to the law of weight, after allowing for the other celestial bodies whose effect could not be set down as zero. Indeed, the projectile's course was being traced between the earth and the moon. As it distanced the earth, the terrestrial attraction diminished: but the lunar attraction rose in proportion. There must then come a point where these two attractions would neutralize each other: the projectile would possess weight no longer. If the moon's and the earth's densities had been equal, this point would have been at an equal distance between the two orbs. But taking the different densities into consideration, it was easy to reckon that this point would be situated at 47-60ths of the whole journey, i.e. at 78,114 leagues from the earth. At this point, a body having no principle of speed or displacement in itself, would remain immovable for ever, being attracted equally by both orbs, and not being drawn more towards one than towards the other.

Now if the projectile's impulsive force had been correctly calculated, it would attain this point without speed, having lost all trace of weight, as well as all the objects within it. What would happen then? Three hypotheses presented themselves.

1. Either it would retain a certain amount of motion, and pass the point of equal attraction, and fall upon the moon by virtue of the excess of the lunar attraction over the terrestiral.

2. Or, its speed failing and unable to reach the point of equal attraction, it

would fall upon the moon by virtue of the excess of the lunar attraction over the terrestrial.

3. Or, lastly, animated with sufficient speed to enable it to reach the neutral point, but not sufficient to pass it, it would reamin for ever suspended in that spot like the pretended tomb of Mahomet, between the zenith and the nadir.

Such was their situation; and Barbicane clearly explained the consequnces to his travelling companions, which greatly interested them. But how should they know when the projectile had reached this neutral point situated at that distance, especially when neither themselves, nor the objects enclosed in the projectile, would be any longer subject to the laws of weight?

Up to this time, the travellers, whilst admitting that this action was constantly decreasing, had not yet become sensible to its total absence.

But that day, about eleven o'clock in the morning, Nicholl having accidentally let a glass slip from his hand, the glass, instead of falling, reamined suspended in the air.

"Ah!" exclaimed Michel Ardan, "that is rather an amusing piece of natural philosphy."

And immediately divers other objects, firearms and bottles, abandoned to themselves, held themselves up as by enchantment. Diana too, placed in space by Michel, reproduced, but without any trick, the wonderful suspension practised by Caston and Robert Houdin. Indeed the dog did not seem to know that she was floating in air.

The three adventurous companions were surprised and stupefied, despite their scientific reasonings. They felt themselves being carried into the domain of wonders! they felt that *weight* was really wanting to their bodies. If they stretched out their arms, they did not attempt to fall. Their heads shook on their shoulders. Their feet no longer clung to the floor of the projectile. They were like drunken men having no stability in themselves.

Fancy has despicted men without reflection, others without shadow. But here *reality*, by the neutralisation of attrative forces, produced men in whom nothing had any weight, and who weighed nothing themselves.

Suddenly Michel, taking a spring, left the floor and remained suspended in the air, like Murillo's monk of the *Cusine des Anges*.

The two friends joined him instantly, and all three formed a miraculous "Ascension" in the centre of the projectile.

"Is it to be believed? is it probable? is it possible?" exclaimed Michel; "and yet it is so. Ah! if Raphael had seen us thus, what an 'Assumption' he would have thrown upon canvas!"

"The 'Assumption' cannot last," replied Barbicane. "If the projectile passes the neutral point, the lunar attraction will draw us to the moon."

"Then our feet will be upon the roof," replied Michel.

"No," said Barbicane, "because the projectile's centre of gravity is very low; it will only turn by degrees."

"Then all our portables will be upset from top to bottom, that is a fact."

"Calm yourself, Michel," replied Nicholl; "no upset is to be feared; not a thing will move, for the projectile's evolution will be imperceptible."

"Just so," continued Barbicane; "and when it has passed the point of equal attraction, its base, being the heavier, will draw it perpendicularly to the moon; but, in order that this phenomenon should take place, we must have passed the neutral line."

"Ah! If Raphael had seen us thus."

"Pass the neutral line!" cried Michel; "then let us do as the sailors do when they cross the equator."

A slight side movement brought Michel back towards the padded side; thence he took a bottle and glasses, placed them "in space" before his companions, and drinking merrily, they saluted the line with a triple hurrah. The influence of these attractions scarcely lasted an hour; the travellers felt themselves insensibly drawn towards the floor, and Barbicane fancied that the conical end of the projectile was varying a little from its normal direction towards the moon. By an inverse motion the base was approaching first; the lunar attraction was prevailing over the terrestrial; the fall towards the moon was beginning, almost imperceptibly as yet, but by degrees the attractive force would become stronger, the fall would be more decided, the projectile, drawn by its base, would turn its cone to the earth, and fall with ever-increasing speed on to the surface of the Selenite continent; their destination would then be attained. Now nothing could prevent the success of their enterprise, and Nicholl and Michel Ardan shared Barbicane's joy.

Then they chatted of all the phenomena which had astonished them one after the other, particularly the neutraliztion of the laws of weight. Michel Ardan, always enthusiastic, drew conclusions which were purely fanciful.

"Ah, my worthy friends," he exclaimed, "what progress we should make if on earth we could throw off some of that weight, some of that chain which binds us to her; it would be the prisoner set at liberty; no more fatigue of either arms or legs. Or, if it is true that in order to fly on the earth's surface, to keep oneself suspended in the air merely by the play of the muscles, there requires a strength a hundred and fifty times greater than that which we possess, a simple act of volition, a caprice, would bear us into space, if attraction did not exist."

"Just so," said Nicholl, smiling; "if we could succeed in suppressing weight as they suppress pain by anæsthesia, that would change the face of modern society!"

"Yes," cried Michel, full of his subject, "destroy weight, and no more burdens!"

"Well said," replied Barbicane; "but if nothing had any weight, nothing would keep in its place, not even your hat on your head, worthy Michel; nor your house, whose stones only adhere by weight; not a boat, whose stability on the water is caused only be weight; not even the ocean, whose waves would no longer be equalized by terrestiral attraction; and lastly, not even the *atmosphere*, whose atoms, being no longer held in their places, would disperse in space!"

"That is tiresome," retorted Michel; "nothing like these matter-of-fact people for bringing one back to the bare reality."

"But console yourself, Michel," continued Barbicane, "for if no orb exists from whence all laws of weight are banished, you are at least going to visit one where it is much less than on the earth."

"The moon?"

"Yes, the moon, on whose surface objects weight six times less than on the earth, a phenomenon easy to prove."

"And we shall feel it?" asked Michel.

"Evidently, as 200lbs. will only weigh 30lbs. on the surface of the moon."

"And our muscular strength will not diminish?"

"Not at all; instead of jumping one yard high, you will rise eighteen feet high."

"But we shall be regular Herculeses in the moon!" exclaimed Michel.

"Yes," replied Nicholl, "for if the height of the Selenites is in proportion to the density of their globe, they will be scarcely a foot high."

"Lilliputians!" ejaculated Michel; "I shall play the part of Gulliver. We are going to realize the fable of the giants. This is the advantage of leaving one's own planet and overrunning the solar world."

"One moment, Michel," answered Barbicane; "if you wish to play the part of Gulliver, only visit the inferior planets, such as Mercury, Venus, or Mars, whose density is a little less than that of the earth; but do not venture into the great planets, Jupiter, Sturn, Uranus, Neptune; for there the order will be changed, and *you* will become Lilliputian."

"And in the sun?"

"In the sun, if its density is thirteen hundred and twenty-four thousand times greater, and the attraction is twenty-seven times greater than on the surface of our globe, keeping everything in proportion, the inhabitants ought to be at least two hundred feet high."

"By Jove!" exclaimed Michel; "I should be nothing more than a pigmy, a shrimp!"

"Gulliver with the giants," said Nicholl.

"Just so," replied Barbicane.

"And it would not be quite useless to carry some pieces of artillery to defend oneself."

"Good," replied Nicholl; "your projectiles would have no effect on the sun; they would fall back on the earth after some minutes."

"That is a strong remark."

"It is certain," replied Barbicane; "the attraction is so great on this enormous orb, that an object weighing 70,000lbs. on the earth would weight but 1920lbs. on the surface of the sun. If you were to fall upon it you would weigh—let me see—about 5000lbs., a weight which you would never be able to raise again."

"The devil!" said Michel; "one would want a portable crane. However, we will be satisfied with the moon for the present; there at least we shall cut a great figure. We will see about the sun by and by."

CHAPTER 9

THE CONSEQUENCES OF A DEVIATION

BARBICANE had now no fear of the issue of the journey, at least as far as the projectile's impulsive force was concerned; its own speed would carry it beyond the neutral line; it would certainly not return to earth; it would certainly not remain motionless on the line of attraction. One single hypothesis remained to be realized, the arrival of the projectile at its destination by the action of the lunar attraction.

It was in reality a fall of 8296 leagues on an orb, it is true, where weight could only be reckoned at one-sixth of terrestrial weight; a formidable fall, nevertheless, and one against which every precaution must be taken without delay.

These precautions were of two sorts, some to deaden the shock when the projectile should touch the lunar soil, others to delay the fall, and consequently make it less violent.

To deaden the shock, it was a pity that Barbicane was no longer able to employ the means which had so ably weakened the shock at departure, that is to say, by water used as springs and the partition-breaks.

The partitions still existed but water failed, for they could not use their reserve, which was precious, in case during the first days the liquid element should be found wanting on lunar soil.

And indeed this reserve would have been quite insufficient for a spring. The layer of water stored in the projectile at their departure, and on which the waterproof disc lay, occupied no less than three feet in depth, and spread over a surface of not less than fifty-four square feet. Besides, the cistern did not contain one fifth part of it; they must therefore give up this efficient means of deadening the shock of arrival. Happily, Barbicane, not content with employing water, had furnished the movable disc with strong spring plugs, destined to lessen the shock against the base after the breaking of the horizontal partitions. These plugs still existed; they had only to readjust them and replace the movable disc; every piece, easy to handle, as their weight was now scarcely felt, was quickly mounted.

The different pieces were fitted without trouble, it being only a matter of bolts and screws; tools were not wanting, and soon the reinstated disc lay on its steel plugs, like a table on its legs. One inconvenience resulted from the replacing of the disc, the lower window was blocked up; thus it was impossible for the travellers to observe the moon from that opening while they were being precipitated perpendicularly upon her; but they were obliged to give it up; even by the side openings they could still see vast lunar regions, as an aëronaut sees the earth from his car.

This replacing of the disc was at least an hour's work. It was past twelve when all preparations were finished. Barbicane took fresh observations of the inclination of the projectile, but to his annoyance it had not turned over sufficiently for its fall; it seemed to take a curve parallel to the lunar disc. The orb of night shone splendidly into space, whilst, opposite, the orb of day blazed with fire.

Their situation began to make them uneasy.

"Are we reaching our destination?" asked Nicholl.

"Let us act as if we were about reaching it," replied Barbicane.

"You are sceptical," retorted Michel Ardan. "We shall arrive, and that, too, quicker than we like."

This answer brought Barbicane back to his preparations, and he occupied himself with placing the contrivances intended to break their descent. We may remember the scene of the meeting held at Tampa Town, in Florida, when Captain Nicholl came forward as Barbicane's enemy and Michel Ardan's adversary. To Captain Nicholl's maintaining that the projectile would smash like glass, Michel replied that he would break their fall by means of rockets properly placed.

Thus, powerful fireworks, taking their starting-point from the base and bursting outside, could, by producing a recoil, check to a certain degree the projectile's speed. These rockets were to burn in space, it is true; but oxygen would not fail them, for they could supply themselves with it, like the lunar volcanoes, the burning of which has never yet been stopped by the want of atmosphere round the moon.

Barbicane had accordingly supplied himself with these fireworks, enclosed in little steel guns, which could be screwed on to the base of the projectile. Inside, these guns were flush with the bottom; outside, they protruded about eighteen inches. There were twenty of them. An opening left in the disc allowed them to light the match with which each was provided. All the effect was felt outside. The burning mixture had been already rammed into each gun. They had, then, nothing to do but to raise the metallic buffers fixed in the base, and replace them by the guns, which fitted closely in their places.

This new work was finished about three o'clock, and after taking all these precautions there remained but to wait. But the projectile was perceptibly nearing the moon, and evidently succumbed to her influence to a certain degree; though its own velocity also drew it in an oblique direction. From these conflicting influences resulted a line which might become a tangent. But it was certain that the projectile would not fall directly on the moon; for its lower part, by reason of its weight, ought to be turned towards her.

Barbicane's uneasiness increased as he saw his projectile resist the influence of gravitation. The Unknown was opening before him, the Unknown in interplanetary space. The man of science thought he had foreseen the only three hypotheses possible—the return to the earth, the return to the moon, or stagnation on the neutral line; and here a fourth hypothesis, big with all the terrors of the Infinite, surged up inopportunely. To face it without flinching, one must be a resolute savant like Barbicane, a phlegmatic being like Nicholl, or an audacious adventurer like Michel Ardan.

Conversation was started upon this subject. Other men would have considered the question from a practical point of view; they would have asked themselves whither their projectile carriage was carrying them. Not so with these; they sought for the cause which produced this effect.

"So we have become diverted from our route," said Michel; "but why?

"I very much fear," answered Nicholl, "that, in spite of all precautions taken, the Columbiad was not fairly pointed. An error, however small, would be enough to throw us out of the moon's attraction."

"Then they must have aimed badly?" asked Michel.

"I do not think so," replied Barbicane. "The perpendicularity of the gun was exact, its direction to the zenith of the spot incontestible; and the moon passing to the zenith of the spot, we ought to reach it at the full. There is another reason, but it escapes me."

"Are we not arriving too late?" asked Nicholl.

"Too late?" said Barbicane.

"Yes," continued Nicholl. "The Cambridge Observatory's note says that the transit ought to be accomplished in ninety-seven hours thirteen minutes and twenty seconds; which means to say, that *sooner* the moon will *not* be at the point indicated, and that *later* it will have passed it."

"True," replied Barbicane. "But we started the 1st of December, at thirteen minutes and twenty-five seconds to eleven at night; and we ought to arrive on the 5th at midnight, at the exact moment when the moon would be full; and we are now at the 5th of December. It is now half past three in the evening; half past eight ought to see us at the end of our journey. Why do we not arrive?"

"Might it not be an excess of speed?" answered Nicholl; "for we know now that its initial velocity was greater than they supposed."

"No! a hundred times, No!" replied Barbicane. "An excess of speed, if the direction of the projectile had been right, would not have prevented us reaching the moon. No, there has been a deviation. We have been turned out of our course."

"By whom? by what?" asked Nicholl.

"I cannot say," replied Barbicane.

"Very well, then, Barbicane," said Michel, "do you wish to know my opinion on the subject of finding out this deviation?"

"Speak."

"I would not give half a dollar to know it. That we *have* diviated is *a fact*. Where we are going to matters little; we shall soon see. Since we are being borne along in space we shall end by falling into some centre of attraction or other."

Michel Ardan's indifference did not content Barbicane. Not that he was uneasy about the future, but he wanted to know at any cost *why* his projectile had deviated.

But the projectile continued its course sideways to the moon, and with it the mass of things thrown out. Barbicane could even prove, by the elevations which served as landmarks upon the moon, which was only 2000 leagues distant, that its speed was becoming uniform—fresh proof that there was no fall. Its impulsive force still prevailed over the lunar attraction, but the projectile's course was certainly bringing it nearer to the moon, and they might hope that at a nearer point the weight, predominating, would cause a decided fall.

The three friends, having nothing better to do, continued their observations; but they could not yet determine the topographical position of the satellite; every relief was levelled under the reflection of the solar rays.

They watched thus through the side windows until eight o'clock at night. The moon had then grown so large in their eyes that it filled half of the firmament. The sun on one side, and the orb of night on the other, flooded the projectile with light.

At that moment, Barbicane thought he could estimate the distance which seperated them from their aim at no more than 700 leagues. The speed of the projectile seemed to him to be more than 200 yards, or about 170 leagues a second. Under the centripetal force, the base of the projectile tended towards the moon; but the centrifugal still prevailed; and it was probable that its rectilineal course would be changed to a curve of some sort, the nature of which they could not at present determine.

Barbicane was still seeking the solution of his insoluble problem. Hours passed without any result. The projectile was evidently *nearing* the moon, but it was also evident that it would never *reach* her. As to the nearest distance at which it would pass her, that must be the result of the two forces, attraction and repulsion, affecting its motion.

"I ask but one thing," said Michel; "that we may pass near enough to penetrate her secrets."

"Cursed be the thing that has caused our projectile to deviate from its course," cried Nicholl.

And, as if a light had suddenly broken in upon his mind, Barbicane answered, "Then cursed be the meteor which crossed our path."

"What?" said Michel Ardan.

"What do you mean?" exclaimed Nicholl.

"I mean," said Barbicane in a decided tone, "I mean that our deviation is owing solely to our meeting with this erring body."

"But it did not even brush us as it passed," said Michel.

"What does that matter? Its mass, compared to that of our projectile, was enormous, and its attraction was enough to influence our course."

"So little?" cried Nicholl.

"Yes, Nicholl; but however little it might be," replied Barbicane, "in a distance of 84,000 leagues, it wanted no more to make us miss the moon."

CHAPTER 10

THE OBSERVERS OF THE MOON

BARBICANE had evidently hit upon the only plausible reason of this deviation. However slight it might have been, it had sufficed to modify the course of the projectile. It was a fatality. The bold attempt had miscarred by a fortuitous circumstance; and unless by some exceptional event, they could now never reach the moon's disc.

Would they pass near enough to be able to solve certain physical and geological questions until then insoluble? This was the question, and the only one, which occupied the minds of these bold travellers. As to the fate in store for themselves, they did not even dream of it.

But what would become of them amid these infinite solitudes, these who would soon want air? A few more days, and they would fall stifled in this wandering projectile. But some days to these intrepid fellows was a centruy; and they devoted all their time to observe that moon which they no longer hoped to reach.

The distance which then separated the projectile from the satellite was estimated at about 200 leagues. Under these conditions, as regards the visibility of the details of the disc, the travellers were farther from the moon than are the inhabitants of the earth with their powerful telescopes.

Indeed, we know that the instrument mounted by Lord Rosse at Parsonstown, which magnifies 6500 times, brings the moon to within an apparent distance of sixteen leagues. And more than that, with the powerful one set up at Long's Peak, the orb of night, magnified 48,000 times, is brought to within less than two leagues, and objects having a diameter of thirty feet are seen very distinctly. So that, at this distance, the topographical details of the moon, observed without glasses, could not be determined with precision. The eye caught the vast outline of those immense depressions inappropriately called "seas," but they could not recognize their nature. The prominence of the mountains disappeared under the splendid irradiation produced by the reflection of the solar rays. The eye, dazzled as if it was leaning over a bath of molten silver, turned from it involuntarily; but the oblong form of the orb was quite clear. It appeared like a gigantic egg, with the small end turned towards the earth. Indeed the moon, liquid and pliable in the first days of its formation, was originally a perfect sphere; but, being soon drawn within the attraction of the earth, it became elongated under the influence of gravitation. In becoming a satellite, she lost her native purity of form; her centre of gravity was in advance of the centre of her figure; and from this fact some savants draw the conclusion that the air and water had taken refuge on the opposite surface of the moon, which is never seen from the earth. This alteration in the primitive form of the satellite was only perceptible for a few moments. The distance of the projectile from the moon diminished very rapidly under its speed, though that was much less than its initial velocity,—but eight or nine times greater than that which propels our express trains. The oblique course of the projectile, from its very obliquity, gave Michel Ardan some hopes of striking the lunar disc at some point or other. He could not think that they would never reach it. No! he could not believe it; and this opinion he often repeated. But Barbicane, who was a better judge, always answered him with merciless logic.

"No, Michel, no! We can only reach the moon by a fall, and we are not falling. The centripetal force keeps us under the moon's influence, but the centrifugal force draws us irresistibly away from it."

This was said in a tone which quenched Michel Ardan's last hope.

The portion of the moon which the projectile was nearing was the northern hemisphere, that which the Selenographic maps place below; for these maps are generally drawn after the outline given by the glasses, and we know that they reverse the objects. Such was the *Mappa Selenographica* of Bœer and Moedler which Barbicane consultled. This northern hemisphere presented vast plains, dotted with isolated mountains.

At midnight the moon was full. At that precise moment the travellers should have alighted upon it, if the mischievous meteor had not diverted their course. The orb was exactly in the condition determined by the Cambridge Observatory. It was mathematically at its perigee, and at the zenith of the twenty-eighth parallel. An observer placed at the bottom of the enormous Columbiad, pointed perpendicularly to the horizon, would have framed the moon in the mouth of the gun. A straight line drawn through the axis of the piece would have passed through the centre of the orb of night. It is needless to say, that during the night of the 5th—6th of December, the travellers took not an instant's rest. Could they close their eyes when so near this new world? No! All their feelings were concentrated in one single thought:—See! Representatives of the earth, of humanity, past and present, all centred in them! It is through their eyes that the human race look at these lunar regions, and penetrate the secrets of their satellite! A strange emotion filled their hearts as they went from one window to the other.

Their observations, reproduced by Barbicane, were rigidly determined. To take them, they had glasses; to correct them, maps.

As regards the optical instruments at their disposal, they had excellent marine glasses specially constructed for this journey. They possessed magnifying poweres of 100. They would thus have brought the moon to within a distance (apparent) of less than 2000 leagues from the earth. But then, at a distance which for three hours in the morning did not exceed sixty-five miles, and in a medium free from all atmospheric disturbances, these instruments could reduce the lunar surface to within less than 1500 yards!

CHAPTER 11

FANCY AND REALITY

"HAVE you seen the moon?" asked a professor, ironically, of one of his pupils.

"No, sir!" replied the pupil, still more ironically, "but I must say I have heard it spoken of."

In one sense, the pupil's witty answer might be given by a large majority of sublunary beings. How many people have heard speak of the moon, who have never seen it—at least through a glass or a telescope! How many have never examined the map of their satellite!

In looking at a selenographic map, one peculiarity strikes us. Contrary to the arrangement followed for that of the Earth and Mars, the continents occupy more particularly the southern hemisphere of the lunar globe. These continents do not show such decided, clear, and regular boundary lines as South America, Africa, and the Indian peninsula. Their angular, capricious, and deeply indented coasts, are rich in gulfs and peninsulas. They remind one of the confusion in the islands of the Sound, where the land is excessively indented. If navigation ever existed on the surface of the moon, it must have been wonderfully difficult and dangerous; and we may well pity the Selenite sailors and hydrographers; the former, when they came upon these perilous coasts, the latter, when they took the soundings of its stormy banks.

We may also notice that, on the lunar sphere, the south pole is much more continental than the north pole. On the latter, there is but one slight strip of land seperated from other continents by vast seas. Towards the south, continents clothe almost the whole of the hemisphere. It is even possible that the Selenites have already planted the flag on one of their poles, whilst Franklin, Ross, Kane, Dumont d'Urville, and Lambert, have never yet been able to attain that unknown point of the terrestrial globe.

As to islands, they are numerous on the surface of the moon. Nearly all oblong or circular, and as if traced with the compass, they seem to form one vast Archipelago, equal to that charming group lying between Greece and Asia Minor, and which mythology in ancient times adorned with most graceful legends. Involuntarily the names of Noxos, Tenedos, and Carpathos, rise before the mind, and we seek vainly for Ulysses' vessel or the "clipper" of the Argonauts. So at least it was in Michel Ardan's eyes. To him it was a Grecian Archipelago that he saw on the map. To the eyes of his matter-of-fact companions, the aspect of these coasts recalled rather the parcelled-out land of New Brunswick and Nova Scotia; and where the Frenchman discovered traces of the heroes of fable, these Americans were marking the most favourable points for the establishment of stores in the interest of lunar commerce and industry.

After wandering over these vast continents, the eye is attracted by still greater seas. Not only their formation, but their situation and aspect remind one of the terrestrial oceans; but again, as on earth, these seas occupy the greater portion of the globe. But in point of fact, these are not liquid spaces, but plains, the nature of which the travellers hoped soon to determine. Astronomers, we must allow, have graced these pretended seas with at least odd names, which science has respected up to the present time. Michel Ardan was right when he compared this man to a "Tendre card," got up by a Scundary or a Cyrano de Bergerac. "Only," said he, "it is no longer the sentimental card of the seventeenth century, it is the card of life, very neatly divided into two parts, one feminine, the other masculine; the right hemisphere for woman, the left for man."

In speaking thus, Michel made his prosaic companions shrug their shoulders. Barbicane and Nicholl looked upon the lunar map from a very different point of view to that of their fantastic friend. Nevertheless, their fantastic friend was a little in the right. Judge for yourselves.

In the left hemisphere stretches the "Sea of Clouds," where human reason is so often shipwrecked. Not far off lies the "Sea of Rains," fed by all the fever of existence. Near this is the "Sea of Storms," where man is ever fighting against his passions, which too often gain the victory. Then, worn out be deceit, treasons, infidelity, and the whole body of terrestrial misery, what does he find at the end of his career? that vast "Sea of Humours," barely softened by some drops of the waters from the "Gulf of Dew!" Clouds, rain, storms, and humours,—does the life of man contain aught but these? and is it not summed up in these four words?

The right hemisphere, "dedicated to the ladies," encloses smaller seas, whose significant names contain every incident of a feminine existence. There is the "Sea of Serenity," over which the young girl bends; "The Lake of Dreams," reflecting a joyous future; the "Sea of Nectar," with its waves of tenderness and breezes of love; "The Sea of Fruitfulness;" "The Sea of Crises;" then the "Sea of Vapours," whose dimensions are perhaps a little too confined; and lastly, that vast "Sea of Tranquillity," in which every false passion, every useless dream, every unsatisifed desire is at length absorbed, and whose waves emerge peaceably into the "Lake of Death!"

What a strange succession of names! What a singular division of the moon's two hemispheres, joined to one another like man and woman, and forming that sphere of life carried into space! And was not the fantastic Michel right in thus interpreting the fancies of the ancient astronomers? But whilst his imagination thus roved over "the seas," his grave companions were considering things more geographically. They were learning this new world by heart. They were measuring angles and diameters.

CHAPTER 12

OROGRAPHIC DETAILS

THE course taken by the projectile, as we have before remarked, was bearing it towards the moon's northern hemisphere. The travellers were far from the central point which they would have struck, had their course not been subject to an irremediable deviation. It was past midnight; and Barbicane then estimated the distance at 750 miles, which was a little greater than the length of the lunar radius, and which would diminish as it advanced nearer to the North Pole. The projectile was then not at the altitude of the equator; but across the tenth parallel, and from that latitude, carefully taken on the map to the pole, Barbicane and his two companions were able to observe the moon under the most favourable conditions. Indeed, by means of glasses, the above named distance was reduced to little more than fourteen miles. The telescope of the Rocky Mountains brought the moon much nearer; but the terrestrial atmosphere singularly lessened its power. Thus Barbicane, posted in his projectile, with the glasses to his eyes, could seize upon details which were almost imperceptible to earthly observers.

"My friends," said the president, in a serious voice, "I do not know whither we are going; I do not know if we shall ever see the terrestrial globe again. Nevertheless, let us proceed as if our work would one day be useful to our fellow-men. Let us keep our minds free from every other consideration. We are astronomers; and this projectile is a room in the Cambridge University, carried into space. Let us make our observations!"

This said, work was begun with great exactness; and they faithfully reproduced the different aspects of the moon, at the different distances which the projectile reached.

At the time that the projectile was as high as the tenth parallel, N. latitude, it seemed rigidly to follow the twentieth degree, E. longitude. We must here make one important remark with regard to the map by which they were takling observations. In the selenographical maps where, on account of the reversing of the objects by the glasses, the south is above and the north below, it would seem natural that, on account of that inversion, the east should be to the left hand, and the west to the right. But it is not so. If the map were turned upside down, showing the moon as we see her, the east would be to the *left*, and the west to the *right*, contrary to that which exists on terrestrial maps. The following is the reason of this anomaly. Observers in the northern hemisphere (say in Europe) see the moon in the south,—according to them. When they take observations, they turn their backs to the north, the reverse position to that which they occupy when they study a terrestrial map. As they turn their backs to the north, the east is on their left, and the west to their right. To observers in the southern hemisphere (Patagonia for example), the moon's west would be quite to their left, and the east to their right, as the south is behind them. Such is the reason of the apparent reversing of these two cardinal points, and we must bear it in mind in order to be able to follow President Barbicane's observations.

With the help of Bœer and Moedler's *Mappa Selenographica*, the travellers were able at once to recognize that portion of the disc enclosed within the field of their glasses.

"What are we looking at, at this moment?" asked Michel.

"At the northern part of the 'Sea of Clouds,'" answered Barbicane. "We are too far off to recognize its nature. Are these plains composed of arid sand, as the first astronomer maintained? Or are they nothing but immense forests, according to M. Warren de la Rue's opinion, who gives the moon an atmosphere, though a very low and a very dense one? That we shall know by and by. We must affirm nothing until we are in a position to do so."

This "Sea of Clouds" is rather doubtfully marked out upon the maps. It is supposed that these vast plains are strewn with blocks of lava from the neighbouring volcanoes on its right, Ptolemy, Purback, Arzachel. But the projectile was advancing, and sensibly nearing it. Soon there appeared the heights which bound this sea at this northern limit. Before them rose a mountain radiant with beauty, the top of which seemed lost in an eruption of solar rays.

"That is—?" asked Michel.

"Copernicus," replied Barbicane.

"Let us see Copernicus."

This mount situated in 9° north latitude and 20° east longitude, rose to a height of 10,600 feet above the surface of the moon. It is quite visible from the earth; and astronomers can study it with ease, particularly during the phase between the last quarter and the new moon, because then the shadows are thrown lengthways from east to west, allowing them to measure the heights.

This Copernicus forms the most important of the radiating system, situated in the southern hemisphere, according to Tycho Brahé. It rises isolated like a gigantic lighthouse on that portion of the Sea of Clouds, which is bounded by the "Sea of Tempests," thus lighting by its splendid rays two oceans at a time. It was a sight without an equal, those long luminous trains, so dazzling in the full moon, and which, passing the boundary chain on the north, extends to the "Sea of Rains." At one o'clock of the terrestiral morning, the projectile, like a balloon borne into space, overlooked the top of this superb mountain. Barbicane could recognize perfectly its chief features. Copernicus is comprised in the series of ringed mountains of the first order, in the division of great circles. Like Kepler and Aristarchus, which overlook the Ocean of Tempests, sometimes it appeared like a brilliant point through the cloudy light, and was taken for a volcano in activity. But it is only an extinct one,—like all on that side of the moon. Its circumference showed a diameter of about twenty-two leagues. The glasses discovered traces of stratification produced by successive eruptions, and the neighbourhood was strewn with volcanic remains which still choked some of the craters.

"There exist," said Barbicane, "several kinds of circles on the surface of the moon, and it is easy to see that Copernicus belongs to the radiating class. If we were nearer, we should see the cones bristling on the inside, which in former times were so many fiery mouths. A curious arrangement, and one without an exception on the lunar disc, is that the interior surface of these circles is the reverse of the exterior, and contrary to the form taken by terrestrial craters. It follows, then, that the general curve of the bottom of these circles gives a sphere of a smaller diameter than that of the moon."

"And why this peculiar disposition?" asked Nicholl.

"We do not know," replied Barbicane.

"What splendid radiation!" said Michel. "One could hardly see a finer spectacle, I think."

"What would you say, then," replied Barbicane, "if chance should bear us towards the southern hemisphere?"

"Well, I should say that it was still more beautiful," retorted Michel Ardan.

At this moment the projectile hung perpendicularly over the circle. The circumference of Copernicus formed almost a perfect circle, and its steep escarpments were clearly defined. They could even distinguish a second ringed enclosure. Around spread a greyish plain, of a wild aspect, on which every relief was marked in yellow. At the bottom of the circle, as if enclosed in a jewel case, sparkled for one instant two or three eruptive cones, like enormous dazzling gems. Towards the north the escarpments were lowered by a depression which would probably have given access to the interior of the crater.

"This plain would then be nothing but an immense cemetery."

In passing over the surrounding plains, Barbicane noticed a great number of less important mountains; and among others a little ringed one called Guy Lussac, the breadth of which measured twelve miles.

Towards the south, the plain was very flat, without one elevation, without one projection. Towards the north, on the contrary, till where it was bounded by the Sea of Storms it resembled a liquid surface agitated by a storm, of which the hills and hollows formed a succession of waves suddenly congealed. Over the whole of this, and in all directions, lay the luminous lines, all converging to the summit of Copernicus.

The travellers discussed the origin of these strange rays; but they could not determine their nature any more than terrestrial observers.

"But why," said Nicholl, "should not these rays be simply spurs of mountains which reflect more vividly the light of the sun?"

"No," replied Barbicane; "if it was so, under certain conditions of the moon, these ridges would cast shadows, and they do not casy any."

And indeed, these rays only appeared when the orb of day was in opposition to the moon, and disappeared as soon as its rays became oblique.

"But how have they endeavoured to explain these lines of light?" asked Michel; "for I cannot believe that savants would ever be stranded for want of an explanation."

"Yes," replied Barbicane; "Herschel has put forward an opinion, but he did not venture to affirm it."

"Never mind. What was the opinion?"

"He thought that these rays might be streams of cooled lava which shone when the sun beats straight upon them. It may be so; but nothing can be less certain. Besides, if we pass nearer to Tycho, we shall be in a better position to find out the cause of this radiation."

"Do you know, my friends, what that plain, seen from the height we are at, resembles?" said Michel.

"No," replied Nicholl.

"Very well; with all those pieces of lava lengthened like rockets, it resembles an immense game of spelikans thrown pell-mell. There wants but the hook to pull them out one by one."

"Do be serious," said Barbicane.

"Well, let us be serious," replied Michel, quietly; "and instead of spelikans, let us put bones. This plain would then be nothing but an immense cemetery, on which would repose the mortal remains of thousands of extinct generations. Do you prefer that high-flown comparison?"

"One is as good as the other," retorted Barbicane.

"My word, friend," continued the matter-of-fact Barbicane, "it matters but little what it *resembles*, when we do not know what is *is*."

"Well, answered," exclaimed Michel. "That will teach me to reason with savants."

But the projectile continued to advance with almost uniform speed around the lunar disc. The travellers, we may easily imagine, did not dream of taking a moment's rest. Every minute changed the landscape which fled from beneath their gaze. About half-past one o'clock in the morning, they caught a glimpse of the tops of another mountain. Barbicane, consulting his map, recognized Eratosthenes.

It was a ringed mountain 9000 feet high, and one of those circles so numerous on this satellite. With regard to this, Barbicane related Kepler's singular opinion on the formation of circles. According to that celebrated mathematician, these crater-like cavities had been dug by the hand of man.

"For what purpose?" asked Nicholl.

"For a very natural one," replied Barbicane. "The Selenites might have undertaken these immense works and dug these enormous holes for a refuge and shield from the solar rays which beat upon them during fifteen consecutive days."

"The Selenties are not fools," said Michel.

"A singular idea," replied Nicholl; "but it is probable that Kepler did not know the true dimensions of these circles, for the digging of them would have been the work of giants, quite impossible for the Selenites."

"Why? if weight on the moon's surface is six times less than on the earth?" said Michel.

"But if the Selenites are six times smaller?" retorted Nicholl.

"And if there are *no* Selenites?" added Barbicane.

This put an end to the discussion.

Soon Eratosthenes disappeared under the horizon without the projectile being sufficiently near to allow of close observation. This mountain separated the Apennines from the Carpathians. In the lunar orography they have discerned some chains of mountains, which are chiefly distributed over the northern hemisphere. Some, however, occupy certain portions of the southern hemisphere also.

About two o'clock in the morning Barbicane found that they were above the twentieth lunar parallel. This distance of the projectile from the moon was not more than 600 miles. Barbicane, now perceiving that the projectile was steadily approaching the lunar disc, did not despair, if of reaching her, at least discovering the secrets of her configurations.

CHAPTER 13

LUNAR LANDSCAPES

AT half-past two in the morning, the projectile was over the thirteenth lunar parallel and at the effective distance of 500 miles, reduced by the glasses to five. It still seemed impossible, however, that it could ever touch any part of the disc. Its motive speed, comparatively so moderate, was inexplicable to President Barbicane. At that distance from the moon it must have been considerable, to enable it to bear up against her attraction. Here was a phenomenon the cause of which escaped them again. Besides, time failed them to investigate the cause. All lunar relief was defiling under the eyes of the travellers, and they would not lose a single detail.

Under the glasses the disc appeared at the distance of five miles. What would an aeronaut, borne to this distance from the earth, distinguish on its surface? We cannot say, since the greatest ascension has not been more than 25,000 feet.

This, however, is an exact description of what Barbicane and his companions saw at this height. Large patches of different colours appeared on the disc. Selenographers are not agreed upon the nature of these colours. There are several, and rather vividly marked. Julius Schmidt, pretends that, if the terrestrial oceans were dried up, a Selenite observer could not distinguish on the globe a greater diversity of shades between the oceans and the continental plains than those on the moon present to a terrestrial observer. According to him, the colour common to the vast plains known by the name of "seas" is a dark grey mixed with green and brown. Some of the large craters present the same appearance. Barbicane knew this opinion of the German selenographer, an opinion shared by Bœer and Moedler. Observation has proved that right was on their side, and not on that of some astronomers who admit the existence of only grey on the moon's surface. In some parts green was very distinct, such as springs, according to Julius Schmidt, from the seas of Serenity and Humours. Barbicane also noticed large craters, without any interior cones, which shed a bluish tint similar to the reflection of a sheet of steel freshly polished. These colours belonged really to the lunar disc, and did not result, as some astronomers say, either from the imperfection in the objective of the glasses or from the interposition of the terrestrial atmosphere.

Not a doubt existed in Barbicane's mind with regard to it, as he observed it through space, and so could not commit any optical error. He considered the establishment of this fact as an acquisition to science. Now, were these shades of green belonging to topical vegetation, kept up by a low dense atmosphere? He could not yet say.

Farther on, he noticed a reddish tint, quite defined. The same shade had before been observed at the bottom of an isolated enclosure, known by the name of Lichtenburg's circle, which is situated near the Hercynian mountains, on the borders of the moon; but they could not tell the nature of it.

They were not more fortunate with regard to another peculiarity of the disc, for they could not decide upon the cause of it.

Michel Ardan was watching near the president, when he noticed long white lines, vividly lighted up by the direct rays of the sun. It was a succession of luminous furrows, very different from the radiation of Copernicus not long before; they ran parallel with each other.

Michel, with his usual readiness, hastened to exclaim,—

"Look there! cultivated fields!"

"Cultivated fields!" replied Nicholl, shrugging his shoulders.

"Ploughed, at all events," retorted Michel Ardan; "but what labourers those Selenites must be, and what giant oxen they must harness to their plough to cut such furrows!"

"They are not furrows," said Barbicane; "they are *rifts*."

"Rifts? stuff!" replied Michel mildly; "but what do you mean by 'rifts' in the scientific world?"

Barbicane immediately enlightened his companion as to what he knew about lunar rifts. He knew that they were a kind of furrow found on every part of the disc which was not mountainous; that these furrows, generally isolated, measured from 400 to 500 leagues in length; that their breadth varied from 1000 to 1500 yards, and that their borders were strictly parallel; but he knew nothing more either of their formation or their nature.

Barbicane, through his glasses, observed these rifts with great attention. He noticed that their borders were formed of steep declivities; they were long parallel ramparts, and with some small amount of imagination he might have admitted the existence of long lines of fortifications, raised by Selenite engineers. Of these different rifts some were perfectly straight, as if cut by a line; others were slightly curved, though still keeping their borders parallel; some crossed each other, some cut through craters; here they wound through ordinary cavities, such as Posidonius or Petavius; there they wound through the seas, such as the Sea of Serenity.

These natural accidents naturally escited the imaginations of these terrestrial astronomers. The first observations had not discovered these rifts. Neither Hevelius, Cassim, La Hire, nor Herschel seemed to have known them. It was Schroeter who in 1789 first drew attention to them. Others followed who studied them, as Pastorff, Gruithuysen, Bœer, Moedler. At this time their number amounts to seventy; but, if they have been counted, their nature has not yet been determined; they are certainly *not* fortifications, any more than they are the ancient beds of dried-up rivers; for, on one side, the waters, so slight on the moon's surface, could never have worn such drains for themselves; and, on the other, they often cross craters of great elevation.

We must, however, allow that Michel Ardan had "an idea," and that, without knowing it, he coincided in that respect with Julius Schmidt.

"Why," said he, "should not these unaccountable appearances by simply phenomena of vegetation?"

"What do you mean?" asked Barbicane quickly.

"Do not excite yourself, my worthy president," replied Michel; "might it not be possible that the dark lines forming that bastion were rows of trees regularly placed?"

"You stick to your vegetation, then?" said Barbicane.

"I like," retorted Michel Ardan, "to explain what you savants cannot explain; at least my hypothesis has the advantage of indicating why these rifts disappear, or seem to disappear, at certain seasons."

"And for what reason?"

"For the reason that the trees become invisible when they lose their leaves, and visible when they regain them."

"Your explanation is ingenius, my dear companion," replied Barbicane, "but inadmissable."

"Why?"

"Because, so to speak, there are no seasons on the moon's surface, and that, consequently, the phenomena of vegetation of which you speak cannot occur."

Indeed, the slight obliquity of the lunar axis keeps the sun at an almost equal height in every latitude. Above the equatorial regions the radiant orb almost invariably occupies the zenith, and does not pass the limits of the horizon in the polar regions; thus, according to each region, there reigns a perpetual winter, spring, summer, or autumn, as in the planet Jupiter, whose axis is but little inclined upon its orbit.

What origin do they attribute to these rifts? That is a question difficult to solve. They are certainly anterior to the formation of craters and circles, for several have introduced themselves by breaking through their circular ramparts. Thus it may be that, contemporary with the latter geological epochs, they are due to the expansion of natural forces.

But the projectile had now attained the 40° of lunar lat., at a distance not exceeding 400 miles. Through the glasses objects appeared to be only four miles distant.

At this point, under their feet, rose Mount Helican, 1520 feet high, and round about the left rose moderate elevations, enclosing a small portion of the "Sea of Rains," under the name of the Gulf of Iris. The terrestrial atmosphere would have to be one hundred and seventy times more transparent than it is, to allow astronomers to make perfect observations on the moon's surface; but in the void in which the projectile floated no fluid interposed itself between the eye of the observer and the object observed. And more, Barbicane found himself carried to a greater distance than the most powerful telescopes had ever done before, either that of Lord Rosse or that of the Rocky Mountains. He was, therefore, under extremely favourable conditions for solving that great question of the habitability of the moon; but the solution still escaped him; he could distinguish nothing but desert beds, immense plains, and towards the north, arid mountains. Not a work betrayed the hand of man; not a ruin marked his course; not a group of animals was to be seen indicating life, even in an inferior degree. In no part was there life, in no part was there an appearance of vegetation. Of the three kingdoms which share the terrestrial globe between them, one alone was represented on the lunar, and that the mineral.

"Ah, indeed!" said Michel Ardan, a little out of countenance; "then you see no one?"

"No," answered Nicholl; "up to this time not a man, not an animal, not a tree! After all, whether the atmosphere has taken refuge at the bottom of cavities, in the midst of the circles, or even on the opposite face of the moon, we cannot decide."

"Besides," added Barbicane, "even to the most piercing eye a man cannot be distinguished farther than three miles and a half off; so that, if there are any Selenites, they can see our projectile, but we cannot see them."

Towards four in the morning, at the height of the fiftieth parallel, the distance was reduced to 300 miles. To the left ran a line of mountains capriciously shaped, lying in the full light. To the right, on the contrary, lay a black hollow resembling a vast well, unfathomable and gloomy, drilled into the lunar soil.

This hole was the "Black Lake;" it was Pluto, a deep circle which can be conveniently studied from the earth, between the last quarter and the new moon, when the shadows fall from west to east.

This black colour is rarely met with on the surface of the satellite. As yet it has only been recognized in the depths of the circle of Endymion, to the east of the Cold Sea, in the northern hemisphere, and at the bottom of Grimaldi's circle, on the equator, towards the eastern border of the orb.

Pluto is an annular mountain, situated in 51° north latitude, and 9° east longitude. Its circuit is forty-seven miles long and thirty-two broad.

Barbicane regretted that they were not passing directly above this vast opening. There was an abyss to fathom, perhaps some mysterious phenomenon to surprise; but the projectile's course could not be altered. They must rigidly submit. They could not guide a balloon, still less a projectile, when once enclosed within its walls. Towards five in the morning the northern limits of the Sea of Rains was at length passed. The mounts of Condamine and Fontenelle remained—one on the right, the other on the left. That part of the disc beginning with 60° was becoming quite mountainous. The glasses brought them to within two miles, less than that seperating the summit of Mont Blanc from the level of the sea.

The whole region was bristling with spikes and circles. Towards the 60° Philolaus stood predominant at a height of 5550 feet with its elliptical crater, and seen from this distance, the disc showed a very fantastical appearance. Landscapes were presented to the eye under very different conditions from those on the earth, and also very inferior to them.

The moon having no atmosphere, the consequences arising from the absence of this gaseous envelope have already been shown. No twilight on her surface; night following day and day following night with the suddenness of a lamp which is extinguished or lighted amidst profound darkness,—no transition from cold to heat, the temperature falling in an instant from boiling point to the cold of space.

Another consequence of this want of air is that absolute darkness reigns where the sun's rays do not penetrate. That which on earth is called diffusion of light, that luminous matter which the air holds in suspension, which created the twilight and the daybreak, which produces the *umbræ* and the *penumbræ*, and all the magic of *chiaro-oscuro*, does not exist on the moon. Hence the harshness of contrasts, which only admit of two colours, black and white. If a Selenite were to shade his eyes from the sun's rays, the sky would seem absolutely black, and the stars would shine to him as on the darkest night. Judge of the impression produced on Barbicane and his three friends by this strange scene! Their eyes were confused. They could no longer grasp the respective distances of the different plains. A lunar landscape without the softening of the phenomena of *chiaro-oscuro* could not be rendered by an earthly landscape painter: it would be spots of ink on a white page—nothing more.

This aspect was not altered even when the projectile, at the height of 80°, was only seperated from the moon by a distance of fifty miles; nor even when, at five in the morning, it passed at less than twenty-five miles from the mountain of Gioja, a distance reduced by the glasses to a quarter of a mile. It seemed as if the moon might be touched by the hand! It seemed impossible that, before long, the projectile would not strike her, if only at the north pole, the brilliant arch of which was so distinctly visible on the black sky.

Michel Ardan wanted to open one of the scuttles and throw himself on to the moon's surface! A very useless attempt; for if the projectile could not attain any point whatever of the satellite, Michel, carried along by its motion, could not attain it either.

At that moment, at six o'clock, the lunar pole appeared. The disc only presented to the travellers' gaze one half brilliantly lit up, whilst the other disappeared in the darkness. Suddenly the projectile passed the line of demarcation between intense light and absolute darkness, and was plunged in profound night!

CHAPTER 14

THE NIGHT OF THREE HUNDRED AND FIFTY-FOUR HOURS AND A HALF

AT the moment when this phenomenon took place so rapidly, the projectile was skirting the moon's north pole at less than twenty-five miles distance. Some seconds had sufficed to plunge it into the absolute darkness of space. The transition was so sudden, without shade, without gradation of light, without attenuation of the luminous waves, that the orb seemed to have been extinguished by a powerful blow.

"Melted, disappeared!" Michel Ardan exclaimed, aghast.

Indeed, there was neither reflection nor shadow. Nothing more was to be seen of that disc, formerly so dazzling. The darkness was complete, and rendered even more so by the rays from the stars. It was "that blackness" in which the lunar nights are insteeped, which last three hundred and four hours and a half at each point of the disc, a long night resulting from the equality of the translatory and rotatory movements of the moon. The projectile, immerged in the conical shadow of the satellite, experienced the action of the solar rays no more than any of its invisible points.

In the interior, the obscurity was complete. They could not see each other. Hence the necessity of despelling the darkness. However desirous Barbicane might be to husband the gas, the reserve of which was small, he was obliged to ask from it a fictitious light, an expensive brilliancy which the sun then refused.

"Devil take the radiant orb!" exclaimed Michel Ardan, "which forces us to expend gas, instead of giving us his rays gratuitously."

"Do not let us accuse the sun," said Nicholl, "it is not his fault, but that of the moon, which has come and placed herself like a screen between us and it."

"It is the sun!" continued Michel.

"It is the moon!" retorted Nicholl.

An idle dispute, which Barbicane put an end to by saying,—

"My friends, it is neither the fault of the sun nor of the moon; it is the fault of the *projectile*, which, instead of rigidly following its course, has awkwardly missed it. To be more just, it is the fault of that unfortunate meteor which has so deplorably altered our first direction."

"Well," replied Michel Ardan, "as the matter is settled, let us have breakfast. After a whole night of watching, it is fair to build ourselves up a little."

This proposal meeting with no contradiction, Michel prepared the repast in a few minutes. But they ate for eating's sake, they drank without toasts, without hurrahs. The bold travellers being borne away into gloomy space, without their accustomed cortège of rays, felt a vague uneasiness at their hearts. The "strange" shadow so dear to Victor Hugo's pen bound them on all sides. But they talked over the interminable night of three hundred and fifty-four hours and a half, nearly fifteen days, which the law of physics has imposed on the inhabitants of the moon.

Barbicane gave his friends some explanation of the causes and the consequences of this curious phenomenon.

"Curious indeed," said they; "for, if each hemisphere of the moon is deprived of solar light for fifteen days, that above which we now float does not even enjoy during its long night any view of the earth so beautifully lit up. In a word she has no moon (applying this designation to our globe) but on one side of her disc. Now if this were the case with the earth,—if, for example, Europe never saw the moon, and she was only visible at the Antipodes, imagine to yourself the astonishment of a European on arriving in Australia."

"They would make the voyage for nothing but to see the moon!" replied Michel.

"Very well!" continued Barbicane, "that astonishment is reserved for the Selenites who inhabit the face of the moon opposite to the earth, a face which is ever invisible to our countrymen of the terrestrial globe."

"And which we should have seen," added Nicholl, "if we had arrived here when the moon was new, that is to say fifteen days later."

"I will add, to make amends," continued Barbicane, "that the inhabitants of the visible face are singularly favoured by nature, to the detriment of their brethren on the invisible face. The latter, as you see, have dark nights of 354 hours, without one single ray to break the darkness. The other, on the contrary, when the sun which has given its light for fifteeen days sinks below the horizon, see a splindid orb rise on the opposite horizon. It is the earth, which is thirteen times greater than that diminutive moon that we know;—the earth which developes itself at a diameter of two degrees, and which sheds a light thirteen times greater than that qualified by atmospheric strata—the earth which only disappears at the moment when the sun reappears in its turn!"

"Nicely worded!" said Michel, "slightly academical perhaps."

"It follows, then," continued Barbicane, without knitting his brows, "that the visible face of the disc must be very agreeable to inhabit, since it always looks on either the sun when the moon is full, or on the earth when the moon is new."

"But," said Nicholl, "that advantage must be well compensated by the insupportable heat which the light brings with it."

"The inconvenience, in that respect, is the same for the two faces, for the earth's light is evidently deprived of heat. But the invisible face is still more searched by the heat than the visible face. I say that for *you*, Nicholl, because Michel will probably not understand."

"Thank you," said Michel.

"Indeed," continued Barbicane, "when the invisible face receives at the same time light and heat from the sun, it is because the moon is new; that is to say, she is situated between the sun and the earth. It follows, then, considering the position which she occupies in opposition when full, that she is nearer to the sun by twice her distance from the earth; and that distance may be estimated at the two-hundredth part of that which separates the sun from the earth, or in round numbers 400,000 miles. So that invisible face is so much nearer to the sun when she receives its rays."

"Quite right," replied Nicholl.

"On the contrary," continued Barbicane.

"One moment," said Michel, interrupting his grave companion.

"What do you want?"

"I ask to be allowed to continue the explanation."

"And why?"

"To prove that I understand."

"Get along with you," said Barbicane, smiling.

"On the contrary," said Michel, imitating the tone and gestures of the president, "on the contrary, when the visible face of the moon is lit by the sun, it is because the moon is full, that is to say, opposite the sun with regard to the earth. The distance separating it from the radiant orb is then increased in round numbers to 400,000 miles, and the heat which she receives must be a little less."

"Very well said!" exclaimed Barbicane. "Do you know, Michel, that, for an amateur, you are intelligent."

"Yes," replied Michel coolly, "we are all so on the Boulevard des Italiens."

Barbicane gravely clasped the hand of his amiable companion, and continued to enumerate the advantages reserved for the inhabitants of the visible face.

Amongst others, he mentioned eclipses of the sun, which only take place on this side of the lunar disc; since, in order that they may take place, it is necessary for the moon to be *in opposition*. These eclipses, caused by the interposition of the earth between the moon and the sun, can last *two hours*; during which time, by reason of the rays refracted by its atmosphere, the terrestrial globe can appear as nothing but a black point upon the sun.

"So," said Nicholl, "there is a hemisphere, that invisible hemisphere which is very ill supplied, very ill treated, by nature."

"Never mind," replied Michel; "if we ever become Selenites, we will inhabit the visible face. I like the light."

"Unless, by any chance," answered Nicholl, "the atmosphere should be condensed on the other side, as certain astronomers pretend."

"That would be a consideration," said Michel.

Breakfast over, the observers returned to their post. They tried to see through the darkened scuttles by extinguishing all light in the projectile; but not a luminous spark made its way through the darkness.

One inexplicable fact preoccupied Barbicane. Why, having passed within such a short distance of the moon—about twenty-five miles only—why the projectile had not fallen? If its speed had been enormous, he could have understood that the fall would not have taken place; but, with a relatively moderate speed, that resistance to the moon's attraction could not be explained. Was the projectile under some foreign influence? Did some kind of body retain it in the ether? It was quite evident that it could never reach any point of the moon. Whither was it going? Was it going farther from, or nearing, the disc? Was it being borne in that profound darkness through the infinity of space? How could they learn, how calculate, in the midst of this night? All these questions made Barbicane uneasy, but he could not solve them.

Certainly, the invisible orb was *there*, perhaps only some few miles off; but neither he nor his companions could see it. If there was any noise on its surface, they could not hear it. Air, that medium of sound, was wanting to transmit the groanings of that moon which the Arabic legends call "a man already half granite, and still breathing."

One must allow that that was enough to aggravate the most patient observers. It was just that unknown hemisphere which was stealing from their sight. That face which fifteen days sooner, or fifteen days later, had been, or would be, splendidly illuminated by the solar rays, was then being lost in utter darkness.

"It is the fault of the Moon."

In fifteen days where would the projectile be? Who could say? Where would the chances of conflicting attractions have drawn it to? The disappointment of the travellers in the midst of this utter darkness may be imagined. All observation of the lunar disc was impossible. The constellations alone claimed all their attention; and we must allow that the astronomers Faye, Charconac, and Secchi, never found themselves in circumstances so favourable for their observation.

Indeed, nothing could equal the splendour of this starry world, bathed in limpid ether. Its diamonds set in the heavenly vault sparkled magnificently. The eye took in the firmament from the Southern Cross to the North Star, those two constellations which in 12,000 years, be reason of the succession of equinoxes, will resign their part of polar stars, the one to Canopus in the southern hemisphere, the other to Wega in the northern. Imagination loses itself in this sublime Infinity, amidst which the projectile was gravitating, like a new star created by the hand of man. From a natural cause, these constellations shone with a soft lustre; they did not *twinkle*, for there was no atmosphere which, by the intervention of its layers unequally dense and of different degrees of humidity, produces this scintillation. These stars were soft eyes, looking out into the dark night, amidst the silence of absolute space.

Long did the travellers stand mute, watching the constellated firmament, upon which the moon, like a vast screen, made an enormous black hole. But at length a painful sensation drew them from their watchings. This was an intense cold, which soon covered the inside of the glass of the scuttles with a thick coating of ice. The sun was no longer warming the projectile with its direct rays, and thus it was losing the heat stored up in its walls by degrees. This heat was rapidly evaporating into space by radiation, and a considerably lower temperature was the result. The humidity of the interior was changed into ice upon contact with the glass, preventing all observation.

Nicholl consulted the thermometer, and saw that it had fallen to seventeen degrees (centigrade) below zero*. So that, in spite of the many reasons for economizing, Barbicane, after having begged light from the gas, was also obliged to beg for heat. The projectile's low temperature was no longer endurable. Its tenants would have been frozen to death.

"Well!" observed Michel, "we cannot reasonably complain of the monotony of our journey! What variety we have had, at least in temperature. Now we are blinded with light and saturated with heat, like the Indians of the Pampas! now plunged into profound darkness, amidst the cold like the Esquimauxs of the north pole. No, indeed! we have no right to complain; nature does wonders in our honour."

"But," asked Nicholl, "what is the temperature outside?"

"Exactly that of the planetary space," replied Barbicane.

"Then," continued Michel Ardan, "would not this be the time to make the experiment which we dared not attempt, when we were drowned in the sun's rays?"

"It is now or never," replied Barbicane, "for we are in a good position to verify the temperature of space, and see if Fourier or Pouillet's calculations are exact."

"In any case it is cold," said Michel. "See! the steam of the interior is

* 1° Fahr. (Ed.)

"The vapor of our breath will fall in snow around us."

condensing on the glasses of the scuttles. If the fall continues, the vapour of our breath will fall in snow around us."

"Let us prepare a thermometer," said Barbicane.

We may imagine that an ordinary thermometer would afford no result under the circumstances in which this instrument was to be exposed. The mercury would have been frozen in its ball, as below forty-two degrees below zero* it is no longer liquid. But Barbicane had furnished himself with a spirit thermometer on Wafferdin's system, which gives the minima of excessively low temperatures.

Before beginning the experiment, this instrument was compared with an ordinary one, and then Barbicane prepared to use it.

"How shall we set about it?" asked Nicholl.

"Nothing is easier," replied Michel Ardan, who was never at a loss. "We open the scuttle rapidly; throw out the instrument; it follows the projectile with exemplary docility; and a quarter of an hour after, draw it in.

"With the hand?" asked Barbicane.

"With the hand," replied Michel.

"Well then, my friend, do not expose yourself," answered Barbicane, "for the hand that you draw in again will be nothing but a stump frozen and deformed by the frightful cold."

"Really!"

"You will feel as if you had a terrible burn, like that of iron at a white heat; for whether the heat leaves our bodies briskly or enters briskly, it its exactly the same thing. Besides, I am not at all certain that the objects we have thrown out are still following us."

"Why not?" asked Nicholl.

"Because, if we are passing through an atmosphere of the slightest density, these objects will be retarded. Again, the darkness prevents our seeing if they still float around us. But in order not to expose ourselves to the loss of our thermometer, we will fasten it, and we can then more easily pull it back again."

Barbicane's advice was followed. Through the scuttle rapidly opened, Nicholl threw out the instrument which was held by a short cord, so that it might be more easily drawn up. The scuttle had not been opened more than a second, but that second had sufficed to let in a most intense cold.

"The devil!" exclaimed Michel Ardan, "it is cold enough to freeze a white bear."

Barbicane waited until half an hour had elapsed, which was more than time enough to allow the instrument to fall to the level of the surrounding temperature. Then it was rapidly pulled in.

Barbicane calculated the quantity of spirits of wine overflowed into the little phial soldered to the lower part of the instrument, and said,—

"A hundred and forty degrees centigrade† below zero!"

M. Pouillet was right and Fourier wrong. That was the undoubted temperature of the starry space. Such is, perhaps, that of the lunar continents, when the orb of night has lost by radiation all the heat which fifteen days of sun have poured into her.

* —44° Fahr. (Ed.)

† —218° Fahr. (Ed.)

CHAPTER 15

HYPERBOLA OR PARABOLA

We may, perhaps, be astonished to find Barbicane and his companions so little occupied with the future reserved for them in their metal prison which was bearing them through the infinity of space. Instead of asking where they were going, they passed their time making experiments, as if they had been quietly installed in their own study.

We might answer that men so strong-minded were above such anxieties—that they did not trouble themselves about such trifles—and that they had something else to do than to occupy their minds with the future.

The truth was that they were not masters of their projectile; they could neither check its course, nor alter its direction.

A sailor can change the head of his ship as he pleases; an aëronaut can give a vertical motion to his balloon. They, on the contrary, had no power over their vehicle. Every manœuvre was forbidden. Hence the inclination ot let things alone, or as the sailors say, "let her run."

Where did they find themselves at this moment, at eight o'clock in the morning of the day called upon the earth the 6th of December? Very certainly in the neighbourhood of the moon, and even near enough for her to look to them like an enormous black screen upon the firmament. As to the distance which seperated them, it was impossible to estimate it. The projectile, held by some unaccountable force, had been within four miles of grazing the satellite's north pole.

But since entering the cone of shadow these last two hours, had the distance increased or diminished? Every point of mark was wanting by which to estimate both the direction and the speed of the projectile.

Perhaps it was rapidly leaving the disc, so that it would soon quit the pure shadow. Perhaps, again, on the other hand, it might be nearing it so much that in a short time it might strike some high point on the invisible hemisphere, which would doubtlessly have ended the journey much to the detriment of the travellers.

A discussion arose on this subject, and Michel Ardan, always ready with an explanation, gave it as his opinion that the projectile, held by the lunar attraction, would end by falling on the surface of the terrestrial globe like an aërolite.

"First of all, my friend," answered Barbicane, "every aërolite does not fall to the earth; it is only a small proportion which do so; and if we had passed into an aërolite, it does not necessarily follow that we should ever reach the surface of the moon."

"But how if we get near enough?" replied Michel.

"Pure mistake," replied Barbicane. "Have you not seen shooting stars rush through the sky by thousands at certain seasons?"

"Yes."

"Well, these stars, or rather corpuscules, only shine when they are heated by gliding over the atmospheric layers. Now, if they enter the atmosphere, they pass at least within forty miles of the earth, but they seldom fall upon it. The same with our projectile. It may approach very near to the moon, and yet not fall upon it."

"But then," asked Michel, "I shall be curious to know how our erring vehicle will act in space?"

"I see but two hypotheses," replied Barbicane, after some moments' reflection.

"What are they?"

"The projectile has the choice between two mathematical curves, and it will follow one or the other according to the speed with which it is animated, and which at this moment I cannot estimate."

"Yes," said Nicholl, "it will follow either a parabola or a hyperbola."

"Just so," replied Barbicane. "With a certain speed it will assume the parabola, and with a greater the hyperbola."

"I like those grand words," exclaimed Michel Ardan; "one knows directly what they mean. And pray what is your parabola, if you please?"

"My friend," answered the captain, "the parabola is a curve of the second order, the result of the section of a cone intersected by a plane parallel to one of its sides."

"Ah! ah!" said Michel, in a satisfied tone.

"It is very nearly," continued Nicholl, "the course described by a bomb launched from a mortar."

"Perfect! And the hyperbola?"

"The hyperbola, Michel, is a curve of the second order, produced by the intersection of a conic surface and a plane parallel to its axis, and constitutes two branches separated one from the other, both tending indefinitely in the two directions."

"Is it possible!" exclaimed Michel Ardan in a serious tone, as if they had told him of some serious event. "What I particularly like in your definition of the hyperbola (I was going to say hyperblague) is that it is still more obscure than the word you pretend to define."

Nicholl and Barbicane cared little for Michel Ardan's fun. They were deep in a scientific discussion. What curve would the projectile follow? was their hobby. One maintained the hyperbola, the other the parabola. They gave each other reasons bristling with *x*. Their arguments were couched in language which made Michel jump. The discussion was hot, and neither would give up his chosen curve to his adversary.

This scientific dispute lasted so long that it made Michel very impatient.

"Now, gentlemen co-sines, will you cease to throw parabolas and hyperbolas at each other's heads? I want to understand the only interesting question in the whole affair. We shall follow one or other of these curves? Good. But where will they lead us to?"

"Nowhere," replied Nicholl.

"How, nowhere?"

"Evidently," said Barbicane, "they are open curves, which may be prolonged indefinitely."

"Ah, savants!" cried Michel; "and what are either the one or the other to us from the moment we know that they equally lead us into infinite space?"

Barbicane and Nicholl could not forbear smiling. They had just been creating "art for art's sake." Never had so idle a question been raised at such an inopportune moment. The sinister truth remained that, whether hyperbolically or parabolically borne away, the projectile would never again meet either the earth or the moon.

What would become of these bold travellers in the immediate future? If they did not die of hunger, if they did not die of thirst, in some days, when the gas failed, they would die from want of air, unless the cold had killed them first. Still, important as it was to economize the gas, the excessive lowness of the surrounding temperature obliged them to consume a certain quantity. Strictly speaking, they could do without its *light*, but not without its *heat*. Fortunately the caloric generated by Reiset's and Regnaut's apparatus raised the temperature of the interior of the projectile a little, and without much expenditure they were able to keep it bearable.

But observations had now become very difficult. The dampness of the projectile was condensed on the windows and congealed immediately. This cloudiness had to be dispersed continually. In any case they might hope to be able to discover some phenomena of the highest interest.

But up to this time the disc remained dumb and dark. It did not answer the multiplicity of questions put by these ardent minds; a matter which drew this reflection from Michel, apparently a just one,—

"If ever we begin this journey over again, we shall do well to choose the time when the moon is at the full."

"Certainly," said Nicholl, "that circumstance will be more favourable. I allow that the moon, immersed in the sun's rays, will not be visible during the transit, but instead we should see the *earth*, which would be full. And what is more, if we were drawn round the moon, as at this moment, we should at least have the advantage of seeing the invisible part of her disc magnificently lit."

"Well said, Nicholl," replied Michel Ardan. "What do you think, Barbicane?"

"I think this," answered the grave president: "If ever we begin this journey again, we shall start at the same time and under the same conditions. Suppose we had attained our end, would it not have been better to have found continents in broad daylight, than a country plunged in utter darkness? Would not our first installation have been made under better circumstances? Yes, evidently. As to the *invisible* side, we could have visited it in our exploring expeditions on the lunar globe. So that the time of the full moon was well chosen. But we ought to have arrived at the end; and in order to have so arrived, we ought to have suffered no deviation on the road."

"I have nothing to say to that," answered Michel Ardan. "Here is, however, a good opportunity lost of observing the other side of the moon."

But the projectile was now describing in the shadow that incalculable course which no sight-mark would allow them to ascertain. Had its direction been altered, either by the influence of the lunar attraction, or by the action of some unknown star? Barbicane could not say. But a change had taken place in the relative position of the vehicle; and Barbicane verified it about four in the morning.

The change consisted in this, that the base of the projectile had turned towards the moon's surface, and was so held by a perpendicular passing through its axis. The attraction, that is to say the *weight*, had brought about this alteration. The heaviest part of the projectile inclined towards the invisible disc as if it would fall upon it.

Was it falling? Were the travellers attaining that much desired end? No. And the observation of a sign-point, quite inexplicable in itself, showed Barbicane that his projectile was not nearing the moon, and that it had shifted by following an almost concentric curve.

This point of mark was a luminous brightness, which Nicholl sighted suddenly, on the limit of the horizon formed by the black disc. This point could not be confounded with a star. It was a reddish incandescence which increased by degrees, a decided proof that the projectile was shifting towards it and not falling normally on the surface of the moon.

"A volcano! it is a volcano in action!" cried Nicholl; "a disembowelling of the interior fires of the moon! That world is not quite extinguished."

"Yes, an eruption," replied Barbicane, who was carefully studying the phenomenon through his night glass. "What should it be, if not a volcano?"

"But, then," said Michel Ardan, "in order to maintain that combustion, there must be air. So an atmosphere *does* surround that part of the moon."

"*Perhaps* so," replied Barbicane, "but not necessarily. The volcano, by the decomposition of certain substances, can provide its own oxygen, and thus throw flames into space. It seems to me that the deflagration, by the intense brillancy of the substances in combustion, is produced in pure oxygen. We must not be in a hurry to proclaim the existence of a lunar atmosphere."

The fiery mountain must have been situated about the 45° south latitude on the invisible part of the disc; but, to Barbicane's great displeasure, the curve which the projectile was describing was taking it far from the point indicated by the eruption. Thus he could not determine its nature exactly. Half an hour after being sighted, this luminous point had disappeared behind the dark horizon; but the verification of this phenomenon was of considerable consequence in their selenographic studies. It proved that all heat had not yet disappeared from the bowels of this globe; and where heat exists, who can affirm that the vegetable kingdom, nay, even the animal kingdom itself, has not up to this time resisted all destructive influences? The existence of this volcano in eruption, unmistakably seen by these earthly savants, would doubtless give rise to many theories favourable to the grave question of the habitability of the moon.

Barbicane allowed himself to be carried away by these reflections. He forgot himself in a deep reverie in which the mysterious destiny of the lunar world was uppermost. He was seeking to combine together the facts observed up to that time, when a new incident recalled him briskly to reality. This incident was more than a cosmical phenomenon; it was a threatened danger, the consequences of which might be disastrous in the extreme.

Suddenly, in the midst of the ether, in the profound darkness, an enormous mass appeared. It was like a moon, but an incandescent moon, whose brilliancy was all the more intolerable as it cut sharply on the frightful darkness of space. This mass, of a circular form, threw a light which filled the projectile. The forms of Barbicane, Nicholl, and Michel Ardan, bathed in its white sheets, assumed that livid spectral appearance which physicians produce with the fictitious light of alcohol impregnated with salt.

"By Jove!" cried Michel Ardan, "we are hideous. What is that ill-conditioned moon?"

"A meteor," replied Barbicane.

"A meteor burning in space?"

"Yes."

This shooting globe suddenly appearing in shadow at a distance of at most 200 miles, ought, according to Barbicane, to have a diameter of 2000 yards. It advanced at a speed of about one mile and a half per second. It cut the projectile's path, and must reach it in some minutes. As it approached it grew to enormous proportions.

Imagine, if possible, the situation of the travellers! It is impossible to describe it. In spite of their courage, their *sangfroid*, their carelessness of danger, they were mute, motionless with stiffened limbs, a prey to frightful terror. Their projectile, the course of which they could not alter, was rushing straight on this ignited mass, more intense than the open mouth of an oven. It seemed as though they were being precipitated towards an abyss of fire.

Barbicane had seized the hands of his two companions, and all three looked through their half-open eyelids upon that asteroid heated to a white heat. If thought was not destroyed within them, if their brains still worked amidst all this awe, they must have given themselves up for lost.

Two minutes after the sudden appearance of the meteor (to them two centuries of anguish) the projectile seemed almost about to strike it, when the globe of fire burst like a bomb, but without making any noise in that void where sound, which is but the agitation of the layers of air, could not be generated.

Nicholl uttered a cry, and he and his companions rushed to the scuttle. What a sight! What pen can describe it? What palette is rich enough in colours to reproduce so magnificent a spectacle?

It was like the opening of a crater, like the scattering of an immense conflagration. Thousands of luminous fragments lit up and irradiated space with their fires. Every size, every colour, was there intermingled. There were rays of yellow and pale yellow, red, green, grey—a crown of fireworks of all colours. Of the enormous and much-dreaded globe there remained nothing but these fragments carried in all directions, now become asteroids in their turn, some flaming like a sword, some surrounded by a whitish cloud, and others leaving behind them trains of brilliant cosmical dust.

These incandescent blocks crossed and struck each other, scattering still smaller fragments, some of which struck the projectile. Its left scuttle was even cracked by a violent shock. It seemed to be floating amidst a hail of howitzer shells, the smallest of which might destroy it instantly.

The light which saturated the ether was so wonderfully intense, that Michel, drawing Barbicane and Nicholl to his window, exclaimed, "The invisible moon, visible at last!"

And through a luminous emanation, which lasted some seconds, the whole three caught a glimpse of that mysterious disc which the eye of man now saw for the first time. What could they distinguish at a distance which they could not estimate? Some lengthened bands along the disc, real clouds formed in the midst of a very confined atmosphere, from which emerged not only all the mountains, but also projections of less importance; its circles, its yawning craters, as capricously placed as on the visible surface. Then immense spaces, no longer arid plains, but real seas, oceans, widely distributed, reflecting on their liquid surface all the dazzling magic of the fires of space; and, lastly, on the surface of the continents, large dark masses, looking like immense forests under the rapid illumination of a brilliance.

Was it an illusion, a mistake, an optical illusion? Could they give a scientific assent to an observation so superficially obtained? Dared they pronounce upon the question of its habitability after so slight a glimpse of the invisible disc?

But the lightnings in space subsided by degrees; its accidental brilliancy died away; the asteroids dispersed in different directions and were extinguished in the distance. The ether returned to its accustomed darkness; the stars, eclipsed for a moment, again twinkled in the firmament, and the disc, so hastily discerned, was again buried in impenetrable night.

CHAPTER 16

THE SOUTHERN HEMISPHERE

THE projectile had just escaped a terrible danger, and a very unforeseen one. Who would have thought of such a rencontre with meteors? These erring bodies might create serious perils for the travellers. They were to them so many sand-banks upon that sea of ether which, less fortunate than sailors, they could not escape. But did these adventurers complain of space? No, not since nature had given them the splendid sight of a cosmical meteor bursting from expansion, since this inimitable firework, which no Ruggieri could imitate, had lit up for some seconds the invisible glory of the moon. In that flash, continents, seas, and forests had become visible to them. Did an atmosphere, then, bring to this unknown face its life-giving atoms? Questions still insoluble, and for ever closed against human curiosity!

It was then half past three in the afternoon. The projectile was following its curvilinear direction round the moon. Had its course been again altered by the meteor? It was to be feared so. But the projectile must describe a curve unalterably determined by the laws of mechanical reasoning. Barbicane was inclined to believe that this curve would be rather a parabola than a hyperbola. But admitting the parabola, the projectile must quickly have passed through the cone of shadow projected into space opposite the sun. This cone, indeed, is very narrow, the angular diameter of the moon being so little when compared with the diameter of the orb of day; and up to this time the projectile had been floating in this deep shadow. Whatever had been its speed (and it could not have been insignificant) its period of occultation continued. That was evident, but perhaps that would not have been the case in a supposed rigidly parabolical trajectory,—a new problem which tormented Barbicane's brain, imprisoned as he was in a circle of unknowns which he could not unravel.

Neither of the travellers thought of taking an instant's repose. Each one watched for an unexpected fact, which might throw some new light on their uranographic studies. About five o'clock, Michel Ardan distributed, under the name of dinner, some pieces of bread and cold meat, which were quickly swallowed without either of them abandoning their scuttle, the glass of which was incessantly encrusted by the condensation of vapour.

About forty-five minutes past five in the evening, Nicholl, armed with his glass, sighted towards the southern border of the moon, and in the direction followed by the projectile, some bright points cut upon the dark shield of the sky. They looked like a succession of sharp points lengthened into a tremulous line. They were very bright. Such appeared the terminal line of the moon when in one of her octants.

They could not be mistaken. It was no longer a simple meteor. This luminous

What a sight!

ridge had neither colour nor motion. Nor was it a volcano in eruption. And Barbicane did not hesitate to pronouce upon it.

"The sun!" he exclaimed.

"What! the sun?" answered Nicholl and Michel Ardan.

"Yes, my friends, it is the radiant orb itself lighting up the summit of the mountains situated on the southern borders of the moon. We are evidently nearing the south pole."

"After having passed the north pole," replied Michel. "We have made the circuit of our satellite, then?"

"Yes, my good Michel."

"Then, no more hyperbolas, no more parabolas, no more open curves to fear?"

"No, but a *closed* curve."

"Which is called—"

"An ellipse. Instead of losing itself in interplanetary space, it is probable that the projectile will describe an elliptical orbit around the moon."

"Indeed!"

"And that it will become *her* satellite."

"Moon of the moon!" cried Michel Ardan.

"Only, I would have you observe, my worthy friend," replied Barbicane, "that we are none the less lost for that."

"Yes, in another manner, and much more pleasantly," answered the careless Frenchman with his most amiable smile.

CHAPTER 17

TYCHO

AT six in the evening the projectile passed the south pole at less than forty miles off, a distance equal to that already reached at the north pole. The elliptical curve was being rigidly carried out.

At this moment the travellers once more entered the blessed rays of the sun. They saw once more those stars which move slowly from east to west. The radiant orb was saluted by a triple hurrah. With its light it also sent heat, which soon pierced the metal walls. The glass resumed its accustomed appearance. The layers of ice melted as if by enchantment; and immediately, for economy's sake, the gas was put out, the air apparatus alone consuming its usual quantity.

"Ah!" said Nicholl, "these rays of heat are good. With what impatience must the Selenites wait the reappearance of the orb of day."

"Yes," replied Michel Ardan, "imbibing as it were the brilliant ether, light and heat, all life is contained in them."

At this moment the bottom of the projectile deviated somewhat from the lunar surface, in order to follow the slightly lengthened elliptical orbit. From this point, had the earth been at the full, Barbicane and his companions could have seen it, but immersed in the sun's irradiation she was quite invisible. Another spectacle attracted their attention, that of the southern part of the moon, brought by the glasses to within 450 yards. They did not again leave the scuttles, and noted every detail of this fantastical continent.

Mounts Doerfel and Leibnitz formed two separate groups very near the south pole. The first group extended from the pole to the eighty-fourth parallel, on the eastern part of the orb; the second occupied the eastern border, extending from the 65° of latitude to the pole.

On their capriciously formed ridge appeared dazzling sheets, as mentioned by Père Secchi. With more certainty than the illustrious Roman astonomer, Barbicane was enabled to recognize their nature.

"They are snow," he exclaimed.

"Snow?" repeated Nicholl.

"Yes, Nicholl, snow; the surface of which is deeply frozen. See how they reflect the luminous rays. Cooled lava would never give out such intense reflection. There must then be water, there must be air on the moon. As little as you please, but the fact can no longer be contested." No, it could not be. And if ever Barbicane should see the earth again, his notes will bear witness to this great fact in his selenographic observations.

These mountains of Doerfel and Leibnitz rose in the midst of plains of a medium extent, which were bounded by an indefinite succession of circles and annular ramparts. These two chains are the only ones met with in this region of circles. Comparatively but slightly marked, they throw up here and there some sharp points, the highest summit of which attains an altitude of 24,600 feet.

But the projectile was high above all this landscape, and the projections disappeared in the intense brilliancy of the disc. And to the eyes of the travellers there reappeared that original aspect of the lunar landscapes, raw in tone, without gradation of colours, and without degrees of shadow, roughly black and white, from the want of diffusion of light.

But the sight of this desolate world did not fail to captivate them by its very strangeness. They were moving over this region as if they had been borne on the breath of some storm, watching heights defile under their feet, piercing the cavities with their eyes, going down into the rifts, climbing the ramparts, sounding these mysterious holes, and levelling all cracks. But no trace of vegetation, no appearance of cities; nothing but stratification, beds of lava, overflowings polished like immense mirrors, reflecting the sun's rays with overpowering brilliancy. Nothing belonging to a *living* world—everything to a dead world, where avalanches, rolling from the summits of the mountains, would disperse noiselessly at the bottom of the abyss, retaining the motion, but wanting the sound. In any case it was the image of death, without its being possible even to say that life had ever existed there.

Michel Ardan, however, thought he recognized a heap of ruins, to which he drew Barbicane's attention. It was about the 80th parallel, in 30° longitude. This heap of stones, rather regularly placed, represented a vast fortress, overlooking a long rift, which in former days had served as a bed to the rivers of prehistorical times. Not far from that, rose to a height of 17,400 feet the annular mountain of Short, equal to the Asiatic Caucasus. Michel Ardan, with his accustomed ardour, maintained "the evidences" of his fortress. Beneath it he discerned the dismantled ramparts of a town; here the still intact arch of a portico, there two or three columns lying under their base; farther on, a succession of arches which must have supported the conduit of an aqueduct; in another part the sunken pillars of a gigantic bridge, run into the thickest parts of the rift. He distinguished all this, but with so much imagination in his glance, and through glasses so fantastical, that we must mistrust his observation. But who could affirm, who would dare to say, that the amiable fellow did not really see that which his two companions would not see?

Moments were too precious to be sacrificed in idle discussion. The Selenite city, whether imaginary or not, had already disappeared afar off. The distance of the projectile from the lunar disc was on the increase, and the details of the soil were being lost in a confused jumble. The reliefs, the circles, the craters and plains alone remained, and still showed their boundary lines distinctly. At this moment, to the left, lay extended one of the finest circles of lunar orography, one of the curiosities of this continent. It was Newton, which Barbicane recognized without trouble, by referring to the *Mappa Selenographica*.

Newton is situated in exactly 77° south lat., and 16° east long. It forms an annular crater, the ramparts of which, rising to a height of 21,300 feet, seemed to be impassable.

Barbicane made his companions observe that the height of this mountain above the surrounding plain was far from equalling the depth of its crater. This enormous hole was beyond all measurement, and formed a gloomy abyss, the bottom of which the sun's rays could never reach. There, according to Humboldt, reigns utter darkness, which the light of the sun and the earth cannot break. Mythologists could well have made it the mouth of hell.

"Newton," said Barbicane, "is the most perfect type of these annular mountains, of which the earth possesses no sample. They prove that the moon's formation, by means of cooling, is due to violent causes; for whilst under the pressure of internal fires the reliefs rise to considerable height, the depths withdraw far below the lunar level."

"I do not dispute the fact," replied Michel Ardan.

Some minutes after passing Newton, the projectile directly overlooked the annular mountain of Moret. It skirted at some distance the summits of Blancanus, and at about half-past seven in the evening reached the circle of Clavius.

This circle, one of the most remarkable of the disc, is situated in 58° south lat., and 15° east long. Its height is estimated at 22,950 feet. The travellers, at a distance of twenty-four miles (reduced to four by their glasses), could admire this vast crater in its entirety.

"Terrestrial volcanoes," said Barbicane, "are but molehills compared with those of the moon. Measuring the old craters formed by the first eruptions of Vesuvius and Etna, we find them little more than three miles in breadth. In France the circle of Cantal measures six miles across; at Ceyland the circle of the island is forty miles, which is considered the largest on the globe. What are these diameters against that of Clavius, which we overlook at this moment?"

"What is its breadth?" asked Nicholl.

"It is 150 miles," replied Barbicane. "This circle is certainly the most important on the moon, but many others measure 150, 100, or 75 miles."

"Ah! my friends," exclaimed Michel, "can you picture to yourselves what this new peaceful orb of night must have been when its craters, filled with thunderings, vomited at the same time smoke and tongues of flame. What a wonderful spectacle then, and now what decay! This moon is nothing more than a thin carcase of fireworks, whose squibs, rockets, serpents and suns, after a

"Light and heat; all life is contained in them."

superb brilliancy, have left but sadly broken cases. Who can say the cause, the reason, the motive force of these cataclysms?''

Barbicane was not listening to Michel Ardan; he was contemplating those ramparts of Clavius, formed by large mountains spread over several miles. At the bottom of the immense cavity burrowed hundreds of small extinguished craters, riddling the soil like a colander, and overlooked by a peak 15,000 feet high.

Around, the plain appeared desolate. Nothing so arid as these reliefs, nothing so sad as these ruins of mountains, and (if we may so express ourselves) these fragments of peaks and mountains which strewed the soil. The satellite seemed to have burst at this spot.

The projectile was still advancing, and this movement did not subside. Circles, craters, and uprooted mountains succeeded each other incessantly. No more plains; no more seas. A never ending Switzerland and Norway. And lastly, in the centre of this region of crevasses, the most splendid mountain on the lunar disc, the dazzling Tycho, in which posterity will ever preserve the name of the illustrious Danish astronomer.

In observing the full moon in a cloudless sky no one has failed to remark this brilliant point of the southern hemisphere. Michel Ardan used every metaphor that his imagination could supply to designate it by. To him this Tycho was a focus of light, a centre of irradiation, a crater vomiting rays. It was the tire of a brilliant wheel, an *asteria* enclosing the disc with its silver tentacles, an enormous eye filled with flames, a glory carved for Pluto's head, a star launched by the Creator's hand, and crushed against the face of the moon!

Tycho forms such a concentration of light that the inhabitants of the earth can see it without glasses, though at a distance of 240,000 miles! Imagine, then, its intensity to the eye of observers placed at a distance of only fifty miles! Seen through this pure ether, its brilliancy was so intolerable that Barbicane and his friends were obliged to blacken their glasses with the gas smoke before they could bear the splendour. Then silent, scarcely uttering an interjection of admiration, they gazed, they contemplated. All their feelings, all their impressions, were concentrated in that look, as under any violent emotion all life is concentrated at the heart.

Tycho belongs to the system of radiating mountains, like Aristarchus and Copernicus; but it is of all the most complete and decided, showing unquestionably the frightful volcanic action to which the formation of the moon is due. Tycho is situated in 43° south lat., and 12° east long. Its centre is occupied by a crater fifty miles broad. It assumes a slightly elliptical form, and is surrounded by an enclosure of annular ramparts, which on the east and west overlook the outer plain from a height of 15,000 feet. It is a group of Mont Blancs, placed round one common centre, and crowned by radiating beams.

What this incomparable mountain really is, with all the projections converging towards it, and the interior excrescences of its crater, photography itself could never represent. Indeed, it is during the full moon that Tycho is seen in all its splendour. Then all shadows disappear, the foreshortening of perspective disappears, and all proofs become white—a disagreeable fact; for this strange region would have been marvellous if reproduced with photographic exactness. It is but a group of hollows, craters, circles, a newtwork of crests; then, as far as the eye could see, a whole volcanic network cast upon this encrusted soil. One can then understand that the bubbles of this central eruption have kept their first form. Crystallized by cooling, they have stereotyped that aspect which the moon formerly presented when under the Plutonian forces.

The distance which separated the travellers from the annular summits of Tycho was not so great but that they could catch the principal details. Even on the causeway forming the fortifications of Tycho, the mountains hanging on to the interior and exterior sloping flanks rose in stories like gigantic terraces. They appeared to be higher by 300 or 400 feet to the west than to the east. No system of terrestrial encampment could equal these natural fortifications. A town built at the bottom of this circular cavity would have been utterly inaccessible.

Inaccessible and wonderfully extended over this soil covered with picturesque projections! Indeed, nature had not left the bottom of this crater flat and empty. It possessed its own peculiar orography, a mountainous system making it a world in itself. The travellers could distinguish clearly cones, central hills, remarkable positions of the soil, naturally placed to receive the chefs-d'œuvre of Selenite architecture. There was marked out the place for a temple, here the ground of a forum, on this spot the plan of a palace, in another the plateau for a citadel; the whole overlocked by a central mountain of 1500 feet. A vast circle, in which ancient Rome could have been held in its entirety ten times over.

"Ah!" exclaimed Michel Ardan, enthusiastic at the sight; "what a grand town might be constructed within that ring of mountains! A quiet city, a peaceful refuge, beyond all human misery. How calm and isolated those misanthropes, those haters of humanity might live there, and all who have a distaste for social life!"

"All! It would be too small for them," replied Barbicane simply.

CHAPTER 18

GRAVE QUESTIONS

BUT the projectile had passed the enceinte of Tycho, and Barbicane and his two companions watched with scrupulous attention the brilliant rays which the celebrated mountain shed so curiously all over the horizon.

What was this radiant glory? What geological phenomenon had designed these ardent beams? This question occupied Barbicane's mind.

Under his eyes ran in all directions luminous furrows, raised at the edges and concave in the centre, some twelve miles, others thirty miles broad. These brilliant trains extended in some places to within 600 miles of Tycho, and seemed to cover, particularly towards the east, the north-east and the north, the half of the southern hemisphere. One of these jets extended as far as the circle of Neander, situated on the 40th meridian. Another by a slight curve furrowed the Sea of Nectar, breaking against the chain of Pyrenees, after a circuit of 800 miles. Others, towards the west, covered the Sea of Clouds and the Sea of Humours with a luminous network. What was the origin of these sparkling rays, which shone on the plains as well as on the reliefs, at whatever height they might be? All started from a common centre, the crater of Tycho. They sprang from him. Herschel attributed their brilliancy to currents of lava congealed by the cold; an opinion, however, which has not been generally adopted. Other astronomers have seen in these inexplicable rays a king of *moraines*, rows of erratic blocks, which had been thrown up at the period of Tycho's formation.

"And why not?" asked Nicholl of Barbicane, who was relating and rejecting these different opinions.

"Because the regularity of these luminous lines, and the violence necessary to carry volcanic matter to such distances, is inexplicable."

"Eh! by Jove!" replied Michel Ardan, "it seems easy enough to me to explain the origin of these rays."

"Indeed?" said Barbicane.

"Indeed," continued Michel. "It is enough to say that it is a vast star, similar to that produced by a ball or a stone thrown at a square of glass!"

"Well!" replied Barbicane, smiling. "And what hand would be powerful enough to throw a ball to give such a shock as that?"

"The hand is not necessary," answered Nicholl, not at all confounded; "and as to the stone, let us suppose it to be a comet."

"Ah! those much-abused comets!" exclaimed Barbicane. "My brave Michel, your explanation is not bad; but your comet is useless. The shock which produced that rent must have come from the inside of the star. A violent contraction of the lunar crust, while cooling, might suffice to imprint this gigantic star."

"A contraction! something like a lunar stomach-ache," said Michel Ardan.

"Besides," added Barbicane, "this opinion is that of an English savant, Nasmyth, and it seems to me to sufficiently explain the radiation of these mountains."

"That Nasmyth was no fool!" replied Michel.

Long did the travellers, whom such a sight could never weary, admire the splendours of Tycho. Their projectile, saturated with luminous gleams in the double irradiation of sun and moon, must have appeared like an incandescent globe. They had passed suddenly from excessive cold to intense heat. Nature was thus preparing them to become Selenties. Become Selenties! That idea brought up once more the question of the habitability of the moon. After what they had seen could the travellers solve it? Would they decide for or against it? Michel Ardan persuaded his two friends to form an opinion, and asked them directly if they thought that men and animals were represented in the lunar world.

"I think that we can answer," said Barbicane; "but according to my idea the question ought not to be put in that form. I ask it to be put differently."

"Put it your own way," replied Michel.

"Here is its," continued Barbicane. "The problem is a double one, and requires a double solution. Is the moon *habitable?* Has the moon ever been *inhabited?*"

"Good!" replied Nicholl. "First let us see whether the moon is habitable."

"To tell the truth, I know nothing about it," answered Michel.

"And I answer in the negative," continued Barbicane. "In her actual state, with her surrounding atmosphere certainly very much reduced, her seas for the most part dried up, her insufficient supply of water restricted, vegetation, sudden alterations of cold and heat, her days and nights of 354 hours; the moon does not seem habitable to me, nor does she seem propitious to animal development, nor sufficient for the wants of existence as we understand it."

"Agreed," replied Nicholl. "But is not the moon habitable for creatures differently organized from ourselves?"

"That question is more difficult to answer, but I will try; and I ask Nicholl if *motion* appears to him to be a necessary result of *life*, whatever be its organization?"

"Without a doubt answered Nicholl.

"Then, my worthy companion, I would answer that we have observed the lunar continent at a distance of 500 yards at most, and that nothing seemed to us to move on the moon's surface. The presence of any kind of life would have been betrayed by its attendant marks, such as divers buildings, and even by ruins. And what have we seen? Everywhere and always the geological works of nature, never the work of man. If, then, there exist representatives of the animal kingdom on the moon, they must have fled to those unfathomable cavities which the eye cannot reach; which I cannot admit, for they must have left traces of their passage on those plains which the atmosphere must cover, however slightly raised it may be. These traces are nowhere visible. There remains but one hypothesis, that of a living race to which motion, which is life, is foreign."

"One might as well say, living creatures which do not live," replied Michel.

"Just so," said Barbicane, "which for us has no meaning."

"Then we may form our opinion?" said Michel.

"Yes," replied Nicholl.

"Very well," continued Michel Ardan, "the Scientific Commission assembled in the projectile of the Gun Club, after having founded their argument on facts recently observed, decide unanimously upon the question of the habitability of the moon—'*No!* the moon is not habitable.' "

This decision was consigned by President Barbicane to his notebook, where the process of the sitting of the 6th of December may be seen.

"Now," said Nicholl, "let us attack the second question, an indispensable complement of the first. I ask the honourable Commission, if the moon is not habitable, has she ever been inhabited, Citizen Barbicane?"

"My friends," replied Barbicane, "I did not undertake this journey in order to form an opinion on the past habitability of our satellite; but I will add that our personal observations only confirm me in this opinion. I believe, indeed I affirm, that the moon has been inhabited by a human race organized like our own; that she had produced animals anatomically formed like the terrestrial animals; but I add that these races, human or animal, have had their day, and are now for ever extinct!"

"Then," asked Michel, "the moon must be older than the earth?"

"No!" said Barbicane decidedly, "but a world which has *grown old* quicker, and whose formation and deformation have been more rapid. Relatively, the organizing force of matter has been much more violent in the interior of the moon than in the interior of the terrestrial globe. The actual state of this cracked, twisted, and burst disc abundantly proves this. The moon and the earth were nothing but gaseous masses originally. These gases have passed into a liquid state under different influences, and the solid masses have been formed later. But most certainly our sphere was still gaseous or liquid, when the moon was solidified by cooling, and had become habitable."

"I believe it," said Nicholl.

"Then," continued Barbicane, "an atmosphere surrounded it, the waters contained within this gaseous envelope could not evaporate. Under the influence of air, water, light, solar heat, and central heat, vegetation took possession of the continents prepared to receive it, and certainly life showed itself about this period, for nature does not expend herself in vain; and a world so wonderfully formed for habitation must necessarily be inhabited."

"But," said Nicholl, "many phenomena inherent in our satellite might cramp the expansion of the animal and vegetable kingdom. For example, its days and nights of 354 hours?"

"At the terrestrial poles they last six months," said Michel.

"An argument of little value, since the poles are not inhabited."

"Let us observe, my friends," continued Barbicane, "that if in the actual state of the moon its long nights and long days created differences of temperature insupportable to organization, it was not so at the historical period of time. The atmosphere enveloped the disc with a fluid mantle; vapour deposited itself in the shape of clouds; this natural screen tempered the ardour of the solar rays, and retained the nocturnal radiation. Light, like heat, can diffuse itself in the air; hence an equality between the influences which no longer exists, now that that atmosphere has almost entirely disappeared. And now I am going to astonish you."

"Astonish us?" said Michel Ardan.

"I firmly believe that at the period when the moon was inhabited, the nights and days did not last 354 hours!"

"And why?" asked Nicholl quickly.

"Because most probably then the rotary motion of the moon upon her axis was not equal to her revolution, an equality which presents each part of her disc during fifteen days to the action of the solar rays."

"Granted," replied Nicholl, "but why should not these two motions have been equal, as they are really so?"

"Because that equality has only been determined by terrestrial attraction. And who can say that this attraction was powerful enough to alter the motion of the moon at that period when the earth was still fluid?"

"Just so," replied Nicholl; "and who can say that the moon has always been a satellite of the earth?"

"And who can say," exclaimed Michel Ardan, "that the moon did not exist before the earth?"

Their imaginations carried them away into an indefinite field of hypothesis. Barbicane sought to restrain them.

"Those speculations are too high," said he; "problems utterly insoluble. Do not let us enter upon them. Let us only admit the insufficiency of the primordial attraction; and then by the inequality of the two motions of rotation and revolution, the days and nights could have succeeded each other on the moon as they succeed each other on the earth. Besides, even without these conditions, life was possible."

"And so," asked Michel Ardan, "humanity has disappeared from the moon?"

"Yes," replied Barbicane, "after having doubtless remained persistently for millions of centuries; by degrees the atmosphere becoming rarefied, the disc became uninhabitable, as the terrestrial globe will one day become by cooling."

"By cooling?"

"Certainly," replied Barbicane; "as the internal fires became extinguished, and the incandescent matter concentrated itself, the lunar crust cooled. By degrees the consequences of these phenomena showed themselves in the disappearance of organized beings, and by the disappearance of vegetation. Soon the atmosphere was rarefied, probably withdrawn by terrestrial attraction; then aërial departure of respirable air, and disappearance of water by means of evaporation. At this period the moon becoming uninhabitable, was no longer inhabited. It was a dead world, such as we see it to-day."

"And you say that the same fate is in store for the earth?"

"Most probably."

"But when?"

"When the cooling of its crust shall have made it uninhabitable."

"And have they calculated the time our unfortunate sphere will take to cool?"

"Certainly."

"And you know these calculations?"

"Perfectly."

"But speak, then, my clumsy savant," exclaimed Michel Arden, "for you make me boil with impatience!"

"Very well, my good Michel," replied Barbicane quietly, "we know what diminution of temperature the earth undergoes in the lapse of a century. And according to certain calculations, this mean temperature will, after a period of 400,000 years, be brought down to zero!"

"Four hundred thousand years!" exclaimed Michel. "Ah! I breathe again. Really I was frightened to hear you; I imagined that we had not more than 50,000 years to live."

Barbicane and Nicholl could not help laughing at their companion's uneasiness. Then Nicholl, who wished to end the discussion, put the second question, which had just been considered again.

"Has the moon been inhabited?" he asked.

The answer was unanimously in the affirmative. But during this discussion, fruitful in somewhat hazardous theories, the projectile was rapidly leaving the moon; the lineaments faded away from the travellers' eyes, mountains were confused in the distance; and of all the wonderful, strange, and fantastical form of the earth's satellite, there soon remained nothing but the imperishable remembrance.

CHAPTER 19

A STRUGGLE AGAINST THE IMPOSSIBLE

For a long time Barbicane and his companions looked silently and sadly upon that world which they had only seen from a distance, as Moses saw the land of Canaan, and which they were leaving without a possibility of ever returning to it. The projectile's position with regard to the moon had altered, and the base was now turned to the earth.

This change, which Barbicane verified, did not fail to surprise them. If the projectile was to gravitate round the satellite in an elliptical orbit, why was not its heaviest part turned towards it, as the moon turns hers to the earth? That was a difficult point.

In watching the course of the projectile they could see that on leaving the moon it followed a course analogous to that traced in approaching her. It was describing a very long ellipse, which would most likely extend to the point of equal attraction, where the influences of the earth and its satellite are neutralized.

Such was the conclusion which Barbicane very justly drew from facts already observed, a conviction which his two friends shared with him.

"And when arrived at this dead point, what will become of us?" asked Michel Ardan.

"We don't know," replied Barbicane.

"But one can draw some hypotheses, I suppose?"

"Two," answered Barbicane; "either the projectile's speed will be insufficient, and it will remain for ever immovable on this line of double attraction—"

"I prefer the other hypothesis, whatever it may be," interrupted Michel.

"Or," continued Barbicane, "its speed will be sufficient, and it will continue its elliptical course, to gravitate for ever around the orb of night."

"A revolution not at all consoling," said Michel, "to pass to the state of humble servants to a moon whom we are accustomed to look upon as our own handmaid. So that is the fate in store for us?"

Neither Barbicane nor Nicholl answered.

"You do not answer," continued Michel impatiently.

"There is nothing to answer," said Nicholl.

"Is there nothing to try?"

"No," answered Barbicane. "Do you pretend to fight against the impossible?"

"Why not? Do one Frenchman and two Americans shrink from such a word?"

"But what would you do?"

"Subdue this motion which is bearing us away."

"Subdue it?"

"Yes," continued Michel, getting animated, "or else alter it, and employ it to the accomplishment of our own ends."

"And how?"

"That is your affair. If artillerymen are not masters of their projectile they are not artillerymen. If the projectile is to command the gunner, we had better ram the gunner into the gun. My faith! fine savants! who do not know what is to become of us after inducing me—"

"Inducing you!" cried Barbicane and Nicholl. "Inducing you! What do you mean by that?"

"No recrimination," said Michel. "I do not complain; the trip has pleased me, the projectile agrees with me; but let us do all that is humanly possible to do to fall somewhere, even if only on the moon."

"We ask no better, my worthy Michel," replied Barbicane, "but means fail us."

"We cannot alter the motion of the projectile?"

"No."

"Nor diminish its speed?"

"No."

"Not even by lightening it, as they lighten an overloaded vessel?"

"What would you throw out?" said Nicholl. "We have no ballast on board; and indeed it seems to me that if lightened it would go much quicker."

"Slower."

"Quicker."

"Neither slower nor quicker," said Barbicane, wishing to make his two friends agree; "for we float in space, and must no longer consider specific weight."

"Very well," cried Michel Ardan in a decided voice; "then there remains but one thing to do."

"What is it?" said Nicholl.

"Breakfast,"answered the cool, audacious Frenchman, who always brought up this solution at the most difficult juncture.

In any case, if this operation had no influence on the projectile's course, it could at least be tried without inconvenience, and even with success from a stomachic point of view. Certainly Michel had none but good ideas.

They breakfasted then at two in the morning; the hour mattered little. Michel served his usual repast, crowned by a glorious bottle drawn from his private cellar. If ideas did not crowd on their brains, we must despair of the Chambertin of 1853. The repast finished, observations began again. Around the projectile, at an invariable distance, were the objects which had been thrown out. Evidently, in its translatory motion round the moon, it had not passed through any atmosphere, for the specific weight of these different objects would have checked their relative speed.

On the side of the terrestrial sphere nothing was to be seen. The earth was but a day old, having been new the night before at twelve; and two days must elapse before its crescent, freed from the solar rays, would serve as a clock to the Selenites, as in its rotatory movement each of its points after twenty-four hours repasses the same lunar meridian.

On the moon's side the sight was different; the orb shone in all her splendour amidst innumerable constellations, whose purity could not be troubled by her rays. On the disc, the plains were already returning to the dark tint which is seen from the earth. The other part of the nimbus remained brilliant, and in the midst of this general brilliancy, Tycho shone prominently like a sun.

Barbicane had no means of estimating the projectile's speed, but reasoning showed that it must uniformly decrease, according to all the laws of mechanical reasoning. Having admitted that the projectile was describing an orbit round the moon, this orbit must necessarily be elliptical; science proves that it must be so. No motive body circulating round an attracting body always occupies one of the foci; so that at one moment the satellite is nearer, and at another farther from the orb around which it gravitates. When the earth is nearest the sun, she is in her perihelion; and in her aphelion at the farthest point. Speaking of the moon, she is nearest to the earth in her perigee, and farthest from it in her apogee. To use analogous expressions, with which the astronomers' language is enriched, if the projectile remains as a satellite of the moon, we must say that it is in its "aposelene" at its farthest point, and in its "periselene" at its nearest. In the latter case, the projectile would attain its maximum speed; and in the former its minimum. It was evidently moving towards its aposelenitical point; and Barbicane had reason to think that its speed would decrease up to this point, and then increase by degrees as it neared the moon. This speed would even become *nil*, if this point joined that of equal attraction. Barbicane studied the consequences of these different situations, and thinking what inference he could draw from them, when he was roughly disturbed by a cry from Michel Ardan.

"By Jove!" he exclaimed, "I must admit we are downright simpletons!"

"I do not say we are not," replied Barbicane; "but why?"

"Because we have a very simple means of checking this speed which is bearing us from the moon, and we do not use it!"

"And what is the means?"

"To use the recoil contained in our rockets."

"Done!" said Nicholl.

"We have not used this force yet," said Barbicane, "it is true, but we will do so."

"When?" asked Michel.

"When the time comes. Observe, my friends, that in the position occupied by the projectile, an oblique position with regard to the lunar disc, our rockets, in slightly altering its direction, might turn it from the moon instead of drawing it nearer?"

"Just so," replied Michel.

"Let us wait, then. By some inexplicable influence, the projectile is turning its base towards the earth. It is probable that at the point of equal attraction, its conical cap will be directed rigidly towards the moon; at that moment we may hope that its speed will be *nil*; then will be the moment to act, and with the influence of our rockets, we may perhaps provoke a fall directly on the surface of the lunar disc."

"Bravo!" said Michel. "What we did not do, what we could not do on our first passage at the dead point, because the projectile was then endowed with too great a speed."

"Very well reasoned," said Nicholl.

"Let us wait patiently," continued Barbicane. "Putting every chance on our side, and after having so much despaired, I may say I think that we shall gain our end."

This conclusion was a signal for Michel Ardan's hips and hurrahs. And none of the audacious boobies remembered the question that they themselves had solved in the negative. No! the moon is not inhabited; no! the moon is probably not habitable. And yet they were going to try every thing to reach her.

One single question remained to be solved. At what precise moment the projectile would reach the point of equal attraction, on which the travellers must play their last card. In order to calculate this to within a few seconds, Barbicane had only to refer to his notes, and to reckon the different heights taken on the lunar parallels. Thus the time necessary to travel over the distance between the dead point and the south pole would be equal to the distance separating the north pole from the dead point. The hours representing the time travelled over were carefully noted, and the calculation was easy. Barbicane found that this point would be reached at one in the morning on the night of the 7th—8th of December. So that, if nothing interfered with its course, it would reach the given point in twenty-two hours.

The rockets had primarily been placed to check the fall of the projectile upon the moon, and now they were going to employ them for a directly contrary purpose. In any case they were ready, and they had only to wait for the moment to set fire to them.

"Since there is nothing else to be done," said Nicholl, "I make a proposition."

"What is it?" asked Barbicane.

"I propose to go to sleep."

"What a motion!" exclaimed Michel Ardan.

"It is forty hours since we closed our eyes," said Nicholl. "Some hours of sleep will restore our strength."

"Never," interrupted Michel.

"Well," continued Nicholl, "every one to his taste; I shall go to sleep." And stretching himself on the divan, he soon snored like a forty-eight pounder.

"That Nicholl has a good deal of sense," said Barbicane, "presently I shall follow his example." Some moments after his continued base supported the captain's barytone.

"Certainly," said Michel Ardan, finding himself alone, "these practical people have sometimes most opportune ideas."

And with his long legs stretched out, and his great arms folded under his head, Michel slept in his turn.

But this sleep could be neither peaceful nor lasting, the minds of these three men were too much occupied, and some hours after, about seven in the morning, all three were on foot at the same instant.

The projectile was still leaving the moon, and turning its conical part more and more towards her.

An explicable phenomenon, but one which happily served Barbicane's ends.

Seventeen hours more, and the moment for action would have arrived.

The day seemed long. However bold the travellers might be, they were greatly impressed by the approach of that moment which would decide all—either precipitate their fall on to the moon, or for ever chain them in an immutable orbit. They counted the hours as they passed too slow for their wish; Barbicane and Nicholl were obstinately plunged in their calculations, Michel going and coming between the narrow walls, and watching that impassive moon with a longing eye.

At times recollections of the earth crossed their minds. They saw once more their friends of the Gun Club, and the dearest of all, J. T. Maston. At that moment, the honourable secretary must be filling his post on the Rocky Mountains. If he could see the projectile through the glass of his gigantic telescope what would he think? After seeing it disappear behind the moon's south pole, he would see them reappear by the north pole! They must therefore be a satellite of a satellite! Had J. T. Maston given this unexpected news to the world? Was this the dénouement of this great enterprise?

But the day passed without incident. The terrestrial midnight arrived. The 8th of December was beginning. One hour more, and the point of equal attraction would be reached. What speed would then animate the projectile? They could not estimate it. But no error could vitiate Barbicane's calculations. At one in the morning, this speed ought to be and would be *nil*.

Besides, another phenomenon would mark the projectile's stopping-point on the neutral line. At that spot the two attractions, lunar and terrestrial, would be annulled. Objects would "weight" no more. This singular fact, which had surprised Barbicane and his companions so much in going, would be repeated on their return under the very same conditions. At this precise moment they must act.

Already the projectile's conical top was sensibly turned towards the lunar disc, presented in such a way as to utilize the whole of the recoil produced by the pressure of the rocket apparatus. The chances were in favour of the travellers. If its speed was utterly annulled on this dead point, a decided movement towards the moon would suffice, however slight, to determine its fall.

"Five minutes to one," said Nicholl.

"All is ready," replied Michel Ardan, directing a lighted match to the flame of the gas.

"Wait!" said Barbicane, holding his chronometer in his hand.

At that moment weight had no effect. The travellers felt in themselves the entire disappearance of it. They were very near the neutral point, if they did not touch it.

"One o'clock," said Barbicane.

Michel Ardan applied the lighted match to a train in communication with the rockets. No detonation was heard in the inside, for there was no air. But, through the scuttles Barbicane saw a prolonged smoke, the flames of which were immediately extinguished.

The projectile sustained a certain shock, which was sensibly felt in the interior.

The three friends looked and listened without speaking, and scarcely breathing. One might have heard the beating of their hearts amidst this perfect silence.

"Are we falling?" asked Michel Ardan, at length.

"No," said Nicholl, "since the bottom of the projectile is not turning to the lunar disc!"

At this moment, Barbicane, quitting the scuttle, turned to his two companions. He was frightfully pale, his forehead wrinkled, and his lips contracted.

"We are falling!" said he.

"Ah!" cried Michel Ardan, "on to the moon?"

"On to the earth!"

"The devil!" exclaimed Michel Ardan, adding philosophically, "well, when we came into this projectile we were very doubtful as to the ease with which we should get out of it."

And now this fearful fall had begun. The speed retained had borne the projectile beyond the dead point. The explosion of the rockets could not divert its course. This speed in going had carried it over the neutral line, and in returning had done the same thing. The laws of physics condemned *it to pass through every point which it had already gone through*. It was a terrible fall, from a height of 160,000 miles, and no springs to break it. According to the laws of gunnery, the projectile must strike the earth with a speed equal to that with which it left the mouth of the Columbiad, a speed of 16,000 yards in the last second.

But to give some figures of comparison, it has been reckoned that an object thrown from the top of the towers of Notre Dame, the height of which is only 200 feet, will arrive on the pavement at a speed of 240 miles per hour. Here the projectile must strike the earth with a speed of 115,200 miles per hour.

"We are lost!" said Michel coolly.

"Very well! if we die," answered Barbicane, with a sort of religious enthusiasm, "the result of our travels will be magnificently spread. It is His own secret that God will tell us! In the other life, the soul will want to know nothing, either of machines or engines! It will be identified with eternal wisdom!"

"In fact," interrupted Michel Ardan, "the whole of the other world may well console us for the loss of that inferior orb called the moon!"

Barbicane crossed his arms on his breast, with a motion of sublime resignation, saying at the same time,—"The will of heaven be done!"

CHAPTER 20

THE SOUNDINGS OF THE "SUSQUEHANNA"

"WELL, lieutenant, and our soundings?"

"I think, sir, that the operation is nearing its completion," replied Lieutenant Bronsfield. "But who would have thought of finding such a depth so near in shore, and only 200 miles from the American coast?"

"Certainly, Bronsfield, there is a great depression," said Captain Blomsberry. "In this spot there is a submarine valley worn by Humboldt's current, which skirts the coast of America as far as the Straits of Magellan."

"These great depths," continued the lieutenant, "are not favourable for laying telegraphic cables. A level bottom, like that supporting the American cable between Valentia and Newfoundland, is much better."

"I agree with you, Bronsfield. With your permission, lieutenant, where are we now?"

"Sir, at this moment we have 3508 fathoms of line out, and the ball which draws the sounding lead has not yet touched the bottom; for if so, it would have come up of itself."

"Brook's apparatus is very ingenious," said Captain Blomsberry; "it gives us very exact soundings."

"Touch!" cried at this moment one of the men at the forewheel, who was superintending the operation.

The captain and the lieutenant mounted the quarter-deck.

"What depth have we?" asked the captain.

"Three thousand six hundred and twenty-seven fathoms," replied the lieutenant, entering it in his note-book.

"Well, Bronsfield," said the captain, "I will take down the result. Now haul in the sounding line. It will be the work of some hours. In that time the engineer can light the furnaces, and we shall be ready to start as soon as you have finished. It is ten o'clock, and with your permission, lieutenant, I will turn in."

"Do so, sir; do so!" replied the lieutenant obligingly.

The captain of the "Susquehanna," as brave a man as need be, and the humble servant of his officers, returned to his cabin, took a brandy-grog, which earned for the steward no end of praise, and turned in, not without having complimented his servant upon his making beds, and slept a peaceful sleep.

It was then ten at night. The eleventh day of the month of December was drawing to a close in a magnificent night.

The "Susquehanna," a corvette of 500 horse-power, of the United States' navy, was occupied in taking soundings in the Pacific Ocean about 200 miles off the American coast, following that long peninsula which stretches down the coast of New Mexico.

The wind had dropped by degrees. There was no disturbance in the air. Their pennant hung motionless from the maintop-gallant-mast truck.

Captain Jonathan Blomsberry (cousin-german of Colonel Blomsberry, one of the most ardent supporters of the Gun Club, who had married an aunt of the captain and daughter of an honourable Kentucky merchant,)—Captain

Blomsberry could not have wished for finer weather in which to bring to a close his delicate operations of sounding. His corvette had not even felt the great tempest, which by sweeping away the groups of clouds on the Rocky Mountains, had allowed them to observe the course of the famous projectile.

Everything went well, and with all the fervour of a Presbyterian, he did not forget to thank heaven for it. The series of soundings taken by the "Susquehanna," had for its aim the finding of a favourable spot for the laying of a submarine cable to connect the Hawaiian Islands with the coast of America.

It was a great undertaking, due to the instigation of a powerful company. Its managing director, the intelligent Cyrus Field, purposed even covering all the islands of Oceania with a vast electrical network, an immense enterprise, and one worthy of American genius.

To the corvette "Susquehanna" had been confided the first operations of sounding. It was on the night of the 11th—12th December, she was in exactly 27° 7′ north lat., and 41° 37′ west long., on the meridian of Washington.

The moon, then in her last quarter, was beginning to rise above the horizon.

After the departure of Captain Blomsberry, the lieutenant and some officers were standing together on the poop. On the appearance of the moon, their thoughts turned to that orb which the eyes of a whole hemisphere were contemplating. The best naval glasses could not have discovered the projectile wandering around its hemisphere, and yet all were pointed towards that brilliant disc which millions of eyes were looking at at the same moment.

"They have been gone ten days," said Lieutenant Bronsfield at last. "What has become of them?"

"They have arrived, lieutenant," exclaimed a young midshipman, "and they are doing what all travellers do when they arrive in a new country, taking a walk!"

"Oh! I am sure of that, if you tell me so, my young friend," said Lieutenant Bronsfield, smiling.

"But," continued another officer, "their arrival cannot be doubted. The projectile was to reach the moon when full on the 5th at midnight. We are now at the 11th of December, which makes six days. And in six times twenty-four hours, without darkness, one would have time to settle comfortably. I fancy I see my brave countrymen encamped at the bottom of some valley, on the borders of a Selenite stream, near a projectile half buried by its fall amidst volcanic rubbish, Captain Nicholl beginning his levelling operations, President Barbicane writing out his notes, and Michel Ardan embalming the lunar solitudes with the perfume of his—"

"Yes! it must be so, it is so!" exclaimed the young midshipman, worked up to a pitch of enthusiasm by this ideal description of his superior officer.

"I should like to believe it," replied the lieutenant, who was quite unmoved. "Unfortunately direct news from the lunar world is still wanting."

"Beg pardon, lieutenant," said the midshipman, "but cannot President Barbicane write?"

A burst of laughter greeted this answer.

"No letters!" continued the young man quickly. "The postal administration has something to see to there."

"Might it not be the telegraphic service that is at fault?" asked one of the officers ironically.

"I fancy I see them."

"Not necessarily," replied the midshipman, not at all confused. "But it is very easy to set up a graphic communication with the earth."

"And how?"

"By means of the telescope at Long's Peak. You know it brings the moon to within four miles of the Rocky Mountains, and that it shows objects on its surface of only nine feet in diameter. Very well; let our industrious friends construct a gigantic alphabet; let them write words three fathoms long, and sentences three miles long, and then they can send us news of themselves?"

The young midshipman, who had a certain amount of imagination, was loudly applauded; Lieutenant Bronsfield allowing that the idea was possible, but observing that if by these means they could *receive* news from the lunar world they could not send any from the terrestrial unless the Selenites had instruments fit for taking distant observations at their disposal.

"Evidently," said one of the officers; "but what has become of the travellers? what they have done, what they have seen, that above all must interest us. Besides, if the experiment has succeeded (which I do not doubt), they will try it again. The Columbiad is still sunk in the soil of Florida. It is now only a question of powder and shot; and every time the moon is at her zenith, a cargo of visitors may be sent to her."

"It is clear," replied Lieutenant Bronsfiled, "that J. T. Maston will one day join his friends."

"If he will have me," cried the midshipman, "I am ready!"

"Oh! volunteers will not be wanting," answered Bronsfield; "and if it were allowed, half of the earth's inhabitants would emigrate to the moon!"

This conversation between the officers of the "Susquehanna" was kept up until nearly one in the morning. We cannot say what blundering systems were broached, what inconsistent theories advanced by these bold spirits. Since Barbicane's attempt, nothing seemed impossible to the Americans. They had already designed an expedition, not only of savants, but of a whole colony towards the Selenite borders, and a complete army, consisting of infantry, artillery, and cavalry, to conquer the lunar world.

At one in the morning, the hauling in of the sounding-line was not yet completed; 1670 fathoms were still out, which would entail some hours' work. According to the commander's orders, the fires had been lighted, and steam was being got up. The "Susquehanna" could have started that very instant.

At that moment (it was seventeen minutes past one in the morning) Lieutenant Bronsfield was preparing to leave the watch and return to his cabin, when his attention was attracted by a distant hissing noise. His comrades and himself first thought that this hissing was caused by the letting off of steam; but lifting their heads, they found that the noise was produced in the highest regions of the air. They had not time to question each other before the hissing became frightfully intense, and suddenly there appeared to their dazzled eyes an enormous meteor, ignited by the rapidity of its course and its friction through the atmospheric strata.

This fiery mass grew larger to their eyes, and fell, with the noise of thunder, upon the bowsprit, which it smashed close to the stem, and buried itself in the waves with a deafening roar!

A few feet nearer, and the "Susquehanna" would have foundered with all on board!

At this instant Captain Blomsberry appeared, half dressed, and rushing on to the forecastel-deck, whither all the officers had hurried, exclaimed, "With your permission, gentlemen, what has happened?"

And the midshipman, making himself as it were the echo of the body, cried, "Commander, it is 'they' come back again!"

CHAPTER 21

J. T. MASTON RECALLED

"It is 'they' come back again!" the young midshipman had said; and every one had understood him. No one doubted but that that meteor was the projectile of the Gun Club. As to the travellers which it enclosed, opinions were divided regarding their fate.

"They are dead!" said one.

"They are alive!" said another; "the crater is deep, and the shock was deadened."

"But they must have wanted air," continued a third speaker; "they must have died of suffocation."

"Burnt!" replied a fourth; "the projectile was nothing but an incandescent mass as it crossed the atmosphere."

"What does it matter!" they exclaimed unanimously; "living or dead, we must pull them out!"

But Captain Blomsberry had assembled his officers, and "with their permission," was holding a council. They must decide upon something to be done immediately. The more hasty ones were for fishing up the projectile. A difficult operation, though not an impossible one. But the corvette had no proper machinery, which must be both fixed and powerful; so it was resolved that they should put in at the nearest port, and give information to the Gun Club of the projectile's fall.

This determination was unanimous. The choice of the port had to be discussed. The neighbouring coast had no anchorage on 27° lat. Higher up, above the peninsula of Monterey, stands the important town from which it takes its name; but, seated on the borders of a perfect desert, it was not connected with the interior by a network of telegraphic wires, and electricity alone could spread these important news fast enough.

Some degrees above opened the bay of San Francisco. Through the capital of the gold country, communication would be easy with the heart of the Union. And in less than two days the "Susquehanna," by putting on high pressure, could arrive in that port. She must therefore start at once.

The fires were made up; they could set off immediately. Two thousand fathoms of line were still out, which Captain Blomsberry, not wishing to lose precious time in hauling in, resolved to cut.

"We will fasten the end to a buoy," said he; "and that buoy will show us the exact spot where the projectile fell."

"Besides," replied Lieutenant Bronsfield, "we have our situation exact—27° 7′ north lat. and 41° 37′ west long."

"Well, Mr. Bronsfield," replied the captain, "now, with your permission, we will have the line cut."

A strong buoy, strengthened by a couple of spars was thrown into the ocean. The end of the rope was carefully lashed to it; and, left solely to the rise and fall of the billows, the buoy would not sensibly deviate from the spot.

At this moment the engineer sent to inform the captain that steam was up and they could start, for which agreeable communication the captain thanked him. The course was then given north-north-east, and the corvette, wearing, steered at full steam direct for San Francisco. It was three in the morning.

Four hundred and fifty miles to cross; it was nothing for a good vessel like the "Susquehanna." In thirty-six hours she had covered that distance; and on the 14th of December, at twenty-seven minutes past one at night, she entered the bay of San Francisco.

At the sight of a ship of the national navy arriving at full speed, with her bowsprit broken, public curiosity was greatly roused. A dense crowd soon assembled on the quay, waiting for them to disembark.

After casting anchor, Captain Blomsberry, and Lieutenant Bronsfield entered an eight-oared cutter, which soon brought them to land.

They jumped on to the quay.

"The telegraph?" they asked, without answering one of the thousand questions addressed to them.

The officer of the port conducted them to the telegraph-office through a concourse of spectators. Blomsberry and Bronsfield entered, while the crowd crushed each other at the door.

Some minutes later a fourfold telegram was sent out—the first to the Naval Secretary at Washington; the second to the Vice-President of the Gun Club, Baltimore; the third to the Hon. J. T. Maston, Long's Peak, Rocky Mountains; the fourth to the Sub-Director of the Cambridge Observatory, Massachusetts.

It was worded as follows:—

"In 20° 7′ north lat., and 41° 37′ west long., on the 12th of December, at 17 minutes past 1 in the morning, the projectile of the Columbiad fell into the Pacific. Send instructions.—BLOMSBERRY, Commander 'Susquehanna.' "

Five minutes afterwards the whole town of San Francisco learned the news. Before six in the evening the different States of the Union had heard the great catastrophe; and after midnight, by the cable, the whole of Europe knew the result of the great American experiment.

We will not attempt to picture the effect produced on the entire world by that unexpected dénouement.

On receipt of the telegram the Naval Secretary telegraphed to the "Susquehanna" to wait in the bay of San Francisco without extinguishing her fires. Day and night she must be ready to put to sea.

The Cambridge Observatory called a special meeting; and, with that composure which distinguishes learned bodies in general, peacefully discussed the scientific bearings of the question. At the Gun Club there was an explosion. All the gunners were assembled. Vice-President the Hon. Wilcome was in the act of reading the premature despatch, in which J. T. Maston and Belfast announced that the projectile had just been seen in the gigantic reflector of Long's Peak, and also that it was held by lunar attraction, and was playing the part of under satellite to the lunar world.

We know the truth on that point.

But on the arrival of Blomsberry's despatch, so decidedly contradicting J. T. Maston's telegram, two parties were formed in the bosom of the Gun Club. On one side were those who admitted the fall of the projectile, and consequently the return of the travellers; on the other, those who believed in the observations of Long's Peak, concluded that the commander of the "Susquehanna" had made a mistake. To the latter the pretended projectile was nothing but a meteor! nothing but a meteor, a shooting globe, which in its fall had smashed the bows of the corvette. It was difficult to answer this argument, for the speed with which it was animated must have made observation very difficult. The commander of the "Susquehanna" and her officers might have made a mistake in all good faith; one argument, however, was in their favour, namely, that if the projectile had fallen on the earth, its place of meeting with the terrestrial globe could only take place on this 27° north lat., and (taking into consideration the time that had elapsed, and the rotary motion of the earth) between the forty-first and the forty-second degree of west longitude. In any case, it was decided in the Gun Club that Blomsberry brothers, Bilsby, and Major Elphinstone should go straight to San Francisco, and consult as to the means of raising the projectile from the depths of the ocean.

These devoted men set off at once; and the railroad, which will soon cross the whole central American, took then as far as St. Louis, where the swift mail-coaches awaited them. Almost at the same moment in which the Secretary of Marine, The Vice-President of the Gun Club, and the Sub-Director of the Observatory received the despatch from San Francisco, the Honourable J. T. Maston was undergoing the greatest excitement he had ever experienced in his life, an excitement which even the bursting of his pet gun, which had more than once nearly cost him his life, had not caused him. We may remember that the Secretary of the Gun Club had started soon after the projectile (and almost as quickly) for the station in Long's Peak, in the Rocky Mountains, J. Belfast, Director of the Cambridge Observatory, accompanying him. Arrived there, the two friends had installed themselves at once, never quitting the summit of their enormous telescope. We know that this gigantic instrument had been set up according to the reflecting system, called by the English, "front view." This arrangement subjected all objects to but one reflection, making the view consequently much clearer; the result was that, when they were taking observations, J. T. Maston and Belfast were placed in the *upper* part of the instrument and not in the lower, which they reached by a circular staircase, a masterpiece of lightness, while below them opened a metal well, terminated by the metallic mirror, which measured 280 feet in depth.

It was on a narrow platform placed above the telescope that the two savants passed their existence, execrating the day which hid the moon from their eyes, and the clouds which obstinately veiled her during the night.

What, then, was their delight when, after some days of waiting, on the night of the 5th of December, they saw the vehicle which was bearing their friends into space! To this delight succeeded a great deception, when, trusting, to a cursory observation, they launched their first telegram to the world, erroneously affirming that the projectile had become a satellite of the moon, gravitating in an immutable orbit.

From that moment it had never shown itself to their eyes—a disappearance all the more easily explained, as it was then passing behind the moon's invisible disc; but when it was time for it to reappear on the visible disc, one may imagine the impatience of the fuming J. T. Maton and his not less impatient companion. Each minute of the night they thought they saw the projectile once more, and they did not see it. Hence constant discussions and violent disputes between them, Belfast affirming that the projectile could not be seen, J. T. Maston maintaining that "it had put his eyes out."

"It is the projectile!" repeated J. T. Maston.

"No," answered Belfast; "it is an avalanche detached from a lunar mountain."

"Well, we shall see it to-morrow."

"No, we shall not see it any more. It is carried into space."

"Yes!"

"No!"

And at these moments, when contradictions rained like hail, the well-known irritability of the Secreatry of the Gun Club constitued a permanent danger for the Hon. Belfast. The existence of these two together would soon have become impossible; but an unforeseen event cut short their everlasting discussions.

During the night, from the 14th to the 15th of December, the two irreconcilable friends were busy observing the lunar disc, J. T. Maston abusing the learned Belfast as usual, who was by his side; the Secretary of the Gun Club maintaining for the thousandth time that he had just seen the projectile, and adding that he could see Michel Ardan's face looking through one of the scuttles, at the same time enforcing his argument by a series of gestures which his formidable hook rendered very unpleasant.

At this moment Belfast's servant appeared on the platform (it was ten at night) and gave his a despatch. It was the commander of the "Susquehanna's" telegram.

Belfast tore the envelope and read, and uttered a cry.

"What!" said J. T. Maston.

"The projectile!"

"Well!"

"Has fallen to the earth!"

Another cry, this time a perfect howl, answered him. He turned towards J. T. Maston. The unfortunate man, imprudently leaning over the metal tube, had disappeared in the immense telescope. A fall of 280 feet! Belfast, dismayed, rushed to the orifice of the reflector.

He breathed. J. T. Maston, caught by his metal hook, was holding on by one of the rings which bound the telescope together, uttering fearful cries.

Belfast called. Help was brought, tackle was let down, and they hoisted up, not without some trouble, the imprudent Secretary of the Gun Club.

He reappeared at the upper orifice without hurt.

"Ah!" said he, "if I had broken the mirror?"

"You would have paid for it," replied Belfast severely.

"And that cursed projectile has fallen?" asked J. T. Maston.

"Into the Pacific!"

"Let us go!"

A quarter of an hour after the two savants were descending the declivity of the Rocky Mountains; and two days after, at the same time as their friends of the Gun Club, they arrived at San Francisco, having killed five horses on the road.

Elphinstone, the brothers Blomsberry, and Bilsby rushed towards them on their arrival.

"What shall we do?" they exclaimed.

"Fish up the projectile," replied J. T. Maston, "and the sooner the better."

CHAPTER 22

RECOVERED FROM THE SEA

THE spot where the projectile sank under the waves was exactly known; but machinery to grasp it and bring it to the surface of the ocean was still wanting. It must first be invented, then made. American engineers could not be troubled with such trifles. The grappling-irons once fixed, by their help they were sure to raise it in spite of its weight, which was lessened by the density of the liquid in which it was plunged.

But fishing-up the projectile was not the only thing to be thought of. They must act promptly in the interest of the travellers. No one doubted that they were still living.

"Yes," repeated J. T. Maston incessantly, whose confidence gained over everybody, "our friends are clever people, and they cannot have fallen like simpletons. They are alive, quite alive; but we must make haste if we wish to find them so. Food and water do not trouble me; they have enough for a long while. But air, air, that is what they will soon want; so quick, quick!"

And they did go quick. They fitted up the "Susquehanna" for her new destination. Her powerful machinery was brought to bear upon the hauling-chains. The aluminium projectile only weighed 19,250lbs., a weight very inferior to that of the transatlantic cable which had been drawn up under similar conditions. The only difficulty was in fishing-up a cylindro-conical projectile, the walls of which were so smooth as to offer no hold for the hooks. On that account engineer Murchison hastened to San Francisco, and had some enormous grappling-irons fixed on an automatic system, which would never let the projectile go if it once succeeded in seizing it in its powerful claws. Diving-dresses were also prepared, which through this impervious covering allowed the divers to observe the bottom of the sea. He also had put on board an apparatus of compressed air very cleverly designed. There were perfect chambers pierced with scuttles, which, with water let into certain compartments, could draw it down into great depths. These apparatuses were at San Francisco, where they had been used in the construction of a submarine breakwater; and very fortunately it was so, for there was not time to construct any. But in spite of the perfection of the machinery, in spite of the ingenuity of the savants entrusted with the use of them, the success of the operation was far from being certain. How great were the chances against them, the projectile being 20,000 feet under the water! And if even it was brought to the surface, how would the travellers have borne the terrible shock which

20,000 feet of water had perhaps not sufficiently broken? At any rate they must act quickly. J. T. Maston hurried the workmen day and night. He was ready to don the diving-dress himself, or try the air apparatus, in order to reconnoitre the situation of his courageous friends.

But in spite of all diligence displayed in preparing the different engines, in spite of the considerable sum placed at the disposal of the Gun Club by the Government of the Union, five long days (five centuries!) elapsed before the preparations were complete. During this time public opinion was excited to the highest pitch. Telegrams were exchanged incessantly throughout the entire world by means of wires and electric cables. The saving of Barbicane, Nicholl, and Michel Ardan was an international affair. Every one who had subscribed to the Gun Club was directly interested in the welfare of the travellers.

At length the hauling-chains, the air-chambers, and the automatic grappling-irons were put on board. J. T. Maston, Engineer Murchison, and the delegates of the Gun Club, were already in their cabins. They had but to start, which they did on the 21st of December, at eight o'clock at night, the corvette meeting with a beautiful sea, a north-easterly wind, and rather sharp cold. The whole population of San Francisco was gathered on the quay, greatly excited but silent, reserving their hurrahs for the return. Steam was fully up, and the screw of the "Susquehanna" carried them briskly out of the bay.

It is needless to relate the conversations on board between the officers, sailors, and passengers. All these men had but one thought. All these hearts beat under the same emotion. Whilst they were hastening to help them, what were Barbicane and his companions doing? What had become of them? Were they able to attempt any bold manœuvre to regain their liberty? None could say. The truth is that every attempt must have failed! Immersed nearly four miles under the ocean, this metal prison defied every effort of its prisoners.

On the 23rd inst., at eight in the morning, after a rapid passage, the "Susquehanna" was due at the fatal spot. They must wait till twelve to take the reckoning exactly. The buoy to which the sounding line had been lashed had not yet been recognized.

At twelve, Captain Blomsberry, assisted by his officers who superintended the observations, took the reckoning in the prescence of the delegates of the Gun Club. Then there was a moment of anxiety. Her position decided, the "Susquehanna" was found to be some minutes to westward of the spot where the projectile had disappeared beneath the waves.

The ship's course was then changed so as to reach this exact point.

At forty-seven minutes past twelve they reached the buoy, it was in perfect condition, and must have shifted but little.

"At last!" exclaimed J. T. Maston.

"Shall we begin?" asked Captain Blomsberry.

"Without losing a second."

Every precaution was taken to keep the corvette almost completely motionless. Before trying to seize the projectile, Engineer Murchison wanted to find its exact postion at the bottom of the ocean. The submarine apparatus destined for this expedition was supplied with air. The working of these engines was not without danger, for at 20,000 feet below the surface of the water, and under such great pressure, they were exposed to fracture, the consequences of which would be dreadful.

J. T. Maston, the Brothers Blomsberry, and Engineer Murchison, without heeding these dangers, took their places in the air-chamber. The commander, posted on his bridge, superintended the operation, ready to stop or haul in the chains on the slightest signal. The screw had been shipped, and the whole power of the machinery collected on the capstan would have quickly drawn the apparatus on board. The descent began at twenty-five minutes past one at night, and the chamber, drawn under by the reservoirs full of water, disappeared from the surface of the ocean.

The emotion of the officers and sailors on board was now divided between the prisoners in the projectile and the prisoners in the submarine apparatus. As to the latter, they forgot themselves, and, glued to the windows of the scuttles, attentively watched the liquid mass through which they were passing.

The descent was rapid. At seventeen minutes past two, J. T. Maston and his companions had reached the bottom of the Pacific; but they saw nothing but an arid desert, no longer animated by either fauna or flora. By the light of their lamps, furnished with powerful reflectors, they could see the dark beds of the ocean for a considerable extent of view, but the projectile was nowhere to be seen.

The impatience of these bold divers cannot be described, and having an electrical communication with the corvette, they made a signal already agreed upon, and for the space of a mile the "Susquehanna" moved their chamber along some yards above the bottom.

Thus they explored the whole submarine plain, deceived at every turn by optical illusions which almost broke their hearts. Here a rock, there a projectile from the ground, seemed to be the much-sought-for projectile; but their mistake was soon discovered, and then they were in despair.

"But where are they? where are they?" cried J. T. Maston. And the poor man called loudly upon Nicholl, Barbicane, and Michel Ardan, as if his unfortunate friends could either hear or answer him through such an impenetrable medium! The search continued under these conditions until the vitiated air compelled the divers to ascend.

The hauling in began about six in the evening, and was not ended before midnight.

"To-morrow," said J. T. Maston, as he set foot on the bridge of the corvette.

"Yes," answered Captain Blomsberry.

"And on another spot?"

"Yes."

J. T. Maston did not doubt of their final success, but his companions, no longer upheld by the excitement of the first hours, understood all the difficulty of the enterprise. What seemed easy at San Francisco, seemed here in the wide ocean almost impossible. The chances of success diminished in rapid proportion; and it was from chance alone that the meeting with the projectile might be expected.

The next day, the 24th, in spite of the fatigue of the previous day, the operation was renewed. The corvette advanced some minutes to westward, and the apparatus, provided with air, bore the same explorers to the depths of the ocean.

The whole day passed in fruitless research; the bed of the sea was a desert. The 25th brought no other results, nor the 26th.

It was disheartening. They thought of those unfortunates shut up in the projectile for twenty-six days. Perhaps at that moment they were experiencing the first approach of suffocation; that is, if they had escaped the dangers of their fall. The air was spent, and doubtless with the air all their *morale*.

"The air, possibly," answered J. T. Maston resolutely, "but their *morale* never!"

On the 28th, after two more days of search, all hope was gone. This projectile was but an atom in the immensity of the ocean. They must give up all idea of finding it.

But J. T. Maston would not hear of going away. He would not abandon the place without at least discovering the tomb of his friends. But Commander Blomsberry could no longer persist, and in spite of the exclamations of the worthy Secretary, was obliged to give the order to sail.

On the 29th of December, at nine a.m., the "Susquehanna," heading N.E., resumed her course to the bay of San Francisco.

It was ten in the morning; the corvette was under half steam, as if regretting to leave the spot where the catastrophe had taken place, when a sailor, perched on the maintop gallant crosstrees, watching the sea, cried suddenly,—

"A buoy on the lee bow!"

The officers looked in the direction indicated, and by the help of their glasses, saw that the object signalled had the appearance of one of those buoys which are used to mark the passages of bays or rivers. But, singularly to say, a flag floating on the wind surmounted its cone, which emerged five or six feet out of water. This buoy shone under the rays of the sun as if it had been made of plates of silver. Commander Blomsberry, J. T. Maston, and the delegates of the Gun Club were mounted on the bridge, examining this object straying at random on the waves.

All looked with feverish anxiety, but in silence. None dared give expression to the thoughts which came to the minds of all.

The corvette approached to within two cables' lengths of the object.

A shudder ran through the whole crew. That flag was the American flag!

At this moment a perfect howling was heard; it was the brave J. T. Maston, who had just fallen all in a heap. Forgetting on the one hand that his right arm had been replaced by an iron hook, and on the other that a simple gutta-percha cap covered his brainbox, he had given himself a formidable blow.

They hurried towards him, picked him up, restored him to life. And what were his first words?

"Ah! trebly brutes! quadruply idiots! quintuply boobies that we are!"

"What is it?" exclaimed every one around him.

"What is it?"

"Come, speak!"

"It is, simpletons," howled the terrible Secretary, "it is that the projectile only weighs 19,250lbs.!"

"Well?"

"And that it displaces twenty-eight tons, or in other words 56,000lbs., and that consequently *it floats!*"

Ah! what stress the worthy man laid on the verb "float!" And it was true! All, yes! all these savants had forgotten this fundamental law, namely, that on account of its specific lightness, the projectile, after having been drawn by its fall to the greatest depths of the ocean, must naturally return to the surface. And now it was floating quietly at the mercy of the waves.

The boats were put to sea. J. T. Maston and his friends had rushed into them!

Excitement was at its height! Every heart beat loudly whilst they advanced to the projectile. What did it contain? Living or dead? Living, yes! living, at least unless death had struck Barbicane and his two friends since they had hoisted the flag. Profound silence reigned on the boats. All were breathless. Eyes no longer saw. One of the scuttles of the projectile was open. Some pieces of glass remained in the frame, showing that it had been broken. This scuttle was actually five feet above the water.

A boat came alongside, that of J. T. Maston, and J. T. Maston rushed to the broken window.

At that moment they heard a clear and merry voice, the voice of Michel Ardan, exclaiming in an accent of triumph,—

"White all, Barbicane, white all!"

Barbicane, Michel Ardan, and Nicholl were playing at dominoes!

CHAPTER 23

THE END

WE may remember the intense sympathy which had accompanied the travellers on their departure. If at the beginning of the enterprise they had excited such emotion both in the old and new world, with what enthusiasm would they be received on their return! The millions of spectators which had beset the peninsula of Florida, would they not rush to meet these sublime adventurers? Those legions of strangers, hurrying from all parts of the globe towards the American shores, would they leave the Union without having seen Barbicane, Nicholl, and Michel Ardan? No! and the ardent passion of the public was bound to respond worthily to the greatness of the enterprise. Human creatures who had left the terrestrial sphere, and returned after this strange voyage into celestial space, could not fail to be received as the prophet Elias would be if he came back to earth. To see them first, and then to hear them, such was the universal longing.

Barbicane, Michel Ardan, Nicholl, and the delegates of the Gun Club, returning without delay to Baltimore, were received with indescribable enthusiasm. The notes of President Barbicane's voyage were ready to be given to the public. The *New York Herald* bought the manuscript at a price not yet known, but which must have been very high. Indeed, during the publication of "A Journey to the Moon," the sale of this paper amounted to five millions of copies. Three days after the return of the travellers to the earth, the slightest detail of their expedition was known. There remained nothing more but to see the heroes of this superhuman enterprise.

The expedition of Barbicane and his friends round the moon had enabled them to correct the many admitted theories regarding the terrestrial satellite. These savants had observed *de visu*, and under particular circumstances. They knew what systems should be rejected, what retained with regard to the formation of that orb, its origin, its habitability. Its past, present, and future had even given up their last secrets. Who could advance objections against conscientious observers, who at less than twenty-four miles distance had marked that curious mountain of Tycho, the strangest system of lunar orography? How answer those savants whose sight had penetrated the abyss of Pluto's circle? How contradict those bold ones whom the chances of their enterprise had borne over that invisible face of the disc, which no human eye until then had ever seen? It was now their turn to impose some limit on that Selenographic science, which had reconstructed the lunar world as Cuvier did the skeleton of a fossil, and say, "The moon *was* this, a habitable world, inhabited before the earth! The moon *is* that, a world uninhabitable, and now uninhabited."

To celebrate the return of its most illustrious member and his two companions, the Gun Club decided upon giving a banquet, but a banquet worthy of the conquerors, worthy of the American people, and under such conditions that all the inhabitants of the Union could directly take part it in.

All the head lines of railroads in the State were joined by flying rails; and on all the platforms, lined with the same flags, and decorated with the same ornaments, were tables laid and all served alike. At certain hours, successively calculated, marked by electric clocks which beat the seconds at the same time, the population were invited to take their place at the banquet tables. For four days, from the 5th to the 9th of January, the trains were stopped as they are on Sundays on the railways of the United States, and every road was open. One engine only at full speed, drawing a triumphal carriage, had the right of travelling for those four days on the railroads of the United States.

The engine was manned by a driver and a stoker, and bore, by special favour, the Hon. J. T. Maston, Secretary of the Gun Club. The carriage was reserved for President Barbicane, Colonel Nicholl, and Michel Ardan. At the whistle of the driver, amid the hurrahs, and all the admiring vociferations of the American language, the train left the platform of Baltimore. It travelled at a speed of 160 miles in the hours. But what was this speed compared with that which had carried the three heroes from the mouth of the Columbiad?

Thus they sped from one town to the other, finding whole populations at table on their road, saluting them with the same acclamations, lavishing the same bravos! They travelled in this way through the east of the Union, Pennsylvania, Connecticut, Massachusetts, Vermont, Maine, and New Hampshire; the north and the west by New York, Ohio, Michigan, and Wisconsin; returning to the south by Illinois, Missouri, Arkansas, Texas, and Louisiana; they went to the south-east by Alabama and Florida, going up by Georgia and the Carolinas, visiting the centre by Tennessee, Kentucky, Virginia, and Indiana, and, after quitting the Washington station, re-entered Baltimore, where for four days one would have thought that the United States of America were seated at one immense banquet, saluting them simultaneously with the same hurrahs! The apotheosis was worthy of these three heroes whom fable would have placed in the rank of demi-gods.

And now will this attempt, unprecedented in the annals of travels lead to any practical result? Will direct communication with the moon ever be established? Will they ever lay the foundation of a travelling service through the solar world? Will they go from one planet to another, from Jupiter to Mercury, and after awhile from one star to another, from the Polar to Sirius? Will this means of locomotion allow us to visit those suns which swarm in the firmament?

To such questions no answer can be given. But knowing the bold ingenuity

"White all, Barbicane."

of the Anglo-Saxon race, no one would be astonished if the Americans seek to make some use of President Barbicane's attempt.

Thus, some time after the return of the travellers, the public received with marked favour the announcement of a company, limited, with a capital of a hundred million of dollars, divided into a hundred thousand shares of a thousand dollars each, under the name of the "*National Company of Interstellary Communication.*" President, Barbicane; Vice-President, Captain Nicholl; Secretary, J. T. Maston; Director of Movements, Michel Ardan.

And as it is part of the American temperament to foresee everything in business, even failure, the Honourable Harry Trolloppe, judge commissioner, and Francis Drayton, magistrate, were nominated beforehand!

Around the World in Eighty Days

Passepartout was not at all frightened.

CHAPTER 1

IN WHICH PHILEAS FOGG AND PASSEPARTOUT ACCEPT EACH OTHER, THE ONE AS MASTER, THE OTHER AS MAN

MR. PHILEAS FOGG lived, in 1872, at No. 7, Saville Row, Burlington Gardens, the house in which Sheridan died in 1814. He was one of the most noticeable members of the Reform Club, though he seemed always to avoid attracting attention; an enigmatical personage, about whom little was known, except that he was a polished man of the world. People said that he resembled Byron,—at least that his head was Byronic; but he was a bearded, tranquil Byron, who might live on a thousand years without growing old.

Certainly an Englishman it was more doubtful whether Phileas Fogg was a Londoner. He was never seen on 'Change, nor at the Bank, nor in the counting-rooms of the "City;" no ships ever came into London docks of which he was the owner; he had no public employment; he had never been entered at any of the Inns of Court, either at the Temple, or Lincoln's Inn, or Gray's Inn; nor had his voice ever resounded in the Court of Chancery, or in the Exchequer, or the Queen's Bench, or the Ecclesiastical Courts. He certainly was not a manufacturer; nor was he a merchant or a gentleman farmer. His name was strange to the scientific and learned societies, and he never was known to take part in the sage deliberations of the Royal Institution or the London Institution, the Artisan's Association or the Institution of Arts and Sciences. He belonged, in fact, to none of the numerous societies which swarm in the English capital, from the Harmonic to that of the Entomologists, founded mainly for the purpose of abolishing pernicious insects.

Phileas Fogg was a member of the Reform, and that was all.

The way in which he got admission to this exclusive club was simple enough.

He was recommended by the Barings, with whom he had an open credit. His checks were regularly paid at sight from his account current, which was always flush.

Was Phileas Fogg rich? Undoubtedly. But those who knew him best could not imagine how he had made his fortune, and Mr. Fogg was the last person to whom to apply for the information. He was not lavish, nor, on the contrary, avaricious; for whenever he knew that money was needed for a noble, useful, or benevolent purpose, he supplied it quietly, and sometimes anonymously. He was, in short, the least communicative of men. He talked very little, and seemed all the more mysterious for his taciturn manner. His daily habits were quite open to observation; but whatever he did was so exactly the same thing that he had always done before, that the wits of the curious were fairly puzzled.

Had he travelled? It was likely, for no one seemed to know the world more familiarly; there was no spot so secluded that he did not appear to have an intimate acquaintance with it. He often corrected, with a few clear words, the thousand conjectures advanced by members of the club as to lost and unheard-of travellers, pointing out the true probabilities, and seeming as if gifted with a sort of second sight, so often did events justify his predictions. He must have travelled everywhere, at least in the spirit.

It was at least certain that Phileas Fogg had not absented himself from London for many years. Those who were honoured by a better acquaintance with him than the rest, declared that nobody could pretend to have ever seen him anywhere else. His sole pastimes were reading the papers and playing whist. He often won at this game, which, as a silent one, harmonized with his nature; but his winnings never went into his purse, being reserved as a fund for his charities. Mr. Fogg played, not to win, but for the sake of playing. The game was in his eyes a contest, a struggle with a difficulty, yet a motionless, unwearying struggle, congenial to his tastes.

Phileas Fogg was not known to have either wife or children, which may happen to the most honest people; either relatives or near friends, which is certainly more unusual. He lived alone in his house in Saville Row, whither none penetrated. A single domestic sufficed to serve him. He breakfasted and dined at the club, at hours mathematically fixed, in the same room, at the same table, never taking his meals with other members, much less bringing a guest with him; and went home at exactly midnight, only to retire at once to bed. He never used the cosy chambers which the Reform provides for its favoured members. He passed ten hours out of the twenty-four in Saville Row, either in sleeping or making his toilet. When he chose to take a walk, it was with a regular step in the entrance hall with its mosaic flooring, or in the circular gallery with its dome supported by twenty red porphyry Ionic columns, and illumined by blue painted windows. When he breakfasted or dined, all the resources of the club—its kitchens and pantries, its buttery and dairy—aided to crowd his table with their most succulent stores; he was served by the gravest waiters, in dress coats, and shoes with swan-skin soles, who proffered the viands in special porcelain, and on the finest linen; club decanters, of a lost mould, contained his sherry, his port, and his cinnamon-spiced claret; while his beverages were refreshingly cooled with ice, brought at great cost from the American lakes.

If to live in this style is to be eccentric, it must be confessed that there is something good in eccentricity!

The mansion in Saville Row, though not sumptuous, was exceedingly comfortable. The habits of its occupant were such as to demand but little from the sole domestic; but Phileas Fogg required him to be almost superhumanly prompt and regular. On this very 2nd of October he had dismissed James Forster, because that luckless youth had brought him shaving-water at eighty-four degrees Fahrenheit instead of eighty-six; and he was awaiting his successor, who was due at the house between eleven and half-past.

Phileas Fogg was seated squarely in his arm-chair, his feet close together like those of a grenadier on parade, his hands resting on his knees, his body straight, his head erect; he was steadily watching a complicated clock which indicated the hours, the minutes, the seconds, the days, the months, and the years. At

Phileas Fogg.

exactly half-past eleven Mr. Fogg would, according to his daily habit, quit Saville Row, and repair to the Reform.

A rap at this moment sounded on the door of the cosy apartment where Phileas Fogg was seated, and James Forster, the dismissed servant, appeared.

"The new servant," said he.

A young man of thirty advanced and bowed.

"You are a Frenchman, I believe," asked Phileas Fogg, "and your name is John?"

"Jean, if monsieur pleases," replied the new-comer, "Jean Passepartout, a surname which has clung to me because I have a natural aptness for going out of one business into another. I believe I'm honest, monsieur, but, to be outspoken, I've had several trades. I've been an itinerant singer, a circus-rider, when I used to vault like Leotard, and dance on a rope like Blondin. Then I got to be a professor of gymnastics, so as to make better use of my talents; and then I was a sergeant fireman at Paris, and assisted at many a big fire. But I quitted France five years ago, and, wishing to taste the sweets of domestic life, took service as a valet here in England. Finding myself out of place, and hearing that Monsieur Phileas Fogg was the most exact and settled gentleman in the United Kingdom, I have come to monsieur in the hope of living with him a tranquil life, and forgetting even the name of Passepartout."

"Passepartout suits me," responded Mr. Fogg. "You are well recommended to me; I hear a good report of you. You know my conditions?"

"Yes, monsieur."

"Good. What time is it?"

"Twenty-two minutes after eleven," returned Passepartout, drawing an enormous silver watch from the depths of his pocket.

"You are too slow," said Mr. Fogg.

"Pardon me, monsieur, it is impossible—"

"You are four minutes too slow. No matter; it's enough to mention the error. Now from this moment, twenty-nine minutes after eleven, a.m., this Wednesday, October 2nd, you are in my service."

Phileas Fogg got up, took his hat in his left hand, put it on his head with an automatic motion, and went off without a word.

Passepartout heard the street door shut once; it was his new master going out. He heard it shut again; it was his predecessor, James Forster, departing in his turn. Passepartout remained alone in the house in Saville Row.

CHAPTER 2

IN WHICH PASSEPARTOUT IS CONVINCED THAT HE HAS AT LAST FOUND HIS IDEAL

"FAITH," muttered Passepartout, somewhat flurried, "I've seen people at Madame Tussaud's as lively as my new master!"

Madame Tussaud's "people," let it be said, are of wax, and are much visited in London; speech is all that is wanting to make them human.

During his brief interview with Mr. Fogg, Passepartout had been carefully observing him. He appeared to be a man about forty years of age, with fine, handsome features, and a tall, well-shaped figure; his hair and whiskers were light, his forehead compact and unwrinkled, his face rather pale, his teeth magnificent. His countenance possessed in the highest degree what physiognomists call "repose in action," a quality of those who act rather than talk. Calm and phlegmatic, with a clear eye, Mr. Fogg seemed a perfect type of that English composure which Angelica Kauffmann has so skilfully represented on canvas. Seen in the various phases of his daily life, he gave the idea of being perfectly well-balanced, as exactly regulated as a Leroy chronometer. Phileas Fogg was, indeed, exactitude personified, and this was betrayed even in the expression of his very hands and feet; for in men, as well as in animals, the limbs themselves are expressive of the passions.

He was so exact that he was never in a hurry, was always ready, and was economical alike of his steps and his motions. He never took one step too many, and always went to his destination by the shortest cut; he made no superfluous gestures, and was never seen to be moved or agitated. He was the most deliberate person in the world, yet always reached his destination at the exact moment.

He lived alone, and so to speak, outside of every social relation; and as he knew that in this world account must be taken of friction, and that friction retards, he never rubbed against anybody.

As for Passepartout, he was a true Parisian of Paris. Since he had abandoned his own country for England, taking service as a valet, he had in vain searched for a master after his own heart. Passepartout was by no means one of those pert dunces depicted by Molière, with a bold gaze and a nose held high in the air; he was an honest fellow, with a pleasant face, lips a trifle protruding, soft-mannered and serviceable, with a good round head, such as one likes to see on the shoulders of a friend. His eyes were blue, his complexion rubicund, his figure almost portly and well built, his body muscular, and his physical powers fully developed by the exercises of his younger days. His brown hair was somewhat tumbled; for while the ancient sculptors are said to have known eighteen methods of arranging Minerva's tresses, Passepartout was familiar with but one of dressing his own: three strokes of a large-tooth comb completed his toilet.

It would be rash to predict how Passepartout's lively nature would agree with Mr. Fogg. It was impossible to tell whether the new servant would turn out as absolutely methodical as his master required; experience alone could solve the question. Passepartout had been a sort of vagrant in his early years, and now yearned for repose; but so far he had failed to find it, though he had already served in ten English houses. But he could not take root in any of these; with chagrin he found his masters invariably whimsical and irregular, constantly running about the country, or on the look-out for adventure. His last master, young Lord Longferry, Member of Parliament, after passing his nights in the Haymarket taverns, was too often brought home in the morning on policemen's shoulders. Passepartout, desirous of respecting the gentleman whom he served, ventured a mild remonstrance on such conduct; which being ill received, he took his leave. Hearing that Mr. Phileas Fogg was looking for a servant, and that his life was one of unbroken regularity, that he neither travelled nor stayed from home overnight, he felt sure that this would be the place he was after. He presented himself, and was accepted, as has been seen.

At half-past eleven, then, Passepartout found himself alone in the house in Saville Row. He began its inspection without delay, scouring it from cellar to garret. So clean, well-arranged, solemn a mansion pleased him; it seemed to him like a snail's shell, lighted and warmed by gas, which sufficed for both these purposes. When Passepartout reached the second story, he recognized at once the room which he was to inhabit, and he was well satisfied with it. Electric bells and speaking-tubes afforded communication with the lower stories; while on the mantel stood an electric clock, precisely like that in Mr. Fogg's bedchamber, both beating the same second at the same instant. "That's good, that'll do," said Passepartout to himself.

He suddenly observed, hung over the clock, a card which, upon inspection, proved to be a programme of the daily routine of the house. It comprised all that was required of the servant, from eight in the morning, exactly at which hour Phileas Fogg rose, till half-past eleven, when he left the house for the Reform Club,—all the details of service, the tea and toast at twenty-three minutes past eight, the shaving-water at thirty-seven minutes past nine, and the toilet at twenty minutes before ten. Everything was regulated and foreseen that was to be done from half-past eleven a.m. till midnight, the hour at which the methodical gentleman retired.

Mr. Fogg's wardrobe was amply supplied and in the best taste. Each pair of trousers, coat, and vest bore a number, indicating the time of year and season at which they were in turn to be laid out for wearing; and the same system was applied to the master's shoes. In short, the house in Saville Row, which must have been a very temple of disorder and unrest under the illustrious but dissipated Sheridan, was cosiness, comfort, and method idealized. There was no study, nor were there books, which would have been quite useless to Mr. Fogg; for at the Reform two libraries, one of general literature and the other of law and politics, were at his service. A moderate-sized safe stood in his bedroom, constructed so as to defy fire as well as burglars; but Passepartout found neither arms nor hunting weapons anywhere; everything betrayed the most tranquil and peaceable habits.

Having scrutinized the house from top to bottom, he rubbed his hands, a broad smile overspread his features, and he said joyfully, "This is just what I wanted! Ah, we shall get on together, Mr. Fogg and I! What a domestic and regular gentleman! A real machine; well, I don't mind serving a machine."

CHAPTER 3

IN WHICH A CONVERSATION TAKES PLACE WHICH SEEMS LIKELY TO COST PHILEAS FOGG DEAR

PHILEAS FOGG, having shut the door of his house at half-past eleven, and having put his right foot before his left five hundred and seventy-five times, and his left foot before his right five hundred and seventy-six times, reached the Reform Club, an imposing edifice in Pall Mall, which could not have cost less than three millions. He repaired at once to the dining-room, the nine windows of which

Jean Passepartout.

open upon a tasteful garden, where the trees were already gilded with an autumn colouring; and took his place at the habitual table, the cover of which had already been laid for him. His breakfast consisted of a side-dish, a broiled fish with Reading sauce, a scarlet slice of roast beef garnished with mushrooms, a rhubarb and gooseberry tart, and a morsel of Cheshire cheese, the whole being washed down with several cups of tea, for which the Reform is famous. He rose at thirteen minutes to one, and directed his steps towards the large hall, a sumptuous apartment adorned with lavishly-framed paintings. A flunkey handed him an uncut *Times,* which he proceeded to cut with a skill which betrayed familiarity with this delicate operation. The perusal of this paper absorbed Phileas Fogg until a quarter before four, whilst the *Standard,* his next task, occupied him till the dinner hour. Dinner passed as breakfast had done, and Mr. Fogg reappeared in the reading-room and sat down to the *Pall Mall* at twenty minutes before six. Half an hour later several members of the Reform came in and drew up to the fireplace, where a coal fire was steadily burning. They were Mr. Fogg's usual partners at whist: Andrew Stuart, an engineer; John Sullivan and Samuel Fallentin, bankers; Thomas Flanagan, a brewer; and Gauthier Ralph, one of the Directors of the Bank of England;—all rich and highly respectable personages, even in a club which comprises the princes of English trade and finance.

"Well, Ralph," said Thomas Flanagan, "what about that robbery?"

"Oh," replied Stuart, "the bank will lose the money."

"On the contrary," broke in Ralph, "I hope we may put our hands on the robber. Skillful detectives have been sent to all the principal ports of America and the Continent, and he'll be a clever fellow if he slips through their fingers."

"But have you got the robber's description?" asked Stuart.

"In the first place, he is no robber at all," returned Ralph, positively.

"What! a fellow who makes off with fifty-five thousand pounds, no robber?"

"No."

"Perhaps he's a manufacturer, then."

"The *Daily Telegraph* says that he is a gentleman."

It was Phileas Fogg, whose head now emerged from behind his newspapers, who made this remark. He bowed to his friends, and entered into the conversation. The affair which formed its subject, and which was town talk, had occurred three days before at the Bank of England. A package of bank-notes, to the value of fifty-five thousand pounds, had been taken from the principal cashier's table, that functionary being at the moment engaged in registering the receipt of three shillings and sixpence. Of course he could not have his eyes everywhere. Let it be observed that the Bank of England reposes a touching confidence in the honesty of the public. There are neither guards nor gratings to protect its treasures; gold, silver, banknotes are freely exposed, at the mercy of the first comer. A keen observer of English customs relates that, being in one of the rooms of the Bank one day, he had the curiosity to examine a gold ingot weighing some seven or eight pounds. He took it up, scrutinized it, passed it to his neighbour, he to the next man, and so on until the ingot, going from hand to hand, was transferred to the end of a dark entry; nor did it return to its place for half an hour. Meanwhile, the cashier had not so much as raised his head. But in the present instance things had not gone so smoothly. The package of notes not being found when five o'clock sounded from the ponderous clock in the "drawing office," the amount was passed to the account of profit and loss. As soon as the robbery was discovered, picked detectives hastened off to

Liverpool, Glasgow, Havre, Suez, Brindisi, New York, and other ports, inspired by the proffered reward of two thousand pounds, and five per cent on the sum that might be recovered. Detectives were also charged with narrowly watching those who arrived at or left London by rail, and a judicial examination was at once entered upon.

There were real grounds for supposing, as the *Daily Telegraph* said, that the thief did not belong to a professional band. On the day of the robbery a well-dressed gentleman of polished manners, and with a well-to-do air, had been observed going to and fro in the paying-room, where the crime was committed. A description of him was easily procured, and sent to the detectives; and some hopeful spirits, of whom Ralph was one, did not despair of his apprehension. The papers and clubs were full of the affair, and everywhere people were discussing the probabilities of a successful pursuit; and the Reform Club was especially agitated, several of its members being Bank officials.

Ralph would not concede that the work of the detectives was likely to be in vain, for he thought that the prize offered would greatly stimulate their zeal and activity. But Stuart was far from sharing this confidence; and as they placed themselves at the whist-table, they continued to argue the matter. Stuart and Flanagan played together, while Phileas Fogg had Fallentin for his partner. As the game proceeded the conversation ceased, excepting between the rubbers, when it revived again.

"I maintain," said Stuart, "that the chances are in favour of the thief, who must be a shrewd fellow."

"Well, but where can he fly to?" asked Ralph. "No country is safe for him."

"Pshaw!"

"Where could he go, then?"

"Oh, I don't know that. The world is big enough."

"It was once," said Phileas Fogg, in a low tone. "Cut, sir," he added, handing the cards to Thomas Flanagan.

The discussion fell during the rubber, after which Stuart took up its thread.

"What do you mean by 'once'? Has the world grown smaller?"

"Certainly," returned Ralph. "I agree with Mr. Fogg. The world *has* grown smaller, since a man can now go round it ten times more quickly than a hundred years ago. And that is why the search for this thief will be more likely to succeed."

"And also why the thief can get away more easily."

"Be so good as to play, Mr. Stuart," said Phileas Fogg.

But the incredulous Stuart was not convinced, and when the hand was finished, said eagerly: "You have a strange way, Ralph, of proving that the world has grown smaller. So, because you can go round it in three months—"

"In eighty days," interrupted Phileas Fogg.

"That is true, gentlemen," added John Sullivan. "Only eighty days, now that the section between Rothal and Allahabad, on the Great Indian Peninsula Railway, has been opened. Here is the estimate made by the *Daily Telegraph*:—

From London to Suez *viâ* Mont Cenis and Brindisi, by rail and steamboats	7 days.
From Suez to Bombay, by steamer	13 "
From Bombay to Calcutta, by rail	3 "
From Calcutta to Hong Kong, by steamer	13 "

From Hong Kong to Yokohama (Japan), by steamer	6	days.
From Yokohama to San Francisco, by steamer	22	"
From San Francisco to New York, by rail	7	"
From New York to London, by steamer and rail	9	"
Total	80	days.

"Yes, in eighty days!" exclaimed Stuart, who in his excitement made a false deal. "But that doesn't take into account bad weather, contrary winds, shipwrecks, railway accidents, and so on."

"All included," returned Phileas Fogg, continuing to play despite the discussion.

"But suppose the Hindoos or Indians pull up the rails," replied Stuart; "suppose they stop the trains, pillage the luggage-vans, and scalp the passengers!"

"All included," calmly retorted Fogg; adding, as he threw down the cards, "Two trumps."

Stuart, whose turn it was to deal, gathered them up, and went on: "You are right theoretically, Mr. Fogg, but practically—"

"Practically also, Mr. Stuart."

"I'd like to see you do it in eighty days."

"It depends on you. Shall we go?"

"Heaven preserve me! But I would wager four thousand pounds that such a journey, made under these conditions, is impossible."

"Quite possible, on the contrary," returned Mr. Fogg.

"Well, make it, then!"

"The journey round the world in eighty days?"

"Yes."

"I should like nothing better."

"When?"

"At once. Only I warn you that I shall do it at your expense."

"It's absurd!" cried Stuart, who was beginning to be annoyed at the persistency of his friend. "Come, let's go on with the game."

"Deal over again, then," said Phileas Fogg. "There's a false deal."

Stuart took up the pack with a feverish hand; then suddenly put them down again.

"Well, Mr. Fogg," said he, "it shall be so: I will wager the four thousand on it."

"Calm yourself, my dear Stuart," said Fallentin. "It's only a joke."

"When I say I'll wager," returned Stuart, "I mean it."

"All right," said Mr. Fogg; and, turning to the others, he continued, "I have a deposit of twenty thousand at Baring's which I will willingly risk upon it."

"Twenty thousand pounds!" cried Sullivan. "Twenty thousand pounds, which you would lose by a single accidental delay!"

"The unforeseen does not exist," quietly replied Phileas Fogg.

"But, Mr. Fogg, eighty days are only the estimate of the least possible time in which the journey can be made."

"A well-used minimum suffices for everything."

"But, in order not to exceed it, you must jump mathematically from the trains upon the steamers, and from the steamers upon the trains again."

"I will jump—mathematically."

"You are joking."

"A true Englishman doesn't joke when he is talking about so serious a thing as a wager," replied Phileas Fogg, solemnly. "I will bet twenty thousand pounds against any one who wishes, that I will make the tour of the world in eighty days or less; in nineteen hundred and twenty hours, or a hundred and fifteen thousand two hundred minutes. Do you accept?"

"We accept," replied Messrs. Stuart, Fallentin, Sullivan, Flanagan, and Ralph, after consulting each other.

"Good," said Mr. Fogg. "The train leaves for Dover at a quarter before nine. I will take it."

"This very evening?" asked Stuart.

"This very evening," returned Phileas Fogg. He took out and consulted a pocket almanac, and added, "As today is Wednesday, the second of October, I shall be due in London, in this very room of the Reform Club, on Saturday, the twenty-first of December, at a quarter before nine p.m.; or else the twenty thousand pounds, now deposited in my name at Baring's, will belong to you, in fact and in right, gentlemen. Here is a check for the amount."

A memorandum of the wager was at once drawn up and signed by the six parties, during which Phileas Fogg preserved a stoical composure. He certainly did not bet to win, and had only staked the twenty thousand pounds, half of his fortune, because he foresaw that he might have to expend the other half to carry out this difficult, not to say unattainable, project. As for his antagonists, they seemed much agitated; not so much by the value of their stake, as because they had some scruples about betting under conditions so difficult to their friend.

The clock struck seven, and the party offered to suspend the game so that Mr. Fogg might make his preparations for departure.

"I am quite ready now," was his tranquil response. "Diamonds are trumps: be so good as to play, gentlemen."

CHAPTER 4

IN WHICH PHILEAS FOGG ASTOUNDS PASSEPARTOUT, HIS SERVANT

HAVING won twenty guineas at whist, and taken leave of his friends, Phileas Fogg, at twenty-five minutes past seven, left the Reform Club.

Passepartout, who had conscientiously studied the programme of his duties, was more than surprised to see his master guilty of the inexactness of appearing at this unaccustomed hour; for, according to rule, he was not due in Saville Row until precisely midnight.

Mr. Fogg repaired to his bedroom, and called out, "Passepartout!"

Passepartout did not reply. It could not be he who was called; it was not the right hour.

"Passepartout!" repeated Mr. Fogg, without raising his voice.

Passepartout made his appearance.

"I've called you twice," observed his master.

"But it is not midnight," responded the other, showing his watch.

"I know it; I don't blame you. We start for Dover and Calais in ten minutes."

A puzzled grin overspread Passepartout's round face; clearly he had not comprehended his master.

"Monsieur is going to leave home?"

"Yes," returned Phileas Fogg. "We are going round the world."

Passepartout opened wide his eyes, raised his eyebrows, held up his hands, and seemed about to collapse, so overcome was he with stupefied astonishment.

"Round the world!" he murmured.

"In eighty days," responded Mr. Fogg. "So we haven't a moment to lose."

"But the trunks?" gasped Passepartout, unconsciously swaying his head from right to left.

"We'll have no trunks; only a carpet-bag, with two shirts and three pairs of stockings for me, and the same for you. We'll buy our clothes on the way. Bring down my mackintosh and travelling-cloak, and some stout shoes, though we shall do little walking. Make haste!"

Passepartout tried to reply, but could not. He went out, mounted to his own room, fell into a chair, and muttered: "That's good, that is! And I, who wanted to remain quiet!"

He mechanically set about making the preparations for departure. Around the world in eighty days! Was his master a fool? No. Was this a joke, then? They were going to Dover; good. To Calais; good again. After all, Passepartout, who had been away from France five years, would not be sorry to set foot on his native soil again. Perhaps they would go as far as Paris, and it would do his eyes good to see Paris once more. But surely a gentleman so chary of his steps would stop there; no doubt,—but, then, it was none the less true that he was going away, this so domestic person hitherto!

By eight o'clock Passepartout had packed the modest carpet-bag, containing the wardrobes of his master and himself; then, still troubled in mind, he carefully shut the door of his room, and descended to Mr. Fogg.

Mr. Fogg was quite ready. Under his arm might have been observed a red-bound copy of "Bradshaw's Continental Railway Steam Transit and General Guide," with its time-tables showing the arrival and departure of steamers and railways. He took the carpet-bag, opened it, and slipped into it a goodly roll of Bank of England notes, which would pass wherever he might go.

"You have forgotten nothing?" asked he.

"Nothing, monsieur."

"My mackintosh and cloak?"

"Here they are."

"Good. Take this carpet-bag," handing it to Passepartout. "Take good care of it, for there are twenty thousand pounds in it."

Passepartout nearly dropped the bag, as if the twenty thousand pounds were in gold, and weighed him down.

Master and man then descended, the street-door was double-locked, and at the end of Saville Row they took a cab and drove rapidly to Charing Cross. The cab stopped before the railway station at twenty minutes past eight. Passepartout jumped off the box and followed his master, who, after paying the cabman, was about to enter the station, when a poor beggar-woman, with a child in her arms, her naked feet smeared with mud, her head covered with a wretched bonnet, from which hung a tattered feather, and her shoulders shrouded in a ragged shawl, approached, and mournfully asked for alms.

Mr. Fogg took out the twenty guineas he had just won at whist, and handed them to the beggar, saying, "Here, my good woman. I'm glad that I met you;" and passed on.

Passepartout had a moist sensation about the eyes; his master's action touched his susceptible heart.

Two first-class tickets for Paris having been speedily purchased, Mr. Fogg was crossing the station to the train, when he perceived his five friends of the Reform.

"Well, gentlemen," said he, "I'm off, you see; and if you will examine my passport when I get back, you will be able to judge whether I have accomplished the journey agreed upon."

"Oh, that would be quite unnecessary, Mr. Fogg," said Ralph, politely. "We will trust your word, as a gentleman of honour."

"You do not forget when you are due in London again?" asked Stuart.

"In eighty days; on Saturday, the 21st of December, 1872, at a quarter before nine p.m. Good-bye, gentlemen."

Phileas Fogg and his servant seated themselves in a first-class carriage at twenty minutes before nine; five minutes later the whistle screamed, and the train slowly glided out of the station.

The night was dark, and a fine, steady rain was falling. Phileas Fogg, snugly ensconced in his corner, did not open his lips. Passepartout, not yet recovered from his stupefaction, clung mechanically to the carpet-bag, with its enormous treasure.

Just as the train was whirling through Sydenham, Passepartout suddenly uttered a cry of despair.

"What's the matter?" asked Mr. Fogg.

"Alas! In my hurry—I—I forgot—"

"What?"

"To turn off the gas in my room!"

"Very well, young man," returned Mr. Fogg, coolly; "it will burn—at your expense."

CHAPTER 5

IN WHICH A NEW SPECIES OF FUNDS, UNKNOWN TO THE MONEYED MEN, APPEARS ON 'CHANGE

PHILEAS FOGG rightly suspected that his departure from London would create a lively sensation at the West End. The news of the bet spread through the Reform Club, and afforded an exciting topic of conversation to its members. From the Club it soon got into the papers throughout England. The boasted "tour of the world" was talked about, disputed, argued with as much warmth as if the subject were another Alabama claim. Some took sides with Phileas Fogg, but the large majority shook their heads and declared against him; it was absurd, impossible, they declared, that the tour of the world could be made, except theoretically and on paper, in this minimum of time, and with the existing means of travelling. The *Times, Standard, Morning Post,* and *Daily News,* and twenty other highly respectable newspapers scouted Mr. Fogg's project as madness; the *Daily Telegraph* alone hesitatingly supported him. People in general thought him a lunatic, and blamed his Reform Club friends for having accepted a wager which betrayed the mental aberration of its proposer.

Articles no less passionate than logical appeared on the question, for geography is one of the pet subjects of the English; and the columns devoted to Phileas Fogg's venture were eagerly devoured by all classes of readers. At first some rash individuals, principally of the gentler sex, espoused his cause, which became still more popular when the *Illustrated London News* came out with his portrait, copied from a photograph in the Reform Club. A few readers of the *Daily Telegraph* even dared to say, "Why not, after all? Stranger things have come to pass."

At last a long article appeared, on the 7th of October, in the bulletin of the Royal Geographical Society, which treated the question from every point of view, and demonstrated the utter folly of the enterprise.

Everything, it said, was against the travellers, every obstacle imposed alike by man and by nature. A miraculous agreement of the times of departure and arrival, which was impossible, was absolutely necessary to his success. He might, perhaps, reckon on the arrival of trains at the designated hours, in Europe, where the distances were relatively moderate; but when he calculated upon crossing India in three days, and the United States in seven, could he rely beyond misgiving upon accomplishing his task? There were accidents to machinery, the liability of trains to run off the line, collisions, bad weather, the blocking up by snow,—were not all these against Phileas Fogg? Would he not find himself, when travelling by steamer in winter, at the mercy of the winds and fogs? Is it uncommon for the best ocean steamers to be two or three days behind time? But a single delay would suffice to fatally break the chain of communication; should Phileas Fogg once miss, even by an hour, a steamer, he would have to wait for the next, and that would irrevocably render his attempt vain.

This article made a great deal of noise, and being copied into all the papers, seriously depressed the advocates of the rash tourist.

Everybody knows that England is the world of betting men, who are of a higher class than mere gamblers; to bet is in the English temperament. Not only the members of the Reform, but the general public, made heavy wagers for or against Phileas Fogg, who was set down in the betting books as if he were a race-horse. Bonds were issued, and made their appearance on 'Change; "Phileas Fogg bonds" were offered at par or at a premium, and a great business was done in them. But five days after the article in the bulletin of the Geographical Society appeared, the demand began to subside: "Phileas Fogg" declined. They were offered by packages, at first of five, then of ten, until at last nobody would take less than twenty, fifty, a hundred!

Lord Albemarle, an elderly paralytic gentleman, was now the only advocate of Phileas Fogg left. This noble lord, who was fastened to his chair, would have given his fortune to be able to make the tour of the world, if it took ten years; and he bet five thousand pounds on Phileas Fogg. When the folly as well as the uselessness of the adventure was pointed out to him, he contented himself with replying, "If the thing is feasible, the first to do it ought to be an Englishman."

The Fogg party dwindled more and more, everybody was going against him, and the bets stood a hundred and fifty and two hundred to one; and a week after his departure, an incident occurred which deprived him of backers at any price.

The commissioner of police was sitting in his office at nine o'clock one evening, when the following telegraphic despatch was put into his hands:—

Suez to London.

ROWAN, COMMISSIONER OF POLICE, SCOTLAND YARD:

I've found the bank robber, Phileas Fogg. Send without delay warrant of arrest to Bombay.

FIX, *Detective.*

The effect of this despatch was instantaneous. The polished gentleman disappeared to give place to the bank robber. His photograph, which was hung with those of the rest of the members at the Reform Club, was minutely examined, and it betrayed, feature by feature, the description of the robber which had been provided to the police. The mysterious habits of Phileas Fogg were recalled; his solitary ways, his sudden departure; and it seemed clear that, in undertaking a tour round the world on the pretext of a wager, he had had no other end in view than to elude the detectives, and throw them off his track.

CHAPTER 6

IN WHICH FIX, THE DETECTIVE, BETRAYS A VERY NATURAL IMPATIENCE

THE circumstances under which this telegraphic despatch about Phileas Fogg was sent were as follows:—

The steamer "Mongolia," belonging to the Peninsula and Oriental Company, built of iron, of two thousand eight hundred tons burden, and five hundred horse-power, was due at eleven o'clock a.m. on Wednesday, the 9th of October, at Suez. The "Mongolia" plied regularly between Brindisi and Bombay *viâ* the Suez Canal, and was one of the fastest steamers belonging to the company, always making more than ten knots an hour between Brindisi and Suez, and nine and a half between Suez and Bombay.

Two men were promenading up and down the wharves, among the crowd of natives and strangers who were sojourning at this once straggling village—now, thanks to the enterprise of M. Lesseps, a fast-growing town. One was the British consul at Suez, who, despite the prophecies of the English Government, and the unfavourable predictions of Stephenson, was in the habit of seeing, from his office window, English ships daily passing to and fro on the great canal, by which the old roundabout route from England to India by the Cape of Good Hope was abridged by at least a half. The other was a small, slight-built personage, with a nervous, intelligent face, and bright eyes peering out from under eyebrows which he was incessantly twitching. He was just now manifesting unmistakable signs of impatience, nervously pacing up and down, and unable to stand still for a moment. This was Fix, one of the detectives who had been despatched from England in search of the bank robber; it was his task to narrowly watch every passenger who arrived at Suez, and to follow up all who seemed to be suspicious characters, or bore a resemblance to the description of the criminal, which he had received two days before from the police head-quarters at London. The detective was evidently inspired by the hope of obtaining the splendid reward which would be the prize of success, and awaited with a feverish impatience, easy to understand, the arrival of the steamer "Mongolia."

"So you say, consul," asked he for the twentieth time, "that this steamer is never behind time?"

"No, Mr. Fix," replied the consul. "She was bespoken yesterday at Port Said, and the rest of the way is of no account to such a craft. I repeat that the 'Mongolia' has been in advance of the time required by the company's regulations, and gained the prize awarded for excess of speed."

"Does she come directly from Brindisi?"

"Directly from Brindisi; she takes on the Indian mails there, and she left there Saturday at five p.m. Have patience, Mr. Fix; she will not be late. But really I don't see how, from the description you have, you will be able to recognize your man, even if he is on board the 'Mongolia.' "

"A man rather feels the presence of these fellows, consul, than recognizes them. You must have a scent for them, and a scent is like a sixth sense which combines hearing, seeing, and smelling. I've arrested more than one of these gentlemen in my time, and if my thief is on board, I'll answer for it, he'll not slip through my fingers."

"I hope so, Mr. Fix, for it was a heavy robbery."

"A magnificent robbery, consul; fifty-five thousand pounds! We don't often have such windfalls. Burglars are getting to be so contemptible nowadays! A fellow gets hung for a handful of shillings!"

"Mr. Fix," said the consul, "I like your way of talking, and hope you'll succeed; but I fear you will find it far from easy. Don't you see, the description which you have there has a singular resemblance to an honest man?"

"Consul," remarked the detective, dogmatically, "great robbers *always* resemble honest folks. Fellows who have rascally faces have only one course to take, and that is to remain honest; otherwise they would be arrested off-hand. The artistic thing is, to unmask honest countenances; it's no light task, I admit, but a real art."

Mr. Fix evidently was not wanting in a tinge of self-conceit.

Little by little the scene on the quay became more animated; sailors of various nations, merchants, ship-brokers, porters, fellahs, bustled to and fro as if the steamer were immediately expected. The weather was clear, and slightly chilly. The minarets of the town loomed above the houses in the pale rays of the sun. A jetty pier, some two thousand yards long, extended into the roadstead. A number of fishing-smacks and coasting boats, some retaining the fantastic fashion of ancient galleys, were discernible on the Red Sea.

As he passed among the busy crowd, Fix, according to habit, scrutinized the passers-by with a keen, rapid glance.

It was now half-past ten.

Detective Fix.

"The steamer doesn't come!" he exclaimed, as the port clock struck.

"She can't be far off now," returned his companion.

"How long will she stop at Suez?"

"Four hours; long enough to get in her coal. It is thirteen hundred and ten miles from Suez to Aden, at the other end of the Red Sea, and she has to take in a fresh coal supply."

"And does she go from Suez directly to Bombay?"

"Without putting in anywhere."

"Good," said Fix. "If the robber is on board, he will no doubt get off at Suez, so as to reach the Dutch or French colonies in Asia by some other route. He ought to know that he would not be safe an hour in India, which is English soil."

"Unless," objected the consul, "he is exceptionally shrewd. An English criminal, you know, is always better concealed in London than anywhere else."

This observation furnished the detective food for thought, and meanwhile the consul went away to his office. Fix, left alone, was more impatient than ever, having a presentiment that the robber was on board the "Mongolia." If he had indeed left London intending to reach the New World, he would naturally take the route *viâ* India, which was less watched and more difficult to watch than that of the Atlantic. But Fix's reflections were soon interrupted by a succession of sharp whistles, which announced the arrival of the "Mongolia." The porters and fellahs rushed down the quay, and a dozen boats pushed off from the shore to go and meet the steamer. Soon her gigantic hull appeared passing along between the banks, and eleven o'clock struck as she anchored in the road. She brought an unusual number of passengers, some of whom remained on deck to scan the picturesque panorama of the town, while the greater part disembarked in the boats, and landed on the quay.

Fix took up a position, and carefully examined each face and figure which made its appearance. Presently one of the passengers, after vigorously pushing his way through the importunate crowd of porters, came up to him, and politely asked if he could point out the English consulate, at the same time showing a passport which he wished to have *visaed*. Fix instinctively took the passport, and with a rapid glance read the description of its bearer. An involuntary motion of surprise nearly escaped him, for the description in the passport was identical with that of the bank robber which he had received from Scotland Yard.

"Is this your passport?" asked he.

"No, it's my master's."

"And your master is—"

"He stayed on board."

"But he must go to the consul's in person, so as to establish his identity."

"Oh, is that necessary?"

"Quite indispensable."

"And where is the consulate?"

"There, on the corner of the square," said Fix, pointing to a house two hundred steps off.

"I'll go and fetch my master, who won't be much pleased, however, to be disturbed."

The passenger bowed to Fix, and returned to the steamer.

CHAPTER 7

WHICH ONCE MORE DEMONSTRATES THE USELESSNESS OF PASSPORTS AS AIDS TO DETECTIVES

THE detective passed down the quay, and rapidly made his way to the consul's office, where he was at once admitted to the presence of that official.

"Consul," said he, without preamble, "I have strong reasons for believing that my man is a passenger on the 'Mongolia.' " And he narrated what had just passed concerning the passport.

"Well, Mr. Fix," replied the consul, "I shall not be sorry to see the rascal's face; but perhaps he won't come here,—that is, if he is the person you suppose him to be. A robber doesn't quite like to leave traces of his flight behind him; and besides, he is not obliged to have his passport countersigned."

"If he is as shrewd as I think he is, consul, he will come."

"To have his passport *visaed?*"

"Yes. Passports are only good for annoying honest folks, and aiding in the flight of rogues. I assure you it will be quite the thing for him to do; but I hope you will not *visa* the passport."

"Why not? If the passport is genuine, I have no right to refuse."

"Still I must keep this man here until I can get a warrant to arrest him from London."

"Ah, that's your look-out. But I cannot—"

The consul did not finish his sentence, for as he spoke a knock was heard at the door, and two strangers entered, one of whom was the servant whom Fix had met on the quay. The other, who was his master, held out his passport with the request that the consul would do him the favour to *visa* it. The consul took the document and carefully read it, whilst Fix observed, or rather devoured, the stranger with his eyes from a corner of the room.

"You are Mr. Phileas Fogg?" said the consul, after reading the passport.

"I am."

"And this man is your servant?"

"He is; a Frenchman, named Passepartout."

"You are from London?"

"Yes."

"And you are going—"

"To Bombay."

"Very good, sir. You know that a *visa* is useless, and that no passport is required?"

"I know it, sir," replied Phileas Fogg; "but I wish to prove, by your *visa*, that I came by Suez."

"Very well, sir."

The consul proceeded to sign and date the passport, after which he added his official seal. Mr. Fogg paid the customary fee, coldly bowed, and went out, followed by his servant.

"Well?" queried the detective.

"Well, he looks and acts like a perfectly honest man," replied the consul.

"Possibly; but that is not the question. Do you think, consul, that this phlegmatic gentleman resembles, feature by feature, the robber whose description I have received?"

"I concede that; but then, you know, all descriptions—"

"I'll make certain of it," interrupted Fix. "The servant seems to me less mysterious than the master; besides, he's a Frenchman, and can't help talking. Excuse me for a little while, consul."

Fix started off in search of Passepartout.

Meanwhile Mr. Fogg, after leaving the consulate, repaired to the quay, gave some orders to Passepartout, went off to the "Mongolia" in a boat, and descended to his cabin. He took up his note-book, which contained the following memoranda:—

"Left London, Wednesday, October 2nd, at 8.45 p.m.

"Reached Paris, Thursday, October 3rd, at 7.20 a.m.

"Left Paris, Thursday, at 8.40 a.m.

"Reached Turin by Mont Cenis, Friday, October 4th, at 6.35 a.m.

"Left Turin, Friday, at 7.20 a.m.

"Arrived at Brindisi, Saturday, October 5th, at 4 p.m.

"Sailed on the 'Mongolia,' Saturday, at 5 p.m.

"Reached Suez, Wednesday, October 9th, at 11 a.m.

"Total of hours spent, 158½; or, in days, six days and a half."

These dates were inscribed in an itinerary divided into columns, indicating the month, the day of the month, and the day for the stipulated and actual arrivals at each principal point,—Paris, Brindisi, Suez, Bombay, Calcutta, Singapore, Hong Kong, Yokohama, San Francisco, New York, and London,—from the 2nd of October to the 21st of December; and giving a space for setting down the gain made or the loss suffered on arrival at each locality. This methodical record thus contained an account of everything needed, and Mr. Fogg always knew whether he was behindhand or in advance of his time. On this Friday, October 9th, he noted his arrival at Suez, and observed that he had as yet neither gained nor lost. He sat down quietly to breakfast in his cabin, never once thinking of inspecting the town, being one of those Englishmen who are wont to see foreign countries through the eyes of their domestics.

CHAPTER 8

IN WHICH PASSEPARTOUT TALKS RATHER MORE, PERHAPS, THAN IS PRUDENT

FIX soon rejoined Passepartout, who was lounging and looking about on the quay, as if he did not feel that he, at least, was obliged not to see anything.

"Well, my friend," said the detective, coming up with him, "is your passport *visaed?*"

"Ah, it's you, is it, monsieur?" responded Passepartout. "Thanks, yes, the passport is all right."

"And you are looking about you?"

"Yes; but we travel so fast that I seem to be journeying in a dream. So this is Suez?"

"Yes."

"In Egypt?"

"Certainly, in Egypt."

"And in Africa?"

"In Africa."

"In Africa!" repeated Passepartout. "Just think, monsieur, I had no idea that we should go farther than Paris; and all that I saw of Paris was between twenty minutes past seven and twenty minutes before nine in the morning, between the Northern and the Lyons stations, through the windows of a car, and in a driving rain! How I regret not having seen once more Père la Chaise and the circus in the Champs Elysées!"

"You are in a great hurry, then?"

"I am not, but my master is. By the way, I must buy some shoes and shirts. We came away without trunks, only with a carpet-bag."

"I will show you an excellent shop for getting what you want."

"Really, monsieur, you are very kind."

And they walked off together, Passepartout chatting volubly as they went along.

"Above all," said he, "don't let me lose the steamer."

"You have plenty of time; it's only twelve o'clock."

Passepartout pulled out his big watch. "Twelve!" he exclaimed; "why it's only eight minutes before ten."

"Your watch is slow."

"My watch? A family watch, monsieur, which has come down from my great-grandfather! It doesn't vary five minutes in the year, it's a perfect chronometer, look you."

"I see how it is," said Fix. "You have kept London time, which is two hours behind that of Suez. You ought to regulate your watch at noon in each country."

"I regulate my watch? Never!"

"Well, then, it will not agree with the sun."

"So much the worse for the sun, monsieur. The sun will be wrong, then!"

And the worthy fellow returned the watch to its fob with a defiant gesture. After a few minutes' silence, Fix resumed: "You left London hastily, then?"

"I rather think so! Last Friday at eight o'clock in the evening, Monsieur Fogg came home from his club, and three quarters of an hour afterwards we were off."

"But where is your master going?"

"Always straight ahead. He is going round the world."

"Round the world?" cried Fix.

"Yes, and in eighty days! He says it is on a wager; but, between us, I don't believe a word of it. That wouldn't be common sense. There's something else in the wind."

"Ah! Mr. Fogg is a character, is he?"

"I should say he was."

"Is he rich?"

"No doubt, for he is carrying an enormous sum in bran-new bank notes with him. And he doesn't spare the money on the way, either: he has offered a large reward to the engineer of the 'Mongolia' if he gets us to Bombay well in advance of time."

"And you have known your master a long time?"

"Why, no; I entered his service the very day we left London."

The effect of these replies upon the already suspicious and excited detective may be imagined. The hasty departure from London soon after the robbery; the large sum carried by Mr. Fogg; his eagerness to reach distant countries; the pretext of an eccentric and foolhardy bet,—all confirmed Fix in his theory. He continued to pump poor Passepartout, and learned that he really knew little or nothing of his master, who lived a solitary existence in London, was said to be rich, though no one knew whence came his riches, and was mysterious and impenetrable in his affairs and habits. Fix felt sure that Phileas Fogg would not land at Suez, but was really going on to Bombay.

"Is Bombay far from here?" asked Passepartout.

"Pretty far. It is a ten days' voyage by sea."

"And in what country is Bombay?"

"India."

"In Asia?"

"Certainly."

"The deuce! I was going to tell you,—there's one thing that worries me,—my burner!"

"What burner?"

"My gas-burner, which I forgot to turn off, and which is at this moment burning—at my expense. I have calculated, monsieur, that I lose two shillings every four and twenty hours, exactly sixpence more than I earn; and you will understand that the longer our journey—"

Did Fix pay any attention to Passepartout's trouble about the gas? It is not probable. He was not listening, but was cogitating a project. Passepartout and he had now reached the shop, where Fix left his companion to make his purchases, after recommending him not to miss the steamer, and hurried back to the consulate. Now that he was fully convinced, Fix had quite recovered his equanimity.

"Consul," said he, "I have no longer any doubt. I have spotted my man. He passed himself off as an odd stick, who is going round the world in eighty days."

"Then he's a sharp fellow," returned the consul, "and counts on returning to London after putting the police of the two continents off his track."

"We'll see about that," replied Fix.

"But are you not mistaken?"

"I am not mistaken."

"Why was this robber so anxious to prove, by the *visa,* that he had passed through Suez?"

"Why? I have no idea; but listen to me."

He reported in a few words the most important parts of his conversation with Passepartout.

"In short," said consul, "appearances are wholly against this man. And what are you going to do?"

"Send a despatch to London for a warrant of arrest to be despatched instantly to Bombay, take passage on board the 'Mongolia,' follow my rogue to India, and there, on English ground, arrest him politely, with my warrant in my hand, and my hand on his shoulder."

Having uttered these words with a cool, careless air, the detective took leave of the consul, and repaired to the telegraph office, whence he sent the despatch which we have seen to the London police office. A quarter of an hour later found Fix, with a small bag in his hand, proceeding on board the "Mongolia;" and ere many moments longer, the noble steamer rode out at full steam upon the waters of the Red Sea.

CHAPTER 9

IN WHICH THE RED SEA AND THE INDIAN OCEAN PROVE PROPITIOUS TO THE DESIGNS OF PHILEAS FOGG

THE distance between Suez and Aden is precisely thirteen hundred and ten miles, and the regulations of the company allow the steamers one hundred and thirty-eight hours in which to traverse it. The "Mongolia," thanks to the vigorous exertions of the engineer, seemed likely, so rapid was her speed, to reach her destination considerably within that time. The greater part of the passengers from Brindisi were bound for India—some for Bombay, others for Calcutta by way of Bombay, the nearest route thither, now that a railway crosses the Indian peninsula. Among the passengers was a number of officials and military officers of various grades, the latter being either attached to the regular British forces, or commanding the Sepoy troops and receiving high salaries ever since the central government has assumed the powers of the East India Company; for the sub-lieutenants get 280*l*., brigadiers, 2400*l*., and generals of division, 4000*l*. What with the military men, a number of rich young Englishmen on their travels, and the hospitable efforts of the purser, the time passed quickly on the "Mongolia." The best of fare was spread upon the cabin tables at breakfast, lunch, dinner, and the eight o'clock supper, and the ladies scrupulously changed their toilets twice a day; and the hours were whiled away, when the sea was tranquil, with music, dancing, and games.

But the Red Sea is full of caprice, and often boisterous, like most long and narrow gulfs. When the wind came from the African or Asian coast, the "Mongolia," with her long hull, rolled fearfully. Then the ladies speedily disappeared below; the pianos were silent; singing and dancing suddenly ceased. Yet the good ship ploughed straight on, unretarded by wind or wave, towards the straits of Bab-el-Mandeb. What was Phileas Fogg doing all this time? It might be thought that, in his anxiety, he would be constantly watching the changes of the wind, the disorderly raging of the billows—every chance, in short, which might force the "Mongolia" to slacken her speed, and thus interrupt his journey. But if he thought of these possibilities, he did not betray the fact by any outward sign.

Always the same impassible member of the Reform Club, whom no incident could surprise, as unvarying as the ship's chronometers, and seldom having the curiosity even to go upon the deck, he passed through the memorable scenes of the Red Sea with cold indifference; did not care to recognize the historic towns and villages which, along its borders, raised their picturesque outlines against the sky; and betrayed no fear of the dangers of the Arabic Gulf, which the old historians always spoke of with horror, and upon which the ancient navigators never ventured without propitiating the gods by ample sacrifices. How did this eccentric personage pass his time on the "Mongolia"? He made his four hearty meals every day, regardless of the most persistent rolling and pitching on the part of the steamer; and he played whist indefatigably, for he had found partners as enthusiastic in the game as himself. A tax-collector, on the way to his post at Goa; the Rev. Decimus Smith, returning to his parish at Bombay; and a brigadier-general of the English army, who was about to rejoin his brigade at Benares, made up the party, and, with Mr. Fogg, played whist by the hour together in absorbing silence.

As for Passepartout, he, too, had escaped sea-sickness, and took his meals conscientiously in the forward cabin. He rather enjoyed the voyage, for he was well fed and well lodged, took a great interest in the scenes through which they were passing, and consoled himself with the delusion that his master's whim would end at Bombay. He was pleased, on the day after leaving Suez, to find on deck the obliging person with whom he had walked and chatted on the quays.

"If I am not mistaken," said he, approaching this person with his most amiable smile, "you are the gentleman who so kindly volunteered to guide me at Suez?"

"Ah! I quite recognize you. You are the servant of the strange Englishman—"

"Just so, Monsieur—"

"Fix."

"Monsieur Fix," resumed Passepartout, "I'm charmed to find you on board. Where are you bound?"

"Like you, to Bombay."

"That's capital! Have you made this trip before?"

"Several times. I am one of the agents of the Peninsula Company."

"Then you know India?"

"Why—yes," replied Fix, who spoke cautiously.

"A curious place, this India?"

"Oh, very curious. Mosques, minarets, temples, fakirs, pagodas, tigers, snakes, elephants! I hope you will have ample time to see the sights."

"I hope so, Monsieur Fix. You see, a man of sound sense ought not to spend his life jumping from a steamer upon a railway train, and from a railway train upon a steamer again, pretending to make the tour of the world in eighty days! No; all these gymnastics, you may be sure, will cease at Bombay."

"And Mr. Fogg is getting on well?" asked Fix, in the most natural tone in the world.

"Quite well, and I too. I eat like a famished ogre; it's the sea air."

"But I never see your master on deck."

"Never; he hasn't the least curiosity."

"Do you know, Mr. Passepartout, that this pretended tour in eighty days may conceal some secret errand—perhaps a diplomatic mission?"

"Faith, Monsieur Fix, I assure you I know nothing about it, nor would I give half-a-crown to find out."

After this meeting, Passepartout and Fix got into the habit of chatting together, the latter making it a point to gain the worthy man's confidence. He frequently offered him a glass of whiskey or pale ale in the steamer bar-room, which Passepartout never failed to accept with graceful alacrity, mentally pronouncing Fix the best of good fellows.

Meanwhile the "Mongolia" was pushing forward rapidly; on the 13th, Mocha, surrounded by its ruined walls whereon date-trees were growing, was sighted, and on the mountains beyond were espied vast coffee-fields. Passepartout was ravished to behold this celebrated place, and thought that, with its circular walls and dismantled fort, it looked like an immense coffee cup and saucer. The following night they passed through the Strait of Bab-el-Mandeb, which means in Arabic "The Bridge of Tears," and the next day they put in at Steamer Point, north-west of Aden harbour, to take in coal. This matter of fuelling steamers is a serious one at such distances from the coal mines; it costs the Peninsula Company some eight hundred thousand pounds a year. In these distant seas, coal is worth three or four pounds sterling a ton.

The "Mongolia" had still sixteen hundred and fifty miles to traverse before reaching Bombay, and was obliged to remain four hours at Steamer Point to coal up. But this delay, as it was foreseen, did not affect Phileas Fogg's programme; besides, the "Mongolia," instead of reaching Aden on the morning of the 15th, when she was due, arrived there on the evening of the 14th, a gain of fifteen hours.

Mr. Fogg and his servant went ashore at Aden to have the passport again *visaed;* Fix, unobserved, followed them. The *visa* procured, Mr. Fogg returned on board to resume his former habits; while Passepartout, according to custom, sauntered about among the mixed population of Somanlis, Banyans, Parsees, Jews, Arabs, and Europeans who comprise the twenty-five thousand inhabitants of Aden. He gazed with wonder upon the fortifications which make this place the Gibraltar of the Indian Ocean, and the vast cisterns where the English engineers were still at work, two thousand years after the engineers of Solomon.

"Very curious, *very* curious," said Passepartout to himself, on returning to the steamer. "I see that it is by no means useless to travel, if a man wants to see something new." At six p.m. the "Mongolia" slowly moved out of the roadstead, and was soon once more on the Indian Ocean. She had a hundred and sixty-eight hours in which to reach Bombay, and the sea was favourable, the wind being in the north-west, and all sails aiding the engine. The steamer rolled but little, the ladies, in fresh toilets, reappeared on deck, and the singing and dancing were resumed. The trip was being accomplished most successfully, and Passepartout was enchanted with the congenial companion which chance had secured him in the person of the delightful Fix. On Sunday, October 20th, towards noon, they came in sight of the Indian coast: two hours later the pilot came on board. A range of hills lay against the sky in the horizon, and soon the rows of palms which adorn Bombay came distinctly into view. The steamer entered the road formed by the islands in the bay, and at half-past four she hauled up at the quays of Bombay.

Phileas Fogg was in the act of finishing the thirty-third rubber of the voyage, and his partner and himself having, by a bold stroke, captured all thirteen of the tricks, concluded this fine campaign with a brilliant victory.

The "Mongolia" was due at Bombay on the 22nd; she arrived on the 20th. This was a gain to Phileas Fogg of two days since his departure from London, and he calmly entered the fact in the itinerary, in the column of gains.

CHAPTER 10

IN WHICH PASSEPARTOUT IS ONLY TOO GLAD TO GET OFF WITH THE LOSS OF HIS SHOES

EVERYBODY knows that the great reversed triangle of land, with its base in the north and its apex in the south, which is called India, embraces fourteen hundred thousand square miles, upon which is spread unequally a population of one hundred and eighty millions of souls. The British Crown exercises a real and despotic dominion over the larger portion of this vast country, and has a governor-general stationed at Calcutta, governors at Madras, Bombay, and in Bengal, and a lieutenant-governor at Agra.

But British India, properly so called, only embraces seven hundred thousand square miles, and a population of from one hundred to one hundred and ten millions of inhabitants. A considerable portion of India is still free from British authority; and there are certain ferocious rajahs in the interior who are absolutely independent. The celebrated East India Company was all-powerful from 1756, when the English first gained a foothold on the spot where now stands the city of Madras, down to the time of the great Sepoy insurrection. It gradually annexed province after province, purchasing them of the native chiefs, whom it seldom paid, and appointed the governor-general and his subordinates, civil and military. But the East India Company has now passed away, leaving the British possessions in India directly under the control of the Crown. The aspect of the country, as well as the manners and distinctions of race, is daily changing.

Formerly one was obliged to travel in India by the old cumbrous methods of going on foot or on horseback, in palaquins or unwieldy coaches; now, fast steamboats ply on the Indus and the Ganges, and a great railway, with branch lines joining the main line at many points on its route, traverses the peninsula from Bombay to Calcutta in three days. This railway does not run in a direct line across India. The distance between Bombay and Calcutta, as the bird flies, is only from one thousand to eleven hundred miles; but the deflections of the road increase this distance by more than a third.

The general route of the Great Indian Peninsula Railway is as follows:—Leaving Bombay, it passes through Salcette, crossing to the continent opposite Tannah, goes over the chain of the Western Ghauts, runs thence north-east as far as Burhampoor, skirts the nearly independent territory of Bundelcund, ascends to Allahabad, turns thence eastwardly, meeting the Ganges at Benares, then departs from the river a little, and, descending south-eastward by Burdivan and the French town of Chandernagor, has its terminus at Calcutta.

The passengers of the "Mongolia" went ashore at half-past four p.m.; at exactly eight the train would start for Calcutta.

Mr. Fogg, after bidding good-bye to his whist partners, left the steamer, gave his servant several errands to do, urged it upon him to be at the station promptly at eight, and, with his regular step, which beat to the second, like an astronomical clock, directed his steps to the passport office. As for the wonders of Bombay—its famous city hall, its splendid library, its forts and docks, its bazaars, mosques,

Mr. Fix on the watch.

synagogues, its Armenian churches, and the noble pagoda on Malebar Hill with its two polygonal towers—he cared not a straw to see them. He would not deign to examine even the masterpieces of Elephanta, or the mysterious hypogea, concealed south-east from the docks, or those fine remains of Buddhist architecture, the Kanherian grottoes of the island of Salcette.

Having transacted his business at the passport office, Phileas Fogg repaired quietly to the railway station, where he ordered dinner. Among the dishes served up to him, the landlord especially recommended a certain giblet of "native rabbit," on which he prided himself.

Mr. Fogg accordingly tasted the dish, but, despite its spiced sauce, found it far from palatable. He rang for the landlord, and on his appearance, said, fixing his clear eyes upon him, "Is this rabbit, sir?"

"Yes, my lord," the rogue boldly replied, "rabbit from the jungles."

"And this rabbit did not mew when he was killed?"

"Mew, my lord! what, a rabbit mew! I swear to you—"

"Be so good, landlord, as not to swear, but remember this: cats were formerly considered, in India, as sacred animals. That was a good time."

"For the cats, my lord?"

"Perhaps for the travellers as well!"

After which Mr. Fogg quietly continued his dinner. Fix had gone on shore shortly after Mr. Fogg, and his first destination was the head-quarters of the Bombay police. He made himself known as a London detective, told his business at Bombay, and the position of affairs relative to the supposed robber, and nervously asked if a warrant had arrived from London. It had not reached the office; indeed, there had not yet been time for it to arrive. Fix was sorely disappointed, and tried to obtain an order of arrest from the director of the Bombay police. This the director refused, as the matter concerned the London office, which alone could legally deliver the warrant. Fix did not insist, and was fain to resign himself to await the arrival of the important document; but he was determined not to lose sight of the mysterious rogue as long as he stayed in Bombay. He did not doubt for a moment, any more than Passepartout, that Phileas Fogg would remain there, at least until it was time for the warrant to arrive.

Passepartout, however, had no sooner heard his master's orders on leaving the "Mongolia," than he saw at once that they were to leave Bombay as they had done Suez and Paris, and that the journey would be extended at least as far as Calcutta, and perhaps beyond that place. He began to ask himself if this bet that Mr. Fogg talked about was not really in good earnest, and whether his fate was not in truth forcing him, despite his love of repose, around the world in eighty days!

Having purchased the usual quota of shirts and shoes, he took a leisurely promenade about the streets, where crowds of people of many nationalities—Europeans, Persians with pointed caps, Banyas with round turbans, Sindes with square bonnets, Parsees with black mitres, and long-robed Armenians—were collected. It happened to be the day of a Parsee festival. These descendants of the sect of Zoroaster—the most thrifty, civilized, intelligent, and austere of the East Indians, among whom are counted the richest native merchants of Bombay—were celebrating a sort of religious carnival, with processions and shows, in the midst of which Indian dancing-girls, clothed in rose-coloured gauze, looped up with gold and silver, danced airily, but with perfect modesty, to the sound of viols and the clanging of tambourines. It is needless to say that Passepartout watched these curious ceremonies with staring eyes and gaping mouth, and that his countenance was that of the greenest booby imaginable.

Unhappily for his master, as well as himself, his curiosity drew him unconsciously farther off than he intended to go. At last, having seen the Parsee carnival wind away in the distance, he was turning his steps towards the station, when he happened to espy the splendid pagoda on Malebar Hill, and was seized with an irresistible desire to see its interior. He was quite ignorant that it is forbidden to Christians to enter certain Indian temples, and that even the faithful must not go in without first leaving their shoes outside the door. It may be said here that the wise policy of the British Government severely punishes a disregard of the practices of the native religions.

Passepartout, however, thinking no harm, went in like a simple tourist, and was soon lost in admiration of the splendid Brahmin ornamentation which everywhere met his eyes, when of a sudden he found himself sprawling on the sacred flagging. He looked up to behold three enraged priests, who forthwith fell upon him, tore off his shoes, and began to beat him with loud, savage exclamations. The agile Frenchman was soon upon his feet again, and lost no time in knocking down two of his long-gowned adversaries with his fists and a vigorous application of his toes; then, rushing out of the pagoda as fast as his legs could carry him, he soon escaped the third priest by mingling with the crowd in the streets.

At five minutes before eight, Passepartout, hatless, shoeless, and having in the squabble lost his package of shirts and shoes, rushed breathlessly into the station.

Fix, who had followed Mr. Fogg to the station, and saw that he was really going to leave Bombay, was there, upon the platform. He had resolved to follow the supposed robber to Calcutta, and farther, if necessary. Passepartout did not observe the detective, who stood in an obscure corner; but Fix heard him relate his adventures in a few words to Mr. Fogg.

"I hope that this will not happen again," said Phileas Fogg, coldly, as he got into the train. Poor Passepartout, quite crestfallen, followed his master without a word. Fix was on the point of entering another carriage, when an idea struck him which induced him to alter his plan.

"No, I'll stay," muttered he. "An offence has been committed on Indian soil. I've got my man."

Just then the locomotive gave a sharp screech, and the train passed out into the darkness of the night.

CHAPTER 11

IN WHICH PHILEAS FOGG SECURES A CURIOUS MEANS OF CONVEYANCE AT A FABULOUS PRICE

THE train had started punctually. Among the passengers were a number of officers, Government officials, and opium and indigo merchants, whose business called them to the eastern coast. Passepartout rode in the same carriage with his master, and a third passenger occupied a seat opposite to them. This was Sir Francis Cromarty, one of Mr. Fogg's whist partners on the "Mongolia," now on his way to join his corps at Benares. Sir Francis was a tall, fair man of fifty, who had greatly distinguished himself in the last Sepoy revolt. He made India his home, only paying brief visits to England at rare intervals; and was almost as familiar as a native with the customs, history, and character of India and its people. But Phileas Fogg, who was not travelling, but only describing a circumference, took no pains to inquire into these subjects; he was a solid body, traversing an orbit around the terrestrial globe, according to the laws of rational mechanics. He was at this moment calculating in his mind the number of hours spent since his departure from London, and, had it been in his nature to make a useless demonstration, would have rubbed his hands for satisfaction. Sir Francis Cromarty had observed the oddity of his travelling companion—although the only opportunity he had for studying him had been while he was dealing the cards, and between two rubbers—and questioned himself whether a human heart really beat beneath this cold exterior, and whether Phileas Fogg had any sense of the beauties of nature. The brigadier-general was free to mentally confess, that, of all the eccentric persons he had ever met, none was comparable to this product of the exact sciences.

Phileas Fogg had not concealed from Sir Francis his design of going round the world, nor the circumstances under which he set out; and the general only saw in the wager a useless eccentricity, and a lack of sound common-sense. In the way this strange gentleman was going on, he would leave the world without having done any good to himself or anybody else.

An hour after leaving Bombay the train had passed the viaducts and the island of Salcette, and had got into the open country. At Callyan they reached the junction of the branch line which descends towards south-eastern India by Kandallah and Pounah; and, passing Pauwell, they entered the defiles of the mountains, with their basalt bases, and their summits crowned with thick and verdant forests. Phileas Fogg and Sir Francis Cromarty exchanged a few words from time to time, and now Sir Francis, reviving the conversation, observed, "Some years ago, Mr. Fogg, you would have met with a delay at this point, which would probably have lost you your wager."

"How so, Sir Francis?"

"Because the railway stopped at the base of these mountains, which the passengers were obliged to cross in palanquins or on ponies to Kandallah, on the other side."

"Such a delay would not have deranged my plans in the least," said Mr. Fogg. "I have constantly foreseen the likelihood of certain obstacles."

"But, Mr. Fogg," pursued Sir Francis, "you run the risk of having some difficulty about this worthy fellow's adventure at the pagoda." Passepartout, his feet comfortably wrapped in his travelling-blanket, was sound asleep, and did not dream that anybody was talking about him. "The Government is very severe upon that kind of offence. It takes particular care that the religious customs of the Indians should be respected, and if your servant were caught—"

"Very well, Sir Francis," replied Mr. Fogg; "if he had been caught he would have been condemned and punished, and then would have quietly returned to Europe. I don't see how this affair could have delayed his master."

The conversation fell again. During the night the train left the mountains behind, and passed Nassik, and the next day proceeded over the flat, well-cultivated country of the Khandeish, with its straggling villages, above which

He knocked down two of his adversaries.

rose the minarets of the pagodas. This fertile territory is watered by numerous small rivers and limpid streams, mostly tributaries of the Godavery.

Passepartout, on waking and looking out, could not realize that he was actually crossing India in a railway train. The locomotive, guided by an English engineer and fed with English coal, threw out its smoke upon cotton, coffee, nutmeg, clove, and pepper plantations, while the steam curled in spirals around groups of palm-trees, in the midst of which were seen picturesque bungalows, viharis (a sort of abandoned monasteries), and marvellous temples enriched by the exhaustless ornamentation of Indian architecture. Then they came upon vast tracts extending to the horizon, with jungles inhabited by snakes and tigers, which fled at the noise of the train; succeeded by forests penetrated by the railway, and still haunted by elephants which, with pensive eyes, gazed at the train as it passed. The travellers crossed, beyond Malligaum, the fatal country so often stained with blood by the sectaries of the goddess Kali. Not far off rose Ellora, with its graceful pagodas, and the famous Aurungabad, capital of the ferocious Aureng-Zeb, now the chief town of one of the detached provinces of the kingdom of the Nizam. It was thereabouts that Feringhea, the Thuggee chief, king of the stranglers, held his sway. These ruffians, united by a secret bond, strangled victims of every age in honour of the goddess Death, without ever shedding blood; there was a period when this part of the country could scarcely be travelled over without corpses being found in every direction. The English Government has succeeded in greatly diminishing these murders, though the Thuggees still exist, and pursue the exercise of their horrible rites.

At half-past twelve the train stopped at Burhampoor, where Passepartout was able to purchase some Indian slippers, ornamented with false pearls, in which, with evident vanity, he proceeded to incase his feet. The travellers made a hasty breakfast, and started off for Assurghur, after skirting for a little the banks of the small river Tapty, which empties into the Gulf of Cambray, near Surat.

Passepartout was now plunged into absorbing reverie. Up to his arrival at Bombay, he had entertained hopes that their journey would end there; but now that they were plainly whirling across India at full speed, a sudden change had come over the spirit of his dreams. His old vagabond nature returned to him; the fantastic ideas of his youth once more took possession of him. He came to regard his master's project as intended in good earnest, believed in the reality of the bet, and therefore in the tour of the world, and the necessity of making it without fail within the designated period. Already he began to worry about possible delays, and accidents which might happen on the way. He recognized himself as being personally interested in the wager, and trembled at the thought that he might have been the means of losing it by his unpardonable folly of the night before. Being much less cool-headed than Mr. Fogg, he was much more restless, counting and recounting the days passed over, uttering maledictions when the train stopped, and accusing it of sluggishness, and mentally blaming Mr. Fogg for not having bribed the engineer. The worthy fellow was ignorant that, while it was possible by such means to hasten the rate of a steamer, it could not be done on the railway.

The train entered the defiles of the Sutpour Mountains, which separate the Khandeish from Bundelcund, towards evening. The next day Sir Francis Cromarty asked Passepartout what time it was; to which, on consulting his watch, he replied that it was three in the morning. This famous timepiece, always regulated on the Greenwich meridian, which was now some seventy-seven degrees westward, was at least four hours slow. Sir Francis corrected Passepartout's time, whereupon the latter made the same remark that he had done to Fix; and upon the general insisting that the watch should be regulated in each new meridian, since he was constantly going eastward, that is in the face of the sun, and therefore the days were shorter by four minutes for each degree gone over, Passepartout obstinately refused to alter his watch, which he kept at London time. It was an innocent delusion which could harm no one.

The train stopped, at eight o'clock, in the midst of a glade some fifteen miles beyond Rothal, where there were several bungalows and workmen's cabins. The conductor, passing along the carriages, shouted, "Passengers will get out here!"

Phileas Fogg looked at Sir Francis Cromarty for an explanation; but the general could not tell what meant a halt in the midst of this forest of dates and acacias.

Passepartout, not less surprised, rushed out and speedily returned, crying, "Monsieur, no more railway!"

"What do you mean?" asked Sir Francis.

"I mean to say that the train isn't going on."

The general at once stepped out, while Phileas Fogg calmly followed him, and they proceeded together to the conductor.

"Where are we?" asked Sir Francis.

"At the hamlet of Kholby."

"Do we stop here?"

"Certainly. The railway isn't finished."

"What! not finished?"

"No. There's still a matter of fifty miles to be laid from here to Allahabad, where the line begins again."

"But the papers announced the opening of the railway throughout."

"What would you have, officer? The papers were mistaken."

"Yet you sell tickets from Bombay to Calcutta," retorted Sir Francis, who was growing warm.

"No doubt," replied the conductor; "but the passengers know that they must provide means of transportation for themselves from Kholby to Allahabad."

Sir Francis was furious. Passepartout would willingly have knocked the conductor down, and did not dare to look at his master.

"Sir Francis," said Mr. Fogg, quietly, "we will, if you please, look about for some means of conveyance to Allahabad."

"Mr. Fogg, this is a delay greatly to your disadvantage."

"No, Sir Francis; it was foreseen."

"What! You knew that the way—"

"Not at all; but I knew that some obstacle or other would sooner or later arise on my route. Nothing, therefore, is lost. I have two days which I have already gained to sacrifice. A steamer leaves Calcutta for Hong Kong at noon, on the 25th. This is the 22nd, and we shall reach Calcutta in time."

There was nothing to say to so confident a response.

It was but too true that the railway came to a termination at this point. The papers were like some watches, which have a way of getting too fast, and had been premature in their announcement of the completion of the line. The greater part of the travellers were aware of this interruption, and leaving the train, they began to engage such vehicles as the village could provide—four-wheeled palkigharis, waggons drawn by zebus, carriages that looked like perambulating pagodas, palaquins, ponies, and what not.

Mr. Fogg and Sir Francis Cromarty, after searching the village from end to end, came back without having found anything.

"I shall go afoot," said Phileas Fogg.

Passepartout, who had now rejoined his master, made a wry grimace, as he thought of his magnificent, but too frail Indian shoes. Happily he too had been looking about him, and, after a moment's hesitation, said, "Monsieur, I think I have found a means of conveyance."

"What?"

"An elephant! An elephant that belongs to an Indian who lives but a hundred steps from here."

"Let's go and see the elephant," replied Mr. Fogg.

They soon reached a small hut, near which, enclosed within some high palings, was the animal in question. An Indian came out of the hut, and, at their request, conducted them within the enclosure. The elephant, which its owner had reared, not for a beast of burden, but for warlike purposes, was half domesticated. The Indian had begun already, by often irritating him, and feeding him every three months on sugar and butter, to impart to him a ferocity not in his nature, this method being often employed by those who train the Indian elephants for battle. Happily, however, for Mr. Fogg, the animal's instruction in this direction had not gone far, and the elephant still preserved his natural gentleness. Kiouni—this was the name of the beast—could doubtless travel rapidly for a long time, and, in default of any other means of conveyance, Mr. Fogg resolved to hire him. But elephants are far from cheap in India, where they are becoming scarce; the males, which alone are suitable for circus shows, are much sought, especially as but few of them are domesticated. When, therefore, Mr. Fogg proposed to the Indian to hire Kiouni, he refused point-blank. Mr. Fogg persisted, offering the excessive sum of ten pounds an hour for the loan of the beast to Allahabad. Refused. Twenty pounds? Refused also. Forty pounds? Still refused. Passepartout jumped at each advance; but the Indian declined to be tempted. Yet the offer was an alluring one, for, supposing it took the elephant fifteen hours to reach Allahabad, his owner would receive no less than six hundred pounds sterling.

Phileas Fogg, without getting in the least flurried, then proposed to purchase the animal outright, and at first offered a thousand pounds for him. The Indian, perhaps thinking he was going to make a great bargain, still refused.

Sir Francis Cromarty took Mr. Fogg aside, and begged him to reflect before he went any further; to which that gentleman replied that he was not in the habit of acting rashly, that a bet of twenty thousand pounds was at stake, that the elephant was absolutely necessary to him, and that he would secure him if he had to pay twenty times his value. Returning to the Indian, whose small, sharp eyes, glistening with avarice, betrayed that with him it was only a question of how great a price he could obtain, Mr. Fogg offered first twelve hundred, then fifteen hundred, eighteen hundred, two thousand pounds. Passepartout, usually so rubicund, was fairly white with suspense.

At two thousand pounds the Indian yielded.

"What a price, good heaven!" cried Passepartout, "for an elephant!"

It only remained now to find a guide, which was comparatively easy. A young Parsee, with an intelligent face, offered his services, which Mr. Fogg accepted, promising so generous a reward as to materially stimulate his zeal, The elephant was led out and equipped. The Parsee, who was an accomplished elephant driver,

There they found themselves in the presense of an animal.

covered his back with a sort of saddle-cloth, and attached to each of his flanks some curiously uncomfortable howdahs.

Phileas Fogg paid the Indian with some bank-notes which he extracted from the famous carpet-bag, a proceeding that seemed to deprive poor Passepartout of his vitals. Then he offered to carry Sir Francis to Allahabad, which the brigadier gratefully accepted, as one traveller the more would not be likely to fatigue the gigantic beast. Provisions were purchased at Kholby, and while Sir Francis and Mr. Fogg took the howdahs on either side, Passepartout got astride the saddle-cloth between them. The Parsee perched himself on the elephant's neck, and at nine o'clock they set out from the village, the animal marching off through the dense forest of palms by the shortest cut.

CHAPTER 12

IN WHICH PHILEAS FOGG AND HIS COMPANIONS VENTURE ACROSS THE INDIAN FORESTS, AND WHAT ENSUED

In order to shorten the journey, the guide passed to the left of the line where the railway was still in process of being built. This line, owing to the capricious turnings of the Vindhia Mountains, did not pursue a straight course. The Parsee, who was quite familiar with the roads and paths in the district, declared that they would gain twenty miles by striking directly through the forest.

Phileas Fogg and Sir Francis Cromarty, plunged to the neck in the peculiar howdahs provided for them, were horribly jostled by the swift trotting of the elephant, spurred on as he was by the skilful Parsee; but they endured the discomfort with true British phlegm, talking little, and scarcely able to catch a glimpse of each other. As for Passepartout, who was mounted on the beast's back, and received the direct force of each concussion as he trod along, he was very careful, in accordance with his master's advice, to keep his tongue from between his teeth, as it would otherwise have been bitten off short. The worthy fellow bounced from the elephant's neck to his rump, and vaulted like a clown on a spring-board; yet he laughed in the midst of his bouncing, and from time to time took a piece of sugar out of his pocket, and inserted it in Kiouni's trunk, who received it without in the least slackening his regular trot.

After two hours the guide stopped the elephant, and gave him an hour for rest, during which Kiouni, after quenching his thirst at a neighbouring spring, set to devouring the branches and shrubs round about him. Neither Sir Francis nor Mr. Fogg regretted the delay, and both descended with a feeling of relief. "Why, he's made of iron!" exclaimed the general, gazing admiringly on Kiouni.

"Of forged iron," replied Passepartout, as he set about preparing a hasty breakfast.

At noon the Parsee gave the signal of departure. The country soon presented a very savage aspect. Copses of dates and dwarf-palms succeeded the dense forests; then vast, dry plains, dotted with scanty shrubs, and sown with great blocks of syenite. All this portion of Bundelcund, which is little frequented by travellers, is inhabited by a fanatical population, hardened in the most horrible practices of the Hindoo faith. The English have not been able to secure complete dominion over this territory, which is subjected to the influence of rajahs, whom it is almost impossible to reach in their inaccessible mountain fastnesses. The travellers several times saw bands of ferocious Indians, who, when they perceived the elephant striding across the country, made angry and threatening motions. The Parsee avoided them as much as possible. Few animals were observed on the route; even the monkeys hurried from their path with contortions and grimaces which convulsed Passepartout with laughter.

In the midst of his gaiety, however, one thought troubled the worthy servant. What would Mr. Fogg do with the elephant, when he got to Allahabad? Would he carry him on with him? Impossible! The cost of transporting him would make him ruinously expensive. Would he sell him, or set him free? The estimable beast certainly deserved some consideration. Should Mr. Fogg choose to make him, Passepartout, a present of Kiouni, he would be very much embarrassed; and these thoughts did not cease worrying him for a long time.

The principal chain of the Vindhias was crossed by eight in the evening, and another halt was made on the northern slope, in a ruined bungalow. They had gone nearly twenty-five miles that day, and an equal distance still separated them from the station of Allahabad.

The night was cold. The Parsee lit a fire in the bungalow with a few dry branches, and the warmth was very grateful. The provisions purchased at Kholby sufficed for supper, and the travellers ate ravenously. The conversation, beginning with a few disconnected phrases, soon gave place to loud and steady snores. The guide watched Kiouni, who slept standing, bolstering himself against the trunk of a large tree. Nothing occurred during the night to disturb the slumberers, although occasional growls from panthers and chatterings of monkeys broke the silence; the more formidable beasts made no cries or hostile demonstration against the occupants of the bungalow. Sir Francis slept heavily, like an honest soldier overcome with fatigue. Passepartout was wrapped in uneasy dreams of the bouncing of the day before. As for Mr. Fogg, he slumbered as peacefully as if he had been in his serene mansion in Saville Row.

The journey was resumed at six in the morning; the guide hoped to reach Allahabad by evening. In that case, Mr. Fogg would only lose a part of the forty-eight hours saved since the beginning of the tour. Kiouni, resuming his rapid gait, soon descended the lower spurs of the Vindhias, and towards noon they passed by the village of Kallenger, on the Cani, one of the branches of the Ganges. The guide avoided inhabited places, thinking it safer to keep the open country, which lies along the first depressions of the basin of the great river. Allahabad was now only twelve miles to the north-east. They stopped under a clump of bananas, the fruit of which, as healthy as bread and as succulent as cream, was amply partaken of and appreciated.

At two o'clock the guide entered a thick forest which extended several miles; he preferred to travel under cover of the woods. They had not as yet had any unpleasant encounters, and the journey seemed on the point of being successfully accomplished, when the elephant, becoming restless, suddenly stopped.

It was then four o'clock.

"What's the matter?" asked Sir Francis, putting out his head.

"I don't know, officer," replied the Parsee, listening attentively to a confused murmur which came through the thick branches.

The murmur soon became more distinct; it now seemed like a distant concert of human voices accompanied by brass instruments. Passepartout was all eyes and ears. Mr. Fogg patiently waited without a word. The Parsee jumped to the ground, fastened the elephant to a tree, and plunged into the thicket. He soon returned, saying,—

"A procession of Brahmins is coming this way. We must prevent their seeing us, if possible."

The guide unloosed the elephant and led him into a thicket, at the same time asking the travellers not to stir. He held himself ready to bestride the animal at a moment's notice, should flight become necessary; but he evidently thought that the procession of the faithful would pass without perceiving them amid the thick foliage, in which they were wholly concealed.

The discordant tones of the voices and instruments drew nearer, and now droning songs mingled with the sound of the tambourines and cymbals. The head of the procession soon appeared beneath the trees, a hundred paces away; and the strange figures who performed the religious ceremony were easily distingusihed through the branches. First came the priests, with mitres on their heads, and clothed in long lace robes. They were surrounded by men, women, and children, who sang a kind of lugubrious psalm, interrupted at regular intervals by the tambourines and cymbals; while behind them was drawn a car with large wheels, the spokes of which represented serpents entwined with each other. Upon the car, which was drawn by four richly caparisoned zebus, stood a hideous statue with four arms, the body coloured a dull red, with haggard eyes, dishevelled hair, protruding tongue, and lips tinted with betel. It stood upright upon the figure of a prostrate and headless giant.

Sir Francis, recognizing the statue, whispered, "The goddess Kali; the goddess of love and death."

"Of death, perhaps," muttered back Passepartout, "but of love—that ugly old hag? Never!"

The Parsee made a motion to keep silence.

A group of old fakirs were capering and making a wild ado around the statue; these were striped with ochre, and covered with cuts whence their blood issued drop by drop,—stupid fanatics, who, in the great Indian ceremonies, still throw themselves under the wheels of Juggernaut. Some Brahmins, clad in all the sumptuousness of Oriental apparel, and leading a woman who faltered at every step, followed. This woman was young, and as fair as a European. Her head and neck, shoulders, ears, arms, hands, and toes, were loaded down with jewels and gems,—with bracelets, earrings, and rings; while a tunic bordered with gold, and covered with a light muslin robe, betrayed the outline of her form.

The guards who followed the young woman presented a violent contrast to her, armed as they were with naked sabres hung at their waists, and long damasceened pistols, and bearing a corpse on a palanquin. It was the body of an old man, gorgeously arrayed in the habiliments of a rajah, wearing, as in life, a turban embroidered with pearls, a robe of tissue of silk and gold, a scarf of cashmere sewed with diamonds, and the magnificent weapons of a Hindoo prince. Next came the musicians and a rearguard of capering fakirs, whose cries sometimes drowned the noise of the instruments; these closed the procession.

It was a young woman.

Sir Francis watched the procession with a sad countenance, and, turning to the guide, said, "A suttee."

The Parsee nodded, and put his finger to his lips. The procession slowly wound under the trees, and soon its last ranks disappeared in the depths of the wood. The songs gradually died away; occasionally cries were heard in the distance, until at last all was silence again.

Phileas Fogg had heard what Sir Francis said, and, as soon as the procession had disappeared, asked, "What is a 'suttee'?"

"A suttee," returned the general, "is a human sacrifice, but a voluntary one. The woman you have just seen will be burned to-morrow at the dawn of day."

"Oh, the scoundrels!" cried Passepartout, who could not repress his indignation.

"And the corpse?" asked Mr. Fogg.

"Is that of the prince, her husband," said the guide; "an independent rajah of Bundelcund."

"Is it possible," resumed Phileas Fogg, his voice betraying not the least emotion, "that these barbarous customs still exist in India, and that the English have been unable to put a stop to them?"

"These sacrifices do not occur in the larger portion of India," replied Sir Francis; "but we have no power over these savage territories, and especially here in Bundelcund. The whole district north of the Vindhias is the theatre of incessant murders and pillage."

"The poor wretch!" exclaimed Passepartout, "to be burned alive!"

"Yes," returned Sir Francis, "burned alive. And if she were not, you cannot conceive what treatment she would be obliged to submit to from her relatives. They would shave off her hair, feed her on a scanty allowance of rice, treat her with contempt; she would be looked upon as an unclean creature, and would die in some corner, like a scurvy dog. The prospect of so frightful an existence drives these poor creatures to the sacrifice much more than love or religious fanaticism. Sometimes, however, the sacrifice is really voluntary, and it requires the active interference of the Government to prevent it. Several years ago, when I was living at Bombay, a young widow asked permission of the governor to be burned along with her husband's body; but, as you may imagine, he refused. The woman left the town, took refuge with an independent rajah, and there carried out her self-devoted purpose."

While Sir Francis was speaking, the guide shook his head several times, and now said, "The sacrifice which will take place to-morrow at dawn is not a voluntary one."

"How do you know?"

"Everybody knows about this affair in Bundelcund."

"But the wretched creature did not seem to be making any resistance," observed Sir Francis.

"That was because they had intoxicated her with fumes of hemp and opium."

"But where are they taking her?"

"To the pagoda of Pillaji, two miles from here; she will pass the night there."

"And the sacrifice will take place—"

"To-morrow, at the first light of dawn."

The guide now led the elephant out of the thicket, and leaped upon his neck. Just at the moment that he was about to urge Kiouni forward with a peculiar whistle, Mr. Fogg stopped him, and, turning to Sir Francis Cromarty, said, "Suppose we save this woman."

"Save the woman, Mr. Fogg!"

"I have yet twelve hours to spare; I can devote them to that."

"Why, you are a man of heart!"

"Sometimes," replied Phileas Fogg, quietly; "when I have the time."

CHAPTER 13

IN WHICH PASSEPARTOUT RECEIVES A NEW PROOF THAT FORTUNE FAVOURS THE BRAVE

THE project was a bold one, full of difficulty, pehaps impracticable. Mr. Fogg was going to risk life, or at least liberty, and therefore the success of his tour. But he did not hesitate, and he found in Sir Francis Cromarty an enthusiastic ally.

As for Passepartout, he was ready for anything that might be proposed. His master's idea charmed him; he perceived a heart, a soul, under that icy exterior. He began to love Phileas Fogg.

There remained the guide: what course would he adopt? Would he not take part with the Indians? In default of his assistance, it was necessary to be assured of his neutrality.

Sir Francis frankly put the question to him.

"Officers," replied the guide, "I am a Parsee, and this woman is a Parsee. Command me as you will."

"Excellent," said Mr. Fogg.

"However," resumed the guide, "it is certain, not only that we shall risk our lives, but horrible tortures, if we are taken."

"That is foreseen," replied Mr. Fogg. "I think we must wait till night before acting."

"I think so," said the guide.

The worthy Indian then gave some account of the victim, who, he said, was a celebrated beauty of the Parsee race, and the daughter of a wealthy Bombay merchant. She had received a thoroughly English education in that city, and, from her manners and intelligence, would be thought an European. Her name was Aouda. Left an orphan, she was married against her will to the old rajah of Bundelcund; and, knowing the fate that awaited her, she escaped, was retaken, and devoted by the rajah's relatives, who had an interest in her death, to the sacrifice from which it seemed she could not escape.

The Parsee's narrative only confirmed Mr. Fogg and his companions in their generous design. It was decided that the guide should direct the elephant towards the pagoda of Pillaji, which he accordingly approached as quickly as possible. They halted, half an hour afterwards, in a copse, some five hundred feet from the pagoda, where they were well concealed; but they could hear the groans and cries of the fakirs distinctly.

They then discussed the means of getting at the victim. The guide was familiar with the pagoda of Pillaji, in which, as he declared, the young woman was imprisoned. Could they enter any of its doors while the whole party of Indians was plunged in a drunken sleep, or was it safer to attempt to make a hole in the walls? This could only be determined at the moment and the place themselves; but it was certain that the abduction must be made that night, and not when, at break of day, the victim was led to her funeral pyre. Then no human intervention could save her.

As soon as night fell, about six o'clock, they decided to make a reconnoissance around the pagoda. The cries of the fakirs were just ceasing; the Indians were in the act of plunging themselves into the drunkenness caused by liquid opium mingled with hemp, and it might be possible to slip between them to the temple itself.

The Parsee, leading the others, noiselessly crept through the wood, and in ten minutes they found themselves on the banks of a small stream, whence, by the light of the rosin torches, they perceived a pyre of wood, on the top of which lay the embalmed body of the rajah, which was to be burned with his wife. The pagoda, whose minarets loomed above the trees in the deepening dusk, stood a hundred steps away.

"Come!" whispered the guide.

He slipped more cautiously than ever through the brush, followed by his companions; the silence around was only broken by the low murmuring of the wind among the branches.

Soon the Parsee stopped on the borders of the glade, which was lit up by the torches. The ground was covered by groups of the Indians, motionless in their drunken sleep; it seemed a battle-field strewn with the dead. Men, women, and children lay together.

In the background, among the trees, the pagoda of Pillaji loomed indistinctly. Much to the guide's disappointment, the guards of the rajah, lighted by torches, were watching at the doors and marching to and fro with naked sabres; probably the priests, too, were watching within.

The Parsee, now convinced that it was impossible to force an entrance to the temple, advanced no farther, but led his companions back again. Phileas Fogg and Sir Francis Cromarty also saw that nothing could be attempted in that direction. They stopped, and engaged in a whispered colloquy.

"It is only eight now," said the brigadier, "and these guards may also go to sleep."

"It is not impossible," returned the Parsee.

They lay down at the foot of a tree, and waited.

The time seemed long; the guide ever and anon left them to take an observation on the edge of the wood, but the guards watched steadily by the glare of the torches, and a dim light crept through the windows of the pagoda.

They waited till midnight; but no change took place among the guards, and it became apparent that their yielding to sleep could not be counted on. The other plan must be carried out; an opening in the walls of the pagoda must be made. It remained to ascertain whether the priests were watching by the side of their victim as assiduously as were the soldiers at the door.

After a last consultation, the guide announced that he was ready for the attempt, and advanced, followed by the others. They took a roundabout way, so as to get at the pagoda on the rear. They reached the walls about half-past twelve, without having met any one; here there was no guard, nor were there either windows or doors.

The night was dark. The moon, on the wane, scarcely left the horizon, and was covered with heavy clouds; the height of the trees deepened the darkness.

It was not enough to reach the walls; an opening in them must be accomplished, and to attain this purpose the party only had their pocket-knives. Happily the temple walls were built of brick and wood, which could be penetrated with little difficulty; after one brick had been taken out, the rest would yield easily.

They set noiselessly to work, and the Parsee on one side and Passepartout on the other began to loosen the bricks, so as to make an aperture two feet wide. They were getting on rapidly, when suddenly a cry was heard in the interior of the temple, followed almost instantly by other cries replying from the outside. Passepartout and the guide stopped. Had they been heard? Was the alarm being given? Common prudence urged them to retire, and they did so, followed by Phileas Fogg and Sir Francis. They again hid themselves in the wood, and waited till the disturbance, whatever it might be, ceased, holding themselves ready to resume their attempt without delay. But, awkwardly enough, the guards now appeared at the rear of the temple, and there installed themselves, in readiness to prevent a surprise.

It would be difficult to describe the disappointment of the party, thus interrupted in their work. They could not now reach the victim; how, then, could they save her? Sir Francis shook his fists, Passepartout was beside himself, and the guide gnashed his teeth with rage. The tranquil Fogg waited, without betraying any emotion.

"We have nothing to do but to go away," whispered Sir Francis.

"Nothing but to go away," echoed the guide.

"Stop," said Fogg. "I am only due at Allahabad to-morrow before noon."

"But what can you hope to do?" asked Sir Francis. "In a few hours it will be daylight, and—"

"The chance which now seems lost may present itself at the last moment."

Sir Francis would have liked to read Phileas Fogg's eyes.

What was this cool Englishman thinking of? Was he planning to make a rush for the young woman at the very moment of the sacrifice, and boldly snatch her from her executioners?

This would be utter folly, and it was hard to admit that Fogg was such a fool. Sir Francis consented, however, to remain to the end of this terrible drama. The guide led them to the rear of the glade, where they were able to observe the sleeping groups.

Meanwhile Passepartout, who had perched himself on the lower branches of a tree, was revolving an idea which had at first struck him like a flash, and which was now firmly lodged in his brain.

He had commenced by saying to himself, "What folly!" and then he repeated, "Why not, after all? It's a chance,—perhaps the only one; and with such sots!" Thinking thus, he slipped, with the suppleness of a serpent, to the lowest branches, the ends of which bent almost to the ground.

The hours passed, and the lighter shades now announced the approach of day, though it was not yet light. This was the moment. The slumbering multitude became animated, the tambourines sounded, songs and cries arose; the hour of the sacrifice had come. The doors of the pagoda swung open, and a bright light escaped from its interior, in the midst of which Mr. Fogg and Sir Francis espied the victim. She seemed, having shaken off the stupor of intoxication, to be striving to escape from her executioner. Sir Francis's heart throbbed; and convulsively seizing Mr. Fogg's hand, found in it an open knife. Just at this moment the crowd began to move. The young woman had again fallen into a stupor, caused by the fumes of hemp, and passed among the fakirs, who escorted her with their wild, religious cries.

Phileas Fogg and his companions, mingling in the rear ranks of the crowd, followed; and in two minutes they reached the banks of the stream, and stopped fifty paces from the pyre, upon which still lay the rajah's corpse. In the semi-obscurity they saw the victim, quite senseless, stretched out beside her husband's body. Then a torch was brought, and the wood, soaked with oil, instantly took fire.

At this moment Sir Francis and the guide seized Phileas Fogg, who, in an instant of mad generosity, was about to rush upon the pyre. But he had quickly pushed them aside, when the whole scene suddenly changed. A cry of terror arose. The whole multitude prostrated themselves, terror-stricken, on the ground.

The old rajah was not dead, then, since he rose of a sudden, like a spectre, took up his wife in his arms, and descended from the pyre in the midst of the clouds of smoke, which only heightened his ghostly appearance.

Fakirs and soldiers and priests, seized with instant terror, lay there, with their faces on the ground, not daring to lift their eyes and behold such a prodigy.

The inanimate victim was borne along by the vigorous arms which supported her, and which she did not seem in the least to burden. Mr. Fogg and Sir Francis stood erect, the Parsee bowed his head, and Passepartout was, no doubt, scarcely less stupefied.

The resuscitated rajah approached Sir Francis and Mr. Fogg, and, in an abrupt tone, said, "Let us be off!"

It was Passepartout himself, who had slipped upon the pyre in the midst of the smoke and, profiting by the still overhanging darkness, had delivered the young woman from death! It was Passepartout who, playing his part with a happy audacity, had passed through the crowd amid the general terror.

A moment after all four of the party had disappeared in the woods, and the elephant was bearing them away at a rapid pace. But the cries and noise, and a ball which whizzed through Phileas Fogg's hat, apprised them that the trick had been discovered.

The old rajah's body, indeed, now appeared upon the burning pyre; and the priests, recovered from their terror, perceived that an abduction had taken place. They hastened into the forest, followed by the soldiers, who fired a volley after the fugitives; but the latter rapidly increased the distance between them, and ere long found themselves beyond the reach of the bullets and arrows.

CHAPTER 14

IN WHICH PHILEAS FOGG DESCENDS THE WHOLE LENGTH OF THE BEAUTIFUL VALLEY OF THE GANGES WITHOUT EVER THINKING OF SEEING IT

THE rash exploit had been accomplished; and for an hour Passepartout laughed gaily at his success. Sir Francis pressed the worthy fellow's hand, and his master said, "Well done!" which, from him, was high commendation; to which Passepartout replied that all the credit of the affair belonged to Mr. Fogg. As for him, he had only been struck with a "queer" idea; and he laughed to think that for a few moments he, Passepartout, the ex-gymnast, ex-sergeant fireman, had been the spouse of a charming woman, a venerable, embalmed rajah! As for the young Indian woman, she had been unconscious throughout of what was passing, and now, wrapped up in a travelling-blanket, was reposing in one of the howdahs.

The elephant, thanks to the skilful guidance of the Parsee, was advancing rapidly through the still darksome forest, and, an hour after leaving the pagoda, had crossed a vast plain. They made a halt at seven o'clock, the young woman being still in a state of complete prostration. The guide made her drink a little brandy and water, but the drowsiness which stupefied her could not yet be shaken off. Sir Francis, who was familiar with the effects of the intoxication produced by the fumes of hemp, reassured his companions on her account. But he was more disturbed at the prospect of her future fate. He told Phileas Fogg that, should Aouda remain in India, she would inevitably fall again into the hands of her executioners. These fanatics were scattered throughout the country, and would, despite the English police, recover their victim at Madras, Bombay, or Calcutta. She would only be safe by quitting India for ever.

Phileas Fogg replied that he would reflect upon the matter.

The station at Allahabad was reached about ten o'clock, and the interrupted line of railway being resumed, would enable them to reach Calcutta in less than twenty-four hours. Phileas Fogg would thus be able to arrive in time to take the steamer which left Calcutta the next day, October 25th, at noon, for Hong Kong.

The young woman was placed in one of the waiting-rooms of the station, whilst Passepartout was charged with purchasing for her various articles of toilet, a dress, shawl, and some furs; for which his master gave him unlimited credit. Passepartout started off forthwith, and found himself in the streets of Allahabad, that is, the "City of God," one of the most venerated in India, being built at the junction of the two sacred rivers Ganges and Jumna, the waters of which attract pilgrims from every part of the peninsula. The Ganges, according to the legends of the Ramayana, rises in heaven, whence, owing to Brahma's agency, it descends to the earth.

Passepartout made it a point, as he made his purchases, to take a good look at the city. It was formerly defended by a noble fort, which has since become a state prison; its commerce has dwindled away, and Passepartout in vain looked about him for such a bazaar as he used to frequent in Regent Street. At last he came upon an elderly, crusty Jew, who sold second-hand articles, and from whom he purchased a dress of Scotch stuff, a large mantle, and a fine otter-skin pelisse, for which he did not hesitate to pay seventy-five pounds. He then returned triumphantly to the station.

The influence to which the priests of Pillaji had subjected Aouda began gradually to yield, and she became more herself, so that her fine eyes resumed all their soft Indian expression.

When the poet-king, Ucaf Uddaul, celebrates the charms of the queen of Ahmehnagara, he speaks thus:—

"Her shining tresses, divided in two parts, encircle the harmonious contour of her white and delicate cheeks, brilliant in their glow and freshness. Her ebony brows have the form and charm of the bow of Kama, the god of love, and beneath her long silken lashes the purest reflections and a celestial light swim, as in the sacred lakes of Himalaya, in the black pupils of her great clear eyes. Her teeth, fine, equal, and white, glitter between her smiling lips like dewdrops in a passion-flower's half-enveloped breast. Her delicately formed ears, her vermilion hands, her little feet, curved and tender as the lotus-bud, glitter with the brilliancy of the loveliest pearls of Ceylon, the most dazzling diamonds of Golconda. Her narrow and supple waist, which a hand may clasp around, sets forth the outline of her rounded figure and the beauty of her bosom, where youth in its flower displays the wealth of its treasures; and beneath the silken folds of her tunic she seems to have been modelled in pure silver by the godlike hand of Vicvarcarma, the immortal sculptor."

It is enough to say, without applying this poetical rhapsody to Aouda, that she was a charming woman, in all the European acceptation of the phrase. She spoke English with great purity, and the guide had not exaggerated in saying that the young Parsee had been transformed by her bringing up.

The train was about to start from Allahabad, and Mr. Fogg proceeded to pay the guide the price agreed upon for his service, and not a farthing more; which astonished Passepartout, who remembered all that his master owed to the guide's devotion. He had, indeed, risked his life in the adventure at Pillaji, and if he should be caught afterwards by the Indians, he would with difficulty escape their vengeance. Kiouni, also, must be disposed of. What should be done with the elephant, which had been so dearly purchased? Phileas Fogg had already determined this question.

"Parsee," said he to the guide, "you have been serviceable and devoted. I have paid for your service, but not for your devotion. Would you like to have this elephant? He is yours."

The guide's eyes glistened.

"Your honour is giving me a fortune!" cried he.

"Take him, guide," returned Mr. Fogg, "and I shall still be your debtor."

"Good!" exclaimed Passepartout; "take him, friend. Kiouni is a brave and faithful beast." And, going up to the elephant, he gave him several lumps of sugar, saying, "Here, Kiouni, here, here."

The elephant grunted out his satisfaction, and, clasping Passepartout around the waist with his trunk, lifted him as high as his head. Passepartout, not in the least alarmed, caressed the animal, which replaced him gently on the ground.

Soon after, Phileas Fogg, Sir Francis Cromarty, and Passepartout, installed in a carriage with Aouda, who had the best seat, were whirling at full speed towards Benares. It was a run of eighty miles, and was accomplished in two hours. During the journey, the young woman fully recovered her senses. What was her astonishment to find herself in this carriage, on the railway, dressed in European habiliments, and with travellers who were quite strangers to her! Her companions first set about fully reviving her with a little liquor, and then Sir Francis narrated to her what had passed, dwelling upon the courage with which Phileas Fogg had not hesitated to risk his life to save her, and recounting the happy sequel of the venture, the result of Passepartout's rash idea. Mr. Fogg said nothing; while Passepartout, abashed, kept repeating that "it wasn't worth telling."

Aouda pathetically thanked her deliverers, rather with tears than words; her fine eyes interpreted her gratitude better than her lips. Then, as her thoughts strayed back to the scene of the sacrifice, and recalled the dangers which still menaced her, she shuddered with terror.

Phileas Fogg understood what was passing in Aouda's mind, and offered, in order to reassure her, to escort her to Hong Kong, where she might remain safely until the affair was hushed up—an offer which she eagerly and gratefully accepted. She had, it seems, a Parsee relation, who was one of the principal merchants of Hong Kong, which is wholly an English city, though on an island on the Chinese coast.

At half-past twelve the train stopped at Benares. The Brahmin legends assert that this city is built on the site of the ancient Casi, which, like Mahomet's tomb, was once suspended between heaven and earth; though the Benares of to-day, which the Orientalists call the Athens of India, stands quite unpoetically on the solid earth. Passepartout caught glimpses of its brick houses and clay huts, giving an aspect of desolation to the place, as the train entered it.

Benares was Sir Francis Cromarty's destination, the troops he was rejoining being encamped some miles northward of the city. He bade adieu to Phileas Fogg, wishing him all success, and expressing the hope that he would come that way again in a less original but more profitable fashion. Mr. Fogg lightly pressed him by the hand. The parting of Aouda, who did not forget what she owned to Sir Francis, betrayed more warmth; and, as for Passepartout, he received a hearty shake of the hand from the gallant general.

The railway, on leaving Benares, passed for a while along the valley of the Ganges. Through the windows of their carriage the travellers had glimpses of the diversified landscape of Behar, with its mountains clothed in verdure, its fields of barley, wheat, and corn, its jungles peopled with green alligators, its neat villages, and its still thickly-leaved forests. Elephants were bathing in the waters of the sacred river, and groups of Indians, despite the advanced season and chilly air, were performing solemnly their pious ablutions. These were fervent Brahmins, the bitterest foes of Buddhism, their deities being Vishnu, the solar god, Shiva, the devine impersonation of natural forces, and Brahma, the supreme ruler of priests and legislators. What would these divinities think of India, anglicized as it is to-day, with steamers whistling and scudding along the Ganges, frightening the gulls which float upon its surface, the turtles swarming along its banks, and the faithful dwelling upon its borders?

The panorama passed before their eyes like a flash, save when the steam concealed it fitfully from the view; the travellers could scarcely discern the fort of Chupenie, twenty miles south-westward from Benares, the ancient stronghold of the rajahs of Behar; or Ghazipur and its famous rose-water factories; or the tomb of Lord Cornwallis, rising on the left bank of the Ganges; the fortified town of Buxar, or Patna, a large manufacturing and trading place, where is held the principal opium market of India; or Monghir, a more than European town, for it is as English as Manchester or Birmingham, with its iron foundries, edge-tool factories, and high chimneys puffing clouds of black smoke heavenward.

Night came on; the train passed on at full speed, in the midst of the roaring of the tigers, bears, and wolves which fled before the locomotive; and the marvels of Bengal, Golconda, ruined Gour, Murshedabad, the ancient capital, Burdwan, Hugly, and the French town of Chandernagor, where Passepartout would have been proud to see his country's flag flying, were hidden from their view in the darkness.

Calcutta was reached at seven in the morning, and the packet left for Hong Kong at noon; so that Phileas Fogg had five hours before him.

According to his journal, he was due at Calcutta on the 25th of October, and that was the exact date of his actual arrival. He was therefore neither behindhand nor ahead of time. The two days gained between London and Bombay had been lost, as has been seen, in the journey across India. But it is not to be supposed that Phileas Fogg regretted them.

CHAPTER 15

IN WHICH THE BAG OF BANK-NOTES DISGORGES SOME THOUSANDS OF POUNDS MORE

THE train entered the station, and Passepartout, jumping out first, was followed by Mr. Fogg, who assisted his fair companion to descend. Phileas Fogg intended to proceed at once to the Hong Kong steamer, in order to get Aouda comfortably settled for the voyage. He was unwilling to leave her while they were still on dangerous ground.

Just as he was leaving the station a policeman came up to him, and said, "Mr. Phileas Fogg?"

"I am he."

"Is this man your servant?" added the policeman, pointing to Passepartout.

"Yes."

"Be so good, both of you, as to follow me."

Mr. Fogg betrayed no surprise whatever. The policeman was a representative of the law, and law is sacred to an Englishman. Passepartout tried to reason about the matter, but the policeman tapped him with his stick, and Mr. Fogg made him a signal to obey.

"May this young lady go with us?" asked he.

"She may," replied the policeman.

Mr. Fogg, Aouda, and Passepartout were conducted to a "palki-gari," a sort of four-wheeled carriage, drawn by two horses, in which they took their places and were driven away. No one spoke during the twenty minutes which elapsed before they reached their destination. They first passed through the "black town," with its narrow streets, its miserable, dirty huts, and squalid population; then through the "European town," which presented a relief in its bright brick mansions, shaded by cocoanut-trees and bristling with masts, where, although it was early morning, elegantly dressed horsemen and handsome equipages were passing back and forth.

The carriage stopped before a modest-looking house, which, however, did not have the appearance of a private mansion. The policeman having requested his prisoners—for so, truly, they might be called—to descend, conducted them into a room with barred windows, and said, "You will appear before Judge Obadiah at half-past eight."

He then retired, and closed the door.

"Why, we are prisoners!" exclaimed Passepartout, falling into a chair.

Aouda, with an emotion she tried to conceal, said to Mr. Fogg, "Sir, you must leave me to my fate! It is on my account that you receive this treatment; it is for having saved me!"

Phileas Fogg contented himself with saying that it was impossible. It was quite unlikely that he should be arrested for preventing a suttee. The complainants would not dare present themselves with such a charge. There was some mistake. Moreover, he would not in any event abandon Aouda, but would escort her to Hong Kong.

"But the steamer leaves at noon!" observed Passepartout, nervously.

"We shall be on board by noon," replied his master, placidly.

It was said so positively, that Passepartout could not help muttering to himself, "Parbleu, that's certain! Before noon we shall be on board." But he was by no means reassured.

At half-past eight the door opened, the policeman appeared, and requesting them to follow him, led the way to an adjoining hall. It was evidently a court-room, and a crowd of Europeans and natives already occupied the rear of the apartment.

Mr. Fogg and his two companions took their places on a bench opposite the desks of the magistrate and his clerk. Immediately after, Judge Obadiah, a fat, round man, followed by the clerk, entered. He proceeded to take down a wig which was hanging on a nail, and put it hurriedly on his head.

"The first case," said he; then, putting his hand to his head, he exclaimed, "Heh! This is not my wig!"

"No, your worship," returned the clerk, "it is mine."

"My dear Mr. Oysterpuff, how can a judge give a wise sentence in a clerk's wig?"

The wigs were exchanged.

Passepartout was getting nervous, for the hands on the face of the big clock over the judge seemed to go round with terrible rapidity.

"The first case," repeated Judge Obadiah.

"Phileas Fogg?" demanded Oysterpuff.

"I am here," replied Mr. Fogg.

"Passepartout?"

"Present!" responded Passepartout.

"Good," said the judge. "You have been looked for, prisoners, for two days on the trains from Bombay."

"But of what are we accused?" asked Passepartout, impatiently.

"You are about to be informed."

"I am an English subject, sir," said Mr. Fogg, "and I have the right—"

"Have you been ill-treated?"

"Not at all."

"Very well; let the complainants come in."

A door was swung open by order of the judge, and three Indian priests entered.

"That's it," muttered Passepartout; "these are the rogues who were going to burn our young lady."

The priests took their places in front of the judge, and the clerk proceeded to read in a loud voice a complaint of sacrilege against Phileas Fogg and his servant, who were accused of having violated a place held consecrated by the Brahmin religion.

"You hear the charge?" asked the judge.

"Yes, sir," replied Mr. Fogg, consulting his watch, "and I admit it."

"You admit it?"

"I admit it, and I wish to hear these priests admit, in their turn, what they were going to do at the pagoda of Pillaji."

The priests looked at each other; they did not seem to understand what was said.

"Yes," cried Passepartout, warmly; "at the pagoda of Pillaji, where they were on the point of burning their victim."

The judge stared with astonishment, and the priests were stupefied.

"What victim?" said Judge Obadiah. "Burn whom? In Bombay itself?"

"Bombay?" cried Passepartout.

"Certainly. We are not talking of the pagoda of Pillaji, but of the pagoda of Malebar Hill, at Bombay."

"And as a proof," added the clerk, "here are the desecrator's very shoes, which he left behind him."

Whereupon he placed a pair of shoes on his desk.

"My shoes!" cried Passepartout, in his surprise permitting this imprudent exclamation to escape him.

The confusion of master and man, who had quite forgotten the affair at Bombay, for which they were now detained at Calcutta, may be imagined.

Fix, the detective, had forseen the advantage which Passepartout's escapade gave him, and delaying his departure for twelve hours, had consulted the priests of Malebar Hill. Knowing that the English authorities dealt very severely with this kind of misdemeanour, he promised them a goodly sum in damages, and sent them forward to Calcutta by the next train. Owing to the delay caused by the rescue of the young widow, Fix and the priests reached the Indian capital before Mr. Fogg and his servant, the magistrates having been already warned by a despatch to arrest them, should they arrive. Fix's disappointment, when he learned that Phileas Fogg had not made his appearance in Calcutta, may be imagined. He made up his mind that the robber had stopped somewhere on the route and taken refuge in the southern provinces. For twenty-four hours Fix watched the station with feverish anxiety; at last he was rewarded by seeing Mr. Fogg and Passepartout arrive, accompanied by a young woman, whose presence he was wholly at a loss to explain. He hastened for a policeman; and this was how the party came to be arrested and brought before Judge Obadiah.

Had Passepartout been a little less preoccupied, he would have espied the detective ensconced in a corner of the court-room, watching the proceedings with an interest easily understood; for the warrant had failed to reach him at Calcutta, as it had done at Bombay and Suez.

Judge Obadiah had unfortunately caught Passepartout's rash exclamation, which the poor fellow would have given the world to recall.

"The facts are admitted?" asked the judge.

"Admitted," replied Mr. Fogg, coldly.

"Inasmuch," resumed the judge, "as the English law protects equally and sternly the religions of the Indian people, and as the man Passepartout has admitted that he violated the sacred pagoda of Malebar Hill, at Bombay, on the 20th of October, I condemn the said Passepartout to imprisonment for fifteen days and a fine of three hundred pounds."

"Three hundred pounds!" cried Passepartout, startled at the largeness of the sum.

"Silence!" shouted the constable.

"And inasmuch," continued the judge, "as it is not proved that the act was not done by the connivance of the master with the servant, and as the master in any case must be held responsible for the acts of his paid servant, I condemn Phileas Fogg to a week's imprisonment and a fine of one hundred and fifty pounds."

Fix rubbed his hands softly with satisfaction; if Phileas Fogg could be detained in Calcutta a week, it would be more than time for the warrant to arrive. Passepartout was stupefied. This sentence ruined his master. A wager of twenty thousand pounds lost, because he, like a precious fool, had gone into that abominable pagoda!

Phileas Fogg, as self-composed as if the judgment did not in the lest concern him, did not even lift his eyebrows while it was being pronounced. Just as the clerk was calling the next case, he rose, and said, "I offer bail."

"You have that right," returned the judge.

Fix's blood ran cold, but he resumed his composure when he heard the judge announce that the bail required for each prisoner would be one thousand pounds.

"I will pay it at once," said Mr. Fogg, taking a roll of bank-bills from the carpet-bag, which Passepartout had by him, and placing them on the clerk's desk.

"This sum will be restored to you upon your release from prison," said the judge. "Meanwhile, you are liberated on bail."

"Come!" said Phileas Fogg to his servant.

"But let them at least give me back my shoes!" cried Passepartout, angrily.

"Ah, these are pretty dear shoes!" he muttered, as they were handed to him. "More than a thousand pounds apiece; besides, they pinch my feet."

Mr. Fogg, offering his arm to Aouda, then departed, followed by the crestfallen Passepartout. Fix still nourished hopes that the robber would not, after all, leave the two thousand pounds behind him, but would decide to serve out his week in jail, and issued forth on Mr. Fogg's traces. That gentleman took a carriage, and the party were soon landed on one of the quays.

The "Rangoon" was moored half a mile off in the harbour, its signal of departure hoisted at the mast-head. Eleven o'clock was striking; Mr. Fogg was an hour in advance of time. Fix saw them leave the carriage and push off in a boat for the steamer, and stamped his feet with disappointment.

"The rascal is off, after all!" he exclaimed. "Two thousand pounds sacrificed!

He's as prodigal as a thief! I'll follow him to the end of the world if necessary; but at the rate he is going on, the stolen money will soon be exhausted."

The detective was not far wrong in making this conjecture. Since leaving London, what with travelling-expenses, bribes, the purchase of the elephant, bails, and fines, Mr. Fogg had already spent more than five thousand pounds on the way, and the percentage of the sum recovered from the bank robber, promised to the detectives, was rapidly diminishing.

CHAPTER 16

IN WHICH FIX DOES NOT SEEM TO UNDERSTAND IN THE LEAST WHAT IS SAID TO HIM

THE "Rangoon"—one of the Peninsular and Oriental Company's boats plying in the Chinese and Japanese seas—was a screw steamer, built of iron, weighing about seventeen hundred and seventy tons, and with engines of four hundred horse-power. She was as fast, but not as well fitted up, as the "Mongolia," and Aouda was not as comfortably provided for on board of her as Phileas Fogg could have wished. However, the trip from Calcutta to Hong Kong only comprised some three thousand five hundred miles, occupying from ten to twelve days, and the young woman was not difficult to please.

During the first days of the journey Aouda became better acquainted with her protector, and constantly gave evidence of her deep gratitude for what he had done. The phlegmatic gentleman listened to her, apparently at least, with coldness, neither his voice nor his manner betraying the slightest emotion; but he seemed to be always on the watch that nothing should be wanting to Aouda's comfort. He visited her regularly each day at certain hours, not so much to talk himself as to sit and hear her talk. He treated her with the strictest politeness, but with the precision of an automaton, the movements of which had been arranged for this purpose. Aouda did not quite know what to make of him, though Passepartout had given her some hints of his master's eccentricity, and made her smile by telling her of the wager which was sending him round the world. After all, she owed Phileas Fogg her life, and she always regarded him throught he exalting medium of her gratitude.

Aouda confirmed the Parsee guide's narrative of her touching history. She did, indeed, belong to the highest of the native races of India. Many of the Parsee merchants have made great fortunes there by dealing in cotton; and one of them, Sir Jametsee Jeejeebhoy, was made a baronet by the English government. Aouda was a relative of this great man, and it was his cousin, Jeejeeh, whom she hoped to join at Hong Kong. Whether she would find a protector in him she could not tell; but Mr. Fogg essayed to calm her anxieties, and to ssure her that everything would be mathematically—he used the very word—arranged. Aouda fastened her great eyes, "clear as the sacred lakes of the Himalaya,"

"My shoes!" cried Passepartout.

upon him; but the intractable Fogg, as reserved as ever, did not seem at all inclined to throw himself into this lake.

The first few days of the voyage passed propserously, amid favourable weather and propitious winds, and they soon came in sight of the great Andaman, the principal of the islands in the Bay of Bengal, with its picturesque Saddle Peak, two thousand four hundred feet high, looming above the waters. The steamer passed along near the shores, but the saveage Papuans, who are in the lowest scale of humanity, but are not, as has been asserted, cannibals, did not make their appearance.

The panorama of the islands, as they steamed by them, was superb. Vast forests of palms, arecs, bamboo, teakwood, of the gigantic mimosa, and tree-like ferns covered the foreground, while behind, the graceful outlines of the mountains were traced against the sky; and along the coasts swarmed by thousands the precious swallows whose nests furnish a luxurious dish to the tables of the Celestial Empire. The varied landscape afforded by the Andaman Islands was soon passed, however, and the "Rangoon" rapidly approached the Straits of Malacca, which give access to the China seas.

What was detective Fix, so unluckily drawn on from country to country, doing all this while? He had managed to embark on the "Rangoon" at Calcutta without being seen by Passepartout, after leaving orders that, if the warrant should arrive, it should be forwarded to him at Hong Kong; and he hoped to conceal his presence to the end of the voyage. It would have been difficult to explain why he was on board without awaking Passepartout's suspicions, who thought him still at Bombay. But necessity impelled him, nevertheless, to renew his acquaintance with the worthy servant, as will be seen.

All the detective's hopes and wishes were now centred on Hong Kong; for the steamer's stay at Singapore would be too brief to enable him to take any steps there. The arrest must be made at Hong Kong, or the robber would probably escape him for ever. Hong Kong was the last English ground on which he would set foot; beyond, China, Japan, America offered to Fogg an almost certain refuge. If the warrant should at last make its appearance at Hong Kong, Fix could arrest him and give him into the hands of the local police, and there would be no further trouble. But beyond Hong Kong, a simple warrant would be of no avail; an extradition warrant would be necessary, and that would result in delays and obstacles, of which the rascal would take advantage to elude justice.

Fix thought over these probabilities during the long hours which he spent in his cabin, and kept repeating to himself, "Now, either the warrant will be at Hong Kong, in which case I shall arrest my man, or it will not be there; and this time it is absolutely necessary that I should delay his departure. I have failed at Bombay, and I have failed at Calcutta: if I fail at Hong Kong, my reputation is lost. Cost what it may, I *must* succeed! But how shall I prevent his departure, if that should turn out to be my last resource?"

Fix made up his mind that, if worst came to worst, he would make a confidant of Passepartout, and tell him what kind of a fellow his master really was. That Passepartout was not Fogg's accomplice, he was very certain. The servant, enlightened by his disclosure, and afraid of being himself implicated in the crime, would doubtless become an ally of the detective. But this method was a dangerous one, only to be employed when everything else had failed. A word from Passepartout to his master would ruin all. The detective was therefore in a sore strait. But suddenly a new idea struck him. The presence of Aouda on the "Rangoon," in company with Phileas Fogg, gave him new material for reflection.

Who was this woman? What combination of events had made her Fogg's travelling companion? They had evidently met somewhere between Bombay and Calcutta; but where? Had they met accidentally, or had Fogg gone into the interior purposely in quest of this charming damsel? Fix was fairly puzzled. He asked himself whether there had not been a wicked elopement; and this idea so impressed itself upon his mind that he determined to make use of the supposed intrigue. Whether the young woman were married or not, he would be able to create such difficulties for Mr. Fogg at Hong Kong, that he could not escape by paying any amount of money.

But could he even wait till they reached Hong Kong? Fogg had an abominable way of jumping from one boat to another, and, before anything could be effected, might get full under weigh again for Yokohama.

Fix decided that he must warn the English authorities, and signal the "Rangoon" before her arrival. This was easy to do, since the steamer stopped at Singapore, whence there is a telegraphic wire to Hong Kong. He finally resolved, moreover, before acting more positively, to question Passepartout. It would not be difficult to make him talk; and, as there was no time to lose, Fix prepared to make himself known.

It was now the 30th of October, and on the following day the "Rangoon" was due at Singapore.

Fix emerged from his cabin and went on deck. Passepartout was promenading up and down in the forward part of the steamer. The detective rushed forward with every appearance of extreme surprise, and exclaimed, "You here, on the 'Rangoon'?"

"What, Monsieur Fix, are you on board?" returned the really astonished Passepartout, recognizing his crony of the "Mongolia." "Why, I left you at Bombay, and here you are, on the way to Hong Kong! Are you going round the world too?"

"No, no," replied Fix; "I shall stop at Hong Kong—at least for some days."

"Hum!" said Passepartout, who seemed for an instant perplexed. "But how is it I have not seen you on board since we left Calcutta?"

"Oh, a trifle of seasickness,—I've been staying in my berth. The Gulf of Bengal does not agree with me as well as the Indian Ocean. And how is Mr. Fogg?"

"As well and as punctual as ever, not a day behind time! But, Monsieur Fix, you don't know that we have a young lady with us."

"A young lady?" replied the detective, not seeming to comprehend what was said.

Passepartout thereupon recounted Aouda's history, the affair at the Bombay pagoda, the purchase of the elephant for two thousand pounds, the rescue, the arrest and sentence of the Calcutta court, and the restoration of Mr. Fogg and himself to liberty on bail. Fix, who was familiar with the last events, seemed to be equally ignorant of all that Passepartout related; and the latter was charmed to find so interested a listener.

"But does your master propose to carry this young woman to Europe?"

"Not at all. We are simply going to place her under the protection of one of her relatives, a rich merchant at Hong Kong."

"Nothing to be done there," said Fix to himself, concealing his disappointment. "A glass of gin, Mr. Passepartout?"

"Willingly, Monsieur Fix. We must at least have a friendly glass on board the 'Rangoon.' "

CHAPTER 17

SHOWING WHAT HAPPENED ON THE VOYAGE FROM SINGAPORE TO HONG KONG

THE detective and Passepartout met often on deck after this interview, though Fix was reserved, and did not attempt to induce his companion to divulge any more facts concerning Mr. Fogg. He caught a glimpse of that mysterious gentleman once or twice; but Mr. Fogg usually confined himself to the cabin, where he kept Aouda company, or, according to his inveterate habit, took a hand at whist.

Passepartout began very seriously to conjecture what strange chance kept Fix still on the route that his master was pursuing. It was really worth considering why this certaintly very amiable and complacent person, whom he had first met at Suez, had then encountered on board the "Mongolia," who disembarked at Bombay, which he announced as his destination, and now turned up so unexpectedly on the "Rangoon," was following Mr. Fogg's tracks step by step. What was Fix's object? Passepartout was ready to wager his Indian shoes—which he religiously preserved—that Fix would also leave Hong Kong at the same time with them, and probably on the same steamer.

Passepartout might have cudgelled his brain for a century without hitting upon the real object which the detective had in view. He never could have imagined that Phileas Fogg was being tracked as a robber around the globe. But as it is in human nature to attempt the solution of every mystery, Passepartout suddenly discovered an explanation of Fix's movements, which was in truth far from unreasonable. Fix, he thought, could only be an agent of Mr. Fogg's friends at the Reform Club, sent to follow him up, and to ascertain that he really went round the world as had been agreed upon.

"It's clear!" repeated the worthy servant to himself, proud of his shrewdness. "He's a spy sent to keep us in view! That isn't quite the thing, either, to be spying Mr. Fogg, who is so honourable a man! Ah, gentlemen of the Reform, this shall cost you dear!"

Passepartout, enchanted with his discovery, resolved to say nothing to his master, lest he should be justly offended at this mistrust on the part of his adversaries. But he determined to chaff Fix, when he had the chance, with mysterious allusions, which, however, need not betray his real suspicions.

During the afternoon of Wednesday, October 30th, the "Rangoon" entered the Strait of Malacca, which separates the peninsula of that name from Sumatra. The mountainous and craggy islets intercepted the beauties of this noble island from the view of the travellers. The "Rangoon" weighed anchor at Singapore the next day at four a.m., to receive coal, having gained half a day on the prescribed time of her arrival. Phileas Fogg noted this gain in his journal, and then, accompanied by Aouda, who betrayed a desire for a walk on shore, disembarked.

Fix, who suspected Mr. Fogg's every movement, followed them cautiously, without being himself perceived; while Passepartout, laughing in his sleeve at Fix's manœuvres, went about his usual errands.

The island of Singapore is not imposing in aspect, for there are no mountains; yet its appearance is not without attractions. It is a park checkered by pleasant highways and avenues. A handsome carriage, drawn by a sleek pair of New Holland horses, carried Phileas Fogg and Aouda into the midst of rows of palms with brilliant foliage, and of clove-trees whereof the cloves form the heart of a half-open flower. Pepper plants replaced the prickly hedges of European fields; sago-bushes, large ferns with gorgeous branches, varied the aspect of this tropical clime; while nutmeg-trees in full foliage filled the air with a penetrating perfume. Agile and grinning bands of monkeys skipped about in the trees, nor were tigers wanting in the jungles.

After a drive of two hours through the country, Aouda and Mr. Fogg returned to the town, which is a vast collection of heavy-looking, irregular houses, surrounded by charming gardens rich in tropical fruits and plants; and at ten o'clock they re-embarked, closely followed by the detective, who had kept them constantly in sight.

Passepartout, who had been purchasing several dozen mangoes—a fruit as large as good-sized apples, of a dark brown colour outside and bright red within, and whose white pulp, melting in the mouth, affords gourmands a delicious sensation—was waiting for them on deck. He was only too glad to offer some mangoes to Aouda, who thanked him very gracefully for them.

At eleven o'clock the "Rangoon" rode out of Singapore harbour, and in a few hours the high mountains of Malacca, with their forests inhabited by the most beautifully-furred tigers in the world, were lost to view. Singapore is distant some thirteen hundred miles from the island of Hong Kong, which is a little English colony near the Chinese coast. Phileas Fogg hoped to accomplish the journey in six days, so as to be in time for the steamer which would leave on the 6th of November for Yokohama, the principal Japanese port.

The "Rangoon" had a large quota of passengers, many of whom disembarked at Singapore, among them a number of Indians, Ceylonese, Chinamen, Malays, and Portuguese, mostly second-class travellers.

The weather, which had hitherto been fine, changed with the last quarter of the moon. The sea rolled heavily, and the wind at intervals rose almost to a storm, but happily blew from the south-west, and thus aided the steamer's progress. The captain as often as possible put up his sails, and under the double action of steam and sail, the vessel made rapid progress along the coasts of Anam and Cochin China. Owing to the defective construction of the "Rangoon," however, unusual precautions became necessary in unfavourable weather; but the loss of time which resulted from this cause, while it nearly drove Passepartout out of his senses, did not seem to affect his master in the least. Passepartout blamed the captain, the engineer, and the crew, and consigned all who were connected with the ship to the land where the pepper grows. Perhaps the thought of the gas, which was remorselessly burning at his expense in Saville Row, had something to do with his hot impatience.

"You are in a great hurry, then," said Fix to him one day, "to reach Hong Kong?"

"A very great hurry!"

"Mr. Fogg, I suppose, is anxious to catch the steamer for Yokohama?"

"Terribly anxious."

"You believe in this journey around the world, then?"

"Absolutely. Don't you, Mr. Fix?"

"I? I don't believe a word of it."

"You're a sly dog!" said Passepartout, winking at him.

This expression rather disturbed Fix, without his knowing why. Had the Frenchman guessed his real purpose? He knew not what to think. But how could Passepartout have discovered that he was a detective? Yet, in speaking as he did, the man evidently meant more than he expressed.

Passepartout went still further the next day; he could not hold his tongue.

"Mr. Fix," said he, in a bantering tone; "shall we be so unfortunate as to lose you when we get to Hong Kong?"

"Why," responded Fix, a little embarrassed, "I don't know; perhaps—"

"Ah, if you would only go on with us! An agent of the Peninsular Company, you know, can't stop on the way! You were only going to Bombay, and here you are in China. America is not far off, and from America to Europe is only a step."

Fix looked intently at his companion, whose countenance was as serene as possible, and laughed with him. But Passepartout persisted in chaffing him by asking him if he made much by his present occupation.

"Yes, and no," returned Fix; "there is good and bad luck in such things. But you must understand that I don't travel at my own expense."

"Oh, I am quite sure of that!" cried Passepartout, laughing heartily.

Fix, fairly puzzled, descended to his cabin and gave himself up to his reflections. He was evidently suspected; somehow or other the Frenchman had found out that he was a detective. But had he told his master? What part was he playing in all this: was he an accomplice or not? Was the game, then, up? Fix spent several hours turning these things over in his mind, sometimes thinking that all was lost, then persuading himself that Fogg was ignorant of his presence, and then undecided what course it was best to take.

Nevertheless, he preserved his coolness of mind, and at last resolved to deal plainly with Passepartout. If he did not find it practicable to arrest Fogg at Hong Kong, and if Fogg made preparations to leave that last foothold of English territory, he, Fix, would tell Passepartout all. Either the servant was the accomplice of his master, and in this case the master knew of his operations, and he should fail; or else the servant knew nothing about the robbery, and then his interest would be to abandon the robber.

Such was the situation between Fix and Passepartout. Meanwhile Phileas Fogg moved about above them in the most majestic and unconscious indifference. He was passing methodically in his orbit around the world, regardless of the lesser stars which gravitated around him. Yet there was near by what the astronomers would call a disturbing star, which might have produced an agitation in this gentleman's heart. But no! the charms of Aouda failed to act, to Passepartout's great surprise; and the disturbances, if they existed, would have been more difficult to calculate than those of Uranus which led to the discovery of Neptune.

It was every day an increasing wonder to Passepartout, who read in Aouda's eyes the depths of her gratitude to his master. Phileas Fogg, though brave and gallant, must be, he thought, quite heartless. As to the sentiment which this journey might have awakened in him, there was clearly no trace of such a thing; while poor Passepartout existed in perpetual reveries.

One day he was leaning on the railing of the engine-room, and was observing the engine, when a sudden pitch of the steamer threw the screw out of the water. The steam came hissing out of the valves; and this made Passepartout indignant.

"The valves are not sufficiently charged!" he exclaimed. "We are not going. Oh, these English! If this was an American craft, we should blow up, perhaps, but we should at all events go faster!"

CHAPTER 18

IN WHICH PHILEAS FOGG, PASSEPARTOUT, AND FIX GO EACH ABOUT HIS BUSINESS

THE weather was bad during the latter days of the voyage. The wind, obstinately remaining in the north-west, blew a gale, and retarded the steamer. The "Rangoon" rolled heavily, and the passengers became impatient of the long, monstrous waves which the wind raised before their path. A sort of tempest arose on the 3rd of November, the squall knocking the vessel about with fury, and the waves running high. The "Rangoon" reefed all her sails, and even the rigging proved too much, whistling and shaking amid the squall. The steamer was forced to proceed slowly, and the captain estimated that she would reach Hong Kong twenty hours behind time, and more if the storm lasted.

Phileas Fogg gazed at the tempestuous sea, which seemed to be struggling especially to delay him, with his habitual tranquillity. He never changed countenance for an instant, though a delay of twenty hours, by making him too late for the Yokohama boat, would almost inevitably cause the loss of the wager. But this man of nerve manifested neither impatience nor annoyance; it seemed as if the storm were a part of his programme, and had been foreseen. Aouda was amazed to find him as calm as he had been from the first time she saw him.

Fix did not look at the state of things in the same light. The storm greatly pleased him. His satisfaction would have been complete had the "Rangoon" been forced to retreat before the violence of wind and waves. Each delay filled him with hope, for it became more and more probable that Fogg would be obliged to remain some days at Hong Kong; and now the heavens themselves became his allies, with the gusts and squalls. It mattered not that they made him sea-sick—he made no account of this inconvenience; and whilst his body was writhing under their effects, his spirit bounded with hopeful exultation.

Passepartout was enraged beyond expression by the unpropitious weather.

Everything had gone so well till now! Earth and sea had seemed to be at his master's service; steamers and railways obeyed him; wind and steam united to speed his journey. Had the hour of adversity come? Passepartout was as much excited as if the twenty thousand pounds were to come from his own pocket. The storm exasperated him, the gale made him furious, and he longed to lash the obstinate sea into obedience. Poor fellow! Fix carefully concealed from him his own satisfaction, for, had he betrayed it, Passepartout could scarcely have restrained himself from personal violence.

Passepartout remained on deck as long as the tempest lasted, being unable to remain quiet below, and taking it into his head to aid the progress of the ship by lending a hand with the crew. He overwhelmed the captain, officers, and sailors, who could not help laughing at his impatience, with all sorts of questions. He wanted to know exactly how long the storm was going to last; whereupon he was referred to the barometer, which seemed to have no intention of rising. Passepartout shook it, but with no perceptible effect; for neither shaking nor maledictions could prevail upon it to change its mind.

On the 4th, however, the sea became more calm, and the storm lessened its violence; the wind veered southward, and was once more favourable. Passepartout cleared up with the weather. Some of the sails were unfurled, and the "Rangoon" resumed its most rapid speed. The time lost could not, however, be regained. Land was not signalled until five o'clock on the morning of the 6th; the steamer was due on the 5th. Phileas Fogg was twenty-four hours behindhand, and the Yokohama steamer would of course be missed.

The pilot went on board at six, and took his place on the bridge, to guide the "Rangoon" through the channels to the port of Hong Kong. Passepartout longed to ask him if the steamer had left for Yokohama; but he dared not, for he wished to preserve the spark of hope which still remained till the last moment. He had confined his anxiety to Fix, who—the sly rascal!—tried to console him by saying that Mr. Fogg would be in time if he took the next boat; but this only put Passepartout in a passion.

Mr. Fogg, bolder than his servant, did not hesitate to approach the pilot, and tranquilly ask him if he knew when a steamer would leave Hong Kong for Yokohama.

"At high tide to-morrow morning," answered the pilot.

"Ah!" said Mr. Fogg, without betraying any astonishment.

Passepartout, who heard what passed, would willingly have embraced the pilot, while Fix would have been glad to twist his neck.

"What is the steamer's name?" asked Mr. Fogg.

"The 'Carnatic.' "

"Ought she not to have gone yesterday?"

"Yes, sir; but they had to repair one of her boilers, and so her departure was postponed till to-morrow."

"Thank you," returned Mr. Fogg, descending mathematically to the saloon.

Passepartout clasped the pilot's hand and shook it heartily in his delight, exclaiming, "Pilot, you are the best of good fellows!"

The pilot proabably does not know to this day why his responses won him this enthusiastic greeting. He remounted the bridge, and guided the steamer through the flotilla of junks, tankas, and fishing-boats which crowd the harbour of Hong Kong.

He took a hand at everything and astonished the crew.

At one o'clock the "Rangoon" was at the quay, and the passengers were going ashore.

Chance had strangely favoured Phileas Fogg, for, had not the "Carnatic" been forced to lie over for repairing her boilers, she would have left on the 6th of November, and the passengers for Japan would have been obliged to await for a week the sailing of the next steamer. Mr. Fogg was, it is true, twenty-four hours behind his time; but this could not seriously imperil the remainder of his tour.

The steamer which crossed the Pacific from Yokohama to San Francisco made a direct connexion with that from Hong Kong, and it could not sail until the latter reached Yokohama; and if Mr. Fogg was twenty-four hours late on reaching Yokohama, this time would no doubt be easily regained in the voyage of twenty-two days across the Pacific. He found himself, then, about twenty-four hours behindhand, thirty-five days after leaving London.

The "Carnatic" was announced to leave Hong Kong at five the next morning. Mr. Fogg had sixteen hours in which to attend to his business there, which was to deposit Aouda safely with her wealthy relative.

On landing, he conducted her to a palanquin, in which they repaired to the Club Hotel. A room was engaged for the young woman, and Mr. Fogg, after seeing that she wanted for nothing, set out in search of her cousin Jejeeh. He instructed Passepartout to remain at the hotel until his return, that Aouda might not be left entirely alone.

Mr. Fogg repaired to the Exchange, where, he did not doubt, every one would know so wealthy and considerable a personage as the Parsee merchant. Meeting a broker, he made the inquiry, to learn that Jejeeh had left China two years before, and, retiring from business with an immense fortune, had taken up his residence in Europe—in Holland, the broker thought, with the merchants of which country he had principally traded. Phileas Fogg returned to the hotel, begged a moment's conversation with Aouda, and, without more ado, apprised her that Jejeeh was no longer at Hong Kong, but probably in Holland.

Aouda at first said nothing. She passed her hand across her forehead, and reflected a few moments. Then, in her sweet, soft voice, she said, "What ought I to do, Mr. Fogg?"

"It is very simple," responded the gentleman. "Go on to Europe."

"But I cannot intrude—"

"You do not intrude, nor do you in the least embarrass my project. Passepartout!"

"Monsieur."

"Go to the 'Carnatic,' and engage three cabins."

Passepartout, delighted that the young woman, who was very gracious to him, was going to continue the journey with them, went off at a brisk gait to obey his master's order.

CHAPTER 19

IN WHICH PASSEPARTOUT TAKES A TOO GREAT INTEREST IN HIS MASTER, AND WHAT COMES OF IT

HONG KONG is an island which came into the possession of the English by the treaty of Nankin, after the war of 1842; and the colonizing genius of the English has created upon it an important city and an excellent port. The island is situated at the mouth of the Canton River, and is separated by about sixty miles from the Portuguese town of Macao, on the opposite coast. Hong Kong has beaten Macao in the struggle for the Chinese trade, and now the greater part of the transportation of Chinese goods finds its depôt at the former place. Docks, hospitals, wharves, a Gothic cathedral, a government house, macadamized streets give to Hong Kong the appearance of a town in Kent or Surrey transferred by some strange magic to the antipodes.

Passepartout wandered, with his hands in his pockets, towards the Victoria port, gazing as he went at the curious palanquins and other modes of conveyance, and the groups of Chinese, Japanese, and Europeans who passed to and fro in the streets. Hong Kong seemed to him not unlike Bombay, Calcutta, and Singapore, since, like them, it betrayed everywhere the evidence of English supremacy. At the Victoria port he found a confused mass of ships of all nations, English, French, American, and Dutch, men-of-war and trading vessels, Japanese and Chinese junks, sempas, tankas, and flower-boats, which formed so many floating parterres. Passepartout noticed in the crowd a number of the natives who seemed very old and were dressed in yellow. On going into a barber's to get shaved, he learned that these ancient men were all at least eighty years old, at which age they are permitted to wear yellow, which is the Imperial colour. Passepartout, without exactly knowing why, thought this very funny.

On reaching the quay where they were to embark on the "Carnatic," he was not astonished to find Fix walking up and down. The detective seemed very much disturbed and disappointed.

"This is bad," muttered Passepartout, "for the gentlemen of the Reform Club!" He accosted Fix with a merry smile, as if he had not perceived that gentleman's chagrin. The detective had, indeed, good reasons to inveigh against the bad luck which pursued him. The warrant had not come! It was certainly on the way, but as certainly it could not now reach Hong Kong for several days; and this being the last English territory on Mr. Fogg's route, the robber would escape, unless he could manage to detain him.

"Well, Monsieur Fix," said Passepartout, "have you decided to go on with us as far as America?"

"Yes," returned Fix, through his set teeth.

"Good!" exclaimed Passepartout, laughing heartily. "I knew you could not persuade yourself to separate from us. Come and engage your berth."

They entered the steamer office and secured cabins for four persons. The clerk, as he gave them the tickets, informed them that, the repairs on the "Carnatic" having been completed, the steamer would leave that very evening, and not the next morning as had been announced.

"That will suit my master all the better," said Passepartout. "I will go and let him know."

Fix now decided to make a bold move; he resolved to tell Passepartout all. It seemed to be the only possible means of keeping Phileas Fogg several days longer at Hong Kong. He accordingly invited his companion into a tavern which caught his eye on the quay. On entering, they found themselves in a large room handsomely decorated, at the end of which was a large camp-bed furnished with cushions. Several persons lay upon this bed in a deep sleep. At the small tables which were arranged about the room some thirty customers were drinking English beer, porter, gin, and brandy; smoking, the while, long red clay pipes stuffed with little balls of opium mingled with essence of rose. From time to time one of the smokers, overcome with the narcotic, would slip under the table, whereupon the waiters, taking him by the head and feet, carried and laid him upon the bed. The bed already supported twenty of these stupefied sots.

Fix and Passepartout saw that they were in a smokinghouse haunted by those wretched, cadaverous, idiotic creatures, to whom the English merchants sell every year the miserable drug call opium, to the amount of one million four hundred thousand pounds—thousands devoted to one of the most despicable vices which afflict humanity! The Chinese government has in vain attempted to deal with the evil by stringent laws. It passed gradually from the rich, to whom it was at first exclusively reserved, to the lower classes, and then its ravages could not be arrested. Opium is smoked everywhere, at all times, by men and women, in the Celestial Empire; and, once accustomed to it, the victims cannot dispense with it, except by suffering horrible bodily contortions and agonies. A great smoker can smoke as many as eight pipes a day; but he dies in five years. It was in one of these dens that Fix and Passepartout, in search of a friendly glass, found themselves. Passepartout had no money, but willingly accepted Fix's invitation in the hope of returning the obligation at some future time.

They ordered two bottles of port, to which the Frenchman did ample justice, whilst Fix observed him with close attention. They chatted about the journey, and Passepartout was especially merry at the idea that Fix was going to continue it with them. When the bottles were empty, however, he rose to go and tell his master of the change in the time of the sailing of the "Carnatic."

Fix caught him by the arm, and said, "Wait a moment."

"What for, Mr. Fix?"

"I want to have a serious talk with you."

"A serious talk!" cried Passepartout, drinking up the little wine that was left in the bottom of his glass. "Well, we'll talk about it to-morrow; I haven't time now."

"Stay! What I have to say concerns your master."

Passepartout, at this, looked attentively at his companion. Fix's face seemed to have a singular expression. He resumed his seat.

"What is it that you have to say?"

Fix placed his hand upon Passepartout's arm and, lowering his voice, said, "You have guessed who I am?"

"Parbleu!" said Passepartout, smiling.

"Then I'm going to tell you everything—"

"Now that I know everything, my friend! Ah! that's very good. But go on,

In his stroll Passepartout came across a number of old natives.

go on. First, though, let me tell you that those gentlemen have put themselves to a useless expense."

"Useless!" said Fix. "You speak confidently. It's clear that you don't know how large the sum is."

"Of course I do," returned Passepartout. "Twenty thousand pounds."

"Fifty-five thousand!" answered Fix, pressing his companion's hand.

"What!" cried the Frenchman. "Has Monsieur Fogg dared—fifty-five thousand pounds! Well, there's all the more reason for not losing an instant," he continued, getting up hastily.

Fix pushed Passepartout back in his chair, and resumed: "Fifty-five thousand pounds; and if I succeed, I get two thousand pounds. If you'll help me, I'll let you have five hundred of them."

"Help you?" cried Passepartout, whose eyes were standing wide open.

"Yes; help me keep Mr. Fogg here for two or three days."

"Why, what are you saying? Those gentlemen are not satisfied with following my master and suspecting his honour, but they must try to put obstacles in his way! I blush for them!"

"What do you mean?"

"I mean that it is a piece of shameful trickery. They might as well waylay Mr. Fogg and put his money in their pockets!"

"That's just what we count on doing."

"It's a conspiracy, then," cried Passepartout, who became more and more excited as the liquor mounted in his head, for he drank without perceiving it. "A real conspiracy! And gentlemen, too. Bah!"

Fix began to be puzzled.

"Members of the Reform Club!" continued Passepartout. "You must know, Monsieur Fix, that my master is an honest man, and that, when he makes a wager, he tries to win it fairly!"

"But who do you think I am?" asked Fix, looking at him intently.

"Parbleu! An agent of the members of the Reform Club, sent out here to interrupt my master's journey. But, though I found you out some time ago, I've taken good care to say nothing about it to Mr. Fogg."

"He knows nothing, then?"

"Nothing," replied Passepartout, again emptying his glass.

The detective passed his hand across his forehead, hesitating before he spoke again. What should he do? Passepartout's mistake seemed sincere, but it made his design more difficult. It was evident that the servant was not the master's accomplice, as Fix had been inclined to suspect.

"Well," said the detective to himself, "as he is not an accomplice, he will help me."

He had no time to lose: Fogg must be detained at Hong Kong; so he resolved to make a clean breast of it.

"Listen to me," said Fix abruptly. "I am not, as you think, an agent of the members of the Reform Club—"

"Bah!" retorted Passepartout, with an air of raillery.

"I am a police detective, sent out here by the London office."

"You, a detective?"

"I will prove it. Here is my commission."

Passepartout was speechless with astonishment when Fix displayed this document, the genuineness of which could not be doubted.

"Listen," said Fix in an undertone.

"Mr. Fogg's wager," resumed Fix, "is only a pretext of which you and the gentlemen of the Reform are dupes. He had a motive for securing your innocent complicity."

"But why?"

"Listen. On the 28th of last September a robbery of fifty-five thousand pounds was committed at the Bank of England by a person whose description was fortunately secured. Here is this description; it answers exactly to that of Mr. Phineas Fogg."

"What nonsense!" cried Passepartout, striking the table with his fist. "My master is the most honourable of men!"

"How can you tell? You know scarcely anything about him. You went into his service the day he came away; and he came away on a foolish pretext, without trunks, and carrying a large amount in bank-notes. And yet you are bold enough to assert that he is an honest man!"

"Yes, yes," repeated the poor fellow, mechanically.

"Would you like to be arrested as his accomplice?"

Passepartout, overcome by what he had heard, held his head between his hands, and did not dare to look at the detective. Phileas Fogg, the saviour of Aouda, that brave and generous man, a robber! And yet how many presumptions there were against him! Passepartout essayed to reject the suspicions which forced themselves upon his mind; he did not wish to believe that his master was guilty.

"Well, what do you want of me?" said he, at last, with an effort.

"See here," replied Fix; "I have tracked Mr. Fogg to this place, but as yet I have failed to receive the warrant of arrest for which I sent to London. You must help me to keep him here in Hong Kong—"

"I! But I—"

"I will share with you the two-thousand-pounds reward offered by the Bank of England."

"Never!" replied Passepartout, who tried to rise, but fell back, exhausted in mind and body.

"Mr. Fix," he stammered, "even should what you say be true—if my master is really the robber you are seeking for—which I deny—I have been, am, in his service; I have seen his generosity and goodness; and I will never betray him—not for all the gold in the world. I come from a village where they don't eat that kind of bread!"

"You refuse?"

"I refuse."

"Consider that I've said nothing," said Fix; "and let us drink."

"Yes; let us drink!"

Passepartout felt himself yielding more and more to the effects of the liquor. Fix, seeing that he must, at all hazards, be separated from his master, wished to entirely overcome him. Some pipes full of opium lay upon the table. Fix slipped one into Passepartout's hand. He took it, put it between his lips, lit it, drew several puffs, and his head, becoming heavy under the influence of the narcotic, fell upon the table.

"At last!" said Fix, seeing Passepartout unconscious. "Mr. Fogg will not be informed of the time of the 'Carnatic's' departure; and, if he is, he will have to do without this cursed Frenchman!"

And, after paying his bill, Fix left the tavern.

CHAPTER 20

IN WHICH FIX COMES FACE TO FACE WITH PHILEAS FOGG

WHILE these events were passing at the opium-house Mr. Fogg, unconscious of the danger he was in of losing the steamer, was quietly escorting Aouda about the streets of the English quarter, making the necessary purchases for the long voyage before them. It was all very well for an Englishman like Mr. Fogg to make the tour of the world with a carpet-bag; a lady could not be expected to travel comfortably under such conditions. He acquitted his task with characteristic serenity, and invariably replied to the remonstrances of his fair companion, who was confused by his patience and generosity,—

"It is in the interest of my journey—a part of my programme."

The purchases made, they returned to the hotel, where they dined at a sumptuously served *table-d'hôte;* after which Aouda, shaking hands with her protector after the English fashion, retired to her room for rest. Mr. Fogg absorbed himself throughout the evening in the perusal of the *Times* and *Illustrated London News*.

Had he been capable of being astonished at anything, it would have been not to see his servant return at bedtime. But, knowing that the steamer was not to leave for Yokohama until the next morning, he did not disturb himself about the matter. When Passepartout did not appear the next morning, to answer his master's bell, Mr. Fogg, not betraying the least vexation, contented himself with taking his carpet-bag, calling Aouda, and sending for a palanquin.

It was then eight o'clock; at half-past nine, it being then high tide, the "Carnatic" would leave the harbour. Mr. Fogg and Aouda got into the palanquin, their luggage being brought after on a wheelbarrow, and half an hour later stepped upon the quay whence they were to embark. Mr. Fogg then learned that the "Carnatic" had sailed the evening before. He had expected to find not only the steamer, but his domestic, and was forced to give up both; but no sign of disappointment appeared on his face, and he merely remarked to Aouda, "It is an accident, madam; nothing more."

At this moment a man who had been observing him attentively approached. It was Fix, who, bowing, addressed Mr. Fogg: "Were you not, like me, sir, a passenger by the 'Rangoon,' which arrived yesterday?"

"I was, sir," replied Mr. Fogg coldly. "But I have not the honour—"

"Pardon me; I thought I should find your servant here."

"Do you know where he is, sir?" asked Aouda anxiously.

"What!" responded Fix, feigning surprise. "Is he not with you?"

"No," said Aouda. "He has not made his appearance since yesterday. Could he have gone on board the 'Carnatic' without us?"

"Without you, madam?" answered the detective. "Excuse me, did you intend to sail in the 'Carnatic'?"

"Yes, sir."

"So did I, madam, and I am excessively disappointed. The 'Carnatic,' its repairs being completed, left Hong Kong twelve hours before the stated time, without any notice being given; and we must now wait a week for another steamer."

As he said "a week" Fix felt his heart leap for joy. Fogg detained at Hong Kong a week! There would be time for the warrant to arrive, and fortune at last favoured the representative of the law. His horror may be imagined when he heard Mr. Fogg say, in his placid voice, "But there are other vessels besides the 'Carnatic,' it seems to me, in the harbour of Hong Kong."

And, offering his arm to Aouda, he directed his steps toward the docks in search of some craft about to start. Fix, stupefied, followed; it seemed as if he were attached to Mr. Fogg by an invisible thread. Chance, however, appeared really to have abandoned the man it had hitherto served so well. For three hours Phileas Fogg wandered about the docks, with the determination, if necessary, to charter a vessel to carry him to Yokohama; but he could only find vessels which were loading or unloading, and which could not therefore set sail. Fix began to hope again.

But Mr. Fogg, far from being discouraged, was continuing his search, resolved not to stop if he had to resort to Macao, when he was accosted by a sailor on one of the wharves.

"Is your honour looking for a boat?"

"Have you a boat ready to sail?"

"Yes, your honour; a pilot-boat—No. 43—the best in the harbour."

"Does she go fast?"

"Between eight and nine knots the hour. Will you look at her?"

"Yes."

"Your honour will be satisfied with her. Is it for a sea excursion?"

"No; for a voyage."

"A voyage?"

"Yes; will you agree to take me to Yokohama?"

The sailor leaned on the railing, opened his eyes wide, and said, "Is your honour joking?"

"No. I have missed the 'Carnatic,' and I must get to Yokohama by the 14th at the latest, to take the boat for San Francisco."

"I am sorry," said the sailor, "but it is impossible."

"I offer you a hundred pounds per day, and an additional reward of two hundred pounds if I reach Yokohama in time."

"Are you in earnest?"

"Very much so."

The pilot walked away a little distance, and gazed out to sea, evidently struggling between the anxiety to gain a large sum and the fear of venturing so far. Fix was in mortal suspense.

Mr. Fogg turned to Aouda and asked her, "You would not be afraid, would you, madam?"

"Not with you, Mr. Fogg," was her answer.

The pilot now returned, shuffling his hat in his hands.

"Well, pilot?" said Mr. Fogg.

"Well, your honour," replied he, "I could not risk myself, my men, or my little boat of scarcely twenty tons on so long a voyage at this time of year. Besides, we could not reach Yokohama in time, for it is sixteen hundred and sixty miles from Hong Kong."

"Only sixteen hundred," said Mr. Fogg.

"It's the same thing."

Fix breathed more freely.

"But," added the pilot, "it might be arranged another way."

Fix ceased to breathe at all.

"How?" asked Mr. Fogg.

"By going to Nagasaki, at the extreme south of Japan, or even to Shanghai, which is only eight hundred miles from here. In going to Shanghai we should not be forced to sail wide of the Chinese coast, which would be a great advantage, as the currents run northward, and would aid us."

"Pilot," said Mr. Fogg, "I must take the American steamer at Yokohama, and not at Shanghai or Nagasaki."

"Why not?" returned the pilot. "The San Francisco steamer does not start from Yokohama. It puts in at Yokohama and Nagasaki, but it starts from Shanghai."

"You are sure of that?"

"Perfectly."

"And when does the boat leave Shanghai?"

"On the 11th, at seven in the evening. We have, therefore, four days before us, that is ninety-six hours; and in that time, if we had good luck and a south-west wind, and the sea was calm, we could make those eight hundred miles to Shanghai."

"And you could go—"

"In an hour; as soon as provisions could be got aboard and the sails put up."

"It is a bargain. Are you the master of the boat?"

"Yes; John Bunsby, master of the 'Tankadere.' "

"Would you like some earnest-money?"

"If it would not put your honour out—"

"Here are two hundred pounds on account. Sir," added Phileas Fogg, turning to Fix, "if you would like to take advantage—"

"Thanks, sir; I was about to ask the favour."

"Very well. In half an hour we shall go on board."

"But poor Passepartout?" urged Aouda, who was much disturbed by the servant's disappearance.

"I shall do all I can to find him," replied Phileas Fogg.

While Fix, in a feverish, nervous state, repaired to the pilot-boat the others directed their course to the police-station at Hong Kong. Phileas Fogg there gave Passepartout's description, and left a sum of money to be spent in the search for him. The same formalities having been gone through at the French consulate, and the palanquin having stopped at the hotel for the luggage, which had been sent back there, they returned to the wharf.

It was now three o'clock; and pilot-boat No. 43, with its crew on board, and its provisions stored away, was ready for departure.

The "Tankadere" was a neat little craft of twenty tons, as gracefully built as if she were a racing yacht. Her shining copper sheathing, her galvanized iron-work, her deck, white as ivory, betrayed the pride taken by John Bunsby in making her presentable. Her two masts leaned a trifle backward; she carried brigantine, foresail, storm-jib, and standing-jib, and was well rigged for running before the wind; and she seemed capable of brisk speed, which, indeed, she had already proved by gaining several prizes in pilot-boat races. The crew of the "Tankadere" was composed of John Bunsby, the master, and four hardy mariners, who were familiar with the Chinese seas. John Bunsby himself, a man of forty-five or thereabouts, vigorous, sunburnt, with a sprightly expression of the eye, and energetic and self-reliant countenance, would have inspired confidence in the most timid.

Phileas Fogg and Aouda went on board, where they found Fix already installed. Below deck was a square cabin, of which the walls bulged out in the form of cots, above a circular divan; in the centre was a table provided with a swinging lamp. The accommodation was confined, but neat.

"I am sorry to have nothing better to offer you," said Mr. Fogg to Fix, who bowed without responding.

The detective had a feeling akin to humiliation in profiting by the kindness of Mr. Fogg.

"It's certain," thought he, "though rascal as he is, he is a polite one!"

The sails and the English flag were hoisted at ten minutes past three. Mr. Fogg and Aouda, who were seated on deck, cast a last glance at the quay, in the hope of espying Passepartout. Fix was not without his fears lest chance should direct the steps of the unfortunate servant, whom he had so badly treated, in this direction; in which case an explanation the reverse of satisfactory to the detective must have ensued. But the Frenchman did not appear, and, without doubt, was still lying under the stupefying influence of the opium.

John Bunsby, master, at length gave the order to start, and the "Tankadere," taking the wind under her brigantine, foresail, and standing-jib, bounded briskly forward over the waves.

CHAPTER 21

IN WHICH THE MASTER OF THE "TANKADERE" RUNS GREAT RISK OF LOSING A REWARD OF TWO HUNDRED POUNDS

THIS voyage of eight hundred miles was a perilous venture, on a craft of twenty tons, and at that season of the year. The Chinese seas are usually boisterous, subject to terrible gales of wind, and especially during the equinoxes; and it was now early November.

It would clearly have been to the master's advantage to carry his passengers to Yokohama, since he was paid a certain sum per day; but he would have been rash to attempt such a voyage, and it was imprudent even to attempt to reach Shanghai. But John Bunsby believed in the "Tankadere," which rode on the waves like a seagull; and perhaps he was not wrong.

Late in the day they passed through the capricious channels of Hong Kong, and the "Tankadere," impelled by favourable winds, conducted herself admirably.

"I do not need, pilot," said Phileas Fogg, when they got into the open sea, "to advise you to use all possible speed."

"Trust me, your honour. We are carrying all the sail the wind will let us. The poles would add nothing, and are only used when we are going into port."

"It's your trade, not mine, pilot, and I confide in you."

Phileas Fogg, with body erect and legs wide apart, standing like a sailor, gazed without staggering at the swelling waters. The young woman, who was seated aft, was profoundly affected as she looked out upon the ocean, darkening now with the twilight, on which she had ventured in so frail a vessel. Above her head rustled the white sails, which seemed like great white wings. The boat, carried forward by the wind, seemed to be flying in the air.

Night came. The moon was entering her first quarter, and her insufficient light would soon die out in the mist on the horizon. Clouds were rising from the east, and already overcast a part of the heavens.

The pilot had hung out his lights, which was very necessary in these seas crowded with vessels bound landward; for collisions are not uncommon occurrences, and, at the speed she was going the least shock would shatter the gallant little craft.

Fix, seated in the bow, gave himself up to meditation. He kept apart from his fellow-travellers, knowing Mr. Fogg's taciturn tastes; besides, he did not quite like to talk to the man whose favours he had accepted. He was thinking, too, of the future. It seemed certain that Fogg would not stop at Yokohama, but would at once take the boat for San Francisco; and the vast extent of America would insure him impunity and safety. Fogg's plan appeared to him the simplest in the world. Instead of sailing directly from England to the United States, like a common villain, he had traversed three quarters of the globe, so as to gain the American continent more surely; and there, after throwing the police off his track, he would quietly enjoy himself with the fortune stolen from the bank. But, once in the United States, what should he, Fix, do? Should he abandon this man? No, a hundred times no! Until he had secured his extradition, he would not lose sight of him for an hour. It was his duty, and he would fulfil it to the end. At all events, there was one thing to be thankful for: Passepartout was not with his master; and it was above all important, after the confidences Fix had imparted to him, that the servant should never have speech with his master.

Phileas Fogg was also thinking of Passepartout, who had so strangely disappeared. Looking at the matter from every point of view, it did not seem to him impossible that, by some mistake, the man might have embarked on the "Carnatic" at the last moment; and this was also Aouda's opinion, who regretted very much the loss of the worthy fellow to whom she owed so much. They might then find him at Yokohama; for it the "Carnatic" was carrying him thither, it would be easy to ascertain if he had been on board.

A brisk breeze arose about ten o'clock; but, though it might have been prudent to take in a reef, the pilot, after carefully examining the heavens, let the craft remain rigged as before. The "Tankadere" bore sail admirably, as she drew a great deal of water, and everything was prepared for high speed in case of a gale.

Mr. Fogg and Aouda descended into the cabin at midnight, having been already preceded by Fix, who had lain down on one of the cots. The pilot and crew remained on deck all night.

At sunrise the next day, which was November 8th, the boat had made more than one hundred miles. The log indicated a mean speed of between eight and nine miles. The "Tankadere" still carried all sail, and was accomplishing her greatest capacity of speed. If the wind held as it was, the chances would be in her favour. During the day she kept along the coast, where the currents were favourable; the coast, irregular in profile, and visible sometimes across the clearings, was at most five miles distant. The sea was less boisterous, since the wind came off land—a fortunate circumstance for the boat, which would suffer, owing to its small tonnage, by a heavy surge on the sea.

The breeze subsided a little towards noon, and set in from the south-west. The pilot put up his poles, but took them down again within two hours, as the wind freshened up anew.

Mr. Fogg and Aouda, happily unaffected by the roughness of the sea, ate with a good appetite, Fix being invited to share their repast, which he accepted with secret chagrin. To travel at this man's expense and live upon his provisions was not palatable to him. Still, he was obliged to eat, and so he ate.

When the meal was over, he took Mr. Fogg apart, and said, "Sir,"—this "sir" scorched his lips, and he had to control himself to avoid collaring this "gentleman,"—"sir, you have been very kind to give me a passage on this boat. But, though my means will not admit of my expending them as freely as you, I must ask to pay my share—"

"Let us not speak of that, sir," replied Mr. Fogg.

"But, if I insist—"

"No, sir," repeated Mr. Fogg, in a tone which did not admit of a reply. "This enters into my general expenses."

Fix, as he bowed, had a stifled feeling, and going forward, where he ensconced himself, did not open his mouth for the rest of the day.

Meanwhile they were progressing famously, and John Bunsby was in high hope. He several times assured Mr. Fogg that they would reach Shanghai in time; to which that gentleman responded that he counted upon it. The crew set to work in good earnest, inspired by the reward to be gained. There was not a sheet which was not tightened, not a sail which was not vigorously hoisted; not a lurch could be charged to the man at the helm. They worked as desperately as if they were contesting in a Royal Yacht regatta.

By evening, the log showed that two hundred and twenty miles had been accomplished from Hong Kong, and Mr. Fogg might hope that he would be able to reach Yokohama without recording any delay in his journal; in which case, the only misadventure which had overtaken him since he left London would not seriously affect his journey.

The "Tankadere" entered the Straits of Fo-Kien, which separate the island of Formosa from the Chinese coast, in the small hours of the night, and crossed the Tropic of Cancer. The sea was very rough in the straits, full of eddies formed by the counter currents, and the chopping waves broke her course, whilst it became very difficult to stand on deck.

At daybreak the wind began to blow hard again, and the heavens seemed to predict a gale. The barometer announced a speedy change, the mercury rising and falling capriciously; the sea also, in the south-east, raised long surges which indicated a tempest. The sun had set the evening before in a red mist, in the midst of the phosphorescent scintillations of the ocean.

John Bunsby long examined the threatening aspect of the heavens, muttering indistinctly between his teeth. At last he said in a low voice to Mr. Fogg, "Shall I speak out to your honour?"

"Of course."

"Well, we are going to have a squall."

"Is the wind north or south?" asked Mr. Fogg quietly.

"South. Look! a typhoon is coming up."

"Glad it's a typhoon from the south, for it will carry us forward."

"Oh, if you take it that way," said John Bunsby, "I've nothing more to say." John Bunsby's suspicions were confirmed. At a less advanced season of the year the typhoon, according to a famous meteorologist, would have passed away like a luminous cascade of electric flame; but in the winter equinox, it was to be feared that it would burst upon them with great violence.

The pilot took his precautions in advance. He reefed all sail, the pole-masts were dispensed with; all hands went forward to the bows. A single triangular sail, of strong canvas, was hoisted as a storm-jib, so as to hold the wind from behind. Then they waited.

John Bunsby had requested his passengers to go below; but this imprisonment in so narrow a space, with little air, and the boat bouncing in the gale, was far from pleasant. Neither Mr. Fogg, Fix, nor Aouda consented to leave the deck.

The storm of rain and wind descended upon them towards eight o'clock. With but its bit of sail, the "Tankadere" was lifted like a feather by a wind an idea of whose violence can scarcely be given. To compare her speed to four times that of a locomotive going on full steam would be below the truth.

The boat scuded thus northward during the whole day, borne on by monstrous waves, preserving always, fortunately, a speed equal to theirs. Twenty times she seemed almost to be submerged by these mountains of water which rose behind her; but the adroit management of the pilot saved her. The passengers were often bathed in spray, but they submitted to it philosophically. Fix cursed it, no doubt; but Aouda, with her eyes fastened upon her protector, whose coolness amazed her, showed herself worthy of him, and bravely weathered the storm. As for Phileas Fogg, it seemed just as if the typhoon were a part of his programme.

Up to this time the "Tankadere" had always held her course to the north; but towards evening the wind, veering three quarters, bore down from the northwest. The boat, now lying in the trough of the waves, shook and rolled terribly; the sea struck her with fearful violence. At night the tempest increased in violence. John Bunsby saw the approach of darkness and the rising of the storm with dark misgivings. He thought awhile, and then asked his crew if it was not time to slacken speed. After a consultation he approached Mr. Fogg, and said, "I think, your honour, that we should do well to make for one of the ports on the coast."

"I think so too."

"Ah!" said the pilot. "But which one?"

"I know of but one," returned Mr. Fogg tranquilly.

"And that is—"

"Shanghai."

The pilot, at first, did not seem to comprehend; he could scarcely realize so much determination and tenacity. Then he cried, "Well—yes! Your honour is right. To Shanghai!"

So the "Tankadere" kept steadily on her northward track.

The night was really terrible; it would be a miracle if the craft did not founder. Twice it would have been all over with her, if the crew had not been constantly on the watch. Aouda was exhausted, but did not utter a complaint. More than once Mr. Fogg rushed to protect her from the violence of the waves.

Day appeared. The tempest still raged with undiminished fury; but the wind now returned to the south-east. It was a favourable change, and the "Tankadere" again bounded forward on this mountainous sea, though the waves crossed each other, and imparted shocks and counter-shocks which would have crushed a craft less solidly built. From time to time the coast was visible through the broken mist, but no vessel was in sight. The "Tankadere" was alone upon the sea.

There were some signs of a calm at noon, and these became more distinct as the sun descended toward the horizon. The tempest had been as brief as terrific. The passengers, thoroughly exhausted, could now eat a little, and take some repose.

The night was comparatively quiet. Some of the sails were again hoisted, and the speed of the boat was very good. The next morning at dawn they espied the coast, and John Bunsby was able to assert that they were not one hundred miles from Shanghai. A hundred miles, and only one day to traverse them! That very evening Mr. Fogg was due at Shanghai, if he did not wish to miss the steamer to Yokohama. Had there been no storm, during which several hours were lost, they would be at this moment within thirty miles of their destination.

The wind grew decidedly calmer, and happily the sea fell with it. All sails were now hoisted, and at noon the "Tankadere" was within forty-five miles of Shanghai. There remained yet six hours in which to accomplish that distance. All on board feared that it could not be done; and every one—Phileas Fogg, no doubt, excepted—felt his heart beat with impatience. The boat must keep up an average of nine miles an hour, and the wind was becoming calmer every moment! It was a capricious breeze, coming from the coast, and after it passed the sea became smooth. Still, the "Tankadere" was so light, and her fine sails caught the fickle zephyrs so well, that, with the aid of the current, John Bunsby found himself at six o'clock not more than ten miles from the mouth of Shanghai River. Shanghai itself is situated at least twelve miles up the stream. At seven they were still three miles from Shanghai. The pilot swore an angry oath; the reward of two hundred pounds was evidently on the point of escaping him. He looked at Mr. Fogg. Mr. Fogg was perfectly tranquil; and yet his whole fortune was at this moment at stake.

At this moment, also, a long black funnel, crowned with wreaths of smoke, appeared on the edge of the waters. It was the American steamer, leaving for Yokohama at the appointed time.

"Confound her!" cried John Bunsby, pushing back the rudder with a desperate jerk.

"Signal her!" said Phileas Fogg quietly.

A small brass cannon stood on the forward deck of the "Tankadere," for making signals in the fogs. It was loaded to the muzzle; but just as the pilot was about to apply a red-hot coal to the touchhole, Mr. Fogg said, "Hoist your flag!"

The flag was run up at halfmast, and, this being the signal of distress, it was hoped that the American steamer, perceiving it, would change her course a little, so as to succour the pilot-boat.

"Fire!" said Mr. Fogg. And the booming of the little cannon resounded in the air.

The *Tankadère* was tossed about like a feather.

CHAPTER 22

IN WHICH PASSEPARTOUT FINDS OUT THAT, EVEN AT THE ANTIPODES, IT IS CONVENIENT TO HAVE SOME MONEY IN ONE'S POCKET

THE "Carnatic," setting sail from Hong Kong at half-past six on the 7th of November, directed her course at full steam towards Japan. She carried a large cargo and a well-filled cabin of passengers. Two state-rooms in the rear were, however, unoccupied,—those which had been engaged by Phileas Fogg.

The next day a passenger, with a half-stupefied eye, staggering gait, and disordered hair, was seen to emerge from the second cabin, and to totter to a seat on deck.

It was Passepartout; and what had happened to him was as follows:—Shortly after Fix left the opium den, two waiters had lifted the unconscious Passepartout, and had carried him to the bed reserved for the smokers. Three hours later, pursued even in his dreams by a fixed idea, the poor fellow awoke, and struggled against the stupefying influence of the narcotic. The thought of a duty unfulfilled shook off his torpor, and he hurried from the abode of drunkenness. Staggering and holding himself up by keeping against the walls, falling down and creeping up again, and irresistibly impelled by a kind of instinct, he kept crying out, "The 'Carnatic!' the 'Carnatic!' "

The steamer lay puffing alongside the quay, on the point of starting. Passepartout had but few steps to go; and, rushing upon the plank, he crossed it, and fell unconscious on the deck, just as the "Carnatic" was moving off. Several sailors, who were evidently accustomed to this sort of scene, carried the poor Frenchman down into the second cabin, and Passepartout did not wake until they were one hundred and fifty miles away from China. Thus he found himself the next morning on the deck of the "Carnatic," and eagerly inhaling the exhilirating sea-breeze. The pure air sobered him. He began to collect his senses, which he found a difficult task; but at last he recalled the events of the evening before, Fix's revelation, and the opium-house.

"It is evident," said he to himself, "that I have been abominably drunk! What will Mr. Fogg say? At least I have not missed the steamer, which is the most important thing."

Then, as Fix occurred to him:—"As for that rascal, I hope we are well rid of him, and that he has not dared, as he proposed, to follow us on board the "Carnatic." A detective on the track of Mr. Fogg, accused of robbing the Bank of England! Pshaw! Mr. Fogg is no more a robber than I am a murderer."

Should he divulge Fix's real errand to his master? Would it do to tell the part the detective was playing? Would it not be better to wait until Mr. Fogg reached London again, and then impart to him that an agent of the metropolitan police had been following him round the world, and have a good laugh over it? No doubt; at least, it was worth considering. The first thing to do was to find Mr. Fogg, and apologize for his singular behavior.

Passepartout got up and proceeded, as well as he could with the rolling of the steamer, to the after-deck. He saw no one who resembled either his master or Aouda. "Good!" muttered he; "Aouda has not got up yet, and Mr. Fogg has probably found some partners at whist."

He descended to the saloon. Mr. Fogg was not there. Passepartout had only, however, to ask the purser the number of his master's state-room. The purser replied that he did not know any passenger by the name of Fogg.

"I beg your pardon," said Passepartout persistently. "He is a tall gentleman, quiet, and not very talkative, and has with him a young lady—"

"There is no young lady on board," interrupted the purser. "Here is a list of the passengers; you may see for yourself."

Passepartout scanned the list, but his master's name was not upon it. All at once an idea struck him.

"Ah! am I on the 'Carnatic?' "

"Yes."

"On the way to Yokohama?"

"Certainly."

Passepartout had for an instant feared that he was on the wrong boat; but, though he was really on the "Carnatic," his master was not there.

He fell thunderstruck on a seat. He saw it all now. He remembered that the time of sailing had been changed, that he should have informed his master of that fact, and that he had not done so. It was his fault, then, that Mr. Fogg and Aouda had missed the steamer. Yes, but it was still more the fault of the traitor who, in order to separate him from his master, and detain the latter at Hong Kong, had inveigled him into getting drunk! He now saw the detective's trick; and at this moment Mr. Fogg was certainly ruined, his bet was lost, and he himself perhaps arrested and imprisoned! At this thought Passepartout tore his hair. Ah, if Fix ever came within his reach, what a settling of accounts there would be!

After his first depression, Passepartout became calmer, and began to study his situation. It was certainly not an enviable one. He found himself on the way to Japan, and what should he do when he got there? His pocket was empty; he had not a solitary shilling—not so much as a penny. His passage had fortunately been paid for in advance; and he had five or six days in which to decide upon his future course. He fell to at meals with an appetite, and ate for Mr. Fogg, Aouda, and himself. He helped himself as generously as if Japan were a desert, where nothing to eat was to be looked for.

At dawn on the 13th the "Carnatic" entered the port of Yokohama. This is an important way-station in the Pacific, where all the mail-steamers, and those carrying travellers between North America, China, Japan, and the Oriental islands, put in. It is situated in the bay of Yeddo, and at but a short distance from that second capital of the Japanese Empire, and the residence of the Tycoon, the civil Emperor, before the Mikado, the spiritual Emperor, absorbed his office in his own. The "Carnatic" anchored at the quay near the custom-house, in the midst of a crowd of ships bearing the flags of all nations.

Passepartout went timidly ashore on this so curious territory of the Sons of the Sun. He had nothing better to do than, taking chance for his guide, to wander aimlessly through the streets of Yokohama. He found himself at first in a thoroughly European quarter, the houses having low fronts, and being adorned with verandas, beneath which he caught glimpses of neat peristyles. This quarter occupied, with its streets, squares, docks and warehouses, all the space between the "promontory of the Treaty" and the river. Here, as at Hong Kong and Calcutta, were mixed crowds of all races,—Americans and English, Chinamen and Dutchmen, mostly merchants ready to buy or sell anything. The Frenchman felt himself as much alone among them as if he had dropped down in the midst of Hottentots.

He had, at least, one resource,—to call on the French and English consuls at Yokohama for assistance. But he shrank from telling the story of his adventures, intimately connected as it was with that of his master: and, before doing so, he determined to exhaust all other means of aid. As chance did not favour him in the European quarter, he penetrated that inhabited by the native Japanese, determined, if necessary, to push on to Yeddo.

The Japanese quarter of Yokohama is called Benten, after the goddess of the sea, who is worshipped on the islands round about. There Passepartout beheld beautiful fir and cedar groves, sacred gaves of a singular architecture, bridges half hid in the midst of bamboos and reeds, temples shaded by immense cedar-trees, holy retreats where were sheltered Buddhist priests and sectaries of Confucius, and interminable streets, where a perfect harvest of rose-tinted and red-checked children, who looked as if they had been cut out of Japanese screens, and who were playing in the midst of short-legged poodles and yellowish cats, might have been gathered.

The streets were crowded with people. Priests were passing in processions. beating their dreary tambourines; police and custom-house officers with pointed hats encrusted with lac, and carrying two sabres hung to their waists; soldiers, clad in blue cotton with white stripes, and bearing guns; the Mikado's guards, enveloped in silken doublets, hauberks, and coats of mail; and numbers of military folk of all ranks—for the military profession is as much respected in Japan as it is despised in China—went hither and thither in groups and pairs. Passepartout saw, too, begging friars, long-robed pilgrims, and simple civilians, with their warped and jet-black hair, big heads, long busts, slender legs, short stature, and complexions varying from copper-colour to a dead white, but never yellow, like the Chinese, from whom the Japanese widely differ. He did not fail to observe the curious equipages,—carriages and palanquins, barrows supplied with sails, and litters made of bamboo; nor the women—whom he thought not especially handsome,—who took little steps with their little feet, whereon they wore canvas shoes, straw sandals, and clogs of worked wood, and who displayed tight-looking eyes, flat chests, teeth fashionably blackened, and gowns crossed with silken scarfs, tied in an enormous knot behind,—an ornament which the modern Parisian ladies seem to have borrowed from the dames of Japan.

Passepartout wandered for several hours in the midst of the motley crowd, looking in at the windows of the rich and curious shops, the jewellery establishments glittering with quaint Japanese ornaments, the restaurants decked with streamers and banners, the tea-houses, where the odorous beverage was being drunk with "saki," a liquor concocted from the fermentation of rice, and the comfortable smoking-houses, where they were puffing, not opium, which is almost unknown in Japan, but a very fine, stringy tobacco. He went on till he found himself in the fields, in the midst of vast rice plantations. There he was dazzling camelias expanding themselves, with flowers which were giving forth their last colours and perfumes, not on bushes, but on trees; and within bamboo enclosures, cherry, plum, and apple trees, which the Japanese cultivate rather for their blossoms than their fruit, and which queerly-fashioned grinning scarecrows protected from the sparrows, pigeons, ravens, and other voracious birds. On the branches of the cedars were perched large eagles; amid the foliage of the weeping willows were herons, solemnly standing on one leg; and on every hand were crows, ducks, hawks, wild birds, and a multitude of cranes, which the Japanese consider sacred, and which to their minds symbolize long life and prosperity.

As he was strolling along, Passepartout espied some violets among the shrubs.

"Good!" said he; "I'll have some supper."

But, on smelling them, he found that they were odourless.

"No chance there," thought he.

The worthy fellow had certainly taken good care to eat as hearty a breakfast as possible before leaving the "Carnatic;" but as he had been walking about all day, the demands of hunger were becoming importunate. He observed that the butchers' stalls contained neither mutton, goat, nor pork; and knowing also that it is a sacrilege to kill cattle, which are preserved solely for farming, he made up his mind that meat was far from plentiful in Yokohama,—nor was he mistaken; and in default of butcher's meat, he could have wished for a quarter of wild boar or deer, a partridge, or some quails, some game or fish, which, with rice, the Japanese eat almost exclusively. But he found it necessary to keep up a stout heart, and to postpone the meal he craved till the following morning. Night came, and Passepartout re-entered the native quarter, where he wandered through the streets, lit by vari-coloured lanterns, looking on at the dancers who were executing skilful steps and boundings, and the astrologers who stood in the open air with their telescopes. Then he came to the harbour, which was lit up by the rosin torches of the fishermen, who were fishing from their boats.

The streets at last became quiet, and the patrol, the officers of which, in their splendid costumes, and surrounded by their suites, Passepartout thought seemed like ambassadors, succeeded the bustling crowd. Each time a company passed, Passepartout chuckled, and said to himself, "Good! another Japanese embassy departing for Europe!"

CHAPTER 23

IN WHICH PASSEPARTOUT'S NOSE BECOMES OUTRAGEOUSLY LONG

THE next morning poor, jaded, famished Passepartout said to himself that he must get something to eat at all hazards, and the sooner he did so the better. He might, indeed, sell his watch; but he would have starved first. Now or never he must use the strong, if not melodious voice which nature had bestowed upon him. He knew several French and English songs, and resolved to try them upon the Japanese, who must be lovers of music, since they were for ever pounding on their cymbals, tam-tams, and tambourines, and could not but appreciate European talent.

It was, perhaps, rather early in the morning to get up a concert, and the audience, prematurely aroused from their slumbers, might not, posssibly, pay their entertainer with coin bearing the Mikado's features. Passepartout therefore decided to wait several hours; and, as he was sauntering along, it occurred to him that he would seem rather too well dressed for a wandering artist. The idea struck him to change his garments for clothes more in harmony with his project; by which he might also get a little money to satisfy the immediate cravings of hunger. The resolution taken, it remained to carry it out.

It was only after a long search that Passepartout discovered a native dealer in old clothes, to whom he applied for an exchange. The man liked the European costume, and ere long Passepartout issued from his shop accoutred in an old Japanese coat, and a sort of one-sided turban, faded with long use. A few small pieces of silver, moreover, jingled in his pocket.

"Good!" thought he. "I will imagine I am at the Carnival!"

His first care, after being thus "Japanesed," was to enter a tea-house of modest appearance, and, upon half a bird and a little rice, to breakfast like a man for whom dinner was as yet a problem to be solved.

"Now," thought he, when he had eaten heartily, "I mustn't lose my head. I can't sell this costume again for one still more Japanese. I must consider how to leave this country of the Sun, of which I shall not retain the most delightful of memories, as quickly as possible."

It occurred to him to visit the steamers which were about to leave for America. He would offer himself as a cook or servant, in payment of his passage and meals. Once at San Francisco, he would find some means of going on. The difficulty was, how to traverse the four thousand seven hundred miles of the Pacific which lay between Japan and the New World.

Passepartout was not the man to let an idea go begging, and directed his steps towards the docks. But, as he approached them, his project, which at first had seemed so simple, began to grow more and more formidable to his mind. What need would they have of a cook or servant on an American steamer, and what confidence would they put in him, dressed as he was? What references could he give?

As he was reflecting in this wise, his eyes fell upon an immense placard which a sort of clown was carrying through the streets. This placard, which was in English, read as follows:—

"ACROBATIC JAPANESE TROUPE,
HONOURABLE WILLIAM BATULCAR, PROPRIETOR,
LAST REPRESENTATIONS,
PRIOR TO THEIR DEPARTURE FOR THE UNITED STATES
OF THE
LONG NOSES! LONG NOSES!
UNDER THE DIRECT PATRONAGE OF THE GOD TINGOU!
GREAT ATTRACTION!"

"The United States!" said Passepartout; "that's just what I want!"

He followed the clown, and soon found himself once more in the Japanese quarter. A quarter of an hour later he stopped before a large cabin, adorned with

Passepartout went out muffled up in an old Japanese robe.

several clusters of streamers, the exterior walls of which were designed to represent, in violent colours and without perspective, a company of jugglers.

This was the Honourable William Batulcar's establishment. That gentleman was a sort of Barnum, the director of a troupe of mountebanks, jugglers, clowns, acrobats, equilibrists, and gymnasts, who, according to the placard, was giving his last performances before leaving the Empire of the Sun for the States of the Union.

Passepartout entered and asked for Mr. Batulcar, who straightway appeared in person.

"What do you want?" said he to Passepartout, whom he at first took for a native.

"Would you like a servant, sir?" asked Passepartout.

"A servant!" cried Mr. Batulcar, caressing the thick gray beard which hung from his chin. "I already have two who are obedient and faithful, have never left me, and serve me for their nourishment,—and here they are," added he, holding out his two robust arms, furrowed with veins as large as the strings of a bass-viol.

"So I can be of no use to you?"

"None."

"The devil! I should so like to cross the Pacific with you!"

"Ah!" said the Honourable Mr. Batulcar. "You are no more a Japanese than I am a monkey! Why are you dressed up in that way?"

"A man dresses as he can."

"That's true. You are a Frenchman, aren't you?"

"Yes; a Parisian of Paris."

"Then you ought to know how to make grimaces?"

"Why," replied Passepartout, a little vexed that his nationality should cause this question, "we Frenchmen know how to make grimaces, it is true,—but not any better than the Americans do."

"True. Well, if I can't take you as a servant, I can as a clown. You see, my friend, in France they exhibit foreign clowns, and in foreign parts French clowns."

"Ah!"

"You are pretty strong, eh?"

"Especially after a good meal."

"And you can sing?"

"Yes," returned Passepartout, who had formerly been wont to sing in the streets.

"But can you sing standing on your head, with a top spinning on your left foot, and a sabre balanced on your right?"

"Humph! I think so," replied Passepartout, recalling the exercises of his younger days.

"Well, that's enough," said the Honourable William Batulcar.

The engagement was concluded there and then.

Passepartout had at last found something to do. He was engaged to act in the celebrated Japanese troupe. It was not a very dignified position, but within a week he would be on his way to San Francisco.

The performance, so noisily announced by the Honourable Mr. Batulcar, was to commence at three o'clock, and soon the deafening instruments of a Japanese orchestra resounded at the door. Passepartout, though he had not been able to study or rehearse a part, was designated to lend the aid of his sturdy shoulders in the great exhibition of the "human pyramid," executed by the Long Noses of the god Tingou. This "great attraction" was to close the performance.

Before three o'clock the large shed was invaded by the spectators, comprising Europeans and natives, Chinese and Japanese, men, women, and children, who precipitated themselves upon the narrow benches and into the boxes opposite the stage. The musicians took up a position inside, and were vigorously performing on their gongs, tam-tams, flutes, bones, tambourines, and immense drums.

The performance was much like all acrobatic displays; but it must be confessed that the Japanese are the first equilibrists in the world.

One, with a fan and some bits of paper, performed the graceful trick of the butterflies and the flowers; another traced in the air, with the odorous smoke of his pipe, a series of blue words, which composed a compliment to the audience; while a third juggled with some lighted candles, which he extinguished successively as they passed his lips, and relit again without interrupting for an instant his juggling. Another reproduced the most singular combinations with a spinning-top; in his hands the revolving tops seemed to be animated with a life of their own in their interminable whirling; they ran over pipe-stems, the edges of sabres, wires, and even hairs stretched across the stage; they turned around on the edges of large glasses, crossed bamboo ladders, dispersed into all the corners, and produced strange musical effects by the combination of their various pitches of tone. The jugglers tossed them in the air, threw them like shuttlecocks with wooden battledores, and yet they kept on spinning; they put them into their pockets, and took them out still whirling as before.

It is useless to describe the astonishing performances of the acrobats and gymnasts. The turning on ladders, poles, balls, barrels, &c., was executed with wonderful precision.

But the principal attraction was the exhibition of the Long Noses, a show to which Europe is as yet a stranger.

The Long Noses form a peculiar company, under the direct patronage of the god Tingou. Attired after the fashion of the Middle Ages, they bore upon their shoulders a splendid pair of wings; but what especially distinguished them was the long noses which were fastened to their faces, and the uses which they made of them. These noses were made of bamboo, and were five, six, and even ten feet long, some straight, others curved, some ribboned, and some having imitation warts upon them. It was upon these appendages, fixed tightly on their real noses, that they performed their gymnastic exercises. A dozen of these sectaries of Tingou lay flat upon their backs, while others, dressed to represent lightning-rods, came and frolicked on their noses, jumping from one to another, and performing the most skilful leapings and somersaults.

As a last scene, a "human pyramid" had been announced, in which fifty Long Noses were to represent the Car of Juggernaut. But, instead of forming a pyramid by mounting each other's shoulders, the artists were to group themselves on top of the noses. It happened that the performer who had hitherto formed the base of the Car had quitted the troupe, and as, to fill this part, only strength and adroitness were necessary, Passepartout had been chosen to take his place.

The poor fellow really felt sad when—melancholy reminiscence of his youth!—he donned his costume, adorned with vari-coloured wings, and fastened to his natural feature a false nose six feet long. But he cheered up when he thought that this nose was winning him something to eat.

He went upon the stage, and took his place beside the rest who were to compose the base of the Car of Juggernaut. They all stretched themselves on the floor, their noses pointing to the ceiling. A second group of artists disposed themselves on these long appendages, then a third above these, then a fourth, until a human monument reaching to the very cornices of the theatre soon arose on top of the noses. This elicited loud applause, in the midst of which the orchestra was just striking up a deafening air, when the pyramid tottered, the balance was lost, one of the lower noses vanished from the pyramid, and the human monument was shattered like a castle built of cards!

It was Passepartout's fault. Abandoning his position, clearing the footlights without the aid of his wings, and clambering up to the right-hand gallery, he fell at the feet of one of the spectators, crying, "Ah, my master! my master!"

"You here?"

"Myself."

"Very well; then let us go to the steamer, young man!"

Mr. Fogg, Aouda, and Passepartout passed through the lobby of the theatre to the outside, where they encountered the Honourable Mr. Batulcar, furious with rage. He demanded damages for the "breakage" of the pyramid; and Phileas Fogg appeased him by giving him a handful of bank-notes.

At half-past six, the very hour of departure, Mr. Fogg and Aouda, followed by Passepartout, who in his hurry had retained his wings, and nose six feet long, stepped upon the American steamer.

CHAPTER 24

DURING WHICH MR. FOGG AND PARTY CROSS THE PACIFIC OCEAN

WHAT happened when the pilot-boat came in sight of Shanghai will be easily guessed. The signals made by the "Tankadere" had been seen by the captain of the Yokohama steamer, who, espying the flag at half-mast, had directed his course towards the little craft. Phileas Fogg, after paying the stipulated price of his passage to John Bunsby, and rewarding that worthy with the additional sum of five hundred and fifty pounds, ascended the steamer with Aouda and Fix; and they started at once for Nagasaki and Yokohama.

They reached their destination on the morning of the 14th of November. Phileas Fogg lost no time in going on board the "Carnatic," where he learned, to Aouda's great delight—and perhaps to his own, though he betrayed no emotion—that Passepartout, a Frenchman, had really arrived on her the day before.

The San Francisco steamer was announced to leave that very evening, and it became necessary to find Passepartout, if possible, without delay. Mr. Fogg applied in vain to the French and English consuls, and, after wandering through the streets a long time, began to despair of finding his missing servant. Chance, or perhaps a kind of presentiment, at last led him into the Honourable Mr.

Followed by Passepartout with the wings on his back.

Batulcar's theatre. He certainly would not have recognized Passepartout in the eccentric mountebank's costume; but the latter, lying on his back, perceived his master in the gallery. He could not help starting, which so changed the position of his nose as to bring the "pyramid" pell-mell upon the stage.

All this Passepartout learned from Aouda, who recounted to him what had taken place on the voyage from Hong Kong to Shanghai on the "Tankadere," in company with one Mr. Fix.

Passepartout did not change countenance on hearing this name. He thought that the time had not yet arrived to divulge to his master what had taken place between the detective and himself; and in the account he gave of his absence, he simply excused himself for having been overtaken by drunkenness, in smoking opium at a tavern in Hong Kong.

Mr. Fogg heard this narrative coldly, without a word; and then furnished his man with funds necessary to obtain clothing more in harmony with his position. Within an hour the Frenchman had cut off his nose and parted with his wings, and retained nothing about him which recalled the sectary of the god Tingou.

The steamer which was about to depart from Yokohama to San Francisco belonged to the Pacific Mail Steamship Company, and was named the "General Grant." She was a large paddle-wheel steamer of two thousand five hundred tons, well equipped and very fast. The massive walking-beam rose and fell above the deck; at one end a piston-rod worked up and down; and at the other was a connecting-rod which, in changing the rectilinear motion to a circular one, was directly connected with the shaft of the paddles. The "General Grant" was rigged with three masts, giving a large capacity for sails, and thus materially aiding the steam power. By making twelve miles an hour, she would cross the ocean in twenty-one days. Phileas Fogg was therefore justified in hoping that he would reach San Francisco by the 2nd of December, New York by the 11th, and London on the 20th,—thus gaining several hours on the fatal date of the 21st of December.

There was a full complement of passengers on board, among them English, many Americans, a large number of Coolies on their way to California, and several East Indian officers, who were spending their vacation in making the tour of the world. Nothing of moment happened on the voyage; the steamer, sustained on its large paddles, rolled but little, and the "Pacific" almost justified its name. Mr. Fogg was as calm and taciturn as ever. His young companion felt herself more and more attached to him by other ties than gratitude; his silent but generous nature impressed her more than she thought; and it was almost unconsciously that she yielded to emotions which did not seem to have the least effect upon her protector. Aouda took the keenest interest in his plans, and became impatient at any incident which seemed likely to retard his journey.

She often chatted with Passepartout, who did not fail to perceive the state of the lady's heart; and, being the most faithful of domestics, he never exhausted his eulogies of Phileas Fogg's honesty, generosity, and devotion. He took pains to calm Aouda's doubts of a successful termination of the journey, telling her that the most difficult part of it had passed, that now they were beyond the fantastic countries of Japan and China, and were fairly on their way to civilized places again. A railway train from San Francisco to New York, and a transatlantic steamer from New York to Liverpool, would doubtless bring them to the end of this impossible journey round the world within the period agreed upon.

On the ninth day after leaving Yokohama, Phileas Fogg had traversed exactly one half of the terrestrial globe. The "General Grant" passed, on the 23rd of November, the one hundred and eightieth meridian, and was at the very antipodes of London. Mr. Fogg had, it is true, exhausted fifty-two of the eighty days in which he was to complete the tour, and there were only twenty-eight left. But, though he was only half-way by the difference of meridians, he had really gone over two-thirds of the whole journey; for he had been obliged to make long circuits from London to Aden, from Aden to Bombay, from Calcutta to Singapore, and from Singapore to Yokohama. Could he have followed without deviation the fiftieth parallel, which is that of London, the whole distance would only have been about twelve thousand miles; whereas he would be forced, by the irregular methods of locomotion, to traverse twenty-six thousand, of which he had, on the 23rd of November, accomplished seventeen thousand five hundred. And now the course was a straight one, and Fix was no longer there to put obstacles in their way!

It happened also, on the 23rd of November, that Passepartout made a joyful discovery. It will be remembered that the obstinate fellow had insisted on keeping his famous family watch at London time, and on regarding that of the countries he had passed through as quite false and unreliable. Now, on this day, though he had not changed the hands, he found that his watch exactly agreed with the ship's chronometers. His triumph was hilarious. He would have liked to know what Fix would say if he were aboard!

"The rogue told me a lot of stories," repeated Passepartout, "about the meridians, the sun, and the moon! Moon, indeed! moonshine more likely! If one listened to that sort of people, a pretty sort of time one would keep! I was sure that the sun would some day regulate itself by my watch!"

Passepartout was ignorant that, if the face of his watch had been divided into twenty-four hours, like the Italian clocks, he would have no reason for exultation; for the hands of his watch would then, instead of as now indicating nine o'clock in the morning, indicate nine o'clock in the evening, that is the twenty-first hour after midnight,—precisely the difference between London time and that of the one hundred and eightieth meridian. But if Fix had been able to explain this purely physical effect, Passepartout would not have admitted, even if he had comprehended it. Moreover, if the detective had been on board at that moment, Passepartout would have joined issue with him on a quite different subject, and in an entirely different manner.

Where was Fix at that moment?

He was actually on board the "General Grant."

On reaching Yokohama, the detective, leaving Mr. Fogg, whom he expected to meet again during the day, had repaired at once to the English consulate, where he at last found the warrant of arrest. It had followed him from Bombay, and had come by the "Carnatic," on which steamer he himself was supposed to be. Fix's disappointment may be imagined when he reflected that the warrant was now useless. Mr. Fogg had left English ground, and it was now necessary to procure his extradition!

"Well," thought Fix, after a moment of anger, "my warrant is not good here, but it will be in England. The rogue evidently intends to return to his own country, thinking he has thrown the police off his track. Good! I will follow him across the Atlantic. As for the money, Heaven grant there may be some left! But the fellow has already spent in travelling, rewards, trials, bail, elephants, and all sorts of changes, more than five thousand pounds. Yet, after all, the Bank is rich!"

His course decided on, he went on board the "General Grant," and was there when Mr. Fogg and Aouda arrived. To his utter amazement, he recognized Passepartout, despite his theatrical disguise. He quickly concealed himself in his cabin, to avoid an awkward explanation, and hoped—thanks to the number of passengers—to remain unperceived by Mr. Fogg's servant.

On that very day, however, he met Passepartout face to face on the forward deck. The latter, without a word, made a rush for him, grasped him by the throat, and, much to the amusement of a group of Americans, who immediately began to bet on him, administered to the detective a perfect volley of blows, which proved the great superiority of French over English pugilistic skill.

When Passepartout had finished, he found himself relieved and comforted. Fix got up in a somewhat rumpled condition, and, looking at his adversary, coldly said, "Have you done?"

"For this time—yes."

"Then let me have a word with you."

"But I—"

"In your master's interest."

Passepartout seemed to be vanquished by Fix's coolness, for he quietly followed him, and they sat down aside from the rest of the passengers.

"You have given me a thrashing," said Fix. "Good! I expected it. Now, listen to me. Up to this time I have been Mr. Fogg's adversary. I am now in his game."

"Aha!" cried Passepartout; "you are convinced he is an honest man?"

"No," replied Fix coldly, "I think him a rascal. Sh! don't budge, and let me speak. As long as Mr. Fogg was on English ground, it was for my interest to detain him there until my warrant of arrest arrived. I did everything I could to keep him back. I sent the Bombay priests after him, I got you intoxicated at Hong Kong, I separated you from him, and I made him miss the Yokohama steamer."

Passepartout listened, with closed fists.

"Now," resumed Fix, "Mr. Fogg seems to be going back to England. Well, I will follow him there. But hereafter I will do as much to keep obstacles out of his way as I have done up to this time to put them in his path. I've changed my game, you see, and simply because it was for my interest to change it. Your interest is the same as mine; for it is only in England that you will ascertain whether you are in the service of a criminal or an honest man."

Passepartout listened very attentively to Fix, and was convinced that he spoke with entire good faith.

"Are we friends?" asked the detective.

"Friends?—no," replied Passepartout; "but allies, perhaps. At the least sign of treason, however, I'll twist your neck for you."

"Agreed," said the detective quietly.

Eleven days later, on the 3rd of December, the "General Grant" entered the bay of the Golden Gate, and reached San Francisco.

Mr. Fogg had neither gained nor lost a single day.

CHAPTER 25

IN WHICH A SLIGHT GLIMPSE IS HAD OF SAN FRANCISCO

It was seven in the morning when Mr. Fogg, Aouda, and Passepartout set foot upon the American continent, if this name can be given to the floating quay upon which they disembarked. These quays, rising and falling with the tide, thus facilitate the loading and unloading of vessels. Alongside them were clippers of all sizes, steamers of all nationalities, and the steamboats, with several decks rising one above the other, which ply on the Sacramento and its tributaries. There were also heaped up the products of a commerce which extends to Mexico, Chili, Peru, Brazil, Europe, Asia, and all the Pacific islands.

Passepartout, in his joy on reaching at last the American continent, thought he would manifest it by executing a perilous vault in fine style; but, tumbling upon some worm-eaten planks, he fell through them. Put out of countenance by the manner in which he thus "set foot" upon the New World, he uttered a loud cry, which so frightened the innumerable cormorants and pelicans that are always perched upon these movable quays, that they flew noisily away.

Mr. Fogg, on reaching shore, proceeded to find out at what hour the first train left for New York, and learned that this was at six o'clock p.m.; he had, therefore, an entire day to spend in the Californian capital. Taking a carriage at a charge of three dollars, he and Aouda entered it, while Passepartout mounted the box beside the driver, and they set out for the International Hotel.

From his exalted position Passepartout observed with much curiosity the wide streets, the low, evenly ranged houses, the Anglo-Saxon Gothic churches, the great docks, the palatial wooden and brick warehouses, the numerous conveyances, omnibuses, horse-cars, and upon the sidewalks, not only Americans and Europeans, but Chinese and Indians. Passepartout was surprised at all he saw. San Francisco was no longer the legendary city of 1849,—a city of banditti, assassins, and incendiaries, who had flocked hither in crowds in pursuit of plunder; a paradise of outlaws, where they gambled with gold-dust, a revolver in one hand and a bowie-knife in the other: it was now a great commercial emporium.

The lofty tower of its City Hall overlooked the whole panorama of the streets and avenues, which cut each other at right angles, and in the midst of which appeared pleasant, verdant squares, while beyond appeared the Chinese quarter, seemingly imported from the Celestial Empire in a toy-box. Sombreros and red shirts and plumed Indians were rarely to be seen; but there were silk hats and black coats everywhere worn by a multitude of nervously active, gentlemanly-looking men. Some of the streets—especially Montgomery Street, which is to San Francisco what Regent Street is to London, the Boulevard des Italiens to Paris, and Broadway to New York—were lined with splendid and spacious stores, which exposed in their windows the products of the entire world.

When Passepartout reached the International Hotel, it did not seem to him as if he had left England at all.

The ground floor of the hotel was occupied by a large bar, a sort of restaurant freely open to all passers-by, who might partake of dried beef, oyster soup, biscuits, and cheese, without taking out their purses. Payment was made only for the ale, porter, or sherry which was drunk. This seemed "very American" to Passepartout. The hotel refreshment-rooms were comfortable, and Mr. Fogg and Aouda, installing themselves at a table, were abundantly served on diminutive plates by negroes of darkest hue.

After breakfast, Mr. Fogg, accompanied by Aouda, started for the English consulate to have his passport *visaed*. As he was going out, he met Passepartout, who asked him if it would not be well, before taking the train, to purchase some dozens of Enfield rifles and Colt's revolvers. He had been listening to stories of attacks upon the trains by the Sioux and Pawnees. Mr. Fogg thought it a useless precaution, but told him to do as he thought best, and went on to the consulate.

He had not proceeded two hundred steps, however, when, "by the greatest chance in the world," he met Fix. The detective seemed wholly taken by surprise. What! Had Mr. Fogg and himself crossed the Pacific together, and not met on the steamer! At least Fix felt honoured to behold once more the gentleman to whom he owed so much, and as his business recalled him to Europe, he should be delighted to continue the journey in such pleasant company.

Mr. Fogg replied that the honour would be his; and the detective—who was determined not to lose sight of him—begged permission to accompany them in their walk about San Francisco—a request which Mr. Fogg readily granted.

They soon found themselves in Montgomery Street, where a great crowd was collected; the side-walks, street, horse-car rails, the shop-doors, the windows of the houses, and even the roofs, were full of people. Men were going about carrying large posters, and flags and streamers were floating in the wind; while loud cries were heard on every hand.

"Hurrah for Camerfield!"

"Hurray for Mandiboy!"

It was a political meeting; at least so Fix conjectured, who said to Mr. Fogg, "Perhaps we had better not mingle with the crowd. There may be danger in it."

"Yes," returned Mr. Fogg; "and blows, even if they are political, are still blows."

Fix smiled at this remark; and in order to be able to see without being jostled about, the party took up a position on the top of a flight of steps situated at the upper end of Montgomery Street. Opposite them, on the other side of the street, between a coal wharf and a petroleum warehouse, a large platform had been erected in the open air, towards which the current of the crowd seemed to be directed.

For what purpose was this meeting? What was the occasion of this excited assemblage? Phileas Fogg could not imagine. Was it to nominate some high official—a governor or member of Congress? It was not improbable, so agitated was the multitude before them.

Just at this moment there was an unusual stir in the human mass. All the hands were raised in the air. Some, tightly closed, seemed to disappear suddenly in the midst of the cries—an energetic way, no doubt, of casting a vote. The crowd swayed back, the banners and flags wavered, disappeared an instant, then reappeared in tatters. The undulations of the human serge reached the steps, while all the heads floundered on the surface like a sea agitated by the squall. Many of the black hats disappeared, and the greater part of the crowd seemed to have diminished in height.

"It is evidently a meeting," said Fix, "and its object must be an exciting one. I should not wonder if it were about the 'Alabama," despite the fact that that question is settled."

"Perhaps," replied Mr. Fogg simply.

"At least, there are two champions in presence of each other, the Honourable Mr. Camerfield and the Honourable Mr. Mandiboy."

Aouda, leaning upon Mr. Fogg's arm, observed the tumultuous scene with surprise, while Fix asked a man near him what the cause of it all was. Before the man could reply, a fresh agitation arose; hurrahs and excited shouts were heard; the staffs of the banners began to be used as offensive weapons; and fists flew about in every direction. Thumps were exchanged from the tops of the carriages and omnibuses which had been blocked up in the crowd. Boots and shoes went whirling through the air, and Mr. Fogg thought he even heard the crack of revolvers mingling in the din. The rout approached the stairway, and flowed over the lower step. One of the parties had evidently been repulsed; but the mere lookers-on could not tell whether Mandiboy or Camerfield had gained the upper hand.

"It would be prudent for us to retire," said Fix, who was anxious that Mr. Fogg should not receive any injury, at least until they got back to London. "If there is any question about England in all this, and we were recognized, I fear it would go hard with us."

"An English subject—" began Mr. Fogg.

He did not finish his sentence; for a terrific hubbub now arose on the terrace behind the flight of steps where they stood, and there were frantic shouts of, "Hurrah for Mandiboy! Hip, hip, hurrah!"

It was a band of voters coming to the rescue of their allies, and taking the Camerfield forces in flank. Mr. Fogg, Aouda, and Fix found themselves between two fires; it was too late to escape. The torrent of men, armed with loaded canes and sticks, was irresistible. Phileas Fogg and Fix were roughly hustled in their attempts to protect their fair companion; the former, as cool as ever, tried to defend himself with the weapons which nature has placed at the end of every Englishman's arm, but in vain. A big brawny fellow with a red beard, flushed face, and broad shoulders, who seemed to be the chief of the band, raised his clenched fist to strike Mr. Fogg, whom he would have given a crushing blow, had not Fix rushed in and received it in his stead. An enormous bruise immediately made its appearance under the detective's silk hat, which was completely smashed in.

"Yankee!" exclaimed Mr. Fogg, darting a contemptuous look at the ruffian.

"Englishman!" returned the other. "We will meet again!"

"When you please."

"What is your name?"

"Phileas Fogg. And yours?"

"Colonel Stamp Proctor."

The human tide now swept by, after overturning Fix, who speedily got upon his feet again, though with tattered clothes. Happily, he was not seriously hurt. His travelling overcoat was divided into two unequal parts, and his trousers resembled those of certain Indians, which fit less compactly than they are easy to put on. Aouda had escaped unharmed, and Fix alone bore marks of the fray in his black and blue bruise.

"Thanks," said Mr. Fogg to the detective, as soon as they were out of the crowd.

"No thanks are necessary," replied Fix; "but let us go."

"Where?"

"To a tailor's."

Such a visit was, indeed, opportune. The clothing of both Mr. Fogg and Fix was in rags, as if they had themselves been actively engaged in the contest between Camerfield and Mandiboy. An hour after, they were once more suitably attired, and with Aouda returned to the International Hotel.

Passepartout was waiting for his master, armed with half a dozen six-barrelled revolvers. When he perceived Fix, he knit his brows; but Aouda having, in a few words, told him of their adventure, his countenance resumed its placid expression. Fix evidently was no longer an enemy, but an ally; he was faithfully keeping his word.

Dinner over, the coach which was to convey the passengers and their luggage to the station drew up to the door. As he was getting in, Mr. Fogg said to Fix, "You have not seen this Colonel Proctor again?"

"No."

"I will come back to America to find him," said Phileas Fogg calmly. "It would not be right for an Englishman to permit himself to be treated in that way, without retaliating."

The detective smiled, but did not reply. It was clear that Mr. Fogg was one of those Englishmen who, while they do not tolerate duelling at home, fight abroad when their honour is attacked.

At a quarter before six the travellers reached the station, and found the train ready to depart. As he was about to enter it, Mr. Fogg called a porter, and said to him, "My friend, was there not some trouble to-day in San Francisco?"

"It was a political meeting, sir," replied the porter.

"But I thought there was a great deal of disturbance in the streets."

"It was only a meeting assembled for an election."

"The election of a general-in-chief, no doubt?" asked Mr. Fogg.

"No, sir; of a justice of the peace."

Phileas Fogg got into the train, which started off at full speed.

CHAPTER 26

IN WHICH PHILEAS FOGG AND PARTY TRAVEL BY THE PACIFIC RAILROAD

"FROM ocean to ocean,"—so say the Americans; and these four words compose the general designation of the "great trunk line" which crosses the entire width of the United States. The Pacific Railroad is, however, really divided into two distinct lines: the Central Pacific, between San Francisco and Ogden, and the Union Pacific, between Ogden and Omaha. Five main lines connect Omaha with New York.

New York and San Francisco are thus united by an uninterrupted metal ribbon, which measures no less than three thousand seven hundred and eighty-six miles. Between Omaha and the Pacific the railway crosses a territory which is still infested by Indians and wild beasts, and a large tract which the Mormons, after they were driven from Illinois in 1845, began to colonize.

The journey from New York to San Francisco consumed, formerly, under the most favourable conditions, at least six months. It is now accomplished in seven days.

It was in 1862 that, in spite of the Southern Members of Congress, who wished a more southerly route, it was decided to lay the road between the forty-first and forty-second parallels. President Lincoln himself fixed the end of the line at Omaha, in Nebraska. The work was at once commenced, and pursued with true American energy; nor did the rapidity with which it went on injuriously affect its good execution. The road grew, on the prairies, a mile and a half a day. A locomotive, running on the rails laid down the evening before, brought the rails to be laid on the morrow, and advanced upon them as fast as they were put in position.

The Pacific Railroad is joined by several branches in Iowa, Kansas, Colorado, and Oregon. On leaving Omaha, it passes along the left bank of the Platte River as far as the junction of its northern branch, follows its southern branch, crosses the Laramie territory and the Wahsatch Mountains, turns the Great Salt Lake, and reaches Salt Lake City, the Mormon capital, plunges into the Tuilla Valley, across the American Desert, Cedar and Humboldt Mountains, the Sierra Nevada, and descends, *viâ* Sacramento, to the Pacific,—its grade, even on the Rocky Mountains, never exceeding one hundred and twelve feet to the mile.

Such was the road to be traversed in seven days, which would enable Phileas Fogg—at least, so he hoped—to take the Atlantic steamer at New York on the 11th for Liverpool.

The car which he occupied was a sort of long omnibus on eight wheels, and with no compartments in the interior. It was supplied with two rows of seats, perpendicular to the direction of the train on either side of an aisle which conducted to the front and rear platforms. These platforms were found throughout the train, and the passengers were able to pass from one end of the train to the other. It was supplied with saloon cars, balcony cars, restaurants, and smoking cars; theatre cars alone were wanting, and they will have these some day.

Book and news dealers, sellers of edibles, drinkables, and cigars, who seemed to have plenty of customers, were continually circulating in the aisles.

The train left Oakland station at six o'clock. It was already night, cold and cheerless, the heavens being overcast with clouds which seemed to threaten snow. The train did not proceed rapidly; counting the stoppages, it did not run more than twenty miles an hour, which was a sufficient speed, however, to enable it to reach Omaha within its designated time.

There was but little conversation in the car, and soon many of the passengers were overcome with sleep. Passepartout found himself beside the detective; but he did not talk to him. After recent events, their relations with each other had grown somewhat cold; there could no longer be mutual sympathy or intimacy between them. Fix's manner had not changed; but Passepartout was very reserved, and ready to strangle his former friend on the slightest provocation.

Snow began to fall an hour after they started, a fine snow, however, which happily could not obstruct the train; nothing could be seen from the windows but a vast, white sheet, against which the smoke of the locomotive had a grayish aspect.

At eight o'clock a steward entered the car and announced that the time for going to bed had arrived; and in a few minutes the car was transformed into a dormitory. The backs of the seats were thrown back, bedsteads carefully packed were rolled out by an ingenious system, berths were suddenly improvised, and each traveller had soon at his disposition a comfortable bed, protected from curious eyes by thick curtains. The sheets were clean and the pillows soft. It only remained to go to bed and sleep—which everybody did—while the train sped on across the State of California.

The country between San Francisco and Sacramento is not very hilly. The Central Pacific, taking Sacramento for its starting-point, extends eastward to meet the road from Omaha. The line from San Francisco to Sacramento runs in a north-easterly direction, along the American River, which empties into San Pablo Bay. The one hundred and twenty miles between these cities were accomplished in six hours, and towards midnight, while fast asleep, the travellers passed through Sacramento; so that they saw nothing of that important place, the seat of the State government, with its fine quays, its broad streets, its noble hotels, squares, and churches.

The train, on leaving Sacramento, and passing the junction, Roclin, Auburn, and Colfax, entered the range of the Sierra Nevada. Cisco was reached at seven in the morning; and an hour later the dormitory was transformed into an ordinary car, and the travellers could observe the picturesque beauties of the mountain region through which they were steaming. The railway track wound in and out among the passes, now approaching the mountain sides, now suspended over precipices, avoiding abrupt angles by bold curves, plunging into narrow defiles, which seemed to have no outlet. The locomotive, its great funnel emitting a weird light, with its sharp bell, and its cow-catcher extended like a spur, mingled its shrieks and bellowings with the noise of torrents and cascades, and twined its smoke among the branches of the gigantic pines.

There were few or no bridges or tunnels on the route. The railway turned around the sides of the mountains, and did not attempt to violate nature by taking the shortest cut from one point to another.

The train entered the State of Nevada through the Carson valley about nine o'clock, going always north-easterly; and at midday reached Reno, where there was a delay of twenty minutes to breakfast.

From this point the road, running along Humboldt River, passed northward for several miles by its banks; then it turned eastward, and kept by the river until it reached the Humboldt Range, nearly at the extreme eastern limit of Nevada.

Having breakfasted, Mr. Fogg and his companions resumed their places in the car, and observed the varied landscape which unfolded itself as they passed along; the vast prairies, the mountains lining the horizon, and the creeks with their frothy, foaming streams. Sometimes a great herd of buffaloes, massing together in the distance, seemed like a movable dam. These innumerable multitudes of ruminating beasts often form an insurmountable obstacle to the passage of the trains; thousands of them have been seen passing over the track for hours together, in compact ranks. The locomotive is then forced to stop and wait till the road is once more clear.

This happened, indeed, to the train in which Mr. Fogg was travelling. About twelve o'clock, a troop of ten or twelve thousand head of buffalo encumbered the track. The locomotive, slackening its speed, tried to clear the way with its cow-catcher; but the mass of animals was too great. The buffaloes marched along with a tranquil gait, uttering now and then deafening bellowings. There was no use of interrupting them, for, having taken a particular direction, nothing can moderate and change their course; it is a torrent of living flesh which no dam could contain.

The travellers gazed on this curious spectacle from the platforms; but Phileas Fogg, who had the most reason of all to be in a hurry, remained in his seat, and waited philosophically until it should please the buffaloes to get out of the way.

Passepartout was furious at the delay they occasioned, and longed to discharge his arsenal of revolvers upon them.

"What a country!" cried he. "Mere cattle stop the trains, and go by in a procession, just as if they were not impeding travel! Parbleu! I should like to know if Mr. Fogg foresaw *this* mishap in his programme! And here's an engineer who doesn't dare to run the locomotive into this herd of beasts!"

The engineer did not try to overcome the obstacle, and he was wise. He would have crushed the first buffaloes, no doubt, with the cow-catcher; but the locomotive, however powerful, would soon have been checked, the train would inevitably have been thrown off the track, and would then have been helpless.

The best course was to wait patiently, and regain the lost time by greater speed when the obstacle was removed. The procession of buffaloes lasted three full hours, and it was night before the track was clear. The last ranks of the herd were now passing over the rails, while the first had already disappeared below the southern horizon.

It was eight o'clock when the train passed through the defiles of the Humboldt Range, and half-past nine when it penetrated Utah, the region of the Great Salt Lake, the singular colony of the Mormons.

CHAPTER 27

IN WHICH PASSEPARTOUT UNDERGOES, AT A SPEED OF TWENTY MILES AN HOUR, A COURSE OF MORMON HISTORY

DURING the night of the 5th of December, the train ran south-easterly for about fifty miles; then rose an equal distance in a north-easterly direction, towards the Great Salt Lake.

Passepartout, about nine o'clock, went out upon the platform to take the air. The weather was cold, the heavens gray, but it was not snowing. The sun's disc, enlarged by the mist, seemed an enormous ring of gold, and Passepartout was amusing himself by calculating its value in pounds sterling, when he was diverted from this interesting study by a strange-looking personage who made his appearance on the platform.

This personage, who had taken the train at Elko, was tall and dark, with black moustaches, black stockings, a black silk hat, a black waistcoat, black trousers, a white cravat, and dogskin gloves. He might have been taken for a clergyman. He went from one end of the train to the other, and affixed to the door of each car a notice written in manuscript.

Passepartout approached and read one of these notices, which stated that Elder William Hitch, Mormon missionary, taking advantage of his presence on train No. 48, would deliver a lecture on Mormonism, in car No. 117, from eleven to twelve o'clock; and that he invited all who were desirous of being instructed concerning the mysteries of the religion of the "Latter Day Saints" to attend.

"I'll go," said Passepartout to himself. He knew nothing of Mormonism except the custom of polygamy, which is its foundation.

The news quickly spread through the train, which contained about one hundred passengers, thirty of whom, at most, attracted by the notice, ensconced themselves in car No. 117. Passepartout took one of the front seats. Neither Mr. Fogg nor Fix cared to attend.

At the appointed hour Elder William Hitch rose, and, in an irritated voice, as if he had already been contradicted, said, "I tell you that Joe Smith is a martyr, that his brother Hiram is a martyr, and that the persecutions of the United States Government against the prophets will also make a martyr of Brigham Young. Who dares to say the contrary?"

No one ventured to gainsay the missionary, whose excited tone contrasted curiously with his naturally calm visage. No doubt his anger arose from the hardships to which the Mormons were actually subjected. The government had just succeeded, with some difficulty, in reducing these independent fanatics to its rule. It had made itself master of Utah, and subjected that territory to the laws of the Union, after imprisoning Brigham Young on a charge of rebellion and polygamy. The disciples of the prophet had since redoubled their efforts, and resisted, by words at least, the authority of Congress. Elder Hitch, as is seen, was trying to make proselytes on the very railway trains.

Then, emphasizing his words with his loud voice and frequent gestures, he related the history of the Mormons from Biblical times: how that, in Israel, a Mormon prophet of the tribe of Joseph published the annals of the new religion, and bequeathed them to his son Morom; how, many centuries later, a translation of this precious book, which was written in Egyptian, was made by Joseph Smith, Junior, a Vermont farmer, who revealed himself as a mystical prophet in 1825; and how, in short, the celestial messenger appeared to him in an illuminated forest, and gave him the annals of the Lord.

Several of the audience, not being much interested in the missionary's narrative, here left the car; but Elder Hitch, continuing his lecture, related how Smith, Junior, with his father, two brothers, and a few disciples, founded the church of the "Latter Day Saints," which, adopted not only in America, but in England, Norway and Sweden, and Germany, counts many artisans, as well as men engaged in the liberal professions, among its members; how a colony was established in Ohio, a temple erected there at a cost of two hundred thousand dollars, and a town built at Kirkland; how Smith became an enterprising banker, and received from a simple mummy showman a papyrus scroll written by Abraham and several famous Egyptians.

The Elder's story became somewhat wearisome, and his audience grew gradually less, until it was reduced to twenty passengers. But this did not disconcert the enthusiast, who proceeded with the story of Joseph Smith's bankruptcy in

1837, and how his ruined creditors gave him a coat of tar and feathers; his reappearance some years afterwards, more honourable and honoured than ever, at Independence, Missouri, the chief of a flourishing colony of three thousand disciples, and his pursuit thence by outraged Gentiles, and retirement into the far West.

Ten hearers only were now left, among them honest Passepartout, who was listening with all his ears. Thus he learned that, after long persecutions, Smith reappeared in Illinois, and in 1839 founded a community at Nauvoo, on the Mississippi, numbering twenty-five thousand souls, of which he became mayor, chief justice, and general-in-chief; that he announced himself, in 1843, as a candidate for the Presidency of the United States; and that finally, being drawn into ambuscade at Carthage, he was thrown into prison, and assassinated by a band of men disguised in masks.

Passepartout was now the only person left in the car, and the Elder, looking him full in the face, reminded him that, two years after the assassination of Joseph Smith, the inspired prophet, Brigham Young, his successor, left Nauvoo for the banks of the Great Salt Lake, where, in the midst of that fertile region, directly on the route of the emigrants who crossed Utah on their way to California, the new colony, thanks to the polygamy practised by the Mormons, had flourished beyond expectation.

"And this," added Elder William Hitch,—"this is why the jealousy of Congress has been aroused against us! Why have the soldiers of the Union invaded the soil of Utah? Why has Brigham Young, our chief, been imprisoned, in contempt of all justice? Shall we yield to force? Never! Driven from Vermont, driven from Illinois, driven from Ohio, driven from Missouri, driven from Utah, we shall yet find some independent territory on which to plant our tents. And you, my brother," continued the Elder, fixing his angry eye upon his single auditor, "will you not plant yours there, too, under the shadow of our flag?"

"No!" replied Passepartout courageously, in his turn retiring from the car, and leaving the Elder to preach to vacancy.

During the lecture the train had been making good progress, and towards half-past twelve it reached the north-west border of the Great Salt Lake. Thence the passengers could observe the vast extent of this interior sea, which is also called the Dead Sea, and into which flows an American Jordan. It is a picturesque expanse, framed in lofty crags in large strata, encrusted with white salt,—a superb sheet of water, which was formerly of larger extent than now, its shores having encroached with the lapse of time, and thus at once reduced its breadth and increased its depth.

The Salt Lake, seventy miles long and thirty-five wide, is situated three miles eight hundred feet above the sea. Quite different from Lake Asphaltite, whose depression is twelve hundred feet below the sea, it contains considerable salt, and one quarter of the weight of its water is solid matter, its specific weight being 1170, and, after being distilled, 1000. Fishes are of course unable to live in it, and those which descend through the Jordan, the Weber, and other streams, soon perish.

The country around the lake was well cultivated, for the Mormons are mostly farmers; while ranches and pens for domesticated animals, fields of wheat, corn, and other cereals, luxuriant prairies, hedges of wild rose, clumps of acacias and milk-wort, would have been seen six months later. Now the ground was covered with a thin powdering of snow.

The train reached Ogden at two o'clock, where it rested for six hours. Mr. Fogg and his party had time to pay a visit to Salt Lake City, connected with Ogden by a branch road; and they spent two hours in this strikingly American town, built on the pattern of other cities of the Union, like a checker-board, "with the sombre sadness of right angles," as Victor Hugo expresses it. The founder of the City of the Saints could not escape from the taste for symmetry which distinguishes the Anglo-Saxons. In this strange country, where the people are certainly not up to the level of their institutions, everything is done "squarely,"—cities, houses, and follies.

The travellers, then, were promenading, at three o'clock, about the streets of the town built between the banks of the Jordan and the spurs of the Wahsatch Range. They saw few or no churches, but the prophet's mansion, the court-house, and the arsenal, blue-brick houses with verandahs and porches, surrounded by gardens bordered with acacias, palms, and locusts. A clay and pebble wall, built in 1853, surrounded the town; and in the principal street were the market and several hotels adorned with pavilions. The place did not seem thickly populated. The streets were almost deserted, except in the vicinity of the Temple, which they only reached after having traversed several quarters surrounded by palisades. There were many women, which was easily accounted for by the "peculiar institution" of the Mormons; but it must not be supposed that all the Mormons are polygamists. They are free to marry or not, as they please; but it is worth noting that it is mainly the female citizens of Utah who are anxious to marry, as, according to the Mormon religion, maiden ladies are not admitted to the possession of its highest joys. These poor creatures seemed to be neither well off nor happy. Some—the more well-to-do, no doubt—wore short, open black silk dresses, under a hood or modest shawl; others were habited in Indian fashion.

Passepartout could not behold without a certain fright these women, charged, in groups, with conferring happiness on a single Mormon. His common sense pitied, above all, the husband. It seemed to him a terrible thing to have to guide so many wives at once across the vicissitudes of life, and to conduct them, as it were, in a body to the Mormon paradise, with the prospect of seeing them in the company of the glorious Smith, who doubtless was the chief ornament of that delightful place, to all eternity. He felt decidedly repelled from such a vocation, and he imagined—perhaps he was mistaken—that the fair ones of Salt Lake City cast rather alarming glances on his person. Happily, his stay there was but brief. At four the party found themselves again at the station, took their places in the train, and the whistle sounded for starting. Just at the moment, however, that the locomotive wheels began to move, cries of "Stop! stop!" were heard.

Trains, like time and tide, stop for no one. The gentleman who uttered the cries was evidently a belated Mormon. He was breathless with running. Happily for him, the station had neither gates nor barriers. He rushed along the track, jumped on the rear platform of the train, and fell exhausted into one of the seats.

Passepartout, who had been anxiously watching this amateur gymnast, approached him with a lively interest, and learned that he had taken flight after an unpleasant domestic scene.

When the Mormon had recovered his breath, Passepartout ventured to ask him politely how many wives he had; for, from the manner in which he had decamped, it might be thought that he had twenty at least.

"And you, my faithful friend."

"One, sir," replied the Mormon, raising his arms heavenward,—"one, and that was enough!"

CHAPTER 28

IN WHICH PASSEPARTOUT DOES NOT SUCCEED IN MAKING ANYBODY LISTEN TO REASON

THE train, on leaving Great Salt Lake at Ogden, passed northward for an hour as far as Weber River, having completed nearly nine hundred miles from San Francisco. From this point it took an easterly direction towards the jagged Wahsatch Mountains. It was in the section included between this range and the Rocky Mountains that the American engineers found the most formidable difficulties in laying the road, and that the government granted a subsidy of forty-eight thousand dollars per mile, instead of sixteen thousand allowed for the work done on the plains. But the engineers, instead of violating nature, avoided its difficulties by winding around, instead of penetrating the rocks. One tunnel only, fourteen thousand feet in length, was pierced in order to arrive at the great basin.

The track up to this time had reached its highest elevation at the Great Salt Lake. From this point it described a long curve, descending towards Bitter Creek Valley, to rise again to the dividing ridge of the waters between the Atlantic and the Pacific. There were many creeks in this mountainous region, and it was necessary to cross Muddy Creek, Green Creek, and others, upon culverts.

Passepartout grew more and more impatient as they went on, while Fix longed to get out of this difficult region, and was more anxious than Phileas Fogg himself to be beyond the danger of delays and accidents, and set foot on English soil.

At ten o'clock at night the train stopped at Fort Bridger station, and twenty minutes later entered Wyoming Territory, following the valley of Bitter Creek throughout. The next day, December 7th, they stopped for a quarter of an hour at Green River station. Snow had fallen abundantly during the night, but, being mixed with rain, it had half melted, and did not interrupt their progress. The bad weather, however, annoyed Passepartout; for the accumulation of snow, by blocking the wheels of the cars, would certainly have been fatal to Mr. Fogg's tour.

"What an idea!" he said to himself. "Why did my master make this journey in winter? Couldn't he have waited for the good season to increase his chances?"

While the worthy Frenchman was absorbed in the state of the sky and the depression of the temperature, Aouda was experiencing fears from a totally different cause.

Several passengers had got off at Green River, and were walking up and down the platforms; and among these Aouda recognized Colonel Stamp Proctor, the same who had so grossly insulted Phileas Fogg at the San Francisco meeting. Not wishing to be recognized, the young woman drew back from the window, feeling much alarm at her discovery. She was attached to the man who, however coldly, gave her daily evidences of the most absolute devotion. She did not comprehend, perhaps, the depth of the sentiment with which her protector inspired her, which she called gratitude, but which, though she was unconscious of it, was really more than that. Her heart sank within her when she recognized the man whom Mr. Fogg desired, sooner or later, to call to account for his conduct. Chance alone, it was clear, had brought Colonel Proctor on this train; but there he was, and it was necessary, at all hazards, that Phileas Fogg should not perceive his adversary.

Aouda seized a moment when Mr. Fogg was asleep, to tell Fix and Passepartout whom she had seen.

"That Proctor on this train!" cried Fix. "Well, reassure yourself, madam; before he settles with Mr. Fogg, he has got to deal with me! It seems to me that I was the more insulted of the two."

"And besides," added Passepartout, "I'll take charge of him, colonel as he is."

"Mr. Fix," resumed Aouda, "Mr. Fogg will allow no one to avenge him. He said that he would come back to America to find this man. Should he perceive Colonel Proctor, we could not prevent a collision which might have terrible results. He must not see him."

"You are right, madam," replied Fix; "a meeting between them might ruin all. Whether he were victorious or beaten, Mr. Fogg would be delayed, and—"

"And," added Passepartout, "that would play the game of the gentlemen of the Reform Club. In four days we shall be in New York. Well, if my master does not leave this car during those four days, we may hope that chance will not bring him face to face with this confounded American. We must, if possible, prevent his stirring out of it."

The conversation dropped. Mr. Fogg had just woke up, and was looking out of the window. Soon after Passepartout, without being heard by his master or Aouda, whispered to the detective, "Would you really fight for him?"

"I would do anything," replied Fix, in a tone which betrayed determined will, "to get him back, living, to Europe!"

Passepartout felt something like a shudder shoot through his frame, but his confidence in his master remained unbroken.

Was there any means of detaining Mr. Fogg in the car, to avoid a meeting between him and the colonel? It ought not to be a difficult task, since that gentleman was naturally sedentary and little curious. The detective, at least, seemed to have found a way; for, after a few moments, he said to Mr. Fogg, "These are long and slow hours, sir, that we are passing on the railway."

"Yes," replied Mr. Fogg; "but they pass."

"You were in the habit of playing whist," resumed Fix, "on the steamers."

"Yes; but it would be difficult to do so here. I have neither cards nor partners."

"Oh, but we can easily buy some cards, for they are sold on all the American trains. And as for partners, if madam plays—"

"Certainly, sir," Aouda quickly replied; "I understand whist. It is part of an English education."

"I myself have some pretensions to playing a good game. Well, here are three of us, and a dummy—"

"As you please, sir," replied Phileas Fogg, heartily glad to resume his favourite pastime,—even on the railway.

Passepartout was despatched in search of the steward, and soon returned with two packs of cards, some pins, counters, and a shelf covered with cloth.

The game commenced. Aouda understood whist sufficiently well, and even received some compliments on her playing from Mr. Fogg. As for the detective, he was simply an adept, and worthy of being matched against his present opponent.

"Now," thought Passepartout, "we've got him. He won't budge."

At eleven in the morning the train had reached the dividing ridge of the waters at Bridger Pass, seven thousand five hundred and twenty-four feet above the level of the sea, one of the highest points attained by the track in crossing the Rocky Mountains. After going about two hundred miles, the travellers at last found themselves on one of those vast plains which extend to the Atlantic, and which nature had made so propitious for laying the iron road.

On the declivity of the Atlantic basin the first streams, branches of the North Platte River, already appeared. The whole northern and eastern horizon was bounded by the immense semicircular curtain which is formed by the southern portion of the Rocky Mountains, the highest being Laramie Peak. Between this and the railway extended vast plains, plentifully irrigated. On the right rose the lower spurs of the mountainous mass which extends southward to the sources of the Arkansas River, one of the great tributaries of the Missouri.

At half past twelve the travellers caught sight for an instant of Fort Halleck, which commands that section; and in a few more hours the Rocky Mountains were crossed. There was reason to hope, then, that no accident would mark the journey through this difficult country. The snow had ceased falling, and the air became crisp and cold. Large birds, frightened by the locomotive, rose and flew off in the distance. No wild beast appeared on the plain. It was a desert in its vast nakedness.

After a comfortable breakfast, served in the car, Mr. Fogg and his partners had just resumed whist, when a violent whistling was heard, and the train stopped. Passepartout put his head out of the door, but saw nothing to cause the delay; no station was in view.

Aouda and Fix feared that Mr. Fogg might take it into his head to get out; but that gentleman contented himself with saying to his servant, "See what is the matter."

Passepartout rushed out of the car. Thirty or forty passengers had already descended, amongst them Colonel Stamp Proctor.

The train had stopped before a red signal which blocked the way. The engineer and conductor were talking excitedly with a signal-man, whom the station-master at Medicine Bow, the next stopping place, had sent on before. The passengers drew around and took part in the discussion, in which Colonel Proctor, with his insolent manner, was conspicuous.

Passepartout, joining the group, heard the signal-man say, "No! you can't pass! The bridge at Medicine Bow is shaky, and would not bear the weight of the train."

This was a suspension-bridge thrown over some rapids, about a mile from the place where they now were. According to the signal-man, it was in a ruinous condition, several of the iron wires being broken; and it was impossible to risk the passage. He did not in any way exaggerate the condition of the bridge. It may be taken for granted that, rash as the Americans usually are, when they are prudent there is good reason for it.

Passepartout, not daring to apprise his master of what he heard, listened with set teeth, immovable as a statue.

"Hmm!" cried Colonel Proctor; "but we are not going to stay here, I imagine, and take root in the snow?"

"Colonel," replied the conductor, "we have telegraphed to Omaha for a train, but it is not likely that it will reach Medicine Bow in less than six hours."

"Six hours!" cried Passepartout.

"Certainly," returned the conductor. "Besides, it will take us as long as that to reach Medicine Bow on foot."

"But it is only a mile from here," said one of the passengers.

"Yes, but it's on the other side of the river."

"And can't we cross that in a boat?" asked the colonel.

"That's impossible. The creek is swelled by the rains. It is a rapid, and we shall have to make circuit of ten miles to the north to find a ford."

The colonel launched a volley of oaths, denouncing the railway company and the conductor; and Passepartout, who was furious, was not disinclined to make common cause with him. Here was an obstacle, indeed, which all his master's bank-notes could not remove.

There was a general disappointment among the passengers, who, without reckoning the delay, saw themselves compelled to trudge fifteen miles over a plain covered with snow. They grumbled and protested, and would certainly have thus attracted Phileas Fogg's attention, if he had not been completely absorbed in his game.

Passepartout found that he could not avoid telling his master what had occurred, and, with hanging head he was turning towards the car, when the engineer—a true Yankee, named Forster—called out, "Gentlemen, perhaps there is a way, after all, to get over."

"On the bridge?" asked a passenger.

"On the bridge."

"With our train?"

"With our train."

Passepartout stopped short, and eagerly listened to the engineer.

"But the bridge is unsafe," urged the conductor.

"No matter," replied Forster; "I think that by putting on the very highest speed we might have a chance of getting over."

"The devil!" muttered Passepartout.

But a number of passengers were at once attracted by the engineer's proposal, and Colonel Proctor was especially delighted, and found the plan a very feasible one. He told stories about engineers leaping their trains over rivers without bridges, by putting on full steam; and many of those present avowed themselves of the engineer's mind.

"We have fifty chances out of a hundred of getting over," said one.

"Eighty! ninety!"

Passepartout was astounded, and, though ready to attempt anything to get over Medicine Creek, thought the experiment proposed a little too American. "Besides," thought he, "there's a still more simple way, and it does not even occur to any of these people! Sir," said he aloud to one of the passengers, "the engineer's plan seems to me a little dangerous, but—"

"Eighty chances!" replied the passenger, turning his back on him.

"I know it," said Passepartout, turning to another passenger, "but a simple idea—"

"Ideas are no use," returned the American, shrugging his shoulders, "as the engineer assures us that we can pass."

"Doubtless," urged Passepartout, "we can pass, but perhaps it would be more prudent—"

"What! Prudent!" cried Colonel Proctor, whom this word seemed to excite prodigiously. "At full speed, don't you see, at full speed!"

"I know—I see," repeated Passepartout; "but it would be, if not more prudent, since that word displeases you, at least more natural—"

"Who! What! What's the matter with this fellow?" cried several.

The poor fellow did not know to whom to address himself.

"Are you afraid?" asked Colonel Proctor.

"I afraid! Very well; I will show these people that a Frenchman can be as American as they!"

"All aboard!" cried the conductor.

"Yes, all aboard!" repeated Passepartout, and immediately. "But they can't prevent me from thinking that it would be more natural for us to cross the bridge on foot, and let the train come after!"

But no one heard this sage reflection, nor would any one have acknowledged its justice. The passengers resumed their places in the cars. Passepartout took his seat without telling what had passed. The whist-players were quite absorbed in their game.

The locomotive whistled vigorously; the engineer, reversing the steam, backed the train for nearly a mile—retiring, like a jumper, in order to take a longer leap. Then, with another whistle, he began to move forward; the train increased its speed, and soon its rapidity became frightful; a prolonged screech issued from the locomotive; the piston worked up and down twenty strokes to the second. They perceived that the whole train, rushing on at the rate of a hundred miles an hour, hardly bore upon the rails at all.

And they passed over! It was like a flash. No one saw the bridge. The train leaped, so to speak, from one bank to the other, and the engineer could not stop it until it had gone five miles beyond the station. But scarcely had the train passed the river, when the bridge, completely ruined, fell with a crash into the rapids of Medicine Bow.

CHAPTER 29

IN WHICH CERTAIN INCIDENTS ARE NARRATED WHICH ARE ONLY TO BE MET WITH ON AMERICAN RAILROADS

THE train pursued its course, that evening, without interruption, passing Fort Saunders, crossing Cheyene Pass, and reaching Evans Pass. The road here attained the highest elevation of the journey, eight thousand and ninety-one feet above the level of the sea. The travellers had now only to descend to the Atlantic by limitless plains, levelled by nature. A branch of the "grand trunk" led off southward to Denver, the capital of Colorado. The country round about is rich in gold and silver, and more than fifty thousand inhabitants are already settled there.

Thirteen hundred and eighty-two miles had been passed over from San Francisco, in three days and three nights; four days and nights more would probably bring them to New York. Phileas Fogg was not as yet behindhand.

During the night Camp Walbach was passed on the left; Lodge Pole Creek ran parallel with the road, marking the boundary between the territories of Wyoming and Colorado. They entered Nebraska at eleven, passed near Sedgwick, and touched at Julesburg, on the southern branch of the Platte River.

It was here that the Union Pacific Railroad was inauguarted on the 23rd of October, 1867, by the chief engineer, General Dodge. Two powerful locomotives, carrying nine cars of invited guests, amongst whom was Thomas C. Durant, vice-president of the road, stopped at this point; cheers were given, the Sioux and Pawnees performed an imitation Indian battle, fireworks were let off, and the first number of the *Railway Pioneer* was printed by a press brought on the train. Thus was celebrated the inauguration of this great railroad, a mighty instrument of progress and civilization, thrown across the desert, and destined to link together cities and towns which do not yet exist. The whistle of the locomotive, more powerful than Amphion's lyre, was about to bid them rise from American soil.

Fort McPherson was left behind at eight in the morning, and three hundred and fifty-seven miles had yet to be traversed before reaching Omaha. The road followed the capricious windings of the southern branch of the Platte River, on its left bank. At nine the train stopped at the important town of North Platte, built between the two arms of the river, which rejoin each other around it and form a single artery,—a large tributary whose waters empty into the Missouri a little above Omaha.

The one hundred and first meridian was passed.

Mr. Fogg and his partners had resumed their game; no one—not even the dummy—complained of the length of the trip. Fix had begun by winning several guineas, which he seemed likely to lose; but he showed himself a not less eager whist-player than Mr. Fogg. During the morning, chance distinctly favoured that gentleman. Trumps and honours were showered upon his hands.

Once, having resolved on a bold stroke, he was on the point of playing a spade, when a voice behind him said, "I should play a diamond."

Mr. Fogg, Aouda, and Fix raised their heads, and beheld Colonel Proctor.

Stamp Proctor and Phileas Fogg recognized each other at once.

"Ah! it's you, is it, Englishman?" cried the colonel; "it's you who are going to play a spade!"

"And who plays it," replied Phileas Fogg coolly, throwing down the ten of spades.

"Well, it pleases me to have it diamonds," replied Colonel Proctor, in an insolent tone.

He made a movement as if to seize the card which had just been played, adding, "You don't understand anything about whist."

"Perhaps I do, as well as another," said Phileas Fogg, rising.

"You have only to try, son of John Bull," replied the colonel.

Aouda turned pale, and her blood ran cold. She seized Mr. Fogg's arm, and gently pulled him back. Passepartout was ready to pounce upon the American, who was staring insolently at his opponent. But Fix got up, and going to Colonel Proctor, said, "You forget that it is I with whom you have to deal, sir; for it was I whom you not only insulted, but struck!"

"Mr. Fix," said Mr. Fogg, "pardon me, but this affair is mine, and mine only. The colonel has again insulted me, by insisting that I should not play a spade, and he shall give me satisfaction for it."

"When and where you will," replied the American, "and with whatever weapon you choose."

Aouda in vain attempted to retain Mr. Fogg; as vainly did the detective endeavour to make the quarrel his. Passepartout wished to throw the colonel out of the window, but a sign from his master checked him. Phileas Fogg left the car, and the American followed him upon the platform.

"Sir," said Mr. Fogg to his adversary, "I am in a great hurry to get back to Europe, and any delay whatever will be greatly to my disadvantage."

"Well, what's that to me?" replied Colonel Proctor.

"Sir," said Mr. Fogg, very politely, "after our meeting at San Francisco, I determined to return to America and find you as soon as I had completed the business which called me to England."

"Really!"

"Will you appoint a meeting for six months hence?"

"Why not ten years hence?"

"I say six months," returned Phileas Fogg, "and I shall be at the place of meeting promptly."

"All this is an evasion," cried Stamp Proctor. "Now or never!"

"Very good. You are going to New York?"

"No."

"To Chicago?"

"No."

"To Omaha?"

"What difference is it to you? Do you know Plum Creek?"

"No," replied Mr. Fogg.

"It's the next station. The train will be there in an hour, and will stop there ten minutes. In ten minutes several revolver-shots could be exchanged."

"Very well," said Mr. Fogg. "I will stop at Plum Creek."

"And I guess you'll stay there too," added the American insolently.

"Who knows?" replied Mr. Fogg, returning to the car as coolly as usual. He began to reassure Aouda, telling her that blusterers were never to be feared, and begged Fix to be his second at the approaching duel, a request which the detective could not refuse. Mr. Fogg resumed the interrupted game with perfect calmness.

At eleven o'clock the locomotive's whistle announced that they were approaching Plum Creek station. Mr. Fogg rose, and, followed by Fix, went out upon the platform. Passepartout accompanied him, carrying a pair of revolvers. Aouda remained in the car, as pale as death.

The door of the next car opened, and Colonel Proctor appeared on the platform, attended by a Yankee of his own stamp as his second. But just as the combatants were about to step from the train, the conductor hurried up, and shouted, "You can't get off, gentlemen!"

"Why not?" asked the colonel.

"We are twenty minutes late, and we shall not stop."

"But I am going to fight a duel with this gentleman."

"I should play a diamond."

"I am sorry," said the conductor, "but we shall be off at once. There's the bell ringing now."

The train started.

"I'm really very sorry, gentlemen," said the conductor. "Under any other circumstances I should have been happy to oblige you. But, after all, as you have not had time to fight here, why not fight as we go along?"

"That wouldn't be convenient, perhaps, for this gentleman," said the colonel, in a jeering tone.

"It would be perfectly so," replied Phileas Fogg.

"Well, we are really in America," thought Passepartout, "and the conductor is a gentleman of the first order!"

So muttering, he followed his master.

The two combatants, their seconds, and the conductor passed through the cars to the rear of the train. The last car was only occupied by a dozen passengers, whom the conductor politely asked if they would not be so kind as to leave it vacant for a few moments, as two gentlemen had an affair of honour to settle. The passengers granted the request with alacrity, and straightway disappeared on the platform.

The car, which was some fifty feet long, was very convenient for their purpose. The adversaries might march on each other in the aisle, and fire at their ease. Never was duel more easily arranged. Mr. Fogg and Colonel Proctor, each provided with two six-barrelled revolvers, entered the car. The seconds, remaining outside, shut them in. They were to begin firing at the first whistle of the locomotive. After an interval of two minutes, what remained of the two gentlemen would be taken from the car.

Nothing could be more simple. Indeed, it was all so simple that Fix and Passepartout felt their hearts beating as if they would crack. They were listening for the whistle agreed upon, when suddenly savage cries resounded in the air, accompanied by reports which certainly did not issue from the car where the duellists were. The reports continued in front and the whole length of the train. Cries of terror proceeded from the interior of the cars.

Colonel Proctor and Mr. Fogg, revolvers in hand, hastily quitted their prison, and rushed forward where the noise was most clamorous. They then perceived that the train was attacked by a band of Sioux.

This was not the first attempt of these daring Indians, for more than once they had waylaid trains on the road. A hundred of them had, according to their habit, jumped upon the steps without stopping the train, with the ease of a clown mounting a horse at full gallop.

The Sioux were armed with guns, from which came the reports, to which the passengers, who were almost all armed, responded by revolver-shots.

The Indians had first mounted the engine, and half stunned the engineer and stoker with blows from their muskets. A Sioux chief, wishing to stop the train, but not knowing how to work the regulator, had opened wide instead of closing the steam-valve, and the locomotive was plunging forward with terrific velocity.

The Sioux had at the same time invaded the cars, skipping like enraged monkeys over the roofs, thrusting open the doors, and fighting hand to hand with the passengers. Penetrating the baggage-car, they pillaged it, throwing the trunks out of the train. The cries and shots were constant.

The travellers defended themselves bravely; some of the cars were barricaded,

Hanging by one hand between the tender and the luggage van, he...

and sustained a siege, like moving forts, carried along at a speed of a hundred miles an hour.

Aouda behaved courageously from the first. She defended herself, like a true heroine, with a revolver, which she shot through the broken windows whenever a savage made his appearance. Twenty Sioux had fallen mortally wounded to the ground, and the wheels crushed those who fell upon the rails as if they had been worms. Several passengers, shot or stunned, lay on the seats.

It was necessary to put an end to the struggle, which had lasted for ten minutes, and which would result in the triumph of the Sioux if the train was not stopped. Fort Kearney station, where there was a garrison, was only two miles distant; but, that once passed, the Sioux would be masters of the train between Fort Kearney and the station beyond.

The conductor was fighting beside Mr. Fogg, when he was shot and fell. At the same moment he cried, "Unless the train is stopped in five minutes, we are lost!"

"It shall be stopped," said Phileas Fogg, preparing to rush from the car.

"Stay, monsieur," cried Passepartout; "I will go."

Mr. Fogg had not time to stop the brave fellow, who, opening a door unperceived by the Indians, succeeded in slipping under the car; and while the struggle continued, and the balls whizzed across each other over his head, he made use of his old acrobatic experience, and with amazing agility worked his way under the cars, holding on to the chains, aiding himself by the brakes and edges of the sashes, creeping from one car to another with marvellous skill, and thus gaining the forward end of the train.

There, suspended by one hand between the baggage-car and the tender, with the other he loosened the safety chains; but, owing to the traction, he would never have succeeded in unscrewing the yoking-bar, had not a violent concussion jolted this bar out. The train, now detached from the engine, remained a little behind, whilst the locomotive rushed forward with increased speed.

Carried on by the force already acquired, the train still moved for several minutes; but the brakes were worked, and at last they stopped, less than a hundred feet from Kearney staiton.

The soldiers of the fort, attracted by the shots, hurried up; the Sioux had not expected them, and decamped in a body before the train entirely stopped.

But when the passengers counted each other on the station platform several were found missing; among others the courageous Frenchman, whose devotion had just saved them.

CHAPTER 30

IN WHICH PHILEAS FOGG SIMPLY DOES HIS DUTY

THREE passengers—including Passepartout—had disappeared. Had they been killed in the struggle? Were they taken prisoners by the Sioux? It was impossible to tell.

There were many wounded, but none mortally. Colonel Proctor was one of the most seriously hurt; he had fought bravely, and a ball had entered his groin.

He was carried into the station with the other wounded passengers, to receive such attention as could be of avail.

Aouda was safe; and Phileas Fogg, who had been in the thickest of the fight, had not received a scratch. Fix was slightly wounded in the arm. But Passepartout was not to be found, and tears coursed down Aouda's cheeks.

All the passengers had got out of the train, the wheels of which were stained with blood. From the tires and spokes hung ragged pieces of flesh. As far as the eye could reach on the white plain behind, red trails were visible. The last Sioux were disappearing in the south, along the banks of Republican River.

Mr. Fogg, with folded arms, remained motionless. He had a serious decision to make. Aouda, standing near him, looked at him without speaking, and he understood her look. If his servant was a prisoner, ought he not to risk everything to rescue him from the Indians? "I will find him, living or dead," said he quietly to Aouda.

"Ah, Mr.—Mr. Fogg!" cried she, clasping his hands and covering them with tears.

"Living," added Mr. Fogg, "if we do not lose a moment."

Phileas Fogg, by this resolution, inevitably sacrificed himself; he pronounced his own doom. The delay of a single day would make him lose the steamer at New York, and his bet would be certainly lost. But as he thought, "It is my duty," he did not hesitate.

The commanding officer of Fort Kearney was there. A hundred of his soldiers had placed themselves in a position to defend the station, should the Sioux attack it.

"Sir," said Mr. Fogg to the captain, "three passengers have disappeared."

"Dead?" asked the captain.

"Dead or prisoners; that is the uncertainty which must be solved. Do you propose to pursue the Sioux?"

"That's a serious thing to do, sir," returned the captain. "These Indians may retreat beyond the Arkansas, and I cannot leave the fort unprotected."

"The lives of three men are in question, sir," said Phileas Fogg.

"Doubtless; but can I risk the lives of fifty men to save three?"

"I don't know whether you can, sir; but you ought to do so."

"Nobody here," returned the other, "has a right to teach me my duty."

"Very well," said Mr. Fogg, coldly. "I will go alone."

"You sir!" cried Fix coming up; "you go alone in pursuit of the Indians?"

"Would you have me leave this poor fellow to perish,—him to whom every one present owes his life? I shall go."

"No, sir, you shall not go alone," cried the captain, touched in spite of himself. "No! you are a brave man. Thirty volunteers!" he added, turning to the soldiers.

The whole company started forward at once. The captain had only to pick his men. Thirty were chosen, and an old sergeant placed at their head.

"Thanks, captain," said Mr. Fogg.

"Will you let me go with you?" asked Fix.

"Do as you please, sir. But if you wish to do me a favour, you will remain with Aouda. In case anything should happen to me—"

A sudden pallor overspread the detective's face. Separate himself from the man whom he had so persistently followed step by step! Leave him to wander about in this desert! Fix gazed attentively at Mr. Fogg, and, despite his suspicions and of the struggle which was going on within him, he lowered his eyes before that calm and frank look.

"I will stay," said he.

A few moments after, Mr. Fogg pressed the young woman's hand, and, having confided to her his precious carpet-bag, went off with the sergeant and his little squad. But, before going, he had said to the soldiers, "My friends, I will divide five thousand dollars among you, if we save the prisoners."

It was then a little past noon.

Aouda retired to a waiting-room, and there she waited alone, thinking of the simple and noble generosity, the tranquil courage of Phileas Fogg. He had sacrificed his fortune, and was now risking his life, all without hesitation, from duty, in silence.

Fix did not have the same thoughts, and could scarcely conceal his agitation. He walked feverishly up and down the platform, but soon resumed his outward composure. He now saw the folly of which he had been quilty in letting Fogg go alone. What! This man, whom he had just followed around the world, was permitted now to separate himself from him! He began to accuse and abuse himself, and, as if he were director of police, administered to himself a sound lecture for his greenness.

"I have been an idiot!" he thought, "and this man will see it. He has gone, and won't come back! But how is it that I, Fix, who have in my pocket a warrant for his arrest, have been so fascinated by him? Decidedly, I am nothing but an ass!"

So reasoned the detective, while the hours crept by all too slowly. He did not know what to do. Sometimes he was tempted to tell Aouda all; but he could not doubt how the young woman would receive his confidences. What course should he take? He thought of pursuing Fogg across the vast white plains; it did not seem impossible that he might overtake him. Footsteps were easily printed on the snow! But soon, under a new sheet, every imprint would be effaced.

Fix became discouraged. He felt a sort of insurmountable longing to abandon the game altogether. He could now leave Fort Kearney station, and pursue his journey homeward in peace.

Towards two o'clock in the afternoon, while it was snowing hard, long whistles were heard approaching from the east. A great shadow, preceded by a wild light, slowly advanced, appearing still larger through the mist, which gave it a fantastic aspect. No train was expected from the east, neither had there been time for the succour asked for by telegraph to arrive; the train from Omaha to San Francisco was not due till the next day. The mystery was soon explained.

The locomotive, which was slowly approaching with deafening whistles, was that which, having been detached from the train, had continued its route with such terrific rapidity, carrying off the unconscious engineer and stoker. It had run several miles, when, the fire becoming low for want of fuel, the steam had slackened; and it had finally stopped an hour after, some twenty miles beyond Fort Kearney. Neither the engineer nor the stoker was dead, and, after remaining for some time in their swoon, had come to themselves. The train had then stopped. The engineer, when he found himself in the desert, and the locomotive without cars, understood what had happened. He could not imagine how the locomotive had become separated from the train; but he did not doubt that the train left behind was in distress.

He did not hesitate what to do. It would be prudent to continue on to Omaha, for it would be dangerous to return to the train, which the Indians might still be engaged in pillaging. Nevertheless, he began to rebuild the fire in the furnace; the pressure again mounted, and the locomotive returned, running backwards to Fort Kearney. This it was which was whistling in the mist.

The travellers were glad to see the locomotive resume its place at the head of the train. They could now continue the journey so terribly interrupted.

Aouda, on seeing the locomotive come up, hurried out of the station, and asked the conductor, "Are you going to start?"

"At once, madam."

"But the prisoners—our unfortunate fellow-travellers—"

"I cannot interrupt the trip," replied the conductor. "We are already three hours behind time."

"And when will another train pass here from San Francisco?"

"To-morrow evening, madam."

"To-morrow evening! But then it will be too late! We must wait—"

"It is impossible," responded the conductor. "If you wish to go, please get in."

"I will not go," said Aouda.

Fix had heard this conversation. A little while before, when there was no prospect of proceeding on the journey, he had made up his mind to leave Fort Kearney; but now that the train was there, ready to start, and he had only to take his seat in the car, an irresistible influence held him back. The station platform burned his feet, and he could not stir. The conflict in his mind again began; anger and failure stifled him. He wished to struggle on to the end.

Meanwhile the passengers and some of the wounded, among them Colonel Proctor, whose injuries were serious, had taken their places in the train. The buzzing of the overheated boiler was heard, and the steam was escaping from the valves. The engineer whistled, the train started, and soon disappeared, mingling its white smoke with the eddies of the densely falling snow.

The detective had remained behind.

Several hours passed. The weather was dismal, and it was very cold. Fix sat motionless on a bench in the station; he might have been thought asleep. Aouda, despite the storm, kept coming out of the waiting-room, going to the end of the platform, and peering through the tempest of snow, as if to pierce the mist which narrowed the horizon around her, and to hear, if possible, some welcome sound. She heard and saw nothing. Then she would return, chilled through, to issue out again after the lapse of a few moments, but always in vain.

Evening came, and the little band had not returned. Where could they be? Had they found the Indians, and were they having a conflict with them, or were they still wandering amid the mist? The commander of the fort was anxious, though he tried to conceal his apprehensions. As night approached, the snow fell less plentifully, but it became intensely cold. Absolute silence rested on the plains. Neither flight of bird nor passing of beast troubled the perfect calm.

Throughout the night Aouda, full of sad forebodings, her heart stifled with anguish, wandered about on the verge of the plains. Her imagination carried her far off, and showed her innumerable dangers. What she suffered through the long hours it would be impossible to describe.

Fix remained stationary in the same place, but did not sleep. Once a man approached and spoke to him, and the detective merely replied by shaking his head.

Thus the night passed. At dawn, the half-extinguished disk of the sun rose above a misty horizon; but it was now possible to recognize objects two miles off. Phileas Fogg and the squad had gone southward; in the south all was still vacancy. It was then seven o'clock.

The captain, who was really alarmed, did not know what course to take. Should he send another detachment to the rescue of the first? Should he sacrifice more men, with so few chances of saving those already sacrificed? His hesitation did not last long, however. Calling one of his lieutenants, he was on the point of ordering a reconnoissance, when gunshots were heard. Was it a signal? The soldiers rushed out of the fort, and half a mile off they perceived a little band returning in good order.

Mr. Fogg was marching at their head, and just behind him were Passepartout and the other two travellers, rescued from the Sioux.

They had met and fought the Indians ten miles south of Fort Kearney. Shortly before the detachment arrived, Passepartout and his companions had begun to struggle with their captors, three of whom the Frenchman had felled with his fists, when his master and the soldiers hastened up to their relief.

All were welcomed with joyful cries. Phileas Fogg distributed the reward he had promised to the soldiers, while Passepartout, not without reason, muttered to himself, "It must certainly be confessed that I cost my master dear!"

Fix, without saying a word, looked at Mr. Fogg, and it would have been difficult to analyze the thoughts which struggled within him. As for Aouda, she took her protector's hand and pressed it in her own, too much moved to speak.

Meanwhile, Passepartout was looking about for the train; he thought he should find it there, ready to start for Omaha, and he hoped that the time lost might be regained.

"The train! the train!" cried he.

"Gone," replied Fix.

"And when does the next train pass here?" asked Phileas Fogg.

"Not till this evening."

"Ah!" returned the impassible gentleman quietly.

CHAPTER 31

IN WHICH FIX THE DETECTIVE CONSIDERABLY FURTHERS THE INTERESTS OF PHILEAS FOGG

PHILEAS FOGG found himself twenty hours behind time. Passepartout, the involuntary cause of this delay, was desperate. He had ruined his master!

At this moment the detective approached Mr. Fogg, and, looking him intently in the face, said,—

"Seriously, sir, are you in great haste?"

"Quite seriously."

"I have a purpose in asking," resumed Fix. "Is it absolutely necessary that

The Frenchman had stunned three with his fists.

you should be in New York on the 11th, before nine o'clock in the evening, the time that the steamer leaves for Liverpool?''

''It is absolutely necessary.''

''And, if your journey had not been interrupted by these Indians, you would have reached New York on the morning of the 11th?''

''Yes; with eleven hours to spare before the steamer left.''

''Good! you are therefore twenty hours behind. Twelve from twenty leaves eight. You must regain eight hours. Do you wish to try to do so?''

''On foot?'' asked Mr. Fogg.

''No; on a sledge,'' replied Fix. ''On a sledge with sails. A man has proposed such a method to me.''

It was the man who had spoken to Fix during the night and whose offer he had refused.

Phileas Fogg did not reply at once; but Fix having pointed out the man, who was walking up and down in front of the station, Mr. Fogg went up to him. An instant after, Mr. Fogg and the American, whose name was Mudge, entered a hut built just below the fort.

There Mr. Fogg examined a curious vehicle, a kind of frame on two long beams, a little raised in front like the runners of a sledge, and upon which there was room for five or six persons. A high mast was fixed on the frame, held firmly by metallic lashings, to which was attached a large brigantine sail. This mast held an iron stay upon which to hoist a jib-sail. Behind, a sort of rudder served to guide the vehicle. It was, in short, a sledge rigged like a sloop. During the winter, when the trains are blocked up by the snow, these sledges make extremely rapid journeys across the frozen plains from one station to another. Provided with more sail than a cutter, and with the wind behind them, they slip over the surface of the prairies with a speed equal if not superior to that of the express trains.

Mr. Fogg readily made a bargain with the owner of this land-craft. The wind was favourable, being fresh, and blowing from the west. The snow had hardened, and Mudge was very confident of being able to transport Mr. Fogg in a few hours to Omaha. Thence the trains eastward run frequently to Chicago and New York. It was not impossible that the lost time might yet be recovered; and such an opportunity was not to be rejected.

Not wishing to expose Aouda to the discomforts of travelling in the open air, Mr. Fogg proposed to leave her with Passepartout at Fort Kearney, the servant taking upon himself to escort her to Europe by a better route and under more favourable conditions. But Aouda refused to spearate from Mr. Fogg, and Passepartout was delighted with her decision; for nothing could induce him to leave his master while Fix was with him.

It would be difficult to guess the detective's thoughts. Was his conviction shaken by Phileas Fogg's return, or did he still regard him as an exceedingly shrewd rascal, who, his journey round the world completed, would think himself absolutely safe in England? Perhaps Fix's opinion of Phileas Fogg was somewhat modified; but he was nevertheless resolved to do his duty, and to hasten the return of the whole party to England as much as possible.

At eight o'clock the sledge was ready to start. The passengers took their places on it, and wrapped themselves up closely in their travelling-cloaks. The two great sails were hoisted, and under the pressure of the wind the sledge slid over the hardened snow with a velocity of forty miles an hour.

The distance between Fort Kearney and Omaha, as the birds fly, is at most two hundred miles. If the wind held god, the distance might be traversed in five hours; if no accident happened, the sledge might reach Omaha by one o'clock.

What a journey! The travellers, huddled close together, could not speak for the cold, intensified by the rapidity at which they were going. The sledge sped on as lightly as a boat over the waves. When the breeze came, skimming the earth, the sledge seemed to be lifted off the ground by its sails. Mudge, who was at the rudder, kept in a straight line, and by a turn of his hand checked the lurches which the vehicle had a tendency to make. All the sails were up, and the jib was so arranged as not to screen the brigantine. A topmast was hoisted, and another jib, held out to the wind, added its force to the other sails. Although the speed could not be exactly estimated, the sledge could not be going at less than forty miles an hour.

"If nothing breaks," said Mudge, "we shall get there!"

Mr. Fogg had made it for Mudge's interest to reach Omaha within the time agreed on, by the offer of a handsome reward.

The prairie, across which the sledge was moving in a straight line, was as flat as a sea. It seemed like a vast frozen lake. The railroad which ran through this section ascended from the south-west to the north-west by Great Island, Columbus, an important Nebraska town, Schuyler, and Fremont, to Omaha. It followed throughout the right bank of the Platte River. The sledge, shortening this route, took the chord of the arc described by the railway. Mudge was not afraid of being stopped by the Platte River, because it was frozen. The road, then, was quite clear of obstacles, and Phileas Fogg had but two things to fear,—an accident to the sledge, and a change or calm in the wind.

But the breeze, far from lessening its force, blew as if to bend the mast, which, however, the metallic lashings held firmly. These lashings, like the chords of a stringed instrument, resounded as if vibrated by a violin bow. The sledge slid along in the midst of a plaintively intense melody.

"Those chords give the fifth and the octave," said Mr. Fogg.

These were the only words he uttered during the journey. Aouda, cosily packed in furs and cloaks, was sheltered as much as possible from the attacks of the freezing wind. As for Passepartout, his face was as red as the sun's disk when it sets in the mist, and he laboriously inhaled the biting air. With his natural buoyancy of spirits, he began to hope again. They would reach New York on the evening, if not on the morning, of the 11th, and there were still some chances that it would be before the streamer sailed for Liverpool.

Passepartout even felt a strong desire to grasp his ally, Fix, by the hand. He remembered that it was the detective who procured the sledge, the only means of reaching Omaha in time; but, checked by some presentiment, he kept his usual reserve. One thing, however, Passepartout would never forget, and that was the sacrifice which Mr. Fogg had made, without hesitation, to rescue him from the Sioux. Mr. Fogg had risked his fortune and his life. No! His servant would never forget that!

While each of the party was absorbed in reflections so different, the sledge flew fast over the vast carpet of snow. The creeks it passed over were not perceived. Fields and streams disappeared under the uniform whiteness. The plain was absolutely deserted. Between the Union Pacific road and the branch which unites Kearney with Saint Joseph it formed a great uninhabited island. Neither village, station, nor fort appeared. From time to time they sped by some phantom-like tree, whose white skeleton twisted and rattled in the wind. Sometimes flocks of wild birds rose, or bands of gaunt, famished, ferocious prairie-wolves ran howling after the sledge. Passepartout, revolver in hand, held himself ready to fire on those which came too near. Had an accident then happened to the sledge, the travellers, attacked by these beasts, would have been in the most terrible danger; but it held on its even course, soon gained on the wolves, and ere long left the howling band at a safe distance behind.

About noon Mudge perceived by certain landmarks that he was crossing the Platte River. He said nothing, but he felt certain that he was now within twenty miles of Omaha. In less than an hour he left the rudder and furled his sails, whilst the sledge, carried forward by the great impetus the wind had given it, went on half a mile further with its sails unspread.

It stopped at last, and Mudge, pointing to a mass of roofs white with snow, said, "We have got there!"

Arrived! Arrived at the station which is in daily communication, by numerous trains, with the Atlantic seaboard!

Passepartout and Fix jumped off, stretched their stiffened limbs, and aided Mr. Fogg and the young woman to descend from the sledge. Phileas Fogg generously rewarded Mudge, whose hand Passepartout warmly grapsed, and the party directed their steps to the Omaha railway station.

The Pacific Railroad proper finds its terminus at this important Nebraska town. Omaha is connected with Chicago by the Chicago and Rock Island Railroad, which runs directly east, and passes fifty stations.

A train was ready to start when Mr. Fogg and his party reached the station, and they only had time to get into the cars. They had seen nothing of Omaha; but Passepartout confessed to himelf that this was not to be regretted, as they were not travelling to see the sights.

The train passed rapidly across the State of Iowa, by Council Bluffs, Des Moines, and Iowa City. During the night it crossed the Mississippi at Davenport, and by Rock Island entered Illinois. The next day, which was the 10th, at four in the evening, it reached Chicago, already risen from its ruins, and more proudly seated than ever on the borders of its beautiful Lake Michigan.

Nine hundred miles separated Chicago from New York; but trains are not wanting at Chicago. Mr. Fogg passed at once from one to the other, and the locomotive of the Pittsburg, Fort Wayne, and Chicago Railway left at full speed, as if it fully comprehended that that gentleman had no time to lose. It traversed Indiana, Ohio, Pennsylvania, and New Jersey like a flash, rushing through towns with antique names, some of which had streets and car-tracks, but as yet no houses. At last the Hudson came into view; and at a quarter-past eleven in the evening of the 11th, the train stopped in the station on the right bank of the river, before the very pier of the Cunard line.

The "China," for Liverpool, had started three quarters of an hour before!

And sometimes a pack of prairie wolves.

CHAPTER 32

IN WHICH PHILEAS FOGG ENGAGES IN A DIRECT STRUGGLE WITH BAD FORTUNE

THE "China," in leaving, seemed to have carried off Phileas Fogg's last hope. None of the other steamers were able to serve his projects. The "Pereire," of the French Transatlantic Company, whose admirable steamers are equal to any in speed and comfort, did not leave until the 14th; the Hamburg boats did not go directly to Liverpool or London, but to Havre; and the additional trip from Havre to Southampton would render Phileas Fogg's last efforts of no avail. The Inman steamer did not depart till the next day, and could not cross the Atlantic in time to save the wager.

Mr. Fogg learned all this in consulting his "Bradshaw," which gave him the daily movements of the transatlantic steamers.

Passepartout was crushed; it overwhelmed him to lose the boat by three quarters of an hour. It was his fault, for, instead of helping his master, he had not ceased putting obstacles in his path! And when he recalled all the incidents of the tour, when he counted up the sums expended in pure loss and on his own account, when he thought that the immense stake, added to the heavy charges of this useless journey, would completely ruin Mr. Fogg, he overwhelmed himself with bitter self-accusations. Mr. Fogg, however, did not reproach him; and, on leaving the Cunard pier, only said, "We will consult about what is best to-morrow. Come."

The party crossed the Hudson in the Jersey City ferryboat, and drove in a carriage to the St. Nicholas Hotel, on Broadway. Rooms were engaged, and the night passed, briefly to Phileas Fogg, who slept profoundly, but very long to Aouda and the others, whose agitation did not permit them to rest.

The next day was the 12th of December. From seven in the morning of the 12th, to a quarter before nine in the evening of the 21st, there were nine days, thirteen hours, and forty-five minutes. If Phileas Fogg had left in the "China," one of the fastest steamers on the Atlantic, he would have reached Liverpool, and then London, within the period agreed upon.

Mr. Fogg left the hotel alone, after giving Passepartout instructions to await his return, and inform Aouda to be ready at an instant's notice. He proceeded to the banks of the Hudson, and looked about among the vessels moored or anchored in the river, for any that were about to depart. Several had departure signals, and were preparing to put to sea at morning tide; for in this immense and admirable port, there is not one day in a hundred that vessels do not set out for every quarter of the globe. But they were mostly sailing vessels, of which, of course, Phileas Fogg could make no use.

He seemed about to give up all hope, when he espied, anchored at the Battery, a cable's length off at most, a trading vessel, with a screw, well-shaped, whose funnel, puffing a cloud of smoke, indicated that she was getting ready for departure.

Phileas Fogg hailed a boat, got into it, and soon found himself on board the

"Henrietta," iron-hulled, wood-built above. He ascended to the deck, and asked for the captain, who forthwith presented himself. He was a man of fifty, a sort of sea-wolf, with big eyes, a complexion of oxidized copper, red hair and thick neck, and a growling voice.

"The captain?" asked Mr. Fogg.

"I am the captain."

"I am Phileas Fogg, of London."

"And I am Andrew Speedy, of Cardiff."

"You are going to put to sea?"

"In an hour."

"You are bound for—"

"Bordeaux."

"And your cargo?"

"No freight. Going in ballast."

"Have you any passengers?"

"No passengers. Never have passengers. Too much in the way."

"Is your vessel a swift one?"

"Between eleven and twelve knots. The 'Henrietta,' well known."

"Will you carry me and three other persons to Liverpool?"

"To Liverpool? Why not to China?"

"I said Liverpool."

"No!"

"No?"

"No. I am setting out for Bordeaux, and shall go to Bordeaux."

"Money is no object?"

"None."

The captain spoke in a tone which did not admit of a reply.

"But the owners of the 'Henrietta'—" resumed Phileas Fogg.

"The owners are myself," replied the captain. "The vessel belong to me."

"I will freight it for you."

"No."

"I will buy it of you."

"No."

Phileas Fogg did not betray the least disappointment; but the situation was a grave one. It was not at New York as at Hong Kong, nor with the captain of the "Henrietta" as with the captain of the "Tankadere." Up to this time money had smoothed away every obstacle. Now money failed.

Still, some means must be found to cross the Atlantic on a boat, unless by balloon,—which would have been venturesome, besides not being capable of being put in practice. It seemed that Phileas Fogg had an idea, for he said to the captain, "Well, will you carry me to Bordeaux?"

"No, not if you paid me two hundred dollars."

"I offer you two thousand."

"Apiece?"

"Apiece."

"And there are four of you?"

"Four."

Captain Speedy began to scratch his head. There were eight thousand dollars to gain, without changing his route; for which it was well worth conquering the repugnance he had for all kinds of passengers. Besides, passengers at two thousand dollars are no longer passengers, but valuable merchandise. "I start at nine o'clock," said Captain Speedy, simply. "Are you and your party ready?"

"We will be on board at nine o'clock," replied, no less simply, Mr. Fogg.

It was half-past eight. To disembark from the "Henrietta," jump into a hack, hurry to the St. Nicholas, and return with Aouda, Passepartout, and even the inseparable Fix, was the work of a brief time, and was performed by Mr. Fogg with the coolness which never abandoned him. They were on board when the "Henrietta" made ready to weigh anchor.

When Passepartout heard what this last voyage was going to cost, he uttered a prolonged "Oh!" which extended throughout his vocal gamut.

As for Fix, he said to himself that the Bank of England would certainly not come out of this affair well indemnified. When they reached England, even if Mr. Fogg did not throw some handfuls of bank-bills into the sea, more than seven thousand pounds would have been spent!

CHAPTER 33

IN WHICH PHILEAS FOGG SHOWS HIMSELF EQUAL TO THE OCCASION

An hour after, the "Henrietta" passed the lighthouse which marks the entrance of the Hudson, turned the point of Sandy Hook, and put to sea. During the day she skirted Long Island, passed Fire Island, and directed her course rapidly eastward.

At noon the next day, a man mounted the bridge to ascertain the vessel's position. It might be thought that this was Captain Speedy. Not the least in the world. It was Phileas Fogg, Esquire. As for Captain Speedy, he was shut up in his cabin under lock and key, and was uttering loud cries, which signified an anger at once pardonable and excessive.

What had happened was very simple. Phileas Fogg wished to go to Liverpool, but the captain would not carry him there. Then Phileas Fogg had taken passage for Bordeaux, and, during the thirty hours he had been on board, had so shrewdly managed with his bank-notes that the sailors and stokers, who were only an occasional crew, and were not on the best terms with the captain, went over to him in a body. This was why Phileas Fogg was in command instead of Captain Speedy; why the captain was a prisoner in his cabin; and why, in short, the "Henrietta" was directing her course towards Liverpool. It was very clear, to see Mr. Fogg manage the craft, that he had been a sailor.

How the adventure ended will be seen anon. Aouda was anxious, though she said nothing. As for Passepartout, he thought Mr. Fogg's manoeuvre simply glorious. The captain had said "between eleven and twelve knots," and the "Henrietta" confirmed his prediction.

If, then—for there were "ifs" still—the sea did not become too boisterous, if the wind did not veer round to the east, if no accident happened to the boat or its machinery, the "Henrietta" might cross the three thousand miles from New York to Liverpool in the nine days, between the 12th and the 21st of December. It is true that, once arrived, the affair on board the "Henrietta," added to that of the Bank of England, might create more difficulties for Mr. Fogg than he imagined or could desire.

During the first days, they went along smoothly enough. The sea was not very unpropitious, the wind seemed stationary in the north-east, the sails were hoisted, and the "Henrietta" ploughed across the waves like a real transatlantic steamer.

Passepartout was delighted. His master's last exploit, the consequences of which he ignored, enchanted him. Never had the crew seen so jolly and dexterous a fellow. He formed warm friendships with the sailors, and amazed them with his acrobatic feats. He thought they managed the vessel like gentlemen, and that the stokers fired up like heroes. His loquacious good-humour infected every one. He had forgotten the past, its vexations and delays. He only thought of the end, so nearly accomplished; and sometimes be boiled over with impatience, as if heated by the furnaces of the "Henrietta." Often, also, the worthy fellow revolved around Fix, looking at him with a keen, distrustful eye; but he did not speak to him, for their old intimacy no longer existed.

Fix, it must be confessed, understood nothing of what was going on. The conquest of the "Henrietta," the bribery of the crew, Fogg managing the boat like a skilled seaman, amazed and confused him. He did not know what to think. For, after all, a man who began by stealing fifty-five thousand prounds might end by stealing a vessel; and Fix was not unnaturally inclined to conclude that the "Henrietta," under Fogg's command, was not going to Liverpool at all, but to some part of the world where the robber, turned into a pirate, would quietly put himself in safety. The conjecture was at least a plausible one, and the detective began to seriously regret that he had embarked in the affair.

As for Captain Speedy, he continued to howl and growl in his cabin; and Passepartout, whose duty it was to carry him his meals, courageous as he was, took the greatest precautions. Mr. Fogg did not seem even to know that there was a captain on board.

On the 13th they passed the edge of the Banks of Newfoundland, a dangerous locality; during the winter, especially, there are frequent fogs and heavy gales of wind. Ever since the evening before the barometer, suddenly falling, had indicated an approaching change in the atmosphere; and during the night the temperature varied, the cold became sharper, and the wind veered to the south-east.

This was a misfortune. Mr. Fogg, in order not to deviate from his course, furled his sails and increased the force of the steam; but the vessel's speed slackened, owing to the state of the sea, the long waves of which broke against the stern. She pitched violently, and this retarded her progress. The breeze little by little swelled into a tempest, and it was to be feared that the "Henrietta" might not be able to maintain herself upright on the waves.

Passepartout's visage darkened with the skies, and for two days the poor fellow experienced constant fright. But Phileas Fogg was a bold mariner, and knew how to maintain headway against the sea; and he kept on his course, without even decreasing his steam. The "Henrietta," when she could not rise upon the waves, crossed them, swamping her deck, but passing safely. Sometimes the screw rose out of the water, beating its protruding end, when a mountain of water raised the stern above the waves; but the craft always kept straight ahead.

The wind, however, did not grow as boisterous as might have been feared; it was not one of those tempests which burst, and rush on with a speed of ninety miles an hour. It continued fresh, but, unhappily, it remained obstinately in the south-east, rendering the sails useless.

The 16th of December was the seventy-fifth day since Phileas Fogg's departure from London, and the "Henrietta" had not yet been seriously delayed. Half of the voyage was almost accomplished, and the worst localities had been passed. In summer, success would have been well-nigh certain. In winter, they were at the mercy of the bad season. Passepartout said nothing; but he cherished hope in secret, and comforted himself with the reflection that, if the wind failed them, they might still count on the steam.

On this day the engineer came on deck, went up to Mr. Fogg, and began to speak earnestly with him. Without knowing why—it was a presentiment, perhaps—Passepartout became vaguely uneasy. He would have given one of his ears to hear with the other what the engineer was saying. He finally managed to catch a few words, and was sure he heard his master say, "You are certain of what you tell me?"

"Certain, sir," replied the engineer. "You must remember that, since we started, we have kept up hot fires in all our furances, and though we had coal enough to go on short steam from New York to Bordeaux, we haven't enough to go with all steam from New York to Liverpool."

"I will consider," replied Mr. Fogg.

Passepartout understood it all; he was seized with mortal anxiety. The coal was giving out! "Ah, if my master can get over that," muttered he, "he'll be a famous man!" He could not help imparting to Fix what he had overheard.

"Then you believe that we really are going to Liverpool?"

"Of course."

"Ass!" replied the detective, shrugging his shoulders and turning on his heel.

Passepartout was on the point of vigorously resenting the epithet, the reason of which he could not for the life of him comprehend; but he reflected that the unfortunate Fix was probably very much disappointed and humiliated in his self-esteem, after having so awkwardly followed a false scent around the world, and refrained.

And now what course would Phileas Fogg adopt? It was difficult to imagine. Nevertheless he seemed to have decided upon one, for that evening he sent for the engineer, and said to him, "Feed all the fires until the coal is exhausted."

A few moments after, the funnel of the "Henrietta" vomited forth torrents of smoke. The vessel continued to proceed with all steam on; but on the 18th, the engineer, as he had predicted, announced that the coal would give out in the course of the day.

"Do not let the fires go down," replied Mr. Fogg. "Keep them up to the last. Let the valves be filled."

Towards noon Phileas Fogg, having ascertained their position, called Passepartout, and ordered him to go for Captain Speedy. It was as if the honest fellow had been commanded to unchain a tiger. He went to the poop, saying to himself, "He will be like a madman!"

In a few moments, with cries and oaths, a bomb appeared on the poop-deck. The bomb was Captain Speedy. It was clear that he was on the point of bursting.

"Where are we?" were the first words his anger permitted him to utter. Had the poor man been apoplectic, he could never have recovered from his paroxysm of wrath.

"Where are we?" he repeated, with purple face.

"Seven hundred and seventy miles from Liverpool," replied Mr. Fogg, with impeturbable calmness.

"Pirate!" cried Captain Speedy.

"I have sent for you, sir—"

"Pickaroon!"

"—Sir," continued Mr. Fogg, "to ask you to sell me your vessel."

"No! By all the devils, no!"

"But I shall be obliged to burn her."

"Burn the 'Henrietta'!"

"Yes; at least the upper part of her. The coal has given out."

"Burn my vessel!" cried Captain Speedy, who could scarcely pronounce the words. "A vessel worth fifty thousand dollars!"

"Here are sixty thousand," replied Phileas Fogg, handing the captain a roll of bank bills. This had a prodigious effect on Andrew Speedy. An American can scarcely remain unmoved at the sight of sixty thousand dollars. The captain forgot in an instant his anger, his imprisonment, and all his grudges against his passenger. The "Henrietta" was twenty years old; it was a great bargain. The bomb would not go off after all. Mr. Fogg had taken away the match.

"And I shall still have the iron hull," said the captain in a softer tone.

"The iron hull and the engine. Is it agreed?"

"Agreed."

And Andrew Speedy, seizing the bank-notes, counted them, and consigned them to his pocket.

During this colloquy, Passepartout was as white as a sheet, and Fix seemed on the point of having an apoplectic fit. Nearly twenty thousand pounds had been expended, and Fogg left the hull and engine to the captain, that is, near the whole value of the craft! It was true, however, that fifty-five thousand pounds had been stolen from the bank.

When Andrew Speedy had pocketed the money, Mr. Fogg said to him, "Don't let this astonish you, sir. You must know that I shall lose twenty thousand pounds, unless I arrive in London by a quarter before nine on the evening of the 21st of December. I missed the steamer at New York, and as you refused to take me to Liverpool—"

"And I did well!" cried Andrew Speedy; "for I have gained at least forty thousand dollars by it!" He added, more sedately, "Do you know one thing, Captain—"

"Fogg."

"Captain Fogg, you've got something of the Yankee about you."

And, having paid his passenger what he considered a high compliment, he was going away, when Mr. Fogg said, "The vessel now belongs to me?"

"Certainly, from the keel to the truck of the masts,—all the wood, that is."

"Very well. Have the interior seats, bunks, and frames pulled down, and burn them."

It was necessary to have dry wood to keep the steam up to the adequate pressure, and on that day the poop, cabins, bunks, and the spare deck were sacrificed. On the next day, the 19th of December, the masts, rafts, and spars were burned; the crew worked lustily, keeping up the fires. Passepartout hewed, cut, and sawed away with all his might. There was a perfect rage for demolition.

The railings, fittings, the greater part of the deck, and top sides disappeared on the 20th, and the "Henrietta" was now only a flat hulk. But on this day they sighted the Irish coast and Fastnet Light. By ten in the evening they were passing Queenstown. Phileas Fogg had only twenty-four hours more in which to get to London; that length of time was necessary to reach Liverpool, with all steam on. And the steam was about to give out altogether!

"Sir," said Captain Speedy, who was now deeply interested in Mr. Fogg's project, "I really commiserate you. Everything is against you. We are only opposite Queenstown."

"Ah," said Mr. Fogg, "is that place where we see the lights Queenstown?"

"Yes."

"Can we enter the harbour?"

"Not under three hours. Only at high tide."

"Stay," replied Mr. Fogg calmly, without betraying in his features that by a supreme inspiration he was about to attempt once more to conquer ill-fortune.

Queenstown is the Irish port at which the transatlantic steamers stop to put off the mails. These mails are carried to Dublin by express trains always held in readiness to start; from Dublin they are sent on to Liverpool by the most rapid boats, and thus gain twelve hours on the Atlantic steamers.

Phileas Fogg counted on gaining twelve hours in the same way. Instead of arriving at Liverpool the next evening by the "Henrietta," he would be there by noon, and would therefore have time to reach London before a quarter before nine in the evening.

The "Henrietta" entered Queenstown harbour at one o'clock in the morning, it then being high tide; and Phileas Fogg, after being grasped heartily by the hand by Captain Speedy, left that gentleman on the levelled hulk of his craft, which was still worth half what he had sold it for.

The party went on shore at once. Fix was greatly tempted to arrest Mr. Fogg on the spot; but he did not. Why? What struggle was going on within him? Had he changed his mind about "his man?" Did he understand that he had made a grave mistake? He did not, however, abandon Mr. Fogg. They all got upon the train, which was just ready to start, at half-past one; at dawn of day they were in Dublin; and they lost no time in embarking on a steamer which, disdaining to rise upon the waves, invariably cut through them.

Phileas Fogg at last disembarked on the Liverpool quay, at twenty minutes before twelve, December 21st. He was only six hours distant from London.

But at this moment Fix came up, put his hand upon Mr. Fogg's shoulder, and, showing his warrant, said, "You are really Phileas Fogg?"

"I am."

"I arrest you in the Queen's name!"

CHAPTER 34

IN WHICH PHILEAS FOGG AT LAST REACHES LONDON

PHILEAS FOGG was in prison. He had been shut up in the Custom House, and he was to be transferred to London the next day.

Passepartout, when he saw his master arrested, would have fallen upon Fix, had he not been held back by some policemen. Aouda was thunderstruck at the suddenness of an event which she could not understand. Passepartout explained to her how it was that the honest and courageous Fogg was arrested as a robber. The young woman's heart revolted against so heinous a charge, and when she saw that she could attempt or do nothing to save her protector, wept bitterly.

As for Fix, he had arrested Mr. Fogg because it was his duty, whether Mr. Fogg were guilty or not.

The thought then struck Passepartout, that he was the cause of this new misfortune! Had he not concealed Fix's errand from his master? When Fix revealed his true character and purpose, why had he not told Mr. Fogg? If the latter had been warned, he would no doubt have given Fix proof of his innocence, and satisfied him of his mistake; at least, Fix would not have continued his journey at the expense and on the heels of his master, only to arrest him the moment he set foot on English soil. Passepartout wept till he was blind, and felt like blowing his brains out.

Aouda and he had remained, despite the cold, under the portico of the Custom House. Neither wished to leave the place; both were anxious to see Mr. Fogg again.

That gentleman was really ruined, and that at the moment when he was about to attain his end. This arrest was fatal. Having arrived at Liverpool at twenty minutes before twelve on the 21st of December, he had till a quarter before nine that evening to reach the Reform Club, that is, nine hours and a quarter; the journey from Liverpool to London was six hours.

If any one, at this moment, had entered the Custom House, he would have found Mr. Fogg seated, Motionless, calm, and without apparent anger, upon a wooden bench. He was not, it is true, resigned; but this last blow failed to force him into an outward betrayal of any emotion. Was he being devoured by one of those secret rages, all the more terrible because contained, and which only burst forth, with an irresistible force, at the last moment? No one could tell. There he sat, calmly waiting—for what? Did he still cherish hope? Did he still believe, now that the door of this prison was closed upon him, that he would succeed?

However that may have been, Mr. Fogg carefully put his watch upon the table, and observed its advancing hands. Not a word escaped his lips, but his look was singularly set and stern. The situation, in any event, was a terrible one, and might be thus stated: If Phileas Fogg was honest, he was ruined. If he was a knave, he was caught.

Did escape occur to him? Did he examine to see if there were any practicable outlet from his prison? Did he think of escaping from it? Possibly; for once he walked slowly around the room. But the door was locked, and the window heavily barred with iron rods. He sat down again, and drew his journel from his pocket. On the line where these words were written, "December 21st, Saturday, Liverpool," he added, "80th day, 11.40 A.M.," and waited.

The Custom House clock struck one. Mr. Fogg observed that his watch was two hours too fast.

Two hours! Admitting that he was at this moment taking an express train, he could reach London and the Reform Club by a quarter before nine, P.M. His forehead slightly wrinkled.

At thirty-three minutes past two he heard a singular noise outside, then a hasty opening of doors. Passepartout's voice was audible, and immediately after that of Fix. Phileas Fogg's eyes brightened for an instant.

The door swung open, and he saw Passepartout, Aouda, and Fix, who hurried towards him.

Fix was out of breath, and his hair was in disorder. He could not speak. "Sir," he stammered, "sir—forgive me—a most—unfortunate resemblance—robber arrested three days ago—you—are free!"

Phileas Fogg was free! He walked to the detective, looked him steadily in the face, and with the only rapid motion he had ever made in his life, or which he ever would make, drew back his arms, and with the precision of a machine, knocked Fix down.

"Well hit!" cried Passepartout. "Parbleu! that's what you might call a good application of English fists!"

Fix, who found himself on the floor, did not utter a word. He had only received his deserts. Mr. Fogg, Aouda, and Passepartout left the Custom House without delay, got into a cab, and in a few moments descended at the station.

Phileas Fogg asked if there was an express train about to leave for London. It was forty minutes past two. The express train had left thirty-five minutes before.

Phileas Fogg then ordered a special train.

There were several rapid locomotives on hand; but the railway arrangements did not permit the special train to leave until three o'clock.

At that hour Phileas Fogg, having stimulated the engineer by the offer of a generous reward, at last set out towards London with Aouda and his faithful servant.

It was necessary to make the journey in five hours and a half; and this would have been easy on a clear road throughout. But there were forced delays, and when Mr. Fogg stepped from the train at the terminus, all the clocks in London were striking ten minutes before nine.*

Having made the tour of the world, he was behindhand five minutes. He had lost the wager!

* A somewhat remarkable eccentricity on the part of the London clocks!—TRANSLATOR.

CHAPTER 35

IN WHICH PHILEAS FOGG DOES NOT HAVE TO REPEAT HIS ORDERS TO PASSEPARTOUT TWICE

THE dwellers in Saville Row would have been surprised, the next day, if they had been told that Phileas Fogg had returned home. His doors and windows were still closed; no appearance of change was visible.

After leaving the station, Mr. Fogg gave Passepartout instructions to purchase some provisions, and quietly went to his domicile.

He bore his misfortune with his habitual tranquillity. Ruined! And by the blundering of the detective! After having steadily traversed that long journey, overcome a hundred obstacles, braved many dangers, and still found time to do some good on his way, to fail near the goal by a sudden event which he could not have foreseen, and against which he was unarmed; it was terrible! But a few pounds were left of the large sum he had carried with him. There only remained of his fortune the twenty thousand pounds deposited at Barings, and this amount he owed to his friends of the Reform Club. So great had been the expense of his tour, that, even had he won, it would not have enriched him; and it is probable that he had not sought to enrich himself, being a man who rather laid wagers for honour's sake than for the stake proposed. But this wager totally ruined him.

Mr. Fogg's course, however, was fully decided upon; he knew what remained for him to do.

A room in the house in Saville Row was set apart for Aouda, who was overwhelmed with grief at her protector's misfortune. From the words which Mr. Fogg dropped, she saw that he was meditating some serious project.

Knowing that Englishmen governed by a fixed idea sometimes resort to the desperate expedient of suicide, Passepartout kept a narrow watch upon his master, though he carefully concealed the appearance of so doing.

First of all, the worthy fellow had gone up to his room, and had extinguished the gas-burner, which had been burning for eighty days. He had found in the letter-box a bill from the gas company, and he thought it more than time to put a stop to this expense, which he had been doomed to bear.

The night passed. Mr. Fogg went to bed, but did he sleep? Aouda did not once close her eyes. Passepartout watched all night, like a faithful dog, at his master's door.

Mr. Fogg called him in the morning, and told him to get Aouda's breakfast, and a cup of tea and a chop for himself. He desired Aouda to excuse him from breakfast and dinner, as his time would be absorbed all day in putting his affairs to rights. In the evening he would ask permission to have a few moments' conversation with the young lady.

Passepartout, having received his orders, had nothing to do but obey them. He looked at his imperturbable master, and could scarcely bring his mind to leave him. His heart was full, and his conscience tortured by remorse; for he accused himself more bitterly than ever of being the cause of the irretrievable disaster. Yes! if he had warned Mr. Fogg, and had betrayed Fix's projects to him, his master would certainly not have given the detective passage to Liverpool, and then—

Passepartout could hold in no longer.

''My master! Mr. Fogg!'' he cried, ''why do you not curse me? It was my fault that—''

''I blame no one,'' returned Phileas Fogg, with perfect calmness. ''Go!''

Passepartout left the room, and went to find Aouda, to whom he delivered his master's message.

''Madam,'' he added, ''I can do nothing myself—nothing! I have no influence over my master; but you, perhaps—''

''What influence could I have?'' replied Aouda. ''Mr. Fogg is influenced by no one. Has he ever understood that my gratitude to him is overflowing? Has he ever read my heart? My friend, he must not be left alone an instant! You say he is going to speak with me this evening?''

''Yes, madam; probably to arrange for your protection and comfort in England.''

''We shall see,'' replied Aouda, becoming suddenly pensive.

Throughout this day (Sunday) the house in Saville Row was as if uninhabited, and Phileas Fogg, for the first time since he had lived in that house, did not set out for his club when Westminster clock struck half-past eleven.

Why should he present himself at the Reform? His friends no longer expected him there. As Phileas Fogg had not appeared in the saloon on the evening before (Saturday, the 21st of December, at a quarter before nine), he had lost his wager. It was not even necessary that he should go to his bankers for the twenty thousand pounds; for his antagonists already had his check in their hands, and they had only to fill it out and send it to the Barings to have the amount transferred to their credit.

Mr. Fogg, therefore, had no reason for going out, and so he remained at home. He shut himself up in his room, and busied himself putting his affairs in order. Passepartout continually ascended and descended the stairs. The hours were long for him. He listened at his master's door, and looked through the keyhole, as if he had a perfect right so to do, and as if he feared that something terrible might happen at any moment. Sometimes he thought of Fix, but no longer in anger. Fix, like all the world, had been mistaken in Phileas Fogg, and had only done his duty in tracking and arresting him; while he, Passepartout— This thought haunted him, and he never ceased cursing his miserable folly.

Finding himself too wretched to remain alone, he knocked at Aouda's door, went into her room, seated himself, without speaking, in a corner, and looked ruefully at the young woman. Aouda was still pensive.

About half-past seven in the evening Mr. Fogg sent to know if Aouda would receive him, and in a few moments he found himself alone with her.

Phileas Fogg took a chair, and sat down near the fireplace, opposite Aouda. No emotion was visible on his face. Fogg returned was exactly the Fogg who had gone away; there was the same calm, the same impassibility.

He sat several minutes without speaking; then, bending his eyes on Aouda, ''Madam,'' said he, ''will you pardon me for bringing you to England?''

''I, Mr. Fogg!'' replied Aouda, checking the pulsations of her heart.

''Please let me finish,'' returned Mr. Fogg. ''When I decided to bring you far away from the country which was so unsafe for you, I was rich, and counted on putting a portion of my fortune at your disposal; then your existence would have been free and happy. But now I am ruined.''

He had found a bill from the gas company.

"I know it, Mr. Fogg," replied Aouda; "and I ask you, in my turn, will you forgive me for having followed you, and—who knows?—for having, perhaps, delayed you, and thus contributed to your ruin?"

"Madam, you could not remain in India, and your safety could only be assured by bringing you to such a distance that your persecutors could not take you."

"So, Mr. Fogg," resumed Aouda, "not content with rescuing me from a terrible death, you thought yourself bound to secure my comfort in a foreign land?"

"Yes, madam; but circumstances have been against me. Still, I beg to place the little I have left at your service."

"But what will become of you, Mr. Fogg?"

"As for me, madam," replied the gentleman, coldly, "I have need of nothing."

"But how do you look upon the fate, sir, which awaits you?"

"As I am in the habit of doing."

"At least," said Aouda, "want should not overtake a man like you. Your friends—"

"I have no friends, madam."

"Your relatives—"

"I have no longer any relatives."

"I pity you, then, Mr. Fogg, for solitude is a sad thing, with no heart to which to confide your griefs. They say, though, that misery itself, shared by two sympathetic souls, may be borne with patience."

"They say so, madam."

"Mr. Fogg," said Aouda, rising, and seizing his hand, "do you wish at once a kinswoman and friend? Will you have me for your wife?"

Mr. Fogg, at this, rose in his turn. There was an unwonted light in his eyes, and a slight trembling of his lips. Aouda looked into his face. The sincerity, rectitude, firmness, and sweetness of this soft glance of a noble woman, who could dare all to save him to whom she owed all, at first astonished, then penetrated him. He shut his eyes for an instant, as if to avoid her look. When he opened them again, "I love you!" he said, simply. "Yes, by all that is holiest, I love you, and I am entirely yours!"

"Ah!" cried Aouda, pressing his hand to her heart.

Passepartout was summoned and appeared immediately. Mr. Fogg still held Aouda's hand in his own; Passepartout understood, and his big, round face became as radiant as the tropical sun at its zenith.

Mr. Fogg asked him if it was not too late to notify the Reverend Samuel Wilson, of Marylebone Parish, that evening.

Passepartout smiled his most genial smile, and said, "Never too late."

It was five minutes past eight.

"Will it be for to-morrow, Monday?"

"For to-morrow, Monday," said Mr. Fogg, turning to Aouda.

"Yes; for to-morrow, Monday," she replied.

Passepartout hurried off as fast as his legs could carry him.

CHAPTER 36

IN WHICH PHILEAS FOGG'S NAME IS ONCE MORE AT A PREMIUM ON 'CHANGE

It is time to relate what a change took place in English public opinion, when it transpired that the real bank-robber, a certain James Strand, had been arrested, on the 17th of December, at Edinburgh. Three days before, Phileas Fogg had been a criminal, who was being desperately followed up by the police; now he was an honourable gentleman, mathematically pursuing his eccentric journey round the world.

The papers resumed their discussion about the wager; all those who had laid bets, for or against him, revived their interest, as if by magic; the "Phileas Fogg bonds" again became negotiable, and many new wagers were made. Phileas Fogg's name was once more at a premium on 'Change.

His five friends of the Reform Club passed these three days in a state of feverish suspense. Would Phileas Fogg, whom they had forgotten, reappear before their eyes! Where was he at this moment? The 17th of December, the day of James Strand's arrest, was the seventy-sixth since Phileas Fogg's departure, and no news of him had been received. Was he dead? Had he abandoned the effort, or was he continuing his journey along the route agreed upon? And would he appear on Saturday, the 21st of December, at a quarter before nine in the evening, on the threshold of the Reform Club saloon?

The anxiety in which, for three days, London society existed, cannot be described. Telegrams were sent to America and Asia for news of Phileas Fogg. Messengers were despatched to the house in Saville Row morning and evening. No news. The police were ignorant what had become of the detective, Fix, who had so unfortunately followed up a false scent. Bets increased, nevertheless, in number and value. Phileas Fogg, like a racehorse, was drawing near his last turning-point. The bonds were quoted, no longer at a hundred below par, but at twenty, at ten, and at five; and paralytic old Lord Albemarle bet even in his favour.

A great crowd was collected in Pall Mall and the neighbouring streets on Saturday evening; it seemed like a multitude of brokers permanently established around the Reform Club. Circulation was impeded, and everywhere disputes, discussions, and financial transactions were going on. The police had great difficulty in keeping back the crowd, and as the hour when Phileas Fogg was due approached, the excitement rose to its highest pitch.

The five antagonists of Phileas Fogg had met in the great saloon of the club. John Sullivan and Samuel Fallentin, the bankers, Andrew Stuart, the engineer, Gauthier Ralph, the director of the Bank of England, and Thomas Flanagan, the brewer, one and all waited anxiously.

When the clock indicated twenty minutes past eight, Andrew Stuart got up, saying, "Gentlemen, in twenty minutes the time agreed upon between Mr. Fogg and ourselves will have expired."

"What time did the last train arrive from Liverpool?" asked Thomas Flanagan.

"At twenty-three minutes past seven," replied Gauthier Ralph; "and the next does not arrive till ten minutes after twelve."

"Well, gentlemen," resumed Andrew Stuart, "if Phileas Fogg had come in the 7.23 train, he would have got here by this time. We can therefore regard the bet as won."

"Wait; don't let us be too hasty," replied Samuel Fallentin. "You know that Mr. Fogg is very eccentric. His punctuality is well known; he never arrives too soon, or too late; and I should not be surprised if he appeared before us at the last minute."

"Why," said Andrew Stuart nervously, "if I should see him, I should not believe it was he."

"The fact is," resumed Thomas Flanagan, "Mr. Fogg's project was absurdly foolish. Whatever his punctuality, he could not prevent the delays which were certain to occur; and a delay of only two or three days would be fatal to his tour."

"Observe, too," added John Sullivan, "that we have received no intelligence from him, though there are telegraphic lines all along his route."

"He has lost, gentlemen," said Andrew Stuart,—"he has a hundred times lost! You know, besides, that the 'China'—the only steamer he could have taken from New York to get here in time—arrived yesterday. I have seen a list of the passengers, and the name of Phileas Fogg is not among them. Even if we admit that fortune has favoured him, he can scarcely have reached America. I think he will be at least twenty days behindhand, and that Lord Albemarle will lose a cool five thousand."

"It is clear," replied Gauthier Ralph; "and we have nothing to do but to present Mr. Fogg's check at Barings to-morrow."

At this moment, the hands of the club clock pointed to twenty minutes to nine.

"Five minutes more," said Andrew Stuart.

The five gentlemen looked at each other. Their anxiety was becoming intense; but, not wishing to betray it, they readily assented to Mr. Fallentin's proposal of a rubber.

"I wouldn't give up my four thousand of the bet," said Andrew Stuart, as he took his seat, "for three thousand nine hundred and ninety-nine."

The clock indicated eighteen minutes to nine.

The players took up their cards, but could not keep their eyes off the clock. Certainly, however secure they felt, minutes had never seemed so long to them!

"Seventeen minutes to nine," said Thomas Flanagan, as he cut the cards which Ralph handed to him.

Then there was a moment of silence. The great saloon was perfectly quiet; but the murmurs of the crowd outside were heard, with now and then a shrill cry. The pendulum beat the seconds, which each player eagerly counted, as he listened, with mathematical regularity.

"Sixteen minutes to nine!" said John Sullivan, in a voice which betrayed his emotion.

One minute more, and the wager would be won. Andrew Stuart and his partners suspended their game. They left their cards, and counted the seconds.

At the fortieth second, nothing. At the fiftieth, still nothing.

At the fifty-fifth, a loud cry was heard in the street, followed by applause, hurrahs, and some fierce growls.

The players rose from their seats.

At the fifty-seventh second the door of the saloon opened; and the pendulum had not beat the sixtieth second when Phileas Fogg appeared, followed by an excited crowd who had forced their way through the club doors, and in his calm voice, said, "Here I am, gentlemen!"

CHAPTER 37

IN WHICH IT IS SHOWN THAT PHILEAS FOGG GAINED NOTHING BY HIS TOUR AROUND THE WORLD, UNLESS IT WERE HAPPINESS

YES; Phileas Fogg in person.

The reader will remember that at five minutes past eight in the evening—about five and twenty hours after the arrival of the travellers in London—Passepartout had been sent by his master to engage the services of the Reverend Samuel Wilson in a certain marriage ceremony, which was to take place the next day.

Passepartout went on his errand enchanted. He soon reached the clergyman's house, but found him not at home. Passepartout waited a good twenty minutes, and when he left the reverend gentleman, it was thirty-five minutes past eight. But in what a state he was! With his hair in disorder, and without his hat, he ran along the street as never man was seen to run before, overturning passers-by, rushing over the sidewalk like a waterspout.

In three minutes he was in Saville Row again, and staggered breathlessly into Mr. Fogg's room.

He could not speak.

"What is the matter?" asked Mr. Fogg.

"My master!" gasped Passepartout,—"marriage—impossible—"

"Impossible?"

"Impossible—for to-morrow."

"Why so?"

"Because to-morrow—is Sunday!"

"Monday," replied Mr. Fogg.

"No—to-day—is Saturday."

"Saturday? Impossible!"

"Yes, yes, yes, yes!" cried Passepartout. "You have made a mistake of one day! We arrived twenty-four hours ahead of time; but there are only ten minutes left!"

Passepartout had seized his master by the collar, and was dragging him along with irresistible force.

Phileas Fogg, thus kidnapped, without having time to think, left his house, jumped into a cab, promised a hundred pounds to the cabman, and, having run over two dogs and overturned five carriages, reached the Reform Club.

The clock indicated a quarter before nine when he appeared in the great saloon.

Phileas Fogg had accomplished the journey round the world in eighty days!

Phileas Fogg had won his wager of twenty thousand pounds!

How was it that a man so exact and fastidious could have made this error of a day? How came he to think that he had arrived in London on Saturday, the twenty-first day of December, when it was really Friday, the twentieth, the seventy-ninth day only from his departure?

The cause of the error is very simple.

Phileas Fogg had, without suspecting it, gained one day on his journey, and this merely because he had travelled constantly *eastward;* he would, on the contrary, have lost a day, had he gone in the opposite direction, that is, *westward.*

In journeying eastward he had gone towards the sun, and the days therefore diminished for him as many times four minutes as he crossed degrees in this direction. There are three hundred and sixty degrees on the circumference of the earth; and these three hundred and sixty degrees, multiplied by four minutes, gives precisely twenty-four hours—that is, the day unconsciously gained. In other words, while Phileas Fogg, going eastward, saw the sun pass the meridian *eighty* times, his friends in London only saw it pass the meridian *seventy-nine* times. That is why they awaited him at the Reform Club on Saturday, and not Sunday, as Mr. Fogg thought.

And Passepartout's famous family watch, which had always kept London time, would have betrayed this fact, if it had marked the days as well as the hours and minutes!

Phileas Fogg, then, had won the twenty thousand pounds; but as he had spent nearly nineteen thousand on the way, the pecuniary gain was small. His object was, however, to be victorious, and not to win money. He divided the one thousand pounds that remained between Passepartout and the unfortunate Fix, against whom he cherished no grudge. He deducted, however, from Passepartout's share the cost of the gas which had burned in his room for nineteen hundred and twenty hours, for the sake of regularity.

That evening, Mr. Fogg, as tranquil and phlegmatic as ever, said to Aouda, "Is our marriage still agreeable to you?"

"Mr. Fogg," replied she, "it is for me to ask that question. You were ruined, but now you are rich again."

"Pardon me, madam; my fortune belongs to you. If you had not suggested our marriage, my servant would not have gone to the Reverend Samuel Wilson's, I should not have been apprised of my error, and—"

"Dear Mr. Fogg!" said the young woman.

"Dear Aouda!" replied Phileas Fogg.

It need not be said that the marriage took place forty-eight hours after, and that Passepartout, glowing and dazzling, gave the bridg away. Had he not saved her, and was he not entitled to this honour?

The next day, as soon as it was light, Passepartout rapped vigorously at his master's door. Mr. Fogg opened it, and asked, "What's the matter, Passepartout?"

"What is it, sir? Why, I've just this instant found out—"

"What?"

"That we might have made the tour of the world in only seventy-eight days."

"No doubt," returned Mr. Fogg, "by not crossing India. But if I had not crossed India, I should not have saved Aouda; she would not have been my wife, and—''

Mr. Fogg quietly shut the door.

Phileas Fogg had won his wager, and had made his journey around the world in eighty days. To do this, he had employed every means of conveyance—steamers, railways, carriages, yachts, trading-vessels, sledges, elephants. The eccentric gentleman had throughout displayed all his marvellous qualities of coolness and exactitude. But what then? What had he really gained by all this trouble? What had he brought back from this long and weary journey?

Nothing, say you? Perhaps so; nothing but a charming woman, who, strange as it may appear, made him the happiest of men!

Truly, would you not for less than that make the tour around the world?

It was no longer a waltz.

Short Stories

Doctor Ox's Experiment

Master Zacharius

A Drama in the Air

Doctor Ox's Experiment

CHAPTER 1

HOW IT IS USELESS TO SEEK, EVEN ON THE BEST MAPS, FOR THE SMALL TOWN OF QUIQUENDONE

If you try to find, on any map of Flanders, ancient or modern, the small town of Quiquendone, probably you will not succeed. Is Quiquendone, then, one of those towns which have disappeared? No. A town of the future? By no means. It exists in spite of geographies, and has done so for some eight or nine hundred years. It even numbers two thousand three hundred and ninety-three souls, allowing one soul to each inhabitant. It is situated thirteen and a half kilometres north-west of Oudenarde, and fifteen and a quarter kilometres south-east of Bruges, in the heart of Flanders. The Vaar, a small tributary of the Scheldt, passes beneath its three bridges, which are still covered with a quaint mediæval roof, like that at Tournay. An old château is to be seen there, the first stone of which was laid so long ago as 1197, by Count Baldwin, afterwards Emperor of Constantinople; and there is a Town Hall, with Gothic windows, crowned by a chaplet of battlements, and surrounded by a turreted belfry, which rises three hundred and fifty-seven feet above the soil. Every hour you may hear there a chime of five octaves, a veritable aerial piano, the renown of which surpasses that of the famous chimes of Bruges. Strangers—if any ever come to Quiquendone—do not quit the curious old town until they have visited its "Stadtholder's Hall," adorned by a full-length portrait of William of Nassau, by Brandon; the loft of the Church of Saint Magloire, a masterpiece of sixteenth century architecture; the cast-iron well in the spacious Place Saint Ernuph, the admirable ornamentation of which is attributed to the artist-blacksmith, Quentin Metsys;

the tomb formerly erected to Mary of Burgundy, daughter of Charles the Bold, who now reposes in the Church of Notre Dame at Bruges; and so on. The principal industry of Quiquendone is the manufacture of whipped creams and barley-sugar on a large scale. It has been governed by the Van Tricasses, from father to son, for several centuries. And yet Quiquendone is not on the map of Flanders! Have the geographers forgotten it, or is it an intentional omission? That I cannot tell; but Quiquendone really exists, with its narrow streets, its fortified walls, its Spanish-looking houses, its market, and its burgomaster—so much so, that it has recently been the theatre of some surprising phenomena, as extraordinary and incredible as they are true, which are to be recounted in the present narration.

Surely there is nothing to be said or thought against the Flemings of Western Flanders. They are a well-to-do folk, wise, prudent, sociable, with even tempers, hospitable, perhaps a little heavy in conversation as in mind; but this does not explain why one of the most interesting towns of their district has yet to appear on modern maps.

This omission is certainly to be regretted. If only history, or in default of history the chronicles, or in default of chronicles the traditions of the country, made mention of Quiquendone! But no; neither atlases, guides, nor itineraries speak of it. M. Joanne himself, that energetic hunter after small towns, says not a word of it. It might be readily conceived that this silence would injure the commerce, the industries, of the town. But let us hasten to add that Quiquendone has neither industry nor commerce, and that it does very well without them. Its barley-sugar and whipped cream are consumed on the spot; none is exported. In short, the Quiquendonians have no need of anybody. Their desires are limited, their existence is a modest one; they are calm, moderate, phlegmatic—in a word, they are Flemings; such as are still to be met with sometimes between the Scheldt and the North Sea.

CHAPTER 2

IN WHICH THE BURGOMASTER VAN TRICASSE AND THE COUNSELLOR NIKLAUSSE CONSULT ABOUT THE AFFAIRS OF THE TOWN

"You think so?" asked the burgomaster.

"I—think so," replied the counsellor, after some minutes of silence.

"You see, we must not act hastily," resumed the burgomaster.

"We have been talking over this grave matter for ten years," replied the Counsellor Niklausse, "and I confess to you, my worthy Van Tricasse, that I cannot yet take it upon myself to come to a decision."

"I quite understand your hesitation," said the burgomaster, who did not speak until after a good quarter of an hour of reflection, "I quite understand it, and I fully share it. We shall do wisely to decide upon nothing without a more careful examination of the question."

"It is certain," replied Niklausse, "that this post of civil commissary is useless in so peaceful a town as Quiquendone."

"Our predecessor," said Van Tricasse gravely, "our predecessor never said, never would have dared to say, that anything is certain. Every affirmation is subject to awkward qualification."

The counsellor nodded his head slowly in token of assent; then he remained silent for nearly half an hour. After this lapse of time, during which neither the counsellor nor the burgomaster moved so much as a finger, Niklausse asked Van Tricasse whether his predecessor—of some twenty years before—had not thought of suppressing this office of civil commissary, which each year cost the town of Quiquendone the sum of thirteen hundred and seventy-five francs and some centimes.

"I believe he did," replied the burgomaster, carrying his hand with majestic deliberation to his ample brow; "but the worthy man died without having dared to make up his mind, either as to this or any other adminstrative measures. He was a sage. Why should I not do as he did?"

Counsellor Niklausse was incapable or originating any objection to the burgomaster's opinion.

"The man who dies," added Van Tricasse solemnly, "without ever having decided upon anything during his life, has very nearly attained to perfection."

This said, the burgomaster pressed a bell with the end of his little finger, which gave forth a muffled sound, which seemed less a sound than a sigh. Presently some light steps glided softly across the tile floor. A mouse would not have made less noise, running over a thick carpet. The door of the room opened, turning on its well-oiled hinges. A young girl, with long blonde tresses, made her appearance. It was Suzel Van Tricasse, the burgomaster's only daughter. She handed her father a pipe, filled to the brim, and a small copper brazier, spoke not a word, and disappeared at once, making no more noise at her exit than at her entrance.

The worthy burgomaster lighted his pipe, and was soon hidden in a cloud of bluish smoke, leaving Counsellor Niklausse plunged in the most absorbing thought.

The room in which these two notable personages, charged with the government of Quiquedone, were talking, was a parlour richly adorned with carvings in dark wood. A lofty fireplace, in which an oak might have been burned or an ox roasted, occupied the whole of one of the sides of the room; opposite to it was a trellised window, the painted glass of which toned down the brightness of the sunbeams. In an antique frame above the chimney-piece appeared the portrait of some worthy man, attributed to Memling, which no doubt represented an ancestor of the Van Tricasses, whose authentic genealogy dates back to the fourteenth century, the period when the Flemings and Guy de Dampierre were engaged in wars with the Emperor Rudolph of Hapsburgh.

This parlour was the principal apartment of the burgomaster's house, which was one of the pleasantest in Quiquendone. Built in the Flemish style, with all the abruptness, quaintness, and picturesqueness of Pointed architecture, it was considered one of the most curious monuments of the town. A Carthusian convent, or a deaf and dumb asylum, was not more silent than this mansion. Noise had no existence there; people did not walk, but glided about in it; they did not speak, they murmured. There was not, however, any lack of women in the house, which, in addition to the burgomaster Van Tricasse himself, sheltered his wife, Madame Brigitte Van Tricasse, his daughter, Suzel Van Tricasse, and his domestic, Lotchè Janshéu. We may also mention the burgomaster's sister, Aunt Hermance, an elderly maiden who still bore the nickname of Tatanémance, which her niece Suzel had given her when a child. But in spite of all these elements of discord and noise, the burgomaster's house was as calm as a desert.

The burgomaster was some fifty years old, neither fat nor lean, neither short nor tall, neither rubicund nor pale, neither gay nor sad, neither contented nor discontented, neither energetic nor dull, neither proud nor humble, neither good nor bad, neither generous nor miserly, neither courageous nor cowardly, neither too much nor too little of anything—a man notably moderate in all respects, whose invariable slowness of motion, slightly hanging lower jaw, prominent eyebrows, massive forehead, smooth as a copper plate and without a wrinkle, would at once have betrayed to a physiognomist that the burgomaster Van Tricasse was phlegm personified. Never, either from anger or passion, had any emotion whatever hastened the beating of this man's heart, or flushed his face; never had his pupils contracted under the influence of any irritation, however ephemeral. He invariably wore good clothes, neither too large nor too small, which he never seemed to wear out. He was shod with large square shoes with triple soles and silver buckles, which lasted so long that his shoemaker was in despair. Upon his head he wore a large hat which dated from the period when Flanders was separated from Holland, so that this venerable masterpiece was at least forty years old. But what would you have? It is the passions which wear out body as well as soul, the clothes as well as the body; and our worthy burgomaster, apathetic, indolent, indifferent, was passionate in nothing. He wore nothing out, not even himself, and he considered himself the very man to administer the affairs of Quiquendone and its tranquil population.

The town, indeed, was not less calm than the Van Tricasse mansion. It was in this peaceful dwelling that the burgomaster reckoned on attaining the utmost limit of human existence, after having, however, seen the good Madame Brigitte Van Tricasse, his wife, precede him to the tomb, where, surely, she would not find a more profound repose than that she had enjoyed on earth for sixty years.

This demands explanation.

The Van Tricasse family might well call itself the "Jeannot family." This is why:—

Every one knows that the knife of this typical personage is as celebrated as its proprietor, and not less incapable of wearing out, thanks to the double operation, incessantly repeated, of replacing the handle when it is worn out, and the blade when it becomes worthless. A precisely similar operation had been going on from time immemorial in the Van Tricasse family, to which Nature had lent herself with more than usual complacency. From 1340 it had invariably happened that a Van Tricasse, when left a widower, had remarried a Van Tricasse younger than himself; who, becoming in turn a widow, had married again a Van Tricasse younger than herself; and so on, without a break in the continuity, from generation to generation. Each died in his or her turn with mechanical regularity. Thus the worthy Madame Brigitte Van Tricasse had now her second husband; and, unless she violated her duty, would precede her spouse—he being ten years younger than herself—to the other world, to make room for a new Madame Van Tricasse. Upon this the burgomaster calmly counted, that the family tradition might not be broken. Such was this mansion, peaceful and silent, of which the

The worthy Madame Brigitte Van Tricasse had now her second husband.

doors never creaked, the windows never rattled, the floors never groaned, the chimneys never roared, the weathercocks never grated, and the occupants never made more noise than their shadows. The god Harpocrates would certainly have chosen it for the Temple of Silence.

CHAPTER 3

IN WHICH THE COMMISSARY PASSAUF ENTERS AS NOISILY AS UNEXPECTEDLY

WHEN the interesting conversation which has been narrated began, it was a quarter before three in the afternoon. It was at a quarter before four that Van Tricasse lighted his enormous pipe, which could hold a quart of tobacco, and it was at thirty-five minutes past five that he finished smoking it.

All this time the two comrades did not exchange a single word.

About six o'clock the counsellor, who had a habit of speaking in a very summary manner, resumed in these words,—

"So we decide—"

"To decide nothing," replied the burgomaster.

"I think, on the whole, that you are right, Van Tricasse."

"I think so too, Niklausse. We will take steps with reference to the civil commissary when we have more light on the subject—later on. There is no need for a month yet."

"Nor even for a year," replied Niklausse, unfolding his pocket-handkerchief and calmly applying it to his nose.

There was another silence of nearly a quarter of an hour. Nothing disturbed this repeated pause in the conversation; not even the appearance of the house-dog Lento, who, not less phlegmatic than his master, came to pay his respects in the parlour. Noble dog!—a model for his race. Had he been made of paste-board, with wheels on his paws, he would not have made less noise during his stay.

Towards eight o'clock, after Lotchè had brought the antique lamp of polished glass, the burgomaster said to the counsellor,—

"We have no other urgent matter to consider?"

"No, Van Tricasse; none that I know of."

"Have I not been told, though," asked the burgomaster, "that the tower of the Oudenarde gate is likely to tumble down?"

"Ah!" replied the counsellor; "really, I should not be astonished if it fell on some passer-by any day."

"Oh! before such a misfortune happens I hope we shall have come to a decision on the subject of this tower."

"I hope so, Van Tricasse."

"There are more pressing matters to decide."

"No doubt; the questions of the leather-market, for instance."

"What, is it still burning?"

"Still burning, and has been for the last three weeks."

"Have we not decided in council to let it burn?"

"Yes, Van Tricasse—on your motion."

"Was not that the surest and simplest way to deal with it?"

"Without doubt."

"Well, let us wait. Is that all?"

"All," replied the counsellor, scratching his head, as if to assure himself that he had not forgotten anything important.

"Ah!" exclaimed the burgomaster, "haven't you also heard something of an escape of water which threatens to inundate the low quarter of Saint Jacques?"

"I have. It is indeed unfortunate that this escape of water did not happen above the leather-market! It would naturally have checked the fire, and would thus have saved us a good deal of discussion."

"What can you expect, Niklausse? There is nothing so illogical as accidents. They are bound by no rules, and we cannot profit by one, as we might wish, to remedy another."

It took Van Tricasse's companion some time to digest this fine observation.

"Well, but," resumed the Counsellor Niklausse, after the lapse of some moments, "we have not spoken of our great affair!"

"What great affair? Have we, then, a great affair?" asked the burgomaster.

"No doubt. About lighting the town."

"O yes. If my memory serves me, you are referring to the lighting plan of Doctor Ox."

"Precisely."

"It is going on, Niklausse," replied the burgomaster. "They are already laying the pipes, and the works are entirely completed."

"Perhaps we have hurried a little in this matter," said the counsellor, shaking his head.

"Perhaps. But our excuse is, that Doctor Ox bears the whole expense of his experiment. It will not cost us a sou."

"That, true enough, is our excuse. Moreover, we must advance with the age. If the experiment succeeds, Quiquendone will be the first town in Flanders to be lighted with the oxy—. What is the gas called?"

"Oxyhydric gas."

"Well, oxyhydric gas, then."

At this moment the door opened, and Lotchè came in to tell the burgomaster that his supper was ready.

Counsellor Niklausse rose to take leave of Van Tricasse, whose appetite had been stimulated by so many affairs discussed and decisions taken; and it was agreed that the council of notables should be convened after a reasonably long delay, to determine whether a decision should be provisionally arrived at with reference to the really urgent matter of the Oudenarde gate.

The two worthy administrators then directed their steps towards the street-door, the one conducting the other. The counsellor, having reached the last step, lighted a little lantern to guide him through the obscure streets of Quiquendone, which Doctor Ox had not yet lighted. It was a dark October night, and a light fog overshadowed the town.

Niklausse's preparations for departure consumed at least a quarter of an hour; for, after having lighted his lantern, he had to put on his big cow-skin socks and his sheep-skin gloves; then he put up the furred collar of his overcoat, turned the brim of his felt hat down over his eyes, grasped his heavy crow-beaked umbrella, and got ready to start.

When Lotchè, however, who was lighting her master, was about to draw the bars of the door, an unexpected noise arose outside.

Yes! Strange as the thing seems, a noise—a real noise, such as the town had certainly not heard since the taking of the donjon by the Spaniards in 1513—a terrible noise, awoke the long-dormant echoes of the venerable Van Tricasse mansion.

Some one knocked heavily upon this door, hitherto virgin to brutal touch! Redoubled knocks were given with some blunt implement, probably a knotty stick, wielded by a vigorous arm. With the strokes were mingled cries and calls. These words were distinctly heard:—

"Monsieur Van Tricasse! Monsieur the burgomaster! Open, open quickly!"

The burgomaster and the counsellor, absolutely astounded, looked at each other speechless.

This passed their comprehension. If the old culverin of the château, which had not been used since 1385, had been let off in the parlour, the dwellers in the Van Tricasse mansion would not have been more dumbfounded.

Meanwhile, the blows and cries were redoubled. Lotchè, recovering her coolness, had plucked up courage to speak.

"Who is there?"

"It is I! I! I!"

"Who are you?"

"The Commissary Passauf!"

The Commissary Passauf! The very man whose office it had been contemplated to suppress for ten years. What had happened, then? Could the Burgundians have invaded Quiquendone, as they did in the fourteenth century? No event of less importance could have so moved Commissary Passauf, who in no degree yielded the palm to the burgomaster himself for calmness and phlegm.

On a sign from Van Tricasse—for the worthy man could not have articulated a syllable—the bar was pushed back and the door opened.

Commissary Passauf flung himself into the antechamber. One would have thought there was a hurricane.

"What's the matter, Monsieur the commissary?" asked Lotchè, a brave woman, who did not lose her head under the most trying circumstances.

"What's the matter!" replied Passauf, whose big round eyes expressed a genuine agitation. "The matter is that I have just come from Doctor Ox's, who has been holding a reception, and that there—"

"There?"

"There I have witnessed such an altercation as—Monsieur the burgomaster, they have been talking politics!"

"Politics!" repeated Van Tricasse, running his fingers through his wig.

"Politics!" resumed Commissary Passauf, "which has not been done for perhaps a hundred years at Quiquendone. Then the discussion got warm, and the advocate, André Schut, and the doctor, Dominique Custos, became so violent that it may be they will call each other out."

"Call each other out!" cried the counsellor. "A duel! A duel at Quiquendone!" And what did Advocate Schut and Doctor Custos say?"

"Just this: 'Monsieur advocate,' said the doctor to his adversary, 'you go too far, it seems to me, and you do not take sufficient care to control your words!"

The Burgomaster Van Tricasse clasped his hands—the counsellor turned pale and let his lantern fall—the commissary shook his head. That a phrase so evidently irritating should be pronounced by two of the principal men in the country!

"This Doctor Custos," muttered Van Tricasse, "is decidely a dangerous man—a hare-brained fellow! Come, gentlemen!"

On this, Counsellor Niklausse and the commissary accompanied the burgomaster into the parlour.

CHAPTER 4

IN WHICH DOCTOR OX REVEALS HIMSELF AS A PHYSIOLOGIST OF THE FIRST RANK, AND AS AN AUDACIOUS EXPERIMENTALIST

WHO, then, was this personage, known by the singular name of Doctor Ox?

An original character for certain, but at the same time a bold *savant*, a physiologist, whose works were known and highly estimated throughout learned Europe, a happy rival of the Davys, the Daltons, the Bostocks, the Menzies, the Godwins, the Vierordts—of all those noble minds who have placed physiology among the highest of modern sciences.

Doctor Ox was a man of medium size and height, aged—: but we cannot state his age, any more than his nationality. Besides, it matters little; let it suffice that he was a strange personage, impetuous and hot-blooded, a regular oddity out of one of Hoffmann's volumes, and one who contrasted amusingly enough with the good people of Quiquendone. He had an imperturbable confidence both in himself and in his doctrines. Always smiling, walking with head erect and shoulders thrown back in a free and unconstrained manner, with a steady gaze, large open nostrils, a vast mouth which inhaled the air in liberal draughts, his appearance was far from unpleasing. He was full of animation, well proportioned in all parts of his bodily mechanism, with quicksilver in his veins, and a most elastic step. He could never stop still in one place, and relieved himself with impetuous words and a superabundance of gesticulations.

Was Doctor Ox rich, then, that he should undertake to light a whole town at his expense? Probably, as he permitted himself to indulge in such extravagance,—and this is the only answer we can give to this indiscreet question.

Doctor Ox had arrived at Quiquendone five months before, accompanied by his assistant, who answered to the name of Gédéon Ygène; a tall, dried-up, thin man, haughty, but not less vivacious than his master.

And next, why had Doctor Ox made the proposition to light the town at his own expense? Why had he, of all the Flemings, selected the peaceable Quiquendonians, to endow their town with the benefits of an unheard-of system of lighting? Did he not, under this pretext, design to make some great physiological experiment by operating *in animâ vili?* In short, what was this original personage about to attempt? We know not, as Doctor Ox had no confidant except his assistant Ygène, who, moreover, obeyed him blindly.

In appearance, at least, Doctor Ox had agreed to light the town, which had much need of it, "especially at night," as Commissary Passauf wittily said. Works for producing a lighting gas had accordingly been established; the gasometers were ready for use, and the main pipes, running beneath the street pavements, would soon appear in the form of burners in the public edifices and the private houses of certain friends of progress. Van Tricasse and Niklausse, in their official capacity, and some other worthies, thought they ought to allow this modern light to be introduced into their dwellings.

If the reader has not forgotten, it was said, during the long conversation of the counsellor and the burgomaster, that the lighting of the town was to be achieved, not by the combustion of common carburetted hydrogen, produced by distilling coal, but by the use of a more modern and twenty-fold more brilliant gas, oxyhydric gas, produced by mixing hydrogen and oxygen.

The doctor, who was an able chemist as well as an ingenious physiologist, knew how to obtain this gas in great quantity and of good quality, not by using manganate of soda, according to the method of M. Tessié du Motay, but by the direct decomposition of slightly acidulated water, by means of a battery made of new elements, invented by himself. Thus there were not costly materials, no platinum, no retorts, no combustibles, no delicate machinery to produce the two gases seperately. An electric current was sent through large basins full of water, and the liquid was decomposed into its two constituent parts, oxygen and hydrogen. The oxygen passed off at one end; the hydrogen, of double the volume of its late associate, at the other. As a necessary precaution, they were collected in separate reservoirs, for their mixture would have produced a frightful explosion if it had become ignited. Thence the pipes were to convey them separately to the various burners, which would be so placed as to prevent all chance of explosion. Thus a remarkably brilliant flame would be obtained, whose light would rival the electric light, which, as everybody knows, is, according to Cassellmann's experiments, equal to that of eleven hundred and seventy-one wax candles,—not one more, nor one less.

It was certain that the town of Quiquendone would, by this liberal contrivance, gain a splendid lighting; but Doctor Ox and his assistant took little account of this, as will be seen in the sequel.

The day after that on which Commissary Passauf had made his noisy entrance into the burgomaster's parlour, Gédéon Ygène, and Doctor Ox were talking in the laboratory which both occupied in common, on the ground-floor of the principal building of the gas-works.

"Well, Ygène, well," cried the doctor, rubbing his hands. "You saw, at my reception yesterday, the cool-bloodedness of these worthy Quiquendonians. For animation they are midway between sponges and coral! You saw them disputing and irritating each other by voice and gesture? They are already metamorphosed, morally and physically! And this is only the beginning. Wait till we treat them to a big dose!"

"Indeed, master," replied Ygène, scratching his sharp nose with the end of his forefinger, "the experiment begins well, and if I had not prudently closed the supply-tap, I know not what would have happened."

"You heard Schut, the advocate, and Custos, the doctor?" resumed Doctor Ox. "The phrase was by no means ill-natured in itself, but, in the mouth of a Quiquendonian, it is worth all the insults which the Homeric heroes hurled at each other before drawing their swords. Ah, these Flemings! You'll see what we shall do some day!"

"We shall make them ungrateful," replied Ygène, in the tone of a man who esteems the human race at its just worth.

"Bah!" said the doctor; "what matters it whether they think well or ill of us, so long as our experiment succeeds?"

"Besides," returned the assistant, smiling with a malicious expression, "is it not to be feared that, in producing such an excitement in their respiratory organs, we shall somewhat injure the lungs of these good people of Quiquendone?"

"So much the worse for them! It is in the interest of science. What would you say if the dogs or frogs refused to lend themselves to the experiments of vivisection?"

It is probable that if the frogs and dogs were consulted, they would offer some objection; but Doctor Ox imagined that he had stated an unanswerable argument, for he heaved a great sigh of satisfaction.

"After all, master, you are right," replied Ygène, as if quite convinced. "We could not have hit upon better subjects than these people of Quiquendone for our experiment."

"We—could—not," said the doctor, slowly articulating each word.

"Have you felt the pulse of any of them?"

"Some hundreds."

"And what is the average pulsation you found?"

"Not fifty per minute. See—this is a town where there has not been the shadow of a discussion for a century, where the carmen don't swear, where the coachmen don't insult each other, where horses don't run away, where the dogs don't bite, where the cats don't scratch,—a town where the police-court has nothing to do from one year's end to another,—a town where people do not grow enthusiastic about anything, either about art or business,—a town where the gendarmes are a sort of myth, and in which an indictment has not been drawn up for a hundred years,—a town, in short, where for three centuries nobody has struck a blow with his fist or so much as exchanged a slap in the face! You see, Ygène, that this cannot last, and that we must change it all."

"Perfectly! perfectly!" cried the enthusiastic assistant; "and have you analyzed the air of this town, master?"

"I have not failed to do so. Seventy-nine parts of azote and twenty-one oxygen, carbonic acid and steam in a variable quantity. These are the ordinary proportions."

"Good, doctor, good!" replied Ygéne. "The experiment will be made on a large scale, and will be decisive."

"And if it is decisive," added Doctor Ox triumphantly, "we shall reform the world!"

CHAPTER 5

IN WHICH THE BURGOMASTER AND THE COUNSELLOR PAY A VISIT TO DOCTOR OX, AND WHAT FOLLOWS

THE Counsellor Niklausse and the Burgomaster Van Tricasse at last knew what it was to have an agitated night. The grave event which had taken place at Doctor Ox's house actually kept them awake. What consequences was this affair destined to bring about? They could not imagine. Would it be necessary for them to come to a decision? Would the municipal authority, whom they represented, be compelled to interfere? Would they be obliged to order arrests to be made, that so great a scandal should not be repeated? All these doubts could not but trouble these soft natures; and on that evening, before separating, the two notables had "decided" to see each other the next day.

On the next morning, then, before dinner, the Burgomaster Van Tricasse proceeded in person to the Counsellor Niklausse's house. He found his friend more calm. He himself had recovered his equanimity.

"Nothing new?" asked Van Tricasse.

"Nothing new since yesterday," replied Niklausse.

"And the doctor, Dominque Custos?"

"I have not heard anything, either of him or of the advocate, André Schut."

After an hour's conversation, which consisted of three remarks which it is needless to repeat, the counsellor and the burgomaster had resolved to pay a visit to Doctor Ox, so as to draw from him, without seeming to do so, some details of the affair.

Contrary to all their habits, after coming to this decision the two notables set about putting it into execution forthwith. They left the house and directed their steps towards Doctor Ox's laboratory, which was situated outside the town, near the Oudenarde gate—the gate whose tower threatened to fall in ruins.

They did not take each other's arms, but walked side by side, with a slow and solemn step, which took them forward but thirteen inches per second. This was, indeed, the ordinary gait of the Quiquendonians, who had never, within the memory of man, seen any one run across the streets of their town.

From time to time the two notables would stop at some calm and tranquil crossway, or at the end of a quiet street, to salute the passers-by.

"Good morning, Monsieur the burgomaster," said one.

"Good morning, my friend," responded Van Tricasse.

"Anything new, Monsieur the counsellor?" asked another.

"Nothing new," answered Niklausse.

But by certain agitated motions and questioning looks, it was evident that the altercation of the evening before was known throughout the town. Observing the direction taken by Van Tricasse, the most obtuse Quiquendonians guessed that the burgomaster was on his way to take some important step. The Custos and Schut affair was talked of everywhere, but the people had not yet come to the point of taking the part of one or the other. The Advocate Schut, having never had occasion to plead in a town where attorneys and bailiffs only existed

"It is in the interests of science."

in tradition, had consequently, never lost a suit. As for the Doctor Custos, he was an honourable practitioner, who, after the example of his fellow-doctors, cured all the illnesses of his patients, except those of which they died—a habit unhappily acquired by all the members of all the faculties in whatever country they may practise.

On reaching the Oudenarde gate, the counsellor and the burgomaster prudently made a short detour, so as not to pass within reach of the tower, in case it should fall; then they turned and looked at it attentively.

"I think that it will fall," said Van Tricasse.

"I think so too," replied Niklausse.

"Unless it is propped up," added Van Tricasse. "But must it be propped up? That is the question."

"That is—in fact—the question."

Some moments after, they reached the door of the gas-works.

"Can we see Doctor Ox?" they asked.

Doctor Ox could always be seen by the first authorities of the town, and they were at once introduced into the celebrated physiologist's study.

Perhaps the two notables waited for the doctor at least an hour; at least it is reasonable to suppose so, as the burgomaster—a thing that had never before happened in his life—betrayed a certain amount of impatience, from which his companion was not exempt.

Doctor Ox came in at last, and began to excuse himself for having kept them waiting; but he had to approve a plan for the gasometer, rectify some of the machinery—But everything was going on well! The pipes intended for the oxygen were already laid. In a few months the town would be splendidly lighted. The two notables might even now see the orifices of the pipes which were laid on in the laboratory.

Then the doctor begged to know to what he was indebted for the honour of this visit.

"Only to see you, doctor; to see you," replied Van Tricasse. "It is long since we have had the pleasure. We go abroad but little in our good town of Quiquendone. We count our steps and measure our walks. We are happy when nothing disturbs the uniformity of our habits."

Niklausse looked at his friend. His friend had never said so much at once—at least, without taking time, and giving long intervals between his sentences. It seemed to him that Van Tricasse expressed himself with a certain volubility, which was by no means common with him. Niklausse himself experienced a kind of irresistible desire to talk.

As for Doctor Ox, he looked at the burgomaster with sly attention.

Van Tricasse, who never argued until he had snugly ensconced himself in a spacious armchair, had risen to his feet. I know not what nervous excitement, quite foreign to his temperament, had taken possession of him. He did not gesticulate as yet, but this could not be far off. As for the counsellor, he rubbed his legs, and breathed with slow and long gasps. His look became animated little by little, and he had "decided" to support at all hazards, if need be, his trusty friend the burgomaster.

Van Tricasse got up and took several steps; then he came back, and stood facing the doctor.

"And in how many months," he asked in a somewhat emphatic tone, "do you say that your work will be finished?"

"In three or four months, Monsieur the burgomaster," replied Doctor Ox.

"Three or four months,—it's a very long time!" said Van Tricasse.

"Altogether too long!" added Niklausse, who, not being able to keep his seat, rose also.

"This lapse of time is necessary to complete our work," returned Doctor Ox. "The workmen, whom we have had to choose in Quiquendone, are not very expeditious."

"How not expeditious?" cried the burgomaster, who seemed to take the remark as personally offensive.

"No, Monsieur Van Tricasse," replied Doctor Ox obstinately. "A French workman would do in a day what it takes ten of your workmen to do; you know, they are regular Flemings!"

"Flemings!" cried the counsellor, whose fingers closed together. "In what sense, sir, do you use that word?"

"Why, in the amiable sense in which everybody uses it," replied Doctor Ox, smiling.

"Ah, but doctor," said the burgomaster, pacing up and down the room, "I don't like these insinuations. The workmen of Quiquendone are as efficient as those of any other town in the world, you must know; and we shall go neither to Paris nor London for our models! As for your project, I beg you to hasten its execution. Our streets have been unpaved for the putting down of your conduit-pipes, and it is a hindrance to traffic. Our trade will begin to suffer, and I, being the responsible authority, do not propose to incur reproaches which will be but too just."

Worthy burgomaster! He spoke of trade, of traffic, and the wonder was that those words, to which he was quite unaccustomed, did not scorch his lips. What could be passing in his mind?

"Besides," added Niklausse, "the town cannot be deprived of light much longer."

"But," urged Doctor Ox, "a town which has been unlighted for eight or nine hundred years—"

"All the more necessary is it," replied the burgomaster, emphasizing his words. "Times alter, manners alter! The world advances, and we do not wish to remain behind. We desire our streets to be lighted within a month, or you must pay a large indemnity for each day of delay; and what would happen if, amid the darkness, some affray should take place?"

"No doubt," cried Niklausse. "It requires but a spark to inflame a Fleming! Fleming! Flame!"

"Apropos of this," said the burgomaster, interrupting his friend, "Commissary Passauf, our chief of police, reports to us that a discussion took place in your drawing-room last evening, Doctor Ox. Was he wrong in declaring that it was a political discussion?"

"By no means, Monsieur the burgomaster," replied Doctor Ox, who with difficulty repressed a sigh of satisfaction.

"So an altercation did take place between Dominique Custos and André Schut?"

"Yes, counsellor; but the words which passed were not of grave import."

"Not of grave import!" cried the burgomaster. "Not of grave import, when one man tells another that he does not measure the effect of his words! But of what stuff are you made, monsieur? Do you not know that in Quiquendone nothing more is needed to bring about extremely disastrous results? But monsieur, if you, or any one else, presume to speak thus to me --"

"Or to me," added Niklausse

As they pronounced these words with a menacing air, the two notables, with folded arms and bristling air, confronted Doctor Ox, ready to do him some violence, if by a gesture, or even the expression of his eye, he manifested any intention of contradicting them.

But the doctor did not budge.

"At all events, monsieur," resumed the burgomaster, "I propose to hold you responsible for what passes in your house. I am bound to insure the tranquillity of this town, and I do not wish it to be disturbed. The events of last evening must not be repeated, or I shall do my duty, sir! Do you hear? Then reply, sir."

The burgomaster, as he spoke, under the influence of extraordinary excitement, elevated his voice to the pitch of anger. He was furious, the worthy Van Tricasse, and might certainly be heard outside. At last, beside himself, and seeing that Doctor Ox did not reply to his challenge, "Come, Niklausse," said he.

And, slamming the door with a violence which shook the house, the burgomaster drew his friend after him

Little by little, when they had taken twenty steps on their road, the worthy notables grew more calm. Their pace slackened, their gait became less feverish. The flush on their faces faded away; from being crimson, they became rosy. A quarter of an hour after quitting the gas-works, Van Tricasse said softly to Niklausse, "An amiable man, Doctor Ox! It is always a pleasure to see him!"

CHAPTER 6

IN WHICH FRANTZ NIKLAUSSE AND SUZEL VAN TRICASSE FORM CERTAIN PROJECTS FOR THE FUTURE

OUR readers know that the burgomaster had a daughter, Suzel, But, shrewd as they may be, they cannot have divined that the counsellor Niklausse had a son, Frantz; and had they divined this, nothing could have led them to imagine that Frantz was the betrothed lover of Suzel. We will add that these young people were made for each other, and that they loved each other, as folks did love at Quiquendone.

It must not be thought that young hearts did not beat in this exceptional place; only they beat with a certain deliberation. There were marriages there, as in every other town in the world; but they took time about it. Betrothed couples, before engaging in these terrible bonds, wished to study each other; and these studies lasted at least ten years, as at college. It was rare that any one was "accepted" before this lapse of time.

Yes, ten years! The courtships last ten years! And is it, after all, too long, when the being bound for life is in consideration? One studies ten years to become an engineer or physician, an advocate or attorney, and should less time be spent in acquiring the knowledge to make a good husband? Is it not reasonable? and, whether due to temperament or reason with them, the Quiquendonians seem to us to be in the right in thus prolonging their courtship. When marriages in other more lively and excitable cities are seen taking place within a few months, we must shrug our shoulders, and hasten to send our boys to the schools and our daughters to the *pensions* of Quiquendone.

For half a century but a single marriage was known to have taken place after the lapse of two years only of courtship, and that turned out badly!

Frantz Niklausse, then, loved Suzel Van Tricasse, but quietly, as a man would love when he has ten years before him in which to obtain the beloved object. Once every week, at an hour agreed upon, Frantz went to fetch Suzel, and took a walk with her along the banks of the Vaar. He took good care to carry his fishing-tackle, and Suzel never forgot her canvas, on which her pretty hands embroidered the most unlikely flowers.

Frantz was a young man of twenty-two, whose cheeks betrayed a soft, peachy down, and whose voice had scarcely a compass of one octave.

As for Suzel, she was blonde and rosy. She was seventeen, and did not dislike fishing. A singular occupation this, however, which forces you to struggle craftily with a barbel. But Frantz loved it; the pastime was congenial to his temperament. As patient as possible, content to follow with his rather dreamy eye the cork which bobbed on the top of the water, he knew how to wait; and when, after sitting for six hours, a modest barbel, taking pity on him, consented at last to be caught, he was happy—but he knew how to control his emotion.

On this day the two lovers—one might say, the two betrothed—were seated upon the verdant bank. The limpid Vaar murmured a few feet below them. Suzel quietly drew her needle across the canvas. Frantz automatically carried his line from left to right, then permitted it to descend the current from right to left. The fish made capricious rings in the water, which crossed each other around the cork, while the hook hung useless near the bottom.

From time to time Frantz would say without raising his eyes,—

"I think I have a bite, Suzel."

"Do you think so, Frantz?" replied Suzel, who, abandoning her work for an instant, followed her lover's line with earnest eye.

"N-no," resumed Frantz; "I thought I felt a little twitch; I was mistaken."

"You *will* have a bite, Frantz," replied Suzel, in her pure, soft voice. "But do not forget to strike at the right moment. You are always a few seconds too late, and the barbel takes advantage to escape."

"Would you like to take my line, Suzel?"

"Willingly, Frantz."

"Then give me your canvas. We shall see whether I am more adroit with the needle than with the hook."

And the young girl took the line with trembling hand, while her swain plied the needle across the stitches of the embroidery. For hours together they thus exchanged soft words, and their hearts palpitated when the cork bobbed on the water. Ah, could they ever forget those charming hours, during which, seated side by side, they listened to the murmurs of the river?

The sun was fast approaching the western horizon, and despite the combined skill of Suzel and Frantz, there had not been a bite. The barbels had not shown themselves complacent, and seemed to scoff at the two young people, who were too just to bear them malice.

"We shall be more lucky another time, Frantz," said Suzel, as the young angler put up his still virgin hook.

"Let us hope so," replied Frantz.

Then walking side by side, they turned their steps towards the house, without exchanging a word, as mute as their shadows which stretched out before them. Suzel became very, very tall under the oblique rays of the setting sun. Frantz appeared very, very thin, like the long rod which he held in his hand.

They reached the burgomaster's house. Green tufts of grass bordered the shining pavement, and no one would have thought of tearing them away, for they deadened the noise made by the passers-by.

As they were about to open the door, Frantz thought it his duty to say to Suzel,—

"You know, Suzel, the great day is approaching?"

"It is indeed, Frantz," replied the young girl, with downcast eyes.

"Yes," said Frantz, "in five or six years—"

"Good-bye, Frantz," said Suzel.

"Good-bye, Suzel," replied Frantz.

And, after the door had been closed, the young man resumed the way to his father's house with a calm and equal pace.

CHAPTER 7

IN WHICH THE ANDANTES BECOME ALLEGROS, AND THE ALLEGROS VIVACES

THE agitation caused by the Schut and Custos affair had subsided. The affair led to no serious consequences. It appeared likely that Quiquendone would return to its habitual apathy, which that unexpected event had for a moment disturbed.

Meanwhile, the laying of the pipes destined to conduct the oxyhydric gas into the principal edifices of the town was proceeding rapidly. The main pipes and branches gradually crept beneath the pavements. But the burners were still wanting; for, as it required delicate skill to make them, it was necessary that they should be fabricated abroad. Doctor Ox was here, there, and everywhere; neither he nor Ygène, his assistant, lost a moment, but they urged on the workmen, completed the delicate mechanism of the gasometer, fed day and night the immense piles which decomposed the water under the influence of a powerful electric current. Yes, the doctor was already making his gas, though the pipe-laying was not yet done; a fact which, between ourselves, might have seemed a little singular. But before long,—at least there was reason to hope so,—before long Doctor Ox would inaugurate the splendours of his invention in the theatre of the town.

For Quiquendone possessed a theatre—a really fine edifice, in truth—the interior and exterior arrangement of which combined every style of architecture. It was at once Byzantine, Roman, Gothic, Renaissance, with semicircular doors,

Pointed windows, Flamboyant rose-windows, fantastic bell-turrets,—in a word, a specimen of all sorts, half a Parthenon, half a Parisian Grand Café. Nor was this surprising, the theatre having been commenced under the burgomasters Ludwig Van Tricasse, in 1175, and only finished in 1837, under the burgomaster Natalis Van Tricasse. It had required seven hundred years to build it, and it had been successively adapted to the architectural style in vogue in each period. But for all that it was an imposing structure; the Roman pillars and Byzantine arches of which would appear to advantage lit up by the oxyhydric gas.

Pretty well everything was acted at the theatre of Quiquendone; but the opera and the opera comique were especially patronized. It must, however, be added that the composers would never have recognized their own works, so entirely changed were the "movements" of the music.

In short, as nothing was done in a hurry at Quiquendone, the dramatic pieces had to be performed in harmony with the peculiar temperament of the Quiquendonians. Though the doors of the theatre were regularly thrown open at four o'clock and closed again at ten, it had never been known that more than two acts were played during the six intervening hours. "Robert le Diable," "Les Huguenots," or "Guillaume Tell" usually took up three evenings, so slow was the execution of these masterpieces. The *vivaces,* at the theatre of Quiquendone, lagged like real *adagios*. The *allegros* were "long-drawn out" indeed. The demisemiquavers were scarcely equal to the ordinary semibreves of other countries. The most rapid runs, performed according to Quiquendonian taste, had the solemn march of a chant. The gayest shakes were languishing and measured, that they might not shock the ears of the *dilettanti*. To give an example, the rapid air sung by Figaro, on his entrance in the first act of "Le Barbier de Séville," lasted fifty-eight minutes—when the actor was particularly enthusiastic.

Artists from abroad, as might be supposed, were forced to conform themselves to Quiquendonian fashions; but as they were well paid, they did not complain, and willingly obeyed the leader's baton, which never beat more than eight measures to the minute in the *allegros*.

But what applause greeted these artists, who enchanted without ever wearying the audiences of Quiquendone! All hands clapped one after another at tolerably long intervals, which the papers characterized as "frantic applause;" and sometimes nothing but the lavish prodigality with which mortar and stone had been used in the twelfth century saved the roof of the hall from falling in.

Besides, the theatre had only one performance a week, that these enthusiastic Flemish folk might not be too much excited; and this enabled the actors to study their parts more thoroughly, and the spectators to digest more at leisure the beauties of the masterpieces brought out.

Such had long been the drama at Quiquendone. Foreign artists were in the habit of making engagements with the director of the town, when they wanted to rest after their exertions in other scenes; and it seemed as if nothing could ever change these inveterate customs, when, a fortnight after the Schut-Custos affair, an unlooked-for incident occurred to throw the population into fresh agitation.

It was on a Saturday, an opera day. It was not yet intended, as may well be supposed, to inaugurate the new illumination. No; the pipes had reached the hall, but, for reasons indicated above, the burners had not yet been placed, and the wax-candles still shed their soft light upon the numerous spectators who filled the theatre. The doors had been opened to the public at one o'clock, and by three the hall was half full. A queue had at one time been formed, which extended as far as the end of the Place Saint Ernuph, in front of the shop of Josse Lietrinck the apothecary. This eagerness was significant of an unusually attractive performance.

"Are you going to the theatre this evening?" inquired the counsellor the same morning of the burgomaster.

"I shall not fail to do so," returned Van Tricasse, "and I shall take Madame Van Tricasse, as well as our daughter Suzel and our dear Tatanémance, who all dote on good music."

"Mademoiselle Suzel is going then?"

"Certainly, Niklausse."

"Then my son Frantz will be one of the first to arrive," said Niklausse.

"A spirited boy, Niklausse," replied the burgomaster sententiously; "but hot-headed! He will require watching!"

"He loves, Van Tricasse,—he loves your charming Suzel."

"Well, Niklausse, he shall marry her. Now that we have agreed on this marriage, what more can he desire?"

"He desires nothing, Van Tricasse, the dear boy! But, in short—we'll say no more about it—he will not be the last to get his ticket at the box-office."

"Ah, vivacious and ardent youth!" replied the burgomaster, recalling his own past. "We have also been thus, my worthy counsellor! We have loved—we too! We have danced attendance in our day! Till to-night, then, till to-night! By-the-bye, do you know this Fiovaranti is a great artist? And what a welcome he has received among us! It will be long before he will forget the applause of Quiquendone!"

The tenor Fiovaranti was, indeed, going to sing; Fiovaranti, who, by his talents as a virtuoso, his perfect method, his melodious voice, provoked a real enthusiasm among the lovers of music in the town.

For three weeks Fiovaranti had been achieving a brilliant success in "Les Huguenots." The first act, interpreted according to the taste of the Quiquendonians, had occupied an entire evening of the first week of the month.—Another evening in the second week, prolonged by infinite *andantes*, had elicited for the celebrated singer a real ovation. His success had been still more marked in the third act of Meyerbeer's masterpiece. But now Fiovaranti was to appear in the fourth act, which was to be performed on this evening before an impatient public. Ah, the duet between Raoul and Valentine, that pathetic love-song for two voices, that strain so full of *crescendos, stringendos,* and *più crescendos*—all this, sung slowly, compendiously, interminably! Ah, how delightful!

At four o'clock the hall was full. The boxes, the orchestra, the pit, were overflowing. In the front stalls sat the Burgomaster Van Tricasse, Mademoiselle Van Tricasse, Madame Van Tricasse, and the amiable Tatanémance in a green bonnet; not far off were the Counsellor Niklausse and his family, not forgetting the amourous Frantz. The families of Custos the doctor, of Schut the advocate, of Honoré Syntax the chief judge, of Norbet Sontman the insurance director, of the banker Collaert, gone mad on German music, and himself somewhat of an amateur, and the teacher Rupp, and the master of the academy, Jerome Resh, and the civil commissary, and so many other notabilities of the town that they could not be enumerated here without wearying the reader's patience, were visible in different parts of the hall.

It was customary for the Quiquendonians, while awaiting the rise of the curtain, to sit silent, some reading the paper, others whispering low to each other, some making their way to their seats slowly and noiselessly, others casting timid looks towards the bewitching beauties in the galleries.

But on this evening a looker-on might have observed that, even before the curtain rose, there was unusual animation among the audience. People were restless who were never known to be restless before. The ladies' fans fluttered with abnormal rapidity. All appeared to be inhaling air of exceptional stimulating power. Every one breathed more freely. The eyes of some became unwontedly bright, and seemed to give forth a light equal to that of the candles, which themselves certainly threw a more brilliant light over the hall. It was evident that people saw more clearly, though the number of candles had not been increased. Ah, if Doctor Ox's experiment were being tried! But it was not being tried, as yet.

The musicians of the orchestra at last took their places. The first violin had gone to the stand to give a modest *la* to his colleagues. The stringed instruments, the wind instruments, the drums and cymbals, were in accord. The conductor only waited the sound of the bell to beat the first bar.

The bell sounds. The fourth act begins. The *allegro appassionato* of the inter-act is played as usual, with a majestic deliberation which would have made Meyerbeer frantic, and all the majesty of which was appreciated by the Quiquendonian *dilettanti*.

But soon the leader perceived that he was no longer master of his musicians. He found it difficult to restrain them, though usually so obedient and calm. The wind instruments betrayed a tendency to hasten the movements, and it was necessary to hold them back with a firm hand, for they would otherwise outstrip the stringed instruments; which, from a musical point of view, would have been disastrous. The bassoon himself, the son of Josse Lietrinck the apothecary, a well-bred young man, seemed to lose his self-control.

Meanwhile Valentine has begun her recitative, "I am along," &c.; but she hurries it.

The leader and all his musicians, perhaps unconsciously, follow her in her *cantabile*, which should be taken deliberately, like a 12⁄8 as it is. When Raoul appears at the door at the bottom of the stage, between the moment when Valentine goes to him and that when she conceals herself in the chamber at the side, a quarter of an hour does not elapse; while formerly, according to the traditions of the Quiquendone theatre, this recitative of thirty-seven bars was wont to last just thirty-seven minutes.

Saint Bris, Nevers, Cavannes, and the Catholic nobles have appeared, somewhat prematurely, perhaps, upon the scene. The composer has marked *allergo pomposo* on the score. The orchestra and the lords proceed *allegro* indeed, but not at all *pomposo*, and at the chorus, in the famous scene of the "benediction of the poniards," they no longer keep to the enjoined *allegro*. Singers and musicians broke away impetuously. The leader does not even attempt to restrain them. Nor do the public protest; on the contrary, the people find themselves carried away, and see that they are involved in the movement, and that the movement responds to the impulses of their souls.

"will you, with me, deliver the land,
From troubles increasing, an impious band?"

They promise, they swear. Nevers has scarcely time to protest, and to sing that "among his ancestors were many soldiers, but never an assassin." He is arrested. The police and the aldermen rush forward and rapidly swear "to strike all at once." Saint Bris shouts the recitative which summons the Catholics to vengeance. The three monks, with white scarfs, hasten in by the door at the back of Nevers's room, without making any account of the stage directions, which enjoin on them to advance slowly. Already all the artists have drawn sword or poniard, which the three monks bless in a trice. The soprani tenors, bassos, attach the *allegro furioso* with cries of rage, and of a dramatic 6/8 time they make it 6/8 quadrille time. Then they rush out, bellowing,—

"At midnight,
Noiselessly,
God wills it,
Yes,
At midnight,"

At this moment the audience start to their feet. Everybody is agitated—in the boxes, the pit, the galleries. It seems as if the spectators are about to rush upon the stage, the Burgomaster Van Tricasse at their head, to join with the conspirators and annihilate the Huguenots, whose religious opinions, however, they share. They applaud, call before the curtain, make loud acclamations! Tatanémance grasps her bonnet with feverish hand. The candles throw out a lurid glow of light.

Raoul, instead of slowly raising the curtain, tears it apart with a superb gesture and finds himself confronting Valentine.

At last! It is the grand duet, and it starts off *allegro vivace*. Raoul does not wait for Valentine's pleading, and Valentine does not wait for Raoul's responses.

The fine passage beginning, "Danger is passing, time is flying," becomes one of those rapid airs which have made Offenbach famous, when he composes a dance for conspirators. The *andante amoroso*, "Thou hast said it, aye, thou lovest me," becomes a real *vivace furioso*, and the violoncello ceases to imitate the inflections of the singer's voice, as indicated in the composer's score. In vain Raoul cries, "Speak on, and prolong the ineffable slumber of my soul." Valentine cannot "prolong." It is evident that an unaccustomed fire devours her. Her *b's* and her *c's* above the stave were dreadfully shrill. He struggles, he gesticulates, he is all in a glow.

The alarum is heard; the bell resounds; but what a panting bell! The bell-ringer has evidently lost his self-control. It is a frightful toscin, which violently struggles against the fury of the orchestra.

Finally the air which ends this magnificent act, beginning, "No more love, no more intoxication, O the remorse that oppresses me!" which the composer marks *allegro con moto*, becomes a wild *prestissimo*. You would say an express-train was whirling by. The alarum resounds again. Valentine falls fainting. Raoul precipitates himself from the window.

It was high time. The orchestra, really intoxicated, could not have gone on. The leader's baton is no longer anything but a broken stick on the prompter's box. The violin strings are broken, and their necks twisted. In his fury the drummer has burst his drum. The counter-bassist has perched on the top of his musical monster. The first clarionet has swallowed the reed of his instrument,

They hustle each other to get out.

and the second hautboy is chewing his reed keys. The groove of the trombone is strained, and finally the unhappy cornist cannot withdraw his hand from the bell of his horn, into which he had thrust it too far.

And the audience! The audience, panting, all in a heat, gesticulates and howls. All the faces are as red as if a fire were burning within their bodies. They crowd each other, hustle each other to get out—the men without hats, the women without mantles! They elbow each other in the corridors, crush between the doors, quarrel, fight! There are no longer any officials, any burgomaster. All are equal amid this infernal frenzy!

Some moments after, when all have reached the street, each one resumes his habitual tranquillity, and peaceably enters his house, with a confused remembrance of what he has just experienced.

The fourth act of the "Huguenots," which formerly lasted six hours, began, on this evening at half-past four, and ended at twelve minutes before five.

It had only lasted eighteen minutes!

CHAPTER 8

IN WHICH THE ANCIENT AND SOLEMN GERMAN WALTZ BECOMES A WHIRLWIND

BUT if the spectators, on leaving the theatre, resumed their customary calm, if they quietly regained their homes, perserving only a sort of passing stupefaction, they had none the less undergone a remarkable exaltation, and overcome and weary as if they had committed some excess of dissipation, they fell heavily upon their beds.

The next day each Quiquendonian had a kind of recollection of what had occurred the evening before. One missed his hat, lost in the hubbub; another a coat-flap, torn in the brawl; one her delicately fashioned shoe, another her best mantle. Memory returned to these worthy people, and with it a certain shame for their unjustifiable agitation. It seemed to them an orgy in which they were the unconscious heroes and heroines. They did not speak of it; they did not wish to think of it. But the most astounded personage in the town was Van Tricasse the burgomaster.

The next morning, on waking, he could not find his wig. Lotchè looked everywhere for it, but in vain. The wig had remained on the field of battle. As for having it publicly claimed by Jean Mistrol, the town-crier,—no, it would not do. It were better to lose the wig than to advertise himself thus, as he had the honour to be the first magistrate of Quiquendone.

The worthy Van Tricasse was reflecting upon this, extended beneath his sheets, with bruised body, heavy head, furred tongue, and burning breast. He felt no desire to get up; on the contrary; and his brain worked more during this morning than it had probably worked before for forty years. The worthy magistrate recalled to his mind all the incidents of the incomprehensible performance. He connected them with the events which had taken place shortly before at Doctore Ox's reception. He tried to discover the causes of the singular excitability which, on two occasions, had betrayed itself in the best citizens of the town.

"What *can* be going on?" he asked himself. "What giddy spirit has taken possesstion of my peaceable town of Quiquendone? Are we about to go mad, and must we make the town one vast asylum? For yesterday we were all there, notables, counsellors, judges, advocates, physicians, schoolmasters; and all, if my memory serves me,—all of us were assailed by this excess of furious folly! But what was there in that infernal music? It is inexplicable! Yet I certainly ate or drank nothing which could put me into such a state. No; yesterday I had for dinner a slice of overdone veal, several spoonfuls of spinach with sugar, eggs, and a little beer and water,—that couldn't get into my head! No! There is something that I cannot explain, and as, after all, I am responsible for the conduct of the citizens, I will have an investigation."

But the investigation, though decided upon by the municipal council, produced no result. If the facts were clear, the causes escaped the sagacity of the magistrates. Besides, tranquillity, had been restored in the public mind, and with tranquillity, forgetfulness of the strange scenes of the theatre. The newspapers avoided speaking of them, and the account of the performance which appeared in the "Quiquendone Memorial," made no allusion to this intoxication of the entire audience.

Meanwhile, though the town resumed its habitual phlegm, and became apparently Flemish as before, it was observable that, at bottom, the character and temperament of the people changed little by little. One might have truly said, with Dominique Custos, the doctor, that "their nerves were affected."

Let us explain. This undoubted change only took place under certain conditions. When the Quiquendonians passed through the streets of the town, walked in the squares or along the Vaar, they were always the cold and methodical people of former days. So, too, when they remained at home, some working with their hands and others with their heads,—these doing nothing, those thinking nothing,—their private life was silent, inert, vegetating as before. No quarrels, no household squabbles, no acceleration in the beating of the heart, no excitement of the brain. The mean of their pulsations remained as it was of old, from fifty to fifty-two per minute.

But, strange and inexplicable phenomenon though it was, which would have defied the sagacity of the most ingenious physiologists of the day, if the inhabitants of Quiquendone did not change in their home life, they were visibly changed in their civil life and in their relations between man and man, to which it leads.

If they met together in some public edifice, it did not "work well," as Commissary Passauf expressed it. On 'change, at the town-hall, in the amphitheatre of the academy, at the sessions of the council, as well as at the reunions of the *savants*, a strange excitement seized the assembled citizens. Their relations with each other became embarrassing before they had been together an hour. In two hours the discussion degenerated into an angry dispute. Heads became heated, and personalities were used. Even at church, during the sermon, the faithful could not listen to Van Stabel, the minister, in patience, and he threw himself about in the pulpit and lectured his flock with far more than his usual severity. At last this state of things brought about altercations more grave, alas!

than that between Custos and Schut, and if they did not require the interference of the authorities, it was because the antagonists, after returning home, found there, with its calm, forgetfulness of the offences offered and received.

This peculiarity could not be observed by these minds, which were absolutely incapable of recognizing what was passing in them. One person only in the town, he whose office the council had thought of suppressing for thirty years, Michael Passauf, had remarked that this excitement, which was absent from private houses, quickly revealed itself in public edifices; and he asked himself, not without a certain anxiety, what would happen if this infection should ever develope itself in the family mansions, and if the epidemic—this was the word he used—should extend through the streets of the town. Then there would be no more forgetfulness of insults, no more tranquillity, no intermission in the delirium; but a permanent inflammation, which would inevitably bring the Quiquendonians into collision with each other.

"What would happen then?" Commissary Passauf asked himself in terror. "How could these furious savages be arrested? How check these goaded temperaments? My office would be no longer a sinecure, and the council would be obliged to double my salary—unless it should arrest me myself, for disturbing the public peace!"

These very reasonable fears began to be realized. The infection spread from 'change, the theatre, the church, the town-hall, the academy, the market, into private houses, and that in less than a fornight after the terrible performance of the "Huguenots."

Its first symptoms appeared in the house of Collaert, the banker.

That wealthy personage gave a ball, or at least a dancing-party, to the notabilities of the town. He had issued, some months before, a loan of thirty thousand francs, three quarters of which had been subscribed; and to celebrate this financial success, he had opened his drawing-rooms, and given a party to his fellow-citizens.

Everybody knows that Flemish parties are innocent and tranquil enough, the principal expense of which is usually in beer and syrups. Some conversation on the weather, the appearance of the crops, the fine condition of the gardens, the care of flowers, and especially of tulips; a slow and measured dance, from time to time, perhaps a minuet; sometimes a waltz, but one of those German waltzes which achieve a turn and a half per minute, and during which the dancers hold each other as far apart as their arms will permit,—such is the usual fashion of the balls attended by the aristocratic society of Quiquendone. The polka, after being altered to four time, had tried to become accustomed to it; but the dancers always lagged behind the orchestra, no matter how slow the measure, and it had to be abandoned.

These peaceable reunions, in which the youths and maidens enjoyed an honest and moderate pleasure, had never been attended by any outburst of ill-nature. Why, then, on this evening at Collaert the banker's, did the syrups seem to be transformed into heady wines, into sparkling champagne, into heating punches? Why, towards the middle of the evening, did a sort of mysterious intoxication take possession of the guests? Why did the minuet become a jig? Why did the orchestra hurry with its harmonies? Why did the candles, just as at the theatre, burn with unwonted refulgence? What electric current invaded the banker's drawing-rooms? How happened it that the couples held each other so closely, and clasped each other's hands so convulsively, that the "cavaliers seuls" made themselves conspicuous by certain extraordinary steps in that figure usually so grave, so solemn, so majestic, so very proper?

Alas! what Œdipus could have answered these unsolvable questions? Commissary Passauf, who was present at the party, saw the storm coming distinctly, but he could not control it or fly from it, and he felt a kind of intoxication entering his own brain. All his physical and emotional faculties increased in intensity. He was seen, several times, to throw himself upon the confectionery and devour the dishes, as if he had just broken a long fast.

The animation of the ball was increasing all this while. A long murmur, like a dull buzzing, escaped from all breasts. They danced—really danced. The feet were agitated by increasing frenzy. The faces became as purple as those of Silenus. The eyes shone like carbuncles. The general fermentation rose to the highest pitch.

And when the orchestra thundered out the waltz in "Der Freyschütz,"—when this waltz, so German, and with a movement so slow, was attacked with wild arms by the musicians,—ah! it was no longer a waltz, but an insensate whirwind, a giddy rotation, a gyration worthy of being led by some Mephistopheles, beating the measure with a firebrand! Then a galop, an infernal galop, which lasted an hour without any one being able to stop it, whirled off, in its windings, across the halls, the drawing-rooms, the ante-chambers, by the staircases, from the cellar to the garret of the opulent mansion, the young men and young girls, the fathers and mothers, people of every age, of every weight, of both sexes; Collaert, the fat banker, and Madame Collaert, and the counsellors, and the magistrates, and the chief justice, and Niklausse, and Madame Van Tricasse, and the Burgomaster Van Tricasse, and the Commissary Passauf himself, who never could recall afterwards who had been his partner on that terrible evening.

But *she* did not forget! And ever since that day she has seen in her dreams the fiery commissary, enfolding her in an impassioned embrace! And "she"—was the amiable Tatanémance!

CHAPTER 9

IN WHICH DOCTOR OX AND YGÈNE, HIS ASSISTANT, SAY A FEW WORDS

"WELL, Ygène?"

"Well, master, all is ready. The laying of the pipes is finished."

"At last! Now then, we are going to operate on a large scale, on the masses!"

CHAPTER 10

IN WHICH IT WILL BE SEEN THAT THE EPIDEMIC INVADES THE ENTIRE TOWN, AND WHAT EFFECT IT PRODUCES

DURING THE following months the evil, in place of subsiding, became more extended. From private houses the epidemic spread into the streets. The town of Quiquendone was no longer to be recognized.

A phenomenon yet stranger than those which had already happened, now appeared; not only the animal kingdom, but the vegetable kingdom itself, became subject to the mysterious influence.

According to the ordinary course of things, epidemics are special in their operation. Those which attack humanity spare the animals, and those which attack the animals spare the vegetables. A horse was never inflicted with small-pox, nor a man with the cattle-plague, nor do sheep suffer from the potato-rot. But here all the laws of nature seemed to be overturned. Not only were the character, temperament, and ideas of the townsfolk changed, but the domestic animals—dogs and cats, horses and cows, asses and goats—suffered from this epidemic influence, as if their habitual equilibrium had been changed. The plants themselves were infected by a similar strange metamorphosis.

In the gardens and vegetable patches and orchards very curious symptoms manifested themselves. Climbing plants climbed more audaciously. Tufted plants became more tufted than ever. Shrubs became trees. Cereals, scarcely sown, showed their little green heads, and gained, in the same length of time, as much in inches as formerly, under the most favourable circumstances, they had gained in fractions. Asparagus attained the height of several feet; the artichokes swelled to the size of melons, the melons to the size of pumpkins, the pumpkins to the size of gourds, the gourds to the size of the belfry bell, which measured, in truth, nine feet in diameter. The cabbages were bushes, and the mushrooms umbrellas.

The fruits did not lag behind the vegetables. It required two persons to eat a strawberry, and four to consume a pear. The grapes also attained the enormous proportions of those so well depicted by Poussin in his "Return of the Envoys to the Promised Land."

It was the same with the flowers: immense violets spread the most penetrating perfumes through the air; exaggerated roses shone with the brightest colours; lilies formed, in a few days, impenetrable copses; geraniums, daisies, camelias, rhododendrons, invaded the garden walks, and stifled each other. And the tulips,—those dear liliaceous plants so dear to the Flemish heart,—what emotion they must have caused to their zealous cultivators! The worthy Van Bistrom nearly fell over backwards, one day, on seeing in his garden an enormous "Tulipa gesneriana," a gigantic monster, whose cup afforded space to a nest for a whole family of robins!

The entire town flocked to see this floral phenomenon, and renamed it the "Tulipa quiquendonia."

But alas! if these plants, these fruits, these flowers, grew visibly to the naked eye, if all the vegetables insisted on assuming colossal proportions, if the brilliancy of their colours and perfume intoxicated the smell and the sight, they quickly withered. The air which they absorbed rapidly exhausted them, and they soon died, faded, and dried up.

Such was the fate of the famous tulip, which, after several days of splendour, became emaciated, and fell lifeless.

It was soon the same with the domestic animals, from the house-dog to the stable pig, from the canary in its cage to the turkey of the back-court. It must be said that in ordinary times these animals were not less phlegmatic than their masters. The dogs and cats vegetated rather than lived. They never betrayed a wag of pleasure nor a snarl of wrath. Their tails moved no more than if they had been made of bronze. Such a thing as a bite or scratch from any of them had not been known from time immemorial. As for mad dogs, they were looked upon as imaginary beasts, like the griffins and the rest in the menagerie of the apocalypse.

But what a change had taken place in a few months, the smallest incidents of which we are trying to reproduce! Dogs and cats began to show teeth and claws. Several executions had taken place after reiterated offences. A horse was seen, for the first time, to take his bit in his teeth and rush through the streets of Quiquendone; an ox was observed to precipitate itself, with lowered horns, upon one of his herd; an ass was seen to turn himself over, with his legs in the air, in the Place Saint Ernuph, and bray as ass never brayed before; a sheep, actually a sheep, defended valiantly the cutlets within him from the butcher's knife.

Van Tricasse, the burgomaster, was forced to make police regulations concerning the domestic animals, as, seized with lunacy, they rendered the streets of Quiquendone unsafe.

But alas! if the animals were mad, the men were scarcely less so. No age was spared by the scourge. Babies soon became quite insupportable, though till now so easy to bring up; and for the first time Honoré Syntax, the judge, was obliged to apply the rod to his youthful offspring.

There was a kind on insurrection at the high school, and the dictionaries became formidable missiles in the classes. The scholars would not submit to be shut in, and, besides, the infection took the teachers themselves, who overwhelmed the boys and girls with extravagant tasks and punishments.

Another strange phenomenon occurred. All these Quiquendonians, so sober before, whose chief food had been whipped creams, committed wild excesses in their eating and drinking. Their usual regimen no longer sufficed. Each stomach was transformed into a gulf, and it became necessary to fill this gulf by the most energetic means. The consumption of the town was trebled. Instead of two repasts they had six. Many cases of indigestion were reported. The Counsellor Niklausse could not satisfy his hunger. Van Tricasse found it impossible to assuage his thirst, and remained in a state of rabid semi-intoxication.

In short, the most alarming symptoms manifested themselves and increased from day to day. Drunken people staggered in the streets, and these were often citizens of high position.

Dominique Custos, the physician, had plenty to do with the heartburns, inflammations, and nervous affections, which proved to what a strange degree the nerves of the people had been irritated.

There were daily quarrels and altercations in the once deserted but now crowded streets of Quiquendone; for nobody could any longer stay at home. It was necessary to establish a new police force to control the disturbers of the public peace. A prison-cage was established in the Town Hall, and speedily became full, night and day of refractory offenders. Commissary Passauf was in despair.

A marriage was concluded in less than two months,—such a thing had never been seen before. Yes, the son of Rupp, the schoolmaster, wedded the daughter of Augustine de Rovere, and that fifty-seven days only after he had petitioned for her hand and heart!

Other marriages were decided upon, which, in old times, would have remained in doubt and discussion for years. The burgomaster perceived that his own daughter, the charming Suzel, was escaping from his hands.

As for dear Tatanémance, she had dared to sound Commissary Passauf on the subject of a union, which seemed to her to combine every element of happiness, fortune, honour, youth!

At last,—to reach the depths of abomination,—a duel took place! Yes, a duel with pistols—horse-pistols—at seventy-five paces, with ball-cartridges. And between whom? Our readers will never believe!

Between M. Frantz Niklausse, the gentle angler, and young Simon Collaert, the wealthy banker's son.

And the cause of this duel was the burgomaster's daughter, for whom Simon discovered himself to be fired with passion, and whom he refused to yield to the claims of an audacious rival!

CHAPTER 11

IN WHICH THE QUIQUENDONIANS ADOPT A HEROIC RESOLUTION

We have seen to what a deplorable condition the people of Quiquendone were reduced. Their heads were in a ferment. They no longer knew or recognized themselves. The most peaceable citizens had become quarrelsome. If you looked at them askance, they would speedily send you a challenge. Some let their moustaches grow, and several—the most belligerent—curled them up at the ends.

This being their condition, the administration of the town and the maintenance of order in the streets became difficult tasks, for the government had not been organized for such a state of things. The burgomaster—that worthy Van Tricasse whom we have seen so placid, so dull, so incapable of coming to any decision—the burgomaster became intractable. His house resounded with the sharpness of his voice. He made twenty decisions a day, scolding his officials, and himself enforcing the regulations of his administration.

Ah, what a change! The amiable and tranquil mansion of the burgomaster, that good Flemish home—where was its former calm? What changes had taken place in your household economy! Madame Van Tricasse had become acrid,

It required two persons to eat a strawberry.

whimsical, harsh. Her husband sometimes succeeded in drowning her voice by talking louder than she, but could not silence her. The petulant humour of this worthy dame was excited by everything. Nothing went right. The servants offended her every moment. Tatanémance, her sister-in-law, who was not less irritable, replied sharply to her. M. Van Tricasse naturally supported Lotchè, his servant, as is the case in all good households; and this permanently exasperated Madame, who constantly disputed, discussed, and made scenes with her husband.

"What on earth is the matter with us?" cried the unhappy burgomaster. "What is this fire that is devouring us? Are we possessed with the devil? Ah, Madame Van Tricasse, Madame Van Tricasse, you will end by making me die before you, and thus violate all the traditions of the family!"

The reader will not have forgotten the strange custom by which M. Van Tricasse would become a widower and marry again, so as not to break the chain of descent.

Meanwhile, this disposition of all minds produced other curious effects worthy of note. This excitement, the cause of which has so far escaped us, brought about unexpected physiological changes. Talents, hitherto unrecognized, betrayed themselves. Aptitudes were suddenly revealed. Artists, before commonplace, displayed new ability. Politicians and authors arose. Orators proved themselves equal to the most arduous debates, and on every question inflamed audiences which were quite ready to be inflamed. From the sessions of the council, this movement spread to the public political meetings, and a club was formed at Quiquendone; whilst twenty newspapers, the "Quiquendone Signal," the "Quiquendone Impartial," the "Quiquendone Radical," and so on, written in an inflammatory style, raised the most important questions.

But what about? you will ask. Apropos of everything, and of nothing; apropos of the Oudenarde tower, which was falling, and which some wished to pull down, and others to prop up; apropos of the police regulations issued by the council, which some obstinate citizens threatened to resist; apropos of the sweeping of the gutters, repairing the sewers, and so on. Nor did the enraged orators confine themselves to the internal administration of the town. Carried on by the current they went further, and essayed to plunge their fellow-citizens into the hazards of war.

Quiquendone had had for eight or nine hundred years a *casus belli* of the best quality; but she had preciously laid it up like a relic, and there had seemed some probability that it would become effete, and no longer serviceable.

This was what had given rise to the *casus belli*.

It is not generally known that Quiquendone, in this cosy corner of Flanders, lies next to the little town of Virgamen. The territories of the two communites are contiguous.

Well, in 1185, some time before Count Baldwin's departure to the Crusades, a Virgamen cow—not a cow belonging to a citizen, but a cow which was common property, let it be observed—audaciously ventured to pasture on the territory of Quiquendone. This unfortunate beast had scarcely eaten three mouthfuls; but the offence, the abuse, the crime—whatever you will—was committed and duly indicted, for the magistrates, at that time, had already begun to know how to write.

"We will take revenge at the proper moment," said simply Natalis Van

Tricasse, the thirty-second predecessor of the burgomaster of this story, "and the Virgamenians will lose nothing by waiting."

The Virgamenians were forewarned. They waited thinking, without doubt, that the remembrance of the offence would fade away with the lapse of time; and really, for several centuries, they lived on good terms with their neighbours of Quiquendone.

But they counted without their hosts, or rather without this strange epidemic, which, radically changing the character of the Quiquendonians, aroused their dormant vengeance.

It was at the club of the Rue Monstrelet that the truculent orator Schut, abruptly introducing the subject to his hearers, inflamed them with the expressions and metaphors used on such occasions. He recalled the offence, the injury which had been done to Quiquendone, and which a nation "jealous of its rights" could not admit as a precedent; he showed the insult to be still existing, the wound still bleeding: he spoke of certain special head-shakings on the part of the people of Virgamen, which indicated in what degree of contempt they regarded the people of Quiquendone; he appealed to his fellow-citizens, who, unconsciously perhaps, had supported this mortal insult for long centuries; he adjured the "children of the ancient town" to have no other purpose than to obtain a substantial reparation. And, lastly, he made an appeal to "all the living energies of the nation!"

With what enthusiasm these words, so new to Quiquendonian ears, were greeted, may be surmised, but cannot be told. All the auditors rose, and with extended arms demanded war with loud cries. Never had the Advocate Schut achieved such a success, and it must be avowed that his triumphs were not few.

The burgomaster, the counsellor, all the notabilities present at this memorable meeting, would have vainly attempted to resist the popular outburst. Besides, they had no desire to do so, and cried as loud, if not louder, than the rest,—

"To the frontier! To the frontier!"

As the frontier was but three kilometers from the walls of Quiquendone, it is certain that the Virgamenians ran a real danger, for they might easily be invaded without having had time to look about them.

Meanwhile, Josse Liefrinck, the worthy chemist, who alone had preserved his senses on this grave occasion, tried to make his fellow-citizens comprehend that guns, cannon, and generals were equally wanting to their design.

They replied to him, not without many impatient gestures, that these generals, cannons and guns would be improvised; that the right and love of country sufficed, and rendered a people irresistible.

Hereupon the burgomaster himself came forward, and in a sublime harangue made short work of those pusillanimous people who disguise their fear under a veil of prudence, which veil he tore off with a patriotic hand.

At this sally it seemed as if the hall would fall in under the applause.

The vote was eagerly demanded, and was taken amid acclamations.

The cries of "To Virgamen! to Virgamen!" redoubled.

The burgomaster then took it upon himself to put the armies in motion, and in the name of the town he promised the honours of a triumph, such as was given in the times of the Romans to that one of its generals who should return victorious.

Meanwhile, Josse Liefrinck, who was an obstinate fellow, and did not regard himself as beaten, though he really had been, insisted on making another observation. He wished to remark that the triumph was only accorded at Rome to those victorious generals who had killed five thousand of the enemy.

"Well, well!" cried the meeting deliriously.

"And as the population of the town of Virgamen consists of but three thousand five hundred and seventy-five inhabitants, it would be difficult, unless the same person was killed several times—"

But they did not let the luckless logician finish, and he was turned out, hustled and bruised.

"Citizens," said Pulmacher the grocer, who usually sold groceries by retail, "whatever this cowardly apothecary may have said, I engage by myself to kill five thousand Virgamenians, if you will accept my services."

"Five thousand five hundred!" cried a yet more resolute patriot.

"Six thousand six hundred!" retorted the grocer.

"Seven thousand!" cried Jean Orbideck, the confectioner of the Rue Hemling, who was on the road to a fortune by making whipped creams.

"Adjudged!" exclaimed the Burgomaster Van Tricasse, on finding that no one else rose on the bid.

And this was how Jean Orbideck the confectioner became general-in-chief of the forces of Quiquendone.

CHAPTER 12

IN WHICH YGÈNE, THE ASSISTANT, GIVES A REASONABLE PIECE OF ADVICE, WHICH IS EAGERLY REJECTED BY DOCTOR OX

"WELL, master," said Ygène next day, as he poured the pails of sulphuric acid into the troughs of the great battery.

"Well," resumed Doctor Ox, "was I not right? See to what not only the physical developments of a whole nation, but its morality, its dignity, its talents, its political sense, have come! It is only a question of molecules."

"But—"

"Do you not think that matters have gone far enough, and that these poor devils should not be excited beyond measure?"

"No, no!" cried the doctor; "no! I will go on to the end!"

"As you will, master; the experiment, however, seems to me conclusive, and I think it time to—"

"To—"

"To close the valve."

"You'd better!" cried Doctor Ox. "If you attempt it, I'll throttle you!"

"To Virgamen! To Virgamen!"

CHAPTER 13

IN WHICH IT IS ONCE MORE PROVED THAT BY TAKING HIGH GROUND ALL HUMAN LITTLENESSES MAY BE OVERLOOKED

"You say?" asked the Burgomaster Van Tricasse of the Counsellor Niklausse.

"I say that this war is necessary," replied Niklausse, firmly, "and that the time has come to avenge this insult."

"Well, I repeat to you," replied the burgomaster, tartly, "that if the people of Quiquendone do not profit by this occasion to vindicate their rights, they will be unworthy of their name."

"And as for me, I maintain that we ought, without delay, to collect our forces and lead them to the front."

"Really, monsieur, really!" replied Van Tricasse. "And do you speak thus to *me?*"

"To yourself, monsieur the burgomaster; and you shall hear the truth, unwelcome as it may be."

"And you shall hear it yourself, counsellor," returned Van Tricasse in a passion, "for it will come better from my mouth than from yours! Yes, monsieur, yes, any delay would be dishonourable. The town of Quiquendone has waited nine hundred years for the moment to take its revenge, and whatever you may say, whether it pleases you or not, we shall march upon the enemy."

"Ah, you take it thus!" replied Niklausse harshly. "Very well, monsieur, we will march without you, if it does not please you to go."

"A burgomaster's place is in the front rank, monsieur!"

"And that of a counsellor also, monsieur."

"You insult me by thwarting all my wishes," cried the burgomaster, whose fists seemed likely to hit out before long.

"And you insult me equally by doubting my patriotism," cried Niklausse, who was equally ready for a tussle.

"I tell you, monsieur, that the army of Quiquendone shall be put in motion within two days!"

"And I repeat to you, monsieur, that forty-eight hours shall not pass before we shall have marched upon the enemy!"

It is easy to see, from this fragment of conversation, that the two speakers supported exactly the same idea. Both wished for hostilities; but as their excitement disposed them to altercation, Niklausse would not listen to Van Tricasse, nor Van Tricasse to Niklausse. Had they been of contrary opinions on this grave question, had the burgomaster favoured war and the counsellor insisted on peace, the quarrel would not have been more violent. These two old friends gazed fiercely at each other. By the quickened beating of their hearts, their red faces, their contracted pupils, the trembling of their muscles, their harsh voices, it might be conjectured that they were ready to come to blows.

But the striking of a large clock happily checked the adversaries at the moment when they seemed on the point of assaulting each other.

"At last the hour has come!" cried the burgomaster.

"What hour?" asked the counsellor.

"The hour to go to the belfry tower."

"It is true, and whether it pleases you or not, I shall go, monsieur."

"And I too."

"Let us go!"

"Let us go!"

It might have been supposed from these last words that a collision had occurred, and that the adversaries were proceeding to a duel; but it was not so. It had been agreed that the burgomaster and the counsellor, as the two principal dignitaries of the town, should repair to the Town Hall, and there show themselves on the high tower which overlooked Quiquendone; that they should examine the surrounding country, so as to make the best strategetic plan for the advance of their troops.

Though they were in accord on this subject, they did not cease to quarrel bitterly as they went. Their loud voices were heard resounding in the streets; but all the passers-by were now accustomed to this; the exasperation of the dignitaries seemed quite natural, and no one took notice of it. Under the circumstances, a calm man would have been regarded as a monster.

The burgomaster and the counsellor, having reached the porch of the belfry, were in a paroxysm of fury. They were no longer red, but pale. This terrible discussion, though they had the same idea, had produced internal spasms, and every one knows that paleness shows that anger has reached its last limits.

At the foot of the narrow tower staircase there was a real explosion. Who should go up first? Who should first creep up the winding steps? Truth compels us to say that there was a tussle, and that the Counsellor Niklausse, forgetful of all that he owed to his superior, to the supreme magistrate of the town, pushed Van Tricasse violently back, and dashed up the staircase first.

Both ascended, denouncing and raging at each other at every step. It was to be feared that a terrible climax would occur on the summit of the tower, which rose three hundred and fifty-seven feet above the pavement.

The two enemies soon got out of breath, however, and in a little while, at the eightieth step, they began to move up heavily, breathing loud and short.

Then—was it because of their being out of breath?—their wrath subsided, or at least only betrayed itself by a succession of unseemly epithets. They became silent, and, strange to say, it seemed as if their excitement diminished as they ascended higher above the town. A sort of lull took place in their minds. Their brains became cooler, and simmered down like a coffee-pot when taken away from the fire. Why?

We cannot answer this "why;" but the truth is that, having reached a certain landing-stage, two hundred and sixty-six feet above ground, the two adversaries sat down and, really more calm, looked at each other without any anger in their faces.

"How high it is!" said the burgomaster, passing his handkerchief over his rubicund face.

"Very high!" returned the counsellor. "Do you know that we have gone fourteen feet higher than the Church of Saint Michael at Hamburg?"

"I know it," replied the burgomaster, in a tone of vanity very pardonable in the chief magistrate of Quiquendone.

The two notabilities soon resumed their ascent, casting curious glances through the loopholes pierced in the tower walls. The burgomaster had taken the head of the procession, without any remark on the part of the counsellor. It even happened that at about the three hundred and fourth step, Van Tricasse being completely tired out, Niklausse kindly pushed him from behind. The burgomaster offered no resistance to this, and, when he reached the platform of the tower, said graciously,—

"Thanks, Niklausse; I will do the same for you one day."

A little while before it had been two wild beasts, ready to tear each other to pieces, who had presented themselves at the foot of the tower; it was now two friends who reached its summit.

The weather was superb. It was the month of May. The sun had absorbed all the vapours. What a pure and limpid atmosphere! The most minute objects over a broad space might be discerned. The walls of Virgamen, glistening in their whiteness,—its red, pointed roofs, its belfries shining in the sunlight—appeared a few miles off. And this was the town that was foredoomed to all the horrors of fire and pillage!

The burgomaster and the counsellor sat down beside each other on a small stone bench, like two worthy people whose souls were in close sympathy. As they recovered breath, they looked around; then, after a brief silence,—

"How fine this is!" cried the burgomaster.

"Yes, it is admirable!" replied the counsellor. "Does it not seem to you, my good Van Tricasse, that humanity is destined to dwell rather at such heights, than to crawl about on the surface of our globe?"

"I agree with you, honest Niklausse," returned the burgomaster, "I agree with you. You seize sentiment better when you get clear of nature. You breathe it in every sense! It is at such heights that philosophers should be formed, and that sages should live, above the miseries of this world!"

"Shall we go around the platform?" asked the counsellor.

"Let us go around the platform," replied the burgomaster.

And the two friends, arm in arm, and putting, as formerly, long pauses between their questions and answers, examined every point of the horizon.

"It is at least seventeen years since I have ascended the belfry tower," said Van Tricasse.

"I do not think I ever came up before," replied Niklausse; "and I regret it, for the view from this height is sublime! Do you see, my friend, the pretty stream of the Vaar, as it winds among the trees?"

"And, beyond, the heights of Saint Hermandad! How gracefully they shut in the horizon! Observe that border of green trees, which Nature has so picturesquely arranged! Ah, Nature, Nature, Niklausse! Could the hand of man ever hope to rival her?"

"It is enchanting, my excellent friend," replied the counsellor. "See the flocks and herds lying in the verdant pastures,—the oxen, the cows, the sheep!"

"And the labourers going to the fields! You would say they were Arcadian shepherds; they only want a bagpipe!"

"And over all this fertile country the beautiful blue sky, which no vapour dims! Ah, Niklausse, one might become a poet here! I do not understand why Saint Simeon Stylites was not one of the greatest poets of the world."

"It was because, perhaps, his column was not high enough," replied the counsellor, with a gentle smile.

At this moment the chimes of Quiquendone rang out. The clear bells played one of their most melodious airs. The two friends listened in ectasy.

Then in his calm voice, Van Tricasse said,—

"But what, friend Niklausse, did we come to the top of this tower to do?"

"In fact," replied the counsellor, "we have permitted ourselves to be carried away by our reveries—"

"What did we come here to do?" repeated the burgomaster.

"We came," said Niklausse, "to breathe this pure air, which human weaknesses have not corrupted."

"Well, shall we descend, friend Niklausse?"

"Let us descend, friend Van Tricasse."

They gave a parting glance at the splendid panorama which spread before their eyes; then the burgomaster passed down first, and began to descend with a slow and measured pace. The counsellor followed a few steps behind. They reached the landing-stage at which they had stopped on ascending. Already their cheeks began to redden. They tarried a moment, then resumed their descent.

In a few moments Van Tricasse begged Niklausse to go more slowly, as he felt him on his heels, and it "worried him." It even did more than worry him; for twenty steps lower down he ordered the counsellor to stop, that he might get on some distance ahead.

The counsellor replied that he did not wish to remain with his leg in the air to await the good pleasure of the burgomaster, and kept on.

Van Tricasse retorted with a rude expression.

The counsellor responded by an insulting allusion to the burgomaster's age, destined as he was, by his family traditions, to marry a second time.

The burgomaster went down twenty steps more, and warned Niklausse that this should not pass thus.

Niklausse replied that, at all events, he would pass down first; and, the space being very narrow, the two dignitaries came into collision, and found themselves in utter darkness. The words "blockhead" and "booby" were the mildest which they now applied to each other.

"We shall see, stupid beast!" cried the burgomaster,—"we shall see what figure you will make in this war, and in what rank you will march!"

"In the rank that precedes yours, you silly old fool!" replied Niklausse.

Then there were other cries, and it seemed as if bodies were rolling over each other. What was going on? Why were these dispositions so quickly changed? Why were the gentle sheep of the tower's summit metamorphosed into tigers two hundred feet below it?

However this might be, the guardian of the tower, hearing the noise, opened the door, just at the moment when the two adversaries, bruised, and with protruding eyes, were in the act of tearing each other's hair,—fortunately they wore wigs.

"You shall give me satisfaction for this!" cried the burgomaster, shaking his fist under his adversary's nose.

"Whenever you please!" growled the Counsellor Niklausse, attempting to respond with a vigorous kick.

The guardian, who was himself in a passion,—I cannot say why,—thought the scene a very natural one. I know not what excitement urged him to take part in it, but he controlled himself, and went off to announce throughout the neighborhood that a hostile meeting was about to take place between the Burgomaster Van Tricasse and the Counsellor Niklausse.

CHAPTER 14

IN WHICH MATTERS GO SO FAR THAT THE INHABITANTS OF QUIQUENDON, THE READER, AND EVEN THE AUTHOR, DEMAND AN IMMEDIATE DÉNOUEMENT

THE last incident proves to what a pitch of excitement the Quiquendonians had been wrought. The two oldest friends in the town, and the most gentle—before the advent of the epidemic, to reach this degree of violence! And that, too, only a few minutes after their old mutual sympathy, their amiable instincts, their contemplative habit, had been restored at the summit of the tower!

On learning what was going on, Doctor Ox could not contain his joy. He resisted the arguments which Ygène, who saw what a serious turn affairs were taking, addressed to him. Besides, both of them were infected by the general fury. They were not less excited than the rest of the population, and they ended by quarrelling as violently as the burgomaster and the counsellor.

Besides, one question eclipsed all others, and the intended duels were postponed to the issue of the Virgamenian difficulty. No man had the right to shed his blood uselessly, when it belonged, to the last drop, to his country in danger. The affair was, in short, a grave one, and there was no withdrawing from it.

The Burgomaster Van Tricasse, despite the warlike ardour with which he was filled, had not thought it best to throw himself upon the enemy without warning him. He had, therefore, through the medium of the rural policeman, Hottering, sent to demand reparation of the Virgamenians for the offence committed, in 1195, on the Quiquendonian territory.

The authorities of Virgamen could not at first imagine of what the envoy spoke, and the latter, despite his official character, was conducted back to the frontier very cavalierly.

Van Tricasse then sent one of the aides-de-camp of the confectioner-general, citizen Hildevert Shuman, a manufacturer of barley-sugar, a very firm and energetic man, who carried to the authorities of Virgamen the original minute of the indictment drawn up in 1195 by order of the Burgomaster Natalis Van Tricasse.

The authorities of Virgamen burst out laughing, and served the aide-de-camp in the same manner as the rural policeman.

The burgomaster then assembled the dignitaries of the town.

A letter, remarkably and vigorously drawn up, was written as an ultimatum; the cause of quarrel was plainly stated, and a delay of twenty-four hours was accorded to the guilty city in which to repair the outrage done to Quiquendone.

The letter was sent off, and returned a few hours afterwards, torn to bits, which made so many fresh insults. The Virgamenians knew of old the forbearance and equanimity of the Quiquendonians, and made sport of them and their demand, of their *casus belli* and their *ultimatum*.

There was only one thing left to do,—to have recourse to arms, to invoke the God of battles, and, after the Prussian fashion, to hurl themselves upon the Virgamenians before the latter could be prepared.

This decision was made by the council in solemn conclave, in which cries, objurgations, and menacing gestures were mingled with unexampled violence. An assembly of idiots, a congress of madmen, a club of maniacs, would not have been more tumultous.

As soon as the declaration of war was known, General Jean Orbideck assembled his troops, perhaps two thousand three hundred and ninety-three combatants from a population of two thousand three hundred and ninety-three souls. The women, the children, the old men, were joined with the able-bodied males. The guns of the town had been put under requisition. Five had been found, two of which were without cocks, and these had been distributed to the advance-guard. The artillery was composed of the old culverin of the château, taken in 1339 at the attack on Quesnoy, one of the first occasions of the use of cannon in history, and which had not been fired off for five centuries. Happily for those who were appointed to take it in charge there were no projectiles with which to lead it; but such as it was, this engine might well impose on the enemy. As for side-arms, they had been taken from the museum of antiquities,—flint hatchets, helmets, Frankish battle-axes, javelins, halberds, rapiers, and so on; and also in those domestic arsenals commonly known as "cupboards" and "kitchens." But courage, the right, hatred of the foreigner, the yearning for vengeance, were to take the place of more perfect engines, and to replace—at least it was hoped so—the modern mitrailleuses and breech-loaders.

The troops were passed in review. Not a citizen failed at the roll-call. General Orbideck, whose seat on horseback was far from firm, and whose steed was a vicious beast, was thrown three times in front of the army; but he got up again without injury, and this was regarded as a favourable omen. The burgomaster, the counsellor, the civil commissary, the chief justice, the school-teacher, the banker, the rector,—in short, all the notabilities of the town,—marched at the head. There were not tears shed, either by mothers, sisters, or daughters. They urged on their husbands, fathers, brothers, to the combat, and even followed them and formed the rear-guard, under the orders of the courageous Madame Van Tricasse.

The crier, Jean Mistrol, blew his trumpet; the army moved off, and directed itself, with ferocious cries, towards the Oudenarde gate.

* * * * *

At the moment when the head of the column was about to pass the walls of the town, a man threw himself before it.

"Stop! stop! Fools that you are!" he cried. "Suspend your blows! Let me shut the valve! You are not changed in nature! You are good citizens, quiet and peaceable! If you are so excited, it is my master, Doctor Ox's, fault! It is an experiment! Under the pretext of lighting your streets with oxyhydric gas, he has saturated—"

The assistant was beside himself; but he could not finish. At the instant that the doctor's secret was about to escape his lips, Doctor Ox himself pounced upon the unhappy Ygène in an indescribable rage, and shut his mouth by blows with his fist.

It was a battle. The burgomaster, the counsellor, the dignitaries, who had stopped short on Ygène's sudden appearance, carried away in turn by their exasperation, rushed upon the two strangers, without waiting to hear either the one or the other.

Doctor Ox and his assistant, beaten and lashed, were about to be dragged, by order of Van Tricasse, to the round-house, when,—

CHAPTER 15

IN WHICH THE DÉNOUEMENT TAKES PLACE

WHEN a formidable explosion resounded. All the atmosphere which enveloped Quiquendone seemed on fire. A flame of an intensity and vividness quite unwonted shot up into the heavens like a meteor. Had it been night, this flame would have been visible for ten leagues around.

The whole army of Quiquendone fell to the earth, like an army of monks. Happily there were no victims; a few scratches and slight hurts were the only result. The confectioner, who, as chance would have it, had not fallen from his horse this time, had his plume singed, and escaped without any further injury.

What had happened?

Something very simple, as was soon learned; the gas-works had just blown up. During the absence of the doctor and his assistant, some careless mistake had no doubt been made. It is not known how or why a communication had been established between the reservoir which contained the oxygen and that which enclosed the hydrogen. An explosive mixture had resulted from the union of these two gases, to which fire had accidentally been applied.

This changed everything; but when the army got upon its feet again, Doctor Ox and his assistant Ygène had disappeared.

CHAPTER 16

IN WHICH THE INTELLIGENT READER SEES THAT HE HAS GUESSED CORRECTLY, DESPITE ALL THE AUTHOR'S PRECAUTIONS

AFTER the explosion, Quiquendone immediately became the peaceable, phlegmatic, and Flemish town it formerly was.

After the explosion, which indeed did not cause a very lively sensation, each one, without knowing why, mechanically took his way home, the burgomaster leaning on the counsellor's arm, the Advocate Schut going arm in arm with

Custos the doctor, Frantz Niklausse walking with equal familiarity with Simon Collaert, each going tranquilly, noiselessly, without even being conscious of what had happened, and having already forgotten Virgamen and their revenge. The general returned to his confections, and his aide-de-camp to the barley-sugar.

Thus everything had become calm again; the old existence had been resumed by men and beasts, beasts and plants; even by the tower of Oudenarde gate, which the explosion—these explosions are sometimes astonishing—had set upright again!

And from that time never a word was spoken more loudly than another, never a discussion took place in the town of Quiquendone. There were no more politics, no more clubs, no more trials, no more policemen! The post of the Commissary Passauf became once more a sinecure, and if his salary was not reduced, it was because the burgomaster and the counsellor could not make up their minds to decide upon it.

From time to time, indeed, Passauf flitted, without any one suspecting it, through the dreams of the inconsolable Tatanémance.

As for Frantz's rival, he generously abandoned the charming Suzel to her lover, who hastened to wed her five or six years after these events.

And as for Madame Van Tricasse, she died ten years later, at the proper time, and the burgomaster married Mademoiselle Pélagie Van Tricasse, his cousin, under excellent conditions—for the happy mortal who should succeed him.

CHAPTER 17

IN WHICH DOCTOR OX'S THEORY IS EXPLAINED

WHAT, then, had this mysterious Doctor Ox done? Tried a fantastic experiment,—nothing more.

After having laid down his gas-pipes, he had saturated, first the public buildings, then the private dwellings, finally the streets of Quiquendone, with pure oxygen, without letting in the least atom of hydrogen.

This gas, tasteless and odorless, spread in generous quantity through the atmosphere, causes, when it is breathed, serious agitation to the human organism. One who lives in an air saturated with oxygen grows excited, frantic, burns!

You scarcely return to the ordinary atmosphere before you return to your usual state. For instance, the counsellor and the burgomaster at the top of the belfry were themselves again, as the oxygen is kept, by its weight, in the lower strata of the air.

But one who lives under such conditions, breathing this gas which transforms the body physiologically as well as the soul, dies speedily, like a madman.

It was fortunate, then, for the Quiquendonians, that a providential explosion put an end to this dangerous experiment, and abolished Doctor Ox's gas-works.

To conclude: Are virtue, courage, talent, wit, imagination,—are all these qualities or faculties only a question of oxygen?

Such is Doctor Ox's theory; but we are not bound to accept it, and for ourselves we utterly reject it, in spite of the curious experiment of which the worthy old town of Quiquendone was the theatre.

The whole army of Quiquendone fell to the earth.

Master Zacharius

CHAPTER 1

A WINTER NIGHT

THE city of Geneva lies at the west end of the lake of the same name. The Rhone, which passes through the town at the outlet of the lake, divides it into two sections, and is itself divided in the centre of the city by an island placed in mid-stream. A topographical feature like this is often found in the great depôts of commerce and industry. No doubt the first inhabitants were influenced by the easy means of transport which the swift currents of the rivers offered them—those "roads which walk along of their own accord," as Pascal puts it. In the case of the Rhone, it would be the road that ran along.

Both new and regular buildings were constructed on this island, which was enclosed like a Dutch galley in the middle of the river, the curious mass of houses, piled one on the other, presented a delightfully confused *coup-d'œil*. The small area of the island had compelled some of the buildings to be perched, as it were, on the piles, which were entangled in the rough currents of the river. The huge beams, blackened by time, and worn by the water, seemed like the claws of an enormous crab, and presented a fantastic appearance. The little yellow streams, which were like cobwebs stretched amid this ancient foundation, quivered in the darkness, as if they had been the leaves of some old oak forest, while the river engulfed in this forest of piles, foamed and roared most mournfully.

One of the houses of the island was striking for its curiously aged appearance. It was the dwelling of the old clockmaker, Master Zacharius, whose household consisted of his daughter Gerande; Aubert Thun, his apprentice, and his old servant Scholastique.

There was no man in Geneva to compare in interest with this Zacharius. His age was past finding out. Not the oldest inhabitant of the town could tell for how long his thin, pointed head had shaken above his shoulders, nor the day when, for the first time, he had walked through the streets, with his long white locks floating in the wind. The man did not live; he vibrated like the pendulum of his clocks. His spare and cadaverous figure was always clothed in dark colours. Like the pictures of Leonardo di Vinci, he was sketched in black.

Gerande had the pleasantest room in the whole house, whence, through a narrow window, she had the inspiriting view of the snowy peaks of Jura; but the bedroom and workshop of the old man were a kind of cavern close on to the water, the floor of which rested on the piles.

From time immemorial Master Zacharius had never come out except at meal times, and when he went to regulate the different clocks of the town. He passed the rest of his time at his bench, which was covered with numerous clockwork instruments, most of which he had invented himself. For he was a clever man; his works were valued in all France and Germany. The best workers in Geneva readily recognized his superiority, and showed that he was an honour to the town, by saying, "To him belongs the glory of having invented the escapement." In fact, the birth of true clock-work dates from the invention which the talents of Zacharius had discovered not many years before.

After he had worked hard for a long time, Zacharius would slowly put his tools away, cover up the delicate pieces that he had been adjusting with glasses, and stop the active wheel of his lathe; then he would raise a trap-door constructed in the floor of his workshop, and, stooping down, used to inhale for hours together the thick vapours of the Rhone, as it dashed along under his eyes.

One winter's night the old servant Scholastique served the supper, which, according to old custom, she and the young mechanic shared with their master. Master Zacharius did not eat, though the food carefully prepared for him was offered him in a handsome blue and white dish. He scarcely answered the sweet words of Gerande, who evidently noticed her father's silence, and even the clatter of Scholastique herself no more struck his ear than the roar of the river, to which he paid no attention.

After the silent meal, the old clockmaker left the table without embracing his daughter, or saying his usual "Good-night" to all. He left by the narrow door leading to his den, and the staircase groaned under his heavy footsteps as he went down.

Gerande, Aubert, and Scholastique sat for some minutes without speaking. On this evening the weather was dull; the clouds dragged heavily on the Alps, and threatened rain; the severe climate of Switzerland made one feel sad, while the south wind swept round the house, and whistled ominously.

"My dear young lady," said Scholastique, at last, "do you know that our master has been out of sorts for several days? Holy Virgin! I know he has had no appetite, because his words stick in his inside, and it would take a very clever devil to drag even one out of him."

"My father has some secret cause of trouble, that I cannot even guess," replied Gerande, as a sad anxiety spread over her face.

"Mademoiselle, don't let such sadness fill your heart. You know the strange habits of Master Zacharius. Who can read his secret thoughts in his face? No doubt some fatigue has overcome him, but to-morrow he will have forgotten it, and be very sorry to have given his daughter pain."

It was Aubert who spoke thus, looking into Gerande's lovely eyes. Aubert was the first apprentice whom Master Zacharius had ever admitted to the intimacy of his labours, for he appreciated his intelligence, discretion, and goodness of heart; and this young man had attached himself to Gerande with the earnest devotion natural to a noble nature.

Gerande was eighteen years of age. Her oval face recalled that of the artless Madonnas whom veneration still displays at the street corners of the antique towns of Brittany. Her eyes betrayed an infinite simplicity. One would love her as the sweetest realization of a poet's dream. Her apparel was of modest colours, and the white linen which was folded about her shoulders had the tint and perfume peculiar to the linen of the church. She led a mystical existence in Geneva, which had not as yet been delivered over to the dryness of Calvinism.

While, night and morning, she read her Latin prayers in her iron-clasped missal, Gerande has also discovered a hidden sentiment in Aubert Thun's heart, and comprehended what a profound devotion the young workman had for her. Indeed, the whole world in his eyes was condensed into this old clockmaker's house, and he passed all his time near the young girl, when he left her father's workshop, after his work was over.

Old Scholastique saw all this, but said nothing. Her loquacity exhausted itself in preference on the evils of the times, and the little worries of the household. Nobody tried to stop its course. It was with her as with the musical snuff-boxes which they made at Geneva; once wound up, you must break them before you will prevent their playing all their airs through.

Finding Gerande absorbed in a melancholy silence, Scholastique left her old wooden chair, fixed a taper on the end of a candlestick, lit it, and placed it near a small waxen Virgin, sheltered in her niche of stone. It was the family custom to kneel before this protecting Madonna of the domestic hearth, and to beg her kindly watchfulness during the coming night; but on this evening Gerande remained silent in her seat.

"Well, well, dear demoiselle," said the astonished Scholastique, "supper is over, and it is time to go to bed. Why do you tire your eyes by sitting up late? Ah, Holy Virgin! It's much better to sleep, and to get a little comfort from happy dreams! In these detestable times in which we live, who can promise herself a fortunate day?"

"Ought we not to send for a doctor for my father?" asked Gerande.

"A doctor!" cried the old domestic. "Has Master Zacharius ever listened to their fancies and pompous sayings? He might accept medicines for the watches, but not for the body!"

"What shall we do?" murmured Gerande. "Has he gone to work, or to rest?"

"Gerande," answered Aubert softly, "some mental trouble annoys your father, that is all."

"Do you know what it is, Aubert?"

"Perhaps, Gerande."

"Tell us, then," cried Scholastique eagerly, economically extinguishing her taper.

"For several days, Gerande," said the young apprentice, "something absolutely incomprehensible has been going on. All the watches which your father has made and sold for some years have suddenly stopped. Very many of them have been brought back to him. He has carefully taken them to pieces; the springs were in good condition, and the wheels well set. He has put them together yet more carefully; but, despite his skill, they will not go."

"The devil's in it!" cried Scholastique.

"Why say you so?" asked Gerande. "It seems very natural to me. Nothing lasts for ever in this world. The infinite cannot be fashioned by the hands of men."

"It is none the less true," returned Aubert, "that there is in this something very mysterious and extraordinary. I have myself been helping Master Zacharius to search for the cause of this derangement of his watches; but I have not been able to find it, and more than once I have let my tools fall from my hands in despair."

"But why undertake so vain a task?" resumed Scholastique. "Is it natural that a little copper instrument should go of itself, and mark the hours? We ought to have kept to the sun-dial!"

"You will not talk thus, Scholastique," said Aubert, "when you learn that the sun-dial was invented by Cain."

"Good heavens! what are you telling me?"

"Do you think," asked Gerande simply, "that we might pray to God to give life to my father's watches?"

"Without doubt," replied Aubert.

"Good! They will be useless prayers," muttered the old servant, "but Heaven will pardon them for their good intent."

The taper was relighted. Scholastique, Gerande, and Aubert knelt down together upon the tiles of the room. The young girl prayed for her mother's soul, for a blessing for the night, for travellers and prisoners, for the good and the wicked, and more earnestly than all for the unknown misfortunes of her father.

Then the three devout souls rose with some confidence in their hearts, because they had laid their sorrow on the bosom of God.

Aubert repaired to his own room; Gerande sat pensively by the window, whilst the last lights were disappearing from the city streets; and Scholastique, having poured a little water on the flickering embers, and shut the two enormous bolts on the door, threw herself upon her bed, where she was soon dreaming that she was dying of fright.

Meanwhile the terrors of this winter's night had increased. Sometimes, with the whirlpools of the river, the wind engulfed itself among the piles, and the whole house shivered and shook; but the young girl, absorbed in her sadness, thought only of her father. After hearing what Aubert told her, the malady of Master Zacharius took fantastic proportions in her mind; and it seemed to her as if his existence, so dear to her, having become purely mechanical, no longer moved on its worn-out pivots without effort.

Suddenly the pent-house shutter, shaken by the squall, struck against the window of the room. Gerande shuddered and started up without understanding the cause of the noise which thus disturbed her reverie. When she became a little calmer she opened the sash. The clouds had burst, and a torrent-like rain pattered on the surrounding roofs. The young girl leaned out of the window to draw to the shutter shaken by the wind, but she feared to do so. It seemed to her that the rain and the river, confounding their tumultuous waters, were submerging the frail house, the planks of which creaked in every direction. She would have flown from her chamber, but she saw below the flickering of a light which appeared to come from Master Zacharius's retreat, and in one of those momentary calms during which the elements keep a sudden silence, her ear caught plaintive sounds. She tried to shut her window, but could not. The wind violently repelled her, like a thief who was breaking into a dwelling.

Gerande thought she would go mad with terror. What was her father doing? She opened the door, and it escaped from her hands, and slammed loudly with the force of the tempest. Gerande then found herself in the dark supper-room, succeeded in gaining, on tiptoe, the staircase which led to her father's shop, and pale and fainting, glided down.

The old watchmaker was upright in the middle of the room, which resounded with the roaring of the river. His bristling hair gave him a sinister aspect. He was talking and gesticulating, without seeing or hearing anything. Gerande stood still on the threshold.

"It is death!" said Master Zacharius, in a hollow voice; "it is death! Why should I live longer, now that I have dispersed my existence over the earth? For I, Master Zacharius, am really the creator of all the watches that I have fashioned! It is a part of my very soul that I have shut up in each of these cases of iron, silver, or gold! Every time that one of these accursed watches stops, I feel my heart cease beating, for I have regulated them with its pulsations!"

As he spoke in this strange way, the old man cast his eyes on his bench. There lay all the pieces of a watch that he had carefully taken apart. He took up a sort of hollow cylinder, called a barrel, in which the spring is enclosed, and removed the steel spiral, but instead of relaxing itself, according to the laws of its elasticity, it remained coiled on itself like a sleeping viper. It seemed knotted, like impotent old men whose blood has long been congealed. Master Zacharius vainly essayed to uncoil it with his thin fingers, the outlines of which were exaggerated on the wall; but he tried in vain, and soon, with a terrible cry of anguish and rage, he threw it through the trap-door into the boiling Rhone.

Gerande, her feet riveted to the floor, stood breathless and motionless. She wished to approach her father, but could not. Giddy hallucinations took possession of her. Suddenly she heard, in the shade, a voice murmur in her ears,—

"Gerande, dear Gerande! grief still keeps you awake. Go in again, I beg of you; the night is cold."

"Aubert!" whispered the young girl, "You?"

These soft words sent the blood back into the young girl's heart. She leaned on Aubert's arm, and said to him,—

"My father is very ill, Aubert! You alone can cure him, for this disorder of the mind would not yield to his daughter's consolings. His mind is attacked by a very natural delusion, and in working with him, repairing the watches, you will bring him back to reason. Aubert," she continued, "it is not true, is it, that his life is mixed up with that of his watches?"

Aubert did not reply.

"But is my father's trade condemned by God?" asked Gerande, trembling.

"I know not," returned the apprentice, warming the cold hands of the girl with his own. "But go back to your room, my poor Gerande, and with sleep recover hope!"

Gerande slowly returned to her chamber, and remained there till daylight, without sleep closing her eyelids. Meanwhile, Master Zacharius, always mute and motionless, gazed at the river as it rolled turbulently at his feet.

CHAPTER 2

THE PRIDE OF SCIENCE

THE severity of the Geneva merchant in business matters has become proverbial. He is rigidly honourable, and excessively just. What must, then, have been the shame of Master Zacharius, when he saw these watches, which he had so carefully constructed, returning to him from every direction?

It was certain that these watches had suddenly stopped, and without any apparent reason. The wheels were in a good condition and firmly fixed, but the springs had lost all elasticity. Vainly did the watchmaker try to replace them; the wheels remained motionless. These unaccountable derangements were greatly to the old man's discredit. His noble inventions had many times brought upon him suspicions of sorcery, which now seemed confirmed. These rumours reached Gerande, and she often trembled for her father, when she saw malicious glances directed towards him.

Yet on the morning after this night of anguish, Master Zacharius seemed to resume work with some confidence. The morning sun inspired him with some courage. Aubert hastened to join him in the shop, and received an affable "Good-day."

"I am better," said the old man. "I don't know what strange pains in the head attacked me yesterday, but the sun has quite chased them away, with the clouds of the night."

"In faith, master," returned Aubert, "I don't like the night for either of us!"

"And thou art right, Aubert. If you ever become a great man, you will understand that day is as necessary to you as food. A great savant should be always ready to receive the homage of his fellow-men."

"Master, it seems to me that the pride of science has possessed you."

"Pride, Aubert! Destroy my past, annihilate my present, dissipate my future, and then it will be permitted to me to live in obscurity! Poor boy, who comprehends not the sublime things to which my art is wholly devoted! Art thou not but a tool in my hands?"

"Yet, Master Zacharius," resumed Aubert, "I have more than once merited your praise for the manner in which I adjusted the most delicate parts of your watches and clocks."

"No doubt, Aubert; thou art a good workman, such as I love; but when thou workest, thou thinkest thou has in thy hands but copper, silver, gold; thou dost not perceive these metals, which my genius animates, palpitating like living flesh! So that thou wilt not die, with the death of thy works!"

Master Zacharius remained silent after these words; but Aubert essayed to keep up the conversation.

"Indeed, master," said he, "I love to see you work so unceasingly! You will be ready for the festival of our corporation, for I see that the work on this crystal watch is going forward famously."

"No doubt, Aubert," cried the old watchmaker, "and it will be no slight honour for me to have been able to cut and shape the crystal to the durability of a diamond! Ah, Louis Berghem did well to perfect the art of diamond-cutting, which has enabled me to polish and pierce the hardest stones!''

Master Zacharius was holding several small watch pieces of cut crystal, and of exquisite workmanship. The wheels, pivots, and case of the watch were of the same material, and he had employed remarkable skill in this very difficult task.

''Would it not be fine,'' said he, his face flushing, ''to see this watch palpitating beneath its transparent envelope, and to be able to count the beatings of its heart?''

''I will wager, sir,'' replied the young apprentice, ''that it will not vary a second in a year.''

''And you would wager on a certainty! Have I not imparted to it all that is purest of myself? And does my heart vary? My heart, I say?''

Aubert did not dare to lift his eyes to his master's face. ''Tell me frankly,'' said the old man sadly. ''Have you never taken me for a madman? Do you not think me sometimes subject to dangerous folly? Yes; is it not so? In my daughter's eyes and yours, I have often read my condemnation. Oh!'' he cried, as if in pain, ''to be misunderstood by those whom one most loves in the world! But I will prove victoriously to thee, Aubert, that I am right! Do not shake thy head, for thou wilt be astounded. The day on which thou understandest how to listen to and comprehend me, thou wilt see that I have discovered the secrets of existence, the secrets of the mysterious union of the soul with the body!''

As he spoke thus, Master Zacharius appeared superb in his vanity. His eyes glittered with a supernatural fire, and his pride illumined every feature. And truly, if ever vanity was excusable, it was that of Master Zacharius!

The watchmaking art, indeed, down to his time, had remained almost in its infancy. From the day when Plato, four centuries before the Christian era, invented the night watch, a sort of clepsydra which indicated the hours of the night by the sound and playing of a flute, the science had continued nearly stationary. The masters paid more attention to the arts than to mechanics, and it was the period of beautiful watches of iron, copper, wood, silver, which were richly engraved, like one of Cellini's ewers. They made a masterpiece of chasing, which measured time imperfectly, but was still a masterpiece. When the artist's imagination was not directed to the perfection of modelling, it set to work to create clocks with moving figures and melodious sounds, whose appearance took all attention. Besides, who troubled himself, in those days, with regulating the advance of time? The delays of the law were not as yet invented; the physical and astronomical sciences had not as yet established their calculations on scrupulously exact measurements; there were neither establishments which were shut at a given hour, nor trains which departed at a precise moment. In the evening the curfew bell sounded; and at night the hours were cried amid the universal silence. Certainly people did not live so long, if existence is measured by the amount of business done; but they lived better. The mind was enriched with the noble sentiments born of the contemplation of chefs-d'œuvré. They built a church in two centuries, a painter painted but few pictures in the course of his life, a poet only composed one great work; but these were so many masterpieces for after-ages to appreciate.

When the exact sciences began at last to make some progress, watch and clock making followed in their path, though it was always arrested by an insurmountable difficulty,—the regular and continuous measurement of time.

It was in the midst of this stagnation that Master Zacharius invented the escapement, which enabled him to obtain a mathematical regularity by submitting the movement of the pendulum to a sustained force. This invention had turned the old man's head. Pride, swelling in his heart, like mercury in the thermometer, had attained the height of transcendent folly. By analogy he had allowed himself to be drawn to materialistic conclusions, and as he constructed his watches, he fancied that he had discovered the secrets of the union of the soul with the body.

Thus, on this day, perceiving that Aubert listened to him attentively, he said to him in a tone of simple conviction,—

"Dost thou know what life is, my child? Hast thou comprehended the action of those springs which produce existence? Hast thou examined thyself? No. And yet, with the eyes of science, thou mightest have seen the intimate relation which exists between God's work and my own; for it is from his creature that I have copied the combinations of the wheels of my clocks."

"Master," replied Aubert eagerly, "can you compare a copper or steel machine with that breath of God which is called the soul, which animates our bodies as the breeze stirs the flowers? What mechanism could be so adjusted as to inspire us with thought?"

"That is not the question," responded Master Zacharius gently, but with all the obstinacy of a blind man walking towards an abyss. "In order to understand me, thou must recall the purpose of the escapement which I have invented. When I saw the irregular working of clocks, I understood that the movements shut up in them did not suffice, and that it was necessary to submit them to the regularity of some independent force. I then thought that the balance-wheel might accomplish this, and I succeeded in regulating the movement! Now, was it not a sublime idea that came to me, to return to it its lost force by the action of the clock itself, which it was charged with regulating?"

Aubert made a sign of assent.

"Now, Aubert," continued the old man, growing animated, "cast thine eyes upon thyself! Dost thou not understand that there are two distinct forces in us, that of the soul and that of the body—that is, a movement and a regulator? The soul is the principle of life; that is, then, the movement. Whether it is produced by a weight, by a spring, or by an immaterial influence, it is none the less in the heart. But without the body this movement would be unequal, irregular, impossible! Thus the body regulates the soul, and, like the balance-wheel, it is submitted to regular oscillations. And this is so true, that one falls ill when one's drink, food, sleep—in a word, the functions of the body—are not properly regulated; just as in my watches the soul renders to the body the force lost by its oscillations. Well, what produces this intimate union between soul and body, if not a marvellous escapement, by which the wheels of the one work into the wheels of the other? This is what I have discovered and applied; and there are no longer any secrets for me in this life, which is, after all, only an ingenious mechanism!"

Master Zacharius looked sublime in this hallucination, which carried him to the ultimate mysteries of the Infinite. But his daughter Gerande, standing on the threshold of the door, had heard all. She rushed into her father's arms, and he pressed her convulsively to his breast.

"What is the matter with thee, my daughter?" he asked.

"If I had only a spring here," said she, putting her hand on her heart, "I would not love you as I do, father."

Master Zacharius looked intently at Gerande, and did not reply. Suddenly he uttered a cry, carried his hand eargerly to his heart, and fell fainting on his old leathern chair.

"Father, what is the matter?"

"Help!" cried Aubert. "Scholastique!"

But Scholastique did not come at once. Some one was knocking at the front door; she had gone to open it, and when she returned to the shop, before she could open her mouth, the old watchmaker, having recovered his senses, spoke:—

"I divine, my old Scholastique, that you bring me still another of those accursed watches which have stopped."

"Lord, it is true enough!" replied Scholastique, handing a watch to Aubert.

"My heart could not be mistaken!" said the old man, with a sigh.

Meanwhile Aubert carefully wound up the watch, but it would not go.

CHAPTER 3

A STRANGE VISIT

POOR Gerande would have lost her life with that of her father, had it not been for the thought of Aubert, who still attached her to the world.

The old watchmaker was, little by little, passing away. His faculties evidently grew more feeble, as he concentrated them on a single thought. By a sad association of ideas, he referred everything to his monomania, and a human existence seemed to have departed from him, to give place to the extra-natural existence of the intermediate powers. Moreover, certain malicious rivals revived the sinister rumours which had spread concerning his labours.

The news of the strange derangements which his watches betrayed had a prodigious effect upon the master clockmakers of Geneva. What signified this sudden paralysis of their wheels, and why these strange relations which they seemed to have with the old man's life? These were the kind of mysteries which people never contemplate without a secret terror. In the various classes of the town, from the apprentice to the great lord who used the watches of the old horologist, there was no one who could not himself judge of the singularity of the fact. The citizens wished, but in vain, to get to see Master Zacharius. He fell very ill; and this enabled his daughter to withdraw him from those incessant visits which had degenerated into reproaches and recriminations.

Medicines and physicians were powerless in presence of this organic wasting away, the cause of which could not be discovered. It sometimes seemed as if the old man's heart had ceased to beat; then the pulsations were resumed with an alarming irregularity.

A custom existed in those days of publicly exhibiting the works of the masters. The heads of the various corporations sought to distinguish themselves by the novelty or the perfection of their productions; and it was among these that the condition of Master Zacharius excited the most lively, because most interested, commiseration. His rivals pitied him the more willingly because they feared him

"Thou wilt see that I have discovered the secrets of existence."

the less. They never forgot the old man's success, when he exhibited his magnificent clocks with moving figures, his repeaters, which provoked general admiration, and commanded such high prices in the cities of France, Switzerland, and Germany.

Meanwhile, thanks to the constant and tender care of Gerande and Aubert, his strength seemed to return a little; and in the tranquility in which his convalescence left him, he succeeded in detaching himself from the thoughts which had absorbed him. As soon as he could walk, his daughter lured him away from the house, which was still besieged with dissatisfied customers. Aubert remained in the shop, vainly adjusting and readjusting the rebel watches; and the poor boy, completely mystified, sometimes covered his face with his hands, fearful that he, like his master, might go mad.

Gerande led her father towards the more pleasant promenades of the town. With his arm resting on hers, she conducted him sometimes through the quarter of Saint Antoine, the view from which extends towards the Cologny hill, and over the lake; on fine mornings they caught sight of the gigantic peaks of Mount Buet against the horizon. Gerande pointed out these spots to her father, who had well-nigh forgotten even their names. His memory wandered; and he took a childish interest in learning anew what had passed from his mind. Master Zacharius leaned upon his daughter; and the two heads, one white as snow and the other covered with rich golden tresses, met in the same ray of sunlight.

So it came about that the old watchmaker at last perceived that he was not alone in the world. As he looked upon his young and lovely daughter, and on himself old and broken, he reflected that after his death she would be left alone without support. Many of the young mechanics of Geneva had already sought to win Gerande's love; but none of them had succeeded in gaining access to the impenetrable retreat of the watchmaker's household. It was natural, then, that during this lucid interval, the old man's choice should fall on Aubert Thun. Once struck with this thought, he remarked to himself that this young couple had been brought up with the same ideas and the same beliefs; and the oscillations of their hearts seemed to him, as he said one day to Scholastique, "isochronous."

The old servant, literally delighted with the word, though she did not understand it, swore by her holy patron saint that the whole town should hear it within a quarter of an hour. Master Zacharius found it difficult to calm her; but made her promise to keep on this subject a silence which she never was known to observe.

So, though Gerande and Aubert were ignorant of it, all Geneva was soon talking of their speedy union. But it happened also that, while the worthy folk were gossiping, a strange chuckle was often heard, and a voice saying, "Gerande will not wed Aubert."

If the talkers turned round, they found themselves facing a little old man who was quite a stranger to them.

How old was this singular being? No one could have told. People conjectured that he must have existed for several centuries, and that was all. His big flat head rested upon shoulders the width of which was equal to the height of his body; this was not above three feet. This personage would have made a good figure to support a pendulum, for the dial would have naturally been placed on his face, and the balance-wheel would have oscillated at its ease in his chest. His nose might readily have been taken for the style of a sun-dial, for it was narrow and sharp; his teeth, far apart, resembled the cogs of a wheel, and ground themselves between his lips; his voice had the metallic sound of a bell, and you could hear his heart beat like the tick of a clock. This little man, whose arms moved like the hands on a dial, walked with jerks, without ever turning round. If any one followed him, it was found that he walked a league an hour, and that his course was nearly circular.

This strange being had not long been seen wandering, or rather circulating, around the town; but it had already been observed that, every day, at the moment when the sun passed the meridian, he stopped before the Cathedral of Saint Pierre, and resumed his course after the twelve strokes of noon had sounded. Excepting at this precise moment, he seemed to become a part of all the conversastions in which the old watchmaker was talked of; and people asked each other, in terror, what relation could exist between him and Master Zacharius. It was remarked, too, that he never lost sight of the old man and his daughter while they were taking their promenades.

One day Gerande perceived this monster looking at her with a hideous smile. She clung to her father with a frightened motion.

"What is the matter, my Gerande?" asked Master Zacharius.

"I do not know," replied the young girl.

"But thou art changed, my child. Art thou going to fall ill in thy turn? Ah, well," he added, with a sad smile, "then I must take care of thee, and I will do it tenderly."

"O father, it will be nothing. I am cold, and I imagine that it is—"

"What, Gerande?"

"The presence of that man, who always follows us," she replied in a low tone.

Master Zacharius turned towards the little old man.

"Faith, he goes well," said he, with a satisfied air, "for it is just four o'clock. Fear nothing, my child; it is not a man, it is a clock!"

Gerande looked at her father in terror. How could Master Zacharius read the hour on this strange creature's visage?

"By-the-bye," continued the old watchmaker, paying no further attention to the matter, "I have not seen Aubert for several days."

"He has not left us, however, father," said Gerande, whose thoughts turned into a gentler channel.

"What is he doing then?"

"He is working."

"Ah!" cried the old man. "He is at work repairing my watches, is he not? But he will never succeed; for it is not repair they need, but a resurrection!"

Gerande remained silent.

"I must know," added the old man, "if they have brought back any more of those accursed watches upon which the Devil has sent this epidemic!"

After these words Master Zacharius fell into complete silence, till he knocked at the door of his house, and for the first time since his convalescence descended to his shop, while Gerande sadly repaired to her chamber.

Just as Master Zacharius crossed the threshold of his shop, one of the many clocks suspended on the wall struck five o'clock. Usually the bells of these clocks—admirably regulated as they were—struck simultaneously, and this rejoiced the old man's heart; but on this day the bells struck one after another, so that for a quarter of an hour the ear was deafened by the successive noises. Master Zacharius suffered acutely; he could not remain still, but went from one clock to the other, and beat the time to them, like a conductor who no longer has control over his musicians.

When the last had ceased striking, the door of the shop opened, and Master Zacharius shuddered from head to foot to see before him the little old man, who looked fixedly at him and said,—

"Master, may I not speak with you a few moments?"

"Who are you?" asked the watchmaker abruptly.

"A colleague. It is my business to regulate the sun."

"Ah, you regulate the sun?" replied Master Zacharius eagerly, without wincing. "I can scarcely compliment you upon it. Your sun goes badly, and in order to make ourselves agree with it, we have to keep putting our clocks forward so much or back so much."

"And by the cloven foot," cried this weird personage, "you are right, my master! My sun does not always mark noon at the same moment as your clocks; but some day it will be known that this is because of the inequality of the earth's transfer, and a mean noon will be invented which will regulate this irregularity!"

"Shall I live till then?" asked the old man, with glistening eyes.

"Without doubt," replied the little old man, laughing. "Can you believe that you will ever die?"

"Alas! I am very ill now."

"Ah, let us talk of that. By Beelzebub! that will lead to just what I wish to speak to you about."

Saying this, the strange being leaped upon the old leather chair, and carried his legs one under the other, after the fashion of the bones which the painters of funeral hangings cross beneath death's heads. Then he resumed, in an ironical tone,—

"Let us see, Master Zacharius, what is going on in this good town of Geneva? They say that your health is failing, that your watches have need of a doctor!"

"Ah, do you believe that there is an intimate relation between their existence and mine?" cried Master Zacharius.

"Why, I imagine that these watches have faults, even vices. If these wantons do not preserve a regular conduct, it is right that they should bear the consequences of their irregularity. It seems to me that they have need of reforming a little!"

"What do you call faults?" asked Master Zacharius, reddening at the sarcastic tone in which these words were uttered. "Have they not a right to be proud of their origin?"

"Not too proud, not too proud," replied the little old man. "They bear a celebrated name, and an illustrious signature is graven on their cases, it is true, and theirs is the exclusive privilege of being introduced among the noblest families; but for some time they have got out of order, and you can do nothing in the matter, Master Zacharius; and the stupidest apprentice in Geneva could prove it to you!"

"To me, to me,—Master Zacharius!" cried the old man, with a flush of outraged pride.

"To you, Master Zacharius,—you, who cannot restore life to your watches!"

"But it is because I have a fever, and so have they also!" replied the old man, as a cold sweat broke out upon him.

"Very well, they will die with you, since you cannot impart a little elasticity to their springs."

Then he resumed, in an ironical tone.

"Die! No, for you yourself have said it! I cannot die,—I, the first watchmaker in the world; I, who, by means of these pieces and diverse wheels, have been able to regulate the movement with absolute precision! Have I not subjected time to exact laws, and can I not dispose of it like a despot? Before a sublime genius had arranged these wandering hours regularly, in what vast uncertainty was human destiny plunged? At what certain moment could the acts of life be connected with each other? But you, man or devil, whatever you may be, have never considered the magnificence of my art, which calls every science to its aid! No, no! I, Master Zacharius, cannot die, for, as I have regulated time, time would end with me! It would return to the infinite, whence my genius has rescued it, and it would lose itself irreparably in the abyss of nothingness! No, I can no more die than the Creator of this universe, that submitted to His laws! I have become His equal, and I have partaken of His power! If God has created eternity, Master Zacharius has created time!"

The old watchmaker now resembled the fallen angel, defiant in the presence of the Creator. The little old man gazed at him, and even seemed to breathe into him this impious transport.

"Well said, master," he replied. "Beelzebub had less right than you to compare himself with God! Your glory must not perish! So your servant here desires to give you the method of controlling these rebellious watches."

"What is it? what is it?" cried Master Zacharius.

"You shall know on the day after that on which you have given me your daughter's hand."

"My Gerande?"

"Herself!"

"My daughter's heart is not free," replied Master Zacharius, who seemed neither astonished nor shocked at the strange demand.

"Bah! She is not the least beautiful of watches; but she will end by stopping also --"

"My daughter,—my Gerande! No!"

"Well, return to your watches, Master Zacharius. Adjust and readjust them. Get ready the marriage of your daughter and your apprentice. Temper your springs with your best steel. Bless Aubert and the pretty Gerande. But remember, your watches will never go, and Gerande will not wed Aubert!"

Thereupon the little old man disappeared, but not so quickly that Master Zacharius could not hear six o'clock strike in his breast.

CHAPTER 4

THE CHURCH OF SAINT PIERRE

MEANWHILE Master Zacharius became more feeble in mind and body every day. An unusual excitement, indeed, impelled him to continue his work more eagerly than ever, nor could his daughter entice him from it.

His pride was still more aroused after the crises to which his strange visitor had hurried him so treacherously, and he resolved to overcome, by the force of genius, the malign influence which weighed upon his work and himself. He first repaired to the various clocks of the town which were confided to his care. He made sure, by a scrupulous examination, that the wheels were in good condition, the pivots firm, the weights exactly balanced. Every part, even to the bells, was examined with the minute attention of a physician studying the breast of a patient. Nothing indicated that these clocks were on the point of being affected by inactivity.

Gerande and Aubert often accompanied the old man on these visits. He would no doubt have been pleased to see them eager to go with him, and certainly he would not have been so much absorbed in his approaching end, had he thought that his existence was to be prolonged by that of these cherished ones, and had he understood that something of the life of a father always remains in his children.

The old watchmaker, on returning home, resumed his labours with feverish zeal. Though persuaded that he would not succeed, it yet seemed to him impossible that this could be so, and he unceasingly took to pieces the watches which were brought to his shop, and put them together again.

Aubert tortured his mind in vain to discover the causes of the evil.

"Master," said he, "this can only come from the wear of the pivots and gearing."

"Do you want, then, to kill me, little by little?" replied Master Zacharius passionately. "Are these watches child's work? Was it lest I should hurt my fingers that I worked the surface of these copper pieces in the lathe? Have I not forged these pieces of copper myself, so as to obtain a greater strength? Are not these springs tempered to a rare perfection? Could anybody have used finer oils than mine? You must yourself agree that it is impossible, and you avow, in short, that the devil is in it!"

From morning till night discontented purchasers besieged the house, and they got access to the old watchmaker himself, who knew not which of them to listen to.

"This watch loses, and I cannot succeed in regulating it,"said one.

"This," said another, "is absolutely obstinate, and stands still, as did Joshua's sun."

"If it is true," said most of them, "that your health has an influence on that of your watches, Master Zacharius, get well as soon as possible."

The old man gazed at these people with haggard eyes, and only replied by shaking his head, or by a few sad words,—

"Wait till the first fine weather, my friends. The season is coming which revives existence in wearied bodies. We want the sun to warm us all!"

"A fine thing, if my watches are to be ill through the winter!" said one of the most angry. "Do you know, Master Zacharius, that your name is inscribed in full on their faces? By the Virgin, you do little honour to your signature!"

It happened at last that the old man, abashed by these reproaches, took some pieces of gold from his old trunk, and began to buy back the damaged watches. At news of this, the customers came in a crowd, and the poor watchmaker's money fast melted away; but his honesty remained intact. Gerande warmly praised his delicacy, which was leading him straight towards ruin; and Aubert soon offered his own savings to his master. "What will become of my daughter?" said Master Zacharius, clinging now and then in the shipwreck to his paternal love.

Aubert dared not answer that he was full of hope for the future, and of deep devotion to Gerande. Master Zacharius would have that day called him his son-in-law, and thus refuted the sad prophecy, which still buzzed in his ears,—"Gerande will not wed Aubert."

By this plan the watchmaker at last succeeded in entirely despoiling himself. His antique vases passed into the hands of strangers; he deprived himself of the richly-carved panels which adorned the walls of his house; some primitive pictures of the the early Flemish painters soon ceased to please his daughter's eyes, and everything, even the precious tools that his genius had invented, were sold to indemnify the clamorous customers.

Scholastique alone refused to listen to reason on the subject; but her efforts failed to prevent the unwelcome visitors from reaching her master, and from soon departing with some valuable object. Then her shattering was heard in all the streets of the neighbourhood, where she had long been known. She eagerly denied the rumours of sorcery and magic on the part of Master Zacharius, which gained currency; but as at bottom she was persuaded of their truth, she said her prayers over and over again to redeem her pious falsehoods.

It had been noticed that for some time the old watchmaker had neglected his religious duties. Time was, when he had accompanied Gerande to church, and had seemed to find in prayer the intellectual charm which it imparts to thoughtful minds, since it is the most sublime exercise of the imagination. This voluntary neglect of holy practices, added to the secret habits of his life, had in some sort confirmed the accusations levelled against his labours. So, with the double purpose of drawing her father back to God, and to the world, Gerande resolved to call religion to her aid. She thought that it might give some vitality to his dying soul; but the dogmas of faith and humility had to combat, in the soul of Master Zacharius, an insurmountable pride, and come into collision with that vanity of science which connects everything with itself, without rising to the infinite source whence first principles flow.

It was under these circumstances that the young girl undertook her father's conversion; and her influence was so effective that the old watchmaker promised to attend high mass at the cathedral on the following Sunday. Gerande was in an ecstasy, as if heaven had opened to her view. Old Scholastique could not contain her joy, and at last found irrefutable arguments against the gossiping tongues which accused her master of impiety. She spoke of it to her neighbours, her friends, her enemies, to those whom she knew.

"In faith, we scarcely believe what you tell us, dame Scholastique," they replied; "Master Zacharius has always acted in concert with the devil!"

"You haven't counted, then," replied the old servant, "the fine bells which strike for my master's clocks? How many times they have struck the hours of prayer and the mass!"

"No doubt," they would reply. "But has he not invented machines which go all by themselves, and which actually do the work of a real man?"

"Could a child of the devil," exclaimed dame Scholastique wrathfully, "have executed the fine iron clock of the château of Andernatt, which the town of Geneva was not rich enough to buy? A pious motto appeared at each hour, and a Christian who obeyed them, would have gone straight to Paradise! Is that the work of the devil?"

This masterpiece, made twenty years before, had carried Master Zacharius's fame to its acme; but even then there had been accusations of sorcery against him. But at least the old man's visit to the Cathedral ought to reduce malicious tongues to silence.

Master Zacharius, having doubtless forgotten the promise made to his daughter, had returned to his shop. After being convinced of his powerlessness to give life to his watches, he resolved to try if he could not make some new ones. He abandoned all those useless works, and devoted himself to the completion of the crystal watch, which he intended to be his masterpiece, but in vain did he use his most perfect tools, and employ rubies and diamonds for resisting friction. The watch fell from his hands the first time that he attempted to wind it up!

The old man concealed this circumstance from every one, even from his daughter; but from that time his health rapidly declined. There were only the last oscillations of a pendulum, which goes slower when nothing restores its original force. It seemed as if the laws of gravity, acting directly upon him, were dragging him irresistibly down to the grave.

The Sunday so ardently anticipated by Gerande at last arrived. The weather was fine, and the temperature inspiriting. The people of Geneva were passing quietly through the streets, gaily chatting about the return of spring. Gerande, tenderly taking the old man's arm, directed her steps towards the cathedral, while Scholastique followed behind with the prayer-books. People looked curiously at them as they passed. The old watchmaker permitted himself to be led like a child, or rather like a blind man. The faithful of Saint Pierre were almost frightened when they saw him cross the threshold, and shrank back at his approach.

The chants of high mass were already resounding through the church. Gerande went to her accustomed bench, and kneeled with profound and simple reverence. Master Zacharius remained standing upright beside her.

The ceremonies continued with the majestic solemnity of that faithful age, but the old man had no faith. He did not implore the pity of Heaven with cries of anguish of the "Kyrie;" he did not, with the "Gloria in Excelsis," sing the splendours of the heavenly heights; the reading of the Testament did not draw him from his materialistic reverie, and he forgot to join in the homage of the "Credo." This proud old man remained motionless, as insensible and silent as a stone statue; and even at the solemn moment when the bell announced the miracle of transubstantiation, he did not bow his head, but gazed directly at the sacred host which the priest raised above the heads of the faithful. Gerande looked at her father, and a flood of tears moistened her missal. At this moment the clock of Saint Pierre struck half-past eleven. Master Zacharius turned quickly towards this ancient clock which still spoke. It seemed to him as if its face was gazing steadily at him; the figures of the hours shone as if they had been engraved in lines of fire, and the hands shot forth electric sparks from their sharp points.

The mass ended. It was customary for the "Angelus" to be said at noon, and the priests, before leaving the altar, waited for the clock to strike the hour of twelve. In a few moments this prayer would ascend to the feet of the Virgin.

But suddenly a harsh noise was heard. Master Zacharius uttered a piercing cry.

The large hand of the clock, having reached twelve, had abruptly stopped, and the clock did not strike the hour.

Gerande hastened to her father's aid. He had fallen down motionless, and they carried him outside the church.

"It is the death-blow!" murmured Gerande, sobbing.

When he had been borne home, Master Zacharius lay upon his bed utterly crushed. Life seemed only to still exist on the surface of his body, like the last whiffs of smoke about a lamp just extinguished.

When he came to his senses, Aubert and Gerande were leaning over him. In these last moments the future took in his eyes the shape of the present. He saw his daughter alone, without a protector.

"My son," said he to Aubert, "I give my daughter to thee."

So saying, he stretched out his hands towards his two children, who were thus united at his death-bed.

But soon Master Zacharius lifted himself up in a paroxysm of rage. The words of the little old man recurred to his mind.

"I do not wish to die!" he cried; "I cannot die! I, Master Zacharius, ought not to die! My books—my accounts!—"

With these words he sprang from his bed towards a book in which the names of his customers and the articles which had been sold to them were inscribed. He seized it and rapidly turned over its leaves, and his emaciated finger fixed itself on one of the pages.

"There!" he cried, "there! this old iron clock, sold to Pittonaccio! It is the only one that has not been returned to me! It still exists—it goes—it lives! Ah, I wish for it—I must find it! I will take such care of it that death will no longer seek me!"

And he fainted away.

Aubert and Gerande knelt by the old man's bed-side and prayed together.

CHAPTER 5

THE HOUR OF DEATH

SEVERAL days passed, and Master Zacharius, though almost dead, rose from his bed and returned to active life under a supernatural excitement. He lived by pride. But Gerande did not deceive herself; her father's body and soul were for ever lost.

The old man got together his last remaining resources, without thought of those who were dependent upon him. He betrayed an incredible energy, walking, ferreting about, and mumbling strange, incomprehensible words.

One morning Gerande went down to his shop. Master Zacharius was not there. She waited for him all day. Master Zacharius did not return.

Gerande wept bitterly, but her father did not reappear.

Aubert searched everywhere through the town, and soon came to the sad conviction that the old man had left it.

"Let us find my father!" cried Gerande, when the young apprentice told her this sad news.

"Where can he be?" Aubert asked himself.

An inspiration suddenly came to his mind. He remembered the last words which Master Zacharius had spoken. The old man only lived now in the old

This proud old man remained motionless.

iron clock that had not been returned! Master Zacharius must have gone in search of it.

Aubert spoke of this to Gerande.

"Let us look at my father's book," she replied.

They descended to the shop. The book was open on the bench. All the watches or clocks made by the old man, and which had been returned to him because they were out of order, were stricken out excepting one:—

> "Sold to M. Pittonaccio, an iron clock, with bell and moving figures; sent to his château at Andernatt."

It was this "moral" clock of which Scholastique had spoken with so much enthusiasm.

"My father is there!" cried Gerande.

"Let us hasten thither," replied Aubert. "We may still save him!"

"Not for this life," murmured Gerande, "but at least for the other."

"By the mercy of God, Gerande! The château of Andernatt stands in the gorge of the 'Dents-du-Midi,' twenty hours from Geneva. Let us go!"

That very evening Aubert and Gerande, followed by the old servant, set out on foot by the road which skirts Lake Leman. They accomplished five leagues during the night, stopping neither at Bessinge nor at Ermance, where rises the famous château of the Mayors. They with difficulty forded the torrent of the Dranse, and everywhere they went they inquired for Master Zacharius, and were soon convinced that they were on his track.

The next morning, at daybreak, having passed Thonon, they reached Evian, whence the Swiss territory may be seen extended over twelve leagues. But the two betrothed did not even perceive the enchanting prospect. They went straight forward, urged on by a supernatural force. Aubert, leaning on a knotty stick, offered his arm alternately to Gerande and to Scholastique, and he made the greatest efforts to sustain his companions. All three talked of their sorrow, of their hopes, and thus passed along the beautiful road by the water-side, and across the narrow plateau which unites the borders of the lake with the heights of the Chalais. They soon reached Bouveret, where the Rhone enters the Lake of Geneva.

On leaving this town they diverged from the lake, and their weariness increased amid these mountain districts. Vionnaz, Chesset, Collombay, half-lost villages, were soon left behind. Meanwhile their knees shook, their feet were lacerated by the sharp points which covered the ground like a brushwood of granite;—but no trace of Master Zacharius!

He must be found, however, and the two young people did not seek repose either in the isolated hamlets or at the château of Monthay, which, with its dependencies, formed the appanage of Margaret of Savoy. At last, late in the day, and half dead with fatigue, they reached the hermitage of Notre-Dame-du-Sex, which is situated at the base of the Dents-du-Midi, six hundred feet above the Rhone.

The hermit received the three wanderers as night was falling. They could not have gone another step, and here they must needs rest.

The hermit could give them no news of Master Zacharius. They could scarcely hope to find him still living amid these sad solitudes. The night was dark, the wind howled amid the mountains, and the avalanches roared down from the summits of the broken crags.

Aubert and Gerande, crouching before the hermit's hearth, told him their melancholy tale. Their mantles, covered with snow, were drying in a corner; and without, the hermit's dog barked lugubriously, and mingled his voice with that of the tempest.

"Pride," said the hermit to his guests, "has destroyed an angel created for good. It is the stumbling-block against which the destinites of man strike. You cannot reason with pride, the principal of all the vices, since, by its very nature, the proud man refuses to listen to it. It only remains, then, to pray for your father!"

All four knelt down, when the barking of the dog redoubled, and some one knocked at the door of the hermitage.

"Open, in the devil's name!"

The door yielded under the blows, and a dishevelled, haggard, ill-clothed man appeared.

"My father!" cried Gerande.

It was Master Zacharius.

"Where am I?" said he. "In eternity! Time is ended—the hours no longer strike—the hands have stopped!"

"Father!" returned Gerande, with so piteous an emotion that the old man seemed to return to the world of the living.

"Thou here, Gerande?" he cried; "and thou, Aubert? Ah, my dear betrothed ones, you are going to be married in our old church!"

"Father," said Gerande, seizing him by the arm, "come home to Geneva,—come with us!"

The old man tore away from his daughter's embrace and hurried towards the door, on the threshold of which the snow was falling in large flakes.

"Do not abandon your children!" cried Aubert.

"Why return," replied the old man sadly, "to those places which my life has already quitted, and where a part of myself is for ever buried?"

"Your soul is not dead," said the hermit solemnly.

"My soul? O no,—its wheels are good! I perceive it beating regularly—"

"Your soul is immaterial,—your soul is immortal!" replied the hermit sternly.

"Yes—like my glory! But it is shut up in the château of Andernatt, and I wish to see it again!"

The hermit crossed himself; Scholastique became almost inanimate. Aubert held Gerande in his arms.

"The château of Andernatt is inhabited by one who is lost," said the hermit, "one who does not salute the cross of my hermitage."

"My father, go not thither!"

"I want my soul! My soul is mine—"

"Hold him! Hold my father!" cried Gerande.

But the old man had leaped across the threshold, and plunged into the night, crying, "Mine, mine, my soul!"

Gerande, Aubert, and Scholastique hastened after him. They went by difficult paths, across which Master Zacharius sped like a tempest, urged by an irresistible force. The snow raged around them, and mingled its white flakes with the froth of the swollen torrents.

As they passed the chapel erected in memory of the massacre of the Theban legion, they hurriedly crossed themselves. Master Zacharius was not to be seen.

At last the village of Evionnaz appeared in the midst of this sterile region. The hardest heart would have been moved to see this hamlet, lost among these horrible solitudes. The old man sped on, and plunged into the deepest gorge of the Dents-du-Midi, which pierce the sky with their sharp peaks.

Soon a ruin, old and gloomy as the rocks at its base, rose before him.

"It is there—there!" he cried, hastening his pace still more frantically.

The château of Andernatt was a ruin even then. A thick, crumbling tower rose above it, and seemed to menace with its downfall the old gables which reared themselves below. The vast piles of jagged stones were gloomy to look on. Several dark halls appeared amid the débris, with caved-in ceilings, now become the abode of vipers.

A low and narrow postern opening upon a ditch choked with rubbish, gave access to the château. Who had dwelt there none knew. No doubt some margrave, half lord, half brigand, had sojourned in it; to the margrave had succeeded bandits or counterfeit coiners, who had been hanged on the scene of their crime. The legend went that, on winter nights, Satan came to lead his diabolical dances on the slope of the deep gorges in which the shadow of these ruins was engulfed.

But Master Zacharius was not dismayed by their sinister aspect. He reached the postern. No one forbade him to pass. A spacious and gloomy court presented itself to his eyes; no one forbade him to cross it. He passed along the kind of inclined plane which conducted to one of the long corridors, whose arches seemed to banish daylight from beneath their heavy springings. His advance was unresisted. Gerande, Aubert, and Scholastique closely followed him.

Master Zacharius, as if guided by an irresistible hand, seemed sure of his way, and strode along with rapid step. He reached an old worm-eaten door, which fell before his blows, whilst the bats described oblique circles around his head.

An immense hall, better preserved than the rest, was soon reached. High sculptured panels, on which serpents, ghouls, and other strange figures seemed to disport themselves confusedly, covered its walls. Several long and narrow windows, like loopholes, shivered beneath the bursts of the tempest.

Master Zacharius, on reaching the middle of this hall, uttered a cry of joy.

On an iron support, fastened to the wall, stood the clock in which now resided his entire life. This unequalled masterpiece represented an ancient Roman church, with buttresses of wrought iron, with its heavy bell-tower, where there was a complete chime for the anthem of the day, the "Angelus," the mass, vespers, compline, and the benediction. Above the church door, which opened at the hour of the services, was placed a "rose," in the centre of which two hands moved, and the archivault of which reproduced the twelve hours of the face sculptured in relief. Between the door and the rose, just as Scholastique had said, a maxim, relative to the employment of every moment of the day, appeared on a copper plate. Master Zacharius had once regulated this succession of devices with a really Christian solicitude; the hours of prayer, of work, of repast, of recreation, and of repose, followed each other according to the religious discipline, and were to infallibly insure salvation to him who scrupulously observed their commands.

Master Zacharius, intoxicated with joy, went forward to take possession of the clock, when a frightful roar of laughter resounded behind him.

He turned, and by the light of a smoky lamp recognized the little old man of Geneva.

"You are here?" cried he.

Gerande was afraid. She drew closer to Aubert.

"Good-day, Master Zacharius," said the monster.

"Who are you?"

"Signor Pittonaccio, at your service! You have come to give me your daughter! You have remembered my words, 'Gerande will not wed Aubert.'"

The young apprentice rushed upon Pittonaccio, who escaped from him like a shadow.

"Stop, Aubert!" cried Master Zacharius.

"Good-night," said Pittonaccio, and he disappeared.

"My father, let us fly from this hateful place!" cried Gerande. "My father!"

Master Zacharius was no longer there. He was pursuing the phantom of Pittonaccio across the rickety corridors. Scholastique, Gerande, and Aubert remained, speechless and fainting, in the large gloomy hall. The young girl had fallen upon a stone seat; the old servant knelt beside her, and prayed; Aubert remained erect, watching his betrothed. Pale lights wandered in the darkness, and the silence was only broken by the movements of the little animals which live in old wood, and the noise of which marks the hours of "death watch."

When daylight came, they ventured upon the endless staircase which wound beneath these ruined masses; for two hours they wandered thus without meeting a living soul, and hearing only a far-off echo responding to their cries. Sometimes they found themselves buried a hundred feet below the ground, and sometimes they reached places whence they could overlook the wild mountains.

Chance brought them at last back again to the vast hall, which had sheltered them during this night of anguish. It was no longer empty. Master Zacharius and Pittonaccio were talking there together, the one upright and rigid as a corpse, the other crouching over a marble table.

Master Zacharius, when he perceived Gerande, went forward and took her by the hand, and led her towards Pittonaccio, saying, "Behold your lord and master, my daughter. Gerande, behold your husband!"

Gerande shuddered from head to foot.

"Never!" cried Aubert, "for she is my betrothed."

"Never!" responded Gerande, like a plaintive echo.

Pittonaccio began to laugh.

"You wish me to die, then!" exclaimed the old man. "There, in that clock, the last which goes of all which have gone from my hands, my life is shut up; and this man tells me, 'When I have thy daughter, this clock shall belong to thee.' And this man will not rewind it. He can break it, and plunge me into chaos. Ah, my daughter, you no longer love me!"

"My father!" murmured Gerande, recovering consciousness.

"If you knew what I have suffered, far away from this principle of my existence!" resumed the old man. "Perhaps no one looked after this timepiece. Perhaps its springs were left to wear out, its wheels to get clogged. But now, in my own hands, I can nourish this health so dear, for I must not die,—I, the great watchmaker of Geneva. Look, my daughter, how these hands advance with certain step. See, five o'clock is about to strike. Listen well, and look at the maxim which is about to be revealed."

Five o'clock struck with a noise which resounded sadly in Gerande's soul, and these words appeared in red letters:

YOU MUST EAT OF THE FRUITS OF THE TREE OF SCIENCE

Aubert and Gerande looked at each other stupefied. These were no longer the pious sayings of the Catholic watchmaker. The breath of Satan must have passed over it. But Zacharius paid no attention to this, and resumed—

"Dost thou hear, my Gerande? I live, I still live! Listen to my breathing,—see the blood circulating in my veins! No, thou wouldst not kill they father, and thou wilt accept this man for they husband, so that I may become immortal, and at last attain the power of God!"

At these blasphemous words old Scholastique crossed herself, and Pittonaccio laughed aloud with joy.

"And then, Gerande, thou wilt be happy with him. See this man,—he is Time! Thy existence will be regulated with absolute precision. Gerande, since I gave thee life, give life to thy father!"

"Gerande," murmured Aubert, "I am thy betrothed."

"He is my father!" replied Gerande, fainting.

"She is thine!" said Master Zacharius. "Pittonaccio, thou wilt keep thy promise!"

"Here is the key of the clock," replied the horrible man.

Master Zacharius seized the long key, which resembled an uncoiled snake, and ran to the clock, which he hastened to wind up with fantastic rapidity. The creaking of the spring jarred upon the nerves. The old watchmaker wound and wound the key, without stopping a moment, and it seemed as if the movement were beyond his control. He would more and more quickly, with strange contortions, until he fell from sheer weariness.

"There, it is wound up for a century!" he cried.

Aubert rushed from the hall as if he were mad. After long wandering, he found the outlet of the hateful château, and hastened into the open air. He returned to the hermitage of Notre-Dame-du-Sex, and talked so despairingly to the holy recluse, that the latter consented to return with him to the château of Andernatt.

If, during these hours of anguish, Gerande had not wept, it was because her tears were exhausted.

Master Zacharius had not left the hall. He ran every moment to listen to the regular beating of the old clock.

Meanwhile the clock had struck, and to Scholastique's great terror, these words had appeared on the silver face:—

MAN OUGHT TO BECOME THE EQUAL OF GOD.

The old man had not only not been shocked by these impious maxims, but read them deliriously, and flattered himself with thoughts of pride, whilst Pittonaccio kept close by him.

The marriage-contract was to be signed at midnight. Gerande, almost unconscious, saw or heard nothing. The silence was only broken by the old man's words, and the chuckling of Pittonaccio.

"See this man—he is Time."

Eleven o'clock struck. Master Zacharius shuddered, and read in a loud voice:—

MAN SHOULD BE THE SLAVE OF SCIENCE AND
SACRIFICE TO IT RELATIVES AND FAMILY.

"Yes!" he cried, "there is nothing but science in this world!"

The hands slipped over the face of the clock with the hiss of a serpent, and the pendulum beat with accelerated strokes.

Master Zacharius no longer spoke. He had fallen to the floor, his throat rattled, and from his oppressed bosom came only these half-broken words: "Life—science!"

The scene had now two new witnesses, the hermit and Aubert. Master Zacharius lay upon the floor; Gerande was praying beside him, more dead than alive.

Of a sudden a dry, hard noise was heard, which preceded the strike.

Master Zacharius sprang up.

"Midnight!" he cried.

The hermit stretched out his hand towards to the old clock,—and midnight did not sound.

Master Zacharius uttered a terrible cry, which must have been heard in hell, when these words appeared:—

WHO EVER SHALL ATTEMPT TO MAKE HIMSELF THE
EQUAL OF GOD, SHALL BE FOR EVER DAMNED!

The old clock burst with a noise like thunder, and the spring, escaping, leaped across the hall with a thousand fantastic contortions; the old man rose, ran after it, trying in vain to seize it, and exclaiming, "My soul,—my soul!"

The spring bounded before him, first on one side, then on the other, and he could not reach it.

At last Pittonaccio seized it, and, uttering a horrible blasphemy, ingulfed himself in the earth.

Master Zacharius fell backwards. He was dead.

The old watchmaker was buried in the midst of the peaks of Andernatt.

Then Aubert and Gerande returned to Geneva, and during the long life which God accorded to them, they made it a duty to redeem by prayer the soul of the castaway of science.

A Drama In The Air

In the month of September, 185—, I arrived at Frankfort-on-the-Maine. My passage though the principal German cities had been brilliantly marked by balloon ascents; but as yet no German had accompanied me in my car, and the fine experiments made at Paris by MM. Green, Eugene Godard, and Poitevin had not tempted the grave Teutons to essay aerial voyages.

But scarcely had the news of my approaching ascent spread through Frankfort, than three of the principal citizens begged the favour of being allowed to ascend with me. Two days afterwards we were to start from the Place de la Comédie. I began at once to get my balloon ready. It was of silk, prepared with gutta percha, a substance impermeable by acids or gasses; and its volume, which was three thousand cubic yards, enabled it to ascend to the loftiest heights.

The day of the ascent was that of the great September fair, which attracts so many people to Frankfort. Lighting gas, of a perfect quality and of great lifting power, had been furnished to me in excellent condition, and about eleven o'clock the balloon was filled; but only three-quarters filled,—an indispensable precaution, for, as one rises, the atmosphere diminishes in density, and the fluid enclosed within the balloon, acquiring more elasticity, might burst its sides. My calculations had furnished me with exactly the quantity of gas necessary to carry up my companions and myself.

We were to start at noon. The impatient crowd which pressed around the enclosed space, filling the enclosed square, overflowing into the contiguous streets, and covering the houses from the ground-floor to the slated gables, presented a striking scene. The high winds of the preceding days had subsided. An oppressive heat fell from the cloudless sky. Scarcely a breath animated the atmosphere. In such weather, one might descend again upon the very spot whence he had risen.

I carried three hundred pounds of ballast in bags; the car, quite round, four feet in diameter, was comfortably arranged; the hempen cords which supported it stretched symmetrically over the upper hemisphere of the balloon; the compass was in place, the barometer suspended in the circle which united the supporting cords, and the anchor carefully put in order. All was now ready for the ascent.

Among those who pressed around the enclosure, I remarked a young man with a pale face and agitated features. The sight of him impressed me. He was an eager spectator of my ascents, whom I had already met in several German cities. With an uneasy air, he closely watched the curious machine, as it lay motionless a few feet above the ground; and he remained silent among those about him.

Twelve o'clock came. The moment had arrived, but my travelling companions did not appear.

I sent to their houses, and learnt that one had left for Hamburg, another for Vienna, and the third for London. Their courage had failed them at the moment of undertaking one of those excursions which, thanks to the ability of living aeronauts, are free from all danger. As they formed, in some sort, a part of the programme of the day, the fear had seized them that they might be forced to execute it faithfully, and they had fled far from the scene at the instant when the balloon was being filled. Their courage was evidently the inverse ratio of their speed—in decamping.

The multitude, half deceived, showed not a little ill-humour. I did not hesitate to ascend alone. In order to re-establish the equilibrium between the specific gravity of the balloon and the weight which had thus proved wanting, I replaced my companions by more sacks of sand, and got into the car. The twelve men who held the balloon by twelve cords fastened to the equatorial circle, let them slip a little between their fingers, and the balloon rose several feet higher. There was not a breath of wind, and the atmosphere was so leaden that it seemed to forbid the ascent.

"Is everything ready?" I cried.

The men put themselves in readiness. A last glance told me that I might go.

"Attention!"

There was a movement in the crowd, which seemed to be invading the enclosure. "Let go!"

The balloon rose slowly, but I experienced a shock which threw me to the bottom of the car.

When I got up, I found myself face to face with an unexpected fellow-voyager,—the pale young man.

"Monsieur, I salute you," said he, with the utmost coolness.

"By what right—"

"Am I here? By the right which the impossibility of your getting rid of me confers."

I was amazed! His calmness put me out of countenance, and I had nothing to reply. I looked at the intruder but he took no notice of my astonishment.

"Does my weight disarrange your equilibrium, monsieur?" he asked. "You will permit me—"

And without waiting for my consent, he relieved the balloon of two bags, which he threw into space.

"Monsieur," said I, taking the only course now possible, "you have come; very well, you will remain; but to me alone belongs the management of the balloon."

"Monsieur," said he, "your urbanity is French all over: it comes from my

"Monsieur, I salute you."

own country. I morally press the hand you refuse me. Make all precautions, and act as seems best to you. I will wait till you have done—"

"For what?"

"To talk with you."

The barometer had fallen to twenty-six inches. We were nearly six hundred yards above the city; but nothing betrayed the horizontal displacement of the balloon, for the mass of air in which it is enclosed goes forward with it. A sort of confused glow enveloped the objects spread out under us, and unfortunately obscured their outline.

I examined my companion afresh.

He was a man of thirty years, simply clad. The sharpness of his features betrayed an indomitable energy, and he seemed very muscular. Indifferent to the astonishment he created, he remained motionless, trying to distinguish the objects which were vaguely confused below us.

"Miserable mist!" said he, after a few moments.

I did not reply.

"You owe me a grudge?" he went on. "Bah! I could not pay for my journey, and it was necessary to take you by surprise."

"Nobody asks you to descend, monsieur!"

"Eh, do you not know, then, that the same thing happened to the Counts of Laurencin and Dampierre, when they ascended at Lyons, on the 15th of January, 1784? A young merchant, named Fontaine, scaled the gallery, at the risk of capsizing the machine. He accomplished the journey, and nobody died of it!"

"Once on the ground, we will have an explanation," replied I, piqued at the light tone in which he spoke.

"Bah! Do not let us think of our return."

"Do you think, then, that I shall not hasten to descend?"

"Descend!" said he, in surprise. "Descend? Let us begin by first ascending."

And before I could prevent it, two more bags had been thrown over the car, without even having been emptied.

"Monsieur!" cried I, in a rage.

"I know your ability," replied the unknown quietly, "and your fine ascents are famous. But if Experience is the sister of Practice, she is also a cousin of Theory, and I have studied the aerial art long. It has got into my head!" he added sadly, falling into a silent reverie.

The balloon, having risen some distance farther, now became stationary. The unknown consulted the barometer, and said,—

"Here we are, at eight hundred yards. Men are like insects. See! I think we should always contemplate them from this height, to judge correctly of their proportions. The Place de la Comédie is transformed into an immense ant-hill. Observe the crowd which is gathered on the quays; and the mountains also get smaller and smaller. We are over the Cathedral. The Main is only a line, cutting the city in two, and the bridge seems a thread thrown between the two banks of the river."

The atmosphere became somewhat chilly.

"There is nothing I would not do for you, my host," said the unknown. "If you are cold, I will take off my coat and lend it to you."

"Thanks," said I dryly.

"Bah! Necessity makes law. Give me your hand. I am your fellow-countryman; you will learn something in my company, and my conversation will indemnify you for the trouble I have given you."

I sat down, without replying, at the opposite extremity of the car. The young man had taken a voluminous manuscript from his great-coat. It was an essay on ballooning.

"I possess," said he, "the most curious collection of engravings and caricatures extant concerning aerial manias. How people admired and scoffed at the same time at this precious discovery! We are happily no longer in the age in which Montgolfier tried to make artificial clouds with steam, or a gas having electrical properties, produced by the combustion of moist straw and chopped-up-wool."

"Do you wish to depreciate the talent of the inventors?" I asked, for I had resolved to enter into the adventure. "Was it not good to have proved by experience the possibility of rising in the air?"

"Ah, monsieur, who denies the glory of the first aerial navigators? It required immense courage to rise by means of those frail envelopes which only contained heated air. But I ask you, has the aerial science made great progress since Blanchard's ascensions, that is, since nearly a century ago? Look here, monsieur."

The unknown took an engraving from his portfolio.

"Here," said he, "is the first aerial voyage undertaken by Pilâtre des Rosiers and the Marquis d'Arlandes, four months after the discovery of balloons. Louis XVI. refused to consent to the venture, and two men who were condemned to death were the first to attempt the aerial ascent. Pilâtre des Rosiers became indignant at this injustice, and, by means of intrigues, obtained permission to make the experiment. The car, which renders the management easy, had not then been invented, and a circular gallery was placed around the lower and contracted part of the Montgolfier balloon. The two aeronauts must then remain motionless at each extremity of this gallery, for the moist straw which filled it forbade them all motion. A chafing-dish with fire was suspended below the orifice of the balloon; when the aeronauts wished to rise, they threw straw upon this brazier, at the risk of setting fire to the balloon, and the air, more heated, gave it fresh ascending power. The two bold travellers rose, on the 21st of November, 1783, from the Muette Gardens, which the dauphin had put at their disposal. The balloon went up majestically, passed over the Isle of Swans, crossed the Seine at the Conference barrier, and, drifting between the dome of the Invalides and the Military School, approached the Church of Saint Sulpice. Then the aeronauts added to the fire, crossed the Boulevard, and descended beyond the Enfer barrier. As it touched the soil, the balloon collapsed, and for a few moments buried Pilâtre des Rosiers under its folds."

"Unlucky augury," I said, interested in the story, which affected me nearly.

"An augury of the catastrophe which was later to cost this unfortunate man his life," replied the unknown sadly. "Have you never experienced anything like it?"

"Never."

"Bah! Misfortunes sometimes occur unforeshadowed!" added my companion. He then remained silent.

Meanwhile we were advancing southward, and Frankfort had already passed from beneath us.

"Perhaps we shall have a storm," said the young man.

"We shall descend before that," I replied.

"Indeed! It is better to ascend. We shall escape it more surely."

And two more bags of sand were hurled into space.

The balloon rose rapidly, and stopped at twelve hundred yards. I became colder; and yet the sun's rays, falling upon the surface, expanded the gas within, and gave it a greater ascending force.

"Fear nothing," said the unknown. "We have still three thousand five hundred fathoms of breathing air. Besides, do not trouble yourself about what I do."

I would have risen, but a vigorous hand held me to my seat. "Your name?" I asked.

"My name? What matters it to you?"

"I demand your name!"

"My name is Erostratus or Empedocles, whichever you choose!"

This reply was far from reassuring.

The unknown, besides, talked with such strange coolness that I anxiously asked myself whom I had to deal with.

"Monsieur," he contined, "nothing original has been imagined since the physicist Charles. Four months after the discovery of balloons, this able man had invented the valve, which permits the gas to escape when the balloon is too full, or when you wish to descend; the car, which aids the management of the machine; the netting, which holds the envelope of the balloon, and divides the weight over its whole surface; the ballast, which enables you to ascend, and to choose the place of your landing; the india-rubber coating, which renders the tissue impermeable; the barometer, which shows the height attained. Lastly, Charles used hydrogen, which, fourteen times lighter than air, permits you to penetrate to the highest atmospheric regions, and does not expose you to the dangers of a combustion in the air. On the 1st of December, 1783, three hundred thousand spectators were crowded around the Tuileries. Charles rose, and the soldiers presented arms to him. He travelled nine leagues in the air, conducting his balloon with an ability not surpassed by modern aeronauts. The king awarded him a pension of two thousand livres; for then they encouraged new inventions."

The unknown now seemed to be under the influence of considerable agitation.

"Monsieur," he resumed, "I have studied this, and I am convinced that the first aernonauts guided their balloons. Without speaking of Blanchard, whose assertions may be received with doubt, Guyton-Morveaux, by the aid of oars and rudder, made his machine answer to the helm, and take the direction he determined on. More recently, M. Julien, a watchmaker, made some convincing experiments at the Hippodrome, in Paris; for, by a special mechanism, his aerial apparatus, oblong in form, went visibly against the wind. It occurred to M. Petin to place four hydrogen balloons together; and, by means of sails hung horizontally and partly folded, he hopes to be able to disturb the equilibrium, and, thus inclining the apparatus, to convey it in an oblique direction. They speak, also, of forces to overcome the resistance of currents,—for instance, the screw; but the screw, working on a moveable centre, will give no result. I, monsieur, have discovered the only means of guiding balloons; and no academy has come to my aid, no city has filled up subscriptions for me, no government has thought fit to listen to me! It is infamous!"

The unknown gesticulated fiercely, and the car underwent violent oscillations. I had much trouble in calming him.

Meanwhile the balloon had entered a more rapid current, and we advanced south, at fifteen hundred yards above the earth.

"See, there is Darmstadt," said my companion, leaning over the car. "Do you perceive the château? Not very distinctly, eh? What would you have? The heat of the storm makes the outline of objects waver, and you must have a skilled eye to recognize localities."

"Are you certain it is Darmstadt?" I asked.

"I am sure of it. We are now six leagues from Frankfort."

"Then we must descend."

"Descend! You would not go down on the steeples," said the unknown, with a chuckle.

"No, but in the suburbs of the city."

"Well, let us avoid the steeples!"

So speaking, my companion seized some bags of ballast. I hastened to prevent him; but he overthrew me with one hand, and the unballasted balloon ascended to two thousand yards.

"Rest easy," said he, "and do not forget that Brioschi, Biot, Gay-Lussac, Bixio, and Barral ascended to still greater heights to make their scientific experiments."

"Monsieur, we must descend," I resumed, trying to persuade him by gentleness. "The storm is gathering around us. It would be more prudent—"

"Bah! We will mount higher than the storm, and then we shall no longer fear it!" cried my companion. "What is nobler than to overlook the clouds which oppress the earth? Is it not an honour thus to navigate on aerial billows? The greatest men have travelled as we are doing. The Marchioness and Countess de Montalembert, the Countess of Podenas, Mademoiselle la Garde, the Marquis de Montalembert, rose from the Faubourg Saint-Antoine for these unknown regions, and the Duke de Chartres exhibited much skill and presence of mind in his ascent on the 15th of July, 1784. At Lyons, the Counts of Laurencin and Dampierre; at Nantes, M. de Luynes; at Bordeaux, D'Arbelet des Granges; in Italy, the Chevalier Andreani; in our own time, the Duke of Brunswick,—have all left the traces of their glory in the air. To equal these great personages, we must penetrate still higher than they into the celestial depths! To approach the infinite is to comprehend it!"

The rarefaction of the air was fast expanding the hydrogen in the balloon, and I saw its lower part, purposely left empty, swell out, so that it was absolutely necessary to open the valve; but my companion did not seem to intend that I should manage the balloon as I wished. I then resolved to pull the valve cord secretly, as he was excitedly talking; for I feared to guess with whom I had to deal. It would have been too horrible! It was nearly a quarter before one. We had been gone forty minutes from Frankfort; heavy clouds were coming against the wind from the south, and seemed about to burst upon us.

"Have you lost all hope of succeeding in your project?" I asked with anxious interest.

"All hope!" exclaimed the unknown in a low voice. "Wounded by slights and caricatures, these asses' kicks have finished me! It is the eternal punishment reserved for innovators! Look at these caricatures of all periods, of which my portfolio is full."

While my companion was fumbling with his papers, I had seized the valve-cord without his perceiving it. I feared, however, that he might hear the hissing noise, like a water-course, which the gas makes in escaping.

"How many jokes were made about the Abbé Miolan!" said he. "He was to go up with Janninet and Bredin. During the filling their balloon caught fire, and the ignorant populace tore it in pieces! Then this caricature of 'curious animals' appeared, giving each of them a punning nickname."

I pulled the valve-cord, and the barometer began to ascend. It was time. Some far-off rumblings were heard in the south.

"Here is another engraving," resumed the unknown, not suspecting what I was doing. "It is an immense balloon carrying a ship, strong castles, houses, and so on. The caricaturists did not suspect that their follies would one day become truths. It is complete, this large vessel. On the left is its helm, with the pilot's box; at the prow are pleasure-houses, an immense organ, and a cannon to call the attention of the inhabitants of the earth or the moon; above the poop there are the observatory and the balloon long-boat; in the equatorial circle, the army barrack; on the left, the funnel; then the upper galleries for promenading, sails, pinions; below, the cafés and general storehouse. Observe this pompous announcement; 'Invented for the happiness of the human race, this globe will depart at once for the ports of the Levant, and on its return the programme of its voyages to the two poles and the extreme west will be announced. No one need furnish himself with anything; everything is foreseen, and all will prosper. There will be a uniform price for all places of destination, but it will be the same for the most distant countries of our hemisphere—that is to say, a thousand louis for one of any of the said journeys. And it must be confessed that this sum is very moderate, when the speed, comfort, and arrangements which will be enjoyed on the balloon are considered—arrangements which are not to be found on land, while on the balloon each passenger may consult his own habits and tastes. This is so true that in the same place some will be dancing, other standing; some will be enjoying delicacies; others fasting. Whoever desires the society of wits may satisfy himself; whoever is stupid may find stupid people to keep him company. Thus pleasure will be the soul of the aerial company.' All this provoked laughter; but before long, if I am not cut off, they will see it all realized."

We were visibly descending. He did not perceive it!

"This kind of 'game at balloons,'" he resumed, spreading out before me some of the engravings of his valuable collection, "this game contains the entire history of the aerostatic art. It is used by elevated minds, and is played with dice and counters, with whatever stakes you like, to be paid or received according to where the player arrives."

"Why," said I, "you seem to have studied the science of aerostation profoundly."

"Yes, monsieur, yes! From Phaethon, Icarus, Architas, I have searched for, examined, learnt everything. I could render immense services to the world in this art, if God granted me life. But that will not be!"

"Why?"

"Because my name is Empedocles, or Erostratus."

Meanwhile, the balloon was happily approaching the earth; but when one is falling, the danger is as great at a hundred feet as at five thousand.

"Do you recall the battle of Fleurus?" resumed my companion, whose face became more and more animated. "It was at the battle that Contello, by order of the Government, organized a company of balloonists. At the siege of Manbenge General Jourdan derived so much service from this new method of observation that Contello ascended twice a day with the general himself. The communications between the aeronaut and his agents who held the balloon were made by means of small white, red, and yellow flags. Often the gun and cannon shot were directed upon the balloon when he ascended, but without result. When General Jourdan was preparing to invest Charleroi, Contello went into the vicinity, ascended from the plain of Jumet, and continued his observations for seven or eight hours with General Morlot, and this no doubt aided in giving us the victory of Fleurus. General Jourdan publicly acknowledged the help which the aeronautical observations had afforded him. Well, despite the services rendered on that occasion and during the Belgian campaign, the year which had seen the beginning of the military career of balloons saw also its end. The school of Meudon, founded by the Government, was closed by Buonaparte on his return from Egypt. And now, what can you expect from the new-born infant? as Franklin said. The infant was born alive; it should not be stifled!

The unknown bowed his head in his hands, and reflected for some moments; then raising his head, he said,—

"Despite my prohibition, monsieur, you have opened the valve."

I dropped the cord.

"Happily," he resumed, "we have still three hundred pounds of ballast."

"What is your purpose?" said I.

"Have you ever crossed the seas?" he asked.

I turned pale.

"It is unfortunate," he went on, "that we are being driven towards the Adriatic. That is only a stream; but higher up we may find other currents."

And, without taking any notice of me, he threw over several bags of sand; then, in a menacing voice, he said,—

"I let you open the valve because the expansion of the gas threatened to burst the balloon; but do not do it again!"

Then he went on as follows:—

"You remember the voyage of Blanchard and Jeffries from Dover to Calais? It was magnificent! On the 7th of January, 1785, there being a north-west wind, their balloon was inflated with gas on the Dover coast. A mistake of equilibrium, just as they were ascending, forced them to throw out their ballast so that they might not go down again, and they only kept thirty pounds. It was too little; for, as the wind did not freshen, they only advanced very slowly towards the French coast. Besides, the permeability of the tissue served to reduce the inflation little by little, and in an hour and a half the aeronauts perceived that they were descending.

" 'What shall we do?' said Jeffries.

" 'We are only one quarter of the way over,' replied Blanchard, 'and very low down. On rising, we shall perhaps meet more favourable winds.'

" 'Let us throw out the rest of the sand.'

"The balloon acquired some ascending force, but it soon began to descend again. Towards the middle of the transit the aeronauts threw over their books and tools. A quarter of an hour after, Blanchard said to Jeffries,—

" 'The barometer?'

" 'It is going up! We are lost, and yet there is the French coast.'

"A loud noise was heard.

" 'Has the balloon burst?' asked Jeffries.

" 'No. The loss of the gas has reduced the inflation of the lower part of the balloon. But we are still descending. We are lost! Out with everything useless!'

"Provisions, oars, and rudder were thrown into the sea. The aeronauts were only one hundred yards high.

" 'We are going up again,' said the doctor.

" 'No. It is the spurt caused by the diminution of the weight, and not a ship in sight, not a bark on the horizon! To the sea with our clothing!'

"The unfortunates stripped themselves, but the balloon continued to descend.

" 'Blanchard,' said Jeffries, 'you should have made this voyage alone; you consented to take me; I will sacrifice myself! I am going to throw myself into the water, and the balloon, relieved of my weight, will mount again.'

" 'No, no! It is frightful!'

"The balloon became less and less inflated, and as it doubled up its concavity pressed the gas against the sides, and hastened its downward course.

" 'Adieu, my friend,' said the doctor. 'God preserve you!'

"He was about to throw himself over, when Blanchard held him back.

" 'There is one more change,' said he. 'We can cut the cords which hold the car, and cling to the net! Perhaps the balloon will rise. Let us hold ourselves ready. But—the barometer is going down! The wind is freshening! We are saved!'

"The aeronauts perceived Calais, Their joy was delirious. A few moments more, and they had fallen in the forest of Guines. I do not doubt," added the unknown, "that, under similar circumstances, you would have followed Doctor Jeffries' example."

The clouds rolled in glittering masses beneath us. The balloon threw large shadows on this heap of clouds, and was surrounded as by an aureola. The thunder rumbled below the car. All this was terrifying.

"Let us descend!" I cried.

"Descend, when the sun is up there, waiting for us? Out with more bags!"

And more than fifty pounds of ballast were cast over.

At a height of three thousand five hundred yards we remained stationary.

The unknown talked unceasingly. I was in a state of complete prostration, while he seemed to be in his element.

"With a good wind, we shall go far," he cried. "In the Antilles there are currents of air which have a speed of a hundred leagues an hour. When Napoleon was crowned, Garnerin sent up a balloon with coloured lamps, at eleven o'clock at night. The wind was blowing north-north-west. The next morning, at daybreak, the inhabitants of Rome greeted its passage over the dome of St. Peter's. We shall go farther and higher!"

I scarcely heard him. Everything whirled around me. An opening appeared in the clouds.

"See that city," said the unknown. "It is Spires!"

I leaned over the car and perceived a small blackish mass. It was Spires. The Rhine, which is so large, seemed an unrolled ribbon. The sky was a deep blue over our heads. The birds had long abandoned us, for in that rarefied air they could not have flown. We were alone in space, and I in presence of this unknown!

"It is useless for you to know whither I am leading you," he said, as he threw the compass among the clouds. "Ah! a fall is a grand thing! You know that but few victims of ballooning are to be reckoned, from Pilâtre des Rosiers to Lieutenant Gale, and that the accidents have always been the result of imprudence. Pilâtre des Rosiers set out with Romain of Boulogne, on the 13th of June, 1785. To his gas balloon he had affixed a Montgolfier apparatus of hot air, so as to dispense, no doubt, with the necessity of losing gas or throwing out ballast. It was putting a torch under a powder-barrel. When they had ascended four hundred yards, and were taken by opposing winds, they were driven over the open sea. Pilâtre, in order to descend, essayed to open the valve, but the valve-cord became entangled in the balloon, and tore it so badly that it became empty in an instant. It fell upon the Montgolfier apparatus, overturned it, and dragged down the unfortunates, who were soon shattered to pieces! It is frightful, is it not?''

I could only reply, ''For pity's sake, let us descend!''

The clouds gathered around us on every side, and dreadful detonations, which reverberated in the cavity of the balloon, took place beneath us.

''You provoke me,'' cried the unknown, ''and you shall no longer know whether we are rising or falling!''

The barometer went the way of the compass, accompanied by several more bags of sand. We must have been 5000 yards high. Some icicles had already attached themselves to the sides of the car, and a kind of fine snow seemed to penetrate to my very bones. Meanwhile a frightful tempest was raging under us, but we were above it.

''Do not be afraid,'' said the unknown, ''It is only the imprudent who are lost. Olivari, who perished at Orleans, rose in a paper 'Montgolfier;' his car, suspended below the chafing-dish, and ballasted with combustible materials, caught fire; Olivari fell, and was killed! Mosment rose, at Lille, on a light tray; an oscillation disturbed his equilibrium; Mosment fell, and was killed! Bittorf, at Mannheim, saw his balloon catch fire in the air; and he, too, fell, and was killed! Harris rose in a badly constructed balloon, the valve of which was too large and would not shut; Harris fell, and was killed! Sadler, deprived of ballast by his long sojourn in the air, was dragged over the town of Boston and dashed against the chimneys; Sadler fell, and was killed! Cokling descended with a convex parachute which he pretended to have perfected; Cokling fell, and was killed! Well, I love them, these victims of their own imprudence, and I shall die as they did. Higher! still higher!''

All the phantoms of this necrology passed before my eyes. The rarefaction of the air and the sun's rays added to the expansion of the gas, and the balloon continued to mount. I tried mechanically to open the valve, but the unknown cut the cord several feet above my head. I was lost!

''Did you see Madame Blanchard fall?'' said he. ''I saw her; yes, I! I was at Tivoli on the 6th of July, 1819. Madame Blanchard rose in a small-sized balloon, to avoid the expense of filling, and she was forced to entirely inflate it. The gas leaked out below, and left a regular train of hydrogen in its path. She carried with her a sort of pyrotechnic aureola, suspended below her car by a wire, which she was to set off in the air. This she had done many times before. On this day she also carried up a small parachute ballasted by a firework contrivance, that would go off in a shower of silver. She was to start this contrivance after having lighted it with a port-fire made on purpose. She set out; the night was gloomy. At the moment of lighting her fireworks she was so imprudent as to pass the taper under the column of hydrogen which was leaking from the balloon. My eyes were fixed upon her. Suddenly an unexpected gleam lit up the darkness. I thought she was preparing a surprise. The light flashed out, suddenly disappeared and reappeared, and gave the summit of the balloon the shape of an immense jet of ignited gas. This sinister glow shed itself over the Boulvard and the whole Montmartre quarter. Then I saw the unhappy woman rise, try twice to close the appendage of the balloon, so as to put out the fire, then sit down in her car and try to guide her descent; for she did not fall. The combustion of the gas lasted for several minutes. The balloon, becoming gradually less, continued to descend, but it was not a fall. The wind blew from the north-west and drove it towards Paris. There were then some large gardens just by the house No. 16, Rue de Provence. Madame Blanchard essayed to fall there without danger: but the balloon and the car struck on the roof of the house with a light shock. 'Save me!' cried the wretched woman. I got into the street at this moment. The car slid along the roof, and encountered an iron cramp. At this concussion, Madame Blanchard was thrown out of her car and precipitated upon the pavement. She was killed!''

These stories froze me with horror. The unknown was standing with bare head, dishevelled hair, haggard eyes!

There was no longer any illusion possible. I at last recognized the horrible truth. I was in the presence of a madman!

He threw out the rest of the ballast, and we must have now reached a height of at least nine thousand yards. Blood spurted from my nose and mouth!

''Who are nobler than the martyrs of science?'' cried the lunatic. ''They are canonized by posterity.''

But I no longer heard him. He looked about him, and, bending down to my ear, muttered,—

''And have you forgotten Zambecarri's catastrophe? Listen. On the 7th of October, 1804, the clouds seemed to lift a little. On the preceding days, the wind and rain had not ceased; but the announced ascension of Zambecarri could not be postponed. His enemies were already bantering him. It was necessary to ascend, to save the science and himself from becoming a public jest. It was at Boulogne. No one helped him to inflate his balloon.

''He rose at midnight, accompanied by Andreoli and Grossetti. The balloon mounted slowly, for it had been perforated by the rain, and the gas was leaking out. The three intrepid aeronauts could only observe the state of the barometer by aid of a dark lantern. Zambecarri had eaten nothing for twenty-four hours. Grossetti was also fasting.

'' 'My friends,' said Zambecarri, 'I am overcome by cold, and exhausted. I am dying.'

''He fell inanimate in the gallery. It was the same with Grossetti. Andreoli alone remained conscious. After long efforts, he succeeded in reviving Zambecarri.

'' 'What news? Whither are we going? How is the wind? What time is it?'

'' 'It is two o'clock.'

'' 'Where is the compass?'

'' 'Upset!'

'' 'Great God! The lantern has gone out!'

'' 'It cannot burn in this rarefied air,' said Zambecarri.

''The moon had not risen, and the atmosphere was plunged in murky darkness.

'' 'I am cold, Andreoli. What shall I do?'

''They slowly descended through a layer of whitish clouds.

'' 'Sh!' said Andreoli. 'Do you hear?'

'' 'What?' asked Zambecarri.

'' 'A strange noise.'

'' 'You are mistaken.'

'' 'No.'

The balloon became less and less inflated.

"Consider these travellers, in the middle of the night, listening to that unaccountable noise! Are they going to knock against a tower? Are they about to be precipitated on the roofs?

" 'Do you hear? One would say it was the noise of the sea.

" 'Impossible!'

" 'It is the groaning of the waves!'

" 'It is true.'

" 'Light! Light!'

"After five fruitless attempts, Andreoli succeeded in obtaining light. It was three o'clock.

"The voice of violent waves was heard. They were almost touching the surface of the sea!

" 'We are lost!' cried Zambecarri, seizing a large bag of sand.

" 'Help!' cried Andreoli.

"The car touched the water, and the waves came up to their breasts.

" 'Throw out the instruments, clothes, money!'

"The aeronauts completely stripped themselves. The balloon, relieved, rose with frightful rapidity. Zambecarri was taken with vomiting. Grossetti bled profusely. The unfortunate men could not speak, so short was their breathing. They were taken with cold, and they were soon crusted over with ice. The moon looked as red as blood.

"After traversing the high regions for a half-hour, the balloon again fell into the sea. It was four in the morning. They were half submerged in the water, and the balloon dragged them along, as if under sail, for several hours.

"At daybreak they found themselves opposite Pesaro, four miles from the coast. They were about to reach it, when a gale blew them back into the open sea. They were lost! The frightened boats fled at their approach. Happily, a more intelligent boatman accosted them, hoisted them on board, and they landed at Ferrada.

"A frightful journey, was it not? But Zambecarri was a brave and energetic man. Scarcely recovered from his sufferings, he resumed his ascensions. During one of them he struck against a tree; his spirit-lamp was broken on his clothes; he was enveloped in fire, his balloon began to catch the flames, and he came down half consumed.

"At last, on the 21st of September, 1812, he made another ascension at Boulogne. The balloon clung to a tree, and his lamp again set it one fire. Zambecarri fell, and was killed! And in presence of these facts, we would still hesitate! No. The higher we go, the more glorious will be our death!"

The balloon being now entirely relieved of ballast and of all it contained, we were carried to an enormous height. It vibrated in the atmosphere. The least noise resounded in the vaults of heaven. Our globe, the only object which caught my view in immensity, seemed ready to be annihilated, and above us the depths of the starry skies were lost in thick darkness.

I saw my companion rise up before me.

"The hour is come!" he said. "We must die. We are rejected men. They despise us. Let us crush them!"

"Mercy!" I cried.

"Let us cut these cords! Let this car be abandoned in space. The attractive force will change its direction, and we shall approach the sun!"

Despair galvanized me. I threw myself upon the madman, we struggled to-

The madman disappeared in space.

gether, and a terrible conflict took place. But I was thrown down, and while he held me under his knee, the madman was cutting the cords of the car.

"One!" he cried.

"My God!"

"Two! Three!"

I made a superhuman effort, rose up, and violently repulsed the madman.

"Four!"

The car fell, but I instinctively clung to the cords and hoisted myself into the meshes of the netting.

The madman disappeared in space!

The balloon was raised to an immeasurable height. A horrible cracking was heard. The gas, too much dilated, had burst the balloon. I shut my eyes—

Some instants after, a damp warmth revived me. I was in the midst of clouds on fire. The balloon turned over with dizzy velocity. Taken by the wind, it made a hundred leagues an hour in a horizontal course, the lightning flashing around it.

Meanwhile my fall was not a very rapid one. When I opened my eyes, I saw the country. I was two miles from the sea, and the tempest was driving me violently towards it, when an abrupt shock forced me to loosen my hold. My hands opened, a cord slipped swiftly between my fingers, and I found myself on the solid earth!

It was the cord of the anchor, which, sweeping along the surface of the ground, was caught in a crevice; and my balloon, unballasted for the last time, careered off to lose itself beyond the sea.

When I came to myself, I was in bed in a peasant's cottage, at Harderwick, a village of La Gueldre, fifteen leagues from Amsterdam, on the shores of the Zuyder-Zee.

A miracle had saved my life, but my voyage had been a series of imprudences, committed by a lunatic, and I had not been able to prevent them.

May this terrible narrative, though instructing those who read it, not discourage the explorers of the air.